# 59 FRONT STREET

## *A NOVEL*

by

## Martin M. Cassity, Jr.

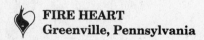

**FIRE HEART**
**Greenville, Pennsylvania**

*Grateful acknowledgment is made to the following for permission to reprint from previously published material:*

*The Richmond Organization—Essex Music International, Inc., excerpts from "Bang A Gong (Get It On)," words and music by Marc Bolan, ©1971 Westminster Music Ltd. Pink Floyd Music Publishers Limited, excerpts from "The Wall," printed by kind permission of Roger Waters, ©1979 Pink Floyd Music Publishers Limited. MCA Music Publishing, excerpts from "Rocky Mountain Way," words and music by Joe Walsh, Joe Vitale, Ken Passerelli, and Rocke Grace, ©1973 Barnstorm Music Inc., Belkin Music Company, and Dutchess Music Corporation. Tiffany and Shore Publishers (Guyasuta), quotations of poems: "God is Talking Now," "Soul Mate," "February 1974," "Mill Street," "Our Rising Sun," all from chapbook, GOD IS TALKING NOW, Tiffany and Shore, ©1990 Martin M. Cassity Jr. Cousins Music, Inc. and Longitude Music, Inc., excerpts from "Barbara Ann," Beach Boys, ©1961 Brian Wilson. Sandra Fadgen, excerpts from "The Child Within," ©1990 Sandra Fadgen (a self-published work). Steven Couture, excerpts from "Lay Low My Sweet Child," ©1987 Steven Couture (a self-published work).*

## ©1993 Martin M. Cassity, Jr.

Cover Artwork © 1988 Martin M. Cassity, Jr.

First Edition—1993
Printed in United States of America

**Library of Congress Cataloging-in-Publication Data**

Cassity, Martin M.
   59 Front Street / by Martin M. Cassity, Jr. -- 1st ed.
      p.      cm.
   ISBN 1-881399-09-5 : $11.95
   1. Man-woman relationships--United States--Fiction.  2. Clergy-United States--Fiction. I. Title. II. Fifty-nine Front Street.
   PS3553.A7995A615  1993
   813' .54--dc20
                                                                  93-44783
                                                                  CIP

### Published by

**FIRE HEART**
A division of Beaver Pond Publishing
P.O. Box 224
Greenville, Pennsylvania 16125

*Doubt is not a pleasant condition, but certainty is absurd.*

—Voltaire (French philosopher)

*... first of all, Beware of the leaven of the Pharisees, which is hyprocrisy. For there is nothing covered, that shall not be revealed; neither hidden, that shall not be known.*

—Jesus Christ (Luke 12: 1-2)

# Chapter One

**S**oap, hot water, Old Spice. Jim Shanley comes out of the bathroom bringing with him the steamy fragrances of his morning shower and shave. There's just enough light in the bedroom, so he doesn't have to turn on the lamp on his dresser. Sharon is still asleep, curled like a comma on her side of the bed, and she doesn't like it when he turns on the lamp, especially on Saturday. During December and January he needed it, but it's now February and the gray light of day is already filtering through the sheer priscilla curtains and drawn shades.

Jim sheds his shabby robe and hangs it on the closet door. Sharon gave him a new robe for Christmas, but he still wears his old red one with the ripped-off pockets and worn-through neck. After hauling on his Levi's and stretching into a plaid flannel shirt—Saturday clothes, favorite clothes—he grabs some white socks from his drawer and sits down on the bed to put on his boots. But the socks have holes in the toes, so he rummages again in his drawer. He finds one of the new pairs that Sharon got for him on her last trip to Marshall's then plops, rather heavily, back onto the bed.

A groan, a yawn, swirls of blond hair, pale-yellow and disheveled. His wife stirs, turns onto her back, and stretches her flannel-clad arms upward over the headboard. She looks up at Jim through squinty eyes. "I need you to come home early today," she reminds in a breathy sleep-glued voice. "I promised Erin and Heather I'd take them to Searstown this afternoon. You know, for spring jackets ... and I really don't want to take Chris; he gets so cranky when I take him shopping."

Pausing, sock in hand, Jim gives a yawn that becomes a sigh. "I'll try, hon, but I have a lot of Sunday school parents to see, with the program tomorrow, plus my regular visits." His reply is perfunctory as if her request never made it to his brain.

Sharon grumbles, rolls away from her husband, and folds her pillow around her head. "Why *you*?" she protests, her voice filled with exasperation. "Why do *you* have to spend every day at the church? Why can't Russ do it? Outreach, outreach. I hate it. We have no Saturday in this family. You do have children, you know? How about outreach to *them*? Your schedule's worse than ever ... even worse than Westover. Is this *ever* going to end?"

Her request, and complaint, finally registers in Jim's mind. A pang of guilt stabs his conscience as he thinks of all the time he spends away from home. He sucks a breath and prepares to defend his busy schedule, but his hollow oft-repeated argument hangfires in his throat—then comes up as a gruff little cough. Now choosing

1

silence over rebuttal, he laces up his boots, plucks his watch, pen, and notepad off the television, and moves around to Sharon's side of the bed where he finds his sweater-vest on her rocking chair. He seeks her face but she remains hidden inside her folded pillow.

*Pit-pit ... pit-pit.* The water dripping off the roof eaves draws Jim to the window. He opens the shade and peers out at the misty morning which cloaks Greeley Hill like a translucent shroud.

Save for sex and suppertime, he and Sharon now live in separate worlds, but he recalls a simpler time fourteen years ago when he was an Air Force lieutenant and she, his new bride. Their love was fresh and free and all-consuming. But time has a way of changing things, not that the years have extinguished their love, but three children together with the regular responsibilities of life have pushed togetherness down on the list. This became especially evident after Jim entered Bible school, then the ministry.

He thinks back to his early years in the ministry when he served God with innocent zeal, childlike faith, and a heartfelt sense of purpose, not to mention a naive trust in those appointed over him. In those days he readily defended the sacrifices he made for his calling and had no qualms about spending time away from home, but now at the age of thirty-six, Shanley knows too much about his office—and *himself.*

Though Jim is a successful and highly regarded pastor, his allegiance to evangelical Christianity is no longer heartfelt. He cares for his flock but he wishes he could turn off the treadmill of religious duty and obligation. On occasion, he sees himself as a visionary called to form a new and simpler church where this would be possible, but more often, he feels like a ship that has broken loose from its mooring and is drifting away in heavy seas.

He sighs and returns his attention to the bedroom. Reaching down, he unfolds Sharon's hiding place but her doll-like eyes are closed in pretended sleep. Her golden hair, baby-soft and fine as corn silk, flows in rivulets over and around her fair Norwegian face. Tawny freckles, faint but large, dapple her square high-boned cheeks like spots on a fawn's back. She snuggles like a long-legged child in her pink floral-print nightgown, but at thirty-three, she's far from a child, and at five-foot-seven, she's almost as tall as Jim. In high heels she is.

As Jim looks at her, the tension of disagreement melts out of his mind along with the disturbing possibilities conjured up in his moment of self-reflection. Sharon seems to sense his changing mood as a flicker of a smile pulls at the corners of her small but cutely full-lipped mouth.

The smile betrays her pretense of sleep and moves Jim to

playfulness. "Let's see if I can find your beautiful thighs and your darling feet," he teases, reaching under the covers to tickle her.

"Honey, don't," she fusses. "Don't. I want to sleep. Let me sleep."

"Oh, you like to be tickled. I know you do."

Wiggling free, Sharon pulls the pale-blue comforter over her head and tightly all around like a zipped-up sleeping bag. Jim tries to grab her through the comforter but the quilted down is too thick, so he reaches underneath. She squeals and rolls over. He falls across her onto the bed.

Now ready to frolic, Sharon comes out, her blue eyes flashing. She pummels Jim with her pillow but he grabs the pillow then her. Rolling, flipping, laughing, they wrestle like yearling cats until all the bedclothes are on the floor and she's sitting on top of him smiling in triumph. "Guess I got you now, don't I?"

"Okay, Shar, that's enough," Jim pants, trying to be serious but unable to erase his simpering smirk. "I give up. You win. I gotta go; I'm late."

"Getting quite a gut on you, mister," Sharon teases. "Some nice handles too, but I bet your ribs are still there. Let's see if I can find them." She pulls up his shirt and digs into his flanks as if she's kneading dough.

Jim squirms and tries to push her hands away. "No, Shar! Don't. I gotta go!"

"Oh, come on, honey. I'm just now having fun. Besides, you started it."

Riding him like a cowgirl, she tickles and teases, as her long cushiony thighs ripple and roll around him. Faint from laughing, he fights back until too weak to move.

Sharon also stills. Eyes, eyes, dusty-blue and dilating. Hungry, seductive eyes—no longer doll-like but wide, womanly, and wanton. No sound, save for steady breathing which mixes a cloud of night breath and toothpaste between them. Ready to go beyond frolic, she pulls her nightgown over her head and flings it onto the rocker.

Naked, naked. Soft female flesh: once trim now plumpish yet still very sexy, perhaps moreso with the added pounds. Ample breasts, ripe pears with a hint of thirtyish sag, not large but larger than when Jim first gazed upon them on their wedding night. He played with them during their year of courting—and petting—but he never saw his wife in the nude until their honeymoon.

Tawny halos, pink nipples, swelling, turning red. This sight turns Jim on. He feels his body shaking under Sharon's straddling weight, but she holds back; she knows how to rein in her passion and ride it to the top.

3

Her aroused nakedness has transformed the room into an enchanted temple of Eros, the bed into a burning altar which gives forth the sweet-and-sour incense of lovemaking: Old Spice and soap, perspiration, female desire, day-old Charlie perfume. Jim can't wait, yet he loves how she makes him wait, heightening his desire, and her own. Helpless, he lets go of time.

When time returns, Jim lies half nude, his blue jeans around his knees, Sharon draped over him.

"Oh, James David," she coos, addressing him formally as she does only in orgasm or anger, "that was *so* good. Just how I like to start my day. Let's go again and again and again. I'm tired of being a pastor's wife. I just want to be wild and naked. I want to screw you all day long."

"I must say, Mrs. Shanley, your mood has certainly changed."

"Sex, sex, your body, I love it more than *any*thing. Let's get real naughty and forget the rest of the world. I feel so earthy and loose. Let's talk about our secret fantasies and make it last, like on Wednesday night."

"Sounds inviting," Jim replies, "but I hafta go. I'm running late. It's fifteen after."

"Oh, all right," Sharon sighs resignedly as she rolls over, allowing Jim to get up. Additional words follow him into the hallway, into the bathroom, "You're no fun. I hate your schedule." She laughs, but he senses more than humor in her complaint.

Jim cat-washes—he always scrubs after sex—then recombs and resprays his sandy-brown hair, carefully fluffing his hard-to-manage cowlick. His blue-green eyes, silent and self-accusing, stare back from the mirror. After clipping an uneven spot in his brushy mustache, he goes back into the bedroom.

Sharon, still naked on her stomach, hugs her pillow under her in a *Playboy* pose. Jim kisses her good-bye, then gives her a love-pat on her large shapely behind. She squeals girlishly but the grimace that comes with it tells him that she still hates his schedule.

Down the hall to the kitchen. Jim swigs down a half glass of orange juice. No time for coffee. He listens a moment to see if the kids are stirring upstairs but hears nothing except the *pit-pit* of the rain. He pulls on his winter jacket, a brown suede jacket, and exits the side door off the kitchen.

Outside, the drizzly rain feels colder than snow as the wind blows the chilly dampness inside Jim's unzipped coat. Guilt and regret slosh about in his stomach together with postejaculation blahs, but it will take something bigger to free him from the shackles of an overbooked life.

\* \* \*

The old mill town of Brendon Falls lies in the valley to the east nestled in the fog along the Nashua River below the dam. It's still early for a Saturday and the rain-slicked streets are a.most empty. Scores of boxy three-story homes and old rowhouses huddle on the hills against the raw wet morning. Most have been converted to apartments with absentee landlords and low-income tenants.

Scattered northward from the dam, nineteenth-century red-brick smokestacks and peak-roofed mill towers, grim, cold, and lifeless, stand as silent reminders of a bygone industrial era. Only Prescott Paper, on the river below the falls, has an active stack, and the white smoke from their boiler room billows upward over the valley until it merges with the low overcast. The soul of the city sighs wistfully—a sad yearning that falls short of hope. The melancholy is so real that Jim can almost touch it and taste it. Yet over the years of living here, he's grown fond of the old town and feels a strange indefinable kinship with the place.

Bypassing the downtown area, he descends South Meadow Road to the lowlands on the west side. The weathered asphalt, frost-heaved, cracked, chalky gray, looks like wet elephant skin between the low banks of dirty leftover snow. On both sides of the road, black and gnarled oak trees lift their naked arms into the fog as if begging God for an early spring, while smaller swamp maples stand leafless in late-winter humility, a crimson blush just beginning to show on their myriad fingertips.

As Jim drives along, worrisome thoughts pop in his mind, *I'm getting old and fat. I'm almost middle-aged. I must cut out desserts and sugar in my coffee. Oh, I forgot to call Dad. I must call him tonight ... and I must remind Sharon to send Gary Bob a card for his birthday—why? Why so busy? She's right. I'm never home on Saturday. But it's not just Saturday, I'm always straight out.*

# Chapter Two

After passing South Meadow Pond, Pastor Shanley ascends to the high ground surrounding Nashoba Reservoir. He turns east on Reservoir Road and quickly arrives at the church, a white, water-stained, cinder-block structure which was formerly an American Legion hall.

The local congregation bought the building in 1977, along with four acres of land, and the following year added a new wing to accommodate their growing ministry. Behind the church, a mixed forest of pine and hardwoods covers the long ridge line that forms the natural northern boundary to the reservoir. This gives the church a rustic country setting, yet the Hadley Hill residential area is only minutes to the east via Reservoir Road.

Dodging potholes, Pastor Jim coasts into the gravel parking lot and pulls his blue 1980 Mustang to a halt in front of the flagpole—five minutes late but still the first to arrive. Inside the church, a faint odor of nicotine mixed with beer and grease still lingers from the old American Legion bar and lounge. Jim clicks on the heat then marches down the hallway to his office. Buzzing, flickering, strobing fluorescence. As usual, the lights won't stay lit. Giving a snort of irritation, he climbs onto his desk and twists both fluorescent tubes until they're fully illuminated. When he comes down, he finds a letter in his in-box from Dr. Logan:

Thursday, Feb. 17, 1983

To: Rev. James D. Shanley      Ref: Easter-Week Pastors'
     Brendon Falls Bible Church            Conference, LBI Campus,
     Reservoir Road                     Nashua, NH, Mar 29-Apr 2.
     Brendon Falls, MA 01519

Dear Pastor Jim,

     I would like for you to speak at the Wednesday afternoon session of our Easter-Week Pastors' Conference. It would also be a pleasure to have you and your lovely wife, Sharon, join me for lunch before the meeting.

     Your ministry at BFBC is a shining example for all of us. We are so thankful for your dedication to our vision. Please call and confirm this date with Amy.

In His Love,

Charles R. Logan
President,
Logan Bible Institute

The phone interrupts his reading. "Is this Jimmy?" asks a familiar female voice.

"Yes, it is," Jim replies. He feels suddenly uneasy as if someone is staring at him. He looks down the hall but the church is empty.

"This is Alison."

"I thought it was you. I heard you guys were back."

"Yep, got back last month," Alison bubbles in her cheery woman-of-God voice. "Pastor wants Ed to teach Missions this semester. Besides, we needed a break from Puerto Rico. We hear great things about your church, Jim. Pastor always speaks so highly of you."

"Well, I'm not exactly a jungle missionary," Jim jokes as he puts Logan's letter back into his in-box, "but I traveled enough in the Air Force. So, how are you?"

"Couldn't be better. The Lord has blessed above and beyond. We're goin' back, of course, but first we need to raise more support. We're praying with Pastor about a return date. Meanwhile, we're soaking up the fellowship here at home base. God is *so* real here and it's *such* a blessing to hear Pastor in person. Just being in his presence inspires us to love holiness and to hate sin, and to be thankful for the grace of God." Alison presents a gushy evangelical facade, but underneath lurks a Dr. Jekyll and Mr. Hyde, and Jim knows them both—Alison, his old friend, and Alison, the pharisee. "But the reason I called, Jim, is about Rebecca Lea. She's a freshman now, and she has to choose a branch ministry for her evangelism practicum."

"Becki's old enough for Bible college?" Jim asks, as if he doesn't know.

"She started this semester," Alison cackles, like a proud mother hen. "She'll be nineteen next month, and Katie Marie's fifteen. They're beautiful young women now, growing in the Lord."

Jim's hand feels sweaty as he grips the phone. "Been that long, huh?"

"Yep, sure has. We went down in August of '79—anyways, like I said, Becki has to do her weekend branch-ministry training, and she's chosen your church."

Jim's heart races but his voice remains calm, "So when's she gonna start?"

"She should be there in about forty-five minutes."

"She's coming *right* now? This week?" Hot, hot. Jim feels heat rushing up into his face.

"Yep, she's on the way. Joe Lareux picked her up twenty

minutes ago. He says he goes down every weekend."

Chaos, confusion, a flood of possibilities. Jim's thoughts whirl and tumble like clothes in a dryer, *Becki, Becki, coming here. I feel old and fat. She can stay with us—no, Sharon will never go for that. Who's she gonna do outreach with? O God?*

"W-well ... she's not on my schedule," he stammers into the phone. "I got nothing on this from Tom Hudson's office."

"That's why I called. Joe says he's got a church family for her to stay with, but I wanted to make sure you knew."

Jim takes a deep breath; he pretends to regain his poise. "No problem," he assures. "We'll take care of her."

He wants to hang up and calm his racing emotions, but Alison goes on, "So how are Sharon and the kids?"

"Doin' fine. They seem to survive my ridiculous schedule."

"You and Sharon must come over next time you're in Nashua. In fact, I'll expect you for supper at least once during the Easter-Week conference. You can bring the whole crew from your church if you like."

Jim feels like he's stuck in Boston traffic with a plane to catch at Logan Airport, but he manages a congenial response, "Okeydoke, we'll take you up on it. Sounds like fun."

"Oh, Jimmy, one more thing," Alison says, her voice becoming secretive and sanctified as if she just emerged from talking with God in the "holy of holies." Jim realizes some God-told-me bullshit is coming. "I believe Rebecca Lea has a special high calling to be a missionary. God showed me in a dream and Pastor confirms it."

"A calling to follow in your footsteps?" Jim retorts, hiding most of the contempt he feels as he thinks of Alison's wild and sinful ways before she came to Christ.

"Well, not exactly but sort of," Alison adroitly equivocates. "But I hope without the problems and lost years I had to go through to get right with the Lord."

"Well, I guess we can never tell," he replies using a favorite styrofoam statement.

"I fear for Becki since evil is so rampant in the world, and it's hard for a young person to hate sin as God commands. But, Jim, if she's cultivated and taught, especially by example, she could be such a soldier for Christ. That's why it'll be good for her to spend her weekends at your church. You know she's always looked up to you, Jimmy, as a spiritual father. It's been tough for her since Derek and I broke up. She gets along with Ed but it's not the same. But that's old news. No need to stir up negative thoughts."

After Alison says that, they exchange good-byes ending the conversation. Jim hangs up then yells down the empty hallway,

"What the heck are you doing, God? My life's crazy enough. I don't need this, not now!"

He feels overwarm almost feverish; he goes over and opens a window. The sweet piercing scent of wet pine drifts into the office, a cool grayish fragrance of green. The indoor-outdoor thermometer next to the window reads 38°. Jim inhales deeply then closes the window all but a crack. He checks his watch: 8:47 a.m. Saturday prayer-outreach is scheduled for 8:30, but the meeting rarely gets going before 9:15. No amount of pastorly persuasion can get people there on time. If he moves the starting time to 9:15—he's tried it—then everyone comes at 9:45. But he still comes dutifully on time or close to it. Such are the ways of born-again Christians.

As Jim sits down at his desk, he hears the main door open and sees Russell Bradley sauntering down the hallway. Ruddy soft-featured face, toasty Scottish smile, laughing eyes on the gray side of green. Russ, his sweat-stained Red Sox cap pushed back on his head—he looks more like a Boston cabby than a church elder—pokes his head into the office and asks Shanley if he wants a coffee. Jim says yes and Russ retreats to the kitchen. Jim soon hears the coughing and huffing of the church's old electric percolator.

When Russ returns, he places two steaming mugs of coffee on the pullout shelf of Jim's army-surplus desk. The mugs, plain, heavy, and eggshell white, are the institutional kind like you find in a hospital cafeteria. Jim picks up his and takes a long swig. He needs a good shot of caffeine to recharge and refocus his brain after Alison's phone call.

Russ, in a burgundy-and-gray argyle sweater and faded corduroys—his typical attire—slips off his orange hunter's vest, tosses it across onto an ancient Canon copy machine, then plops into Jim's broken recliner which has one arm missing and is stuck in the open position. (The black vinyl LA-Z-BOY once occupied a place in the Shanleys' living room, then the basement TV-room until Sharon threw it out.) Once comfortable, Russ reaches for his cup of coffee, clutches it to his bosom, and inhales deeply.

Jim wants to talk about Alison's call but he's never shared his Becki-feelings with anyone. So he willfully turns his attention to church business, "Well, Russ, you wanna hear about the latest incident at the teen center?"

No response. Russ simply sits there savoring the rich aroma of his coffee. No rush. No sense of urgency. Never in a hurry. Russ Bradley, unlike Shanley, lives like a man with no clocks. He works as a shop foreman at Stromberg Tool & Machine, but he never says much about his job except that he wishes he didn't have to work at all. "Do I have to?" he finally replies fussily, his face twisting into a half grimace. "I'd rather sit back and think about baseball season, and speaking of the Red Sox, did you hear that 'the Eck' may be going on the trading block?"

Jim takes a swig from his mug. "Don't think I did," he replies with half his attention. He normally likes to talk baseball with Russ but on this morning there's little room for the Red Sox in his thoughts.

"But it figures," Russ goes on. "Here's a guy who goes 13-13 on a mediocre team and they want to trade him. That's why the Sox'll never win it all. They don't know how to handle pitchers. Even in '67 and '75, it was the pitching that came up short—but anyway, what's happening with Barry and Leslie?"

"Well, I guess a couple of the teenagers got out of hand last night. At least, Leslie thinks they—"

"Oh, before I forget," Russ interjects, leaning forward for emphasis, "Joe called. He said he's bringing a new girl from the college this—"

"I'm one step ahead of you, Russ," Jim quickly cuts in, almost choking on his coffee as Becki roars back to the front of his mind. "He's bringing Rebecca Reinhardt. Her mom just called." Jim coughs. He's stirred, ready to go on, but he pauses to swallow and clear his throat.

"Anyway," Russ elaborates, "Joe says she'll be coming the usual six weekends to get her credits. He asked if Bev and I could put her up. He said he would stay with the Bufords this—"

"I've known Becki since she was a kid," Jim interrupts again, toasting the air with his mug. "I went to Bible school with her mom and her stepfather. You know, Alison and Ed Landreth?"

"Oh, the missionaries that come to raise money every year or so, and we send 'em fifty bucks a month?"

"That's them," Jim affirms. He pushes his desk chair back a bit as if he needs more room to vent his anxious feelings but his words do not convey the true reason for his anxiety. "Alison says Becki has a special call from God—wishful thinking. She sounds just like Logan. They think these kids get a calling by osmosis. They enroll at LBI, profess allegiance to Logan's vision, and visit branch churches on weekends. It's so much bullcrap! None of 'em ever like it here except Joe and he's different. He's more like us. Becki won't stay long. She'll be gone in three weeks I bet."

"No reason to get worked up," Russ replies. "I agree. Logan's training program *is* bullshit. I've been saying that for three years, but it's no big deal. We have students down all the time. Bev and I will take care of her. You don't have to get involved at all."

Hot emotion rises into Jim's face. "My schedule's already so bleepin' tight. Any new thing makes me feel like I'm drowning. Becki's a sweet kid, least she was four years ago, but I can't make a missionary out of her."

"Okay, okay; why the hell are you in such a lather? I said I'd take care of it." Russ seems to realize that Becki is more than a scheduling problem, but he does not dig. Instead, he settles back into the recliner, sucks on his coffee, then backtracks to the teen ministry, "Now what about Leslie and the teenagers?"

Jim, upset with himself for being so affected by Becki, doesn't reply but swings his chair away from Russ and gazes out into the gray morning. The muted rumble of a Boston & Maine freight train invades the office, through the open window, as it creaks slowly westward on its daily trip along the reservoir. The engine whines while the cars jerk along, their flanged wheels screaking on the rusty rails. The fog, the gloom, the drip-drip of the rain soften the sound as if the train is a memory—a memory that soothes Jim's spirit as it takes him back to Texas, back to the old Missouri Pacific depot in Longview where his dad took him to see the *Eagle* on its way to Houston; the *Eagle* didn't stop in his hometown of Gilmer. Only freight trains came to Gilmer, often pulled by steam locomotives. He liked the steam engines the best. Terrible black behemoths they were, huffing, chuffing, hissing. But the grimy-faced engineers smiled and tossed Tootsie Rolls to the kids.

As the rumble of the train fades into the distance, Jim rotates his chair back toward Russ, takes a drink of coffee, then says, "I guess Leslie's really pissed this time. You know how women overreact, and especially Leslie. You should've heard her when she called last night: 'Pastor, I need help. The devil's taking over, and Barry's not here. I just caught Kevin kissing Cathy in the toolshed, and her *bra* was off. Pastor, she's so young. This is a disgrace, a dis*gusting* disgrace to God.'"

Russ laughs and Jim too. "But she's ticked," Jim elaborates. "She wants tighter rules, like no more walks in the picnic area, and no more tight jeans or low-cut shirts, and she wants Kevin banned altogether. She's gonna talk to Stan, and she says she'll quit if we don't adopt her new policies."

Russ places his coffee on the desk, then takes off his hat and runs his callused yet delicate hands through his burnt-auburn hair. He gives an omniscient smile and says, "Tight, tight ... that word fits Leslie perfectly. She's so tight, it would take a year of foreplay to loosen her up, but there's not a man around with *that* kind of patience, certainly not Gerald; she castrated him long ago." They both laugh again.

"You got that right," Jim agrees gesturing with his cup. "I feel sorry for Jerry. Not that she's ugly—she is sort of with her froggy eyes and flat chest—but it's more like her soul's on ice. We've got some nice warm gals in this church who I wouldn't mind crawling under the covers with, least in my fantasies, but Leslie wouldn't turn me on if she danced *naked* on my desk." Jim says *"neckid."*

This sets off another round of snickers and snorts. The ribald jesting releases the rest of Jim's anxiety over Alison's call—at least for the moment. He wouldn't dare joke in such an off-color manner with anyone but Russ with whom he takes off his "pastor" mask, yet he still hides the deeper secrets of his heart.

"But this does present a problem," Jim says after sobering. "Stan's been wanting a crackdown ever since he caught Haley smoking pot on the tracks out back, and what about Friday night chaperone if Leslie quits?" Russ replaces his cap and clears his throat but says nothing. "So whaddeya think?" Jim prods, patting his forehead to make sure his cowlick is in place.

Russ still doesn't reply but sits up on the side of the recliner. His paunchy belly rolls out over his belt as if he has a half-inflated beach ball under his sweater. He crosses his legs ankle-on-knee. He fiddles with the cuff of his corduroy trousers, then with the laces of his sneakers. "What the heck are you doing, Russ?" Jim asks with growing impatience though his tone is still good-natured. "I can't spend all day watching you sit there in a trance."

Seemingly unaffected by Jim's prodding, Russ hauls himself slowly to his feet, picks up his mug, and gulps the last of his coffee. He lazily pats his paunch and looks down at Jim with a squinting bemused smile. "You want my advice, Jim? Well, I think we should do nothing, absolutely nothing. This will pass soon enough, even if Stan does go on one of his crusades. Let's face it; no amount of rules will stop teenagers, or adults, from kissing and petting. Love and passion are too far beyond us to even comprehend, much less control."

"That's easy enough to say," Jim rebuts, now becoming a bit aggravated by Russ's laissez-faire attitude. "If it was up to you, we wouldn't even have leaders in this church, much less leadership. But I don't trust God that much. Besides, everybody expects me to take action. You don't catch the heat like I do. This could really set Stan off. You know how he feels about teenagers fooling around? He'll have all the parents in an uproar."

"Well, that's how I see it," Russ maintains. "If you have a good plan that'll stop boys from kissing and fondling girls, then by all means implement it."

No rebuttal. Despite his annoyance, Jim knows that Russ's right. "Okay, we'll let it ride, but what about Leslie?"

No response. Russ takes his empty mug and heads out of the office. But as new voices sound down the hall, he leans back in, an impish twinkle in his eyes, a wry leprechaun grin on his lips. "You know, Jim; I bet Leslie wishes *she* was in the toolshed with a secret lover. Of course, she'd never admit it." Russ laughs.

"Come on, Russ; you're no help." But Jim grins in spite of himself.

Russ sobers. "No, seriously, Jim, even though Leslie acts cold and we make fun, I think she loves the kids, in her own way, and she gets a charge out of being a chaperone. She'll never quit, so just let it be, Jim. Let it be." After saying that, Russ turns and strolls lazily to the kitchen.

Jim gets up, closes the door, then goes over to the windows, his favorite spot when in his office—but not for long, as a firm double knock sends him back to his desk; he knows it's Stan Campbell, his head elder. Jim tells him to come in. Campbell pulls up a straight-backed wooden chair and sits down in front of the desk. He smells of Aqua Velva and fuel oil. His boots are covered with grime from his job at Prescott Paper. "So how's it going at the mill?" Jim asks.

Stan gives a proud union-boss grin. "Well, Pastor Jim, if I can jus' get the guys to hol' the line, we're gonna get a good raise this go roun'. The white collars are usin' the carrot 'steada the stick. They're offerin' some 'ticin' 'centives, but no way is it our fair share." As always, Stan butchers the English language yet he speaks in a huge authoritative voice which goes with his huge authoritative body. He's an oak of a man, and his massive frame overwhelms Jim's small office as Abraham Lincoln's statue over-whelms the Lincoln Memorial. At forty-seven, Stan Campbell, despite his ineloquence and blue-collar background, still commands and intimidates every scene he enters.

"So you have the '82 growth report?" Jim asks, turning to church business.

Stan's proud grin gives way to fawning soberness, his usual attitude around Pastor Jim. "I jus' gotta bring it to Angela so she can type it an' correct my spellin'. I'm good at 'rithmitic but spellin', I never took it ser'ous at school like I shoulda. But we're growin' each month an' souls are gettin' saved. God's honorin' our faith."

Stan sits erect like a soldier, like an eager servant, but with wild gray hair, a rugged rocklike face, and an aura of holy authority, he could pass for Moses, especially with his Charlton Heston physique. But Jim never confuses him with Moses. Though Campbell's outward behavior always conforms to the Bible and evangelical norms, Jim sees through his self-righteousness zeal. Moreover, he knows too much about Stan's home life to ever call him a prophet or a saint. Nonetheless, Stan's soldierly dedication to the church and to Dr. Logan's worldwide vision makes Jim feel guilty about his own waning religious fervor—whereas Russ Bradley makes him feel good about his growing disenchantment with evangelical Christianity.

"But, Pastor Jim, the devil's not givin' up," Stan declares as he knits his bushy pepper-colored eyebrows and squints out into the gray morning. "In fac', I gotta 'lert you to a dangerous trend that's developin'." Concern clouds his rugged face as if he's a cavalry commander who just spotted Indians on a far ridge line.

"So you talked with Leslie?" Jim replies, presuming the problem.

"She called, but that's jus' parta what I'm seein'."

"So what else are you seeing?"

Stan turns back toward Pastor Jim and looks right at him. Deep-set dark eyes, deep-set and blue. Dark sapphires embedded well back in a craggy cliff. Jim has often searched these blue eyes for friendship, for longing. Sometimes he sees a glimmer of warmth, a glimpse of a little boy, but when he pursues it, he always runs into an intimidating cold wall.

Stan reaches up with his Goliath-like hand and pulls down on his jaw as if trying to drag his weathered cheeks off the end of his dimpled chin. His sharp-featured face looks like it was carved from an outcropping of pale granite giving him a rock-hard handsomeness which has not softened with middle-age. Finally, he answers Jim's question, "It's more what adults are doin'—not so much doin', but what they 'peer to be doin'. The Bible says in Thess'lonins 'to 'void all 'peerances of evil.' That's what I'm uh seein'. I'm seein' the 'peerances of evil."

"Whaddeya getting at?" Jim asks. He realizes that Stan's on a crusade of some sort.

"You know the verse, Pastor Jim, the one that says the devil is a roarin' lion?"

"That's 1st Peter 5:8," Jim answers crisply. "'The devil, like a roaring lion walketh about seeking whom he may devour.'"

Stan grins with delight at Shanley's mastery of the Bible then goes on. He gestures with uplifted hands as if he's shooting a basketball. "It's like this, Pastor. Lucifer wants to keep new b'lievers worldly so they won't never be soldiers. If we want teenagers an' new Christians to grow into soul-winners, we hafta set a stan'ard of righ'chiness. We hafta set the sample. If they see 'peerances of evil 'mong the reg'lars, it tempts 'em jus' as much as real sin 'cuz of evil 'maginin' ... an' I'm noticin' lots of poor samples from folks who know better."

"Like what?" Jim queries, drumming the desktop with a ball-point pen. He feels strong conviction contrary to Stan's but he suppresses it.

Campbell motions, a broad sweep of his brawny pythonlike arm, as if he's on Mt. Sinai looking down at a multitude of sinful souls. Setting his face like iron and narrowing his eyes, he lifts his nose as if he's sniffing. "I'm seein' lots of reg'lars, 'specially women, sittin' in cars out front, smokin', listenin' to rock music, an' gossipin'." Stan never ignores sin in the camp; when he picks up the scent of iniquity, he becomes merciless and cold with a "Book 'em, Danno," spirit like Jack Lord from *Hawaii Five-0*. If Stan were there in John Chapter Eight when the Pharisees brought the adulterous woman to Jesus, he would've surely cast the first stone. "Now, if it was jus' babes in Christ or Spanics, I could understand, but I'm seein' reg'lars like Jodi 'n Janet 'n Sylvia ... 'n the Black gym teacher, uh ... Tony Liggons."

Stan hugs his massive chest revealing, on his right bicep, a death's-head skull clenching a bloody pirate dagger between its teeth. The hideous scarlet-and-blue tattoo is half hidden under his short-sleeved madras shirt—he wears short sleeves all year as if to show that cold does not affect him. He shrugs off the tattoo as a reminder of his worldly past, as something he picked up in the Navy, but Jim thinks he's proud of it because during softball season Stan rolls his sleeve so everyone can see it.

"Not that cig'rettes 'n rock music mean nuthin'," Campbell goes on, "but it's a first step. It lets in demons of lust that tempt an' draw 'em back, back to movies 'n gossip 'n flirtin' an' havin' a beer or two, an' missin' church to follow their selfish ways. An' lust will root deeper 'n deeper 'til they fall into fornicatin'. It's the 'ception of Lucifer, an' he's got a few already. I'm not mentionin' names, but I hear the scuttlebutt."

Inflating with righteous indignation, Stan speaks more vehe-mently, rolling his huge hands in front of him. "I know, Pastor Jim, 'cuz I walked many a day in the devil's power 'til I got saved. Lucifer's crafty. He lurks in darkness. He rules the night jus' like the Viet Cong, ambushin' an' deceivin'. If Satan brings down our reg'lars, who's gonna train the troops? Who's gonna win the lost an' save 'em from hell? The stakes are high in this war!" Stan served two tours on a PT boat on the Mekong River, and he often compares spiritual warfare with the war in Vietnam; the degree of success is certainly the same.

Jim doodles on a legal pad in front of him. "So you think this's why the kids were kissing in the toolshed?" he asks. While awaiting a reply, he silently reminds himself that Campbell is the last person on earth to ask about kissing.

Stan scrubs his wooly head with his knuckles. There's still a hint of auburn in his prematurely gray locks. The back of his thick work-roughened hand is dappled with large freckles. He has smaller freckles on his arms but only a few on his face. "Well, Pastor Jim," he replies, "when they see reg'lars flirtin' an' bein' suggestive, an' married men goin' for coffee with young flirts, it's jus' no good. It's not Bible. We gotta be careful, startin' with 'peerances. No wonder we got 'bellus behavior at the teen center."

"So whaddeya wanna do, Stan?" Jim asks.

Stan fawns with sudden deep humility like Uriah Heep before Mr. Wickfield. "It's not my place to set up no battle strategy. God speaks to you, Pastor. I'm jus' here to obey the orders that come down from the Lord."

"But you must have ideas to share with me?" Jim prods, still doodling.

"Well, if you insist," Stan responds, his aroused ego showing through his facade of humility like an erect penis in tight pants. "I got a plan that'll 'tack the devil, an' defeat him." He gestures fervently but awkwardly, his huge hands hacking the air with herky-jerky Frankensteinian movements. "We need hard messages from the pulpit to make us hate sin and evil 'peerances. We need special classes on the docturns of holiness 'specially 'bout the husband bein' the head of the wife. We need docturns that'll make us sober 'n serious, that'll cleanse us of loose flirtin' spirits of lust! An' we need fervent prayer to bind the demons, to 'lease the angels ... so we can *win* this war!" Stan's eyes burn with pious indignation. He seems ready to preach all morning but he checks himself, sits back, and waits for Pastor Jim to reply.

"Sounds good," Jim lies. "Why don't you develop your plan with specifics and bring it to staff meeting tomorrow night." He knows that Stan's fervor will wilt when it comes to writing his proposal.

"I'll get right on it," Stan replies eagerly as he hoists his Buyanesque body out of the chair. "But, Pastor Jim, forgive me for persistin', but you can start this fight right now from the pulpit. Jesus loves us an' died for us but we gotta 'cept his Word an' act on it. We mus' warn the flock or we'll surely get his heavy hand of chastiment.... And we can start prayin' about it this morning, soon as I move the chairs in."

Stan shakes Jim's hand then executes an about-face, strides out of the office, and cuts a quick left into the new wing.

Jim goes the other way, down the main hallway, and pushes open the swinging door into the kitchen, now alive with laughter and the aroma of coffee and glazed donuts. Barry Buford, Angela Thornton, and Jodi Donovan are seated at the table, while Russ and Sylvia Cahill lean against the counter.

Jim jokes with them in an exaggerated Texas dialect—he does have a Texas drawl but eighteen years living outside of Texas has diminished it somewhat—and he adds some Old South Negro for effect, "Whatch yawl doin' in heah? We done had the meetin' ... an' awh reckon yawl done missed ever'thang. Yahssir, we is finished an' yawl done missed it."

"Whatcha mean *we*?" mocks Jodi D. "*We* is awl right heah."

"Awh declawer, Jodi," Jim teases. "Yuh cain't getah nuf canyuh? Can yawl mahgin' it? She's uh taychin' heah awl week an' then sure-a-nuf she's back heah on Sadahday fah mower."

"After spending five days with 1st- and 2nd-graders," Jodi retorts, dropping her mock drawl, "I need to see some adult faces. Maybe I'll see some on visitation?"

A chorus of boos erupt from the gathering as Barry Buford teases back, "That makes us the greatest in the kingdom, Jodi. Thanks for the compliment."

Back and forth they banter. Jim senses the unspoken bond of love that he often feels when they simply have fun and forget themselves—and their mission. But the feeling ends abruptly as the kitchen door swings open. Stan announces that it's twenty after and time to start; everyone marches out and heads for the new wing.

Jodi, the last to leave, looks at Jim with yearning eyes as if she wants to tell him something but she doesn't. Instead, she clears the table, placing the coffee mugs on the counter and tossing the empty donut bag into the trash, and follows the others. As she departs, Jim tells her that he'll be right down—to wait for him.

He wonders about Jodi, but the thought is quickly washed away as the realization of Becki's imminent arrival roars back into his mind like a West Texas flash flood.

# Chapter Three

As Jim comes out of the kitchen, the main door opens down the hall: Joe Lareux, a short pouty-faced brunette. Becki, Becki, in a gray ski jacket. Eyes down, she follows Joe into the church.

Jim's heart pounds; he feels awkward and nervous. He pulls in his gut. As she comes closer, he notices a white *Pink Floyd* sweat shirt under her unzipped coat.

"Pastor, I brought your old buddy with me," Joe explains, presenting Rebecca to Jim. "She says she used to hang around with you before this church was even here."

Shy grin, dimples. Becki looks up, but when her eyes meet Jim's, she quickly averts them. Hips canted, she rests her arm on a faded black-denim shoulder bag, gripping the strap like a paratrooper. Also like a paratrooper, she wears boots but not the black military kind. They're scuffy brown Timberlands. Jim knows they're Timberland boots because he wears Timberlands himself, and he was with her when she bought hers five years ago.

Becki's chocolate-colored hair is chin-length just reaching the collar of her jacket. She looks older to Jim but she still has the ruddy glow of high school in her cherub face. "Long time no see," he says as he shakes her hand. He uses a convenient cliché to mask his uneasiness. "Guess we had some fun times in the old days, huh?"

"Yeah, I remember," Becki replies. "You always came over to see Mom 'n Ed but ended up helping me with my homework so we could play Atari pinball. You could beat Mom 'n Ed, and Katie, but you never beat me. I was wicked good." Her grin broadens, showing her crooked teeth, but she continues to avert her eyes. Her voice is velvety soft with a moist undertone, still girlish, though a bit thicker than before. She's also slightly taller and more fully filled out, not fat but tending toward chunky.

"Y-you've ... you've grown up," Jim stammers fumbling for words as his spirit gropes for solid ground. "You look like your mom now."

"Everybody says that," she quips. "I'm just younger and cuter, that's all."

Rebecca seems just as offbeat and cocky as ever, and she *is* cute—when animated and playful—yet she's hardly a candidate for homecoming queen, or Miss Congeniality. Oval face, snub nose, cupid mouth, chubby cheeks, naturally frowny countenance. Her prettiness is utterly commonplace—except for her big blue eyes. The rings about her pupils are liquid azure like sunny January sky, giving her eyes an unfathomable, enchanting quality, particu-

18

larly against her fair skin, dark eyebrows, and brown bangs.

Despite her flaws, Jim sees her as adorable. He wants to hug her but he doesn't dare. Instead, he says, "How d'you like college? Better than high school?"

Becki drops back into a slight frown; she doesn't seem thrilled with the checklist questions. Nonetheless, she answers politely without revealing herself, "I'm glad to be home 'cause Puerto Rico is the pits. But college seems mostly like a lot of work so far."

She nervously fidgets her feet, moving her left boot backward then forward into her right instep; then shifting her weight, she sketches a square on the carpet with the toe of her right boot. She performs this routine twice in quick succession.

Jim recognizes this cute adolescent gesture—he's seen her nervous foot-shuffle many times—as an indication that she's impatient, or ill at ease, or both. So he quickly concludes the conversation, "Anyway, kiddo, welcome to Brendon Falls. It's good to have you with us." He doesn't know if he's lying or not. Normally, he knows when he's lying.

Turning to Joe, Jim says, "Take her on down to prayer meeting. I'll be there in a few."

Joe and Becki head down the hall and hang a right into the new wing, Joe in front, she behind him, her low-hung womanly buttocks shifting from side to side in her washed-out blue jeans. On first impression, Becki gives no hint of the missionary calling Alison talked about. Jim is glad.

He escapes into the men's room, into the ammoniac smell of urine and industrial cleanser. Exhilaration, fever, butterflies. His thoughts race, *I can hardly believe this. I wonder what she's thinking. Having her around after four years is so different—it's almost scary. I wonder if I seem old to her.*

But after flushing the urinal, Jim willfully pushes her to the back of his mind and heads to the prayer meeting where he joins the others who are seated around a large conference table.

They hold hands and bow their heads. Pastor Jim starts, "Dear Lord Jesus, bless everything we're doing this weekend. Bless our outreach teams today, and bless our Sunday school program tomorrow. And, God, I guess you know we're desperately dependent on you." Jim's prayer is superficial, save for the last sentence which issues from his heart.

Then Barry, in a corpulent voice, "O Father in heaven, there are so many lost souls in this town. Help us share the gospel with them that they might accept Christ and be saved. O Father, keep us ever mindful of the reality of hell and the certain condemnation of every person who rejects your son."

Next a high-pitched reedy voice, Angela Thornton: "Dear Jesus, please watch over the marriages in this body. Keep our families together. O Jesus, touch all the unsaved husbands. Help the women to be faithful wives and godly testimonies in their homes, and bless all the children."

After Angela, silence. Jim doesn't feel like praying again so he waits and listens to the buglike buzzing of the fluorescent lights—all at once, thunder: "Aw'mighty God 'n Father we come to you as humble soldiers on your battlefield." Stan's unmistakable voice booms out. "Dear Lord, we ask you to send your holy angels to mount a 'tack 'gainst Lucifer's latest 'ceptions 'n 'vices—"

Stan drones on. Jim thinks about Becki. But his thoughts race toward forbidden territory, so he forces his mind to focus on other things, *I can't stand these meetings anymore. I share my feelings with God but group prayer out loud, it bores me to death. Yet this is Logan's war cry—pray for finances, souls, growth, missionary teams ... like God's waiting up there and He doesn't make a move until He hears our petitions. If that's how He runs the universe, we're all in deep shit—I feel blah. Sex in the morning, it drains me. Sharon's like a cat in heat since she got her tubes tied—bet I know what Russ's thinking, "Wish this meeting was over so we can go to McD's for breakfast," or he's checking out Sylvia's thighs.*

*Syl does give a nice shape to those green cords—and Angie? I can't figure her. One day she's like Leslie, hating sin and praying for marriages, and the next, she's free-spirited and flirty like a spring nymph—what's bugging Jodi? I've always wanted to know her but we never really talk, we just kid around—and Barry? He's so boyish yet hidden, and Stan controls him like a father. Janet's so different. I still can't believe she married Barry. Sharon says he's—but who knows?*

Jim looks up at the clock on the wall. It says 9:37 a.m. The old office clock is large, round, and brown, and across the face is the word "Lathem" in script writing. The red second hand is stuck at seven, stuck at thirty-five seconds into the minute; it quivers and jerks but proceeds no further.

Stan finishes. Angela begins again. Sleepiness fills the room. Russ nods. Jodi's face is almost on the table. Drowsy, drowsy. Jim feels it too. He can no longer keep Rebecca out of his mind. He lifts his head and looks at her as she sits directly across the table, head bowed, her soft maiden face half hidden under her feathered helmet of hair. *What's she doing here? Can't be Alison's missionary fantasy, or can it? Look at her sitting there with her head humbly bowed, but she won't pray out loud. She'll never play this game. I wonder if she's still a virgin. I shouldn't think such thoughts, but most missionary brats have their panties off by nineteen but then again, she's different. She's always been different, like a wild rose in a garden of clones. Any girl who wears boots and Pink Floyd into church is not following a crowd, good or bad.*

Heavy eyelids. Jim is falling asleep, or is he? *Look at her, so demure, a picture of peace, so adorable, so innocent, yet so ripe and inviting, so—*

Without warning, Becki looks up and gives Jim a devilish half-grin, as if she knows everything he's thinking. Naked, naked. He feels utterly exposed as if she's reached over and pulled a rip cord that released his clothes. Jim quickly bows his head and pretends to pray; shame burns his face. But Becki's eyes, her sky-blue eyes. *O Lord, I feel her eyes. She's staring at me.*

It's Jim's recurring nightmare. He's sitting nude next to his pulpit on Sunday morning. Everyone's pointing and laughing at his chalky-pale skin, his knobby knees, his hairless chest, his potbelly, his timid little penis cringing between his legs. His nightmare is coming true, but this time it's Becki who's laughing and pointing at his ugliness.

Yet in the midst of his shame, Jim senses her eyes beckoning. He doesn't want to look at her. He wants to stay down, look away, look anywhere, but Becki draws him with an irresistible, enchanting call, like a Siren's song.

Too much. He gives himself to her eyes, to those purling pools of liquid blue. He plunges into her depths. Swirling azure gives way to murky fog. Time ceases. Space flees away. The others, the table, the room, the world recede into a ghostly ethereal setting.

Suddenly, monsters! Horned Neanderthal heads, bull-like bodies. Two dreadful Minotaur-like creatures, dark fire-breathing specters in the murk. Jim watches with fear and awe as the two monsters wrestle and snort like lovers nearing climax. Blood, blood: the smaller monster thrusts with its horns and gores the larger. Crimson life pours out turning the fog into a red mist. The wounded Minotaur moans and staggers in seeming disbelief then topples to the ground. A fiery sword comes up out of the bleeding wound. The victor stares at it then falls upon it, and they both fade from view.

Now the bloody cloud becomes a "horror of darkness" and thickens around Jim as if he's fallen into the bowels of hell. He sees nothing. He waits a thousand years—or so it seems.

Finally, light, and color. Misty pink, cerulean blue, caramel-brown. Becki's dreamlike face, like a blooming flower, reappears extinguishing the rufescent murk. Jim takes her hand and they frolic in a beautiful meadow at the edge of a great forest. A spring zephyr whispers through the trees kissing their faces. The air is filled with the sweet fragrances of honeysuckle and lilacs. Jim is still naked but his shame has fled away; he feels as if he has the body of Adonis. Becki smiles then melts tenderly into his arms. She purrs with happiness. Heaven has come down.

Warm, sunny, blue above—but not for long. Strobes of lightning, crashes of thunder, black clouds, screams of wind! A violent storm blows up about them. Electricity charges the air. Flying creatures, primeval creatures, fierce and foreboding like great pterodactyls, soar overhead under vaulted ice-crystal towers. A bolt of lightning ignites a bush at the edge of the forest. Jim and Becki flee to the safety of this fire.

Chemistry. Chemistry. Hot vibes, and magic. Rebecca's *Pink Floyd* sweat shirt lifts magically from her and becomes an angelic rock band playing a sexy blues beat. Then the rest of her clothes melt away, and her chunky body begins to writhe to the rhythm— ever so slightly at first then more vigorously until her girlish breasts bounce to the raunchy tempo.

In the midst of this second darkness, in the midst of tempest and danger, Jim is again swept into Becki's eyes, and into her dance. They shimmy and shake about the fire. They move as one yet apart until hot phallic life breaks loose between them and her cupid face grimaces in sweet agony. The music climaxes with them, then shifts to a pulsing primal rhythm—like rap music.

Suddenly, Russ and Sylvia and the others are back: phantom faces, naked bodies, gyrating in Bacchic frenzy about the burning bush. All are back except Stan who cowers nearby among the trees, a hoary-headed ogre lurking in the shadows.

Finally, the conference room comes back into focus. Jim feels faraway. He hears a voice praying, a distant distorted echo, as if he's underwater. *What the hell was that?* he exclaims to himself. *I must've drifted off. It was like a fairy-tale nightmare, so terrible yet beautiful. A heavenly hug then sex with our eyes. Is that possible? But more than sex, she loved me, she knew me. I danced in her eyes—stop it! This isn't right. It's obscene and perverted. Besides, she didn't feel it. She couldn't have? Maybe she did look up at me but the rest is fantasy. This is not good. This is way too sexual. I can't think of her like this. O God, this is—*Jim suddenly realizes that everyone is watching him as he speaks in a mumbling whisper, like a drunk slurring in his beer, just loud enough to be heard but not understood. His senses recovered, he quickly closes the prayer meeting with a canned benediction.

"For a moment there, Jim, we thought you'd lost it," Jodi kids as everyone stretches and yawns. "Sounded like you were speaking in tongues or something. What'd you have in your coffee this morning anyways?"

Jim banters back, "It's the anointing of the Holy Spirit which you don't have, Jodi. It comes down only on prophets and kings." He doesn't dare tell her the real reason for his drunkenness. If he did, she'd know for sure that he'd lost it.

Laughs and chuckles ripple about the table, but briefly as everyone is restless to leave like schoolkids waiting for the bell. Jim hears Becki snicker with the others but dares not look at her again. Instead, he gets down to business and assigns outreach teams, and gives out the names of the Sunday school parents. Everybody then files out of the room. Rebecca leaves with Russ.

# Chapter Four

Dancing sunshine, dancing on the window sill, dancing on the desk. It calls to Pastor Jim, as does the frisky wind playing among the pine trees outside his office windows. Out of his wing tips into his sneakers. He sheds his coat and tie, dons his parka, and heads out the back entrance and across the picnic area. The pine-needle carpet is spongy and wet underfoot with a few lingering patches of melting snow. Despite a chilly edge to the wind, which has blown Saturday's rain out to sea, the morning feels more like April than February. As usual, Jim arrived at the church early to finish his Sunday message—often a wasted effort because he frequently changes his sermon as he stands at the pulpit.

Winter deadfall decorates the picnic tables and cooking pit. Jim strips a pine branch then, with a sharp *crack*, snaps off the end to make a walking stick. At the south boundary of the church property, he crosses a crumbling stone fence and descends to the black cinder muck of the B&M right-of-way. The rusting branchline coils eastward: a giant steel serpent cutting through the granite slope to reach the high trestle that spans the Nashua River north of the dam. A rotting shrub-choked sidetrack parallels the main track halfway to the river. Grimy ballast, diesel smoke, ties soaked in creosote. Jim inhales the familiar railroad smells as he crosses the tracks and, using his stick, climbs the slippery slush-covered embankment which overlooks the reservoir. A pallid sheet of late-winter ice covers the state-owned lake but sunshine and underwater currents have opened a narrow channel along the rocky north shore. Under the brilliant cloudless sky, the water in the channel looks dark green except near the rocks where swirling gusts of wind send transient wavelets and bursts of ripples racing to and fro, creating an excited mosaic of sparkling color, yellows, greens, violets, blues, mixing, reflecting. The sunny colors flicker and vibrate like the shimmering foreground in a Monet painting.

Jim goes down a rough trail, through scattered pines, oaks, and birch clusters, to a narrow gravel beach. To the east, piles of granite stone form the mile-long north dike. The large rocks were blasted out of the ridge eighty years ago to make way for the dam, the sluice, and the railroad cut. The beach is at the west end of the dike where it merges with the natural steep slope to the west. After pulling a few cockleburrs from the cuffs of his dress pants, Jim drops his pine staff, picks up some rocks, and casts them one at a time on a low trajectory into the lake. Each skips several times; one even skips onto the ice. Finally, he retires to his favorite spot: the west end of the beach where a large oak has toppled across into the water.

Jim sits down on the knee-high trunk of the dead tree and soaks up the sun until rustling sounds in the underbrush to his left draw his attention. A gray squirrel, her bushy tail quivering instant with life, scurries about gathering her previously hidden breakfast. Now comes squawking from overhead. Fluttering plumage, flitting color. Violet, blue, gray, and black. A pair of bluejays jump about in the branches of a large maple tree taunting the squirrel with raucous squawks of *jay-jay* and melodic cries of *kweedle-kweedle*. The jays jauntily cock their crested heads up and down, taunting, teasing, as if they're old friends with the squirrel. The squirrel, sitting up, chatters back at the birds then rushes to a new spot and does the same. They seem to be having fun.

A carefree sense of abandon takes the reins of Jim's soul. Nature is alive about him, breathing, pulsing, teeming: the animals, the trees, the sky, the water, the wind—all of creation. No more Sunday, no more February. A feeling of tranquility and transcendent awareness sweeps him across the horizon into the beyond. But his peace is short-lived, for the creation also opens a door within, into the mystery of "Jim Shanley." A paradox but true. If he goes far enough over the horizon, he ends up inside of himself, as in Joseph Campbell's *Inner Reaches of Outer Space.*

*Becki, Becki, why are you here in my private place?* Jim asks as he opens this door into his deepest self. *It's dangerous for you to come here. This is my place of yearning. You shouldn't be here looking down into my soul, into its unexplored depths, into dreams and fairy tales that can never come true. Why do you invade my intimacy? Go away! We can't be "buddies" anymore. I knew when you were fourteen. Go away! You're no longer a little girl in pigtails and Disney T-shirts. It's good that you went to Puerto Rico. We both dodged a bullet. But now it's worse because you've grown into a woman. I see your seductive smile and the soft glow of your ripe young body. I see your ready hips and your upturned breasts. I sense your dirty-sweet hunger for discovery and arousal, and erotic release. You're now just another chapter in my insatiable sexual imagination. We've never touched, but you must go before we do. Forget the past. You're bad for me. You make me have sinful fantasies. I love Sharon—all else is confusion.*

Self-condemnation, like a giant hand reaching out from the church, grips Jim's conscience. He feels fearful, anxious. Clouds, clouds, no more blue. Ranks of clouds invade the sky, fleecy whiteness boiling and billowing over violets and grays. They chase the sun as if God is displaying Jim's inner turmoil in the heavens. Sinister shadows skim over the empty beach. A chill burst of wind buffets his soul. He shudders and pulls his parka around him. He retreats inside the hood as his heart contracts in like manner within his bosom.

He huddles on the darkening beach like a hooded monk until the cold forces him to move. He gets up and throws more rocks into the now-black water—none skip. *But why can't we be close? I was always drawn to her, to her tempestuous spirit, to her shy vulnerability, to her affection for animals, to her distance from people, to her quiet aura of sadness, to her rebellious resistance to Alison's arbitrary rules. True, she was a brat at times and mean to me, but I saw through her petulance, her insolence. I cherished her as a wonderfully strange little girl, but yesterday was so disturbing, so terrible, yet so beautiful and irresistible. Must I flee these thoughts? Oh, how I want to think them, again and again—BUT IT'S WRONG! This is not God! It's twisted and sick. It's my flesh. It's sin! SIN! SIN! SIN! Jesus would never dance with us. He didn't make a place for this. The Bible leaves no doubt: Flee fornication! Flee youthful lusts! Thou shalt not commit adultery!*

He agonizes. He paces. He kicks the gravel. *Jim, you're a putrid excuse for a Christian, much less a pastor. You're in the flesh. Lust rules your mind. You say the right things. You pretend to be devoted, but your thoughts are filthy and foul. You've forsaken the Word of God. If people knew how fucked up you are, the church would empty in five minutes. If Stan knew, or Logan, they'd strip you of command. If Sharon knew, she'd claw your eyeballs out, and if Becki could read your perverted mind, she wouldn't set foot around here. You're such a phony. Who are you to counsel people about God when you can't even control your own lust?*

Exhausted, numb, drained: Jim feels like an escaped convict who has run with his ball and chain before the baying bloodhounds until he can run no more. He slumps back down on the oak tree and stares at the expanse of water and ice before him. A skein of Canadian geese honk overhead and splash down in the open channel. Snowy breasts, smoky backs, long black necks, white cheeks. They look like ushers from a lost wedding party.

*I wish I was like the geese, free to fly on the wind, and to go with my instincts. They never feel guilty and agonize over trying to do the right thing.* But Jim is too tired to hold onto the wish. Instead, he quietly surrenders to reason and reality as they cuff him and lead him back to the safe-and-secure prison of duty, honor, and godly sobriety. *Why am I so torn up over nothing? This is all in my imagination. Becki doesn't want me. This is insane! I've been out of control for 24 hours over a daydream—let go! Let it pass! Let her work with Russ. Love her as a daughter only—from a distance. Think on Sharon and the kids. Concentrate on ministry goals. Becki will be gone in a few weeks. Stop feeding this fantasy!*

Jim's anxiety slowly dissipates, giving way to a resigned peace. His 24-hour Becki-frenzy is over. Oh, she's still there, a thorn in his mind, a fantasy in his heart, but now he has a plan, a resolved Bible-based policy, to deal with her. He's back on top—in control. The day is sunny and pleasant once more. He unzips his parka and pushes the hood back.

He sighs and thinks back to a simpler time when all his days were sunny. He sees a dusty road stretching like a long red scar through the East Texas countryside, through piney woods and cow pastures. The August heat is like a sauna bath. A buzzard scrolls the thermals overhead. The smell of cow manure and fresh-mowed hay hangs in the sultry air along with the buzz of summer insects.

Jim pictures a white farmhouse set back from the road amid the pines. It has a gray roof and red chimney and a porch that rests on cinder blocks. A blue Chevy pickup sits in the dirt driveway. On the door of the pickup are painted letters: UPSHUR COUNTY ROAD DEPT. Behind the house stands a green barn and a chicken coop with a sheet-metal roof. In front of the house a dozen chickens scratch for bugs in the bare ground which is shaded by a large chinaberry tree. A black-and-white mutt sleeps under the porch along with two tiger cats, while a boxy evaporative cooler drones in the living-room window.

A sandy-haired cowlicked boy bursts barefoot out of the house with a baseball glove and a ball. The cats look up sleepily, the chickens squawk out of his way, but the dog jumps up and follows. The boy's burr-cut hair shines in the bright sun. A bit later, a pretty dark-haired woman comes out. She has another glove and two red baseball caps. The boy runs excitedly up to her and she puts one of the caps on his head. She dons the other one and they play catch in the shade of the chinaberry tree. After tossing the ball back and forth for a while, the boy playfully throws it far beyond the woman and tries to beat her to it. He gets there first, grabs the ball, but she catches him and they both fall laughing into a patch of grass. The boy lies back on the woman's lap. She strokes his head and they talk and laugh and—

"Pastor Jim, I figured I'd find you here," Joe Lareux declares as he crashes out of the underbrush, jerking Jim out of his childhood memories. Short, stocky, and wearing a gray bomber-style jacket, Joe looks like a baby rhino, especially with his large no-neck head.

"There *is* a trail, you know?" Jim replies jokingly.

"I like breaking new trails," Joe kids back as he strolls out toward the water.

Jim stretches and shifts on the log. "What are you doin' here so early?"

"Oh, I had to coordinate with Carl on the music for the program," Joe answers, "but I couldn't take it anymore."

"Carl got on your nerves, did he?"

"That's an understatement," Joe quips as a gust of wind whips a curtain of black hair over his round face. He pushes it to the side then saunters over and plops down on the old oak tree, next to Jim. "Angie and I wanted to spice things up for the junior high skit, so we put together the song 'Good News,' you know, from *The Second Chapter of Acts*. Well, Carl says it's too worldly. It does have a rock tempo and a rich guitar, but the lyrics are pure gospel." Joe reaches down between his scuffed boots and picks up two round stones the size of large marbles.

"Sounds like Carl," Jim replies. "He and Stan see any song with a strong beat as the devil's music, and they're always looking for secret Satanic messages, ever since the rock seminar last fall in Nashua. Remember when the guy came from California and played the *Beatles* records backwards?"

"Yeah, I was there. It's like everybody says that Lucifer's leading kids astray with rock music, but they never bring out the fact that most top-forty songs are about love and heartache, passions of *this* life to be sure, but still, they touch me more than most gospel, and it's rare to find a hit song without artistic merit. Now some lyrics *are* pretty gross, and some of the stars, like Ozzy Osbourne and *Kiss,* are disgusting, and will do anything to make up for their lack of talent, but they're a noisy minority. And I seriously doubt they're Satanic."

Jim sighs, then says, "As an LBI pastor, I hafta take an official stance against it, of course. But off the record, I like a lot of the groups, though I'm pretty ignorant about pop music."

Jim and Joe have talked just enough to know they're on the same wavelength but they've never opened up. Bashful about going further, they sit silent for a bit. Jim leans forward resting his chin on his closed fist while Joe shakes the rocks in his hand as if he's rolling dice. The aroma of sun-warmed cowhide radiates from Joe's jacket. Finally, Jim sits up and ends the silence, "So whaddeya gonna do after graduation, Joe? Got any plans?"

"I have a few options, Pastor, but I don't know. I'm not sure I want—" Joe pauses; his face drops.

"Not sure you want what?" Jim asks.

Joe rolls the stones in his hand more deliberately, clicking them like Humphrey Bogart's steel marbles in *The Caine Mutiny* court martial. His countenance clouds as if he's preparing to confess a crime. "I'm not sure I want to, Go into all the world....

I'd rather keep my job at Alexander's and get my own place, and still come here on weekends."

Leaning back a bit, Jim crosses his outstretched legs and hugs his arms about his chest. He feels a quickening in his soul, a greater sense of kinship to Joe. "So, what soured you on the vision?"

"Mainly, Pastor Jim, I don't feel like I belong anymore. All the seniors are hyped about going out on a missionary team. They profess such assurance while I have doubts about everything, even *God*. And I see so many contradictions. Jesus says, 'Love your enemies,' but Dr. Logan says that just wars are sanctioned by God, even Vietnam. The Bible says, 'Make a joyful noise unto the Lord,' but Dr. Logan says that rock music is demonic. The first commandment in the Bible says, 'Be fruitful and multiply,' but the Christian attitude toward sex is strict and hush-hush and negative, like our sex drive is evil and shameful. Even in marriage, it's still hush-hush, like it's to be tolerated instead of enjoyed."

Joe sighs and shakes his head. He clicks the stones in his hand. "Jesus says a rich man can hardly enter the kingdom of God, but Logan and most Christian leaders are wealthy and ride around in limousines. Jesus says you can't serve God and mammon, yet we take offerings at *every* service, and exhort people to give and give. It's confusing and disheartening. I can hardly get out of bed for class. Coming here is the only thing that keeps me going ... and smoking *pot* during the week. I get high a lot. I can't help it. I've lost it. Maybe I'm not even saved—this is crazy. Why am I pouring my doubts and dirty laundry on you like this? I'm sorry for being so negative. I'm hardly a soldier of God."

"What's a *soldier of God*?" Jim shoots back. "You're simply saying what you feel. That's *more* than I can do."

Joe shifts the stones to his left hand and holds them quietly. His color returns. His spirits lift a bit. "Russ said you had ears to hear me, but I guess I was afraid to talk face to face. I never talked to a *pastor* like this."

"*Pastor, pastor* ... sometimes I hate that word," Jim replies as he sits up and twists sideways on the tree trunk, and begins to pry up a piece of bark between them. "Shit, I'm no different, except maybe the marijuana part. We all doubt; we just don't dare admit it." Jim's confession of doubt is a no-no for an LBI pastor. He'd like to go further and tell Joe everything about his own growing disenchantment with Dr. Logan, but he's not ready to expose himself *that* much, except through suggestion and innuendo.

A chuckling smile cups Joe's moonish face but he doesn't reply, so Jim adds, "Bet you never heard that from a *pastor*."

"You can say that again," Joe quickly affirms, sounding

relieved. "I almost wish you were God, the way you accept me just as I am."

"You'd take that back if it ever came true," Jim jokes as he continues to fiddle with the bark, trying to work it free without breaking it. "I'm a real prick sometimes, but speaking of wishes, what would you wish for if you could have your wildest dream come true?"

Joe stands up and takes a few steps toward the water. Grunting with his whole body, he throws the stones in quick succession high into the air. Both drop into the open channel short of the ice with muffled piercing plunks, like pistol shots fired with a silencer. Joe sweeps his hair off his face then turns back toward Jim. "Well, if I could write my own story, I'd have a warm loving wife with puppy-dog eyes and I'd form a rock band and touch hearts with my guitar like Jimmy Page—and I'd get high whenever I like."

"Sounds good to me," Jim says, looking up, "if you'd just leave out the pot."

"I sneak my joints now," Joe explains sheepishly. "I go to my car each morning and take a couple of hits to get me going." Joe softens. His face fills with longing. "But mainly, I just want a girl who really wants me. You know, real love, like in love songs, like in the movies."

Jim grins knowingly. "You mean like: 'I just want a she who wants me so I can be ... by myself, but not alone'?"

"What are you, a poet or something?"

Jim returns his attention to the loose bark. "Nawh—well, in a way. That's just a verse I wrote down. But we all want that kind of love, Joe. To me, it's the greatest thing, in *this* life anyway. Yet I'm not sure anyone has it."

"But you have it, Pastor, you and your wife?"

"Yeah, in a way we do, but in a way we don't. Sharon and I, we have a special closeness and lots of fun times, but still, I feel there's *more* ... and I'm not sure if anyone has ever possessed it, at least since Eve was taken out of Adam."

"That's my problem," Joe sighs. "I'm always after the impossible."

Jim's heart is moved by the longing in Joe's voice. He wants to talk about Becki but he doesn't dare, so he keeps the focus on Joe, "I can see why you're not into the LBI missionary hype. Most students would never confess such a dream. Why do you stay, feeling as you do?"

Joe puts his foot up on the tree and leans forward with his arms crossed on his knee. He reminds Jim of a baseball manager watching a game from the dugout steps. "What makes anyone stay?

But, Pastor Jim, I guess—"

"Cut this 'Pastor' bullshit. Just call me 'Jim.' We left the formalities a long way back." Jim grins broadly, his face warming into a blush.

Joe gives a quick embarrassed laugh. "Okay, if you want. Uh ... well, anyway, J-i-i-mmm." Joe draws out Shanley's first name as if getting used to saying it. "I guess I stayed because I didn't want to let God down, or Dr. Logan, but finally last summer, I got up the nerve to leave, but then I heard you speak at summer conference. I liked what you said. I wanted to hear more so I stayed, and signed up to come here weekends."

Pastor Jim finally breaks off a concave section of bark. A beetle scurries for cover. The wood underneath is dank and dark and earthy-smelling with many bored-out engravings that look like hieroglyphics. "That's good to hear," he says to Joe as he traces the insect tunnels with his finger. "I'm never sure if my heart gets through, but maybe you're just crazy like me and Russ?"

"Could be," Joe agrees. "Who knows what crazy is? I just know that when I'm here, I don't have to get high to survive. I like being with Russ. I can talk about anything, even about being horny and looking at chicks. He helps me relax. He's got the same feelings. He's like me."

"You're like Russ," Jim snickers. "Now I *know* our common ground is radical."

"Cut it out," Joe laughs. "I mean it. I'm serious."

"Sorry, I couldn't help it. But go on. I'll be good now."

Joe waits while the humorous interlude fades then says, "I can't talk to the guys at the dorm. They just look at me with condescending pity like I'm blind Bartimaeus on the Jericho Road, but with you and Russ, like right now, I can share my *true* feelings. You may not agree, but you treat me like a person instead of a spiritual organism in an evangelical Petri dish."

Tossing the bark away, Jim wipes the rotten pulp off his hands. "Pretty good sermon, Joe. I wish I had it on tape. I'd play it ever' time I get down on myself—like twenty minutes ago."

"It's the truth, Jim. You and Russ, this church. You're the only glimmer of hope in my quest so far."

"Most Christians would never admit they're still on a quest. After all, we're supposed to have the truth already. But tell me more about it."

Knitting his crescent-shaped eyebrows, Joe gazes intently into the distance as if waiting for his story to rise over the Worcester Hills. He looks jolly almost matronly, somewhere between a Lou Costello and a Danny DeVito—neither ugly nor handsome but appealing in a droll and elfish way. Finally, his brown eyes relax and he begins, "Well, I grew up in Methuen. My mother wanted me to be a doctor. I did well in school ... football jock, National Honor Society, popular with girls, and I continued to shine at UMASS, into my senior year. Then one day I drew a large Dali-like picture of a hand reaching up for a question mark. After taping it on my dormitory door, I left college with one suitcase and my guitar. My mother flipped."

"Would've been hip in the '60s. You were ten years late?"

"Yeah, I guess it was '77 when I left Amherst."

"So what brought that on?"

Joe heads back to the water. Jim grabs his walking stick and follows. "I got sick of it," Joe says. "Grades, credentials, connections, trying to get laid. I always had to prove myself." They walk east toward the dike. The geese are still cavorting in the waves but farther out, near the ice. "Competition was God. It was insane like trampling each other in a mad rush for *no*where. Love was demoted to a sociosexual need to be enjoyed, but never to be embraced at the expense of career or money goals. So I left, with no degree, no applause ... and *no* regrets."

Reaching the dike, they begin to negotiate the granite rocks, grayish-white, blue-speckled, sun-gilded stones ranging in size from small bricks to man-sized boulders and slabs. After about fifty feet, Jim becomes impatient and hops, holding his pine stick in the air, from rock to rock toward the lake. He goes as far as he can then sits down on a large slab near the water. Joe follows hurling his barrel-shaped body across the stones. "So what'd you do after UMASS?" Jim asks after Joe plops panting beside him.

Joe explains between breaths, "Well, Jim ... I guess ... well, that's when I really began my quest. I hoped to find a community of souls where love and getting to know each other was the most important thing."

There's no ice around the dike and the waves gurgle and suck as they lap about the rocks. The mossy-algal-fishy odor of the fresh-water lake blows up into Jim's face. It reminds him of the pond back home where he used to go fishing. "And that led you to Logan?" he asks Joe.

"Eventually ... but only after I bummed around the country three years. I worked a lot of jobs, played in a few bands. I met lots of musicians. They looked different, talked different, but they all had the same insane drive for money, fame, and status. I also checked out a number of religious groups. I tried a fundamentalist Baptist ministry—I got saved and baptized, but they were strict and military: short haircuts, no guitars, no blue jeans, and the girls couldn't wear makeup. And every sermon was about sin and hell and the second coming. Then the Episcopal Church—they were wishy-washy about everything and more into liberal politics than God. Then I checked out the Moonies, and the Way, even the Hare Khrishnas. Let's face it; I was desperate. Finally in 1979, around Christmas, I came home and I heard Dr. Logan on the radio talking about love and oneness in Christ. He emphasized grace and forgiveness rather than judgment. I went up to Nashua to check it out. There was such a sense of movement and purpose on campus, and everyone seemed kind and loving, and Dr. Logan, he seemed like a modern-day St. Paul. So I enrolled at the college."

Jim pushes his pine staff into the water until it comes to rest on another large slab about two feet under the surface. Green algae covers the submerged slab like a mucky carpet. Little bubblelike spots of shadow and sunlight dance about the end of the stick. Further out, he sees more algae-covered rocks sloping down into inky blackness. As he peers into the depths, he replies, "So how long were you zealous for the—" Plashing and flapping, the geese take to the air. After circling, they head north. Jim and Joe watch them until they disappear over the trees on the ridge line.

Jim doesn't finish his question. Instead, Joe says, "What about you, Jim? How'd you get hooked up with Pastor Logan? You graduated from the Air Force Academy and M.I.T. And you were an officer and a meteorologist. You're certainly not a typical LBI disciple."

"Let's go over there where it's less windy," Jim suggests, "and I'll try to fit the pieces together for you." Moving back from the water, they sit down on the sunny side of a large boulder that has found its way beyond the dike to the foot of the railroad embankment.

"Why'd you come to Brendon Falls?" Joe asks as they get comfortable.

"Well, Sharon and I liked New England ever since my graduate-school days at M.I.T. We were also stationed for a while at Westover AFB in Chicopee, just north of Springfield. So when I got back from Guam in '73, I took a job with a private weather service in Bedford, working for a fellow I knew at M.I.T. We ended up in Brendon Falls only because we got a good deal on our house."

"So you just wanted the comfy suburban life, huh?"

Jim leans back against the rock. "Well, I certainly wasn't on a quest. I had a good job, a good marriage, healthy kids. I did have a gnawing sense of unease, but I ignored it."

"Didn't you have some kind of vision that got you into God? I heard you preach on it."

"In a way, but it's hard to describe. Let's see, how to tell this?"

"You weren't into religion back then?"

"Oh, I went to church with Sharon, and I professed to be born-again, mainly to please her and her parents, but that was the extent of it. Then one day out of the blue it happened."

"You mean the mystical calling thing?" Joe asks, his eyes opening wide with curiosity. He locks his arms about his knees and shifts to face Jim.

"Yeh, it just happened. I wasn't searching, but still it came. It was a year after we got here. I was working swing shift. I got home about midnight. Sharon was asleep. I built a fire in the fireplace and sat down in my old recliner and began to read the Bible."

"I thought you just professed to be born-again because of your wife?"

"True," Jim says. "But I was just curious enough to investigate the book for myself. Anyway, I was reading First Corinthians, you know, 'Eye hath not seen nor ear heard' and then...."

"Go on, go on," Joe prods eagerly. "I have to go set up the PA."

"Well, it was very quiet except for the logs popping and settling, and then—" Jim suddenly stops to Joe's dismay. "I'm not telling this right," he says as he pulls an old index card out of his wallet and hands it to Joe. "Here, read this." The ink is faded but legible:

### FEBRUARY 1974

SHE SLIPS IN UPON ME OUT OF MIDNIGHT MURK
THAT SHIVERS SILENT OVER EDSEL ROAD
AS I READ PAUL BY THE FIRE IN MY ABODE.
"NEITHER HAVE ENTERED INTO THE HEART...."
HEAVEN'S HOLY BREASTS DRAW ME THROUGH THE BARS
OF MY BEING AS WILD SEARCHING LIPS UNFOLD
MY SECRET AND LIFT ME BREATHLESS TO BEHOLD
MY LOVE GODDESS ON A CROSS IN THE STARS.

"FEAR NOT, GOOD SHEPHERD. I AM COME TO SHOW
THE THINGS THAT ARE FREELY GIVEN TO YOU."
I FEAST FULL ON HER FIRE OF COMPASSION PURE.
I DRINK DEEP HER BITTERSWEET NECTAR FLOW.
I DROWN IN HER ROYAL RAGING SEA OF BLUE
COSMIC CHRIST THAT HOLDS ALL AND MAKES ME SURE.

- - - - - - - -

"It's like you had *sex* with an angel?" Joe remarks.

"I think it was God," Jim replies. "I wrote this the next morning. I've showed it to no one, except Sharon and Russ. God was so female, not macho like the God of Moses. She was kind and tender, yet passionate and carnal, like a mother-sister-best friend-lover all at the same time. Needless to say, I don't share this story with very many people."

Joe returns the card, goes up on one knee. "So this is why," he muses softly.

Folding the card, Jim puts it back into his wallet. They both become silent. Joe gazes out over the lake. Jim rests his head back against the rock and looks up into the sky.

"Oh no, it's twenty after!" Joe declares, jumping to his feet. "I gotta go." After giving Shanley a playfully punch on the shoulder, he hustles up the slope toward the church as Jim hauls himself slowly to his feet.

At the top of the embankment, Joe turns and yells back to Jim, "I want to hear the rest of your story sometime!" He then disappears into the railroad cut and all is quiet again.

Before going back, Jim looks once more at the sky, the water, the ice. The wind whips the trees, bringing a verse to mind:

> *The wind bloweth where it listeth, and thou hearest the sound of it, but canst not tell from where it cometh, and where it goeth; so is every one that is born of the Spirit.*

# Chapter Five

B y the time Pastor Jim has changed his shoes and put on his tie, the church is alive with chattering voices. He opens his office door just enough to whiff the oversweet fragrances of Sunday morning Christianity—perfume, cologne, aftershave, fabric-softener, freshly showered born-again bodies moving in all directions. Mothers and fathers deliver crying babies to the nursery. Giggling children run from Sunday school buses to their class-rooms. Clumps of murmuring teenagers clog the corridors. Teachers and staff members hurry about, accomplishing last-minute tasks. First-time visitors, with fish-out-of-water faces, grope awkwardly toward the sanctuary, politely accepting handshakes of greeting. And a steady stream of women squeeze through to the ladies' room for a last pee before service. "Okay, time to start!" Stan Campbell declares, taking charge like a traffic cop. "Sunday school to the new wing! Ever'body else, this way!" Then to the reluctant teenagers, "Come on, kids! Get amovin'!"

Jim closes the door. The clamor in the hallway soon gives way to quiet, then a double knock. Jim opens again. Stan, wearing a cheap gray suit and a faded red tie, enters the office and reports like a first sergeant, "God's amovin', Pastor Jim. We got over ninety people out there, an' lots of new faces."

"Here to see their kids," Shanley asserts. "We'll be back to sixty next week."

"Well, if jus' one soul gets saved, it's worth it." Stan replies, declaring the never-questioned justification for all Christian endeavor.

Ignoring Stan's hype, Jim turns to practical concerns, "Ushers all set?"

"Yeah, I got Russ 'n Calvin workin' the service, an' Barry's makin' the rounds outside. I'll be in my reg'lar spot in the back, near the door."

"Okeydoke, we'll run a short service, then we'll turn it over to Carl for the Sunday school program." At BFBC (Brendon Falls Bible Church), as with all LBI (Logan Bible Institute) branches, there are no church bulletins. Dr. Logan teaches that printed order-of-service bulletins hinder the Holy Spirit.

After a short prayer, Stan exits, and Carl Baker, the BFBC Sunday school chief, comes in. "So, is the program all set?" Pastor Jim asks as he shakes Carl's limp uncallused hand; it feels skinny and bony, and overlong.

"Most definitely," Carl answers, giving a meek little grin. Beady-eyed and bald, he peers down at Jim through wire-rimmed

John Lennon glasses. The glasses rest halfway down his narrow jutting nose which looks like a beak.

"Good," Jim replies. "After the offering, I'll speak for twenty minutes, then I'll turn it over to you, and your teachers can march the kids in. Does that fit your schedule?"

"Most definitely, Pastor, that's what I expected." He again uses his pet positive phrase. Carl, an obsequious Digital nerd in his mid 30s, has worked his whole life to be less than mediocre. Thin, sallow, and sickly-looking, he reminds Jim of an undernourished praying mantis. Despite Carl's expertise on Bible curriculums for children, Jim never liked the idea of making him Sunday school director, but Stan insisted, and Jim acquiesced when no one else wanted the position.

"I like the way you're on top of things, Carl," Jim lies. Carl lusts for praise, especially from Pastor Jim. Compliments spur him to action beyond the call, and Jim takes full advantage. "The Sunday school's running smoother than ever, and you've done a great job with this program." In truth, Jim despises Carl, and his heart recoils against this buttery falseness, but when Jim is caught up in running the church, expediency takes priority over honesty.

After Carl, Russ Bradley sticks his head in and says, "I gave Cal the combination so he can handle Sunday offerings." Russ is dressed the same as Saturday except he's holding his Red Sox cap instead of wearing it.

"Good," Jim replies. "But he'll need a key to the closet door, to get to the safe."

"I'll have one made and give it to him before next Sunday."

Russ turns to go but Jim stops him, "Wait, Russ. There's one other thing."

"What's that?" Russ asks, stepping back into the office doorway.

"I'm taking you up on your offer to work with Becki each weekend. You can get Sylvia and Joe to help if you like. She'll only be here five more weeks at the most—looks like you survived so far?"

Russ grins lazily. "No problem, I like working with Becki. Besides, I'd hardly call it work. We spent the afternoon at Cal and Joanne's, and after supper, we played Space Invaders and Pac-Man. Then she and Sheila listened to records and tapes half the night."

"Sounds like she made herself right at home?"

"I'll say. She's already like a big sister to Sheila, but she doesn't seem very enthused about outreach and visitation. She's certainly different from the hyperspiritual types that usually come down from Nashua. She's shy, but she's also witty and funny when she gets going." Russ departs. Jim closes the door. Russ's perfect description of Rebecca tugs at his heart, but with a strong exertion of will, he chases her out of his mind—in accordance with his new policy of dealing with her which he just resolved down at the lake.

Quiet, then piano, then singing. The service is starting in the main auditorium. Jim slips on his blue blazer, checks his hair—at the mirror behind his desk—grabs his Scofield Bible, and heads into the hallway, where he runs immediately into Sharon. She gives him a coy smile and says, "I just have a second. My class is climbing the walls. But I wondered if we can take the kids to Pewter Pot after, and stop at a few stores, since we didn't go yesterday?"

"I guess so," Jim says. "But I'll have to ask Russ to do outreach for me."

"It's done. I just asked him ten seconds ago. He said he would."

"Shar-*ron*?"

"Well, I didn't tell him. I just asked ... as a friend."

"You're always one step ahead. What am I gonna do with you?"

"I can't help it that I'm so creative—oh, by the way, I saw Becki with Bev and Sheila in the parking lot. She does look like Alison now, but she still dresses like a tomboy, like out of the bargain basement, and she still talks like a groupie. Should I ask her to come with, and Sheila too?" Sharon gives a quick little grimace.

"N-no, that's okay," Jim replies, scrambling for words. "She's goin' with Russ. They're all going to McDonald's after church. Joe's goin' too." Jim is presuming but it sounds good.

"Okay, it'll just be us then."

Sharon gives Jim a quick but inviting kiss then strides gracefully into the new wing, her corn-yellow hair bouncing on her neck. Her aggressive hips roll from side to side. Her green skirt swishes above her nylon-covered calves. She seems especially tall in the narrow hallway. *Why would I ever want another women?* Jim asks himself as he marvels at his wife's pelvic potency, bold and assertive through the pleats.

Jim heads for the main hall where the assembled body of believers is singing "Amazing Grace." The singing is louder now because everyone knows the words; at BFBC there are no songbooks—another Logan-LBI tradition. As he turns the corner, Leslie Burton almost runs him over. "Oh, Pastor!" she exclaims. "I'm sorry, but it must be the Lord. We must keep the teenagers out of that old shed. I don't know what happened to the lock. But they're going out on the path as well, even down to the tracks. They've been impossible lately. It must be the warmer weather."

Leslie, stern, willowy, yet somehow regal, stands nose to nose with Pastor Jim. Frog eyes, pungent perfume, purple angora sweater. No way to ignore her presence. And she speaks rapidly in a grating voice—like an IBM printer. Jim can detect nothing soft about her, save for the sweater which hides her fried-egg bustline. With her tawny hair pulled into a tight bun, her frog eyes seem to bug out all the more. Before he can break away, Leslie shifts gears and proceeds to tell him—in less than 30 seconds—how she's finally realizing her full godly potential as a woman and a mother and a wife, and how Jerry and the kids are changing as well, making the whole mood in their home more spiritual.

After escaping from Leslie, Pastor Jim enters the main auditorium through a swinging glass door. When BFBC bought the building, Stan Campbell's remodeling team, working with Sharon and Beverly, converted this former Legion function-room into a cozy sanctuary. They covered the ugly aqua tile with brown carpet, panelled the walls halfway, and papered above with a beige floral-print wallpaper. Also on the walls, Sharon hung cherrywood wall sconces with real candles and hurricane globes, and she adorned the windows with blue priscilla curtains—her favorite kind.

Jim likes the way the hall is finished: no longer a party room yet not like a church, but more like a large colonial living room. Nonetheless, the old smoke-yellowed ceiling gives silent testimony to the many Legion parties and pub nites. And he can still detect the disgusting tobacco-alcohol smell; they've scrubbed and scrubbed but they can't get rid of it.

Jim strides briskly to the low dais where Joe Lareux is leading the song service. Behind Joe on the wall is a seven-foot wooden cross which dominates the small stage. Also on the stage are three mate's chairs and a hefty oak pulpit. Jim sits down in the middle chair. He opens his Bible, as if studying, then lifts his eyes just enough to scan the singing faces before him. He quickly locates Becki between Beverly Bradley and Sheila. Becki looks the same as yesterday except her hair is flying about in silky tangles as if she just got out of bed. Arms folded, eyes down, she seems bored with the singing. *No, no, Jim,* his conscience admonishes, *don't let your eyes betray you. Remember what you decided down by the reservoir?* Jim looks away and determines to not look at Becki again.

The song service ends and everyone sits down. Joe comes over to Pastor Jim and whispers, "I asked Sylvia to sing during the offering."

"No, I'd rather have Angie play during the offering," Jim replies hushedly. "Then Sylvia can sing before I speak, and Carl will take over at half past."

Nodding his agreement, Joe returns to the lectern, "Okay, everybody, listen up. Today at two-thirty, we have outreach and visitation and tonight at seven we'll be back here...." The packed room feels warm and stuffy, and the usual latecomers are still trickling in. Jim, directing his attention to Stan who is stationed at the back of the room, lightly brushes his forehead: a signal. Immediate response. Stan shoots out of his seat, adjusts the thermo-stat, then opens the middle and rear windows about an inch. The blue curtains stir as welcome fresh air circulates into the sanctuary.

"Monday at 7:30 p.m.," Joe goes on, "we have our LBI college-extension class taught by Pastor Shanley. This semester's course is entitled: King David and His World. It's a study of 1st and 2nd Samuel. On Tuesday at 7:30, we have our regular midweek service, and on Saturday morning, we have prayer meeting and outreach. We also operate a teen center on weekends and a Christian academy during the week, and we run two Sunday school buses on Sunday. If you have questions, please see Stan Campbell or Russ Bradley after service. Okay, let's all stand for another song."

Angela plays the piano, Joe leads, the body sings, "This is the *day.* This is the *day,* that the Lord...."

Jim stands as well. As he does, he nods for Stan to come forward. Stan springs to his feet and marches to the stage with the ramrod dignity of a British brigadier. He always tries to carry himself in a soldierly manner, especially when in front of a crowd, yet with his huge frame and less-than-graceful gait, he seems more monstrous than military. Campbell seems to take pride in being disciplined, calm, self-possessed, even when he laughs. Jim often wonders if he loses control with his wife, Doris, or if he also copulates by the numbers. "After this song, I want you to take the offering," Jim whispers to Stan. "You can also bring up a few of the points we talked about yesterday morning, but don't be long-winded. I still hafta speak before Carl takes over at eleven-thirty."

The body continues to sing and clap to the familiar Sunday school chorus. The collection of smiling souls could well be a Norman Rockwell painting. Grays, browns, blues, reds, greens, even yellows, and paisley and plaids and flowers and solids. Coats and ties, flannel shirts, faded jeans with holes in the knees. Dressy blouses, dressy skirts, suede pants, knit sweaters, patched denim jackets, and worn corduroys. Blond hair, black hair, red, brown, and gray, with a sprinkling of bald heads, and a few hats. Tall folks, short folks, fat, thin, and average. Ruddy Irish dimples, pointy Polish chins, puffy alcoholic pallor, scattered olive and copper cheeks. Blue eyes, brown eyes, green and hazel, some wearing glasses, some red from drink—and a few pairs of white eyes set in burnt umber. Ski jackets, poplin vests, trench coats, parkas, wind-breakers, wool coats, and a few fake furs—some on the people, some on the chairs, some on the floor, but only a few on the coatrack in the hallway. Big Bibles, little Bibles, black, white, and red Bibles. Leather Bible cases, plastic Bible cases, some zippered, some with velcro snaps. Dog-eared notepaper, pencils, pens, file cards, bookmarks. King James Bibles, Living Bibles, Thompson Chain, and NIVs, some in the hand, some on the floor with purses and handbags, but most on the chairs during the singing.

The BFBC flock is mostly white and lower middle class with a lot of Irish blood—Pastor Jim is half Irish himself but not from New England; his great-grandfather's family came from Galway to Chicago in 1881 and his grandfather moved to Ft. Worth in 1922—intermixed with Polish, German, French-Canadian, Italian, and Greek. Many are descended from the European immigrants who came to work in the textile mills. In addition there's a small but increasing number of Hispanics and Blacks and Koreans.

The song ends and Stan marches to the pulpit amid coughing, shuffling, and clearing of throats, together with hushed whispers and wrapper crinkling, as each body member gets seated, settled, and sneaks in that last comment, or Life Saver. Stan, truculent, somber, itching to do battle, waits behind the lectern holding the microphone in his mammoth hand.

In the bizarre booming revival of evangelical Christianity, where repentance, conversion, and zealous devotion to Jesus are the crucial criteria, Stan Campbell, though an uneducated mill foreman from South Boston, has become a champion, a chieftain. His disadvantaged, delinquent, and sinful past—he often testifies of his rebellious youth and his worldly ways in the Navy—is now an asset, like his tattoo, for it shows how far he's come with the Lord. Despite his clipped Southie dialect and frequent malaprop-isms, his ranting exhortations to give all in the great war against Lucifer have made him a popular lay preacher. When all is quiet, he begins, "Let us pray: O God, O heavenly Father, draw us together into the utter ser'ousness of this hour...."

Pastor Jim shifts restlessly in his chair. He can hardly stomach Stan's high-and-mighty prayers. *Why'd I tell him to preach?* he asks himself. *He'll run over. I'll be lucky to speak at all?* The clock on the back wall says 10:55. Jim's eyes wander from the clock to the pink and purple flowers in the wallpaper, to the nicotine stains overhead, then to a hemispherical heat detector in the ceiling that reminds him of a shiny metallic tit with an erect nipple.

Finally, Jim scans the crowd of bowed heads. *This place is packed. Must be a hundred at least. There's Sylvia and Frank. She*

41

*drinks for pain, but he's an alcoholic and a smart-ass to boot. I can't stand him. He's always full of professions and promises but he never follows through. And there's Ernie and Sarah. He doesn't like going places with her, especially to church—he's a "home Baptist" from West Virginia. He's just here to see Jennifer sing, but I like him. I like hearing his hillbilly stories. Sarah comes to every service chirping hyperspiritual news, but I like her better at home. She's good in the kitchen. And there's Aunt Agnes filling two seats on the front row: Agnes J. Hanratty. She's so fat I don't see how she gets up once she sits down. And Cal and Joanne in the back with little Shane. Newlyweds. When was their wedding? August? Cal looks like a kid except for his boozy eyes. Joanne is so stoic and burdened. She seems a lot older than twenty-one. Little Shane must be two months now. She never puts him in the nursery. And over here, Herschel and Thelma Hightower. He's the only Black guy I ever knew with freckles.*

Stan is still praying. Jim sighs and continues to look over his flock. *There's shy Melissa Baker, Carl's living widow, an island in a sea of people. I feel sorry for her. And Tony Liggons, my laughing Black cleanup hitter. He's fun to be with. I wish summer would hurry up. Things are less hectic during softball season. Can't miss Elmer Kowalski. He's always sleeping, and exhaling Old Grand-Dad fumes over three rows. He's disgusting. He's wrinkled as a raisin, and look at those ugly red bags under his eyes.*

*And two chairs over is Mary LeBlanc. She's so small and skinny, and tight-faced. She can't be over thirty, but she looks like a shriveled old maid, and she's such a pious prude. I doubt she ever had an orgasm. Her pussy is probably dried up from disuse—shit, my mind is guttering out right in church. But it's true. She makes Leslie Burton seem like a party animal. And there's Freddie and Juanita: getting married in June, or is it August? I don't know much about Freddie except he's got a cute face, and he's Stan Campbell's nephew. But Juanita, I've known since she was a teenage townie. Have to admit, she's turned into quite a woman, dark and ravishing, and built like a model, but Sharon says she's bedding more than Freddie. I believe it. She's a sly one. Stan calls her "a connivin' bitch an' a deceitful Spanic"—that's one thing we agree on.*

*O God, I have to look.* Jim can't help but look at Becki. *She's not praying I bet. Looks like she's fiddling with a cassette tape of some sort.* He stares at her for a long moment hoping that she'll look up at him, but she doesn't. *She's still playing with that damn tape. What's wrong with her? She knows I'm up here. She doesn't give a shit about me. Glad I let go of that fantasy this morning—O God, I wish we could talk and spend some time together. Oh, how I wish—STOP IT!* Jim wrenches Becki out of his mind and turns his attention back to Stan.

Having finished his prayer, Stan opens his big Bible. He uses a large-print edition so he doesn't have to wear his reading glasses. "Please turn to 1st Peter Chapter Five," he says. His deep resonant timbre reminds Jim of Sherm Feller at Fenway Park. The rustle of flipping pages fills the room. "I jus' want to read verse eight:

> **Be sober, be vigilant, 'cuz our a'versary, the devil, like a roarin' lion walketh 'bout seekin' whom he may devour.**

"Now today is a special day for our Sunday school and— KEVIN! Move up here right now! I wan'cha on the front row. You need this more than anyone! HALEY! You sit still an' open your Bible! How yuh gonna be a woman of God, when yuh horse around durin' the readin' of the Holy Word?" Stan, like a sharp-eyed hawk, spots the two teenagers giggling in the last row and comes down swiftly upon them, his talons flashing. Kevin trudges sheepishly to the front dragging his leather jacket, while Haley looks down at her now-open Bible. Her face flashes crimson then white. A severe hush falls over the assembly.

Stan begins again, "Today we're havin' our Sunday school program. Our kids are learnin' the Bible an' how to live for Jesus. But we only got 'em for an hour each week. So I mus' share the warnin' of this verse. The devil's goin' 'round like a roarin' lion. Now if you was a lion in Afirka an' you was hungry an' you came on a herd of ant'lope, which ones would you 'tack? The lion always 'tacks the young ones, an' so does the devil. He's cunnin' 'n deceitful. He tempts young people. He stirs their fleshly passions. He leads them into sin, into drugs 'n stealin' 'n pornology ... an' bein' 'bellus 'n pomiscous. That's the devil's world! Now do yuh want Lucifer to take our kids down into his world of sin 'n damnation! And to *hell* when they die!"

The flock responds with murmurs of "No, no," and "God have mercy."

"That's the beauty of the Word," Stan goes on. "It tells us 'zachly how to save our little ones from Satan. 'Be sober, be vigilant,' that's how we defeat him, by forsakin' our evil ways an' not allowin' 'peerances of sin or evil 'maginin'. 'Be sober' means more than not drinkin'. It means to be ser'ous 'bout your walk with God. How canyuh protect your kids from evil when lots of you jus' come to church once a week or once a month? You gotta get ser'ous to win this war! Howyuh gonna save your kids from Satan, when you don't never obey the Word yourself, an' you jus' watch TV an' go to worldly movies an' read worldly books 'n magazines?"

Pausing in a militant devil-defying pose, Stan stares back and forth as if he's daring anyone to challenge him. Some lean forward almost foaming with fervor to "get right." Others slink back to hide. Jim feels nothing but impatience as Stan takes more of *his* time. There's no sound, save for the buzzing of the lights and the whir of the furnace fan echoing through the heating ducts. Nothing moves, except the curtains breathing in and out.

The quietness grows ominous like the dark calm before a tempest—"BE VIGILANT!" Stan suddenly roars, his gray locks flying wildly about his pulsing temples. "THAT MEANS TO BE READY FOR THE DEVIL! IT MEANS TO GIVE *ALL* FOR THE LORD! AN' TO STOP GIVIN' IN TO THE LUSTS OF YOUR FLESH! It means to come to ever' service, an' to stop bein' lazy 'n lukewarm, an' loose in your thoughts!"

Shouts of Right on! and Amen! erupt from the body as Stan's convincing condemnation hooks like a deep-sea lure into the bathyal monsters of self-hatred and God-guilt, drawing the flock into the almost-sexual frenzy of religious masochism. They now crave to hear how sinful they are.

And Stan does not disappoint them. "IT'S NO *WONDER* YOUR KIDS ARE INTO DRUGS 'N ALC'HOL, AN' CIG'RETTES!" he thunders, slamming his meaty sledgehammer fist on the lectern again and again. The pulpit resounds shaking the stage, shaking the building, shaking the souls of the flock. "THEY SEE YOU GIVIN' IN TO THE DEVIL! THEY SEE YOU SIPPIN' MICH'LOBS ON THE COUCH AN' SMOKIN' MAR'BOROS! AN' THEN YOU GO PARTY AT NIGHT, AN' SMOKE MARYAUNA! No *wonder* the kids are speer'mentin' with 'licit sex when you adults are flirtin' 'n dancin' to rock music. How canyuh have a godly home when the kids see you bein' lazy an' always sleepin' late on Sunday! How canyuh 'spect young people to give their lives to Jesus, when you don't give your ties an' offerin's to God? Lotta yuh don't give nothing to God 'cept *pocket change,* but your kids see you spendin' on stereos 'n TVs, an' cars 'n furniture, an' mic'owaves, even gamblin' an' bettin' on the horses! And you fathers! You let your kids go to *hell* in public school 'cuz you won't pay twition for 'em to come here to our academy. An' you ladies disobey your husbands, an' spend 'n spend on new clothes, then you *rob* God on Sunday to pay for your lust!"

Stan takes a quick breath, then gesturing with his whole body, finishes with a series of bellowing shouts, his face swelling red— his finish is pure Logan. "NO *WONDER* YOU'RE LOSIN' YOUR KIDS TO THE DEVIL AN' DROWNIN' IN DEBT! GOD'S NOT

MOCKED! WHAT YOU *SOW* YOU SHALL ALSO *REAP*! God'll never bless your pocketbook 'less you give your ties! We need a revival of holy dedicatin' that'll spread over this town! WE MUS' PUT GOD *FIRST,* STARTIN' TODAY! AN' YOU WIVES MUS' BE HUMBLE 'N SUB*MISSIVE* 'STEADA 'BELLUS 'N GOSS'PY! WE MUS' GO TO THE CROSS AN' LAY DOWN OUR LIVES TO JESUS. OUR KIDS'LL SEE US LOVIN' THE LORD AN' THEY'LL FOLLOW OUR HOLY SAMPLES! THAT'S HOW WE'RE GONNA WIN! WE'RE GONNA *FIGHT* THE DEVIL, AN' WE'RE GONNA *BEAT* HIM!"

A storm of applause resounds through the room. Campbell stands at the pulpit drinking in the adoration. Jim has seen it a thousand times but it still amazes him how born-again believers love to be convicted of sin. After everyone settles, Stan relaxes and jokes his way into the offering, "Now that oughta get ole 'Benezer Scrooge into a givin' mood!" The flock laughs with collective release as Russ and Calvin come forward with the baskets.

Stan is a master at breaking the severe mood of his exhortations with humor, just enough to maintain his friendly, fatherly, hero popularity—he knows when to laugh, when to be sober. After praying for the offering, he marches triumphantly off the stage like Elijah leaving Mt. Carmel.

Angela plays "Have Thine Own Way Lord." Russ and Cal pass the baskets. Money noise competes with the music. Purses, pocketbooks, wallets. Popping snaps, ripping velcro, fingers rummaging in handbags. The jingle and clink of dimes, quarters, nickels. The crisp rustle of new ten-dollar bills, the soiled silence of well-worn dollars. Clicking of pens, flipping of checkbooks, tearing and folding of checks. The sounds of Christian cash flow. Jim hopes for a large offering—they need $975 on Sunday morning to break even—yet he's never felt right about passing baskets.

After the offering, Joe leads the body in a song then calls Sylvia up for her solo. Sylvia, her feline eyes flashing a hidden wildness and her dark cinnamon-splashed hair cascading well past the shoulders, looks like an Indian princess in her beltless navy-and-burgandy dress. She's actually half Sicilian, half Irish, but with her tawny complexion, she could pass for a Native American.

As Angela accompanies, she sings C. Austin Miles' beloved song, "In the Garden," one of the few hymns that Jim likes, "I come to the garden alone while the dew is still on the roses...."

Singing in a rich contralto voice, Sylvia's longing soul pours out like a "river of living water." The masochistic zeal stirred up by Stan's message evaporates off the faces of the flock. Spirits lift like flowers rising on their stems in the morning sun. Desperate unseen hands reach out to touch, becoming cords of love threading from heart to heart, weaving the body into a moment of oneness, while real fingers on real hands fidget on laps, twisting, turning, opening, closing, as when lovers talk about forever. Teenagers, even Kevin and Haley, are captivated and give their childlike eyes to Sylvia. Love and compassion well up in Pastor Jim's bosom.

"He tells me I am his own ... and the joy we share as we tarry there, none other ... has ever known." Warm applause momentarily breaks the spell as Sylvia slips quietly back to her seat like a doe slipping from a meadow back into the tree line.

"Thank you, Sylvia, for that solo," Pastor Jim says as he finally arrives at his pulpit with seven minutes showing on the clock. "That hymn always touches me ... and I also want to thank Stan for his inspiring message. It makes us all want to serve with greater dedication." *Why'd I say that?* Jim silently scolds himself. *That's such a lie. Why do I always stroke Stan's ego?* He sighs then quickly directs his attention back to his flock. "I'm going to be brief this morning since we have our—" Laughter and exclamations of disbelief cut him off. "No, really, I'm serious," Jim jokes. "I mean it. I'm only going to talk for an hour and a half this week." The assembly erupts in hee-haws, catcalls, and boos.

"Let's pray," Jim half-shouts above the still-rippling laughter. Prayer is always a sure way to bring in soberness. After the short petition to God, Jim looks out over the expectant faces of his flock. As he does, he's again moved with compassion. His minister mask cracks and falls away. He jettisons his planned sermon from Isaiah in favor of a passage in Luke. "Please turn to Luke 13:34," he tells the congregation. He then reads the verse:

> O Jerusalem, Jerusalem, which killest the prophets, and stonest them that are sent unto thee, how often would I have gathered thy children together, as a hen doth gather her brood under her wings, and ye would not!

"This morning I want to pose a question.... Why did Jesus come? Some would quickly reply that Jesus came to pay for our sins and to save us from hell. Of course, this's true but I submit that there's a bigger reason. Others may say, as Stan pointed out earlier, that Jesus came to deliver us from sin, from the miserable experience of serving our fallen nature ... to deliver us from alcohol, drugs, idolatry, lust, and unbelief, and certainly he came to do this. Others may say he came to make us soldiers of God so we'll go into all the world and preach the gospel, and we all know that this is Christ's great commission ... but I still submit there's a bigger more wonderful reason." The flock tunes into Pastor Jim's heart as the spirit of oneness, briefly present during Sylvia's song, returns.

Jim takes a glass of water from inside the lectern and drinks a bit to lubricate his throat which has been dry since his talk with Joe down by the lake. "Now this verse tells us the main reason. Look at it again: 'How often would I have gathered thy children together as a hen doth gather her brood under her wings.' I think Jesus came because he wants to be *with* us and to *gather* us to himself, not just to save us from hell, not just to change our behavior, not just to train us as missionaries. These are simply by-products of his true purpose."

Holding the mike in his right hand and whipping the cord behind him with his left, Jim moves to the front of the platform— he preaches more powerfully, "I believe the ultimate reason, the passionate burning reason, that brought Jesus to Earth is that he loves us and wants us to be his bride. He wants to have us and to hold us forever, to take us in his arms in the mystery of oneness, which I think is the *highest* good! The mystery of *oneness* that we all felt during Sylvia's song! The mystery of *oneness* that we all dream about when we sit alone and look at the sunset! The mystery of *oneness* that passes knowledge in Ephesians 3:19! That knits our hearts together in Colossians 2:2! That makes a man leave his father and mother and cleave unto his wife in Ephesians 5:31! That makes a 'friend love at all times' in Proverbs 17:17!"

Bouncing like a boxer, Pastor Jim punches home his conclusion with short compact combinations, "And finally, the mystery of *oneness*, that speaks within us and all creatures, that says we're connected, not separate! The mystery of *oneness* that makes little children trust! That makes a kitten purr! That makes a faithful dog wait day after day at the door of her dead master! The mystery of *oneness* that makes us search for eye contact in the checkout line at Kmart, that causes us to dream of happiness year after year without assurance, without answers, and against all odds! To dream of escaping hatred and wars and heartache, and lies and loneliness, and the fear of death! The mystery of *oneness* that causes us to dream of a great coming day, the 'day of our Lord,' when GOD WILL CAST OUT FEAR AND GATHER ALL HEARTS! AND JESUS WILL TAKE *US* AS HIS BRIDE!"

Without giving time for applause, Jim offers a short prayer, a minute of silence for unsaved people to receive Christ, then retires to the back of the room and sits down next to Stan.

After a short break to darken the room and to move furniture, microphones, and stage props, Joe introduces Carl and the Sunday school program commences. Parents, their cameras ready, jockey for position as the children march in. "Great sermon, Pastor," Stan whispers obsequiously to Jim. "It balanced my message so well. It's 'portant for the body to get both the love an' justice of God, an' durin' the invitation, I saw three hands go up for salvation. We're sure beatin' the devil today." Jim thanks Campbell then tells him that he liked his sermon as well which is a lie. He no longer cares for Stan's pharisaical ranting except when attendance or the offerings are down—then he tolerates it for the sake of results. Jim even preaches an occasional "get right" sermon himself, but much less frequently than in the early years of his ministry when he scorched the pulpit every other message.

The Shanley children are in the program. Chris sings with Sharon's kindergarten class. Heather plays her flute with the sixth grade. And Erin has the part of Martha in the junior high skit about the raising of Lazurus. Jim watches until Erin's skit is almost over then heads for his office to grab his briefcase in hopes of making a fast getaway.

As he passes the ladies' room, a cloud of cigarette smoke pushes Sylvia Cahill out the door into the hallway. She looks down sheepishly but Jim doesn't mention her smoking. He just says that he enjoyed her song. She blushes like a shy virgin, but she's hardly a virgin. She has three little girls and they all look like her, except they don't have sadness in their eyes like their mommy.

Sylvia thanks Jim then gives him a hug. Her hair smells like smoke but it feels silky soft against his cheek. Her slender body presses warm against his. Her breasts squeeze up against his chest. Lust, lust. He pictures her getting out of the shower and drying her tits with a towel. But a pang of guilt quickly chases this illicit imagination. Jim is glad she can't read his thoughts.

At BFBC, brother-sister hugging, in Christ, is normal, expected, but there are only a few women that Jim likes to hug, and when he hugs them, his thoughts often go beyond brother-sister, as with Sylvia. Despite her reserved Christian demeanor, her soul is spirited and passionate. Jim feels it when he hugs her. He feels it when she sings. She's much more than a body, but that's what makes her body so provocative. *Why'd she marry a twerp like Frank?* he asks himself as Sylvia heads back down the hall toward the main auditorium. *I don't blame her for hanging around with Russ—not one bit.*

Becki, Becki. When Jim enters his office, he finds Becki Lea sitting boldly at his desk looking at his family snapshots which he keeps on his desk. He's startled but not surprised. Ever since he's known her, she's always taken great liberty with his things.

"Oh, hi, Jimmy," she greets him in a self-possessed voice. "I got wicked bored so I came to use your copy machine. Russ said I could. I had to make a copy of the lyrics off Sheila's tape cover. It's a *Fleetwood Mac* album."

"Yeh, I think I heard him sing once," Jim lies, trying to hide his ignorance.

"No, silly; *Fleetwood Mac*'s not a person. They're a group. You know: Mick Fleetwood, John McVie, Lindsey Buckingham, Stevie Nicks? They did the song 'Dreams' that I used to play all the time. What are we gonna do with you, Shanley? You're as square as Ronnie Howard on *Happy Days*. You even look like him."

Becki laughs and returns her attention to the framed snapshots on the desk. As she studies them, she gives a quick scrunchy-faced grimace—mouth twisted, nose lifted, eyes squinted. This familiar contortion of her features, which she uses to express various emotions from mirth to disgust, makes Jim feel warm and tingly inside, like when a playful kitten makes a cute gesture, and you want to pick up the squirming little cat and hug her to your neck. "These are wicked good," Becki remarks. "Must be recent, huh? I like this one of Erin. Her hair's getting so much auburn in it, and she wears it long now. And Heather, she looks like Jennifer from *Family Ties*, don'tcha think? And Chris is wicked cute now. Remember when he was newborn, and looked like a monkey? I just saw him earlier, outside with Sharon before church. I can tell he's sweet on me already—is this your dad in this picture with Sharon?"

"Yeh, that's him," Jim replies, rushing in between her rapid-fire questions, "from this past Christmas when we went to Texas."

"Oh yeah, I forgot," Becki teases. "That's why you talk so weird. You say 'yawl' and 'thang' and 'neckid' like J.R. from *Dallas*." She giggles but quickly sobers and becomes quiet.

Jim waits then queries, "What are you looking at?"

"Nothing really," she replies concernedly. "I was just thinking about your dad ... how he must be sad living alone all these years, after your mom died."

"I guess he is sometimes, but he's kind of used to it I think. Besides, Gary Bob lives with him ... you know, my younger brother? He never got married."

"Definitely *weird*," Becki kids, her playful spirit returning. "Gary Bob and James David. It's like you both got two first names." She laughs but quickly shifts to good-bye. "I gotta go. I don't wanna miss my ride. Joe 'n I have to split right after church. He has to stock shelves at Alexander's this afternoon." Rebecca blows out the door leaving Jim in her wake. But his thoughts follow her, twirling and tumbling like a swirl of autumn leaves caught in a whirlwind.

# Chapter Six

The sweet country aroma of burning wood welcomes Dr. Logan as he enters his lavish Blantyre office through a private entrance. Just back from his Monday taping session at Moody Coliseum, he heads to the other end of the spacious room and warms his hands at the fireplace. The domed Austrian clock on the mantel says 3:50 p.m. For a minute he watches the logs popping and snapping amid the orange flames then he retires to his private washroom where he dabs his cheek with a washcloth to remove a leftover splotch of TV makeup. Despite deep laugh lines, puffy eyes, and gray frost in his ginger-colored hair, Charles Logan doesn't look bad for 56; he looks more like a man in his late 40s.

Located in southernmost New Hampshire, Logan Bible Institute (LBI) sprawls over 96 acres of the old Bancroft estate which straddles the Nashua-Hollis line along the Nashua River, the same river that passes through Brendon Falls, 85 winding miles to the south (but only 45 straight-line miles).

In 1898, Jonathan Bancroft, a British textile magnate, built a granite mansion for his young American bride. He called it *Blantyre Castle* after his uncle's Scottish home. Bancroft died in 1932, but his wife lived in the house until her death in 1963. Her son sold the estate to the LBI corporation in 1971, and Logan converted it into a Bible college and ministry headquarters. With verdant woods and rolling meadows, the main campus has the lush foxhunt atmosphere of an English manor, especially in summer. Yet the western (Hollis) side has a Scottish highland character with steep hills and granite outcroppings.

The doctor exits the bathroom and pours himself a cup of coffee at a marble-topped refreshment table adjacent to his desk. Linen napkins, china cups, two trays of pastries, a sterling silver coffeepot, small spoons. The table is replenished several times a day by the Blantyre kitchen staff. Moving over to his large Regency desk, Logan sits down and buzzes his personal secretary, Amy Brannigan. He asks her to get Mary Beth Hudson on the line.

Marble pilasters under Ionic capitals, antique oak wainscoting, Prussian-blue wallpaper, Palladian windows under swag-topped gold draperies, a Louis XVI living-room set arranged in front of the fireplace. The office has a French neoclassic atmosphere that would make Napoleon himself feel at home. Though most of the Blantyre rooms retain John Bancroft's British motif, Logan has redone his office to suit his own tastes. Amy buzzes back. Logan picks up: "Mary Beth, it's good to talk to you."

"Yes, it's been a while," Mary Beth replies, her voice restrained.

"Tom talked with me this morning," Logan says, "and—"

"I appreciate your concern, Pastor," Mary Beth cuts in, "but Tom is blowing this whole thing out of proportion."

Many LBI'ers still refer to Logan as "Pastor," but the LBI Handbook instructs staff and students to address him as "Dr. Logan." Though he never completed college, he has several honorary degrees, including a D.D. and LL.D. from John Clarke School of Theology, a small divinity school in Pennsylvania.

Logan swivels his chair sideways and leans back. "Oh, don't get me wrong, Mary Beth. I'm not taking sides. Tom is just concerned, that's all. I thought we might have a chat and talk this out, the three of us." His voice is commanding yet gritty as if he has sand in his throat.

"Well, there's nothing to talk about," Mary Beth insists, her voice rising. "Michael was just another senior in remedial English Comp. Besides, I haven't seen him since January, since he graduated and went to Lawrence, and—"

"Whoa, whoa," Logan interrupts, "I'm not accusing you and Michael of anything. We're all in this together. We've been friends since Biddeford. I know your heart is pure, but I also know how couples sometimes fail to communicate. That's why God has given us the body of Christ, and pastors and elders."

"Oh, I know, Pastor; I'm sorry," she apologizes, her voice calming a bit. "I know I've been cruel and hateful to Tom but it's just me. It's not another man. We'll be all right. I just need to sort out some things and straighten out my own walk with the Lord."

"I understand perfectly, Mary Beth. We all need to spend time alone, so we can hear God's voice."

"So you still want me to come in to talk?"

"No. If you two can work it out, that's fine. But remember, I love you both, and I'm here if you need me."

As Logan hangs up, a slender boyish-faced man in a tan sandpiper sweater enters through the private doorway. He moves with grace and efficiency, like a cat. It's Matthew Garrett, Logan's administrative assistant who has an adjoining office. Garrett is one of two people with carte blanche access to Logan's inner office— Amy is the other. He drops a file on Logan's desk and says, "Here's the schedule for Easter Week." A fast riser, Garrett went right from Bible college to Logan's staff. He's ordained but has never pastored a church. With brilliant ice-blue eyes and soft but well-defined facial features, he's more pretty than handsome.

"That was Mary Beth Hudson," Logan tells Garrett, ignoring the file.

"So, Doctor, is she coming in?" Garrett replies. "Tom buzzed me while you were gone to see if you'd caught up with her."

Dr. Logan swings his chair straight and takes a sip of coffee. He gestures with his cup. "No, she denies everything. It'll be a frosty day in Hades before she comes clean on this. She's been chasing my nephew since he was a sophomore. Mary Beth's a hard worker, but sometimes I think she's more of a liability than an asset, especially as a teacher. When it comes to young men, she's a *damn* seductress, and a liar to boot."

"She *is* different," Garrett chuckles. "I've always heard gossip about her and her male students. I took English Lit from her my junior year—of course, she didn't get far with me."

They both laugh, but the doctor quickly sobers. "But this time it's Michael. I just hope she lets go of it now that Tom's making a stink. Michael doesn't need this gossipy shit following him to Lawrence, and he certainly doesn't need a forty-year-old college teacher chasing him. He's got enough problems. If he wasn't so damn good-looking—it's the Montanaro curse."

They converse a bit longer then Garrett returns to his own office. On his way out he snaps on a Roman-style torchere lamp by the door. The office is already softly illuminated, by wall sconces mounted on the marble pilasters, but the additional light is helpful since the February afternoon is giving way to evening. Moving on to other business, Logan buzzes Amy and asks her to have Pastor Beckman come down. While he waits, he slips on his reading glasses and looks over Garrett's Easter-Week file.

Of Scotch-Irish descent, Charles Robert Logan grew up in Brunswick, Maine. His Presbyterian parents rarely went to church so he had little chance to cultivate his religious inclination. He dropped out of school in the eleventh grade. It was during the war, and he left to work with his father at the Bath Ironworks. In 1947 he married Priscilla Montanaro, his high school sweetheart, and they moved to Portland where he got a job in the parts department at a small Chevy dealership. The owner was so impressed with Logan that he promoted him to salesman and he soon became the best on the floor. In 1956, after shifting from Chevrolet to New York Life, Logan sold a policy to the pastor of Bethel Baptist Church in Gorham. He became friends with the minister and was soon converted. Priscilla also "got saved." Priscilla's Italian-Catholic parents denounced Logan and disowned Priscilla.

But Logan found his stride as a born-again Baptist and was soon selling more salvation than insurance. In 1960, after a two-year correspondence program from Moody Bible Institute, he started his own church in Biddeford—as a branch of Bethel Baptist.

Preaching powerfully and seeking converts day and night, he acquired a hundred followers by 1963. The next year, after declaring that he'd seen a vision of the "Great White Throne Judgment" and that God had called him to form a worldwide ministry for the "last" days, Logan split from the Baptist church, bought a Biddeford school, and incorporated the LBI ministry. From the outset, the directors saw Logan as an infallible prophet of God and gave him absolute power. By the time he moved to Nashua in 1971, he had 1500 followers, mostly blue-collar and country folks.

A burst of fluorescent light and the sound of clicking keyboards, from Amy's outer office, draws Dr. Logan's attention as a lean sinewy figure suited in black enters through the large oak doors at the other end of the room. "So, Dick, do you have the institute projections for next year?" Logan asks as Richard Beckman pulls up one of the yellow Louis Phillipe armchairs. Pastor Beckman is Logan's chief of staff and has been with the ministry from the start.

"Well, Pastor, I've got some prelim—"

"Have some coffee and a Danish," Logan interrupts. "It's fresh from the kitchen." While Beckman goes to the refreshment table, the doctor stands, stretches, then removes his suit coat.

"It's amazing, Dick, how you can eat pastry and never gain," Logan kids as they sit down again. "Look at this gut." He pats his portly stomach which seems ready to pop his suit vest. "I've put on ten pounds since Christmas. I'll be ashamed to wear my swim trunks in Florida, especially if Amy comes. She doesn't have an extra pound on her. It's funny. I never worried about my weight with Pris. Of course, I was younger then and she was my age." Logan's wife died of breast cancer in 1975. A great throng attended her funeral, even her parents. But behind the scenes, Priscilla's family blamed Logan, declaring the cancer was God's judgment because Logan led Priscilla away from the true Church.

"Metabolism," Beckman grunts through a mouthful of cheese Danish. "My metabolism is high. I need to gain weight, but even if I eat desserts all day, I never put on an ounce." Though Beckman is ten years younger, he and Logan have been friends since the late '50s. Yet in recent years, as the ministry has grown, his demeanor around Logan has become more official and less chummy.

"Not me," Dr. Logan quips. "If I even look at a doughnut, I gain a pound, especially during the winter."

"So you're flying to Orlando?" Beckman asks.

"Yeah, on March 14th. Bob and Tricia are coming too. We'll be back for Easter Week." Logan has no family with him save for his oldest son, Robert, and Robert's wife, Patricia—Bob directs the LBI media department—but Logan's nephew Michael Montanaro is nearby in Lawrence, Mass. Ironically, Michael is from Priscilla's side of the family. Logan's other children, two daughters and a son, sided with Priscilla's parents in the family feud and remain aloof from their dad.

Logan sips his coffee then chuckles and says, "Remember when we took the train to Florida, Dick? You brought Gladys and we had adjoining Pullman compartments, and Pris got sick from sunburn."

"That was a crazy trip all right," Beckman replies, giving a tight twist of a grin which is the biggest smile he can give with his lipless mouth. "Gladys Katherine Jordan, she's the only woman I came close to marrying. We dated for four years then she runs off with that bastard from Tennessee, that Pentecostal evangelist who came for summer conference back in '66."

"Yeah, Gladys was a good choir leader," Logan kids, lifting his coffee cup. "And she had a nice pair of hips, but she could be a real airhead at times. Maybe God blessed you by taking her away." They both laugh, then Logan sighs nostalgically. "But those were good ol' days, Dick. Now everything is so rush-rush."

"Well, at least you still go to Florida," Beckman replies, still chuckling. "March can be a long month around here."

Lipless mouth, close-cropped hair, rough pockmarked complexion, small dark eyes behind steel-rimmed glasses. Beckman looks more reptile than human, not to mention his lizardlike physique. And his personality and character fit his appearance perfectly. Though outwardly congenial, he's actually cold and cunning, and will stop at nothing to advance LBI goals.

After another bite of Danish, he gets down to business and hands his boss a blue binder. "These are preliminary figures," he explains, his voice clogged with pastry, "but certainly ballpark."

Logan puts on his glasses, thumbs through the report. He likes what he sees and gives a triumphant grin. "That's a lot of new recruits. You really anticipate 325 freshmen, not counting married couples?"

Beckman drinks from his coffee cup then replies, "Well, Jerry has 275 applications already, and three weeks to go."

Though pleasantly surprised at the size of the increase, Logan expects growth. Since moving to Nashua twelve years ago, his religious empire has grown rapidly, especially in New England where he's established LBI branches in Manchester, Merrimack, North Berwick, Lewiston-Auburn, Fitchburg, Lawrence, Lowell, Brockton, Millbury (Worcester), Gardner, North Adams, Pittsfield, and Brendon Falls—and he still operates a branch in Biddeford, his former headquarters. He also has active churches in the larger cities, Boston, Portland, Providence, Springfield, but the ministry has grown faster in the depressed mill towns. Preaching on radio and TV, and from many pulpits, Logan promises salvation, prosperity, and a return to righteousness. He proclaims that the woes of the region are spiritual, that people have forgotten God, that the Catholic and Protestant churches have forsaken the Bible, and that God has raised up LBI to bring Christ back to the people. During the late '70s, he began to set up branches down the East Coast (New London, Waterbury, Poughkeepsie, Newark, Long Island, Trenton, Harrisburg, Baltimore) and to send out overseas missionary teams (El Salvador, Panama, Puerto Rico, Korea, Taiwan, Finland, Uganda, Brazil, the Philippines). At present, he has thirty branch churches, fifteen missionary teams, a daily radio network, and a weekly television program. Altogether, the LBI ministry has 6500 active members, plus 12,000 listeners and viewers on the radio-TV donation lists.

The doctor hands the binder back to his chief of staff then learns forward resting his elbows on the desk. His grin fades. "What about housing?" he asks concernedly. "We're already three to a room, and I'm not psyched about building more dorms."

Beckman takes a quick drink of coffee then sets his cup and saucer on Logan's desk. "We can squeeze them in," he assures with a confident, almost complacent air. "First, we go to four in a room. We'll still meet the codes. Then we convert the large storage room at the gym into a barracks-style dorm for the guys."

"You mean the big room at Mather? It doesn't have heat, does it?"

"No, not now, but that's easy to fix." After stuffing the last of his pastry into his mouth, Beckman pulls a yellow legal pad from his leather portfolio and goes around to Dr. Logan's side of the desk. Placing the pad in front of Logan, he draws a quick diagram. "Now right here, Pastor, see this main duct?" Beckman points with his pen. "It feeds the shower rooms. We cut in right here and bleed off into the new dorm. It won't be toasty, but it'll be warm enough. Besides, a spartan environment will build character ... and weed out the weaklings."

"That's most creative, Dick," Logan declares, his words punctuated by a haughty snort.

"Well, this is stopgap to be sure, but why build new dorms until we absolutely must? I'd rather collect interest than pay it."

The doctor gives a cackling snicker that makes his potbelly shake. "No argument there. So, what's the gross ... for next year?"

Pastor Beckman returns to his chair where he whips out a pocket calculator and punches it with his long bony forefinger.

"Well, if we increase tuition to ninety-five, and room and board to a thou? Of course, we're losing 140 grads, but then adding married, off-campus, and part-timers, plus extension schools. Let's see ... four million, possibly four and a quarter. That's compared to three and a half this year. Now subtracting expenses, we should clear around nine hundred thou."

"But what about new teachers?" Logan asks as he swigs down the last of his coffee.

A shrewd half-grin twists again onto Beckman's slotlike mouth. "Not needed—not this year anyway. We'll just increase the size of our freshman sections and move the larger classes into the gym, or over to Knox."

Logan removes his glasses and rubs his eyes. "You're telling me we can absorb a *thirty* percent increase without increasing expenses? There's got to be a catch, or a trick?"

"No, n-no," Beckman reassures, "no trick, just arithmetic. It's going to take about sixty out of the kitty, for furniture and remodeling, but our overall cost will only go up ten percent."

Logan replaces his glasses. "Sounds convincing, Dick. I guess I can't get used to having the college in the black, after taking a beating so many years. But go ahead, take what you need. Just tell Jerry about it."

Beckman stands and prepares to leave. "I wish I could be as positive on the church side of the ledger. I don't have the final figures from Jerry, but with the Moody mortgage and the new TV time, and the Cessna deal, we're looking tight. No panic, but we should perhaps take a closer look at the proposal Matt and I shared with you last month."

"I could've figured as much," the doctor replies, his voice showing concern again. "As soon as you get the projections from Jerry, we'll talk about the big picture, but I don't see how the news could be terribly bad. After all, we're growing faster than ever?"

Without replying, Beckman turns to go, but Logan halts him, "Oh, Dick, did you ever catch up with Morgan?—you know, the newspaper guy in Pittsfield?"

Beckman leans on the chair he just vacated. "I talked to him once, and I think we have an understanding, but I'll know more on Friday." As LBI chief of staff, Pastor Beckman oversees all areas of the ministry, but he devotes much of his time to dealing with dissidents and adversaries. A genius at manipulation, he wins some with the carrot, and brings others into line with the stick, all the time exuding a spirit of icy invincibility that strikes fear into LBI's detractors. Ruthlessly loyal to Logan, Rich Beckman is the Heinrich Himmler of Logan Bible Institute. He even looks like Hitler's

Waffen S.S. czar.

"I'm sick and tired of Caldwell *bad*-mouthing us," Logan declares hitting his fist into his hand with moderate emotion. "That *bast*ard is spreading a lot of gossip that goes all the way back to Biddeford. Morgan even brought it up in the interview. We certainly don't want that crap in print. We're going good in the Berkshires. We don't need some *cry*baby Baptist screwing things up. It a*mazes* me, Dick. Churches are lukewarm and dying, and we come in and start winning souls, and even give them the converts. But they still attack us. They're a bunch of jealous and ungrateful infighters and *back*biters, and most of them don't even have seventy-five members in their church, not active members anyway. And Caldwell's the ringleader."

"Well, I think that fire's under control," Beckman assures the doctor. "I told Morgan that we're not perfect, anymore than any church, but that we came to Pittsfield to help the community, and to serve the people."

"And?" Logan asks, cocking his head curiously.

Beckman, as if bowing to his boss, bends his serpentine body over the chair. A sly chuckle accompanies his answer, "Morgan asked for specifics on what we're doing to help the community. I told him we'd already committed to a quarter-page ad every Saturday for thirteen weeks. He hemmed and hawed, and said that's not what he meant ... but he *got* the message."

"What's that costing us?"

"A buck and a quarter per week, or $1625 in all. The Pittsfield team is picking up half the tab, but it's worth it, double worth it— to advertise in the *Eagle*."

"And Caldwell?"

"Well, he's been more friendly lately," Beckman replies, a cocky glint in his beady eyes. "Some of our people knew him back in Portland and they've got some juicy stories. I sent Caldwell a nice letter suggesting that we cooperate in our evangelism efforts, and I just happened to mention our mutual friends, to uh ... let's say, re*mind* him of his roots."

Logan folds his arms around his barrel-shaped chest. "Cooperate, yes ... cooperate," he says half under his breath. "That's the key word, Dick. Wherever we go, we want to *cooperate*."

Pastor Beckman says no more, but gives a departing high sign, strides briskly to the massive oak doors, and slithers through into the outer office.

# Chapter Seven

A playful gust of wind hurries through the pine trees sending the snowflakes scurrying. Some of the flakes settle on the snow-clad branches, some balance delicately on the wires overhead, while others spiral to the mantle of white below. The gently falling snow gives Jim a peaceful feeling. Spring is only two weeks away but winter prevails on this Tuesday morning creating a Christmas card scene outside his office windows. Even Stan Campbell's junk pile at the corner of the drive-around looks like a sculptured work of art. Stan talks about hauling the stuff away but never does, so the pile grows with bus tires, school desks, bookshelves, tables, chairs, an old air conditioner, and other items.

The public schools have declared a "snow day," but at Brendon Falls Christian Academy (BFCA), K-6, morning assembly is just getting over. Jim hears the commotion in the hallway as twenty-seven prattling pupils, like quacking ducklings, disperse to their classrooms behind their teachers.

After the children pass, Beverly Bradley pops in, drops her daily attendance sheet into Jim's in-box, smiles, and departs. Bev, a grayheaded energetic 39-year-old, with a perky big-sister personality, teaches fifth and sixth grades, and serves as assistant principal. But in practice she runs the school—she's the only state-certified faculty member—while Jim runs the church, or rather it runs him. Mrs. B., as the kids call her, is matronly and schoolmarmish, especially with her saddle-bridge half-eye glasses, yet she's still reasonably attractive. She and Russ are the same age, but her prematurely gray hair—a cool gray that looks almost blue, especially under the fluorescent lights—makes her look older.

Jim sits down at his desk. He sighs and sips his coffee. He scans his calendar book:

Tuesday 3-8-83: Send '82 Growth Report to Nashua (Stan). Men's Prayer Bkfst, Sat. 3-19 (Stan & Russ). 2PM = hosp. visits. Increase ins. liability. Call on yellow pages. 7:15 PM, pick up Elmer & Agnes for svc. Wednesday 3-9-83: New BFCA brochure. 9:30 AM = Sarah Johnson (counseling). Spring special events to B-board. Call Amy = final coord on Pastors' Conference. Finalize teen skate/3-12 (Barry). Sched Baby Dedication 3-20 (Joanne, Thelma). New Sunday school curriculum (Carl). 7PM = PTF. Thursday 3-10-83: 9AM = bldg inspector. Stan list: lock on shed, grass in front, sign loose. 3PM = Worcester Jail visits....

*No way; I can't get into this,* Jim says to himself as he swivels his attention back to the window and its thick mist of hoary white. He gazes wide-eyed at the dime-sized flakes: darting, twirling, floating, down, down, peacefully down. The forecast calls for a change to rain, for a wet and windy afternoon, but for now the snowfall is soft, soothing, almost hypnotic.

The snowflakes etch traces on the screen of Jim's mind like shooting ice-crystal stars, falling, falling, until the long tendrils of white weave together into a snowy fabric, a downy-soft curtain. Retreating within this curtain, he thinks about Becki, *She didn't come this past weekend. No explanation ... just told Joe she wasn't coming. Face it. She doesn't give a shit about me—oh, maybe she's fond of me as a leftover friend, father figure, but the romantic thing was all in my mind, pure fantasy. Two weekends of practicum training were enough. I knew she wouldn't last. I had her figured right. I'm glad I came to my senses.*

His eyes drift from the window to the wall. Cascading color: pink, yellow, lilac, tawny brown. The flowers in the blue-sage wallpaper are now colorful snowflakes cascading down onto the carpet. Eyes, eyes, blue eyes, and a bantering grin. A face appears in the waterfall of color, distorted at first, then well-defined. "J-Jodi, what are you doing out, in here?" Jim asks.

"What am I doing?" she mocks, gesturing at Jim with a handful of papers. "I'm standing here talking to the pastor, to the principal of the school, who seems to be a space case today. In fact, he's been a space case for the last few weeks."

"Awh, come on, I was just daydreaming. You could've knocked?"

"I did. What am I supposed to do, knock all day? I've got kids waiting. I have to teach when I'm here. I don't have an office to daydream in."

"Speaking of teaching ... since when can you teach in scruffy blue jeans and old boots?"

"You're fishing, Jim. You can't get me on that one. I was at the meeting when you fought against the dress code. Besides, it's snowing. Why should I wear a dress and heels when you can wear pants and boots?"

Jim swigs his coffee and searches for a logical comeback. Finding none, he laughs and says, "You're impossible, Jodi Donovan—so whaddeya doin' in here?"

Sheathing her sword, Jodi laughs as well then explains, "I need to run off these spelling sheets. The machine in Angie's office is out again, and the Mita man can't come until tomorrow."

"Be my guest," Jim replies, gesturing toward the old Canon copier.

Jodi, her back to him, commences and a chemical odor soon fills the office. As Jim listens to the whirring, clicking, and clunking of the primitive wet-copy process, he speaks to himself, *She'd never banter with Stan, much less Dr. Logan. They'd be outraged at her disrespect and familiarity, at her failure to give "double honor" to delegated authority, but I'm glad she cuts up with me. I don't want "double honor."*

Thirty-one, slender, Irish, and brunette. Graceful jockish legs. Jodi slouches at the machine like a relaxed marionette. Boyish hips: small, high, compact. Faded Calvin Klein's, more white than blue. She's almost as tall as Sharon, but with shoulders tilted one way and pelvis another, Jodi doesn't look tall. When finished, she kills the machine, collects her papers, then without turning around, speaks in a shy voice, "Jim, I need to...."

"Need to what?" Jim asks gently. He senses her mood change.

Jodi turns toward him but averts her eyes. "I uh ... I need to talk."

Compassion, fond affection. Warm feelings stir Jim's heart as Jodi stands poignantly before him. "Okeydoke, let's do an early lunch at the diner. Can you get away at eleven?" Based on Sharon's latest pillow-talk gossip, he suspects what Jodi wants to talk about.

"Yeah, my kids go to music with Angie. I'll tell her, in case we're late." Jodi smiles sheepishly then adds, "We can even take *my* car. How does *that* grab you?"

"Now I *know* you're desperate," Jim kids as Jodi laughs and departs.

Quickened for action, Pastor Jim downs the last of his coffee then heads for Angie's office which is around the corner in the new wing. As he enters, he runs into Doris Campbell coming out with her distribution items in her hand. "What's with this weather?" Doris asks, rolling her large hazel eyes up to him. "I like snow but it gets old in March. I can't believe we actually came in today. I bet we're the only school open in the whole state."

Jim moves inside the doorway as Doris rotates into the hall. "Could be," he replies with a grin, "but you can blame it on Bev. I delegate that decision to her. I hafta come in anyway."

Doris brushes a burnt-auburn cheek wisp back toward her ear. "Actually, it's a good thing we did have school," she bubbles. "God's honoring our faith already. Tommy and Kimberly invited Jesus into their hearts during assembly. We caught Satan off guard for sure."

"That's great," Jim replies halfheartedly. Doris often tries to sound evangelical like her husband but she lacks the gut conviction, so she comes across chirpy and flaky—like Lucy Ricardo.

"So, Jim, what are you doing for lunch?" Doris asks, shifting to a subject where she's more at home. "You want to go to Bergson's? Or did Sharon bag you a lunch?"

"No, I didn't bag it today. But I can't go to Bergson's either. I'm going to lunch early today ... to the diner with Jodi."

"Well, I must say, Pastor, you *are* a popular fellow. Guess I'll have to take a number."

"I guess you will," Jim teases. "But don't despair. You may get a *low* number."

"Your humor is such a consolation, Rev. Shanley," Doris wisecracks over her shoulder as she walks briskly back to her class of third- and fourth-graders. Watching her go, Jim thinks about Stan Campbell divorcing his first alcoholic wife to marry Doris who's seventeen years younger than her husband. Of course, that was before Stan was born-again; it's after you're saved that you must walk the "straight and narrow." And Doris and Stan are careful to do that before their peers in the church. Only a few, including Jim, know that behind the pretense, Doris is unhappy and has a secret drinking problem of her own.

Jim goes on through the mail room into Angela's cluttered office where she's typing furiously at a table next to her desk, amid coffee mugs, stacks of paper, file folders, boxes, two telephones, crumpled napkins, and an empty McDonald's bag. Angie's familiar Windsong fragrance stakes out the room as her territory. As she works, she clenches a pencil between her teeth. Before Jim hired Angie back in '79, he had asked Sharon to be the church-school secretary but she declined, preferring to keep her part-time position at Brenner & Williams, a Brendon Falls law firm. At least, that was her announced reason. Truth is, as Sharon now admits, she didn't want to take orders from her husband.

When Angela sees Jim, her face lights up. "Well, this *is* a happening," she declares after taking the pencil from between her teeth. "You haven't been this far into my office since the Christmas party." From the inflection in her voice, Jim realizes that her playful side is in command, as opposed to her pious side which predominates at prayer meetings.

"A burst of energy came upon me. I decided I'd come see you today."

Pushing back from her worktable, Angie gives a sporty grin and removes her Liz Claiborne designer glasses—everyone in the church knows they are designer glasses because she made a point of showing them off when she got them. "Don't you have a class at nine? I thought you taught math to the fifth- and sixth-graders?" Her voice is high-pitched and hoarse as if she has a perpetual cold.

Jim pulls up a chair. "No, that's Monday, Wednesday, and Friday."

"Well, I'm almost finished with Stan's report. I can bring it to you."

"That's all right," he teases. "I think I'll just watch my *lovely* secretary at work. I like how you bite on that pencil. You have such intensity, like you're writing a passionate novel."

Angie blushes but quickly changes the subject, "Did you know, Jim, that fast food is more nourishing than people think? I saw it night before last on *Chronicle*." Her hands glide in the air as if she's conducting an orchestra, her fingers moving as if she's still typing. "Larry's always bugging me because I go to McDonald's. He says I should eat a lighter lunch, and that's why I'm putting on weight. If he had his way, I'd be eating Stouffer's Lean Cuisine every meal, but I'm not putting on weight, not really—oh, I'm a little plump on my behind but that's because I sit on it all day."

To Jim, Larry and Angela seem like a mismatch as do most of the couples in the church. The Thorntons also live on Greeley Hill but in a more expensive neighborhood up near the new hospital. They have no children. Larry, a nattily dressed investment broker and fitness nut, is a professing atheist who only comes to church for potluck suppers and special events. Jim finds him obnoxious, and he figures that Angie took the church secretary job because of loneliness and boredom. She certainly doesn't need the money; in that respect she's unique among the BFBC regulars.

"Well, Angie, if you want an expert opinion," Jim kids in reply to her comment about her weight, "I think your figure is very healthy, regardless of what you eat, or how you sit."

"Oh, cut it out, Jim. I must say, you're in a *rare* mood. I haven't heard flattery from your lips for a while." Angie's cheeks stain pinker than before. A frisky-kitten glint dances in her green eyes— she has soft hazel-flecked green eyes but the hazel is hardly noticeable until you get close.

Replacing her glasses, and the pencil, she resumes typing. As she blisters the keys on the Olympia electric, her modest bust lifts then lowers inside her pink blouse, and a fallen curl bounces on her forehead. She has pretty swept-back hair, tawny-orange like the color of apricots. Though fair-skinned and freckled, she's better looking than the average redhead, but her pointy nose, overlong with little nostrils, prevents her from being a knockout. Under the typing table her nylon-clad legs are slightly spread inside a knee-length corduroy skirt.

Jim tries to refrain but he can't stop his roving eyes; they move inside her skirt, inside her thighs. *Oh, Angie, open a little wider,* he exhorts, but only to himself. *Let me see your crotch.* It's hard for Jim to picture Angela getting off with Larry. She seems warm and wet and sensual, while her husband seems antiseptic and packaged and dry. *Having sex with Larry Thornton must be about as exciting as getting cash at an ATM.*

Pinch of guilt. Jim has no control when it comes to looking at ripe female flesh—acting, yes, but looking, no. Dr. Logan teaches that the Holy Spirit gives a Christian man brotherly love without sexual desire, but it has never worked for Jim. At thirty-five, Angie's still most provocative, and he often fantasizes about her; he wonders about the color of her bush and how her breasts hang. After all, Jim has only seen two real-life women in the nude, Sharon and his mother—or three, counting his cousin Charlotte who was twelve and going through puberty, but she had hair.

Angie finishes the report and hands it to Jim. "Glad you came over," she says as he gets up to depart. "It's nice to get some attention, even if you are a big *tease.*"

Jim grins and gives her a mock salute. "Don't worry, we'll talk again one of these days. Meanwhile, keep blushing. It makes you look like a bashful vir—I mean like a *rose* in bloom."

"Oh, get out of here!" she sports, giving a girlish giggle.

\* \* \*

Pastor Jim brushes four inches of fluffy snow off the windshield and rear window of Jodi's gray '79 Honda then climbs inside, into the smell of a smoker's car. Jodi takes off across the snow-covered parking lot, steering with one hand, while she shifts, punches the radio buttons, and rummages for cigarettes with the other. The radio blares something about Reagan calling the Soviet Union an evil empire, jumps abruptly to a Jordan's Furniture commercial, then stops at John Cougar Mellencamp doing "Hurt So Good." Half the contents of Jodi's purse fall out into her lap but she finally finds her Winstons. She lights one, inhales deeply, then opens the window a crack. Smoking is prohibited on church property, so getting a nicotine fix upon leaving is the norm for BFBC smokers. They also take cigarette breaks in the rest rooms and in parked cars. This violates the no-smoking policy but is an accepted practice, except when Stan Campbell is around.

"Let's go to McD's instead of Park Street," Jodi suggests as she turns the radio down a notch. "It's closer. We'll go through drive-thru and talk in the car."

"I can live with that," Jim says. "Besides, you're driving."

East on Reservoir Road, then down the hill to Coachlace Plaza. They arrive in five minutes despite the snow.

"Welcome to McDonald's," the speaker crackles impersonally. "Can I take your order?"

Jodi spouts their order, "Big Mac, large fries, Quarter-Pounder, two milks, two hot-fudge sundaes, one with nuts."

"Six forty-four, first window please," the speaker crackles again.

They pull into a parking spot and dig into the McDonald's experience. While eating, they make small talk without getting much deeper than the snow. When finished, Jim runs in for coffee while Jodi disposes of the trash. On the way he expels several burps of pickled aftertaste, a taste that is uniquely McDonald's. On his return, he begins with a question, "So, Jodi, what's on your mind?"

Jodi brings her steaming cup to her lips then places it on the dash. The hot vapors fog the windshield. Gazing pensively at the rising steam, her eyes cloud with hazy sadness. Jim waits. He watches the snowflakes hitting the windshield. They come down as pristine works of art but on impact flatten into smushy blops of ice. They hold a moment, then melt and run off as plain water. It reminds him of the downside of growing up—the giving up of one's uniqueness to conform to the human herd.

Finally, Jodi replies, "You probably think I'm a together person, being married and teaching and having an energetic fourteen-year-old like Brenda, but really, Jim, you don't know me, not the *real* me."

"Maybe not," Jim replies, "but I see the hurt in your eyes. I've been around. I know Kyle enough. I can tell your life is no rose garden."

"You can say that again. But now things are coming to a head and I have to talk to someone, and I can't tell my mom or my family. They just preach at me. I'm not even sure how you'll—"

Jodi stops abruptly and picks up her cup.

"Take your time," Jim says. "I'm not goin' anywhere." He thinks about what Sharon has already told him about Jodi. He feels deceitful. He wishes he hadn't heard the gossip. Jodi picks at a spot of red paint on her jeans. Her fingernails are short, well-manicured, but unpolished. She seems hesitant. "This isn't a confessional," Jim reassures. "We're just friends talking in a car."

Framed by a chin-length pageboy, Jodi's face is lean and ordinary. The rings and crow's-feet about her blue eyes—actually more lavender than blue—along with the flecks of gray in her hair, make her look older than thirty-one. "My life's been mainly unhappy," she goes on, after gathering her courage. "My parents split up when I was five. I never had a father or a man I could trust, and Kyle's the worst. We got married six months after he got back from Vietnam. I was pregnant with Brenda. My mom's Catholic, and his parents are too, not devout about God, but strict when it comes to babies out of wedlock. So we had little choice. I was just seventeen. I think the war screwed up Kyle's mind because our marriage has been hell. A week after the wedding, he's out all night goin' to bars and parties, and he hasn't changed since ... and now he's chasing my cousin Ruthie since she started working with him at NyPro."

Jim sips his coffee then responds, "Sounds like a lot of the marriages around this town. So why'd you stay with him all this time?"

Abandoning her coffee to the dash, Jodi restarts the engine then lights up a cigarette. The pungent odor of the burned-out match fills the front seat then fades behind the milder aroma of tobacco smoke. She sucks intently on her Winston—so intently that the cracks in her lips push through an old application of pink lipstick.

After exhaling, she replies to Jim's question, "I felt like a failure as a wife. So I stayed and tried to make it better. Kyle, he'd beat me up then beg for forgiveness. He was so pitiful, and Mom said, 'You took vows. You can't leave as long as he's working.' When I got saved and came here, I prayed for God to change him, but after three years, there's been no change. Oh, he's a little better during softball season. That's the only thing he likes about the church. But overall, it's just the same old shit."

Pastor Jim loosens his tie and shifts slightly so as to rest his arm on the back of Jodi's seat. Staring wide-eyed at the foggy windshield, she seems weary and heavy laden as she yawns out a puff of smoke. The tumbling plume disintegrates over the dashboard then slowly rises and exits over the top of the slightly open window. "Why come to me now if this has been goin' on so long?" Jim asks. "There's more to this, right?"

Jodi's eyebrows knit with mild irritation. She leans forward and places her still-burning cigarette in the ashtray. "Let me finish, Jim. You're getting ahead of me. Of course, that's not all. There's more. I've got dirty laundry of my own, and—"

"Let me guess," Jim blurts impatiently, anxious to get Sharon's gossip on the table, and to clear his conscience. "You're involved with someone at church? at the school? another teacher?"

Jodi's irritation flashes into rage: "YOU *KNOW* ALREADY! That's not right! This is personal! It's for *me* to tell! It really pisses me off that my personal life is all over the damn church!"

"It's okay, Jodi," he quickly pleads. "I'm not against you. I'm not against you and Tony; really, I'm *not*." After fourteen years with Sharon, Jim is good at backpedaling.

Jodi seethes, her nostrils flaring then closing like the gills of a fish. "This makes me so mad! I try to tell you, Jim, and *you* come out with it like you're playing with me. You should've told me. It's not fair!"

"Okay, Jodi, okay. You're right. I should've shown you all my cards." Jodi's indignation hangs in the air freezing them into silence. Snatching up her Winston, she takes several determined drags; the smoke mingles with the anger. Jim anxiously drinks his coffee until it's gone.

After several minutes—that seem like hours—her fierce scowl softens. Then comes a hint of a sheepish grin. Jim knows he's regained her trust. He breaks the silence, "Aren't you a sly little *fox*. You and Anthony Liggons. Now that's an affair. No wonder you've been volunteering to help with P.E. since November."

They both chuckle as Jodi's grin breaks wide. "But still, Jim, it pisses me off. I thought pastors never listen to gossip?"

"How can I help it? I sleep with Sharon. She tells me all the chitchat."

Jodi mashes her cigarette in the ashtray. "Yeah, I guess that figures. But I hate the word 'affair.' This is more, much more. But I'm just shy about goin' on." She compresses her lips as if thinking. "It's like this ... how can I say it? Oh f-f-fuck—*fuck it*. I need another cigarette." She fumbles for her Winstons. "Pardon my language, but I've got to have a smoke in my mouth before I can go deeper. I'm *some* role model for the kids, huh, cussing like a sailor and having nicotine fits? Sure you want to know the *real* me?"

"You're funny, Jodi," Jim teases, ignoring her question. "I can tell the F-word's not a new word for you"—it isn't new for him either, but as a pastor, he of course has dropped it from his vocabulary, but not his thoughts. "In fact, I bet you knew every four-letter word by the time you were six, having grown up in *this* town."

"Come on," she teases back. "I'm not *that* bad."

They both snicker as Jodi lights up. She then sobers, kills the engine, and goes on with her story, speaking reflectively, "After about four years of being married and abused, and being left alone all the time, I started goin' to Clancy's myself, and guys would pick me up."

"Lonely frustrated wives meeting men at a bar ... that's also pretty normal around here."

"But, Jim, I hated it—not that I did it much, maybe four or five times. But it made my skin crawl. I wanted to be loved, understood, talked to. I wanted what I never got with Kyle. But I didn't find it at Clancy's. After screwing around with a drunk horny guy, I felt even worse ... like dirty and discarded, like a used rubber. So I quit going out, but I was still lonely. That's the *main* reason I came to this church." Jodi's openness moves Jim. Her confession makes him feel closer to her. He always feels closer to confessed sinners than to victorious saintly Christians, because he knows *he's* not a victorious Christian—despite his righteous facade.

Jodi draws on her cigarette until the tip glows red-hot, then she slowly exhales. The smoke coils up around her head like a gray serpent then slips out the window. A blissful smile gathers up the corners of her mouth as if she's smoking a joint instead of tobacco. A gentle brightness, soft like summer moonlight, comes into her eyes and pink color warms her cheeks, but the high is not chemical. "Now Tony, he changed everything ... the sky, the clouds, the trees, even the snow seemed happy. Tony's not like other men. He tells me what he's thinking. He listens, he understands me, and when he holds me, it's like going to *hea*ven. I want to be with him all the time. He fills my thoughts, my dreams. He stirs me and makes me happy—more than God *ever* did." As Jodi talks about Tony, Jim longs to tell her about Becki but he doesn't dare.

Dark, dark. Just as quickly as it brightened, Jodi's face goes dark. Her forehead furrows. Her eyes fall. "At least, that's how it used to be," she wistfully laments as if speaking of her own death. "Now it's like *tor*ture. The end's coming. Now love is a fuckin' *curse*. And I hate myself for getting in so deep."

"What happened?" Jim asks. "Did Claudia find out?"

"Well, yeah. Tony denies it but she's heard the gossip. She knows. But she's just part of the problem." The pink color has drained out of Jodi's cheeks leaving a chalky pallor.

"Is it because he's Black?"

"That doesn't help any. Kyle knows. He's guessing, but he's guessing right. He calls me a 'nigger-*lovin*' bitch' and his bigoted lounge-lizard buddies look at me like I'm trash. He's so two-faced. He's buddy-buddy with Tony on the softball field, but off the field, Tony's a 'nigger.' But still, race is more of a subplot in all this."

To Jim, Tony Liggons hardly seems colored. A large-boned, athletic, and handsome Negro, with an associate's degree in physical education, he seems much different from the poor Blacks that hang around downtown.

"So what's the main plot, Jodi?" Jim asks. "What gives you this sense of doom?"

"It's more like what's happening inside of us. It's too intense. It's like we have to be together all the time or not at all. I hate the hiding and the lying. Our love can never fit. I feel so guilty and cut off, like God is punishing us." Jodi gestures, cigarette in hand. Ashes dribble down her blue shirt onto her lap. She notices but does not wipe them off.

"So whaddeya gonna do?" Jim asks.

"I don't have to do anything," she replies, her face like stone, her voice detached and distant. "He's goin' to break it off. We're together, but we're absent. Our dream is withering on the vine. I try to keep a happy front but my soul feels like it's soaked in formaldehyde. I'm in a cold slippery pit that has no bottom, just sloping sides of slime ... and I *know* I'm goin' down."

Jodi's raw nakedness now shakes Jim. He feels uncomfortable, almost panicky. She flips her cigarette out the window then takes a deep shuddering breath. "I feel like I'm in a fish bowl, Jim. Everyone knows and talks behind my back, yet they pretend all is well to my face ... but I see the looks. The other night Kyle hit me and gave me a drunken lecture on adultery and the purity of the white race. He says it's a disgrace to God that I want a nigger more than him. It's like he's saying what everyone else is thinking."

Jodi leans forward as if she's going to vomit. Her words choke out in gasps, "Now I'm so afraid. I cringe waiting for the final blow. I know I deserve it. I'm *such* a liar, *such* a cheat. I feel *so* guilty, so *fuckin'* guilty! Why does love always fuck things up? I had to tell you, Jim, and you probably—O God! What can I do!" She breaks into heavy sobs and falls across into Jim's arms. Compassion and affection dispel his panicky discomfort. He holds her close until her crying diminishes to quivering congested sighs.

"Oh, Jodi," Jim consoles. "I wish I could tell you it's right, or it's wrong, or how to make it fit, but I can't. A few years back I would've quoted scriptures to you about adultery, fornication, and forgiveness, but now, to admonish your heart would be like standing at the rim of the Grand Canyon and telling the Colorado River that it's in the wrong place. True love is so much bigger than us, so rare, so fleeting. It's like the blue asters that come in the fall. I see them when I walk in the woods. Even in October, I see them blooming amid the fallen leaves. They're so beautiful, so magical, yet they have no enduring place in the dying woods. When I go back in November, they're always gone except for the memory."

"I like it when you talk to me," Jodi replies into his breast. "It makes me feel better even if things *are* fucked up forever. I never expected you to be so open with me. I knew you wouldn't condemn me to hell, but I half-expected a pastorly scolding over this."

Jim responds with a quip, "Guess you're getting to know the *real* me, huh?"

They both chuckle in spite of all, as Jodi retreats to her side of the car. She coughs several times, a hacking smoker's cough, then blows her nose on a McDonald's napkin. Finally, she starts the car and they head back to the church.

The snow is coming down in large feathery flakes, like great white butterflies. As yet, it has not changed to rain. Jim hopes it won't. He likes snow better than rain.

# Chapter Eight

Pastor Shanley parks his Mustang behind the Campbells' blue Datsun. Stan and Doris live in a three-bedroom ranch on Candace Street in the Acre district east of the river. Neglect and disrepair. The gray clapboard house needs paint and roof shingles—the wind has blown away a lot of them exposing black squares of roofing paper—and the yard looks like the deep rough at a third-rate golf course. Stan's old pickup is not around.

Doris, wearing her raggedy aqua breakfast coat, meets Jim at the door. "Sorry I didn't make it in, Jimmy. Jus' one of those days for me. I-I, I'm glad you came." The lapel of her robe is stained with egg and the buttons are missing, but she keeps it closed with three safety pins.

"No problem," Jim fibs. "You gave me an excuse to leave early. You know how Fridays are?" Normally true, but this Friday afternoon he's in a rush because Sharon's parents are coming for the weekend.

Doris is buzzed, as expected, but reasonably coherent for a stay-at-home drinking day. Swaying slightly, she escorts Jim through the foyer into the kitchen. "Snow went fas', huh?" she says as she toddles over to get the coffee. "Hard to believe we had a storm on Tuesday; think it was Tuesday? Was it? Think it was?"

"Yeh, it snowed Tuesday," Jim affirms, "but the sun works fast in March."

"You're a weatherman, aren't you, Jim honey? That's righ', an' a pashor too." Jim removes his coat, loosens his tie, and sits down at a breakfast table in a sunlit nook off the kitchen. He's immediately welcomed by Midnight, the Campbells' gray-coated tomcat, who jumps purring into his lap.

Doris brings Jim his coffee in a blue "Pastor Jim" mug that she gave him years before but keeps in her own cupboard for his frequent pastoral visits. She then grabs her jug of wine, her glass, her cigarettes, and a crystal ashtray, and plunks down across from him. "So where's Stan?" Jim inquires.

Doris fires up a Salem Light, takes a drag, then exhales upward across the table. "He's at a union meeting," she replies. "If it's not the damn church, it's the damn mill. He's never home. You know that, honey. You know he's the vice president of the Paperworkers of America. He ish. I tol' you that. An' you're a pashor an' a deshent pershon." She handles the beginning of each line of thought but after a sentence or two loses the signal and her words begin to garble and slur. But Jim is used to it, and if he had to choose between sober and drunk for Doris, he'd choose drunk because the wine takes away her flaky evangelical pretense. He's known her since the fall of '75 when the church started in his living room, and he's one of the few who's intimate with her "wino" side. Stan wasn't involved until the following year. In fact, Doris and Jim often discussed ways to win Stan over, but since he joined and became superzealous, they've discussed ways of slowing him down.

Hefting the green Carlo Rossi wine jug, Doris fills her glass. Her disjointed rambling is strangely poetic: "It's my cross. I bear it daily, Jimmy honey, being married to an older man. He treats Paula like she's still the wife, an' all these years, I'm a child, a damn toy. After twelve years, I'm still the babysitter, see, but Junior's grown-up. *I'm* the baby now. Paula's the *real* wife, see ... 'caush I'm barren like Hannah, an' no Shamuel's coming for me. You always shay, Jim, if you love, it'll come back, but it never works with Stan, an' now he won't let Ruthie come over, an' you know, Jimmy, she'sh my friend like you, an' David's jusha mixed up kid. He ish, Jimmy. You know that, an'...."

She rambles on. Jim sips his coffee, strokes the cat. He's been in the Campbells' kitchen fifty times but he can never appreciate the design or the decor; he can tell the room is yellow but not much more. Cabinet doors ajar, drawers open, cup towels thrown about. Dirty dishes, pots, pans, utensils: in the sink, on the counter, on the cooking island. Doris's lack of motivation is all around. Also on the counter: an open box of Post Raisin Bran, a bowl of half-eaten raisin bran, a gooey cutting board, an open loaf of Italian bread, a Mr. Coffee coffeemaker, a family-size bottle of DeMoula's ketchup, a giant box of Fab detergent, two bags of unsorted groceries, piles of circulars, coupons, magazines, plus four Bibles, a large bottle of Rolaids, three cartons of Salem Lights, a wet sponge, a half-eaten bag of Hershey's kisses, two ashtrays brimming over with butts and ashes, and a small boom box behind a stack of Neil Diamond tapes.

Spilled milk, ketchup, and coffee grounds decorate the countertop, while spots of syrup, grease, and dried gravy dapple the breakfast table. Tracked-in mud splotches the gray-tile floor. Waist-high trash fills the corner at the end of the counter along with a knee-high stack of *Boston Herald* newspapers. Dirty laundry falls out of an overflowing basket in the door of the utility room. Foul odors abound. Old tobacco ashes, cheap wine, greasy day-old bacon, barbecued chicken, rancid cat food, decomposing garbage—all mixed with the latest: fresh coffee, cigarette smoke, and Doris's cheap perfume.

*How does she stand it in here?* Jim wonders as Doris goes on talking and smoking and sipping her wine. *Somebody needs to come in with a wheelbarrow and a fire hose. Look at her, damp and*

*dumpy and radiating bleakness, and half soused, while her hus-*
*band preaches about the power of the Holy Spirit, and expects the*
*church to be as clean as a hospital.* Jim stares with disgust at the
half-eaten bowl of raisin bran. He can't see it that well but he
imagines the soggy flakes floating in slimy milk and clinging to the
sides. Half-eaten cereal is one of his pet peeves and he often gets on
Sharon and the kids about it. Too much. He returns his attention to
the breakfast nook, to a deacon's bench under the window. It's piled
with stacks of old magazines: *Reader's Digest, Time, American*
*Legion Magazine, Vogue, Cosmopolitan.* And right on top, ironically, are several issues of *Good Housekeeping.*

Midnight stretches, jumps off Jim's lap, and struts out of the
room. As Jim rubs cat hair off his pants, his thoughts drift, *I should*
*get home. Nana and Pop are probably there already. Sharon'll be*
*pissed if I'm late. She's been cooking for two days.... I've still heard*
*nothing from Becki. Forget it. She's had all the training she wants,*
*at least in Brendon Falls.*

Doris stops talking to light another Salem. Jim takes the
opportunity to respond, "What can I say, Doris? We've talked.
We've prayed. What more can we do? Stan is set in his ways."

Drooping like a wilted daffodil in a narrow-necked vase,
Doris seems on the verge of tears but she fights them back with a
quick sip of wine and a casual dignified drag on her cigarette. Next
to Janet Buford, Doris is the best-looking of Jim's teachers and,
despite her pointy Polish chin, would be the prettiest if it weren't for
her drinking. She doesn't look like an alcoholic—not yet. But her
eyes are red-tinged and she has puffy pouches beginning to show
underneath them. "Jimmy honey, my life is *so* banal, such a drag,"
she laments. "You know, honey, I love my class, my kids, but they
don't know about it, see ... how it all goesh shour when you're
nineteen and married. My name, m-my name, used to be Myshzak.
You know that, Jimmy honey, an' I gave it up for Campbell. Jesush
ish with me, but still I shuffer. Stan shays ish becaush I still pray to
Mary an' think like a Catholic. You know, honey, I tol' you that. Ish
my crossh for God. I shuffer. O Jesush, Joseph, an' Mary. I shuffer
alone for God ... ish *all* for God."

Silence. Doris smokes and drinks. Pitiful yet poignant, she
reminds Jim of a tragic character from a Faulkner novel. Cigarette
smoke gathers like morning fog above the table. Her hazel eyes
reflect many colors, autumn colors, as rays of late afternoon
sunshine dance on her face. Pinprick freckles, so small they look
like blush makeup until you get close, dust her cheeks and nose. Her
wavy burnt-auburn hair is cut in a bob with short bangs that spill
over her forehead. Frisky side wisps play about her temples and tiny

maple leaf earrings sparkle in her ears.

Jim watches her smoking and sipping. Carnal curiosity. His thoughts descend to his dick. Naked, naked. He undresses her in his mind until she's sitting there nude, her breasts pendulous over the table. Lust, lust—*guilt*. He kills the fantasy.

But Doris doesn't. After a long last pull on her second Salem, she crushes it out in the ashtray then reaches for Jim with her eyes. Intently gazing, she peruses his face, his hands, his body. He feels suddenly uneasy—like a prey being stalked by a predator. She often flirts but has never looked at him with such aggressive eyes, yet her pupils don't seem dilated. He senses mixed vibes coming from her. She takes his hand and caresses it tenderly. Her hands are small and soft, her touch gentle. But her yeasty breath is disgusting. Jim again pictures her naked breasts. Another pang of guilt grips his conscience but he doesn't stop her.

Now Doris slides out of her chair and comes around to his side of the table, and massages his back and his shoulders and neck. Jim doesn't know what to do, so he closes his eyes.

Lips, tongue: smoky, wet, wine-flavored. Doris locks her mouth onto his. Swirling sensations race through him as if he's falling in a dream and he's unsure where he'll land, or if he will. Her kiss is clumsy and rough, and conveys little sexual urgency as if she is kissing first, and hoping that lust will follow. Jim chokes on her yeasty-wino-cigarette breath, but he does not push her away.

After kissing him, Doris steps back from the table, unsnaps the safety pins on her robe, and lets it fall to the floor, leaving her naked except for bikini underpants—lacy light-green underpants.

Purple fascination captures Jim despite the bad taste she left in his mouth, despite the alarms ringing in his conscience. Her body is certainly fuckable, but it's a B-minus at best, not nearly as sexy as he has imagined over the years of knowing her. Her figure is slender but her flesh has no tone. It hangs in baggy folds about her thighs, hips, and midriff, as if her skin is too big for her body. Her small egg-shaped breasts droop like half-filled water balloons. They're smaller than Sharon's but the tips are nice: pink nipples with bunny-brown areolas, as if each tit has been dipped in light chocolate and topped off with a small strawberry.

Jim would love to play with her pretty nipples but any thought of going farther is quickly waning. His dick is only semihard. This is the first time since he started the church that one of his women has gone beyond playful sporting and has actually taken off her clothes. But it will take a lot more fire to get him to commit adultery. There's something strange about Doris. It's like she's trying to seduce herself rather than him. Then again, the confused vibes may derive from her inebriated condition. But whatever the reason, she doesn't have that crazy melting "I crave it" look that Sharon gets when ravenous for orgasm.

Doris moves closer. The heat of her nakedness warms Jim's face. He feels suddenly fevered, confused. His heart races—then comes a blast of yeasty breath. SHARP REVULSION! Guilt! Guilt! He grabs his coat, bolts from the table, and runs out of the house.

* * *

A haloed sun hangs low in the western sky, veiled by feathery clouds—precursors of a rainy weekend. But the storminess has already arrived in Jim Shanley's mind, *Wasn't my fault, or was it? It's like I took advantage of her drunkenness to look at her body. It's sick. Why didn't I stop her? She won't tell Stan. She never talks to him. But what the hell is happening to me, lusting and lusting? I've lost control of my thought-life.* But as he drives, he gradually escapes the shackles of self-condemnation. *Stop making such a big deal out of this. Doris is just hurting and crying out for love and attention. What happened today is just part of the risk of being friends with a lonely woman.*

Multistory brick buildings, street-level storefronts, many boarded up. When Jim emerges from his introspective battle, he finds himself downtown, stuck in traffic on High Street. He hardly remembers coming up Chestnut or crossing the bridge or driving down from the Campbells' hillside neighborhood. High Street, old and rather narrow for a main street, is also Route 72, the only way through town. The time-temperature sign in front of Comfed Savings says 5:42 PM and 56°. Dozens of ruddy-faced teenagers are swarming the sidewalks on this mild Friday evening. The guys stand awkwardly in twos and threes, their hands thrust into their pants pockets. They look but shyly keep their distance from clumps of gum-chewing girls in tight jeans. Jim often comes down on Fridays to invite the kids to the teen center, but not on this Friday.

Finally, he turns left, breaking out of the traffic, and heads west on Sterling Road. The gathering dusk hides the Worcester Hills in purple haze, but the sky breathes red, pink, and orange through a wash of milky gray. Jim likes sunsets. The warm quiet hues soothe his nerves and slow the racing engine inside him, a calming effect he especially needs on this evening. After a mile or so, he veers off onto Greeley Hill Road which ascends the hill from the east. Right on Pilgrim, left on Mayflower, then right on Edsel Road. Four houses, five, the Shanleys live in the sixth house on the

right, a white full-dormered Cape with a central chimney and a pair
of red maples out front.

\* \* \*

"But Sheila needs to know, Mom. I gotta *call* her. It's her
birth—"

"That's enough, Heather," Sharon declares. "I *said* to drop it.
We'll talk about it later. Let's eat in peace for a change. I worked
hard on this meal and I'm going to enjoy it, if I can."

But peace lasts less than a minute. "Howcum we can't eat in
here eber' night?" Chris asks in his chirpy chipmunk voice. "I like
habin' real na'kins 'stead of paper ones. An' my chair in the kitchen
is broken. The back part is fallin' off, an' I always hab to sit against
the wall by Heather's old Bubble Yum. It's pink an' hard, all stuck
under the table. It's yech-eeee."

"It's not *my* gum," Heather shoots back, taking out her
festering frustration on her brother. "I'm not a slob like you,
Christopher."

"Yes, it is," Chris insists, a devilish glint sparking in his blue
eyes as he seizes the opportunity to get into his sister. "I saw yuh.
'Member? Dad said spit it out, an' you *per*-tended to frow it in the
trash but you sabed it an' stuck it under the table. I saw *yuh.*"

"I did no such thing," Heather rebuts, not that she cares so
much, but if Chris says one thing, she has to say the opposite.

"Yes, you did!" Chris emphatically counters, holding his
ground. "'Cuz you jus' put it in your mouph, an' you wanted to sabe
the sweet part, but you forgot it an' it got hard. I saw *yuh.*"

"Mo-*ommm,*" Heather pleads, calling for reinforcements.

"Christopher Martin, that's *enough,*" Sharon intervenes in a
firm motherly tone. "Forget the gum. Now, eat your broccoli and
carrots."

"But, Maw, I don't *like* broc'li," Chris complains pushing out
his lower lip. "It's yechy. It rots. It's like eatin' a stinky ol' tree, an'
I ardie ate mos' of my carrots."

Heather, her bright aqua eyes opening wide, takes advantage
of Chris's defensive posture. "Umm, you're *so* infantile, Chris. No
wonder Mrs. Buford puts you on the first row at assembly, an' your
baby legs are so short your feet don't even touch the floor." She
beams in apparent triumph, having delivered what she thinks is the
final blow.

Chris crumbles into a defeated pout, but within seconds
recovers into a cocky smirk and finishes his sister with a lower
blow, "Lease, I don't hab a big roly-poly *bum* hangin' outa my gym

shorts like you, Hea—".

"Knock it off!" Jim abruptly orders in a military voice. "If I hear another word, you're both going to your room, with no dessert." Immediate quiet—as if he pushed a mute button. Even Erin puts on a meek face and she wasn't involved. Jim's not angry, just emphatic, but the kids know they better obey quickly, because after his command voice comes the quiet voice that pronounces punishment.

Heather and Chris can be so cruel to each other, yet when they watch TV downstairs and he gets sleepy, he lays his head in her lap. In a blue chambray shirt and frosted purple jeans, Heather is all tomboy, her blond hair cutely short with downy bangs. She's only eleven but already bigger than Erin, not fat, but taller and stouter. A budding jock, she plays soccer in the Worcester community league. She loves kittens and snowy days, and she always cries during sad movies. She hates homework and fancy dresses and formal occasions. She's a lot like her dad.

Christopher Martin, five and a half with reddish hair somewhere between the red of a rusty nail and the orange of a ripe pumpkin, is the family cutup. All Pedersen, he has high Norwegian cheeks and more freckles each year. He has on camouflaged fatigue pants and a white, now gravy-splashed, GI Joe shirt.

Hot dishes, delicious aromas, fogged windows. A plume of steam still rises from the pot roast though not as much as when it was first placed on the table. Sharon's parents cancelled at the last minute, but since the table had been set for two days, Sharon decided to eat in the dining room anyway. She prepared all week as if God were coming. A furious fit of cleaning, cooking, and arranging presages a visit from her mom just as surely as a falling barometer presages a storm. It seems to Jim, in fact, that Sharon fears her mother *more* than God. He's always wondered at the reverence that Nana Pedersen receives, especially since Sharon is closer to her father.

Jim sits near the window at the end of the polished pine table. He remembers the argument. They could've saved $325 on an off-brand table from Furniture Warehouse but Sharon insisted on going to the Ethan Allen Gallery at Searstown. She loves early-American furniture and the house is full of it—not all Ethan Allen of course. Only the rocking chair in their bedroom and the coffee table and end tables in the living room are Ethan Allen, along with the dining room table which usually resides under the window where it supports a doily and a vase of artificial flowers, but not tonight. China, crystal, gleaming silverware. The table is set with Sharon's best along with cranberry place mats and matching napkins. In the center, a nosegay of purple rockcress nestled in ferns adds a scent of spring to the setting. Sharon rarely uses a tablecloth. "Why get a beautiful table if no one sees it?" she always says.

She normally keeps her silverware hidden away in a rich-smelling velvet-lined box, purple velvet, on the bottom shelf of her pine hutch—also colonial but not Ethan Allen. Her china and crystal also stay in this tall pine sideboard, on the upper shelves behind glass-windowed doors. The hutch stands against the wall opposite Jim—behind Sharon. Taupe wallpaper, light-blue curtains, and an oval rug on the hardwood floor complete the room, along with a brass chandelier that has hurricane lamps and scrolled arms. The Shanley dining room seems right out of Old Sturbridge Village save for Heather's muddy soccer ball by the hutch and Jim's black Samsonite attaché case in the corner.

Sharon's menu is likewise colonial in taste: Yankee pot roast, scalloped potatoes, carrots, broccoli, popovers, apple cider, grapenut custard pudding. Jim takes his popover and breaks it open releasing a cloud of steam along with the rich aromas of melted butter and egg pastry. Crisp and golden brown on the outside, hot, soft, and yellow on the inside, it resembles a cream puff but isn't sweet. Jim has liked popovers since he ate them as a boy at Grandma Shanley's in Ft. Worth. As a matter of fact, she taught Sharon how to make them. (Grandma Shanley died three years after Jim and Sharon were married.) Jim always pokes a hole in his popover at the beginning of the meal and pushes butter inside, so the butter will be melted when he's ready to eat it.

As Jim breaks his popover, Erin breaks the silence, "Mom, I just love your china and the Waterford crystal. It's a shame we only use it for Nana and Pop, and on Christmas, or like when Pastor Logan and the Hudsons came last fall."

Erin, ruddy-cheeked, thirteen, and dressed in a navy-and-white check dress, sounds so ladylike. She reminds Jim of Sharon, or she acts like Sharon. She looks like him. Into clothes, cooking, and pretty things, she has long copper-brown hair and a pug nose—not as pug as Heather but definitely "Shanley." Like her mother, Erin loves to shop and to dress up. As a little girl, she wrote her daddy love notes every day, and still does on occasion. "When I get married," she goes on to say, "we'll use china and sterling every meal, with linen tablecloths and flowers and candlelight."

"Sounds romantic," Sharon counsels her oldest, "but after you're married five years with two kids and another on the way, you'll change your tune. Everyday dishes in the kitchen will do just fine."

Erin draws her lips into a tight sophomoric smile then rebuts,

"Not me, Mom; I'll never give in to the dreary routine. I want to live like Princess Diana my whole life."

"Who's gonna be your Prince Charles, Billy McArthur?" Heather teases as she works her tongue free within a mouthful of potatoes. "Umm, I saw you talkin' to him when we picked you up at the liberry?"

"Heather, don't talk with you mouth full," Sharon instructs.

"Not hardly," Erin denies matter-of-factly. "He's in tenth grade. Besides, he's not even a Christian. He's Catholic. He says our church is a cult."

"I saw him too," Chris chimes in. "He's got big zits all ober his face. He's *gross*."

"Don't be so cruel, Christopher," Sharon interjects. "You'll probably have pimples yourself someday."

"Yeah, Chris, you're gonna get wicked awesome zits for sure," Heather quickly agrees, speaking through another mouthful of food. "'Cuza all those Snickers an' M&M's you eat."

"Shut up, Heather," Chris fires back. "Mom said not to talk with your mouph full—"

"Doesn't matter how Billy looks," Erin maintains, cutting Chris off and cleverly shifting the attention away from herself. "I don't like him anyway, but I know who *Heather* likes."

Taunting, teasing, the kids continue to banter, with Sharon acting as referee. Jim turns his attention to eating, but not for long as his wife looks over the children and gives him an affectionate wink. Doris, Doris, pang of guilt. Wine-flavored kiss, yeasty breath, green underpants, droopy tits. Doris's naked body flashes into his mind. Guilt. Guilt. *If Shar knew what happened today, she wouldn't wink at me—nor would Stan. I took advantage of a married woman just to see her boobs. I took advantage of her drunkenness. I could've stopped her but I didn't. I'm turning into a sleaze. And not just with Doris. It's always happening at the school. If I'm not looking at Janet, I'm flirting with Angie, and I still think about Becki, even though she's out of the picture ... but it's different with Becki—or is it?*

Jim quietly wallows in self-condemnation until Heather turns the table conversation back to Sheila Bradley's birthday party. Sharon's need for a fatherly ruling rescues him. "I don't know, Heather," she says. "You'll have to ask your father." Sharon always defers to her husband on the gray areas of Christian conduct, not because she sees him as more qualified, but so she can say, "It was Jim's decision," when Nana Pedersen second-guesses her.

"Umm, umm, can we, Dad?" Heather pleads, straining impatiently for a yes. "Can we? It's rated PG. It is." Erin nods in agreement.

"Can you what?" Jim asks, having missed the question.

"Can Erin an' I go see *Tootsie* with Sheila tomorrow? Her dad's gonna take us. Please, can we?"

"Can you see *who*?" he asks again, now looking to Sharon for help.

"You know, Dad, the movie at Searstown," Erin answers before Sharon.

Finally, Sharon explains, "Bev's having Sheila's party tomorrow. You know, we've been talking about it. It's a pizza party then all the girls are staying over at the Bradleys' for a slumber party. Erin and Heather are going of course, but there's a new complication. Before pizza, Russ wants to take the kids to a movie at Sears—"

"Doesn't sound complicated to me," Jim declares abruptly. "Sounds like fun. I don't see why you need my say on that."

"Would you let me finish?" Sharon retorts, rolling her eyes and giving an exasperated sigh, as if to say, "You know nothing about being a Christian mother in the 1980s." She doesn't actually say it, but Jim gets the message.

"Sorry, dear; I wasn't paying attention. But go on. I'm listening."

"Anyway, the movie's called *Tootsie*," Sharon elaborates, her voice assuming that hushed newzy tone it gets when she's sharing gossip. "Now when Leslie Burton found out that Russ was taking the kids to the movie, she became upset and told Bev that Wendell and Lisa couldn't go. Of course, Leslie's against all movies so that was no surprise, but then she got on the phone this afternoon and warned all the other mothers. She says the movie's off because a man dresses up like a woman, and it has homosexual over—"

"It does not!" Erin interrupts, gesturing vehemently with uplifted hands. "It's a comedy. You know, he's an actor in the story, he's not *gay*. It's Dustin Hoffman. He's adorable, like wicked cute. My friends in school, they're all—"

"Hold your horses, Erin," Jim admonishes. "Don't forget, you're in a public school now. You can't do things just because your friends do. Besides, this is only a movie, not your whole life."

"Anyway," Sharon continues, "all the mothers except Jodi Donovan backed out. They said their kids can go to the pizza party after, but not to the movie, and—"

"I think that rots!" Heather exclaims, cutting her mother off.

"Mrs. Burton is such a prude!" Erin declares simultaneously.

"How can she *be* like that?" Heather whines, going on with her complaint. "Mrs. Burton never lets Lisa do *any*thing. And now, she's messin' up Sheila's birthday. It's not fair, Daddy!"

"Okay, this is getting out of hand," Sharon declares. "We can't discuss this in front of you kids. Daddy and I will talk it over ... and tell you later."

"But, Mo-*ommm*," Heather protests. "This is wicked important! It's her *par*ty. If we don't go, it'll be ruined. I gotta call an' tell her. We've waited *all* day."

"Settle down," Jim commands. "You girls can wait another half hour. We haven't even had dessert yet, and Mom made grapenut custard. I bet Chris is ready?"

"Yeah," Chris agrees. "I want my puddin'. I'm tired of hearin' 'bout Sheila's stupid party. An' I get the blue bowl. I awhready got first dibs on it."

The girls finally calm as Sharon stands and issues orders, "Okay, let's get these dishes into the kitchen and be careful. These are the best we have. Then you can take your pudding downstairs and watch *The Waltons*, so Daddy and I can—"

"I wanna watch *Flintstones*," Chris declares. "I'm tired of *The Waltons*. Erin 'n Heather always get to watch their shows."

"No, we don't," Heather rebuts. "Umm, you're always hoggin' the TV ever' afternoon to watch *GI Joe* and *Scooby Doo*. We get to pick at night."

"But I'm gettin' robbed," Chris insists. "*The Waltons* come on eber' night an' last a whole hour, an' I gotta go to bed at nine o'clock."

"Okay, cool it," Sharon warns, "or you'll go to your rooms, and no one will watch TV, or go to any parties or movies. You girls watch *The Waltons* now, but let Chris have it at eight for *The Dukes of Hazzard,* and I don't want any more back talk. Now let's get these dishes." The bickering quickly ceases, and after several trips to the kitchen, Heather and Chris emerge, pudding in hand. Erin follows. They all disappear into the hallway and clomp down the stairs to the basement TV-room.

The movie issue diverted Jim's attention but festering guilt still fouls his conscience like dirty dishwater in a stopped-up sink. As he sits waiting for his wife, he feels another pang of shame for allowing Doris's drunken advance and for gazing upon her naked flesh. Sharon soon brings in a pot of coffee and two more dishes of pudding. Her brown polka-dotted dress swishes as she walks.

She clears Erin's place and sits down to Jim's left. After pouring the coffee, she breathes a sigh of relief as she takes off her mother hat and relaxes into their aftersupper quiet time. She sugars and stirs her coffee then takes a bite of dessert, drawing the pudding slowly off her spoon as if sucking on a Popsicle. She gives a curious grin, her lips creamy with custard, and says, "You've been rather quiet and pensive, Jim, like you're in another world. Even the kids noticed. Is there something on your mind?"

"Nawh," Jim calmly lies despite a pinch of guilt. "I'm just tired I guess." *Shit, she reads me like a book,* he declares silently then quickly changes the subject. "So, when did your mom call?"

"Oh, around two. Pop's got a bad cold. He doesn't feel like driving." The Pedersens live in Cobleskill, New York, thirty minutes west of Albany, and three hours west of Brendon Falls.

"Sorry they can't make it," Jim lies again, but this time it's a nice white lie. He never feels relaxed when the Pedersens visit. He has nothing against Sharon's parents except her mom is overbearing and legalistic, mainly with Sharon. Nana and Pop actually treat him rather well, but he senses that their kindness derives more from courteous respect rather than fond affection—not because they're unloving people, but because they and Jim have always related superficially and have never gotten to know each other on a heart-to-heart level.

Sharon, between bites of dessert and sips of coffee, reports the latest news from her mom—Pedersen gossip is not of great interest to Jim but he listens dutifully, as if making up for his unchristian behavior with Doris. Nana's Aunt Julia is coming in August for the annual family gathering. It's her first time to leave Norway. Mor is so excited about Julia that she can't sleep which makes her more cantankerous than ever. (Mor is Nana's mother, Sharon's grandmother.) Dottie isn't pregnant after all. (Dottie, actually Dorothy, is Sharon's cousin in Toronto.) She's been married eight years without child and Nana is concerned. Uncle Olaf is still in Brooklyn on 61st Street. He's been in the same house for 44 years. Nana says it's time for him to move upstate, that it's not healthy for him to stay there alone—after all, Helga's been gone for four years. Pop's having trouble hearing the TV and keeps on turning the volume up. Sharon's mom says he won't go for a hearing aid because he's too proud and stubborn.

Sharon goes on for some time then sighs and lazily pulls a last mouthful of grapenut custard. "I guess it's best," she confesses as she shifts from gossip back to real life. "I'm not up to having Mom around this weekend."

Jim looks at his wife's cute cherry-rose lips, all creamy with pudding. Sharon, Sharon, no more Doris. He feels a surge of desire as he thinks of his wife's other mouth, her other lips. All the confusion and guilt of the day quickly drain out of his conscience as if Sharon reached in and pulled the plug. She's in the mood as well, for she gives him a sexy side-glance and says, "Let's go to bed early and stay *up* all night. How does that sound, Reverend

Shanley?"

"Sounds like the best part of this day is yet to come," he replies giving a flirty grin as he boyishly scrapes the remnants of custard out of his pudding dish. "I've just got a few things to do downstairs in my office." His silver spoon rings against the china dish.

Sharon warms both cups with a fresh shot of coffee then sips silently for a time. Doll-like face, diffused, dreamlike. She always looks pretty to Jim, but especially when he knows that she has sex on her mind. Her dusty-blue eyes seem most provocative within the soft shadows cast by her bangs and side wisps, as if a summer breeze has blown her hair forward around her cheeks.

"So, do you want to let the kids go to the movie, or what?" she asks after a couple of minutes.

Jim senses that she already knows his answer is yes, and agrees with it, but he also knows from past experience that she'll likely debate the issue so that any parental endorsement of marginal Christian behavior will appear to be his—with her reluctant acquiescence. "Why not?" he says, gesturing with his coffee cup. "If it's good enough for Russ, it's good enough for me. Especially if Leslie Burton's that vehement against it. If she's warning mothers about it, it must be a great flick." Grinning, Jim takes a swig of coffee.

"Come on, Jim," Sharon objects. "Don't be so hard on Leslie. She's trying to serve the Lord in her own way, even if she is a bit legalistic. Besides, she's not the only Christian against the movie. I kind of talked to Mom about—"

"Good night, Shar! Why'd you do that? Can't you let sleeping dogs lie?"

Sharon retreats into her sheepish I-know-I-did-it-but-I-can't-help-it look. "I know, honey, I know. But she does keep up on these things, and she called just as I hung up with Leslie. I had to see what she thought about it."

"I know what she thinks. But go on."

"Well, Mom's church in Cobleskill puts out a monthly movie sheet. She says that *Tootsie* is borderline for Christians and that it wouldn't be wise for the girls to go, after so many mothers have expressed concern. Mom feels that the pastor's children have to set the example, so their behavior must be above reproach."

Hot feeling flares in Jim's gut. "I'm gettin' sick and tired of people calling the kids, 'pastor's kids'! Why can't they just be 'kids'? Now that I know Leslie *and* your mom are against this, I want Erin and Heather to go all the more! It's like every Christian mother within a thousand miles has to butt her damn nose into Sheila's party plans! Why don't they mind their own damn business!"

"Watch your language," Sharon admonishes religiously—but without conviction.

"Pharisees need strong language!" Jim retorts, slapping the table. Coffee spurts up. The dishes rattle. "It's just bleepin' ridiculous that something *this* simple, kids goin' to a movie, has to go before the Great White Throne of Christian opinion! Where the hell was your mom and Leslie, and all the Christian matriarchs, when Jesus was plucking corn on the Sabbath, or hanging around with Mary Magdalene, or eating and drinking with Peter and John and all the worldly fishermen in the bars of Capernaum?"

Sharon wipes up the coffee. She tries to act miffed but she can't contain her secret agreement, and a ruddy 'amen' grin flushes onto her face. Jim knows from her previous confessions—mainly during sex—that his maverick spirit fires every nerve in her body. She loves his wild rebellious side though she always counsels him to control it, except in bed—suddenly: Heather. She enters the dining room carrying Samantha, the Shanleys' Siamese cat.

Flashing her shiny blue eyes, Sam gives a humanlike mew that means she's ready for supper. With a pale-fawn body, long black legs, and a serpentlike tail, she looks more like an organ-grinder's monkey than a cat. She demands royal treatment and she gets it, mainly from Heather who interprets her wide range of meows. Sam rules the basement as "her territory" and has her own cat-door through a basement window.

"What's all the yelling up here?" Heather asks expectantly. "We can hear Dad shouting over the TV?"

"Your father just got a little excited," Sharon answers, her grin receding to a wifely smirk.

"So can we, or what?" Heather inquires. "What's the decision? Can we go?"

Sharon tries to be judicial, but instead spills the news: "After you feed Sam, go get Erin to help in the kitchen. After the dishes are all done, we'll give you the official word.... But as you probably heard, Daddy's on your side."

Heather's face jumps into joy. She runs over and hugs her father, almost crushing Sam between them. As the cat utters wails of protest, Heather squeals out her delight, "Oh, Daddy! You're the *best* dad of all! I knew you'd let us. You're not like Mrs. Burton at all. You saved Sheila's birthday!"

She then scoots into the kitchen with the cat. "Sam's wicked hungry," she bubbles, her voice flying back through the open door. "D' we have any more Fancy Feast tuna? That's all she's eatin' this week. Oh, here's some"—then talking to Sam, "Umm, you're a good kitty. Now eat your supper then you can come down an' I'll brush your back an' you can sleep on my lap; that is, after I call Sheila."

Back through the dining room, into the hall. Heather dashes down the stairs taking three steps at a time. Sharon and Jim trade smiles as they hear her breathlessly sharing the good news with Erin. It makes Jim feel good to see the kids happy, even if it's a simple childlike happiness over a movie. But is there any other kind? he wonders as he reflects on how adults rarely display such exuberance.

Jim stretches and starts to get up, but Sharon stops him, "While you're granting requests, honey, you said you'd have an answer on the new couch; you know, for the basement? If I have to look at that shabby yard-sale sofa another week, I'm going to throw up." Smirking coyly, she plays with her empty coffee cup as if she's fondling a wine glass at a nightclub.

At this point, Jim's in no mood to oppose her—as she well knows—but he is in a mood to flirt, so he kids, "It can't be *that* bad, Shar. That sofa doesn't nauseate me at all. In fact, I think I can sit on it the rest of my life without even getting queasy."

"James David, you stop playing with me," Sharon protests, trying to stop a laugh.

Jim gives a teasing grin. "Okeydoke, I'll be serious now. How much does it cost?"

Sharon balls her napkin and hurls it at her husband, but with her girlish all-wrist motion it shoots out sideways toward the window. "Oh drit!" she curses in Norwegian, her face red with mirth. "You're so *im*possible. You *know* how much it costs. We've talked about this since January."

"Oh yeh, but I think I forgot anyhow."

"Okay, one *last* time," she says, trying to look annoyed—but failing. "It's normally $625, but through March 20th, we can get it for the low price of $499."

"I'm glad we get the *low* price," Jim jests as he toys with a piece of potato on his place mat. "But while we're remembering things, weren't you going to contribute $250 yourself, you know, from all those extra hours typing up the Gallagher depositions? Didn't you have four hundred bucks coming the last week of February? I haven't heard much about that lately."

Jim smirks and tosses his chin cockily toward his wife. She looks down with a girlish grin and smooths her dress; she speaks toward her fingers, "I uh—well, I spent it on necessities."

*Ding-ding-ding.* He drums his spoon on the rim of his empty pudding dish. "So the $150 a week I give you isn't enough?"

"N-no, not that. These were uh ... like new *un*expected

necessities."

"You mean like new *spring* necessities? Like a new coat, and shirts and skirts, and the dress you wore last Sunday?"

"You almost got it, dear. Keep guessing."

"All that, plus your Easter outfit that no one has seen yet?"

"Now you got it!" Sharon gushes like a schoolgirl.

Unable to resist her frolicsome spirit, Jim gets up and hugs her from behind. She wiggles playfully. "So after spending $400 on clothes," he replies, "you want $500 for the couch?"

"You got it, Reverend. That's the big picture."

Speaking into the back of her head, he makes an offer, "Okay, you win. I'll let you put $350 on MasterCard, but you have to pay the rest."

"Make it $400," Sharon counters. "I'll pay $100, and we have a deal."

"Okay, okay, it's a deal," Jim agrees. "But you better hope the church keeps growing, or we'll never pay off our MasterCard, or Sears."

"Don't fret, honey; it's just money. Besides, we're saving $125, and you get to enjoy the new couch as much as me. It's a win-win situation. You can't ask for more." Sharon beams over her successful salesmanship.

Jim playfully tousles her hair and chucks her cheek. "I don't know what to do with you, woman. You're too much." Sharon's logic is beyond him. When he tries to follow her arguments, he always ends up tied in knots.

Quietness. He massages her shoulders. She purrs with contentment. Chemistry, chemistry: warm, romantic, and so sexual, no doubt, no doubt—unlike the confused emotions he felt at Doris's house. Sharon comes up and melts into Jim's arms. She gives him a lingering wet kiss, more tongue than lips. Love and desire connect them as she snuggles close. Sharon, Sharon, heart and body. Eyes and tits and hips and cunt. Sharon's cunt, the only cunt he's ever fucked—despite the many playful cunts in his life, despite the many horny cunts in his fantasies. Cunt, cunt. The word is dark, potent, and wanton. It's aggressive, fierce, shocking, and selfish, yet it burns to satisfy. Cunt, cunt. It's hot-blooded and ravenous. It takes no shit. It describes a woman best, at least the women that Jim cares to know, though he would never use this obscene word around his wife, or anyone—not even Russ.

"This is my preview of coming attractions," Sharon whispers in her breathy bedroom voice. "The main show starts at ten p.m., mister, and it's *X*-rated."

"It's a date but I don't know if I can wait," Jim kids as he lets go of her and heads for the hallway.

"Oh, honey, remind the girls to come up after *The Waltons*. I need them to help finish up in the kitchen. I'm not used to doing dishes this late. This has been *such* a crazy day."

"You can say that again," Jim quickly agrees as he jauntily descends the stairs to the basement.

\* \* \*

Twenty minutes later, Jim gropes into his dark basement-office after watching the end of *The Waltons* with Chris and the girls. As usual, John Boy's moralistic musing summed up the meaning of the episode. Jim finally finds the string and pulls on a naked lightbulb that hangs over his makeshift butcher-block desk.

The desk sits against an unfinished Sheetrock wall amid file cabinets, bookcases, and tables piled with papers, notebooks, and ministry tracts. Unlike the TV-room, which is panelled, carpeted, and warmed by a wood-burning stove, his home office remains unfinished, musty, and dank. Pine-scent air fresheners and a low-power electric heater fight against the chilly cavelike environment—but with little success. On the long desk he has an Apple IIc personal computer and a touch-tone phone, both crudely wired to a jack in the kitchen above. Jim sits down to the right of the computer and looks over his weekly domestic checklist which is written on a legal pad:

> Call Dad. Empty ashes. Bring in wood. PAY BILLS. SET UP INCOME TAX. Haircut. FIX WIPERS ON MUSTANG. Gray suit to cleaners. Oil change on both cars. Go to Bank. Buy floppy discs, envelopes, razor blades . . .

Before he gets to the bottom of the list, the phone rings. Incoming calls are always for Erin or Heather, so he doesn't answer. But seconds later, Erin pokes her head into the office and says, "It's for you, Dad. It's Becki Reinhardt."

"Okay, I've got it," Jim responds with prosaic calmness. "You can hang up." But as he picks up the phone, the realization that it's Becki slams home as if he's been shot with a stun gun. Anxiety, anxiety, erupting emotion. Hot blood rushes up into his face. His heart races right behind it catching in his throat. His mind tumbles like a TV with no vertical hold, but he manages to speak, "Hello."

"Jimmy, this is Becki," comes her soft voice.

"How you doin'?" Jim asks in a reflexive response.

"Okay, I guess. I just wanted to call. Sorry I didn't make it last weekend. I had to go to a banquet with Mom 'n Ed, for the Puerto Rico team—su*per* dull. But I'll be there in the morning. I like coming to Brendon Falls. Russ is wicked nice and Bev too. And Sheila 'n I are good buddies already."

Jim, thinking this is the extent of her news, feels his emotions stabilizing. "I'll call Russ and let him know," he tells her, his voice official and pastorly. "He can use your help. He's taking a bunch of kids to the movies for Sheila's birthday. Erin and Heather are going too."

"Yeah, should be fun," Becki says halfheartedly. "Sheila told me about it two weeks ago, the last time I was down."

"Okeydokey, thanks for letting me know," Jim replies, assuming the conversation is over. "And tell your mom and Ed that I said hello. I'll see you in the morning at prayer meeting."

Silence. Becki doesn't say good-bye. "Oh, Jimmy, there *is* one more thing," she remarks after a long pause. "I was just wondering—"

"Wondering what, Becki?"

"I was just wondering if, maybe like, well—can I be on *your* outreach team, instead of goin' with Russ?"

Mass panic. Joy, hope, fear. Run, run. Jim's thoughts tear wildly through the streets of his mind like terrified citizens in a Godzilla movie.

He barely hears the rest of Rebecca's words as she fires away with machine-gun bursts of rationale behind her request: "Mom 'n I talked. It'll be better for me, like I'll learn a wicked lot with you. It's neat working with Russ, and with Sylvia, but you're a *real* pastor, and I can help. I'll keep your lists, and hold your cards and stuff. It'll be a good experience for me. It'll help me prepare for the mission—for the future.... So how 'bout it, Shanley? Think we can be a team?"

Jim's brain is still down, waiting to be rebooted, but his heart replies, "I guess so, kiddo. I usually go by myself, but you can hang with me tomorrow if you like."

Becki's voice lights up, "*Great*—so I'll be there in the morning, Jimmy, at the regular time. I'm glad you see the wisdom of it. I was wicked nervous about asking, since you're so busy and all, but we'll make a good team ... like soldiers for God."

After hanging up, Jim slowly scans his basement office looking for his lost peace. He does not find it. *O God!* he cries in his soul. *This is not good! Why are you stirring this pot?*

# Chapter Nine

Sheets of windblown rain, steely gray and ghostly, whip across the parking lot. A sodium security light, like a strange Cyclopean eye, stares at Jim from the other side of the lot. The light casts an eerie amber glow into the chilly downpour. It normally goes off at daybreak but not on this stormy Saturday.

*Shunk-a-ca-shunk ... shunk-a-ca-shunk.* The wipers on the Mustang work only in intermittent mode, so they struggle to keep pace with the pelting raindrops, like a drumbeat that's too slow for the song. *What's taking her so long?* Jim asks himself as he reaches back and grabs the newspaper off the backseat. He scans the front page:

*BRENDON FALLS BANNER* ... Saturday, March 12, 1983 ... Rain today, clearing colder on Sunday ... REAGAN CONDEMNS RUSSIA, SAYS SOVIET UNION IS FOCUS OF EVIL IN MODERN WORLD ... OPEC PROPOSES FIRST EVER CUT IN OIL PRICES ... DUKAKIS APPLAUDS ECONOMIC UPTURN, SAYS HIS POLICIES ARE WORKING ... LECH WALESA DEMANDS LEGAL STATUS FOR SOLIDARITY ... CHIEF REILLY PROPOSES NEW BYLAW TO STOP TEEN-LOITERING ON HIGH STREET.

All at once: Becki. She dashes out of the church. Her boots splash on the puddled sidewalk. Her black shoulder bag bounces against her side. She hurdles the small lake at the end of the sidewalk, opens the door, and hops into the car—all in one motion.

"Wicked wet out there," she declares as she pulls a handful of blue BFBC outreach tracts out of her bag and gives them to Jim. He places them on the gearshift module, tosses the newspaper into the back, and throws the Mustang into gear. They exit from the flooded east entrance leaving a wake in the shallow water.

Becki fingerfluffs her hair, but there's no fluff left. The humidity has taken it all. Her locks hang flat and straight like a brunette mop. Yet her face radiates a happy glow as if they're leaving on vacation. Eager butterflies swarm in Jim's stomach. He can't believe she's with him—and for an entire day of outreach.

"I thought maybe you got lost in there or something," he says as they accelerate eastward on Reservoir Road. "Have trouble finding the box?" After prayer meeting, he sent her back to his office to get more tracts.

No answer. Becki's busy rummaging in her purse. She fishes out a pack of Wrigley's Big Red gum, pops a piece into her mouth, and offers Jim a stick. He takes it and puts it into his shirt pocket. She stuffs the wrappers into the ashtray then replies in a juicy gum-clogged voice, "No, it was right where you said on the shelf behind your desk, but I had to call Sheila and tell her I wouldn't be over until tonight. I told Russ at prayer meeting, but since it's Sheila's birthday and she invited me and all, I wanted to tell her myself. She says Erin 'n Heather are sleeping over too."

"Sounds like fun, but better you than me—a half-dozen girls in one room?"

"Should be wild. I'm a little old for slumber parties, but Sheila 'n I get along good, and I'm looking forward to seeing Erin 'n Heather. Last time I did anything with them, they were little kids—but outreach is more important. After all, we have to remember why I'm here, like I said on the phone last night."

Jim smiles under his mustache at Rebecca's profession of evangelical purpose. "Come on, Jimmy," she playfully protests. "Stop lookin' at me like that. I'm serious. I'll be nineteen next week. I have to do *some*thing with my life, you know?" She tries to hold a soldierly face but blushes and dimples in spite of herself.

"You repeat your mom's words very well," Jim teases. "She's probably been bugging you all year about getting your life together with—"

"Shanley, you're just as *bad* as ever," Becki cuts in, with obvious but unconfessed agreement. "You think you know so much." She scrunches her face in teasing defiance, then she laughs, her blue eyes sparking with delight.

Magic, magic. A happy gush of warm elation wells up into Jim's bosom. He gives Becki a playful jab on the shoulder. "I do," he chuckles. "At least enough to see that you haven't *changed* since you were fifteen. You may look more grown-up, but you act the same. You even make that sassy face like when you were twelve."

"At least, I didn't get old and wrinkled and paunchy, like *you*," Becki banters between smacks of her gum as she checks the glove compartment. Peanut M&M's, Snickers, Heath Bars. "Well, looka here," she chortles. "I figured you'd still have goodies in there—do I know you or what?" She stuffs a handful of the "trick or treat" size candy into her ski jacket then slips quietly into her shy I-showed-you-too-much mood.

Jim pulls an old T-shirt from under his seat and rubs the fog off the side window. Silence prevails save for the familiar sounds of driving in the rain. Pelting drops pepper the windshield like hundreds of tapping fingers. The crippled wipers oscillate with their hesitant percussive tempo. The defrost fan moans over the low muted buzz of the four-cylinder Ford engine. Oncoming cars go by with a slow-building, wet-ripping, quick-passing, *waaassshhh—SHOOM!* Becki's hair smells damper than it is. To Jim, the odor is like wet fur. He also detects her lilac-scented shampoo and the faint but distinct fragrance of Moonlight Lace perfume, her favorite since she was thirteen.

He thinks back to his Bible-college days when he commuted to Nashua and spent many afternoons and evenings at Ed and Alison's cottage on campus. Jim got to know the Landreths when he took New Testament Survey with Alison in the spring of his first year. Like Jim, they were older, adult students—as with most Bible colleges, LBI has a sizable minority of older change-of-career "God called me" students—and he felt more comfortable with them than with the pimple-faced just-out-of-high-school crowd. The campus cottages are normally reserved for LBI staff, but Ed, shortly after his conversion, made a large contribution to Dr. Logan (about ten thousand dollars from the sale of his Kenworth when he left his truck-driving job). So the Landreths were treated more like staff members than students.

In those days, Jim loved Becki as a daughter but she treated him more like a buddy. They were unusually close—that is until she got older. But when she was 11, 12, 13, even 14, she confided in him about almost everything. Then she turned fifteen and stopped sharing, and the guessing game started. Jim recalls those confusing months back in '79, right before she left for Puerto Rico. Forbidden feelings. He sensed romantic love between them, but they never kissed or confessed. He recalls the ecstasy and the agony and the guilt—and the tormenting questions: Does she love me? Does she want me? What's wrong with me? I can't be in love with a 15-year-old? God, why won't you take these feelings away?

After she moved, he missed her dearly, yet he was relieved to be free of temptation. Except for a few letters and birthday cards, they fell out of touch, and Jim banished the idea of romance with Rebecca to the impossible drawer of his memory. He still thought about her, fantasized about her, but only as a player in a fairy tale that could never come true. But her unexpected return, and especially her desire to go with him on outreach, has now reopened the drawer and resurrected all the questions and possibilities.

As they descend Reservoir Road toward Coachlace Shopping Plaza, four years melt to minutes. Jim inhales her perfume, her presence. His soul rejoices, but does not stop at joy. Bolts of lust fire like depth charges deep within his psyche. His recent Dionysian Becki-vision roars back into his mind. He again pictures her dancing naked, her breasts bobbing in the firelight. Alarms go off. His conscience warns, *Turn back, turn back. This road leads to ruin.* But the magic of the moment washes the warning away. He's playing with matches around gasoline, but it does not matter. Reason and Rebecca can never be in his life at the same time.

\* \* \*

While Rebecca visits the ladies' room, Jim orders two McDonald's Big Breakfasts. He sits in a booth by a bay window. He doctors then sips his coffee. The windblown rain pitters against the panes. The drops collect into beads that grow large then abruptly run down like tears. Becki emerges from the rest room. After a self-conscious search to locate Jim, she strides quickly to their table. Upon sitting down, she sheds her ski jacket uncovering, to Jim's surprise, a stylish border-print sweater, cream in color.

"That's a nice sweater," he says giving a happy half-grin. "But what happened to your *Pink Floyd* sweat shirt?" He hopes she dressed up for him, but even if true, he knows she'll not admit it.

"Oh, it's in the wash," Becki replies. "I like it but I wear it too much. Besides, a rock-band shirt might scare away the natives who need to be saved." She laughs.

Jim laughs too, then gestures with his coffee. "Not the natives in this town. *Pink Floyd* rates pretty high around here. But I like you better in the sweater. It really brings out your blue eyes."

Becki quickly averts her eyes, her cheeks warming with color. "Cut it out, Shanley. You're so full of it." Compliments always make her self-conscious, but the smirk on her mouth tells Jim that she's glad he noticed. Gush of warm joy, up, up. Jim feels high like he's on a drug. For a moment he fears that he's dreaming, that he'll soon wake up and she'll be gone. But the moment passes, and she's still there, smirking fondly.

They open their Big Breakfasts. "Seems strange having you around again after four years," Jim remarks. "Like goin' back in time. Those were crazy days, huh? Your backyard was like a zoo, with the rabbits and ducks, and hamsters."

"Yeah, remember when we made the rabbit hutch, and I put straw down your shirt and you sneezed all through supper?" They both laugh as Becki's smirk breaks into a wide toothy grin, but she quickly turns her attention to buttering her English muffin.

Large round front teeth. Crooked overlapping eyeteeth. Becki has always been shy about smiling broadly. In the old days she talked about getting braces but it's evident that she never did. Nonetheless, Jim sees her smile as irresistible. She smiles with her mouth, her dimples, her nose, but mostly with her eyes. Her face is plain and countryish, like a full-cheeked peasant girl—chubby-cheeked but not fat-faced—yet her large sky-blue eyes make her countenance enchanting and extraordinary, at least to him. When frolicsome, her eyes sparkle with teasing mirth, yet in the blue depths under the sparkle, they're somehow sad, and aware.

While in the ladies' room, she doctored her appearance with a light touch of makeup and a quick brush of her hair; Becki uses makeup as Sharon does, just a bit here and there. Her complexion is fair but her cherub cheeks have a ruddy youthful glow. Her nose and upper cheeks are sprinkled with small freckles, faded from lack of sun. In the summer they're more noticeable.

Becki and Sharon have the same cupid mouth, small, angelic, full-lipped, though Becki's lips tend to puff out because of her natural pout. Otherwise, their faces are very different—and most would rate Sharon as more attractive. When you look at Sharon, the impression is one of squareness, of porcelain angularity, a sculptured prettiness, but when you look at Becki, the impression is one of roundness, of fullness—a chipmunky cuteness.

It's a toss-up whether the brushing in the bathroom made Becki's hair better or worse. Her bangs are now cockeyed as if she's wearing a moppy wig, canted a bit on her head. But Jim still sees her hair as attractive even when it's wrecked by rain. He especially likes the color, a warm chocolate brown—not dark chocolate, but a moderate hue—with honey-blond highlights. As with her freckles, her highlights are less noticeable in winter, but they still flash here and there like sunlight shining through maple syrup.

"So, kiddo, whaddeya been doin' these past four years?" Jim asks around a mouthful of hash browns.

Becki peels the lid from her orange juice, then replies, "Not a wicked whole lot except living in a hot miserable town and going to school with missionary brats and South Island spics. I survived, but I didn't like it. Mom 'n Ed, and Pastor, they always talk about how important the Puerto Rico team is for winning souls, and maybe it is. But still, I'm glad to be back." She swigs her orange juice.

"That bad, huh?"

"Well, we lived in Guayama on the south side of the island—su*per* dull. It was like the other side of the world. Everyone spoke Spanish, and we could hardly pick up any tunes or TV, and the geckos were dis*gust*ing. They crawl on the ceiling and walls. You know, the yechy little lizards with bug eyes and big feet?"

"Yeh, we had 'em on Guam," Jim replies. "So did Ed run the school, or what? Your mom said you had a combined ministry with a Baptist missionary group and—"

"Come *on,* Jimmy," Becki interrupts, bursting with frisky boldness. "I don't wanna talk about the fuckin' Puerto Rico team. I hear this shit *all* day at home. It's wicked *bor*ing."

Shock, lightning, wonder. Electricity races through Jim; he's wounded, yet thrilled. He watches in awe as Becki shoves her muffin into her mouth, but his response is unspoken, *You certainly don't sound like a missionary to me. I never heard you say "fuck" before—and you say it with* <u>such</u> *authority.*

"So, Shanley, does my language offend you?" she kids, her voice thick with bread.

"Well, I must say, young lady, you've spiced up your vocabulary a bit."

"Should've heard me last year," Becki boasts after chugging the last of her orange juice to wash down her muffin. "I'm much tamer now, but I hate boring conversations." She contorts her face in feigned disgust. "I like to talk about fun things."

Jim takes a bite of scrambled eggs. "Like what?" he asks.

"You know: movies, rock music, getting buzzed on beer, running on the beach with Skip, or riding on Manny's motorcycle—now that's not boring, I tellyuh." Warm color stains her cheeks giving added connotation to her words, and arousing Jim's carnal curiosity. He's excited by the thought that Rebecca's high school years in Puerto Rico were neither cloistered nor ascetic.

"Who's Manny?" he asks, after killing his coffee.

Using her girlish fingers and short unpolished nails, Becki opens her milk; she gestures with it. "Oh, Manuel, he's Maria's older brother; he's got a Camaro and a Harley cycle—but he's in the Air Force now. Maria's my friend; her real name is Consuelo Annamaria Sanchez, but everybody calls her Maria. Her dad mows the lawn and stuff at the mission school. She's Catholic but never goes to church. Mom says she's unsaved and a bad influence."

Becki's quick shift from Manny to Maria fuels Jim's curiosity. Maybe she rode more than Manny's Harley? Maybe she rode his *hot* rod as well? Becki, Becki, panties, pussy, pubic hair. Jim's thoughts descend to her crotch. The very idea of Becki having a dark womanly cunt, ripe and ready to fuck, is almost too volatile to consider—it makes him quiver inside. Her eyebrows are naturally dark, somewhat darker than her hair, so he figures her bush is the same, but he's never seen her in the nude—and he's seen her in her panties only once, one time when she ran from the bathroom to her room without her robe. But whether a virgin or not, she's no longer a child—despite her adolescent teeth. Jim has known from a distance. He's known in his fantasies. But now, Becki sits fleshed-out before him, immediate and palpable. Her bosom is modest, perhaps even small, yet her figure overall is chunky and weighs in on the plump side of perfection, not portly but packing just enough heft to give a husky "umph" to her ripe and ready pubescence, like the succulent fullness of a September plum.

Jim wants to pursue the Manny thing, but he doesn't dare. So he says, "How about Skip? Did you ride his motorcycle too?"

"Not hardly," Becki laughs. "Skipper's my puppy, my dog. But he's not a puppy anymore." She goes on about her pet pooch. As she does, she shovels eggs and sausage into her mouth in between gulps of milk, scarcely pausing to breathe.

As Jim downs his own breakfast, he thinks how Becki has always loved to eat. He suspects she loves sexual pleasure as well, but he has no firsthand knowledge of her carnal appetites. He wonders if she lusts for guys and gets off in wet dreams or in her bubble bath. He pictures Manny, dark-skinned and virile, fucking her on a moonlit night under the palm trees. Illicit thoughts: hot, hot, too hot. Jim swigs his orange juice. To think of Becki coming—with or without a guy—makes him weak in the knees.

After talking about Skipper, Becki rests her head on her hand and lazily toys with a leftover piece of sausage on her polystyrene plate. Her hair drapes about her hand like a bunched curtain. Shanley sips his juice. His carnal curiosity fades behind feelings of affection. He senses love between them, but she breaks the spell. Stabbing the morsel of meat with her fork, she pops it into her mouth then grabs her milk carton and aggressively drinks the last of her milk. Head back, she gulps until she gets it all. When she comes down, her upper lip is cutely covered with a milk-mustache. "I see you still get milk on your lip like a ten-year-old," he teases.

"So, I like milk; it keeps me young. After all, I'm not middle-aged and over the hill, like *you,* Shanley." Becki laughs. Jim chuckles, then excuses himself and heads to the men's room.

After taking a leak, Jim washes his hands and looks in the mirror. *Becki's right. I'm getting wrinkles all over and I have bags under my eyes. And my nose is crooked. I should've never boxed at the academy, and it's so bulbous and red. It looks like a potato. I look like Karl Malden. And my skin is sickly like I've never been in the sun. My mustache is too long and scrubby, and it looks washed-out like the color of dirty dishwater. I'm certainly not tall, tan, and handsome. I'm more like short, pallid, and past prime, and with this damn cowlick, my hair looks like an abandoned bird nest. All I have are my eyes, and they even seem to be losing their luster. Why would Becki want—what the hell am I thinking?*

When Jim gets back, he finds Becki busily breaking up the styrofoam boxes and cups into little pieces and arranging them into artistic patterns on the table. After completing her composition, she wads her napkin and playfully tosses it like a basketball toward Jim's orange juice cup. "Ta-dah!" she exclaims as it goes right in. "Am I good or what?"

*We've both gone mad,* Shanley says to himself as he goes for more coffee. But after coming back with his second cup and her first, they return to reality, and he restarts their conversation, "So now that you're back in Nashua, is life any better?"

"Oh, it's a little better," Becki replies, "but I'm tired of living at home. Ed's all right but Mom never lets up. She's on me about goin' to service. She's on me about playing my stereo. She bugs me about doin' my chores. I love her, but she's a real pain."

"So why doncha move out?" Jim asks, after taking a swig of his coffee. He gestures with his cup.

Becki takes a drink of her own heavily creamed and sugared coffee. Three empty sugar packets and two empty nondairy creamers testify to its sweetness. "Where am I gonna go? I don't have any money except what I make at Burger King and babysitting, and I give half of it to Mom."

"Well, you can always move into the dorm," Jim suggests tongue-in-cheek.

"*Never.* Are you *kid*din'?" Rebecca's face twists with revulsion as if she just tasted something rancid. "Mom's bad enough but she's nothing compared to those legal*istic* dorm mothers. You can't have *any* cassette tapes, except for gospel and Pastor's sermons, and you have to sign out every time you leave." Jim smiles under his mustache. "Stop *put*ting me on, Shanley," she protests, giving a knowing grin as she realizes that he's trying to get her going.

Silence. Becki sips her coffee. Now comes a reflective mood. "I'm kind of treading water I guess," she says, looking pensively into her cup. "Everybody in Nashua is so hyped on God like foaming at the mouth. I feel closer to God when I'm alone listening to tunes, or walking in the woods with Skipper. I've made a few friends at college, like Joe ... but mainly I keep to myself."

Jim leans back and hugs his chest. "What about Katie?"

"Oh, we get along okay. But Katie has her own high school friends. We don't do much together. I'm in a different place.... I think about getting a real job or going to a secular college, but somehow it seems even worse than where I'm at. Mom says, 'Re*becca Lea,* you must re*spond* to your calling. You must do some*thing* with your life,' and Ed says it too, and Pastor always preaches it at chapel." Becki sighs resignedly and takes a slow drink of coffee. "As I get older, I feel more and more boxed in, like eventually I'll have to give in and take some yechy job I hate just to live? Sometimes I feel like running away and being wild and unwashed, like a hippie."

Her honest sharing makes Jim feel warm inside, though he knows she won't divulge her feelings for him—whatever they are. "So, Becki, is there anything you really want to do?" he asks.

"I wish—oh, it's a crazy dream, but I'd like to work with a rock band. Joe and I talk about it in the car. But I can't sing or play an instrument. Still, I'd like to be part of the chemistry, like touching people with music and love and God—of course, Mom would disown me."

"You really get into it, huh, like into *Pink Floyd*?"

"Yeah, I guess I do," Becki affirms, looking wide-eyed out the window. "But it's not just Roger Waters, even though *The Wall* album is maybe the best, but I also like *Foreigner*, the *Eagles*, *Fleetwood Mac*, Dan Fogelberg, Pat Benetar, Rod Stewart—a lot of different groups."

"So you're a regular groupie?"

"Not really. I don't get into the rah-rah concert scene, and all the hype. I like listening alone; it makes me feel like...."

"Like what?"

"Like there's got to be *more*."

"More what?" Jim asks, wrinkling his brow inquisitively.

Becki leans forward on her elbows. Holding her half-empty styrofoam cup with both hands, she sloshes the coffee around as if trying to read something on the bottom of the cup. Her voice is contemplative, "You know, *more*—more than being a goody-goody and going to class, and pleasing Mom, and going on a team, or getting married, and getting a job and buying a house."

"So you're serious about being wild and unwashed?"

"I dunno.... Sometimes I wish for a nice house in the country with kids and lots of animals. It certainly seems better than goin' on a missionary team, but still, there's got to be more than marriage and settling down. Besides, I'd rather just live with a guy." Becki gives a mischievous smirk. "That is if he's young and cute—but seriously, there's got to be more to life than duties and routines."

"You sound like Joe Lareux," Jim says, wiping his mouth with a napkin.

"Well, he and I talk about it," Becki replies. "I don't wanna live like a robot. I wanna feel alive each day, like in touch with myself and others. But I always felt this way, and I think you do too. At least, you preached about it the first week I came down."

"Yeh, maybe so ... but I was talking about heaven. You know, *after* death."

"But what's the point of living, if all we do is perform like trained circus seals to get our fish? There's got to be more in *this* life."

"Why?" Jim asks.

"I can't explain it," Becki says after chugging down the last of her coffee. "It's something I feel. I feel like we ought to be wicked free like the birds. Jesus says, 'The truth shall make you free.' We need a movement on this earth that will free everyone, so people don't have to spend their whole life kissin' ass and workin' super-dull jobs just to get money."

Becki gives a snort of disgust then goes on, "That's what Christians should be into instead of playing church every Sunday and judging each other, and dividing up into so many groups. Evangelicals, Pentecostals, Fundamentalists ... they all say they believe the Bible, yet they won't even *talk* to each other. Like Mom says that Jerry Falwell is a great preacher, but she says that Billy Graham has compromised his faith because he has Catholics on the platform at his crusades, and she says that Jimmy Swaggert hinders Christian growth because his preaching on tongues is unbalanced."

Becki gestures with her empty cup. "It's crazy, Jimmy. If the truth is supposed to make us *free*, then howcome Christians are so rigid and bowed down, and separated from each other? And most local churches are filled with bickering and infighting, and they fire the pastor every three years—or have a church split. The Baptist church in Guayama split twice while we were there. I know 'cause they helped run our school, and they were always bitching at Ed about money. They said the LBI team didn't contribute enough toward expenses. It shouldn't be like this. It shouldn't. We need a *wick*ed big change. We need to get back to what Jesus said about love and freedom."

*God, she's more like me than I thought,* Jim declares to himself. *It's like she's reading the wishes of my own heart.* But before he can form a reply that fits this realization, his mind is taken by a more potent wish. Becki sighs reproachfully then yawns and stretches, raising her arms. Her modest bust lifts against her sweater.

Hidden peaches, warm and nippled. Jim imagines her youthful breasts hanging free, then in his hands. He fondles them and loves them. Too much. He escapes to his watch; it says 11:21 a.m. "Well, Miss Reinhardt, I guess we better go. I told Joanne McClusky we'd drop by before she leaves for work."

As if she doesn't hear, Becki goes on with her previous line of thought, "I think about these things when I'm alone listening to tunes, but what can I do?" She gives a shrug of resignation. "In real life, it all comes down to money. Without cash or plastic, you can't do a fuckin' thing."

"That's the bottom line," Jim agrees. "Money makes us all slaves, but it's especially tough when you're young and have no credentials—but really, Becki Lea, we gotta go. It's almost eleven-thirty. Joanne's expecting us."

"You go ahead, Jimmy. I'll meet you at the car. I've gotta go to the bathroom."

"You just went when we came in?" Jim kids her.

"Yeah, but you know me. Milk, orange juice, coffee ... and rain. I always pee a lot on rainy days." Becki gives a girlish grin then heads for the rest room.

Jim can't help but watch as she goes: low-slung moonish hips over short legs, chunky haunches that give a delicious tightness to her blue jeans. From the hips up she's shaped like Sharon, yet when they stand side by side, they look quite different, because of Sharon's long thighs.

Becki goes into the ladies' room. Jim heads for the parking lot, shaking his head: *She's too much. "You know me ... I pee a lot on rainy days." O Jesus, how am I gonna deal with this? She turns me on. She makes me laugh. She drives me crazy. My emotions are already drained and we've only been together for an hour.*

Outside, the rain has slackened to a mist, but the raw March wind still moans overhead whipping the empty halyard on the McDonald's flagpole. The snap fastener hits the hollow aluminum pole. *Ding. Ding. Ding.* It rings like a ship's bell. Jim looks up at the flagpole then at the ragged clouds scudding by overhead.

He ponders the situation, *Maybe she really loves me and wants me? Maybe she's missed me all this time?* His heart rejoices at the thought, but his joy is quickly tempered by doubts. *Or does she actually want to be a mission—no way, I can't see her following in Alison's footsteps, but maybe she's just bored and wants to get away from Nashua, and I'm just the least painful alternative until something better comes along?*

As Jim ambles across the wet asphalt to the Mustang, Becki's voice catches up to him, "Hey, Jimmy, let me drive. Whenever we do outreach, I'll be your driver so you can look over your visitation cards and stuff." She hurries over at a fast walk, bouncing stiffly from foot to foot. It warms Jim's heart to see that Becki has not outgrown her happy-girl quickstep, a cute antimated gait—stiff legs, wagging head, swinging arms, springy feet—like the Eveready *ENERGIZER* Bunny but with no drum, and she does it without conscious intent. Jim hasn't seen this bouncy and most unladylike manner of walking—though wonderfully endearing to him—since she was fourteen, since she stopped expressing her feelings. She must be in a *very* buoyant mood to display her happiness in such a juvenile fashion. Jim hopes that *he* is the reason.

He tosses her the keys, but grins warily. "Whaddeya grinning at?" she banters. "I'm a good driver. You taught me, remember?"

Jim starts around to the passenger side. But Becki does not move; she simply stands there looking down at the car keys. Going back, he touches her gently on the shoulder. She melts into his arms, hugging herself to his bosom. He holds her tightly, caressing her back. He feels her warm body snuggling into his. Her soft hair presses against his cheek. No words—but no words are needed.

Magic, magic. Jim feels elated, euphoric as if he's been sprinkled with stardust, like the feeling he got on Christmas Eve when he was a boy, but more intense, like a whoosh, like a drug, like a dream, as if he's died and gone to heaven. *O God, she does love me,* he declares happily to himself. *I'll never be the same after today.*

Jim wants to kiss her lips, but before he pursues the wish, Becki breaks the spell, "Okay, let's cut the mushy stuff. We have visits to make. After all, we must remember why we're here."

"It's coming back vaguely," Jim quips as he gives her a peck on the forehead. "Oh yeh, I remember ... it had something to do with a church." He playfully tickles her ribs.

"Jimmy Shanley, you cut it out!" Becki squeals, as she quickly escapes and hops into the driver's seat.

After getting in on the passenger side, Jim comments on an administrative detail—to bring himself back to earth, "Oh, before I forget it, I never received your practicum forms from Pastor Hudson's office. You can't get credit for your weekends here unless I sign them. Maybe you should check on it this week."

"No need to," Becki replies, giving a mischievous grin. "I never turned 'em in."

With that, she fires up the Mustang, fires up the radio, backs up, and guns out of the parking lot. The tires spin and squall on the wet asphalt as "Another One Bites the Dust" by *Queen* blares over the speakers.

# Chapter Ten

"Now, Pastor Jim, you gotta hawler out for whatcha want," Ernie Johnson exhorts as he pushes more bread and baloney onto Jim's plate.

"No, no, I'm stuffed," Jim protests to no avail as Ernie dumps a helping of potato salad next to the bread.

Ernie gives a warm redneck smile showing his tobacco-stained false teeth—from chewing tobacco not cigarettes. His country-green eyes beam with delight behind thick-framed Clark Kent glasses that cant sideways on his large nose.

"Here, take a messuh these here beans," Ernie insists. "Lemmie getcha more lettuce an' tomaters, an' you's aneedin' may'naise I reckon. Now lemmie see—woman! Whatcha do with that there jar? Fetch the may'naise an' the milk back outah the icebox. We's got a feller astarvin' out here—now I'm plum awhshamed, Pastor Jim, that we hain't got nuthin' hot pared up. I never knowed yuh to come over this early, but if yawl take a hankerin' to come back this ev'in', Sarah's gonna have a mighty fine supper."

Sarah, chubby, cheerful, with a ball-shaped body on birdlike legs, brings out the mayonnaise then begins to clear the dirty dishes. She seems most at home in her cluttered cubbyhole kitchen where she scurries about like a field mouse getting ready for winter. Her hillbilly meals are always sumptuous, whether hot or cold, and Jim often partakes of her West Virginia menu. The Johnsons moved to New England six years ago when Ernie got his job at Blaylock Concrete in Worcester. Jim no longer visits out of evangelical duty but because he and Ernie have become friends, though Ernie rarely comes to church—he professes faith in Christ, and the Bible, but feels spiritually inferior to his Pentecostal hyperactive wife, not that he says he feels inferior but Jim suspects so.

Located on Water Street in old Germantown, just up from the river, the Johnson home reminds Jim of an ongoing rummage sale. Every room is wall-to-wall clutter—boxes, paper bags, clothes, odds and ends. One can scarcely see the walls much less the furniture. Ernie's relationship with Sarah seems more dutiful than heartfelt, at worst a smoldering toleration of each other, at best a bantering brother-sister fondness, but Jim does not sense much passion between them. In fact, Ernie acts like a man who's serving time, and he's always happy to have visitors to joke with, to share his redneck yarns with, and Pastor Jim is his favorite visitor.

Becki sits on the floor in the middle of the sun-splashed dinette-living room. She's playing Donkey-Kong with Jennifer, both having quietly slipped away from the table after one sandwich.

Jennifer is Heather's age and looks like Sarah, except not as hefty. Facing the TV, Rebecca sits crosslegged with her back to Jim. Her *Pink Floyd* sweat shirt has ridden up above her waist exposing her soft white lower back as it runs down inside her jeans. Jim can't help but notice her pale-blue panty elastic peering out. He wishes he could see all of her panties. Red lights flash in his conscience. He wrestles with the wayward wish but the match ends in a draw.

Saturday, March 26, 1983. Jim continues to fantasize about romance with Becki but has yet to try to kiss her. He doesn't have the nerve. Despite her display of affection at McDonald's two weeks ago, doubts concerning her feelings and intentions still torment him, tempering his joy. On this Saturday, in fact, his emotions are stuck between hurt and anger. She's been obnoxious all day—at times, insolent.

After Jim and Ernie finish their lunch, Sarah brings out cookies and ice cream for everyone, and Ernie, his dentures clicking, shares a story about his younger days in West Virginia— how he outran the police in his '56 Buick, with his trunk full of Kentucky moonshine. He soon has everyone laughing.

* * *

2:20 p.m. The Mustang departs from the Johnsons' duplex and bombs up Water Street. Becki taps the steering wheel keeping time to Bob Seger and the *Silver Bullet Band*. Her soft bangs bounce over a sporty pair of Ray-Ban sunglasses. Downshifting, she turns left and zooms south on Maple Avenue. She negotiates the winding street as if racing in the French Grand Prix. Her driving is bold, brash, alive with sexual vibes. Despite her foul mood, and his wounded spirit—wounded by her barbs and insults—Becki still excites Jim. He hates her impudence when it hurts him, yet he loves her cocky wild side from which it comes. He just wishes her brashness would include him instead of cutting against him.

Though Jim only sees Becki on Saturdays, she's taken center stage in his life and weighs heavy on his mind all the time, sometimes as a cozy blanket of happy expectancy, and other times as an albatross of guilt and anxiety. His Christian conscience declares his Becki-fantasies to be utterly sinful, while his rational mind dismisses them as quixotic yearnings. But his heart is undaunted. In spite of his inner conflicts, and her impossible mood swings, he lives for Saturday, for the ecstasy and agony of being with her.

After his first Saturday with Becki, Jim told Sharon that Becki had come with him on outreach, as part of her practicum training, but that it was a one-time thing—that in the future, she would do outreach with Russ or Joe. So, as Jim and Becki speed along in the Mustang, Sharon doesn't know that her husband is in the midst of his third Saturday with young Miss Reinhardt.

Shanley's non-Becki life is like the moon in the daytime: it's there if you look for it. He and Russ talk often, but Jim has yet to tell him—or anyone—about Becki. But Russ knows. At least, Jim thinks so from the way that Russ grins at him. Jodi drops by Jim's office with donuts almost every morning. As expected, Tony broke it off and the gossip has diminished. Jodi is hurt yet relieved. But her pain seems bigger than Tony. Behind her bantering, she seems somehow burdened with the ache of all hearts. Jim is growing to know and trust Jodi almost as much as Russ, but her cosmic sadness fills him with a sense of foreboding.

Stan's February fit of righteous fervor died quickly, and for most of March, he's been hyping the LBI Easter-Week Pastors' Conference which starts this Tuesday, March 29th. As for Doris: since her drunken advance, she's apologized to Jim five times, "I lost my mind, Jim. God knows, I'm not like *that*."

On the home front, Erin and Heather saw *Tootsie* and lived through it. Nana questioned Sharon on the matter. She, of course, said it was Jim's decision, which satisfied her mom. Jordan's delivered Sharon's new couch, and Samantha, enraged at the violation of her territory, promptly peed on it. Only Heather's desperate pleas saved the cat from being sent to the humane society.

Becki whips the Mustang into a parking spot on the east side of the town common. Her abrupt turn and screeching halt sends a pile of ministry tracts flying from the gearshift module onto the floor. Jim, after releasing his hold on the door grip to which he tightly clung during their wild wide, picks them up. In front of the car stands a large granite arch with engraved words:

**WAR MEMORIAL PARK**
**Established 1877.**
**Land bequeathed by Cyrus A. Buchanan (1815-1874).**
**Philanthropist and founder of Buchanan Carpets.**

Now known as Central Park, the common is deserted save for two elderly women walking on the far side. "You should've never bought a Ford, Shanley," Becki complains after removing her sunglasses. "This Mustang's wicked weak. It has *no* get-up. But I guess it fits your perso*nal*ity, huh?" She chuckles, then cuts a loud fart like an exclamation point to accentuate her complaint. She laughs derisively, so hard her face turns red.

"That's real *lady*like," Jim snaps, his annoyance growing, not because she farted but because he senses it was directed toward him—a sharp insult that well describes her daylong disrespect for his feelings. Becki cracks her window to let in some air.

"Well, that's what I think of this car," she chortles. "We should ditch this clunker and get a real sports car like a Datsun 280ZX. Then we can really cruise."

"You're cruising just fine," Jim contends, gesturing at Becki with the blue gospel tracts he holds in his hand. "You're gonna get us killed, or arrested."

"Awh, come *on*," she taunts. "Where's your spirit of adventure, Shanley? You're wicked *bor*ing today. Stop acting like an old shit!"

Her stinging barb rips Jim's heart, and his patience. He wants to slap her but instead hops out and stomps into the park. After venting several sighs of frustration, he goes back to the car only to find the doors locked. He storms around to the driver's side. "Come *on*, Becki, open up! You're acting like a *damn* twelve-year-old!"

"*Me?* Look who's talking. You started this, Jimmy! I can't believe you're acting so rowdy and adolescent, when we're supposed to be on outreach." Becki flips on the radio. Michael Jackson's "Billie Jean" blasts from the speakers; she opens her window a little more so Shanley can hear it full force.

"Dammit, Becki Lea! Get outa my car! You're gonna run down the battery!"

Becki scowls, narrowing her eyes into a defiant I'm-in-no-hurry look. "So what! Let it run down!" She angrily thrusts her hands into the pockets of her unzipped ski jacket.

The shouting match rages a while, then Becki closes her window. Jim hurls the tracts—that he's been holding in his hand—at the closed window, then huffs away: *She hasn't grown up! She still acts like a fucking infantile! I never saw such blatant contrariness, calling me boring one minute and adolescent the next. She's selfish, impossible, and implacable. She's worse than Alison.*

Becki is indeed a petulant package of contradiction, and her bratty side would send most people running the other way. For that matter, most would conclude, at least from outward observation, that she possesses none of the attractive qualities that a young woman should have, and is therefore unworthy of any man's devotion. But love, as anyone who has been smitten will attest, is not like that. It's unpredictable and irrational, and is undeterred by obvious flaws and detractive traits, or perhaps the heart sees more clearly than the mind. Either way, Jim is hooked; his love and longing for Becki aren't based on reason.

A few minutes pass then the door of the Mustang swings open.

He returns to the car. Pouty-faced and sullen, she gets out but says nothing. Jim kneels near her to collect the gospel tracts. Becki gives a huffy sigh then yawns and stretches as if Jim's presence is putting her to sleep. When she lifts her arms, her sweat shirt rises like a curtain giving him a peek at her belly dimple as it lifts out of her Levi's along with her panty waistband which cutely bisects it. Lust stirs, despite the smoldering argument. He's seen her navel before, when she was younger—swimming, and when she wore a halter top—but now her belly is so womanly, a plumpish cushion of white custardy flesh. The glimpse is over quickly but Jim continues to stare as he stands up. He scans up to her bustline. He pictures her breasts nestled inside her bra—pain, lightning, piercing eyes!

Becki discovers his gaze and nails him with a silent but lacerating command: "Keep your fuckin' eyes off my body!"

Cold steel stabs Jim's heart. A tide of shame drowns his lust. Rebecca, scowling fiercely between contempt and disgust, pulls the shade, locks the door, and slams down the steel mesh. The exchange is quick, sharp, and silent, but acrimony hangs between them like smoke after a gunfight. She lifts her chin haughtily. She sniffs the air. She paws the pavement with her boot. Her mood has shifted abruptly from impudence to pious indignation—as if Jim's lustful staring vindicates her insolent behavior before, and shows him to be the guilty party in their daylong discord. Becki is short, five-foot-two at best, but she holds herself erect like Queen Victoria.

While Jim licks his wounds, they cut diagonally across the sun-washed, shadow-splotched common. The ancient oatmeal-textured sidewalk is cracked and water-stained. Jim looks up at the once-stately-but-now-sickly-and-amputated elm trees; he feels just as sickly: *I'm out of my mind. She doesn't want romance with me. She just comes down because she has nothing better to occupy her time. My feelings are out of touch with reality. Besides, I'm breaking my vows and half the commandments in the Bible. But what am I to do? She makes me go crazy—even when she's shitface. O God, I'm fucked.* Resigned to the impossibility of his situation, he forces his attention to the statues along the sidewalk. Most are memorials to Civil War heroes, but nearest to them are three large statues of local leaders. To his surprise, Becki goes over to read the inscriptions; he joins her:

**Silas Eliot Brendon (1634-1703):** First white settler and owner of Nashoba Plantation. Established grist mill and trading post near the falls in 1668. Traded with Nashaway Indians. Survived massacre of February 10, 1676, during uprising of Wampanoags, Nashaways, and Nipmunks under Chief Philip of Pokanoket. Served as emissary to the

Nashaways during peace negotiations. In 1679 petitioned the General Court for permission to settle eighteen families on Nashoba Plantation thus establishing the village of Brendonville within the Town of Lancaster.

**Josiah Ebenezer Buckingham (1799-1867):** Industrialist and town father. Established Buckingham Mills in 1839. Perfected looms for weaving coachlace and counterpane quilts. Introduced gingham loom in 1844. Served on founding commission that incorporated Brendonville as Town of Brendon Falls in 1846. Served as selectman until 1857, then as mayor until his death in 1867. Instrumental in bringing Worcester & Nashua Railroad to Brendon Falls in 1852, and Boston & Hudson Railroad in 1859.

**Horatio Erastus Hinton (1838-1911):** "Mr. Brendon Falls." Mayor (1876-1894). Developed subdivision plans for Germantown, Green Street, the Acre, and Hadley Hill, along with the layout for War Memorial Park. Supervised the introduction of electric lights and the Brendon Falls Street Railway. Formed the Textile-Wire Zoning Board. Oversaw the construction of Chestnut Street bridge, Wekepeke Brook pipeline, the town sewage system, and Front Road depot and overpass. Served in Congress (1894-1906). Saved Nashoba Dam/Reservoir Project, and oversaw its completion. Served on the staff of General Philip Sheridan during the War to Preserve the Union. Decorated for valor at Battle of Cedar Creek.

"Is that why they call the high school, Silas Brendon?" Becki asks, addressing Shanley as if he's a tour guide. There's no intimacy in her voice or softening of her frowny face, but to have her talk at all brings a measure of solace to Jim's wounded soul.

He says yes in reply to her question, then as they resume walking, he goes on about the history of the town, explaining how the immigrants came to work in the textile mills, and the Irish lived on Hadley Hill, and the Polish on Green Street, and the Germans in Germantown, but nowadays everybody's mixed together. Since Becki is three-quarters German herself—both sets of her grandparents came over from Germany shortly before WWII, though Alison's father is actually French—Jim elaborates about the Germantown section of Brendon Falls hoping to get a response from her, but she says nothing more.

On the far side of the park they cross under a row of large maples and emerge onto Church Street. The weather is just cold enough for winter jackets but with the sunshine it seems much warmer. Pastor Jim usually spends an hour or so talking to folks downtown then visits homes and apartments within walking distance of the common. In the early years of his ministry he sought converts by sharing the gospel on the streets and by knocking on doors, but he's long since abandoned the hard-line you-gotta-get-saved approach. The BFBC tracts still contain the Biblical plan of salvation, but Jim spends most of his time talking with people he already knows.

Turning north onto High Street, Jim and Becki enter the gutted and emaciated austerity of a once-proud main street. Sun-splashed asphalt, brick, and concrete. Beaux-arts motif, bas relief, dull brick colors, buffs, browns, reds, stacked several stories high. Timeworn storefronts, dirty plate glass, many boarded up. Frayed and rusted awnings. Scores of weather-faded signs, ghostly epitaphs to Saturdays long gone: F.W. Woolworth, Newberry's, A&P, J.C. Penney Co., Brendon National Bank, Donlan's Furniture, Selkirk Motors, Bergman Shoes & Leather Goods, Straub Appliances, Morelli's Meat Market, Brendon Falls Hotel, Ritz and Tivoli Theatres. Other signs are living epitaphs to the now dying: Leger's Bakery, Stefano's Men's Shop, Halperin Hardware, Kennedy's Pharmacy, Leavitt's Jewel Shoppe, Rakowski Carpets. And some signs are newly painted for the prosperous few: Flanagan's Liquor, Bancrofts' Steakhouse, Roux's Market & Deli, Reeds' Music Store, Comfed Savings, Brenner & Williams, *Brendon Falls Banner,* Bergson's Restaurant, Clancy's Pub, Theo's Tavern, Pauline's Variety Store.

Jim feels the heavy soul of the old factory town sighing about him. It's like the sad haunting feeling he got when his mom took him to visit Uncle Clyde at the old-soldiers' home in Tyler—the feeling of being in a place the rest of the world has forgotten.

Brilliant flashes of sun, like flashbulbs, reflect off the cars as they huff and snort up High Street. Most do not stop but go right through following Route 72. Grotesque shadows accompany the cars, darting, dancing, stretching, shrinking, reaching like fingers, hands, arms, feeling along the street and the curb. Other shadows, not moving, not feeling, but hopeless and murky, hold the doorways, alleyways, and boarded-up storefronts.

Life-ravaged souls are scattered here and there, solitary, in pairs, with leathery faces: florid, pallid, olive, and black. Some trudge along the sidewalk. Some spit tobacco by the parking meters. Some lounge on the liars' bench across from the bank and talk about yesterday. Other faces, innocent and soft, gather in flocks. Ruddy, young, pimpled, with yearning eyes, they stand outside Flanagan's, Bergson's, Pauline's. Teenage townies: they chew gum and smoke cigarettes, and talk about tomorrow.

In front of Halperin Hardware, Jim and Becki run into Larry Thornton coming out with a spreader and a bag of fertilizer. Larry, trim and tan and dapperly dressed in a blue cardigan and sand-pale slacks, seems out of place in downtown Brendon Falls. Perfect,

perfect. Everything about him seems preppy and precise, even his dulcet radio-announcer voice.

Jim shakes hands with Larry then introduces Becki. Larry says hello yet scarcely acknowledges her presence, but as usual, he taunts Jim, "Down trying to convert people again, huh? I must say, Jimbo, you're worse than my wife, and you're an M.I.T. grad?" He gives a cynical one-syllable laugh then opens the trunk of his Mercedes. After tossing in the lawn-care items, he dusts his hands, gives a thumbs-up, and departs. Jim again wonders why Angela married such a cold perfectionist bastard.

"He won't be laughing and making *fun* when he meets God," Becki declares, briefly breaking her silence. Her tone is so pharisaical, Jim looks twice to make sure that she's not Alison.

"Hey, Pastor Jim," a voice calls from behind them. Jim and Becki turn as a middle-aged hippie-looking fellow comes out of Kennedy's Pharmacy. Next to him is a young woman with long ash-blonde hair that hangs in crimped locks beyond her shoulders. It's Harry Hinton and his live-in girlfriend, Judy Kerrigan.

Judy is Jodi Donovan's cousin and Ruthie Myszak's younger sister. Ruthie's married to Doris Campbell's younger brother, David Myszak, but they're separated. Ruthie cats around and is currently involved with Jodi's husband, Kyle. David now lives with Nina Ramirez, Juanita's cousin. Juanita, of course, is engaged to Stan Campbell's pretty-boy nephew, Freddie Bergman. A tangle of relationships, but typical for Brendon Falls.

"So, what are you guys up to?" Jim asks as he shakes Harry's hand.

Harry hooks his thumbs inside a big coiled-serpent belt buckle that barely holds his fortyish paunch. "Oh, nothing much. We're just getting medicine for Cam—"

"Cami has an ear infection," Judy explains, interrupting Harry. "We jus' hafta to give her these drops. She's home sleepin' now. Ruthie's watchin' her." Judy, short, braless, and freckled, with pale-violet eyes, pulls the prescription bottle out of the bag and holds it up. "See, it's a special antib'otic for babies—oh, is this your daughter, Pastor Jim?"

"Oh, n-no," Jim replies feeling suddenly old—and guilty. "My girls are at home. This is Becki. She's a student at the Bible college in Nashua. She comes down on weekends to help us with our street ministry." Becki shakes their hands, says hello, but does not enter the conversation.

With Harry's black leather vest, which sports a large skull on the back, and Judy's Janis Joplin look—paisley pants, loose tank top, and faded denim jacket—not to mention their beaded bracelets and necklaces, they both look right out of the '60s, as if they just returned from Woodstock.

Harry runs his hand through his long Indian-style hair which is held in place with a beaded headband. "Well, you need all the help you can get in *this* town," he quips, his voice mellow and lazy. "I think all the other churches have given up. Religion sure gave up on me, long ago ... except for you, Pastor Jim."

A delinquent dropout at sixteen, Harry lost his good name—he's descended from the renowned Hinton family of textile and political fame—and ran off with the Hell's Angels. He spent fifteen years on the road finally landing in a California prison. Two years later he returned to Brendon Falls, got married, tried to settle down, but after five years and three kids, took off again, this time with Judy. After three years with a Vermont cycle clan, they returned in 1980—Harry, tired and forty; Judy, nineteen and pregnant. They moved into a run-down house on Mill Street where Judy miscarried at four months, but Cami arrived a year and a half later.

"I think religion gives up on all of us," Jim says in response to Harry's remarks. "But I hope God doesn't. Jesus said, 'I'll never leave thee nor forsake thee.' That's my only hope."

"Your church *is* different," Judy says. "I hated goin' to St. John's, an' Sister Bernice, she scared the fuck outa me at CCD. Pardon my French, but she—"

"I quit church for good in fifth grade," Harry cuts in mirthfully, his blue eyes twinkling. "Mrs. Bailey, she caught me lifting Mary Lou Straub's dress at Episcopal Sunday school. She almost twisted my ear off, but it was worth it to see those frilly pink panties." Everyone laughs except Becki who gives a half grin but quickly reassumes her pious face. "After that I didn't set foot in a church for thirty years, not 'til we came up to your place. I expected the roof to fall but it didn't."

As Jim and Becki depart, Judy says, "You come see us now, Pastor Jim. We're gonna get plenty of donuts, the glazed ones you like, an' you come too, Becki. We enjoyed meetin' yuh."

After seeing middle-aged Harry with young Judy, Jim feels better about his chances with Becki: *Maybe I'm overreacting to her rebuff in the park and to her bitchy mood all day? After all, no one's forcing her to hang around with me. She asked to come on outreach with me, and I sure felt more than friendship when she hugged me at McDonald's week before last. Maybe she has her period or something? We hafta give this more time.*

As they continue up the almost-deserted sidewalk, curiosity breaks Rebecca's silence but not her self-righteous mood, "So how long have you known *them*?"

"Oh, two years or so. They've only come to church twice but I go see 'em a lot."

"Are they married or what?" Becki asks, giving a haughty toss of her head.

"No, they're not married," Jim answers matter-of-factly.

"Harry looks like a *Deadhead*," Becki says as they pause in front of the old Ritz Theatre. "And Judy, she's so much younger and she dresses like Pat Benatar. How'd they ever get together?"

"It's a strange tale ... kind of a riches-to-rags story." Jim doesn't elaborate but turns his attention to some time-faded coming-attraction posters. The movie house has been closed for years but a few of the cobwebbed display cases still have marquee posters hanging in them.

"*So,* are you gonna tell me about them or what?" Becki asks impatiently.

"Oh, you really want to hear it?" Jim teases, hoping to break her snooty mood and rouse her to playfulness; he's now fully recovered from the wounds suffered back at the park. "Well, one of these days I'll tell you."

"Jimmy *Shanley,* you better cut it out." The use of his full name is her official notice that more teasing will not lead to frolic but to another fight.

Jim is annoyed by her unrelenting pissy-face disposition but he's no longer threatened. He's won his bout with discouragement—at least for this Saturday. So, as they browse in the paper-littered runway under the old marquee, he drops his teasing tact and briefly relates Harry's story. "So what crime did he commit?" Becki asks after Jim finishes. "It must've been wicked bad if he went to jail?" Her dark eyebrows knit with contempt.

"Nothing terrible ... he was dealing stolen goods I think."

Jim stops and studies a discolored poster for the movie *Patton* starring George C. Scott. The helmeted general's "arrogant bastard" command presence reminds him of Stan Campbell. A few steps to Jim's right, Becki seems fascinated by an old billing for the movie *Carnal Knowledge* which shows Ann-Margret kissing Jack Nicholson. Jim joins her in front of the provocative poster.

Becki stares at the kissing movie stars but goes on about Harry, "What about his real wife? Did he divorce her? And what about the kids? Does he support them?"

*God, she sounds just like Alison,* Jim declares to himself as he digests Rebecca's gossipy questions. *Perhaps she has a missionary calling after all?* He's seen flashes of pharisee in Becki before, even as a child, but this is the first time he's seen her probe for sin in order to incriminate and condemn. Finally, he replies aloud, "Harry's still married. But beyond that, it's none of my business and none of yours either."

"Whaddeya mean?" Becki retorts. "Don'tcha think the shepherd should know what's goin' on in the flock?"

Jim doesn't respond, though he surely would if Erin or Heather were this nosy and judgmental. But this is Becki. He puts up with shit from her that he'd never tolerate from others. She does not press her question but rather turns her full attention to the *Carnal Knowledge* poster. Her brow still furrowed in self-righteous scorn, she stares at the faded movie billing then reaches over and runs her finger across the glass clearing a path through the accumulated grime, as if she's trying to touch Ann-Margret's face.

*What the hell is she doing?* Jim wonders.

Becki lifts her dirty finger and scowls at it reproachfully as if it's covered with fecal matter. "Yech ... dis*gusting*," she whispers, exhaling the words slowly on her breath. Jim doesn't know if she means the movie, Harry, or himself. And to add to the puzzle, she speaks as if addressing herself. She looks for a long moment at her dirty finger, as if hypnotized by the uplifted digit, then abruptly breaks her gaze, wipes her finger on her jeans, and returns to her previous line of questioning, "So Harry 'n Judy are into free sex, huh, like *hippies*?"

"I thought all godly sex was free?" Jim mocks, venting his annoyance with a bit of sardonic wit—he knows it'll set her off. "If it isn't free, then I think it's called prostitution."

"You *know* what I mean," Becki snarls. "God speaks through the Bible, and you know what the Bible says about sex. It's wicked sacred and nothing to joke about, and you ought to tell 'em. It makes me f-ing mad how people ignore God and sleep around like *dogs!*"

Normally, such an outburst about sexual sin would throw Jim into guilt, but now her antics seem hyper, almost comical, as if she's condemning herself. *Maybe she wants to fuck me and hates herself for having such sinful desires?* He quickly dismisses the possibility and chases it back to the realm of quixotic dreaming. Nonetheless, simply thinking about it excites him.

"Wicked lost; those two are *lost*," Becki declares, passing sentence on Harry and Judy.

Jim smirks under his mustache, his quixotic fantasy lingering deliciously in his mind. "Very true. According to religious scorecards, they are surely hellbound, but sometimes I think Harry and Judy are the most saved couple around."

"Awh, come *on*, Jimmy! He's just a lazy selfish male. God won't let him get away with this. He's gonna reap what he's sowing."

After a few more pointed exchanges, they leave the old
marquee and continue up High Street. At Pauline's Variety they
turn right on Mill Street which runs east over the hill then down to
the Nashua River. Mill Street, lined with old rowhouses and
dilapidated three-deckers, is the poorest street in town except for
the Fitch Road Projects. Years ago it was an elegant avenue which
ran to the main gate at Buckingham's North Mill. The brick many-
windowed factory is still there but it's been abandoned for decades.
Most of the old textile mills in Brendon Falls have been converted
to new uses, warehouses, plastic factories, even apartments, but a
few, like Buckingham's North Mill, lie empty and ghostly behind
crumbling walls, rusting gates, and hip-high weeds, and are visited
only by rats and cats, and teenagers looking for adventure.

Jim knows most of the people who live on Mill Street but only
a few come to church. He plans to visit Cal and Joanne McClusky
who live about halfway up the hill not far from Harry and Judy. But
they never make it to the McCluskys' apartment, because Jim spots,
in the cobblestone alleyway behind Pauline's, three Blacks in the
midst of a wine-enhanced debate: T. Willy Jones, Richard Sam
Washington, and Herschel Hightower. Herschel, of course, comes
to church—he's the freckled mulatto married to Thelma—but Jim
knows the other two almost as well. He and Becki stop at the
entrance to the alley. But the three men, some fifty feet away, are
too occupied to notice them.

T. Willy, an unkempt potbellied Vietnam veteran, leans on a
wooden cane—and a wooden leg. His left leg, shattered by a mortar
round during the Tet offensive, was amputated below the knee.
Wearing a ragged topcoat and a wide-brimmed straw hat, he looks
sixty but he's only forty-three. Inside his coat, a buttonless corduroy vest hangs open framing his huge stomach. But Richard Sam
Washington, better known as "Slick Dick" or just "Slick," is spiffed
to a gaudy hilt in a lavender pencil-striped shirt, plaid trousers,
white loafers, and a sueded-pigskin sport coat. For added swagger,
he wears a pair of wraparound sunglasses and a Scottish-style wool
cap. Short, stocky, and built like a boxer, Slick fancies himself a
ladies' man and does all he can to live up to his nickname. Herschel
H., known downtown as "Professor" because he has one year of
college and seems to be an expert on every subject, is the youngest
yet the tallest of the three. Though his skin is lighter, an ashy brown,
and his freckles testify to white blood, his features are more Negro
than Caucasian. Just off work from the diner, he still wears his white
kitchen outfit plus a blue parka.

As they banter, Willie and Slick drink from wine bottles
concealed in paper bags. "Gentlemans, the way I knows it," T.

Willy declares in his raspy "Satchmo" voice, "when you hits forty, you ain't gonna want it more'n once a week."

Slick takes a swig then rebuts, "Shit, whatchew talkin' 'bout, man? You's a simple motherfucker! Jus' cauz you done let you' self go. It don't mean nuthin' a'*tall* 'bout me. *Shit,* I gets it up as good as any 20-year-ole."

"The way I sees it, Mr. Slick," T. Willy comes back, pointing with his cane, "your cattin' ways *ain't* gonna last. Foe you knows it, you's gonna be keepin' your black ass home mos' ever' night."

Slick lifts his chin defiantly. "Get *off* this shit. I got a fuckin' uncle back home who turned seven'y-five lash year, an' he's never slowed up a lick. Age ain't no 'cauz to worry." Then he turns to Herschel and says, "Isn't that right, Professor?" Slick and T. Willy both chug down some wine as they await Herschel's response.

Herschel laughs and says, "I don't rightly know. But I doubt age slows a man if he's got a good woman who likes to get it on." Herschel's the only sober one in the group.

"You goddam *right!*" Slick declares, giving a smile of triumph; his teeth shine brightly out of his ebony face. "See, Mr. Willy, you's a dumb motherfucker! I'll be out cattin' when you's long gone, ole man."

Slick suddenly spies Pastor Jim. "Hey, there's my main man! Come on over heah, Pastor Jim. These Black motherfuckers need some ah *God's* wisdom, mos' especially Mr. T. Willy Jones." Amid more laughing and bantering, Jim and Becki go over. Jim introduces Becki then jokes with them for five minutes or so. Becki, of course, doesn't join in but Jim notices a few flickers of response playing about her mouth, in spite of herself.

Leaving the alley, Jim and Becki cross Mill Street into Flanagan's parking lot where several groups of teenage townies are gathered. The liquor store itself faces High Street and sits back like a supermarket. A foursome of familiar faces are gathered about Ernie Johnson's blue '79 Malibu. Jim knows it's Ernie's Chevy because it has a Carter-Mondale sticker on the bumper and Ernie's son Kevin is leaning against the driver's-side door. Also present are Cathy Rosinski, Haley Cameron, and Billy McArthur. The rhythmic beat of the *Eagles* and "Heartache Tonight" is pumping through the open front window.

"So your dad finally gave in?" Pastor Jim kids Kevin.

Puffing on a cigarette, Kevin replies out of the side of his mouth, cowboy-style, "I reckon so, Chief." He calls Pastor Jim, "Chief." "Hain't had the car for a month, since that night Mrs. Burton ratted on—"

"She's a real dink!" Cathy cuts in. "We weren't doin' nuthin' wrong."

"Sometimes, she can be fuckin' nice," Haley says, exhaling a stream of tobacco smoke over the roof of the Chevy. "Like when she plays pool with us, but she usually ends up yellin' at us."

Next comes a squeaky Beaver Cleaver voice, Billy McArthur, "I don't have to worry about it. My mom won't let me go to the teen center anyway. She says your church is a cult. But they don't have anything at St. John's anymore. They even closed the gym because they can't get insurance."

Pastor Jim introduces Becki to Billy. She already knows the others from the teen center. Kevin takes a last drag on his Marlboro, flips it onto the asphalt, and crushes it with his cowboy boot. He then focuses on Becki like a young pooch who just spotted a sleeping cat. Burly, brown-eyed, and seventeen, Kevin is a developing clone of his father, and he flirts with any gal he meets, as long as she has apples up front and a full caboose in the rear. "Check it out," he drawls. "So yuh done come back for more, huh, Miss Becki? I thought maybe I scared you off when I got awl rowdy durin' our game of eight ball last week?" A gifted bullshit artist with a "good ol' boy" personality, Kevin reminds Jim of Foghorn Leghorn, the bossy bigmouthed rooster in the TV cartoons.

Rebecca descends from her pious pedestal to toy with Kevin's advance. She scrunches her face then gives a foxy smirk. "You were kind of off-the-wall. But I cooled you down on the Ping-Pong table. You didn't show me much, least at Ping-Pong—but I like your music. What station is that?"

"WCGY 93.7," Cathy offers proudly. She speaks toward Kevin as if trying to regain his attention.

Kevin pushes his hands into the pockets of his scuffed leather jacket—Fonzie-style. He ignores Cathy and continues to flirt with Becki, "Now what's a cute little religious gal like you doin' in this here town?"

Becki's reply is instant and cutting, "Because of superlost souls like you, Kevin." Her sharp and witty counterquip punctures his inflated "cock of the roost" persona and arouses a chorus of hoots and taunts from the other teenagers. Becki purses her lips. Her smirk becomes catty, cocksure.

Kevin quickly retreats to a safer subject, "So you get into the *Eagles,* do yuh?"

Becki's catty smirk gives way to a friendly grin. "Yeah, in a way, I have all their albums at home." Though she artfully rejected Kevin's flirting, she does not reject *him.* Moreover, the exchange has finally broken her pharisaical mood. Jim is glad for that.

The conversation now becomes more inclusive as they all

complain to Pastor Jim about the sorry state of life in Brendon Falls. A closet rebel himself, Jim agrees with most of their grievances yet he knows that the teens will soon grow up and join the adult society they complain about. But he still admires their blatant honesty and unprostituted souls.

As the discussion runs out of gas, Haley reaches into the car and grabs Kevin's cigarettes from the dash. Giving a sigh of displeasure, she says, "Hey, Kev, we're out of fuckin' smokes." She wads the red-and-white Marlboro pack and tosses it at Kevin.

He snaps the wadded pack out of the air with one hand. "I believe it, gal. You done awhready smoked up half a pack. Howcum I gotta supply yuh anyhow?"

"'Cause I'm *all* out," Haley says, giving him an impudent toss of her strawberry locks. Dressed in an untucked shirt and worn corduroys, with a tan sweater tied jock-style about her neck, Haley Cameron is a saucy sixteen-year-old with cherry lips and sad hazel eyes. She's the oldest daughter of Barbara Sims and lives in the projects on Fitch Road. "Come on, Kev, I'm gonna pay you back. You know I'm always broke on Saturday. So *cut* the shit, okay?"

Kevin fishes into the pocket of his Western-style shirt and pulls out another soft-pack of Marlboros, but it too is empty. He crushes it as well then tosses both wadded packs onto the front seat of the Malibu. "See, woman, that's the difference," he says to Haley. "I kin take 'em or leave 'em. I don't have no nico fits like you, but here take this change and run over to Clancy's. Getcha some outa the machine."

Haley takes the change from Kevin and counts it, fingering each of the coins in her cupped hand, a slender pretty hand with graceful fingers. Pastor Jim has known Haley and her family since his ministry began; he knows that her sassiness and vulgarity hide a love-starved soul. "I need another fuckin' quarter," she fusses after counting the change. "They went up, you know?"

"Well, check this shit," Kevin grumbles good-naturedly. "I hain't got another cent. I know you're broke, Cath. How 'bout you, Billy boy? Why don'tcha break open your piggy bank?"

"We already broke it at McDonald's, remember?" Billy reminds Kevin.

Pastor Jim pulls out his wallet and gives Haley a ten-dollar bill. "Here, take this. Get yourself three packs and get some Peanut M&M's as well, and two packs of Big Red gum, and any other candy you want." Haley gives Jim a shy grin that quickly breaks wide into a beaming smile which shatters her brazen tough-girl facade. As the others shout their candy preferences after her, she takes off for Clancy's.

Billy McArthur peers up curiously at Pastor Jim through little Poindexter glasses. "I thought smoking was a sin at your church?" he says.

A young fifteen, Billy is slight, slouched, and nerdy with a pitted-acne complexion. But even with pimples, he's a pretty young man in a choirboy sort of way. He wears a Boston Celtic cap and a black *AC-DC* sweat shirt. He hangs around with Kevin and Cathy, and Jim has seen nothing to substantiate Heather's rumor that he's sweet on Erin, and even if he is, he'll have no opportunity to see her outside of school—Sharon will never allow Erin to hang out downtown, much less have a Catholic boyfriend.

"In a way it is," Jim answers Billy. "It's certainly not a healthy habit."

"So why'd you give her the money?" Billy asks. "If it's not a good thing?"

Jim shrugs and lifts his upturned hands, giving an I-don't-know gesture. "Hard to say. I just wanted to, I guess. I don't like cigarettes, Billy. They're dirty and they cause cancer, but I can't see God getting into a panic over them and—"

"What about *pot*?" Cathy Rosinski cuts in, with more than academic interest. "I saw you get superpissed when Mrs. Burton found that roach in the ladies' room." Cathy, an insecure broken-home runaway with mouse-brown hair and ruddy Polish cheeks, lives with her barfly aunt on Mill Street, down by the river. She works as a waitress-trainee at Bergson's. She's dressed in her usual simplicity: khaki sweats and dirty-gray sneakers.

Jim is moved with compassion as he looks into Cathy's abandoned-puppy eyes which are round and blue and gray-flecked, and ringed with dark lashes. She looks like a youthful Debra Winger. Jim has been fondly concerned for Cathy since he first met her on the street two years ago. "Oh, I remember all right, Cath. I was pissed that night for sure. But I think drugs and alcohol are worse because they make you drunk, while cigarettes—"

"That's right," Cathy comes back, interrupting him. "That's why I don't give a shit about cigarettes, but weed gets me out of this boring life." She blushes and gives a revealing grin. "That's why I torch up. I can't afford it much, but I sure love the *whoosh* it gives me. But I guess God's not too keen on me gettin' high, huh?"

"That's for sure," Kevin affirms, gesturing with his thick hands. "Like how you got stoned on St. Paddy's Day, plus all those beers. You didn't even know your name. I bet that gotcha on God's shitlist, right, Chief?"

"No doubt about it," Billy chirps in ahead of Pastor Jim. "You'll go to hell for that—or at least purgatory."

115

"Enough already," Cathy retorts. "I've seen you guys a lot worse."

"Okay, okay," Pastor Jim says, patting the air with his hands like a cop slowing traffic. "If you'll settle down, I'll tell you what I think." He likes to share with the teens because he can speak more freely—beyond the bounds of LBI doctrine. "Drugs kill us like slow suicide and liquor is perhaps the worst, but even if drugs were safe, I wouldn't use them myself. I don't like being drunk—not that smoking pot puts us on God's shitlist. Whether it's a sin or not isn't the big issue with me. I see love and closeness to each other as the main thing, and if we're fogged up on chemicals, how can we share our true hearts? I'd rather be honestly unhappy with you than to ride a phony high with you. Natural highs are rare, but they do come—in God's due season."

"So I'm supposed to stop gettin' stoned?" Cathy asks. "And wait for God to bring something good to break this sucky life? I'm not into waiting and staying down, not if I have money for a joint. God's too slow for me."

"God *is* slow," Shanley agrees. "I get tired of waiting myself. I'm not telling you what to do. I can't live your life for you. I'm just telling you what I think. Look at the story of Job that we discussed at the teen center. He was a good man, yet he lost everything. He went through hell on earth and never knew why, just like we don't know why life gets so shitty sometimes. But God finally blessed Job with happiness. But it's no fun waiting. So I'm not shocked to see you or anyone turning to drugs even though drugs kill us and cut us off from each other."

"It's like *Pink Floyd* filling up the empty spaces," Becki adds spontaneously. "We all need love and good times, and we want to like ourselves instead of feeling crummy. We need something to get off on in this yechy life. But we don't wait like Job. We try to fill our empty spaces with phony highs—but it doesn't work. But I think God understands how much we ache."

Jim can scarcely believe how warm and considerate Becki sounds. She seems a different person from the one he's been with all day. Her words touch him as if she's speaking from within his own heart; his spirit soars, *O Jesus, I know she loves me. How did I get so caught up with sexual anxiety? Romance will come in due season if it's meant to be. If not, spiritual intimacy will suffice.* A transcendent peace spreads through his soul, like a beautiful dye diffusing in warm water.

"That's exactly right, Becki," Jim affirms buoyantly, no longer speaking to himself but to everyone. He gestures like a musical conductor. "If not with drugs, then we try to fill our empty places with something, anything—like being a jock, or making straight A's, or the Red Sox, or driving fast cars, or finding fast sex, or getting married to the wrong person, or accumulating money and credentials ... or even religion."

Billy again looks puzzled. "Even religion?" he asks.

"That's right, Billy," Pastor Jim answers. "You see, a lot of people try to move God with a formula—if I get saved, go to church, and live according to the Bible, then God will bless. I used to think that myself, but I've long since found out that I can't move God no matter how much I pray or serve." Jim is sharing convictions he'd never preach from his pulpit. "Sometimes good things happen, sometimes bad things. I suspect that everyone has found this out, but many churchgoers refuse to admit it. They maintain that God responds to their prayers and to their correct Biblical choices. They profess to be blessed and happy even when they're miserable inside. They call it 'walking by faith,' but to me, it's phony and propped up, just as phony as getting happy on alcohol or pot."

"You're saying that gettin' high and goin' to church is the *same*?" Cathy asks in amazement.

"Well, in a way, but not exactly," Pastor Jim explains. "They're just two different ways of coping with pain, guilt, and uncertainty, and the fear of death. Some go to drugs. Others go to church—not that everyone who goes to church is phony. Some of us admit that God is beyond our control. But drugs and religion have more similarities than most Christians would *dare* to admit."

Billy's face fills with wonder. "*Far* out. I never heard a priest talk like this. But it makes sense what you're—"

Red hair, cherry lips, a paper bag full of goodies. Haley is back, abruptly ending the rap session.

They all dig into the bag. Haley pulls out three packs of Winstons, pockets one, tosses one to Kevin, rips open the third. Becki pops a piece of Big Red into her mouth. The rest have some form of chocolate. Even Kevin stuffs in a handful of Milk Duds before opening his cigarettes. But Haley is sucking smoke like a newborn who just found her mother's tit. After a few deep drags she exhales and says, "So, Jim, are you gonna take us to the mountains this year, to that place in Maine by the lake?"

"Maybe in the fall?" Jim replies around a mouthful of Peanut M&M's.

"I'm going this year," Billy says, his squeaky voice clogged with half of a Snickers bar. "My mom can't say no again. It's not like I'm converting to your church or anything. Maybe you can talk to her, Pastor Jim?"

"Whoa there, Billy boy," Kevin says before Jim can reply.

**117**

"I've done been there, see, like three trips. It kin get plum physical. Yuh gotta be a man to go up Shutdown Mountain. I'm not sure you'll make it, boy."

Undaunted, Billy quickly counters, "If you lugged *your* fat ass up there, Kev, it'll be a piece of cake—"

Suddenly, a godlike voice: "OKAY, KIDS! You'll have to move on now!" It's Steve Flanagan approaching from the liquor store. "This lot is for our customers. It's not a public park. We can't have you loitering around and playing your loud music, and making a mess." The other groups of townies are rapidly dispersing.

Pastor Jim has never liked the Flanagan brothers, especially Steve who is the youngest and seems to delight in chasing the kids away. "Now hold on, Steve," Jim objects. "They're not hurting anything. Besides, you have fifty empty parking spots, and they're way out here almost on the side—"

"You stay out of this, Pastor Jim," Flanagan interrupts. "I don't want any trouble with you. We pay taxes to maintain the common. The kids can hang out down there. How can we run this store with all the loud music and profanity? It disturbs the peace and hurts our business."

Jim feels hot emotion: "Just what is your business anyway, Steve? Getting rich at the expense of the alcoholics in this town, while you ignore the needs of the youth—so they *too* will grow up to be regular customers?" Jim knows he's out of line legally but he can't contain himself. He feels that the kids are unfairly treated by the town merchants and the town government, and he knows that his own BFBC teen ministry is the only adult-sponsored teen program in Brendon Falls. He feels like smashing Flanagan in the face. But instead, he wads his yellow M&M's bag and tosses it at him.

"GODDAMMIT, PASTOR JIM!" Flanagan shouts as the teenagers look on spellbound. "I don't go up to your church on Sunday and loiter in your parking lot! So stop gettin' on my case for insisting on my rights as a property owner! I don't know *why* you waste your time down here anyway, always talking with the rowdies and the riffraff. Most ministers stay in their churches where they belong. But that's your business. I got no quarrel with you talking with whoever, or handing out your blue cards, but just don't do it on *my* fuckin' property!"

"Whoa now, Stevie boy," Kevin jumps in. "Look who's usin' profanity! Betcha if I pop some twenties an' fetch several cases of Coors for a party, you'd sure enough change your tune."

"You'd be wise to cool it, Kevin," Flanagan warns. "Or I'll call your dad."

"Just let us alone, YOU *FUCK*WAD!" Haley shouts as she

backs away toward the car.

Police, police: a B.F.P.D. squad car pulls up with officer Bradley Selkirk at the wheel. Officer Brad, ruddy, fat, and macho, with dark glasses and curly blond hair under a baseball-style police hat, makes a radio call then issues his orders, "Come on, kids, let's get a move on it."

"We hain't doin' nuthin' wrong!" Kevin protests.

"Okay, Kevin, let's cool it now," Pastor Jim counsels. "Do what he says and get everyone into the car." It actually warms Jim's heart to see the kids stand up to Flanagan and Selkirk, but he sees no point in anyone getting arrested over it. Kevin hustles everyone into the Malibu and they take off. As they drive out onto High Street, Haley yells obscenities out the back window.

"What about this brunette?" Selkirk asks, referring to Becki.

"She's not with them," Jim explains. "She's with me."

After emphasizing how bad the teen situation is getting, Flanagan thanks Officer Selkirk and returns to his store, leaving Jim, Becki, and the policeman in the parking lot, with Selkirk still in his cruiser. "So, Brad, you got rid of them," Jim remarks derisively. "I guess you feel real proud of yourself?"

"I'm just doing my job, Pastor Jim," Officer Brad replies. "I have to enforce the no-loitering and trespassing laws. You have your rights, but so do the merchants. So stop encouraging the kids to think they can gather anywhere they want. We get more calls to disperse teenagers than anything in this town."

"Doesn't that tell you something, Brad?" Jim asks. "About the *town,* maybe?"

"That's *enough,* Pastor Jim. I don't need your religious and philosophical bullshit. I'm a police officer. I've got nothing against you or any minister. In fact, I go to church myself, in Hudson, when I'm not on duty. But I'm sworn to enforce the laws in this town. So, you and the young lady get a move on it." With that, Officer Selkirk makes another radio transmission and departs.

Jim and Becki cross the street to the other sidewalk. Becki talks excitedly about the standoff in the parking lot. Noisy exhalations, noisy gum, slangy words: "wicked, super, yechy, sucky." Beaming, laughing, dimples, pimples, rosy cherub cheeks. No more insolence, no more piety, no more adult propriety. She skips on one foot as if playing hopscotch, then does her happy-girl quickstep, imitating the *ENERGIZER* Bunny. Tacky tomboy clothes, fluffy chocolate hair, raunchy street-lingo: "asshole, fartface, fuckwad." Becki, Becki: buoyant, sassy, coltish, crude—and most unladylike.

Jim marvels. His head spins—but his heart soars.

It's 4:32 p.m. They've been downtown for two hours.

# Chapter Eleven

**T**error, gasping, no breath, dark, dark. Pastor Jim plunges through the thick tropical undergrowth. Thorny brambles lacerate his face and arms setting them on fire with salty pain. Yet he still hears the creature crashing through the jungle behind him. Finally, Jim breaks out of the rain forest and sloshes frantically through ankle-deep water and waist-high swamp grass.

Silver, silver. The grass looks silver in the moonlight. His lungs burn. His heart pounds. He gulps the sultry air. But he cannot elude the haunting nightbeast. The swamp gives way to a grassy savanna. With a last surge of adrenaline, he bursts onto the dry prairie. But the galloping hoofbeats pursue relentlessly, drawing closer until he can hear the monster snorting. A large acacia tree looms ahead in the ethereal murk. Jim sprints toward the spreading canopy of limbs and foliage, but as he approaches, the tree explodes in a blaze of blue fire knocking him onto the ground.

When he looks up, he sees fluorescent eyes and ape-like nostrils, and sharp curved horns. "O GOD, NO!" he screams. He looks for the tunnel of death, but instead, he sees Sharon's face.

"Jim, Jim, wake up," Sharon urges as she leans over him.

With a sigh of relief, Jim finally escapes the dream. "This thing was chasing me," he explains, his voice thick with sleep. "It was like a bull with a gorilla's face, and it was breathing fire." He usually doesn't remember dreams, but he recalls every detail of this one, especially the appearance of the monster since it's similar to the Minotaur creatures that he saw in his phantasmal Becki-vision at prayer meeting last month.

"Sounds like my nightmare," Sharon says, "except I'm always running down a dark alley trying to escape from a mad rapist."

She laughs and playfully tweaks Jim's nose then waltzes back to her closet where she pulls off her robe and takes out her new Easter dress. It's pale-orange and pretty with ruffles about the waist. At least, it looks orange to Jim; she calls it apricot. "Better get moving, hon," she bubbles as she slips into the dress—she's in an ebullient holiday mood. "We have to pick up Barry and Janet at nine if we expect to be in Nashua by ten-fifteen."

\* \* \*

Wednesday, March 30, 1983. As Jim rolls out of bed in Brendon Falls, Rebecca Lea is in her room in Nashua getting ready for class. Having overslept, she's already missed Dr. Logan's eight o'clock chapel. Just out of the shower and wrapped in a yellow robe, she stands at her makeshift dresser, an old chest of drawers with a mirror propped on top. She's applying a spot of peach cover-up to a large inflamed pimple on her chin. She knows the pimple well for it appears a week before her period each month then erupts like a solar flare the day before her cramps start. Her frowny look is more severe than usual, partly because it's morning, and partly because she's disgusted with her pale full-cheeked face as it stares back at her out of the mirror—not to mention the bloaty blahs from her approaching period.

The door opens behind her. "Oh, Becki," comes an adolescent voice. "Can I borrow your new sweater, the one with the fancy border?" Katie comes over next to her sister.

"Why d'you always have to wear *my* stuff?" Becki whines, speaking to Katie's reflection in the mirror. "Half of my clothes are in your closet—howcome you're not in school?"

"We go at nine this week, because of the conference. So can I borrow the sweater, or what?"

Becki does not reply as she puts another dab of makeup on her pimple. Katie, lean-faced with shoulder-length hair the color of ripe wheat, watches impatiently. She's a bit taller than Becki but not as chunky. She looks like their father, Derek. She's definitely a Reinhardt, while Becki takes after Alison's (Chavin) side of the family—except for her blue eyes. "Well, can *I?*" Katie asks again, her tone sharper, more demanding.

"No!" Becki snaps. "You can wear your *own* stuff." A huffy sigh follows her pointed words.

Katie gives a frown more fierce than Becki's, and her voice has just as much bite, "Well, you can take your sweater and stick it you know *where.*" Fuming, she departs and slams the door behind her.

Becki pads over to her stereo and pops in a Rod Stewart tape. "Da Ya Think I'm Sexy?" sounds through the speakers. She then goes to her closet intending to take off her robe, but instead, she pulls the border-print sweater off its hanger and yells above the music, "KATIE! KATIE MARIE! COME BACK IN HERE!"

When Katie comes in, Becki tosses her the sweater. For a moment they stare at each other, still frowning, but the frowns quickly melt into grins. "Thanks," Katie says. "I knew you had a heart—somewhere in there." Giving a mock salute, she departs.

But Becki's friendly spirit is short-lived as Alison marches in on Katie's heels: "Rebecca, I'm going over to catch Pastor's message at the morning session but I—turn off that stereo! How can I talk to you when you have worldly music blaring?" Becki flips off the tape deck. Alison sighs then goes on, "I need you to sign two application forms."

"Applications for what?" Becki asks suspiciously.

"For the dormitory next fall. Ed says dorm space'll be tight because of all the new students coming in September. So we want to reserve you a room ahead of the rush."

"No way, Mom. I toldjuh I'm not moving into the dorm ... no way."

"Oh yes, you are," Alison insists with motherly firmness.

"No, I'm not!" Becki exclaims testily, moving back to her mirror to escape Alison's stern face. But she feels her mother's eyes burning the back of her head. Her own face in the mirror seems dull and fat and blemished, even more disgusting than before; her mom's disapproving eyes have this effect on her.

Unzipping her calfskin jacket, Alison follows her daughter across the room. "Well, it's either the dorm or Puerto Rico. If you don't move into the dorm, then you're coming back with us in August."

Becki, scowling defiantly, puts a touch of pink lipstick on her lips. "I don't have to obey you, Mom, not anymore. I *am* nineteen, you know?"

They glare at each other in the mirror, blue eyes blazing against brown. Except for the eyes, Alison looks much like Becki, short, bouncy, and cupid-faced, with low-slung hips. She also has the same chocolate-brown hair but her highlights are auburn rather than honey-blond. "I don't care if you're thirty-five, young lady. As long as *I'm* supporting you, then you'll do as *I* say." Alison punctuates her declaration with an indignant snort.

"Well, whoopie-*do*—then I don't need your fuckin' money."

"You check your foul mouth! How dare you use that word in this house!"

Becki compresses her lips. "Well, I don't," she maintains, sassily holding her ground. "I can make it without your money." She closes her lipstick and replaces it amid the cluttered array of bottles, jars, and tubes on her dresser.

Alison coils her body, lifts her hand, thrusts her chin, as if to strike her daughter. Becki winces anticipating the blow, but Alison attacks with words instead, "You know nothing! You have no sense of responsibility! You can't even do simple chores around this house, much less make a living. You have no humility. You show no respect for authority. The world's a cold place. You wouldn't last two weeks on your own!"

Rebecca tosses her head impudently. "I can move to Boston and live with Amelia. I'll work as a waitress and make plenty of money." She picks up a rat-tail comb and sweeps it angrily through her still-wet hair.

"Right?" Alison growls sarcastically. "You really think my sister wants an insolent nineteen-year-old living in her apartment? She has her own life, you know?"

"She already invited me when she called on my birthday," Becki rebuts, still speaking into the mirror. Her scowl is so sharp that her knit brow looks like a knife blade.

Alison sighs and retreats a few steps. She now seems more discouraged than angry. "I don't know what to do with you, Becki. I was so proud of you when we first got back. You went to every service and never missed a class. You seemed so devoted to the Lord. And on your own you chose a field practicum and started doing weekend evangelism with Jim in Brendon Falls, and—" *Clatter, clink, clink.* Tall can falling. Bottles, jars knocking about.

When Alison says, "With Jim in Brendon Falls," Becki knocks over a can of hair spray with an errant sweep of her comb, but she quickly recovers the hair spray, and her poise, then watches in the mirror as her mom continues her lamentation, "But lately you've reverted to your old ways. You miss church and cut classes. I have to fight with you to get you out of bed." Shaking her head, Alison gestures with uplifted hands. "Your dirty mouth is coming back, and your flippant attitude, and you seem addicted to rock music again. You watch worldly movies and TV shows instead of studying. And now you've got this *crazy* idea about dropping out of college and goin' to live with your unsaved aunt. You're *im*possible, Rebecca Lea. You have a new direction every three months. If you don't settle down and anchor yourself in the Lord's work, you're goin' to learn the hard way about life, and bring the whole family into disgrace."

"Just like *you,* huh, Mom?" Becki mocks, her words filled with stinging contempt.

"I give up!" Alison exclaims, her temper erupting again. "Go ahead, Miss *Know*-it-all, do what you want. I wash my hands. I'm not even goin' to pray for you anymore. I give *up!*"

Alison tosses the application forms on Becki's unmade bed and storms out. But she hasn't given up, for no sooner than she closes the door, she swings it open again, "I'll be back at ten and you *better* be in class, young lady. And before you go, you straighten this room. It looks like the inside of a Goodwill dumpster. I'm sick of seeing your clothes piled everywhere. And make your bed and take those mugs and glasses to the kitchen and get that *pizza* box out of here. And I don't want you wearing jeans today. Jim and Sharon are coming and I want you to look nice. We're all goin' to hear Jim speak at the afternoon session then the Brendon Falls team is coming over for spaghetti before we go to service. So you have a full day ahead of you, Miss *Rein*hardt—and before you start throwing your age around, you better start acting like a Christian woman instead of a bratty child! And wipe that pout off your face before I *slap* it off! I don't care if you're *fifty*! And don't forget to feed Skipper; he's in the side yard. I'll see you at eleven."

Cursing under her breath, Becki grabs the dormitory papers from her bed and stuffs them into the top drawer of her study desk—unsigned. As soon as she hears her mom leave, via the kitchen door, she flips on the stereo. "Do Ya Think I'm Sexy?" again reverberates through the room—this time cranked to full volume.

\* \* \*

9:10 a.m. Gray Ford Grenada. Sunny but unseasonably cold. After picking up the Bufords—they live in a rental house on Green Street not far from the paper mill—Jim heads north on Route 72 then east on Route 117. Bubbly conversation. They exchange evangelical pleasantries and party-line comments—as born-again Christians do when they first get together, especially for a big event like the annual LBI Easter-Week Pastors' Conference. Reaching Route 495, Pastor Jim eases into northbound traffic. A gust of wind buffets the car. The Shanleys' Grenada is no luxury car but it's more than adequate despite a balky heater which pours most of the heat on the front passenger side. As they head north through the rolling hills of Bolton, the ebullient chatter gives way to quiet.

"So, Sharon, who's got the kids?" Janet asks from the back-seat after five miles of silence. Sleek, alluring, and tempestuous, with raven-black hair and a breathy voice, Janet Buford—formerly Janet Poulos—is the youngest of Jim's teachers and the best-looking.

Sharon removes her sunglasses and shifts around to face Janet. "Oh, they're with Bev 'til Friday. Cathy Rosinski's babysitting the entire crew tonight so Russ and Bev can come up for the main service at Moody."

Despite the cold, Sharon and Janet are dressed in striking spring outfits. Sharon's apricot dress is topped by a new trench coat, fawn-brown and double-breasted, while Janet wears pastel-blue under a gray stadium jacket. Every LBI event is a fashion show but especially the Easter-Week conference where it's traditional for the ladies to show off their Easter stuff. "And who's subbing for you?" Sharon asks Janet.

"Well, Leslie offered but I don't need her getting heavy on my kids. So Doris is covering for me while Leslie and Angela give

Doris's class art and music projects."

"I think that's wise," Sharon says, her tone judicial yet diplomatic. "Leslie's more suited for older kids." She then turns her attention to Barry, "So, Barry, how'd—"

"Hey, Jim," Janet cuts back in. "You guys mind if I smoke?"

"Go right ahead," Jim replies over his shoulder as Janet unzips her pouchy purse and takes out a pack of Merit Lights. As he returns his attention to the road, he catches Sharon giving a quick condescending frown.

"What were you saying, Sharon?" Barry asks curiously, his voice just as corpulent as his physique.

"Oh, I was just wondering how you got the day off. Doris says you and Stan are working a lot of overtime."

"With Stan Campbell, all things are possible," Barry replies kiddingly. Curly black hair, fat face, bulging brown eyes. Barry Buford reminds Jim of a young Jackie Gleason. He's a deacon in the church and, despite his Pillsbury Doughboy physique, plays a fine first base on the BFBC "Crusader" softball team.

"No, seriously," Barry says, now giving a straight answer to Sharon's question, "Stan juggled the boiler-room schedule for me. He says the anointed atmosphere in Nashua helps us grow spiritually, so I should spend time on campus whenever I can. Besides, he wants me to tape Pastor Jim's message this afternoon so we can listen to it on the way back tonight. He and Doris are coming up for the evening service and we'll be riding back with them. And we're spending the day with Matt and Pamela. Stan says that's good so we can see all the campus and meet some of the faculty. Of course, Stan wants me to enroll full—"

"*Stan, Stan,* that's all I hear," Janet complains, bursting the congenial bubble of polite Christian conversation.

Jim, surprised but not shocked, glances back to see what's coming next. Janet's dark-hazel eyes flash like lightning through her square-framed glasses. She sucks hard on her cigarette then vents a fierce stream of smoke up toward her partially opened window. After uttering a contemptuous grunt, somewhere between a groan and a growl, she vents her feelings as well, "I don't give a shit what Stan feels! And it'll be an f-ing cold day in hell before I move into a cramped one-room apartment so I can face five hundred shit-eating smiles each morning at breakfast! Pardon my language, but Stan Campbell really *pisses* me off!"

Silence. Icy tension. A Janet-Barry fight seems imminent. Janet's refusal to submit to male authority, as commanded in the Bible, has given her a "difficult woman" tag. A liberated LBI wife—she's a rare case. Jim doesn't agree with most of her feminist

125

views yet he admires her spunk. And he sees how she loves her kindergarten class—her little ones. He sees them gather daily at her bosom where she protects them like a mother bear.

Though of Greek descent, Janet has an Asian sweep to her eyes with shadowy crescents underneath that make her look old enough, but not old. Nonetheless, despite her gypsylike beauty and untameable spirit, she has an aura of wistful resignation, as if she knows she can never escape the walls about her.

*Wish I could share my feelings so honestly,* Jim says to himself, siding with Janet in his thoughts. *Bet she'd love to hear about my '74 experience, that the Holy Spirit was a goddess. I'd love to tell her about it—in bed. Shit, why can't I think about her without pulling down her underpants? I'm her pastor. I'm supposed—it's no use. She's gotta have the blackest-meanest bush in the church. Why the fuck did she marry Barry? It's hard to imagine him pumping her to the seventh heaven, especially after what Sharon told me about him, and they're spending the day with the Garretts. I wonder if it's really true about Barry and—*

"Stan can be overbearing but he means well," Sharon says, breaking the icy silence—and Jim's wayward train of thought. "And I think—well, we can respect his opinions without putting him on a pedestal." While she speaks, she nervously fingers her necklace of small white shells. Sharon is a master at diplomacy, and her maneuver defuses the acrimony a bit, at least enough for conversation to resume.

"You can always commute to Nashua," Jim says to Barry. "I did, you know?"

"I'd never go through that again," Sharon quips.

"That's an option," Barry replies simultaneously, "but Stan says if I'm going to Bible college, I need to live daily in the fullness of the body to—"

"You and Stan can live daily in the fullness of the body," Janet shoots back—this time with more humor than acid. "I'll live daily in the fullness of a Dutch colonial in the country."

As the interstate unrolls like a wide double-ribbon through Westford and Chelmsford, Janet's pungent personality salts the conversation, not allowing them to settle back into pleasant Christian platitudes—just as her cigarette smoke disturbs the perfumy fragrances in the car. Jim is glad. He's never liked polite evangelical chattiness. They get off at Exit 35 in Lowell and head north on Route 3. Jim unbuttons his suit vest. His gray pinstripe is his dressiest suit but it seems smaller every time he wears it. He doesn't look forward to the conference. He's prepared a sermon, "The Sure Mercies of David," but it's watered-down to stay within the LBI fences. He'd like to declare his true feelings, his hopes and fears and doubts and dreads, but he's far away from that kind of courage. He doesn't even look forward to seeing Becki because she's always cool to him in the presence of a crowd. He looks forward to nothing in Nashua—except leaving.

Before going back to Brendon Falls, he and Sharon are going on a two-day getaway to Vermont. Sex, sex. Wanton women in his head, wanton wife in his bed. Pussy, pussy, Sharon's pussy. Jim wants to fuck it and fuck it, with his cock, with his hand, his tongue, his arms, his legs, his whole body. He wants to pull back her cunt flap like a tent door and go inside and hide there and never come out. No matter the conflicts and confusion, and fantasies and fears, swirling in his brain, Jim forgets all when fucking his wife. Despite—or perhaps because of—Becki, he and Sharon have reached new pinnacles of conjugal pleasure. Their sex life has always been good—once they got past the first month of virginal awkwardness—and it's the one area of their marriage that has survived the onslaught of life's responsibilities, but in the last six weeks they seem to have broken through into a new dimension of carnal knowing. Jim often counsels married couples who have sexual problems but he cannot identify, for his marriage bed has been uniquely blessed, and he takes it for granted more than he knows—yet events are shaping up to teach him just how much.

Though Jim fantasizes about Becki, he doesn't see his wife as a can't-have-Becki consolation prize. Romance with Rebecca is a far-fetched dream that may never come true. He's far away from her cabbage patch. He can't even peep through the fence without arousing her wrath. Besides, if she ever does let go, angels will have to hold him, for he disintegrates just at the thought of kissing her. One tender Becki-embrace at McDonald's raptured him into ineffable bliss. To actually fondle her flesh would be an out-of-body experience. But Becki on weekends, with her clothes on, now that's very believable. In fact, it's happening.

Sharon, Becki, wife, fantasy. Conflict, confusion, no vacancy in his heart. Two women, many women. Hips, lips, hairy twats. Warm eyes, cozy souls. Females, females. How many can he love? Does he have a choice? How can Becki fit into his future? Forget the future. Forget everything past Friday. In the real world, Sharon is his only "Lady Jane." She's not a fairy tale. She's real, and she's going to fuck him in Vermont.

\* \* \*

Pastor Jim turns north on Brooke Drive. West campus now lies on both sides of the road. His stomach swirls. Butterflies, butter-flies. Logan intimidation, religious stage fright, LBI peer pressure. Jim must perform and excel and look good, even if he has to fake it, which he does. He weighs himself in the balances and finds himself wanting. His mind knows better but his stomach doesn't. His growing disenchantment with home base, which gives him rebellious boldness in Brendon Falls, makes him feel even greater anxiety in Nashua. The LBI God-squad in his conscience—not the God of love and freedom he hopes for, but Logan's God—accuses him of thought treason. He feels like Benedict Arnold just waiting to be found out.

When they reach "Blantyre Gate," used by pastors, faculty, and distinguished guests, a security guard waves them through wrought-iron gate doors which hang on massive granite gateposts.

A cobblestone driveway curves up the hill through a Victorian setting of terraced lawns, manicured hedges and gardens, Italian fountains, and stately trees. Blantyre Hall, a cross between a Scottish baronial castle and a San Francisco Bonanza King man-sion, commands the top of the hill with its ivy towers, columned portico, and rose-colored parapets. In front, on a freshly painted flagpole, flies an American flag and a large LBI banner. The flags give the old Bancroft mansion an embassy-like touch. The Italian fountains are dry and littered with leaves. Jim always notices the cherubs, how they have spigots for penises. In the summer, water spurts from the spigots as if the cherubs are pissing. He wonders again why they have dicks at all, if angels are sexless and there's no intercourse in heaven; at least, that's how Logan preaches it.

Before reaching the castle, they turn off, crest the hill, and descend into another world—east campus, a modern academic quadrangle: academic halls, residence halls, roadways, sidewalks, lawns. Beyond the quadrangle is Cotton Mather Gymnasium which is surrounded by fenced athletic fields still splotched with snow. Finally near the east gate looms the silver-gray dome atop the brand-new Dwight L. Moody Coliseum. Used for church services, conferences, varsity basketball, and TV production, it looks like a small version of the Astrodome. Moody is Logan's pride and joy, but he had to remortgage the entire property to build it.

They drive around the quadrangle. Coveys of sun-washed, wind-chilled students march zealously to and from class, books and Bibles in hand. Fawning apple-polishers, puffing clouds of white breath, gather around teachers to ask high-sounding questions. Others stand in twos and threes eagerly expounding on Logan's latest spiritual theme. Jim can't hear them of course, but based on his own student days, he surmises what they're saying. A stream of young bodies stride in and out of the John Wesley Student Union complex, women in skirts, men in coats and ties, only a few in Levi's or cords. Wholesome devout faces, happy positive faces. There's never "a discouraging word" on campus—at least not openly. Jim looks for Becki but doesn't see her. They drive by the new Priscilla Logan Memorial Chapel, a white country-style church with a high steeple, which gives the quadrangle the distinct flavor of a New England town common.

Across from the chapel, in the middle of the square, is a flagpole, a fountain, and a reflecting pool—with no cherubs. The plumbing, however, has never worked properly, and over the decade of its existence, the fountain has become an ugly basin of cracked and weed-invaded concrete. Only rain and melting snow fill the pool. It freezes in winter and stinks in summer.

Pastor Jim turns off on Cottage Row, an old tree-lined road that runs behind the castle. A half mile down this bumpy cobblestone road are six turn-of-the-century Chautauqua-style houses and several caretaker cottages. Logan has converted most to faculty-staff apartments. Only the smaller cottages are single-family. After a quick stop at the Garretts' where they leave the Bufords with Pam, Jim and Sharon proceed to the Landreths' cottage. Behind a red picket fence, it's white with green shutters and gingerbread trim. It's the most charming of all the staff houses.

Into the drive. They get out. Alison meets them at the gate along with an excited tawny-brown shepherd dog. "So good to see you guys," Alison gushes cheerily as she hugs Sharon, then Jim. "It's been so long. Come on in. I've got coffee on the stove—no Skipper! STAY! You stay in the yard and wait for Becki."

Quaint Victorian decor. Cozy aromas of coffee and hot muffins. The timeworn kitchen is the same as Jim remembers: small, yellow, and grease-stained, with turn-of-the-century oak counters and cabinets, plus a 1920s-era gas stove. The Shanleys sit down. Alison fills the terra cotta mugs, places a tray of blueberry muffins on the table, then sits down herself. They sit in rush-seated ladder chairs around a warped pine table. The fourth chair is missing and its place is filled by a vinyl-backed folding chair.

Wearing a trendy plum-colored sweater, Alison looks youthful and collegiate. Jim thinks how much she resembles Becki. Except for telltale wrinkles about her eyes, she could pass for Becki's sister—but in truth, she's thirty-eight.

They sugar and cream their coffee and start on the muffins. As they do, Alison shares news about Papa Chavin, Becki's grandfather. She says her mom just called and said that Papa won't have to have a gallbladder operation after all, that the doctors can correct the problem by changing his diet. Jim has met Papa Chavin once. He's a gusty old Frenchman with a large red nose and a Marshal Foch mustache. Becki adores him.

Alison, of course, sees the improved diagnosis as an answer to prayer since she had placed her father's name on the LBI prayer list. Jim and Sharon agree, but Jim's agreement is polite and perfunctory, unlike the old days when he believed in the power of prayer to heal and change circumstances. Jim still prays, but he doubts his prayers do anything other than communicate his feelings upward—which may be all that God wants.

After talking a bit longer about Papa Chavin, Sharon hoists her beige shoulder bag onto her lap and pulls out the latest pictures of Erin, Heather, and Chris, and the conversation shifts to mother-mother talk. Jim tunes out as his attention drifts relaxedly about the kitchen: to the soiled once-white curtains, to the worn linoleum floor, to the old Coca-Cola clock that groans with pain the last ten minutes of each hour. The familiar setting brings to remembrance his friendship with Becki in former days, slowly at first then faster the memories come, one after another like a train coming out of a tunnel, until the fullness of "Becki the child" roars into his mind.

She's eleven again. Ruddy fat cheeks, summer freckles, toothy smile, big innocent eyes, mischievous mop of brunette hair. Teasing, giggling, running. Bashful, pensive, curious. Happy among her animals. Sobbing over unjust punishment. Jim recalls the innocent love they shared, and how she would run out to the car when he drove up. But a pang of regret stabs him as he remembers the change. He sees Becki at fourteen and fifteen. New feelings. He recalls fighting them, and hating himself.

Alison's voice brings Jim back to the present, "Well, here we are sitting around my kitchen table ... just like old times, huh, Jimmy?"

"You can say that again," he replies, glad that Alison cannot read his thoughts. "We spent many an afternoon at this old table." There was a time when Alison and Jim were close. They sat together in class, took walks on campus, and had long talks. But when she became "Alison the missionary," she stopped looking at him honestly and began to avert her eyes with quick calculating side-glances. She learned, like all Loganites, to profess without knowing. Sharon, though congenial with Alison, detests her I'm-a-missionary-and-you're-not air of superiority, and she still resents the attention that Jim gave Alison and Becki in the old days. Nonetheless, for Jim's sake and the ministry's, she tolerates Alison in small doses, plus she picks up the latest Nashua gossip.

"I've always loved this cottage," Sharon says gesturing with her mug. "I like the Welsh sideboard and the old stove, and the porcelain sink fixtures. It's all so charming. I'd like to get an older home in the country that I can fix up and decorate, you know, one that has character like this place." Sharon smiles at Jim. She often talks to him about getting a house in the country but the idea has never advanced beyond the dream stage. "So how'd you guys get back into this house, anyway? I bet everybody on campus wants to live here?"

"Yep, that's for sure," Alison chortles through a mouthful of muffin. "But the Lord is *so* faithful. When we left, Bob Logan and Tricia had just married, so Pastor put them in here. When we found out we were coming back, we prayed we could get this cottage again but we saw no way, especially since we'd be here less than a year, and Tricia's my friend so I didn't want to press the issue with Pastor." As with most of Logan's longtime followers, Alison fondly refers to the doctor as "Pastor," like she's calling him by his first name. Sharon, and even Becki, also use this possessive and less formal title at times. But Jim rarely does. He's never felt comfortable, or honest, calling him, "Pastor."

Alison gets up to get the coffeepot but continues her testimony, "Well, our prayers were answered. Bob 'n Tricia moved off campus the very week we got back. Bob built a house in Hollis, you know, not far from Pastor's villa." Shortly after Dr. Logan moved his headquarters to Nashua, he built himself a large country home in the hills on the Hollis side. Now ten years later, his son has done the same, albeit on a smaller scale.

After sitting down, Alison goes on with God-is-great news, telling how God has blessed their finances, the Puerto Rico team, Ed's teaching, their marriage, Becki's walk with the Lord, Katie's progress in school, and various other things. To Jim, her words seem hollow, superficial, as if echoing up out of an empty well.

*I wonder if God's really blessing Alison's marriage,* he thinks to himself. *I wonder if Ed's faithful to her. He surely wasn't in the old days, but now he's a pastor so he probably toes the line—shit, I got butter on my suit trousers and I'm preaching in a few hours. They'll think I dribbled in my pants. And this vest is so tight I can hardly breath. I gotta do something about this gut.*

"So you're going back to Puerto Rico in the fall?" Sharon asks Alison as the Coca-Cola clock begins its ten-minute groan toward 11:00 a.m.

Alison nods her head as she swallows her last bite of muffin. "Yep, that's the plan. Actually, we'd like to go in August. It just depends on how fast we raise the money." Her tone becomes superior and fills with disdain. "Pastor wants us to set up a separate

LBI school. You know how it is working with other churches. They can't seem to discern Pastor's vision for the world. They don't understand grace or the seriousness of sin, or the sacredness of the blood.... They just *don't* sense the anointing." Her haughty exclusive attitude turns Jim's stomach. He abhors the idea that LBI'ers are more in tune with God than other Christians.

But after a pause to sip her coffee, Alison changes the subject and her tone. "So, you'll be back for supper with your gang from Brendon Falls? I think Pastor's coming by to greet your team."

"You really think you can handle a wild bunch of mill-town Christians?" Jim jokes.

"Come on, Jimmy," Alison laughs. "We used to have thirty or—"

All at once: Becki. Red-faced, wind-chafed, and hugging a load of books, she bursts into the kitchen. Skipper follows, jumping, sniffing, wagging, clicking his claws on the linoleum. Rebecca utters a quick, "Hi, everybody; I kinda figured you'd be here," then grabs one of the remaining muffins and prances to her room, Skipper clicking after her.

Alison chuckles and shakes her head. "I don't know what I'm going to do with that girl. It's hard to believe she's nineteen. Sometimes she acts more like a 13-year-old, and her moods change faster than the weather."

*You sure got that right, Alison,* Jim declares in his thoughts.

"But I think it's good that she's spending weekends at your church," Alison adds. "I can tell she's gaining an appreciation for what it means to 'win the lost.'"

*Sounds like wishful thinking,* Jim replies, but only to himself, as he and Sharon get up to leave.

Alison walks them to their car. "Enjoy your lunch with Pastor," she exhorts. "It's a blessing to just be in his presence. And, Jimmy, I'm looking forward to your message this afternoon. I'll find you, Sharon. We can sit together."

\* \* \*

The flags on the Blantyre flagpole pop and snap in the gusty wind, drawing Pastor Jim's attention upward to the red-tile roof of the old mansion, and to the Victorian towers. Memories, memories. Mixed emotions wrestle in his gut—pride, fear, self-consciousness. The massive mahogany door creaks open and he and Sharon go in. Dark-panelled walls, thick columns, high-beamed ceiling. The spacious Tudor-style entry hall exudes an intimidating aura of baronial authority. It even smells severe like the polished-wood smell in a courtroom. To their left, a set of golden-oak doors lead to the reception lounge. They enter and ask for Amy Brannigan.

Emerging from her office, Amy welcomes the Shanleys then escorts them upstairs where Dr. Logan is still doing radio. Amy walks briskly before them, her heels resounding sharply on the polished parquet floor—back through the entry hall, past the fluted oak columns, underneath a wrought-iron chandelier with a half-dozen pairs of shaded Tudor lamps. Jim can't help but focus on Amy's high compact hips; she's built like a fashion model.

Halfway down the main hallway, which is lined with ornate Elizabethan chairs, they ascend a winding oak staircase to the second floor. With an upward sweeping balustrade and plush blue carpeting, the stairway seems right out of the Old South, right out of *Gone With the Wind*. Jim's been up these stairs many times, yet they still make him feel small, like one foot tall.

Amy takes them to the Blantyre radio room where an overflow crowd of Logan-disciples, the ever-present "peanut gallery," is flocked around Logan, his son, and a half-dozen visiting pastors. After thanking Amy, Jim and Sharon slip in and stand in the back of the room—not a studio but a pastel-green double drawing room with gold-embellished woodwork and a high Palladian window that overlooks east campus. The radio calls are patched through from the media center at Moody Coliseum. On the wall opposite the window hangs a large rectangular mirror between portraits of Jonathan Bancroft and his young wife. Dr. Logan and the other pastors are at the far end of the room where three sofas form an open horseshoe around a low microphone table.

"Our last caller is Marcia from Lawrence, Massachusetts," Robert Logan announces.

"Yes, Marcia, please go ahead," Logan intones in his gritty sandpaper voice. The doctor, in a tailored blue suit, red tie, and blond-framed glasses, looks and conducts himself like a professional and caring radio counselor.

"Pastor, I listen ever' day," Marcia says respectfully, but nervously. The call is fed through speakers on the wall. "You're a gifted man of God, but I never had the courage to call 'til now. I'm havin' a bad time, an' I need help?"

Logan drops an octave, becoming hushed and holy. "Marcia, I knew you'd call today. I was up early, walking and praying in the woods behind my house, and the Lord spoke to my heart about a woman, a Massachusetts woman ... with deep problems in her marriage."

"Oh, Pastor, that's me. You're truly a prophet of God. My marriage is—well, it's just so bad, so impossible. My husband, he's an alcoholic an' I'm losin' hope." To Jim, she sounds like a blue-collar Irish-American, like so many in Brendon Falls. Her marriage sounds familiar as well.

"Tell me about it, Marcia," Logan counsels.

"He just goes away for days then comes back," she explains. "I can never predict. He can't keep a job so I hafta work. I have two teenage girls and a ten-year-old boy ... and they're runnin' with a bad crowd."

"Are you born-again, Marcia?"

"Oh yes, Pastor; I got saved at Calvary Baptist in Lowell, when I was fifteen ... but I live in Lawrence now, on Farley Street."

"Do you fellowship regularly with a body of believers?"

Marcia's response is meek and apologetic, "I've tried a few churches but I never keep goin'. I hafta work an' all, but I know it's no excuse. I should put God first."

The doctor removes his reading glasses, rubs his eyes and thick tobacco-colored eyebrows. "I do understand, Marcia," he replies, his voice now gentle and fatherly. "I feel your hurt and I want to help you. Jesus said, 'Come unto me all ye that are heavy laden and I will give you rest.' Do you believe that, Marcia?"

"Oh yes, Pastor; I do, and I know *Christ* is my only hope."

"Are you ready to follow Jesus into his rest?" Logan asks.

"Oh, yes. That's what I want. That's why I called."

"You see, Marcia, Satan is robbing you. He plants lazy thoughts in your mind. He lies and says you don't need to go to church. But we love you in the Lord and must tell you the truth from the Word. In Hebrews 10:25, God warns not to forsake 'the assembling of ourselves together.' If you want God's rest and healing for your marriage, Marcia, and protection for your children, you *must* come under the covering of the body of Christ. On your own, you don't have a chance in this evil age."

"Oh, Pastor, I jus' know it's true, what you're sayin'."

Now Dr. Logan commends her, "Marcia, you're very sensitive to the Spirit. And you're so humble and teachable. I know God is pleased with you." He pronounces "God" as if it's "Gawd."

"So, what should I do, Pastor? Should I come up to Nashua for church?"

Logan replaces his glasses and sits forward a bit. "Yes, Marcia, when you can, but we also have an active branch ministry right there in Lawrence with Pastor Michael Montanaro. They meet at the YMCA across from the common on Thursday and Sunday. If you truly want to save your husband and your children from the devil's devices, come to the YMCA at seven tomorrow night and Pastor Montanaro will speak to you personally."

"Oh, Pastor," she replies exuberantly, "I feel so much better. I'm glad I called. I'll be at the Y for church tomorrow night. I want a new life that'll be pleasin' to God. I do."

Dr. Logan prays for Marcia then hands the microphone to his son. "Again today," Robert Logan declares in his dulcet voice, "we have witnessed the power of God's anointing upon our beloved pastor as he reaches out to the lost, to the misfortunate, to believers who seek the fullness of Christ. *The LBI Hour* proclaims the good news of salvation to one and all, but as most of you know, our radio outreach costs more than ever as we add new stations all over America. We desperately need your support to keep this program on the air. If you believe in the Bible, if you believe in bringing people to Jesus, please send your generous gift today to: *The LBI Hour*, Logan Bible Institute, Nashua, NH 03060, or give us a call at 1-800-LBI-HOUR. You may use MasterCard or *VISA,* and remember all gifts are tax deductible. And for any gift of twenty dollars or more, we will send you Dr. Logan's recent three-tape series: 'How Christ Can Redeem Your Marriage.'"

Finally, Dr. Logan closes with a promo for the evening service, "Tonight at 7:30 at our new Dwight L. Moody Auditorium, I'll be speaking on: 'The Secret to Winning in Life.' I encourage you folks in New England to come for this Easter-Week service which is also the highlight of our annual pastors' conference. As believers, we must learn to appropriate the *power* of the cross, the *power* of the finished work, so we can declare to the devil: 'Take your hand off my body. I'm not going to submit to sickness. I refuse it. I take *authority* over illness and disease. I'm not going to submit to alcohol. I refuse it. I take *authority* over the spirit of alcohol. I'm not going to submit to lust. I take *authority* over the spirit of lust.' Yes, tonight, I'll show you how to exercise God's authority over Satan. So come, and bring your family and your friends.... Until next time, this is Dr. Charles Logan. May God bless—"

Cheering drowns his last words, along with shouts of amen, praise God, wow, hallelujah, amazing, and thank you, Jesus. As Logan gets up, students, missionaries, and other LBI'ers surge about him. The Shanleys remain in the back, but Dr. Logan spots them and beckons for them to come up. Jim and Sharon, squeezing through familiar and unfamiliar faces, make their way to the front where Logan greets them with fatherly hugs. Jim smells coffee breath and Mennen Skin Bracer as the doctor scrapes his stubbly beard against Jim's cheek.

After the hugs Logan gives Jim and Sharon a plug in front of the other pastors, "Not only is Pastor Shanley an Air Force Academy grad and one of *our* finest, but he's an excellent judge of women, wouldn't you gentlemen agree?" Affirming laughter erupts right on cue. "She's the secret to Jim's success; right, Sharon?" Sharon blushes into a smile of agreement. "But seriously, and this is for all of us. It's so vital to have the Lord's peace and joy in our homes. Proverbs 31:10 says, 'Who can find a virtuous woman? For her price is far above rubies.' A Spirit-filled wife is the key to victory in the Christian home." Sharon's blush deepens—she loves praise but hates the attention that comes with it. "Mrs. Shanley is such a wife, devout, dedicated, and holy, and pure in all her motives. She shepherds her children, and she's faithful to her husband in thought and deed. So many people take their vows lightly these days, but not Sharon, or Jim. Their home is filled with God's righteousness. They're a fine testimony for all of us!"

Dr. Logan is a master at cultivating goodwill through creative compliments and positive reinforcement. His bold body language, aura of assurance, and fatherly demeanor cultivate a spirit of trust within the flock—at least in those who don't see him behind closed doors, and few do. Though his fiery sermons condemn sin in the church, he rarely criticizes one-on-one. Personal reprimands come through channels, rarely from Logan directly. With a public persona that combines the charming sophistication of Robert Schuller with the down-home simplicity of Oral Roberts, Logan has a persuasive I-made-it-with-God-but-I'm-still-like-you air about him.

But he looks like a short Spiro Agnew—long patrician face, squinting eyes, aristocratic nose—except his hair is lighter, his eyebrows bushier. He even combs his hair straight back like the former vice president. About Jim's height but heavier, the doctor seems vigorous and healthy with a tanned just-back-from-Florida complexion. All this, plus his Seiko watch, Lucien Piccard cuff links, and a gold diamond-studded executive ring, gives him the look of a victorious man of God. He looks well-to-do and he is, not rich like Falwell or Swaggert or Schuller—but rich enough.

Nevertheless, Logan cannot completely hide his blue-collar, country roots. He takes backhand bites when he eats—he never moves his fork to his right hand after cutting his meat. He also talks with his mouth full, and his shirts and lapels are often stained with food. He shaves carelessly, leaving uneven patches of missed whiskers, and his face is often razor-nicked. Some are offended at these signs of Logan's boorish background, but Jim finds them comforting as reminders of his humanity. Yet there is one aspect to Pastor Logan's person which Shanley finds quite disturbing, but the doctor uses to considerable advantage: he has dark-brown hypnotic eyes—so dark that he seems to have no pupils.

# Chapter Twelve

"Well, if it isn't Jim and Sharon Shanley," Matthew Garrett jokes in his charming headwaiter voice. "I haven't seen you two since New Year's Eve."

"Jim's a busy man," Logan interjects. "His church in Brendon Falls is one of our fastest-growing branches."

"I guess we're busy enough," Jim remarks modestly as he shakes Garrett's hand. He's known Garrett since Bible school but they've never been close. He's always sensed something secretive, perhaps even sinister, behind Matt's engaging personality.

Sharon also shakes Matt's hand and smiles politely. "I thought you were with the Bufords?" she says. "We dropped them off an hour and a half ago."

"I know," he replies, returning her smile. "Pam called. That's where I'm headed." Garrett then turns his attention to Logan, "Doctor, may I see you a moment in my office before I go?"

"Please excuse me," Logan says to the Shanleys. "And do make yourselves at home. I'll be right back." Garrett and Logan depart via the private entrance near Logan's desk.

Jim and Sharon sit down in front of the fireplace on one of the richly upholstered sofas. The Louis XVI living-room set includes two maroon-and-gray sofas and a matching wing chair and ottoman, all arranged around a low center table with winged lions for legs. On the fireplace mantel next to a domed clock are a few of Dr. Logan's treasured items: a small bust of President Reagan, a framed photograph of Logan and Pat Robertson on the set of the *700 Club*, and an autographed photo of the doctor and Jerry Falwell at the dedication of Moody Coliseum. On the opposite wall, between east-facing Palladian windows, hangs a large portrait of Douglas MacArthur bracketed by a pair of Napoleonic battle scenes.

The fire, along with a bowl of pink flowers on the center table, adds some warmth to the room, but overall, the lavish office seems cold and disconcerting to Jim; he much prefers his army-surplus desk and broken LA-Z-BOY. He's been in Logan's office many times but the stately neoclassic setting still intimidates him.

While Sharon thumbs through Christian-resort brochures she found on the end table, Jim strolls to the other end of the office where a trio of south-facing windows create a sunlit pattern of stretched ovals on the plush magenta carpet. Behind Logan's desk hang a number of honorary degrees between Wedgwood cameo plaques. To the right of the sunshiny windows and just beyond the doctor's refreshment table stands a hickory case clock with a large brass pendulum artfully revealed through a smoked-glass door. Jim is tempted to take a pecan Danish from the tray of pastries on the goodie table, but he refrains since it's time for lunch. Besides, he doesn't want Dr. Logan to catch him munching on the V.I.P. food. Though Pastor Jim is the speaker for the afternoon session, he does not consider himself a V.I.P. At least, he isn't getting a $2500 honorarium like Jerry Falwell received when he came to dedicate Moody in '81. Jim is getting nothing—except lunch.

Next to the case clock is a tall bookcase with glass doors and a Grecian pediment. Jim scans the shelves. Fine volumes, some vellum bound and gilded, some recent and hardbacked, a few paperbacks. Books on theology, philosophy, church administration, mass media, marketing, and surprisingly, or maybe not, a number on warfare and military history.

Though never in the army, Dr. Logan is a military buff. Jim recalls the last time the doctor spoke at BFBC—October of last year—and had supper beforehand with the Shanleys; on that occasion, he talked with Jim on three subjects: the Red Sox, the Air Force Academy, and WWII. Logan assumes that Jim, as a former officer, is gung-ho military, but Jim lost any fervor he had for war when his best friend at the academy, a pilot, was killed in Vietnam. Nonetheless, his display of military knowledge gets him lots of brownie points with the LBI chief, as does his baseball savvy.

No sound, but the pendulous ticking of the case clock, the occasional popping of the fire. Logan's been gone ten minutes. Jim feels self-conscious as if he's invading the doctor's privacy, as if he's browsing in his bedroom. Nevertheless, he opens the glass doors and quickly thumbs through a few of the books: *The Day of Doom* by Michael Wigglesworth, *The Power of God* by Thomas Aquinas, *The Mind of Napoleon* by J. Christopher Herold, *American Caesar* by William Manchester, *Public Opinion and Propaganda* by W. K. Agee, *The Theory and Practice of Manipulative Communication* by G. N. Gordon. On the inside flyleaf of the last book is a handwritten inscription: "Dear Pastor. This book describes the ideas we've talked about. Please read it and keep it for your library. Your faithful servant, Matthew Garrett." Sticking out from the middle of this volume, like a bookmark, is a faded newspaper clipping. Jim takes it out and reads it:

**Heirs Lose Suit Against Chauffeur**—Glenwood, New Jersey. Yesterday in Sussex District Court, a jury of three men and seven women found for the defendant, Matthew A. Garrett, against the family of Helen J. Thomason, deceased. The jury declared Mrs. Thomason's last will and testament to be legal and binding. Said will gives Garrett $95,000. The heirs contested this bequest which was added only weeks before Mrs. Thomason's death—she died last November (1974) after a long illness. The remainder of her estate, along with the sprawling Thomason farm in Colesville, was left to the family. The trial ran four days. Judge Claibourne Stahl presided.

Garrett (26) served as Mrs. Thomason's chauffeur-kitchen steward from July 1972 until her death. A native of Florida, Garrett moved to New Jersey in 1960, graduated from Pequannock High School in 1966, attended culinary arts school in New York, then worked in various restaurants until hired by Mrs. Thomason. Mr. Garrett, who has aspirations of entering the ministry, said he would likely use part of the money for college and seminary training.

*So that's it,* Jim says to himself. *No wonder Garrett's been in tight with Logan from the first day of Bible school. Money, money, shrewd ideas—that got him into the club.* Awareness, knowing. The eyes of Jim's mind open wider and for a moment he sees Logan as a power-hungry religious charlatan, a perception he entertains more and more, especially when talking with Russ Bradley, but one he's rarely entertained in Nashua, certainly not in Logan's office.

But as quickly as his eyes are opened, self-doubt closes them: *You have no right, Jim. You're snooping in the affairs of an overseeing pastor. You're being sneaky and deceitful.* Confusion and guilt replace conviction in his gut. Like a thief leaving a crime scene, Jim hurriedly replaces the newspaper article, closes the bookcase, and returns to the couch, where Sharon makes him forget he ever left her side.

She surprises him with an eager embrace and a long passionate kiss. Jim quickly surrenders to her sweet lips and darting tongue. "I'd like to screw you right here in front of the fire," she whispers wantonly after coming up for air. "I'd like to take you down on this red carpet and *ride* you until we both go nuts."

"Not a bad thought. What's got into you?"

"Oh, I was just wishing we were already at the motel. I can't re*sist* you in that suit. It's tight you know. I want to unzip you and pull out your dick. I'm in love with it. I want to look at it and touch it and stroke it. I want to give it *double* honor. I can see you getting hard right now. Oh, Jim, it makes me wet my panties."

"Well, whaddeya expect? That kiss would turn a monk to a rod of iron, not to mention your horny language."

"That's the idea," Sharon flirts, gobbling her husband with her dusty-blue eyes.

Logan's return abruptly ends the conjugal foreplay. After poking the fire, he sits down across from them. His presence makes Jim feel tense again, but not as much as when snooping in the bookcase—thanks to Sharon's lips. "Sorry I was gone so long," he apologizes. "I had to take an unexpected call." The doctor sighs, leans back, and crosses his legs. "Let's see ... we've got ten minutes until lunch, but it's good to rest a moment. I miss having quiet times with my special friends—so, Jim, what d'you think about the Red Sox this year?"

Jim chuckles uneasily. "Well, sir, I can't see them winning, especially if they trade Eckersley?" He says "cain't" instead of "can't." Jim's Texas drawl becomes more pronounced when he's nervous. As he replies, he fingers the "68" on his gold USAFA class ring. He rarely wears the ring, but he never goes to Nashua without it.

"Yeah, this season does look rather bleak," Logan agrees. "I just got back from Florida and the team looks old and flat. It's hard to believe that this is Yaz's last year. I also heard the Eckersley rumors, but I doubt they'll get what they want for him.... I wish I had more time to get down to Fenway."

"I can well imagine, sir," Jim replies respectfully. "I can barely keep up with one church. I don't know how you do it with so many branches and teams." Jim feels more comfortable—no, comfortable is not the word, not with Logan; he feels more correct, in line—addressing the doctor as "sir" as if he's back at Westover AFB, a weather officer briefing the SAC wing commander.

Logan sits quietly a moment stroking his ill-kempt beard; it's ginger brown like his hair. Jim notices his hands. They're delicate with slender fingers, smooth skin, and manicured nails—unusual hands for a middle-aged, potbellied, barrel-chested man. Logan slowly nods his head and gives a closed-mouth smile of triumph. His smile is so pronounced that his puckered chin resembles a small pillow nested within a triple set of V-shaped laugh lines.

"It's a team effort, Jim," the LBI chief explains in his grainy voice. "We have an army of loyal soldiers and prayer warriors. Being a military man yourself, you know a general can't win without seasoned troops on the line. It's faithful soldiers like you and Sharon that give us the victory. It's not *my* doing."

Dr. Logan softens and turns to Sharon: "So, Sharon, how are the children? Erin, Heather, and ... Chris, if I remember correctly?"

Sharon gives a proud-mother grin. "It's amazing, Pastor, how you remember names. But the kids are fine, growing fast, but doing fine."

Pastor Logan's ability to "call his sheep by name" is not a gift. He and Garrett work hard at it—as all LBI pastors are encouraged to do—studying the LBI church directories, and Garrett always includes pertinent names, photos, and bio-notes in his daily briefing package. Like a political candidate running for office, the doctor always projects a caring image. Perhaps he does care, at times, for some, but regardless, he always seems kind and concerned because of good packaging. "They were so well-behaved the last time we were down," Logan elaborates. "Erin's such a little lady, and Heather, she's going to be a soccer star for sure. And Christopher, that young fellow's smart as a whip. He has quite a vocabulary for a five-year-old."

"It was fun having you," Sharon warmly responds, "and Amy and the Hudsons. I hope you'll come again." Though Jim's suspicions are growing, his wife's faith in Logan remains solid. When Jim first went to Bible college, she was wary of the LBI chief, but over the years, she's become one of his biggest fans, not in a rah-rah fashion like Alison, but in a quiet trusting way.

All at once, eyes, eyes: dark as night and penetrating. The doctor stares right at Jim who instantly feels the irresistible allure of this hypnotic gaze, as if God himself is inside Logan's head looking out at him. Jim's nagging Logan-suspicions disappear faster than electricity during a power outage. The feeling is not one of responding to love, but of submitting to undeniable authority—like having his fears calmed by a tranquilizing drug.

"Tell me, Jim, how's the battle going in Brendon Falls?" Logan says, his voice gentle and mesmerizing.

"Everything's going great," Jim lies, half-lies, but it doesn't feel like a lie. He's so captivated he can't feel his real life—the stress, the busy schedule, the doubts and confusion, the lusts of his flesh, the Becki-conflict.

"I know it's good on paper. Tom shows me your growth reports and Jerry says that Brendon Falls gives more per capita than any branch, but how about you personally? You and Sharon?" Logan relaxes his gaze. His eyes fill. His concern seems genuine. "Are you taking enough salary to live comfortably? Do you get away for relaxed times together? We're in a worldwide ministry. We face strenuous demands. But we must take time to rest just like the Lord. If we're burned out, we have nothing to offer. I care for you and Sharon, and I want the best for you and your flock."

"Things couldn't be better," Jim assures him. "Finances, family, Sharon and I. The Lord is blessing us. In fact, we're going to Manchester, Vermont for a little vacation before we go back to Brendon Falls. And we're stopping in Brattleboro on the way."

Logan nods his head approvingly. "Glad to hear that things are A-OK, Jim. There's so much false profession, even right here at home base, but I sense that you and Sharon are truly fulfilled in your walk with the Lord—oh, before I forget, I want to invite you to a get-together out at my place after church tonight, just a few special friends for a rap session and a relaxed time around the fire.... Come to think of it, you can even sleep over in one of our guest rooms and save the expense of a motel." Logan gestures with a beckoning motion of his hand. "And I'll have Ellie prepare you a big breakfast in the morning. How's that sound?"

Before Jim or Sharon can respond, the doctor gives a broad grin—fait accompli—and says, "On second thought, I insist. I'm not giving you a choice. Just follow me after service tonight." The Shanleys agree—to Logan's delight. They're too caught up in his charisma to refuse.

* * *

Jim and Sharon, following Dr. Logan, weave through the empty tables and join the others near the fireplace. Like a ship captain, Logan takes his meals with his staff and invited guests, but today many of his lieutenants are escorting visiting pastors and their contingents, all of whom are dining in the faculty room at John Wesley Cafeteria. So the doctor's Blantyre party requires but one table. In addition to the Shanleys, the group includes Tom Hudson, Rich Beckman, Amy Brannigan, Michael Montanaro, and a student/secretary, Molly Gibson. To eat at Dr. Logan's table is a high honor among LBI'ers. In nine years, Jim has lunched with him five times.

After a flurry of greetings and introductions, they sit down. Blue-damask tablecloth and napery, gold crystal stemware, English bone china, sterling silverware—Reed & Barton no less. The table is set in royal fashion, and in the center an arrangement of pink roses between two oil lamps adds an artistic touch.

The dining room itself, like a turn-of-the-century British officers' club, boasts polished panelling, mahogany columns and beams, leaded Tudor windows, and an elegant Persian carpet which covers the dark hardwood floor. Over the long arched fireplace, a bigger-than-life portrait of Teddy Roosevelt hangs between smaller oval portraits of Queen Victoria and Prince Albert. Shaded candlestick lamps, on the columns, provide a soft yellow light. Lamplight, firelight, foggy light from steamed-up windows. The subdued radiances and gray shadows give the room an English-winter ambience, like a January day in a Charles Dickens novel.

After a brief prayer, two student-servants, a husky bow-tied waiter and a tidy little waitress in a white blouse, bring out the salads. The students are polite, proficient, and meekly obeisant. Like all LBI operations, the Blantyre kitchen is run by a professional chef and a crew of student helpers. Logan is a master at using student labor. He hires only enough staff to train and oversee the students who serve throughout the campus as waiters, waitresses, janitors, groundskeepers, radio-TV jockeys, secretaries, clerks, chauffeurs, gofers, librarians, assistant coaches. Some even teach at LCA (Logan Christian Academy, K-12). Some are assigned to the doctor's household and live at his country villa as do many of the student-secretaries. They all serve eagerly "as unto the Lord." The work is called Doorkeeper Duty, from Psalm 84, verse 10: "I had rather be a doorkeeper in the house of my God, than to dwell in the tents of wickedness." All resident students have an assigned job. Joe Lareux, for example, duplicates audiotapes for Robert Logan, but Becki has no assigned task since she still lives with her parents. Doorkeeper Duty is considered a practicum, for academic credit, which frees Logan from having to pay the students as employees. Only his handpicked student-secretaries and varsity athletes receive compensation, not money but tuition credits.

The waitress pours a sparkling nonalcoholic wine. Logan is adamant against alcohol but he enjoys the white look-alike in his goblets. While eating their salads, Logan and his party engage in small talk about the dining room, the dinnerware, the cold weather, the conference schedule, and they exchange flattering comments on apparel and hairdos. Soon the food arrives—baked cabbage stuffed with salmon, roasted new potatoes, green beans with browned butter, sauteed carrots, cloverleaf dinner rolls—and the earnest eating commences. Chattering food-clogged conversation continues amid the sounds of dining: silver ringing on china; hungry mouths sucking, smacking, swallowing; rustling of clothing and napkins; satisfied stomachs grunting, groaning. Jim finds it curious that these LBI staffers display the same hunger as the heathen when it comes to masticating. He wonders if the same is true when they copulate—if they copulate.

As the meal progresses, Dr. Logan takes over the conversation and gives a rambling discourse on various subjects: the prayer life of Watchman Nee, the dangers of the New Age movement, the certain damnation of homosexuals, the folly of forming friendships with unsaved people, the importance of re-electing Ronald Reagan, the lousy officiating at the postseason basketball tournament in Laconia where the LBI squad placed fifth out of twelve teams. Speaking from the head-end of the table, his voice thick with food, Logan gestures above his plate with his right-hand knife and backhand fork, as if stabbing the air.

"Did everyone meet Molly?" the doctor asks, interrupting his monologue to introduce Molly Gibson. "She came to us from Pastor Bowman's ministry in Boston. Amy says she's already one of the best girls in the office. That's what I like to see, a young woman who gives her heart to Jesus, and her talent to a ministry that means business for God." Reaching in front of Amy, who's sitting to his left, Logan gives Molly a paternal pat on the shoulder. Molly blushes and smiles sheepishly as melting butter drips off her roll and runs down her girlish fingers. Everyone nods in affirmation of Logan's praise, except Amy, who draws her lips into a tight reluctant smile and looks down at her unfinished cabbage.

*Now that's a delicious bod,* Jim says to himself praising Molly for what moves *him* most, *a bit hefty but every pound of her is so nice.* A plump Irish honey with big green eyes and long brown hair, Molly has a seasoned yet expectant look, as if life has stolen her innocence but not her hunger. Her full figure seems to want out of her blue skirt and beige blouse. Despite a supreme effort to suppress sexual thoughts in Logan's presence, Jim undresses Molly in his mind: *Red nipples, dark bush, deep belly dimple. She acts so shy, but I bet she's not shy when she gets off.* Warning bells, shame, self-rejection. *What the fuck is wrong with me? I know the other men at this table aren't thinking dirty thoughts, certainly not Dr. Logan.* Jim picks up the last of his roll and nibbles on it.

The dessert arrives—apple tarts and orange custard—and Logan begins to preach about Biddeford and the early days. Everyone tunes in except for Amy. She seems distant as she eats her custard. Soft gray eyes. Quiet oval face, sculptured and rather delicate. Dark-blond hair, stylishly bobbed. Amy Brannigan is polite, professional, but hidden. She's thirty-four, and has been an LBI secretary since her student days, and Logan's personal secretary for the past six years. A gold bracelet on her wrist and a diamond-studded butterfly pin on the lapel of her dark tweed suit testify to her financial well-being, yet she has a cynical air about her that contrasts sharply with the zealous spirit on campus, as if the perks of her position no longer excite her.

In spite of Logan's profession of Spirit-filled celibacy since Priscilla's death, Amy reminds Jim of a bored wife. He has often wondered about her and the other sugarplums that follow Logan around, but no one dares to speculate about Dr. Logan's sex life, or lack of it. It's considered a sin of rebellion, "a sin unto death," to gossip about an overseeing pastor, and Jim never does, except behind closed doors with Russ Bradley. Not that he fears chastisement from God—he did in the early years—but even a closet rebel has to be in a bold frame of mind to think of Logan as a fornicator when the doctor preaches so vehemently against sexual sin.

"We had nothing," Logan declares, his face heating with passion, "no money, no reputation, no radio or TV, just a small group of disciples in an old schoolhouse in Biddeford. But we prayed, we worked, we preached. We went door-to-door. We lived in cramped apartments and gave all our money to the Lord's vision—and thought *nothing* of it. That's why we're going into all the world while most churches are dead. Most ministers don't *dare* preach the whole Bible. It's not just a Sunday thing. It's our life! It's all-out war against Lucifer!"

"Amen!" Logan's Italian nephew exclaims excitedly.

A "Right on!" follows from Tom Hudson. Molly, like a starry-eyed groupie, looks on spellbound. The Shanleys nod their agreement but Jim feels nothing but his presermon butterflies, and self-disgust for his wayward thoughts, for not being like the others, for not *wanting* to be like the others. Besides, he's heard the Biddeford story ten times. Pastor Beckman also nods approvingly yet he seems preoccupied. Beckman looks so much like a reptile that Jim expects to see a forked-tongue dart out of his mouth.

Dr. Logan pushes back from the table and pounds on the corner rattling the dishes. "Most Christians don't really believe! Is it any wonder they can't resist the demons of alcohol, drugs, and lust! They don't even go to *church,* much less give their *lives* to God! But we're different! We're soldiers! We're going *all* the way with Christ!" Affirming amens sound around the table.

Logan smooths his receding hairline then moves forward and eats his dessert. As he eats, his preaching passion drains out of his patrician face back down into his barrel-shaped body.

Taking Logan's cue, everyone quietly finishes their dessert, until Tom Hudson can no longer contain his fawning spirit, "That's why I liked your message this morning, Pastor. I never understood what Jesus meant when he said Satan wants to sift us, but you made it *so* clear, and—"

"I always knew Lucifer was more cunning than we dared admit," Michael Montanaro cuts in. "But I need to be reminded. I see Satan deceiving people daily in Lawrence. You couldn't have said it *better.*"

"Oh, Pastor, your message jus' helped me *so* much," Molly adds shyly in her clipped South Boston brogue. "I jus' never realized that the devil's keepin' a catalog on all my sinful tendencies."

Molly's remarks seem innocent and freshmanlike, but Jim can barely stomach the obsequious behavior of the two pastors. They're *yes*-men of the first order. Pastor Hudson, clad in a tacky out-of-season sport coat, is tall, blond, and handsome, but stiff and unnatural like a department-store mannequin. As director of Evangelism and Missions, he carries out Logan's orders to the letter, and he and Mary Beth often accompany the doctor on trips to branch churches. Pastor Montanaro, on the other hand, is dark, heavy-boned, and rakishly good-looking, and he's sharply dressed in a Giorgio Armani suit. With black curly locks that fall forward over a face of bronze, he looks like a cross between "Fonzie" and John Travolta. Yet, like Tom, his intelligence does not match his looks. It took him five-and-a-half years to finish Bible school and Jim doubts he would've been ordained if Logan were not his uncle.

Sharon once gossiped about Michael, telling Jim about his reputed affairs with older women, including a liaison with Mary Beth Hudson. But since the Hudsons came, with Logan, to the Shanleys' house for supper last fall, Sharon hasn't shared one word about Michael, or Mary Beth.

No more remarks. An opening, but Shanley says nothing. He has no desire to follow the lead of Hudson and Montanaro. Sharon is also quiet. She never joins in with the "peanut gallery."

Taking advantage of this lull, Pastor Beckman stands and says, "Please excuse me. I have a meeting at one with the Baltimore team." But before leaving, he turns to Dr. Logan: "Pastor, I talked with Jerry. He finished the computer simulations."

"Fine," Logan replies as he wipes a spot of custard off his shirt. "Tell him to bring the printouts with him tonight."

\* \* \*

"Before I turn this session over to Pastor Shanley," Dr. Logan says to the assembled throng, "I want to take a few minutes to amplify a point I brought up yesterday." Eager to hear Logan's counsel, everyone sits up straight in their coats and ties, dresses and skirts—that is except for Rebecca Reinhardt. Jim finally finds her halfway up on his left with Alison, Ed, Katie, and Sharon. Slouching in her seat like a tenth-grader at study hall, Becki is wearing her usual Levi's and boots, but she does have a fleecy lavender top. Probably Alison's idea Jim thinks—not the jeans but the lavender top. Becki looks bored with a tinge of sadness in her face. To Jim's right and closer, he spots Barry, Janet, Matt Garrett, and Pam. Joe Lareux isn't here; he works on Wednesday afternoons.

Pastor Jim is sitting on the dais in the John Knox lecture hall, the largest classroom on campus. Semicircular with elevated seating and a central rostrum, the hall reminds him of John Houseman's Harvard lecture hall in *The Paper Chase*, except John Knox is new and contemporary, and has that acrylic aerospace smell. Jim's butterflies are fluttering wildly, more like moths, as rushes of adrenaline surge in his gut. But now he's more psyched than nervous as he prepares to preach on King David. He especially likes David because the famous shepherd-king was weak and sinful, yet still made it with God.

"Yesterday," Logan goes on, "I opened the conference by discussing Lucifer's two-pronged attack on Christian leaders, money and sex, and I finished by quoting 2nd Timothy 2:22 which commands us to 'Flee also youthful lusts.' Now, as pastors and leaders and Bible students, you men and women are God's elite. You're on the front lines. You're a threat to the devil's dominion so he saves his most vicious and seasoned demons to attack you." A sense of holy awe captures the assembled LBI'ers at the mention of demons. "When you were babes in Christ, you could get by with relaxed attitudes and sloppy discipline, but *no more.* Now that you're leaders, you must work harder than ever to defend yourself. Lucifer is the fallen angel in Luke 10:18. He knows you better than you know yourself. He knows how to seduce you."

Like sudden wind-stirred waves rising on a peaceful lake, vibes of self-consciousness radiate through the body of believers. Anxious hands fidget on laps, leaf through notebooks, adjust ties, check hairdos, cover nervous coughs, and prepare to record their own condemnation. Jim too feels self-conscious but remains outwardly calm. He isn't afraid of the devil or demons, but he is afraid of Logan when he's condemning lust. But Becki looks the same— slouched, detached, slightly sad.

The doctor takes a drink of water—two glasses of ice water are always placed on Logan's pulpit by student-servants—then moves to the front of the dais where he paces slowly back and forth. "Now God never intended for fleshly passion to have preeminence over the highest love, the *love of God.* In heaven we'll be free from the flesh. There'll be *no* sex there, just pure divine love.... But for this earthly life, God has created sexual passion so we'll 'be fruitful and multiply' in Genesis 1:28, and become 'one flesh' in Ephesians 5:31. But this passion is for the marriage bed and only for the marriage bed. Outside of holy vows, sexual stimulation, actual or imagined, is a 'vile affection' in Romans 1:26." A hot flash of guilt sears Jim's conscience as if Logan is speaking directly to him—as if he knows all about his Becki-feelings. "You must discipline your will. It's better to be *over*cautious than to play in the den of dragons in Jeremiah 10:22. You must flee the nest of the ravenous bird in Isaiah 46:11. You must run from the chamber of Jezebel in Revelation 2:20 and the den of Delilah in Judges 16:18."

Dr. Logan salts and peppers his message with Bible quotes, in and out of context, not so much to buttress his rhetoric but to move the flock into the mystical realm like a tribal shaman chanting before a battle or a hunt—for he realizes that his spiritual authority is not rooted in cerebral response to logical argument but rather in collective soul-response to ritual, mystery, symbols, and charisma. To claim to know the mysteries of life, death, salvation, and judgment, to claim to represent the Most High God, gives one mystical authority over other humans, but only if the flock is persuaded beyond reason, beyond credo. They must feel the awe, the fear, the spell, the anointing—the erotic call of the supernatural.

Logan stops pacing and slowly scans the room. His dark eyes seem to pierce into the secret chambers of each heart. Though Jim is sitting behind the lectern, he still feels the doctor's convicting eyes. "This morning I prayed before the Lord," he goes on, his voice becoming hushed and holy. "And the Spirit showed me that some of you have been flirting outside of marriage and lusting in your mind, and a few of you, God forbid, are secretly reading pornography to feed your lust, and I know of four students, here today, who have actually committed fornication—and are still living in this most dreadful *sin*." The body gives a collective gasp. The hall becomes silent, like the inside of a submarine under attack. No one dares breathe lest the next depth charge bear their name. Logan professes to have the "gift of knowledge" by which he discerns the secret sins of the flock—and most believe it. Jim no longer believes it, but he feels the collective fear nonetheless.

"Yes, there are four," Logan affirms, "who are living in the sin of Samson and Delilah in Judges 16:4. You have fouled your bodies outside of the covenant. And I know, God forbid, of three married people who are having affairs like David and Bathsheba in 2nd Samuel 11:4. You are betraying your family, your calling, your Savior. But Jesus loves you and shows me the sin, so I can lead you to repentance, so God's holy fire can purge us of this cancer."

Shifting the microphone to his left hand and hewing the air with his right, he preaches more forcefully—but short of yelling. "Listen to me pastors! You must *never* be alone with any woman other than your wife! Not in your office, not in your car, not *even* in a restaurant. You must *flee* from all temptation, like Joseph in the house of Potiphar in Genesis 39:12. You must cut off immediately any questionable relationship. Any friendship that stirs passion is not a godly friendship. You must discipline your mind with study and prayer. You must *never* entertain sexual fantasies! You must obey ... or Satan will draw you into the pit of serpents in Isaiah 11:8!" Guilt, guilt, Becki-guilt. The doctor's convicting words rip into Jim's brain like a fusillade of fiery darts; he feels ashamed and confused, and upset with himself for letting Logan get to him.

Eyes riveted on Logan, everyone sits forward on the edge of

their seats. But not Becki. Still pensive, faraway, she scribbles absentmindedly in her notebook. Jim tries to look away but he can't. He stares at her cute chipmunky face, which is half hidden under her feathery bangs, then drops his gaze to her shirt, to her waist, to her crotch. The harder Logan preaches about sexual restraint, the more Jim wants Becki to pull down her pants, to spread her creamy thighs, to show him her panty-clad mound of pubic darkness. He wants her pussy. He wants to finger it, to fuck it, to eat it. He wants to make love to it until she passes out from ecstasy. He wrestles but he can't cleanse his mind. He *hates* himself.

Logan slowly scans the guilt-blanched faces before him. "Give yourself to higher love," he counsels in a plaintive and burdened voice. "The Lord is grieved when he sees you give in to your lower nature, when he sees you flirting over coffee, or lusting for your secretary. The Lord is grieved when you give your holy temple in fornication, or when you masturbate over pornography and 'spill your seed on the ground' in the wicked sin of Onan in Genesis 38:9. Is it any *won*der you feel so wretched and guilty afterward? It breaks Jesus' heart. He must look away from your filthy *sin*-fouled body. Do you want to *grieve* the Lord who died for you?" Dr. Logan's voice breaks as if God's sorrowful heart is pouring through him. "As your shepherd, I love you, but I must preach the truth. I want you to win over lust. There is a way. I know, because I fought the same battle, and the Lord has given me com*plete* victory." Going on, he explains how prayer and faith and consecration have delivered him from lust, and have given him a celibate yet joyful walk with the Lord.

The doctor has been speaking for fifteen minutes, but Jim does not care. He doesn't even know if he can still talk, much less deliver a message. He abhors himself. He feels uprooted and fragmented. His convictions have drained out of him like dirty oil out of a crankcase. Logan has pulled his plug—again.

Dr. Logan concludes with a time of silence for prayer, repentance, and rededication. He then gives a two-minute break in place. Everyone stands and stretches, but the mood remains sober and pentitent. There is little talking.

After the body is seated and settled, Logan says, "I'm delighted this afternoon to introduce one of our most distinguished graduates, Pastor Jim Shanley. Many of you know Pastor Shanley, but for those who don't, let me tell you a little about him."

Jim tunes out. He can't bear to hear Logan's laudatory remarks, but when he tunes back in a long minute later, the doctor is still praising him, "And even before he graduated, he pioneered his own church in Brendon Falls, Massachusetts. His church, though still small, is one of our fastest-growing branches. Jim is also a gifted street preacher and spends many hours winning souls. He has three beautiful children, and his lovely wife, Sharon, is with us today. Sharon would you please stand."

The body applauds as Sharon stands.

Jim begins to feel better but for the wrong reason. Religious pride inflates his ego. Logan has him hooked. This will not be a day to preach about the grace and mercy of God toward sinners. Jim takes the King David sermon notes out of his Bible, folds them, and puts them into the breast pocket of his suit coat.

"Pastor Shanley is a true inspiration to me, to all of us," Logan declares completing the introduction. "He epitomizes the sacred ideals of our worldwide vision. Let's give him a warm welcome."

Jim strides proudly to the pulpit and waits as spirited applause continues for some time, as if he's just slain Goliath and turned back the Philistines in the valley of Elah. Even Becki sits up in her seat as if she expects something.

But Jim has nothing for her, or for any seeking heart. Instead, for some forty minutes, he proceeds to pound home the party line— that the key to victory in the local church is total commitment to the LBI vision and absolute allegiance to Dr. Logan. He makes a few passing remarks about love and oneness in Christ, but his heart is not in it—just his pious ego.

With many interruptions for applause, and a standing ovation at the conclusion, Jim feels even more like a conquering hero after his sermon—but later he feels like a forty-dollar whore.

# Chapter Thirteen

Jim Shanley heads across the backyard. He hunches his shoulders against the cold and thrusts his hands into the pockets of his overcoat. The primrose light of day is fading from the evening sky. A dying waft of wind stings his face: an icy kiss blown through the trees. Reaching the back edge of the yard, he wades through weeds and low bushes over to Becki's long-vacant rabbit hutches. The elevated pens look as he feels—timeworn, empty, and overgrown with weeds.

Spaghetti, French bread, tossed salad, strawberry shortcake. Alison prepared a simple but abundant buffet-style meal. But the shortcake was the only good thing that happened to Jim at supper. Hurt, hurt, oversensitive, overreact. Becki was chilly to him, as she normally is when a crowd's around, and after his hectic, emotional, self-rejecting day, he has no confidence to see through it. Her frowny aloofness makes him insecure, desperate for the slightest sign of affection—which only chills her farther—until she can crush him with one word or one icy dart of her eyes, and at supper she did just that.

*Accept it,* Jim laments to himself. *I'm old and married. Logan's right. The Bible's right. There's no way. But what about all the special times we had right here with the rabbits, talking, laughing, having fun? Is it all wiped away forever because I now want her as a woman? Why does she turn cold when people are—*

"This whole campus gives me the creeps," a familiar voice declares. Jim turns around as Russ Bradley saunters over to him.

"Yes, it can be a bit unsettling," Jim replies in an understatement. "So, what's going on inside?"

"Well, Logan's the main attraction," Russ answers derisively. "He's shooting the shit in the living room, and everyone's going ga-ga. Stan and Barry are more excited than male puppies going through puberty. But Logan reminds me of an asshole colonel we had at Chu Lai—Colonel George Kramer. He lived nice and comfortable in Da Nang and came down once a week to inspect. He had a war-hero reputation from his first tour ... Bronze Stars, Purple Heart, all that shit, and everyone kissed his ass, but he didn't give a shit about the troops, he just got off on the adulation. That's how I see Logan. It's no different." Russ's potbelly is straining to get out of a corduroy vest. He's wearing a three-piece suit—Russ in a suit: a rare sight, that occurs only in Nashua.

"So all our people are with the doctor, huh?"

Russ hitches his thumbs over his belt and under his paunch. "Well, all but Doris, Janet, and Jodi. They snuck out for a smoke, and Joe, he's helping Becki and Katie with the dishes. But Bev and Sharon, the Bakers, the Burtons, Mary LeBlanc, and uh ... Barbara Sims—and the Landreths, of course—they're all right there eating it up with Stan and Barry. And Logan's got his covey of starry-*eyed* whores who follow him around ... and that *fag*gy guy, Garrett, the one who carries his briefcase. They're all going ga-ga." Jim's feelings about Logan are unanchored and blow with the wind, generally toward increasing skepticism, but Russ's opinion of the LBI president is solidly settled on the negative side, though he doesn't talk about it except to Shanley.

Jim wants to tell Russ about Becki, to share his hurt, his hopes, his fears, his inner conflicts, but he doesn't. Instead, he tries to be humorous, "So, Russ, where's your Red Sox cap? You look far out in that suit and tie. Logan's a big Bosox fan, you know? Maybe if you went to a few games with him, you'd start liking him."

But Jim's phony jesting falls flatter than a week-old McDonald's Coke. "It's not funny, Jim," Russ declares. "Logan's got power over people. He walks into a room, reaches for his zipper, and everyone's on their *fuck*ing knees with their mouths wide-open. I never know where he's coming from. I don't know how the hell he ever got into you. I know the story, but I still can't figure it. You're as different from him as night from day."

"Dammit, Russ!" Jim shoots back. "You don't hafta *rip* him all the time! So he gets caught up in his popularity, but you make him sound like Jim Jones. We have no evidence. Why d'you always think *evil* of the guy?" Russ doesn't reply except with a shake of his head and a resigned sigh. He then turns and ambles back to the cottage. Jim's defense of Dr. Logan is actually a defense of his own lack of conviction. He has no balls when it comes to Logan as his afternoon performance attests. Sometimes the doctor seems so good and kind, but other times he seems like the devil himself—but either way, Jim's still on his knees with the others. Maybe his mouth is closed, but he's still on his knees.

Twilight, getting colder. Jim shivers. He feels dejected, apprehensive, fearful, not over Logan, maybe some, but moreso over Becki and how she occupies his thoughts and has the power to make him happy and hopeful, or to crush him and fill him with a sense of doom. With a sinking I-missed-my-train feeling, he looks up into the darkening sky. He needs to share Becki and he missed his chance. But he can't open up—even to Russ. To love a 19-year-old girl is too bizarre, *way* out of line for a married pastor.

Jim feels utterly alone. No one knows him, not really, not his deepest hopes and fears and heartaches, not even Sharon, certainly not Sharon. No one feels what he's feeling, except God? Maybe

God? If God? *Who the fuck are you, God?* he cries silently into the gathering darkness. *Jehovah, Jesus, Lord, Father, Love Goddess. Fuck it! I need more than Bible verses and night visions. I hurt. I hurt. I'm out of control.* Jim stays until he sees the first stars, twinkling pinpricks of light that grow large then blurry then swirly with halos, like Van Gogh's *Starry Night.* After wiping his eyes with his handkerchief, he trudges slowly back to the house.

Inside, everyone is leaving. Jim tosses the car keys to Sharon so she can warm up the Grenada while he combs his hair and takes a leak. When he comes out of the bathroom, he runs head-on into Becki coming out of her room. Pink denim, kneesocks, dressy sandals. She has ditched her jeans for a skirt, and she clutches a gray envelope purse in her hand. No time to think—he confronts her: "So what's bugging *you?* You treat me like I have the plague."

Becki doesn't reply but assumes a defensive shy-turtle pose—pouty face down, shoulders hunched. "Go ahead and act like a spoiled two-year-old!" Jim snaps, venting his hurt and aggravation. "I don't have time for your games!"

Becki's frown deepens into a scowl. She nervously opens and closes the velcro snap on her purse. "I don't hafta tell you *any-*thing," she declares angrily. "You always wanna know what I'm *fee*ling, and you keep on looking at me to see if I'll *smile* at you. You're wicked insecure. It makes me sick. Just let me alone!"

Jim seeks her face, but she rotates away from him. "I thought you and I were a team?" he complains, spitting his words into her honey-maple locks as they tumble onto the collar of her ski jacket.

"We *are,*" she fumes, speaking toward her purse. "But that doesn't mean I gotta tell you my feelings ever' time you get insecure. I spend every Saturday with you. Doesn't *that* tell you something. I hate it when you get this way!"

"Yeah, we're a great team. One minute, you're friendly and funny and loving, and the next, you're like a porcupine! That's not a team! That's *shit!*"

Becki wheels up and faces him, her blue eyes blazing with indignation. "Stop it, Jimmy! Stop acting like an insecure baby. I'm gonna be with you in three days. So stop asking for more. And stop trying to manipulate me. You always want to be in control, but you weren't in control today, were you? You're so fuckin' two-faced! You really *PISS* ME OFF!" When she says *"PISS* ME OFF!" she blows hot toothpaste breath into his face. "Why didn't you tell Pastor Logan and all the other pastors that going to church is just as phony as smokin' pot, like you tell the kids downtown? You been kissing ass all day. You're spineless, wicked spineless, like a jellyfish! Who are you to question my moods! I don't have to explain anything to you, Jimmy Shanley! So let me alone! I'll see you on Saturday, but I don't wanna be around you now—while you're acting like a spineless jellyfish!" She pushes by him and storms awkwardly down the hall, her thick-heeled sandals clomping noisily. She exits the kitchen door, slamming it so hard that the whole house shakes. Now only Skipper remains behind and he comes over and licks Jim's hand. Skipper's tongue is wet and sticky and has that "dog" smell but Jim doesn't mind. He's glad for the friendly attention though it gives him little solace.

*  *  *

Ten minutes later. Jim and Sharon are in bumper-to-bumper church traffic crawling across campus toward Moody Coliseum. The sidewalks are crowded with students going down on foot. Jim's argument with Becki in the hallway was no fun but it didn't hurt him like her coldness at supper. He much prefers her passion, even in anger, to her chilly indifference. *It'll be better on Saturday,* he says to himself. *Becki always acts cold in front of people, but she'll warm up when we're alone together. I can't wait.*

Red brake lights illuminate Sharon's face. She seems preoccupied. Jim suspects the reason. "You're having second thoughts about going to Pastor's, huh?" A parking attendant in an orange Day-Glo vest directs the Shanleys into the staff-faculty lot with a wave of his light-baton.

"Yes, I am," Sharon affirms giving a quick twist of her mouth, an expression that could be a sneer, could be a smirk. "I like being with Pastor but you and I haven't had a moment alone since this morning in his office." Now she smirks openly, coquettishly. "I've been ready ever since that kiss. Your penis has been flying around in my mind all day, like a jet plane with no wings."

"You wanna skip service," he teases, his spirits lifting at the thought, "and do it right here in the car like that night in Chicopee at the Starlite Drive-in, or last July on our way home from summer conference?"

They both chuckle, then she leans close and whispers into his ear, "Sounds inviting. It's always wild in the car ... but I'd rather sit on a big bed and play in each others undies and see who gives in first. Let's leave right after church, and go straight to Brattleboro. If we hurry we can be at our motel by ten-thirty."

Sharon's flirting excites Jim, elevates his mood, lifts him above guilt and anxiety and Becki-woe. Sex with Sharon is like a good drug, better than any drug. And he needs a fix to make him forget this day. He'd like to leave right now. But he doesn't dare back out on Logan. He explains as diplomatically as he can, but his diplomacy is about as smooth as Nikita Krushchev pounding his shoe at the UN, "It's too late, honey. We told Dr. Logan we'd be there. Besides, I already canceled the motel. But no big deal, his guest room will do just fine."

Sharon, bristling, pushes away to her side of the car. "Drit! Why'd you do that? Those afterservice raps can go on forever. It's our vacation, Jim. I'm tired of clucking around with pastors' wives. Just tell Pastor we decided to go on to Vermont tonight. He'll understand. He's always got a crowd around. He won't miss us."

Down, down. Jim's mood plummets again: a quail shot down while taking flight. He pulls into a parking spot, cuts the engine; he gives a bothered sigh. "No sense in getting upset, Shar. We *told* him we'd be there. We can't back out now. Besides, I can't just grab him on the stage, not during the middle of a service."

"YOU ALWAYS PUT THE DAMN CHURCH AHEAD OF ME!" Sharon shouts, flashing into sudden fury. "And before the church it was Bible school! Before that, the Air Force! I bet if Becki Reinhardt wanted you, you'd drop everything! Alison tells me that you two are a *team* now. How sweet? I didn't want to bring it up on our vacation, but dammit, James David, you give me no choice! And you said outreach with Becki was a *one-time* thing! What a crock! Being married to you is impossible enough without you THROWING BECKI-*SHIT* IN MY FACE AGAIN!" Sharon hops out, slams the door, and hurries across the parking lot to the main entrance. Jim watches until she disappears inside.

Fear! Fear! Pangs of Fear! No more Saturdays? No more Rebecca? Waves of heat then cold sweep up and down his body finally focusing as a burning fever in his face. *I don't fuckin' believe it! It's like Sharon's psychic or something. Maybe Alison? But she doesn't know. It's my secret. Maybe Sharon's just pissed because I'm showing Becki fatherly attention again? No, n-no, this is sexual jealousy like she caught us in bed. If Becki finds out that Shar—shit! I'm getting sick.* Jim rolls down the window; the cold night flows in. Stunned and numb, he stares over the steering wheel at the Bible-carrying Christians converging on Moody Coliseum which looms before him like a giant UFO. *Look at 'em, so squeaky clean and good and happy—so pious. I hate their fuckin' faces!*

The frosty air settles Jim's stomach but not his angst. His first impulse is to take control, *I'll run in and smooth things, and we'll go straight to the motel—no way, not in front of everyone.* Too late. He can do nothing until after church. If Sharon vents her rage with Alison, or Rebecca, it'll surely torpedo everything. He'll never spend another Saturday with Becki, or another minute for that matter. And he's *powerless* to stop it, helpless. He hates the feeling even more than he hates the squeaky-clean faces going into the coliseum. Under normal circumstances, Sharon would not talk about a fight with Jim, except with her mom. But this knowing is of little consolation. Fighting over Becki is not a normal circumstance. After a deep shuddering breath, Jim closes the window, starts the engine, turns on the heat. He sits and sulks.

But as he sits there, a strange peace pervades his rattled psyche, the peace of resignation. Destiny has forced him into a brief experience of "letting go." He feels drained and tired but strangely serene. It's a warm penetrating sensation like taking a hot bath. The car has become a womb, a warm escape.

* * *

7:35 p.m. Pastor Jim reluctantly grabs his Bible and hauls himself out of the warm Grenada. He sighs, exhaling a cloud of white vapor. As he walks across the parking lot, he puts on his pious pastor-face, but it does little good. Anxiety. No more peace. His peace is behind him locked in the car. His gut tightens. He feels suddenly guilty about everything as if God is grading him and giving him all F's. He looks about him at the LBI faithful swarming toward the domed edifice like honeybees returning to their hive: *I'm not like these Christians. They're sold out to God. But I'm a fake. I'm sold out to myself, to my own flesh.*

Reaching the main sidewalk, he merges into the flow and is swept inside, into a long crescent-shaped lobby. Perfume, paper, new clothes, curing concrete. The coliseum still smells like damp cement, at least the underside. Familiar faces, smiley born-again faces. Jim exchanges polite greetings but sees none of his BFBC flock. Booths line the walls, booths manned by LBI students in red-white-and-blue jackets. You can buy Logan's books, booklets, and sermon tapes, along with Bibles, tracts, and gospel literature. You can subscribe to *Choose Ye This Day*, the LBI magazine. You can pledge support for missionary teams. You can buy Jesus buttons, bumper stickers, wall plaques, LBI pennants, pins, posters, mugs, cards—even photos of Dr. Logan. The eager student workers—they all have a wholesome freshly scrubbed look like *Mickey Mouse Club* mouseketeers—busily stuff merchandise into white paper bags that make crinkling sounds. Also in the lobby, a snack bar sells coffee, milk, soda, donuts, snacks, but you can't take food up into the auditorium—the blue-uniformed ushers will stop you.

Jim feels like a fish out of water—no, he feels like he's in water but no longer a fish. He stations himself near the rest rooms hoping that Sharon will appear alone and he can rescue the situation. She doesn't show but Tom Hudson does. Beaming with LBI pride, he packs a Thompson Chain Bible and two of Logan's sermon tapes. Jim asks if he's seen Sharon. Tom says that the BFBC people are sitting up front in the V.I.P. section where Matt Garrett seated them.

Tom also tells him about a shortcut to the stage. So Jim follows him through a side door, down a flight of stairs, through a long tunnel-like corridor, up a flight of stairs, through the locker rooms, athletic offices, the Sunday school department, the radio-TV studios, and finally up another flight of stairs that leads backstage. Tom stops at the pastors' lounge to wait for Dr. Logan. Jim goes on stage and takes a seat in the last row of the pastors' section. Out of breath, he feels like he's just run an obstacle course.

The Moody stage is almost as big as the entire sanctuary at BFBC. Logan always seats ten to twenty pastors on the platform when he preaches, but on this special night there are already fifty, and the front row, reserved for the highest brass, is still vacant. Pastor Shanley greets those around him, but it only increases his sense of falseness. He hates pastor-pastor small talk. It stinks with phony concern, false humility, and party line. He's talked with his LBI peers hundreds of times, but he's never said anything of substance, nor have they. In truth, they're strangers to him. Also on the stage, to Jim's left, the LBI musicians tune up, emitting a chorus of discordant honks, twangs, blats, and blares.

The auditorium is filling toward its capacity of 3100. Anxious to find his wife, and Becki, Jim focuses his attention on the V.I.P. section to his right front where he locates both of them. Sharon is sitting between Doris and Beverly, with Alison, Becki, and Katie next to them. Stan and Russ and the rest of the BFBC contingent are also in this row but farther down. Upon spotting Jim, Sharon gives him "the finger" with her eyes. But Becki doesn't look up at all. Down, down, Jim's stomach sinks. Helpless, helpless. He can't deal with it. He looks away.

Sitting in Moody Coliseum is like sitting in a great blue egg—blue like the heavens. A truncating wall behind the stage cuts the egg dividing the horseshoe-shaped amphitheater from the smaller administrative portion of the building. Tiers of adobe-red seats rise in sloping sections from the central floor. Toffee-brown carpet is everywhere, even on the walls, creating a hi-tech sound-soaking environment, but the acrylic "new" smell is almost intoxicating. Bible-verse banners hang throughout, while missionary flags circle a high suspended scoreboard. In like fashion, on the high wall behind the stage is a large American flag surrounded by state flags, one for each state with an LBI branch. Below them hangs an LBI banner—a blood-red cross superimposed on a blue map of the world. The flags, the festive setting, the platform of officers, the fervent body of believers create an almost-military atmosphere.

Peach, pink, aqua, lemon, lilac, lavender. Blooming through winter grays, browns, and plaids, the LBI ladies, like spring flowers, paint a pretty mosaic of pastel color. In the first two rows of staff seating alone there are enough Easter dresses to have a fashion show. The LBI men are also well-dressed, yet are hardly noticeable. But there are exceptions to the fashion parade—some in casual attire, some shabbily clad.

The LBI regulars seem to accept the poorly dressed members of the congregation, but in fact, they look down on them as lost souls or immature believers. Logan teaches that proper dress is a sign of spiritual maturity. Pastor Jim is different; he feels closer to God in blue jeans than in a suit. Yet the BFBC flock always dresses up for Nashua events—even Russ Bradley.

At 7:50 p.m., the LBI treasurer and song leader, Jerry Crenshaw, approaches the lectern. Crenshaw, a nattily dressed Ted Koppel look-alike, seems a natural for his money job but a poor choice for song leader. After a brief scan of the agenda notes, he asks everyone to enter into an attitude of prayer. The hustle-and-bustle quickly gives way to quiet piety. Latecomers enter reverently as ushers direct them to the few remaining seats.

Jim glances at Becki in the V.I.P. section, and to his surprise, she's staring right at him with big eyes. She quickly looks down. To catch Becki gazing at him normally gives him a rush but he's too anxious about Sharon to feel good about it.

While the body prays, Dr. Logan and his entourage, Tom Hudson, Rich Beckman, Bob Logan, Ed Landreth, and Matt Garrett, quietly file onto the stage and sit down on the front row of the pastors' section. A few minutes later, Crenshaw gives the announcements, then leads the opening song service: "It's Bubbling"—"This Is the Day"—"Somebody Touched Me"—"This Little Light of Mine." Then hymns of worship: "Jesus, We Just Want to Thank You"—"Where He Leads Me I Will Follow"—"The Old Rugged Cross." Finally, the flock lifts holy hands and worships in four-part harmony.

Crenshaw sits down and Dr. Logan steps to the pulpit. The crowd buzzes expectantly as if they can wait no longer for his message. But he makes them wait as he announces, "We have a young woman here tonight, a student, who wants to share her testimony." He often calls people up without prior notice. All the coeds freeze hoping it won't be them, yet at the same time, they lust for such personal attention from the ultimate Christian. Logan waits as if to tease them. Finally, he says, "Molly Gibson, please come up." Blushing and smiling, Molly sidels out of the staff section and comes forward, swinging her robust figure inside a lemon-yellow dress. As she hurries up the stairs onto the platform, her lush mahogany locks bounce on her back. "We're all so proud of Molly," Logan declares as he puts his arm around her waist in fatherly fashion. "She's from Pastor Bowman's church in Boston, and not only has she given her heart to the Lord and done well in her studies, but she's also one of our top-notch secretaries at Blantyre."

Logan hands her the microphone and steps back. "Well, gosh," Molly begins nervously, "I don't know what to say. I jus' can't believe I'm up here. Gosh, I didn't expect this." She laughs. The body laughs with her. She relaxes a bit. "But I jus' wanna thank God tonight for leadin' me to Pastor Bowman, an' to Dr. Logan. I'm twenty-one now, but when I was in high school back in South Boston, I got into drugs 'n stealin', an' lots of trouble...."

Molly shifts her weight to one leg, canting her provocative hips underneath her yellow dress. Her backside draws far more of Jim's attention than her testimony: "My dad's an alcoholic, an' my mom, she didn't know what to do with me. I dropped out in eleventh grade an' ran with a bad crowd. Then I met Pastor Bowman at Carson Beach; he gave me a tract an' led me to the Lord. He encouraged me to finish school. Now I'm here at college an' I have a new life. I'm *so* happy here. Ever'body's got so much love. I jus' thank God. I uh—I guess that's all." As the body applauds, Molly gives Logan a big hug then returns to her seat.

Next, Dr. Logan calls up Becki's stepfather, Ed Landreth, to take the offering. Pastor Landreth, ruddy, redheaded, and moustached, with friendly eyes and a hefty Burl Ives body, still looks more like a truck driver than a missionary. He led a double life at Bible school, spending his days in class and his nights carousing around. Alison often lamented to Jim that she was cursed the day she met Ed. Yet Jim liked him, and they often talked and watched TV ballgames together. In those days, Ed was a man of few words. He loved the outdoors and hated crowds and paperwork. But after graduation, he changed, reformed, assumed a pastor persona. He, like Alison, can now spout the LBI line with the best of them.

"We're moving around the world to save souls," Ed declares, his voice husky and full, like the husky voices that say "breaker, breaker" on CB radio. "And Pastor has a calling to go into new countries with new teams, to go on more radio and TV stations, and to go into more cities and towns in America. Let's give because we believe in Pastor's sacred vision!" Ed goes on another five minutes, praising Dr. Logan and emphasizing the dire need of funds. Finally, he finishes by saying, "If you wish to give to the Moody Building Fund, please use a building-fund envelope or write Moody on the bottom of your check, and remember for any Moody gift of $200 or more, we'll place an engraved plaque with your name and the name of a deceased loved-one on the 'Wall of Remembrance' in front of the coliseum."

*Can you imagine a "wall of remembrance" in front of our old Legion hall?* Jim chuckles cynically to himself as he thinks of all the ingenious ways that Logan raises money: regular offerings, special offerings, radio-TV offerings, missionary offerings, building funds, branch-ministry tithes, seminars, conferences, tape sales, bookstore receipts, Moody concessions, tuition, room and board, student union, cafeteria, faculty club, snack bars, vending machines, athletic events, and fund-raising drives from candy bars to flea markets. Yet there's never enough. Jim has never heard it said, "We have plenty, so we won't take an offering tonight."

After the offering, Dr. Logan returns to the pulpit—this time to preach. He starts by telling an amusing story about the Easter Bunny and cold New England weather which sets off a roar of laughter. The anecdote is actually corny, but the body always responds to Logan's humor as if he's Johnny Carson. As everyone settles, he slips on his glasses and says, "Please open your Bibles to Romans eight ... and go to verse eleven." He reads the verse:

> **But if the Spirit of him that raised up Jesus from the dead dwell in you, he that raised up Christ from the dead shall also quicken your mortal bodies by his Spirit that dwelleth in you.**

"Paul tells us here that the miracle of resurrection, the mystery of Easter, not only gives us victory over death and delivers us to glory, but also gives us the power to win in *this* life. Tonight, I want to show you how to appropriate this power, so you can win daily with Christ, and store up heavenly rewards at the same time."

Charming, reasonable, persuasive, Logan goes on for ten minutes about the believer's sure inheritance. But just as it seems that his sermon is going to be relaxed and dispassionate, he pauses, sniffs the air like a bloodhound picking up a scent, and marches boldly to the front of the platform. Whipping the microphone cord behind him, he paces back and forth. "WE HAVE THE TRUTH in John 8:32!" he shouts as he slashes the air with compact karate-chop gestures. "We have the *only* Savior of the world in John 4:42! It's time for us to claim our finished-work victory! Jesus is not a mediocre Savior! And he has no pleasure in MEDIOCRE CHRISTIANS!" Cheering applause resounds through the amphitheater.

Riding the response like a drug, Logan stops center stage and flies into a rage; showers of spittle accompany his words: "THE SPIRIT THAT RAISED UP JESUS DWELLS IN *US*! WE *ARE* THE SONS OF GOD in John 1:12! WE MUST SET THE STANDARDS FOR THE HUMAN RACE! WE MUST FOLLOW OUR CAPTAIN ACROSS THE JORDAN in Joshua 5:13!"

His face red and mottled, the doctor roars and rants until it seems he will collapse from lack of wind. Then after a quick breath, he drops into a quiet fatherly voice, "But there is no fear because perfect love casts out fear in 1st John 4:18, and you're the apple of God's eye in Psalm 17:8." He cuddles the mike near his mouth as if making love to it. "Jesus will soothe your wounds with the balm of Gilead in Jeremiah 8:22, and will lead you home to Shiloh in Joshua 18:1. He shall deliver you from Gog and Magog in Ezekiel 38:2. The Lord will feed you at the fig tree and give you tender grapes in Song of Solomon 2:13. He will give you the north wind which is sweetly spiced with spikenard and saffron."

Confusing cloudy phrases, enchanting verses out of context, even obvious contradictions do not bother Dr. Logan. He's tuned to the collective libido of the body, to their instinctive fears and longings. He rides this psychic energy until he can harness it, just as a broncobuster rides a wild mare until the horse is broken and submissive. Arousing then subduing the wild animal is everything to Logan, far more important than homiletics and hermeneutics.

He enthralls the flock with his charisma, his voice, his gestures, his hypnotic eyes. He ventures deep into the primal caves of *Eros* and *Phobos* where only witch doctors and wild lovers dare to descend. That's why LBI services are packed with fervent worshipers aroused to a drunken almost-sexual frenzy, while most mainline ministers, Protestant and Catholic, present dry structured sermons to lifeless congregations in half-empty churches.

Logan retreats to the lectern and begins to preach vehemently again, pounding the pulpit with deliberate, hammerlike blows, "We have peace that passes all understanding in Philippians 4:7, love that passes knowledge in Ephesians 3:19, and 'joy unspeakable and full of glory' in 1st Peter 1:8! The unsaved pretend to have victory through money, worldly education, and positive thinking, but they're liars! When the tempest comes, their lives will crumble, but God will deliver you from the wild bulls of Bashan in Psalm 22:12! We have God's Holy Bible which gives us the sure answers to life's mysteries, as testified by angels and apostles. We *have* the truth! OUR SEARCH IS *OVER*!" Cheering approval erupts in a rising crescendo which peaks in deafening noise then descends in spasms and spurts of applause. Spirits soar as the body senses that this is the night they'll finally discover the secret of making Christianity work for them. But Jim's spirit does not soar. He's heard the promises a thousand times yet to him Christians seem no more blessed than the unsaved. In fact, it's been his experience—both in his own life and from counseling others—that being "born again" usually brings more misery than miracles, and certainly more stress and pretense.

But the assembled multitude, now entranced and malleable in their pastor's hands, anticipates enlightenment as a woman anticipates orgasm and gives her body and soul to her seducer. Logan, however, has no intention of satisfying. Instead, he becomes caustic, condemning, "Most people are losers! And tragically most believers—even many of you here tonight!" Jim senses the sinister shift in the sermon as the LBI chief now preaches to make the flock hate itself, but moreso to make the flock *love* hating itself. Logan craves it, gets off on it—and it gets results, producing disciples who, rejecting their own instincts, blindly give total allegiance to him and his worldwide vision. It's the key to his power, the barb on the hook which the body has already swallowed.

"YOU'VE FORSAKEN THE GOD OF ISRAEL by the river Chebar in Ezekiel 10:22!" Logan roars as he races wildly about the stage. "You commune with worldly friends! Instead of witnessing to them, you join them as they make cakes to the 'queen of heaven' in Jeremiah 7:18! You are gone away backward in Isaiah 1:4! You crucify the Son of God afresh and put him to open shame in Hebrews 6:6! YOU MAKE GOD *SICK*!" Burning with righteous indignation, he bobs and weaves and jabs the air as he cuts loose with barrage after barrage, like bursts of machine-gun fire.

Finally, after five minutes of fury, he calms and retreats to the lectern where he wipes the spittle off his chin with a folded handkerchief. Sweating profusely, he slips off his suit coat. Flash: Jerry Crenshaw is there to take it as if shot out of a cannon. "You'd better listen, and you'd better listen well," Logan goes on, his timbre quiet but severe. "Jesus is calling each of you to his army, but you refuse to hearken. If you can't go overseas, you should serve in a branch ministry, and we have thirty churches to choose from. You have *no* excuse. What will you say at the 'judgment seat' of Romans 14:10? You'll have to confess that you wasted your life following owls, satyrs and wild beasts in Isaiah 13:21. And what will you say to the damned as they go wailing into the 'lake of fire' in Revelation 20:15?"

The doctor removes his glasses and places them on his Bible—an ominous sign. "That's why I preach the whole Bible. I don't water it down like 'teachers with itching ears' in 2nd Timothy 4:3. I love you in God's truth. I want you to win at the Bemas Seat."

No applause, no cheers. Crushed silence fills the coliseum, the crushed silence of souls who've measured themselves against the Word and have come up short.

Fire, fire: Logan bolts from the pulpit, charges to the front, as if struck by lightning. The congregation gives a collective gasp. "YOU HAVE GONE A WHORING AFTER THE HEATHEN in Ezekiel 23:30!" he thunders. "YOU ARE POLLUTED WITH THEIR IDOLS! YOU BOW DOWN TO THE FALSE GODS OF EGYPT! To cigarettes and beer and marijuana and rock music! You live like the drunken daughters of Astoreth in Judges 2:13! Like the wild jackals in Isaiah 13:22! You don't take charge with positive faith! You let your emotions control you! No wonder YOU'RE LAZY, FAT, SLOPPY, AND *ALWAYS* UNHAPPY!"

Again, nothing but silence from the body of believers.

Logan prowls the stage, whipping the mike cord decisively as a cat whips its tail. "I'm not preaching this to be nice! It's easy to cheer for the loving gentle side of God, and rightly we should, but it takes a *real* soldier to cheer for chastisement! And yet the Bible says, If you endure chastening, God dealeth with you as with sons! SO, COME *ON*! LET'S GET OUT OF THIS PITIFUL SPIRIT!"

The doctor pummels the air as if he's punching the devil's face. The crowd roars to its feet applauding and shouting until the coliseum vibrates from the noise. The flock always rebels when Logan first sets the hook but as he draws them deeper into self-hatred, they cheer his condemning words and beg for more. And he gives them more: "You fornicate with Molech in the valley of Hinnom! You bow to the devils of Sodom in Genesis 19:5! Why do you think this terrible new plague called AIDS is sweeping the gay community! GOD HATES HOMOSEXUAL SIN AND HE WON'T TOLERATE IT! Others of you play on the hole of the asp in Isaiah 11:8 and masturbate in the temple of Chemosh in 1st Kings 11:7! COME *ON*! GROW UP AND GET RID OF THAT BABY STUFF! GET SOME GUTS! IT'S TIME TO FOLLOW A HIGHER PAS-SION! I would never gratify my flesh before the Mother of Harlots in Revelation 17:5, or touch my genitals in the night! NEVER! *NEVER!* I live in heavenly bliss far above such lewd and thankless behavior! GLORY BE TO GOD!" Roaring, shouting, wild ap-plause. Thunderous response shakes the coliseum.

But Pastor Jim only smells the foul stink of guilt and shame. He stands and applauds with the others yet he's not so affected by the doctor's condemnation as at the afternoon session. His own conscience has already made him feel as guilty as he can feel. But unlike most of the flock, he no longer takes pleasure in despising himself. Logan bows his head and lifts his right arm in a holy "Heil

Hitler" salute to God. Soon the auditorium is a sea of arms—all lifted to heaven. He now has total control as if the mesmerized flock is an extension of his own body. Finally, Logan seats everyone.

As Jim sits down, he once more pictures Sharon confronting Alison and Becki, and Becki leaving forever. He once more feels the urgent need to smooth things with his wife but he can't. Logan is going full blast again, ranting, condemning, exhorting. His grainy voice is now a painful buzz in Jim's brain like having a tooth filled without Novocain.

*I liked God better before I was born-again,* he declares to himself. *Before I knew anything about the Bible or winning souls, or the Holy Spirit giving victory over lust.*

Jim thinks back to such a time, to a warm moonlit night in his memory. He hears crickets, locusts, and frogs, together with the whisper of the wind in the trees and the distant yelping of a coyote. He sees the farmhouse; the gray roof looks silver in the moonlight. He pictures the pretty dark-haired woman; she's tucking the sandy-haired cowlicked boy into bed. After kissing him good-night, she hands him a worn-looking teddy bear and reaches for the lamp but the boy stops her, "Mama?"

"What is it, honey?" she replies.

"D'you think second grade is too ol' to sleep with Pooh?" The boy says "thank" instead of "think."

"Do you still like to sleep with him?"

The boy ponders a moment then says, "Yeh, I guess I do."

"Well then, I reckon second grade's not too old."

She reaches for the light but the boy stops her a second time, "Oh, Mama?"

"You're sure enough full of questions tonight, young man," she laughs as she sits down on the side of the bed and tweaks the boy's nose. "So, what else is on your mind?"

"Howcum I jus' go to Sunday school on Easter and Mother's Day?" He looks up at his mom concernedly. "Most of my friends at school go ever' Sunday."

"Would you like to go every Sunday?" she asks, giving a knowing smile.

The boy smiles back showing his new front teeth. "No ... I don't think so. I always feel funny like everybody's lookin' at me. It's all right, the coloring and stuff, but I like stayin' home best."

The dark-haired woman laughs. "Me too. I'm grown-up but I still feel a bit funny at church. I suppose we'd feel better if we went a lot. I guess we should go more ... maybe?"

The boy sobers; his face clouds. "Some of the kids at school said if I don't start goin' more often, God's gonna give me to the devil, and send me down to *hell*."

"Oh, so that's what set all this off?"

"I told 'em God loves me whether I go or not. Does He, Mama?"

"I reckon He does, honey," she answers, her voice now warm with motherly compassion. "At least, I hope so. I like to think"—she too pronounces it "thank"—"that Jesus loves us all the time."

"Me too, Mama," the boy responds, his face brightening. "I hope God loves us a *whole* bunch, even when we go fishin' on Sunday."

The woman hugs the boy then gets up; she gives a chuckling laugh. "Sometimes I think Jesus would rather go fishing with us than put on a coat and tie for church and all. Now you get to sleep. You've got school tomorrow."

"I know, Mama, but leave the door open a crack, okay?" She agrees then switches off the lamp and leaves the room. The boy turns on his side and gathers Pooh Bear to his bosom.

Jim hears the wind whispering in the trees; he hears the mournful whistle of a faraway train—"YOU HAVE *NO* EXCUSE TO SIN!" Dr. Logan bellows, jolting Shanley out of his childhood memories. "YOU REFUSE TO GIVE ALL! YOU PLAY GAMES WITH GOD! So you remain weak, impotent, and poor, and you complain that life is hard! WELL, YOU'LL GET NO PITY FROM ME! I'M *SICK* OF YOUR BELLYACHING! I'M *SICK* OF YOUR UNBELIEF!" The body roars to its feet. The tumult is continuous, as in the closing seconds of a Boston Celtics game.

Logan, lobster red, soaked with sweat, looks like a boxer in the 14th round. But he rants on, rushing from side to side and beating the air furiously, "I FACE TEMPTATION DAILY BUT I DEFEAT THE DEVIL WITH THE WORD OF GOD! I HAVE *FAITH* IN THE PROMISES! I TRIUMPH THROUGH THE FINISHED WORK OF CHRIST! That's why I'm up at five every day. That's why I'm keen and always ready to win souls! That's why I can work longer than any of you, EVEN LATE INTO THE NIGHT! THIS IS HOW I'VE BEEN CELIBATE FOR *EIGHT* YEARS WITHOUT ONE LAPSE INTO SEXUAL SIN! I LIVE IN A *HIGH*ER LOVE! I MADE THE CHOICE! *GLOR*Y BE TO GOD! You think angels are going to come and carry you to victory! That's not how it is! You have to exercise your free will! GOD DID HIS PART! HE *DIED* FOR YOU! HE *ROSE* FOR YOU! HE *LIVES* IN YOU! WHAT MORE CAN HE DO! IT'S UP TO *YOU* TO GO TO THE CROSS!" The delirious throng roars and howls, and leans forward as if ready to charge the platform. The thunderous acclamation seems ready to lift the domed roof.

"SURRENDER IS THE KEY! YOU MUST SURRENDER TO GOD! YOU MUST *OBEY* THE WORD! The Bible says don't forsake 'the assembling of ourselves together' in Hebrews 10:25, SO *OBEY* THE WORD AND COME TO EVERY SERVICE! The Bible says to 'study to show yourself approved' in 2nd Timothy 2:15, SO *OBEY* THE WORD AND COME TO BIBLE COLLEGE! The Bible says to bring your tithes into the storehouse in Malachi 3:10, SO *OBEY* THE WORD AND GIVE TEN PERCENT!"

Purple-faced, swollen with fury, Logan looks like an erect penis thrusting for climax. The pulsing veins on the side of his head protrude like black snakes. "The Bible says to 'preach the gospel to every creature' in Mark 16:15, SO *OBEY* THE WORD AND WITNESS TO YOUR FAMILY, YOUR FRIENDS, YOUR NEIGHBORS! The Bible says we are complete in Christ in Colossians 2:10, SO *OBEY* THE WORD AND ACCEPT YOUR FINISHED-WORK VICTORY OVER SIN AND LETHARGY AND LUKEWARM ATTITUDES! The Bible says to 'seek ye first the kingdom of God' in Matthew 6:33, SO *OBEY* THE WORD AND COME WITH ME INTO ALL THE WORLD! LET'S LIVE FOR JESUS! LET'S FIGHT IN GOD'S ARMY! LET'S GO AND GO AND GO FOR GOD ... UNTIL WE DROP!"

The doctor punches the air violently then goes limp with fatigue before the wildly cheering congregation. For a long while he stands silently before them—drinking in their adoration.

# Chapter Fourteen

Pastor Shanley fights through traffic to Dr. Logan's private exit where a buzzing crowd of devotees is assembled. He pulls in behind Logan's limousine, a black Lincoln Continental with a trunk-mounted flying-wing antenna and vanity plates that say: GOSPEL. Jim feels cold. The heat in the Grenada is just coming up. Sharon has been silent since they got into the car, but as the heat comes up, so does she, "Well, James David, I hope you're *satisfied*. Our va*c*ation, and we spend it sitting in traffic."

Bothered sigh, condemning eyes. The church service did not cool Sharon's hot discontent. This dismays Jim. He wants to make up, to talk calmly, to do damage control, and he's not even sure of the damage, of whether she talked with Alison, Becki, or what.

"We never have a *real* vacation like normal people," Sharon goes on. "You know, going away for a week. I've given up on that. But I was looking forward to these two days. Why don't we just charter a *bus* and take everyone to Vermont? Then you and Becki can sit together and talk about winning souls. If people only *knew* what I go through. Being married to you is *shit*. You make me so damn—"

"Come on, Shar," Jim cuts in, scrambling to defuse her wrath. "Would you just *cool* it. It's gonna be all right. Pastor's guest room will be better than a motel, and it's not what you think with Rebec—"

"I don't want to hear about that spoiled bitch! She's a conceited *brat,* and selfish and conniving and crude! She's even worse than her mom! She's been taking you for a ride since she was eleven! And now that she's got that fat butt, you follow her around like a *horny male dog*! It makes me sick! I hate her roly-poly face and her ugly teeth! I can't stand her corny jokes and her constant bragging. I don't know what you see in her. She's a discredit to womanhood. All she talks about is rock music and TV shows ... and she dresses like a *damn* scarecrow!"

"You got it all wrong, Shar. There's nothing—"

"Just shut up!" Sharon declares, her eyes flashing like a cat ready to attack. "I've had enough of your *bull*shit, Jim!"

"WELL, FUCK *YOU* THEN!" Jim shouts, abandoning his peace initiative. "You're the bitch, not Becki! Besides, I don't have to answer to you anyway!"

"I *said* shut up! I don't want to hear it! And when did you start using such *fil*thy language? I guess you've picked up her gutter talk as well."

"Shar-*ron!* It's not—"

"I'm not kidding, Jim! One more word and I'm getting out!"
"But it's not—"

Sharon opens the door. Jim shuts up. She closes the door.

Hot tension, unconsummated indignation. Sharon, her eyes filling, pulls a tissue out of her coat pocket and dabs her tears but she does not break. Jim feels frustrated, helpless, guilty, and fearful—all at the same time. *Maybe she already spilled her gut to Alison? If not, she still could. I just wish we could talk this out.* Now comes a surge of rage. *Shit! Who does she think she is? She's always messing up my life! Who is she to judge me? She's no saint. I feel like slapping her fuckin' face.* But he refrains. He's only slapped Sharon twice in fifteen years. She's swung at him many times but has only landed a few blows because he grabs her arms and holds on, which makes her so mad that she turns blue.

Sudden action in front of the Grenada: a uniformed man of ursine proportions lumbers out of Dr. Logan's private exit. He has a face like a bulldog, arms like tree trunks. It's Lucas Simpson, Logan's security chief, bodyguard, and driver. As the crowd cheers, Dr. Logan emerges behind Simpson with Amy Brannigan by his side. Following them are Rich Beckman and Tom and Mary Beth Hudson.

The doctor, in a gray overcoat, smiles broadly and waves—like a Southern senator on his way to an election-night victory party. As he nears the limo, the crowd surges about him giving him kudos and hugs and handshakes. But with Simpson's help, Logan and his entourage get into the car, and the limo speeds away followed by Matt Garrett's BMW—Garrett, parked to the side, guns in ahead of the Grenada—then Jim and Sharon, and another half-dozen cars behind the Shanleys.

Like a presidential motorcade they head back across campus, down Cottage Row, then west on a narrow asphalt road that ascends into the wooded hills on the Hollis half of the property. Finally, they turn off and pass a security gate that looks like a Fotomat booth. A guard waves each car through with a crisp military snap of his arm. A long winding driveway goes up to the top of the hill.

The villa itself, an oversized log chalet between a pair of motel-like dormitories, resembles a giant bug with its wings spread. Wide cornices, steep roof-lines, overhanging gable ends, many lights. It looks more like a ski lodge than a private home. The house is officially named "Craggy Heights" after the high ridge upon which it sits, but everyone calls it "the villa."

Jim parks in the drive-around. While he gets the bags out of the trunk, Sharon runs quickly ahead to join Tom and Mary Beth. Once inside, Jim is escorted upstairs by Ellie Burns, Logan's matronly housekeeper. She takes him to a large guest room which is indeed more luxurious than most motel rooms. Logan lives in the central chalet along with his security chief while his staff secretaries, student houseservants, and a small cadre of hired servants live in the dormitories. Amy Brannigan has a suite of rooms in the north dorm wing, as does Rich Beckman. The doctor likes to surround himself with staff and other loyal devotees—day and night. But at the same time, he protects himself with a computerized security system that monitors the entire property with video cameras and automatically locks all doors into his central chalet at 11:00 p.m.

Before going downstairs, Jim stops on the balcony that over-looks the spacious prow-shaped living room. Western motif, beamed cathedral ceiling, log walls, stone fireplace at the prow end, floor-to-ceiling windows on both sides of the fireplace. He's been to the villa a number of times but the layout still fascinates him. Above the mantel is a shaggy buffalo head with curved horns and orange eyes. The black bearded bison gives Jim a sense of foreboding, for it brings to mind the bull-like beast in his nightmare. From his balcony perch, he watches the LBI faithful file by the food tables.

Chips, dips, finger-sandwiches, crackers, cheese, brownies, cookies. Coffee, hot chocolate, cider, soda. After getting food and beverage, they mix and mingle cocktail party-style standing amid the rustic twigwork furniture which is arranged about the large room as in a hotel lobby. About forty people are present not counting the servants. Logan prefers open raps with larger crowds—like in the old days—but Lucas Simpson insists on limiting access to the villa. A bow-tied household student comes in from the deck with an armload of firewood and puts it on the fire. Sparks fly up; the new logs pop, snap, and burst into flames.

Amy Brannigan mixes quietly, and issues orders to the servants. Wearing a pink dress with a lace collar, she conducts herself like a wife. But Jim cannot bring himself to think of her as any more than a hostess, not on this night, not after Dr. Logan's blistering sermons and professions of celibacy. The idea of Logan fucking outside of marriage, Amy or any of the young honeys that work at Blantyre, now seems far-fetched like the lurid headlines in the tabloid racks by the check-out counters at Stop & Shop.

But Logan himself has yet to appear. The doctor's after-service ritual is always the same—shower, change, retire to his home office where Jerry Crenshaw gives him a report on the money receipts and Ellie Burns serves him a glass of V-8 juice mixed with yogurt. No Becki either. Freshmen are rarely invited. Besides, she's never liked to group around Pastor or sit fawningly at his feet. But Jim does spot Sharon, by the fireplace. *Shit; look at her joking with Hudson. And Ed and Alison are with them. Alison's gonna wonder why I'm not with Sharon. Or maybe Shar's already done me in?* Anger, fear, jealousy, regret. Flares of emotion shoot off like Roman candles in his stomach but he can do nothing, so the flares burn out leaving a smoldering sense of anxiety and impotence—there's no peaceful resignation like earlier in the car.

*Look at her laughing with Hudson like she just met him at a bar. I bet that obsequious bastard would like to pump Sharon with his big Aryan cock.* The thought bothers Jim but not nearly so much as the possibility of losing his Saturday-time with Rebecca.

Finally, he goes downstairs, grabs a brownie and a coffee, and browses around the back perimeter of the room, under the loft. He has little desire to mix, and no desire to go near Sharon, so he pretends to be occupied with the Fredric Remington reproductions on the walls. *Why'd I say yes to Logan?* Jim thinks regretfully as he looks at the cowboy-and-Indian scenes. *That was so fucking dumb. Sharon and I could be at the motel right now, crotch to crotch on the bed, and my Becki-life wouldn't be hanging by a thread. I blew it big time. Now I'm stuck and—*all at once, Mary Beth Hudson. She interrupts Jim's thoughts as she joins him at the back of the room, as if she too wants to get away from the crowd, perhaps from Mike Montanaro who's huddled with a group of fawning students near the food tables.

Mary Beth, handsome-faced with a greyhound body and a she-wolf psyche, seems an overmatch for her wooden-headed husband. For that matter, she's an overmatch for most of the LBI sycophants including Logan's dashing but slow-witted nephew. She, like Janet Buford, seems too liberated to be an LBI woman. She and Jim exchange comments about the Remington paintings. He senses that Mary Beth has more serious things to talk about, but before she can, Molly Gibson and Pastor Bowman come over to congratulate Pastor Jim on his afternoon message.

Jim finds Molly to be a person he'd like to have as a friend, and not just for her body. She is sexy to be sure, yet she also seems sensitive and genuine, and more intelligent than she let on at lunch—but she does seem starved for affection which explains her starry-eyed attachment to Logan. But Jim can't stomach George Bowman whom he's known since Bible school. Bowman, an LBI clone all the way, never talks, he just echoes.

Now noticed by his fellow LBI'ers, Jim begins to mingle, moving from group to group, making ministry talk. Cookie-cutter Christians all around. Loganites. Masked evangelicals. Shallow, haughty, filled with pretense. His people in Brendon Falls seem much more real and down-to-earth. Jim despises himself for participating in such perverse and jaded conversation. Team news, branch news, Logan's latest sermon. Who got saved, who got baptized, who repented and came back to the body. Campus news, Logan's latest class, who's teaching what—this semester, in the summer, in the fall. Russia, Israel, Middle East oil, the Lord is coming. Family news, good gossip only. Sons, daughters coming to Bible college, going out on a team. Brother, sister, Mom, and Pop, winning in Christ, walking in the Spirit, living above the common level of life. Except for the new and naive, no one really shares; they just strut their evangelical egos and utter snide high-sounding remarks accompanied by cool smirks. They speak in an elitist we-are-the-ultimate-Christians-with-the-ultimate-pastor spirit. With drinks and munchies in hand, they look and act like middle class snobs at a suburban country club, except there's no alcohol—but Logan's faithful don't need alcohol to get drunk.

Overload, overload: Jim feels suddenly out of touch, out of focus. Distorted smiling faces jump out at him like grotesque images from a house of mirrors—swollen mouths, fat lips speaking empty words of praise: "Great message this afternoon, Jim. We loved it. You were *so* anointed"—"You really touched me today, Pastor Shanley. Your sermon changed my life"—"Oh, Pastor, your teaching was *so* timely, and it prepared our hearts for Dr. Logan's message tonight"—"I hear great things about your church, Jim. Do come to Lawrence soon and speak to my people"—"I'm so glad you and Sharon could come up. Your marriage is *such* a testimony to the Lord"—"Oh, Pastor Shanley, let me give you a hug in the Lord. You're *such* a darling. We love your portion"—"I met your head elder, Stan Campbell, at service tonight. What a man of God. You've got a great team in Brendon Falls, Jim. Keep up the good work. We're *so* proud of you."

Shanley is out of balance, out of tune, stressed to the limit, but he still has enough conviction to detest what he's hearing. Fire ignites inside him, *Shit, this isn't Christ! I see more Jesus in the townies at Flanagan's than these country-club pharisees could generate in a thousand years! What the fuck is wrong with me? Why do I put up with this? I've had enough! Next time I see Dr. Logan, I'm going to tell him how I really feel. I can't tell another lie. I can't play this fuckin' game anymore! This is it! I gotta go outside. I need some air.*

After running upstairs to grab his coat, Jim heads for one of the side doors that lead out onto the deck. But a fatherly voice stops him, "Jim, can I see you a minute?" Turning around, he sees Dr. Logan coming toward him. The doctor, in a blue alpine sweater, looks refreshed, relaxed, and sporty, yet very much in charge.

They shake hands; their eyes meet. Naked, naked, sinner, traitor, hot blush of shame. Jim's new resolve fizzles faster than Alka-Seltzer in a glass of water. He feels exposed, guilty, inferior, as if Logan knows his rebellious thoughts. The doctor's gaze, dark, dark, no pupils, seems to confirm what Jim feels. Too much. Jim starts lying the moment his lips move, "I-I, I was just going out on the deck to see the view. I understand you can see the lights of Nashua and east campus ... the whole valley."

"It *is* quite splendid. That's why we chose this ridge to build on. It's the highest spot on the property, you know." Logan pats Jim on the shoulder in paternal fashion. "Your teaching this afternoon, Jim, was truly inspiring, and it fit so well with my theme tonight. I've heard many favorable comments—great job."

Jim fawns nervously like a puppy at suppertime. If he had a tail, it would surely be wagging. "Well, I—well, thank you, sir," he stammers. "But it was nothing compared with tonight. Your message was *truly* hallmark. The anointing was overwhelming. My people were blown away. I'm sure many lives were changed and won over to God." His lies getting bigger and bigger, he goes on praising the LBI chief for some time.

Logan beams, giving his V-shaped victory grin. "I'm glad to hear my message touched you, and your team," he replies after Jim finally stops. "But, Jim, the main reason I came over, I'd like for you to come to my office after the rap session. We're having an important policy meeting and I'd like for you to sit in, since you're staying over anyway." Shanley, still fawning and wagging, readily accepts.

Excusing himself, Logan moves about the room, mixing with the flock. As Jim watches the doctor grinning, beaming, receiving kudos, hugs, more praise, his own self-esteem crashes to a new low for the day, which seems impossible. He's just whipped off a dozen lies—all after vowing to tell the truth. But he had no chance. Logan castrated him with his eyes before he knew what happened. Jim now wants to get out of there more than ever, to go outside, to hide his face, but he doesn't dare. He has to make a show of enthusiasm for the rap session.

After mingling for a bit, Dr. Logan sits down in a maroon recliner, the only nonrustic piece in the room. He signals and the lights dim. Everyone gathers around on the sofas and chairs while the overflow sprawls on the Navajo rug at Logan's feet. Molly G. is close enough to touch her beloved pastor—like Lazarus' sister Mary at the feet of Jesus. Logan likes the bewitching effect of low lights, flickering flames, and dancing shadows. The mood is almost eerie, like telling ghost stories around a campfire late at night. All eyes are fixed on Pastor. The LBI faithful see him as a special prophet of God called to prepare the world for the coming of Christ.

But Jim doesn't give a shit about the second coming. He just wants to rescue his Saturday-time with Becki. He feels an urge to grab Sharon, to take her up to their room, to cool her down, to bed her down, to get her attention off of Becki. But when he sees her seated front-row-center with the Hudsons and Landreths, he quickly dismisses the idea and waits for a chance to slip outside.

The doctor starts the rap with a quick summary of his sermon points then throws it open for questions. Fawning favor-seeking hands go up all over the room. Logan picks Pastor Bowman: "Dr. Logan ... why are most churches so dead, while we're sending teams all over the world to save and disciple the lost?"

Narrowing his eyes, Logan replies in a hoarse but still authoritative voice, "An excellent question, George. I'd say the answer is twofold." Pastor Bowman's face shines with toadyish delight; to be complimented by Pastor in front of a group is perhaps the highest honor for a Loganite, especially when he calls you by your first name. "Number one: most churches try to operate as a democracy instead of a kingdom. And number two: most churches do not obey the Bible." Logan pauses as a houseservant hands him a glass of water. He takes a sip then gestures with the glass. "You see, God never intended that the Church be a democracy. The Catholics have the right idea. They just got off on the Virgin Mary thing. Let's take the Lord's Prayer. Jesus did not say, 'Our father who art in heaven, thy *democracy* come.'" Everyone laughs heartily, including Logan.

Taking advantage of the commotion, Pastor Jim slips out unnoticed. He hauls on his overcoat as he goes. It's dark on the deck. Amy doused the outside lights earlier so people could see the view. As Jim's eyes adjust, he notices someone at the far end of the deck where it curves around the prow of the chalet—a dark figure dimly visible in the light coming from the tall windows.

Pulling on his gloves, Jim heads that way. As he approaches, he sees a hooded, rather statuesque woman. Cloaked in a long cape, she stands at the railing on the other side of a wooden bench. She faces away toward the valley. In her graceful ungloved hand is a lighted cigarette. She doesn't move, though she surely hears his footsteps on the planks. Jim usually avoids solitary women, but curiosity compels him to stop by the bench. He cannot imagine one of Logan's ladies smoking in such a sacred spot—and during a rap session. "Quite a view, huh?" he says to her.

Turning around, she surprises Jim. She's no woman, no Logan lady; she's Matthew Garrett. Garrett does not reply to Jim's question but stares right at him Logan-style, though his eyes are not dark but a brilliant Nordic blue; yet they look pearl gray in the dim light. Icy eyes, chalky pallor, shadowy features. Garrett looks like a hooded specter. He seems mysterious, unsettling, almost macabre—like Peter O'Toole in *Lawrence of Arabia*. He takes a long pull on his cigarette; the fiery tip lights up his boyish face with a red glow which makes him seem even more macabre.

As a self-assured smile plays at the corners of his mouth, Matt puts out the cigarette then flicks the butt over the rail with smooth nonchalance. Finally, after exhaling a cloud of smoke and winter breath, he says, "Things are never what they seem ... are they, Jim?" His voice is calm, deliberate, yet filled with irony and foreboding. Before Jim can reply, Garrett turns, hurries down a stairway, and disappears into the darkness.

Calm, cold, moonless. The black starry night seems suddenly ominous. The lights of east campus flicker in the valley below— and Nashua beyond. A touch of frost shivers on the wooden railing like a sprinkling of stardust. Matt Garrett's face and words linger in Jim's mind. A shiver runs up his back. He hunches his shoulders against it and pulls his overcoat tightly around him.

Footsteps. High heels. Jim turns. Dark hair, a gray midlength coat—Alison. His heart plummets, *This is it. Sharon got to her. Besides, she was at Logan's afternoon tirade. She heard his warning against unhealthy relationships. She's coming to end my fantasy, to tell me that it's not wise for her daughter to spend Saturdays with me—and she's right. This is God's judgment. I've been expecting it all day and now it's here.*

Nonetheless, Jim does his best to hide his sinking heart. As Alison comes closer, he sees that her coat is not gray but light blue. Her brunette hair is feathery, wispy; it frames her face. She looks too Becki-ish to be a Logan lady.

Alison gives a demure smile and pushes her hands deep into her coat pockets, schoolgirl fashion. "Sure is cold out here, Jimmy," she says. "Hard to believe it's spring." She also sounds like Rebecca. Her voice is just more adult, a bit lower and thicker.

"I guess after four years in the Tropics, New England can be a shock to your system?" Though Jim speaks calmly, his wet underarms remind him of the high stakes at hand.

"Yep, that's for sure," she affirms with a laugh as she leans back against the deck railing. "It's not so bad now, but back in January we almost froze." She looks up. "Just look at those stars, Jimmy. They're like twinkling diamonds, and so bright. They remind me of those nights when we used to talk in the backyard."

*What the fuck is goin' on here?* Jim asks himself. *She certainly isn't acting like a concerned mother. But it has to be Becki. She's*

**174**

*not gonna leave a Logan rap to talk about the stars. But why doesn't she come out with it?*

"You know, Jimmy," Alison reflects, "you've been a true friend, like a brother to me, all these years. I miss talking to you. I saw you slip out a while ago so I decided to join you. Besides, I know you 'n Sharon are having a bit of an argument, and I wanted to build you up."

*THAT'S IT! IT'S OVER!* Jim exclaims but only to himself. *I'm tired of waiting for the inevitable. Let's get this out onto the fuckin' table.* He takes Alison by the shoulders and holds her in front of him as if he's going to shake her.

"That's why you left the rap and came out here?" he asks in obvious disbelief. "You found out Sharon and I were fighting, and you wanted to con*sole* me with sisterly affection?"

"Yep, that's right," Alison replies matter-of-factly as she straightens Jim's tie in wifely fashion. Her brown eyes are fixed on her moving hands.

Jim sighs—half in wonder, half in dismay. *I don't fuckin' believe it,* he declares silently. *She's making me dig for my own condemnation. It's no great mystery where Becki gets her contrariness.* Then he speaks out loud challenging her, "I know you better than that, Alison. That's not the *only* reason you came out here, is it? There's something else, right?"

"Yep, I guess there is," Alison confesses, withdrawing from his grasp. She moves to the railing and speaks into the night, "I never could fool you, could I, Jimmy? I really wanted to talk with you about Rebecca Lea."

*AH HA! JUST WHAT I THOUGHT!* Jim shouts to himself, his heart racing madly. Yet despite the storm breaking within, he maintains outward calm. "So ... what about her?" he asks innocently. He now waits for the axe, for the dreaded words which will dash his Becki-hopes.

Alison turns around and faces him yet averts her eyes. "Well, I'm—" she starts then stops. A faint almost imperceptible smile alights on her lips then flies quickly away.

"You're what?" Jim prompts.

"I'm worried," Alison says speaking down at her ungloved hands which are clasped in front of her like fig leaves. "I fear she's being drawn away from her calling. She's so young and impressionable, you know?"

Jim's pounding heart shakes his whole body. "What makes you think that?"

Alison lifts her eyes and her hands. She blurts her reply as if trying to explain in one breath, "She says she'll never move into the dorm, that she wants to move to Boston instead and live with Amelia, my unsaved sister—you met her once. I love Amelia but she's liberal and rebellious toward God and she's got a lot of funny feminist ideas. She could ruin Becki. So I wondered, Jim, if you'd encourage her to move into the dorm. She'll listen to you. I told Becki if she doesn't, she has to go back to Puerto Rico with us, but it's like talking to the wall."

Jim can hardly believe his ears. She isn't blowing the whistle on him at all. She just wants his help. Sharon didn't talk with Alison, or at least she didn't divulge that her fight with him was over Becki. But this truth is slow to register as if his emotions are wood chips tossed into the air—that haven't come down yet. He starts to reply but Alison has more, "Rebecca looks up to you, Jimmy. She loves going to Brendon Falls. You're the only father figure in her life. She gets along with Ed, but it's not the same. I'm glad she can be with you each week. You're a good influence on her."

Relief, relief, reprieve. Her words finally sink in. Jim is so relieved he almost wets his pants. He feels like a condemned man who just received a stay of execution—and more than a stay. Alison has exonerated him. To have her support his Saturday-time with Becki is remarkable good fortune. But he doesn't celebrate openly. Instead, he gathers his faculties and says, "No problem, Alison. I'll have a chat with her. She won't be moving to Boston if I can help it." His tone is pastorly and assuring.

Giving a coy grin, Alison moves closer and fingers the lapel of his coat. "Now, Jim, you know how to do it. Let it come up naturally so it won't seem like you're counseling her. Besides, there's no rush. We won't be leaving until August." Her eyes narrow into a calculating half-squint that to Jim seems forced. "But whatever you do, don't tell her I talked with you. You know, be 'wise as a serpent' and 'harmless as a dove.'"

"Don't worry, Alison," Jim assures again. "I'll take care of it." He feels buoyant with renewed Becki-hope, so buoyant he fears he may float off the deck at any moment.

"I knew I could count on you, Jimmy," Alison replies. "You're an answer to prayer." She hugs him, gives him a kiss on the cheek, and turns to go. But after a few steps, she whirls and comes back: "Oh, Jimmy, there is *one* more thing?"

"What's that?" Jim asks.

"Well uh ... Ed...." Alison hesitates, looks down, then goes on in an apologetic tone. "Ed ... well, he wants me to ask you something. He was going to talk to you earlier, but he felt shy about it, so I said I'd ask you."

"Ask me what?" Jim says with half his attention. He's floating, floating, feeling no pain.

"You know how Ed's raising support so we can have our own school for the Puerto Rico team?" She nervously picks at her thumbnail—just like Becki.

"Yeh, you were talking about it this morning."

"Anyway ... well, he was just wondering if the church in Brendon Falls could increase our monthly support? Ed feels *really* bad, having to ask like this, since you've been sending fifty dollars a month for so long, but it's so hard to raise support." Alison drops her head like an ashamed beggar. "Even ten or twenty more a month would be a real blessing, but please don't feel obligated, Jimmy."

Jim grins broadly under his mustache. "I tell you what, kiddo. Let's make it simple. We'll just double it and make it an even hundred." He's so elated about the turn of events, he would give three hundred without a thought. "I may have to rob Peter to pay Paul, but we can swing it."

"Oh, Jimmy, that's more than I *ever* expected!" She throws her arms around him. "Ed's gonna be excited to hear about this. You're a true friend, Jimmy. I'll never forget how you've helped us. You'll always be a special part of the Puerto Rico team. I'll have Ed send you the paperwork next week ... and thanks again for helping me with Rebecca Lea." After giving him another peck on the cheek, Alison turns and strides briskly down the deck, her high heels resounding, her Becki-like hips swinging under her coat. Jim watches her until she disappears inside.

Savoring his reversal of fortune, Jim leans back against the railing and looks up into the starry night. He takes a deep breath. The frosty air now seems refreshing like a cold drink on a hot day. A small voice tries to speak to him from deep within, but the words get lost in the good news of the moment. Now if he can just cool his wife, reassure her regarding Becki, he'll have everything under control. And Vermont—they're leaving in the morning—is the perfect place for reconciliation. Jim chuckles. He's sure that Sharon will make up with him before they get to the motel in Manchester.

* * *

Dr. Logan tosses Rich Beckman's report onto his desk then leans back in his chair, takes off his glasses, and rubs his tired eyes. "So, Dick, you're saying the problem is quality, not quantity?"

Beckman strokes his pocked face with his bony fingers then replies, "That's it, Pastor. That's it exactly."

"You see, Doctor," Jerry Crenshaw explains, "converting the masses is not enough, not in the long run. Even though our people

**177**

give more per capita than most ministries, our current economic base cannot support our expanding expenditures. When we reach out to the masses, we end up demographically with people on the downside." Crenshaw not only looks like Ted Koppel, but he talks like him as well: big words but no feeling.

"So our people are *too* poor?" Logan asks, replacing his glasses.

Crenshaw gives an intellectual nod of his Howdy Doody head. "To put it bluntly, yes. Historically, our members have been working class people, lower middle class for the most part. We've never had many white-collar members, and the situation is deteriorating. Take New England which accounts for 55% of our domestic membership. Most of our branches are in old mill towns which are now falling into the lowest strata of society with increasing numbers of Blacks, Latinos, and Orientals—along with poor whites. Many are unskilled immigrants who can't even work blue-collar or pink-collar jobs. Our churches still have Caucasian majorities for the most part, but the ratio is changing to reflect the deteriorating demographics and unless—"

"You can say that again," Michael Montanaro cuts in. "When I go to DeMoulas in Lawrence, I feel like I'm on a refugee boat, and it's getting that way in the church." Snorts, snickers, derisive laughter. The others get a kick out of Michael's condescending humor.

"Not that we want to discriminate against the less fortunate," Crenshaw elaborates after calm returns, "but for their sake, for our sake, we must reach the higher-income brackets." He pulls a notepad from his pocket. "Consider tonight's offering. We had a standing-room crowd but the offering was only $15,238. We had about three hundred checks between $10 and $30, plus an equal number of $10 and $20 bills. That's a weekly or half-weekly tithe for most of our people, but there were only nine checks over $100, and only *one* over $500—"

Logan, chuckling, interrupts him, "Florence Bentley, right?"

"You got it," Crenshaw confirms, giving a dry smirk. "A nice beige-and-blue Baybank scenic check for $750—a nice seascape with seagulls."

"Good ol' Florence," Pastor Beckman jokes. "She's as faithful as a milk cow and just as ugly." Everybody laughs except Logan. But he smiles so it's safe. Jim also joins the contemptuous mirth, but his heart is nauseated. Besides, he feels that Rich Beckman is the last person to call anyone ugly.

Logan, Crenshaw, Beckman. They're doing the talking with a few comments from Mike Montanaro, Tom Hudson, Ed Landreth, and Robert Logan. But Jim has nothing to offer as they sit around Logan's desk with Lucas Simpson watching the door. Dr. Logan's home office looks much like his office at the castle, as if he took his Blantyre office, reduced it by half, and moved it up to Craggy Heights. It's the only room in the villa done in a non-Western motif. It even has Napoleonic battle-scene prints on the walls. Jim wonders why Logan invited him. He also wonders why Matt Garrett is absent, especially after their strange encounter on the deck. But most of his thoughts are above and beyond ministry matters, as he relishes his revived Becki-dreams.

"Okay, that's enough," Logan says putting the joke to rest. "Let's not be too hard on her. If it weren't for Florence, we'd still be in Biddeford, and Moody would just be a dream." Everyone instantly sobers.

"Seriously now," Beckman says. "We must find more Florence Bentleys, people with money who believe in the Bible, who believe in the kingdom of God, who believe in our vision."

"That's precisely what I was getting at before," Crenshaw follows. He gestures with a felt-tip pen as if writing on an imaginary blackboard. "Matt and I ran a series of computer simulations with different church populations. The results show that a large body of poor people is always a liability, never an asset. Of course, as I said, we want to reach everyone for the Lord, and large crowds are important, especially on TV, but we must look at fiscal reality. People of color, plus poor whites, will never fund our vision. We need affluent supporters—doctors, lawyers, executives, heirs of wealth. We must reach out to them using the resources here at home base and in our branch churches. We must increase their numbers in our radio-TV audience. If we don't, we'll drown in a sea of red ink within five years."

Logan, leaning forward, knits his brow. "Aren't you being overpessimistic, Jerry? The last three years have been the best ever and we're finally out of the red on the institute. Besides, we've always shepherded the poor. It's the essence of the gospel. Look at Jesus. All his followers were poor. He even warns about the rich."

"True enough," Jerry replies without emotion. "But Jesus didn't have an exploding TV budget, or a coliseum to pay for, or an airplane on order. Things were different in Bible times, but we're approaching the 21st century, and we must utilize modern technology. The devil's certainly using a hi-tech arsenal to enslave souls. Just look at prime-time TV, the movies, the music, video games, porno cassettes, flashy ads for beer—"

"Okay, okay," Logan cuts in. "I know all that. Just tell me about the money situation."

"Yes sir, that's what I'm coming to." Crenshaw takes a computer printout from his briefcase and quickly scans it with his felt-tip pen. "Let's see. If we project expenditures against revenues, we find that unless we have a significant upscale shift in our membership, we'll go into the red in fiscal '85, and stay in the red thereafter, which means a scale-down of our vision for '85 and beyond, even if the college remains in the black."

Becoming visibly disturbed, Logan removes his glasses, sets them aside—again an ominous sign. He picks up Beckman's stapled papers, rolls them into a tube, and smacks his open hand. "We've been in the red many times," he declares, his voice still powerful but hoarse from fatigue and anxiety—it's now more gravelly than grainy. "But we never bowed down. The body responded and gave and gave, and we triumphed, like when we bought Biddeford, or first came here to Nashua. I'm a soldier! I *thrive* on crisis! I de*test* unbelief! God always honors faith!"

"You're absolutely right, Doctor," Crenshaw replies, backpedaling in masterful yes-man fashion. "God does honor faith, and I too detest negativity. But the Bible also instructs us to be good stewards"—he cleverly returns to the problem—"and God may withhold future blessing if we don't plan wisely."

"Yes, yes, we must be good stewards," Logan impatiently agrees. "But tell me, Jerry ... how much do you see us in the red by '85?"

Crenshaw scans through the pages of the printout. Dr. Logan fidgets, folding and unfolding his hands. Building paranoia blotches his Florida tan. His dark eyes dilate and dart rapidly from Crenshaw to Beckman, and around the room, as if all his enemies are gathered outside the villa preparing to launch an all-out attack. The doctor looks suddenly mad, but also afraid. Jim feels a mixture of fear, revulsion, and pity—perhaps like David when he looked upon King Saul's insanity. Finally finding the figures, Crenshaw reads from the printout, "We'll be short $125,000 in '85, $280,000 in '86, $615,000 in '87, and in '88 it goes up to—"

"That's *enough!*" Dr. Logan shouts. Alarm, turning white, gasping panic. He grabs the neck of his sweater and opens his mouth in a silent scream as if Lucifer is choking him, as if the air has been sucked out of the room. The assembled pastors hold their collective breath, including Shanley.

Logan turns red then blue, but just as he seems on the verge of collapse—*WHOOSH! ka-BOOM!* The air rushes back into the office like the concussion wave from a bomb. Logan, his eyes wild with black fire, springs to his feet and hurls Beckman's report at Crenshaw. "DAMMIT, JERRY! THAT'S NOT GOIN' TO HAP-

PEN! THEY WANT TO BRING ME DOWN! BUT I'M A FIGHTER NOT A LOSER! MY FAITH WILL CRUSH SATAN! THEY'LL NEVER GET ME! *NEVER!*"

Bobbing, weaving, raging like a lunatic, Logan beats the air then slams his fist again and again on the desk. "The Bible says to 'walk by faith,' AND DAMMIT TO HELL, THAT'S HOW I'M GOIN' TO WALK! I was walking by faith before you *gut*less bastards were even saved! So don't tell me we're goin' under! I don't want to hear it! DO YOU UNDER*STAND* ME! NOT AN-OTHER WORD!" Saliva spews from his mouth like hot rain, peppering heads, faces, clothes, but no one dares reach for a hankie. "I'm not discouraged by defeatist talk from a bunch of doubters with computer projections! We're goin' *up,* not down! We're goin' on *more* stations, not less! We'll send *more* teams, not less! We'll buy *three* planes, not just one! I'm sick of your sissified unbelief! I never again want to hear the terms 'cutback' and 'scale-down'! *NEVER AGAIN!* DO YOU UNDERSTAND ME! We're goin' forward on all fronts, always!" The doctor slams the desk again then slumps into his chair like a sulking child. Hot blood pounds in his swollen face as if his head is a huge veiny heart.

Silence. An electric charred-wood smell permeates the air as if lightning has struck. Jim has seen several Logan tantrums, the throwing and spitting and cursing, but this one is especially infantile. The doctor teaches that the Holy Spirit governs the church by filling the leaders with wisdom, patience, and love. But behind the scenes, unbeknown to most of the flock, he runs his church based on what *he* wants and if he doesn't get it, he resorts to temper tantrums and vitriolic bullying. This is another contradiction which has dampened Jim's evangelical fervor over the years.

"It's okay, Pastor," Dick Beckman says breaking the silence. The soothing words seem out of place coming from Beckman's reptilian mouth. "It's going to be all right. Everything's under control. There'll be no cutbacks, no retreat from our goals. Our problem arises not because of defeat but because of *over*prosperity, because your faith, your great vision, has given us many victories, and has taken us beyond our wildest dreams. Most churches don't dare to adventure in faith, as we have."

"I didn't mean to suggest we'd ever lose ground," Crenshaw apologizes as he finally dares to reach up, with a neatly folded handkerchief, and wipe the spit off his forehead. "Losing is not an option. We simply have to choose between regional victory and global victory. If we're going to reach the world, we must acquire more affluent supporters. That's all we're trying to say. There's no risk to our current prosperity. We simply want you to know that the vast capital we need to implement our global vision over the next fifteen years can never be raised from our current economic base. We cannot get 'blood out of a turnip' to use a cliché."

The lines of tension in Logan's forehead relax. His face brightens. His eyes soften. Lucas Simpson hands him a damp towel and a box of tissues. Logan wipes the spit off his chin, the sweat off his brow, then takes a handful of tissues and blows his nose. After rubbing his eyes, he replaces his glasses. "Don't scare me like that," he quips—but the message is serious. "From now on, I just want *good* news."

Laughter, relief. The doctor, grinning triumphantly, sits forward and resumes his role as commander in chief. "Of course, we want the world. We'll launch a three-pronged attack, one from home base, one through the branch ministries, one through our radio-TV outreach. We'll call it 'Project Malachi' from Malachi 3:10, and we want a first class program with emphasis on the loving, forgiving side of God."

"Precisely," Pastor Beckman adds, a cunning glint in his beady Himmler eyes. "We must remember that the rich fear death just as much as the poor. And they have many sinful habits and psychological problems. They're plagued by guilt, especially wealthy women who feel guilty about having money in a world filled with less-fortunate people—which is to *our* considerable advantage." A chorus of snickers and chortles fills the office.

Then Crenshaw says, "We'll start a file on donors who have given a single gift of $500 dollars or more."

"Good starting point," Logan agrees. "Tom, you have the branch pastors do the same, and, Bob, you scan our media lists."

"If we have to," Beckman adds, "we can buy lists of donor names from Jerry Falwell and Pat Robertson. It'll cost us, but it might be worth it in the long run."

* * *

12:47 a.m. Pastor Jim finally gets upstairs to the guest room. Sharon is sleeping soundly on her stomach. He quickly undresses and crawls into bed. *What a long day,* he sighs to himself. *But my talk with Alison turned it all around. She likes it that Becki comes down on Saturdays—course, she wouldn't say that if she knew my fantasies. But why should I be ashamed of impossible dreams? Nothing's happening between me and Becki, not in real life, except I'm caring for her and watching over her. I am a good influence. Now, I just have to convince Shar ... and she can't stay pissed at me, not in Vermont.*

Jim's exhausted but his emotions are wired. His thoughts race from Sharon to Alison to Logan's tantrum, to fucking Sharon in Vermont, to fucking Becki in the woods behind—he kills the thought. How can he reassure Sharon if he's screwing Becki in his mind? He tosses, he turns. He folds and unfolds his pillow. He needs to get off. He slips his hand under his wife's nightgown. Warm flesh. No panties. But Jim quickly reconsiders. She'll be in a better mood after a good night's sleep. He rolls over and stares at a blue-tinted security light on a pole in front of the villa. He thinks about masturbating—with his left hand so he won't disturb Sharon—but with a great exertion of will, he quells the urge, electing to save his rocks to make their reconciliation at the motel even better. He lies still. His penis shrivels to its usual thumby size. Finally, a hundred years later, or so it seems, he falls into a fitful sleep.

* * *

As Jim and Sharon wind their way up Route 9 west of Brattleboro, late-morning sunshine bathes the hills, splashing over the road, the woods, the meadows, the outcroppings of rock. The sunny day invades the shadows, dappling, daubing, dancing, creating a patchwork quilt of light and dark, and quickening the soft spring colors: olive, mint, primrose, rust, amber, buff, and many grays. The sky is high and blue, and cloudless save for a few scribbles of cumulus over the far horizon. The day seems mild but leftover patches of snow among the pines testify to the lingering chill in the air. The radio is tuned to "easy listening" WSRS. Sharon, her legs crossed, taps her knee keeping time to the chugging tempo of Neil Diamond's "Cracklin' Rosie."

Out of Nashua—finally. Jim and Sharon have not settled their argument, but Sharon seems remarkably pleasant as she talks about her fanciful wish of getting an old house in the country and how Alison's kitchen has given her some new ideas. Jim hopes for an easy reconciliation but his buoyant confidence of last night, after talking with Alison, has given way to growing anxiety. Yet his wife's mood is promising, and simply being out of the LBI hype and into sweaters and blue jeans has relaxed the tension between them—or so Jim thinks.

12:00 noon. The news replaces the music. Seizing the moment, Jim snaps off the radio. "So, honey, are you ready to end this silly spat? I'm sorry about yesterday but there's no point in taking this to Manchester with us." He speaks in an optimistic tone hiding his anxiety behind a "fait accompli" grin. And to emphasize the reasonableness of his overture, he gives her a "why not?" gesture with his upturned hand.

Sharon tosses her head to the side as she does when she feels she's the innocent party—which is every time they fight. "You make it sound so trivial," she replies. "But I think it's more than a 'silly spat' ... don't you?" She takes off her sunglasses and begins to clean them with a tissue.

Jim's grin disappears. "Whaddeya mean?"

"What do you *think* I mean?" she bristles as she rubs the blue Serengeti lenses between her fingers and thumb.

Jim starts to reply, to tell her about Alison's endorsement of his ministry-time with Becki, but quickly reconsiders. Sharon despises Alison almost as much as Becki. He tries to think of a better tact, but Sharon interrupts before he can, "This is our old fight, Jim—all over again. I was so *glad* when they moved. Alison, Alison. Becki, Becki, Becki. *Damn* those names! And now they're back. But it's worse because Becki's got tits and hips to go with her devious little mind. She doesn't give a *shit* about you! She's just like her mom. She just wants your time, your attention, your money, your ga-ga adoration, and she's getting it. It's just plain wrong. Besides, you have no business chumming around with a single woman half your age, and you *know* it!"

Down, down, demolished. Sharon's more pissed than Jim thought. His optimistic pretense collapses. He feels panicky, threatened. His thoughts thrash about inside his head like terrified chickens trying to escape a weasel in a dark henhouse. But he does not give up. Letting go of everything except Becki, he fights like a cornered rooster, and Sharon is the weasel; she has the power to end his Saturday happiness. Becki, Becki. It's only been a month, but Jim yearns to be with her. He needs her—even if they never become lovers. He cherishes her. She's given him new life and he must fight to save it. He must get Sharon's blessing, or at least her passive assent. Nothing else matters. No holds barred. He must break her bold assertiveness and put her on the defensive.

"Well, what about you, Sharon?" he counters. "You looked *real* cozy with Tom Hudson last night. Maybe I'm the *one* who should be jealous?" His voice is strong and accusing, and he shakes his finger at his wife as if she's an adulteress taken in the act.

Hot, hot. Sharon's blue eyes burn hot with indignation. "Get *off* it, Jim! We've known Tom and Mary Beth for two years. We were talking ministry talk. One of his secretaries is leaving on a team in June, so he asked me if I'd like a part-time typing job. That's hardly—"

"Offered you a job, did he? That sneaky sonovabitch! So you two can *fool* around in his office like you were doin' last night."

"That's enough, Jim! You have no right."

"I know you, Shar. You're no saint. I know your naughty lust-fantasies."

"Yeah, in bed with you. It's not the same, and you *know* it! So stop twisting things!"

"Well, the way you were flirting, I'm surprised you didn't take the bastard up to our room. You probably soaked your panties *fanta*sizing about his penis!"

"HOW *DARE* YOU ACCUSE ME LIKE THAT!" Sharon explodes, almost choking on her fury. She gestures awkwardly. She hurls her words like stones. "DAMMIT, JAMES DAVID, I'M NOT OVERSEXED LIKE *YOU*! You have the hots for half the women in the church, and now you've added Becki to the list! How dare you suggest I'm like that! I don't take vows lightly! HOW *DARE* YOU!" Her screaming barrage ends, but her blazing eyes continue the attack clawing Jim's face like fiery blue talons. Clawing, clawing, silently clawing.

Hurt, hurt. Rage gives way to hurt feelings and raw nerves. Tears dribble down Sharon's dappled cheeks. She wipes her eyes with the tissue then fidgets nervously with her sunglasses. Guilt gnaws on Jim's conscience but his desperate purpose is accomplished. "I'm sorry, honey," he apologizes. "Really, I am. I'm sorry. That was unfair I admit ... but, Shar, it's not what you *think* with Becki Lea. She needs me, and I just want to help her. She needs someone to father her, to watch over her. I know she takes advantage, but she's not all bad. She's just been through a lot. How would you like to have Alison as a mother?"

Sharon puts on her sunglasses and gazes straight ahead at the road. She bites her underlip, a sign she's feeling insecure. After a shuddering breath and several sniffles, she says, "I just have one question, Jim—and don't you dare lie to me." Sharon blows her nose then asks the question: "Are you in love with her?"

Jim reaches over and caresses her shoulder. "It's not like that, honey," he lies, without hesitation. "You're my only wife. You have my heart. No one, not *even* Becki, can change that."

"Well then," she blurts between sniffles, "do you think about her as a woman, now that she's grown up? I doubt she wants you, but if she ever did, would you take her to a motel?"

"N-no, no way," Jim declares. This is his biggest lie but he tells it eagerly, emphatically, despite his guilty conscience; he's down to his last ounce of mendacity but he senses a breakthrough. "I could never. She's like a daughter. I uh—don't get me wrong, I do look at women, but never Becki." Sharon calms a bit as if she believes him; he's sure she wants to.

"I love you, Shar," he says tenderly after a long moment of silence, "and I cherish our friendship too. I'll always want you."

This is *not* a lie. Jim does love his wife. A mystery but true. A mystery he can't comprehend and often rejects—the dilemma of loving two women. It violates all the rules. His love for Becki is a fire out of control, but it has not consumed his long-held feelings for Sharon. In fact, in Jim's wildest fairy tale, he gets them both, but for the moment he just prays that Sharon will accept Becki as his outreach assistant on Saturdays.

And his prayers are answered. "Well, I still don't like it," Sharon replies speaking ahead toward the curvy highway, "but if you want to put up with her shit once a week, that's up to you, but just don't rub it in my face anymore. And if I ever hear—"

"Now, Shar," Jim cuts in teasingly, "why would I seriously pursue Becki or any woman when I'm married to a sex goddess?" Buoyed by her apparent acquiescence, he shifts to flirting to close the sale—and it works.

Sharon smirks, in spite of herself. "Here it comes, the Shanley bullshit," she kids back. She removes her sunglasses and turns toward him; her eyes soften. "You're impossible, Jim. You're too much." Her smirk breaks into a wide blushing smile. The storm clouds have cleared. The ice is melted. Peace is at hand.

"Well you *are*," he repeats. "You *are* a goddess in the bedroom."

Sliding across the seat, she cuddles close and whispers, "And I want to be the *only* one. So just know this, Mr. Hot Pants. If I ever catch you in bed with Becki, or any woman, I'll kill you both."

Sharon laughs but Jim believes her. She gives him a nibbling but inviting kiss on the side of his mouth. Then becoming more serious, she says, "I'm sorry for getting so upset, but I love you too much to share you."

Sharon becomes quiet, but a coy grin still playing about her rosy mouth tells Jim that she wants to flirt and get into verbal foreplay, her usual mood after making up. Their best sex comes after fights, and the motel's only an hour away. *I don't believe it,* Jim thinks happily. *We're on our way to a sexfest, and Saturday I'll be with Becki Lea—with Sharon's consent and Alison's support. I can't believe I pulled this off.* He notices a cluster of crows on the highway in front of them. As the Grenada approaches, the crows fly up over the road, cawing raucously and flapping their big black wings. The day is still sunny but the blue sky is now dappled with fleecy fair-weather clouds. A prick of lingering guilt signals up from his conscience, but it has no chance; he feels too good.

# Chapter Fifteen

Sunny but cool. 2:05 p.m., Good Friday. East out of North Adams, up, up, up, toward Horseshoe Curve. The Shanleys' one-night stand in Vermont is over—or so Jim thinks. Sharon dozes, her cheeks ruddy warm as if she's still savoring her night of carnal pleasure. *It's a good thing I can hold back,* Jim says to himself. *How can she come so many times, and still want more? I wonder if Becki—O God, I can't think about it.*

Sharon stirs. She stretches downward into her crotch and clasps her thighs around her hands. Her voice is sleepy, wanton, "Oh *drit,* I'm having a wet dream. I never saw such a mean penis. I love it. I want it."

"Who?" Jim asks curiously; lust stirs his soul but not his burned-out body.

No reply, just dusty-blue dilating eyes. One-track mind. Sharon wastes no time. Blue stand-collar blouse. Fingers, buttons, front-hook bra. Her tits roll free inside her shirt, but she leaves the collar buttoned at the top. One nipple, like the pink nose of a kitten, peers out. Jim's penis is exhausted but not his imagination—or his fingers. He reaches over and runs his fingertip around her tawny areola. She sighs. Her nipple grows bigger begging to be twisted. He doesn't disappoint her; it feels like a bumpy gumdrop.

"Oh *drit,* I can't wait," Sharon whispers lustfully. "I have to finish my dream. You can help." She pulls down her jeans and underpants just enough to give Jim access to her crotch. Creamy midriff, belly dimple, curly pubic jungle. Beige panties, juicy slit, swollen clit. "Oh, right there. Do me. Do me."

Heavy breathing, rocking pelvis, determined doll-like face. Horseshoe turn, the car swerves. "Drit, let me do it," she pants.

Quickly adjusting her seat, Sharon reclines as far as she can. Her corn-yellow locks tumble onto the sloping seat back. Higher, higher they ascend the Hoosac Range. Higher, higher, Sharon ascends in wanton fantasy, moaning, groaning, grimacing—then she abruptly stops. Jim is winded just from watching. He teases her between breaths, "I must say, honey, that was a quiet finish."

"I'm *not* done," she sighs breathlessly, her eyes ablaze with unsated desire. "*Too* good. O God ... I want to keep this high." She tucks her chin and grimaces back from the edge, postponing her climax. Her open shirt, still buttoned at the top, A-frames her naked breasts. Her ginger-colored bush, bisected by the panty waistband, looks up the slope of her plumpish belly like a furry beast. A trucker would have quite a view, not a problem on Route 2, but Jim doubts she'd mind; she's drunk on sex. The car is warm like a locker room and smells the same: smoky, sweaty, yet delicate. There's no mistaking the pungent fragrance of his wife's pussy.

"I'm goin' to make this last all the way home," Sharon boasts. "Then I'm goin' to take you, mister, where you've *never* been." As she brags about her sexual prowess, she fingers her pubic hair and plays with the elastic waistband of her underpants.

"You're gonna diddle yourself for two hours?" Jim teases. His mind's ready to fuck her, to turn off on the next side road, but his flesh is too fatigued. His dick is still blah and deflated from their last go at the motel four hours ago, and he barely got it up for that. Sharon's sexual stamina surpasses his by a wide margin.

"Oooh, nice," she sighs as she squeezes her thighs into her crotch. "I can stay here a *long* time." Her voice is dreamy, entranced, dripping with eros. "I still see his penis. It's hot and so big. It's burning up my brain. I love young guys who are sweaty and strong and well-hung. I want them to fuck me and fuck me. Fucking, screwing, there's nothing like it. I crave it. I *just* crave it! I live for this feeling—oh, James David, talk to me dirty, tell me a naughty story. I want to get real earthy in my mind. You can start by guessing who's in my dream."

When drunk on lust, Sharon loves for Jim to make up lewd stories, like *Penthouse* Forum erotica, involving her and some illicit lover, usually someone they know. He doesn't mind since the naughty-talk sessions usually lead to their longest and wildest sex. When sober she'd never admit to such sinful excursions, but when sexually high, the imaginary escapades excite her to no end, renewing her hunger again and again until she wrings every ounce of pleasure out of her aroused flesh.

Jim takes a guess, "It's Tony Liggons?"

"A nice thought," Sharon replies, giving her husband a co-quettish side-glance, "but he's not in *this* dream."

Jim runs down the naughty-lover list: Stan, Russ, Kevin Johnson, Mr. Brenner, Ed Landreth, Tom Hudson, her sister's husband, even Richard Gere. Sharon smirks and flirts, but says no to each, then anxious to get on with it, she makes it easy, "He's a young Italian hunk, and he ate with us Wednesday at noon."

"I thought you said he was empty-headed?"

"Maybe so, but I'm sure not thinking about his brain." Sharon fingers her belly dimple then lifts her breasts one at a time, staring at each erect nipple as if it's an eye. Finally, she sighs and says, "Come on, Jim."

"I thought you could wait all day?"

"I can, but I want to go higher. I want to get *real* naughty."

"Why don't you tell me your dream? That should do the

trick."

"No, you make it up. It happened in Nashua. That's all I'm saying."

"Okay, gal, you asked for it.... It's summer. You're working in Tom Hudson's office. It's late afternoon; you're typing a last letter. Tom and the others are gone. You've been horny all day. You're buzzing and fantasizing. You can't bear the thought of driving back and waiting 'til bedtime. The door's closed. No one will know. You feel sinful but you can't resist. You hafta get off. You push down your pantyhose and panties, and lift your skirt. Oh, *sweet* anticipation, then the door—it's Michael Montanaro. You drop your skirt and move forward under the desk. He comes over and starts to flirt. Nothing new, he teaches at summer session and flirts with you each week. You feast on his muscular body, his bronze face, his sexy eyes."

Jim stops. "D-don't stop," Sharon protests as she mashes her tits roughly. "I'm just starting to feel naughty and earthy. I *love* naughty sex. It feels so good when it's sinful and I fight the temptation, and fight it, and fight it. Sinful sex, I love it. It gets me *so* high ... and it makes me come so hard when I finally give in."

Jim goes on with his erotic tale, "You stare at him, he at you. A black curl falls over his forehead. You smell his cologne. You feel feverish. You fight the urge, but the more you fight the more you want him. You push back. Michael sees your panties around your ankles. You slowly lift your skirt and spread your creamy thighs. You show him all you've got. His eyes flare with desire. He moves closer. You unzip him. Out bobs a dark pulsing cock. It's hairy and hard, and nine inches long. Resting on the arms of the chair, he comes down. You guide his dick to the door but you stop him there, teasing him and yourself. You rub his knob back and forth until it's oozy wet just inside your pussy lips. Your clit swells until it's ready to burst with unsated lust. You need to come so bad. Throbbing, throbbing, his cock is so hot and tempting in your hand. But you resist the fiery sensations and searing need—"

"Oh, I can't *wait!* I can't!" Hands, fingers, denim, cotton, ginger pubic hair. Sharon shoves her jeans and panties down over her knees and spreads her cushiony thighs. Eyes closed, she goes crazy on her clitoris—grimacing, gasping, groaning, gyrating, opening, closing. "O GOD! Help me! Oh, I'm dying! Oh, James David! Oh, fuck me, Michael! Pump me! Pump me! Oh, fuck me hard, you dark hairy bastard! You sweaty Italian hunk! Ram me! Take me! Rape me! Ravage me! Mount me like a wild horse! Oh, hurry, hurry! Yes! Yes! God, here it goes! Oh, glory! I'm gonna go! OH! OH! OH!" She thrusts and recoils again and again, like a cannon firing all its rounds in quick succession. Her long thighs thrash uncontrollably, slamming her wide-spread knees against the door and the radio; her flab shimmies. "OH! OH! AAAAAAAAH! Aaaaaah! ... oooh!" Panting, panting, silent panting.

Deerfield River, picnic tables, Mohawk Trail State Forest. Sharon didn't exactly make it two hours, but ten minutes isn't bad, not for a pastor's wife—who is devout, demure, and very discreet, at least in the daylight.

\* \* \*

"I'd like to be a fly on Logan's shoulder," Russ says as he relaxes back into the broken recliner. "I bet I'd see more than Bible verses." He takes some coffee, not drinking but sucking, then stares at the steam rising from his mug.

Jim steeples his hands under his chin. "It *is* hard to believe, Russ. How can he be celibate with all those sexy women around him? Yet he sounds so convincing from the pulpit, like he's purer than the Pope. But Amy's been with him since I can remember, and all his secretaries are sweet young sugarplums, like that girl, Molly, who gave the testimony, and they flock around him like nymphs around a Greek god."

"He's a liar," Russ chortles scornfully. He pushes his Red Sox cap back on his head; a swatch of rusty-brown hair rolls lazily onto his forehead. "That pious bastard's no more celibate than a barnyard rooster. I bet he porks a lot of young pussy with his old pecker—enough to keep him crowing anyway."

Russ, his brows arched in amused contempt, slowly nods his head and gazes beyond Jim out the window, out at the sunny but chilly Saturday morning. His smoky-green eyes are full of laughter, yet they remain compelling, sensitive, perceptive. With ruddy soft cheeks above a shadow of beard, and a relaxed grin under a handsome nose, he reminds Jim of Captain B. J. Hunnicut on *M\*A\*S\*H,* except Russ has no mustache. Jim sips his coffee then says, "When I'm sitting here with you, I can easily believe it. A horny 'God' figure plus infatuated women equals sex behind the scenes. But when I'm with Logan, I can't even imagine him having a lust thought, much less screwing his secretaries."

Russ narrows his eyes. He speaks out the window as if addressing the pine trees. His voice is firmer, more serious, "So Logan secretly bangs his office girls ... or maybe not? But that's not what bothers me. Everybody lies about sex, but what concerns me, Jim, is what you said about the late-night meeting, the Malachi thing. Let's face it, the whole LBI system is rooted in money, power, and ambition. No wonder Logan preaches so much about obeying authority. No wonder he's into marketing. No wonder he runs his services like Hollywood productions. No wonder he promotes Nashua like it's a *damn* theme park. No wonder he has sly characters like Garrett and Beckman on his staff. Handlers, spin artists, enforcers. He's more power crazy than Reagan *or* Dukakis."

Russ blows out his cheeks as if he's whistling but no whistle comes out. He then gives a toasty grin and goes on, now speaking toward Jim instead of the trees, "And to top it off, Logan makes everyone dress up like they're going to a wedding. I only went to college one semester, in 1963 at U of M, and I only learned one thing—that I can remember anyway. I learned it from my English professor, an eccentric fellow by the name of Larkin. He said, 'Never trust a man when he's wearing a tie.' That's sound advice if you ask me." They both laugh.

"But seriously, Jim, you and I, and Joe and Jodi and Sylvia, and a number of others here in Brendon Falls, we're going in the opposite direction from Logan, at least in our hearts. But what the hell can we do? We may have a separate corporation on paper but not in fact. Nashua's very clever when they set up branch ministries. They divorce themselves from financial responsibility but they maintain control of the board of directors, and our church is no exception. They've got you and me outnumbered three to two, with Logan and Beckman on the board, and Stan. Though I doubt Logan has much desire to get involved locally as long as we send in our monthly money. But someday I fear things are going to blow sky-high, especially since Stan and Carl, and Barry and Leslie, maybe half the church, they worship the bastard. But if a storm is coming, let it come in due season. I don't see any point in taking matters into our own hands.... Of course, the way our budget is getting tighter each month, the due season may come sooner than we think. And it's the Nashua money that's making it tighter."

Jim swivels his chair toward Russ. "Well, I hope the storm holds off. I'm in no hurry to go back to the weather station. And as long as we're part of LBI, Logan's the boss whether we like him or not, whether he's celibate or not ... or godly or money crazy, or just misguided." But Jim doesn't tell Russ his biggest reason for wanting to maintain the status quo with Nashua. He now has a clear track with Rebecca, so this is no time to rock his relationship with Logan. In fact, his heart is beating with anticipation since Becki and Joe are due for prayer meeting in fifteen minutes.

"But Logan *pisses* me off!" Russ exclaims, suddenly venting his rancor. He pushes his mug toward Jim, so hard he spills his coffee. "The way he takes advantage of those starry-eyed girls.

Whether he fucks them or not, he keeps them like concubines and glories over them like a king glories over his harem—and not just girls, but *all* the students; in fact, the whole damn body! He's devious and cruel and dictatorial. He's like Hitler but *worse* because he does it in the name of God! And he—"

A knock on the door stops Russ in midsentence.

Lavender eyes, faded jeans. "Oh, am I interrupting something?" Jodi Donovan asks innocently, but the smirk on her face betrays her pretense.

Russ hops up and ushers her into the office. "No, you're just in time," he quips. "I was just telling Jim what I thought of you, Jodi, and I got so worked up I started to preach, but now I've lost my anointing so you may as well come in. Besides, I have to help Stan fix a light out front." They all laugh then Russ departs.

After closing the door, Jodi pulls a Dunkin' Donuts bag out from behind her, tosses it to Jim, then parks herself sidesaddle on his desk. "We saved two for you," she teases. "We don't want to get fat without you, Jim."

"Thanks a lot," he replies. "I've already moved two holes on my belt since you started bringing me donuts."

She laughs then settles into a shy but affectionate grin. The more time Jim spends with Jodi, the more he trusts her. He likes her honesty and courage. She's a lot like Janet, just older and not as pretty, nor as adamant about women's lib, though she surely stands up for herself. Surprisingly, Jim does not fantasize or feel much sexual desire for Jodi. Ever since their talk at McDonald's, she has seemed more like a sister to him. She leans toward Jim and doodles on his yellow legal pad with a red pen.

"So, how was your honeymoon getaway?" she asks.

Jim opens the donut bag and takes out a large overly-glazed donut. "Well, once we got out of Nashua it was good. In fact, real good." His jaunty grin says more than his words. The glaze on the donut is dry so when he breaks it in two, crusty flakes of sugar crumble onto his sweater-vest and onto his lap. "It seems like Sharon and I get along just fine in bed ... better than ever. But sometimes I think that's the only place we see eye to eye."

Jodi draws stick men with smiley faces. "Ah, heavenly bliss in the marriage bed. Now, that's something I'm still waiting for— but you didn't like Logan's big doin's in Nashua?"

Jim dunks his donut into the last of his coffee, takes a bite, then replies in a pastry-clogged voice, "I was so glad to get out of there. I feel inferior around Logan. He always treats me nice, and I see through most of his bullshit, but he still intimidates me." As with Russ, Jim now shares his true Nashua sentiments with Jodi.

"I'll say," Jodi confesses, twirling the pen like a baton. "I'm never around Dr. Logan that much but just being around him at Alison's house was enough. He got there just as I was getting my strawberry shortcake. I felt like he was watching me. I felt guilty for having dessert at all. And when Doris, Janet, and I came back in after smoking in the car, we got nothing but pious I'm-goin'-to-pray-for-you looks from him and his Nashua gang."

The phone rings. Jodi answers, "Brendon Falls Bible Church.... Yeah, he's right here." She hands the phone to Jim, blows him a kiss, then departs.

"Jimmy honey, I'm so glad I got you now," comes Doris Campbell's inebriated voice. "My marriage ish so bad. I need to talk. I love you, Jimmy honey—"

"I know you do," Jim interjects. "I'll come by later. I promise. I have visits up your way anyway. So, what put you in the dumps?" He immediately regrets asking the question.

"Stanley says I'm a poor excuse. You wouldn't believe what he'sh saying. He saysh I'm a poor excushe. Thash righ', Jimmy honey. Ever shince we went to Nashua on Wednesday. He'sh been yelling at me 'bout how we mush have a godly home an' how I'm ruining it with my drinking. But ish not true, Jimmy honey. You know I don't drink anymore 'shept a little wine on bad daysh."

"Okay, okay, Doris, I'll—"

"And he hollers an' says I'm a slob." Doris rambles right over Jim's attempt to stop her. "An' he says the house ish a pigsty. He saysh the cat shit is stinking up the housh. But you know, Jimmy honey, I clean Midnight's box at leash once a week. You wouldn't believe what he'sh saying, Jimmy honey. He'sh ashamed to take me to Nashua becaush I'm a gosship. But Alishon an' Tricia an' Mary Beth, an' all my friends in Nashua, they gosship more than me. Thash righ'. An' he saysh I'm not in the Spirit becaush I still pray to the Virgin Mary, an' I still smoke, but you know, Jimmy, I've cut way down. I hardly smoke at all. I'm doing good."

Doris pauses. Jim quickly assures her that he'll be over and ends the call before she can get going again; she seems very drunk for so early in the day.

Moments later, Stan Campbell, speak of the devil, gives his patented double knock and opens the office door. Towering wide-shouldered in the doorway, he gives Pastor Jim an obsequious grin. "The secur'ty light out front is fixed," he reports. "Russ 'n I, we jus' went up an' cleaned the 'lectric-eye box. A bird had crapped on it. That's why it wouldn't turn off the last few days."

Wearing greasy Prescott Paper coveralls and holding a gray hard hat, Stan looks like a roughneck on a West Texas oil rig. Jim detects a flicker of friendliness in his dark-blue eyes but it quickly disappears as a dutiful frown takes over his craggy features.

Stan pulls a pair of pliers and a screwdriver out of his pocket. Both tools are spotted with fresh orange rust. "Pastor Jim, I found these lyin' in the grass by the bicycle rack. Russ said Bev 'n Jodi prob'ly left 'em there last week, 'cuz he saw 'em out there fixin' April Cam'ron's bike."

He shakes his hoary head and gives an exasperated sigh. "The women in this church," he goes on to say, "they take tools outa the closet, outa the shed, an' jus' leave 'em lay. I'm findin' stuff *all* over. And things outa the kitchen. I find coffee mugs an' spoons in mos' all the classrooms. You know how *women* are? They're always gabbin', an' they don't think orderly. So they hardly never put things back. There's gotta be more order 'round here. God's not the author of confusion. Ever'thing in this church has a proper place. We gotta get stric' on this."

*Shit, who is he to talk about putting things away?* Jim says emphatically to himself. *His house looks worse than* Sanford and Son? He then responds aloud to Stan's complaint—his usual response—"Why don't you write this up as a policy proposal, Stan, and we'll talk about it at staff meeting in a week or so."

"Good idea," Stan replies. "The teachers gotta learn that this church is God's house, so we gotta keep it lookin' good." He then shifts abruptly to a new subject, "Oh, by the way, Pastor Jim; Pastor Hudson called me yesterday 'bout that new fund-raisin' program."

Jim searches in the side drawer of his desk for a packet of visitation file cards. "How'd he find you, Stan? I thought you're at the mill until six this month?"

"Oh, I got out early," Stan explains as he puts on his gray safety hat. "I came over to hold down the fort, since you were gone. It's a good thing 'cuz Bev was goin' crazy. She's got a lotta head knowledge, but no *wo*man's gonna control a flock of teachers 'n kids without a man.... But anyways, Pastor Hudson says he needs a list of our 'fluent donors, anyone who's given a gift of three hun'erd or more."

Jim gives a snorting laugh as he checks another drawer for the outreach cards. "That list'll be very short, but if you like, you can take care of it yourself. It'll be good experience for you. Angie's got the records and if you have questions, you can ask Russ." Jim has no desire to be involved with Logan's latest money project.

"No problem. I was hopin' you'd let me get involved. I wanna stay tuned to what's goin' on in Nashwa." As Stan replies, he paddle-wheels his thick freckled hands.

Jim finally finds the cards in the pocket of his jacket. "Okay,

Stan, the whole project can be your baby. Just tell Hudson that you're going to be our local director for Project Malachi. He'll brief you on everything you need to know."

Stan eagerly accepts, then excuses himself and heads for the conference room to set up for prayer meeting. But before Jim can get up, he returns. "Oh, Pastor, one more thing."

"What's that, Stan?"

"Your message, Pastor Jim, your afternoon teachin' in Nashwa, it was a haw'mark sermon. Barry played the tape on our way home Wednesday night. I always knew you were loyal to Dr. Logan an' his vision for the world, but I never heard you make it so clear. It did my heart good ... an' Dr. Logan's main message 'spired me like never before. It changed my life."

Having said that, Stan gives a half salute, whirls awkwardly, and disappears into the new wing.

# Chapter Sixteen

"**C**ome *on,* old man," Rebecca yells back from the "big rock" as Pastor Jim emerges from the tree line behind her. About a mile from the church via the meadow, a bit longer following the tracks, the "big rock" is a large outcropping of granite high above the Nashua River.

Jim hustles through the underbrush and joins her on the ledge. "Can't keep up with me, can you, Shanley? Guess old age is catching up with you, huh?" Becki's cheeks and nose are flushed pink, partly from the chill in the air but mainly from running.

Jim pants to get his breath. "I could've beaten you. I didn't know it was a race."

"Yeah, right; you *always* say that," Becki teases around a pink wad of gum. Jim laughs and gives her a bantering love-tap on the shoulder. She playfully punches him back. She's been friendly and frisky all day. She even gave him a warm embrace in his office after prayer meeting. And she shows no indication she even remembers their Nashua fight, and Jim certainly hasn't reminded her. Needless to say, his hopes are up, his spirits high. Becki, Becki. Drunk on Becki. Despite the counsel of his conscience, his heart is intoxicated with romantic dreams and youthful passions. Danger, risk, uncharted waters—yet he's never felt so alive.

Rebecca plops down on the rock and hangs her boots over the edge, not the main cliff but the upper tier. The big rock has two tiers like a giant porch step. The lower ledge, about four feet below them, runs out some fifteen feet to the main dropoff. Jim sits down beside her, on her left. Becki takes her gum out of her mouth, throws it high beyond the cliff, then shoves her fingers into the front pocket of her Levi's. She has some difficulty because her jeans are tight. Finally, she comes out with a crumpled pack of Big Red that holds one piece of gum. She breaks it in two and offers Jim half. He declines so she puts both halves into her mouth. She then puts her hands into the pockets of her ski jacket and gazes wide-eyed at the wooded hills on the other side of the river. As her mouth works vigorously on the fresh gum, her face assumes its natural pout, but her frowny countenance seems softer than usual.

A gentle but chilly breeze kisses Jim's face yet he feels warm after hiking over from the church. Advancing clouds have reduced the sun to a fuzzy yellow spot in the western sky, too dim to cast shadows. Easter promises to be a rainy Sunday. Gentle breeze, cool and gray. Peaceful, peaceful. Escaping to the big rock is a welcome change of pace after a hectic day of outreach. From prayer meeting, they went to Ernie Johnson's where Sarah made them a big hillbilly breakfast: ham, eggs, home fries, grits, lots of toast and jam. Then downtown to talk with the townies. Then to Mill Street, to Cal and Joanne's apartment, where they spent most of their visit playing with Baby Shane. Then across the street to Harry Hinton's where Judy gave them coffee and donuts. Becki held little Cami and seemed right at home. Jim saw no sign of Rebecca's ugly pharisee side that she displayed downtown last Saturday. Next, across the river to see Doris Campbell—she gave them more coffee and her usual drunken monologue. Becki said little, but made immediate friends with Midnight. Finally, to the projects on Fitch Road where they visited Sunday school parents, mostly Hispanics in crowded apartments filled with dark-skinned, big-eyed children, and the spicy aromas of Puerto Rican food.

Jim takes in the view: the river, the dam, the trees, the trestle. The old B&M trestle stirs his train fascination. Stove-black with spots of rust on its riveted girders, it crosses high above the river, supported by five steel towers that look like oil derricks. On the far side the tracks plunge into a tunnel which bores through the high ridge east of the river. Adolescent daredevils have decorated the old bridge with spray-paint graffiti: SBHS CLASS OF '82—SUSIE 4EVER—ELVIS LIVES—LIFE SUCKS!—BOB LUVS KAREN—and many others. Beyond the trestle is Nashoba Dam which holds back Nashoba Reservoir. The granite-faced dam, which is 175 feet high and 1050 feet long, looms massively before them like a blue-gray mountain; it was constructed at the turn of the century to augment the Boston water supply. The river, after exiting the generator gates in the bowels of the dam, foams up into a large circular pool then flows north again toward the falls. Jim and Becki's rock perch is some 200 feet above this part of the river— well above the trestle and a bit higher than the dam.

Pine trees dominate near the dam, but downriver toward the falls (northward), the woods become mixed. The pines are green of course while the hardwoods still display winter umbers and grays under a mist of soft red, the red of new buds. The river itself is dark gray almost black. Just beyond the falls, smoke and steam drift up from the Prescott Paper smokestack. The northeast breeze tilts the plume toward Hadley Hill behind them. There's a hint of oily odor in the air but not the rancid stink of raw-pulp mills.

"Jimmy, do trains still go on that bridge?" Becki asks, her natural frown giving way to an inquisitive face; her velvety voice seems relaxed and intimate.

"There's one that does," he answers. "An old freight train with a blue engine. It comes out in the morning and goes back in the evening. When I first came to Brendon Falls there were commuter trains too but they quit running five years ago."

Becki grins up at Jim with loving eyes. When he smiles back, she blushes and her dimpled grin breaks wide showing her crooked teeth and her gum. Magic, magic, wonder and joy. Warm elation floods Jim's bosom as if his heart is immersed in a hot tub. He hopes she feels it too but he knows she won't tell even if she does. He longs to hug her, to kiss her, to hold her tight. But he dares not. Instead, he slips his arm affectionately around her and gives her a quick squeeze. Her toothy smile gives way to a sheepish half-grin, as if she's trying not to grin. When Jim sees this bashful expression, a flash of knowing tells him that she too feels the warm love-feeling. His expectations soar.

But the sense of shared bliss doesn't last long, as Becki, reassuming her pouty face, pulls her hands out of her pockets and begins to pick at her thumbnail. This worries Jim a bit making him think that his quick one-arm hug bothered her. He still feels good but no longer elated—pigeons, pigeons, perhaps a dozen: gray, white, blue, and mottled brown. They circle over the dam, over the trestle, then fly up under the trestle, under the black girders, where they roost. The stout-bodied birds break the introspective love tension as Becki talks about Maria's pigeons in Puerto Rico, about how they live in a pen behind the house, how they poop worse than chickens and stink, and how the babies hatch out of eggs.

Rebecca seems relieved to direct attention away from herself as if the love vibes between her and Jim were too intense like a spotlight on her heart. Jim doesn't know for sure since she's confessed nothing as yet, but he senses it to be so.

After talking about Maria's pigeons, Becki stares pensively across the river. She chews her gum more slowly. She seems older.

"I wonder what it was like in this town a long time ago," Jim says a bit later, "when the textile mills were goin' full blast and the dam was just built, and trains were coming from all over."

Becki crosses her legs and folds her hands in her lap. "Yeah, I think about the olden days too, like what people thought and felt back then."

"It seems like life was better in those days, more honest or something?"

"It's sad to think they're all dead now ... or wicked old and ready to die."

"And this town died with them. It's like this place has a past, but no future."

"I hated history in high school. It was boring, like su*per* dull ... just facts and dates and shit like that. But I like reading stories that are set in olden times like *Anne of Green Gables* and *Huckleberry*

*Finn* and *Jane Eyre*."

"You've read *Jane Eyre?*" Jim teases, briefly breaking the nostalgic mood.

Becki gives Jim her sassy scrunched-face look then banters back, "Well, I'm not illiterate, you know? I didn't spend *all* my time listening to rock music ... even though my grades never showed it."

They continue to talk about the past gradually gravitating to their own experiences. As they talk, Jim feels the warm elation filling him again. He shares about his boyhood in Texas, about Gary Bob, his father, and about his mom and how he cried when she died. Rebecca talks about her dad, and how it hurt when her mom left him to marry Ed. Jim tells her once again—this time giving more detail—how he met Sharon in New York City when he was a first classman at the Air Force Academy, and had come east with the baseball team. Then Becki asks Jim about the '60s, about the Vietnam War. He tells her that when he first got to Guam and started giving weather briefings to B-52 bomber crews, it didn't seem any different than any other flight briefings, but after several crews didn't come back, the reality of the war impacted upon him.

Becki stretches then bounces her boots against the rock, as if her limbs have fallen asleep. Jim, after picking up a small stone from the ledge beside him, goes on about Vietnam, explaining that he was a hawk at first, but after many planes didn't come back, and especially after his academy roommate Ronnie Samuelson, a fighter pilot, was killed near the DMZ, he began to hate the war. Becki replies that she was too young to appreciate the antiwar activism, but she likes the music of the '60s, and when she listens to Jimmy Hendricks or *Jefferson Airplane,* or Janis Joplin or John Lennon, she gets the feeling that something big was happening back then. Jim rolls the golf-ball-sized stone between his palms.

Becki then talks about Jesus and what he said about war and loving your enemies, and how churches and ministers justify killing by classifying wars as "just" or "unjust." This in turn leads to a discussion of other contradictions between the teachings of Jesus and the doctrines of Dr. Logan. Becki's radical convictions seem almost identical to those of Joe Lareux, convictions that Jim is embracing more and more, and being with Becki is accelerating his shift away from evangelical orthodoxy. But on this cloudy afternoon, the day before Easter, he doesn't care; he just wants to be with Becki as much as he can, as close as he can.

He tosses the rock into the air a few times then holds it quietly. Their conversation slows as well until all is still. The muted whine of a downshifting truck wafts across from Route 72. They stare at the sound without seeing it. The narrow highway parallels the river but is largely hidden behind trees. As the truck sound fades, Jim turns his attention to Rebecca's hands which are again folded demurely on her lap. Small, soft, and high-schoolish, with short unpolished nails, they're far from pretty by modeling standards but to him they're beautiful, almost holy. He longs to take her hand, to hold it affectionately, but he doesn't dare. He's never held her hand except at Saturday prayer meeting where she now sits next to him instead of across the table. Buoyed by the hopeful signs he's seen all day, he thinks she might want him to hold her hand, to take that first step toward romance, but he's not ready for an answer to the big question. For her to reject his advance would crush him.

Becki doesn't seem to notice Jim looking at her hands. She's still gazing into the distance, her eyes filling with a curious and sad longing. "What are you thinking about?" Jim asks as he pockets the rock, and his hands.

"Oh, I dunno. Just something."

"Just what?"

Becki doesn't respond as she continues to stare wide-eyed at the wooded high ground across the river. She chews her gum slowly, deliberately. Seconds tick by, maybe a minute. Finally, she sighs and replies, speaking over the cliff, "Why does it have to be like this?" Her voice, though still soft and youthful, is now filled with an adult sense of resignation.

"Like what?" Jim asks.

"Why does life have to be so yechy? Why does it have to suck so much, and be so sad?" Becki gestures, opening her folded hands like the petals of a flower.

"Sad? What is sad?"

"You know, people keep hoping for happiness. But they don't get it—not even Christians. It's like everyone just grows old and dies without their dreams coming true, least not in this life."

"How d'*you* know? You're only nineteen."

"I know I'm nineteen, but I knew when I was seven."

"How's that?"

Becki rubs her lower lip with the side of her thumb. Her feathery bangs ripple in the breeze. Her countenance seems misty and wistful. "I just know ... 'cause I like sad songs better."

"Sad songs?"

"Yeah, songs about hurt and heartbreak. They feel right and true, but upbeat songs seem false ... just as false as Michael Jackson singing a Pepsi commercial."

"I'm not sure that proves it," Jim asserts. He thinks how Becki's mood has shifted but he doesn't mind her wistfulness as long as he's included.

"No wonder people smoke pot," she sighs, ignoring his assertion as if too engrossed in her own train of thought. "I don't blame Maria or Manny for getting stoned, or Joe, or Cathy and the teenagers. Life can be wicked depressing."

"So, did you smoke pot in Puerto Rico?" Jim asks, arching his eyebrows.

"Yeah, I partied. I smoked a few J's. Everyone did, even the LBI brats."

"How about now ... with Joe?" Becki doesn't reply. Instead, she takes her gum out of her mouth and throws it high above the cliff, but this time the pink wad falls short landing on the lower ledge; it bounces and stops a few inches from the edge.

Jim doesn't press for an answer but spins the question in his mind, *Smoking weed with Joe? She's got more sense than that? Or does she? But I bet she sure partied with Manny? He probably got her high and fucked her in his Camaro? Shit, I'd like to hear her confess—but no way is she gonna tell me about it even if she did.* But the thought turns Jim on. He feels light-headed. His penis lifts against the fly of his jeans. *O God, I can't think on this.*

Colder, getting dark, the breeze is stronger. Jim shifts his weight on his hips as one butt cheek is pinched against an uneven spot in the rock. He should go back to the church so Barry can pick up teenagers around town; he usually helps at the teen center on Saturday night. But he's too intoxicated on Becki to end this time with her. So he zips his jacket and stays put.

Becki gazes into the distance. The wind tosses her hair, opening and closing her bangs like curtains on a window. Her brown locks seem darker, no honey-blond: maple syrup, without sunlight. The raw April air has drawn pink color into her cherub cheeks. On her chin is a scabby pimple, actually several pimples clustered together. Her cupid lips are chapped and the cracks show through the remnants of her lipstick. Plain-faced, pouty-faced, she'll never stand out in a crowd, yet to Jim she's beautiful and enchanting. At her temple, where a man has a sideburn, she has a downy-soft tuft of hair like the fine hock feathers on a young goose. Out of this silky earlock comes a wayward wisp that frolics in the breeze, playing on her cheek. Jim watches this feathery wisp dancing among her faded winter freckles.

Feelings, feelings. His heart overflows with such force that he fears for a moment that his bosom will burst. He knows, as much as he knows that his name is Jim Shanley, that he loves her, desperately, unreservedly, madly, agonizingly—a love that pervades his soul as sunshine pervades a summer day. Flash! He imagines Becki turning and kissing him tenderly then lustfully.

Flash! He pictures her with him in bed naked under the covers. Flash! He sees Becki on top of him, humping, humping, until she comes with screams of joyful release. Flash! He sees himself inside her heart where he feels everything she feels—her joys, her sorrows, her aches, her fears. Flash! He *is* "Becki" and she *is* "him."

Becki dimples into a smirk and gives Jim a glance as if she knows his thoughts. Her blue eyes seem warm, loving, inviting. Elation, elation: *O God, she does love me. I've sensed it all day. She wants to hug me and kiss me. I feel it. O God!* Jim's Becki-passion, like a breaking wave, courses through his soul, hot like the color scarlet, fragrant like roses, crashing like thunder. It rushes, roars, pounds, quickens. His heart lurches, *O Lord, I love her! I hafta tell her. I've waited five years—since she was fourteen, since she was fifteen, since she left for Puerto Rico.*

Rebecca has returned her gaze to the other side of the river where early lights twinkle on the hills. Hot, hot, no turning back. Hope and dread clash in Jim's gut, banging and crashing like dueling knights. His heart is in his throat, hammering to get out. Hot, hot. He feels feverish in spite of the chill wind. His soul shakes in a delirium of anxious anticipation. He takes a deep breath then says, "Becki Lea."

"Yeah?" she replies.

"You know what?"

"What?" Becki says, shifting uneasily as if she *knows what*.

Jim hesitates then lets go, haltingly at first, then bolder, faster, "I just ... I ... well, I just want you to know, Becki, that you're the apple of my eye. You're the most special person on earth to me. I love you. I love being with you. I want to be with you forever. I want to hug you. I want to take care of you. I love you *dearly*."

Blue eyes, blank and big, then a snort and a scowl. No more pink, Becki's face goes white. She hops down onto the lower tier of rock. Jim follows. She goes out to the edge like she's going to jump but she doesn't. Instead, she tucks her chin and hunches her shoulders assuming her shy-turtle pose as if trying to draw her head into her shell. Without looking up, she snarls a reply, "I don't love you *that* way, Jimmy. You're old enough to be my father. I don't wanna be your lover. To even think such a thing is *sick!*"

Shock! Shock! Shooting pain! Hot naked pain! Her words pierce Jim's heart again and again like the fangs of fiery serpents. Ache, ache, burning ache. Now comes the heavy hurt as the vipers release their deadly venom into his blood, *O Jesus! O God! Why did I open my fuckin' mouth! Now I know what I didn't wanna know. O God! I'm so fuckin' outa tune with reality! She doesn't <u>love</u> me. She doesn't <u>want</u> me. It was all in my mind!* Shame and regret rip his conscience like a pair of twisting knives.

Shell shock. Burning tension. Silent standoff. Jim seeks Becki's face, but she turns like a barber's pole keeping her back to him. He feels like jumping off the cliff himself, but instead backpedals to lies and half-truths; he spouts his words into the back of her downturned head, "It's not what you think, Becki Lea. I care for you that's all. I want to be close to you. I didn't mean any harm. I didn't mean I wanted you to go to b—"

"Knock it off, Jimmy Shanley," she snaps, cutting him off. "Your feelings are *sin*ful and *wrong*. I don't wanna hear your feelings. So knock it off, o*kay*."

Jim, his stomach knotting then sinking, stares at the nape of her fair neck which is now splotchy pink with emotion between her fluffy helmet of hair and the collar of her jacket. *What I feared Sharon would do, I've done myself,* he laments silently, as he gestures at the sky. *I've ruined everything. She'll never come back now.* Hope gushes from his mortally injured psyche like blood spurting from a sucking chest wound. *Oh fuck, I'm dying! I can't bear the thought of her leaving. I've got to smooth this over. I need her near me, even if I have to act like her brother the rest of my life.*

Jim meekly tries again, with the same lies and half-truths, "I mean it, Becki. I care for you. It's not what you think. I don't expect anything from—"

"I said *knock* it off!" Becki rebukes sharply. "I don't wanna hear it!"

"WELL, YOU'RE *GONNA* HEAR IT!" Jim erupts, shocked at the exploding boldness of his own voice, at the sudden rage in his soul. Instead of finishing him, her sharp rebuke has set him on fire. He's now a wounded animal, fighting to save his Becki-life at any cost—like Thursday in the car with Sharon.

"You better knock it off!" Becki growls. "Because I'm about to get mad!"

"WELL, I'M ALREADY MAD!" Jim roars. She walks away. He follows. "But I love you, Becki Lea! I do! I LOVE YOU DAMMIT! I HAFTA SAY IT!"

"I don't want you to love me! Not like *that*!"

"Like *what*!"

"I don't want to be the *girl* and you the *guy*, love like *that*!"

"WHAT THE FUCK ARE YOU TALKING ABOUT!" Jim shouts, as if he doesn't know.

Rebecca sucks a deep breath and whirls around. Her face ignites starting with her eyes, "I DON'T WANNA BE YOUR *LOVER*, JIMMY SHANLEY! DO YOU UNDERSTAND! I DIDN'T COME HERE TO *FUCK* YOU!" Her screaming voice echoes off the hills, the dam, and up and down the river, then reverberates inside Jim's brain like a resounding gong. "Just because I had a teenybopper crush on you once doesn't mean I want a romance with you now! I came here to do God's work. I'm not a starry-eyed schoolgirl anymore. Besides, I never had *sexual* feelings for you, even back then!"

"Who said anything about sex?" Jim evades, his voice calmer in hopes of cooling her down. "I just said you're the most special—"

"BUT *SEX* IS WHAT YOU MEANT!" Becki squalls, her angry voice now filling with a sense of hurt and betrayal. "You don't love me like before. You just want my body, now that I have one. You just want me in bed!" Bursting into tears, she runs over, and collapses against the ledge where they were sitting before. She buries her face into her folded arms and sobs and sobs.

Her tears disarm Jim. He wants to comfort her, to hug her, but he doesn't dare. Finally, she lets go of the ledge and sobs out a question, "Why? Why? Why does every beautiful relationship get fucked up by sex? I thought you were my *friend*?"

Still gasping and crying, she falls into Jim's arms. He's asked the same question a hundred times, but he still has no answer so he says nothing. He just holds her tightly. Becki's warm body melts into his embrace but he now feels only paternal love and tender compassion. Fear of losing her has chased lust out of his shaking soul. He loves her. He loves her. *O Jesus, don't let her go,* he prays desperately. *I need her even if I never see her naked.*

Jim smells her hair, her hot breath, her stale perfume. Her tears soak through his vest and shirt. Her crying subsides to sniffles and choking whimpers; he gives her his handkerchief.

"I just don't want anything to mess up our team," Becki says after snuffling and wiping her nose several times. "The devil's trying, but we can't let him."

Jim's heart leaps back from the edge of death. "You mean you still want to hang around with me?"

"Yeah, it's wicked important what we're doin', especially with the teenagers. I wanna tell people about God's love instead of scaring them with judgment and hell. But we must have an understanding, Jimmy: I love you as a special friend, but we can't be intimate with each other. It's impossible and it's wrong. You're married. I care for Sharon and the kids. Besides, I don't wanna do it with you. We can never be lovers. You have to accept that, okay?"

"Oh, I do; it's okay, Becki," Jim readily agrees. At this point he'd cut off his dick to keep her in his life. "What we have is more special anyway. It's God's love. It's not a flesh thing." She doesn't reply but she seems convinced as she relaxes her head against his breast. He pats her shoulder in a fatherly manner.

Murky darkness is descending. The lights on the other side of the river reflect like twinkling stars in the water below them. Jim's sense of reprieve overshadows his disappointment, *Now that I know the door is closed, I can let go of my fairy-tale fantasies once and for all. And my carnal desires will diminish, like right now. I can live with this. And I—BWAAAAAAHWONK!*

A diesel horn blasts through the valley. Jim and Becki both jump as the brassy sound shatters the stillness. Rumbling. Rumbling. Heavy rumbling shakes the hillside; the rock ledge trembles beneath them.

Lumbering out of the darkness like a huffing prehistoric dragon, a blue locomotive, its Gyralite oscillating, roars onto the high trestle, pulling two boxcars, three flatcars, two covered hoppers, and a large tank car. Puffing clouds of oily smoke, the ancient long-nosed diesel pulses, pops, and wheezes—in addition to its heavy diesel whine—as it trundles across the old railroad bridge. The oscillating headlight dances on the rocks above the tunnel entrance. The cars, following slowly but obediently, wobble, screak, and jerk along. No caboose, but behind the tank car, there's a FRED—a flashing rear-end device. The tunnel swallows the engine then the cars. Jim and Becki gaze at the tunnel as the rumble recedes eastward into the bowels of the ridge line, taking the flashing amber light with it.

They share a few comments about the train, then Jim says, "Really, Becki, I'm sorry if I upset you. If you like, I'll take you to Russ's house now. Maybe you'd like to call it a day? I can help Barry by myself tonight."

"Are you kidding?" Becki chortles, her face brightening like a lightbulb coming on. "I'm hungry. We haven't eaten real food since breakfast. Let's go to Bergson's, then I'm gonna beat you at Ping-Pong when we get to the teen center."

Up, down, up, down, then up again. No control. Jim feels like he's trapped on a roller coaster, and it never stops to let him off. Even when his life seems peaceful and orderly, it's just cranking up to the top for the next wild ride.

# Chapter Seventeen

"**M**an, it's in the *fuck*ing air!" Joe exclaims cutting Jim off. "Like angels all around. You don't preach like a Bible teacher, simply *re*hashing the bullshit, but you de*clare* like a witness, like a prophet, like you've seen it with your own *fuck*ing eyes." Joe, as he speaks, unfolds another Sunday school chair, places it in line with the others, then slaps the steel seat twice as if to punctuate his words.

Pastor Jim sighs and leans back against the pool table. He's becoming annoyed at the frequent interruptions. Joe can't seem to wait to make his next point, and he's speaking faster, louder than normal, and using a lot of profanity. After recovering his train of thought, Jim goes on with his story, "It was crazy after that night. I never felt such—"

"I hope you don't mind," Joe cuts in again, "but I smoked half a joint in the car before I came in. Lately I'm dead to God, like dead *shit*. Staying at Barry's is a drag; he brings me down. I know it's Easter but I was in a spiritual coma when I woke up this morning. I needed a boost so I can feel the *fuck*ing anointing."

Jim shakes his head. "So you think pot tunes you into God?"

*Squeak. Screak.* Joe pops open another folding chair. "Hey, when I'm straight, I'm always filled with fucking doubts but one or two hits and I'm a be*liever,* not in Logan's bullshit, but in 'Jesus the man.'"

Jim snorts derisively. "I don't buy it, Joe. I think it's bogus."

"*Bogus?* How the hell can you say that? How can you condemn what you've never tried?" Joe gives Jim a condescending look, as if he should be ashamed for never smoking pot. Joe's expression reminds Jim of how the upperclassmen at the Air Force Academy looked at him when he confessed that he was still a virgin.

"I've never tried dog shit either," Jim declares, hitting the side of the pool table for emphasis. "I don't want some chemical high that *fries* my brain. If I'm gonna get high, I wanna be high on *love,* like with people I care about, or like what happened to me that night. I wasn't taking anything. I wasn't trying to alter my consciousness, yet I felt love and God like never before, like being in heaven."

Joe's moonish face blotches with color. "But what if certain drugs, like pot, enable you to turn on like that whenever you want? What if weed lights up the *fuck*ing tunnels in our mind so we can go through into Shekinah glory, and commune with the *fuck*ing angels?" Joe has a chair in each hand and he jerks them up and down noisily. "Why wait for a fucking vision that comes once in a lifetime, if ever? I can see heaven when I want. Marijuana gives me faith. It takes me out of this hellish life. It should be legal, like wine. How can you dismiss drugs if they *do good*? Besides, all our fucking feelings are chemical—even orgasm is an opiate shooting into the brain. What the hell? Didn't you read Timothy Leary?"

Jim gives an exasperated sigh. "Why should I? He's just a guru for the drug culture. Look what drugs did to Janis Joplin and Lenny Bruce."

"Well, what's better? Dying honest or *living a lie!*" Joe hurls both chairs into the rows he's already set up. Metallic crashing reverberates through the teen center.

"I don't need this shit!" Jim snaps, his annoyance igniting into anger. "I'm goin' to my office."

"No! No! I'm sorry," Joe apologizes, becoming suddenly contrite. "Stay, finish. I like what you're saying. Just because we disagree on drugs doesn't mean we can't agree on God?" Jim doesn't reply but he stays—Sunday, April 3rd. Easter morning. Rainy and raw. It feels like February. Jim arrived at 8:30 and found the church empty except for Joe in the teen center. Carl phoned to say he'd be late and asked Joe to set up for Sunday school.

The animosity in the air gradually dissipates, like smoke when you open the windows. Finally, Jim smiles at Joe and says, "You know I can't stand marijuana, and if anyone else finds out, like Stan. Now he'd wring your neck. But if you—well, just don't smoke it on the property, okay?"

Joe picks up, very gingerly, one of the thrown chairs and unfolds it. "Oh, I won't anymore," he replies sheepishly—and straightly as if Jim's angry rebuff sobered him a bit. "Besides, I only had a few tokes. I'm okay now. I'm not high like stoned out of my mind, so go ahead. I want to hear it. I do.... I won't get on your case anymore."

Jim has his doubts but after a sigh he leans once more against the pool table and goes on, "Like I say ... I felt like I was in God, and God was in me, and God was female. She was wild and uninhibited like a lover yet kind and gentle like a mother. It was like being swallowed by the cosmos, yet having it all happen inside me. It was like sex ... but better. It was beyond the physical, and there was no fear or jealousy or guilt. The intimacy was inclusive, bigger, like I felt connected to all hearts. I felt love and compassion for people. Everyone I saw ... my wife, my kids, my friends, the people at the weather station, strangers on the street, people in cars, teenagers, old people. Whites, Blacks, everybody. I felt a drawing, a wonder, like I wanted to know them, really *know* them, and share their hopes and dreams and dreads and hurts. It's like I knew everyone was good inside despite all the hate and greed and outward badness. It's like I knew the walls are a lie, a lie that says we're ugly and unfit, and must hide from each other behind fig leaves and facades."

"That's some love trip," Joe quips as he picks up the other chair. "No wonder that poem you wrote was so far out. Maybe you *don't* need pot? Maybe you're a natural mystic?"

Jim stretches then hops up and sits on the side of the pool table, dangling his suit-clad legs and wing-tip shoes. He gives a chuckling snort. "I don't know, but the feeling was beautiful and warm. I never knew such bliss. I was euphoric for days, maybe a week, before I came down. Sharon, bless her heart, she thought I was having a breakdown. But even after the ecstasy faded, it was still there inside me. The Love Goddess had changed me. No, *change* is not the word. She opened me up inside. It was like a spiritual earthquake, like a great awakening in my heart, like I knew that *love* was everything, that connecting with God, and with other hearts was all that really mattered. Everything else in life diminished. All the American dream stuff—duty, honor, country, money, career, credentials, climbing the ladder, being the best, having a nice house—it all became so trivial and phony and superficial, like a Budweiser commercial playing over and over again."

Joe, noticeably more relaxed, sits down in one of the Sunday school chairs. He extends and crosses his stocky legs. He takes a deep breath then squeezes against it with his arms. Garish aqua shirt, sleeves rolled. Ugly brown tie. He's dressed tackily. His boots are caked with mud. His hair is getting long, just over his ears. A non-issue at BFBC, but Logan preaches that long hair is a symbol of rebellion. To see Joe rebelling more strongly against Nashua makes Jim feel closer to him, despite the pot.

"But it still puzzles me," Joe replies. "You were in such a pure realm of love and living from within, while LBI is dogmatic and structured. How'd you ever connect up with Pastor Logan?"

Jim gestures in storyteller fashion: "Well, about two weeks after my heart vision, I talked with Pastor Vickers at Valley Baptist where Sharon was a member and I went occasionally. I told him I had a visitation from the Holy Spirit, without getting too specific of course. I knew he couldn't handle the news that God was a warm sensual female who made love to me." They both chortle, Jim so hard that he almost falls off his perch on the pool table. But he quickly regains his balance and his soberness. "No, I was actually ashamed to tell him everything. By this time I was having a lot of second thoughts about what had happened to me."

"So, he hit you with the follow-the-Word shit?" Joe asks.

"Well, not exactly, but in a way. He said God was calling me to the ministry and the love I felt was the Spirit filling me so I'd have compassion for the lost. He knew Logan, so he recommended LBI. He cautioned about getting carried away with feelings. He said that 'ecstatic rapture'—I think that's the term he used—was godly only when it conforms to Bible doctrine, and that the devil often deceives people through their emotions."

"That sounds like Logan," Joe says.

"No kidding. It's the safe thing to say. Sharon told me the same thing, and her mother, though Shar wasn't so enthused about the 'God is calling you' part. But anyway, I knew Vickers and I were tuned to different signals. He talked about people being depraved but I saw them as beautiful and precious, just hidden behind fig leaves. And the love he spoke of seemed dry and canned, whereas the love I'd felt was rapturous and all-consuming and I had no need to check it against the Bible. But as my vision became more memory than immediate, I began to lose confidence. It's like I still hoped but I'd lost the knowing. So when I went to see Vickers, I had a lot of self-doubt. After all, I had no religious training or credentials. Who was I to say anything about spiritual matters? So I took his advice and enrolled at LBI in the fall of '74. I kept my job at the weather station, working odd shifts, and commuted to Nashua."

"But still, Jim, you're different," Joe asserts. "Nashua didn't change you. I can tell. Anyone can tell."

Jim slides off the table. He picks up a pool cue, holds it like a staff, tip pointing up. "Yeh, I've always felt different. Russ says it too. When I'm with Logan, I feel funny in my stomach and I wonder if I'm doin' the right thing, but that's not how it was when love visited me that night. It was beautiful and perfect with no fear or pressure. Now after nine years, I still feel different. I want to follow the Love Goddess but I'm afraid to." Jim taps the cue stick a few times on the tile floor. As he does, he notices muddy footprints around the pool table. Some are Joe's but most are sneakers—teenagers. Barry didn't mop very well, if at all.

Joe's face lights. "So you're a spiritual libertarian? You think we should follow love in our hearts without checking our actions against the Bible, or Logan's latest message?"

"Yeh, that's how I see it. I don't have the balls to do it, or even to preach it, but somehow it seems so right, so pure, to live from within—or at least to express our innermost feelings. It's the only true liberty, and the only way we can really know each other. How can we be one with each other, like Jesus prayed in John seventeen, if we always hide our hearts behind party-line facades?" Jim replaces the stick in the rack at the end of the table then strolls over and looks out at the rain. He elaborates in a voice out the window, "I hint about this in my sermons, but I always deliver it in evangelical wrapping. That's why you can hear my heart yet I still satisfy Stan and Carl and all the Loganites. I preach a double message. I don't share my doubts about Logan except with Russ and Jodi, and now with you"—Jim also shares his doubts with Becki, and he'd like to talk about her, about how she stirs up feelings he hasn't known since the Love Goddess, but he's careful to exclude her, not wanting to focus attention on his relationship with her, especially after her emotional "I don't wanna fuck you" declaration on the big rock yesterday—"and I get confused myself, not in my heart, but when I try to make my feelings fit. Sometimes I think I'm wacko, way out there, like the people who thought the earth was flat." Jim chuckles at himself as he stares at the wet pine trees in the picnic area behind the church.

"I don't see you as wacko," Joe replies, a sense of adventure in his voice that goes beyond the pot. "You're more like Columbus, like on the cutting edge of truth. You want to escape the shackles of orthodox religion and sail to a new world where we can be in love with God, the God who lives within—without all the damnation and duty and 'get right' bullshit.... But I don't have the balls to live it either. The idea of following *my heart* scares the shit out of me."

"No kidding," Jim muses, half to himself, half to Joe. "We all ache for such freedom and honesty, but none of us dare to—"

"I bet we'll have a dozen babies today," sounds a female voice, interrupting Jim. "The only good thing about workin' the nursery on Easter, I don't hafta get dressed up." Puffy eyes, plain features, ash-blond hair formed into an unkempt pony tail. It's Barbara Cameron—no, Sims; it used to be Cameron. Ambling over, she plops down in one of the Sunday school chairs. A shabby raincoat covers all but the cuffs of her corduroys and a pair of worn sneakers. She has a mug of coffee and a bag of peanuts. Her mouth seems lazy and tends to hang open. Outside of church she can found working at the diner, or at Clancy's Pub where she forgets the diner.

A number of BFBC members frequent Clancy's. If the Holy Spirit doesn't move them at church, they can count on Clancy's where the spirits never fail. Pastor Jim and Joe return from the window to where Barbara is sitting. She complains to Jim about the low Pamper supply in the nursery, advising him that there's only a half box left. She says she told Stan about it last Sunday.

But before Jim can reply, another voice echoes through the teen center, "Pastor, can I see you a minute?" It's Carl Baker.

Excusing himself, Jim goes into the corridor with Carl. In a dirty shirt with no tie, Carl looks flustered and disheveled—most unusual for him. He has a day's growth of beard and the monkish fringe around his bald dome is uncombed. He explains that Melissa needs counseling regarding a problem. Jim asks Carl if he's already talked with her about it. "Most definitely, Pastor," Carl answers in his usual confident tone, but Jim senses discouragement in his body language, especially his posture; his tall bony insectlike frame seems bowed and canted, as if burdened with anxiety.

"We believe in being open with each other," Carl goes on. "We've been talking about it all night—in fact, we've been discussing it since we got back from Nashua Wednesday night."

Jim tells Carl to have Melissa wait in his office. After a visit to the men's room, Jim meets her there. Wearing a blue dress with a white belt and lace collar, she's seated in one of the wooden office chairs. Not wanting the desk between them, he pulls up another chair and sits down facing her obliquely.

Melissa, petite, prim, and pretty, with blue eyes and porcelain cheeks, looks like a china doll as she sits in ladylike repose, hands in lap, ankles crossed. Her short black hair is still sleep-mussed, and her face is red from recent tears. She holds a wad of tissue, and on her lap is a pink muff-style handbag. Her voice is whispery and thick as if her throat needs to be brushed out: "I hate to bother you, Pastor Jim, but Carl and I had a long talk"—Jim suspects it was a fight—"and he feels I should tell you everything."

As Jim considers Melissa's forlorn face, his heart is moved. Sharon has told him gossip about her but not recently, so he doesn't rush to conclusions. "You don't hafta talk about it unless you really want to," he says to her. "This isn't the Catholic Church, you know?"

"Oh, I know, Pastor Jim. My parents are French-Canadian and strict Catholics. I went to St. Jerome's in Worcester when I was a girl, and I hated going into that booth thing to confess to the priest. But it's different talking to you. You're more like a friend." She dabs her bleary eyes with the wad of tissue. "I'm so ashamed about this. I never told anyone except Doris"—Doris Campbell is Melissa's best friend in the church—"and I finally told Carl, but not until Wednesday night on our way back from Nashua. After Dr. Logan's message, I knew I had to get right."

Jim pulls down his suit vest where it has ridden up over his paunch—he's wearing his tan corduroy suit, not very dressy for Easter but more comfortable for driving, as the Shanleys are leaving after church for Sharon's parents' in Cobleskill. "I'm not sure I'll have any answers," he replies to Melissa, "but I'll gladly listen." *After what I've been through this week,* he adds silently to himself, *I know I have no answers.*

Shaking her head slowly, she begins, "I've had this secret sin since I was eleven ... but last summer it really got out of hand. It was

**211**

August so I wasn't teaching"—Melissa teaches home economics at Silas Brendon High School—"and Carl's niece Wanda came to stay for a month." Melissa's eyes fill. She begins to sniffle. "Wanda's fifteen, no fourteen then, and I started having these feelings for her, bad feelings, like how I'm supposed to feel for Carl. We always watched *General Hospital* together, and one afternoon we watched it in my bedroom. We were on the bed and I sort of rubbed Wanda's back and I-I—"

Melissa begins to cry, hanging her head and rocking forward.

Quickened with compassion, Jim leans closer and caresses her shoulder. She sobs and coughs and sputters, then blows her nose. When she lays her petite hands back on her lap, Jim holds them both with one of his and says, "I think I get the picture, Melissa. You don't hafta go into details if it's too painful for you."

"I know, Pastor Jim," Melissa replies between sniffles. "But I have to confess it, all of it. It's not like we did anything bad at first. We just rubbed backs. But then my feelings got really out of hand, and I knew the devil was tempting me. The same thing used to happen when I was a teenager and my friend Janice slept over, but with Wanda it was worse."

"Why is that?" Jim asks, letting go of her hands so she can wipe her nose.

"Because now I know about sinful desires and how to follow them. I knew my feelings for Wanda were off, so I vowed to not watch TV on the bed with her anymore. But the next week she came in right after her shower and lay down on the bed, and one thing led to another and we uh, w-we...." Melissa shudders, shakes, then sobs out the dreaded words, "We had *pleasure* together and she's just a child. And it was *all* my fault! It was *so* awful!" She hangs her head in shame. Tears rain onto her lap making dark spots in the light blue fabric of her dress. Jim takes her hand. Her tears feel hot on his skin.

"This all happened last summer," Melissa goes on between sobs and whimpers. "But I didn't tell Carl until this week. He says Lucifer is attacking because we're on the battlefield. I don't know what's wrong with me, Pastor Jim. I should get feelings for Carl, but I never do. I'm *such* a failure as a wife. I keep thinking about Wanda and I feel so wretched because I know what the Bible says about being a lesbian, and I don't know if I am or not? I miss Wanda and I wish we could be close, if only we didn't have this physical thing. It makes it impossible."

Jim knows her inner conflict very well, certainly more than she realizes. He replies tenderly, "It seems that physical feelings always complicate things. But even if it is a sin, what you did with Wanda, I still think your affection for her is a good thing. I know this sounds like double-talk but love seems to always produce contradictions. I used to see things as black-and-white, especially when it came to sexual sin, but now everything's getting sort of gray." He gives a resigned chuckle. "See, I told you I had no answers." Melissa looks at Jim curiously, then grins and gives a snuffly snicker. "But I think you have a good heart, Melissa," he adds, becoming serious again. "And I like talking to you, and being your friend, even if we don't have the answers."

\* \* \*

By the time the Shanleys arrive in Cobleskill the rain has diminished to a chilly mist. Three-and-a-half hours of driving: Worcester, Mass. Pike, Springfield, the Berkshires, New York State Thruway, Albany, Interstate 88, Route 30, finally back roads. Sharon napped from Springfield to Albany. The kids also slept except for Erin. She's had her nose buried in a *Sweet Valley High* romance the entire trip. The Pedersens actually live in the farm country south of Cobleskill. They moved upstate in 1971, from Valley Stream on Long Island. Sharon was born in Brooklyn but they moved to Long Island when she was eleven.

As Jim turns off on Jacob's Hill Road, Heather and Chris wake up. Heather yawns then cuddles back against the door, but Chris looks up and says, "How much longer, Daddy?"

"Not much," Jim replies. "Maybe ten minutes?"

The youngest Shanley sits up and scans for familiar sights. "There's the green fence!" he excitedly announces as he crawls over Heather toward the window. "Lemme hab the window. I gotta see. We're almos' there."

"Get off me, you twirp!" Heather growls.

"Why do I hafta sit in the middle?" Chris complains. "It's not fair."

"Now let's be sweet," Sharon admonishes. "It's Easter and Susie's going to be there, and Crystal and Little Alf and Baby Tim. Let's comb your hair, Chris, and put on your tie. You girls sit up and start getting—"

"Umm ... do I have to sit at the kids' table?" Heather asks, her forehead furrowed by a sleepy scowl. "Why does Erin get to sit with the grown-ups?"

"I doughwanna wear a tie," Chris declares at the same time. "Howcum we habta wear Sunday clothes all day on Easter?"

Erin, looking down her nose, marks her book and moves as far away from her fussing siblings as she can. "You two are so *child*ish," she observes in a condescending teenage tone.

Chris reluctantly leans forward so Sharon can tend to him. "Christopher Martin!" she exclaims. "Look at *you*." His mouth is covered with chocolate as is the front of his blue dress shirt. "I told you not to bring those chocolate eggs with." Pulling a Wash 'n Dry out of her purse, Sharon scrubs him while he squirms and moans with displeasure. In addition to his new shirt, Chris has a new white blazer, and fortunately for him, it's folded in the back window.

The Shanley girls are also decked out for Easter—Erin in a lavender drop-waist dress, Heather in a white cuff-collar top and pink polka-dot skirt, while their mom wears the same apricot outfit she wore to Nashua on Wednesday.

As the Grenada crests Jacob's Hill, a rolling valley spreads out before them. The distant hills look purple in the mist while the nearby fields show a hint of green. Budding trees and a few conifers gather in groves between the grassy meadows. The wet fields glisten with a milky translucence as if covered with cobwebs.

Six cars in the driveway. Two-story farmhouse, old and white, with a large connected barn—but Alfred Pedersen is not a farmer; he's a cost analyst for the New York Thruway Authority in Albany. A quiet graying man, his frame is slender, his manners refined, and he has dusty-blue eyes like Sharon. Alf, or "Pop" as Sharon and the kids call him, is sensitive and kind but seems resigned and rather sad, even when he smiles. When at home, he keeps to himself in his barn office—he's remodeled part of the barn into a den-office—or puttering around outside. The Shanleys pull into the driveway.

Pop, clad in a dark overcoat and a Ben Hogan cap, comes out to greet them along with his two dogs, Harry and Grover—actually Harry Truman and Grover Cleveland. Both are mutts and getting on in years. Jim asked Alf once why he gave them presidential names. His answer was simple yet most profound: "Well, Jim ... how would you like to be called 'Spot'?"

Pop gives everyone hugs and handshakes while the dogs whine and wag excitedly. Before going inside, Pop points out a new birdhouse that he put up in front of the barn—"Vaer saw goo, vaer saw goo!" Nana Pedersen shouts from the porch, summoning them to the dinner table. "Vaer saw goo, vaer saw goo!" She speaks urgently, raucously, like a squawking jay. Sharon instantly herds the kids toward the house. Nana comes halfway down the walk and greets everyone with kisses all around. "Come on, come on," she urges. "Dinner's ready. The children will catch cold. It's so damp and raw. We just about froze at sunrise service. Alf, why didn't you *say* they're here? Everyone's waiting." She casts her words toward Pop as if it's all his fault—even the weather at sunrise service.

Alf doesn't defend himself except to say, "Now, Gretta, we

have plenty of time. The Lord is not coming today." Square-faced with high mottled cheeks and strawberry hair, Gretta Pedersen is shorter but heavier than her daughter, not chubby but stocky and large-boned. She's matronly yet pretty in a country sort of way— though she was never as pretty as Sharon—and she's stylishly attired for Easter in a tulip-print dress and lilac blazer.

After a quick visit upstairs to deposit coats and to visit the bathroom, the Shanleys join the rest of the clan in the dining room and exchange hugs, handshakes, greetings, and pleasantries. "Yah, yah, dis one, he's my favorite," Mor teases affectionately as she hugs Jim then holds onto his arm. "You know vaht, Sharon? I tell you sumpting. Maybe I steal dis young man from you? Yah, yah." Sharon blushes at her grandmother's teasing as everybody laughs.

Mor's real name is Elsa Jensen. Grayheaded, ruddy-faced, and full of vigor, she lives with Gretta and Alf, and still does much of the cooking and housework. She, like Gretta, is a stocky large-boned Norwegian. To Jim, she seems younger than her eighty years, especially her eyes which are emerald green, like a tropical sea on a sunny day.

"Just think," Nana says as the laughing subsides. "We were so concerned about Jim's soul and now he's pastoring his own church. He's putting us all to shame." Everyone heartily agrees; Jim's face warms with embarrassment. Finally, they all sit down and get ready to eat. Jim is glad to be out of the spotlight.

Also present for Easter is Elsa's other daughter, Erika Knudsen. Unlike her sister Gretta, Erika is shy and slightly built, but she has the same strawberry hair. A widow, she lives in Cobleskill. Her one daughter, Dorothy, is Sharon's barren cousin who lives in Toronto. Debbie and Robert are there of course, and Mark and Leslie. Debbie is Sharon's sister. Slim with long blond hair, she has two kids: Crystal (5) and Timmy (10 months). Debbie is quiet, like her dad. Jim likes talking with her—not to mention looking at her perfect legs. Freckled and redheaded, Sharon's brother Mark is a grown-up version of Chris Shanley. He has two children: Susie (11) and Little Alf (3). Completing the group is Mor's brother Olaf who's up from Brooklyn. Short, bald, and barrel-shaped, with huge hands and a bulbous nose, he looks like a cross between Elmer Fudd and Nikita Khrushchev. He smells of cigars and speaks with a deep nasal voice, and like Mor, has a heavy accent. The rest were born or brought up in America and have no accents, but they still use pet Norwegian phrases like "vaer saw goo" and "voo'dahn gawr day" and "tahk fra mahtin."

China, crystal, silver. The Pedersen Easter table is set with Nana's best, along with a vase of daffodils in the center. Over the table hangs a wagon-wheel chandelier with frosted globes, while on the wall behind the table is a painting of an old bearded fellow praying over a loaf of bread. Underneath the painting is a plaque that says: Prayer Changes Things. Pop, like the fellow in the painting, says grace, then comes the food: fresh ham, mashed potatoes, gravy, peas, carrots, creamed cabbage, homemade bread, applesauce, and cider to drink. Mor manages the food and exhorts everyone to eat, especially the men: "Vaht do you need, Olaf. I get you more ham—Bobby, you need sumpting?—Vaht is dis, Gretta? Vee need more gravy—Jimmy, you vant more potatoes? Debbie, pass Jim the potatoes—Erika, voor aer Alf's vater? Vould you get his vater, and turn on dee kahffer?"

Uncle Olaf, grunting and groaning like a barnyard sow, gets as much food on his face as into his mouth. In between bites he says, "I tink dis summer, Alf. I come and vee look. I tink it's time. I vant to move." Olaf has said this at every family gathering since his wife Helga died, but Jim figures that Olaf will die on 61st Street.

Bob, an IBM nerd—Jim finds him obnoxious and figures that Debbie could've done a lot better—shares his latest riddle, "If a chicken and a half can lay an egg and a half in a day and a half, how many eggs can one chicken lay in one day?" Everyone quickly gives up, except Mark who pulls pen and pad out of his pocket, and after covering the notepad with algebraic formulas, ends up in a private debate with Bob over the correct answer.

Leslie, with Sharon's help, tends the children's table in the kitchen. Debbie is occupied with little Timmy who's in a high chair at the main table. Pop says little except a few remarks about the weather, his dogs, and the Jews—how they control all the money in the state. And for the 27th year in a row, he and Olaf lament about the Dodgers moving to Los Angeles, agreeing that Brooklyn will never be the same.

As the meal culminates, the talk gravitates toward church chitchat and finally becomes a gossipy dialogue between Nana and Erika: "It's *such* a shame about Lars Torkelsen—It's the traveling—I feel so sorry for Laila—Lars is having a midlife crisis—Is he *ever*. He's trying to preserve his youth. The girl's but a child—Now his brother has the nerve to suggest that divorced people should be accepted as members—Not to worry. I think Pastor Johansen put that issue to rest this morning." Nana and Erika are both active in the Lutheran Brethren Church, in Cobleskill. Alf is a deacon, but he never talks about church affairs at home.

Finally, it's time for coffee and dessert—chocolate pie, two cream cakes, tons of Norwegian cookies: krumkake, sandkake, fattigmann. Things always loosen up during dessert. Even Nana tells an off-color joke. She has a risqué side that only comes out when she's high on sugar. "There was this fat farmer," she explains. "He was so obese that he went to the doctor and said, 'Doc, I'm so fat I can't see my wee-wee. So when I pee, I miss the toilet.' The doctor told the farmer that he must diet. The farmer looked with amazement at the doctor and said, *'What color?'*"

Everybody howls, especially Olaf who keeps on saying, "Vaht color? I can't see my vee-vee." Turning beet red, he laughs and roars and rumbles until tears come. Finally, he hugs his arm around Nana and says, "I tell you sumpting, Gretta. Dat is funny. Vaht color? I tink dat is funny."

Easter with the Pedersens. Outside, it's still gray and gloomy, and getting dark, but no one notices—except Jim. Though he laughs with everyone, his thoughts are faraway.

\* \* \*

Nashua, seven hours later, actually Hollis. The afterservice rap at Craggy Heights is over and the villa is secure for the night. Easter Sunday has just turned into Monday. Dr. Logan's central chalet is empty save for himself and Molly Gibson. The room is dark except for a fire in the fireplace.

Molly, clad in a turquoise dress, dances near the hearth. The fire casts monstrous terpsichorean shadows of her movements on the log walls and cathedral ceiling. Her dark tresses, glistening like polished mahogany, fly about her shoulders and tumble carelessly down her back. She seems filled with life, like a frisky heifer bounding about a barnyard. She's unskilled as a dancer, almost clumsy, especially with her portly hip-heavy figure, but Logan doesn't mind. In fact, he finds her most provocative as he watches from a sofa in the middle of the room.

Warm onyx pullover, khaki slacks, shoes off. The doctor is relaxed and comfortable as he lies full-length on the rustic couch, his head resting on a large pillow. He beckons to Molly with a "come here" motion of his hand. She stops dancing, scurries over, and plops onto her knees before him. Logan reaches back and turns on a table lamp so he can see her better. The shaded lamp gives off a soft gold light. Molly is flushed and out of breath and still sucking on the Life Saver he gave her before she started dancing.

"So, Molly, did you have a good week?" he asks hoarsely as he turns more onto his side. His grainy sandpaper voice is tired and croupy from all the extra preaching of Easter Week.

"Jus' the best ever," she bubbles between breaths as she rocks back against her heels, her hands on her thighs. "I never expected so much attention from you like being invited to lunch, or being called up to talk on Wednesday night—I was so nervous—an' then tonight when you asked me to stay after the rap. I jus' never expected it."

Logan caresses Molly's shoulder. His tone is kind and fatherly. "Well, I'm glad this busy week is over so we can relax and get to know each other. After all, you've been living up here since January and I've scarcely taken time to talk with you."

"Oh, Pastor, that's okay," Molly replies, crunching the last of her Life Saver. Her big green eyes spark with enchantment. "You're a busy man. You can't spend time with all the secretaries, but I knew you liked me, even last semester, because you always looked at me, and when you asked me to move into your house-dorm, it made me feel special since most people jus' see you when you preach."

"So ... how do you feel about being here alone with me?"

"Well, at first, when you asked me to wait up, I got butterflies. I jus' felt kinda weird about being in the chalet late at night, but now that everyone's gone, I feel more relaxed."

"But just now, did you feel self-conscious ... dancing in front of me?"

Molly gives a sheepish little laugh. "Sorta, yeah, in a way."

"You do seem bashful, but you're very pretty, and I like your shy grin."

"Awh, I'm nuthin' special. I'm jus' ordinary, really."

Logan gently strokes Molly's cheek. She bashfully drops her eyes. "Oh, Molly, you're *far* from ordinary. You're very special, my dear. You're a gift from God. You see, God made some 'vessels unto honor' and some 'vessels unto dishonor.' You're a vessel of honor in my house, a chosen vessel of mercy, fit for the master's use—"

"Yeah, we jus' studied about that," Molly interjects as she looks up at Logan with adoring eyes.

Logan, taking full advantage, runs his hand through her hair then fondles her ear, her neck, her cheek. His worn-out voice drops into a seductive whisper, "You're one of my special ones, Molly. I knew from the first time I saw you. I'm going to take care of you and teach you all about God and life. I want to help you bloom and prosper in your womanhood. I want you to know the fullness of your calling. You see, Molly, God is sovereign which means He can give us special blessings which to some might seem sinful, but in truth are righteous and good for his chosen ones. Your coming here is no accident. You're *truly* a gift from God.... And you're so beautiful, Molly, your heart, your spirit, your face ... and your body is bountiful and *over*flowing with life, like a juicy vineyard *rich* with succulent grapes."

Dreamy-eyed with infatuation, Molly leans forward and gives Logan a hug, then a quick but sensual nibble on his lips. "Oh, *Pas*tor, you're a gift too," she sighs, her inhibitions melting in response to his verbal aphrodisiac. "I've wanted to get closer to you since the first time I heard you preach."

Right on cue with a masterful sense of timing, the doctor adroitly reaches around and unzips her dress.

After their lovemaking which satisfied him but not her—he fucked her in a furious two-minute rush as if purging her of sin—Logan stands and zips up his corduroys. Still breathing heavily, he says, "We'll have more special times, you and me ... but it's *our* secret, okay?"

"Oh yes, I wanna," Molly replies readily—she seems happy to have been fucked by him despite the abrupt one-sided nature of the act. "I do. Jus' whenever."

Getting up from the sofa, she pulls on her underpants. Her copious hips strain against the pink nylon briefs. A doughy bulge of saddlebag fat peers out through a rip in the side where the nylon has split away from the leg elastic. She then gets halfway into her crumpled turquoise dress, and gathers her bra, her pantyhose, her belt, and her pumps. Holding the front of her dress over her loose breasts, she pads barefoot out of the great room, down a hallway, and through a fire door that opens into the dorm wing. The steel door swings open with a whoosh then clicks shut, locking behind her.

Dr. Logan gazes at the vacant hallway. Silence, silence. The dread side of midnight now envelops the villa. Silence and loneliness. He sighs then grabs his shoes and heads for his suite, walking in his socks.

He leaves behind him the disheveled sofa, the lamp on the table, and the dying embers of a once-roaring fire—now just props on an empty stage. Easter Week is over.

# Chapter Eighteen

Thursday, August 18, 1983. The rental truck grinds and roars down High Street. Jim Shanley, his elbow out the window, shifts up, shifts down, then up again. Shimmering heat rises from the asphalt. Exhaust fumes drift in the sultry air along with the stench of garbage. Overhead, an amber disk of sun glares hotly through a dirty haze. Jim adjusts his sunglasses against the brightness. He checks the rearview mirror. Becki is still behind him in the Mustang; her moppy hair hangs disheveled and wilted about her head. In addition to her own things, she has a lot of secondhand stuff that Alison bought for her at the August tag sale on campus: furniture, dishes, odds and ends. So the truck is half full.

Sweaty, sticky, sweltering. The back of Jim's shirt is wet. He likes hot weather but not driving in it, much less wrestling a U-HAUL in traffic. But he's too happy to notice his discomfort. To have Rebecca move to Brendon Falls is beyond all his expectations.

April, May, June, July, now August. After the reluctant green light from Sharon and the Easter Eve fight on the big rock, Jim and Becki's relationship settled into a platonic weekly routine—at least seemingly so. Yet during their many Saturdays together, Jim has grown to love and desire Becki more than ever. Despite her changeable moods, her selfish immaturity, and her professed unavailability for romance, he still sees her as beautiful and provocative and precious beyond words—and worthy to fight for, to lie for, to do anything for. Of course, he's been careful to keep his feelings to himself. He even senses that her heart is growing closer to his. Occasionally, unsated lust, along with the tormenting prospect of unrequited love, throws him into a slough of guilt and discouragement, but overall, it has been a good five months, as the magic of being with Becki usually keeps him above the realm of reason.

And to make matters better: on the third day of August, Alison and Becki had a climactic showdown over the dormitory thing. (Jim, despite his Easter-Week promise to Alison, had never brought up the dorm issue with Becki since he knew it would only make her angry with him.) Alison delivered a final ultimatum: move into the dorm or go back to Puerto Rico. Becki again refused, declaring she was moving to Boston to live with Amelia. Alison then delivered the low blow which turned out to be a most providential plot twist for Jim. Alison called her sister and said if Becki came to Boston, she'd come without money or family blessing. The plan worked as Aunt Amelia withdrew her invitation, telling Becki it would be wiser to wait until she finished college. After hanging up, Becki lit into her mom for interfering with her life.

They fought like cats, pawing, clawing, hissing, crying. Then the twist: in the midst of this fight, Becki declared that if she couldn't go to Boston, she'd go to Brendon Falls and work full-time with Jim, and if he couldn't pay her, she'd work at McDonald's. To Becki's surprise, her mom agreed and immediately called Jim to see if it was okay. Jim, most receptive to the idea—actually out of his mind with excitement—said yes ten different ways, explaining to Alison that Becki could work as a teacher's aide at BFCA, and that he'd find her a place to live.

At the end of High Street, Jim breaks out of traffic, Becki Lea following. They take a right then a left putting them on Reservoir Road. The balky truck lurches as he shifts through the gears. So, except for romance, everything has fallen into place to preserve, enhance, and enlarge Jim's time with Becki. Of course, when Sharon found out Becki was moving down, the Shanleys had a big fight of their own, but after Jim swore his schedule would not change, Sharon cooled down.

Yet overall through the summer, he and Sharon have had few fights over Becki. In fact, Becki often babysits on Sunday so Jim and Sharon can go out to eat after church. Becki takes the kids home in the Mustang and makes them tuna fish sandwiches, and Sheila Bradley usually comes along. Fun big sister. The kids like Becki. And Sharon is even friendly to her. They talk and laugh with each other, but Jim knows that underneath the sweet facade, Sharon hates Becki with jealous eye-clawing hatred. But she's hidden it well all summer—not honest, but good for peace.

Also good for peace is Jim and Sharon's red-hot sex life which has continued into the summer, not that he burns for Becki and screws Sharon—except occasionally on Saturday night after being with Becki all day. Another reason for peace at home is Jim's support for Sharon's new job. In June she began working one day a week for Tom Hudson—typing for Project Malachi. Jim takes care of the kids on Tuesday so she can go to Nashua. He still wonders if Sharon has the hots for Hudson. Unsated lust, amorous yearnings? Maybe this is why she's so insatiable in bed? But she's never confessed, even during her naughty fuck-fantasies, and Jim has never pressed her about it. As long as she doesn't oppose his time with Becki, he sees no reason to rock the status quo.

Otherwise, it's summer in the church. Softball, lazy time. Attendance down, regulars away, academy out of session. Joe Lareux graduated but didn't go out on a team. He kept his job at Alexander's and got a place in Nashua, and has continued to commute to Brendon Falls on weekends, bringing Becki with him until now. Pastor Jim did have a baptism service in July. He performed it but didn't like it. He's never been enthused about dunking new converts in cold water, especially when many come up gagging and coughing. At BFBC there's no baptismal tank, so they do baptisms in Angela Thornton's swimming pool. After the baptism they had a picnic at the church; in fact, during the summer, there's a church picnic every three weeks. Nashua is also more relaxed. Right after the July conference, Dr. Logan and Amy B. departed on their annual trek to visit missionary teams, accompanied by enough staff and students—most pay their own way—to insure that the doctor will have his "peanut gallery" of zealous Loganites wherever he stops. To Jim, it seems like a yearly vacation, since they jet all over the world and stay in posh hotels.

Before reaching the church—a half mile from the church to be exact—Jim and Becki turn left on Taylor Street, then more turns, more narrow streets. Up, up, they go, up Hadley Hill. Reaching the top, they arrive at a tree-lined dead-end street with a tight turn-around circle: Front Street. Freshly patched potholes pockmark the gray, weathered asphalt. There are only five houses, four clustered near the entrance to the short street, while the fifth, a turn-of-the-century-style three-story home, sits by itself near the crest of the hill.

Hip-roofed with dormer windows, and facing northwest directly down Front Street, the boxy house commands the high ground beyond the dead end. Two red-brick chimneys anchor the hips of the roof like a pair of devil's horns. Dirty-white trim, railed country porch, moss-green paint, peeling here and there from narrow clapboards. The old place has an aura of peaceful neglect and comfortable laziness as if a retired farmer in overalls should be rocking on the large porch. A huge oak tree in the front yard gives added country flavor, as does a faded red barn behind the house. The old barn, with vertical-plank walls and a gambrel roof, stands amid broken fences and high weeds. The only nonrural aspect to the setting is an ugly wooden fire escape, like permanent scaffolding, which zigzags up the driveway side of the house.

No farmer, no rocking chair, no overalls, but Barry Buford is waiting on the porch steps in his Prescott work pants and a white BFBC softball jersey. Jim halts the truck in the turnaround so Becki can go ahead of him up the curved gravel driveway which is over a hundred feet long. She puts the Mustang in the parking nook to the right of the house (right as seen from the street) then with Barry directing, Jim backs the U-HAUL up to the front porch. When Jim gets out and looks up at the peeling facade and the many windows, he senses a strange deja vu feeling as if he's greeting an old friend. The third-story (attic) dormer windows seem like a pair of sad eyes looking down at him. The trimwork, circles, swirls, and a bit of gingerbread, plus the bedpost porch columns with scrolled capitals, give the house a Victorian flavor, but it's not overly ornate or garish. An old kitchen stove—with a sprung-open oven door—sits on the porch along with a rolled-up rug and a dead TV. A number of the baluster posts in the porch railing are broken or missing, like a white comb with missing teeth. Rusted script letters under the peak of the porch spell out the address: *Fifty-Nine*.

How did Jim find out about 59 Front Street? This too fell right into place. Judy Kerrigan told him that her sister Ruthie had just moved into a place on Hadley Hill where another apartment was vacant. Judy called Ruthie and got the owner's name. Jim then called the owner, a Mrs. Courtney, who said she had a two-room apartment for $285. When he told her it was for a young woman who was coming to work with the church, she cut the rent to $250.

The BFBC board—actually Jim and Russ, since Stan rarely gets involved with the academy—has allocated $140 per week for Becki's teacher's-aide job, but it's plenty since Jim is paying her rent and telephone. He hasn't told Sharon about this. In fact, he opened a separate checking account with Bank of New England in Hudson so she won't find out—the Shanleys do their regular banking at Comfed on High Street. When Jim went to Hudson to open the account, he felt like a deceitful shit but he's long since left the realm where conscience can affect his Becki-decisions.

Jim has seen the old house often since you can see it from the meadow on the way to the big rock. For that matter, most of the meadow—which crowns Hadley Hill—belongs to Mrs. Courtney. Jim talked to her yesterday when he picked up the keys. Though she lives in the house, on the first floor, he had to get the keys yesterday since she's away today with her daughter. Short, shriveled, and white-haired, with bright turquoise eyes and little tortoise-shell spectacles, Mrs. C. loves to talk and turned his brief stop into an hour-long visit. Jim found her kneeled among the leafy squash vines in her backyard garden. Wearing an old-fashioned sunbonnet, she was attacking the soil with a hand cultivator that looked like a claw. When he finally got her attention—she's hard of hearing— she peered up at him and said, "In *my* day, young man, no 'spectable soul would be let out without a hat." But after fussing at Jim for being bareheaded, Mrs. C. gave him a tour of the grounds then took him to the barn and showed him her purple 1938 Packard. She also took him down to the spooky rock-walled basement to see the fuse box and the ancient oil-fired furnace.

When she walked him back to his car, she talked fondly about the history of the house, explaining that Winston Hadley, an "English chap," cleared the hill and built a home in the mid 1700s—

that's why it's called Hadley Hill. The original structure burned down in 1901 and the current house was built in its place. The hill remained rural until the 1920s when the town built out to it. Yet even when she bought the place in 1962, it was still known as Hadley Farm. Only when she converted to apartments did the house get a numbered address. Jim asked about the name of the street since it seemed odd to have "Front Street" as a dead end at the top of a hill. Mrs. C. explained that in the old days there was one road that ran from downtown up to Hadley Hill; it was called "Front Road." But when they subdivided the hill for development, they abandoned the old road save for a stretch at the bottom and a little piece at the top. The stretch at the bottom became part of Reservoir Road and the little piece at the top became "Front Street."

Pastor Jim unlatches the back of the U-Haul. As he does, Barry kids him about being late. Jim blames it on Becki, she blames it on him, and the three of them banter and laugh as they go up to unlock Becki's apartment, #4 on the second floor which is the first door on the left at the top of the stairs. The apartment is hot and stifling, and musty and dusty, and smells of new carpeting.

An ugly radiator guards each room—old-fashioned steam radiators: black-knobbed, gun-metal gray. Faded buff wallpaper covers the walls. Victorian swirls, circles, and lines embellish the thickly painted woodwork which is yellow from smoke and age. A bug-filled Capiz shell fixture adorns the ceiling in the living room-bedroom. The brown carpet is new but cheap, perhaps $5 a yard at Sears. In the kitchen—a large kitchen which was once a regular room—ugly linoleum covers the floor; it's pea green and worn to the black near the sink. The pine cabinets are also cheap, and poorly installed—the units cant downward from the corner as if the workman was drunk when he put them in. Becki opens the windows. Some are stuck so Jim helps her. When the old windows slide up, the counterweights clunk inside the frame. There's a view from every window, since the house is near the top of Hadley Hill.

Back to the truck. Unloading, lifting, then up the stairs. Jim and Barry carry the furniture and heavy boxes. Becki takes the smaller items. Up and down, up and down, the same porch plank creaks, the screen door squeaks then bangs, and the oak staircase moans with age. With each trip the apartment gets smaller and more cluttered and smells increasingly of cardboard and sweat.

Becki's hair hangs limp and moppish. It's a lighter summery shade of brown, with sun-bleached highlights. Her face is flushed and blotchy from heat and exertion. Perspiry smudges of dirt accent her summer freckles. And her snubby nose is lobster red from sunburn. Yet to Jim, she seems adorable and sexually exciting, and he can hardly take his eyes off of her. Normally, she reacts when he gazes at her, but on this hot afternoon she doesn't seem to mind. She's friendly and frisky and filled with teasing mirth. Since her decision to move down two weeks ago, Jim has noticed a change, like a letting down of her guard, not that she's said anything to retract her Easter Eve denial of romantic feelings, but her sporty butt-wiggling spirit seems to be doing just that. Nonetheless, having been burned before, he's reluctant to read too much into her friskiness, yet he can't help but be encouraged, especially after her unilateral decision to move down.

As they work, Jim tries to suppress his upwelling carnal desires. But he has no chance. Rebecca's summer-ripened body is blooming with that youthful "fuck me" glow that girls get at puberty and lose in their twenties. And when she bends over to pick up her stereo speakers, her ragged polo shirt, which has no buttons, falls away from her chest revealing her pendulous breasts as they slope shyly into her bra. Jim sees all but the nipples. His prick responds instantly, lifting against the left pocket of his pants. To him, the white slopes are the most enticing aspect of a woman's tits because the slope makes you anticipate the nipple. To actually see the nipple is too intense, almost frightening, except during actual lovemaking. Though on the small side of average, Becki's breasts are certainly big enough, and tempting beyond description.

In addition, when she reaches up to put her flea-market iron on the top shelf of a kitchen cabinet, her armpit shows through a rip in her shirt. The crotch of her arm is raw, pink, and goosefleshy, and sports a sweaty whiskery shadow. Her naked underarm makes Jim think of her other more pubescent crotch which he has never seen.

Moreover, each time he goes up the stairs, it seems that Becki is two steps ahead of him, swinging her beefy hips in his face. Her haunches fill her Levi's with that nubile fullness that only a woman's ass can accomplish, and her thighs connect into her bum like a pair of plump sausages, rounded and tempting inside their tight blue-denim skins. Her hips will never make it into *Playboy*—they're too low and fat for modern times; high compact buttocks are now the standard—but they're unspeakably sexy to Jim, like the haunches of a Venetian odalisque, or a Renior nude. He wants to grab them and squeeze them—no, no, much more than that, he wants to peel off her jeans and finger her pussy until she blacks out from orgasmic pleasure.

Finally, they bring up the last item, a secondhand sleep-sofa which is broken down like a swayback mare. The ugly plaid cushions smell of mildew. But their own sweaty bodies outstink the mildew. Sweaty, grimy, grubby, even Becki. Jim's old USAFA gym shirt is clingy wet but not soaked like Barry's softball shirt. Rebecca isn't wet with sweat but she does exude a damp perspiry glow, along with a singular scent. Jim's nose focuses on this most familiar smell. Beyond BO, Becki's flesh has a unique scent, slightly salty, delicately female, yet faintly fragrant like fresh bananas. Her room in Nashua always smelled of this singular aroma even when she wasn't in it. It intoxicates him. Oh, Becki, Becki. Jim wonders how long he can endure having her just five minutes from the church. But he eagerly awaits the test.

* * *

Buddy lowers his block-shaped head over the table right into Becki's face and says, "With whipped cream?" His voice is raspy, his manner gruff.

"Yes," Becki replies, shying back from the waiter. But he doesn't hear so he leans closer and repeats the question. She answers in a louder firmer voice. This time he understands and shuffles away. He goes behind the counter to a glass case full of pies. Buddy, half blind, half deaf, his gray hair dyed sooty-black, slides open the glass case and puts his face close to each pie until he finds a pecan pie. He then lowers his head into a drawer to get a pie cutter. He goes through the same process to get dishes, forks, to squirt Cool Whip, to get two coffees, and to put it all on a tray.

Above the pie case, a long mirror on the wall makes the diner look bigger. Over the mirror near the kitchen door is an old-fashioned Coca-Cola poster that shows a leggy brunette sitting on a beach while a hand reaches in from outside the picture to offer her a Coke. Over the kitchen door itself hangs a Western-style schoolhouse clock, but in ten years Jim has never seen the pendulum move or the hands. The clock always says 2:25 a.m—or p.m?

Jim and Becki have already finished their hot dogs and fries and are preparing to eat their dessert. Sharon and the kids are in Cobleskill for the Pedersen family gathering so Jim has no pressing deadlines. He'll be driving out to join them Sunday after church. Buddy shuffles back to Jim and Becki's booth. Square-face, wide-set eyes, flat pug nose, no chin. He looks like a Pekingese dog. He squints as if it helps him to see better but the expression is grotesque because he closes one eye more than the other. His disposition is perpetually sour. Jim has never seen him smile or make small talk.

Buddy—Jim doesn't know his last name—is in the running for the ugliest person in town along with Aunt Agnes and Ernie Kowalski. But considering his handicaps, he does a better than average job as a waiter. He doesn't write his orders but memorizes them, even for parties of four or more. And unlike the waitresses, he wears no uniform, just a dress shirt and slacks plus an old yellowed apron which is always dirty with ketchup, gravy, and egg.

The Park Street Diner, like Buddy, has a unique personality. Across from the new fire station and the elevated Conrail tracks, the fluted stainless-steel diner is shaped like a shoe box with a kitchen sticking out the back and a small vestibule on the front. It looks right out of the '40s or '50s with large train-style windows and a red border just below the flat roof. Three of the windows sport spider-web cracks where they've been hit by rocks. A '40s-era neon sign on the roof lights up at night with pink letters but four of the letters don't light, so the sign says PA_K _TREE_ DINE_ instead of PARK STREET DINER. The sickly green walls inside give Jim the feeling that he's inside a lima bean with windows.

Decades of cigarette burns frame the rose-formica table where he and Becki are sitting, and the underside feels like the roof of a cave from all the petrified gum. The food is greasy but tolerable as long as you order safe items, not safe in the sense of healthy, but menu items that are hard to screw up—coffee, toast, hot dogs, BLTs, desserts. Jim knows all the safe items, and all the waitresses, including three from the church: Joanne McClusky, Juanita Ramirez, and Barbara Sims. In fact, Juanita met Freddie Bergman (Stan's nephew) at the diner. He was a short-order cook but couldn't handle the pressure, so Flanagan fired him and hired Herschel Hightower. John Flanagan, the eldest of the three Flanagan brothers, owns the diner as well as Clancy's Pub and the liquor store, but he spends most of his time at the liquor store.

In five months of Saturday outreach, Jim and Becki have eaten at the diner many times. They always sit in the same booth, the second from the far end, away from the rest rooms, so they don't smell urine when the bathroom doors open. Otherwise, the eatery has typical "greasy spoon" smells: coffee, bacon, hamburger, french fries—all of which seem especially strong on this muggy evening as the ancient air conditioning is having little success in circulating, much less cooling, the sultry air. But the tile floors are mopped daily, the tables are wiped between customers, and the prices are the lowest in town. You pay at an old-fashioned cash register, the kind where the numbers pop up and a bell rings. Sister Bessie, who must be eighty, runs the register.

In their booth near the window is a jukebox selection console which says: "Three songs: 25¢," but the system hasn't worked in years. The song selections are pre-*Beatles*: Elvis, Ricky Nelson, Brenda Lee, Chubby Checker, Ray Charles, Roy Orbison. Becki always flips through the old titles and teases Jim, "Now these are your songs, Shanley—right out of *Happy Days*." Jim likes the lazy Norman Rockwell tempo at the diner. But, like the town itself, the old eatery has an aura of sad longing. No hype, no glitz, no promotions, it's dying, like so many things "American." It's already dead in fact—Flanagan only runs it as a tax write-off. Yet to Jim, it seems more honest than McDonald's, and the "go-go '80s America" that McDonald's represents.

Jim and Becki eat their pecan pie. Rich, sweet, crunchy. Jim likes to chew it slowly and wash it with sips of coffee, but on this evening he isn't enjoying it as much, for Becki seems to have left her mirthful spirit back at 59 Front Street. It's not that she's indignant with him, a more normal reason for quiet aloofness, but she seems disheartened. Her blue eyes are forlorn and heavy under her matted bangs. Leaning forward, elbow on table, head on hand, she's just picking at her pie.

He suspects the reason. "Feeling a bit homesick, huh?" he says in a gentle voice. "Well, it's a big move to actually be away from home and living by yourself for the first time."

Looking up at Jim, Becki's eyes fill, but she quickly returns her attention to her pie, without replying, as if embarrassed by her childlike display of emotion. Compassion, tender feelings. *O God,* Jim says to himself, *I have so many different feelings for her. I love her as a woman—right or wrong—like earlier when I saw her tits inside her shirt. I love her as a friend. I want to know her soul as much as her body. I love her as a father. I want to meet her needs and protect her. But right now I want to take her home and hold her to my bosom and comfort her like a baby.* He reaches over and caresses her head. She doesn't look up but cuddles against his hand like an affectionate cat.

Jim's loving caress seems to quicken Becki's spirit, for she scrunches her face at him then quips, "Me homesick, are you kidding? I'm glad to be free and to have my own place. I was just missing Skipper a little bit, that's all." Jim gives her a knowing smile. Becki laughs then digs into her pie, shoveling in big bites between gulps of coffee.

"Jimmy," she says a minute later, speaking in a pie-clogged voice.

"What?" he asks.

"There's uh...." She hesitates as she stuffs in another bite. "There's something I really need."

"What's that?"

"You know, I'm gonna be working with Jodi and you in the daytime, and we'll be doin' outreach on weekends, but what about weeknights?"

"Well, what about them?"

Becki finishes her pie, swigs her coffee, then wipes her sticky mouth with her napkin. "Katie's taking my TV to Puerto Rico. So how can I watch *Cheers* and *Dallas* and *Knot's Landing*? The TV was in my room, but it's actually Mom's and she says Katie gets to have it since I brought the new stereo with ... so I guess I need a TV, Jimmy."

Jim gives a fatherly chuckle. "Well, I guess we can go over to Sears one of these days and have a look around."

"Let's go tomorrow," she quickly suggests, taking full advantage of the moment. "That way I won't miss *Dallas* tomorrow night." Jim grins at her Sharon-like maneuvering but doesn't reply. Yet Becki seems satisfied as if she perceives his unspoken yes.

Leaning back, she gazes out the window at the sky; the setting sun hangs over the fire station like a dirty red ball. "Shanley, you know what?" she says in a voice toward the sun.

"What?" he asks, after downing his last swallow of coffee.

Becki gives her sassy scrunchy face then a mischievous smirk. "I like *color* TVs the best," she chortles girlishly.

"Get *outa* here," he kids. Dimpling, blushing, laughing, Becki shows her crooked teeth. Jim shakes his head then laughs with her. He can't help but love her. For Jim Shanley, loving Rebecca Reinhardt is like breathing.

\* \* \*

A large black-and-yellow butterfly flits across the grassy hilltop with Jim and Becki in hot pursuit. Unable to catch it, they chase each other, laughing, frolicking, finally sprawling into the short grass just off the pathway. Becki loves to run and romp. She, like Heather, runs like a tomboy, not like Sharon who runs awkwardly with her knees together. Jim yearns to tickle Becki but her exposed flesh is too tempting to touch. Flesh, flesh, Becki-flesh: youthful, ripe, abundantly exposed. Calves, knees, thighs, cute midriff paunch. Her Red Sox T-shirt has ridden up above her ribs, and she's wearing shorts, corduroy cutoffs.

After catching their breath, they sit up. Becki's cherubic face, red from running and too much sun, has that hot-weather cuteness that makes a college girl look like a high-schooler again. Pink spots of peeling dot her snubby nose complementing the summer freckles on her cheeks. Knees up, legs slightly spread, she leans back on her hands while Jim sits with his arms hooked about his denim-clad knees. Her T-shirt has fallen back over her midriff but her bare legs are almost touching his. Her feet, clad in cotton socks and dirty-white sneakers, do touch—her right foot anyway—the outside of his Pony running shoe. He feels electricity at the touch point, as if a current is flowing from her foot into his. Rebecca, noticing a white blob of milkweed spittle on the swell of her well-shaped calf, leans forward, wipes it off, then rests back on her hands again. To see her bare legs is a rare treat for Jim. She never wears shorts. Her self-deprecating comments explain why, "My skin is so white, Jimmy. I never tan. Yech. I just burn and my legs are short and my knees are knobby, and my thighs are wicked disgusting. All my fat goes there. I must weigh 125. I'm afraid to weigh myself."

True, Becki's genes have given her milky-pale skin and chunky thighs, yet to Jim, her legs are sexually provocative to the point of being unbearable. Her luminous knees, though not gracefully rounded or dimpled, are hardly knobby, especially compared to his own bony knees. Her upper legs are indeed soft and marshmallowy and a bit bulbous—much like Sharon's except shorter—but they're certainly not fat enough to be disgusting. In fact, as Jim studies the dent of flesh where her cutoffs dig into her cushiony inner thigh, he feels hot spurts of blood filling his penis. *Oh, to be Becki's shorts.* The thought dries his mouth. He has to look away. Being Becki's buddy is becoming increasingly frustrating for Jim, especially with her frisky and coquettish spirit of recent days.

Saturday, August 20, 1983. Jim and Becki are in the meadow behind 59 Front Street. A pathway, perhaps an old cowpath, runs from the barn up to this grassy knoll. Instead of doing outreach, Jim came over to help Becki with the last of her unpacking, and they're taking a midday break. Doing things other than outreach is not unusual. They've not advertised it, but they've done fun things all summer—walks around the lake, to the big rock, shopping trips, trips to Buckner's Farm for ice cream. A few times they've gone to the movies at Searstown, and once they took off to Boston for a Red Sox game. That's where Becki got her Red Sox T-shirt. Jim bought it for her.

A hot bright breeze blows from the southwest. The sky is hazy, more amber than blue. Around them, lush summer grass ripples lazily in the light wind—together with milkweed, chickweed, daises, buttercups, Queen Anne's lace, yellow dabs of dandelions, and patches of pursalene. Becki likes the buttercups best. The wall of trees on three sides gives them an added sense of privacy. The cool green of the pines contradicts the hot humid day. But the foliage of the hardwoods has dulled down from the liquid green of early summer when new leaves unfurled moist and bright. The oak leaves are now drier, darker, middle-aged, beginning their curl toward autumn. The maples even show hints of red here and there.

A few glowing goldenrods and nodding asters also signal that summer is past prime. The June wetness is gone from the insect hum. The buzzing undertone of crickets, grasshoppers, and other bugs is now a dry rasp that reminds Jim of Texas; August is the one month when New England can seem like Texas. The dry-grass smell makes him think of September in Gilmer—of sticker burrs, football, new teachers, and green blackboards.

Becki sits forward, a silly elusive expression on her face as women get when they're thinking thoughts they have no intention of divulging. She fingers a patch of clover between her spread legs, evidently looking for the four-leafed variety. The breeze fluffs her browny-blond hair. Her uncombed locks, held to her head by a Nike sweatband, seem wanton and reckless, like her new untamed spirit. In bright sun her highlights look so light that she almost seems dirty-blond instead of brunette.

For a time they sit silently as the fragrance of honeysuckle circulates about them having blown on the wind from the woods. Finally, Becki gives up her search for a four-leafed clover and looks up at Jim. She squints against the sun, a boldness sparking in her eyes; there's something sensual about her lower lids. They seem to bow upward. Jim senses her spirit swimming toward him. He feels vibes of prurient passion as if she's going to pull down her shorts and show him her pussy. His heart skips a beat then thumps excitedly in his bosom. But he has misread—by a wide margin— the extent of her desire to show herself.

"See, Jimmy, when I take a bath, I shave this part down here. That's why it feels bristly. But up here I don't shave." She points at the halo of tawny unshaven hair on her upper legs. To Jim, it looks like the downy fuzz of a boy's beard. To talk about shaving her legs is a far cry from showing her genitals, but it's still the most intimate revelation that she's ever made to him about her body, and it sends another shot of hot blood into his swelling prick which is straining to get out of its bent position imposed by his lifted legs. He must straighten his leg, but before he can move, Becki stands up.

"My legs are burning underneath," she declares. "I got a wicked bad rash from the grass." Turning around, she shows him. Sure enough, on the back of her lower thighs and behind her knees, she's covered with red bumpiness like poison ivy. "I'm going back to put on my jeans," she says, to Jim's relief. Becki in shorts: too much, unless she is ready to take them off. And he, despite the positive signs of the past three weeks, is not about to ask her.

As they head back to the house, a gray-bellied cloud unscrolls overhead briefly covering the sun. The sudden shade gives the meadow a silver sheen. *Building cumulus,* Jim says to himself. *We may have a storm this afternoon.*

* * *

Two hours later. Pastor Jim and Rebecca—she's now in jeans—are back outside. While in the house they had baloney sandwiches, Cheetos, and Pepsi, then he helped her hang her bulletin board, her animal pictures, her potted plants, and her Rod Stewart poster. He also helped her put up copper-colored curtains on her bedroom windows. Sitting on a stone wall on the south side of the meadow just inside the tree line, they've just rubbed on some stinky repellent out of a yellow squeeze bottle to ward off the gnats, blackflies, and mosquitoes that hang back in the woods during the hot part of the day. The pesty insects are not as bad as earlier in the summer but are still bothersome. During their time inside, Jim's passion over Becki's bare legs subsided. Her mood has settled as well—or so he thinks.

They sit near an opening in the rock fence where the path comes out—the path that leads through the woods to the church picnic area. The church sits atop the same ridge line as Hadley Hill. (Hadley Hill is simply the highest point on the ridge before the terrain slopes steeply downward to the Nashua River.) Becki is talking about her early childhood in New Bedford. Mottled sunshine and shadow play on her face and hair. The changing light patterns give her an aura of softness and childlike innocence as she tells how her dad took her and Katie for walks in the park where they fed popcorn to the squirrels, and how he brought stuffed animals, teddy bears and bunnies and other animals, home to her from his job at Woolworth's. They were rejects, damaged or made wrong at the factory, but she loved them nonetheless and still has many of them, as Jim well knows from helping her unpack.

The old stone wall is constructed of various-sized granite rocks which are carefully laid and fitted—more carefully than most New England rock fences which usually look like long piles of rocks rather than squared-off walls—to a height of three feet and a width of two feet. Green on gray: lichens and moss dapple the raw tints of the granite with different hues of green. Woodbine clings to the fitted rocks, the topmost tendrils turning as if to embrace the top stones. Away from the wall, on the meadow side, the rich clusters of the barberry are changing from orange to red, while on the woods side, the poison ivy is now dappled with yellow and brown, and the stems of the pokeweed are turning purple. Pine roots, like buried ribs, run along and under the fence; these roots are especially noticeable where they cross the path.

After a lengthy pause, Becki gets that squinty look with her

232

eyes, this time not from looking at the sun. The expression is inquisitive, curious in nature, like a detective, and yet devilish as if her spirit is sparking with sudden mischief. She shifts abruptly to a new subject that quickly dispels her aura of innocence: "So, Shanley, when's the first time you saw a girl in the raw?"

Jim chokes on the question, yet manages to blurt a two-sentence response about how he saw his cousin Charlotte in the nude. Becki then takes over the conversation and begins to confess her own naughty experiences. She's a bit bashful at first but seems compelled to talk about it as if a prurient wind is blowing in her soul.

As she speaks, she scrapes the large rock she's sitting on with a small pointed stone. Except for a few blushing glances, she carefully averts her eyes and speaks down toward her fingers as she works on the rock. She says it was Mell, her friend Carmella, who taught her about sex and men, that Mell had a bunch of *Hustler* magazines and pictures of naked guys hidden in her basement, and they often looked at them. Jim remembers Mell from his Nashua days. A heavyset Italian girl with dark eyes, she was a cutup and a flirt—and past puberty at eleven and a half.

"Paul lived next door to Mell," Becki explains. "He wore glasses and had lots of pimples." As she talks about Paul, her velvety voice becomes whispery and secretive yet somehow proud. "He was tall and older like fifteen, but he acted like a kid, and Mell bossed him around. Well, it was summer and I was thirteen. It was hot and Mell's mom was gone. We got bored, so we went down and looked at dirty pictures and told dirty jokes until we got into a wicked naughty mood. Now Mell, she was like the boss and she said, We're goin' to play a dirty game. I was glad but scared. Mell told Paul we'd pull down our panties if he'd show us his dick."

New, wild. Jim gulps. Uncharted territory. Earthy, wanton. He can scarcely believe his ears. He can't use his old Becki-map. She seems loose and trancy as if drugged. And her prurience turns him on even more than her bare legs in the meadow. The thought of what she's going to confess sets off tremors of excitement in his stomach, in his penis. He often senses sexual vibes in her animated playfulness, and on occasion she kids obliquely about sexual things, but this is the first time he's seen her openly lewd, yet he loves it and quickly gets drunk on her bawdy spirit, even though he dares not expect anything save frustration and added fuel for his fantasies, along with a bad case of guilt when he gets home. He shifts on the rock to give his swelling dick room in his crotch.

Chuckling into a devilish smirk, Becki tosses the stone away and lifts her legs up onto the wall. She embraces her upfolded legs pulling her knees toward her bosom until her thighs press against her shirt. "Anyway," she elaborates, now speaking down into the intimate chamber between her knees and bosom, "Paul, he said he would, if we'd show our boobs too. Mell said, It's a deal. When she said that, my face got hot. I almost ran but I didn't. We had on shorts and tank tops, and Paul had cutoffs. For a minute we giggled and joked, and I thought maybe Mell was kidding, but then she faced toward Paul and dropped her shorts and underpants to the floor, then me, then Paul. We stared at each other a minute, then sat down in a circle like Indians in a teepee. My skin was so fuckin' white compared to Mell. We pulled off our bras and tops too. Mell's boobs hung all over, but I didn't have much to show."

Jim starts to make a comment but he can't talk; mucus has dried like library paste in his throat. Becki, blushing naughtily, leans back and glances down at her bustline. She then gives Jim her sassy scrunchy-faced look accompanied by a snicker, as if to remind him that she's now at least ample. "So me 'n Mell, and Paul, we just sat there showing our fur. Mine was brand new, but Mell, she had thick black hair and a whole lot of it. Paul's pecker was little and floppy and pink on the end, but it was *so* fuckin' cute. I was hoping he'd get a hard-on like the guys in Mell's pictures, but it stayed little like a mouse." Becki swallows hard as if realizing how much she's exposing herself. "My heart was beating wicked fast. I wanted to touch it but I got scared. So, I jumped up, put on my clothes, and ran home. And I never told anybody ... except Maria." Jim's dick is far from floppy in his pants. He wonders if she notices.

Becki is flying and goes on confessing. She shares about Puerto Rico where she smoked pot at Maria's house and they read dirty comic books and racy novels and *Playgirl* and *Penthouse,* and looked at X-rated pictures that showed everything. She took a bunch home and hid them under her mattress. Her mom caught her reading *Playgirl* once and told Becki she was sinful and oversexed and filled with impure thoughts. Alison ripped up the magazine but didn't find the rest that Becki had hidden.

"Well, isn't it unusual for a girl to look at porno?" Jim asks baiting her. "I thought girls were more into the lovey-dovey side of sex?" He knows full well that Sharon, when aroused, gets just as wanton and lewd and wild as he, moreso in fact, though he's not aware of his wife ever reading smutty magazines. But she certainly gets high on verbal erotica.

Becki gives a ribald grin. "Not this girl, I tellyuh. I always liked looking at dirty pictures, even when I was ten."

Her answer excites Jim to no end. Naughty Becki: earthy, bawdy. So opposite from Becki Lea the wholesome Christian girl, from Becki Lea the pious pharisee. It amazes him that such contradiction can live in the same person. But knowing himself, and Sharon, it shouldn't. He wonders again if Becki masturbates. He suspects she does. If she gets turned on enough to talk about it, she must do something about it when alone, but no way could he ever ask her about such a taboo subject.

In his younger days Jim could hardly imagine girls getting horny and getting off, even though he did, at least twice a week, despite the guilt, from the time he was thirteen until he got married. Nor could he imagine them looking at pornography, though he did, every scrap he could get his hands on. The girls he knew in high school, at least most of them, seemed so good and pure in their soft pleated skirts and frilly white blouses. Oh, he made out with a few, and even fondled Betty Sue Barnett's tits in tenth grade, but she was different. She was Jason's little sister and considered to be loose. Jason was Jim's older friend, two years older. He lived in town and Jim often went over to his house after school. Betty Sue was the first girl Jim ever kissed, but he never got into her panties, or saw her naked. He never even saw her breasts in fact; he just felt them up while they were still inside her shirt.

Leaves rustle overhead in the freshening wind, but it's too high up to touch them. Becki goes on about her high school days in Puerto Rico. The LBI team had a cabin on the beach. Nobody used it much. Manny took Becki and Maria there in his Camaro. He usually dropped them off because he had to work, but sometimes he stayed. "Manny, he was old," Becki says, "like four years older and wicked good-looking. He had wavy hair and a tattoo of a heart on his arm. He wasn't lazy like the other spics. He had a good job at the Holiday Inn." Jim asks her if she liked that cabin better than Mell's basement. "I'm not tellin'," she replies, giving a blushing sidelong glance as if she's remembering something too embarrassing, or too good, to talk about. Letting go of her legs, Rebecca leans back on her hands and slowly opens and closes her knees. She looks feverish, and not from the weather. Jim, feasting on her crotch, imagines the tight denim taking on the shape of a swelling pussy. She catches him staring. He quickly turns away and looks toward the meadow. Normally fuel for a fight, but not this day. Becki seems to want Jim to look and appreciate that she's nubile and ripe and turned on to guys—as long as he's not the guy.

*O God, she wants it,* he declares to himself. *She wants to fuck. It's just not me, that's all—what a curse. But I bet she'd like to impale herself on Manny's cock or make it with hunky guys at the college, even Joe Lareux. She's got that hot crazy glow like Sharon gets when she needs to come. O God, if she is a virgin, she doesn't wanna be I bet.* Jim wants to pull down her jeans and screw her right there on the wall. But he's still too gun-shy to initiate. Though her new frolicsome spirit has encouraged him, and has led to flirting, wrestling, and romping sessions, and now to a red-hot confession, he's still too afraid of rejection to make the first move—he has no desire to get zapped again like in April. After all, she might be confiding in him simply as a buddy, and her antsy-pantsy prurience is no more than a safety-valve rush of pent-up eros. She has to tell someone, so she tells him, as if he's Maria or Mell. To dismiss her wantonness in such a fashion may not be rational, but Jim is never rational when it comes to Rebecca.

Nonetheless, he's so turned on that his overfull gonads are aching. Blue balls. Blue balls. Becki, Becki, Sharon, Sharon. He'll go home and fuck Sharon—no, Sharon's still in Cobleskill. He'll have to jerk off in the shower. Becki, Sharon, rabbit, rabbit. He's saved by a rabbit. A small bunny hops out of the underbrush and starts munching grass at the edge of the meadow.

Becki sees it. "Look, Jimmy, it's a baby cottontail." Slowly slipping off the stone wall, she tries to sneak up on the cute little critter, but the bunny scampers back into the woods. When Becki returns to the wall, she quickly withdraws into her quiet I-showed-you-too-much—in this case, *way*-too-much—mood.

They sit pensively for a time. Jim's hard-on quickly gives way to guilt as if the whole conversation was his fault. Becki looks ashamed as well, but Jim interprets it as disgust with him. But his session of self-hatred is short-lived, as a rumble of thunder rolls over the meadow and a gust of cool wind whips through the trees bringing with it the aroma of rain.

They run into the meadow, to the top of the hill, just in time to see black clouds boiling in from the west. The chill wind raises goose bumps on their bare arms. Lightning splits the darkening sky. Thunder booms. A strong gust whips the grass. The trees heave and thrash. Now comes the rain: big icy drops, then a deluge.

Run, run—against wind and rain. Jim and Becki dash back to the house, but by the time they get to the front porch, they're soaked. The rain roars on the porch roof and pours off the eaves, while thick ropes of water, like long liquid snakes, twist off the roof where the eaves come together. Panting, laughing, they drip on the wide porch planks. Becki's hair, now wet and dark, is plastered down under her Nike sweatband. Her soaked Red Sox T-shirt is molded to her like a second skin. Her breasts slosh and shiver in her very visible bra as if she's wearing a bikini swimsuit and just came out of the pool. But the cold rain has cooled Jim's lust, though his swollen testicles still ache. They feel like baseballs between his legs.

The talk on the fence was bawdy, lascivious, and undeniably

sinful for two soldiers of Christ, yet it seems to Jim that Becki's prurient sharing has somehow brought their relationship into a new place, as if they've crossed a deep and dangerous Rubicon, whether she fucks him, flesh to flesh—that would be the ultimate—or just talks about her sexual experiences and fantasies. Either way, it's a perilous and illicit place, and they're over there *together*.

* * *

Two outs. Three-and-two on the batter. Pastor Jim, playing second base, crouches hoping for a ground ball. Kyle Donovan pitches—a screaming line drive. Jim's stomach sinks. No chance. No chance. Like a shot the ball heads for left-center field. Tony dashes, makes a futile dive, but can't come up with it, and the winning run scores easily from second base. It's all over. Softball is over for another year. The red-shirted Flanagan players go crazy, hugging, jumping, yelling, diving into a pile of ecstatic entwined bodies around home plate—as if having an orgy. But the white-shirted BFBC Crusaders trudge dejectedly off the field.

Shanley hates to lose to any team, but to be eliminated by Steve Flanagan's team is the worst-possible playoff scenario. After bagging the equipment and throwing it into Stan's pickup, the BFBC players follow Pastor Jim to the shade of a large oak tree for a team talk. The tree is beyond the left-field fence not far from the river. It's the last Sunday of August, not hot like last week, but warm enough and rather humid. The sweaty, dirty, defeated Crusaders, in blue hats, grimy shirts, and gray dust-covered pants, sit and sprawl under the tree, bitching and moaning among assorted gloves and personal bats. Tony Liggon's pants are ripped open exposing his mocha-colored knee which sports a juicy red strawberry. Kyle Donovan, his huge beerbelly hanging out from under his too-small shirt, seems devastated as if his life has ended—it has, at least until next season. "Those fuckin' *um*pires!" he mutters bitterly. "They took it from us in the sixth innin'. If it wasn't for those *blind* bastards we woulda never gone to extra innin's!" The crushing defeat has removed all restraint on language.

Sharon and all the BFBC fans wait in the parking area. The meeting is for players only. That is except for Rebecca Lea. She keeps score at all the games, and scorebook in hand, she always comes to the postgame meetings as if she's a player. Pastor Jim, trying to console the team, explains that finishing third out of eight teams is not so bad and that having Jesus Christ is far better than any trophy. But his words ring hollow. The players smile weakly but are not moved except when Kyle cuts in and says, "We'll get those fuckers next year!" When he says that, everybody exclaims, "Yeah! Yeah!" And there's a burst of vows—vows of revenge.

After the team meeting Barry Buford asks Pastor Jim if he can talk with him alone, so they walk down to the river. Despite last week's cloudburst, the river is low as it normally is in late summer. The mucky riverbank is littered with debris especially old tires and rusty shopping carts. Jim has always wondered how so many shopping carts end up in the Nashua River when Stop & Shop is on the other side of town. "So what's on your mind, Barry?" he asks as he picks up a rock and tosses it into the river. "Are you still ticked off about batting seventh instead of third?"

Barry doesn't answer but gazes wide-eyed into the water. The water is murky, mossy, dirty-green. He takes off his Crusader cap and wipes the sweat off his brow. His curly black locks tumble onto his forehead. He fidgets with the hat, he gives a sigh. There's no sign of his boyish smile. His mood seems somber and heavy like a dark November day. Jim quickly realizes that Barry has much bigger things on his mind than his spot in the batting order. Finally, after replacing his hat, he says, "Jim, you remember the Monday night course you taught in the spring? The one about David and Jonathan?" His voice is filled with apprehension.

"Yeh, I remember," Jim replies.

"Well, you know how you said that David was your favorite guy in the whole Bible next to Jesus ... because he lived from his heart?"

"Yeh, King David, I like how he followed God with gut feelings."

"That's my problem. I've got these feelings, see, but I don't know if they're coming from my own deceitful heart, or from God who's living *in* my heart?" Barry's pudgy face darkens as if a war is raging inside him. He begins to breathe rapidly in short panicky spurts as if he's approaching orgasm or death—or both.

"What kind of feelings?" Jim asks, his voice dry and cracking. Barry's distress is shaking him up a bit.

White, white, ashy white. Barry blanches then gasps as if he can't breathe. His fat eyes bulge like they're about to pop out of their sockets. Finally catching his wind, he quickly blurts, "I can't! I can't! I *just* can't!" He then takes off running, back by the oak tree, back toward the softball field. As he approaches the parking area, he slows to a waddling trot. Jim watches until he gets into his white Toyota and speeds away on Water Street.

Turning back to the river, Jim gazes at the murky green water flowing slowly and slowly. It's late August and the river is low and lazy.

# Chapter Nineteen

The phone rings. Pastor Jim answers. It's Russ: "I have the preliminary figures for the 3rd quarter, Jim, and they're worse than I expected. Looks like September's going to take the whole quarter into the red."

"What happened?" Jim asks. "We haven't done any big spending since May?"

"It's the money going to Nashua, especially the extra for the bullshit Moody fund, plus the hundred a month to the Landreths?"

"So, what d'you suggest we do?" Jim feels a pang of anxiety as he now does about anything that can conceivably threaten his Becki-rich status quo.

"Nothing now," Russ says, chasing Jim's anxiety. "We have enough cash to go for a while, but if things don't turn around the last quarter, we'll have to act in January. I'll give you the summer figures at church tonight.... Oh, and I just want to wish you and Miss Reinhardt well on your afternoon projects." Russ laughs. Jim still hasn't confessed his true Becki-feelings to Russ, but Russ acts as though he has.

Tuesday, September 27, 1983. Cloudy and rainy. Jim is just back from Bergson's, where he lunched with Doris, Bev, and Leslie. Barbara Sims was the main topic at lunch as the three women politely roasted her for drinking and being tacky, and for bringing up foulmouthed children who show no respect for God or their teachers. Of course, the BFBC ladies referred to Barbara's faults as prayer needs. Jim didn't like the condescending tone of the conversation but he offered no defense of Barbara. His thoughts were elsewhere, dwelling on matters that might've been—he fears anyway—the gossip topic had he not been present.

He swivels his chair toward the open window. Leaning back, he listens to the collective *shhhhh* of the peaceful September rain. He likes rainy-day sounds, the *pit-pit-pit* of water dripping off the eaves and the muted adhesive *rrrr-ip* of cars passing on Reservoir Road. He feels butterflies of anticipation; Becki will be finished with her teacher's-aide duties in twenty minutes. As a part of her job, she accompanies him on his afternoon visits, or helps him with other ministry projects. Jodi lets her go at 1:30 p.m. Jim arranged Becki's schedule this way and it's perfect for him. He now has an official reason to be with her on weekdays as well as Saturdays, without taking any additional time away from home. And on many days his afternoon "project" is hardly ministry related.

\* \* \*

239

Musty darkness, pink denim, bare calves, white socks, new Reebok sneakers. Becki, shifting her hips and swishing her skirt, hurries up the stairs. Jim follows. Reaching her door, she puts in the key and pushes it open. Bathsheba is waiting and rubs against Rebecca's legs as hungry cats do when you first get home. Leftover breakfast-smells fight the litter box for control of Jim's nostrils, but he ignores both as he tunes in to the unique background scent, the unique scent of Becki herself; it's like banana oil with a pinch of salt. Not strong, yet it now brands the apartment as her own.

Becki tosses her keys and teaching satchel onto the counter, hangs her shoulder bag on a chair, and picks up her kitten—all in one motion. Bathsheba is five months old and black as coal, with yellow eyes and big pointy ears. Cuddling the cat, Becki kisses her nose, tickles her tummy, and talks baby talk. The purring kitten places her paw on Becki's chin then wiggles, wanting down. Becki puts her down and she makes a beeline for her dish by the refrigerator. Becki opens a can of Nine Lives tuna, scrapes some into the dish, pours some Kitten Chow into her dry-food bowl, then replenishes her water. After returning the Kitten Chow to the cupboard, she puts a plastic lid on the Nine Lives can, puts it in the fridge, washes her hands, dries on a dish towel, opens both kitchen windows, skips into her room, peels off her jacket, flips on her stereo, and closes the door. "The Long Run" by the *Eagles* sounds through the door. And all this happens in less than a minute, as if a honey-brown whirlwind just blew into the apartment.

A greasy skillet on the stove plus leftover sausage and French toast glued to a syrupy plate by the sink tell Jim that she made an equally quick morning departure. Alison's old Coca-Cola clock hangs above the refrigerator. It says 2:01 p.m., having just completed its end-of-hour groaning cycle. Jim slips out of his sport coat, pulls off his tie, and sits down at the kitchen table. The garage-sale table has one short leg, so it rocks when he leans upon it. On the table is a section of the *Worcester Sunday Telegram*. The newspaper is full of holes where Becki has cut out coupons. Bathsheba eats her food; she jerks her head as cats do when they eat meat.

The fishy metallic cat-food stink fills the kitchen. Jim opens the window a bit wider. The lacy white curtains balloon over the table as fresh air blows in. He leans closer to the south-facing window and inhales the sweet fragrance of the meadow grass. It reminds him of the hayfields back home. The rain has just stopped but the *drip-drip* of water continues, from the roof above. Behind the house the wet and wilted cornstalks in Mrs. Courtney's vegetable garden hang limp despite a freshening breeze. The ripe pumpkins look like orange basketballs half hidden in their leafy vines. Behind Becki's door "The Long Run" gives way to "Heart-ache Tonite." *What's taking her so long?* Jim asks himself.

At BFBC everyone has resumed their busy routines: working, planning, pushing, pressing—Stan, Carl, Barry, the teachers. Same goes for Logan, Garrett, Beckman, Hudson, all the troops in Nashua. Autumn brings rededication to ministry goals. Russ isn't pushing or pressing, but even he has left summer behind.

But not Jim Shanley, he's still living in August. He's happy and having fun—at least a good part of the time—but he feels like he's playing hooky from life, like how he felt in fifth grade when he'd fake a sore throat so he could stay home and sort his baseball cards and watch *Amos 'n Andy* and *My Little Margie* on the Shanleys' new Motorola television. He liked staying home, but he felt guilty about having fun when the other kids were in school. Actually, Pastor Jim is just as busy as Stan and the others, perhaps moreso, but now his hectic schedule revolves around Rebecca. The ministry is important only insofar as it provides opportunity to be with Becki and gives official sanction to their togetherness.

And being with Becki continues to be an emotional roller-coaster ride, but he feels the overall trend is up—though she's still said nothing to rebut her April denial of romantic intentions. Not all is rosy of course. At times, Jim burns with impatience waiting for Becki to make a move. He wonders how she can frolic and flirt and talk lewdly with him without having at least a twitch in her twat for *his* dick. He wants to kiss her more than ever, but he's still too afraid to initiate. Doubts, doubts, lingering doubts. He won't truly believe she wants *him* until she grabs him and unbuckles his belt.

Sometimes he knows he has to make it with her or die, but on other days he feels laid-back and patient, like he could be with her fifty years without fucking or fooling around—if necessary to preserve their relationship. Occasionally their changing moods and contradictory passions become so unbearable that they snap at each other or fume for an afternoon, and Becki still acts like a spoiled brat at times, but they've yet to have a full-scale fight.

Doubts, doubts, bigger doubts. Torment. Terror. The most ominous cloud in Jim's mind is not the fear of unconsummated love but the fear that she will leave his life, that their relationship won't last, whether consummated or not. He still has horrible sobering moments when he concludes that his charmed life with Becki is doomed, headed for a dead end, bound to conclude unhappily. He's married. He's the pastor. He's old. She's nineteen and a half. Their flirting, their prurient talks, his deceit and lying, it's all wrong—sinful, selfish, perverted, foolhardy, *way* out of bounds. She can never fit. To think otherwise is pure fantasy. God and Sharon will never allow it—not in the long run. But one look into Becki's blue eyes and he doesn't give a shit about the long run or consequences or making it fit. He's just glad for the short run, for hazy September days with Becki at his side. There's no such thing as tomorrow— or winter.

The sound of Becki's door grabs Jim's attention. The *Eagles* tape has finished. Becki says nothing but he knows she wants him to come in. Bathsheba scoots in ahead of him and jumps onto the unmade bed. In addition to Rebecca's unique scent, the room smells of perfume, pizza, and hair spray.

Becki, sporting her usual pouty face, stands at her mirror, clad in Levi's, white socks, and an untucked shirt. The rectangular mirror is propped on top of her chest of drawers next to a small lamp which has a parchment shade and a pump-handle switch. The lamp stands amid the usual female clutter, moreso for Becki. Bottles, jars, tubes, aerosol cans. Nivea, Sure, Revlon, Avon, Noxzema, Oil of Olay, Sally Hansen. Brushes, combs, a hand-held mirror, two Nike sweatbands, a floppy makeup kit, two packs of Big Red gum, a blue Kmart mug half full of ancient coffee. A wooden jewelry tree holds necklaces, pendants, lockets, and a gold cross, while a shallow dish contains hair clips, straight pins, earrings, Tic-Tac breath mints, pennies, paper clips, pushpins, Life Savers, barrettes, wadded gum wrappers, and her '82 class ring. Finally, in the center of this clutter, sits a round ceramic music box topped by a lady mouse in a blue-checked dress and white bonnet.

The makeshift dresser is the same one Becki had in Nashua. The shirt is her dad's. It's white with blue and pink windowpane stripes, so faint you can scarcely see them. It's big on Becki but not like a tent. Derek Reinhardt is not a big man; he's slightly built, with a shy *Mr. Peepers* (Wally Cox) personality. Jim has met him a few times. Becki rolls her sleeves to three-quarter length then flips up the collar. The shirttail hangs like a curtain over her moonish butt. She likes her dad's old shirt. It's her "bum around" shirt. As she rolls her sleeve, Jim notices her Timex watch that he gave her for Christmas when she was fourteen. She rarely wears the watch, or jewelry, but she does wear the Timex when teaching.

After adjusting her shirt, Becki fiddles with her bangs. She still wears her hair in a chin-length blow-dry cut. Her hair, like the leaves, changes color in the fall, going back to a darker brown. But on this last Tuesday of September, sun-kissed memories of summer still highlight her fluffy locks, giving them a honey-maple warmth. Satisfied with her bangs, Becki leans closer and dabs peach cover-up on her chin to hide a budding pimple. Jim suspects that it's the start of her monthly menstrual cluster. She told him all about it during one of their earthy talks—how they come a week before her period. Sometimes Becki shares openly about her cycle, "Shit, Shanley, I got my period" or "I'm so wicked unpredictable," but other times she bristles if he even mentions it.

Jim, moved to playful affection, steps up next to Becki and makes faces in her mirror. She tries to hold her frowny face but she can't, so she gives him her sassy scrunchy look then a dimpled grin. Electric surge of joy. Jim's heart soars as he realizes that she's in an extra good mood. When at her mirror she normally doesn't like him looking over her shoulder.

Becki twists the top of her mouse music box, winding it up. It plays the "Do-Re-Mi" song from *Sound of Music*. The top goes round and round, and the mouse too. Grinning amusedly, like a little girl, Becki watches then leans against Jim as he gives her a quick one-arm hug. Flares of happiness shoot off inside his stomach. Magic, magic. He feels hot, then chills, then light-headed. It's beyond understanding—and far beyond words.

Jim has confessed his true feelings to no one except Becki— during their Easter Eve fight. But Russ knows, and Jim thinks that Jodi knows as well. Angela seems concerned, or jealous, about Becki but she's said nothing. Doris does talk about it, but only on her drunk days. Sharon's not thrilled about Becki's daily presence at the church, but she's made little fuss to Jim about it—of course, she doesn't know that he and Becki often spend the afternoon doing fun things unrelated to the ministry. Sharon's continuing acquiescence puzzles Jim. Maybe she's satisfied as long as his schedule is unchanged? Or perhaps she's putting her heart in the sand? Or perhaps she's confident that Becki has no romantic intentions? Or perhaps she's secretly forming a relationship with Tom Hudson? She still works on Project Malachi every Tuesday. Whatever the reason, the Shanley household seems unaffected, and Jim and Sharon's hot sex life has continued unabated into the fall. Such is the mystery of Sharon Shanley.

The BFBC regulars seem to have accepted Rebecca, seeing her move to Brendon Falls as a good thing—for the church at least. Jodi likes her as a helper but moreso as a friend—and the kids in Jodi's class love having her as a teacher. Carl Baker likes her as a substitute Sunday school teacher and Barry likes her as a Saturday-night teen chaperone. The teenagers like Becki because she relates to them as a peer rather than an authority figure. Stan welcomes her as a "soldier from Nashwa." Since she's the daughter of a front-line LBI missionary, Stan treats Becki with special respect. He even took opportunity to praise her at church, "'Fore I take the offerin',

I wanna interduce one of our new staffers, Miss Becki Reinhold."
Stan has yet to get her name right. "She's been helpin' on weekends
since March, but last month she moved down from Nashwa an'
she's gonna be with us full-time now, workin' in the 'cademy an'
helpin' on outreach. We're real proud to have Becki with us. To see
a young woman who's dedicated to Jesus, an' to winnin' souls, does
my heart good. I pray that you high school an' junior high girls will
follow in Becki's footsteps."

As the music box runs down, Becki turns to her new but
unmade sofa bed which is covered with a tangle of blue pillows,
blue sheets, a gold blanket, a red afghan, and a pink flannel
nightgown. When Jim sees the ruffled floral-print gown twisted
among the bedclothes, his heart heaves forward, *O Lord, I want to
sleep with her and hold her close all night. I want to feel her snuggly
softness.*

"Watch this, Jimmy," she says mirthfully as she wiggles her
hand under the afghan. Bathsheba, biting, kicking, grasping, attacks her hidden hand. Jim has seen the kitten perform at least ten
times, but Becki still goes through this routine every time she
makes the bed. No mystery how the bedding gets so tangled.

Also, no mystery how Becki got the new sofa bed. In August
when she and Jim went to Sears to get her a TV set, they also got
the sofa and moved the old swayback into the kitchen. Plain but
adequate, the beige sleep-sofa cost $299 on sale. He's also given
her the keys to the church car. The church has a red Ford Escort that
Angela and the academy teachers use for official business during
the day. Becki gets to use it after hours. She simply has to replace
the gas. And Jim gives her an occasional list of church supplies to
buy, or letters to mail, to justify her using the ministry vehicle.

Pizza smell: a greasy day-old pizza box sits on her ugly flea-
market coffee table along with an empty one-liter Pepsi bottle, a
half glass of flat Pepsi, wadded napkins, a TV guide, a TV remote,
a *Rolling Stone* magazine, and a red 1983 calendar book. The table
is displaced against the wall, between the radiator and the east-
facing window, to make room for the unfolded bed. In the corner
beyond the radiator—to the right of the bed—is a big overstuffed
green chair with fat rounded arms. It's moss-green like the house.
No one sits in this chair; it's strictly a catchall holding a perpetual
pile of clothes and stuff. It reminds Jim of a giant toad frog
crouching in the corner. Becki pulls the blankets and sheets off the
bed. The kitten fights the moving bedcovers, but just as she's being
dragged over the edge, she scurries off the bed, jumps onto the back
of the green chair, and begins to groom herself. Jim helps Becki fold
the bed, converting the room back into a living room.

After moving the coffee table to its daytime position, Becki opens the east—actually northeast—facing window. The copper-colored curtains stir slightly. The rainy day has turned sunny. The temperature has warmed to 71°. Jim knows because a Taylor indoor-outdoor thermometer hangs behind the sofa next to the north windows. He gave it to Becki but she rarely checks it. But for Jim, knowing the temperature is like knowing the time. Becki picks up her new Reeboks from the middle of the floor and tosses them over in front of the green chair. She then clears the pizza box and other stuff from the coffee table and heads for the kitchen. Bathsheba bounds after her, attacking her stocking feet.

Jim sits down on the sofa. Becki's new 14" color TV stares blankly at him from the top of the stereo cabinet directly across the room. Behind the TV is a brick chimney and plugged fireplace—there's an opposing plugged fireplace in the kitchen, behind the refrigerator. A dark-oak mantel supports two antique kerosene lamps along with numerous knickknacks and a vase of wilted daisies. The kerosene lamps are a gift from Papa Chavin.

Pictures, posters, hanging plants, knickknacks, bookshelves full of books, boxes, stuffed animals. Becki has enough stuff to fill three rooms. Jim thinks how she's always kept her room cluttered, even as a child. His attention shifts to her new Reebok sneakers by the green chair. Moved with Becki-curiosity, he leans over, picks one up and smells the inside, inhaling the rubbery plastic new-shoe smell together with her perspiry foot odor. Jim loves to smell her shoes, her clothes. He wants to take her into his senses, all of her. He longs to know her as much as he knows himself.

Huffing, coughing. He hears Becki's—used to be Amelia's—electric percolator. Then he sees Becki go into the bathroom off the kitchen. Bathsheba returns and jumps onto his lap. He strokes her back; she purrs loudly. Becki got the kitten from Connie, Mrs. Courtney's daughter. Pets are not normally allowed at 59 Front Street, but Mrs. C. made an exception for Bathsheba.

Becki, Becki, Becki in the bathroom. Carnal curiosity. Jim tunes his ears. He hears her buckle, her zipper, the rustle of clothing, then the hissing tinkle of female piss spewing into the toilet. *Oh, I love the sound of a girl peeing,* he says to himself, *especially if the girl is Becki Lea. It's so different from the heavy gurgle when a man takes a leak. And to think what's just above her peehole. Shit, I wonder if we'll get into a naughty talk today. I love it but I can't stand it at the same time. How long can this go on?* He hears the pop of elastic as she pulls up her panties then the screak of the tank lid on the toilet, then the flush—the trip lever is broken so she has to reach into the back to flush. But she doesn't come out. He hears water running in the bathroom sink.

To the left of the mantel hangs Becki's big bulletin board which is covered with pictures, mementos, newspaper clippings, programs, ticket stubs, dried corsages, and other keepsakes, all held in place by clear pushpins. Jim gets up to take a closer look. As he does, Bathsheba jumps off his lap and returns to her perch on the green chair. While at the B-board, he notices Becki's closet door ajar to his left. Temptation. He can't resist. He opens it. Out comes her salty-banana scent mingled with the dank smell of shoe leather and the sweet fragrance of fabric softener. Her wardrobe is neither new nor fancy. Much of it is Alison's old stuff. And Becki's favorite items rarely make it to the closet, but cycle from the laundry to the green chair. Her yellow robe hangs on a hook on the back of the closet door. Jim fondles it; it feels like a thick beach towel.

At his feet, her *Pink Floyd* sweat shirt spills out of an overfull laundry basket. Again he can't resist. He sifts among the dirty jeans, socks, and shirts, until he finds a pair of beige cotton briefs. Pussy, pussy. They've been intimate with Rebecca's pussy, covering it, feeling the heat of it. Cotton panties: they look softer, more girlish than the nylon kind that Sharon wears. Jim wants to examine them, smell them, but he doesn't dare. Instead, he pictures her softly pressed pubic hair as she rolls her panties down her marshmallowy thighs, softly pressed pubic curls—flattened yet springy—how a woman's bush looks after spending the day inside a panty crotch.

Behind the laundry basket are sneakers, pumps, sandals, slippers, boots, piled like so many dead bodies without regard for matching pairs. Finally, in the dark shadows behind the footgear, he spies a red shopping bag full of magazines, like rock-music or movie magazines. Curiosity stirs. He reaches—noise, doorknob. Bathroom door: Becki, Becki. Jim quickly closes the closet and retreats to the bulletin board. He feels a brief but heavy wash of guilt for invading her privacy, especially for digging in her laundry to see her dirty underpants.

When Becki comes in, he's innocently perusing her B-board. She comes over next to him and says, "That picture there, Jimmy, is me and Manny when he took me to his high school alumni party. Mom just about croaked when I asked to go to a worldly dance, but after two weeks of begging, she gave in. And this is Skipper when he was a pup, and over here, that's me at graduation. My hair wouldn't lay down so Mom pinned my cap thing on. It made my hair stick out worse. We just had nine graduates. I wish I went to a regular school instead of a Christian one. Regular schools are more fun.... And this is my tassel. See, it says '82."

(Sound of helicopter.) HERE! YES, YOU! STAND STILL, LADDIE!

"Wicked good dynamics," Becki declares, her mouth clogged with potato chips and dip. "I like how the drums bang in here. Listen to his guitar, Jimmy. He's using a reverb. It gives a superneat percussive echo, like a marching beat."

Well, well, when we grew up and went to school, there were certain teachers who hurt the children anyway they could by pouring their derision on anything we did, exposing every weakness however carefully hid.

3:25 p.m. *Pink Floyd*, *The Wall*. 100-watt Pioneer system. Becki, head on hand, feet toward the stereo cabinet, lies on her side on the carpet. Jim sprawls in like fashion facing her. Between them is a yellow shoe box of music tapes, along with two coffee mugs, now empty; a bag of Chips Ahoy cookies, also empty; a large half-full bag of Lay's potato chips; a thing of onion dip, almost gone; and two glasses of Pepsi, almost empty. They both have a blue bed-pillow. She's already played part of a Pat Benatar album plus a hodgepodge tape she recorded off the radio. The tape is dubbed so "Rocky Mountain Way" plays two times at the start. Jim asked why. She replied, "Because I like Joe Walsh's bluesy beat. It makes you want to move your butt." She blushed as if she were talking about fucking. Rock music is big to Becki, like an erect penis in her life, and the only penis—as far as Jim knows. Her blushing response made him think they'd get into a suggestive talk, but no such luck. Her mood is philosophical: poetic rather than erotic.

Nonetheless, he much prefers her poetic free-spirited side to her pious pharisaical side, or to her bratty adolescent side—Becki, Becki, so many sides, and Jim has seen them all, yet he still can hardly believe how much her mood seems to change from day to day, from hour to hour.

As *The Wall* album plays, Becki makes comments here and there. She's in her element. She can quote and interpret rock lyrics better than Jim can quote and interpret the Bible, and she usually nails more truth. Speaking in a reflective tone as if she's thinking out loud, her velvety voice conveys surprising authority and conviction—as does the music. Jim listens, says little. In the realm of rock music, he's still a learner and her teaching touches him more than any class he ever took at college—LBJ, M.I.T., or the Air Force Academy. The tape plays on:

> We don't need no education. We don't need no thought control. No
> dark sarcasm in the classroom. Teacher, leave them kids alone. HEY,
> TEACHER! LEAVE THEM KIDS ALONE! All in all, it's just another
> brick in the wall. All in all, you're just another brick in the wall.

"My school in New Bedford was right down the street," Becki
remarks as she scoops some dip with a large chip. "I was six and
Mom walked me the first day. When she left, I cried and felt sick
in my stomach. My school was old and brick and dirty-lookin'. We
had to line up and Miss Hoffman said, 'Don't talk!' Keith 'n Freda
were my best friends. They lived on my street, but Keith had to stay
back in 2nd grade, and Freda, they put her in the advanced reading
group. I was just average. So during 3rd grade, I didn't see my
friends as much. I liked some of my teachers but I still got that sick
feeling, especially during tests, or when we got our report cards
because Mom always showed mine to Papa Chavin. I doubt Jesus
would ever have report cards. He always taught kids on his knee."

> If you don't eat your meat, you can't have any pudding! HOW CAN
> YOU HAVE ANY PUDDING, IF YOU DON'T EAT YOUR MEAT!

"When I was nine," Becki goes on, "we moved to Nashua, but
it was no better at LCA. If you did your homework and behaved and
learned your Bible verses, then all the teachers patted you on the
back, and you were looked up to as good and godly. It's like schools
turn friends into phonies, especially girls, 'cause they want recognition and the cutest boyfriends. In Nashua I could never be myself,
'cept with Mell."

> Mother, do you think they'll drop the bomb? Mother, do you think
> they'll like this song? ... Mother, should I run for president? Mother,
> should I trust the government? ... Hush now, Baby, Baby; don't you
> cry.... Mama's gonna keep you right here under her wing; Mama's
> gonna keep Baby cozy and warm.

Becki sips her Pepsi then gives a sigh. "All mothers say that.
They don't ever tell their kids that grown-ups are money crazy and
cruel and want to turn you into slaves and soldiers. Mothers don't
talk about divorce and loneliness ... or cancer and car wrecks and
Hitler killing six million Jews. They just say it's gonna be *all right*.
When I was eight, I had a bad nightmare about dying. I ran to Mom
and she said, 'You have Jesus in your heart, so God's angels are
watching over you'—a comforting thought, I hope it's true. But it
was like Mom was talking about fuckin' Santa Claus. At the time
it soothed my fears, but she really didn't know any more about

death than me, but mothers never admit that—now that's good acoustic guitar. Fuckin' Roger Waters, he can make a guitar talk in a dozen languages, and listen to the keyboard, Jimmy ... nothing fancy just several sustained notes, but it sets the mood."

*She knows as much about rock as Joe,* Jim says to himself. *And she knows this tape verbatim, and she's saying exactly what I'm feeling. We ought to play this at church and let her talk about it. But that'll never happen. Stan won't allow rock music in the building, much less at service—O Jesus, Becki is so pretty and alive, and so full of breath. And I can see her tummy inside her shirt, where a button is missing. Why can't we unfold the bed and listen to the rest of this under the covers, in the afterglow of lovemaking? Forget it. She'll never make a move, nor will I. God help us.* Jim kills the thought with four chips and a swig of soda.

> "You wanna take a bath? Whaddeya watchin'? Hello? Are you feelin' okay?" ... Day after day, love turns gray like the skin of a dying man, and night after night we pretend it's all right, but I've grown older and you've grown colder, and nothing is very much fun anymore.

Becki, looking down, becomes suddenly wistful. "When people get married, their love dies. They start screaming and hitting and cheating on each other, but they always put on a lovey-dovey act for the kids and the relatives. When Mom left Dad, everybody thought it would shock me and break my heart, but it wasn't any fuckin' surprise. I knew. Lots of times they thought I was sleeping, but I heard Mom bitching at Daddy and calling him a coward and a 'no 'count' because he dropped out of college and went to work at Woolworth's." Becki munches a chip and stares wide-eyed at the carpet as if she's thinking about her dad.

> Oh, babe, don't leave me now; don't say it's the end of the road; remember the flowers I sent? I need you. How could you go when you know I need you? ... need you? ... need you? ... need you? How can you treat me this way?

"Listen to that piano and the heavy breathing," Becki says as she crunches another potato chip. "It sets the melancholy mood for this part, and the TV in the background. Pink's goin' through hell here but it doesn't do a bit a good to beg. My dad begged, even in front of Ed. It was pitiful. I almost hated him for it. He should've stood up for himself and called Mom a bar-hoppin' whore 'cause that's how she met Ed. Of course, they weren't Christians then, but still, she had no right. Ed treats me okay, but I'm glad I'm outa his house. I hate how he 'n Mom act so devout like they're both so good, now that they're saved and serving God. Yet they still crack jokes about Dad being a mouse and not a man. It makes me want to kill 'em both, and Katie still cries when they make fun of him.''

Rolling onto her back, Becki hugs her blue pillow to her bosom. Her disheveled hair cascades off her head breaking like rapids onto the carpet; her honey-maple locks are darker than the carpet which is sort of a cocoa-brown. Not much makeup, just a little leftover lip gloss and mascara, plus the cover-up on her chin. Becki's fair complexion is oily and dotted with pigment blemishes in addition to her fading freckles. Too many flaws to draw a photographer, not to mention her teeth, but Jim could gaze at her for a thousand years without getting enough. The budding pimple on her chin now seems redder, like a pinprick of blood under the peach cover-up. She seems to be oozing with muliebrial ripeness, with juicy fertility, as if her hormones will soon gush out of her pores if she doesn't get sexually active soon.

As the music plays, Jim wonders again if she's ever had a hard cock in her young cunt. He wonders why she's not dating. If he's just a buddy then why doesn't she go out? Likewise, he still wonders if she masturbates. Although sexual self-gratification is an unmentionable sin for a young LBI woman—for the LBI men it's a shameful "thorn in the flesh" yet it's confessed and tolerated, but for the women, who are reputed to be chaste in thought and deed, it's unmentionable—he can't see Becki going back to her room and reading the Bible every night, especially after witnessing her prurient moods over the past two months. He imagines her thrashing wildly on her sofa as she thumbfucks herself with her Levi's around her ankles. Jim sighs. Even when she's serious, far from flirting, Rebecca Reinhardt's sex appeal goes off the chart. No more music. Side one clicks off; she hops up and turns the tape:

> Hey, you, out there on your own, sitting naked by the phone, will you touch me? Hey, you, with your ear against the wall, waiting for someone to call out, will you touch me? Hey, you, would you help me to carry the stone? Open your heart I'm coming home. But it was only fantasy. The wall's too high as you can see. No matter how he tried, he could not break free, and the worms ate into his brain. Hey, you, out there on the road always doin' what you're told, can you help me? Hey, you, out there beyond the wall, breaking bottles in the hall, can you help me? Don't tell me ... there's no hope at all?

"Now they go from acoustic to distorted wailing and thundering drums," Becki explains. "It's good dynamics and the transition goes right along with Pink's mood change. Pink's talking about breaking out but it's only a dream. He's still behind his wall, and the worms are eating his brain. The worms are fearful thoughts that make us say the proper expected thing, even when we feel just the opposite. The worms take over our mind and make us liars. Everybody has worms in the head except Jesus, and they crucified him 'cause he wouldn't let the worms eat his brain. It's like me at Burger King. I had to be nice to my boss when I felt like giving him the bird, or like when Pastor used to come to Puerto Rico, and I had to say all the right things and not hang around with Maria 'til he left. The worms always say, 'If you do this or say that, you're gonna be rejected.' So I always said the right thing, except with Maria—I told her all my shit." Becki's honest musing stirs Jim's soul. He just hopes it was the worms, and not her heart, that made her deny any romantic feelings for him on that gray evening back in April up on the big rock.

> I got nicotine stains on my fingers; I got a silver spoon on a chain; I got a grand piano to prop up my mortal remains. I got wild starring eyes, and I got a strong urge to fly—but I got no place to fly to, fly to, fly to.... When I pick up the phone, there'll still be nobody home.

Becki sits up and crosses her legs under her. She pulls the pillow into her lap. After killing the last of her Pepsi, she belches and gives a quick snorting laugh, but it doesn't break her poetic mood: "Now a whole orchestra comes in with brass and woodwinds and strings, and all that shit. In the story, Pink's hurting bad. He has lots of money and stuff, but no matter how he tries, he can't get his wife back ... just like Mell's Uncle Vincent." Becki gestures with her empty Pepsi glass. "He was a doctor, and he had a pretty wife and a big house and three cars. One day he came home early and caught his wife boffing the guy from across the street. So Vinnie beat her up and tore up the whole house. He even ripped the cabinets off the kitchen walls. Mell 'n I saw it two days later. Uncle Vinnie lost his license and became an alcoholic and a recluse. Mell says he lives in Maine and doesn't even come for Christmas."

> Hello, hello? Is there anybody in there? Just nod if you can hear me. Is there anybody home? I hear you're feeling down. Well, I can ease your pain, get you on your feet again. Relax, relax, need some information first, just the basic facts. Can you show me where it hurts? There is no pain. You are receding like distant ship smoke on the horizon. You are only coming through in waves. Your lips move but I can't hear what you're saying. When I was a child, I had a fever. My hands felt like two balloons. Now I've got that feeling once again. I can't explain, you would not understand. This is not how I am. I have become comfortably numb. When I was a child, I caught a fleeting glimpse out of the corner of my eye. I turned to look but it was gone. I cannot put my finger on

it now. The child is grown, the dream is gone, I have become comfortably numb.

"Now the string section comes in wicked good," Becki says as she rolls her empty glass between her hands. "They're trying to psyche Pink up and get him goin'. They don't care about Pink. They just want him to do the show, to get him away from his true heart until it's like 'distant ship smoke on the horizon' ... just like how Mom gets on my case to do something with my life, or like when Katie gets into one of her superdepressed spells and won't come out of her room, and Ed goes in and yells at her and says, 'You're not gonna amount to anything unless you come out of your room and face life. You'll never get a husband 'cause you got nothing to offer'—now listen to that lead, Jimmy. That's a fuckin' *great* guitar lead, like his heart is screaming with pain." Rebecca sighs with resignation. "It's like the show is everything. You must have a title and a pedigree. You have to sell yourself and nobody wants you if you're just a mutt, except Jesus. He loves people even if they have no reputation, like Mary Magdalene and blind Bartimaeus. It's like Pink says. We get numb in the head, like super numb, because every day you go to a show ... and you put on a show, and you don't see anything wrong with it 'cause of the worms, and that's the main difference between kids and grown-ups."

> There must be some mistake? I didn't mean to let them take away my soul. Am I too old? Is it too late? Where has the feeling gone? The show must go on.

Becki puts down her glass then gestures as if preaching: "The worms ate Pink's mind and stole his soul, and it started way back 'cause the worms controlled his school. It's fear versus feelings, and feelings always lose 'cause the worms say emotions are dangerous and must be checked. Even our best impulses must bow to the worms." Jim can't believe she sees the human disease so clearly, and yet she's infected with it—as he is.

> You cannot reach me now, no matter how you try. Good-bye cruel world, it's over, walk on by. Sitting in a bunker hid behind my wall, waiting for the worms to come. Perfect isolation here behind my wall, waiting for the worms to come. Waiting, waiting, waiting, waiting, waiting, waiting.... Would you like to see Britannia rule the world, my friend? All you have to do is follow the worms.

Jim rolls onto his back and looks at the ancient buff-colored wallpaper then the water-stained ceiling then the unlit Capiz shell fixture. The only light in the room is coming from the windows and the small lamp on Becki's dresser. She preaches on. Her voice, her voice. Soft, liquid, high-schoolish, yet so convincing. He's drunk on Becki's voice: "Now check this, Jimmy; we get a choir singing and amplified plucking, like it's a religious or patriotic thing. In the story, Pink's like a Nazi and everyone's marching. They want to feel connected and march like an army and sacrifice all for Britannia. They want to be so committed that nothing can stop 'em, but it's all part of the show. They're not really connected. They still have their wall, but the worms promise happiness once Britannia rules the world, so they gladly follow the worms. That's how it is in Nashua. Everybody cheers for God's army to rule the world. But I like talking to God by myself."

> I wanna go home, take off this uniform, and leave the show. I'm waiting in this cell because I hafta know, hafta know. Have I been guilty all this time?

Becki jabs the air like she's closing a sermon: "Now comes a miracle. Pink's heart gets out! He defies the worms and tells his *true* feelings! And the music changes. The orchestra takes over."

> Good morning, worm, your honor. The Crown will plainly show the prisoner who now stands before you was caught red-handed showing feelings of an almost human nature—this will not do.... The evidence before the court is incontrovertible. There's no need for the jury to retire. I sentence you to be exposed before your peers! Tear down the wall! Tear down the wall! Tear down the wall!

Jim turns back onto his side, propping his head on his hand. Becki seems enthralled; her blue eyes flash. "The worms take Pink to court. They can no longer control him so they reject him, just like the people rejected Jesus for Barabbas. The head worm sentences Pink to be 'exposed before his peers' which brings down the wall, just like the veil ripped in the temple when Jesus was crucified. They kick Pink out of the show and force him into truth. He's still alone but now he's honest and ready for love ... 'cause the worms are *out* of his brain!" After a deep breath, Becki uncrosses her legs, leans back on her hands, and listens to the last song. She has said a lot. Jim hopes it's true—only time will reveal how *much* he hopes it's true:

> The ones who really love you walk up and down outside the wall. Some hand in hand, some gathered in bands, the bleeding hearts and the artists make their stand, and when they've given you their all, some stagger and fall. After all, it's not easy ... banging your heart against some mad bugger's wall.

\* \* \*

Talking lazily, almost dozing, Jim and Becki are on the sofa. On the night table a clock radio with revolving white numbers says 5:26 p.m. Outside, the day is waning. *Pink Floyd* has been finished for an hour, but no rush. Sharon's in Nashua and the kids are at the Bradleys'. Sharon normally gets back just in time for church.

Rebecca yawns and stretches then gets up and collects the mugs and glasses and stuff from the floor. The moment she moves, Bathsheba, who's been sleeping on the back of the green chair, stretches as well, arching her back until her black body looks like the Greek letter omega. Becki disappears into the kitchen and the kitten, as usual, chases after her.

Jim crosses his legs, ankle on knee. He picks at some lint on the floppy cuff of his gray pants and plays with the laces on his wing tips. Weekday pastor clothes: polyester slacks, blue dress shirt. He much prefers denim and flannel. *We've got forty-five minutes*, he says to himself. *If we leave here by six-fifteen, we'll have time to stop at McD's on our way to pick up Elmer and Agnes.*

Becki scrapes more cat food into Bathsheba's bowl then pads back in, still in her stocking feet. Stopping at her dresser, she grabs her gum, pops a piece into her mouth, then gives a juicy grin and tosses a stick to Shanley. He thanks her and puts it in his shirt pocket. He likes gum okay but not as much as Becki. He chews it mainly when he's outside, like mowing the lawn or playing softball, so the pieces she gives him end up on his dresser at home. Becki, as if quickened by the shot of sugar, turns on her heel and does her happy-girl quickstep, over to the closet. She whips her butt sassily like a filly horse. Jim doesn't need a shot of sugar. The sight of her low-hung haunches brings him to full alertness.

*Maybe her mood is changing?* he says to himself, still hoping that she'll get into a prurient spirit. He figures if she's ever going to make a move, it will be when she's drunk out of her mind on erotic talk. A long shot, or maybe not, but Jim's weighing of odds is academic for Rebecca is far away from a naughty-girl mood as she reaches up and grabs a big hatbox from the shelf of her closet. She brings it over, sets it on the coffee table, then flips on the ceiling light. Somewhere between pink and purple in color, the box looks like a drum and says Filene's on the top.

"I never showed anybody this stuff except Mom 'n Katie," she says, her voice juicy thick with fresh gum. "And Oma saw some of it." (Becki calls her paternal grandparents, Oma and Opa, as is customary in German families.) She sits down and opens the box. Jim sits forward next to her and peers inside. Dolls, all kinds, at least a dozen. Bundles of letters and cards. A purple ring box. He also spies two diaries, blue with brass locks. The letters are tied with thick red yarn. Bathsheba scurries in from the kitchen, jumps up on the coffee table, and soon is in the box.

"No! No!" Becki playfully scolds as she fishes the kitten out. Bathsheba tries three more times, then tires of the game and returns to her regular spot on the green chair.

Becki takes a chubby dark-haired doll from the box. "Now this is Baby Jessica," she says talking slowly around her gum; her voice is cozy and nostalgic. "Amelia gave her to me when I was five." She adjusts Jessica's arms and legs and seats her on the coffee table. Next, she takes out a Heidi doll, then other German and Swiss dolls, then Barbie and Ken dolls, then Nina, a talking doll.

Jim's passions settle back toward peace and paternal affection. He's not into dolls but it warms his heart that she wants to show him her prized childhood possessions. As she looks down into the box, her hair hangs forward. He stares at her cupid mouth through the wispy curtain of brown. Her leg touches his. Dimples, dimples. Becki beams then emits a happy laugh as if sensing Jim's loving gaze. Magic, magic, his heart melts. For a moment he knows they love each other forever despite all—whether they ever have sex or not. He tries to hold onto such glimpses, to store them for days of doubt, but such moments are fleeting and untenable.

After the dolls, Becki takes out the purple jewelry box which holds a heart pendant that her dad gave her for eighth-grade graduation. She talks about it for a minute then sets it on the coffee table. Next, the letters. Without untying the bundles, she takes them out, briefly comments about who-when, then stacks them on the coffee table next to the pile of dolls. The biggest bundle is from her dad, like twelve years' worth, with smaller bunches from Oma, Carmella, Amelia, Papa Chavin, and Maria, plus a few letters from Manny, in U.S. Air Force envelopes. Near the bottom of the box, Jim spots a small batch of cards and letters that he sent her in Puerto Rico. Becki takes his letters out and sets them with the others, but makes no comment about them—or the diaries.

After emptying the box, she picks up Maria's letters again and bounces the bundle on her open palm. Her nostalgic coziness suddenly fades—as does Jim's brief moment of knowing. She chews her gum with deliberate determination. Her eyes seem contemplative, her spirit disturbed. She speaks toward the letters in her hand, "Shanley, you know how you always say it's good to share what we really feel? Well, there's two things that bug me."

Jim's spirit rears up preparing for hurt feelings and self-defense. "What two things?" He slides back on the sofa away from her. He nervously fingers his mustache.

"Two things that you teach. You want me to say what I feel or what?"

"Go ahead; I'm listening." Jim relaxes his defenses a bit. He's relieved to know it isn't a Jim-loves-Becki-and-it-bothers-her problem.

"You know how you preach that lesbians are damned?"

"That's what the Bible says ... unless they repent." Jim's thoughts race through the files of his mind, *What the fuck is she getting at? She's not a lesbian, not in a million years.*

"Well, you know how I told you that Maria and Manny and me, we used to go out to the beach and fool around and stuff?" Becki, still sitting forward, speaks away from him.

From his position on the sofa behind her, Jim gazes at the elastic trusswork of her bra that wraps her back underneath her bum-around shirt. The strap makes a provocative crease in her soft girlish flesh, especially as it curves under her left arm. Suddenly, sex with Becki is important again. He feels an urge to unsnap her bra then to reach around and fondle her dangling breasts, but he doesn't dare. Instead, he gives a flirtatious snicker and spins her question back at her, hoping to stir her prurient side, "You mean the cabin where you got high and looked at dirty magazines?"

Rebecca replies—but obliquely—"One day Manny had to work, so he took Maria and me out to the beach and left us all afternoon. Nobody was around, so we got stoned and looked at some raunchy pictures that Maria brought with her. After that we went swimming in the nude and laid out in the sun ... and Maria touched my nipples and I touched hers." Flares of lust and erotic expectation shoot off in Jim's gut sending tingling signals to the tip of his dick, but to no avail. Despite the risqué subject, Becki is not being prurient, she's simply making a point.

She shifts sideways to face Jim, her countenance taking on an expression of adverse inquisitiveness: "And that's all we did, Jimmy. And I have no desire to fuck her or any woman. So, does fondling Maria mean I'm damned? Do we hafta repent, or what?"

"Nawh, I think you'd have to go farther to be a lesbian."

Becki tosses her head testily and pops the bundled letters against her hand. She squints with determination. "How *much* farther?" she presses. She sounds like a defense lawyer and Jim feels like a prosecution witness with a shaky testimony. He realizes again that she's sharper than Alison or Sharon give her credit for. "Where do you draw the line, Jimmy? Fondling tits and ass is okay but play with the cunny and you're damned?"

"Lesbians aren't damned," Jim rebuts, sweeping the air with his hand, "if they forsake it and ask God to forgive them." He's fishing, quoting doctrine, defending his ego against her combative cross-examination, but his words are far from his heart.

"But what if they don't?" Becki persists. "What if they do it again?"

"They can still be forgiven, if they isolate it and confess it, and don't practice it." His response is pure Logan, right out of his LBI classnotes.

"Isolate it, practice it, what the fuck does that mean?" she scoffs. "It's okay once a month, once a week, but *twice* a week and you're over God's limit?"

Jim throws up his hands in exasperation. "I don't *know.* I'm not fuckin' God." Becki has him; she's tied him into a knot—with his own words. But he isn't angry, abashed but not angry, for he knows that her adversative bantering is just a more serious way of teasing him. This is confirmed as Becki scrunches her face at him then gives a cocky grin of triumph. A wave of playful affection quickly washes away his exasperation. He gives her a teasing love-slap on her thigh. "You think you're so smart, you little tiger, you."

"I am, at least smart enough to get *you* coming and going." Becki dimples, her grin breaking wide until Jim can see her gum buried in her cheek pocket.

For a few minutes they kid each other mirthfully, then Becki sobers as her mood shifts back to adverse inquisitiveness. Clearing her throat, she moves on to the second thing that bugs her. "Jimmy, remember when you told Kevin 'n Cathy that drugs are false?" As she speaks, she drums Maria's letters against the table.

"Yeh, I remember. That's the day we got into it with Flanagan, and Brad Selkirk came in his police car." Jim strokes his chin apprehensively.

"Right. Well, if drugs are so bad and sinful, howcome when me 'n Maria got high, we always talked about real things, and got wicked free? And howcome people like to get stoned and buzzed on beer, but they don't like to go to work, or to school ... or to church?"

"Sounds like you've been talking to Joe Lareux again?"

Becki frees her gum from her cheek with a sweep of her tongue. A devilish glint sparks in her eyes. After a cycle of rapid chewing, she replies, "Well, we talked about it a lot when I used to ride with him. I even lit up with—"

"You still smoke that shit!" Jim snaps angrily, cutting her off. The possibility that she's playing with him to get a reaction is no longer a comfort.

"Don't pee in you pants, Shanley. I'm not a pothead. We just did it a few times and sometimes Joe had beer in his trunk. It wasn't anything really, just a few times when we felt like getting fogged before facing the sucky life in Nashua. It's hard goin' to college, especially a strict Bible college."

"Well, I don't agree with Joe when it comes to pot. You know how I feel about drugs."

"But how can *you* know?" Becki counters, smacking her gum and swirling it around in her mouth. "You're so square. You've never smoked it, not even one joint. How can you judge it?"

"Good God, Becki, you sound *just* like Joe. But marijuana fucks you up, and beer too. And you *know* it."

"Well, what are people supposed to do when they grow up and find out that life sucks, and they hate their job and they're super lonely ... and all they have to look forward to is death?"

"That's why we have the church, remember?"

"Oh, *swell.* Come to church and sing and pray, and it'll be all better. It's no different! Besides, *you're* the one who said goin' to church was like smoking pot."

"Dammit, Rebecca Lea! You know what I mean. Stop twisting every fuckin' thing I say. Just drop it, okay." She has him by the balls which aggravates him even more.

"Okay, okay," Becki huffs. "But *you're* the one who's always talking about freedom and following the heart, but you never do. You're all talk." Their emotions are hot but not exploding—like when they fought about love and sex on the big rock back in April.

Jim slaps his thigh. "But drugs and booze are a lie. And drunkenness is a sin. Just look at what it's done to the people in this town. That's one LBI doctrine I *do* endorse."

"Well, maybe so," Becki shoots back, almost losing her gum. "But freedom's the issue, not sin?"

She gives a sigh of exasperation and throws Maria's letters onto the coffee table. They bounce off onto the floor. Bathsheba, like a panther pouncing on her prey, flies off the back of the green chair and attacks the red yarn around the letters.

Jim is distracted as the kitten bites the yarn and digs into the bundle of letters with her hind legs, but he quickly regains his train of thought. "Freedom *is* the issue," he argues, "freedom from the slavery of drugs. You can't be free without responsibility. God's liberty is never lawless." His reply is pure party line, pure Logan.

Becki contorts her face disgustedly then starts throwing her stuff back into the hatbox. "Well, Jimmy, it's bigger than just drugs. How can you be free if you just keep rules and stifle yourself so you can be cool and correct and goody-goody, like the nerdy Bible dinks in Nashua? You think *free*dom means to obey?"

"Yeh, it does," Jim replies dogmatically. "But to obey freely, in the power of the Holy Spirit."

"That's a fuckin' contradiction!" Becki exclaims, scowling and chomping her gum. "You dan't be *free* and obey at the same time. If you have to obey and be responsible, you're a slave. Jesus said, 'Know the truth and the truth shall make you free.' So why aren't we free? Why can't we fly like the birds, instead of always having to obey some *super*impossible commandment?"

*What the fuck? J*im thinks to himself. *This argument is upside down. I'm arguing against the very freedom I yearn to see in her, especially in her sex life, and she's arguing for it, yet she'll never follow her heart, anymore than me. We're fucking out of tune with reality. Besides, why waste passion on Christian dogma. Fighting over "us," now that's worth it, but not arguing over doctrines. Bantering is one thing, but having a real fight over sermon topics is insane. I'm tired of arguing. I'd much rather get her flying like a bird, flying on prurient talk.*

"I guess it's beyond us?" he replies to Becki as he tries a long-shot maneuver hoping to effect a mood shift. "I sure don't have the final answers. But I do have a question."

"Yeah, what's that?" Becki snorts huffily as she throws the last doll back into the box.

Jim gives a flirty grin under his mustache. "What did you like best with Maria, smoking pot or looking at pictures of naked guys with hard-ons?"

His X-rated zinger, shooting out of the blue, catches Becki off guard, disarming her. She fights to hold her face but fails. Her scowl breaks open into a revealing grin. "You don't know what kind of pictures we had? I never said?"

"Well," Jim snickers, "you just told me you weren't into women ... right?"

Rebecca chortles coquettishly and rolls her eyes. "Let's just say ... pot's a lot easier to control." Carnal excitement stirs Jim's soul, and his penis, as Becki's naughty-girl spirit finally surfaces. To think of what happened at that beach cabin dries his mouth. He suspects that the teenybopper experiences in Mell's basement were like a Sunday school picnic in comparison.

Oh, how he wants to let her run with this volatile subject—but it's too little too late. It's time to leave for Tuesday night service. They're already twenty minutes behind schedule, and they have to eat and pick up Elmer and Agnes on the way.

\* \* \*

Burping Big Mac aftertaste, Jim and Becki pull up at Riverview Apartments, an elderly housing project on Mill Street. The project is a converted rowhouse just up from the river and right across from where Cathy Rosinski lives. On the car radio Bonnie Tyler sings "Total Eclipse of the Heart." It's 7:18 p.m. Despite their fast eating and Becki's fast driving, they're still ten minutes behind schedule.

Pastor Jim gets out, but Elmer and Aunt Agnes are already coming down the walk. Elmer, a stooped little drunkard, drags his crippled leg but still beats Agnes to the car. As Jim waits, he concludes that Elmer is even uglier than Buddy at the diner. In addition to being wrinkled like a prune, he has fat protruding lips, a convex receding brow, and bushy eyebrows that look like hairy W's pasted above his eyes. The lack of order in his silver hair gives him a drowsy just-out-of-bed look as if he merely awoke for the trip to the church—where he'll resume his nap. His pocked and bulbous nose, ruddy and veiny from alcohol, looks like an IBM print ball, and wiry tufts of white hair jut out disgustingly from his cavernous nostrils. He wears a shabby '50s-era suit, brown, overlarge, no buttons on the coat. Yet he does have twinkling blue eyes, when they're open, and he's always friendly to Pastor Jim. But Jim has nothing but dutiful Christian concern to offer him. In truth, he'd never choose to spend one minute with Elmer Kowalski.

Reaching the car, the old man smiles, shakes Jim's hand, mutters something about the weather, then crawls into the back-seat. Jim also gets into the back as Elmer quickly fumigates the Mustang with whiskey breath.

They wait as Agnes waddles down the sidewalk in her huge black overcoat; it's scarcely cool enough for a jacket, much less a winter coat. Old-fashioned nylons stretch tightly over her elephant-like legs, muddy-brown nylons like Jim remembers on elderly colored women back in Texas. Shifting her heavy-jowled corpulence from side to side, Agnes moves like Jabba the Hut. Wild shocks of gray hair stick out from under her blue yarn cap. Pale bloated face, sunken eyes, tiny nose, wide mouth. She looks like a whitewashed orangutan. In fact, most orangutans would rank ahead of her in a beauty contest. Her high-top orthopedic shoes remind Jim of the football cleats he wore in high school.

*Women really lose it with age*, he remarks to himself. *They go from being the most beautiful creatures on earth to being the most disgusting. God, it's impossible for me to picture Agnes as young and sexually attractive—shit, am I ever fucked and far away from Jesus. I have no compassion for old people.* As she shuffles closer, he sees the hairy mole on her chin and the old-fashioned red rouge on her cheeks—so red it looks like clown makeup. Her teeth are stained from tobacco and she's missing one tooth on top.

"You wanna drive tonight, Agnes?" Becki quips after turning down the radio. Agnes gives a raucous laugh then, huffing and puffing, lowers herself into the front seat. The Mustang sinks down almost to the street. As they drive, Agnes talks about her son Albert who's 48 and lives in Cleveland, and works for Conrail, and has a young wife and two kids. She speaks in a truncated squawk like a muted trumpet. She says her grandkids call every Sunday and that Albert is buying a house soon and then she'll be moving to Cleveland to live with them.

Jim's heard this rosy prediction ten times over the past two years but it's yet to come true. He doubts it ever will. Agnes's floral-scented perfume is strong and oversweet—it smells like Kitty Litter Maxx, the deodorized cat litter that Sharon gets for Samantha's box—but it does take the edge off Elmer's whiskey breath. Jim sighs with relief when they finally pull into the church parking lot.

* * *

"Tonight, I want you to open your Bibles to Galatians Chapter Five," Pastor Jim says to the BFBC regulars gathered for Tuesday night service. "Now, let's read verses one, five, and six:

> **Stand fast, therefore, in the liberty with which Christ hath made us free, and be not entangled again with the yoke of bondage.... For we through the Spirit wait for the hope of righteousness by faith.... For in Christ Jesus neither circumcision availeth anything, nor uncircumcision, but faith which worketh by love.**

"In these verses Paul is telling us that all godliness and true righteousness comes from within us, not from doctrines, rules, and traditions that are outside of us...." Jim proceeds to preach a forty-minute message about love, liberty, and motivation, contradicting the conservative LBI line which he spouted earlier in his bantering with Becki. In his sermon he declares that following Christ means to let go of all rudders except for love which constrains from within, that fear of chastisement, or hell or the devil, is not godly motivation nor is hope of reward or achievement. Furthermore, he declares that following our God-given instincts and affections with no thought of tomorrow, with no thought of consequences, but simply living in the "now of joy," is what it means to "walk in the Spirit," and liberty in Christ means to do what our redeemed human spirit wants from within—from deep within our fountain of being—and anything else is slavery or prostitution of one form or another.

Becki's face lights up when Jim pounds the pulpit to drive home this point, for it's the very point she made during their afternoon bickering.

Finally, he declares that true faith "works by love"—that true faith means to trust the leading of love from within one's heart. Jim is not convinced of the veracity of his sermon, but it's his only hope because he now knows he cannot change his heart.

While he preaches, a great weight seems to lift from the thirty-five assembled souls as if they glimpse, for a moment at least, the profound possibility that godliness is not complicated, arduous, and adult, but simple, instinctive, and childlike—that living from within is godly not sinful, and that the "real me," the "interior me," can come out without fear or shame.

As Jim looks upon the trusting faces, he's so moved that he almost lets it all hang out, but he doesn't. To appease Stan and the Loganites, he spends the last five minutes explaining that God's love in your heart will never lead you outside of Bible doctrine. This, of course, shoots the hell out of true freedom. Nevertheless, his sermon goes farther than any he's ever preached on the idea of spiritual authority coming from within. He hopes the flock will get the meat of his message and shuck the last five minutes.

Refreshments in the teen center. Hyper kids, just out of junior church. The adults talk, laugh, eat, and sip coffee. The kids yell, run, and fight. Tuesday night routine. Tuesday night regulars: Beverly B., Barry, Janet, Doris, Barbara, Angela, Sylvia, Jodi D., Joanne, Carl, Sarah, Thelma, Leslie B., and a few teenagers and teenyboppers. Tuesday night always draws more women than men. Lukewarm husbands rarely come to midweek service and some, like Herschel Hightower, have to work.

Leslie B. takes Jim aside and asks him to pray for her husband. She speaks hurriedly and hushedly—as if ashamed—explaining that Gerald has "fallen into sin," that he's once more given in to his "fleshly obsession with pornography." She says she's concerned for her son Wendell, since he's at an age when Satan tempts with impure thoughts. Jim tells Leslie that he'll pray for Gerald, and Wendall, but as she departs, he thinks, *I don't blame Jerry for reading porno. If I was married to Leslie, I'd be reading it too.*

Stan is bustling with excitement because one of the fellows at the mill came to service with his wife, and they both raised their hands for Christ, and they're coming back on Sunday. Russ is there but not excited. He simply smiles and gives Jim a binder that contains the preliminary third-quarter financial figures, and he tells

Jim that Barry needs $35 for new pool sticks.

Becki jokes with Jodi then groups with Erin, Heather, and Sheila. She even makes small talk with Sharon, but she says little to Jim. She still doesn't show him attention or hang by his side when a crowd is present. Who would believe she spends thirty hours a week with him?

9:47 p.m. Jim's the last to leave—except for Stan. He follows Sharon and the kids, he in the Mustang, they in the Grenada. Becki left earlier taking the Escort home. The night is damp and foggy especially in the lowlands around South Meadow Pond.

Long day. Becki, Becki, now Sharon. Jim is tired and drained, yet he feels good about his sermon: *God wants us to live from within—I should preach this every message. But I'd feel a lot better if I knew it was true.*

# Chapter Twenty

Laughing, teasing, rollicking: Heather and Erin and Sheila Bradley, who's sleeping over. They all have a case of the Friday night giggles as they tromp down from their room to help in the kitchen. September 30th, last day of the month. Jim and Sharon's aftersupper "quiet time" is over.

Jim takes a last swig of coffee from his black M.I.T. mug, excuses himself, and goes down to the basement where Chris has wisely escaped to watch *Hogan's Heroes*. Entering his office, Jim plops down at his desk—after the usual groping for the light.

October church schedule, first-time visitor cards, Sunday school names. He pulls a few visitor cards for Saturday visits but quickly loses his concentration. Blue eyes, sassy smirk, frisky hips. Becki, Becki. It's no use; he can't wait until morning to see her.

He hurries upstairs, changes into jeans and sneakers, then hustles through the kitchen, pulling on his old USAFA baseball warm-up as he goes. He tells Sharon that Barry needs him at the teen center—a very believable lie. She sighs, sucks a breath, but before she can protest, he's out the door. And ten minutes later, he's at 59 Front Street knocking on Rebecca's door. Extra time, extra time. The thought of spending Friday night with her outside their normal schedule fills Jim with a sense of adventure—and risk. He's crossing another forbidden line.

"Who is it?" comes Becki's shy-sleepy-apprehensive voice.

"It's me," he replies.

The security bolt slides open, then the door. Untucked bum-around shirt, faded jeans, stocking feet, yawny pouty face. Becki, standing hipshot against the open door, stares blankly at Jim. Bathsheba crouches behind her in the feline on-guard position, but when the cat sees that it's only Jim, her attention turns to food and she rubs against Rebecca's legs.

With no makeup and her disheveled hair pressed flat on one side, Becki looks like a half-awake farm girl just back from milking the cows in the morning. But Jim, despite her homey hayseed look—or perhaps because of it—sees her as adorable, huggable, angelic, and his heart races excitedly in hopes that she'll go along with his bold proposal. "Whadda *you* doin' back here?" Becki asks, her voice no longer shy or apprehensive but still sleepy. "Didyuh forget something this afternoon or what?"

"Yeh, I think I might have," Jim teases.

"What'd you forget? I don't see anything of yours around here." She yawns again, stretching her arms over her head, then lazily wraps her legs around the open door and presses her bosom against it—a most provocative pose.

Jim chuckles. "Well, I think I misplaced this cute brunette. She's short but real pretty. I'm not sure but I think I might've left her here." Becki almost smirks but kills it with her frown. In fact, her frown becomes more severe; she seems bothered.

Jim's racing heart sinks as he fears his scheme has fallen flat from the outset, but he presses on since her first response is usually a bothered look. Of course, when she playfully initiates, she expects him to kid back at once, and he always does, but when he teases first, she always acts annoyed—and sometimes she is. He probes to find out, "I'm goin' to the teen center, and I was hoping to find this cute young gal so I can take her with me."

Becki rubs her lip with her thumb then gives her patented scrunchy-faced grimace. "But this's my night to watch *Dallas* and *Falcon Crest,*" she replies fussily. "And I hafta fold my laundry and do my hair." Her disturbed tone seems forced. Jim hopes that it is.

"Well, it's windy and wild out there, and getting dark," he says. "I hate to walk the path by myself on an eerie night like this."

"So you have your car. Why don'tcha drive to the church?"

"I like the path better, especially when you're walking with me—like by my side."

Now comes a dimpling grin. "Well, I guess it won't kill me to miss my shows one week, but let's not make a habit of this. I have *no* free time, you know, since I moved down." Jim steps inside. The Coca-Cola clock is groaning. Without looking, he knows it's almost seven. Despite her bitching, Becki seems eager—no longer sleepy. After quickly feeding Bathsheba, she puts on her sneakers, tucks her shirt, fluffs and sprays her hair, dabs on some perfume, brushes her teeth, grabs a light jacket—her tan one with snaps—and they're off. Jim has a plan: make an appearance at the teen center then go have fun, but he must make it look good.

* * *

Barry greets Pastor Jim and Becki with some surprise but he's glad to see them since Leslie's gone to pick up kids on the other side of town. The pop-country song "Elvira" booms through the teen center—Stan okayed the *Oakridge Boys,* despite the fast beat, because they also do gospel albums. A crowd is gathered at the pool table where Kevin Johnson has just assumed his victory strut after beating Haley Cameron. But Ping-Pong is Jim's game and he quickly organizes a tournament with Kevin, Haley, Cathy Rosinski, Haley's sister Teri, plus Becki, Brenda Donovan, and Billy McArthur. Billy finally got permission to come to the teen center after his mom caught him smoking pot with Cathy R. in their garage. Wendell Burton, Leslie's bug-eyed 13-year-old, is also part of the lineup. Wendell, poor kid, looks more like a frog than his mom. To make the tournament interesting, Pastor Jim—no big worry, he knows he'll win—promises a trip to McDonald's for the champ. No one's ever defeated him except Kevin who's done it twice in three years.

Jim taught Becki to play in the old days back in Nashua, and she's not bad for a girl. She even beats Kevin on occasion, but her big goal is to beat Jim. And on this night she's in rare form. Wild, aggressive, rowdy with the paddle, she hits screamers left and right. Teasing, taunting, bobbing, weaving, she finishes off her opponents with ease; Kevin gets only six points. Jim, meanwhile, beats Billy and Haley, and squeaks by Cathy. So it's Pastor Jim and Rebecca for the prize. As everyone gathers to watch, Becki rolls her sleeves and stuffs a piece of Big Red into her mouth.

As usual, Jim lets her get ahead. He likes to come from behind and beat her; it makes her so mad—he loves it. But this time he finds his uphill strategy tough to pull off. Becki is wired and reckless and playing with abandon. She reaches fore and aft, to the side. She slams, then softly taps. Bouncing from foot to foot, she bobs and weaves and works her gum—and taunts Jim, "Look at him. He's nervous. Look at him. He knows he's goin' to lose!"

The teenagers, and Barry, root for her. The *Oakridge Boys'* "Fancy Free" blares down from the ceiling speakers. Becki is both—fancy and free. A honey-brown blur, she whips about the table, darting, dipping, advancing, then stepping back. Offense, offense. She presses Jim, keeping him on the defense. It's all he can do to pull even at twenty. But not to worry, he quickly puts her on the ropes with a hot serve that she hits high off the fluorescent lights.

Game point. But two lucky shots turn the tide again; both hit the net, teeter on top, and just fall over. She then returns his next serve with a blistering backhand slam that he never sees.

"TA-DAH! I'M THE BEST!" Becki shouts as the ball rockets off the table, ricochets off the window sill, and bounces to the other end of the room. It's all over. Pastor Jim has lost. Winded and flushed but smiling from ear to ear, Becki raises her arms in triumph and teases him unmercifully, as do the others.

Finally, the excitement subsides as the teens break up into smaller groups and Rebecca retires to the ladies' room. Jim follows Barry to the chaperone desk. Barry has never spoken about their strange talk by the river after the softball game. In fact, since that August afternoon, he hasn't talked to Jim at all except about ministry business. Barry takes the October teen-ministry schedule out of the desk drawer and hands it to Jim for his approval. It shows the regular Friday-Saturday teen center schedule plus special events like bowling, roller skating, movies, and a Halloween hayride. Jim, scarcely looking at it, scrawls his name at the bottom and gives it back to Barry. He just wants to be with Becki—that's his October schedule.

Excusing himself, Jim heads for the men's room and runs into Becki in the hallway. She blushes. The message in her eyes is starkly sexual. "Now I want my prize," she teases, then coming closer, she whispers, "Let's go someplace where we can get ice cream with lots of chocolate on it." She blows hot breath into his ear. It tickles and sends electric chills up his spine. Happy Becki: she does her cute *ENERGIZER* quickstep, back into the teen center.

Becki, Becki—too much. Jim goes into the men's room. Love, lust, magic. No guilt—at least for now. No thought for Sharon, the kids, his pastoral position. Becki fills his mind, fires his hopes, pounds in his heart—hot thunder. *O God*, he prays wantonly as he stands at the urinal. *Let this be the night. I love her. I need her. I want her so*. Before leaving, he takes a deep breath and collects his wits. His plan is working perfectly, but he must be patient.

8:15 p.m. Jim and Becki leave the teen center, escaping out the back door. The air is thick with pine needles and sodium light. They chase their shadows through the picnic area to the path where all shadows disappear in the windy darkness. When they walked over an hour ago, they still had a bit of light, but now it's pitch dark. They walk hurriedly through the fresh carpet of pine straw.

Windy, spooky, scary. It's only a half mile to the meadow but it seems like ten. Black trees, like many-armed creatures, jump out at every turn, their gnarled and twisted limbs swaying in the wind. Pine trees creak overhead like ship masts in a gale. Autumn leaves roar and rattle on the oaks, maples, and birches, while new-fallen leaves scurry across in front of them. Above the trees the lights of the town reflect off the low clouds giving the overcast a reddish glow. The smell of rain is in the air, but it's warm for late September; they scarcely need their jackets. The night is terrible, eerie, foreboding, like how you feel in a haunted house on Halloween, or like the spooky autumn scene in *To Kill a Mockingbird* when Boo Radley saves Scout from Mr. Ewell.

Halfway to the meadow, Becki becomes suddenly bold, leaves the path, and bolts due south crashing downhill through the underbrush. Jim follows. Running, slogging, slashing, stumbling. Bushes, brambles, gripping vines. They soon break out of the woods, cross the railroad tracks, and ascend the embankment that overlooks the reservoir. Whitecapped waves gurgle and splash over the rocks below them. Farther out, the windblown lake looks like frothing blood under the ruddy overcast. A gust of wind blows Becki's bangs up off her forehead. She pulls her gum and throws it down toward the rocks; it disappears in the wild darkness.

Breathing hard, they stand in the wind, not talking, not touching—then another burst of energy: Becki takes off, back across the tracks, uphill through the woods to the path, and up the path to the meadow. Jim, his lungs on fire, tears after her. He sucks in the night. Leaves, pine needles, earth, the lake. Wild primal scents. Water, wind, clouds, rain, and Becki—Becki, Becki. She's just as stormy as the night, and just as scary. She's like an animal in heat. The thought makes him weak in the knees, so weak he can hardly run. In eight months he's yet to kiss her lips, much less get into her panties, but on this tempestuous night, he feels near, at the gate. The feeling is consuming, heavenly, out of this life, but oh, so terrifying. Jim wonders if he would survive such intimacy.

He wants, he craves. His wanton prayer is being answered, or is it? He can never read her for sure. But it has to be *him*. How can this wildness be for another? He's never sensed such sexual energy coming from her toward him, save for his phantasmal Becki-vision back in February, the first day she came.

Running, panting, they emerge into the meadow. Becki scurries halfway up the hill and throws herself into the windswept grass. The clouds give a reddish cast to all of Hadley Hill, like the rufescent glow inside a photographer's darkroom. Jim's lungs burn for air. His heart overflows with awful expectancy. "You're too much," he gasps as he leans on his shaking knees like a sprinter after a race. "You're sure enough a wild and crazy gal tonight!"

"I like being crazy!" Becki pants, her face feverish and red—red from the clouds, red from hot blood. "I feel fuckin' good, like *buzzed* all over."

"You mean like pot?" Jim asks, his carnal curiosity raging.

"Whew, God! I think it's better. I feel so alive I can't stand it, like I have a thousand wild demons in me, and they all want out *wick*ed bad."

Jim gulps inside as he grasps her meaning. Too hot—he doesn't dare respond lest he chase her wildness. Becki sheds her jacket, wads it into a pillow, then lies back on it, knees up, legs spread, as if she's giving birth. Her denim-clad crotch looms big in the darkness; it seems two feet wide. Her shirttail has ridden above her waist. She has no belt and the top button of her jeans is undone but the Levi's still dig into her pillowy midriff. Behind the open waist button, her deep belly dimple, tinted red by the clouds, heaves up with each panting breath. Jim gulps again. Lightning flashes on the western horizon, and in his brain. His thoughts rush ahead then slam back on themselves like thunder, *I feel it, I feel it. She's gonna pull down her pants. God, is she ever horny—NO WAY! She'd never. This is all imagination. Sharing her sexual exploits is one thing, but actually getting off with me—no! never! It ˙ the running. She's just flushed and excited.* Hope, fear, conflict, confusion.

Jim's too scared to make a move. So he collapses on his back beside her and looks up at the tattered and windblown clouds.

But not for long. Becki, Becki. He can't keep his eyes off her. He turns onto his side and watches her bosom lift then fall. He smells her perspiry BO through her shirt. In fact, he smells her whole body coming through her clothes: ammonia, salt, sugar, bananas. Becki sweat, Becki scent, Jim's favorite fragrances on the whole earth. That's why her closet smells so special, and her clothes, her bed, her room, her bathroom, her whole apartment.

He even imagines he smells her shadowy fount, her fleshy double-lipped wellspring of wantonness, hot, wet, and pubescent inside her panties. Not really, but the scent is forever fixed in his mind from Sharon, and he figures he'd surely smell Rebecca's cunt if he put his head between her legs—what a thought!

Pussy, pussy, pubic hair. Legs, hips, tummy, tits. O God! Becki's crotch, Becki's flesh, Becki's body odor, hot Becki breath— Jim loves everything about her. He can't get enough.

As if reading his thoughts, Becki slowly closes her legs, then opens, then closes. The sight intoxicates Jim. Drunk, drunk, pass out, faint, weak, spinning—his head is spinning. He's falling then floating. Insane, wild, insane. Smoke, fire—he's on fire.

He loves her, he loves her. He loves Becki Reinhardt. Him in her, she in him, he feels that close. He's crazy to kiss her, to take off her clothes, to fuck her and fuck her until they scream into heaven, and the earth moves beneath them. Becki, Becki, young, fierce, feral, and nubile, and slowly opening and closing like a fertile flower beside him. She's so vulnerable, hot, and precious. She's so—it's beyond him. Love, lust, bursting heart, but Jim can't move. He's frozen to the ground.

Doubts, like diving bats, attack again: *She doesn't want me! She's thinking about Manny or some other hunky guy in her mind. I'm twice her age. All the doors are closed. She can't be my wife. She won't be my lover. She'll never ride my cock, not even in secret—or will she?* Flash. Another burst of lightning. Silver clouds boil upward in the west, swirling, billowing, advancing behind rolling barrages of thunder. The lightning chases, for the moment, the batlike doubts. *But she spends all her time with me. She flirts with me. She talks dirty with me. It is me! It is! It has to be!*

*Come on, Becki Lea, whaddeya waiting for? Confess that you've wanted me all along. Admit that your pious denial on the big rock was just fear and pride talking, that you weren't denying me, but rather your own heart—and body.* No more sweet missionary facade. No more goody-goody professions. No more pious denials. He wants to hear her confess that she loves to get off, that she craves the rushing high. He wants to hear her beg for hard cock, for his cock. Then he'll unleash her pent-up passion, her bucking animal-wildness. Moaning, groaning, grinding, panting, raging, thrashing and thrusting and thrusting, until she howls and goes berserk, until her pent-up eros explodes all over the meadow, and all over him.

But he doesn't dare—he's frozen—make the first move. He doesn't dare kiss or try to undo buttons. Love, passion, hope, fear, doubt. His emotions clash hotly and cannot unite for action. Becki must kiss *him*, come after *him*. It has to be. He wants her, he craves her. But he loves her too dearly to lose her. Becki has to make the first move—and she does, but not toward Jim. Jumping up, she takes off again, her shirttail and jacket trailing like a tail behind her.

He gives chase. She sprints down the hill past Mrs. C's garden and around the house to the Mustang; she hops in and fires up the engine—she now has her own set of keys. Jim, staggering and breathless, plops into the seat on the passenger side.

The radio's going full blast on the "oldies" station. "Barbara Ann" by the *Beach Boys* rocks and rolls through the car and out Becki's open window. "So, Jimmy, you ready for some good eating," she asks buoyantly, "like burgers and fries, and I still have to get my prize? After all, I beat you *good*—and I want a *wick*ed lot of chocolate on it." She shifts into reverse but suddenly stops, puts the car in neutral, and locks on the brake. Announcing she has to get her purse, she scampers up the walk, hurdles the porch steps in a single bound, and bombs through the front door. The screen door doesn't latch so it blows back and forth in the wind squeaking and banging and keeping time to the *Beach Boys*: "Ba-Ba-Ba, Ba-Ba-bar-Ann, Ba-Ba-Ba, Ba-Ba-bar-Ann."

Winded and drained, and numb all over, Jim speaks to Rebecca in his mind, *Becki, Becki, I love you so ... but I can't figure you. I can't.* Then he stops thinking.

\* \* \*

Rain and thunder. Rain pitter-pats against the window while thunder rumbles in the distance, now a gentle receding thunder as the worst of the storm is over. Becki licks at the ice cream on her underlip but it escapes and oozes down onto her chin. Jim wishes he could lick it off for her, but she reaches up with her finger and pushes the cold vanilla sweetness into her mouth. Park Street Diner. Second booth from the end, their regular booth. Juanita Ramirez is their waitress. They've already downed their hamburgers and fries. Jim is stuffed—this is his second supper—yet he's far from sated. Now he sips his coffee while Becki attacks, with a long spoon, a mountainous chocolate sundae which is in an old-fashioned glass dish with flower-petal lobes. The dish reminds Jim of the sundae dishes at the soda fountain at Gravitt's Pharmacy back in Gilmer.

Rebecca, disheveled and covered with grass stains and dried perspiration, looks like a soccer player after a game, except she has no sweatband. She played soccer on the J-V team in Nashua when she was fourteen and Jim went to a few of her games. Though short, she's agile and fast and would've surely made the LCA varsity team, but her move to Puerto Rico cut her soccer career short.

Becki's honey-highlighted hair huddles down over her forehead, ears, and temples like a wind-tossed haystack. Dirty, dampish, no body, just wayward locks and jutting tufts. Underneath this mussy mop, her cherub face blooms warm and perspiry through freckles and blemishes and adolescent blotches. With her usual oily complexion and a few zits on her nose, she looks very highschoolish, like seventeen. Since Tuesday, the fertility pimple on her chin has become a cluster of three. Jim figures her period is on the way. He now knows her cycle as well as Sharon's.

If Becki ever needs makeup, she needs it this night. But Jim likes her better without it. He likes her raw natural complexion, the reds, pinks, violets, grays, and tawny browns. Warm colors and cool. They blend and shimmer and make her face active and alive and true, and bring out her sky-blue eyes—blue eyes that make her beautiful in spite of her common country features, an enchanting blue that is liquid yet bright, as if God melted and bottled the blue of heaven itself then painted her irises until He had perfect azure halos about her pupils.

Becki's eyes, the barometer of her tempestuous spirit as they blaze with anger, or sparkle with mirth, or deepen with sadness, or darken with mystery, or dilate with prurient fascination. Jim sees her eyes as more sexual than her body—hungry blueness: bold, erotic, seductive, yet also poignant and vulnerable, like open windows on her wanton soul. He longs to drown in Becki's eyes, to die in Becki's eyes, then to rise again and live forever in Becki's eyes. Whenever he thinks of her, he sees her eyes.

Normally after showing her wild side, she withdraws and becomes cool and distant, but not on this night of wind and thunder. Just looking at her, as she eats her ice cream, she seems demure, wholesome, and composed, but in truth, her spirit is just as untamed as in the meadow except her flirting is now verbal instead of romping. Jim's fervor is also undiminished as he feeds on the titillating mood of the conversation which has become personal and prurient much like that afternoon six weeks ago on the stone fence.

Becki, averting her eyes, gives him only occasional glances as she spoons her Ping-Pong prize but her bashfulness is not from ice, but fire, not because of withdrawal, but because of bold venturing into forbidden territory, like a modest but sexually hungry maiden slowly stripping before her first lover; not that she sees Jim as her lover—perhaps? likely? long shot? perhaps for this night? The questions remain but for the moment he embraces hopeful possibilities. At best, he'll be invited into her bed when he takes her home. At worst, it's all a heavenly fantasy, but the best fantasy he's ever had. Either way, she's playing her part well.

And she wasted no time in the opening act. When they arrived thirty minutes ago, Becki tossed her floppy purse—a fawn-brown hobo bag that she ran back in to get—on the table next to the jukebox selector console, wiggled out of her jacket, slid all the way into the booth, and sat sideways, her back to the window. A devilish glint danced in her eyes. Jim quickly discovered why. Her dad's old shirt was buttoned with only one button and she had ditched her bra.

Becki acted as if it were nothing but as she played with the string on her hobo purse, she gave Jim a knowing grin like she knew that he knew. Looking on in awe, he wondered if it was a come-on signal or just her liberated spirit. But he said nothing. He didn't dare. He tried to look away, to calmly reason, to stop the hot and surging river. But even before Juanita came to take their order, he gave up and dove into the flood. Unthinkable, unheard of—Becki without a bra—it's like him preaching on Sunday morning without his pants. Her breasts, though ample, are not so big as to demand support—her youthful chest muscles give them a natural high-perch—but she's always been very modest about her tits. Even when she was eleven, and had nothing but cute bumps of baby fat, she wore a flat training bra.

Now at the end of the meal, Jim again focuses on her girlish breasts as they nestle warmly, like baby bunnies, on her chest, soft, white, cuddly, and enticingly hidden by her barely buttoned shirt. Her cleavage is shallow but tantalizing as it diverges downward like the dimple of a baby's ass. He yearns to reach in and lift them out one at a time and to fondle them until she forgets her ice cream. When she breathes, her uptilted nipples press up against the inside of the shirt, not clearly but clear enough as they make two enticing bumps in the fabric, circled by dimly defined areolar shadows and nubile receding curves.

Becki takes a huge bite of sundae and spills some chocolate syrup on her shirt near her cleavage. As she swallows she looks down at the spot of syrup. When she lifts her eyes, she discovers Jim staring; a rush of pink stains her face but she does not object. On the contrary, her shyness quickly gives way to a wanton smirk as if she's proud of her maidenly breasts and their power to stir a man— especially an older *married* man. She returns to her sundae but Jim continues to stare, now at her face.

*"What?"* she gushes-smiles-blushes as if feeling the heat of his gaze.

"Whaddeya think?" he teases, his own face warming.

"So you noticed, huh?" Becki flirts.

"How can I not notice? You're almost out on the table."

Becki, half-turning, tucks her chin into her shoulder then rolls her eyes up to Jim in a sensual side-glance—but she does it all at once, in one provocative gesture. "So tell me, Shanley, you like what you see, or what?"

Hot question: Jim almost chokes on his coffee but he's not actually that shocked. Normally, he'd be shocked out of his mind but not on this night. He gives her a sporty grin then adds fuel to the flames, "Just undo that last button, gal, and I'll tell you." Becki is hot and he has no desire to cool her off. He's lost in fantasy—or perhaps reality—and he wants to whet her carnal appetite, to feed it and feed it until she gets so horny she'll fuck the first hard cock she sees, even if it's his. She takes another bite of sundae then swabs her ice-creamy lips with her tongue as if she's French kissing an imaginary mouth. Jim can almost taste her darting tongue. His penis, already hard, stretches farther down his leg.

Silence, searing silence. A more compelling erotic spell comes over them. Wanton exhilaration, no rules. Jim feels rushes of adrenaline. He and Becki have already crossed many forbidden lines; they're deep in scarlet sin even with their clothes on. But Jim's conscience is unplugged, his Bible closed. He still senses risk and fear and danger but now it only adds to the sexual high.

"I'm not gonna unbutton *anything*," Becki finally replies. She tries to look serious as she digs out another bite of sundae but she can't turn off her fountain. "I just undo the last button for my *se*cret lovers." Her voice brims with naughty-girl delight. She scrunches her face sassily then gives a big openmouthed grin showing her crooked adolescent teeth. Her blush is deeper, almost crimson.

Jim smiles incredulously. "You've got secret lovers?"

She turns toward the window, tosses her nose in the air, and gives an indignant "umph," as if piqued. "And *why* is that so hard to believe?" she asks, gesturing with her spoon as if it's a band-leader's baton. "I *am* college age, you know?" She tries to look adult but the best she can do is her frowny face, yet her pretended pout can't erase the sporty mirth playing about her mouth.

Outside, raindrops run down the window. All is black except for a few lights at the fire station and a pair of Conrail signals on the elevated tracks, both red, not to mention the distorted reflections from inside the diner: pinks, greens, and grays, and people color and fluorescent white and stainless steel, and Becki's honey-brown hair running down with the rain.

Jim sips his coffee. Becki stares out the window. He stares at her reflection, then at her. She's sober-eyed as if thinking but her faint smirk, which continues to tease her lips, tells him that her bawdy mood is still very much alive. He stares. His desire grows deeper, darker, as deep and black as the stormy night outside.

Love, lust, obsession. Girl, woman, mystery. Fever, wonder, magic. Female, female. Becki, Miss Becki, soft and cupid-faced, yet so adult. Jim craves to explore the blood-hot source of life in her panties, the dark evidence of her womanhood, her pussy, her pubic hair, her clitoris, her black tunnel of love and birth—her dark underbelly, the seat of her mystery and pleasure and power, that draws him, thrills him, scares him, and makes her so different from a man.

Becki, Becki. Her hot presence carries him, sweeps him into the swarthy depths of her. Breasts, curves, cunt, cunt, hairy cunt. Fierce, dark, mean, Becki's cunt, unrelenting, demanding, desperate for more, desperate to score, desperate to make a man—especially an older man—crave her youthful potency.

But not just her body. Jim craves to know her and know her until all ways of knowing her are exhausted. A knowing that goes beyond getting hard-ons over naughty talk, that goes beyond Becki's cuddle-bunny, pretty-dress, Sunday school goodness, beyond her pious put-ons, beyond her bratty adolescent insolence, beyond all her games and facades. A knowing that is feral, fierce, earthy, and instinctive, and beyond all rules, rites, duties, and vows.

Jim longs to explore the forbidden chambers and uncharted passageways deep within her soul that make her feel and think and act as a female. His carnal curiosity is rooted in a larger wonder, the wonder of her womanhood. The miracle of the womb, waiting for seed, fertile soil, primal connections to Mother Earth and origins. Earth, birth, energy and aura, maternal power, a mystical calling that transcends yet demands malehood, mating, and orgasmic completion. He still feels it with Sharon. After years of intimacy and discovery, he's yet to exhaust the mystery of his wife's muliebrity. She still intrigues him, amazes him. And he feels it with Angela, Janet, Sylvia, Sharon's sister Debbie, any woman that turns him on, Molly Gibson, Amy Brannigan, even high school girls, especially high school girls, Cathy Rosinski, Brenda Donovan, even Betty Sue Barnett back in Gilmer—Jim will always think of her as a teenager.

He's always felt an awe around girls, a magnetism, a desire to uncover, even as a small boy, like when he was six years old playing with his cousin Charlotte in his wading pool. She was twelve with long blond curls and big hazel eyes, and she wore a blue bikini. Even though he knew nothing about sex, he had an urge to touch Charlotte, to see her nakedness, especially between her legs. She must've felt it too because she took him into the barn, into the hayloft where they pulled off their bathing suits and stared at each other. Jim recalls her skinny-girl nakedness, her fried-egg tits, and he'll never forget her soft muff of fawn-colored pubic hair. She was just getting her puberty bush. It looked like overgrown peach fuzz.

But just as he was enjoying the sight, his father came into the barn and caught them. Charlotte started crying and Jim too. His dad scolded Charlotte, "You're a naughty girl. You're old enough to know better." After that Jim always thought of Charlotte as a "naughty girl." She came to visit each summer, and he liked her the best of all his relatives.

Returning from the window to her ice cream, Becki shovels in several spoonfuls. "So, Shanley, didyuh ever hear the washing-machine joke?" Her voice is clogged with ice cream and as she speaks, she gives him a quick inviting glance, just enough to let him know that her dirty-sweet mood has not diminished.

"No, but I'm game," Jim replies. He knows it has to be a dirty joke.

"Well, John 'n Mary are lovers. But they're wicked shy, so they have code words for everything, like his prick, they call it 'the laundry,' and her cunny, they call it 'the washing machine,' and when they make love, they call that 'doin' the wash.'" Becki pauses. She smirks and toys with her ice cream—and with Jim.

"Okay, okay, tell me the rest," he says impatiently. She has him and not just with the joke. She snickers, blushes. Jim's thoughts race, *I can't believe we're talking like this. It's like verbal foreplay with Sharon? This whole night has to be a dream?* But it isn't. Becki's moist and velvety voice is very real and deeper than usual, and dark and trancy and rich. Listening to her is like eating Jell-O chocolate pudding, the dark smooth kind that melts in your mouth. Jim loves her voice when it's seductive. He could listen to Becki all night, even if she simply recites the ABCs.

Finally, Becki rests her spoon in the dish and goes on. She gestures with her girlish hands. "One night John 'n Mary, they were on the couch watching a racy movie and John got wicked horny, so he said, 'Mary, you wanna do some wash?' And Mary, she said, 'Not now, honey.' Then the movie got racier and racier, and John, he was in a bad way so he said, 'Mary, my laundry needs to be washed wicked bad.' But Mary said, 'Let's wait, honey, 'til the movie's over.' So John, he got up and went into the bathroom and when he got back, Mary said, 'I can't wait either. You can put your laundry in now.' But John said, 'It's too late, honey. I already did my laundry—*by hand.*'" Blushing scarlet, Becki laughs. Jim's throat goes dry. He gives a sigh that becomes a chuckle then a chortle. His heart thumps. His face feels hot. Becki, Becki, dirty joke—no doubt now, he concludes. She has fucking on her mind.

At this point Juanita comes with the check, briefly disrupting their bawdy mirth. Jim and Becki quickly sober and make small talk with her. Juanita looks so sweet and prim in her gray-checked, white-aproned uniform and she says all the right words, but Jim senses something terribly plastic about her. After a minute or so, Juanita leaves returning to her duties behind the counter.

"She's marrying Freddie, right?" Becki asks as the prurient mood reasserts itself.

"Yeh," Jim replies, "in December. They rescheduled it from last June."

"So, Shanley, tell me, do yuh think Juanita gets it on behind Freddie's back, you know, with a lot of guys?" Becki speaks matter-of-factly as if the question is your routine everyday question, but a flirty half-grin pulling at the corners of her mouth gives away her seductive intent.

Becki, Becki. Too much. Jim has seen a lot of looseness and naughtiness in her since she moved down but nothing like this. How can she have such a fixation about fucking without doing it—with him? When they get in the car, she's going to kiss him, attack him. The thought makes him shake with anticipation. He picks up his coffee cup and holds it in front of him with both hands. He's beginning to wonder if he'll live to see the first day of October.

But live or die, Jim has no desire to break the spell, so he tosses the hot question back in the same lewd packaging; he pushes his uplifted cup to emphasize each point. "Well, she's 24. Her voice is low and sensual. She's got a full bosom and a sexy heart-shaped ass ... and she's had her own apartment for three years. So what d'you think, Miss Reinhardt?"

"Sounds like a fun way to live," Becki quips as she fishes for unmelted ice cream in the chocolate-vanilla glop at the bottom of her dish. "That's the neat thing about having my own place, you know. Now I can have guys over and nobody will know, not even you, Shanley."

"Like who?" Jim asks, playing along.

Becki cocks her head proudly. "Well, like maybe ... Stephen, to name one."

"And who is Stephen?" Jim asks curiously.

Finding one last bite of ice cream, Becki lifts it, but instead of eating it, she gestures with it. "Oh, he lives upstairs in the attic apartment and he's got wicked pretty eyes like Richard Gere. He works for Digital in Maynard, and last week we kinda talked on the porch."

"So that makes him your secret lover?"

"No, that part doesn't, but uh ... well, there's more to it."

Becki sucks the last bite of sundae off her spoon as if she's sucking something better. Jim watches wide-eyed. She swirls it around in her mouth like she wants to savor it, caress it, melt it with her tongue. Her voice is creamy with melted ice cream as are her lips. Angelic lips, rosy and cute. They make Jim think of her other mouth which he figures must be just as creamy in her underpants. Tantalizing thought: a hot burst of blood swells his hard-on.

"Like what?" Jim replies. "Did Stephen come to your apartment to borrow an egg and give you some sausage in return?"

No holding back. Jim wants to get Becki so randy that her lustful imagination juices not only her pussy lips but her panty liner as well. He knows she wears them because there's always an open package in her bathroom.

"Well, not to borrow an egg," Becki responds coyly, "but he did stop by in a way, not exactly, but sorta."

"What do you mean, not exactly, but sorta?"

"I uh—well, I sort of had this dream about him."

*O God, what an opening!* Jim exclaims to himself, then he teases her, "You're a virgin and a nice Christian girl, and you had a dream about a guy who lives in the attic?"

"Who says I'm a virgin?" Becki shoots back as if it's an insult, a blow to her sexual pride. She gives an impudent toss of her honey-maple locks then sassily scrunches her face at Jim. "You think you know so much about me, but you don't know *all* my secrets, Jimmy Shanley."

"I know you well enough, girl. You still have that cherry glow." He's playing with her of course, hoping she'll answer the question he's posed in his mind so many times.

No more ice cream, but Becki spoons some chocolate syrup out of the bottom of her dish; she gives a chocolate-covered grin.

"Well, that's *one* secret I'm not telling.... Maria, she always said that sex is like a drug, and once you taste it, you can't get it outa your mind. She's sure right about that, I tellyuh."

Now comes a dreamy look as if Becki's recalling the rush of her first orgasm. Their eyes meet. Jim senses meltdown.

Quickly possessing herself, Becki averts her eyes, her dreamy expression dropping back to a coy smirk. But Jim presses her, "So you made it with Manny, huh? Or just came close?"

"I'm not saying," Becki replies with feigned modesty, but her feint is not convincing.

Jim stares at her as she stares into her empty dish. Her smirk almost breaks but she reins it in. He jumps at the opportunity. "So he really turns you on, huh?"

"Jimmy Shanley, you cut it out!" she gushes-blushes, her face splitting wide. "Stop being so curious about me. I said I'm not telling." She fiddles in her dish. She tries once more to retire behind a mask of modesty but she can't kill the coquettish mirth in her face—as if she knows their talk is going to get even more prurient.

Taking the cue, Jim comes in from a different angle, "So, Becki Lea, are you going to tell me about Stephen, the dream you had about him?"

"O God," Becki banters, "you can't handle it, Shanley. I know you. It'll make you wicked jealous, and just get you all hot and bothered."

"Me jealous and bothered, over *you*?"

"Yeah, over *me*. I see you lookin' all the time." She narrows her eyes into her cute detective look as if she's deduced all of his lustful hopes, plans, and strategies.

"Maybe so, but still I want to hear about your wet dream."

"I didn't say it was *wet*," Becki declares, pretending indignation at the suggestion. "Girls don't have wet dreams." Yet her eyes spark with naughty elation as if the word "wet" really turns her on— as if savoring the fact that *her* sex dreams are never dry.

"Don't be so technical," Jim counters. "You know what I mean."

Becki rolls her eyes. "You think I'm gonna tell yuh *that*?"

"Why not? You've been talking dirty and suggestive all night, about 'doing it by hand' and 'putting the wash in' and all kinds of sexually explicit stuff? Telling about an erotic dream seems to fit right in if you ask me."

No reply. Becki places her elbow on the table, leans forward, and rests her head on her hand. She continues to play in the puddle of chocolate at the bottom of her dish. She stares wide-eyed into the syrup—then comes a sudden burst of wanton delight: "Okay, so it *was* a wet dream, but it happened in my sleep, like I can't help that. It's not like how guys are. I don't give in to lust every time I get a little bit bothered."

"So d'you ever do it when you're awake?" Jim asks without thinking. "The wash, I mean?" Becki doesn't reply but picks up her sundae dish and licks the remaining chocolate off the inside, off the lobes that look like flower petals.

*O God, I don't believe I asked her that*, Jim exclaims to himself. Taboo subject, unmentionable, but her X-rated mood and dirty joke have opened the door. The thought of Becki masturbating makes his head swim. *But why is it such a big deal? If Sharon does it, why not Becki? According to Kinsey, 4 out of 10 college-age single girls do it regularly, and 6 out of ten have done it at least once. I'd lay odds Rebecca's one of the four?* At the Air Force Academy, Jim and his fellow cadets studied *The Kinsey Report* more zealously than any textbook.

The question hangs like a sword—no, like a pulsing penis—over the table. Finally, Becki grins and chortles an oblique reply, "Your mind really *is* in the gutter. You hafta know everything about me, don'tcha, Jimmy Shanley, even what goes on in my fuckin' panties? Good God, I can't even fantasize and get horny over guys, without telling you." As she replies a flare of lust springs into her eyes, dilating them. Seeing this, Jim knows that she's wet between her legs.

"Well, you started this with your joke," he banters, his cock now a railroad spike in his jeans, so hard that it hurts. And his balls are swollen to the limit; they ache like they're in a vise.

"Well, I guess—" Becki starts then quickly stops.

"You guess what?"

"Nothing. I don't guess anything."

"But you said, 'I guess'?"

"I don't mean 'I guess.' I mean the answer is ... mostly no."

"Mostly no? What the fuck does that mean?"

Becki purses then folds her cupid lips. "I'm not telling," she insists.

"Okeydokey," Jim kids, relaxing his pursuit. "No biggie; you don't have to confess. Let's change the subject and talk about the visits we're gonna make tomorrow." He pulls some outreach cards out of his jacket pocket as if he means it. Becki waits. She blushes. She gives a sporty grin. Jim grins back but says nothing. Now he has *her*. He has her going, and he loves it.

"Well, maybe it happened once or twice when I was in Puerto Rico," she finally admits, unable to let go of such a delicious topic, "back when I was young and rebellious and curious."

"Once or twice, huh, and that was it?"

"Let's just say I have good self-control."

"So I guess that's why you took Maria's magazines home? So you could test and develop your self-control against the *biggest* and *hardest* and *most* sinful temptations?" Hot, wild, X-rated: Jim is using his whole arsenal; he wants to tempt Becki beyond any magazine.

Becki sucks her empty spoon like a pacifier then gives a sassy smirk. "Wouldn't you like to know?" Putting her spoon down, she wiggles as if a shiver is going up and down her spine. She wipes her mouth with a napkin, but not the smirk. "I can live without it, you know? I'm not like *you,* Shanley. You could never be single."

They're now wallowing in wantonness and drunk on prurience, moreso than most lovers during actual intercourse. Jim rarely gets this high with Sharon and certainly not with his clothes on. And Sharon would surely have her legs spread by now. On and on they go with verbal foreplay until he fears he will faint.

Finally, at 10:35 p.m., they stagger out like two drunks—especially Jim. Blue balls. Blue balls. Ache, ache, he can hardly walk. His nuts feel like bowling balls between his legs. *O God!* he cries in his soul. *I can't take it! I can't flirt like this without goin' all the way. I hafta fuck her. I'm goin' crazy. I want her. I want her forever, no matter the cost!* The yearning is final, like death—and he knows it.

Windy, colder. The rain has stopped. The wind has shifted into the northwest. Lots of leaves and small branches have blown down in the storm. A loose piece of fluted siding near the top of the diner screaks in the wind while an overturned trash can rolls and clatters on the other side of the street in front of the fire station.

The night is still charged and ominous as if the biggest event is yet to happen. Becki hops into the Mustang. Jim gets in on the passenger side.

* * *

Male to female, bush to bush, they sit facing each other, her legs over his. Her naked flesh looks silver in the flickering light from the TV. Her small hands trembling with anticipation, she takes his stocky rock-hard penis and guides it toward her honeypot until the head goes inside—into the honey.

Now Jim takes over. Teasing, teasing, he moves his swollen glans slowly up and down, in and out, making sweet sucky-oozy sounds. She leans back on her hands. She breathes in long drafts. She watches with ravenous eyes, holding back her eruption, holding and holding, as the musky, smoky, perspiry smell of aroused genitals wafts up over the bed.

"O God, let's *go!*" she cries after a long minute, that seems like an hour. Her words ride hot bursts of breath. Her face twists with sweet agony. "That feels *so* good. I can't wait any longer."

Too much. She pushes up onto Jim's lap and takes his full shaft into her hungry vagina. Her folded tummy fat hugs his paunch. Lifting her haunches then coming down, she fucks him slowly, then faster and faster until they're both thrusting violently, flesh slapping flesh.

Finally, they collapse gasping on the bed. Orgasmic high; seconds tick by, maybe thirty—shock, shock! Sharon bolts to her feet.

"YOU DE*CEIT*FUL BASTARD!" she screams. "YOU WERE THINKING ABOUT BECKI! I KNOW IT! I KNOW IT!" Sharon towers like a full-thighed Amazon over the bed. She gestures furiously as if throwing rocks at Jim. Her pear-shaped breasts bounce wildly on her chest. "YOU WERE FUCKING HER IN YOUR MIND! I KNOW! I KNOW YOU WERE!"

Guilty, guilty! But Jim fights back anyway in a futile effort to put his wife on the defensive. "Well, what about *you!* Your thought-life's not exactly pristine! You're always gettin' off on other guys, like Michael Montanaro, and Tony Liggons, and all the guys on the softball team!"

"NOT LIKE *THIS!*" Sharon roars back. "I may fantasize but I've never flirted around! And I certainly don't take men to the diner and try to seduce them with suggestive language! You weren't at the teen center, were you! YOU HAD THAT LITTLE BITCH AT THE DINER TONIGHT! DIDN'T YOU!"

Dead, dead, Jim is dead. No alibi, no excuse. He says, "Yes."

Arms, hands, fingernails. Hitting, scratching, burning pain. Insane with fury, Sharon attacks, screaming, wailing, slugging, scratching. Jim grabs her flailing arms but she breaks free and rages around the room. With one wild swing of her arm she sweeps everything off her dresser. Bottles and jars crash against the wall and floor. She knocks everything off his dresser as well. She storms to the door. She sobs-yells, "Never again! Never again! 'Follow the heart,' I hate it! 'Follow love'! You're not following *love*! YOU'RE FOLLOWING BECKI'S *CUNT*! I'll never let you touch me again! YOU *BAST*ARD! YOU LYING *BAST*ARD!"

Sharon grabs her Westclox windup off the TV and hurls it at Jim, but the clock shoots out sideways—she can never throw straight—and shatters the big mirror on her dresser. A thousand pieces of glass crash down into the night. She then departs—for the guest room most likely—slamming the door violently behind her.

Jim, his tongue-lashed ego stinging with pain, stares after her as the flickering light from the silent television plays upon the closed door. Finally, he gives a pitiful sigh, snaps off the TV, flops onto the bed, and lies there: naked, empty, blah, and smelling of sex. *What the fuck? How does she know who I'm thinking about? How'd she find out I was at the diner? If I'd thought of Shar instead of Becki there would've been no fight—yeah, right. Why didn't she say anything before? No mystery—when she comes right out of sleep into arousal, she has nothing on her mind but orgasm—fuck it!*

*Women and sex. They're all bitches, and liars too! They want it just as much, but they use it like a weapon. Becki turns cold and Sharon turns hot—she fucks me then fries me. Nailed by two wet cunts in less than an hour, and I love them both. But Becki, O God! I never wanted anyone like her, and she's off-limits.*

*I'm guilty, so fucking guilty, but what about them? They act like they never had an illicit thought even while they're creaming their panties. What the fuck, God? I don't have a chance. Loving and wanting a hot pussy—it's a curse. I wish the fuck I had no sex drive!*

Hurt, hurt, fatigue. Jim's brain is shutting down. He's too exhausted to reason or realize significance. He expects to hear the kids coming down to investigate but he hears nothing. The house is deathly quiet, except for the alarm clock—ticking, ticking on the floor.

# Chapter Twenty-one

The ticking clock on the floor pounds in Jim's head like a galloping horse. He gets up and turns on the lamp on his dresser; it's 1:40 a.m. The house is quiet. Glass is everywhere. He tiptoes around it and finds his shorts then quickly hauls on his Levi's. After popping on his Pony sneakers, he grabs a flannel shirt and takes off out the door. Strobes of lightning, screams of wind. The sky is charged with storminess. Fast-moving clouds, red and low, stream up from the river toward Greeley Hill. No jacket, but Jim feels warm, almost hot.

He drives fast. The wind buffets the car. Thunder crashes overhead. *Pink Floyd* booms over the radio. Thick red fog envelops the lowlands. The Mustang headlights probe the rufescent murk like a pair of bloody laser beams. Blue, blue, pang of fear—Jim sees blue lights following. He pushes the pedal to the floor. When he looks again, they're gone. Faster, faster, the Mustang pierces the night. Reservoir Road, Taylor Street, Hadley Hill, 59 Front Street. He zooms up the driveway, hops out, runs up the walk and through the door. Becki waits at the top of the stairs, naked save for her daddy's shirt. Jim bounds up the stairs into her arms. Cinnamon and sugar: her lips taste hot and sweet. She unbuckles his belt; they collapse to the floor. Their time has come, or so he thinks.

*KA-BOOM! KA-RAACK!* Blue, blue, electric blue. A lightning strike explodes like a smart bomb over Hadley Hill. The explosion blows open the front door. Jim hears howling wind then fierce snorting then hooves on the porch. Becki flees into her apartment. Terror, terror. Fiery eyes, hairy face, curved horns.

A Neanderthal bull-monster paws at the foot of the stairs. Panic, panic. Jim struggles to get up but his pants are tangled about his ankles. The beast charges up the stairs. Terror, terror. Gasping from fright, Jim hops, staggers into Becki's kitchen.

He closes and bolts the door. He breathes a sigh of relief—but it's not Becki's kitchen. "You feast on strange women in Proverbs 5:3!" Dr. Logan shouts. "You fornicate with Molech in the valley of Hinnom! You play with the hole of the viper in Isaiah 11:8!"

No kitchen but Moody Coliseum, and Pastor Jim stands center stage before a packed house. The scene is foggy as if the ruddy clouds have come in from outside. Jim, naked and ashamed, tries to pull up his jeans but he can't move his arms. His flannel shirt is his only cover. But Logan nods, and Jerry Crenshaw races over and rips it off his back. Becki is no longer an adult but a sweet little girl. She stands next to Logan in a pink Sunday school dress. Behind the pulpit and to the side towers Stan Campbell who's dressed as a Roman soldier, tufted helmet and all; he stands at attention next to a large wooden cross. Nailed to the cross is Becki's bum-around shirt. Logan pauses from his preaching then bends down and puts his arm around Becki. She gives him a Shirley Temple smile and a kiss on the cheek, then presents him with a bouquet of buttercups. The body roars and cheers.

"I MADE THE DECISION!" Logan cries above the cheering. "I made the choice! Glory be to God! Jesus loves his bride and he'll deliver her, just as he's given victory to little Rebecca, dear *sweet* Rebecca. But as for *you,* Jim Shanley, you still live in defeat and wallow in filthy abominations! And you call it following love! YOU CAN'T FOLLOW YOUR HEART! THE HEART IS *WICK*ED AND DE*CEIT*FUL!" Derisive jeers and laughter break out except Sharon and the kids are crying in the front row, along with Nana Pedersen. Jim feels three thousand fingers pointing at him. Hoping for mercy, he looks back at Logan, but Logan's face crumbles away like a breaking clay mask. His shoulders burst out of his suit like the Incredible Hulk. Bloody horns spike up out of his head. He becomes a Minotaur. Stan also becomes half bull, half Neanderthal. Jim turns back to the body, but all he sees is a multitude of bull-monsters. Even Becki has changed into a cute baby Minotaur, as she stands there in her frilly pink dress.

"YOU THINK GOD'S GOING TO DO IT ALL, DON'T YOU, JIM SHANLEY!" The Logan-Minotaur bellows. The body of Minotaurs roar as well, creating a thunderous tumult. "That's not how it is! You must exercise your free will, Jim Shanley! You must repent and go to the cross! You're using grace as a license to sin! Your life is lewd and lascivious and mired in lust! You're obsessed with carnal pleasure! You crave young flesh, forbidden flesh! You're oppressed by demons of lust! Your tongue is nasty and foul, an instrument of Lucifer! God is not mocked! If you don't get right, He'll vomit you out of his mouth in Revelation 3:16! And I don't blame him, BECAUSE YOU DESERVE IT, JIM SHANLEY! YOU DESERVE IT! You, you! Yes, *you*, Jim Shanley! You deserve it! Deserve it! Deserve it! Deserve it!"

The words "Deserve it! Deserve it!" echo through the auditorium, coming back again and again. Finally, Pastor Jim cries out, "I REPENT! I REPENT!" He falls on his face but he has no face, just a hairy ape-like snout. He too has become a monster. On the cross, Becki's shirt is now a serpent. Coiled about the vertical beam, it sticks out its red forked tongue—"O God! O God!" Jim cries desperately. He rolls to the other side of his bed. He feels feverish, dirty, and dishonest; he trembles. He feels guilty and humiliated.

The sheets are tangled around his naked body.

The nightmare made him sick. Tiptoeing through broken glass, he heads to the bathroom, but only takes a piss. The bathroom floor is freezing. He looks at his watch—3:15 a.m. Back to the bedroom. He turns on his dresser lamp—after retrieving it from the floor; the bulb somehow survived Sharon's rage—then checks the thermometer by the window; it's 31° outside. *Shit, I should go flip the main furnace switch so the heat'll kick on.* But the basement seems far away, like on a different continent. So instead, Jim fishes into his dresser for his flannel pajamas, puts them on, and crawls back into bed. But he leaves the lamp on. He shivers. He feels miserable and cold, and fearful and nauseated. Summer is over.

* * *

Pastor Jim, puffy-faced and groggy, drives slowly up Front Street. Under his shirt four Band-Aids cover a patch of clawlike lacerations on his chest where Sharon scratched him. Bright sun, but chilly and breezy. Thin layers of ice top the puddles. Jim has on his winter jacket for the first time since May. Fresh brushstrokes of yellow, red, amber, and auburn highlight the trees but green still predominates. A few maple leaves twirl and tumble down in front of the car like big yellow snowflakes. The Mustang crawls up the curved driveway. A light frost glistens on the lawn and on the cars in the parking nook, on Ruthie's Chevette, the church Escort, Kyle Donovan's Honda, the Browns' pickup, and Stephen's Subaru.

Becki's nightdream lover is the only tenant Jim has yet to meet. Ruthie lives on the first floor across from Mrs. C. and Sergeant Brown and his wife live across from Becki. Sergeant Brown is stationed at Ft. Devens. Jim parks next to the Escort and trudges slowly to the door; he feels ugly.

The old house is quiet except for kitchen sounds coming from Mrs. Courtney's apartment along with the smell of frying bacon. Jim knocks on Rebecca's door—nothing. He knocks again. Out comes a sleepy voice, "Awh, uh, my alarm, it didn't go off." He tells her he'll wait in the car but to hurry because it's a quarter to nine.

*Every Saturday*, he sighs as he goes back down, *I have to wait on her like she's a fuckin' celebrity.* But her tardiness is only an added aggravation. His heart is heavy and slowly sinking because he knows she'll be distant and cold, colder than the weather.

Her mood changed in the car as they drove home from the diner. She scarcely spoke but he felt the chill and his hopes of fucking her fled quickly back to the realm of fantasy. She didn't even invite him up but ran right inside, saying she was tired. So he

285

went home and fucked Sharon, and got her wrath as well.

After starting the Mustang, Jim goes around to the passenger side. He's still in shell shock from last night. Love, lust, foolish venture. Naughty Becki, hot Becki, dirty jokes, verbal foreplay. Cold Becki in the car, pain, pain. Then Sharon and nightmares, and fucking and fighting, and guilt, and more guilt. As he waits, his conscience convicts him again making his heart sink farther.

Jim knows he deserves to be rejected by Becki, by Sharon. He feels sleazy like a sex criminal. *And I'm the pastor,* he thinks. *What a fuckin' joke!* He despises himself. He knows he must repent and "get right" and return to reality. But he despises this thought almost as much. Prayer, outreach, Saturday duties. He feels like running. He feels like hiding. He doesn't want to see the church, or his office, or the eager faces of Saturday soldiers. But he has to.

Stress, stress, Jim hates the feeling—the have-to, ought-to tension that comes in the pit of your stomach when authority is watching and you must compete and perform and be good. It's like the first day of school, or going out for the team, or coming back to the Air Force Academy after a weekend pass, or trying to please the SAC wing commander at Westover or his boss at the weather station, or trying to impress Dr. Logan. *God, I hate getting it up,* he declares to himself. *But I have to. I gotta face reality.*

Suddenly: brown hair and puffs of white breath. Becki Lea comes out carrying her hobo bag and her outreach portfolio—she now keeps all the BFBC master visitation lists. Pulling her jacket around her, she plods slowly, head down, no bounce in her step. Her hair is a dirty thatch of straw, sticky and stiff from too much hair spray; it needs to be washed. She's still wearing her lightweight tan jacket; she never thinks about the weather until she's in it.

Sneakers, denim-clad thighs—flash: no more jeans. Naughty Becki flashes into Jim's mind. Surge of lust. Naked flesh, creamy thighs, rolling, rocking. She's on top of him panting toward orgasm. But the fantasy quickly gives way to sick greenish guilt that coats the walls of his conscience like slimy gall. He abhors himself, *What the fuck is wrong with me? I can't stop. I can't look at her without thinking about her cunt. I'm depraved.*

Becki opens the driver's-side door. She has little chunks of sleep in her eyes. Her complexion is pale, as if her blood has been drained and her cheeks stone-washed. Her blue eyes meet Jim's, but she quickly averts them as if ashamed. Tossing her stuff into the backseat, she plops into the driver's seat. "What are *you* gawkin' at?" she growls, her voice sulky and truculent. Her forehead furrows more deeply, her pout becoming a scowl.

"Nothing," Jim replies. "Whaddeya mean?"

leaves. The others are in their Sunday best, save for Russ who never dresses up except for Nashua.

Russ seems more concerned about his Red Sox cap which he holds gingerly as he picks at a loose thread under the bill. "I think we should table this until June," he remarks. "I see no point in starting a video college during the middle of the year." Now comes an impish grin. "Of course, getting a VCR might be good. We can rent movies from that new video store in Lancaster, like *The Graduate*—remember Mrs. Robinson? Or *The Last Picture Show*— now that was a great flick. Or even *Body Heat* with Kathleen Turner—now she'd get people to attend, especially the men."

Snickers, snorts, coughs, chuckles versus stony looks from Stan, Leslie, and Carl. "Come on; let's get serious," Carl admonishes, speaking in his usual monotone. "This is not a time for worldly jesting. We're talking about the future of our church."

"That's right," Barry Buford adds, suppressing a chuckle. He ...es to mimic Stan's indignant frown, but only succeeds in pushing ...fat eyes out a bit farther, until the whites are showing all around. ...ree with Carl and Stan. I've wanted to take college classes for ...time now, but I can't move to Nashua because of my job"— ..., Jim declares to himself; *Janet won't go; that's the real* ...—"so expanding our extension program will give me oppor- ...d I've talked to Cal and Joanne, and Freddie and Juanita, ...ra Sims. They all want to take college courses."

...speaks in a hefty voice, more hefty than even a month ...l he puts on weight like a bear preparing for hiberna- ...of his tie is half hidden by a roll of neck fat. He looks ...e Gleason than ever, like Ralph Kramden in his bus- ... And like Kramden, Barry speaks with boyish ...the readiness of body members to sign up for the ...But Jim knows from experience that when it's ...exuberance will not suffice.

...her bunned head and rolls her bullfrog eyes. ...of staff meeting already. We still have to ...g food drive. There *are* poor people in this ...eople who don't even have the necessities ...m the gospel for their souls and food and ...ow do you think the Lord feels when he ...his? Let's play the tape." Leslie has ...the shiny marble-sized spheres swing ...d.

...r Jim replies, thinking how Leslie's ...ings on her person. Then he turns ...promo tape, Stan?"

"I saw you lookin' at me."

"So?"

"I'm not a sexual object, you know?"

"Well, are you a sexual person?" Jim presses scornfully as he vents his own guilt and aggravation and hurt. "Do you ever have sexual desires? Do you like getting off, or do you have a problem like being secretly frigid?" He knows these subjects will not play on the morning after, but he's already resigned to the coming explosion so he primes the charge—like a misbehaving child who knows he deserves a spanking and wants to get it over with.

"That's kind of personal, don'tcha think?"

"It didn't seem too personal last night?"

"Forget about last night!" Becki snarls, contorting her face defiantly. "I hate what happened last night! Maybe I do want sex, but it's none of *your* business. It's personal, between me and my husband someday. I don't want it in some heated rush, like some horny animal. I want it to be God's way, the right way—so *knock* it off, Shanley! OKAY! I know what you're thinking, and I'm wicked sick of it! Just *sick* of it!"

"So, what am I thinking?" Jim asks.

"You're not thinking, you're *lust*ing, and don't deny it!"

"Okay, so I'm looking, but it's more than lust. Didyuh ever hear about love? Oh, pardon me, I forgot. You don't need love, or sex." Jim pauses then sticks the knife in, "And speaking of lust, what about you, Miss Becki Braless? You were no *saint* last night?"

Glaring straight ahead, Becki grabs the top of the steering wheel with both hands. Her countenance tightens with reproach. Fire ignites in her eyes. Her temple pulses. But she holds back her rage as if preparing her defense—and God's. Meanwhile, she vents a safety-valve burst of indignation. Her voice wavers just enough for Jim to know that greater wrath is yet to come. "Don't accuse *me*. It's *your* fault. You always get me goin', and get me talking about filthy suggestive stuff, stuff I'm ashamed of. That's not love, and it's happening more and more, and it's...."

"It's what?" Jim prods. "Come *on*, Becki, spit it out."

Acrimony fills the car: gas fumes waiting for a spark. Becki gives Jim a withering glance but no reply. She grips the steering wheel so tightly that her knuckles turn white. Her round cheeks slowly blotch as if the final wrath of God is rising in her body. A red maple leaf tumbles down onto the windshield catching in the wiper mechanism. Flash—"IT'S SIN! IT'S SIN! IT'S SIN!" she blazes, her words sudden, painful, piercing, like three pistol shots.

*Bang! Bang! Bang!* Each bullet lodges deep in Jim's bosom. Hot and heavy agony engulfs his heart. Nonetheless, he continues to twist the knife, "How do *you* know, Miss Pious Panties!" He's cutting his own tombstone.

"Because God says so! That's why!"

"So He came down and talked to you about it, huh?"

"He didn't have to! He wrote it in the Bible! It's in the Bible, and you know it! And you know what Pastor says about fooling around. You just want me to give in to lust without considering consequences, or love or God, or being married. Well, I'm not *like* that. It's wrong and you can't get away with it, Jimmy. Nobody can. God's truth doesn't change to fit your fantasies. You can flirt and talk dirty all you want, but—" Becki stops midsentence. She lets go of the steering wheel. Silence. She takes a deep breath, holds it until blue with indignation, then she detonates: "BUT IT'S STILL *SIN* AND I HATE IT! AND GOD HATES IT TOO! HOW YOU GET NASTY AND LOOSE AND GET ME GOIN', AND GET ME THINKING ABOUT SINFUL STUFF! LOVE IS *PURE,* NOT NASTY AND DIRTY! YOU JUST WANT ME TO GIVE IN LIKE A SLUT! YOU JUST WANT MY BODY! YOU JUST WANT ME IN BED! AND DON'T YOU *FUCKIN'* DENY IT!" Blue, purple, red with rage, she beats the air with her fisted hands.

"OKAY, DAMMIT! I DO WANT YOU IN BED!" Jim roars almost gagging on his erupting passion as his pent-up heart blasts through his self-pity and self-hate. "You're right! I do want your body! I *DO*! I *DO*!" He pounds the dashboard furiously like it's a pulpit, hitting it so hard that the blue vinyl splits wide from the blows, like an axe wound in a human head. "I *DO*! I *DO*! I want you more than any woman on earth! But I love you! I love you, Becki Lea! Dammit, doncha get it! Even if we never go to bed, I love you! I love you more than—"

"YOU DON'T LOVE *ANY*ONE, JIMMY SHANLEY, EX-CEPT YOURSELF! You don't even love who you're supposed to love, like God 'n Sharon!" Becki heaves and pants as if breathing fire; her face scrunches, her eyes fill, her nostrils flare. "You think nothing of breaking your vows! Well, I'm not gonna help you! God doesn't take it lightly! You're a deceitful dirty-mouthed bastard! I don't wanna fuck you! AND I *NEVER* WILL! Pull your head out, Jimmy! Nothing has changed! I toldjuh last April we could never be lovers! Just 'cause you got me goin' and talking about dreams and Puerto Rico and personal stuff—which I shoulda never done—doesn't mean I want *YOU*! Nothing has changed! What are you, dumb in the head! How many times do I have to say it! I hate your dirty lustful spirit! It makes me want to puke! You need to get right with God! I don't even want to be with you when you're like this!"

"Like what!" Jim asks angrily.

"Like a dirty old man! That's what!" Along with her hot words, Becki spews a shower of hot spittle all over Jim.

"Well, what about you, *Saint* Rebecca? I guess you're clean and pure, huh, like the *wash*? Like when you do it by hand, like in your bed last night after I dropped you off?" Jim is locking his coffin; he knows he's *finished.*

Blur. Arm. Hand. *KA-WHAAP!* Becki slaps Jim sharply. "YOU'RE A FUCKIN' LIAR, SHANLEY!" Shock wave of hurt. His cheek burns. "You're always thinking nasty stuff about me! And fantasizing! Well, I'm not *like* that! I'm not loose and gutter-minded like you, always thinking about sex and dirty stuff! HOW *DARE* YOU ACCUSE ME! I OUGHTA RIP YOUR FUCKIN TONGUE OUT! I DON'T HAFTA TAKE THIS SHIT!"

Breaking into tears, Becki grabs her purse and portfolio o the backseat, bursts out of the car, and strides defiantly towar house. Halfway to the porch, she stops and screams out a sc "FUCK *YOU,* JIMMY SHANLEY! I HATE YOUR GUT hurls the portfolio back toward the car. It comes open, di outreach cards and visitation lists all over the yard. She t up the steps, hurries inside the house, and slams the d

Jim's face burns as does his heart. Hauling him car, he chases down the loose cards and papers as wind. The storm door didn't latch when Becki blows back and forth, squeaking, whining October, but Jim Shanley does not need a ca seasons are changing.

*   *   *   *

Carl Baker's hairless head r a polished ceramic egg. His file fawning grin. "Most definitely Word daily, and if we get L

"I don't think it's wis Saturday," Beverly cuts peering over her half-e tip of her nose. "It's blue-gray hair give

Angela has bility of workin books and pa

"Bev afternoon." boy is wind-te

Stan nods to indicate yes, then gives a glossy brochure to each staff member. On the front is a picture of Dr. Logan teaching an LBI class, and above the picture in bold blue letters is the title: EDGE. After putting on his reading glasses, Stan briefly explains the handout then starts the recorder. Dr. Logan's sandpapery voice fills the room:

> I want to talk with you about our new video college. We call it Evangelical Dynamic Growth Emphasis or EDGE. The acronym EDGE is most appropriate because this video extension program will give your local church the edge over Satan and his devices, the edge over your flesh and its sinful tendencies, the edge over liberal churches that preach lukewarm messages, and the edge over the world system that tempts the believer and draws many away. Our EDGE curriculum not only allows your local branch membership to take LBI courses and to graduate, but it will also make your ministry the most dynamic force for Christ in your community....

Everyone seems to be listening except for Russ and Joe. Russ is still occupied with his cap while Joe, as if somewhere else in his mind, gazes out the window at the fading pink in the evening sky.

All BFBC staffers—officers, elders, deacons—are supposed to come to staff meeting. Academy teachers are also expected to attend, but Janet never comes, and Doris only half the time. Stan told Pastor Jim before the meeting that Doris is under the weather. Jim never discusses Doris with Stan, but he figures the weather she's under comes in a green Carlo Rossi jug. As the tape drones, Jim stares at the wall clock. It says 6:42 p.m., and 35 seconds, but the red second hand is still crippled; it quivers at seven but can't make it to eight. Jim feels the same on this second Sunday of October, like he's stuck at seven and can't go forward—or backward. He hasn't talked with Becki for nine days. She normally comes to staff meeting and sits to his left where she takes notes for him, but not this Sunday or last. He sees her at school but from a distance.

Cool days, crisp days, fallish. Honking skeins of southbound geese arrive daily, taking up temporary residence on the reservoir. The nights are frosty in the meadow and all the summer flowers have died. Only goldenrods and asters remain. The meadow seems sad without buttercups, even sadder without Becki. Jim knows he can get her back by apologizing and denying-denouncing his romantic feelings. But he feels she should accept her share of the blame for the verbal orgy that took place at the diner. After all, she was as coquettish and sexually suggestive as a woman can get, short of kissing and fondling. Yet he knows that she's right. She can never be his lover. He's married. He's too old. She must save her passion for her future husband. God will never permit it.

Jim now accepts this as reality, except when he walks by the stone fence, or goes to the big rock, or sits by the lake, or drives by the diner—or eats or sleeps or breathes. No. No. A thousand times, no. His head may accept it but not his heart. Despite Rebecca's vehement affirmation of her April denial, he agonizes daily, *Becki wants me? Becki wants me not?*

The tape plays. Logan introduces Jerry Crenshaw, the project director for EDGE. As with most initiatives coming out of Nashua, Jim smells Rich Beckman's sly ingenuity and Matt Garrett's shrewd strategies. All LBI classes are videotaped anyway so Crenshaw simply has to reproduce the tapes and sell them to the branch ministries. The branch churches will have to promote their local college classes to get enough students to cover cost.

Russ described it well, over coffee in Jim's office, "It's just another scheme to squeeze more money out of the LBI sponge." Crenshaw called in September and Pastor Jim turned it over to Stan. Nashua's goal, of course, is to convince each branch to buy a full load of classes, so here comes the rah-rah tape.

Crenshaw, his glib Ted Koppel voice crackling through the cheap Panasonic recorder, goes on for some ten minutes explaining the details of EDGE implementation.

On the Sharon front, it took Jim six days to get back into her good graces, and back into her bed. As it turns out, she had called the teen center on that hellish Friday night and Leslie "big mouth" Burton told her she had seen the Mustang at the diner. Sharon called the diner and talked with Juanita, so Jim was dead on arrival, except his wife fell asleep and her hormones got the best of her—when sexually sober, Sharon refers to her sex drive as "hormones." During the Shanley peace negotiations, Sharon at first demanded that Jim spend no more time whatsoever with Becki and five days of apologizing, arguing, promising, and lying failed to budge her. But what fervent pleading could not achieve, Sharon's hormones accomplished in five minutes—a week of celibacy was too much.

She came to the guest room at one a.m. and quickly made her demands like a court clerk administering an oath. But she wanted more than promises. She could never make it as a nun, nor could Becki, and yet *he's* the one with the "lust problem"—but anyway, Jim swore he'd never again cut into family time, that Becki and he would conduct ministry business only, as he had agreed all along, and that there would be no more "Friday nights at the diner." Then during foreplay, Sharon added a final condition: if he breaks his promise, he must see Dr. Logan for counseling. Jim readily agreed.

Peace with Sharon, but he's only halfway back. Until he reconciles with Rebecca, there can be no peace in his heart.

The Friday night diner incident has proved to be much less volatile as a gossip item than it could've been. Leslie Burton knows that Jim ate with Becki at the diner and that Sharon was looking for him, but that's hardly news. Juanita overheard Jim and Becki talking, but not as much as Jim feared. What she related to Sharon was incriminating—enough to set Shar off, her jealous and seasoned mind jumping to the correct Jim-Becki conclusions—but quite mild to an unbiased ear, certainly mild compared to the raunchier portions of Jim and Becki's conversation. Moreover, Juanita's reputation among the women in the church does not make her a reliable source for gossip about the pastor.

Becki's absence at outreach and staff meetings has scarcely been noticed, except by Russ and Jodi, both of whom know more than Jim has confessed. But what they know is gleaned through their closeness to Jim, and Becki, through sensitivity and heart awareness rather than gossipy chitchat.

Finally, the promo tape stops, and Campbell starts, "The beauty of the EDGE curr'culum is that it satchers us with the Word. We may be ahead of the dead churches in this town but we can do better. We have too many lazy Christians in our ranks." Stan mauls the air with his huge pawlike hands. "An' no dis'spect to you ladies, but we got too many men stayin' home an' babysittin' when they oughta be hearin' the Word. The Bible says that the *husband* is the spiritual head in the home, not the wife." Truth is, it rankles Stan to even have women at staff meeting. "We gotta make a choice. We can settle back and be backsliders 'n pleasure-seekers an' dwindle down to nuthin', or we can hear the Word daily an' get on fire to win souls! I pray the Word'll be preached here 24 hours a day 'til our flesh is cruc'fied an' sin is 'radicated from our midst. That's why we need the EDGE program now!"

"So, what does it cost?" Beverly asks, unmoved by Stan's zealous preaching.

"How can we talk about cost right now?" Carl jumps in fervently as he fans his EDGE brochure back and forth in his skinny insectlike hand—yet compared to Stan, Carl is calm and clinical.

"Carl's right," Stan agrees. "How much is it worth to save a soul from hell?"

"But still, we need to know the bottom line," Russ asserts, now giving his full attention to the discussion. "Besides, how can we send more money to Nashua when we're in the red locally?"

Stan runs his thick fingers through his hoary hair then gives an exasperated sigh as if to say, "You folks jus' don't get it, do you?"

But he doesn't actually say it. Instead, he cools and says, "It's on the back of the brochure, Russ. For each three-hour course we pay $500, but it's really a deal 'cuz we can use the course over an' over, year after year. Now we also have to buy three VCRs. But if we buy through Nashwa, we can get 'em for $475 each."

"How can you talk about spending more money on Nashua stuff," Jodi complains, "when the teachers here are getting Depression-era wages? After taxes I barely get $175 per week." The meeting has degenerated into a debate. Pastor Jim has no energy or inspiration to participate, so he sits back and listens.

Stan replies to Jodi, "We're talkin' 'bout a one-time 'vestment, Jodi. An' this's for trainin' an army to win souls."

But Jodi is not convinced. "What about my first- and second-graders? Don't they have souls?"

"The $1500 for the VCRs may be a one-time allocation," Russ remarks simultaneously with Jodi, "but we still have to buy new courses each semester at $500 a whack, right?"

"Now, Jodi, you're being paranoid," Carl declares. "This won't affect the academy budget."

Stan answers Russ, "Right, but we're gonna develop a video lib'ary, so our new members—an' we'll be convertin' a lot more—they'll take the old courses. We'll come out ahead."

"But, Carl," Beverly says, supporting Jodi, "we have budget requests each year that get voted down, like the lab equipment and the computer, and paving the basketball court."

"I agree with Carl," Barry says with a burst of exuberance. "Let's vote on it."

"Bev's right," Jodi says at the same time as Barry. "Our money should go to our kids. They're the future of this church, not some Nashua fantasy about converting this whole town."

"How can we be soldiers," Stan asks, "if we're thinkin' 'bout our own pocketbook? I work a full-time job and I take no money from the ministry. Jesus calls us to lay down our lives."

"But I can't go on Friday nights," Leslie says, seemingly concerned that she might miss out on the LBI classes. "Can't we have the video college on Monday, Wednesday, and Thursday?"

"Who's going to keep the books?" Angela asks again. "I'm not."

"I have to go turn on the PA for service," Joe announces as if waking up.

"Are you suggesting that our teachers shouldn't be paid?" Beverly asks Stan.

Stan, ignoring Beverly, replies to Leslie, "We'll try to do that, Leslie. We'll try to keep Friday night open."

"Stop by the kitchen and plug in the coffee," Russ says to Joe above the debate.

"What about you, Carl?" Leslie asks. "Don't you think it's a good idea to keep Friday nights open?"

"Okay, okay," Pastor Jim says, finally taking charge. "This is going nowhere and we've only got ten minutes. It seems to me there's a more basic issue here. What's our goal anyway? To teach the Bible and train up Christian soldiers and saints? Or is it to love and get close to people whether they get right, or not?"

This question opens a can of clashing convictions. Jim and his staff rarely argue theology, at least not openly. In the LBI system it's assumed a priori that everyone accepts Dr. Logan's Bible-based philosophy. But this meeting is proving to be different.

"The Bible is very clear on this," Carl asserts, sweeping the air with his mantis-like arm which seems all bone and no flesh inside the sleeve of his suit coat. "'In the beginning was the *Word*.' So doctrine has to be preeminent and it must be taught categorically like Dr. Logan says."

Barry, his face turning red with emotion, or lack of air, supports Carl, giving the standard LBI line, "The Bible commands us to save people from hell. Millions are perishing without Christ. We have to save them and teach them the Word, and train them to be soul-winners."

Leslie nods approvingly. "I agree," she says. "We must put the Bible first. Sound doctrine is the seed and love is the fruit."

"No way," Jodi rebuts. "Love comes from within, not from studying the Bible. I had love in my heart when I was a little girl, long before I knew any Bible doctrines."

Barry counters Jodi, "But Dr. Logan says we can't trust our hearts because—"

"Don't tell us what Dr. Logan thinks," Jodi comes back, her emotions rising. "Tell us what *you* think, Barry! What *you* think ... how *you* feel, in *your* heart." Pen in hand, she gestures sharply at Barry as if the ballpoint is the handle of an invisible whip.

"But fallen humans cannot love with true love," Carl refutes Jodi. "The natural heart is deceitful and wicked in Jeremiah 17:9. Only after we invite Jesus into our hearts, can we truly love with Christ's self-denying love. This love comes from the Word and the Holy Spirit. We must be born-again to love with true love."

"I never liked that verse," Angela says as if thinking out loud. "It must be translated wrong. I don't think my heart is wicked. I give in to temptation sometimes, but I'm not wicked."

Stan lifts his big black Bible and declares, "'Blessed are they that hear the Word of God an' keep it' in Luke 11:28. It's all in here.

295

This is the Word of Aw'mighty God! We can't love without it, or marry or raise children, or rule a home or run this church or face death, or have any hope or be anointed. The highest form of love is learnin' docturns together. We need Bible teachin' ever' night 'steda worldly talkin' 'n chitchat. This holy book is *all* I need."

"Amen to that," Carl agrees. "'Faith comes by hearing' in Romans 10:17, 'and hearing by the Word of God.' Anything you do apart from the Bible is sin because it's outside of faith. If your life doesn't conform to the Word, you're either unsaved or a backslider. You're out of fellowship with God."

"I've got no quarrel with the Bible," Russ counters. "But I put loving and being close to people ahead of *any* book. The Bible may have a lot to tell us, but I can't hug it on cold nights or laugh with it or cry in its arms, or make love to it. I want intimacy with people, not doctrines. If God is love, He has to be bigger than a book, bigger than rules and concepts, bigger than being 'lost' or 'saved' or 'backslidden.' Doctrines and categories may be good to a point, like in helping us define our faith, but not when they get in the way of love, and separate people in the name of God."

Barry rebuts Russ, "But without the Word, we'd be sinning *all* the time, like Carl says. And we have to separate the lost from the saved. The lost are going to hell. They're out of fellowship with God, like Dr. Logan says. We can preach the gospel to the lost, but we can't be close to them, not if we're close to God."

"We've been studying the same doctrines for years," Jodi declares, contradicting Barry, and Carl. "Yet we just keep on sinning and sinning. Maybe the problem is our definition of sin?"

"That's 'zachly why we need the Word ever' day an' ever' night," Stan proclaims. "We mus' study an' pray an' rededicate 'til the devil has no power over us. The docturns are good; we jus' don't study 'em enough, or obey 'em."

Russ rebuts Stan, "I think we're too busy already. How can we fit in fifteen hours of college each week?" Russ, his hand fisted, hits the conference table with moderate emotion—but short of anger. "Busy, busy, rush-rush, push-push, produce, achieve, conquer, grow, grow, grow. We're becoming a business, an assembly line, a big organization. I don't have the answers but I came here six years ago for one reason. I felt love when Pastor Jim preached. It wasn't his doctrines. And I felt love from you folks too. That's why I stayed. Now we're *so* busy we scarcely have time to give each other a smile, much less touch hearts."

"That's not what Jesus says," Carl rebuts. "He says, 'Go ... and teach them to observe all things I have commanded you.' We need the Word daily. We need a strong structure to obey the Lord, to keep us from sinning, so we can claim our finished-work victory."

"That's right, Carl!" Stan exclaims. "We're in a war with Satan. And the Word is our sword. We mus' use it might'ly. This is all-out war!"

"Okay, so it's a war," Russ comes back. "I believe that, but Jesus was also in the war and my Bible tells me that he took on the flesh of a poor carpenter and just went around loving and healing and doing good. He didn't have a big organization with professional money-raisers and tracts and brochures, and busy hyped-up rush-here-rush-there schedules ... and some new let's-push-harder program every three months—"

"But he died to save souls from hell," Barry declares, cutting Russ off.

"True, Barry," Russ goes on, "but he didn't have a big organization that was propped up with money and marketing, and fear and lies. He just hung out with common people like Peter, James, and John, and Mary Magdalene, the hooker. He didn't bow down to celebrities and dignitaries, and kiss up to winning personalities. He got closest to losers and sinners and outcasts ... and children. Everywhere he went, he had kids playing around him and crawling on him." Russ gestures with his Red Sox hat, so vehemently that it almost flies out of his hand. "But we treat kids like they're in the way, like they're in the way of progress, in the way of business. We don't even like having them in church, because they talk and cut up. Well, Jesus never told kids to shut up or to be still, or to go to the nursery. Now *that* ought to tell us something about our priorities. If Jesus walked in here and saw us having this high-and-mighty staff meeting, he'd break it up, and turn over this table ... just like he did when he cleared the temple."

"But Mary Magdalene repented?" Angie says as if concerned about the Lord's reputation. "Jesus didn't hang around with her while she was still doing it, did he?"

"I beg to differ, Russ," Carl says simultaneously with Angela. "If the Lord walked in, he'd say preach the Word 'in season, out of season,' and 'study to show thyself approved.' He'd tell us to go forward with the EDGE program."

"Of course not," Leslie answers Angie. "He cast seven demons out of Mary Magdalene, demons of lust. She was a believer after that."

Joe Lareux sticks his head into the conference room. "It's seven-thirty," he announces. "There's only about fifteen people out there so far, but I'm going to start the songs anyway ... in about two minutes."

Pastor Jim tries to end on an amicable note, "This *is* a change

... but I think it's good to have some healthy discourse now and then." From the look on Stan's face, and Carl's, he's not sure they agree it's healthy. "But if you're looking for my opinion, you'll just have to listen well when I preach." Jim chuckles then closes with a short prayer.

\* \* \*

9:02 p.m. Jim is in his office. The service is over. Stan's clean-up crew is vacuuming. Russ and Carl are helping Bev and Leslie convert the classrooms from Sunday school setup back to weekday setup. Sharon stayed home. In fact, only 27 turned out, not unusual for Sunday nights in the fall. But the low offering, $97.45, is disturbing, especially in the light of Russ's recent report. Jim never expects much on Sunday night—most members tithe on Sunday morning or Tuesday night—but they usually get at least $175.

Becki came to church but kept her distance of course. Jim preached on Job and now he feels like Job. *Shit, she jokes with Jodi and Barry after service but she doesn't even look at me. She's perfectly happy without me. She could live the rest of her life without me and it wouldn't bother her at all—God, I miss her! How come she doesn't miss me?* Jim gets up. He paces. He agonizes. He stops at the window. He checks the thermometer. It's 37°. The chilly autumn weather continues but it feels even colder in his office. He gives a resigned sigh. *Accept it. She doesn't love you the same. She wants a young husband, not an illicit fling with a married*—a knock, the door opens. Frog eyes. Pungent perfume. Leslie Burton. *O Lord, not her. Why can't it be Becki?*

Leslie hands Jim an LBI form letter. "Pastor, Angie asked me to give this to you. She had to leave right after service. She said it came Saturday but she forgot to give it to you at staff meeting." Leslie gives a dutiful grin then departs. The letter is a computer-generated reminder from Jerry Crehshaw's office that BFBC is late with its monthly WMF (World Missionary Fund) donation.

*Fuck this!* Jim exclaims to himself as he wads the letter and slams it into his trash can. *Hasn't been a week and they're already pushing. It's all computerized. Our past record doesn't mean shit. Haven't been late for seven years 'til last month. I sure don't see any grace here—and why don't they call it what it is, a ten percent tax, a tithe? Besides, if Crenshaw has a problem, why not give me a call instead of this computerized bullshit! He's just a skinny big-headed brown-noser. I can't stand the little fucker.*

Bristling with irritation, Jim storms out of his office to the men's room where he finds Russ Bradley at the urinal. "You're just the person I need to see," Jim declares venting his rancor. "I just got an overdue notice from Crenshaw. If those bastards don't cool it about money, I'm gonna take this ship—" Russ immediately nudges Jim then puts his finger to his mouth, making a "shhhh" sign, but he utters not a word. Jim quickly sees the reason.

Carl Baker, the toilet flushing behind him, swings open the door to the stall and marches out. He grins and gives a friendly, "Hi guys," then washes his hands, makes a few comments about the chilly weather, and departs.

Russ smirks impishly and says, "Loose lips sink ships ... especially when Carl Baker's in the shitter." They both laugh then Russ becomes serious and tells Jim that he already saw the overdue notice from Crenshaw, that it's a reminder they'll have to take action if things don't improve by year's end.

After exiting the men's room, Russ goes out the front door while Jim grabs his suit coat and briefcase and heads out the back. As he unlocks the empty, cold, Becki-less Mustang, a wave of heavy sadness washes over him.

* * *

Jodi Donovan laughs as she stuffs the last of her donut into her mouth. A shower of crumbs cascades down her white knit shirt. 2:10 p.m., 6th period, but no one is teaching. The day started chilly but has warmed into a toasty afternoon, and the overheated building has zapped all scholastic energy. Besides, it's Friday. To kill the last hour, Bev and Angie have the kids in the main hall for games and singing. Jodi took the opportunity to escape to Jim's office.

She wipes the crumbs from her shirt then looks down sheepishly, her laugh relaxing into a secretive smile. "Guess who called me Wednesday night?" she says.

"I don't believe it," Jim replies, lifting his coffee mug. "He didn't, not Tony? I wondered why you're so frisky and charged up today."

"Yeah, he called. I couldn't believe it either."

"So what'd he say?"

"He said he wanted to see me."

"And?"

Jodi grins, her cheeks dimpling. "I met him at Searstown yesterday after school. He and Claudia split up you know—at least for now. That's why they haven't been to church. Tony's living with his uncle in Ayer—anyway, he and I took a long ride. It was exciting, but scary too." Jodi's lavender eyes show hope, hurt, and unquenchable warmth.

"Well, good for Tony," Jim says. "He's got more balls than I thought."

Jodi doesn't reply; she seems occupied as if thinking. Shifting her weight on the edge of the desk, she cranks her neck to look out the window. Jim takes a slow drink of coffee. After gazing for a bit, Jodi makes a few remarks about the weather, about how Indian Summer is coming for the weekend. Finally, a bold twinkle flashes in her eyes, then comes a knowing grin and a pink rush, "Well, Jim, I guess you know that Becki Reinhardt loves you."

Shock, choke, coughing. Jim chokes on his coffee. His heart soars then spins out of control like a crippled fighter plane. Hot face, clammy hands; he can't swallow. He's suspected since summer that Jodi knew about Becki but this is the first open discussion of her. "How d'you know?" he asks, after recovering enough to talk.

"Because I see it in her eyes when I mention your name, or when you come into class for some reason. Believe me, Jim, she misses you like crazy. I'm not sure if this is good news or bad, but you know it's true."

"W-well, uh ... well, uh—" The office door opens; Beverly sticks her head in and says that little Paul Sims is having a temper tantrum in the main hall. Jodi leaves to attend to him.

*Becki, Becki; oh, Becki!* Jim exclaims to himself, his heart still soaring and spinning. *She does love me! She misses me! O God, I can't wait to make up with her, to talk with her, to spend time with her. I don't care if she accepts her share of the blame or not. I just want to be with her.*

His heart soars higher and higher until he fears it will burst with joyous anticipation. But then it peaks and falls into a screaming dive, hurtling, hurtling toward the ground until he's terrified. He knows he'll crash and burn—but at the last second, just above the treetops, he pulls out and recovers a measure of emotional stability. He swivels his chair and gazes out the window at the sunny day, at the hazy-blue sky, at the pine trees swaying lazily in the warm breeze. A leftover green-and-black dragonfly hovers outside his office windows.

*Yes, yes,* Jim cries happily to himself, *Indian Summer is indeed coming for the weekend.*

\* \* \*

"Hello," comes Rebecca's soft voice.

"Becki Lea," Jim says, his heart in his throat. The confidence he had after talking to Jodi five hours ago has given way to fresh anxiety; he fears Becki may crush his renewed hopes.

"Yeah," Becki replies, her voice becoming quiet now that she knows it's Jim.

"I uh ... well, I miss you on outreach and all," Jim says imploringly. No response, just bothered silence on the other end, or so it seems to him. "Really, Becki, I'm sorry about everything. It was all my fault. I know I got carried away. I'm sorry for getting you upset ... but it's no reason to break up the team. I know things are the same, like we agreed last spring. I accept that."

Still no response. A sudden shiver of fear shoots up Jim's spine but he pops the question anyway, "So, Becki, d'you want me to pick you up for outreach in the morning? It's Saturday, you know?"

"I know it's Saturday," Becki says; she still sounds like a bothered mouse.

Jim's heart pounds: a kettledrum in his throat. "Well, what d'you say? D'you wanna go or what? We've got lots of people to see?"

Silence, then a faint reply, like a feather falling into a cloud, "Yeh, I guess." Becki seems determined to show no emotion.

"Good," Jim says, "I'll pick you up at the regular time." Then, with a sudden burst of boldness, he adds, "Are you sorry too?"

"I guess," comes her mouselike answer—"But it was mostly *your* fault!" she chortles, her voice becoming suddenly happy and alive with teasing mirth.

"Oh *yeh*?" Jim kids back as relief spreads through his soul like a narcotic. The fourteen-day fight is over.

After bantering a bit longer, Jim again tells her that he'll pick her up at the regular time, but Becki doesn't want to hang up. She keeps on bubbling, laughing, and telling him everything she's done in the past two weeks. She goes on and on. Her voice sends waves of elation gushing up again and again into his bosom until he's drunk with joy.

It's Friday night in Jim's basement. Above him, one naked lightbulb is burning.

# Chapter Twenty-two

Mrs. Courtney's apartment is dark and Victorian, and smells of honeysuckle-scented air fresheners. Lace curtains deck the windows while family photos abound on the walls. The Airwick air fresheners, shaped like little mushrooms, are placed throughout her apartment as if Mrs. C. is determined to cover up the fusty-cheesy odor that seems to prevail in the homes of elderly people. In the living room is a boarded-up fireplace. A domed clock on the mantel says 10:20 a.m. The brass-ball pendulum revolves like a merry-go-round, first one way, then the other. The clock is similar to the one in Dr. Logan's office.

Mrs. C., after giving Becki her rent receipt, notices Jim looking at the clock. "Eh, me youngest," she says, "he brought it from Germany after the war." Mrs. C.'s ruddy round face is full of puckers and wrinkles—she looks like a pink walnut with glasses.

"I'm German, you know," Becki proudly announces upon hearing that the clock is from Germany. "Both sides of my family came from Wiesbaden. Dad was born there. He came to America when he was a baby, but Mom, she was born in New Bedford. I'm not all German though, 'cause Papa Chavin, he's French."

But Becki's soft voice is too soft for Mrs. Courtney's deaf ears. "What's that you say, Miss Becki? I've had quite enough of your mafflin'. Don't mumble like a bashful child. *Speak* your mind. I'm an old deaf woman, mind you." Mrs. C. speaks with a raucous Irish brogue mixed with New England millworker dialect.

Rebecca, blushing and dimpling, fidgets her feet, placing the heel of her right Reebok sneaker onto the toe of the left, then vice versa, left on right. As she executes her nervous foot-shuffle, several repetitions, she explains again about her German backround—at higher volume. Mrs. C. understands this time: "I suspected as much. Eh, if not a Scottish lass, 'twas certain you mus' be a fraulein—now, Miss Becki, why are you dancin' your feet about like me rug is hot? You settle yourself an' act your age."

Becki's blush deepens; her dimpled grin breaks wide, showing her crooked teeth. She's embarrassed at the attention though she's used to Mrs. C.'s playful scoldings. She self-consciously fingers her rent receipt then stuffs it into her jeans. Jim gives her rent money each month and she pays Mrs. C., but Becki has worked out a deal so she can pay half, twice a month. She's shrewd when it comes to stretching dollars, a trait she inherits from Alison.

Mrs. C. toddles toward her kitchen insisting that they stay for coffee and muffins. They follow her into the kitchen but Jim

"I saw you lookin' at me."

"So?"

"I'm not a sexual object, you know?"

"Well, are you a sexual person?" Jim presses scornfully as he vents his own guilt and aggravation and hurt. "Do you ever have sexual desires? Do you like getting off, or do you have a problem like being secretly frigid?" He knows these subjects will not play on the morning after, but he's already resigned to the coming explosion so he primes the charge—like a misbehaving child who knows he deserves a spanking and wants to get it over with.

"That's kind of personal, don'tcha think?"

"It didn't seem too personal last night?"

"Forget about last night!" Becki snarls, contorting her face defiantly. "I hate what happened last night! Maybe I do want sex, but it's none of *your* business. It's personal, between me and my husband someday. I don't want it in some heated rush, like some horny animal. I want it to be God's way, the right way—so *knock* it off, Shanley! OKAY! I know what you're thinking, and I'm wicked sick of it! Just *sick* of it!"

"So, what am I thinking?" Jim asks.

"You're not thinking, you're *lust*ing, and don't deny it!"

"Okay, so I'm looking, but it's more than lust. Didyuh ever hear about love? Oh, pardon me, I forgot. You don't need love, or sex." Jim pauses then sticks the knife in, "And speaking of lust, what about you, Miss Becki Braless? You were no *saint* last night?"

Glaring straight ahead, Becki grabs the top of the steering wheel with both hands. Her countenance tightens with reproach. Fire ignites in her eyes. Her temple pulses. But she holds back her rage as if preparing her defense—and God's. Meanwhile, she vents a safety-valve burst of indignation. Her voice wavers just enough for Jim to know that greater wrath is yet to come. "Don't accuse *me.* It's *your* fault. You always get me goin', and get me talking about filthy suggestive stuff, stuff I'm ashamed of. That's not love, and it's happening more and more, and it's...."

"It's what?" Jim prods. "Come *on*, Becki, spit it out."

Acrimony fills the car: gas fumes waiting for a spark. Becki gives Jim a withering glance but no reply. She grips the steering wheel so tightly that her knuckles turn white. Her round cheeks slowly blotch as if the final wrath of God is rising in her body. A red maple leaf tumbles down onto the windshield catching in the wiper mechanism. Flash—"IT'S SIN! IT'S SIN! IT'S SIN!" she blazes, her words sudden, painful, piercing, like three pistol shots.

*Bang! Bang! Bang!* Each bullet lodges deep in Jim's bosom. Hot and heavy agony engulfs his heart. Nonetheless, he continues to twist the knife, "How do *you* know, Miss Pious Panties!" He's cutting his own tombstone.

"Because God says so! That's why!"

"So He came down and talked to you about it, huh?"

"He didn't have to! He wrote it in the Bible! It's in the Bible, and you know it! And you know what Pastor says about fooling around. You just want me to give in to lust without considering consequences, or love or God, or being married. Well, I'm not *like* that. It's wrong and you can't get away with it, Jimmy. Nobody can. God's truth doesn't change to fit your fantasies. You can flirt and talk dirty all you want, but—" Becki stops midsentence. She lets go of the steering wheel. Silence. She takes a deep breath, holds it until blue with indignation, then she detonates: "BUT IT'S STILL *SIN* AND I HATE IT! AND GOD HATES IT TOO! HOW YOU GET NASTY AND LOOSE AND GET ME GOIN', AND GET ME THINKING ABOUT SINFUL STUFF! LOVE IS *PURE,* NOT NASTY AND DIRTY! YOU JUST WANT ME TO GIVE IN LIKE A SLUT! YOU JUST WANT MY BODY! YOU JUST WANT ME IN BED! AND DON'T YOU *FUCKIN'* DENY IT!" Blue, purple, red with rage, she beats the air with her fisted hands.

"OKAY, DAMMIT! I DO WANT YOU IN BED!" Jim roars almost gagging on his erupting passion as his pent-up heart blasts through his self-pity and self-hate. "You're right! I do want your body! I *DO*! I *DO*!" He pounds the dashboard furiously like it's a pulpit, hitting it so hard that the blue vinyl splits wide from the blows, like an axe wound in a human head. "I *DO*! I *DO*! I want you more than any woman on earth! But I love you! I love you, Becki Lea! Dammit, doncha get it! Even if we never go to bed, I love you! I love you more than—"

"YOU DON'T LOVE *ANY*ONE, JIMMY SHANLEY, EX-CEPT YOURSELF! You don't even love who you're supposed to love, like God 'n Sharon!" Becki heaves and pants as if breathing fire; her face scrunches, her eyes fill, her nostrils flare. "You think nothing of breaking your vows! Well, I'm not gonna help you! God doesn't take it lightly! You're a deceitful dirty-mouthed bastard! I don't wanna fuck you! AND I *NEVER* WILL! Pull your head out, Jimmy! Nothing has changed! I toldjuh last April we could never be lovers! Just 'cause you got me goin' and talking about dreams and Puerto Rico and personal stuff—which I shoulda never done—doesn't mean I want *YOU*! Nothing has changed! What are you, dumb in the head! How many times do I have to say it! I hate your dirty lustful spirit! It makes me want to puke! You need to get right with God! I don't even want to be with you when you're like this!"

"Like what!" Jim asks angrily.

"Like a dirty old man! That's what!" Along with her hot words, Becki spews a shower of hot spittle all over Jim.

"Well, what about you, *Saint* Rebecca? I guess you're clean and pure, huh, like the *wash*? Like when you do it by hand, like in your bed last night after I dropped you off?" Jim is locking his coffin; he knows he's *finished*.

Blur. Arm. Hand. *KA-WHAAP!* Becki slaps Jim sharply. "YOU'RE A FUCKIN' LIAR, SHANLEY!" Shock wave of hurt. His cheek burns. "You're always thinking nasty stuff about me! And fantasizing! Well, I'm not *like* that! I'm not loose and gutter-minded like you, always thinking about sex and dirty stuff! HOW *DARE* YOU ACCUSE ME! I OUGHTA RIP YOUR FUCKIN' TONGUE OUT! I DON'T HAFTA TAKE THIS SHIT!"

Breaking into tears, Becki grabs her purse and portfolio out of the backseat, bursts out of the car, and strides defiantly toward the house. Halfway to the porch, she stops and screams out a sobbing, "FUCK *YOU,* JIMMY SHANLEY! I HATE YOUR GUTS!" She hurls the portfolio back toward the car. It comes open, disgorging outreach cards and visitation lists all over the yard. She then storms up the steps, hurries inside the house, and slams the door.

Jim's face burns as does his heart. Hauling himself out of the car, he chases down the loose cards and papers as they blow in the wind. The storm door didn't latch when Becki ran inside and it blows back and forth, squeaking, whining, banging. It's now October, but Jim Shanley does not need a calendar to know that the seasons are changing.

* * *

Carl Baker's hairless head reflects the fluorescent lights like a polished ceramic egg. His file-clerk face rearranges itself into a fawning grin. "Most definitely," he replies. "We need to hear the Word daily, and if we get LBI college credits then—"

"I don't think it's wise to open our classrooms every night and Saturday," Beverly cuts in, arching her brows into triangles and peering over her half-eye glasses as they perch precariously on the tip of her nose. "It's difficult enough with the Sunday school." Her blue-gray hair gives her an air of seasoned practicality.

Angela has a wary look as if pondering the disturbing possi-bility of working under Carl and Stan. "Who's going to keep the books and paperwork?" she asks.

"Bev's right," Jodi agrees. "We can't move desks every afternoon." Jodi has on a sweat shirt and a denim jacket; her page-boy is wind-teased. She looks like she just came in from raking leaves. The others are in their Sunday best, save for Russ who never dresses up except for Nashua.

Russ seems more concerned about his Red Sox cap which he holds gingerly as he picks at a loose thread under the bill. "I think we should table this until June," he remarks. "I see no point in starting a video college during the middle of the year." Now comes an impish grin. "Of course, getting a VCR might be good. We can rent movies from that new video store in Lancaster, like *The Graduate*—remember Mrs. Robinson? Or *The Last Picture Show*— now that was a great flick. Or even *Body Heat* with Kathleen Turner—now she'd get people to attend, especially the men."

Snickers, snorts, coughs, chuckles versus stony looks from Stan, Leslie, and Carl. "Come on; let's get serious," Carl admonishes, speaking in his usual monotone. "This is not a time for worldly jesting. We're talking about the future of our church."

"That's right," Barry Buford adds, suppressing a chuckle. He tries to mimic Stan's indignant frown, but only succeeds in pushing his fat eyes out a bit farther, until the whites are showing all around. "I agree with Carl and Stan. I've wanted to take college classes for some time now, but I can't move to Nashua because of my job"— *Lie, lie,* Jim declares to himself; *Janet won't go; that's the real reason*—"so expanding our extension program will give me opportunity. And I've talked to Cal and Joanne, and Freddie and Juanita, and Barbara Sims. They all want to take college courses."

Barry speaks in a hefty voice, more hefty than even a month ago. Each fall he puts on weight like a bear preparing for hibernation. The top of his tie is half hidden by a roll of neck fat. He looks more like Jackie Gleason than ever, like Ralph Kramden in his bus-driver's uniform. And like Kramden, Barry speaks with boyish exuberance about the readiness of body members to sign up for the EDGE curriculum. But Jim knows from experience that when it's time to pay tuition, exuberance will not suffice.

Leslie B. tosses her bunned head and rolls her bullfrog eyes. "We've wasted half of staff meeting already. We still have to discuss the Thanksgiving food drive. There *are* poor people in this town, you know? Poor people who don't even have the necessities of life. We need to give them the gospel for their souls and food and clothing for their bodies. How do you think the Lord feels when he sees us wasting time like this? Let's play the tape." Leslie has pendulous gold-ball earrings; the shiny marble-sized spheres swing about when she moves her head.

"Good idea, Leslie," Pastor Jim replies, thinking how Leslie's earrings are the only pendulous things on her person. Then he turns to Stan. "Are you all set with the promo tape, Stan?"

politely declines. After their two-week fight he's anxious to be alone with Becki. But Mrs. C. won't take no for an answer. "Hear, hear, young man," she fusses. "You sit right down. If you leave here 'fore eatin' me best crumpets, I'm gonna have a *crow* to pluck with you. You young'uns these days, I declare. You jus' rush 'n bustle about, an' you never sit yourself and eat. I'm sure you've not had a whit of breakfast. I hope to goodness. But eh ... who listens to me anymore? I'm jus' a stupid old fool in this world."

Jim quickly yields to her insistent invitation and he and Becki sit down. The table is round and covered with a crocheted lace tablecloth. It reminds him of the tablecloth that Grandma Shanley put on her dining room table in Ft. Worth each Christmas.

The aroma of percolating coffee soon fills the kitchen which is cozy and quaint much like Alison's old kitchen in Nashua except the stove is modern. Mrs. C., wearing a floral-print housedress and a pink pinafore apron, hustles about muttering under her breath. Her tight little mouth seems twisted into a perpetual sneer, but she has warm twinkling eyes behind her tortoise-shell spectacles.

Despite her cantankerous nature, Jim likes her, and Becki has grown fond of her as well. Mrs. C. loves by fussing just as Becki loves by bantering and being witty. Mrs. C. teeters and totters as if she's tipsy on wine, but it isn't alcohol. She calls it her "rheumatism." A touch of rouge warms her cheeks and her long white hair is bundled on top of her head. Becki offers to help but Mrs. C. won't hear of it. After a dozen trips in and out of cupboards, the stove, the refrigerator, she finally sits down bringing with her a plate of hot well-buttered English muffins; she calls them crumpets but they look like English muffins to Jim.

"Now, Miss Becki, you fold your collar an' roll your sleeves," Mrs. C. fusses as soon as she sits down. "Goodness *me*. How can I make a lady of you, if you wear your blouse like a beatnik? And it's such a pretty blouse." Becki has a new shirt, beige with drop shoulders and embroidered trim. Mrs. C. calls her, "Miss Becki," and Jim, "young man"—though she knows he's a minister and married and past 35. The coffee is rich and strong but not strong enough for Mrs. Courtney. She gets up and grabs a dark long-necked bottle from the kitchen counter.

"A soul needs a spot of Baileys to liven up this brew," she says as she toddles back to her chair. She offers Jim and Becki some but they both decline. Refusal of alcohol is a Christian knee-jerk reflex for Jim, though he never liked liquor much, even when he was younger, except for a beer every now and then.

Mrs. C. stirs her spiked coffee then takes a swig. "It's like summer out, a good day to see the colors," Jim says, filling the silence with a bit of small talk as he glances out the window at the trees beyond the parking nook. "And the maples down by the lake look like they're on fire."

"Quite right, young man," Mrs. C. agrees for a change as she spreads jam on her muffin. "'Tis a splendid day for a walk in the meadow, when a soul can be let out without mufflin' up." She takes a huge bite of her crumpet. As she chews it, her dentures click.

"You mean you still walk in the meadow?" Becki teases.

Not waiting to swallow, Mrs. C. snaps a reply, "Eh, what are you blatherin' about, you little puppy you? I been hikin' 'round this lake near 70 years, and I was jus' yesterday clearin' me garden, and I took a stroll to the top of the hill, and a very jolly stroll it was. I may not walk as fast as I used to, but I can walk just as far."

Mrs. C. goes on for a bit about her active life then begins to grumble about the sorry state of the town. Punching the air with her second muffin, she complains that all the factories are gone, but no one wants to work anyway, and that all the houses are run-down and filled with "no 'counts 'n Cambodians, 'n Puerto Ricans on welfare." She laments that St. John's Church has been overtaken by Puerto Ricans and there are only a few true Catholics left in the whole town. "The priest is a left-wing tub of guts," she says. "I don't go anymore 'cept on High Holy Days ... an' Massachusetts is dyin' as well, an' Washington's in the hands of *low-lived* dogs 'cept for Ronnie, of course. Eh, I like Ronnie Reagan. He's a jolly fine chap, an' cute too, with a good Irish name."

After a quick drink of her spiked coffee, Mrs. C. starts bragging about the good old days, "Eh ... when I first came to Brendon Falls, there were dozens of hot smokestacks 'n factories. The whole town was boomin'. It was the most prosperous town in the region with lots of new three-story homes, an' large families. The streets downtown were cobblestone ... an' the shod hooves clomped an' the carriage wheels clattered an' the horses snorted. Gentlemen an' ladies would go by in buggies 'n coaches 'n new-fangled motorcars, but the workin' people drove buckboards. There were scores of wagons and a few lorries haulin' an' deliverin' an' goin' this way 'n that. Children ran about an' yelled, an' dogs barked. The women wore bell-bottom dresses and *every*one wore hats, like God in*tend*ed. The trolleys rang their bells an' work whistles blew at the mills for each shift, an' train whistles blew as trains were comin' 'n goin', freight trains, passenger trains. The station was bustlin'. An' church bells rang an' hammers banged as new buildings were goin' up. The air smelled of bakin' bread an' cabbage stewin'—oh, there were foul smells too, like coal smoke 'n wool dyes, 'n horse manure 'n sewage, but it wasn't a great stink, save in the summertime."

Mrs. C. spreads a spoonful of raspberry jam on her third muffin. Becki's on her second but Jim's mostly sipping his coffee, out of a pearl-gray cup adorned with bluebirds and butterflies.

"Young man, you eat away now," Mrs. C. cackles upon noticing the half-eaten muffin on his plate. "Eh, there's still a half-dozen crumpets a beggin' on the platter." After scolding Jim, she settles and returns to the past, telling them about her trip over from Ireland when she was a "young lass." Her name back then was Murphy. She had one sister and two brothers and they lived in Cork in the South of Ireland. Her mother got them up in the middle of the night to catch the train to Dublin. It was November and foggy and the steamship had three smokestacks and it took eight days. Her "Papa" met them at Ellis Island in New York and they rode the train to Boston then changed to another train that took them out to Brendon Falls. Right before they arrived, her father said, Pack away now an' muffle up; we're jus' a bit farther, after the tunnel.

"Ecod, we came out of the tunnel onto the trestle and I saw the dam," Mrs. C. declares, gesturing with both hands, so much so that she shakes a glob of jam off her muffin and it falls onto the lace tablecloth. "It was gray and high an' still new, an' bigger than the ship, a right terrible sight for a nine-year-old lass to see. It was sunny that day an' the river was green, and I saw the millworks. There was a lot of smoke, an' white houses on the hills. After we crossed, I saw the reservoir for the first time, an' then the train turned straightaway to the station."

Jim asks about the train. Mrs. C. says it was a gray locomotive that huffed and hissed geysers of steam, and when they walked by it, she felt the heat and saw water running out of it. "The station was crowded," she explains, "an' folks were bustlin' about, intent 'n nervous like millin' insects. Baggage men were pullin' 'n pushin' carts. We got milk 'n rolls 'n honey at the food counter, then we went outside. Lots of people were new like us, and each family was sponsored by their mill. Papa led us to the Buckingham carryall where we loaded up an' headed for the river."

"So that's why it says Buckingham up on the smokestack at the paper mill?" Becki asks. "You know, the faded white letters with the B at the top?"

Mrs. C. gives Rebecca a grin and a wink. "Ay, quite right you are, me dear lassie. Prescott Paper used to be Buckingham Mills which was our mill, an' the biggest an' the best. If you drive around this town an' look at the old mills, you'll see other famous names ... like Hinton Brothers Yarn, an' Buchanan Carpets, an' Ladbury Gingham. But now they're all converted to plastic companies an' warehouses. They're not worth a damn farthing nowadays. This town used to be famous for its factories. Now it's known for its run-down apartments an' alcoholics."

"You mean Hinton Brothers, like Harry Hinton?" Becki inquires.

Jim answers her, "It was his great-grandfather I think—"

"Oh, goodness me," Mrs. C. cuts in. "The Hinton brothers were such decent chaps, an' Mayor Hinton, he made this town. He died in 1911, the same year I got here. The whole town turned out for the funeral and all the mill owners came in their shiny black coaches... an' Mr. Buckingham's coach was the *most* elegant of all. His coachman had a tall black hat and a stock collar—not the original Mr. Buckingham, mind you, but his son."

"So your father was here working already?" Jim asks.

"Ay, bedad he was. He lived in the bachelor house 'til he could send for us, an' when we got here we all moved into Buckingham Four, the long rowhouse by the river, an' we stayed there, in unit #16, 'til I was eleven, then we moved up here to Winter Street. All the streets on Hadley Hill were new 'n muddy, and all us kids, we went to St. John's School. Ay, the neighborhood was like bein' back home in Ireland with dogs barkin' an' chickens squawkin' an' horses neighin' an' pigs squealin' ... an' we always had tea 'n barmbrack at four o'clock in the afternoon, an' I always put lots of milk 'n sugar in me tea, and everybody seemed right jolly in*deed*."

Mrs. C. shifts a bit in her chair then gazes out the window. Wistful eyes. Her face clouds. Speaking solemnly, she tells the rest of her story, the downside of living in Brendon Falls. She went to work at Buckingham when she was 14. All the girls started at 14. She worked as a spinner in the woolen mill and hated it. She met her future husband, Mr. Courtney, one summer day while "bathing in the river." He was a "dashing young chap with blazin' red hair" who worked at Hinton Brothers. He left for one year to fight in the Great War. When he came home from France, they got married and they lived with Mrs. C.'s parents on Winter Street. Within five years Mrs. C. had three children, two sons and a daughter, but Mr. C. catted around with the "slatternly girls at the pubs," then the factories failed, many for good, and Mrs. C. had to take in laundry. Then WWII and her eldest son was killed at Anzio. Mr. C. never got over it: "he jus' hung out at the VFW, an' got all screwed with liquor most every day, an' could scarce hold a job 'til he died in 1961."

"So why did the factories die out?" Becki asks.

Mrs. C. sighs and slowly shakes her head. "Well, after a time the owners turned into greedy tubs of fat, an' wanted to suck us dry, not Mr. Buckingham, mind you, but he died and his nephew took over. The younger Buckingham was not worth a quid of Tullamore. He jus' wanted profits, an' his wife, she was a drunken old harridan that treated us like serfs. So we organized and had a strike for fair wages, an' 'fore you know it, the mill closed down. The mayor formed a commission an' the mill reopened for a while, but durin' the depression it all fell apart an' Buckingham relocated to North Carolina where he could hire folks for a *bit a nuthin'*."

* * *

"Just save it, okay!" Ruthie exclaims. Jim isn't trying to convert her, but Ruthie takes offense anyway. "I've heard it all from Doris 'n Stan, and Doris knows better than to start, and Stan's the biggest fuckin' hypocrite in this town. Is it any wonder that David's loose in the head? So jus' save it, Preach, okay!"

Ruthie and Judy could pass for twins except Ruthie has short cropped hair with stubby bangs that just tickle her forehead. Judy tries to cool the conversation with mundane pleasantries but her sister is in a slow burn. Harry simply smiles a knowing smile as he sips from a huge *Black Sabbath* coffee mug. "I hope there *is* a God," Ruthie goes on. "But I don't want to hear about him from fuckin' hypocrites!" She sweeps up her Virginia Slims, her Bic lighter, and sashays to the door, flaunting her well-shaped hips which are tightly clad in blue corduroy pants. She brandishes her sexy butt as if it's a .357 Magnum. To Jim, it's almost that intimidating, yet he can readily see why the men in town love to fuck it.

At the door Ruthie turns, her face florid with outrage: "Mama was a Catholic and it drove her to drink! And they called Daddy a sinner 'til he left! You pretend to be different, and loving 'n all, but you only save people so you can lord it over 'em and take their time 'n money! You ain't no better than the fuckin' priests! In fact, you're worse!" Her violet eyes flashing, she turns on Rebecca, "And you, Miss Holiness, you priss around this town so pure 'n pious! Go ahead, be a nun, but you ain't foolin' me. I got two aunts and a cousin who took vows, three horny bitches and they didn't change. They were *boffin'* their brains out within six weeks, gettin' more cock than I ever thought of—with priests and any other sugar daddy they could find. I know 'cuz I overheard 'em sayin' that the greatest blessing of God this century was *the pill*. I can't keep you from living upstairs, but jus' stay away from me with your born-again *bull*shit! Both of you!"

Ruthie stomps out and slams the door behind her—so hard the dishes rattle in Judy's cabinets. Acrid silence smolders in Ruthie's

wake. Judy looks down ashamedly. Becki blushes crimson as if
she's naked. Jim starts to make a witty remark but it catches like
phlegm in his throat. Harry sips his coffee with the same knowing
smile. "Don't mind her none," he says. "She's just got a wild hair
up her ass. She's a frustrated broad like most gals now'days ... but
actually, she's not a bad kid if you can get onto her good side."
Somehow Jim knows this already.

* * *

Mill Street is lined with stately oaks and beeches, and sickly
elms—and sickly run-down houses. Becki pulls into the driveway
at #23. She cuts the engine then grabs a tract, rips it in two, wraps
her gum in the blue paper, and stuffs it into the ashtray. Jim twists
the rearview mirror toward him so he can comb his cowlicked
bangs. He fixes them in place with a shot of Vitalis Super Hold
which he keeps in the glove compartment. Finally, they get out and
walk up a crumbling sidewalk to a dilapidated three-decker, ashy-
yellow in color, more from dirt than paint.

Ruthie's outburst is now a bad memory, several hours old—
getting yelled at is one of the hazards of outreach though it hasn't
happened as much in recent years since Pastor Jim abandoned his
hard-line approach—and Jim and Becki's ears have had time to
cool as they spent an hour downtown then made a number of other
visits, the last to Ernie Johnson's where Sarah served them a late
lunch. Fried chicken, corn bread, mashed potatoes, green beans in
bacon grease, and apple pie. It was better than any restaurant. Also,
Ernie told Jim that Kevin and Cathy had the canoe down at South
Meadow Pond and if he and Becki wanted to use it later, they could
have it anytime after four-thirty.

Jim knocks on the McCluskys' door. Joanne answers and
ushers them into the living room where Calvin, a boyish-looking
couch potato, is watching Doug Flutie and the Boston College
Eagles. Jim smells rotting garbage and beer and nicotine. Dirty
first-floor apartment, thirdhand furniture, cheap rug mottled with
food stains and cigarette ash. A sluggish housefly, attracted by the
sticky residue of a spilled beverage, crawls about on the coffee
table. Cal sits forward to greet Pastor Jim and Becki. His potbelly
rolls almost to his thighs, but he's not a large man just paunchy in
the gut. Blond hair, blunt features, bashful blue eyes. He seems
embarrassed, ashamed of the house—and himself. Cigarette in
hand, Bud Light on the coffee table, he wears a ragged T-shirt and
a pair of Prescott Paper dungarees. Though he's only twenty-five
and looks younger, he already has a late-30s alcoholic personality

that ranges from mellow to melancholy.

Joanne, just back from the diner, is still in her gray-checked waitress uniform. Baby Shane, naked except for a Pamper, crawls over and pulls himself up onto his mother's legs. He's a chubby baby with no hair save for a cap of blond fuzz. Joanne picks him up and playfully kisses his protruding belly button. Shane screeches with delight. She and the baby then sit down on the couch next to her husband. Jim sits in a shabby love seat. But Becki sprawls on the floor and toys with Shane's stacking clown.

Baby Shane cannot resist. Leaving his mom, he ventures around holding onto the coffee table, his head wobbling as he goes. When he gets to the other side, he plops down butt first to play with Becki. She makes funny faces and tickles his fat tummy. He laughs and drools on her hand. Then, shrieking with delight, he grabs two of the colored stacking rings and shakes them wildly over his head with his monkeylike arms. Shane loves it when Rebecca comes over because he gets all of her attention.

Cal hasn't been to church for a month, but Jim doesn't feel like pushing him, so they talk about Doug Flutie then about the Red Sox and Carl Yazstremski's last game, when he ran around Fenway Park and touched the hands of the fans.

After a while, the sports talk dies out and Joanne asks Pastor Jim to come into the kitchen to see the curtains she's making for the church nursery. They're folded neatly on a small table next to her sewing machine. She unfolds one; it's light blue and ruffled, and it's decorated with ducks and puppies and kittens and rabbits. Jim suspects there's another reason Joanne called him in there. He sees hurt in her eyes—pretty gray eyes, flecked with green.

"Pastor Jim," she says. "I uh...." She hesitates, looking down shyly.

"I know," Jim consoles. "It's okay."

"I-I, I just don't...." Again she falters. She looks up at him, her eyes welling. She lifts the ruffled curtain and hugs it, like a security blanket, to her cheek.

"It's okay, Jo," he reassures in a gentle voice. "You can tell me."

"It's Cal. I'm such a failure. Our marriage, it's so ... well, it...."

"It stinks," Jim says, helping her past the hard part. "Your marriage stinks and you're ready to throw in the towel, but you're ashamed because we had a big church wedding just one year ago, and all your family plus the church and everyone said that you two were the *perfect* couple."

Joanne runs her hand through her curly auburn locks. "I can't tell Mom," she sighs, confirming Jim's assessment. "She'll *die*. I can still hear her and Dad bragging to the relatives when Shane was born, 'Jo waited and married a good Christian man, and now God has rewarded with a beautiful grandson.'"

Jim pats her on the shoulder then replies, "But you can tell me; I won't die." *In fact, I'm not surprised,* he adds silently.

Joanne, holding back her tears, stares wistfully out the window at the hazy October day. In the backyard stands a big maple tree ablaze with amber-gold color, a warm and painterly gold like the first rays of morning sun. A little burst of wind brings down a flurry of leaves. "Cal, he never talks," she laments in a hushed voice out the window toward the falling leaves. "We don't talk anymore. He goes to the mill then to Clancy's. And Doris says that one night he went home with her brother's wife"—*I guess Kyle's not the only one getting into Ruthie,* Jim says to himself; *she may hate our church but she sure loves our men*—"and weekends are even worse because he's camped out on the couch watching TV and stuffing his face, and drinking one beer after another. When I say we need to talk, he just mumbles and tells me to stop nagging. He spends so much on booze, I have to work to pay the rent, and I'm afraid for Shane because when Cal's on that couch, it's like no one else exists. He won't go to church anymore and he complains when I go. He says a woman's place is in the home and I'm gone too much.... Sometimes, Jim, I think God has chosen me for suffering, like Job."

Joanne embraces Pastor Jim; he expects her to cry but she doesn't. He's known Cal and Jo since they were in high school, and they seemed reasonably happy as teenagers—but then they grew up, paired off, and got married.

\* \* \*

The lengthening shadows of late afternoon send Jim and Becki laughing and running to the meadow. Happiness bubbles in Becki's laugh and shines in her eyes. They sit on the stone fence but not for long as she puts leaves down his shirt and takes off for the top of the hill. He catches her, tackles her, then tickles her until she squeals with delight. Finally, they lie quietly in the warm grass.

Jim is drunk on joy, the joy of being with Becki. The human realities of outreach are behind them and the day now seems like a fairy tale in progress. Unfettered by fear or frustrated lust, he feels free and transcendent as if the Love Goddess herself has lifted them to a realm beyond want. Not that his love has become platonic. On the contrary, he loves her more than ever, in every way, all the way. But he's so happy to be with her again, it's as if they've already spent a day in bed and have satisfied each other over and over, and now float on updrafts of afterpleasure.

Birds twitter. Crickets chirp. Little brown grasshoppers, survivors of the frost, hop about in the grass. And a small yellow butterfly flits by as if inviting Jim and Becki to play. Overhead, wispy mare's tails sail through the heavens, an armada of ancient sailing vessels, while nearer to earth, cottony cumulus drift above the meadow like fleecy white airships. Warm puffs of wind kiss the lips of Jim's soul stirring the poet within him. Always there, the poetry, but especially on this Indian Summer evening. Becki smiles. Paradise opens. Jim cries out—without voice:

> *O sweet sadness, veiled and virgin, fold and fold upon yourself 'til you burst and become forever. O sweet Goddess ... come, possess your chosen vessel, rend the cerulean veil, show us your mysteries, "the things that are freely given." O sweet death, swallow us in thy "royal raging sea." Cleanse us of the foul stain.*

A hazy disk of sun, dirty and orange, seems suspended above the Worcester Hills—as if time has stopped. The meadow smells of autumn. Dry, spicy, earthy, yet vaguely sweet. The woods are fragrant and dank with falling leaves and pine needles. Nature has wrapped Jim and Becki in that cozy wistful feeling that comes only on warm autumn days. Ripe pumpkins, wilted cornstalks, hornets on rotting apples or buzzing over spilled ice cream at Buckner's Farm. Words cannot describe it but Jim feels it each fall. There's an indefinable something in the air, a collective awareness that autumn even at peak is a sorrowful time, a time to die. The ambers and ochres and golds and reds will soon give way to umbers and purples and grays. But the pine trees, after giving up their brown needles, will remain green—perhaps to offer hope of life after death. The message of the trees consoles Jim more than any preacher.

Jim and Becki stroll hand in hand through the meadow. She too seems magically beyond fear and want and the stress of making feelings fit. The buttercups are long gone but late-blooming goldenrods, like yellow flames, light up the far side of the meadow. Becki also finds a few lingering asters near the stone fence. They walk farther down along the fence. As they come into a low place where the ground is always damp, she says, "Look, Shanley."

Before them are a pair of beautiful purple flowers, long and tubular with delicately fringed petals. They seem almost blue as they bloom fresh and cool in the waning sunshine. And they seem hauntingly aware of Jim and Becki's presence as if they'll soon speak about love and sadness. A late-season honeybee lands on one of them and plunges inside. The flower seems to close around the bee. Becki kneels down for a closer look. Soon the bee emerges and goes into the other flower. Finally, heavy with pollen, it comes out and buzzes happily away.

Jim goes down on one knee across from Becki. When he does, she looks up with an enchanting I-love-you smile. Her eyes brim with affection. He smiles back.

Gush of joy. Love quickens Jim. Warm bliss wells up, then speaks out loud, "Do you love me, Becki Lea?"

No reply. Becki shyly averts her eyes.

Jim's heart races with anticipation, yet surprisingly he feels no apprehension about her silence. He drops to both knees. He gazes at her, loving her and loving her. He asks again, "Do you, Becki?"

Rebecca reaches out and touches the blue petals ever so gently. A smile trembles on her lips. Without looking up, she says, "Yes." Time ceases. No movement, not even a whisper of a sound. But Jim's heart races, jumps, turns flips, then settles and fills his bosom with melting waves of love and elation.

Becki dimples, her smile breaking wide. Feathery tendrils of honey-brown hair soften her face. Becki, Becki, so common, so flawed, so human, and worth little on the market of human exchange, but to Jim Shanley, there is no pearl of greater price.

Finally, Becki looks up, her smile more intimate than any kiss. Jim stands and gathers her up into his arms. She melts into his embrace. He kisses her on the head but does not seek her lips. Fire, awe, touching, trembling. But for now he seeks nothing more. To know she loves him raptures him more than a hundred orgasms. Ecstasy. Ecstasy. His soul can go no higher short of death.

*My knees, my knees,* he cries within. *I'm gonna faint. I love her so. O God, I love her forever! I do! She's more part of me than my name—in fact, she is my name.*

* * *

The pond shimmers in the moonlight. The distant sounds of traffic waft over the water as if from another world. Jim kisses Becki on the cheek. *O Lord, I could stay here forever,* he says in his heart as they cuddle in the canoe, half-lying down, half-propped up against the seat cushions. Her lilac-scented locks press softly against his cheek. Her warm cotton-clad bosom presses sweet affection into his. Jim's heart exults again and again. A thousand shooting stars streak the heavens. Fireworks light the night—yet it's all inside of them, inside of Jim and Becki.

Eyes closed, she snuggles into his shoulder. Amber moonlight dusts her face, giving her countenance a dreamy aura. Jim senses love as never before, as if every heart he's ever touched is somehow beating inside Becki's bosom. It has been a once-in-a-lifetime evening, an evening of wonder, of being a child again.

The joy of reunion has taken them beyond the flesh into a magical realm—no fear, no jealousy, no lust-driven panic for physical union. To cuddle so closely and not be compelled to kiss, to force their intimacy farther, to foreplay, to lovemaking—to sudden guilt, another fight—is indeed a miracle for Jim. But on this night he *knows*, so he can rest, and trust. He senses that Becki *knows* as well. They *know* that their love, like a great and peaceful river, will in due season take them to the "royal raging sea," without fear, without forcing.

Oh, to possess this knowing, to keep it in the daylight of life's duties and demands, a bridge too far, but for now there is no harsh glare of day—but only moonlight and magic. The night sky is ruled by the Hunter's Moon: hazy, haloed, and amber-white—and pear-shaped; some call it gibbous. It's Jim and Becki's moon and it smiles down upon them, down, down through the feathery clouds.

Jim senses "eternity" on this warm October night. The peace is unfathomable, bottomless. The waves gently rock the canoe, swaying and lapping, lulling, lulling, to the dreamy edge of sleep where the heart can speak and the mind does not interfere:

*O Becki, Becki, is there more? But how can God be more than this? Show me a higher God? I know of none in any church or creed who ravishes my soul with such heaven ... and hell is no more and no less than your absence. Is this truth but a dream? Must I hide like a thief and worship ... a lesser God?*

# Chapter Twenty-three

"**D**ad! Dad! Phey're here!" Chris shouts in his toothless six-year-old voice. "It's time to go! 'Member, we're goin' to McDonald's an' phen to get our tree!"

Saturday, December 10, 1983. Jim is on the couch downstairs watching the Celtics. He rarely watches basketball but Sharon and the girls have been Christmas shopping all day with Bev and Sheila. He stayed home with Chris. No outreach, but he isn't missing anything since Becki's also shopping all day—with Jodi.

Two hours later Jim and Chris pull a prickly Scotch pine through the door while Sharon and the girls supervise. Heather and Chris are so excited you'd think it was Christmas Eve. Erin's excited too but she's learning to "act" her age. The red-and-green stand is already screwed in place. Jim did that in the garage. All Christmas trees are created with trunks too thick for the stand. He knows this fundamental truth from past years of sawing and hacking in the living room and having Sharon say, "Honey, you're getting splinters and that gooey stuff on the carpet."

The Shanley tree always goes up the second Saturday of December, a Pedersen tradition of course. Jim secures it with piano wire to make it Samantha-proof; she brought down the last tree trying to get the birds on the upper branches. Now the lights and another fundamental truth: Christmas-tree lights never work the first time especially the old series-wired bubble lights. But after Jim and the kids go through each string ten times, unscrewing, testing, rescrewing—and after he curses the whole idea of bringing a tree into the house—he lucks out and the lights come on.

Jim must go to the teen center. This time it's legit. Besides, Becki won't be there anyway; she's having Jodi over for supper. So he leaves the rest of the tree decorating to Sharon and the kids.

Cloudy, cold, not freezing but close. The night sky over Brendon Falls is red and low obscuring the tops of the hills. *What the hell happened to Christmas anyway?* Jim asks himself as he descends South Meadow Road. *It's just a series of obligations. But I used to love it when I was a kid.*

He fondly recalls such a Christmas, a raw wintry Christmas. He even feels the chilly mist blowing into his face. He smells wet pine and woodsmoke. The winter landscape lies ashen like the face of a dying woman. Rolls of winter hay huddle in the fields like giant spools of yarn. He sees the white farmhouse and the scene inside. Greens, reds, whites: Christmas colors. Blues, yellows, purples too. Shiny wrapping paper, ribbons, bows, toys, tissue paper, open boxes, new clothes, candy, nuts, oranges, apples. Lazy flames dance inside a potbellied stove. A Christmas spruce sparkles with ornaments, lights, and icicles. A tiger cat is asleep on the TV set while a calico kitten runs among the piles of wrapping paper, batting the bows. The sandy-haired cowlicked boy shows the dark-haired woman a large blue box. On the box is a baseball player and the words: CADACO-ELLIS ALL-STAR BASEBALL.

The boy, dressed in jeans and a St. Louis Cardinal warm-up, is taller, his shoulders broader. The dark-haired woman is thin and pale but she smiles with motherly affection. A blondheaded man lies on the couch reading a newspaper. On the floor near the tree is another boy, much younger, with reddish-blond hair. He's busily laying out track for a windup train. The black-and-white dog looks on; the dog is now gray about the face. The blond-haired man gets up, and he and the boys collect the wrapping paper, and stuff it into a large box. Then the man goes over to the dark-haired woman. She smiles and takes his hand. He turns the wheelchair and rolls her into the kitchen. The boys follow, and the dog.

Jim, as he remembers, feels a warm tug on his heart. He wishes he could relive that day. But the first drops of rain peppering the windshield bring him back to the present. A gust of wind buffets the Mustang, southeast wind, ocean wind. This storm will be rain. The low is "tracking inside" as they say in the weather business.

Jim and Becki usually help at the teen center on Saturday night; it's part of their routine. Without her there's little incentive to go to the church. He's only going because Barry is especially shorthanded. Leslie, who now chaperones on Saturday as well as Friday, is in Nashua with Stan and Doris for Dr. Logan's Lay Leadership seminar. Carl and Melissa also went up with the Campbells. It cost $65 each. Stan wanted Russ and Barry to go as well, but Barry had to work during the day, and when Russ saw the list in Jim's office, he said, "No way, Jim. I'm not going unless you go." Truth is, Jim doesn't give a shit who went to Nashua. He just wants to get this Becki-less Saturday over with.

By the time he gets to the church the rain is coming down hard. He splashes around to the back, parks next to Joe's old Buick, and hustles inside. As he hangs up his jacket, he hears Kevin Johnson's Foghorn Leghorn voice, "Well, check this out. If it ain't the chief hisself, an' I reckon he's got a hankerin' to take us on. So, Billy boy, fetch me them paddles." Soon, Kevin, Billy, Cathy, Haley, and Teri, plus Kevin's little sister Jennifer, are gathered for Ping-Pong. Pastor Jim says a quick hello to Barry, grabs some paper, and scrawls out the brackets. As he does, Kevin says, "Ah, Chief, hope yuh don't mind havin' this here minah chil' playin'. You see, I got roped into babysettin', kinah like."

"Cut it out, Kev," Jennifer protests. She tosses her head defiantly causing her pigtails to swing about. "I'm gonna be twelve on Christmas Day. I got the same birthday as Jesus an' I'm plum prouda that. Mama says it's a sign that God chose me special." Her remarks set off a round of loud bantering and teasing among the teenagers.

Jim finishes the brackets, calls for order. As he does, Joe Lareux and Brenda Donovan enter the teen center from the main hallway; they each have a guitar. "What's all the commotion?" Joe kids as he and Brenda squint against the bright fluorescent light. "We can hear you in the main sanctuary."

When Jim kids them back about hiding out so much, Brenda blushes and gives a shy smile. Built like Jodi, but with Kyle's pudgy no-chin face, she's a frisky heifer with dark hair and slate-blue eyes; she wears her hair up high, above her ears.

While Pastor Jim conducts the Ping-Pong tournament, Joe and Brenda go to pick up kids for the video movie, *The Gospel Road* with Johnny Cash and June Carter, which starts at 8:00 p.m. One beneficial spin-off of Stan's EDGE proposal—the BFBC leadership, in a compromise decision, has decided to offer one EDGE video course for the spring semester—was the acquisition of a VCR from Jerry Crenshaw. So the teen ministry now rents videocassettes instead of reel movies, which saves a lot of money.

After Joe and Brenda return with a carload, everyone grabs a folding chair. Burst of noise. Clanging, squeaking, metallic banging. The teenagers quickly set up their chairs in front of a 24" TV which is on a stand in front of the pool table. Barry kills the lights and starts the movie. Pastor Jim sits down also but hardly notices the flick. Becki, Becki. She's too heavy on his mind.

October, November, December. Jim's roller-coaster ride rushes on, but now the ups and downs are steeper, more frequent. He still hasn't kissed Becki's lips but he's never known such elation, or torment: "Why are you pouting? I just wanted to hug you and you turn into a porcupine!"—"Why d'you have to chew gum all the time? It's disgusting. Look at me, Becki Lea! Stop fiddlin' with your hands. I feel like I'm with a *damn* ten-year-old!"—"DON'T ACCUSE *ME*, YOU PRICK-TEASIN' WHORE! You're the *one* who's flirting and wiggling your ass!"—"I'm sorry! I'm sorry! I didn't mean it! I just lost my temper"—"I LOVE YOU, DAMMIT! If you don't want love, fine! I'm outa here, and this time I'm *never* coming back!" —"It's uh, I uh—you knew I'd be back. It's so neat taking walks with you, Becki. I feel so close, like you're part of me"—"I must say, young lady, you sure know a lot about it. The

action in that cabin must've been hotter than your sugar dreams"—
"No, Sharon was the first. I hardly dated when I was at the academy
... but I fondled Betty Sue Barnett back in high school, but just her
breasts. She was Jason's sister."

Becki, Becki. Jim loves her so, wants her so. Yet at times he
wants to run and never stop. Whoosh! Rush of heart, rush of fear.
No grip, no grip. Falling, falling—like Alice falling down the rabbit
hole. 59 Front Street, it's heaven, it's hell, it's a battlefield: "I just
want to be with you, Jimmy. I want to go where you go, and do what
you do"—"Sharon doesn't understand you, Shanley, not really, not
like *I* do"—"I like rainy days; but they make me sad. Let's go to the
lake and see the ducks before they go away"—"You look funny,
Shanley. You got milk shake all over your mustache"—"I'll be a
crab if I want! I just got my period. So *lay* off, okay!"—"Wouldn't
you like to know? Well, I'm still not saying what we did at the cabin.
But it was better than church, I tellyuh"—"I have wicked good
control but I still like to think about it. I like reading the forum part.
I even thought up a good one: I'm on the couch and sort of dozing
and my mind gets away from me; you know, when a girl needs
relief, but not Rolaids? And I—O Jesus, I have this yummy dream
and just when I'm ... there's a knock and it's Stephen from
upstairs"—"I'll never do it with you, Jimmy Shanley! Nothing has
changed! I toldjuh! I toldjuh all along! I hate your lust problem!"—
"HOW *DARE* YOU CALL ME A WHORE! YOU'RE DEMON
POSSESSED! I know the real you, Jimmy! And I hate it how you
are! Your mind's always in the gutter!"

Folksy guitar, bearded robe-clad figures: Christ and his disciples. Johnny Cash's country rendition of Jesus' life continues on
the teen center television, but Jim senses nothing but flashes of
color, bites of sound. The movie has become an unbearable distraction. Besides, he needs to take a piss. He tiptoes out of the darkened
teen center and heads to the men's room in the old wing, to the
privacy of a urinal.

Love, hate, guilt, love. Love, hate, guilt, love. Faster, hotter,
cycling, cycling. Jim and Becki's hide 'n seek romance roars down
destiny's track like a steam locomotive approaching the red. But
instead of kissing and fucking, they fight and slash at each other
with scathing words, then Jim goes home hating himself. Guilt,
guilt. His conscience stinks like a backed-up toilet. Becki too feels
shame for she cowers away from him like a bat turning from light.
But even worse is a dreadful sense of impending doom. Yet in a day
or two they make up, and even without kissing, their reunion is
heavenly, like on that enchanting October night in the moonlight.
Warm affection, playful kidding, tender talk—without wanting

more. But after a few days comes a cozy sleep-together feeling—
it's too much for their unsated flesh.

Becki always starts it. Bitchy, restless, then bashful. That's the
sign her carnal side is stirring. Then she gets randy and they flirt and
talk suggestively until drunk with desire, like their raunchy talk at
the diner the last day of September. Becki loves the thrill and risk
of flirting on the edge of forbidden pleasure. Wanton teasing.
Buzzed on eros. Who'd believe it from a blushing Christian girl
who's seemingly chaste, pure, and serving God? The contrast is too
much for Jim to bear, as is the thought of her having a dark menacing
bush between her white cushiony thighs. It makes her irresistible.

As Jim shakes the excess piss out of his penis, it swells in his
hand, his hot blood catching up with his hot thoughts. When he
thinks about Rebecca, a good erection is only a touch away. When
with her, no touch is needed. He thinks about jerking off into the
urinal but quickly kills the idea—to jerk off in the church would be
an ultimate sin—and stuffs his half-stiff rod back into his jeans.

Becki loves to get high on erotic talk. But they never finish
what she starts or even make it personal except during their fights.
She always remains self-possessed, tethered to her conscience, and
never goes beyond fevered cheeks and crossing of legs—at least
not in front of Jim. He's also tethered, at least more than he realizes.
Naughty talk, confession, fantasy. Lust, lust, higher, higher. Then
the crash. Fears, doubts, a thousand reasons, mostly unspoken,
some too scary to contemplate. It's wrong. It's sinful. It's unfair to
Sharon, to the kids, to the church, to everyone. I'm a Christian, I'm
a pastor. Married, too old, too young. Consequences, consequences. Naked, naked. Naked flesh, Jim and Becki, male and
female. No, no, we can't. People are watching. God is watching.

But there's something even bigger that stops them—bigger
than will power, or mutual guilt, or fear of God, or fear of Sharon,
or Alison, or Logan, or others—a bigger more essential aspect of
God, or them, or both, something beautiful yet terrible. Naked,
naked, fucking, fucking. People are watching. God is watching.
No, no. *We* are watching. Terror, shrieking, self-disclosure. Ugly!
Ugly! I hate you! I hate myself! I *abhor* myself! It's like the "Big
Bang" is taking place inside them but it has no way out. They're
petrified of their own brightness, their own glory, glory that's
noble, heroic, majestic, divine, yet their light is also black and
wanton and selfish—dark like death. Demonic, ghastly, nefari-
ous—too terrible to look upon. Adam loves Eve, but only behind
fig leaves. Fig leaves, fig leaves. Damn the fig leaves! But they
can't let go. To let go means falling naked into the abyss, or into the
hands of God, like dying or being born. And Jim and Becki aren't

ready to discover the true nature of God, or *themselves,* not yet—
and it isn't their choice anyway.

Jim dries his hands on a paper towel then smells them as if he
expects to smell jism, as if he actually jacked off into the urinal. He
associates the smell of masturbation cum with sin and guilt more
than any smell. He's felt guilty about it since seventh grade, since
his friend Jason (Jason Barnett, Betty Sue's brother) taught him
how to jack off. Jason was older, a ninth-grader. Jim's rational side
knows better—he never rants against masturbation like Logan—
but solitary sex still shames his psyche, and he's glad he rarely has
to resort to it, thanks to Sharon.

To his office. He turns on the lights—buzzing, half-lit fluorescence. Jim has wrestled with enough lights for one day so he goes
to the kitchen. No perked coffee. He puts water on for instant.
Outside, the rain continues to fall, drumming on the cowling over
the kitchen exhaust fan. Jim likes the sound of the rain; it's honest
and soothing. The kitchen smells of coffee grounds and discarded
milk cartons. Friday's school-day trash has not been emptied.
There are crumbs on the table along with dried rings of coffee and
a Dunkin' Donuts bag, all left over from Saturday morning prayer
meeting. Inside the bag are two fossilized donuts. He tosses the bag,
and donuts, into the trash.

At home Jim doesn't know what to make of Sharon. She's
outwardly pleasant, still passionate in bed, yet he senses that her
Becki-wrath is building. He keeps the peace by diligently adhering
to her schedule demands, and so far he's walked the tightrope very
well. She still goes to Nashua every Tuesday to work for Tom H.
And, according to Doris, Tom and Mary Beth are close to splitting
up over Michael Montanaro.

But Jim doubts anything is going on between Tom and Sharon.
In one sense the thought of her fucking Tom infuriates and humili-
ates him, but in another sense he wishes she would, so he won't feel
so damn guilty over Becki. Jim sees Sharon as such a saint, such a
faithful wife and mother. It torments him. She and the kids are
innocent and pure, like the Ingalls on *Little House,* while he's a
lecherous gutter-minded liar filled with adulterous intentions.
Sometimes he imagines scenarios that will give him Becki without
destroying his godly standing such as Sharon running off with Tom,
or even more bizarre is the sick notion that his wife will die young
and he'll marry Becki. But this sick idea serves no purpose but to
make his guilt unbearable—*SSSSSSSH.* Whistling, spouting steam.
The water is ready. Jim grabs a mug, a spoon, a jar of Taster's
Choice, and makes a cup of coffee. After adding milk and sugar, he
sits down at the table and listens to the rain.

The whole thing makes Jim and Sharon schizo about their marriage, as when you deny the approach of death in a terminally-ill loved one. Becki still babysits and Sharon is still outwardly nice to her. Insane but happening. The only place he and Sharon get out of their insanity and into each other is in bed. As paradoxical as it may seem, Jim's love-war with Becki hasn't altered his desire for his wife—or his love. His guilt obscures it, but it comes out in the bedroom. So alike, Sharon and Becki, yet so different, like Tonya and Lara in *Doctor Zhivago*. He and Sharon saw that movie before they got married, and Sharon hated Zhivago for loving Lara.

Jim's mind is desperate for a good ending that will make it all fit, but his heart doesn't give a shit about fit. He just wants Becki forever, and Sharon too, for that matter, just as Jacob had Leah and Rachel. But if he has to choose, he has no choice. Unfaithful husband. Disloyal father. Sharon, Erin, Heather, Chris. They matter, they matter dearly. That's why the torment. Traitor, traitor. Yet Jim's conscience can't turn him. He's traveling an uncharted increasingly narrow road. The signs warn: DANGER AHEAD. DEEP GORGE. BRIDGE IS OUT. But he has no reverse or brakes. In fact, he has no steering wheel.

At the church it's business as usual, as if Jim and Becki are caught in a raging hurricane and everyone else is living in relative calm in the eye of the storm. Only Jodi is privy to Jim's heart; they pour out to each other like cellmates in a mental ward. Jim knows that Russ knows as well, but he's yet to openly share Becki with Russ. Jim and Becki have become a gossip topic, not hot, but certainly warm. Doris keeps Jim posted, on her drunk days—though he evades her pressing efforts to get him to confirm or deny his feelings for Becki. Nonetheless, he knows he can't keep his Becki-fire banked forever under the guise of ministry duties.

But for now, no one has hard evidence of scandal—there *is* none so far—and LBI'ers, in accordance with Dr. Logan's teaching on submitting to authority, are most reluctant to openly question a pastor's behavior. Besides, no one in the church would dare accuse Pastor Jim as long as Stan Campbell supports him. And Stan doesn't seem concerned. Ignoring the scuttlebutt, he stays on the bridge, like a good first mate, and keeps his eyes on the ministry itself. Attendance is up and the church has accepted nine new members since September. The BFBC ship is on course and making good speed—just like the *Titanic*.

Door, door, swinging door. Maroon sweats, hiking boots. It's Joe Lareux. Jim comes back from his thoughts. Joe gives a grunt then says, "So this is where you went? I was wondering." His eyes are keen and clear; he seems to be sober. He reheats the water on the stove and grabs the Lipton tea bags on the counter. Joe's hair is now well over his ears. The long hair actually improves his appearance because it diminishes his large head and short "rhino" neck.

Joe prepares his tea. Jim makes another cup of coffee. They joke and exchange small talk. But after a few sips of his tea, Joe becomes serious and confesses that something is bothering him. Speaking honestly, like the rain, he gets right to the point. His voice, like his face, is mellow and round. He says he has a crush on Brenda Donovan, or maybe he loves her. This doesn't shock Jim; Joe and Brenda are always together, playing the guitar, riding in the car.

Jim sits down again while Joe leans against the counter. Joe says it hasn't bothered him too much, loving a tenth-grader and flirting and having fun. As a matter of fact, he says it's Jim's recent preaching on "following the heart" that freed him to get close to Brenda, and he says it's the most beautiful thing that's ever happened to him. At least until last night.

"You saw Brenda last night?" Jim asks. "I thought you had to work?"

"I did. This happened without Brenda."

"How's that?"

Joe takes a swig of his tea then explains, "Well, when I got home from work, I got high in my apartment. I don't usually get stoned after work but I was bummed. Alexander's sucks this time of the year; you know, the December food-buying craze. Anyway, I was on my second J, and I was staring at the floor by my bed. I saw this ant. It was a beautiful ant, red and green and shiny, and its legs were strong and knotty-looking. It soon disappeared into a crack between the boards. I got down and looked into the crack. I saw the ant crawling and then another ant, and the inside of the crack was bigger than I ever realized, like a canyon with a road at the bottom, and at the end of the road was a tunnel and the ants went into it." Jim, slowly sipping his freeze-dried coffee, wonders where this tale is leading.

"Anyway, after the ants were gone," Joe goes on, his eyes growing large as he talks, "I turned on my stereo and listened to *Led Zeppelin*. I can really get into Jimmy Page when I'm stoned. I must've stayed up 'til one o'clock.... Now this is what troubles me. When I fell asleep, I had this dream. I was down on my knees again looking into the crack on my floor, looking at the ants. But they were no longer ants, but Brenda and me. She was running naked down a long street and I was down there too, and I was chasing her with a knife, but it wasn't a knife. It was a plaster-cast penis, my penis. As we ran, the sky turned black like Judgment Day, and I saw more ants but they were flying, swarms of big flying ants like giant termites, and they had glowing tails like fireflies, but when they came closer they weren't ants. They were demons with fiendish batlike faces and fangs and claws, and big red eyes. I knew I was damned."

Jim gives a quick laugh, one syllable's worth. "Now that's quite a story," he declares pushing his mug toward Joe. "Sounds like something out of an X-rated horror comic. Maybe you'll believe me now and lay off that weed."

Joe laughs too, but uneasily. "No, it's not the pot. Marijuana doesn't make you hallucinate. It's the dream. It's like God's telling me that my feelings for Brenda are *way* too sexual." Joe drinks his tea, slowly sucking it with his lips.

"Well, Joe, I doubt God damns people in dreams ... but who knows? I'm beginning to think I know less about God every day. But I can't blame you for liking Brenda. After all, she's cute and lovable, and has that soft innocent sex appeal that girls get right after puberty. But most people would not agree, at least about the sexual attraction part."

"That's for sure," Joe replies, giving a chuckling snort. Jim chuckles as well. They go on for a while lamenting back and forth about the unfairness of so many doctrines and attitudes that are never honestly weighed against reality in any Christian church, or in Christianized Western culture, like how sex with teen girls is taboo and called rape even though most girls are hungry to mate at fourteen, and how it's no longer socially acceptable for teenage women to marry, and how self-control and celibacy are championed as virtues, while giving in to one's sex drive is condemned as sinful and foolhardy except in marriage where it's tolerated, and how the Western psyche has been ashamed of erotic pleasure since St. Augustine, whereas in primitive cultures the maturing of the penis and the vagina and the awakening of sexual desire were celebrated without shame, and how fear is the bottom line in Western sexuality: fear of God, fear of self, fear of losing career and social status, fear of pregnancy, fear of disturbing the moral order of marriage and family, and now fear of AIDS. Of course, neither Jim nor Joe would dare voice such opinions in regular LBI circles.

Joe kids that he would've had a better chance with Brenda if they both lived in the Stone Age. Jim agrees. They laugh—then an unexpected turn. Jim begins to compare Brenda to Becki. All at once he becomes a great keg of liquid truth that flows out all over the kitchen and all over Joe, who listens and sucks his tea, a knowing twinkle in his brown eyes. He seems more relaxed as if relieved that the spotlight has shifted from Joe-Brenda to Jim-Becki. When Jim is finished, Joe gives a crooked grin. "I figured you were turned on to Becki. She says funny things about you when she's stoned. She smokes grass with me, you know ... not so much lately but when we used to ride together."

"That's what I hear," Jim replies, his heart springing to attention. "Doesn't exactly thrill me but I guess she's more into your shit than I am." Jim tries to look blasé but curiosity rages in his gut. "So, what'd she say about me?" he asks, unable to constrain himself.

Joe snickers. "Oh, not much ... but she pees like a fucking cow."

Alarm, alarm, anxiety. Jealousy heats Jim's face. "You saw her take a piss?"

"I'll say," Joe replies, chuckling and shaking his head as if he can't believe it himself.

*Maybe Becki does want Joe?* Jim worries to himself. *Maybe he already fucked her?* His stomach churns but he maintains outward calm. He lifts his mug. He's afraid to ask but he has to know. "So, Joe, when did this happen?"

"Oh, different times. Sometimes on the way back to Nashua we'd stop on a side road and listen to tunes and share a joint and a six-pack. When Becki gets tanked on beer, she has to pee and she doesn't care where." Joe swigs down the last of his tea then gives a wolfish grin. "Does she ever have a nice ass. It's big and round and white, but *so* nice. It's hard to believe she can pack it into her pants so well." Dry throat. Tingling dick. Jim feels a tingling at the tip of his penis as if it's contracting even smaller than its usual thumby size; it feels like a grub worm. He gulps but doesn't reply. Joe has seen her naked butt. He cringes to think what else Joe has seen, or done. He hopes Joe will stop talking about it—no, that's a lie. Becki, Becki: naked, moaning, begging Joe to put it in. Jim has to hear it, hear it all.

Joe continues with his story, which turns out to be mild, hardly X-rated. "But the time I remember most, Jim, was more recent ... October I think. Anyway, Becki took me to the cliff above the river. The one by the train trestle. After two joints and four beers she was flying. She usually doesn't get wasted, but that day she was in a sucky mood and got drunk like she wanted to forget everything. Then she says, 'I gotta pee wicked bad.' Next thing I know, she squats right on the rock maybe five feet away and hisses and pisses and makes a puddle that runs over the edge to the ledge below. When she's buzzed, she gets fucking loose, and to be honest—I hope you don't take offense—but her fat ass looked so nice I felt like plugging her right there on the rock. But she never comes on to me. She treats me like a brother. She'd fit a lot better into my life than Brenda, but that's not how things are."

Jim sighs with partial relief; he's no longer so jealous, except he wishes he'd seen Becki's naked behind instead of Joe.

"So, what'd she say about me?" Jim asks.

"Sure you want to hear it?" Joe teases.

Jim blushes and gives a short embarrassed laugh. "Whaddeya think? If you don't hurry, I'm gonna make a puddle of my own right here on the floor."

Joe pushes his hair back off his face. His voice drops an octave to that secretive tone that men reserve for dirty jokes. "Well, like I say, she was wasted. I doubt she knew what she was saying, but she got to talking about you, about how you had little feet for a guy, and short legs. Then she giggled and said, 'I bet he's got a little pecker too. I doubt Jimmy has five inches.'" Joe chortles. Jim laughs; he can laugh since he knows he has six, exactly six. Sharon has measured it several times. She's always amazed at how much it grows from soft to hard. Jim's dick grows a lot, unlike his friend Jason back in Gilmer, the one who taught him to jerk off. Jason's penis hung long and ropey all the time, and when it got hard, it scarcely grew in length; it just filled out and got thicker.

Brenda, Brenda. The door swings open and Brenda spills into the kitchen. She breathlessly announces that Teri Cameron is sick, that she threw up in the bathroom and Barry needs Joe to take her home. Brenda quickly adds that she'll come along to help. She seems eager as if looking forward to the trip back when she and Joe will be alone in his old Buick. Excusing himself, Joe leaves with Brenda.

Jim goes to the window and gazes into the dark rainy night. He doesn't know whether to feel good or bad over what he's said and heard. But either way, his Becki-heart is getting out. Now he's told two—Jodi and Joe.

* * *

Pastor Jim pulls his jacket tightly around him and exits the teen center. He's the last to leave except for Barry who's mopping the floor. The night is Edgar Allen Poe: bleak, haunted, ominous. The pelting rain has formed a small lake in the drive-around. The downspouts gurgle and gush. The wind moans through the pine trees. Red clouds scud by overhead. The air smells like wet snow, cold, ozonic, astringent, like inhaling the color blue. The raindrops even dash and swirl like snowflakes as gusts of wind whip them around the security light. The swaying tree branches cast weird terpsichorean shadows on the back of the church as if a band of goblins and ghosts have come forth to haunt. The Mustang glistens wet and strangely pink in the honey-ochre light, and seems ten miles away.

Jim dashes through the rain, splashing, sloshing toward his car—wait; what is that? He sees a dark shadowy thing moving, gliding through the picnic area. Then he loses sight of it as the rain blinds him. He wipes his eyes and peers again into the darkness but the strange form has disappeared. Wet, wet, getting drenched, he feels like he's stepped into a cold shower with his clothes on. Water runs off his brow. Again he wipes his eyes but sees nothing save trees and blackness and quivering sodium light—and water. Water, water. A carpet of water covers the picnic area.

Jim turns to get into the car—no, there it is again, coming closer, a black phantom, a dark specter, floating, hovering out of the night. Fear grips Jim's soul. His heart beats faster than the rain. His imagination runs wild. Fiery eyes, flaring nostrils, curved—no, it's walking, it's a man; at least, he's dressed like a man.

Black raincoat, drenched. A solitary hatted-figure. Who can be out there? He's coming closer. Jim's fear shifts, perhaps prematurely, from nightmare to real world. Slowly the intruder comes, mysterious, dignified, gracefully slender, almost catlike.

The rain pours. Jim waits, getting wetter. *Squish-ka-squish. Squish-ka-squish.* The mysterious hatted-figure advances through the heel-deep water, through the dancing shadows, into the tremulous light, then back into the shadows. Closer, closer. Head down, collar up, hands in his pockets, this strange night-visitor comes closer until Jim can see that his hat is a dark Humphrey-Bogart-style fedora, but his black raincoat is actually fox-brown and trendy, over light-colored pants and pointy-toed Italian-style boots.

"Can I help you?" Shanley asks, politely challenging the intruder. No response, nor does the man look up. He comes closer. He has a red feather in the band of his hat and he wears a stylish white neck-scarf. Jim challenges again, "This is *church* property. Can I help you!" This time his tone is stern, military.

Face, face, the man looks up—a pale boyish face. "I know it's a church, Jim," Matt Garrett wisecracks above the roar of the rain. "You can sheathe your sword. This isn't an army base, you *know*?" Jim gives a self-conscious smile of surprise and bewilderment—but not of relief.

"Good God!" Jim exclaims as they shake hands. "What the fu—hell are *you* doin' out here?" He's glad it's not a prowler but Garrett's presence rearouses his nightmarish fears. Despite the humor, Garrett seems foreboding like Poe's night-visitor, the "grim, ungainly, ghastly, gaunt, and ominous bird of yore," who spoke not hope but—"Nevermore."

But Garrett does not quote "The Raven." Instead, he says, "Pam and I came down to see Barry and Janet. I came to pick up Barry. I just thought I'd take a look around the property while I was waiting."

Jim grins uneasily under his wet mustache. "Well, you sure picked a lousy night to tour the grounds."

Pelting rain, puffs of winter breath, penetrating Nordic eyes. Garrett stares at Shanley as if he's X-raying him, as if he's casting a spell—like that night on Logan's deck. Water pours off the brim of his hat in a steady stream. In the shivering sodium light, Matt's face looks ashen, ethereal, shadowy, as if he's indeed a ghost who's come to haunt the night. Finally, he gives a cocky smile and says, "I like walking on dark stormy nights. Don't you, Jim?"

"Sometimes, but right now walking to my car is enough." Jim is cold and waterlogged. He wants to go home. He has to take a leak. "Go on in," he suggests to Matt. "Barry's almost done."

"I am," Garrett replies. "But first I want to grab a smoke." Matt heads for his car which is parked at the corner of the drive-around near Stan's junk pile; the black BMW is hardly noticeable in the dark shadows.

Jim opens the door of the Mustang but before he can get in, Garrett turns and yells, "Hey, Jim!"

"Yeh!" Jim yells back above the downpour.

"D'you know what the monkey said when he got his tail caught in the lawnmower!"

"Nawh, I guess not! What did he say!"

Jim waits. The wind moans, the shadows dance. The rain pours. "IT WON'T BE LONG NOW!" Matt shouts after opening the door of his BMW.

A gust of wind blows an icy burst of rain into Shanley's face. *It won't be long now—clever, real clever; ha, ha. What the fuck is he saying?* An ominous shudder races up Jim's spine. He shivers. He slides his cold soaked body behind the wheel of the Mustang. Water squishes out of his suede jacket as if it's a chamois cloth.

Jim drives slowly around the building. His still-crippled wipers can't keep up with the rain. He gives a beep as he passes Matt's car. Flash of flame, flicker of orange. Garrett lights a cigarette briefly illuminating his ghostly countenance.

* * *

Jim twists the fluorescent bulb. The lights flicker then come on. "What time is it?" he asks Becki. He doesn't feel like fishing his watch out of his pocket—his watchband is broken.

Becki pulls back the sleeve of her ski jacket and looks at her Timex. "Twenty 'til six," she replies.

Jim hops down, peels off his trench coat, his suit coat, unbuttons his vest, then plunks down at his desk. Becki, her blue-plaid skirt hiked to her knees, sits Jodi-style on the side of the desk. Outside, the squalling wind and rain drives the December darkness against the windows of Shanley's office. The storm windows are loose, and they rattle with each strong gust. The rainstorm abated some during the day but has now returned full force—actually, it's a second low moving up the front. Sharon and the kids stayed home, so Jim left early and picked up Becki on the way.

Preparing for staff meeting, he scribbles a few notes on his Christmas-week schedule, but he can't concentrate with Becki's legs close enough to touch. She's digging around in Jim's collection of pens, pencils, and markers, which he keeps in an old wooden mug. Finding a purple marker-pen, she grabs one of his personalized memo pads and begins to decorate his name with festoons of flowers and stars and leaves and birds. Jim senses vibes of playful affection. The mood is cozy, relaxing. He gives up on the schedule in his hand. He looks up as does Rebecca. Their eyes meet and she dimples into an "ah shucks" smile. This sets off warm geysers inside Jim's bosom. He longs to hug her—*BAM! BAM! Knock! Knock! Knock!* Frantic knocking shatters the cozy mood.

Becki opens the door. It's Barry. Unshaven, uncombed, he seems nervous, confused, distraught. His attire is equally confused: Sunday pants under a ragged sweat shirt and a Silas Brendon letter jacket that's way too small. His black hair is dirty, sweaty, and matted down as if he's been wearing a football helmet. His huge winter belly pushes out under his shirt; he looks eight months pregnant. Becki, sensing Barry's need to talk, grabs her stuff and departs.

Barry sits down across from Jim but does not relax. Instead, he balances his Doughboy physique on the front of the chair in an "on guard" position. His bulging eyes scan warily from side to side as if he expects a screaming devil to spring upon him. The ammoniac stink of sweat fills the room. Barry, his face pasty white like on that day by the river, wrings his hands anxiously as if he's Lady Macbeth trying to wash the blood off her hands. He seems on the verge of hysteria. His panicky state rattles Jim, who picks up a Bic Clic ballpoint pen and nibbles on it. Barry leans closer, looking right at Jim. "That's why, that's the reason," he mutters. His eyes seem frightened, desperate, pleading, bewildered, like a wounded animal. He's so close Jim could almost reach across the desk and touch his fear-blanched face.

"Whaa...." Jim's words catch in his dry throat.

He clears, but before he can speak, Barry blurts a confused confession: "I-I know. I do. Stan, he can't know. Nobody knows. Stan doesn't. He can't, and Doris. And Janet, she can't know either. But I have to tell. I have to confess before God. My heart is wicked. I'm fucked. It's true. I'm perverted. I'm *wretch*ed." His voice drops to a pitiful whisper. "Jim, Jim, I-I...." A gasp, a moan, a breaking sob. "O God ... I'm in love with a *man*."

Barry falls forward onto the desk, sobbing, gasping, shuddering. Jim wants to comfort him but he's riveted to his chair. Barry's tears soak Jim's memo pad smearing Becki's purple flowers and birds. Jim waits, nibbles his ballpoint pen, tries to collect his wits.

December darkness, squalling rain. The windows rattle—and Barry cries. After a minute or so, he stands halfway, pulls a wrinkled well-used hankie from his pocket, then sinks backward into the chair. He blows his nose and wipes his tear-blotched face. The panic, the tension, the insanity seem to be gone, but he looks ashen and half alive, as one looks after vomiting. His fat jowls are viscous, ready to ooze off his pudding face. His whole body is blubber. No muscle, no bone. His skin strains to hold his corpulence together. At least, it seems so to Jim. He pictures Barry's hide ripping open and his fat gushing out like jelly out of a jelly doughnut. Barry pushes his hands and his handkerchief down into his crotch as if covering himself with fig leaves. He sighs resignedly then gazes out the window at the stormy night. He has no expression save for a blank I-know-I'm-damned look. Finally, like a death-row inmate confessing to a priest before his final walk to the electric chair, he relates his story. His protruding eyes are as big as cue balls and just as white. Only his lips move. His hands seem frozen over his genitals as if he has no clothes.

Jim listens and nibbles—he's already chewed half the clicker off his Bic pen. As usual, Sharon's gossip is right on target. Barry says he's in love with Matt Garrett and they've been meeting romantically for over a year—after services in Nashua, at conferences, weekday mornings in Brendon Falls when Janet is teaching, plus secret rendezvous at the 495 rest area in Westford.

Barry's voice is hoarse and snuffly: "Matt is the sweetest, most gentle soul. I couldn't help but love him. He called me beautiful and ravishing, and vowed that our love was holy and forever just like Jonathan and David, and when he touched me, my heart shuddered and caved in." Jim gazes at Barry's lips. Lips, lips, Barry's lips: fat and blue and boyish, talking, telling all, as if they're somehow detached and can therefore speak objectively.

Barry goes on to say that he's been turned on to boys since he was twelve, and he even fantasized about making it with the guys on his football team, and by the time he was seventeen, he despised himself. He says he cares for Janet and that sex with her is pleasant, but nothing stirs him like Matt Garrett's boyish body. He says he pretended to be straight until Matt brought him out: "I couldn't resist Matt's tender words ... or his sensual kisses. Now I'm so reprobate and deceitful and unclean."

It's all beyond Jim. *How could he want Garrett over Janet?* he asks himself. *O God, to get in bed with that she-tiger—but to kiss Matt Garrett? It's disgusting. And why does Janet stay if she gets no passion from Barry? Human sexuality, I can't figure it, but who am I to judge? Wanting Becki doesn't fit either?*

Somber blackness descends over Barry like an executioner's hood, until he's nothing but eyes, lips, and a chairful of sagging corpulence. "Abomination, I knew it was abomination," he says detachedly as if about to carry out his own execution. "I knew God was disgusted with me. I felt the conviction. I puked my guts on the ground, but still I went on. I knew God would deal with me ... and *now* He has. Last night Matt picked me up here, after I closed the teen center, and we went to Mister Disco, a gay bar in Boston. We go there a lot, but it was terrible. He left with another guy. I had to take the train back in the rain, then a cab from Ayer. I was cold and soaked, just like my heart. And I lied as usual to cover up. I told Janet I was out with Joe Lareux. My whole life is a lie, and now it may as well be *over*." Barry says no more but simply stares out at the storm from within his hood of black resignation.

Jim slips on his pastor face. "It's never too late to repent, Barry," he counsels, making tight little gestures with his half-chewed pen. "Love covers a multitude of sins. If you isolate this sin and forsake—SCREW THIS!" Jim shouts, bolting out of his chair—and his pastor facade. "Screw it all!" He punches the air. "It's all a lie! Truth is, Barry, I don't know *shit* about your situation! I never had desires for a guy, but who am I to say anything? My life is more messed up than yours. I don't even know what sin is anymore.... I just hope that love is somehow the highest good. That's all I know."

Barry, taken by surprise, seems relieved to hear Jim's admission. The black gloom fades from his pudding face. Jim considers telling him about Becki, but before he can complete the decision, a double knock comes at the door. It's Stan. He says that leaves are clogging the downspout by the main entrance, and he needs Barry to hold the ladder. Barry leaves with Stan.

Jim digs his watch out of his pocket. It's ten after, almost time for staff meeting. Before going down, he visits the men's room where the pungent odor of Christian piss clears his nostrils like a strong shot of Vick's Inhaler; the men's room always reeks on Sunday evening. *Barry and I, now we can really talk*—or so Jim thinks as he stands at the urinal.

* * *

Stan announces that Barry won't be at staff meeting because he's got an upset stomach—Jim chuckles under his breath at this news. Stan then slips on his glasses and reads from a legal pad. Becki, sitting to Pastor Jim's left, takes notes. "We got soda cans all over the teen center. I found a basketball outside in the mud. An' I found cig'rette butts by the sidewalk out front."

The mention of cigarettes sets Stan off. He waves the yellow pad, fanning the air. "How can we lead people to God when the first thing they see is a bunch of filthy *butts* by the main entrance? How many times do we hafta say it? There's *no* smokin' on church property! I'm gettin' sick 'n tired of how all the women around here hafta go suck a cig'rette ever two hours! I'm always findin' ashes in the ladies' room. They should be prayin' 'steada smokin', so God can deliver 'em from tobacco. That's how *I* quit."

Stan gives an exasperated sigh, cooling a bit, then returns his attention to the list. "I found dirty coffee mugs all over, most with lipstick on 'em. There musta been six in Angie's office alone, plus a box of stale donuts in the teachers' mail room. And, let's see ... the safe closet wasn't locked. The kitchen trash hasn't been emptied for four days. I got enough stuff this afternoon to fill ten 'spection lists." Shaking his hoary head, he drops the pad, his massive hands falling on top of it, *BAM!* A heavy fleshy, *BAM!* "We gotta show 'tention to details. We been goin' good since summer. We can't let Lucifer outsmart us now. So let's get with it!"

Nervous coughing, clearing of throats. "Before we get into the Christmas schedule," Pastor Jim says, moving the meeting to a milder subject, "I've got a draft here of the '84 budget. I'll pass it around, but first I need to write in the '83 figures. So, Russ, if you'll read them off?" The tension in the air slowly relaxes like a wind-up toy running down.

"Okay," Russ replies, "Angie's got the main copy, so these may not be in order. Let's see, bus transportation: $4135. Auto transportation, that's mainly the Escort: $2782. Food, clothing, shelter fund—for the poor—$875. Teen ministry: $1944. Softball program: $635. Tithes to Nashua: $8731, and—"

"That's not *ties* to Nashwa," Stan cuts in to clarify—as usual, he says "ties" instead of "tithes." "The money we send goes to WMF, to the mission'ry fund, since we don't have our own mission'ries, 'cept what we send to Alison 'n Ed."

Russ acknowledges Stan's remark with a nod then goes on, "Telephone: $1727. Fuel oil: $2315. Electricity: $2918. Insurance: $2104. Moody fund: $6392. EDGE program: $463. Ed Landreth: $1050. Mortgage: $3874. Pastor's salary: $22,800. Pastor's expense account: $5325. Other salaries, teachers-secretarial: $37,830. Office supplies: $2146—"

A rap on the door; it's Barbara Sims. She tells Pastor Jim that Sharon's on the phone, that it's urgent.

Jim hurries to his office. His heart races, bracing for bad news. The kids? His dad? It is bad, but not so close to home. Sharon says that little Shane McClusky choked on a piece of Christmas candy and they took him to Hinton Regional but then had to medevac him to Mass. General.

As Jim comes out, he runs into Stan coming down the hall. He quickly briefs Stan then hurries out the back way to the Mustang. When he gets to the car, he's surprised to find it running with Becki in the driver's seat.

"How'd you know I'd be leaving?" Jim asks her.

Becki's eyes are keen, her voice sober, "Why would Sharon call during staff meeting unless it's wicked bad? You can't go by yourself. So tell me where we're going."

"Head for the Mass. Pike," Jim instructs. "We're going to Boston."

The Mustang rears and roars then zooms around the church fording the deep puddles. Becki whips out onto Reservoir Road and they quickly leave the lighted parking lot behind as they speed away into the black and stormy night. The rain pelts the windshield. The headlights pierce the fog.

Nothing gets by her—Rebecca is like that.

# Chapter Twenty-four

Pastor Jim lays his hand on the child and prays, but his prayer is just as limp and lifeless as Shane's dead body. Joanne holds her son. His little arms and legs hang down like the limbs of a rag doll. His eyes are closed. His skin feels cold. His face is ashy-white like candle wax. A nurse helps Joanne. The young doctor looks on regretfully, but with no words. He's already spoken all the dreaded words. Though the wailing is over, Calvin whimpers and tells the baby good-bye. But Joanne, still in her gray-checked waitress uniform, stands silent, stoic, and remote. Mute pain and resignation lie naked in her eyes. She, like Job, has surrendered to the certain hand of God, who "giveth" and "taketh away." After his prayer, Jim tries to console with Bible promises.

A minister in the midst of death, a Minister of the Gospel no less, but Pastor Jim's "good news" from the Bible rings hollow as if he's reading the classified ads from the *Sunday Globe*. Why is he talking? The scene speaks for itself. Joanne's tear-blotched face says more than a thousand sermons. Jim feels false then witless then awkward—then awestruck. Why did they call him, mother and dad and dead child, to this room of death equipped with nurses, doctors, and a crib with white sheets? Monitors, machines, wires, blinking red lights, LCD readouts, tubes, tape, i.v. bottles. Stainless steel cabinets, trash receptacles, a table by the crib. On the table: an open box of Pampers, a cylinder of Handi-wipes. A room with four beige walls and nursery-style decals, bunnies and birds and puppies and kitty cats and trees and flowers and squirrels, and a happy-face toy box full of reds and yellows and blues, and teddy bears and tactile blocks and locking beads and rattle keys and chime balls.

It seems a tragic twisted version of the Christmas story: Joseph and Mary, the babe, the wise men, the presents, and the animals. But is it? One window, one door, but Shane used neither when he left—if he left.

\* \* \*

With a sweep of his hand Pastor Jim tries to smooth his cowlicked bangs. After being in the rain then drying, his hair is like a crown of straw. Buddy brings the food, one hamburger, one cheeseburger, and a large platter of fries, then a minute later, shuffles back with two milks and a bottle of ketchup. He carries the ketchup in the pocket of his dirty apron. Before leaving, he bends down into Jim's face, close enough to kiss, and says, "Is that all?"

His voice is gruff. His breath smells of onions. Jim answers yes, nodding to make sure, and Buddy shuffles away.

10:37 p.m. Becki's in the bathroom. Jim sits in their regular booth. There are perhaps a half-dozen people in the diner; it's slow between ten and two, then comes the bar crowd. Buddy's working this end, Juanita the other. They know. They have to know. News travels fast in Brendon Falls. Besides, Joanne was working at the diner when she got the call. Buddy never says anything anyway, and Juanita just waves a greeting and gives a smiley-face like all is well. Death is like that. It's like fucking. Everyone thinks about it, but no one talks about it, except in jest.

Wailing, weeping, sobbing. The worst was in the family room when Cal and Joanne told their parents, and everyone went into hysterics. Rebecca didn't cry, but she was shook, as was Jim.

An emotional day—Jim's feelings have been reeling since his session with Barry. Becki was quiet all the way back from Boston, quiet and subdued. When they got to 59 Front Street, she wasn't ready to go home; she didn't want to be by herself. ·

The ketchup is in a plastic squeeze bottle with a white pop-up cap. Dried ketchup cakes the cap like a bloody scab. The label says: Give Heinz A Squeeze. Jim obeys and squirts some to the side of the french fries making a puddle on the platter. The aroma of the hot fries stirs his appetite. Hot fries, large, thick, golden brown, with the skins on. He takes a big one, dips it in the ketchup, then snacks on it like a candy bar.

He leans over to the window and looks out. The rain has stopped but the window is still wet. It's turning colder. After two days of rain and ocean air, the old mill town is clammy, dank, and blah, and smells like London. The streets and gutters are begrimed with mud and silt and catch-basin detritus. Across the street the fire station lies dark and buttoned up save for a light in a side office.

No traffic, except for a Poulos' Pizza truck bouncing along through the puddles and potholes. The bars are open but it seems that Sunday drinkers go in and never come out. The cherry-red taillamps of the pizza truck flicker and jump and distort as they move amid the water droplets on the window. Jim follows the red lights until they turn off Park Street onto Chestnut. Baby Shane is dead—and so is the town.

Becki returns. She tosses her hobo bag onto the seat, sheds her jacket, and slides into the booth. After a few remarks about her rain-dampened hair and the filthy state of the ladies' room, she turns her attention to her cheeseburger, and they eat without talking much.

Sunday clothes, makeup, no bangs. Though pouty-faced as usual, Rebecca seems older to Jim, and she has on a different perfume, not Moonlight Lace. Her hair is parted, her bangs swept to one side. He can see her forehead, a rare sight. And her hair is darker, more chocolately. Her makeup gives her skin a dry matte texture instead of her usual oily adolescent look. Her eyes are outlined with mascara and toned with eye shadow. Darker eyes, they seem deeper, and strikingly unfamiliar. The blue in them seems farther away, exotic, charming, provocative, as if Jim is peering into the future. But in addition to looking older, she looks wilted and drained. Her eye shadow is bleeding into the crevices and there are mascara smudges where she's rubbed her tired eyes. She has on her beige shirt, the one with the embroidered border. She's been wearing it since morning service along with her plaid skirt. She's also wearing a pewter teddy-bear pin and star earrings.

After their burgers and fries, they order the usual: coffee and pecan pie. "Did you see him?" Becki inquires a bit later as they finish their dessert.

"Yeh, I did," Jim replies. "I touched him too, while I was praying."

She sips her coffee then says, "What was it like?"

"It was kind of weird being in there, kind of like a dream. He was mainly, what I recall, he was just limp, real limp ... his arms, his legs."

"Did you hold him?"

"No, I just touched his head. Calvin held him, then Joanne."

"Was his skin cold?"

Jim takes his last bite of pie. After chewing, he answers, "Not like ice or anything, but sort of cold. It's hard to explain. It's not like touching anything else. It was like—well, his color was gone. He was pale like the color of mushrooms, not the brown ones but the grayish-white kind."

Becki toys with the crust of her pie. She seems sad. Not heartbroken sad but reflective, wistful. She had grown fond of Baby Shane during their many Saturday visits, but it's more like she's reflecting on the mystery of death itself. Her bangs fall. She sweeps them back to the side, first with one hand, then the other. She leans back in the booth. She hugs her arms about her bosom and gazes out the window with a faraway look. Outside, it's raining again, not hard, just a few streaks on the window.

"Whaddeya thinking about, Becki?" Jim asks.

"It's just wicked sad, that's all," Becki replies, her voice filled with a sense of resignation.

"What is?"

She sighs and answers out the window, "That we have to die. Everything has to die. Birds, flowers, family, friends, and Skipper and Bathsheba, and Baby Shane ... and me." Jim doesn't reply but slowly drinks his coffee. He feels empathy and wonder at Becki's contemplative mood. "There was this hill in Puerto Rico not far from our house," she goes on. "And there was this open area at the top and you could see the ocean wicked good. There was this old concrete bunker up there and they used to have cannons and stuff. Nobody ever went there except me and Skipper. It was my special place, Jimmy ... where I could go and think about it."

"Think about what?" Jim asks.

"Death and God and stuff, not like in church, but like I was on a desert island and had to think it out for myself ... without pastors and teachers."

"So did you figure it out?"

Becki pushes her bangs back. She continues to speak out the window. "Sorta, maybe ... in a way. You see, there was this one day. It was windy and the ocean was blue-green and the waves were white and coming onto the beach. The sun was getting low and there were lots of puffy clouds goin' by. I was sitting on the concrete bunker thing petting Skipper, and I got this superstrong feeling, like God was talking to me, or maybe it was like a knowing."

Jim downs the last of his coffee. "You mean like an inkling ... like an intuitive feeling?"

"Well, it's hard to—but I guess I just knew. I knew, I uh—"

"You knew what?"

"I just knew I was gonna die."

"So ... everybody dies?"

"No," Becki replies out into the night. "It was like God was telling me that I'd never get old, that I was gonna die young. So when somebody dies, I think about it."

"Come on; I bet you outlive me by twenty years, maybe thirty?"

Becki brings her attention back into the diner. She picks up the piece of crust from her plate, pops it into her mouth, and washes it down with a swig of coffee. "No, really, I felt it. I felt God speaking to me ... and I think Skipper sensed it too. Dogs know about death, don'tcha think, Shanley?"

"I've heard that, like how dogs can sense when their master is dying.... But I still doubt that you'll die before me. I'm seventeen years ahead of you, you know?"

Buddy appears with the check and a pot of coffee. Placing the check on the table, he bends down over Jim's cup until his eye is almost in it. "More coffee?" he asks. Jim says yes. Buddy lifts the cup right to his eyes and pours. He then repeats the process with Becki and shuffles off.

Jim doesn't like to entertain the idea of Becki dying before him, but as they doctor their fresh coffee, he takes her premonition more seriously, "So does it scare you to think about it, what God told you?"

Becki looks right at Jim. Her eyes seem sad and honest and searching. They're still unfamiliar but only because she rarely looks directly at him with sober intent. Blue, blue, sky-blue and seeking. Her eyes shine steadily into his like yearning blue lamps—naked, aggressive, phallic, as if she's coming into him with her eyes. Too much. He looks down at his coffee as she replies, "I wasn't afraid up on my special hill with Skipper when it was sunny and bright and the wind was warm, but it's different today. It's dark and rainy and cold, and Shane choked on candy. Now it's scary to think about because we don't know anything for sure, like what it feels like to die, or where we go."

"But what about faith?" Jim says without looking up.

"That's what Mom 'n Ed always say, and Pastor in his classes. Faith is a cop-out and a catchword if you ask me. If you have great faith, Pastor Logan calls you up on stage and everybody cheers. But why should we *cheer* for somebody who pretends to know things we can't possibly know ... like what happens when we die, or who goes to heaven? It's like cheering for a liar. 'Have *faith*' ... that's what all Christians say. Profess your faith. Profess to believe in Jesus and the Bible, and keep professing no matter what, then peace will come ... but I still get wicked scared sometimes, like today."

Jim, ignoring his heart, gives a party-line response, "Well, it takes time. Remember, 'Faith comes by hearing and hearing by the Word of God'?"

"I know, I know," Becki comes back. "I've heard that a *zillion* times. But when I sat on my hill and looked at the ocean and the clouds, I knew I couldn't."

"You couldn't what?"

"I couldn't just choose to believe. I had to feel it. Sometimes I do, sometimes I don't. To say I do when I don't is a lie, even though Mom 'n Ed 'n Pastor, they call it faith, and you too, Jimmy, at least when you're acting religious, like tonight." Becki isn't pissed. She's just being painfully honest as if Shane's death has given her a desire to get real about what Christians *actually* know versus what they *profess* to know.

Jim doesn't reply but holds his cup to his lips with both hands and slowly sucks coffee into his mouth. Becki rolls her sleeves as if getting ready to preach. Her arms are soft and fair like arms you'd expect to see raised in eleventh-grade English. He wishes they could cuddle up somewhere and forget about death. But she's not finished. "So, Shanley," she asks, "do you believe that Shane's with God?"

Jim lowers his cup just enough to talk. "Yeh, I think he is."

"But do you *know* he's with God?" Becki presses, her eyes saying more than her lips.

"Whaddeya mean, *know*?" Jim asks. His coffee cup is so close he feels heat on his nose.

"*Know*, like you *know* you're sitting here with me."

"I uh ... I think, I hope, but uh—"

"You don't *know* for sure, d'yuh?"

Jim stares at the mocha liquid in his cup, then replies, "No, I guess not ... not for sure."

Not an ego triumph or a bantering victory, Becki's simply asking the hard questions about death and dying, and she's disrobing Shanley in the process. She shifts back to Baby Shane, "D'you think he suffered?"

"Maybe, but not too long. I guess until he lost consciousness."

"D'you think it was like that burning feeling, like when you're swimming and you stay under as long as you can?"

"Yeh, it's probably like that when you choke to death." *She's not beating around the bush,* Jim adds to himself. *She's looking right at it ... and not flinching.*

Becki gestures over her empty pie plate as if she's kneading the air. "Sometimes I try to imagine what it's like to drown, or to fall from a high building, or to crash in an airplane, or to get shot in the stomach ... or to be electrocuted."

"That's kind of morbid, doncha think?" Jim asks.

"Yeah, but when the scary death-feelings come, I imagine all the possibilities. It's wicked terrifying, like no control. Yet it's a release too, like I'm in God's hands—the *real* God."

Becki takes a swig of coffee and swishes it around in her mouth. Then her mood suddenly shifts. She pushes her cup and saucer away, grabs her hobo bag, and starts rummaging. She reminds Jim of Jodi D. searching for cigarettes. Gum wrappers, three empty packs of Big Red, but no gum. She continues to rummage, pulling things out and placing them on the table. Two combs, a brush, several wadded tissues, sunglasses, a checkbook, her beige wallet. A floppy makeup kit, a little round mirror with a handle, a thing of green Tic-Tacs, a zippered case, oblong with flowers on it—Jim knows it's for Kotex—a pocket-pack of Kleenex, a "Garfield" key ring with all her keys, a white pocket-Bible, and a bottle of Jontue perfume.

*So that's the new fragrance,* Jim concludes to himself.

She also brings up two ballpoint pens, several loose lipsticks, a bottle of aspirin, a crushed orange box of Luden's cough drops, three barrettes, a half-eaten pack of Peanut M&M's, and finally a small Ziploc freezer bag which contains a Bic lighter, a small white envelope, and a roach clip. When Becki pulls out the Ziploc bag, she smiles sheepishly and says, "I just got half a J left."

Silence. Jim does not reply but smirks at her under his mustache.

"What?" she finally says, dimpling and blushing.

"You better not let Officer Brad catch you with that," he teases.

Becki playfully scrunches her face at Jim then banters back, "Stop lookin' at me like that, Shanley. I hardly ever get high. I'm not like Joe. I only smoke it when life gets super sucky and boring— maybe twice since I moved down."

"So tell me, Miss Reinhardt, where d'you get it?"

"Oh, Joe gets 'em for me, or Amelia; and Joe rolls 'em for me so I don't have to."

"Your mother would croak."

"No kidding. She caught me smoking it once ... me 'n Maria, on the patio in back of our house. I got grounded for two months. After that we just got stoned at Maria's house or at the beach. And that's why Mom freaked when I said I was goin' to Boston to live with Amelia." Returning to her hobo bag, Becki digs among the dregs at the bottom. "Ahah," she says as she finally finds a piece of gum. Not Big Red, but Dentyne. It's wrinkled, dirty, and ancient, as if it's been in a time capsule, but she pops it right into her mouth. She then holds her bag by the edge of the table and sweeps all her stuff back into it. As she does, she kids, "You're funny, Shanley."

"I know," Jim agrees, taking it as a compliment. He gives a proud little smirk.

"No, silly; I mean you *look* funny."

"Whaa ... that's a real nice thing to say."

"Your hair, Jimmy. I mean your hair, the front of it; it's sticking up like you got butch wax on it. Like I always say, you're right out of *Happy Days.*" Becki gives a snickering laugh; she blushes and smacks her gum.

Jim reaches across and gives her a playful jab on the shoulder. Magic, magic, gush of elation. His heart melts. He senses warm affection in her teasing as he sensed back in his office before Barry's intrusion. And considering the somber atmosphere of the night, he's glad to see some levity and playfulness in her.

But her mood change proves to be short-lived as Buddy comes over with his coffeepot and warms Jim's cup. Becki declines more coffee but Buddy's presence seems to sober her. "So, Jimmy, d'you think we should confess our doubts?" she asks returning to serious talk—though she remains more animated and less reflective, as if the activity and teasing plus the gum has energized her. She gestures up and down with her hands and fingers like she's playing a harp. "Or should we say, 'He's with the Lord, he's with the Lord,' like Joanne's mom kept on saying ... like fifty times?"

Jim stirs his coffee, then responds to her question, "Well, when it's just you and me, I think we should say what we feel."

"But what about when you preach, or like at the hospital?" Becki presses.

Jim moves his spoon in tight little circles as if still stirring his coffee. "If I got up on Sunday morning and confessed my fears and uncertainties, I'd be gone by nightfall. People don't want to hear this ... what we're talking about. They think about these things, but they don't want to hear it from their pastor."

"I figured as much," Becki declares pointedly, her blue eyes shining boldly into Jim's face. He has a party-line comeback but it sounds too canned in his mind so he says nothing.

"I've heard it all my life," Becki goes on. "If you're saved, you don't have to be afraid of death, but if you're not saved, if you're a Moslem or a Moonie, or a Jew or a Buddist, or an atheist or a whatever ... or even a Catholic, then you *better* be afraid because you're going to hell when you die. But in truth, we have *no more* assurance than those other religions."

Becki continues sharing and preaching. Her eyes, her eyes. Jim surrenders to her eyes. He no longer cares what she's saying, though what she's saying rings true to his heart. Her blue eyes are loving him. That's all that matters when facing death—or life. He imagines himself cuddled close to her in bed, listening, listening.

No clocks, no schedules, just angelic Beckiness, cozy and warm, and forever blue. A few lonely raindrops splatter against the window, but Park Street is empty and dark.

\* \* \*

Jim turns the key and pushes. *It's bolted,* he says to himself. *Why? It's never bolted?* He starts to go around but the kitchen door swings open. Pink robe, blond hair; fire, fire, two coals of blue fire!

"YOU'RE *WORSE* THAN AN ALCOHOLIC!" Sharon explodes, her words lacerating like hot shrapnel. "SHANE'S DEAD AND YOU'RE AT THE DINER *FLIRT*ING WITH THAT CONNIVING LITTLE HUSSY! And you're the *pastor* of the church! How could you, Jim! I was at the McCluskys 'til midnight waiting for you. How can you do this to Cal and Joanne? And to *me!* I saw the Mustang at the diner! Bev saw it too! HOW *DARE* YOU!"

"But Shar," Jim meekly protests. "It's not what—"

"I DON'T WANT TO HEAR YOUR SHIT! It's one-thirty in the morning! You're addicted! You're sick! Everyone is grieving, but not *you*! All *you* think about is screwing Becki, fucking a teenage brat! It's perverted! It's incest! And I'm going to tell her! AND PASTOR TOO!" Sharon slams the door and bolts it again.

Numb, numb, shock, fear. Jim staggers. But where's the pain? Then it comes, searing, stinging, crimson red, as when you cut yourself with a razor blade. You feel a sharp clean slice but the pain is delayed. His thoughts race confusedly: *Over, over; God, it's over! The wind, the wind, it's fuckin' cold. But I'm innocent. Why? Why? Not now? I'm innocent! I can't get the key in the ignition. Shane, Becki, diner, it wasn't! I'm innocent! No, no, I'm guilty, guilty! I'M SO FUCKIN' GUILTY! Sin! Sin! Pastor, father figure. Incest! Sick! Sick! Sick! It can't go on! Turn on the heat. I need the heat. Sharon, Logan, Doris, gossip, Alison, LOGAN, LOGAN. Sharon's gonna tell Logan, and Becki. SHIT! I'm fucked! Becki's gonna leave. She'll never stay. Never! Never! Stan, Leslie, Carl, Matt Garrett—"It won't be long now." I hafta cry but I can't. How can I preach? Red clouds, I see two stars. Puddles, potholes, wet leaves. Where the fuck am I goin'? Russ, Russ—I need Russ.*

The telephone booth in front of the diner is drafty, cold, and wet. The door doesn't close. Jim dials then puts in a dime, *ding-ding,* then comes the ring. One, two, three rings. "I wanna suck your Tootsie Pop," says the graffiti sticker on the face of the phone. "I'm waiting for you at 465-4278." It's signed: "Munchie Boy."

Four rings, five, then Russ's sleepy voice, "Whaallo, hello, whaa?" Jim tells him he needs to talk, about Becki, about everything. Russ says he'll be right down.

Jim heads for the Mustang in the parking lot. As he does, he runs into Ruthie Myszak and Kyle Donovan. Seeing Jim, Kyle hurries ashamedly into the diner but Ruthie stops on the steps and slurs out a drunken complaint. Her words ride on white clouds of beer breath, "Jeezush fuckin' Mary. Cain' ge-away. Ever'where I fuckin' go! I tol'juh, I doughwanna. I tol'juh. Where ish the swee' li'le nun? Alwaysh clomping up the stairsh. Doughstar. I ain't gonna let no fuckin' priesh damn me!"

Jim scarcely hears Ruthie; his senses are overloaded. He walks away, but her words chase him, "J-jush walk righ' away an' not shay nuhin'! You're no fuckin' priesh! I tol'juh! Y-you're nuhin', jusha cun'-lickin' sugar daddy! Betcha goin' righ' now to pork that swee' li'le nun. You dough fool me!"

Hunkering down into his trench coat, Jim trudges around the

diner into the parking lot. The icy wind takes his breath like a slap of cold water in the morning. At his feet the puddles are beginning to freeze, while in the sky above, the stars play hide 'n seek among fast-moving orange-glowing clouds. The parking lot is a collage of wet, grimy, half-frozen newspapers, maple leaves, potato chip bags, straws, cigarette butts, cigarette packs, styrofoam cups, and candy wrappers, all smashed flat and plastered down among the oil spots and potholes as if they've been pasted there by some sick surrealistic artist—some local Max Ernst. The loose piece of siding on the diner creaks in the gusty wind. Jim doubts that Flanagan will ever fix it. The Mustang is parked on the back side facing Walnut Street. He gets in and starts the engine. Cobwebby, confused, shell-shocked. His mind can't focus or reason. His nerve endings are frayed and shorted out from overfiring. And his emotions are drained—into a two-liter bottle and locked in the trunk.

He waits. The heat comes up. He wriggles out of his coat. Occasional gusts of wind buffet the Mustang, while in front of the car a few lonely snowflakes hurry along under the streetlight. The old-fashioned lamp has a shade over it that looks like a Mexican sombrero with a corrugated brim. The bulb is clear, not frosted, and gives off a pale-copper radiance. Two headlights in the rearview mirror, approaching slowly. Russ pulls his white Fairmont around driver to driver, and rolls his window: "So, you want to go in?"

"No," Jim says. "The bar crowd's in there. I've got enough insanity already."

"Okay, I'll be right back." Russ gets out and moseys across to the diner. Upon his return he joins Jim in the Mustang and places two large coffees and some napkins on the dashboard—next to the crack where Jim smashed the dash during his October Becki-rage.

The plastic lids make a screaking noise as they come off, and round spots of windshield fog form above each cup. The steamy aroma of coffee fills the car along with the smell of Russ's parka. His military-looking parka smells like tent canvas. "Feels like February out there," Russ remarks through a yawn.

"Quite a change," Jim replies, his voice now tired and raspy. "We almost drowned going to Boston."

"So you went to the hospital, huh?"

"Yeh, it was intense. I don't wanna go through that again."

"Bev says everyone's in shock. It's a fucking hard thing to go through. It's like we all have an hourglass and the sand is running out."

"And Baby Shane didn't get much sand."

They drink their coffees. The mood is somber, filled with a sense of foreboding, partly because of Shane but mainly because

Jim fears the worst—that Sharon will blow the whistle on Becki, that this time he won't be able to stop her. Russ puts his cup on the dash then massages his face with both hands like you do in the shower after turning off the water—as if he's trying to wake up. Jim sips and watches the lonely snowflakes winging by under the street-light. He feels a sleepy shudder as your body shudders when you're camping and it's chilly and you sit up late by the fire. The hot cup feels good in his hands.

"I appreciate you coming, Russ," Jim says after a minute.

Russ gives a leisurely grin that becomes a chuckle. "No problem," he says. "This gives me a reason to call in sick so we may as well make a night of it." In the dim light from the streetlamp, the day-old stubble on Russ's chin looks dark gray instead of auburn as does the swatch of hair tumbling out under the lifted bill of his Red Sox cap. But there's enough light to see that his eyebrows are arched mischievously and his eyes are twinkling. He seems sud-denly boyish, impish, as if he relishes the idea of skipping work. Jim feels less panicky. Russ's presence always calms him as if he's Luke Skywalker and Russ, his Yoda. Even his voice is soothing, neither low nor high but baritone rather, and mellow.

The car's too warm. Jim kills the engine then kills his coffee in several gulps. He's already overdosed on caffeine but this extra shot revives him enough to tell his story. He goes all the way back to when Becki was eleven. He tells Russ everything including the dilemma of still loving Sharon, but if he has to choose, he'll choose Becki. As he talks, the lonely flakes of snow diminish then stop altogether. Russ stares ahead, sipping his coffee, listening without expression. Finally, Jim tells about Sharon's angry threats at the door and how he fears it's all coming to a head.

In typical Bradley fashion, Russ does not respond but simply gives Jim one of his elfish grins then goes for more coffee.

While he's gone, Jim walks across Walnut Street to a vacant lot and takes a piss under some trees. As the cold wind bites his pecker, he looks up through the naked branches at the now-cloudless sky. The stars shimmer brightly. They don't have to advertise to get his attention; he's always been drawn to the stars. Yet they make him feel a strange ineffable loneliness as if each star is a yearning and broken heart.

Back at the car they open their fresh coffees and Russ resumes his wide-eyed gaze. Waiting for Russ is like waiting for the ice to melt off the reservoir. It always does, but only in due season. Russ strokes his chin. His hand is callused yet he has graceful fingers like a surgeon or a pianist—so different from Stan Campbell's huge meathooks. Finally, he sighs and speaks into the distance as if addressing the streetlight or even the stars, "Well, Jim, I guess you know this is hardly news to me. And I may be damned for saying it, but I think it's good that you love Becki. I see how happy she is. She loves you, Jim, and wants you—whether she admits it or not."

"How d'you know?" Jim asks, giving a grin—his first in two hours.

"It's written on her face," Russ explains, his eyes warm and filled with knowing. "I've seen it ever since she came last winter, and when you guys are together, I can feel it. I've known all along. It's beautiful. Of course, I doubt I can find many that'll agree with me. Loving Becki breaks all the rules, and stirs up a lot of shit, but even the pious bitches that whisper and put you down behind your back, I bet they wish they had such a beautiful love in their own lives. They're fucking jealous."

*Shit, he sounds like Jodi,* Jim declares silently. *He's with me more than I thought and he sees that Becki loves me and wants me.* This confirmation sends his heart soaring up with Russ's words— toward the stars. *Of course, she does. Jodi can see it. He can see it. I can see it, even Joe. Anybody can, if they just look—BUT SO WHAT? Shar's gonna ruin it all. She's gonna confront Becki and go to Pastor?* Jim's joy quickly fizzles and plummets back to reality like a burned-out Fourth of July skyrocket. Worry and guilt. His conscience speaks, "But, Russ, what about me and Shar?"

Russ gives his friendly leprechaun grin, then replies, "I think it's good that you love her too. You and Sharon, you have a childlike closeness. It's no wonder you have good sex."

"Come on, Russ, you're just as fucked as I am," Jim quips, his words riding a sigh of exasperation. "Nobody's gonna buy that, certainly not Logan, or any normal Christian. I'm in fuckin' deep shit and you're telling me fairy tales." Jim tries to put on a death-row face but ends up smirking. Russ Bradley is impossible. He would've been a good person to have on the *Titanic,* to spend your last hours with.

"I like fairy tales," Russ teases, gesturing with his coffee. But then he sobers and adds the disclaimer, "I don't say I'm right about any of this, or that I speak for God. This is just how *I* feel—so why do you have to see Logan anyway?"

"Well, I doubt Sharon will cool down, until we get Logan's view on all this," Jim replies.

"So, big deal. He's not going to pull the rug on you now, not over a jealous wife. Not after we sent the bastard over $15,000 this year. Preaching is one thing but priorities are another. And who knows whether Sharon will scare Becki away? Women are fucking unpredictable. It might send Becki running right into your arms.

She may want you more than you think. I'm not saying things are rosy, but it's not time to jump off the dam ... not yet."

Jim rolls his head back then stretches and grips the top of the steering wheel, and twists. The exercise gets the ache out of his arms. *Good, good, beautiful and good,* he quips ironically to himself. *Me loving two women. Me wanting a 20-year-old outside of marriage. Russ is way out, even more radical than me. No normal Christian would dare profess such heresy.* Nonetheless, Jim feels more hopeful, not that he sees any way out, but at least the doom seems further away.

Russ takes off his parka and throws it into the back, spilling half his coffee in the process. He wipes his pants—actually Stromberg coveralls—with a napkin. He then settles and looks right at Jim. His eyes are contemplative, like Becki's four hours ago. "I guess reality is too much for people sometimes," he says.

"What reality?" Jim asks, his voice a hoarse whisper. His throat is burning.

"The reality of birth and frolic and sex and love, and eating and sickness and death ... and hugging and sorrow and laughing and yelling and rage."

Jim sits forward, picks up his coffee. "What the hell are you saying, Russ?" he asks after a few quick swallows. The hot liquid soothes his raw throat.

"It's like we try to hide it," Russ replies pushing his cup toward Jim.

"Hide what?"

"That we're wild and instinctive ... that we're animals. But I think it's good that we're animals. I do."

"Animals? What the fuck are you talking about?"

"Just let me finish, Jim, and you'll see.... Maybe my reality is actually insanity, but no matter, I like it better than the propped-up socially correct reality that is sold daily in the markets of human exchange." Russ's eyes ignite with indignation. He's no longer a friendly leprechaun. "I think it's wrong to call it 'sin nature'! We're *ashamed* of ourselves. We hide our bodies, our burps, our farts, our puke, our shit ... and orgasm is locked away behind ritual and taboos and vows. No one is supposed to see it or talk about it, or admit such ecstasy or loss of control occurs in their life, especially the moaning and thrashing and gasping! And cocks and cunts must *never* be seen, as if humans don't have them except in X-rated smut where there's no love. Is it any *wonder* we're fucked-up sexually? Same goes for death, we pretend it doesn't exist." He's nailing some of the same points that Jim and Joe discussed last night in the church kitchen, but Russ has a way of bringing it out of the hallowed halls of philosophy and religion into the practical realm of everyday life. His preaching is also fogging the windshield; Jim turns on the engine and the defrost.

Russ takes a quick swig of coffee then places his cup on the dashboard. "It's like we're regimented right out of the womb," he goes on, now gesturing with both hands. "From a child, we're told, 'Don't yell, don't run, don't reach, don't take big bites, don't talk back, don't talk to strangers. Do your homework, be the best, comb your hair, say your prayers. Cool it, calm down, control yourself, and *be careful* with girls. Get a job, go to college, join the army, save your money, fight, fight, win, win.' And most of us learn about fucking from dirty jokes and naughty-talk sessions with the older guys down the block. And—"

"That's how I learned," Jim interjects. "I was in third grade, and my friend Jason, who lived in town, he was in fifth grade and he took me down into his basement, way back into a dark corner behind the hot-water heater and there he told me the facts of life in graphic detail. I felt guilty for just knowing."

Russ sighs, then goes on, "It's a *damn* shame that we have to learn about life's most beautiful experience in such a perverse way. That alone should tell us that there's something fucked about our society, and things are getting worse. Whatever happened to happiness and carefree running and yelling and having fun? Or just being lazy? We have all kinds of computers and time-saving technology today and it was supposed to give us leisure, but instead, we use the extra time to improve, to push, to pursue goals, to get the fucking *edge*. I always hated that word and now that Logan's using it, I hate it even more. We're all busy trying to get ahead, and born-again Christians are pushing the hardest of all. Nobody's waiting on the Lord, *nobody,* not even for a second. It's like *Pink Floyd.* We all have our place in the 'machine' and the 'machine' is all important, but in the process, we've lost the mystery."

"What mystery?" Jim asks after soothing his throat with more coffee.

"The mystery of being fully alive ... of being spontaneous, of feasting on the moment, of falling in love with reckless abandon. We're afraid of being human, afraid of what we really are. It's no wonder that people are sad and depressed and ticking like time bombs. We all wear a happy face to school, to work, to church, to Grandma's house, even to war. Then we come home and scream and rage and feel guilty, and get drunk—on one drug or another."

"So should we be afraid of what we are?"

"Well, according to Logan and the Pope and the police ... yes."

"But should we?" Jim presses. This has been his question for years.

"Are you afraid of a cuddly-playful kitten?" Russ asks.

"No," Jim responds.

"How about a hungry she-lion in the wild who's ready to rip and claw any warm-blooded creature that moves in order to feed and protect her cubs?"

"Fuckin' A; I'd need a gun."

Russ does not reply so Jim asks a question of his own, "What about Becki? Is she the kitten, or the lion?"

"Both," Russ responds without hesitation. "And if she weren't, you wouldn't want her so desperately. All the wise counselors, they say tame the animal so we can be loving, well-balanced, and productive. And Logan and Falwell, and Pat Robertson and Robert Schuller, and Lee Iacocca and Dale Carnegie, and Dear Abby and Oprah and Donahue, and Nightingale-Conant, and a thousand others, they tell us how—for money of course—but nobody really tames the animal. We just pretend to be tame, pretend to be socially correct, so we can get pseudo-love and applause from our ego-support groups ... whether it's LBI or IBM or Digital or KKK, or the Democratic Party or my mother's family or the U.S. Army or gay rights, or the *fuck*ing Red Sox diehards. Maybe this's how God wants it, but it seems *fuck*ing false to me, like selling my soul. We all spout some party line. I do it too, but I hate it!" Shaking his head, Russ gives a disgusted snort but says no more.

Jim feels hot; he turns off the engine. He agrees totally with Russ's description of the human disease of which his predicament is a symptom, but he doubts if either is curable. He drinks more coffee. The hot liquid feels good going down but the overdose of caffeine is sending him into orbit. His eyes hurt as if he's looking into hi-beam headlights and his head aches as if a screw is being screwed into the bridge of his nose. "Well, d'you think it's all predestined?" Jim asks, restarting the conversation.

Russ picks up his coffee from the dash. "Why do you ask that?"

"Remember, I told you about that spiritual experience back in '74, like a visitation of the Holy Spirit, but God was like a love goddess? Well, ever since that night, I've had this feeling that I was on a predestined journey of some sort. I used to think it was a call to preach, but now it seems bigger and somehow connected to Becki, but it even goes beyond her as if history itself is leading to something big ... but then again maybe I'm just lost in a fairy-tale fog like you, Russ?" Jim gives Russ a playful punch on the shoulder; they both laugh.

"I don't know if it's all planned by God or not," Russ says, his laugh subsiding. "I guess, I hope—let's put it this way. If it's up to us, I see no hope of a happy ending. But back to the love experience you had with the Holy Spirit, I've felt it myself. It's like a sexual thing, but it's also spiritual. I can't explain it. I just know that when I'm with Sylvia—"

"So you *do* have a thing with Sylvia?" Jim asks—as if he doesn't know.

"Well, maybe it's not like you and Becki, but maybe it is. I have cozy feelings for a number of women in the church: Angela, Jodi, Janet, Melissa ... a few others."

"God, Russ, you're just as oversexed as me."

They both chortle then Russ elaborates, "When Sylvia and I go on Sunday school visitation, we always hurry through our visits so we can sit and talk, or go out to eat, or walk by the lake. That's when I feel it. It's love, but the word has been watered down. It's more like an ache to know her, to really know her ... like I want to get inside her skin and live with her and look out through her eyes, like I can't know myself 'til I know Sylvia—that kind of knowing." Russ lifts his gaze to the streetlight. A tinge of wonder glistens in his eyes. "When we sit and talk, and Syl is relaxed and smoking and laughing, it's like the mystery unfolds, and all I see are dark eyes and dark hair and blushing smiles and pretty hands, and sexy legs and white socks and penny loafers. I love the way she walks and how she talks with her hands, and how her voice is warm and dark and rich—like hot fudge."

Warm bursts of Becki-love bathe Jim's heart. He knows exactly what Russ means, and Russ has more to say, "Sylvia can be cozy and calm then fierce and filled with fire. She can be cold and religious then sad or drunk or both. She tells me little things, like about Kimberly spilling her milk or sewing Frank's softball pants, or how the song 'The Rose' makes her cry. She makes me feel alive. The more I'm with her the more I want to get naked and go all the way. One day we did, and it was like being in heaven for a whole afternoon, but now something stops us. It's like we've met the beast within and we don't dare unlock the cage again."

"Well, what about Bev?" Jim asks, wondering if Russ feels guilt as he does.

"We get along. We have good sex, sometimes great, but it's like we've backed off into the ought's and ought not's, and routines and duties of life. It was better when we first got married. Sometimes I feel so out of tune ... with the whole thing."

"What whole thing?"

Russ's eyes narrow but remain tender. "You know, the whole idea of 'one and only.' I can never choose who to love or how much to love them. I've always been attached to other girls, not a great number but just a few special ones who I see a lot. I feel it with Angie when we work on the books, or joking with Jodi on Saturday mornings, or Cathy when she babysits. There's something, it's calling us, but we never get there. I see the want in their eyes, but we never get there."

"You mean you never get their panties off?" Jim asks. "Or you never get their hearts to come out?"

"Both.... It's always both. But the love we're yearning for is ... how can I say it? It's just bigger that's all, bigger than church or saving souls or America, or any cause." Russ's eyes now spark with an indefinable knowing. "It's bigger than one husband, one wife, or raising kids in a nice suburban house behind a white picket fence. And it's bigger than the macho bar scene, the boozy-druggy Budweiser playboy porno bullshit—it's not *that*. It's primal and male-female, but it's even bigger than sex. It's somehow spiritual, as if getting into a warmhearted woman is getting into God."

After a lengthy pause, Russ shakes his head and gives a resigned sigh. "Or maybe, Jim, we're just oversexed and over thirty-five, and the women at the church are bored and horny? Maybe the ache to know them is just pent-up lust which has no higher purpose than making babies and propagating our genes? Maybe God wants us to be monogamous and faithful to our wives, and maybe being a virtuous Christian is the highest good? I hope for more ... but who the fuck knows? I don't."

Action, action. Russ nods his head toward the street. "Look," he says.

Dogs in front of the car, two canines under the streetlight: one small terrier-like mutt, and a larger dog that looks part Doberman. The small dog, after sniffing and wagging, tries to mount the larger dog. Russ chuckles. "Now, Jim, they don't seem to care if it has a deeper meaning. Course that little guy's getting frustrated. That bitch is making him jump. Seems like a woman's cunt is always high and lifted up ... and she lords it over the man and makes him work hard to get up to it."

"No kidding," Jim quips. "That's how I feel with Becki. She wiggles her tail and when I respond, she stops wagging and turns around and bites me."

The short mutt humps and thrusts with his little pink prick but he gets nothing but cold air and a bit of leg. The sight is hilarious and Jim and Russ fall into a fit of laughter until they're howling and coughing and choking. Watching that male pooch thrust his wet cock at three-thirty in the morning is too much, as if God has a sense of humor and is trying to show that even a man's greatest frustration should not be taken too seriously. Finally, the dogs give up and trot away toward the dumpster behind the diner.

Snorts, chuckles. Coughing, clearing. The fit slowly subsides and quiet returns to the car. Leaning back, Jim drums his fingers on the top of the steering wheel. The laughing, like liquor, has freed him of any remaining inhibitions. He takes the conversation into even deeper waters, "Well, what about Jesus? What d'you think he would say if he were sitting in the backseat this whole time?"

Russ downs his last swallow of coffee and wipes his mouth with a napkin. He gives a bemused chuckle then a princely almost cocky grin. "Well, if Logan's right, he'd smoke us with fire right on the spot, but if Jesus is like me—I wish—he'd tell us how much he loves Mary Magdalene and how precious it is to snuggle with her and to look into her eyes."

This leads to Jim's biggest question, a question he always wanted to ask at Bible school but never had the guts. "So, Russ, d'you think Jesus ever had sex with Mary Mag ... or any woman?"

Russ wads the napkin into a ball. "I don't know. But if he's like me, he did, or he sure wanted to. How could he hang around with her, and that other Mary, and Martha and Joanna and Susanna? And I'm sure there were others, good-looking girls ... how could he be with them and not want to fuck them? After all, he was a man with a penis and testicles. Then again, maybe Logan's right, and Jesus never had sex or even yielded to lust in his thoughts?"

A flare of boldness flashes in Russ's eyes. His brow wrinkles with mocking scorn. He gestures with a long sweeping motion of his arm. "Actually, Jim, I think Jesus is more like us than we realize, but he's been sissified and castrated and misrepresented by the Church. Let's face it. If you want people to feel guilty and sinful and deserving of damnation, what better way to do it than to tell them that Jesus was celibate and never lusted. Everybody's hung up and confused by their sexual feelings, even within marriage, and no one can control their sex drive, not really, so every time a person gets horny and they masturbate or fornicate or fantasize, they *hate* themselves and they crawl on their face to the Church for salvation and cleansing; they readily submit to every doctrine and every pastor, so they can be *like* Jesus and get rid of lust and impure thoughts. They hate themselves for having sexual pleasure, and yet it's *God* who created it. It's twisted. It's such a fucking lie. You don't see animals feeling guilty about fucking and orgasm, like those dogs just now. Sex is natural and instinctive, and it's the most glorious experience we have. It should be lifted up, not condemned, and banished to the gutter. No *wonder* the Church has so much power over people. Why do you think Logan screams about sexual sin so much? The Church isn't built on *love*. It's built on sexual guilt and shame—yet *sex* is how we got here! Even the Pope!"

"Radical!" Jim exclaims. "I've thought about this a lot and it makes sense, but if I ever preached it, off with my fuckin' head." He makes a cutting motion against his throat. "This conversation would be utter blasphemy in Nashua."

Russ, his face hot with indignation, pulls off his Red Sox hat and beats it against the dash. "Who the fuck cares what Logan thinks! I can't prove it, but I bet he bangs half his secretaries. It's no accident that they're all luscious and sweet-assed. 'The Holy Spirit gave me victory over lust,' he claims. What a crock! Why would God take away the most real thing about us? And if He did, I certainly wouldn't call it *victory*. Logan's no different. I bet he gets more cunt than any of us.... And I think priests and pastors, and monks and nuns and missionaries, have been secretly fucking and sucking and jerking for centuries! They condemn and promise deliverance from lust, but they never escape themselves. And many of them suppress it and suppress it until it comes out perverted, sick, and sadistic, without love ... then they hide it under robes and coats and ties, and vows of celibacy and matrimony. Why can't we let go of the *bull*shit and just scream it out, 'If you love someone and you love to be with them, and you like to hug and tease them and laugh with them, then it's good, good, forever good, to get laid with them! And you don't have to hide it with clever games and disguises!'"

Russ shoves his wadded napkin into his empty cup, then sighs and settles a bit. "But who knows?" he confesses. "Maybe I'm fucked up, and I'm just trying to justify my sins?"

"Maybe so?" Jim croaks, his throat burning. "Maybe you're fucked, maybe not? But whatever, we're sure in the same boat."

"Dammit, Jim, all I know is how I feel. We've been through a lot of shit and I fear there's a lot more coming. So we might as well be naked with each other. After all, I didn't link up with you because of your wise counsel, or your great morality, or your sound doctrines. I'd rather be honestly sinful—if we are—than to be a phony fucking saint."

Jim feels drained, almost faint; his turbulent emotional state and the late hour are catching up with him. The streetlight is again obscured by fog on the windshield.

"How much choice do you have, Jim?" Russ says, shifting back to Jim's dilemma after a long moment of silence.

"What d'you mean?" Jim asks, his voice a croupy whisper; his throat is closing down.

"Let's say you go to Dr. Logan and repent, and make a vow to be a good Christian and a good husband and to obey the Bible as

Logan teaches it. Let's say you agree to end it with Becki, and to preach the LBI party line like all the ass-kissing pastors who sit on the stage at Moody Coliseum. Do you think you could abide by such a vow?"

"Well, not for long," Jim replies. "At least, I haven't been able to do it so far."

Russ snorts then gives a wry grin. "So I'd say the question for us is not 'if' but rather 'how long?'"

When Russ says "how long?" it reminds Jim of Matt Garrett. So he tells Russ about the strange encounter in the rain, and also about Barry's confession.

"Not only is Garrett a faggot, but he's a sly fucking devil," Russ replies. "He's creepy and strange, and he's even got power over Logan. He's a short-haired Rasputin." Russ goes on for some time about Logan and Garrett. Jim makes a few croupy comments here and there.

Finally, at 4:25 a.m., Russ grabs his parka, gives Jim a fond pat on the shoulder, and gets out. As he warms his car, he rolls down his window and says, "If you still can't get in, Jim, you can sleep at our house. I'll leave the back door open."

Russ pulls out of the parking lot. Jim wheels the Mustang and follows, as they both head for Greeley Hill. Now there are three who know all: Jodi, Joe, and Russ. Jim feels confident that Russ is with him to the end of the journey whatever that means, and after their talk, he suspects it may mean a lot more than he ever thought.

When Jim gets home, the door is unbolted, but he finds a note on the kitchen table:

*You have to sleep in the guest room ...*
*until we see Pastor.*

# Chapter Twenty-five

Doris looks furtively around the restaurant as if she and Pastor Jim are spies behind enemy lines. "I knew it, I knew it," she whispers to Jim. "But I won't tell. I won't tell a soul. I love you, I do. You know that." She leans back and takes a long self-satisfied draw on her cigarette; she waits a moment, then exhales a curly stream of smoke upward over the table.

Jim sighs but says nothing more. He's now naked before Doris, but he's not convinced of the wisdom of his confession.

Bancrofts' Steakhouse. Wednesday, December 14th. Pastor Jim and Doris have just finished their lunch. Doris caught up with Jim after Shane McClusky's committal service at Buchanan Memorial Cemetery. Jim dislikes religious death rituals yet Shane's funeral seemed more honest to him than Cal and Joanne's wedding. The weeping and sobbing under the green graveside canopy struck him somehow as a truer expression of the human condition. Doris, handsomely attired in a Sherlock Holmes suit of brown wool, arrived at the restaurant sober but she's quickly correcting that situation as she pours her fourth glass of Pinot Chardonnay. She doesn't usually drink in public but the emotion of the funeral along with Jim's confession has taken her mind off Christian propriety.

Above them, a dark-cypress ceiling fan slowly circulates the aromas of hot rolls, coffee, charbroiled beef, deep-fried seafood, along with the perfumy fragrances of the arriving lunch crowd, mostly white-collar professionals from other towns, many from Digital Maynard or Digital Hudson. Behind the mahogany bar a long mirror doubles the size of the old dining room. Above the mirror, an 18th-century mural, like a comic strip, depicts the downside of drunkenness. Bancrofts' is rustic, informal, and offers the only fine dining in Brendon Falls. Plank floors, dark panelled walls, beamed ceiling, heavy oak tables. The restaurant retains the authentic Yankee atmosphere of its 200-year history. The establishment has had many owners and many names but it began in 1797 as a roadside inn in the old village of Brendonville when High Street was a winding dirt road known as Groton Way.

The current owners, Benjamin and Martha Bancroft, are distant relatives of Jonathan Bancroft who built Blantyre Castle in Nashua. Present-day Bancrofts' is famous for prime rib but their seafood is equally tasty. Doris had fried scallops, Jim, fried shrimp—so many that he had to unbutton his suit vest to make room.

Because of the funeral the rest of the academy school day has been cancelled. Sharon took the kids home, while Becki went shopping with Jodi. Becki's leaving on Friday for a week in New Bedford, to see her Dad and grandparents, so she wanted to finish her Christmas shopping. She's been cozy and warm with Jim since their serious talk about death on Sunday night but he's too anxious to enjoy her—too anxious about Logan, too anxious about Sharon.

He doubts that Sharon has followed through—as yet anyway—on her threat to talk to Becki. If she had, Becki wouldn't be so friendly. But he hasn't brought it up with either. He and Sharon are going for counseling with Dr. Logan next Tuesday, the 20th. He's concerned about seeing Logan, but more concerned about Sharon counseling Becki.

Jim had no intention of confessing to Doris but as they ate their lunch, he discovered she knew a lot of half-truths concerning him and Becki, so he let go and shared all, even though he knew he was possibly opening floodgates that he could never close. He also told Doris she's the only person who knows the whole truth. This is a lie of course but he had to win her allegiance, and he has.

Despite her flaky-Christian, closet-wino personality—she still apologizes to Jim for her one-time drunken advance back in March—Doris has always been kind to him, never mean-spirited or calculating, and he prefers to have her as a friend and confidante rather than a guessing busybody. He needs her in his corner, especially since she always knows the latest church chitchat. And she wastes no time bringing him up to date. According to Doris, the news of Sharon's Sunday night wrath has spread from Bev to her, but no further, and gossip in general is at a low ebb in the church because of Shane and Christmas.

After finishing his coffee and giving the waitress his American Express card, Jim asks Doris if Stan ever talks about him and Becki. "No, Jimmy honey," she replies, now feeling the full effect of her wine. "He won't talk about it; no, he won't. An' when I brought it up, he shaid, 'You're a meddling woman with evil imaginations, an' if you ever gosship about leaders in the church again, God's going to strike you dumb.' He shaid it, Jimmy honey. He did."

* * *

"Okay, okay," Becki admits. "She called last night, but that's all I'm saying."

"I knew it," Jim replies huffily. "So, what'd she tell yuh?"

"I don't wanna talk about it I *said*. I'm wicked tired. So drop it."

Jim's thoughts race crazily like mice running in a maze,

*Sharon must've gotten to her good? Why'd she wait four days to call? No, maybe it's just a mood swing? But she was so warm to me? And today—fuck, she's like ice. Now I have to see Logan, and he's gonna tell me I'm guilty and Sharon's innocent. Becki's gonna split, I know it. She'll probably stay in New Bedford. It can't go on. I have to face it. I'm a hypocrite and a deceitful husband, and I'm betraying the kids. But even if Becki does come back, Logan's gonna tell me to stop doing ministry work with her. Gossip or no gossip, everyone's gonna know. Alison, Stan, the whole ministry, they're gonna find out. I'm cooked. It's over. Yet Russ is hopeful— fuck, he's in a fairy tale, and Jodi too. There's no way out.... But I love her so. Why? Why? Why does it have to be wrong? Why do we have to stop loving each other ... to love God?*

His panicky thoughts, exhausted and battered from banging walls, slow to a stagger then collapse without getting out of the maze. He stares over the steering wheel at the railroad tracks then up into the midday sky where the December sun is low and blinding; he lowers the visor. The wind is cold but the ground is bare and Becki's train is late. The MBTA commuter-rail station in Ayer is just a wind shelter behind Carlin's Bar, but it's the most convenient place to get a train to Boston; Ayer is twenty-five minutes north of Brendon Falls. Becki is meeting Amelia in Boston then driving with her to New Bedford. She's coming back on Christmas Eve—at least, that's the plan.

Jim smells the lilac fragrance of Becki's just-washed hair. It reminds him of that enchanted moonlit night in October when they cuddled close in the canoe. Torture, torture. She slowly chews her gum and gazes straight ahead. Inert, inert, no expression. Her face is like a cloudy day without rain. Silence. Jim can't stand it. He presses her, "Well, Sharon must've said something to get you into such a cold mood?" No response, except for a few don't-bother-me wrinkles on Becki's brow. Now desperate, he claws the wall, "I didn't hafta bring you up here, you know?"

"So I owe you a smile, as cab fare?" she snarls impudently.

"No, but you could at least be kind."

"Why should I be kind to *you*?" Becki snaps, sinking her fangs into his heart. "You think life's been kind to me? Besides, your motives are selfish. You just do things for me so you can throw it in my face, like I owe you."

She returns to her distant gaze. She works her gum slowly, determinedly. Jim feels like Napoleon at Waterloo. Resigned, abandoned. It's over. He feels his soul draining out. Nothing left to lose. His heart becomes suicidal. He has to know. "So what about it, Becki Lea? What about *us*?"

Becki stops chewing, takes her gum out of her mouth, wraps it in a tissue, and stuffs it into the ashtray. She then folds her hands neatly on her lap and slowly turns toward Jim. Her blue eyes are cold, calm, and lethal. She speaks in a self-possessed manner but her words drip with venom, "*Us?* What d'you mean, *us*?"

"I mean *us, you* and *me* ... *us,* the past ten months? Hanging around together, talking, loving each other? Flirting, getting suggestive, doing everything together ... at least everything short of actually doin' it?"

"You got it all wrong, Shanley," Becki rebuts coldly. "As usual, you're twisting everything to fit your fantasies. There's no *us*. You're asking the *wrong* question."

"So what's the *right* question?" Jim asks, his voice rising. Becki frowns more severely, her face now hot with color, hot with growing indignation. Yet she gives no response.

"Dammit, Becki, tell me!" Jim demands, slamming the top of the steering wheel with the heel of his hand.

Fire ignites in Becki's eyes. "WHAT ABOUT SHARON!" she rages. "What about Sharon and the kids! That's the *right* question! Don'tcha think!"

"DAMMIT, REBECCA LEA!" Jim shouts, thrusting his upturned hands toward her. "Doncha get it! I love you *more* than Sharon! That's why I get insecure and go crazy—like now!"

Becki slaps the air with the back of her hand as if slapping Jim. "Beautiful, fuck*ing* beautiful! So what about God? and the Bible? and the church?"

"I LOVE YOU MORE! I LOVE YOU MORE THAN ALL OF IT! I LOVE YOU MORE THAN I LOVE GOD!" *KA-WHAAP!* He smashes the dash with his fist. The angry blow splits even wider the old wound in the blue-vinyl pad. "But I hate myself for it, more than I hate the devil! Especially when you're pissy-faced like today! Loving you is a curse, Becki Lea! A fuckin' curse!"

Silence, smoke, smoldering emotion. Becki gazes again into the distance. A flicker of a smile plays at the corner of her mouth but quickly darts away—a frightened butterfly—leaving her face a cold frowny rock. A heavy sense of foreboding now squeezes all hope out of Jim's heart like a cruel hand crushing the life out of a trembling bird. He even wonders if he imagined the faint smile; his heart sinks—*BWAAAAHWONK! BWAAAAHWONK!* The train, the train. The diesel horn blares, loud like a fire horn, yet melodic like a muted harmonica. Becki grabs her shoulder bag, reaches into the back for her travel bag, then hurries toward the train. Her travel bag is a fat purple roll-bag, so overpacked that the seams and zipper seem ready to burst. The strap is broken on her denim shoulder purse so she carries it like a huge football—stop, stop. What's this? Becki suddenly stops and runs back. Jim's sinking heart lurches and leaps into his throat. He opens the window.

"Don't forget to feed Bathsheba!" she shouts above the throbbing whine of the old round-nosed diesel. Without another word she dashes back to the train. Jim's heart plummets again. Becki gets in line behind a half-dozen others who are boarding. Her brunette locks blow in the wind. Her hammy denim-clad hips cant against the weight of the overpacked purple bag.

*O God, such sweet hips,* Jim laments to himself. *Hips, hips— but no hope. I have no hope. So young, so shy, so high-schoolish, yet such a cruel cold woman. She's impossible and so fuckin' proud. I have no hope. But I love her more ... more than Sharon, more than God, more than the Love Goddess. It's crazy. It's killing me. It's gonna take me down. It's love without pity, or reprieve. I can't escape. She's too—I have no words.*

Rebecca disappears up the stairway into the fluted commuter coach. It's silver-gray, with a broad maroon stripe, but it looks dull and drab from dirt and grime. The conductor boards right behind Becki. After two quick horn bleats, the round-nosed diesel whines to full power. *Clic-clac, clic-clac, clic-clac.* The train rolls out. *BWAAAAHWONK! BWAAAAHWONK!* Jim watches until it disappears under the overpass. The horn blasts slowly fade until there's nothing but empty tracks. Becki's gone.

Jim loves trains—but he hates this one.

\* \* \*

Sharon wiggles out of her coat and tosses it into the backseat. "Right on the coffee table," she says. "Red sour balls. Any baby would grab them. Doris was right. Something was bound to happen with Joanne working and leaving him like that."

Baby Shane has been dead just over a week but empathy has already given way to judgment, and Calvin bears most of the blame, though no one dares talk about it except in their most intimate conversations. Jim fears he'll be the next to face this merciless jury, and he doubts they'll be silent for long once the news of his Becki-love hits the fan. And he sees no way of stopping it, now that Logan has heard Sharon's allegations.

Pulling off her low-heel dress shoes, Sharon spreads her haunches and folds one leg under. When comfortable, she cocks her head like a hen as if waiting for Jim to voice his agreement. When he says nothing, she goes on talking about Shane. As she talks, she flutters her fingers as if she's typing. White cardigan, words, sunglasses. Hands, Sharon, more words. Camel-colored shirt, spruce-green pleats, pantyhose, hands typing in the air, baby-fine hair: corn-yellow and feathered. Jim gathers his wife into his senses—but not her words. Despite his depressed mood, her provocative spread-leg pose is hard to ignore, especially after nine days in the guest room.

Finally, as they pass through the hills of Littleton, Sharon ends her analysis and says, "It's hot. I'm turning down the heat."

The highway rolls under the Grenada, a great conveyer belt, wide and rushing and stretching far ahead where it becomes a pair of gray filaments before disappearing over the haze-shrouded hills. Rolling hills, sprawling valleys. Grays, browns, evergreens. The frozen December landscape begs for a mantle of snow. Where the interstate cuts through the hills, blue-white ice flows from the man-made cliffs: frozen waterfalls. The morning sky is milky with cirrus but the clouds seem aimless and sterile. "Why the long face, honey?" Sharon asks after taking off her sunglasses. "You look like you're on the way to face a firing squad?"

"Well, in a way I am. You wouldn't give me a chance to ex—"

"Why should I? You agreed to see Pastor?"

"That was almost three months ago. I-I, I'm not ... it's not what—"

"It's not uncommon, you know," Sharon declares, barrelling right over his stuttering attempt to exonerate himself. "Mom says it happened to Pop when they first moved upstate—a girl in the office. She says middle-aged men are afraid of getting old. So they get infatuated with younger women."

"You sound like Ann Landers," Jim counters. "Besides, I'm not middle-aged"—brake lights ahead. Jim slows to 60 mph, and just in time. Blue flashing lights, cars pulled over, troopers in Smokey Bear hats. It's a speed trap. After ten years on this route, Jim knows their ways.

"Mom says the first step to recovery is honesty with yourself," Sharon goes on, after they pass safely by. As she speaks, she pushes her sunglasses at her husband. "She thinks you should spend all week with us in Cobleskill instead of rushing in for Christmas dinner and rushing out the next day.... She's right, Jim. You need to get away from it all, from the church, from your busy schedule, and—"

"And Becki?" Jim cuts in, completing Sharon's sentence.

"Especially Becki," Sharon affirms. "You're so involved with her you can't see the forest for the trees. You can't see your problem. You can't be honest with yourself."

"You talk like I'm hooked on drugs. It's hardly the same thing."

"Well, I think it *is* the same. You have an unhealthy infatuation for a girl who's hardly more than a teenager. It's not love, least not anymore. You're obsessed with her. She even agrees."

"It's not unhealthy or obsessive—how d' you know she agrees?"

Sharon gives a triumphant grin. "She said so last Thursday when I talked to her on the phone."

*There it is again,* Jim thinks regretfully, *that fuckin' phone call. That's what messed up Becki's mind.*

"Well, what else did you two talk about?" he asks out loud.

"That's between her and me," Sharon replies.

"So you're on her side now?"

"No, she's still a conniving brat who takes advantage. She gets a charge out of having an older man get all excited over her."

"She said that?"

"No, of course not. She's not about to admit her games. But that's how young women are, at least the flirty ones, like Becki. They like to control older men; it builds their ego."

"God, you and your mom have it all figured out. You're *worse* than Ann Landers. You should start your own column."

"Maybe we will," Sharon quips giving another triumphant grin. "But really, Jim, you must face your weakness."

"Weakness? Loving someone in Christ is a weakness?"

"It's not love, and it's not in Christ," Sharon asserts. "You just think it is, like Joe Lareux thinks he talks with God when he's high on—"

"No way, Shar!" Jim protests angrily. "You're twisting—you got it all wrong."

Sharon, unmoved, takes a tissue from her purse and cleans her sunglasses. Jim hates it when she treats him as an emotionally sick person as if his Becki-love is merely a symptom of a midlife crisis. He'd rather have her yell at him and call him a sinner. He wants to fight back but he knows he has no chance in this debate so he swallows his rebuttal. Sharon shifts, unfolding her leg from under her. She then replaces her glasses and turns on the radio.

Blip, blip, blip. Guardrails, drain gratings, lanemarkers, light stanchions, green exit signs. Blip, blip. Fast lane. 75 mph. Westford, Chelmsford, finally Lowell, where they leave Route 495.

As they head north on Route 3, Jim's thoughts shift ahead to Nashua, *Should I tell Logan the truth?—no way, not in front of Sharon. I have to deny it. Maybe he'll believe me—and it's not really a lie. I haven't done anything except in my thoughts. I haven't even kissed her. But so what? Becki may still leave because of*

*Sharon. Fuck, I hate this.*

* * *

A cold breeze breaks the morning calm. The flags in front of Blantyre Castle flutter lazily. Jim and Sharon walk under the columned portico. Jim feels anxious, almost nauseated. The freezing air stings his face. He pushes the heavy door. Sharon goes first. Blond hair, fur collar, wool winter coat.

*O God, I wish we were making love instead of this,* Jim sighs to himself. *Sharon, Becki, I love Becki more. No, not more, but different—or is it? Maybe I am sick?*

The entry hall smells of polished oak and Christmas balsam. Resounding heels. Jim hears Amy before seeing her. She approaches from the other end of the hall making her way around a huge Christmas tree which stands opposite the stairway. Amy greets the Shanleys with her usual businesslike politeness. She says that Dr. Logan is delayed at Moody and that Pastor Hudson needs Sharon for a minute in the Project Malachi office.

*I doubt a minute will be enough,* Jim quips to himself as a vision of Hudson fucking his wife flashes into his mind. But his conscience quickly changes the channel, shifting his thoughts back to his own depressing situation.

Wreaths on the doors, garland around the fluted columns, garland up the winding balustrade, soft red lights on the tree. The castle, all decked out for Christmas, seems almost warm—but not warm enough to make Jim feel any better. Amy ushers him into Logan's office where Matt Garrett is sitting in front of the fireplace with Molly Gibson. Molly, taking dictation, sits across from Garrett. They both rise to greet Jim. Molly smiles and says she remembers Jim from Easter Week. She seems subdued; the starry brightness is gone from her green eyes. Matt dismisses her and Jim takes her place on the other sofa.

"Pastor's delayed at Moody for a retake," Garrett says.

Jim yawns, more out of apprehension than drowsiness. "Yeh, Amy told me. So who's doin' radio?"

"Jerry and Bob ... Bob Logan—I thought Sharon was coming with you?"

"Oh, she is. She's upstairs in the Malachi office. She'll be down in a few."

A silver metallic Christmas tree stands by the French doors that open onto the terrace. Red balls, no lights. Jim doesn't like it. There's also a potted poinsettia on the center table in front of the

359

fireplace. Otherwise, the office is the same: lavish, Napoleonic, blue and magenta, and splashed with morning sun.

Garrett, trendily dressed in a double-breasted blue blazer, a gray V-neck sweater, and a paisley neck scarf, looks like a New York yuppie on a weekend getaway. His tan windowpane slacks are held up by ribbon suspenders with button-on leather ends. And he wears a gold neck medallion; it looks like an ancient coin on a chain. His dark hair, wavy on top but slick and clean on the sides, matches his trendy New Yorkish clothes. He seems very relaxed in Logan's office, as if sitting in his own living room. "Would you like coffee and a Danish?" he asks Jim. "Or some hot cider?"

"Whatever," Jim replies. The marble-topped refreshment table is not set with goodies so Matt, as if dialing room service, picks up a phone from a new communications console on the end table.

After placing his order with the Blantyre kitchen, Matt says, "Sorry I startled you, Jim ... on that rainy night. Was it Saturday before last? I lose track?" He smiles at Jim but his smile doesn't reach his eyes. He crosses his legs. Jim notices that he's wearing the same pointy-toed boots.

"No problem," Jim replies. "I'm just not used to people walking out of the woods on dark stormy nights."

For a few minutes they exchange pleasantries and small talk, then Garrett stares right at Jim. Eyes, eyes, Nordic eyes: calm, strong, icy cold. A sense of uneasiness sweeps over Jim. He can't help but submit. His stomach knots; his hands feel clammy; his suit vest feels too tight. "So you're keeping busy?" he asks Matt, trying to make more small talk, but his voice wavers.

"Radio and TV, that's the big push," Garrett replies. "We have a number of new stations and—" He stops midsentence as a bow-tied student waiter arrives with a large tray. With him come the aromas of fresh coffee, buttered pastry, and hot cinnamon.

Jim recognizes the young waiter as Randall Scowcroft, Ed Landreth's cousin. He looks eighteen but he's actually in his mid 20s. Short black hair, lustrous brown eyes, cute features, six-foot gangly physique. Randy's much better looking than his older cousin. He nods to Garrett and gives Pastor Shanley a polite, "Good to see ya." Against the wall is a folding food-service stool. Randy takes it and slings it open then sets the tray on it. Jim has talked with him a few times at Alison's in the old days, when Randy was a part-time student at Fitchburg State and worked at Kentucky Fried Chicken in Leominster. Ed and Alison always pestered Randy about coming to Bible school and getting his life together with God. Now after six years their persistence has evidently paid off.

Randy has a just-showered I'm-a-good-Christian air about

him, and the demeanor of an eager dog. His fawning behavior before Garrett strengthens the intimidating you-must-submit atmosphere in the room. After asking their preferences, he serves them almond Danish and hot cinnamon cider in goblet-style mugs. It *is* like room service except Randy gets no tip. He turns to leave but Garrett stops him, "Oh, Randy, would you get some logs for the fire?"

A coiling plume of steam rises from Jim's mug. The aroma is spicy, pungent, and somehow more exotic than Sharon's Christmas cider. He starts to sip but it's too hot so he places the mug on the end table and starts on his Danish. Matt does sip but quickly exclaims, "Whew, hot."

Randy soon returns with three logs. After poking and stirring, he places the logs on the fire. He moves with holy purpose as if serving Pastor Garrett will help win souls to Christ. "Will that be all, sir?" he asks obsequiously.

"Yes," Matt replies. "But do tell Peter there'll be six—oh, Jim, do you want to join us for lunch?" Jim tells him thanks but they must go right back. "Okay ... so it'll be six at Pastor's table. And do remind Peter that Dr. Logan must have decaf at lunch ... and he wants Cheri, the new waitress, to serve our table. And Pastor Beckman is still on his salt-free diet." Randy nods obediently to each of Garrett's requests then turns and marches dutifully out of the office.

Fit of crackling, flurry of sparks. The new logs catch fire. Jim looks at the flames, then at Garrett. *To think that Barry kissed those lips,* he says to himself. *He does have boyish skin but still he has a beard. Seems fucking disgusting ... but who am I to say anything about sexual feelings? I'm up to my neck in unresolved passion.*

Matt stares into his steaming mug. He runs his finger around the rim as if reflecting on a serious matter. After a bit, he gives a cocksure grin and brings up the very subject Jim's thinking about, "So Barry told you, I understand?"

"Yeh, he did," Jim says, feeling even more uncomfortable as he considers the bizarre possibility that Garrett can read his mind. "I guess that explains a lot. So, you guys—"

"It was just a misunderstanding," Matt interjects abruptly, "that's all."

Jim has questions about Garrett and Barry but right now he's only conscious of his own sin, *Off, off, totally off—it's wrong to be with Becki, to lust, to love her.* Even if Garrett were a practicing pederast and delighted in debauching little boys, Jim would still see him as righteous, while he sees himself as perverted and iniquitous. Nashua has this effect on one's psyche. Jim takes a bite of Danish but can barely get it down his dry throat. He reaches for his cider but it's still too hot. He doesn't want to open up about his love-triangle situation but Garrett's eyes beckon. "Guess you know why we're here?" Jim says as if Matt pushed a start button in his brain.

"Yes, I know," Matt acknowledges. "I was with Pastor when Sharon called."

Garrett wants him to say more. Jim feels it. Garrett's presence has a power of its own, like a magnetic field. His manner is friendly but his spirit threatens—like Logan, like Beckman, like all of them at once. Maybe Russ is right, but at this moment Jim has no power to think evil of Garrett—or Logan. Again come the eyes, brilliant-blue and penetrating; they seem almost luminescent.

"So how much does Dr. Logan know?" Jim asks, pretending to be calm, but he's not convincing.

"Well, he knows all about you and Rebecca Reinhardt."

"You mean what Sharon told him when she called?"

"No, I mean what Joe Lareux told him. Joe came in last week. He was a bit stoned, but he had a lot to say."

Jim tries to hold his poise but his lips panic, "You mean Pastor knows how I *really* feel?" Fever, fever. Hot flashes burn Jim's face. Blood pounds in his temples. *Joe, Joe, how could you? That fuckin' pot makes you crazy.* His thoughts race and screech and spin out of control, finally exploding in flames along with his fragile Becki-hopes and all his rehearsed explanations. The dikes give way flooding his bosom with emptiness. His pounding heart slowly sinks into this dire sea. His masks are gone. He's naked save for the scarlet shroud of shame that cloaks, yet reveals him.

Jim tries to reason, to speak, "I uh, I uh...." But he can't engage his mind. His brain is still burning out of control.

Garrett, calmly turning his attention to his Danish, seems unaffected as Jim's composure crumbles. A few pieces of almond sprinkle onto Matt's slacks. He brushes them away with a girlish backhand flick of his wrist. The fire in Jim's head slowly burns out and his reason returns; he feels numb; he wants to run and hide. He cringes to think what Logan will—too much. After drinking some cider, Garrett speaks, slowly, calmly, "Yes, Jim, Pastor knows all, but I think you're about to be pleasantly surprised."

"Whaddeya mean?" Jim asks, his voice now working but thick with anxiety.

"Take a sip of your cider and you'll understand."

"What has cider got to do with it?"

"Just drink it."

Jim has no strength to seek further explanation, so he picks up his mug and takes a swig. "This stuff is spiked," he remarks with surprise. "How uh? How do you—"

"How do I get rum in my cider when it's against the rules for everyone else?" Matt gives a Cheshire-cat smile and toasts the air with his mug. "You know the verse, Jim ... milk is for babes while strong meat is—" Noise, a door opens; it's Dr. Logan, and Rich Beckman. They come in through Logan's private entrance.

Jim stands and greets them. He feels numb, shell-shocked. Dr. Logan tells him to sit down, that he'll be right back. The doctor then beckons for Garrett and the three LBI leaders disappear, again through the private door. Jim sinks back onto the Louis XVI sofa. He inhales the rustic fragrance of the burning wood in the fireplace. The fire is the only pleasant aspect of this entire experience.

Jim's shock and shame slowly give way to resignation. Love, hope, anxiety, guilt, shame; dread, panic, despair; finally, resignation. His emotions have been through this cycle a hundred times since Becki arrived ten months ago.

Mennen aftershave. Dr. Logan returns, unaccompanied except for the bracy scent of his aftershave. "Do you want anything else, Jim?" he asks.

"No thank you, sir," Jim replies respectfully. "This is plenty." He can't believe he's sipping rum and cider in Logan's office.

After poking the fire, the doctor sits down in the spot vacated by Garrett. He smiles at Jim but his smile seems more dutiful than warm. His suit, like Jim's, is a gray pinstripe but the gray is darker, the pinstripes more widely spaced. But they both have red ties and tight button-straining vests—though Logan's paunch is bigger than Jim's.

"Is Sharon with you?" Logan asks, raising his bushy eyebrows.

"She's up in the Malachi office," Jim replies. "But she should be down anytime now."

Dr. Logan clears his throat. His brow creases into a slight frown. He acts like a stern father preparing to discipline a wayward son. But Jim feels like a convicted felon about to be sentenced. Despite Garrett's strange prediction, he does not expect Logan to be surprising or pleasant. But he gets a short reprieve as the doctor picks up the phone from the end table. "Molly, I'm back," he says. "Please hold all calls, and when Sharon Shanley comes down, have her wait until I buzz for her."

Dark hypnotic eyes: black headlights, hi-beams. Logan turns them on. Blinded and overwhelmed by the darkness, Jim readily submits. Garrett's gone, Logan's here. But they're plugged into the same bewitching power. Besides, Jim is now resigned to his dire fate. He's eager to plead guilty, to get everything out. He has no desire to lie, or the strength. After all, Joe's already told him everything. Logan strokes his bristly chin a few times then gets right to the heart of the issue, "So, Jim, tell me ... are you in love with Rebecca Reinhardt?" The doctor speaks in his usual grainy voice—and with his hands.

"Yes, I am," Jim replies. He can't believe he's confessing to Logan yet he feels a strange peace. It always appears when he gives up. Perhaps it comes from truth or death—or both?

"Have you had intercourse with her?" Logan asks.

"No, I haven't," Jim answers.

"Do you want to?"

"Yes ... I love her deeply, all of her."

Logan slowly nods his head then strokes his chin again. "Do you fantasize about her? I mean in a sexual, lustful way?" His voice is judicial but with an undertone that seems carnally curious almost prurient.

"Yes, I do," Jim says, ignoring Logan's carnal curiosity. He can see no sin in his judge.

"You know what the Word says, Jim. So tell me ... what do you think you should do, when the Bible says to *flee* youthful lusts?"

"I don't know. I just know I love Becki."

"Do you believe that the Bible is the Word of God?"

"Well, I uh ... I guess, but I trust my heart more ... or maybe I should say my heart is stronger than my mind."

"If I, as your pastor, tell you that you must break off your relationship with Becki, will you do it?"

"No, I won't."

"Why not?"

"Because I love her too much. Even if I vowed to obey you, I know I couldn't."

"You love her more than the Word of God?"

"I don't know; I guess I do." Jim is stark naked, yet he has no desire to cover up.

"So you see this relationship as good ... as a godly thing?"

"I don't know. Sometimes I think it's a bad thing and I feel guilty, but other days, I feel really sure about it; but either way, I still love her."

Dr. Logan slowly nods his head as if digesting Jim's scarlet-hot confession. Then he picks up the phone and buzzes Molly. Jim figures that he's heard enough and is ready to pass sentence. When Sharon comes in, the doctor stands and gives her a warm greeting and a fatherly hug. She takes a seat beside Jim on the sofa. After sitting down, Logan gives a friendly relaxed grin and slowly rubs his hands together in wise-counselor fashion. He speaks slowly in a kind paternal voice, "Sharon, I know you're concerned about your husband's relationship with Rebecca Reinhardt ... but after talking with him, I don't think you have anything to fear. Your marriage is strong. Jim's ministry is strong. You're a beautiful woman of God and a devoted wife, and Jim loves you very much. So, uh ... well, you two go on home and enjoy each other. Enjoy your Christmas."

Shock, shock, relief. Jim can scarcely believe his ears. Garrett is right.

Sharon's face colors with apparent gladness but she holds back her smile. Though she trusts Logan as her pastor, and as an overseeing prophet who speaks for God, she queries to make sure she heard him right, "You mean it's okay for Jim to do outreach with Becki?"

Logan gives his V-shaped victory smile. Sharon, anticipating his answer, smiles as well, as does Jim. The doctor confirms, "As long as Jim doesn't neglect you and the children, I see no harm in it. In fact, I think God, in his sovereignty, has given Jim and Becki a unique ministry together. Jim assures me that nothing romantic or sexual has happened between them, and I'm sure God will keep their relationship pure. I would not give such liberal counsel to most couples but I feel that you two are especially mature in the Lord."

* * *

Perfume, soft hair, warm breath. Sharon snuggles against Jim's shoulder. She feels cozy and inviting. Shoes off, she curls her long nylon-covered legs up into the seat. The midday sun is low and haloed behind a veil of cirrus. It's still cold, well below freezing, but it always seems warm driving home from Nashua, driving into the sun, and away from Logan and Beckman and Garrett.

Jim is relieved but puzzled, *Maybe it's a test? I can't believe this turnaround. Oh, Becki Lea, come home. We have to patch things up. It's okay. We have a green light from Pastor himself— fuck, I can't believe it. Maybe Logan's just giving me rope to hang myself? Maybe he really cares? No, no, it's strange, he's not like Russ. Maybe it's true? Logan's inner circle? Money, perks, power, Molly, Barry, Garrett, Amy ... and spiked cider. Maybe "all things are lawful" for his inner circle ... even sin? But I'm not part of his—*

"Well, do you want the good news or the bad?" Sharon teases, interrupting her husband's thoughts. Her voice is sleepy. Her dusty-blue eyes are soft and liquid.

"Give me the good news," Jim says.

Sharon nibbles his ear then whispers into it, "I can't wait."

"I can't either," he flirts. "So how can you have bad news?"

She smirks bemusedly. "Because we have to wait. We have to wait five more days until you come to Cobleskill on Christmas—until Christmas night."

"Whaa ... what? Why—whaddeya talking about?"

Sharon's smirk opens into an "awh shucks" smile. "I just got my friend," she sighs, shaking her head and chuckling. "I had a feeling this might happen."

"You just got it right now?" Jim asks.

"No, I found out in the ladies' room right before we left. And my cramps are starting."

"Well, we've done it plenty when you had your—"

"I know, but it's never as good. And after waiting so long, I want this one to be *real* good."

"But you only have two heavy days?" Jim says.

"I know," Sharon replies, "but I'm leaving with the kids for Cobleskill tomorrow."

"Oh yeah, I forgot—what a blessing."

"In a way it is, Jim. Waiting will make it incredible, even better than Manchester—that is, if you can work it into your schedule ... to stay a few days in Cobleskill."

"Sounds inviting, but what am I supposed to do until Christmas?"

"Well," Sharon flirts. "You still have a good right hand don't you?"

"What about you?" Jim quips, returning the question. "What've you been doin' while I've been in the guest room?"

"I'm not telling," she teases. But her saucy snicker tells more than words.

He knows full well, but he kids her anyway, "I thought you said that good girls don't—"

"Who says I'm *good*?" she cuts in, giving a naughty chortle. When it comes to carnal pleasure, Sharon has a way of nailing it—she does.

# Chapter Twenty-six

The gray afternoon shivers and gives way to evening; the smell of snow is in the air. Pastor Jim and Becki make their way, rather quickly, down High Street. The Mustang purrs along puffing white exhaust. The time-temperature sign at Comfed Savings says 4:02 p.m. and 28°. Sparse traffic, empty sidewalks. It's Christmas Eve and the bleary-eyed face of the old mill town seems especially sad. There are few last-minute shoppers, except at Flanagan's where everyone is stocking up on holiday booze for presents and parties—and lonely times.

Spirals of garland wrap the lampposts along with tiny Christmas lights, winking red and green. When Jim first came to Brendon Falls, there was much more in the way of Yuletide decorations, but budget cuts and the increasing secularization of the season have reduced the town's observance of Christ's birth to twinkling lights on lampposts. Besides, why try to create a festive shopping mood when thirty percent of the stores are boarded up?

Right on Chestnut, left on Reservoir. They head up the hill. The cold winter sky, gray, vague, and seamless, stretches over them like a vast sheet of dull aluminum. Rebecca Lea is back and she's just as cold as the winter sky. She's even more distant and sulky than the day she left. Jim was hoping for a cozy hug and a warm smile, but the moment she got off the train, his stomach sank.

Gray ski jacket, knit gloves, black. No hug. No grin. Stone face. Becki mumbled a "hi" but said little else. As Jim drove down from Ayer—she didn't want to drive—he made a few witty remarks but they all fell flat. He turned on the radio but she snapped it off. He asked about her week in New Bedford and got nothing but terse yes-and-no answers. He told her about the trip to Nashua, about the good outcome anyway. She had no response except, "You got any gum?" After that they rode in silence.

Not only is Becki sullen and aloof, but she has that cobwebby just-home-from-vacation aura about her: rumpled and dirty clothes, sleepy don't-bother-me eyes, neglected oversprayed hair, and she smells of stale perfume and unbathed flesh. Her bangs hang dirty and matted over her dark eyebrows which are drawn into their usual frown. *Why the hell did she come back?* Jim asks himself. *Like a miracle, I get a clear track from Logan—and Sharon. But so what if Becki's still fucked? This's gonna be a frustrating night.*

Finally, as they turn left on Taylor Street, Becki vents her displeasure, "It just pisses me off, Shanley."

"What does?" Jim asks.

367

"You."

"*Me?* Whaddeya mean?"

"Your problem!" Becki snaps. "You know what I mean." She grabs the gloves on her lap and beats the air. "You 'n Sharon fight over me and it makes people think I'm-I'm—well, it makes me wicked mad! It's *your* problem, Jimmy Shanley, not *mine*. I'm just here for the ministry. There's nothing more. Fuck, I hate it how you twist things, trying to make something out of nothing!" Her angry outburst cuts to the quick of Jim's heart. Nonetheless, he prefers fire over silence. She gives a huffy sigh then calms a bit. She rubs her lower lip with her thumb as if mulling over the situation. "Pastor's right ... what he said to you and Sharon. God put us together for a ministry. That's all. She's got nothing to worry about. I told her on the phone. She knows. But still, I get caught in the middle."

Right off Taylor Street, then another right, then a left. Up, up, they go, negotiating the narrow streets. Spits of white. The first snowflakes fall furtively from the pewter sky, one here, one there. Jim steers the Mustang up Front Street then up the frozen driveway. Becki starts to get out but he tells her to wait. Hoping to chase her sour mood, he pulls a white paper bag out of his coat pocket. Her scowl relaxes a notch into a look of pained tolerance. A good sign— or so he thinks. Red-script lettering on the bag says Leavitt's Jewel Shoppe. Inside is Becki's Christmas present, unwrapped. Jim gives her the bag. She reaches inside; the paper crinkles as does his heart. She pulls out a small blue-velvet box and opens it to find a 14-karat sapphire pendant and matching earrings. She mumbles a mouse-like "thanks." Inert blankness. Her look of pained tolerance fades to no expression at all. No smile. No dimples. *Nothing.*

Jim feels like slapping her, but instead, he swallows his hurt and plans his revenge, *I'll teach her. I'll go to the fuckin' Christmas Eve service without her.*

Rebecca puts the blue box into her jacket, gathers her stuff, and hops out. As she does, she says, "Bathsheba, I been waiting all week to see her. I hope you fed her, Jimmy." Her voice comes down to Jim as if he's a servant boy. He doesn't respond except with a heavy sigh of hurt feelings that she doesn't hear, for she's up the sidewalk and into the house before his sigh gets all the way out.

The snow is coming down more steadily; a dusting of white already covers the sidewalk and frozen lawn like sugarcoating on a cake. Jim gazes at the falling snow, soft, sifting down, a mist of tiny flakes. His eyes fill but the tears won't come. He feels like going up and blasting Becki but he has no strength for open war. So his angst simply festers in his gut making him nauseated, *Maybe God's chastising me? And Logan gave me enough rope so my sin could find me out—the hard way. I wish I was in Cobleskill with Sharon. I should've let Becki get home on her own. This isn't ministry business. There's no outreach today. I should leave right now and go to the church. Why wait? I should teach her a lesson.*

No revenge. No lesson. Despite his unspoken threats, Jim hauls himself out of the Mustang and trudges up the snow-dusted walk, following the swirly-patterned prints of Rebecca's Reeboks: apostrophes in the powdery white. He pauses by the porch and looks up into the gently falling snow; the fine flakes tickle his face. The sky is darker, a purplish gray like slate. The house is deserted. Mrs. Courtney is at her granddaughter's in Hartford for the whole week. The Browns went home to Kentucky for the holidays. And Stephen moved out on the 15th—so much for Rebecca's dream lover. And Ruthie's red Chevette is not around; Jim figures she's out celebrating with Kyle.

Up the stairs. Becki's door is closed but unlatched. Jim goes in and finds her cuddling and kissing Bathsheba. "Oh, my baby, my baby," she gushes while the cat rubs against her face emitting mewy feline sounds. "Oh, I know," Becki coos as if she understands the mews and meows. "I missed you too."

Jim plops down at the kitchen table. *Oh, to be Becki's cat,* he mutters under his breath. After a few more kisses and hugs, Becki puts Bathsheba down and takes a can of Friskies Sea Captain's Choice from a bag on the counter. Jim, after feeding the cat all week, knows all the flavors in the bag. *Rrrrr-up.* Becki tugs the pull-tab, opening the can. While scraping it into the dish, she says, "Be sure and remind me, Jimmy. We hafta get cat food. There's only one can left. The stores'll be closed tomorrow, and I need milk too—oh, and I need to borrow some money; I mean cash. You can deduct it out of my January rent check. I'm flat broke."

Jim sighs and rolls his eyes, upward. Naked circle of garish light: he stares at the fluorescent ceiling fixture. "Don't worry about it," he says. "I'll buy the stuff." He feels like an abused husband-father-little brother-servant, but he can't leave. Love or lust or obsession, or whatever it is—at the moment he's not sure—has him hooked, a fish dangling on a line, and Becki holds the pole.

She goes into the bathroom, closes the door. He hears the faucet going at high volume, but it stays on longer than she needs to wash cat food off her hands, so he knows she's taking a pee. If he's in the kitchen, she always turns on the water to camouflage. The apartment looks like Christmas—a three-foot tree on the night table by Becki's sleep-sofa, a balsam wreath on her bedroom door, a big red bow on the fridge—and would smell like Christmas as well if not for the litter box. Jim cleaned it yesterday but one shot of cat urine and the stink is back, especially in the kitchen. The toilet flushes. The sink faucet goes off. Out of the bathroom into her room. Seconds later, Billy Joel, and "Tell Her About It," sounds through Becki's closed door. Jim wishes he could "tell her about it," but he has no balls left; her rebuff in the car crushed them. All week long the place seemed so lonely without Becki, but her present foul mood makes it worse than lonely. Sickening. Nauseating. Guilt and anxiety slosh about in his gut along with festering anger and self-pity. Tuesday's good fortune in Nashua now seems like delayed judgment, like a divine setup to teach him a lesson.

Jim pulls up the shade and looks out the window; it's snowing harder. The meadow is white. The gray sky now shows a hint of red as darkness descends over Hadley Hill. Playful gusts of wind send swirls of powder scurrying along on the roof of the barn. He feels the swirling coldness as if the wind is blowing inside him.

On the far peak of the barn, a rusted weathercock swings back and forth but points generally northeast. The Christmas Eve service, which is followed by a potluck supper, starts early so everyone can get home by nine o'clock. LBI churches do not conduct midnight services except for New Year's Eve in Nashua. But this year Pastor Jim also has Freddie and Juanita's wedding which he must weave into the schedule. *Why do they have to get married on Christmas Eve?* he complains to himself as he looks out at the storm. *I don't feel like doing a sermon, much less a fuckin' wedding—fuck, I can't even think anymore without saying "fuck." Who am I to be preaching and doing a wedding? If people knew my thoughts—fuck, I'd rather go home and die in my sleep.*

Jim sits back in his chair. Gray suit, paisley tie, Dingo boots. It seems as if he's been in his pinstripe suit the whole month of December. It feels tight, and hot as the kitchen radiator hisses and clanks to life. He wiggles out of his overcoat. As he does, Bathsheba hops up on the table. Jim pets her until she's purring loudly and licking his hand. Fishy breath, fishy tongue. Yech. He puts her on the floor. No way. She immediately jumps back up and gives a sassy toss of her snakelike tail, as if to say, "Hey, buddy, this is *my* house. I'll go where I want, if you don't mind." She then struts defiantly to the center of the table where she proceeds to groom herself.

Jim gives a pained chuckle, *I don't believe it. This cat is taking on Becki's personality. I don't have any say around here.*

The bedroom door opens. Rebecca, wrapped in her yellow bathrobe, pads barefoot to the bathroom. She carries a hair dryer, a curling brush, and a gray toilette case: personal items just unpacked from her travel bag. Jim also spies a pair of pale-blue panties in the pocket of her robe—he has an eagle eye when it comes to spotting her underwear. She closes the door until it latches—there is no lock—but then she pokes her head out. "Jimmy, why don'tcha make us some coffee?" She sounds almost friendly. Jim likes it when she says "us." But as he fills the electric percolator, he dismisses the hopeful thought as premature. He plugs it in. It coughs and wheezes. In the bathroom, the shower comes on.

Ten minutes later, Becki comes out, her hair towel-dried but still wet. She pads back to her room. Her face has a freshly scrubbed hot-water ruddiness; it makes her look younger, like thirteen. Yet she whips her low-hung hips under her robe as proudly as any woman. In her wake she leaves a fragrant plume of perfumed powder and soap and lilac-scented shampoo. Jim wishes she would take off her robe and join him on the old swayback sofa in the corner of the kitchen but the wish quickly sours in his guilt-ridden gut, his conscience telling him he shouldn't be there at all, not when she's taking a shower. He sighs, hoists himself to his feet, and goes into the bathroom himself. When he closes the door, Becki yells from her room, "Don't be long, Jimmy! I still hafta do my hair!"

Yellow stream, foamy bubbles. Jim pisses sideways into the toilet. The odor of urine wafts up joining the muggy bath fragrances. He holds the toilet seat with his left hand and aims with his right; a thick rose-colored lid cover prevents the seat from staying up by itself. A matching rug, oval-shaped, lies on the black tile floor. A sprinkling of body talc on the rug and floor testify to Rebecca's recent aftershower ritual. Also on the floor is a white bathroom scale, the one that tells Becki she weighs 125 pounds—more likely 122 or 123. She exaggerates on the chunky side when speaking of her weight. On the back of the toilet is her hair dryer, her gray toilette kit, a book of matches touting Flanagan's Liquor Store—she uses matches instead of air freshener—and a ceramic bowl of decorative soap bars, different colors, different shapes.

As Jim expels a few last squirts of urine, draining his bladder, he checks the trash basket to see if Becki is over her period—she is. There are no ball-like wads of toilet paper, just a thin tissue-wrapped panty liner, and a strip of waxy paper off a new one. *She may've come back bitchy,* he says to himself, *but it's not because of her period. I figured as much since her pimple is dried up—shit, I keep track of her cycle as if we're screwing four times a week. I'm fuckin' nuts. I should check in at Worcester.*

He shakes his thumby dick then lowers the seat gently. It bangs if he drops it, which gets Becki upset, and she's shitface enough already. After zipping his fly, he reaches into the back and flushes. It's no big job to replace the flush mechanism but he's never gotten around to it, or reporting it to Mrs. Courtney, nor has

Becki. To the mirror, which hangs like a picture over a naked spindly-legged sink. Jim rubs the steam fog off the framed looking-glass then checks his carefully combed cowlick. On the sink is Becki's curling brush; it's plugged into an extension cord which is stapled to the wall and runs up to the ceiling fixture. When the house was converted to apartments, the bathroom was carved out of a large closet. No outlets were added—typical for Brendon Falls. No heat either—but enough heat comes from the kitchen.

Jim washes his hands to get the fishy smell off where Bathsheba licked him. A pair of purple towels hang on the rack by the bathtub, one dry and neat, the other damp and disheveled. He dries on the damp one. Becki-temptation. As usual, he can't resist. He smells up and down the soft terry cloth inhaling all the Becki-smells he can, soap, shampoo, underarm odor, all mingled with her faint but unique salty-banana scent. *Ahah,* he declares to himself as he locates an area of vaginal odor near the bottom of the towel. Pungent, smoky, so muliebrial, so Sharon-like. It's unmistakable: *Oh, to be this towel and to be pressed against Becki's cunt.*

Jim is fascinated, attracted, turned on by anything that touches her pussy. It draws him like nothing else, yet he's never even seen it. Waves of guilt. *This is sick. I'm turning into a degenerate. Besides, I'm invading. If she wanted me to smell her body, she'd let me smell the real—but I can't help it. I love her forever. This towel is sacred. This bathroom is a temple of worship. I'm losing it. How much longer? I'm drowning in lust. I deserve to be abused. Logan's letting me hang myself. I knew it, I knew—O God, change Becki's mood! I want to flirt and laugh and—*

"Come on, Jimmy, I hafta do my hair!" Becki yells impatiently, breaking his train of thought—a runaway train.

"Be right out," Jim tells her through the door. He replaces the towel on the rack, exactly as it was. A still-dripping pink shower curtain forms a circular cubicle within the old-fashioned four-legged bathtub. A wire basket hangs on the side of the tub; it contains an egg-shaped bar of soap, a razor, a tube of Soft Sense shave gel, and a squeeze bottle of Pert shampoo.

In the tub itself, Jim sees several strands of brown hair among the beads of water. More temptation. He leans down for a closer look, and sure enough spots a few circles of pubic hair, a darker brown, burnt umber. *Look at that,* he says to himself. *It is the same color as her eyebrows.* Cunt, cunt. He's obsessed with her cunt. *O God, help me. When I'm around her, my mind gutters out every five minutes. I can't help it. I wanna see her nakedness. I wanna know her completely. I wanna fuck her ... but I'll be lucky to get a smile. I love her. I want her. But she treats me like shit.*

No hope, no hope. He sighs. He exits the bathroom into the kitchen, into the aromas of coffee and Jontue perfume. Becki, still in her bathrobe, leans against the counter with a mug of coffee. "This is *too* strong," she complains after taking a sip. She frowns and pushes the blue mug at Jim. "How many scoops did you put in?"

"Three, I think? Maybe three and a half?"

"God, Jimmy, it's *two* 'n a half. How many times do I hafta tellyuh? This tastes like paint remover." She pours the coffee into the sink, shakes her head in disgust, and marches into the bathroom.

4:51 p.m. The Coca-Cola clock groans as does Jim's heart, but Becki's hair dryer quickly drowns out the clock.

\* \* \*

Pastor Jim, alone in his unlit office, looks out at the snowstorm. It's dark on this side, the east side, of the building but the nightglow of the storm gives the snow-clad pine trees a ruddy cast. The capricious wind sends a swarm of flakes clittering against the storm windows; the little sounds are muted and hollow like fingernails tapping on a wooden box. Otherwise, the thick falling snow brings only quietness, eerie quietness, to the outside world.

Inside the church, the combined wedding and Christmas Eve service is over. In the teen center a covered-dish eat-on-your-lap supper is in progress. The potluck also serves as an informal reception for Freddie and Juanita. Jim still hears bubbly chatter as stragglers walk by on their way to the new wing. BFBC regulars, Christmas crowd, wedding guests. The sanctuary was packed for the service and now everyone is in the teen center, except for Pastor Jim, who has escaped to the dark solitude of his office. (At BFBC weddings are incorporated right into the preaching service, usually the last thing—another LBI custom and a clever way to get potential converts into church; Jim once looked at weddings as evangelistic opportunities, but no more.) Juanita, in a traditional white gown, was ravishing as usual, while her attendants looked very Christmasy in cherry-red dresses.

But Becki, her brown hair glistening in the candlelight, her face dreamy-soft under her feathered bangs, captured Jim's attention as if she were the only one present for the service. Dressy pink shirt, argyle sweater-vest, wine-colored skirt, charcoal riding boots. Attired in spiffy new clothes—Christmas presents from New Bedford—she sat halfway back with Jodi and Brenda. As Jim conducted the service, he looked at Becki again and again hoping for a smile or a nod, but she gave him neither. Each no-response aggravated the sinking lovesick nausea in his stomach.

After the service, Becki disappeared and Jim still doesn't know her whereabouts. To add to his hurt, she's wearing her old earrings, the little stars. He's seen no sign of the new sapphire earrings he gave her, or the pendant. As far as he knows, they're still at home in the white paper bag.

At the wedding-party photo session, Freddie smiled like a cutie-boy high-schooler, but Juanita got all the attention, and all the kisses. She looked like a movie star and acted the same. Jim wanted to slap her, especially since she ratted on him when Sharon called the diner that stormy September night. He's never said anything to Juanita about it, and she always acts the same toward him: plastic and syrupy, filled with platitudes. Weddings annoy Jim anyway, as much as TV commercials and shopping malls and theme parks—and church services at Moody Coliseum. He hates the ceremonial pretense and the rah-rah pseudo-festive atmosphere.

*Who am I to declare a couple to be husband and wife?* he asks himself as another gust of wind sends a volley of snowflakes clittering against the window. *Marriage is okay, love is a dream, but I hate weddings. There's something so bogus about them—Becki, Becki, where the hell are you? Is she with Jodi or Brenda or—fuck it! What does it matter? She's shitface anyway.*

Jim gives a heavyhearted sigh then goes over and flips the light switch. Buzzing, flickering—*fuck it, God! Can't you make any-thing easy?* He climbs up on—"Oh shit!" he cries as he bangs his shin. He fiddles with the lights; they come on; he comes down.

He slumps into his chair and utters a silent prayer, *Fuck you, God! You got me into this. I wasn't looking for a church, or Becki Reinhardt.* He halfway expects some kind of judgment to fall upon him. He's never used the F-word on God before. But nothing happens, nothing changes. The festive chatter continues down the hall. The snow continues to fall. He still feels hurt and frustrated.

Jim stares wide-eyed at the unfinished paperwork on his desk, work put off until after the holidays. Clipped to his calendar book is a folded note; he reads it:

```
JIM
     THE CHURCH IS CLEAN BUT I WON'T BE THERE
TONIGHT. SHEILA'S HAD THE FLU ALL WEEK. SHE'S
BETTER BUT BEV'S WORN OUT. SO I'LL SEE YOU IN THE
MORNING. ALSO REMIND BECKI THAT SHE'S INVITED FOR
CHRISTMAS DINNER. YOU'RE INVITED TOO IF YOU'RE
GOING TO BE AROUND BUT I FIGURED YOU'D BE GOING
TO NEW YORK SINCE YOU AND SHAR MADE PEACE. I HAD
```

A HUNCH THAT LOGAN WOULDN'T BE TOO HARD ON YOU.
OH, I ALMOST FORGOT. THE LAST QUARTER IS GOING
TO BE EVEN WORSE. ALL THE MONEY GOING TO NASHUA
IS DRAINING US DRY. WE'VE GOT TO TALK WITH STAN
ON THIS, BUT IT CAN WAIT UNTIL AFTER THE FIRST.

RUSS

*So that's why I didn't see Russ at service,* Jim concludes to himself.

Now comes a knock, a teasing smirk, a tray of food; it's Jodi Donovan. "Make room, Jim, I'm coming in to hide with you."

She quickly converts his desk into a supper table. On the tray are two styrofoam plates heaped high. Twin plumes of steam rise from the plates, filling the office with the savory aromas of a Christmas dinner. Turkey and dressing, candied yams, scalloped potatoes, baked ham, baked beans, green beans, creamed corn, cranberry sauce, coleslaw, lots of gravy. Also on the tray: buttered rolls, two milks, two coffees, two pieces of Boston cream pie. "I figured I'd bring the regular," Jodi says. "Juanita's family has a ton of Puerto Rican food out there, but this is no time to experiment."

"You got that right," Jim kids. Jodi's hospitality and teasing spirit make him feel better—no, it's her innate solitude and sad awareness that make him feel better. It's always there, a deepness, a knowing, behind the bantering. And like Russ, she never tries to bullshit him. She pulls up a chair and sits to Jim's left at the side of the desk. No Calvin Klein's, but a chestnut-brown dress with a red belt. Jodi looks very ladylike. Her gray-flecked brunette hair is blown up and back—quite a change from her moppy pageboy. She also wears a pearl necklace and matching earrings. The only blemish to her appearance is an ugly cold sore on her lower lip.

"You look dressy tonight," Jim says. "You're beating the hell out of the dress code."

"Well, it *is* Christmas," Jodi snickers as she opens her milk carton.

"I appreciate you bringing this, but what inspired you to give me room service? I thought Brenda—"

"Oh, she went with Becki and Joe to Bergson's."

"*Becki* went to Bergson's?" Jim asks anxiously.

Jodi's mouth is too packed with turkey and dressing to reply. Disappointment, jealousy. Another cold wash of hurt chills Jim's gut. *Fuck, she doesn't even want to be in the same building with me. And she's with fucking Joe who ratted to Logan. That asshole. He's probably lusting over her right now—"wanted to plug her right there on the rock"—he's a damn traitor and he'd probably love to get Becki buzzed and fuck her in the backseat of his Buick. And who knows what she'll do in her pissy frame of mind?* He hasn't seen Joe since he found out from Garrett that Joe had ratted on him. But it's not Joe's betrayal so much, but his professed attraction for Becki and her going with him that bothers Jim. His stomach is too upset to eat, especially after hearing this; he picks at his food.

Jodi swallows, takes a drink of milk. Finally, she replies, "Becki, she was bored, and Joe says he gets sick on potluck. Of course, Brenda, she had to go with. I didn't feel like churchy chitchat, so here I am." *Brenda, Brenda, Joe and Brenda.* The fact that Brenda is with Joe and Becki, after Jodi declares it for the second time, finally breaks through Jim's jealous reaction. He feels better about Joe, but Becki's going still bothers him. He takes a small bite of turkey, just a nibble of white meat.

"So how'd you know I was in here?" Jim asks.

Jodi, her fork in one hand, a roll in the other, gives an omniscient half-grin, just enough to show her dimples. "Well, your face was so long up there during the wedding, I thought your chin was goin' to scrape the carpet. So I figured I'd come cheer you up. I knew Sharon was gone, and you don't like eating potluck on your lap, so you had to be in here." She laughs then shovels in a bite of potatoes, a bite of turkey; she pushes food onto her fork with her roll.

Jodi eats. Jim nibbles. After a minute or so, she slows her pace of eating. Sober face. Her lighthearted mood has given way to seriousness. "You're hurting, aren't you, Jim, and not over Shane?" Her tone is resigned yet curious.

Jodi already knows about Becki's cold departure a week ago Friday and about Jim and Sharon's trip to Nashua. But Jim pours it all out again, then brings her up to date as he describes Rebecca's icy return this afternoon. Talking it out settles his stomach just enough to eat but he's well behind Jodi who's already half finished with her Boston cream pie. She rolls her fork above her pie and looks out at the dark stormy night. "So it's the uncertainty, huh?" she says in a voice out the windows. "That's why you're so desperate and flipping from love to hate? I know Becki can be a real bitch, but if you really love her—and I know you do—you have a damn weird way of showing it. I feel for you, Jim, but I think a lot of your pain is self-inflicted. I'd say *you're* the problem, not Becki."

*"Me?"* Jim says incredulously. "That's a crock of shit. She's the one who's hating and flipping and acting like a spoiled brat, not *me*? I've been honest and loving. I've poured out my heart and laid

down my life."

"Yeah, you're so fuckin' kind," Jodi mocks, not angrily but with enough sharpness to pierce Jim's Becki-facade. She gives a snorting sigh and takes a quick bite of pie. Their language has become foul, filled with four-letter words, which is quite a change from even a year ago, when "goodnight" and "heck" and "crap" were the strongest words ever uttered in Jim's office—except maybe for Russ Bradley. Jodi swallows her pie, swigs her coffee. "You make a nice legitimate-looking nest to hide her in? You call that honest, Jim? How would you like to be a 20-year-old girl in love with a married minister twice your—"

"You don't know she loves me, Jodi. She never told you that?"

"Come on, Jimmy. Why does she spend thirty hours a week with you? Whaddeya think it is, *missionary* zeal?"

"Get off it, Jodi," Jim declares, now irritated—no, he's frustrated. "Don't mess with my mind. If she loves me, she has a *damn* poor way of showing it. This afternoon she was so insolent, I felt like slapping her. You'd think she'd grow up but she keeps reverting into a bratty adolescent. And she treats me like I'm her little brother, or worse. In fact, she hasn't said a kind word to me for nine days."

Hunger. Jim's rising emotions stimulate his appetite; he takes several quick bites, ham, potatoes, beans. Jodi returns to her dessert. "So, it may be ninety days," she says, her voice thick with pie. She pushes the back of her fork at him for emphasis. "Or nine hundred? Who knows? Or perhaps never?"

"What the hell are you saying?" Jim asks, after swallowing.

Seeming to ignore his question, Jodi wipes her mouth with a napkin, takes a drink of coffee, then looks past Jim, gazing wide-eyed toward the windows. She gently touches the cold sore on her lip with her forefinger. As she does, a shadow comes over her face like a dark cloud passing over the sun, but with Jodi the darkness comes up from within. She gives a weary sigh. "I feel so fuckin' old, Jim. I'm thirty-two you know, but I feel sixty sometimes, and with these dark circles and wrinkles"—she points at her eyes—"I look like a corpse in the morning."

"Well, I'm five years older than you and seventeen years older than Becki Lea," Jim replies, trying to steer her back to Becki.

But Jodi seems more into her own woes than Jim's. Besides, she's like Russ; she can never be steered in conversation—or life. She gazes out toward the snowy night as if she can see out but she can't because the office lights are on. "My hair's getting so gray. And I smoke so much, my breath is awful. I'm getting so skinny and my tits are shriveled up to nothing, and Tony, he never—well, he called to say Merry Christmas but it was nothing, just a fuckin' cordial gesture. After six weeks of flirting, he's gone home to Claudia. He's backed off, gone again." Jodi's tone is rancorous, resentful, as if Tony fucked up her life, or God, or herself—or all three.

Jim sops the last of his gravy with a roll then starts on his pie. "Well, I guess it's my turn now?" he replies, still trying to steer.

But Jodi goes on as if she doesn't hear him, "Mom and Grandma Kerrigan, they expect Kyle and me for Christmas dinner, and Brenda, like we're a happy little family. Yet everyone knows that Kyle's screwing Ruthie, but on Christmas they all pretend 'for *family's* sake' except when they're alone in the kitchen. Then they call Ruthie a slut and a disgrace to the family. But I feel sorry for her. Getting laid under Kyle's grunting body is not exactly romantic. He fucks like a boar hog rooting in the ground." Jodi kills the last of her coffee, then adds, "I hate snow."

"I thought you liked winter?" Jim says, giving up trying to get her back to Becki.

"I used to ... but now every snowfall just stirs up painful memories." Jodi places her empty styrofoam cup upside down on her empty pie plate. She stares at it as if it's a crystal ball. She takes a deep breath and slowly exhales. Her eyes grow large. A peacefulness seems to come over her. She speaks as if she's getting a message from the cup, "There's nothing else, Jim, nothing else to live for, but still, we never give in to it ... not completely." Her voice is no longer indignant but gentle, resigned, tinged with wonder.

"Give in to what?" Jim asks as he wads his dirty napkin.

Jodi's eyes are lavender and hazy and peaceful, like the reflection of a summer evening on a tranquil pond. She answers obliquely, "We yearn to soar on the wind, to let the tempest sweep us away, but instead, we play it safe. Love scares us, so we put walls around it and try to make it fit. We call it marriage, but love can't live in cages."

"Maybe so, Jodi? But my marriage was okay until Becki. And Shar and I, we still have good sex when we're not fighting. But Becki, I never knew such—it's too big. It's beyond anything I ever knew. I can't describe it. I-I, it's—*she's* the one that doesn't fit."

Jodi crushes her cup with the heel of her hand, until it's flat on the pie plate. "I'm outa here," she says. "I need a smoke, and I have to pee." She stands and stretches, gathers everything onto the tray, and heads for the door. But then she turns back around, and stands there bouncing the tray against her legs.

"What?" Jim asks.

Jodi's eyes flash as if a gust of wind has stirred the water in the tranquil summer pond. She gives a bold smirk. "I bet Becki wants you so bad, Jim, that she has to wring her panties out every time she gets back from outreach."

Hope, disbelief, X-rated shock. Jim's mind, like an anchored ship in heavy seas, lists one way then the other. His thoughts race to weigh Jodi's assertion against all stored data on Becki's feelings but they quickly get tangled in a jungle of contradiction as if he's playing speed chess blindfolded. By the time he collects his senses, Jodi's on her way out. But he speaks anyway, as the door closes behind her. "Jodi, you're crazy. But I hope you're right ... or do I?"

\* \* \*

The clock on the teen center wall says 7:51 p.m. Becki still isn't back. Freddie and Juanita, and their guests, have departed for a more festive celebration at the VFW. Those who remain are gathered near the Christmas tree. Regulars, nonregulars, sitting, standing, talking, drinking coffee, nibbling Christmas cookies, trying to corral excited children.

The tree has red balls, red lights, and a shiny star on top—the one in the main sanctuary has blue balls and blue lights. Pastor Jim says hello to Thelma Hightower and Curtis Sims as they pass him headed for the kitchen, each carrying a tray piled high with utensils, dishes, food warmers, condiments, and other potluck items. Jim then drifts about the room. He feels better about mixing now that most of the strange faces have departed. Everyone has something to say, and he lets them do most of the talking.

"You done right good, Pastor Jim," Ernie Johnson declares. "I like your Bible preachin', but I reckon I'm the biggest backslider here—an' a glutton to boot. I had a hankerin' there'd be a heapuh good food, an' I done made a *pig* outa myself." Ernie, his face red with good humor, is wearing Dickies overalls, his usual attire.

"The Lord ain't gonna hold back his daily bread jus'cuz a soul's adoin' poorly," Sarah says to Ernie. She peers at her husband through a pair of granny glasses which seem ready to slide off her owlish nose. Her fat pear-shaped body is covered by a turtleneck dress. It looks like a tent. Sarah's cheeks are pouchy like a rodent but her voice is birdlike to match her legs, and nose. "A mighty healin's acomin' in our church, Pastor," she says, turning her attention to Jim. "I seen it in a vision day 'fore last." She glances toward the ceiling as if tuning into a heavenly signal. "There was a red-haired harlot. She was covered with sores an' pus an' fixin' to die. She cried out to the Lord, an' I seen this here angel acomin', a six-winged seraph, an' his eyes were on fire an' he hovered a spell over the harlot, an' her skin turned right pretty, like the skin of a chil' ... an' the six-winged angel said, 'Doncha fret none. The devil ain't gonna fetch you no more.'"

A few steps over from Ernie and Sarah, Larry Thornton is making a pitch to Carl Baker about a new mutual fund, while Angela sits with a mug of coffee, her curvaceous legs crossed under a blue ruffled dress. As Jim steps closer, he catches a glimpse of her salmon-colored bra cups inside the V-neck of her dress—his eyes are always ready for such opportunities. "So I guess Sharon and the kids went to Albany, huh?" Angie says to Jim, toasting him with her mug.

"Please don't misinterpret my presence, Jimbo," Larry quips before Jim can reply to Angie. "It's important to be eclectic in our tastes and to sample the different religious myths and traditions. You don't have to believe in the virgin birth to appreciate the civilizing influence of Christianity." Larry wears a dapper lambswool vest and a silk tie. Quite a contrast with Ernie's overalls. Neither comes to church but Jim feels closer to Ernie, light-years closer.

"I'm working on him, Pastor Jim," Carl brags giving a tight little grin—*I'd say it's the other way around, Carl,* Jim rebuts silently—"but I do agree with Larry that it's good to have an open mind. Most definitely ... that is, until you find Christ." Carl's beady eyes have a sheen of purpose, but it seems more like lust for money than love for the lost.

Jim makes his way around the Christmas tree where he finds Sylvia Cahill sitting with Melanie, her youngest, on her lap. "I'm really getting into worldly songs, Jim," Sylvia remarks as he sits down beside her. "Now more than ever, since Joe's been helping me." Jim starts to answer but before he can, little Melanie crawls off her mom's lap onto his. "I like popular music," Sylvia goes on. "Especially rock songs that have poetic lyrics, but I don't know if it's God's will? I don't—so where's Russ and Bev? I guess Sheila's still sick? That flu's goin' around. Mel just got over it."

"Yep, dat's right," Melanie declares, looking up at Pastor Jim with her big brown eyes. "I ardie had de flu 'n I barfed all ober de rug 'n Ginger wuz lickin' it, 'n her tail was waggin'." Melanie, in a green-and-white Christmas dress, feels soft and cozy and frilly, and her dark curly locks smell sweet like baby shampoo.

After returning Melanie to her mom, Jim excuses himself and runs immediately into Aunt Agnes, waddling across from the other side of the room with a cup of cider and a huge gingerbread cookie. "Oh, Pastor, I talked to Albert in Cleveland, an' he's lookin' at a nice four-bedroom place. So this may be my last Christmas here." Agnes gives a big ugly smile and emits wheezing jets of short-breathed laughter. *God, is she ever revolting,* Jim thinks. *Look at those gray rolls of fat and that big gap between her front teeth. How am I supposed to love her? O Lord, why'd you make so many ugly and pitiful people? And here comes another one.*

"Merry Christmas, Pastor," Elmer Kowalski says, grinning up at Jim like a hoary-headed gnome, his raspy old voice just as wizened as his face. "This snow reminds me of the Christmas of '44. I was fightin' with Georgie Patton in Europe and—uhgaruhhh— we rode in trucks for three days and nights to relieve Bastogne. Uhgaruhhh." Elmer keeps making disgusting hawking sounds as if he's trying to bring up phlegm. "We almost froze and our battalion got lost—uhgaruhhh—and by the time we got there, all the fightin' was over. I never even got out of my duece-'n-a-half."

Sickly and emaciated, Elmer looks like a bag of bones in his shabby brown suit, as if he's wasting away.

"I hope this skull on my vest isn't scaring anybody off, Pastor Jim," Harry Hinton jokes as he turns to show the dirty-gray death's head on his back. They both laugh and Judy too. Then Harry becomes more serious. "I liked what you said before the wedding, about how God doesn't want anything from us like good works, but He just wants to be close to us like a lover. That's *my* only chance ... for sure."

Judy, sitting with Cami on her lap, asks Jim a question, "Ruthie says Joseph 'n Mary, they weren't never legally married? Is that—" Cami suddenly starts to cry; she waves her dimpled arms, her chubby red face contracting, quivering. "She's teethin' an' cranky," Judy explains. "We'd better get home an' get her to bed."

Pastor Jim tells Harry and Judy good-night then goes to the other end of the teen center where he talks for a while with Herschel Hightower and Gerald Burton—mainly about the snowstorm.

Jim wears no clerical collar but the title of "Pastor" still wraps his neck like a warning label. Only a few, like Jodi and Russ, really know him. Sometimes he feels like getting up and boldly declaring his Becki-love, so he'll find out who really loves him. But most of the time, as on this Christmas Eve, the trusting faces of the flock make him feel ashamed of his Becki-love, as if he's betraying the church and placing it in jeopardy.

Finally, at eight-twenty, Jim departs the teen center, heads for his office. "So the head doctor gave you a clean bill of health?" comes a secretive voice from behind him. "That should close a few mouths." Jim turns. It's Doris Campbell coming out of the ladies' room; she smells like cigarettes. They grin knowingly at each other but she changes the subject, "The wedding was beautiful, don't you think, Jim? And it was a good idea to turn off the lights. Candlelight is so romantic. But I feel bad for Juanita. She's in for a letdown. Freddie tries but he's lazy and irresponsible, and can't hold a job."

Doris pauses, looks furtively up and down the hall, then she steps closer and whispers, "Your secret is safe with me, Jim, and I think—" *Swish, swish.* Noisy skirt, scurrying feet. Doris hustles back into the ladies' room.

Jim quickly realizes why as he sees Stan and Barry and Frank Cahill coming in through the hallway entrance near Angela's office. They each have a snow shovel and are covered with snow. With no coat or gloves, Stan looks like the Abominable Snowman with a tie. After stomping their feet and stowing the shovels in the corner, Barry and Frank head into the old wing, but Stan sees Jim and comes down the hall like a warrior returning from battle.

Stan's hair is covered with melting snow. His face and hands are lobster red. "Paasssss-tor Jim, jus' the man I was goin' to see," he says exuberantly. "All the walks are shoveled an' I wanted to brief yuh on our plowin' sitchiation." Stan cups his cold hands and blows into them. "Frank's got a guy. He's private but he also plows for the town. He wants forty bucks a whack. I told Frank to have him here at six a.m., an' Barry would meet him."

With a sweep of his huge hand, Stan pushes his wet hair back off his forehead. Drops of water run down his brow. His craggy face looms over Jim like a granite cliff on a rainy day. The melting snow makes his gray hair look darker, younger.

"Sounds good to me," Jim replies. "The fellow we had last year charged fifty."

"And he's a pima-don, Pastor Jim. He couldn't get it through his head that we never cancel. We *never* cancel. We're the only church that held services during the 'Blizzard of '78.' I remember it well, climbin' over fifteen-foot drifts an' droppin' down to the door, jus' six people, but we sure whupped on the devil that night ... an' I was jus' a babe in Christ." Stan's sapphire eyes gleam excitedly like glassy volcanic rock. He gets off on storms and wars, or any crisis that requires heroic action.

"So how'd it go earlier?" Jim asks as they go into the men's room. The men's room in the new wing is bigger, with two stalls and three urinals.

No reply. No sound, save for the spattering of piss on porcelain. But as they flush, Stan's authoritative voice rises above the gurgling rush of the urinals, "We ran 75 people through in 35 minutes, an' I sent the overflow into the main sanc'uary since there was too many in the teen center."

"That's fast," Jim remarks as they wash their hands. "Who'd you have on the line?"

"Mary 'n Thelma, an' Leslie 'n Gerald ... an' also Barbara Cameron."

Jim pulls a a paper towel out of the Erving dispenser—a khaki-brown institutional paper towel. "You mean Sims?" he says to Stan.

"Yeah, Barbara Sims, she was helpin', an' Nita's dad had a crew workin'." Stan's voice drops into a bassy whisper—heavy with breath. He sounds like Darth Vader. "Truth is, the Spanics, they got in the way. If it wasn't for them, we coulda served ever'body in twenty-five minutes. They don't know our system an' they let people cut in, an' they kept on yakin' with ever'body in line. An' nobody can understand them 'cuz they talk half Spanic an' half English, an' they talk fast like squawkin' blackbirds. An' they all wear the same cheap perfume. It's *dis*gustin'. It smells like the insect repellent we used in Vietnam." They both laugh, Stan harder than Jim. "In fact, they remind me of gooks, 'cept gooks are smarter. I never knew a Spanic who could think on his feet. I know 'cuz we got a bunch of 'em doin day-labor down at the mill, an' they're all lazy an' overpaid. They're even *worse* than the colored guys back in Boston."

Stan leans over the sink toward the mirror and adjusts his snow-dampened tie. Jim throws back a safe reply, "Well, they still need God?" He has no energy or inspiration to get into a discussion about which race makes the best Christians. Stan's prejudicial attitude actually turns him off.

Campbell pulls out a pocket comb and runs it through his wet hair. "Mos' certainly," he affirms, abandoning his whisper. "We're called to preach the gospel to ever' creature, even the immigrams. They can be saved but it's hard. I've talked with Nita's folks. Spanics have a weird kind of Catholism. They got heathen blood an' pagan ways. They got magic 'n witchcraft in their thinkin' ... and they breed like rabbits. All Cath'lics need to be saved, like Dr. Logan says, but the Spanics are the hardest to reach ... an' even when they get saved, they don't make good soul-winners. Now *Irish* Cath'lics, they're more like us. I know 'cuz I witness to my mom a lot, an' I think she may be saved in her heart."

Pocketing his comb, Stan's disdain shifts from Puerto Ricans to women. "Pastor Jim, I haven't put my foot down or nuthin', but I'm not too happy 'bout this marriage. I feel sorry for Freddie. He's got no balls. I feel like wringin' his fool neck sometimes, but it's not his fault. He's been a baby all his life 'cuz *women* have ruined him, mainly my sister but also Doris ... an' now Nita. His father was a no-good drunk so Freddie never had a Christian man to teach him 'bout the 'ceitful ways of females. Nita's gonna eat him right up. She 'minds me of Doris's slutty sister-in-law, that Ruthie bitch, an' bein' a Spanic, Nita's not gonna take care of Freddie like a woman ought. Women these days, they don't know their place, Pastor Jim. They're too uppity an' sassy-faced. It goes against the Bible."

Campbell gives a proud-peacock grin then, hitching his thumbs inside the waist of his suit pants, puffs out his massive chest like a tom turkey. His swelling presence is overwhelming yet pompous to the point of being funny.

Jim chuckles under his breath and heads for the door, but Stan stops him, "Oh, Pastor Jim, I jus' want you to know I'm *with* you on the battlefield no matter what. I know that the women been gossipin' 'bout your personal life, but it's nobody's bus'ness 'cept you an' God ... an' I'm glad Dr. Logan set them straight. I know you're gonna win with God. The devil's after all of us. I gotta fight him ever' day myself."

Jim leaves the men's room with mixed emotions. Stan's vow of allegiance does not comfort him.

On the way to his office, Jim runs into Frank Cahill in the hall. A gaunt pasty-faced alcoholic, Frank seems too small for his heavy wool parka and thermal boots. He pumps Jim's hand and tells him about the new snowplow guy. His high-pitched whine grates on Jim's already-frayed nerves.

Playing dumb, Jim thanks Frank and pats him on the back. Frank gives an embarrassed hayseed smile. "This is gonna be *my* year, Pastor," he proudly declares. "No more playin' around. I'm goin' *all* the way with God. Stan and I talked. He says it's more important for a man to take Bible classes. So startin' second semester, Sylvia's stayin' home with the girls and I'll be comin' on Mondays." Jim tells him he'll be looking for him.

*Yes,* Jim mutters to himself as he heads into the old wing. *I'll look for Frank, but I won't see him, unless we hold class at Clancy's Pub. I hope he doesn't come to class. I don't wanna see his fucking face anymore than I have to.*

Jim finds the lights on in his office. Barry Buford stands by the windows with a mug of hot chocolate. Packed into a too-small tuxedo, he looks like a penquin; he served as one of Freddie's ushers at the wedding.

"Would you like to go skiing, Pastor Jim?" Barry asks with boyish enthusiasm. "I have lift tickets for Crotched Mountain. You can bring Sharon, *or Becki.*" When he says *"or Becki,"* he smirks as if to say I know the whole story.

Jim gives a one-syllable laugh. He pulls off his tie and tosses it onto his desk. "You know I can't ski, Barry. The few times I tried back in Colorado, I almost killed myself."

*Barry must know all about Becki,* Jim concludes to himself as he lies back on the LA-Z-BOY. *Garrett must've told him? Maybe Stan knows too? But so what? It all may be of no consequence. The way Becki's treating me, I doubt this scandal will ever get past the rumor stage.*

Barry sips his hot chocolate then gives a teddy-bear grin. "Not to fear, Jim," he reassures. "I've got some short skis. They'll be perfect for you." His black curly hair is still wet with melted snow, from helping Stan shovel the walk.

Jim unbuttons his suit vest then folds his hands behind his head. "Well, maybe after New Year's. But only on a weekday when it's not crowded. I don't want a bunch of people gawking at me when I fall."

Barry laughs but quickly sobers. He sets his mug on the desk. His eyes fill with determination, the whites bulging out. His fat voice drops an octave. "Matt says I'm inhibited; he says I have an unhealthy submissive attitude toward Stan. He says I need to come out. So *I'm* not hiding anymore. What you preach is right, Jim, and Matt agrees. He says we should follow our hearts and tell it like it is. It's like you say ... people can never get close if they hide. We *must* challenge the lies and force people out, and I'm starting with myself."

Jim feels suddenly nervous, as if someone's playing with a loaded gun. "Well, Barry, it's one thing to preach it, but another to live it."

"Well, I'm going to live it!" Barry declares brashly in a burst of bravado; he paces determinedly back and forth. "I'm going to practice what I preach. In fact, I already started this afternoon."

"Whaa? How? You did what?"

Barry flaps his arms as if they're wings: a penguin trying to take flight. "I told Janet *every*thing about me and Matt," he explains zealously. "She went ballistic, screaming and crying. Then she slapped me and kicked me in the nuts, and took off in the car. I had to ride down with Stan, but it was worth it. I didn't tell Stan though. Matt says I shouldn't. He says that Stan's not ready to hear it. But I had to tell you, Jim. And I also want you to know that I'm with you *all* the way.... Well, I better go. I have to help Stan clean and set up for church." With that, Barry grabs his cocoa and leaves.

*So that's why I haven't seen Janet tonight. Fuckin' Barry knows too much, and he's acting crazier than Joe Lareux ... even without pot.* Jim sighs and pulls his watch; it's 8:38 p.m. He smells gunpowder—or maybe it's sweat?

# Chapter Twenty-seven

9:15 p.m. Pastor Jim sits at his desk doing nothing except hoping that Becki will come back to the church before he leaves. There are several wadded napkins on the desk, left from his supper with Jodi, plus a plastic spoon. In preparation for his departure, he collects them. Yet he's reluctant to go.

A double knock on his door. His heart leaps then falls as Stan Campbell enters. Jim's brain knew it was Stan's knock but his heart is tuned to Rebecca. "The doors are locked," Stan reports. "And we mopped 'n vacked, an' set up for church. Barry's gonna be here at six to brief the new plow guy, an' to shovel the walks. I'll be down at seven to get the buses goin'." His voice is hoarse but his spirit seems gung ho, pugnacious. Jim gives him a tired half-grin, a word of thanks, and a feeble high sign. Stan wishes Jim a Merry Christmas, wheels on his heels, and departs.

Jim slumps back into his chair. He hears Stan leave the building, the main door clicking shut behind him. *Fight, fight, duty, doors, snowplowing, mop, vac, buses, souls. How does Stan get off on it week after week? Or maybe I've just lost it?* He gives a weary sigh. *But what does it matter? Becki's not coming. I've been trying to make something out of nothing this whole year, and Jodi and Russ are living in the same fuckin' fantasy.*

He pushes back from his desk and yawns to his feet. He hauls on his overcoat, slips on his gloves, grabs his attaché case, and heads out the back door into the storm; he picks up a snow shovel on the way. The wind is stronger. The swirling gusts have sculptured the snowdrifts into wavelike ridges and valleys, like sand on a summer beach. The Mustang is buried. Tossing the briefcase into the backseat, he fires up the engine, then shovels out.

Back to his office. Jim dials Becki's number: no answer. Melting snow drips from his bangs; he wipes away the wetness with the back of his hand. He dials again: still no answer. He agonizes. *Where the fuck is she? Why?—let go, accept it. She doesn't want to be with you.* Jim douses the lights and goes to the windows. He takes a deep breath. He gazes at the wintry scene. A strong gust of wind rattles the storm windows and sends a burst of flakes against the glass. His frustration slowly subsides leaving nothing but a lingering lovesick ache. Finally, he gives a resigned shrug and turns to go. He notices his paisley tie on the desk; he stuffs it into his overcoat pocket then trudges out.

Stan shoveled earlier but the storm has covered the sidewalk again. Jim's Dingo boots sink into the fresh snow—WHITE!

WHITE! Burning white! White burning cold slaps into his face, down his neck. Giggling, snow flying, gray poplin, black gloves.

"No! No! Stop it!" Jim cries happily, his heart bursting with joyous relief. "You just wait!" He feels wet coldness going down inside his shirt. Brown hair, girlish giggling. White breath, short of breath. Arms, gloves, more snow. He feels more snow going down, this time down his back.

Her ambush a smashing success, Becki takes off toward the picnic area, her skirt billowing behind her, along with a plume of giggles and winter breath. Jim pursues plowing through the calf-deep mantle of white. The air is thick with snowflakes and sodium light. She hits a deep drift and falls squealing into the snow. He dives after her grabbing her about the waist but she wiggles loose.

"TA-DAH!" Becki exclaims triumphantly as she ends up on top of Jim like a victorious wrestler. "I gotcha good, didn't I!" Her cheeks and nose are red from the cold, and she's covered with snow. Jim is also freezing and covered with snow, but Becki's haunches, as they straddle him, feel deliciously warm, moreso than anything he's ever felt.

*O God,* he exclaims happily to himself, *she's in Sharon's favorite position.* Rebecca looks down at him, a teasing smirk on her lips, a wad of gum in her mouth; her eyes spark with playful affection. Jim grins so big his face hurts. His fortunes have reversed so fast his heart has whiplash.

"You didn't expect me, I bet," Becki gushes breathlessly. "Joe just dropped me off." As she pants trying to catch her wind, she warms his face with puffs of white breath, Big Red cinnamon breath—and beer breath.

"You're *drunk,*" Jim snickers.

"No, just a little buzzed. I'm not drunk, just happy."

"Happy? So you did miss me this week, huh?"

"No way," Becki teases, giving her sassy contorted face. "I'm always happy on Christmas Eve."

Jim playfully tweaks her nose then pulls her to him. Her chunky softness feels heavy on his chest but oh, so heavenly. Jontue, lilac shampoo, beer breath. He lifts his knee between her legs, not all the way—he doesn't dare—but enough to feel the grip of her cushiony thighs. He inhales her. Pounding, pounding, heart to heart, his soul is flying, *I must've died. I'm in heaven. Oh, dear Becki. She loves me. And her soul is fucking me. O God, my knee's gonna catch fire!* But before it does, Becki jumps up and hurries to the Mustang which is still running in the drive-around. Jim follows, at a fast walk. He pinches himself to see if he's dreaming.

* * *

Rock 107. Big Red gum. The radio blares. Rebecca, her mouth working violently on a fresh wad of gum, hits the driveway at 35 mph. Snow explodes in all directions but they make it to the top fishtailing all the way. Bursting with buoyant delight, she grabs her hobo bag and hops out into the storm. Jim follows with the groceries. The sky is red and low and thick with snow. The oak tree in front waves its frosted arms against the night. Reaching the porch, they stomp their feet and hustle inside. Jim is eager and expectant despite the counsel of his rational mind, *Come on, Jim, don't expect her mood change to lead to anything. Just because she's frisky and friendly again doesn't mean anything has changed.*

The apartment smells of coffee grounds, Christmas tree, and litter box. The Coca-Cola clock is groaning. It's 9:53 p.m. Jim drapes his overcoat on a kitchen chair, his paisley tie hanging out of the pocket. He and Becki are damp from the snow but not wet.

Tossing her gloves on the table, Becki greets Bathsheba then opens one of the new cans of cat food and puts some in her dish. She covers the can with a red-plastic lid and puts it in the fridge. Then executing a happy half-pirouette, she spins over to the sink and washes her hands. Her new skirt, calf-length with accordion pleats, fans outward. Animated, girlish, bounce in her step, ruddy glow in her cheeks. Jim has seen such mood swings before, scores of times. Nonetheless, he can scarcely believe the change in her since they were last in her kitchen, since she snapped at him over the too-strong coffee. Becki quickly puts away the rest of the groceries—more cat food, bread, soda, milk, and a special treat: two quarts of eggnog. "Let's go in my room," she says as she folds the bag and puts it under the sink. Jim loves those words. Becki pops a tape into the stereo. The *Eagles'* "Witchy Woman" begins to play on low volume. The thermometer by the window says 25° outside, 65° inside. Jim cranks the radiator so more heat will come up—the living-room radiator doesn't heat as well as the kitchen one.

Becki sheds her ski jacket and slings it onto the green chair. She fingerfluffs her damp locks then plunks backward onto the sofa, putting her feet on the flea-market coffee table. Melting snow drips off her new boots onto a *Rolling Stone* magazine. Jim takes off his suit coat and sits down to Becki's right on the other side of the pillows, two bed pillows, and her "Garfield" throw-pillow. To his right is the tabletop Christmas tree which is decorated, over-decorated, with lights, ornaments, and little animals. For a minute they just sit there as if in a cinema waiting for the show to start. Jim hopes it's a love story with a happy ending. The radiator pops and hisses. He thinks how it would be nice to unplug the old fireplace but Mrs. Courtney has already said no on that. On the stereo "Witchy Woman" gives way to "Lyin' Eyes."

Finally, Becki gives a sheepish grin and says, "Shanley, take a look under the Christmas tree." He looks and finds a present: thick, cylindrical, about a foot long, wrapped in red paper, a green bow on each end. The wrapping paper has pictures of Santa Claus on it. He picks it up; it reads: TO SHANLEY ... FROM BECKI.

"Ah, let's see," he kids her. "It feels like two rolls of toilet paper."

"Get outa here," she snickers. "Just open it."

Jim unwraps the Santa Claus paper. Inside are layers of tissue wrapping. "It *is* toilet paper," he teases. Bathsheba hears the rustling paper and shoots in from the kitchen to check it out. Jim wads the red paper and throws it on the floor. The cat attacks the crinkly paper then goes crazy on the ribbons.

"You probably won't like 'em," Becki says apprehensively. Inside the tissue paper is a clear zippered case. Inside the case are tan bedroom slippers. Jim unzips the case and takes them out. Real leather. The smell reminds him of his softball glove. Quickly removing his Dingo boots, he puts on the slippers and prances about the room as Bathsheba escapes to the back of the green chair. Becki blushes self-consciously, but happily. "Come on, Shanley; you make such a big deal out of opening presents and stuff."

While Jim prances, Becki looks on with shy but glad eyes, her cupid lips slightly parted in an embarrassed but sweetly endearing smile. Becki, Becki. Blushing, smiling, pink wad of gum. Crooked teeth, disheveled bangs, happy blue eyes. Jim exults. *O God, I love her!* he exclaims in his heart. *She's such a child, but I love her, I love her! This is the best Christmas ever.* His overflowing heart sweeps him back to the sofa. He folds Becki into his arms and holds her with all his strength, all his being. "I love you, Becki Lea," he whispers tenderly. "I love you forever. I just want to be with you, no matter what we do, no matter what we call it." Becki does not reply but hugs him back placing her head on his shoulder.

Bliss, bliss, moment of bliss—but then she wiggles playfully away. "Now you're gonna get it," Jim declares with a rollicking laugh. He grabs her and tickles her ribs until she falls squealing and squirming onto the pillows. Retaliation. Without warning, she cuts a rippling fart. This makes her giggle so hard that she turns redder than the Santa Claus paper. Her gum falls out onto the floor.

"Well, that's real Christmasy," he teases.

"Serves you right," Becki retorts, looking up through tears of laughter. Finally, she sobers, sits up, and looks for her gum. Feeling under the couch, she finds it stuck to a dust bunny. "Yech," she says as she wraps the gum et al in a scrap of the tissue wrapping.

The room now seems warm. Becki rolls her argyle sweater-vest up over her head and throws it on the green chair. Jim likewise sheds his suit vest. "Jimmy, can you get some eggnog?" she asks, pushing her hair back. "I'm too weak from laughing."

To the kitchen. He gets two of Becki's blue Kmart mugs down from the cupboard. While he's pouring, Becki closes her door and says, "Don't come in 'til I say."

Jim looks curiously at the closed door and sips from his mug. Rich, cold, smooth, spicy. The eggnog tastes sort of like melted ice cream. He goes over and peers out the east-facing window into the stormy night. The snow-fogged lights of the old mill town sprawl in the distance like the coals of a dying campfire.

"You can come in now," Becki announces.

"Okeydoke," Jim says. The mood in her room is romantic, enchanting, enticing. "Desperado" plays on the stereo. The ceiling light is off and the dresser lamp, the one with the parchment shade and pump-handle switch, casts a soft honey-yellow glow over the room. Becki sits on the couch as before, but she's now wearing a coy grin, along with Jim's sapphire pendant and matching earrings.

Jim hands her a mug and sits down. "Whereyuh been hiding those?" he kids.

She playfully sticks out her lower lip giving an exaggerated pouty face. "I was pissed before, and I had every right to be." She swigs her eggnog; it leaves a creamy mustache on her upper lip. She licks it off, curling her tongue sensually.

Despite the counsel of his rational mind, Jim's loins lurch with lust. Becki's carnal ripeness always turns him on but especially after two weeks of celibacy. Except for one soapy masturbation in the shower—Tuesday evening after flirting with Sharon on the way back from Nashua—he's had no sexual release for two weeks. *Oh, I want to suck her sweet lips, and tongue,* he sighs to himself.

But he doesn't. Instead, he sips his eggnog and says, "So that's why you took off with Joe and Brenda?"

Becki hops up, sashays over to turn the *Eagles* tape. She replies over her shoulder, "Partly, but I don't like potluck suppers anyhow. They're boring, like super dull. Everyone walks around with phony grins saying 'hi' and 'how are you?' and horny men are always undressing me with their eyes. Now if they were young and cute, I might've stayed." She gives a coquettish laugh. "But it's always the older married guys, or some dorky nerd with thick glasses. Besides, the church was so crowded tonight with the wedding, and Juanita's such a priss. She thinks she's Princess

Diana, but she's really nothing, and her whole family smells like the Fitch Road Projects. You know how those moldy hallways smell ... sorta stinky sweet like cheap cologne? It's disgusting. It's the lowest ones that come here, you know? At least, Manny 'n Maria, they have a little class."

She gives a saucy toss of her head then saunters back to the sofa and sits down. Assuming her previous relaxed posture, she quietly sips her eggnog as "One of These Nights," the first song on side two, plays on the stereo. The lyrics speak of demons and desires, and fever and turning on. Becki looks down shyly into her mug; her cheeks pulse warm as if she's fantasizing about her own demons. Jim gives her a knowing smirk. She responds with dimples and a revealing grin. "Cut it out, Shanley," she gushes. "You think you know so much about me."

"Well, maybe I do?" he flirts, pushing his mug at her playfully. "Maybe I can read your mind?"

"Not a chance. If you could, you wouldn't be so calm, mister." Becki gives him a wanton roll of her eyes.

*What an opening,* Jim declares to himself. *She wants to flirt and get prurient. Maybe this is the night?* The thought parches his throat, overwhelming his psyche as direct sunlight overwhelms the eyes. He wets his throat with a swig of eggnog. "So you went to Bergson's?" he asks, retreating to safer ground.

"Yep, we had burgers and hot pumpkin pie. Then we sipped Michelobs and listened to tunes in Joe's car, and the snow was coming down. Joe's radical, even more than me, but I like what he has to say, and so does Brenda."

"Brenda's only fifteen, you know?"

"So?"

"Well, did she drink too?"

Becki sips slowly from her mug, again leaving a mustache, but this time she ignores it. "No, Brenda was mainly teasing Joe and kinda snuggling close to him. She's sweet on him, you know. Now that would stir some hot fuckin' gossip if it got out, even more than Tony 'n Jodi. Especially since Brenda's a minor and Joe's almost twice her age."

"Well, I'm almost twice your age?" Jim replies boldly.

Becki gives her scrunchy-faced grimace then a smirk. "So, we're not lovers or anything?" But Jim immediately knows her denial is a tease rather than a pious closed-door refutation like she professes when she's in a prudish mood, like in the car last week, or during their many love-hate blowouts since October.

"Yeh, I've noticed," he plays along. "I guess I'm stuck being a father figure."

"Fuck that too!" she exclaims—the freer Becki gets, the more she says "fuck." "I hate that father-figure bullshit. Mom always says, 'Jimmy's like a *father.*' Fuck that. I've already got two dads. Besides, I hate labels." She sips her eggnog. She gives a chuckling laugh. She wipes her mouth with the back of her hand.

"What's so funny?" Jim asks.

"Oh, nothing. I'm just thinking about some bigger gossip that's goin' around."

Jim drinks from his mug then gestures with it. "Like what? Whoyuh thinking about?"

Becki blushes. "I'm not saying?"

Jim knows she means *them.* He tries to make her admit it but she isn't about to. So after a bit of bantering, he moves back to Joe and Brenda, "So Brenda, she just watched you guys drinking?"

"Well, maybe she took a few sips, but that's all—and no pot."

"*Pot?* You had marijuana?" Jim pretends to be alarmed. But in truth he doesn't care, not on this night; if pot will help get her panties off, he hopes she did smoke it.

Becki laughs teasingly then dimples into a toothy grin. "Don't have a fuckin' fit, Jimmy. It wasn't me; it was Joe. He just smoked a couple of J's. I'm giving up weed myself. And I can't drink a lot of beer 'cause it makes me pee all the time." She sobers a bit but a sporty pink glow remains on her cheeks. "But I like how Joe gets radical about music and God when he's stoned—oh, maybe I did take a hit or two. But it was nothing."

"That sounds more like you, Becki Lea," Jim kids. "I can't imagine you turning down a free joint."

Becki's blush deepens but she doesn't reply.

The *Eagles* tape plays on. Otherwise, quietness, as they finish their eggnogs. Becki places her empty mug on the coffee table then rests her head on the back of the couch. She stares across the room as if watching TV. She fiddles with her shirttail, rolling it, unrolling it; it came out when Jim tickled her. Clasping his hands behind his head, he too relaxes back into the sofa. He places his stocking feet on the coffee table next to Becki's boots. His socks are white cotton and thick. That's why he likes Dingo boots. If he wears his wing tips, he has to wear dark dress socks, the thin kind, and he much prefers the thick white athletic kind.

Rebecca gazes wide-eyed across the room. Jim gazes at Rebecca. Cute, cherubic, fair-skinned. Chunky, hippish, nubile. She has such a "farm girl" look, somehow horny and wholesome at the same time. Short, common, blemished. She could pass for a German peasant girl in a WWII newsreel. Childlike, fallow, yet yearning for seed, ready to make babies, many babies. Despite her fluffing efforts, her hair remains a wind-tossed thicket of tangled locks and feathery tufts. It has taken on the toasty chocolate color it assumes each winter; her highlights are darker: less honey, more maple. Her face is windburned, raw, and blotchy, her lips chapped. Except for the rosy glow on her cheeks, her complexion is wintry-pale and dominated by violets and grays. The tawny sun-tones of summer have faded. Her freckles are likewise faint.

Becki changes with the seasons just like the trees, and Jim knows her changes so well. To him, her contrasts are inexhaustible. He could paint her face, her body, her moods, every month, every week, and each painting would be a masterpiece of heart and Eros, of line and hue and heft and shape, of shadow and light and subtle blending, all Becki, but all different—like Claude Monet and his many *Grainstacks*.

Her gazing blue eyes seem poignant, full of soul, yet the sparkle in them seems mirthful, mischievous, seductive. She looks dreamy-faced, a bit trancy, and it's more than beer or pot—at least, Jim fantasizes that it is, *Maybe she has no intention of going past flirting with me, but I know that look, that horny glow. I've seen it on her a dozen times in ten months, and I see it all the time with Sharon, and Angela and Sylvia ... but I never see it on Leslie or Mary LeBlanc. Perhaps their pussies have dried up just as juicy plums dehydrate into shriveled prunes? Women, sex, I can't figure it. I just know I don't want a dry crusty cunt. I want a pussy that's hot, buttery, and swollen with want—sin, sin.* Jim's thoughts shift abruptly as his conscience cuts in. *This is sin and it's going nowhere. You shouldn't be here this late. You shouldn't be here at all.*

The *Eagles* tape ends. Becki puts her mug on the coffee table and picks up the *TV Guide*. Sudden sinking. Jim fears her coquettish mood is over, that she doesn't want to flirt anymore, even on the safe side of eros. But worse, he's afraid her cold mood is returning. The warning from his conscience reinforces this fear, as if God is now ready to teach him the lesson he failed to learn earlier. He sits forward. He stretches. He sighs to remind Becki of his presence. No response. A chilly gust sweeps into his gut snuffing out his joy.

Jim's Becki-emotions have no roots but blow back and forth across his field of dreams like tumbleweed on shifting winds. *Oh fuck, her mood is changing. Sex always gets in the way. She always knows when I'm lusting. O God, why have these feelings if we can't—but it'll never happen, even if Jodi's right? Becki may like to flirt and get naughty, but she'll never go all the way with me. Besides, God won't allow it. It is sin. Who am I kidding?* Guilt, shame, self-rejection. Jim is discouraged, ready to leave.

Then a miracle—or so he thinks. "Do you like my new riding

boots?" Rebecca asks. "I got 'em from Papa Chavin." Jim starts to reply, but before he can, she snatches the pillows from between them, shifts on the sofa, and puts her boots on his lap. "Help me, Jimmy. Help me get them off." Jim's sinking heart bucks, jolts, then races upward like a fast elevator. The smell of new leather fills his nostrils. He grabs her boot under the heel and pulls it off as she lifts her leg, then the other. Under the boots she has gray kneesocks. Becki prefers kneesocks to pantyhose, even in cold weather.

She relaxes back into the pillows, which are now behind her, and to Jim's surprise, she leaves her stocking feet on his lap. Her knees are lifted and slightly spread, but her billowy skirt covers her legs like a wine-colored tablecloth. The warm pleated fabric looks something like flannel. Jim doesn't know what to do or say. He just knows her feet are scorching his thighs. But Becki solves the problem: "Oh, Shanley, do give me a foot massage. I need my feet rubbed after wearing my new boots—but no tickling."

Jim's face heats; his throat contracts. This is the first time she's ever offered her body to be caressed. He feels hesitant, awkward, nervous, as if Jesus and Alison and Logan and Sharon are all in the room. Yet it feels so good to fondle her girlish feet—like petting a pair of cuddly kittens—that his heart quickly settles into a sweet place: *I'm fondling her and she likes it. I feel her loving me ... loving my touch. She loves me. She wants me. O God, I feel it.*

Eros unplugs Jim's conscience and sends hot blood into his penis. He feels it growing against his leg. "You like having your feet rubbed?" he asks Becki, his voice gentle yet seductive.

"Oh *yeah;* I like it," she purrs. "Do my toes and my instep. Yeah, right there." Her feet are adorable, small and slender, and so soft in her socks, yet they're a bit damp and stinky. Her foot odor is familiar to Jim, like how her sneakers smell, yet it's tempered some by the leathery odor of her new boots. Becki leans back further into the pillows, half-sitting, half-lying down. She talks for a bit about her trip to New Bedford. Her voice is cozy, almost drowsy. The snowstorm moans about the house. Bathsheba sleeps on the green chair. Love, wind, snow, cozy warmth, tender touching, tender talking. Five minutes, six, then quiet. Becki's face glows soft and warm in the honey-amber light. She watches Jim with lazy liquid eyes. A sleepy-cat smile rests on her lips.

Now it comes, an erotic spell. It descends over them as if they're falling into a wet dream. Wiggling her toes within his grip, Becki begins to play footsies with his hands pushing her big toe into his open grip as if she's kissing and probing his mouth with her tongue. He in turn strokes her big toe as if it's a penis. Finally, she breaks the silence with a question, "Do you like my legs, Jimmy?"

"They feel fine to me," Jim replies as he moves up and caresses her stocking-covered calves, her cheerleader calves, firmly muscled, nubily curved, gracefully tapering to small ankles—not cushiony soft like most of her body.

"No, not down there, up here," Becki says, pulling her skirt back over her lifted knees and bunching the fabric in her crotch. Jim's heart rears. He gulps at the sight. Thighs, thighs, cushiony thighs. Thighs, thighs, naked thighs. Naked ivory-vanilla flesh with splashes of pink and violet, all tinted honey-yellow by the lamp. Full, plumpish, baby-fattish: her upper legs are much like Sharon's, just shorter and more youthful. Becki's adolescent flab still has that soft, smooth, postpubescent texture, while the years have given Sharon doughy wrinkles and waves. Jim loves what he sees, especially Rebecca's relaxed adductors: spongy rolls of fish-white flesh—whiter than the rest—that hang a bit with gravity, a delicious bit. On the left one, just outside her bunched skirt, is a dark dime-sized birthmark. She's far from a *Playboy* centerfold, yet her chunkish body turns Jim on more than any Barbie Doll cover girl.

"So you like 'em or what?" Becki asks, giving Jim a bold smirk. "You never said last summer when I got that rash?" Her eyes are no longer lazy, but dancing, and devilish.

"I-I, yeh, I like 'em," Jim stammers. "Better than ever." Becki begins to slowly open and close her knees. Jim is in disbelief; it has to be a dream. His prick is so hard that it's lifting his suit pants off his leg. Becki's feet are still propped on his thigh, her toes less than an inch from his swelling malehood. He fears-hopes that she'll touch it. He can't get enough. His eyes run again and again from her knees down her inner thighs until they disappear under her bunched skirt. *O God, Becki,* he cries silently. *Let me see your panties.*

God hears his prayer, or Becki, or both. Giving a naughty-girl grin, she slowly lifts her skirt and spreads her legs wider until her cotton-veiled crotch looms large and damp: a pale-blue moon between her marshmallowy thighs.

*O God!* Jim exclaims in his soul. *Her crotch is so big, like the door to a house. It's amazing how big girls are between their legs, and you never notice 'til they spread them.*

Wider, wider. Becki spreads still wider, pushing her knee into the back of the sofa, the other out over the coffee table, until Jim can see the elastic on each side of her panty crotch along with the tawny-pink junctures of her groin which are shadowy and goosefleshy, like hairless armpits. Cutely folded underneath her crotch are two white cushions of gluteal flesh that bulge out of her underpants. Intimate odors waft up. Jim's heart pounds in his penis. He longs to probe with his finger, but before he can gather the courage, she suddenly hops up and does her happy-girl quickstep, toward the kitchen. Halfway there she wheels around and teases him, "You like looking at me, don'tcha? Bet you'd like for me to pull 'em off? Well, I'm not gonna. I may give you a quick peek at my panties, but that's *all* I'm showing." Becki then pads through the kitchen to the bathroom—wiggling her hips coquettishly as she goes.

Jim reaches into his trousers and shifts his erection to give it more room. His head spins, *O Jesus, I'm gonna come in my pants. Is she ever a prick-teasing flirt. I missed my chance. But it's like I couldn't move. I have no guts. But how does she do it? Sharon would've never got up without firing her gun. She would've pulled my hand into her panties.*

Upon her return, Becki reassumes her earlier position on the sofa, her feet propped on the coffee table. Taking opportunity, Bathsheba hops off the green chair onto her lap. Becki strokes the cat. Jim sighs, resigning himself to the probability that their sexual flirting is over—unconsummated as usual, though they went farther than they've ever gone—but a hint of a smirk flitting about Becki's mouth suggests otherwise. Jim's nose itches; he rubs it which starts a cycle of short gasping snorts followed by a hard sneeze.

"I won't say what *that* reminds me of," Becki teases, reacting quickly to the sneeze with a shot of prurient wit. A rush of pink stains her cheeks. Her blue eyes flash with naughty intent. "Looks like you're in a bad way, Reverend?"

"What makes you think that, young lady?"

Becki gives a sassy grin but does not look up from the cat. "Well, it's kind of obvious, unless you have a fuckin' pickle in your pocket. You're not exactly fleeing youthful lusts, are you, Reverend? Guess looking under my skirt was too much for you, huh? Especially since my goodies are off-limits to you?"

Becki looks up at Jim, her eyes wide and wanton. A euphoric rush sweeps through him like a drug. She must feel it too because her eyes flash excitedly as if she's also erect—female-style—in her panties. She doesn't have a pickle in her "pocket" either, but she crosses her legs under Bathsheba as if she needs one. Her randy spirit reminds Jim of Sharon's uninhibited horniness during his risqué stories—and Sharon never escapes such moods except through orgasm; the thought takes his breath.

"You think you're such a hot ticket," Jim banters. "Maybe I'm thinking about a mature woman ... who's experienced and knows how to satisfy a man?"

"You mean like Sharon?" Becki replies.

"That's right, and maybe a few others."

"Yeah, like Angela. I see you looking at her at school. I bet you'd like to ball her in your office, right on your recliner. But you don't have the guts. I know you, Shanley ... better than anyone."

"Least she's not a kid like you, Becki Lea. I'd have to take you away for a month, just to teach you how to come with a man."

"Ha, that's a laugh," she brags. "I'd take you places Sharon never took you." Eros sparking in her eyes, Becki stokes the fire. "She may be good, but I'd be the *best* you ever had. Too bad you're in the wrong generation. I don't want no middle-aged pecker that hangs at nine o'clock. I want a young cock, a high-noon man."

"You don't want me, huh? You'd have trouble convincing a jury, young lady. You're not exactly Mother Theresa tonight?"

"Flirting and getting buzzed on sexy talk is one thing, but doin' is another. I like to fool around and get you going, Shanley, but if I really came on to you, you'd never live through it." Jim shudders at the thought. Becki speaks in a bantering timbre but a husky and throaty undertone tells him that her words are arousing her as much as him. "I know you so well, Jimmy. You been thinking naughty thoughts about me all week, I betcha?"

"Well, what about you, Miss Chastity?" Jim replies sassily. "What's on your mind? A cold shower then prayer and Bible study, followed by a nice celibate dream?"

Becki gives a proud smirk and a roll of her eyes. "So what's wrong with a celibate dream? I can live without it, you know? I don't let sex rule me ... like guys do. I know how to draw the line. I may like to fantasize and get horny—after all I'm a normal healthy girl—but I don't get into a heated panic. I have self-control. I'm not like *you,* Jimmy. I know how to hold back my demons."

"So you take Logan seriously when he screams against—"

"Are you kidding?" Becki replies, cutting Jim off. "Knowing it's a sin, that's what gets me going. Resisting temptation—oh, that gets me *wicked* high. But if I give in quick like a guy—whoosh, it's over."

*I can't believe this conversation,* Jim declares to himself. *I never saw her this wild and prurient. This has to be a wet dream.* But he has no desire to wake up. His conscience is not only unplugged but it's banished to the basement of his psyche. "So you think resisting is better than the 'whoosh'?" he asks Becki.

Becki grins lustfully, her blush deepening. "What d'*you* think?"

The grin together with a flare of desire in her eyes tells Jim all he needs to know. "Well, why fight it then?" he asks. "Women can go more than once—at least, Sharon does."

"No *shit,*" Becki mocks, shaking her head with pretended indignation. "I *am* past puberty, you know? I know how to get there when it's time ... and as many times as necessary, like four times once."

"Sounds like quite a fantasy, young lady. Was I in it?" Jim doesn't dare rest his hand on his lap; one touch and his penis will explode.

Becki gives a sassy toss of her head then quips, "Get real, Shanley, I don't fantasize about *old* guys. Besides, it wasn't a fantasy. It was Manny."

"I thought you said—"

"You said it, Jimmy, not me."

"You mean you—"

"That's right. I lost my cherry summer before last when I was eighteen. Does that shock you, Shanley?" Becki's expression is proud and unspeakably provocative.

"Nawh, it's no fuckin' surprise," Jim replies. "After being with you this year, I'm shocked you made it *that* far."

Normally, the thought of Becki fucking Manny would torment Jim, but not on this night. If her Manny-memories will help get her clothes off, then he's glad she did fuck him. "So how'd it happen?" he asks. "I thought you had self-control?"

"I'm not saying," Becki flirts. "Besides, you can't handle it."

"*Me?* You're the one I'm worried about. You certainly don't sound like a sweet young missionary?"

"Well, I guess you don't know much about sweet young missionaries, d'yuh?"

Jim crosses his legs to vary the position of his hard-on. He needs to take a piss but he's not about to move lest he break the prurient mood. "So how long were you and Manny together?"

"Hardly at all," Becki replies, smirking. She can't help but give a few details. "It was June. I had just graduated. Manny was just a friend, just Maria's big brother. But then I went with him to his alumni dance, and two days later he took me to the beach cabin without Maria, and that changed everything—and *how*. But it just lasted a few weeks, maybe a month, then he left for the fuckin' Air Force." She gives a dreamy look of remembered pleasure that tells Jim she wishes it had gone on longer.

"And that was your only love affair?" Jim asks.

"That was it. He wrote a few times but then the letters stopped. Maria said he had a girlfriend near his base in Ohio. I didn't get on with any other guys. Besides, we were coming back."

"Well, I guess God was watching over you."

Becki snorts then quips, "Yeah, I'm still *thank*ing him."

"Your mom would kill you if she knew. Or did she find out?"

"No way. You're the only one I ever told except Maria. I told

Maria all about it. But even if Mom finds out, she has no right to criticize. Amelia said that Mom was gettin' laid in tenth grade. And like I toldjuh, she picked up Ed at a bar."

The conversation rapidly cools then gives way to silence. Becki directs her attention to Bathsheba as the cat stands up and stretches in her lap. Jim hears sleet pinging against the storm windows; the snow is mixing. Becki's flushed complexion slowly returns to normal. His hard-on reluctantly softens. *O God, I can't believe this night,* he cries out in his soul. *So good but so frustrating. I can't believe she pulled up her dress ... and I never saw her go this far into naughty talk. She loves the panty-soaking rush of flirting on the edge, but she'll never make the first move. I should've grabbed her and kissed her. But it's too late now. Her mood is swinging the other way. It always ends like this. Now, I'll have to go home and get my rocks off by myself. Solitary sex, what a bummer. I'll be with Sharon tomorrow night, but I can't hold this for 24 hours. I got a bad case of blue balls—like time bombs.... But all things considered, I guess this night is ending much better than it started.*

Jim, now free to take a leak without missing anything, heads for the bathroom. Bathsheba chases him attacking his white socks. He pours some Friskies into her dry dish, then goes into the bathroom where he takes his usual position at the side of the toilet.

His dick is limp but still long. He likes his penis best when it hangs semisoft after an erection. It still isn't big, maybe average, but it feels big in his hand since much of the time it stays thumby small and timid-looking. For a moment nothing comes out. The eye of his penis burns like cum is going to shoot out but the piss wins and a hot yellow stream spurts forth tinkling into the john. When Jim is horny and loaded, pissing is like a mini-orgasm, but more of a tease than a—"Be sure and shake it good, Reverend," comes a soft but curious voice through the door.

SHOCK! SHOCK! Then the knob, then the door. Pink shirt, purple skirt, gray kneesocks, girlish hands on canted hips. Ruddy cheeks, silly grin, cute disheveled bangs. Large curious eyes, blue, blue, and staring. FLASH! FLASH! Hot, cold, pounding fever! No. No. Yes! Yes! Yes! Time ends, space explodes!

Jim hears angels singing. He sees the face of Lucifer. His mind closes down. His thoughts swirl into a vortex, draining out of his head into his body then into his prick, where he pisses them out into the toilet. He pisses. Becki stares. The smell of urine wafts up. The Coca-Cola clock groans. Bathsheba crunches her Friskies. A hundred years later—or so it seems—as he finishes peeing, his brain reboots itself and he regains a measure of composure.

"Oh, it's cute, Jimmy," Becki speaks first. "I wanna touch it."

She sounds like a teenybopper with a bad case of penis-fascination.

"Suit yourself, gal," Jim flirts, still in disbelief over the abrupt turn of events. He gives her a blushing grin then lets go of his prick allowing it to dangle freely out the fly of his suit pants.

Becki hesitates, a brief look of panic coming over her face. She seems eager yet nervous at the same time. She advances timidly, like a child wading through water. She takes his penis in her girlish hand; she cups it gently as if it's a pet bird. Her touch sends a hot current through Jim's body. An awful expectancy grips his soul. He feels excited to the point of being terrified, but his penis is too overwhelmed to lift with his hopes.

Becki lets go and reaches into her gray toilette kit on the back of the toilet. "I got something for it," she explains.

*Does she want to play doctor or does she want to fuck?* Jim as) s himself. *Even with my dick in her hand, she's still teasing and bantering.* She rummages among her toilette articles a few seconds then pulls out a blue foil packet, a Trojan condom. "Where'd you get that?" he asks as hot blood heats his face.

"Amelia gave 'em to me," Becki replies, touting her sex appeal. "Guys are always checking me out, you know? Amelia says a girl should keep a few skins for *un*expected pleasures, especially these days." Giving a sexy grin that's also proud, she rips open the foil packet then unfurls the condom filling the bathroom with that raw latex smell unique to rubbers. "*Yech;* these things are stinky and greasy."

Whatever her intention, Becki wastes no time. She strokes the underside of Jim's prick until it grows to full erection over the toilet. *O Lord, no doctor ever touched me like this,* he exclaims to himself. She then slips the rubber over his swollen glans and rolls it down his shaft, like a pro.

Rebecca steps back like an artist admiring her work. "Oh, Jimmy, you have a *nice* dick. Not the biggest ... but not bad for a *pas*tor." A breathy shortness in her voice tells Jim that her adolescent silliness has given way to sober adult lust, that the animal desire aroused during their prurient conversation has reawakened and must be satisfied—despite her claims of being able to "live without it." Her face becomes determined; her pupils dilate. She can't take her eyes off his erection. All at once, she peels the rubber off his penis like she's pulling a sock off her foot. "We don't need it, not really. I just got over my period on Thursday."

Jim's heart jolts and jolts, *O Lord, this is it. She's serious. I see it in her eyes. She's got that crazy melting look just like Sharon gets when she's ready to fuck. I can't stand up.* He quickly lowers the lid and sits down on the toilet facing Rebecca. He unbuckles his pants and opens the fly of his underpants as wide as it will go. The full six inches of his turgid manhood rises up out of his jockey briefs like a Boeing 727 lifting off the runway. His tight overfull testicles also escape along with several shocks of hazel-brown pubic hair.

Becki, now all business and all woman, tosses the rubber into the waste basket. "I can't wait *any* longer," she declares.

Finally after ten months, their lips meet. She screws her aggressive mouth onto Jim's. Bold, reckless, savage, she probes deep and hard with her phallic tongue. Beer, gum, eggnog: she tastes sweet. Jim caresses her crooked teeth with his own tongue. Withdrawing, she nibble-bites his lip, so hard he fears he's bleeding. Then she kisses him again, pushing her tongue into him, into him.

Jim quivers with anticipation, *O Jesus, does she ever want it!*

Breaking for air, Becki returns her attention to Jim's cock. Her pupils are big, fully dilated: a feral cat on the prowl. Eyes like a cat, but filled with lightning, with starbursts of lust. She fondles him sensually—girlish fingers, womanly touch.

"Oh, *Shan*ley," she pants, her voice a trancy whisper. "I love how a guy's dick feels when it's hard, like how you get a thick blue vein and pimply bumps like a hot cucumber. It fuckin' turns me *on,* I tellyuh. And on the end it's so big and round like a purple mushroom. I wish I could keep it here under my pillow—oh fuck, am I ever sinning in my mind." Becki dances her fingers down his thick shaft then combs them through his pubic hair. Finally, she fondles his balls.

"I want you, honey," Jim exclaims breathlessly, his feelings erupting. "I do. I do. I love you *so!*"

Grabbing her boldly by the shoulders, he pulls her to him and gives her another passionate kiss. Becki makes a mewing sound that becomes a moan; she gives her whole body to the kiss—too much. She straightens up and quickly unbuttons her shirt; her hands tremble. Then she reaches around and unsnaps her brassiere. She leaves her shirt on, but lifts her loose bra cups allowing her breasts to roll free underneath them.

"Oh, Becki Lea, they're *beautiful,*" Jim sighs as he gazes upon her twin cupfuls of mammary flesh, white, high-perched, and proud—youthful tits like you'd see in the girls' locker room after tenth-grade gym class. Though higher and a tad smaller, they're shaped like Sharon's, not hemispherical or conical but in between, like a pair of gibbous moons. And they have just enough heft to hang deliciously when she leans forward. Needless to say, Jim loves them immediately. Her dusky-pink areolas are goose-bumpy with little glands and her swelling nipples are raspberry red—red with hot blood.

Becki sighs deeply as if ready to swoon. "O *Jesus,* I feel my heart beating in my breasts, in the tips." She leans forward resting her weight on the sink and the back of the toilet; her tits fall forward toward Jim. Her soft midriff bulges cutely over her skirt waist. Her disheveled brunette hair shrouds her head: a wanton aura. Her open shirt hangs like pink side-curtains.

Becki gazes hungrily at Jim; their eyes lock. They breathe in unison. Bolts of desire shoot from Jim's brain, through his body, up his penis—then back again.

Becki, Becki, fertile Becki: nubile, ripe, ready to nourish. She purses her lips then wets them sensually with her tongue. Her face seems misty, softly indistinct, as if the bathroom is filled with dreamy blue fog—azure blue, like her eyes. Blue, blue, and Jontue, and latex, and bathroom smells, and hot sugared-out breath. The moment is transcendent and glorious as with the Love Goddess, yet it's naughty and nasty and earthy and erotic—but with no inhibition or guilt. In fact, the risqué naughtiness and sense of sinful temptation make the moment brazen and venturous beyond words.

Jim runs his finger around Becki's areolas teasing her aroused nipples. Swelling raspberries: they bud and bud, growing before his eyes. *Oh, look at that! Is she ever horny! She wants to fuck. Look at them swelling. O Jesus, I'm in heaven!*

More sighs and mewing sounds. Becki's sex demons cry for release. She steps over by the tub. She pulls up her skirt, and with a wiggle of her haunches, pushes her panties over her hips and down her legs until they fall like a wrinkled cloth onto her stocking feet. But she keeps her skirt on, as if she wants to hide her cunt a bit longer to tease and tantalize, to make it more enticing.

*I'm dreaming; I'm dreaming,* Jim raves to himself. *Now she's gonna sit on my lap—O glory, I can't wait.*

Becki steps out of her underpants then advances toward him, slowly but aggressively. She utters a guttural cry somewhere between a grunt and a growl. Blue, blue, sky-blue and staring. She devours Jim with her wild staring eyes—*RRRRRRING!*

*What the hell!* Jim cries out in his thoughts. *O GOD! NOT THE PHONE! NO!*

*RRRRRRING!*

Becki continues her bold advance as if ignoring the phone. *RRRRRRING!* The phone screams for attention.

"Oh fuck!" Becki curses, now fighting the interruption.

*RRRRRRING!*—FLASH! FLASH! OH NO! White! White! Becki's face blanches as if she just plunged off a high dive into ice water.

*NO! NO!* Jim screams in his heart. *BECKI, NO!*

But it's too late. She hustles into her room to answer, as if the phone is her conscience calling.

Electric sparks, breaking glass, darkness, darkness. The erotic spell, like a crystal chandelier crashing down onto a dance floor, shatters into a million pieces of broken desire. Jim's feelings spin out of control as self-disgust kills his passion. He can't find the horizon. His penis stalls and shudders then flops belly-down onto the runway. Disappointment explodes in his brain. Shame, shame. He inhales guilt and shame, as a soul-crushing miasma floods the apartment like foul-smelling smoke from a just-doused fire.

"That's great, Mom; who else?"—Jim hears Becki talking sweetly to her mom with the television going. Sick, sinful, caught with Becki—he feels disgraced, as if Alison has walked in on them. He hates himself, and Alison: *Fuckin' Alison, she always calls after eleven, to get the lower rates. She's such a miserly bitch.*

A drop of pre-cum oozes like a tear out the eye of Jim's deflating penis as if to mock his and Becki's unconsummated lovemaking—as if to sum up without words their ten months together. He takes a piece of toilet paper and wipes it off with a disgusted swipe as if trying to clean the scum off his soul. He wads the toilet paper into a ball. His pants still down to his ankles, he shivers amid the chilly bathroom smells. He feels filthy, foul, defeated, nauseated. *I rot, I stink! I hate my fuckin' cock! I'm putrid! I hate my sex drive! I have no control. It always turns heaven into hell.*

But Becki's Merry Christmas voice, coming in from her room, sounds relaxed, cheerful, very matter-of-fact, and sexually inert as if she's never lusted or gotten off in her life: "Oh, nothing, Mom, just watching the news.... Yeah.... Oh, we just got back from church.... Jimmy.... Yeah, he brought me home.... No, it's snowing wicked hard up here. Oh, about four this afternoon.... Yeah.... No.... No, it's probably at the post office. I got one of those yellow things. Yeah.... Amelia.... Fine.... Yeah, with Dad, and we went to the Cape one day, and I went shopping with Oma and Amelia.... No, that was Grandma Chavin. No.... I know. Yeah, lots of stuff.... Well, a shirt and a skirt and riding boots.... No, from Papa—"

Tuning Becki out, Jim slips his despicable little penis back into his shorts and hoists himself up from his rose-colored throne of near-sex, which has now become a judgment seat. He lifts the toilet lid and tosses the wad of toilet paper into the john. He hauls up his suit pants and zips up then reaches into the back and flushes.

When he turns around, he spies Rebecca's panties still on the floor by the tub. A flimsy handful of faded blue cotton and overstretched elastic, they form a twisted figure eight on the rose-colored rug.

An X-rated impulse pops into Jim's depraved will: *I may be scummy, but I'm never too scummy to go lower.* He despises himself. Nonetheless, after closing the door, he picks up the panties: plain full-size briefs, the modest kind that cover the belly-button. They seem suddenly huge in his hands, like an unfurled flag, much bigger than the skimpy double-doughnut of cloth that lay on the rose-colored rug. He examines them as if handling the Holy Grail. The crotch is damp, her panty liner soaked.

*Oh, was she ever horny,* he laments to himself. *I bet we'll never get this close again.*

Jim wraps the panty shield in toilet paper and tosses it in the trash, but he wads the panties in his hand. He then opens the bathroom door and pads furtively over to the kitchen table where he shoves them into the pocket of his overcoat—burying them under his paisley tie.

After this obscene act, he slips quietly into Becki's room where she's still talking to her mom. Hips canted and facing the TV, she stands in front of the green chair. Jim knows Becki-the-lover is long gone and Becki-the-saint will blame him for their near-fuck, and at the moment his guilt-ridden conscience tells him that he deserves the blame.

Becki's pink shirt is neatly retucked and rebuttoned. She looks calm, collected, and pure: as pure as the snow falling outside. As she talks, she twists the coiled phone cord around her forefinger. The telephone itself is half buried in the pile of clothes on the green chair. On the TV, Barry Burbank, the Channel 4 weatherman, is explaining why the snow has changed to rain in Boston.

Suddenly, Becki hands Jim the phone. "Mom wants to talk to you," she explains curtly without eye contact. She then plops onto the sofa, grabs the TV remote, and dits through the channels.

*Alison, Alison,* Jim says guiltily to himself before putting the phone to his ear. *How can I talk to you after leading your daughter to the edge of fornication?*

He doesn't want to hear her bubbly God-is-great missionary voice; he feels shitty enough already. But he has no strength to refuse, so he puts his brain on autopilot and says, "Hello."

"Merry *Christ*mas, Jimmy," Alison chirps. "I hear you've got a lot of snow?"

"About a foot," Jim replies perfunctorily. "But I'm sure it's hot down there?"

"Yep, it's in the 80s every day," she affirms. "You and Sharon should come down. We have beach weather all year. I do miss the snow sometimes, especially at Christmas ... but it's *so* important for us to be here. The Lord is blessing us so much, Jimmy. We'll be starting our own school next year. Ed's looking at a building and Pastor's going to double the size of our team over the next three years. The money you send is reaching lots of Puerto Rican kids with the gospel. We can't thank you enough—so I guess Sharon and the kids went to your in-laws?"

"Yeh, they went to Cobleskill on Wednesday. I'm going over tomorrow afternoon, after our service here."

"So how many did you have tonight, at your Christmas Eve service?" Alison asks.

*Shit, I hate these questions,* Jim complains to himself, but he answers anyway, "Oh, about ninety, I'd say."

"That's *fabulous*," Alison bubbles. "I remember your first Christmas Eve service back in '77. There were maybe twenty people. The Lord has rewarded your faithfulness, Jimmy ... and remember, Ed and I are be*hind* you one hundred percent."

After exchanging good-byes, Jim gives the phone back to Becki. She talks a few more minutes then tells her mom good-bye. She digs the telephone out of the pile of clothes and hangs up the receiver.

Her composed face instantly gives way to a blushing frown. She glances furtively at Jim then assumes her "indignant porcupine" posture. He doesn't know if it's shame, or anger, or both.

Hoping for a quick reconciliation, Jim gives in to guilt and apologizes as if the entire episode was orchestrated by him. When Becki doesn't respond, he approaches her gently and tries to put his arm around her.

"*Stop it,* Shanley," she snarls, twisting away from him. "Just go away." Her face contorts into a hateful scowl.

"Well, Becki, I think we should talk about it," Jim responds—his tone is still conciliatory.

Becki picks at her thumbnail; she fidgets her feet. "I don't wanna talk about it."

Jim realizes that his penitent approach is getting nowhere; he fumes inside. He feels like a fool for apologizing, especially since he knows it's a lie to accept all the blame. Bathsheba wisely heads for the kitchen, while on the television, *Saturday Night Live* replaces the news, but they'll be hard pressed to put on a Christmas Eve skit to match the action at 59 Front Street.

"Okay, okay, so I have a problem," Jim says with growing anger. "I'm sorry; I know it leads to trouble, but you've got the *same* problem, young lady, and tonight proves it!"

"It's *your* problem, Shanley, not *mine*," Becki rebuts sharply. "You took advantage. Now just go away!"

"Dammit, Rebecca Lea!" Jim shouts, throwing up his arms

behind her turned back. "So it's wrong and doesn't fit, but we can't pretend it doesn't exist! You always put your head in the sand. I love you. I want you. Doncha get it! You drive me *crazy*! What am I supposed to do?"

"WHY DON'TCHA GO HOME AND *JERK OFF*!" Becki roars, whirling around, her eyes hot with reproach. "Fingering off and fuckin' and wet dreams! That's all you wanna talk about! Your mind's always in the gutter, Jimmy Shanley!" She beats the air with her fists; she spews hot spittle in Jim's face. "You always get me goin'. You always want me to talk about sex fantasies, or the wild things I did with Manny and Maria, or to confess about playing with myself before I go to bed. Why don't you grow up, Shanley. I'm not a kid anymore. I already sowed my wild oats. That's *all* in my past, before I got serious with God. It's all dirty and sinful, and I'm not *proud* of it. But I'm not like that anymore, do you understand! I don't sit around fantasizing like you, Jimmy. It's perverted. It's sin. It's all rebellious teenager stuff! Can't you get off it! I'm not *like* that! Not anymore!"

"Well," Jim counters, "who was that horny brunette in the bathroom then?" Instead of roaring back, he pierces her pious profession with a sword of sarcasm. Becki turns away reassuming her porcupine posture. Undaunted, he spits his words into the side of her downturned face, "Was that *you* by chance, or your long-lost *twin* sister?"

No reply. But Jim knows a storm is coming because the blood vessels in Becki's temple are knotting and quivering and turning blue, like varicose veins. He retreats just in time as she comes up screeching and preaching, her face a fist of florid rage, her words scathing and contemptuous, "What happened in there will *never* happen again AS LONG AS I LIVE! But it wasn't *my* fault! You started it, Jimmy, when you put your knee between my legs in the snow! You took advantage 'cause you knew I was buzzed on beer! I should've never let you get me goin'!"

Becki gestures berserkly as if fighting off a swarm of hornets. "You're so fuckin' oversexed, Shanley! It's *all* you think about. Sex! Sex! Sex! You're an animal! You're selfish! You don't give a shit about my feelings or what God says in the Bible! Every time we're together, you just wanna get me goin'. And tonight you did. Well, con*grat*ulations. But it's not what you think. I'm wicked ashamed about this. But it's *your* fault! You kept after me and after me! I should've stopped this filthy trend when it started last August! Nothing has changed! So just go home, and don't come back until you repent and get your thinking straight! I don't wanna talk dirty with you ever again! Do you understand me! *NEVER!* I'M NOT

LIKE THAT! Not really. You just take advantage and make me do things I'm ashamed of! I don't want to do it in some wild horny rush! Especially with a married man who's too old for me! I'm gonna do it God's way. I'm gonna save myself for my husband— and you can forget it, Jimmy Shanley, 'cause I'll *never* marry you!"

"You don't know that for sure," Jim rebuts.

"YES, I DO!" Becki howls, her face now pale with wrath. "I'll never marry *you*, even if Sharon dies! SO JUST ACCEPT IT, OKAY!"

She again turns a cold shoulder, but her hot fury hangs in the air like toxic fumes after an electrical explosion.

Jim's sarcastic sword has certainly set Becki on fire but he feels no better for it. In fact, he feels battered and abused like he felt in the kitchen before they left for church—the night has come full circle.

Giving a weary sigh, he grabs his Dingo boots, plops onto the sofa, and zips them on. He then collects his vest, his suit coat, his new slippers, and heads for the kitchen, but before getting there, he turns and asks a practical question, "So you want me to pick you up in the morning? The Escort's at the church, you know?"

"I'll walk, thank you," Becki replies icily.

"Okay, suit yourself. But you may never see me again."

"Yeah, right," Becki mocks. "I've heard *that* before."

# Chapter Twenty-eight

Jim Shanley, waiting for the Mustang to warm up, watches the snow and sleet hitting the windshield. The crippled wipers swing back and forth hesitatingly, *shunk-a-ca-shunk...* *shunk-a-ca-shunk.* The snowflakes hug the glass like crumpled starfish before the wipers sweep them away. The ice pellets are like small diamonds. Some bounce but most are captured by the film of melted snow. Finally, the engine is warm and he backs down Becki's driveway through the deep drifts. He's glad it's downhill.

*This whole day—what a fuckin' abortion!* Jim exclaims to himself as he gingerly steers the car down Front Street. *It was so beautiful when she gave me the present and we hugged on the sofa. How can something so good turn out so bad? Sex always ruins it and tonight—oh shit! Things really got out of—why can't I control myself? I can't help it. I want her. O God, why can't I go back and sleep with her? How come David and Jacob and all the Bible guys had more than one woman? Why was it right then, but not now? O Jesus, I can't stand it. And tonight she was wild and crazy, even hornier than me. She would've been on my lap if Alison hadn't called. But as it is, I never even saw her pussy.*

Nonetheless, Jim has evidence of her aggressive passion. Evidence, evidence, incriminating evidence. He reaches into his pocket and feels her damp panties, cotton evidence, the proof that she gave in to lust—at least for a while. Savage kisses, wanton eyes, proud tits, budding nipples. His loaded penis rears up again. *Oh fuck, my nuts are about to detonate. I've got to get home and get off. Maybe I am sick and oversexed, but I can't help it.*

He descends Hadley Hill through a blur of snow and sleet and haloed streetlights. The going is difficult on the narrow streets. Reaching Reservoir Road, he turns left. As he does, his conscience reacts. Shame, shame, powerful shame. The thought of getting off alone now makes him sick with self-hate. Masturbation makes Jim despise himself more than any sexual act, especially when illicit lust drives him to it. Not only does it seem dirty and sinful and weak, but it's humiliating, like being homeless.

*Come on, Jim,* his conscience convicts, *Becki is right. You've given yourself to a filthy trend. You've been controlled by lust since she came last February. You've turned away from the Lord, not because you can't help it, but because you don't <u>want</u> to help it. You have no faith, no prayer life. You've forsaken the Word for a romantic fantasy. You love carnal pleasure more than God. And now you want to go home and fuck Becki in your mind ... and come*

*all over your sheets. How low can you go? You better get right
before it's too late. You're deceitful and filled with iniquity. You've
betrayed Sharon and the kids and the church, and you've sinned
against Becki. She's just a child, an innocent flower trying to
bloom. She's vulnerable to fatherly affection, and you've taken
advantage to satisfy your lewd appetites. You have no business
seeing her sexual side, or even thinking about it.... But God will help
you, Jim, if you'll honestly repent. But you must let go of Becki, and
let her live her own life. You must love her with pure love.*

His erection softening, Jim resolves to pray his lust away. To
the church. Prayer, prayer, holy power. He must conquer his flesh.
He bursts through the snow dam at the entrance to the parking lot
and fishtails the Mustang to the front door. Stomping his feet, he
enters and flips on the heat. The main sanctuary is dark save for the
lighted Christmas tree on the dais which dimly illuminates the large
room with cool blue light. Two heart-shaped arrangements of
mums and baby's-breath bracket the stage—leftover flowers from
Freddie and Juanita's wedding. Jim marches willfully to the stage
and falls on his knees before the large cross on the wall.

*O God, forgive me. Fill me with your Holy Spirit. Cleanse me,
empower me. Fill me with love that's unselfish and pure, so I can
love Becki as a sister in Christ. Take my lust away.* Jim prays hard
but his prayer comes from his head not his soul.

After a few minutes, he loses his concentration. He looks up
at the cherrywood cross. There are black-ringed knots in the wood:
racoon eyes. His thoughts drift. Girlish breasts: white and pendulous. Jutting nipples: little red raspberries. Becki's aroused body
storms back into his mind.

*Oh, no—help me, Jesus!* Jim prays—to no avail. Truth is, he
doesn't want Jesus, he wants Becki. He wants to finish what they
started. He wants to twist those budding nipples that he teased but
didn't touch. His penis is harder than ever in his pants.

Jim sees Becki lifting her skirt and squatting over him, her
cushiony thighs spread wide. He sees her fierce darkness, her cunt
coming down, swollen with want. He can almost smell her unsated
desire. In fact, he can. He pulls her panties out of his overcoat and
inhales them, filling his nostrils, his lungs, with the smoky myrrh-
like odor of her pussy. The lust-dampened underpants are a living
Bible, an undeniable testimony to Rebecca's wanton side. Unzip,
unzip. He must unzip. *NO! NO! Not in the church. I can't.*

His conscience fights the fire. He tries again to pray. But the
harder he tries, the more she takes his mind. Becki, Becki, sweet
Christian Becki, so wholesome, so childlike. No, no, dark and
furious and feral and female. So adult, so X-rated. Cunt hair, cunt

hair, dark, dark, fiercely dark between white baby-soft thighs.

Jim's conscience overloads then shuts down. He unbuckles, unzips, wheels up from his kneeling position. His suit pants fall to his ankles. He throws Becki's underwear onto the carpet to the left of the pulpit then quickly whips off his overcoat and suit coat. Now in a delirium of anticipation, he pushes down his jockey shorts and grips his cock as it reaches for the ceiling.

He now prays in earnest, but you'll not find his prayer in any prayerbook: "O *God,* give me Becki's body! I love her! I want her! Give me her pussy, her hairy pussy! I wanna *fuck* her body! I wanna *fuck* her soul!" His lust-crazed voice echoes off the walls of the empty sanctuary, his words more fervent than any he's ever uttered from this dais. "O *Jesus,* let her *ride* me until she comes a hundred times! I wanna give her hot love until she passes out from pleasure!"

Shuffling forward, Jim jacks off over her panties, bobbing, weaving, thrusting and thrusting, as if he's preaching a powerful sermon. His thick pole feels like a burning log in his hand. Becki's trancy face flashes in his mind. Fiery pleasure, like a scorching wind, rips through his body rushing to the knob of his thrusting cock. His swollen gonads bounce on his groin. He grimaces against the rising tide. Hotter, higher, rushing, rushing, converging upward to the peak. "Oh, Becki, Becki! AH, *GOD!* AAAAAAH!" With a howling cry he explodes in sinful ecstasy ejaculating a hot rope of cum into the air like wild water from a runaway fire hose. But he quickly reins in his spewing penis and shoots most of his long pent-up load onto Becki's panties. Gasping, shuddering, he thrusts and thrusts covering the pale-blue cotton with spurt after spurt of stringy white jism—as if he'll never empty his aching testicles.

Finally, he collapses panting onto the stage. He cuddles into a fetal position. Warm euphoria spreads through his drained and breathless body giving him a sense of utter peace and completeness. Eyes closed, he hugs his bosom as if he's hugging Rebecca. He feels like he's suspended in warm water, like he's back in the womb, and she's there with him. Floating, floating, cocooned in love.

Time passes, perhaps a minute, but he has no sense of it. Orgasm takes him out of time, and place. He opens his eyes. Three splotches of yellow, dark dancing moths. But as he focuses, they turn into windows, curtains, flitting shadows of falling snowflakes. The Priscilla curtains glow yellow from the security light in the parking lot. There's no sound save for his breathing and the occasional snow-muffled rush of a car passing on Reservoir Road. But there are many smells: acrylic carpet, polished pulpit, ancient beer and nicotine, wedding flowers, the Christmas tree—but all are subordinate to the newest odor, freshly ejaculated semen.

Jim's groin itches. He reaches down—gooey wetness. Guilt, guilt, crushing guilt. "Oh shit, my hand." Reality crashes in upon him like water pouring into the bowels of a sinking ship. *O Lord Jesus! What have I done? Not on Christmas? Not in the church? No it can't be?* Dirty, wet, fetid. He feels filthy, slimy, like scum on raw sewage. His jerk-off jism smells funky and mildewy like the stink of a sour dishrag. He's smelled it a thousand times, yet it never fails to make him feel depraved. He closes his eyes hoping it's all a nightmare; he can't bear to look at his sin-fouled body.

But when Jim opens again, he's still there on his side, lying in his putrescence. His dripping dick, like a smoking gun, testifies to his unspeakable deed. He watches it wilt and droop below his disgusting paunch which seems especially fat, like a roll of blubber. He hates his body, especially his dirty little dick. He rolls onto his back. As he does, he cuts a sick bubbly fart, and a rotten-egg smell rises up around him as if he farted out his decadent soul.

Finally, he sits up, reaches into his pants for his handkerchief, then wipes his stomach, his groin, and his drippy deflated penis. He tosses the cum-fouled hankie on top of Becki's panties. He then stands and pulls up his pants, but shame brings him down again. He falls on knees, on his face, at the foot of the cross.

Sick, sick, sinful, sick. Dirty, depraved, despicable, degenerate. Cold shivers. Blah emptiness. Jim despises himself as never before: *O Lord, help me, deliver me. I'm sick. My life is obscene. My feelings are out of control. It's not love. It's sin! It's sin! I've been off all year. I can't be with Becki. I must flee. I must tell her. Oh, Sharon, forgive me. You're right. I am obsessed. Look where it's taken me. O Lord, my heart is wicked. The Bible's right. My heart is lecherous and sneaky and dirty. I've tried to seduce Becki all year with flirting and lewd talk. She's right. It's all rebellious teenage stuff. She's repented but I haven't. I'm still wallowing in the mire of lust and gutter talk. O God, forgive me for trying to drag Becki into the gutter with me. Why am I so weak? O Lord, why can't I think pure thoughts like other Christians? Why am I so messed up sexually? O Jesus, I've neglected your work to chase Becki. I've lost all devotion to my calling. My language is filthy. I never said the F-word this much in my whole life, even before I was saved.*

*O God, I've spent a whole year trying to seduce a sweet and righteous girl who loves me as a friend. O Lord, I want to get right! If there's still hope for me, show me a sign. Please, God, give me a sign ... a sign that it's not too late, a sign that you accept my confession and my vows of repentance.*

\* \* \*

The Christmas tree twinkles on the night table. The pump-handle lamp glows softly on the dresser. Bathsheba sleeps on the back of the green chair, but Becki is still wide awake on the sofa, her feet propped on the coffee table, the Garfield pillow in her lap. *Saturday Night Live* is still on, now an off-color skit about Santa Claus coming down the chimney to deliver presents and finding not only cookies and milk but also a horny wife home alone. Becki chuckles but quickly kills it with a frown of pious indignation.

Firing the TV remote like a pistol, she changes to a Jimmy Stewart movie, the one they show every Christmas about the small-town banker. She zaps again and gets Ebenezer Scrooge and Tiny Tim. After a dab of Dickens, she dits to channel 66 and a Lionel Ritchie video of "All Night Long." Giving up, she zaps the TV off. She can't stand Lionel Ritchie.

Becki pads across the room and digs through her shoe box of rock tapes. She picks a few, but instead of playing one, she sighs and throws them all back. Restless, restless, no attention span.

To her dresser. She removes her earrings then pulls a pink hairbrush through her disheveled hair. The brush pulls painfully through the tangles. She grimaces. She leans close to the mirror and fingers her dried chin-pimple. Disgusted with her hair and face, she returns to the sofa with the intention of unfolding her bed. She moves the coffee table then tosses the bed pillows and one sofa cushion onto the green chair. She hesitates, then replaces the cushion and the pillows. Bathsheba opens one eye as if to say, "What the fuck are doing, girl? Are you going to bed or what? Make up your mind." As if she hears her cat, Becki ponders a few seconds then goes back to the stereo and flips on the *Eagles* tape which is already loaded. Don Henley's voice fills the room.

She pads over to the Christmas tree. She removes a red ornament from the top and places it at the bottom. She moves a teddy bear from the bottom to the top, a mouse from the left to the right, and a reindeer from the back to the front. Finally, she leaves the tree and plunks longwise onto the sofa like a bored high-schooler.

She picks up the *Rolling Stone* magazine from the coffee table and flips through it. She lifts her leg onto the back of the sofa. Her skirt falls back exposing her pudding-soft inner thigh as it hangs with gravity. Noticing her flab, Becki gives a disgusted snort, drops her leg off the back of the couch, and crosses it over her uplifted knee. Unable to read, she tosses the magazine back on the coffee table and listens to the *Eagles'* rendition of "Witchy Woman."

Bouncing her free foot to the music, she feels a curious swooping pulling at her innards as the Indianlike drumbeat and suggestive lyrics rekindle her smoldering passions. An unwelcome spurt of lust spirals through her tired but unsated body. Becki again senses the searing need that came so close to conquering her less than an hour ago, a need that's been building for weeks and became an unbearable temptation during her prurient talk with Jimmy, a need that made her lose control and walk in on him. But for the phone call, she would've surely given in to sin. Despite her strong will, she could've never put out that fire by herself.

Horny, hot, too close. No way. But her mother's call was like cold water on the flames, a cold shock that awakened her conscience. Her cheery evangelical voice made Becki feel slutty and oversexed, as if her mom was somehow a witness to her unspeakably lewd behavior in the bathroom. And the fight with Jimmy suppressed her carnal desires even further.

But now it's all coming back like a rush as her demons break out of the corral to which shame had chased them. Becki knows she can't sleep without a cold shower or a session of sinful fantasy. Her religious side and good-daughter pride demand the former, especially after her profession of continence to Shanley. But her young sexually-starved flesh cries for the latter. The idea of yielding sends a shiver of delight down her spine then to her pantyless crotch where her frustrated clitoris swells again at the thought. Temptation—but a wave of guilt stops her.

"No, no, forget it," Becki declares, hopping up and tromping over to kill the suggestive song. "Not now, not after coming to my senses. This's been happening *too* much since summer. It's no accident Mom called. I'm not *kid*ding—what I said to Jimmy. Besides, I've been good this whole month." She speaks out loud as if to Satan, as if he's in the room with her.

Stepping determinedly to her closet, Becki unbuttons, proceeding with her intention of showering and going to bed. But before she can slip out of her shirt, her mind gets away. She pictures Shanley's penis hanging from his fly, then growing, then in her hand. She flees to her dresser but the thought meets her there. She picks up the hairbrush but doesn't use it. With a strong exertion of will, she forces Jimmy out of her thoughts, but her lust demands a fantasy. Manny, Manny. His dark Hispanic cock flashes onto the screen of her mind. Canting her hips, she slouches in front of her mirror trying to throttle the libidinal current coursing up from the core of her womanhood, but it builds into a burning sweetness that makes her dizzy and demands surrender. A shadow of annoyance crosses her face then gives way to a naughty-girl glint.

Her self-control melts like butter in a microwave oven. Flirting, naughty talk, kissing, fondling. She got too close to the edge with Jimmy. Besides, it's been too long. She has to come. The thought makes her shake inside. No more choice, but she'll give in to Manny, not Jimmy. She's not about to confess to Shanley, even in a fantasy fuck, not on this night, not after their fight.

Now resigned, Becki lets a flood of Manny-memories take her mind, torrid memories of their beachhouse fling in the summer of '82, memories that torment when she fights temptation yet fuel her fire when she gives in. But she wants more than memories to whet her craving. She quickly lowers the window shades then digs in her closet and comes out with a red shopping bag.

She sprawls on the floor and empties the bag covering the carpet with pages out of *Hustler, Playgirl, Penthouse*, and Spanish-captioned photos of hunky guys with hard-ons. Mounting the dark beast within, she leaves guilt, shame, and piety behind as she devours the slick dog-eared, fingerworn pages. The scene is silent save for the sleet pinging on the storm windows. Next, she flips through a stapled collection of *Penthouse* "Forum" pages savoring the orgasmic paragraphs. She feasts on erotica with a zeal that a young missionary should have for the Bible. Few would believe it. But such is the secret life of Rebecca Reinhardt.

Finally, she unfolds a large poster like her Rod Stewart poster but Becki's star is no music idol. He's a rugged thirtyish porno stud in a provocative ithyphallic pose. She spreads the four-foot poster on the floor then sits crab-style at his feet and rakes his virile sun-bronzed body with her lusting eyes. Mustache, square jaw, cute features. He looks like an X-rated Burt Reynolds. But she's not looking at his face. His hefty prick seems ten inches long. It's mocha brown, almost blue, but the glans is baby pink and points at the sky. And underneath he has the bags of a baby bull. His pubic forest is the meanest she's ever seen, black, thick, and billowing, like smoke from burning crude. She studies every detail of his turgid male genitals, gazing, feasting, fantasizing.

Cock, cock. Becki can't get enough. She loves to look at hard cock. She studies every ridge, every pimple, every vein, every crease, every hair. Swarthy, menacing, almost brutal in its masculine potency, the poster penis excites her like an aphrodisiac as it sharpens her memory of Manny's dark Mediterranean prick.

Her pulse skitters erratically. She feels oozing dampness between her legs. Miss Reinhardt's gun has been loaded since she pulled up her skirt on the sofa and showed Jimmy her panties, and it's now recocked and ready to fire. But she doesn't rush for the trigger. She wants to get all the erotic pleasure her sex drive can give her, and when she hasn't come for some time, her pent-up lust can take her to astounding heights before breaking loose. In fact, her demons have already taken her far beyond sweet romance or marriage or making it fit. She's now like an animal in heat and would fuck any hard cock without taking thought.

Her experience has become purely sensual, primal, and self-gratifying—and unspeakably sinful for a "good" Christian girl. Yet it's this very wantonness, the lure of forbidden sex, that makes her fantasy fucks irresistible and mind-blowing. Only wild and sinful fantasies can make Rebecca come.

"O *Jes*us, this's too good to waste," Becki sighs under her breath. Hopping up, she takes a tape from her shoe box and pops it into the stereo. The bluesy roadhouse beat of Joe Walsh and "Rocky Mountain Way" blares through the speakers. Hot squalling guitar, sexy Southern piano, wave after wave of splashing cymbals. It's a perfect song for a horny girl who wants to ride her lust without letting it go. She strips off her shirt and bra and flings them onto the sofa; her naked breasts heave out into their natural hang. Rocking her hips to the raunchy beat, Rebecca sways and spins to the music.

> Spent the last year, Rocky Mountain way.
> Couldn't get much higher.
> Out to pasture, think it's safe to say,
> Time to open fire ...

The room careens about her, the lamp, the Christmas tree, the sofa, Bathsheba sleeping on the green chair. The wind excites her nipples making them tingle as they jut out stiffly. She unsnaps, unwraps her skirt, leaving her nude save for her kneesocks.

> And we don't need the lady crying
> Because the story's sad ...
> 'Cause the Rocky Mountain way
> Is better than the way we had.

Becki twists and twirls about her "high noon" poster cock. She bumps and grinds her haunches. She does her happy-girl quickstep, then the boogaloo, the twist, the frug, the funky chicken. She whips her wine-colored skirt like a bullfighter's cape.

> Well, he's telling us this and he's telling us that.
> He changes it every day, says it doesn't matter.
> Bases are loaded and Casey's at bat.
> Playing it play by play, time to change the batter.

Her tits joggle, her midriff shakes, her flank fat shimmies, and the sapphire pendant bounces on her chest like a sacred amulet. She pants for breath. Finally, she sails her skirt onto the green chair and stops over her porno star, but her hips go on rocking to the music.

> And we don't need the lady crying
> Because the story's sad,
> 'Cause the Rocky Mountain way
> Is better than the way we had.

Now sexually entranced, she's no longer disgusted with her flabby thighs but she's proud of her womanly physique and its power to arouse the male penis, like the one pictured below her, or like Manny's in her mind. Becki caresses her body lovingly as if soaping up in the shower. She admires her burnt-umber bush as it undulates like a stormy patch of primal night within her slabby rolls and shelves of ivory-vanilla flesh. Without moving her feet, she bangs her hips to the sexy beat as if against invisible walls. Closing her eyes, she breathes in long lustful sighs. She gyrates her pelvis as if fucking, and in her fantasy she's doing just that.

"Oh, Manny," she sighs, "you're *so* big. I love your cock. I love to ride it. Oh shit, I love to fuck. I need to fuck."

The music settles as Joe Walsh comes in with a talking box plus a percussive "E" on the synthesizer. Becki reins in her pelvis until her hips roll ever so slowly to the suppressed blues rhythm. Manny, Manny. She's fucking him slowly. Lifting off, coming down, teasing herself. Go, go, it's time. Fire, fire. It's been too long. Her clit screams for attention but she skillfully refrains, until her haunches begin to quiver with involuntary tremors.

Weak-kneed and hair-trigger hot, Becki sits down on her porno stud, her legs spread like a cowgirl right over his cock. Her pussy, like a bursting fully-ripe plum, is wide-open and juiced to overflowing. Watching with wanton eyes, she teases the periphery of her swollen vulva as she slowfucks Manny in her mind. Slowly in, slowly out. Hotter, higher. Sweet torture. She grimaces like a baby about to cry—all at once the music explodes. Wailing guitar, crashing cymbals, wild piano, pounding drums. And just in time. Even Mount St. Helens could not hold forever.

Rebecca gives a shuddering gasp and goes wild on her clit with the side of her thumb. Stroking, stroking. Now she feels it, building, building, the "good feeling," the scarlet-hot and surging pleasure that she's craved since she was fifteen. Head back, eyes closed, her breath coming in long surrendering moans, she masturbates for dear life as she fucks Manny furiously in her mind. "Oh! Oh! Oh! ... O *God*! Oh, *Man*ny!" Her short knobby-kneed legs open and close like butterfly wings. Her cushiony thighs roll and jiggle like

Jell-O then come together squeezing, enhancing, prolonging each pang of pleasure. Her beefy hips bounce on the poster making sweaty-slappy sounds. Becki feels the hysteria of delight rising within her. She claws for the hot and final joy—higher, higher, but her mountain seems to have no peak. It's too big, like a breech birth. Her fingers ache; she wishes she had Maria's vibrator.

Insane for orgasm, knowing she must come or die, she hurls her chunky body forward onto the poster, onto her fast-moving hand. Her face is mashed to the floor. Her heart hammers in her chest. Fingerfucking herself from underneath, Becki desperately humps the porno stud like a sex-crazed man fucking a sex doll.

Flash! Shanley, Shanley. She's suddenly in a new fantasy: "Oh, *Shanley,* I want you! Want you! I'm gonna screw your brains out!" She's now fucking Jimmy on the kitchen floor just outside the bathroom door. Her fantasy is savage, almost violent.

The music rages. Her hefty haunches hump faster and faster. Hotter, hotter, higher, higher. Becki shakes as if she's having a seizure. Spread-eagle and writhing wildly, she rocks off the poster kicking porno pictures in all directions. Sensing her climax, she arches her back raising her head off the floor. Her neck muscles stiffen. Her face tightens into a fist of anticipation like a sprinter breaking the tape, "OH! OH! OH! O God, I'm *com*ing!"

Gasping, moaning, she stretches her legs straight out behind her like a gymnast and comes and comes as a million glowing stars burst inside of her. "OH! OH! AAAAAAAAAH!" Hot rushes of ecstasy in Rebecca's veins explode again and again in her brain then run back through her body as warm melting waves of liberation. "Oh, wicked *nice*! Oooh ... *nice*." Rolling onto her back, she sobs with relief as her body continues to shudder with uncontrollable spasms as if her climax will last all night.

Finally, she lies still. Dreamy, dreamy. Melting sweetness. Becki floats on clouds of invisible warmth. Seconds slip by then minutes. "Rocky Mountain Way" is followed by Bette Midler and "The Rose." Bathsheba jumps off the green chair, comes over, and licks Becki's perspiring brow. It's forty minutes past midnight on Christmas morning, and young Miss Reinhardt has fornicated her way into the holiday by fucking two men in her mind.

* * *

At the church Pastor Jim is still on his face behind his pulpit making vows of repentance. The mildewy stink of semen is on him, all around him. It lingers like the smell of dead fish, reminding him again and again of his sin. Too much. He hauls himself to his feet,

417

exits through a side door, and goes into the teen center men's room.

He disrobes and runs hot water until it's steaming. He stands sideways so he won't see his face in the mirror—he hates his fucking face. He grabs a fresh bar of Ivory soap from the cabinet under the sink plus a large sponge. Lathering from neck to ankles, Jim scrubs his sin-fouled body, especially his genitals which he scrubs until raw and red. He dries with paper towels then throws them into a pile on the floor as if they're radioactive. Finally, he uses the corner of the sponge to spot-clean his vest, pants, shirttail, and Dingo boots.

Jim quickly dresses then goes to the kitchen where he dons a pair of yellow dishwashing gloves and finds a white kitchen-size garbage bag and a twist tie. Returning to the men's room, he stuffs the dirty paper towels into the plastic bag, then heads back to the main sanctuary, back to the stage, where he picks up his cummy handkerchief and Becki's desecrated panties and puts them into the same bag. He seals the bag with the twist tie.

He picks up his suit coat from the floor and slips it on—after making sure it was out of range during his sinful explosion. Then he marches back through the teen center and out into the windy, snowy night. The snowflakes are larger. The sleet has ended. Jim wades through the snow to the dumpster, lifts the lid, and throws the bag inside. *BANG!* The heavy steel lid crashes down.

His adrenaline now flowing, he runs-slogs his way back to the church. He's back in the battle—on God's side. He feels cleaner, like half purged. He goes to the utility closet, fetches a bucket and fills it with hot water plus Lestoil Heavy Duty Cleaner and Parson's Lemon Fresh Ammonia Cleaner. He takes the bucket to the main auditorium along with a spray can of Lysol disinfectant and a can of Woolite rug cleaner, and a handful of rags. He turns on the overhead lights. Clean, clean, clean. Overclean. Overkill. With his bucket of lemon-pine-ammonia suds Jim purges the scene of his lewd act, rubbing, scrubbing, rescrubbing. When finished, he sprays the carpet with Woolite. While waiting for it to foam up, he puts everything away, exactly as it was, except for the Lysol spray.

Ten minutes later, he's back on stage vacuuming the foamy rug cleaner. The high-pitched pneumatic whir of the Air-Way vacuum is soothing to his spirit. The church also has a large industrial vac but he doesn't feel like wrestling with it. Jim has always liked the sound of vacuum cleaners since he was a boy. He's not sure if it's the sound itself or the awareness that dirt is being sucked up. A sense of peace and righteousness begins to well up from within—"SHUT THAT FUCKING THING OFF!" Shanley jumps as if shot. Turning, he sees wild stoned eyes, windblown hair, and an untucked shirttail hanging under a bomber jacket.

It's Joe Lareux. Shock, guilt, shame. It all returns. Jim feels naked, embarrassed as if caught in the very act; his heart pounds in his face. After killing the vacuum, he scrambles for his senses, starts to utter a greeting, but Joe cuts him off, "Good thing I saw the Mustang. I've been looking for you for all night, you *ass*hole!" Jim quickly realizes that Joe's visit is not friendly. "Go ahead and clean and vacuum and scrub, but you'll never purge *this* pulpit!"

*He knows!* Jim exclaims silently, his face burning with humiliation. *But how?*

Joe pulls his pocket Bible as if it's a handgun. "'How long halt ye between two opinions'!" he rails, reading the words of Elijah. "'If the Lord be God, follow him. But if Baal, then follow him.' I'm getting the fuck outa here! I have to follow the angels. YOU'RE A *FUCK*ING HERETIC, JIM! This ministry is a cloud without water! You can't put your heart ahead of the *Word*. It's anathema! It's antichrist! You're a 'black wandering star.'" Joe's moonish face is florid with wrath; he jabs the air with his Bible. "You're leading people astray. You're trying to justify your lust for Becki. It's not of God. She's an idol, just like Brenda! Face it, Jim. Lucifer has you by the balls! Your shit is weak! YOU *MUST* REPENT AND FORSAKE THE WAY OF BAALIM!"

Each condemning barrage sends a shudder through Jim's guilt-ridden conscience like a pile driver pounding a post into rancid muck. He sees that Joe is flying on pot, but after his unspeakable sin, he's ready to receive chastisement from any source. He fidgets nervously with the wand of the vacuum cleaner. He gives a feeble response, "I know, I agree, but—"

"SAVE IT!" Joe shouts. "I don't want to hear your shit! I'm outa here!" Without another word Joe strides fervently out of the sanctuary then out the front door—he's gone.

Jim's face burns with shame: *I feel like he beat me up and threw me in an alley. But I deserve it. He's right. I hafta face it. It's the truth, even if he is stoned. I hafta face—*

"Sign! Sign! O Lord Jesus, this is a sign!" Jim exclaims out loud. He gestures fervently with uplifted hands as if preaching. "This is my sign! I'm forgiven! Joe's the sign I prayed for. O God, you *did* hear my plea. I have a clean slate. O God, you snatched me out of the mouth of the dragon. Now I see why Logan gave me a green light with Becki. It was the only way, but it's working for good because I now see my deceitful heart and how Satan has used lust to lead me astray. O God, you've opened my eyes."

Jim finishes vacuuming then sprays the whole scene with Lysol. Clean, clean. Lemon, pine, ammonia, and disinfectant. The sanctuary now smells as clean as a hospital. He senses a new and sacred pureness around him and in him. His sin is purged. After hauling on his overcoat, he kills the lights and departs.

2:05 a.m. Jim drives north on South Meadow Road. It's still snowing but not as hard. The storm may have changed to rain in Boston but not in Brendon Falls. No traffic. Peaceful, peaceful. The wooded lowlands lie dark and silent as if asleep under their cottony mantle of white. He hears nothing except the muted groaning of the Mustang tires on the packed snow.

Samantha meets Jim at the door. She mews hungrily and pushes against his legs. He's only been gone eleven hours but it seems like eleven years. He feeds her then goes right to bed. He feels renewed, right with God—ready to soldier.

* * *

Christmas morning. 10:10 a.m. The church is beginning to buzz with eager Christian voices. Pastor Jim, showered, shaved, and dressed in fresh clothes—his tan corduroy suit—stands by his office windows looking out at the new-fallen snow. Despite only four hours sleep, he feels fervent and energetic—and *clean*.

The clouds are breaking. Slanting shafts of winter sun glisten on the drifted snow, casting long shadows and waking up the vivid colors that make day different than night: arctic blue, sunny gold, forest green, pearl-white over indigo, and myriad shades of gray and violet. Occasional avalanches of snow shudder off the shoulders of the heavy-laden pine trees and crash to the ground filling the air with fleeting clouds of sparkling white. Jim is unspeakably ashamed of his secret sin, his vile and secret sin, but on this bright cold Christmas morn, he sees his shame as an asset, for it drives him to serve—to show God that he means business.

To the door. He opens it a crack to spy on the early arrivals, and just in time. Laughing, chewing, chocolate hair. Cupid face, red from cold. It's Rebecca Lea coming in the door with Jodi and Brenda. *Ahah, she didn't walk, she rode with Jodi,* Jim declares to himself. Jodi and Becki are talking-joking but Brenda is sober and sleepy-eyed. Becki's hobo bag hangs from her crooked elbow as she cradles her blue Thompson Chain Reference Bible to her bosom. Alison gave her the large reference Bible for high school graduation but she rarely brings it to church. She normally uses the small pocket-Bible she keeps in her purse.

Jodi and Brenda head for the auditorium but Rebecca makes a beeline toward Shanley's office—or so he thinks. He quickly closes the door. *She's coming to confront me. Good; I agree that we can't do outreach anymore. Now's my chance to tell her I've repented.* His heart racing, he waits for the knock, but it never comes. He opens again, ever so slowly, just enough to see Becki talking with Carl Baker. Under her ski jacket she's dressed modestly in Alison hand-me-downs: a scoop-neck sweater, a delicate blouse with a frilly collar, and a corduroy skirt. The sweater is primrose yellow, the blouse white, the skirt nutmeg brown. And she has a gold cross around her neck and a red ribbon in her hair. She looks right out of the 1950s, like Betty Anderson from *Father Knows Best.* And her demeanor is just as prim and proper as her looks.

"Sure, no problem," Becki says, speaking upward to Carl who's a foot taller than she. "I subbed for Sharon twice already. I kind of figured you might ask me to teach her class since she's gone this week. Besides, I know most of the kids anyhow ... from school." Becki's wad of gum is hidden, safely tucked into her cheek.

Carl gives an approving mission-accomplished smile. "Great, I knew I could count on you, Becki. Here's your curriculum packet, but mainly I just want you to explain the Christmas story as it relates to John 3:16." Carl's smile reminds Jim of the salesclerk at Stefano's Men's Shop. His name is Enrico and he always gives an upbeat I-made-the-sale grin as he rings up Jim's Levi's.

"Sharon already has them learning scripture verses?" Becki asks as she places the buff-colored packet inside the front cover of her Bible; she cocks her head curiously as if impressed and interested.

Carl's sallow face colors with pride. He steps closer. His spindly praying-mantis body seems to curl over Becki's chunkish figure. "Most definitely," he brags. "Our five-year-olds know more verses than most adults."

Becki dimples and looks down demurely. "Yeah, I guess John 3:16 is perfect for today. It'll show the kids that God is serious about sin and salvation, and that Christmas means more than getting presents from Santa Claus." Her voice is honey-rich, angelic, filled with humility.

"Exactly," Carl affirms, nodding his shiny bald dome. "Our kids must learn that Santa Claus is make-believe while Jesus is real. They must know the truth."

Ruddy-cheeked, wind-chapped, little makeup. Rebecca glows with evangelical cheerfulness and Sunday morning piety. She looks fresh and natural and healthy—and seventeen, especially with the red ribbon in her hair. There's no hint of her usual frowniness. Her hair is freshly shampooed and softly feathered, which is unusual; she rarely washes her hair two days in a row, even for church. She looks so innocent and lamblike, so pink and pure and wholesome, like an Iowa farm girl at a 4-H fair. She could pass for Little Bo Peep. Jim can't believe she's the same Becki who flirted so wantonly with him last night, and showed him her panties, and—kill it! Newly commissioned "thought police" charge out of his conscience to abort the prurient train of thought; he's now "walking in the Spirit."

"So Sharon's class still meets in classroom four?" Becki asks Carl.

"Most definitely," he replies, "the last room before the teen center."

With a swish of corduroy she turns to leave, but Carl stops her, "Oh, Becki, I've been meaning to tell you ... I uh—well, I appreciate how you lay down your life for the Lord, and for the church. You're very mature in Christ for a college-age woman, and I mean that as a compliment." He speaks in a patronizing tone, yet there's an odd tremor in his voice as if Becki makes him nervous.

"Oh, it's nothing really," Becki replies, giving a blushing "awh shucks" smile. "I like teaching Sunday school and helping the kids learn about God." Her humble words convey Christian congeniality and sisterly appreciation, but she shifts her weight and fidgets her feet as if she's anxious to leave, to get away from Carl and his compliments.

"No, I don't mean subbing for Sharon," Carl elaborates. "Oh, I do mean that too, but I mean the way that you come to every service and every Bible class, and how you teach all week and do more outreach than any woman in this church ... and I know it's not for the money." Becki averts her eyes; her blush deepens. "And you never complain or gossip or meddle. I know Pastor Jim is proud of you, but I want you to know that we're all proud of you. Your life is *such* a testimony for the Lord. And you're a godly role model for all our girls, especially the teenagers. I know that one day you'll go out on a team just like your mom, but while you're here, I just want you to know that you're a fine soldier for Christ."

Having said that, Carl gives Becki a clumsy Christian embrace knocking his glasses sideways on his pointy nose.

Becki responds with a self-conscious laugh, then she thanks Carl for his vote of confidence and heads into the new wing. Pastor Jim feels an impulse to follow her, to tell her that he's repented, but he decides to wait for a quieter more settled time.

Closing the door, Jim sits down at his desk. *I can't believe how sweet and godly Becki sounds,* he thinks to himself. *Watching her at church, you'd never suspect*—abort it! His Spirit-filled conscience again corrects the wayward drift in his thoughts, redirecting his attention to the ministry, to his pastoral duties. He's asked Barry to lead songs since he doubts Joe Lareux will show for church. But he's not sure if Joe will actually follow through on his vow to leave. Barry's no musician but he can carry a tune and operate the PA. Jim prefers to have Sylvia lead songs, but Stan long ago declared, "No woman's gonna lead songs in *this* church."

Suddenly, a knock and a navy-blue dress, and a furious spectacled face, fierce, feline, blazing with passion. Jim's heart jumps. Dark, raven-haired, beautiful. He cringes as she slams the door. Her angry presence ravages the room.

She comes at him like a she-tiger ready to strike, but she does not spring, she simply leans over the desk and claws him with her fiery hazel eyes, and scathing words, "You really *piss* me off, Jim!" She's so close he can taste her perfume. "I'm not into gossip and I don't give a shit about Stan's holier-than-thou Christianity, but I thought you and I were on the *same* wavelength!"

Jim tries to reply, "Whoa, whaa—"

"You've known for *two* weeks," she snarls, cutting him off. "And you kept it from me. You call that friend*ship!*" Her hot breath fans his face.

Shrinking back into his chair, he tries again, "Wait a min—"

But she doesn't wait. "When the chips are down, you're a typical male! You're conceited and proud! You're a slave to testosterone! You have to preserve the illusion of male superiority, as if God speaks through the testicles. If I had a penis, my convictions would be respected. But since I've got nothing between my legs but a birth canal, I don't rate. The women in this church have enough trouble without you supporting every bizarre notion that springs up in the diseased male psyche. Your 'follow the heart' bullshit is *so* chauvinistic. It's okay for a man to follow his heart, but a woman has to follow a *male* heart. What a crock! You're just as bad as Stan Campbell!"

She sucks a quick breath then nails Jim with her primary complaint. "What the fuck are you doin', telling my husband that loving a guy is okay!"

"I-I uh ... I didn't exactly—"

Janet Buford steams right over him again, her eyes like blow-torches. "I'm the most liberated Christian in this church and I'm not afraid to stand up for women's rights, but I'm not a radical feminist, nor a lesbian. I draw the line when it comes to homosexuality, and especially when it's *my* husband. I know all about you and Becki"— *I doubt it,* Jim quickly interjects to himself—"and I think it stinks what you're doing to Sharon and the kids, but at least it's normal chemistry, like male-female, but guys balling guys, that's Sodom and Gomorrah stuff!"

"If you'll just cool it," Jim implores—but Janet's gone as quickly as she came. Yet he finishes his statement anyway, addressing the stinging silence in the wake of the slamming door, "Believe me, Janet, things are gonna change, starting today."

Normally such a blast would leave Jim wounded, but Janet's wrath, as with Joe's, simply reinforces his new resolve. He adds several afterthoughts, *She's off base on women being equal—the Bible's clear on that—but she's right on the gay part. I can't play games with Barry when it comes to sexual sin.*

* * *

"GOD HATES FORNICATION!" Pastor Jim bellows. "IT DESECRATES THE TEMPLE OF GOD!"

He pauses to catch his breath. He slips out of his coat and tosses it to Barry. He reaches inside the lectern for his glass of water. Thirty minutes of vehement preaching. His face is throbbing, his shirt soaked. After sipping from the glass, he reads the last two verses of his sermon text—John 3:19-20:

> And this is the condemnation, that light is come into the world, and men loved darkness rather than light because their deeds were evil. For everyone who doeth evil hateth the light, neither cometh to the light, lest his deeds should be reproved.

Jim steps to the side of his pulpit. The mood is grave. There's not a sound in the sanctuary. Lemon, pine, ammonia. The smells of his late-night cleaning session still waft up from the carpet at his feet, not thick and strong, but tenuous like dissipating fog, yet enough to jog Jim's memory, to jar his conscience, to fuel his self-disgust which comes out as righteous indignation directed at his flock. He drops into a quiet but stern tone, "Every Christmas we talk about peace and joy and good tidings, but most of you don't have peace and joy. Most of you struggle and fail over and over again. Why? Because it's not enough to give intellectual assent. You must open up to the glory of Christ's incarnation ... but you refuse the glory and shut out the light. You love darkness more than light because your deeds are *evil*. You love sinful pleasure *more* than God. The light exposes your lust and your depraved carnal nature, and you don't want anyone to see the real you ... but *God* knows.

"AND *GOD* IS NOT MOCKED!" Jim roars becoming heated again. "He knows what goes on in hidden chambers. You love the dark since it covers your flirting and suggestive jesting and solitary perversions—and your fornications! And if you're not doin' it, you're *think*ing it ... like how you men lust and undress women with your wicked eyes! Don't you think God knows your filthy thoughts! And some of you women are just as bad, going to Clancy's to satisfy your lascivious spirit! And you have families at home! GOD HATES IT! IT MAKES HIM PUKE AND HE'S GONNA VOMIT YOU *RIGHT* OUT OF HIS MOUTH in Revelation 3:16!"

Pastor Jim slaps his open Bible, again and again, driving home each word: "LUST! LUST! LUST! SEX! SEX! SEX! How can you receive the light when you feast on carnal pleasure!"

He moves aggressively to the front of the dais. He beats the air. "LUST! LUST! LUST! Your thought-life is obscene! But is it any wonder when you feast on lewd movies and magazines, and videos and rock music!"

Guilt and self-condemnation sweep the sanctuary. Many look down ashamedly, like Frank Cahill and Brenda D., and Calvin McClusky and David Myszak, and Angela and Doris and Ernie and Mary LeBlanc. Gerald Burton hangs his head like a condemned convict, his face blanched white. Others look right at Jim with pleading eyes, like Melissa and Kevin and Sylvia, and Aunt Agnes and Cathy R., and Joanne McClusky. Some seem excited, holier-than-thou, like Stan and Leslie and Sarah—and Pastor Jim himself. A few, like Jodi and Russ, seem unaffected. Elmer is also unmoved; he's been asleep since the offering. And a few seem defiant, like Haley C. and Curt Sims and Nina Ramirez, and Kyle Donovan, who glowers at Jim from the last row. Kyle came in late and alone. Unshaven, bleary-eyed, and clad in a wrinkled logger's shirt, he looks like he just rolled out of Ruthie's bed.

*This is too much,* Jim counsels himself as he retreats to his pulpit. *I must balance this. I must bring in love and forgiveness.*

He pauses over his Bible; his mood softens. After loosening his tie, he reaches into the back of the lectern for another sip of water. But he misses the glass and his hand closes around the spray can of Lysol.

FLASH! FLASH! Thrusting cock, wild spurts of cum. The whole sinful night replays in Jim's mind. Filthy, blah, wet. Shame, shame—*I hate myself!*

Pastor Jim's compassion scalds away turning to hot steam. He explodes in a furious fusillade of fire and brimstone, "GOD HATES SIN! THAT'S WHY JESUS CAME! The 'whole world lieth in wickedness' in 1st John 5:19! AND GOD HATES IT!" Moving to the side, Jim pounds his pulpit, so hard that his fist becomes numb. "LUST! LUST! LEWD TALK! AND FILTHY

JESTING! GOD HATES IT *ALL*! HE HATES SUGGESTIVE TALK in Ephesians 4:29! HE HATES FLIRTING in Ephesians 5:4! HE HATES LUST in James 1:14 and 2nd Timothy 2:22!"

Excited to a frenzy of masochistic fervor, the flock claps and cheers each verse as Pastor Jim howls and pounds: "GOD HATES FORNICATION in 1st Thessalonians 4:3! GOD HATES WHOREMONGERS in Hebrews 13:4! GOD HATES LOOSE WOMEN in Jeremiah 3:1-3! GOD HATES VILE AFFECTIONS in Romans 1:26! GOD HATES ADULTERY in Exodus 20:14! GOD HATES MASTURBATION in Genesis 38:9! AND *MOST* OF ALL, GOD HATES HOMOSEXUALITY in Romans 1:27!" Hot blood swells Jim's face. His knees shake, from passion and fatigue. "That's why God brought the flood in Genesis 6:5! That's why God rained fire and brimstone on Sodom and Gomorrah in Genesis 19:24! And that's why God's bringing a new judgment upon lust and perversion today! Do you think that AIDS is an accident!"

Jim gulps a deep breath then storms about the stage as he explodes in a final fireball of pious indignation, "'KNOW YE NOT THAT THE UNRIGHTEOUS SHALL NOT INHERIT THE KINGDOM OF GOD' in 1st Corinthians 6:9!" The congregation cheers. "NEITHER FORNICATORS!" More cheering. "NOR ADULTERERS!" Another roar from the flock. "NOR EFFEMINATE!" Now deafening applause. "NOR ABUSERS OF THEMSELVES!"

The body members roar to their feet. Pastor Jim stands limp and drained. He waits for the ovation to stop but it goes on and on, together with many amens and hallelujahs.

Finally, Jim asks everyone to bow in prayer, quieting the flock. He hands the microphone to Barry, tells him to give the invitation, then grabs his coat and exits the sanctuary.

Stan Campbell follows him through the glass door. "That's a haw'mark message, Pastor Jim. The best Christmas sermon ever. I never heard it this good." Stan, his blue eyes beaming, wraps his huge Frankensteinian hand around Jim's shoulder. "It's a *mile*-stone, a turnin' point. This's a new era for BFBC."

Puffed with pious pride, Jim heartily agrees, then heads for his office. Stan's voice follows him down the hall, "Now you go to your wife an' rest up. You deserve it. And don't worry 'bout nuthin'. I'll see you Tuesday evenin'."

Jim quickly visits the men's room; he wants to leave before the crowd gets out since he has to be in Cobleskill by three-thirty.

When he comes out of the bathroom, he runs into Russ who gives him a twinkle-eyed elfish grin, and a wry quip, "So it's that

426

bad, huh?"

Jim chuckles into a laugh, but he's flying too fast to be affected by dry humor—or truth.

Russ pulls on his parka then adds, "Like I said in my note, we've got to talk on this money thing, but it can wait. Besides, I've got Bev and Sheila and Becki in the car, and they're all hungry for Christmas dinner."

Russ ambles on out, the back way.

After a quick stop at his office to get his briefcase, Pastor Jim exits the same way, just as Russ's white Fairmont pulls around the building. But Jim doesn't notice the car; he just sees red ribbon and feathery brown hair through the rear window.

# Chapter Twenty-nine

S haron Shanley presses her warm full-buttocked body against her husband; her flesh is soft and satiny white, and fragrant from bubble bath. The mood is enchanting as they snuggle in the nude bathed by the yellow glow of the bedside lamp.

"Oh, James *Dav*id, how I needed that," Sharon purrs, her dusty-blue eyes dreamy with afterpleasure. "I thought my head was going to blow off on that last one. Oh, honey, just hold me close." Her cheeks pulse pink then pearl, like evening clouds in the last rays of the setting sun.

"Certainly better than our first time," Jim quips after a lengthy silence. "Remember, it was like pushing a limp wiener through a zipped-up zipper?" This witty remark, along with his laugh, breaks the amorous mood.

Sharon sighs and relaxes her embrace. "Come on, honey. How can you joke after being so turned on just two minutes ago? Why are men so unromantic after?" She tries to look disturbed but fails as a grin chases her brief frown.

"Well, it *was* like a hot dog and a zipper," he kids, patting his wife playfully on her naked behind.

Now they both chuckle at the recollection. "We were just nervous," she says. "It was our honeymoon. It's a big step to go from petting to sex. Besides, they all knew we were doing it."

"They?"

"You know, after the wedding, Mom, Dad, your dad, Gary Bob ... Mor, Debbie, Mark, my whole family. They knew we were going to a motel to do it ... to have sex."

"So, they knew we were coming in here tonight? Pardon my pun."

"Yeah, but who's curious after fifteen years?"

Sharon rolls onto her back and grabs a box of Kleenex from the night table. She takes some then hands the box to Jim. After swabbing her crotch, she throws the soppy wad into the trash. *Thung!* It makes a resonant thud in the empty metal can. Knees up, their legs form a big naked W across the bed, her long cushiony thighs rising above his to make the W lopsided. Jim's legs are rather monkeyish—skinny, short, sharply knobbed knees, with just enough hair to look masculine.

Jim wipes his deflated penis. It's no longer a "dirty little dick," but righteous and godly, having just performed its husbandly duty. Likewise, the smell of sex seems natural and good. Sharon's pungent female fragrance overwhelms his cummy male smell—

testifying that it was not his hand but his wife's vagina that pumped his penis to orgasm. Husband-wife. Marriage bed. Godly, no shame or disgust. What a difference a day makes.

They talk and kid a bit more about their honeymoon, then Sharon says she's cold and sits up on the side of the bed and retrieves her new flannel nightgown from the floor; it's her Christmas present from Jim. "Guys have it easy, you know?" she says speaking away from the bed as she slips the baby-blue gown over her head.

Jim pulls his old gray-plaid pajamas down over his lifted legs. He could've used new pajamas for Christmas but Sharon gave him two shirts and a tie. "How's that, hon?" he asks in response to her assertion about guys.

Sharon stands so her nightgown can fall full-length, then turns and fluffs her pillow. "Well, all you have to do is wipe off, but I have to carry your goo around inside me, and it oozes out for two days. No wonder I'm never dry."

"Awh, come on, Shar," Jim teases, giving her a boyish smirk, "you should consider it an honor."

She doesn't reply but waggles her tongue at him as if to say, "You could never hack it as a woman, James David, not for one day." Lying down again, she pulls the sheet and blanket over them, then a red-and-blue barnyard quilt that Mor made.

The Pedersens' upstairs guest room has gray wallpaper and a wide-planked carpetless floor. The floor is icy cold on winter mornings but there's a braided throw rug on each side of the bed. The room smells musty and old yet faintly floral. The windows have small colonial panes and blue Scottish-lace curtains. At the foot of the bed is an oak blanket chest that Mor brought from Norway when she came to America in 1928.

Sharon twists over and turns off the lamp. "So did you tell Becki?" she asks after getting comfortable again.

"Not yet," Jim replies. "I was gonna tell her before church this morning but Carl asked her to take your Sunday school class, so I didn't get a chance. But I'll tell her Tuesday." He's already told his wife of his decision to stop doing outreach with Becki, but of course, he didn't tell her what prompted his decision.

Sharon's voice takes on that intuitive tone it gets when she shares a gut feeling: "I knew Pastor had a good reason. I guess he's wiser than we realize. Instead of condemning you, he let God bring you to your senses, and it didn't even take a week." She gives a teasing chuckle. "I could say I told you so, but I won't."

Jim gives her a playful jab on the shoulder. She laughs and snuggles close to him. Cozy silence, but not for long as Sharon shares some family concerns. She's worried about Heather who came in coughing after playing in the snow with Susie. The kids aren't sleeping well in the same room with Sue and Little Alf. Mark and Leslie are being inconsiderate, leaving right after Christmas dinner and expecting Pop and Nana to watch their kids while they vacation in Montreal. Pop has spent the whole week hiding in his barn office with Harry and Grover; he talks more to the dogs than to the family.

Cozy, homey, wifely, motherly, hot breath on his neck. Cuddling with Sharon in her parents' home gives Jim a secure it's-all-better-now feeling, especially after his personal vows of repentance. It's like they've gone back to a simpler time—before Becki, before LBI, before Brendon Falls. They're in the Air Force, home for the holidays. Erin is a toddler, Heather an infant, Chris not yet born. Life is young and full of promise. The upstairs room is pitch dark as is the cold moonless night outside. A gust of wind buffets the old farmhouse, but Jim Shanley feels toasty warm.

\* \* \*

Monday morning finds Jim and Heather and Chris sledding at Jacob's Hill. Sue and Little Alf are also along. Erin stayed at the house to read. Susie Pedersen, a short unkempt teenybopper with a pudgy face and straggling mouth, is a female version of Uncle Olaf, while Little Alf, just turned four, is a tidy square-faced lad with a demeanor much like his namesake grandfather.

It's well below freezing but the bright sunshine makes it seem warmer. Heather is still coughing but otherwise seems energetic and full of health. The snow is good for sledding: five inches with ice underneath; upstate New York didn't get as much from the Christmas Eve storm as New England. Jim feels like a kid again, boisterous, bold, alive, and free—so different from real life. He can never be a kid again in real life because of women and sex. He can be a Spirit-filled Christian adult—his current status and ongoing ambition—but never a kid. Cursed be the day he passed puberty.

By eleven a.m. they're all snow-covered, snow-burned, red-faced, runny-nosed, and ready to go home. On the walk back, down Jacob's Hill Road, Heather and Susie run ahead while Jim follows with the boys. Chris is full of questions: "Daddy, howcum snow is white?"—"Howcum Nana puts mud on her freckles in the baffroom?"— "Daddy, howcum Harry 'n Grober lift their legs when they pee? An' they always pee on a tree or sumptin'? Crystal's dog neber does that?"—"Howcum God has long hair? I thought only girls were supodz to hab it long?"

And Little Alf has questions of his own: "Unka Jim, howduzda sun know whereda go when it comes up?"—"Howcum Unka Owaf hasta go to his room to smoke his ceegars?"—"Unka Jim, why duz Unka Owaf burp at da table? Mommy says we're not supodz to do dat?"—"Unka Jim, howduz Jeezus get inda my heart? Duz he come inda my nose ... or inda my mouff?"

Jim responds as best he can, but his answers fall far short of the innocent honesty and childlike wonder conveyed in the questions.

*Some questions have no answers,* he says to himself. *But we adults invent answers anyway, especially if we're Christian adults.* His talk with the boys pricks his heart as he considers his own Christmas Eve vow to adhere to Christian dogma, to Christian answers, but after his wild spree of carnal sin, he doesn't dare listen to his heart. His rational and religious side is firmly in control.

Back at the house they put their boots and wet clothes by the fireplace. Erin is curled up on the sofa with her new Anne Shirley books: *Anne of Avonlea, Anne of the Island,* and *Anne of Windy Poplars.* Chris got a radio-controlled GI Joe tank for Christmas, and he and Little Alf send it after Harry and Grover who have a barking fit. Heather and Susie escape to the basement with Heather's new softball mitt and bounce a tennis ball off the wall.

The house smells of burning wood, coffee, and nokkelost cheese. Mor and Nana are fixing lunch: homemade vegetable soup and cold cuts, and nokkelost and gjetost, plus assorted rolls and buns, and the usual Norwegian cookies. The kitchen windows are fogged. The mood in the house is cozy, Christmasy, Scandinavian.

"Let's take a nap after we eat," Sharon whispers to Jim as she sets the table. After two weeks apart, they can't stay away from each other. Godly, proper, no guilt. Jim senses that his sex drive is finally governed by the Holy Spirit.

\* \* \*

Pastor Jim exits the Mass. Pike at Auburn and heads north on Route 290. The day is cloudy, gloomy, drizzly. The snow is melting. Worcester's fog-shrouded skyline looms ahead. Morning traffic on 290 is like the chariot race in *Ben-Hur.* Cars, trucks, buses: zooming, darting, grinding, growling, jockeying for position. Jim falls behind a behemoth dump truck which is belching black smoke through twin stacks and kicking up a storm of mud and salt. He pushes the windshield washer three times but only manages to smear the brown mist into an opaque film. Giving up, he reins in the Mustang, and retreats to the rightmost lane.

Tuesday, December 27th. Christmas in Cobleskill is over, at

least for Jim. Sharon and the kids are coming back on Friday. He passes the Holy Cross football stadium. His thoughts turn to the church, to his revived religious goals, *I can't let up. I have to hit hard again tonight. I'll pick up where I left off Sunday. I can't wait. I'll read it right out of the Word ... what God did to Sodom, what Moses did to fornicators and queers. I'm gonna wake people up and get 'em in line. 1984 is gonna be different: no more lazy lukewarm attitudes toward sin. We're goin' all-out for God!*

Then, as he exits onto Route 72, Jim begins to rehearse for his most immediate mission, *"You're right, Becki, I have a weakness. We must put an end to this"—no, that stinks. It sounds like I'm rejecting her. Let's see, "We'll always love each other in Christ and we'll be together at church, and you can still babysit, but we can't"—no, that minimizes the problem. Let's see, "We've been cl se a long...."* He rehearses until he has the perfect words. He's resolved, ready, in control—no turning back. Yet something deep inside is hurting, crying, screaming, dying. *It's my "old man," my "sin nature,"* he rationalizes to himself. *I'm finally going to the cross. I'm finally "dying unto self." That's why it hurts.*

After a quick stop at home to feed Samantha, Jim heads for 59 Front Street, his stomach knotting with anxiety. He's not sure Becki will let him in, but he hopes she'll receive him once she hears that he's repented before God.

He parks behind the Escort, next to Kyle's Honda. *The nerve of that guy,* Jim declares indignantly to himself. *It's 9:30 on a Tuesday morning and he's still in Ruthie's bed, still shacked up with that slut. He ignored my sermon as if it means nothing. Who is he to ignore God? No wonder Jodi gave up on him.*

Jim gets out, stretches into his jacket, shoves his flannel shirt into his Levi's, then marches determinedly up the slushy unshoveled sidewalk. The melting snow on the house drips off the eaves and pitter-patters on the porch roof. The east wind blows a chilly mist into his face along with the oily smell of the Prescott smokestack. He stomps his Timberland boots on the porch but to no avail. No amount of stomping can dislodge the snow from the deep waffle-iron treads. Up the stairs. He knocks—no answer. He knocks again—no answer. Finally, a weak voice: "Who is it?"

"It's me!" Jim loudly announces. He's puzzled at Becki's faintness of voice.

"It's locked but not bolted," comes her weak voice again. "Use your key." He flips through his keys until he finds it, then goes in. Bathsheba meets Jim at the door eagerly rubbing against his legs as if famished. Darkness, quietness. Rebecca is still in bed. The gray morning sneaks in around the window shades dimly defining her room; the light is weak and without color, like a night scene in a black-and-white movie. Frowny-faced, her eyes barely open, she lies on her back under the covers, two pillows under her head.

"What's goin' on?" Jim queries. "Are you sick or something?"

Becki coughs, wheezes, then answers in a croupy whisper, "I feel wicked hot. I got diarrhea. I stayed up too late. I ate too much. Now my stomach *kills,* and my throat." Jim raises the window shade so he can see her better. Her eyes are dull and heavy-lidded, her skin chalky, her lips blue-gray and cracked. She has dark pockets under her eyes. And her hair looks like seaweed at low tide. Becki squints against the intruding light, the frown on her brow becoming more pronounced. She moans, curls away into a fetal position. Jim asks if she wants to go to the doctor. She shakes her head, "No." He asks if she wants him to stay. She nods, "Yes."

To the kitchen, messy kitchen. Bathsheba follows, mewing, rubbing. Melting boot tracks follow as well. Mingled odors, stale, greasy, sour, join the sharp stink of cat piss. Dirty dishes on the table, in the sink, on the counter. Also on the counter: a greasy skillet, a dried slice of tomato, a wilted head of lettuce, an open bag of hamburger rolls, an overturned glass of milk. There are pawprints in the milk, and up and down the gray formica countertop.

Too warm. Jim closes the radiator. He peels off his jacket and throws it on the swayback sofa. He finds a leftover can of Nine Lives tuna in the fridge and feeds Bathsheba; she usually turns up her nose at cold cat food but she gobbles this right down. Jim then grabs a kitchen chair, goes back to Rebecca's room, and parks at her bedside.

She's still on her side curled away from him. He touches her forehead; her skin feels pasty and hot, but not burning. He hikes the sheet and blanket up over her shoulder. Her red afghan is wadded into a tangle at the foot of the bed. The bedroom is just as messy as the kitchen and smells of stale McDonald's french fries. The coffee table looks like a giant unemptied McDonald's tray. The beige sofa cushions are piled helter-skelter around the green chair which is overflowing with clothes, as always. Becki's yellow shoe box of music tapes is on the floor in front of the stereo. A half-dozen cassettes are scattered about it along with her Garfield throw-pillow, the *TV Guide,* the TV remote, the *Rolling Stone* magazine, a blue mug, and an empty eggnog carton. Jim figures that the McDonald's debris is a day or two old and that her late-night meal came from the kitchen, but he suspects that her sickness is not from eating too much but from the flu bug going around.

Rebecca's hip-heavy figure fills the sofa bed like a beached dolphin. There's no sound except the *drip-drip* of melting snow and her croupy breathing. The gold blanket is Alison's; it's cheap, acrylic, and worn. The satiny nylon binding is torn loose and hangs over Becki's shoulder like a shiny frayed ribbon.

Jim wrestles in his mind: *No, I can't. I can't tell her now; not when she's sick.... But why not? She has to know, sick or not. Besides, it might make her feel better. She'll be glad to hear that I've repented, that I now agree with her.*

"Becki Lea, I hafta tell you something," he says gently but piously. "You don't hafta talk. Just listen. Now about Christmas Eve, it was *my* fault. I let things get out of hand. In fact, I've been giving in to selfish and sinful fantasies all year. You know I love you, and I always will, but you're right. I have a problem, and it's messing up our friendship. I hafta face it. I want our love to be pure, in Christ only. So, I don't think ... well, we shouldn't—"

FLASH! FLASH! Flailing arms. Flying bedclothes.

Becki bolts upright, tries to get up, but doesn't make it. Jim jumps just in time. Vomit! Vomit! Vomit everywhere! Heaving, retching, she barfs all over the side of the bed, the chair, the carpet. Some splatters onto Jim's boots and blue jeans. Chunky with undigested food, her vomit is gray and orange and gravylike; it looks like cream of mushroom soup mixed with Russian dressing. But her last heaves bring up nothing but yellow slime that looks like nasal snot. The room reeks. Jim's gut contracts like a closing fist. He can almost taste the sour-caustic puke. He gags almost barfing himself.

Becki, ashen-faced, near to fainting, moans pitifully as she totters on her hands and knees over the edge of the bed. Bathsheba, having scurried in from the kitchen, sniffs the hot stinking puddle on the carpet then escapes to the back of the green chair.

Panic, fear, compassion, revulsion. Shock, brainlock, then a frenzy of mental activity. Jim's frantic thoughts race after his rattled emotions like pups chasing a covey of quail. Panic: *Do something dammit!* Fear: *Call Russ.* Compassion: *Hold her.* Revulsion: *This is gross. Gotta clean this shit up, and quickly.* Compassion: *Help her; she's gonna fall off into the vomit.* But Becki doesn't fall. Instead, she curls, shaking and whimpering, into a ball on the other side of the bed, her head at the foot. She hugs the afghan.

Instinct, instinct. Jim's psyche finally shuts down all thoughts except for the immediate. Moving around the bed, he gently caresses her head and tells her to lie still, that he'll be right back. He vaguely remembers what Sharon did when Heather had the stomach flu in November. To the bathroom. He wets a washcloth with hot water, grabs a bath towel. Back to the bedroom. He quickly clears the pile of clothes off the green chair and kicks the sofa cushions out of the way. Bathsheba takes off for the kitchen.

*Oh shit!* Jim exclaims to himself as he helps Becki into the chair. *It's all over her nightgown and inside it too.* She has on a buff-colored flannel gown with a brown bow on the neck, and there's a stream of orange puke down the front. Lifting her legs, Becki curls back, shivering and shaking, into the overstuffed chair.

Jim quickly searches her chest of drawers: panties, white socks, bras. *No.* Next drawer: Levi's, cords, shorts, sweaters. *No.* Next drawer: *Ahah*—nightgowns, nightshirts, pajamas. He grabs the top gown, a pink ruffled one with flowers on it.

"Now we have to get this stinky thing off," he explains to Becki as he sits her up in the chair, her head wobbly like a baby's.

"I jus' wanna lie dow'," she protests, her voice slurred and wheezy and faint.

"Don't try to talk, Becki," Jim instructs. "Just lean forward. Now lift up. That's it ... good girl." He pulls the gown from under her buttocks, lifts the barf-fouled garment over her head, and tosses it toward the kitchen, leaving her naked save for her white knee-socks.

Becki's deathly-pale body, flabby, floppy, helpless, hot to the touch, looks baby-fattish and childlike. It's the first time Jim has seen her this naked, but the experience is not sexual in the least. Her limp ashen presence is a far cry from the wanton woman that fondled him in the bathroom three days ago.

Her breasts seem smaller, more girlish, as they overhang her folded paunch. Her legs are together hiding her bush. Her chunky thighs seem wider, her flab more fluid: two heaping mounds of tapioca pudding. Only a few tufts of dark pubic hair peek above the converging rolls of white flesh.

Jim cleans the vomit from her face, her neck, her tits, her midriff. Goose bumps come up in the wake of the washcloth. Her nipples swell as well—from the chill. Next, he dries her gently with the towel. Tender affection, compassion, warmth. A dam breaks in his heart flooding his bosom. *O Lord, I don't want her to be sick. I love her. I love her so!* He slips the clean nightgown over her head then helps her put her arms into the sleeves.

As Becki curls again into the chair, Jim moves quickly to fix a new place for her to lie down. He pulls the gold blanket off the bed, the red afghan, the blue sheet, the top one. They're okay, as are the pillows. He piles them in the corner by the closet. But the bottom sheet is covered with vomit. Stripping it off, he tosses it the other way, toward the kitchen, putting it with the stinky gown. The thin foam-rubber mattress is also soaked. No time. He knows that stomach flu makes you throw up more than once. He quickly pulls the mattress off the bed, folds the springs and frame back into the sofa, replaces the cushions, and makes up a new bed lengthwise on the couch, using the good sheet and gold blanket.

He then helps Becki over from the green chair. After tucking her in, he covers her with the afghan. Eyes closed, she groans, shifts onto her side, pushing her butt against the sofa back.

Jim caresses her head, kisses her gently on the cheek, then returns to his cleaning. He rolls the thin mattress and takes it into the kitchen along with the puke-covered sheet and clothes. He grabs some Tide detergent and a bucket from under the sink. While the bucket is filling with hot suds, he takes a roll of paper towels, swabs-blots the puddle of vomit on the floor, wipes it off the chair, and throws the dirty towels into a plastic bag. Then using the bucket and a sponge, he scrubs the barfy area of carpet along with his boots and the cuffs of his jeans; he also scrubs the chair. In three days he's done more scrubbing than in the past five years. Finally, he rinses out the bucket and places it on the floor by Rebecca's head.

And just in time, as she begins to gag and retch again, vomiting a handful of brownish-green bile into the bucket. Jim holds her, steadies her. She dry-heaves several more times then falls back onto her pillow, panting, shivering, whimpering, her face grayer than the weather outside. He wipes her mouth and chin then tucks her back into the makeshift bed. *O Lord,* he prays, *let this be the last one.*

Becki looks up pleadingly. "I'm thirsty," she moans, her voice having no more weight than a dandelion puff. Her sickly eyes are dull and dark like the ocean on a cloudy day, more gray than blue.

Jim can't give her water or any liquid, not yet, but he remembers what Sharon gave Heather. To the fridge. He pulls a tray of ice and wraps four cubes in a clean washcloth. Using the greasy skillet as a hammer, he crushes the ice on a cutting board. After twisting the washcloth tightly around the crushed ice, he secures it with a twist tie and gives it to Becki, along with another bath towel. He pulls his chair over to her side and begins a bedside vigil.

Becki sucks on the small pink ice bag wetting her cracked lips and parched mouth; her breathing is shallow, throaty, thick. Jim strokes her disheveled mop of hair, her pallid cheek. He also speaks tender words of affection and encouragement, but not many since he wants her to sleep, but sleep doesn't come. Every thirty minutes or so, she gags and vomits and dry-heaves. Each time she barfs up a little more slime, like a spoonful. He holds her, helps her.

Gray, white, hint of green. Her complexion drains and drains until her cheeks are almost the color of the green slime she's vomiting up. Weaker, weaker. She can no longer hold the washcloth to her lips. The ice melts but Jim continues to dampen her lips with the baggy wet cloth. Drained and queasy himself, he's becoming concerned, almost scared.

But finally, after two hours and five cycles of vomiting, Becki falls into a shallow fitful doze that gradually deepens into much needed sleep.

Bathsheba, sensing that the commotion is over, comes in and curls up at the end of the sofa by Becki's feet. Jim washes out the bucket but keeps it by the couch just in case. He then sits a bit longer watching Rebecca sleep.

Half on her stomach, half on her side, she presses her cheek into the blue pillow distorting her face. A matted lock of brunette hair hangs over the side of her face. Her nostrils are caked with dried mucus. Her mouth is open and her breath smells like a dead rat. But her respiration, though still croupy, is deeper, more regular, like snoring but without the grating rumbling nasal stridulation—Becki never snores when she sleeps; at least, Jim has never heard her.

*Sickness is such a mystery,* he thinks to himself. *It's like a preview of death. I hate being sick, especially vomiting. But it's like we have no control. We all get sick. We all die. It's because of sin, but it's bigger than sin. Even the holiest Christians get sick, even Billy Graham. It's scary. It's awful. Yet it's honest and somehow comforting, strangely comforting.*

*Oh, Becki, Becki,* Jim thinks on, now addressing her silently in his thoughts. *You're such a child yet so much a part of me. I love being with you even when you're sick. It's heaven. I can't explain it. You make me happy. You make me feel so alive. Even if you were sick, or paralyzed, for your whole life, I would take care of you and feed you and read to you and dress you ... and pay for it until I had no money left, and every moment would be beautiful. I love looking into your face, like now when you're sleeping, and touching your hair even when it's dirty and matted. It seems so right to be here with you, just like it seems right when a bird is flying, or a fish is swimming, or a deer is running. It's like you and I were created to be together. Can this be? Is this what love is? Is this where the magic comes from?*

As Jim sits there gazing at her sickly and plain face—but beautiful to him—his new religious resolve fades like darkness at dawn. He knows he can never tell her what he came to tell her.

Finally, he kisses her cheek, picks up Bathsheba, and retires to the kitchen, closing the door so the cat won't bug her. Bathsheba tries to get back in for a bit then gives up and jumps up on the old swayback couch where she licks her sleek black coat.

The kitchen is okay but Bathsheba prefers to sleep with Becki—just like Jim.

* * *

Becki shoves a piece of Big Red gum into her mouth then grabs the TV remote. "Come on, Becki," Jim banters as she dits up and down the dial. "How can we keep up with the movie, if you keep changing channels?"

Becki scrunches her face teasingly. She waves the remote like a magic wand. "I hafta see what else is on. I don't wanna miss anything."

Needless to say, she's feeling better; she's still wheezy, queasy, congested, and weak, but her fever has broken and her feisty spirit has returned. There's now a sparkle in her eyes and a hint of color in her cheeks. Her voice is still croupy but stronger. They're both on the sofa. Becki lies on her side, her head on Jim's lap; she's in her yellow robe and half under the afghan. They're watching *The Asphalt Jungle* on Channel 38 but she keeps zapping to the network shows, *The A-Team, The Mississippi,* and *Just Our Luck.* In the movie the bad guys seem like good guys which encourages Jim's heart. Besides, he likes Marilyn Monroe who's young and innocent in this old flick.

Becki slept all afternoon. While she slept, Jim washed her dishes, cleaned the kitchen, scrubbed the mattress, emptied the litter box, took her trash down, took the puke-covered sheet and gown to the laundromat, and went to Stop & Shop where he bought ginger ale, saltine crackers, chicken noodle soup, cat food, Comtrex, drinking straws, and Big Red gum. It came to $11.68; he paid for it with a twenty. By nature he hates domestic chores, but when it comes to Becki Lea, he doesn't mind. He loves taking care of her. He'd take care of her forever, if he could.

When she awoke, Jim cleared the McDonald's stuff off the coffee table, moved the table closer, and gave her crackers and ginger ale. That's what his mom always gave him when he was a boy and got sick. When Jim gave Becki the ginger ale, she sat up and said, "I feel dizzy but I'm wicked thirsty." She wanted to guzzle the bubbly soda but he made her sip it slowly through a straw. "This cracker tastes yechy," she fussed, nibbling on a saltine. As she fussed, she assumed her usual pouty face, a good sign. After eating two crackers and sipping a juice glass of ginger ale, she lay back on the pillow.

While Bathsheba licked the unfinished crackers, Jim waited and watched, the bucket in position. Five minutes later, Becki sat up, leaned forward as if to retch, but instead belched out a big burp and announced, "I gotta pee." Getting up, she headed to the bathroom, unsteady on her feet but she made it on her own. When she returned, she put on her robe, brushed her hair, and lay back down, her breath smelling of Crest toothpaste; the change was refreshing.

About six-thirty, Jim made chicken noodle soup for her. He ate a bowl as well. Becki sipped, slurped the steamy liquid, and sucked the long noodles into her mouth. She finished most of the bowl and kept it down, along with five crackers. After eating, she lay down and said, "I feel a chill. Will you sit with me?" That's when she put her head on Jim's lap.

Tucking the covers around her, Jim caressed her back, her shoulders, her hair, her face. Heaven, heaven. He sensed her soul loving him, like on that October day by the blue flowers. *Oh, this feeling is so beautiful,* he declared happily to himself. *It's so different than lust yet somehow the same. It's my heart, but the liquid waves of heat are the same.* Finally, Becki zapped on the TV.

Now it's 8:30 p.m. and she's still lying on Jim's lap as they watch the movie. Her brown hair is straight and stringy, her face blah and drained, her eyes filled with chunks of sleep, her nostrils caked with mucus. And the pimple patch on her chin is a dried scab. But she's still adorable to Jim, more angelic and precious and enchanting than words can express.

Nonetheless, he speaks words, silent words in his heart, *Oh, Becki Lea, I wish you could live with me forever and be my wife for all eternity. I want to be with you every day. I want to see you and touch you, and hear you and smell you and taste you. I want to know you and know you. I wish we could have our own place where you and I could laugh and love and live together—I wish.*

Pastor Jim never made it to Tuesday night service. He called Russ earlier and told him to have Stan preach in his place—so much for the new get-tough policy. He called while Becki was eating her noodle soup.

"You're gonna stay here, Shanley, and play hooky from church?" she chided after he hung up. "You call that forsaking all for Christ?" But her girlish grin told Jim that she was glad he skipped church to stay with her.

# Chapter Thirty

Pastor Jim pulls into the Park Street Diner and stops by the phone booth in front. He leaves the engine running. The fire station is buttoned up tight, so is the town. Up and down the deserted streets, pole-mounted streetlamps punctuate the darkness, their capped cones of copper light shivering against the black moonless night. Cold, calm, full of stars. The clouds have broken.

Jim coughs, he clears, he coughs again. He takes off his gloves, fishes into his Levi's for his watch; it's 9:24 p.m. He fingers the bandless timepiece. *Gotta get this fixed. I can't keep it in my pocket forever.* The watch is an old Waltham that Sharon gave him for his twenty-third birthday. He's had numerous digital and battery-powered watches since, but the Waltham has outlasted them all. He shoves it back into his jeans then flips on the heater fan. He feels heat blowing on his feet—about time. It's been ten minutes since he left the church. He coughs. His throat tickles. He pulls, out of his jacket pocket, a crumpled red box of Pine Bros. cough drops. He pops the last one into his mouth. The cherry-flavored glycerin drop is soft and melty sweet, yet chewy tough like Dots candy when you sink your teeth into it.

Monday, January 2, 1984. The Christmas snow is now hard and crusty, and yellow with dog piss. Becki is over her flu, but Jim has been to hell and back since Friday—fever, vomiting, chills, queasy, weak, blah, nagging cough. Sharon and the kids returned just in time to nurse him. He hasn't preached since Christmas, and his voice just gave out thirty minutes ago while teaching Monday night Bible class. He chews the cough drop. It sticks to his teeth like licorice. Reaching inside his sweater-vest, he takes a letter from his shirt pocket; now the light:

> DEC. 28, 1983
>
> JIM,
>     I'M IN ST. LOUIS. I LOOKED UP A GUY I MET BACK IN '78. HE'S GOT A CHRISTIAN BAND THAT MEANS BUSINESS FOR GOD. SORRY I BLASTED YOU BUT I STILL THINK YOU SHOULD PRAY SERIOUSLY ABOUT THE DIRECTION OF YOUR MINISTRY AND ABOUT YOUR RELATIONSHIP WITH BECKI. THE TIME IS GROWING SHORT, JIM. WE CAN'T WASTE OUR LIVES PLAYING GAMES.
>
> JOE L.

Russ's Fairmont, then a blue Datsun. Jim stuffs the letter into his pocket and hops out. He exchanges a few smirky remarks with Russ and Stan—about their tardiness, about losing his voice at Bible study—as men do when greeting one another. Into the diner. They grab the last booth. Russ and Stan sit opposite Jim, their backs to the rest of the diner. Buddy shuffles over with three glasses of water. They order coffees all around, and a giant plate of fries.

Forget staff meetings, business meetings, corporation meetings. The real ministry decisions are made over french fries at the Park Street Diner. No hooks on the coat-tree—they were broken off long ago. Russ perches his Red Sox cap on the jukebox selector thing. Stan tosses his khaki windbreaker into the booth behind him along with Russ's parka. Jim wads his jacket on the seat beside him, then takes a sip of water to kill the tickle in his throat.

As always, Campbell dominates the booth with his pompous Stalin-like presence. But his tan polo shirt is tacky, too small, and out of season. His shirt pocket, overloaded with tracts, a notepad, and a Bic-Clic pen, sticks out like a square tit.

Herschel Hightower pops his chubby mulatto face out of the kitchen and waves at the three BFBC elders. At the lunch counter Elmer Kowalski eats a bowl of chili with a VFW buddy. Elmer, clad in his shabby brown suit, dangles his short legs from the stool. Jim knows they're eating chili because he shook their hands on the way in. At the other end of the diner, Barbara Sims waits on three Oriental men; they look Thai or Vietnamese, but could be Cambodians. Bessie isn't at the register, but a new girl: frumpy, fiftyish, thick glasses, graying brown hair. Jim doesn't know her.

"Well, Pastor Jim, it's good havin' you back on the battlefield," Stan says as he embarks on a bit of rah-rah apple-polishing. He fawns in his finest Uriah Heep manner which includes many servile gestures and grimaces. "I like preachin' but I can't hardly fill your shoes. Ever'one's still buzzin' 'bout your Christmas message. It was def'nitely haw'mark. Dr. Logan preached the same theme Saturday night at the New Year's Eve service. Too bad you missed it, but I got the tape. I'll bring it with me to church tomorrow night, so you can take it an' listen to it. 1984's gonna be a banner year, even better than—" Suddenly a gray-checked uniform: Barbara Sims.

She tells Pastor Jim that April has been sick all day and won't be coming to school. Academy classes resume tomorrow. Russ and Jim tell her about their own bouts with the flu. Russ got it but only a mild case. Stan never gets sick; at least, he never admits it.

Puffy eyes, poorly combed hair, wrinkled uniform. As usual, Barbara has that just-crawled-out-of-bed look. She does have a sweet smile and nice straight teeth, but they're piss-yellow from tartar which spoils her smile somewhat. And her mouth, when relaxed, hangs open a bit, not grotesquely like a stroke victim but enough to make her seem more stupid than she is. One of the Oriental men signals. Barbara notices and heads for the other end, but after a few steps, she returns, leans over the table, and whispers, "We get more slant eyes 'n spigs in here nowadays than regular people." Her breath is bad—sour, yeasty, cigarette-smoky.

Stan wags his thick forefinger. "Tell me about it," he says. "Mos' all our loadin'-dock guys at the mill are immigrams. Don't get me wrong, I'm for interrogation of the races an' equal op'tunity, but mos' of 'em are unsaved, an' they never fought in our wars or nuthin'." Russ snickers at Stan's misuse of the language then takes a quick swig of water. Jim snickers as well but suppresses it under a cough. Mispronounciations, double negatives, malapropian blunders: Stan Campbell butchers English worse than Yogi Berra.

"And they tip lousy, worse than Blacks," Barbara adds, her tone naive, common, her hazel eyes childlike. She reminds Jim of the poor white folks who lived in tarpaper shacks back in Upshur County when he was a boy. She shakes her head. "I'll be lucky to get a buck-fifty from these guys. And they chatter like magpies an' you can't understand nuthin'. And more are comin' all the time. When I was a kid, we jus' had a few coloreds, but then more came, then the Puerto Ricans, and now the boat people. I feel surrounded at the projects. There's more foreigners than whites. This whole town is goin' down ... but I been handing out tracts to 'em."

"Good; keep it up," Stan commends her. "God says, 'Preach the gospel to ever' creature,' in Mark 16:15. The immigrams are hard to convert. They got weird ideas and pagan customs. But Jesus is still their only hope."

A blush of Christian pride warms Barbara's face. After a few more comments she excuses herself and strides back to the other end, her ash-blond ponytail bouncing on her neck like a dirty dishrag. Nice hips but no breasts. She has the chest of a chicken.

But Jim scarcely notices. He can never lust on a queasy stomach. Besides, he has no desire for Barbara anyway, not because she's a holy prude like Leslie or Mary LeBlanc—Barb's too simpleminded to be pharisaical—but she seems to have no carnal-flirtatious side as if her sex drive is dormant.

Cunts and sex. The more Jim learns, the less sense it makes. Barbara, Doris, Melissa, Becki, Sharon, Betty Sue Barnett. Sharon's hot sexuality had skewed his understanding, but now he's realizing that the spectrum of female sexual response is much broader than he thought, that each woman is unique when it comes to lusting and fucking, and fits no label or category.

Buddy arrives with coffee, and a few minutes later, shuffles back with a large platter of fries, three plates, and a bottle of ketchup. Hot thick fries with the skins on, the diner's only claim to fame. Jim munches. Hot, but no taste. His taste buds are dead from the flu; everything tastes bland, insipid, gray. Russ eats slowly, salting and savoring each french fry as if it's a slice of apple.

Stan squeezes the ketchup bottle as if he's choking a goose, until his plate is red with Heinz. He then attacks the potatoes, picking up several at a time with his huge fingers. He swabs the fries in ketchup then stuffs them into his cavernous mouth. Grunting, groaning, gulping black coffee, he eats lustily like the Cyclops in the movie *Ulysses*. As Stan chews, he throws his head back showing his enormous elliptical nostrils; they're dark and deep like mine shafts, and are filled with shocks of bristly gray hair. Despite his handsome rock-featured face, he's hardly attractive when eating. Moreover, his vulgar table manners contradict his Christian-leader facade. Like Dr. Logan—though Logan nearly succeeds—Stanley Campbell cannot hide his boorish roots.

"Why'd the Polack need five guys to make popcorn?" Stan jokes, his husky voice thick with potato. Jim and Russ offer a few absurd answers but quickly give up. Stan's sapphire eyes spark with amusement, with triumph. He flashes a cocky grin then chortles the punch line, "'Cuz he needed *one* to hold the pan an' *four* to shake the stove." Jim and Russ laugh briefly but Stan laughs until his craggy face is redder than the ketchup on his plate. Finally, he settles, sucks a breath, then stuffs three more fries into his huge mouth. He washes them down with coffee then says, "She's right, you know?" This remark sets off a flurry of table talk.

"Who?" Russ asks while salting a potato.

Stan reaches for more fries. "Barbara Cameron," he answers.

"You mean Sims?" Jim corrects as he coughs and takes a sip of water—yech.

"Yeah, Sims," Stan agrees.

"She's right about what?" Russ asks Stan.

Stan sucks his ketchupy fingers. "About this town ... 'bout it goin' down."

"It's already down if you ask me," Pastor Jim remarks.

"But it's gettin' worse," Stan asserts. "They're even 'plyin' to join the union."

"Don't you think loading-dock workers should be in your union?" Russ asks. "We get all the guys to sign up at Stromberg, after they do their six months. I'd think you'd want more members, the way unions are losing clout?"

Stan cants his hoary head as if the idea is absurd. His tone

443

becomes more derisive, more condescending. "Come on, Russ. They don't hardly speak English."

*Look who's talking,* Jim interjects, but only in his thoughts.

"So conduct your meetings in Spanish and English," Russ counters Stan.

"'Gainst the bylaws," Stan grunts.

"You can change bylaws, you know?" Russ rebuts.

"We'd hafta have a different transmuter for each minor'ty," Stan replies.

"You mean translator?" Jim says between coughs, this time speaking aloud.

"Right," Stan goes on. "We'd hafta have a Spanic an' a Viennese an' a Korean, maybe a Cambod'an. Who knows? No way. It's too confusin' with so many—"

"Or you could teach them English," Russ interjects.

Stan chuckles through a belch. "Come on, Russ. You're puttin' me on?"

"You're just a bigot, Stan," Russ kids—but Jim knows that Russ is more serious than he lets on.

"Not really, they can't help it," Stan says, swabbing a fry until it's red.

Jim sips his coffee; it tastes like chalk. "Who can't help it?" he asks Stan.

"The Spanics 'n gooks, an' all of 'em," Stan says. "They don't want our ways."

"How d'you know, Stan?" Russ asks.

"It's in their blood," Stan explains. "'Cuza the curse of Ham in Genesis 9:25."

Russ gestures toward Stan with a french fry. "The curse of what?"

"You know, the curse. Ham saw Noah naked, so God cursed his seed."

"His seed?" Russ asks, playing dumb.

"You know, his 'cendents, the niggers ... an' all the darkskins 'n gooks."

Russ chuckles. "Never heard you say 'nigger,' Stanley. Guess that proves it?"

Stan lifts his cup, and his rocklike chin. "Proves what?" he asks defensively.

"That you're a bigot," Russ responds.

"No way," Stan rebuts. "It jus' shows I go by the Bible."

Russ has Stan going and he continues to bait him, "So you think it's okay for you, a church elder, to use a white-trash word?"

"I never say it around 'em," Stan defends himself. "Truth is,

I love 'em—with the love of Christ."

Russ grins mockingly. "You *love* them? Now I've heard everything, Stan."

"It's true. I do. I wanna lead 'em to God. There's no greater love than that."

"Well, I don't," Russ confesses. "But I got no beef against the Blacks, or the boat people, or any of them, except we get taxed to pay for their welfare."

"That's 'cuza the curse," Stan says. "They're lazy an' they breed like rabbits."

"So you think whites are superior?" Russ asks, baiting Stan some more.

Stan snorts derisively then replies, "Among the unsaved they are, 'cuza the curse. The Bible says it, Russ."

"But, Stan, the Jews said the same thing about the Samaritans?" Russ counters.

"You mean the Good Smerton in Luke ten?" Stan asks, holding three fries.

"Yeah, him too," Russ replies.

Stan stuffs the fries into his mouth. "Well, he's different. He was saved." Stan speaks with his mouth open; the gunky half-chewed fries swirl disgustingly about his tongue, like wet concrete in a cement mixer.

"How d'you know?" Jim asks Stan, from the sidelines.

"'Cuz he took care of the wounded guy in the ditch," Stan explains.

"So the curse of Ham is off if a Black or Hispanic accepts Christ?" Russ asks.

"Of course," Stan affirms. "If you're saved, you're a child of God—like *us*."

Russ gives an impish grin then presses his point, "Even Juanita?"

"I doubt Nita's saved," Stan reacts. "She's a lyin' jezebel, an' lazy. She comes to church, but she's a deceitful female, like so many of 'em. She's gonna ruin Freddie."

"So where are they living?" Russ asks.

"At Nita's apartment. She's too good for my sister's attic."

Russ gives a breathy sigh as if to say, "Come on, Stan. Your sister's attic is a rathole. And Juanita may be deceitful, but Freddie's the lazy one. I haven't heard about him working lately." But Russ doesn't say it, for he doesn't want to get Stan going on one of his "uppity women" tirades; at least, that's what Jim suspects.

Stan swabs the last two fries and stuffs them clumsily into his mouth, splattering ketchup onto Russ's argyle sweater. Seeing what he's done, Stan apologizes to Russ. "No big deal," Russ replies, wiping the spot with a napkin, yet he wastes little time getting Stan back. Moving closer to the window, Russ leans away from Stan and cuts a loud rumbling fart. Russ laughs. Jim grins.

Stan chuckles but quickly sobers into a smug grin as if to say, "Burping is okay for Christians but farting is too much. I have more control than that." But he doesn't actually say it. He, like Russ, is careful, for the sake of the church, to stay on the bantering side of the line. In fact, someone looking on would conclude that Stan and Russ are friends, but looming underneath their baiting is an iceberg of animosity.

Pastor Jim leaves to take a leak. When he returns, he slides into the booth and says, "Okeydoke, let's get down to business; we can't bullshit all night. We hafta deal with this budget thing."

While Russ digs his paperwork out of an ancient leather case—it looks like a WWII spy satchel—Stan signals for Buddy. Buddy doesn't see the signal of course but Barbara does. She tells Buddy and he shuffles over and lowers his sooty-black head almost into Stan's mouth. After getting instructions, he departs but shortly returns with fresh coffee all around.

Jim picks up the glass sugar dispenser—it's the old-fashioned cylindrical kind with a hole in the top, like a little silo—and pours three spoonfuls into his coffee, along with a lot of milk, but it doesn't help; his coffee still tastes chalky. Nonetheless, he sips it to soothe the tormenting tickle in his throat.

Finding his report, Russ places it on the table before him and smooths it with his hands. The stapled papers are wrinkled, dog-eared, water-spotted, as if he typed it in the shower. Russ starts but Stan interrupts him, "'Fore we get into money talk there's one other thing."

"Go ahead," Pastor Jim says muffling a cough. "Let's hear it."

Stan gestures with his uplifted cup. "I jus' wancha to know that it's not true."

"What's not true?" Russ asks.

Knitting his thick brows, Campbell swigs some coffee then pushes the cup and saucer to the side. He spreads his mottled paws on the rose-colored table and stretches, throwing his head back and hunching his thick oarsman shoulders. His muscles tighten until his undersized knit shirt is ready to burst. His cumbrous hands seem to cover the entire tabletop and his skull-dagger tattoo seems alive on his bulging pythonlike bicep. Finally, he replies, "You know, the rumors that been spreadin' 'bout Barry 'n Pastor Garrett?" Stan relaxes his muscles. "I talked to Barry. He says Janet's all 'cited an' confused 'bout the scuttlebutt goin' 'round, but there's not nuthin' to it, not nuthin'. You think Dr. Logan's gonna have a *queer* workin' at Blant'er Castle? An' I've known Barry since he was sixteen. He's no pervert. He's normal as any guy. Besides, it's not possible for a saved man to be a fag. The Holy Spirit won't allow it. The women in this church, they can't live without gossip, an' I'm married to the biggest one of all. I oughta wring her neck."

Jim and Russ do not contest Stan's innocent verdict for Barry and Garrett despite what they know. After what Jim's been through over Christmas, he has no desire to stir any shit lest he discover it to be his own. And Russ never plays the pharisee. Stan takes another drink of coffee, wipes his mouth with the back of his hand, then says, "Okay, I'm ready. Let's hear the bad news."

Russ begins but pauses again as Stan pulls out his notepad and pen, then reaches around behind him and fishes his glasses out of his jacket. He props them on his nose like a librarian. The gray frames match his hoary hair; they even have the same reddish-blond flecks. Russ waits. He blows out his cheeks. He gives a sleepy-cat sigh. When Stan is settled, Russ proceeds but with no sense of urgency, "Well, let's see here. Now with corrections for the bills Angie paid last week, let's see ... where's that—"

"Come on, Russell," Stan prompts impatiently. "Want me to look?"

"Calm down; it's here somewhere," Russ replies as he flips to the second page, then the third. "I uh—oh yeah, here it is." He scans down to a circled number. The number is thickly penciled in next to a typed number which has been crossed out. The soft pencil-lead has smeared badly making the new number almost illegible. "Yes, this is the figure. As of December 31st—so it's for all of '83—we're in the red by $7560—"

"Can't be?" Stan interjects concernedly. He bounces his Bic-Clic on the pad.

"Oh, but we are," Russ affirms. "Let's see; 1st quarter, up $2700. 2nd quarter, we broke even, and most of the 3rd, but then the bottom fell out. September was down $990. October, $3140, and November, $2880. Now, let's look over here, December, yeah ... we're down $3250 in December.... And if we project ahead based on this rate of red ink, our cash reserves will be depleted by February 1st."

Campbell writes it all down with awkward strokes, his blockish scrawl eighth grade at best. Russ goes on—he's approaching the main issue indirectly—"Now offerings are only down 11%, but fourth-quarter delinquent tuition is up 65%. The problem is tuition versus salaries, but we can't lay off teachers during the school year. We have to cut elsewhere, so I propose ... or I think ... well, we have

447

no choice. We have to—"

"Come on, Russ, spit it out," Stan urges, his apprehension growing.

But Russ is in no hurry. His pace remains relaxed, resigned—and his voice: "Like I say, we have no choice. So this is what we must do. Starting this month, we must suspend all donations to Nashua for six months and—"

"Whaa! What! We can't do that!" Stan objects vehemently. He shakes his head so hard that his glasses almost fall off his nose. "We can't cut off home base jus' cuz our parents are diligent on their twition. God'll never honor it! The Bible says don't stop givin' but give 'til it hurts, an' it'll come back a hunerdfold, an' to bring your ties to the storehouse an' God will bless. That money is for WMF, for mission'ries. We got LBI teams all over. They're dependin' on us, an' we pledged that money to Moody. It's our promise to Dr. Logan. We can't back out *now*."

"Whoa, whoa," Jim says to Stan. "Nothing's been decided. Let Russ finish."

Stan, adjusting his glasses, apologizes for his lack of restraint—to Pastor Jim, not to Russ—then sits back, like a "good doggie" awaiting permission to eat.

Russ sips his coffee then goes on, "I also propose some additional cuts. One: suspend our support to the Landreths. Two: put a lock on all office phones. Three: lower our thermostats to 66°. Four: put a freeze on all major purchases. Five: postpone painting the old wing." He goes on for a few minutes. Finally, he tosses the report over to Stan, sits back, and waits for the rebuttal.

And it comes quickly. "That's not it," Stan argues, picking up the wrinkled report. He doesn't raise his voice yet his tone is hot with righteous indignation and cocksureness. "The problem's on the givin' side, not the spendin' side. If we start slashin' our budget, we're goin' down. It's a 'featist attitude." He flips through the report disgustedly. He turns up his nose as if it's fetid. "We don't need no reports. We need hard preachin' on givin' an' sackerfice like Neh'miah when he 'spired the people to build the walls of Jerusalem. They had nuthin' an' enemies were 'tackin', but he prayed an' rallied the people to victory." Stan grimaces with disdain and tosses the report back to Russ. "We jus' need to pray an' work harder. We need to organize better. We can't let losses in the 'cademy sink the *whole* church. If parents don't pay their twition on time, we gotta expend their kids. We can't let 'em rob God month after month."

Russ spews coffee. Jim chokes as well at the hilarious malapropism but turns it into a cough. Butcher, butcher. Stan butchers the language, especially when worked up. But he's undaunted, or too excited to notice. He preaches on, whipping his ballpoint like a baton, "Mos' all our converts are Spanics an' poor whites. It's the Malachi problem. We gotta win the 'fleunt. We're not bein' 'gressive on the battlefield. Take Nita's fam'ly. They're lazy 'n sloppy. They're not even 'sponsible at home. How can we 'spec 'em to be soldiers at church? The men got no dis'pline, an' the women are 'bellus 'n slutty an' whorin' all over. They *never* make good reg'lars." A wild spit curl tumbles onto Stan's forehead; he sweeps it back awkwardly but decisively. "We gotta visit ever' homeowner in this town. We gotta win more 'fluent fam'lies 'steada cuttin' off Nashwa. We gotta—" *BLAHWAAAANK! BLAHWAAAANK!*

Everybody jumps, except Buddy. Elmer spins off his stool. The diner vibrates: dishes, glasses, windows. Again and again comes the deafening blast as if they're inside a foghorn: *BLAHWAAAANK! BLAHWAAAANK!* Lights, action across the street: B.F.P.D. squad car, more cars, men running, doors opening. Finally, the fire trucks roll out, their red lights flashing.

Barbara Sims, like an excited child, jumps into an empty booth and presses her nose to the window. "It's a fire!" she exclaims.

"No shit," Herschel quips as he hangs over the counter. "They're sure not goin' to a parade."

Gears grinding, sirens wailing, the two pumpers, one new, one ancient, accelerate up Park Street behind the police car. The fire chief's sedan follows. The old fire truck growls, bangs, roars, like Dick Van Dyke's car in *Chitty Chitty Bang Bang*. At the end of Park Street, they turn left on Chestnut and the flashing lights disappear under the Conrail overpass; the sirens fade.

"Probably a furnace fire, with this cold weather," Russ surmises to Jim and Stan as quiet returns to the nearly empty diner.

"I bet it's one of those room heaters at the projects," Stan asserts. "Those people aren't careful. Some Spanic kid prob'ly left a newspaper lyin' on one an' it caught fire, an' her mother's out drinkin', or worse."

Stan swigs some coffee, takes off his glasses, and resumes his previous argument, "No way can we do it. We can't expand by cuttin' Nashwa. We gotta *fight* the devil. We gotta preach hard 'til ever'one's givin' their ties. The Bible commands it in seventeen different places. How can b'lievers ignore it? Lotta reg'lars don't even give 10%. I saw Angie's book when I was doin' the Malachi Project. Lotta folks jus' toss in a dollar, an' they think they're doin' God a favor. We gotta show people from the Bible, about the curse of Malachi three. If they don't give, they're gonna get laid off or they're gonna get sick ... or worse things. We gotta put the fear of God in 'em—but it's true! We can't prosper 'til we put God first!

We can't cut home base. It'll send a bad signal. We're part of a worl'wide ministry an' we're the best branch in New England. An' Dr. Logan's dependin' on us. The Landreths are dependin' on us."

While Stan rants and gestures with his folded glasses, Pastor Jim stares down at his cup until it fills the panorama of his mind—eggshell white, green stripe around the rim, around the saucer. The ceramic is thick, designed for wear rather than looks. He picks up his steel spoon—it's scratched, tarnished, from ten thousand washings—and stirs his khaki-colored coffee then watches the bubbles going round and round.

*My stomach still feels weird,* Jim says to himself. *Like cold slimy water is sloshing in my gut. I knew Stan would preach his fuckin' head off. I've heard it all before.... I don't feel like goin' in tomorrow. Maybe Jodi will bring donuts—oh, Becki, Becki, I wish I was with you. You were so pretty at Bible class, especially when you looked up and smiled at me. I wish Stan would shut up. Money talk is so monotonous and meaningless now, and cold and ugly.*

Walls, ceiling, grease-clogged exhaust fan. Jim looks up. Cobwebs adorn the corners of the ceiling. A few of the gray filaments drift on the rising convection currents but he sees no spiders. He figures they died from exposure. Compared to the walls and ceiling, the long mirror behind the counter looks spotless as if someone just cleaned it with Windex, but the mirror panels are warped just enough to distort the reflected images like in a house of mirrors. When Barbara Sims comes out of the kitchen, her reflection in the mirror has a grotesque pointy head and big knockers that jut out—Jim knows *that* is a distortion. But not the buxom brunette in the '40s-era Coca-Cola poster: her bikini-clad boobs are no distortion, yet time and smoke have discolored the old ad, turning her white swimsuit ash-gray, her skin yellow. The old schoolhouse clock still says 2:25; it's always 2:25 at the diner.

Having completed their meal, the three Oriental guys head over to the cash register where the frumpy new girl rings up their bill. Barbara clears their table. She notices Pastor Jim looking and waves two one-dollar bills.

At the counter, Elmer and his friend have a *Brendon Falls Banner* and are laughing at a picture of Boy George on the entertainment page. They grab Buddy and show him the androgynous leader of *Culture Club.* Buddy puts his face right down on the newspaper. He shakes his head with disgust and shuffles away. As he does, he mutters under his breath, "Fuckan' *maf*adite."

"You're overreacting, Stan," Russ calmly rebuts after Campbell finishes his ten-minute argument. "We're not withdrawing our spiritual support"—Russ isn't lying, at least not about himself; he withdrew his spirit from Nashua long ago—"but these measures are just stopgap to get us to summer. Let's face it. We either suspend payments to Nashua, or we stop paying our teachers and Pastor Jim, and stop running our Sunday school buses. It's not going to kill the other branches to pick up the slack. After all, since '77, we've sent some $70,000 to home base. Crenshaw showed me the blue list at summer conference, and like you say, Stan, we're at the top ... per capita anyway."

"How much will suspending Nashua save us?" Jim asks—as if he doesn't know.

"Well, about $1400 per month," Russ replies. "Roughly $700 in tithes, $500 to Moody, and $100 to Alison and Ed, plus smaller amounts to EDGE and special events."

Pastor Jim fingers his mustache as if thinking, but in truth, he decided on a compromise the first week of December when Russ first alerted him to the size of the deficit. Jim knows Stan will agree because the compromise plan will stroke Stan's ego which, as always, is like a horny dick. It just takes a few strokes to make it swell. And once swollen with pride, Stan must assert himself until he gets off on a good surge of cocky self-righteousness, which around Pastor Jim translates into obsequious obedience.

Jim clears his throat of bothersome phlegm, then says, "I think we can meet in the—" Distraction, distraction.

Officer Brad Selkirk waddles into the diner drawing Jim's attention. Selkirk, almost as wide as he is tall, is accompanied by a new female cop, a thirtyish redhead with a shovel-shaped ass which seems to want out of her tight uniform trousers. Brad acknowledges the BFBC elders with a wave of his black baseball-style hat, then he and the lady cop saunter down to the other end. His police revolver hangs halfway down his hip under his jacket. He reminds Jim of Sheriff Roscoe P. Coltrane on *The Dukes of Hazzard*.

"Looks like Selkirk's got a girl trainee," Russ quips after twisting around to check out the policewoman. "I bet he likes these long cold nights when he can teach her how to *hand*le his gun."

Russ laughs. Jim has a coughing fit. But Stan sobers like an Indian chief preparing for war. Pious eyes. His deep-seated blue eyes stare down his heavy wedge of nose. "I've had enough of your *fil*thy jestin', Russell," he declares. "How can we set the sample for the church if we're sackerligious? You know Ephesians 4:29 as well as me, what it says about *cor*rupt communication." Campbell kids about many subjects. He even has his own witty punch lines, mostly ethnic like his Polack joke, but he never jokes about sex. When it comes to copulation, he only quotes the Bible.

Over the line. Stan and Russ seem ready to have it out.

Tension, tension, as if the iceberg of animosity is coming up—but Barbara Sim's sudden appearance defuses the situation. "The fire was in the maint'nance garage at the projects," she proudly announces to the three BFBC leaders. "Brad jus' told me. And my apartment's okay. The garage is behind Building Six. That's Nina's building. But nobody got hurt or nuthin'."

"Wha'd I tellyuh," Stan chortles, quickly forgetting his disgust at Russ's off-color quip. "I knew it was the projects. Maybe it wasn't a heater but it's the same thing. Do I know this town, or what?" Beaming with I-told-you-so pride, he gives a cocky half-grin that exudes an air of conquest.

Russ raises his cup and toasts Stan in a gesture of derisive concession as if to say, "You're omniscient, you're omnipotent, you're righteous ... you must be the messiah of Brendon Falls." But he says nothing out loud. Instead, he arches his eyebrows, rolls his eyes, and gives a resigned shrug.

Jim coughs and sneezes; he pulls his hankie and blows his nose. His throat tickles, torments, as if he has poison ivy lining his larynx. "Okay, let's get back on track," he says after a quick drink of coffee. "I think I have a compromise that will solve this budget problem.... Let's implement Russ's plan, but only for two months. And on the preaching side, Stan, you'll be our standard-bearer. I'd like for you to take every Sunday offering and to give a teaching on stewardship each time, and I'd like for you to visit each family in the church, not to badger, but to share our needs, to reemphasize our local and worldwide vision, and to inspire our members to lay down their lives for the Lord. After all, you have the gift of exhortation, probably more than any leader in the church."

"*Per*fect idea, Pastor Jim," Stan heartily agrees, his ego quickly inflating until it throbs with hot pride. "Matter of fact, I been wantin' to preach more. An' I guess two months won't hurt our standin' in Nashwa, long as you explain to Dr. Logan." He raises his hands in a primal gesture of reassurance. "God's gonna come through, guys. You watch. If we jus' b'lieve. We gotta b'lieve the promises 'cuz greater is he that's in us than he that's in the worl', an' faith is the substance of things hoped for. Now I must say, Pastor Jim, you've got a real gift, yourself, when it comes to settlin' disputes." Stan gives a big shit-eating grin, showing his teeth which are handsomely set but gray in color.

"Okay, that's that," Jim declares. "We send no money for January or February, and we resume on March 1st. I'll get a letter out to Dr. Logan and to Alison.... Now let's get onto other business. Let's look at Beverly's academy list. Starting second semester, she wants to teach ABEKA pre-algebra to grades five and six—"

Stan is suddenly up and ready to go; he shoves his glasses into the case, the case into his jacket. He has little interest in the school. Jim suspects his lack of education makes him self-conscious about discussing scholastic matters—except for Bible courses.

But as usual, Campbell covers himself well, "Almos' ten-thirty. I'm a workin' man, you know." As he stands, he picks up the check. Russ tries to get it back but Stan says, "Relax, I'm payin' this week."

Wadding his windbreaker, like a Baggie, in his mammoth hand, Stan strides to the cash register; he moves with his usual awkward-soldier gait. *Ding. Ding.* The old-fashioned cash register springs open. After paying, he spends a minute witnessing to the new cashier. He then gives her a BFBC tract and departs.

As Stan marches by on the outside, he looks up and salutes Jim and Russ, then folds his Frankensteinian frame into his little Datsun and speeds off into the night. As he leaves, the fire trucks pull in across the street.

Buddy brings fresh coffee in a Pyrex pot. He fills Russ's cup but Jim declines; he has just enough water to soothe his cough. He's tired, weak, and wheezy, with no voice, but he needs to talk, to hear how Russ feels about things. Russ, Jodi, no more Joe—but Joe is schizo anyway, like Angie, Barry, and Doris, and Jim himself. Russ and Jodi are no longer driven by pious pressures. They never say the "right" thing. They always tell Jim what they really feel. They no longer crucify the heart in the name of God.

But before removing their ministry masks, Jim and Russ quickly dispose of Bev's academy list, approving everything that costs less than forty bucks and tabling the rest. Then comes Russ's warm Scottish smile: "So you and Sharon finally got it together, huh?"

"I'll *say,*" Jim replies, his voice now croaky like a frog. "She just about wore me out. It was good. It was sort of like going back in time, being at her mom's, being with the kids. Shit, if it was just Sharon and the kids, life would be okay, but—"

"Miss Becki," Russ cuts in, finishing the sentence for Jim. "She complicates the plot. You have no control when it comes to her. She makes you happy. She fills you with sweet yearning. She thrills you. She threatens you. She hurts you. She scares the hell out of you."

Jim sighs. He sips his water and gazes out the window into the cold January darkness. "You got it, Russ. I couldn't have said it better myself."

Park Street is empty. The fire station is buttoned up once again. A Conrail freight train trundles slowly by on the elevated tracks behind the fire station. Conrail runs through the heart of Brendon Falls while the B&M runs by the reservoir—both are marginal branchlines. The two railroads meet west of town where they share a small switching yard. Locomotives fascinate Jim especially at night, the headlights, the lighted numbers, the droning throb of the diesel engines. Massive and lumbering, they seem like primeval fire-breathing beasts, somehow out of place, out of time.

"Your Christmas message," Russ remarks, drawing Jim's attention back inside. "That was Becki, right?" Jim doesn't answer but Russ doesn't need one. He grins broadly and gestures with his cup. "So you two must've had a hell of an episode last week?"

"You can say that again," Jim confesses. He feels his face warming into a blush; he looks down and fingers his water glass.

Russ gives a wry chuckle. "Well, that *was* some fire-and-brimstone performance. Rougher than Logan, or Campbell. People are still shaking. It's amazing what guilt can do when it gets loose in the pulpit."

Jim takes a drink of water. For a long moment he holds his glass and his thoughts. Finally, he looks up at Russ with a shy smile and says, "You know me pretty well I guess?"

"Let's just say I know myself," Russ replies. His smoky-green eyes are tender and relaxed. Jim senses love in them. Russ's whole countenance is compassionate and calm, yet aware and tinged with portent, like Nashoba Reservoir in the early morning. At dawn the lake is often calm as glass, but a whisper of wind, a burst of ripples scurrying across—they speak of a stormy day ahead.

Trusting his naked heart to Russ's friendship, Jim opens the spigot; his words pour out in croupy spurts, "She's too much, Becki Lea. She's such a tease. She makes me laugh ... but she can be so mean to me, and selfish and sullen, and stubborn and pious—like she's frigid. She has to get her way. Then she flips. O *God,* she gets naughty and sassy and sexy. She flirts until she craves it, until she's creaming her panties, then she swirls about me like a dust devil, saucy, spirited, impulsive, and kicking up dirt and sand and rocks until I can't see. She's so ripe, so alive, so beyond, yet so much a part of me. Her fire consumes me, but it's like God always stops us, and I feel guilty for lusting, invading, so I-I, well, it's like I have no control, like I have no grip on things. It's like driving with no road map, or no road. It's a dream-come-true, yet it's a fuckin' nightmare. It's like being hooked on drugs."

"What the fuck can I say to that, Jim? It's crazy. It's irrational. It doesn't fit no matter how you shoehorn it, and you can't kill it or will it away. It's like me and Sylvia, but you're in over your head. I'm just neck deep."

"You got that right. I can't even obey my own preaching. I vowed to repent, to end it, but I only made it three days. When Becki was sick last week, she was so vulnerable, so soft, so cozy. Her eyes were big and innocent and brimming with affection. I felt her heart loving me. I melted, and my new resolve died on her couch. I wish that night could've lasted forever. Then I got sick. Now I don't have the strength to repent, even if I wanted to—and I don't."

Russ picks up his Red Sox cap and fingers it fondly. "The way I see it, your Becki-love is like Christ. It has no place to lay its head. Yet I think people see the glory of it, but only a few of us are insane enough to admit it, much less embrace it. Let's face it, Jim, concerned Christians have to deny it and crucify it. It violates all the rules, but moreso, it exposes the falseness of their own relationships, and the phoniness of their neatly packaged and propped-up lives. No one wants to deal with love outside their understanding, outside their control. If it doesn't fit, they must condemn it, and reject it as an ungodly thing. They're not about to consider it with an open mind."

"So why's everyone so hush-hush about it?" Jim asks. "About me and Becki?"

Russ stretches and yawns like an old dog. He puts on his baseball cap and stares down into his half-empty coffee cup as if it's a million miles away; his eyes grow big as if he's staring through to another dimension. "I'm sure there's plenty of talk behind closed doors, but who's going to openly challenge a pastor? Especially after Logan said it's okay for Becki to do outreach and ministry work with you."

"So what goes with Logan, anyway?" Jim asks, giving a yawn of his own that ends as a clipped cough. "I still can't figure it. Why would he endorse my time with Becki after I confessed that I want to have sex with her?"

"I don't know," Russ replies pushing his cap back on his head. "It puzzles me too. But I'm sure he has a sound tactical reason. Don't forget ... Logan and Garrett and Beckman, they don't think like rank-and-file Christians. Their ambitions go far beyond preventing fornication and preserving Christian virtue. Their game is power and control, so the issue is allegiance, not who's fucking outside the rules. They don't give a shit what you do with Becki, or what you preach, not really ... as long as you're loyal, as long as you stand with Logan, as long as you support him and openly respect his authority. But if you break ranks, then he'll use anything he can against you, and believe me, he'll take *no* prisoners. I don't trust any of those cocksuckers in Nashua. I never have. And it's going to be interesting to see how they react to this two-month cutoff of funds."

455

"You think Dr. Logan's gonna come down on us over this?"

"I don't know ... but I tend to doubt it."

"Why is that?" Jim asks.

"Nashua's too cagey to get bothered over losing three grand as long as they see us as a long-term asset. I have a hunch the bastard will stay with the carrot as long as he can. He's a fucking shrewd businessman, and Garrett and Beckman too. They're all sly codgers." Russ sips his coffee then gestures at Jim with his uplifted cup. "Say you ran a lumberyard, Jim, and one of your best contractor accounts was overdue, would you send a bill collector right over?"

"Not hardly," Jim replies. "I'd be nice as long as there was any hope of future business on the account."

"Exactly," Russ affirms. "Once you pull the gun, it's over.... See, that's the difference between us and the big shots in Nashua. Whether it's God or the devil, you and I are into love and intimacy. We've glimpsed the glory of hearts and souls and bodies coming together. The rewards of being shrewd: power and money, and prestige, and adulation, all the shit that gets you applause and high standing—well, that shit doesn't move us anymore, if it ever did. But Stan, he's still in it deep. He's still a wheeler-dealer. He's always persuading, promoting, selling. He's always got to be on top, in control—or at least look like he is. He's trying to be another Logan. He has Bible answers for everybody, chapter and verse, but it's false. It's fucked up and—"

Russ stops midsentence and kills the last of his coffee.

"Go on," Jim prods.

"You've been to Campbell's house, right?"

"Too many times to count."

"Did you ever see such a messy dirty place?" Russ replies. "How can he put down Juanita and the Puerto Ricans for being lazy and sloppy when his own house looks like the inside of a dumpster?"

Sudden passion. Fire ignites in Russ's eyes. He begins to preach—in a loud whisper lest anyone hear him. He chokes the column of air above his coffee cup as if choking Campbell's neck. "And the arrogant bastard has the gall to say he loves them. Well, *I* don't call it love. It's a code word for shame and control and bigotry. He *shames* them into submission. He's power hungry. That's why he defends Nashua. He smells opportunity like a vampire smells blood. But Campbell is no Logan, and he's certainly no Matthew Garrett. He's small potatoes, just a two-bit thug wrapped in the pretense of Christian repentance and goodness. He hasn't changed from the old days in Southie. He's just as corrupt as ever. His con game is different, that's all. I can't stand the cocky fucker! No wonder Doris is miserable. I've never felt one bit of warmth from him. He's so fucking false and propped up. He just wants power and adoration. That's why he agreed to your compromise. It puts him in the limelight. And, if any shit should arise over this, he looks good in *both* camps!"

Russ's vehemence stirs Jim. He feels like preaching himself but he's too croupy. Besides, Russ is telling it as good as it can be told, "Campbell's idea of church is to plug everyone into Carl Baker's organizational chart so each person will know their place in the pecking order like so many tools in a toolrack, and everyone will perform their duties like caged squirrels running on their respective wheels. That's not *God*. Least not any God I want to know. I hate it! It's far away from love!"

Russ leans forward for emphasis, placing his elbows on the table. He sucks a breath then goes on, "And this money bullshit, it's getting out of hand. $16,000 to Nashua in one year, from a branch church with fifty members. That's *fuck*ing insane. Why should *we* give ten percent of our offerings to Nashua? They don't do *shit* for us. And why should *we* pitch in to pay off the Moody mortgage? They talk like it belongs to all of us, but we sure don't have a key to the place. Money, money. It all flows to Nashua. Logan rants about love and winning the lost, but in the final analysis, every LBI decision is based on two questions: what will it cost? and what will it bring in?—and you can be sure the green light that Logan gave you on Becki is somehow connected to this thinking. It's no different from GM or Prudential or IBM, or the Mafia for that matter.... And Stan is so concerned about Nashua, Nashua, Nashua. But Nashua doesn't give a shit about Stan, not really. They just see him as an uneducated zealous boor—*fuck* Nashua! People need to be loved not exploited, not shamed into servitude. It's not right! It's far away from the Jesus I read about!"

"Nashua, or money?" Jim asks between coughs.

"Both!" Russ declares. "They go right together. Nashua, Logan, Campbell, money! Production, profits, power! Just like any greedy corporation!"

Russ tries to hold his voice to a loud whisper but is hardly succeeding. "But it's *worse* 'cause they do it in the name of God and justify it with the Bible. They call it salvation and sanctification but those are just catchy code words that sell the programs. Nashua's not into *help*ing people. They're into seducing and controlling and intimidating people, especially naive guilt-ridden souls! And once they get them they turn them into whores ... not dollars and sex, but people sell out for prestige, reputation, to attain their goals, to get the edge on others! They sell out to get ordained, to get appointed to a team, to get a cute and sexy wife. It's the same as any worldly organization—pay your dues and you get the goodies. Yet they say, 'Look what God has done'! But in truth, they should say, 'Look what money and fear and guilt and kissing ass and deceitful manipulation have done'! No *wonder* Jesus said, 'You can't serve God and mammon'! I tell you, Jim, we're marching to a different drumbeat. They're in another *fuck*ing universe from us. I've always known it. And we can't play this fucking game forever."

Russ takes off his cap, pushes his rusty locks back off his forehead, then gazes out the window. Jim downs the last of his water.

Quietness descends over the booth like a strange drug of calm.

After a minute, Russ speaks again, as if addressing the darkness, "It can't go on. Even if they don't come down on us over the money thing, something has to give. It's only a matter of time, Jim ... only a matter of time."

"How long do we have?" Jim asks.

"I don't know," Russ replies. "But I hear the bomb ticking."

# Chapter Thirty-one

Pastor Jim coughs. He blows his nose. He wheels out of his desk chair and goes to the windows. The thermometer says one-below zero. Not a breath of wind, and not a cloud, except for a billowing plume of smoke and steam, puffy like cumulus, rising beyond the pine trees. *Looks like Stan and Barry are stoking this morning,* he remarks to himself as he stuffs his hankie into the back pocket of his dress slacks. The Prescott furnace roars full blast on cold days—Stan says they fire the furnace mainly to make steam for heating and keeping the pipes thawed—but Jim usually can't see the smoke from his office because the wind normally blows it to the other side of the river. The morning sun, still low behind the trees, paints the wooly plume honey-gold and shimmering rose, and brushes in shadows of blue and gray and deep purple.

Otherwise, the January morning lies cold and dead and dank and dirty, like the inside of a meat locker. The drive-around is washboardy with rutted ice and is bordered on the woods side by a dirty rocklike wall of old plowed snow. In the middle of the drive-around, Jim spies a spot of red on the ground, crushed and frozen down; it looks like a discarded Winston pack, probably Jodi's.

The pine trees, more gray than green, shiver and wait, not for spring but for more snow. Under the trees, discarded tires, desks, and chairs peer out from Stan's snow-covered junk pile: faces trapped and frozen black. *It's hard to believe what has happened since we last had school,* Jim says to himself as he returns to his desk. *It has to be a dream—oh, but it wasn't. Sin, sin, sin ... on Becki's couch, in Becki's bathroom, on the stage by the pulpit. I'm so fuckin' helpless. I have no will power left. Oh, Becki, you're too much. I want to hold you, kiss you. I love you more than ever. Why do I have to sit here and sort this shit?* A pile of neglected paperwork, two weeks' worth, waits impatiently on his desk. He shoves it away knocking over the mug of pencils and pens; a few roll out.

But as soon as he pushes one pile of papers away, Angie bounces in and plops another batch in front of him. "Thanks a lot," Jim whines to his secretary, but he gives her a smile.

"Okay, Jim, it's Tuesday morn*ing,*" she chirps. "Holidays are *ov*er. Time to get rolling. You must tell me *all* about your Christmas break ... maybe later, huh?" Before Jim can reply, Angie gives a jaunty toss of her swept-back hair and bops out of the office, her wide hips swinging under a flowing beige skirt.

*What is she so bubbly about? If I actually told her what happened over Christmas, she wouldn't be so bubbly I bet ... or then again she might get off on it. You can never figure women out when it comes to talking about sex. They either run like hell, like you pulled a gun on them, or they tune right in and get more prurient than you.* Jim picks up his calendar book in hopes that it'll be blank—no such luck. He adds another item: "Send letter to Logan, and Alison, about money situation." He circles the entry for emphasis.

Brown skirt, yellow sweater, sky-blue eyes, blushing cheeks. Jim's heart jumps excitedly as Becki spills into the office. She tosses a folder on Jim's desk and says, "Jodi needs you to sign these." Brunette, pneumatic, Alison's clothes. Becki fluffs her hair then gives her sassy scrunchy-faced expression, wrinkling her nose, pursing her lips.

*Good mood! Good mood!* Jim exclaims happily to himself. *She's in a good mood. I can't wait 'til afternoon.*

Becki comes around next to him, close enough to touch. Jim's heart exults. His face breaks wide, but he covers his excitement with a cough and a question, "What are they?"

"Some kind of P.E. forms," Becki replies, cocking her hips. Her voice is cozy, moist, more than usual. Her canted hip is almost in Jim's face, so close he can feel the heat. "The guy at Silas Brendon says we need these to use the gym." Becki, Becki, Jontue, lilac shampoo. Jim can't resist; he gives her a love-swat on the butt.

Becki gives a spirited giggle then executes a playful pirouette toward the door. But instead of leaving, she whirls around, leans over the desk, and places a red Tootsie Roll Pop on Jim's open calendar. Oh, Becki Lea, pink, proud, blooming like a rose. Love-magic, elation, cute snubby nose. Lips, dimples, crooked teeth.

Jim's heart gushes then melts. Becki's eyes are sunny and glad, and brimming with affection. She pretends to depart, closing the door, then playfully opens it again. "So how about it, old man?" she flirts. "You coming over today? I'm baking cookies."

"Oh, I don't know?" he replies teasingly. "I'm real busy. But I guess I can fit you in ... say around two-thirty."

"Oh, you can," she banters. "That's wicked nice of you." With that, she gives him another scrunchy face, sticks out her tongue playfully, and departs.

Jim picks up the Tootsie Pop as if it's Rebecca's heart—and in a way it is. Despite her moods and games and clever devices, he can't help but see her heart as precious, the most precious of all hearts. Elation and joyful anticipation flood his bosom. He unwraps the red wax paper. The cherry sweetness melts in his mouth. *God help me,* he thinks-prays out the window. *She drives me crazy. I love her. I want her more than ever. I want her heart, her soul, her body.*

*I want her lips. I want to kiss her. I want to finish what we started
Christmas Eve. I'll never be the same. I can never repent of this. O
God! I'm hooked forever!*

\* \* \*

2:34 p.m. Pastor Jim is running late. The thought of spending
the afternoon at 59 Front Street stirs happy butterflies in his
stomach, especially after Becki's warm playfulness in his office.
He can't wait. He would've preferred to go home with her at one-
thirty but he had an afterlunch meeting with Beverly to go over the
items he and Russ approved-disapproved at the diner last night.

The day is sunny but still frigid. The cold air penetrates Jim's
polyester dress pants as if they're made of tissue paper. He hops into
the Mustang, fires up the engine, but when he tries to go, the car
stalls. He restarts, and tries again, but it stalls again. The Mustang
is balky on cold days. Normally, it still goes, but not if the
temperature is below 15°. In severe cold the engine requires a five-
minute warm-up—no getting around it. So Jim starts it a third time
and waits. He loosens his tie. He pulls his suede jacket around him;
he wishes he'd worn his overcoat. *Calm down,* he counsels himself.
*There's no rush. Sharon's in Nashua all day.*

Pastor Jim's first day back at the office was a loss, but he did
get the letters out to Logan and the Landreths regarding the BFBC
budget crisis. And Janet came by and apologized. She said she
overreacted, that Barry was back to normal. But her words lacked
the oaklike honesty with which she normally speaks. Also, Leslie
B. grabbed Jim in the hall and bragged about how his fiery
Christmas message convicted Gerald so much that he burned all his
adult magazines and had a talk with Wendell about cultivating pure
thoughts. Jim listened politely to Leslie but had no ears to hear her;
his Christmas-morning zeal is long gone.

Jodi didn't bring donuts but she did stick her head in long
enough to read Joe's letter. Her response was interesting: "Joe's a
liar, Jim. He didn't leave because of your 'heart' message. He's
running because of guilt. Brenda told me all about it. They got into
each other pretty good over Christmas, not all the way, but enough
to shake them both up. It's no wonder Joe got stoned out of his mind.
Brenda's relieved that he left, and so am I. Maybe someday but not
now. Their situation is even more radical than you 'n Becki. At
least, Becki's an adult. I guess in the realm of the heart, love is the
same—I hope so—but in our society, fifteen is a *far* cry from
twenty. They'd never survive the pressure, nor would I."

Jim then told Jodi about Christmas Eve—not everything but

close. She chuckled and replied, "Quite a little missionary, huh? Maybe you'll believe me now."

Jim coughs. He blows his nose. He still has lingering symptoms from his weekend bout with the flu but he feels much better than last night at the diner. After pocketing his hankie, he shifts into gear and the Mustang responds. But as he wheels around the building, Barry Buford hails him down. Barry is securing the muffler on the old International bus. Red-faced from cold, hooded in a heavy parka, he looks like a fat Inuit. He briefs Jim on the muffler repairs then talks about the January teen schedule.

After talking ministry business a few minutes, Jim brings up Becki—no response from Barry. Then Matt—still no response. *Guess we won't be talking after all,* Jim says to himself as Barry mumbles something about skiing. "Yeah, yeah, maybe," Jim replies with half his attention.

Barry gives a thumbs-up sign and says, "See you at church tonight. This is going to be a great year for God."

*Shit, he sounds like Stan,* Jim says to himself as he pulls out of the parking lot onto Reservoir Road. *Everybody's responding to my Christmas message except me. But I can't—oh, Becki, I'm fucking addicted. I'll do anything to be with you.*

Eager, expectant, he guns the Mustang up the frozen driveway at 59 Front Street and hustles inside. He bounds up the stairs, his Dingo boots clomping like horse's hooves on the oak treads. Rebecca's door is slightly ajar. Jim knocks: no answer. He enters.

Tight jeans, beefy buttocks, bum-around shirt, unlaced Timberland boots. Sleep-sofa open, bedclothes on the floor, blue laundry basket on the bed, piles of folded clothes. Becki, her back to Jim, folds her laundry as Bathsheba cavorts among the piles. Becki's recently removed school clothes are on the green chair.

Jim says, "Hi." The cat looks up but Becki doesn't respond. He starts to say more but all he can manage is a silent gulp. As a deer smells danger, Jim senses pious indignation pervading the room. He can't see Becki's face but he feels her scowl. His heart freezes into a stone, then falls over as dead.

Whirling brown locks, fisted hands. Becki spins, but Jim's shocked psyche experiences the scene in slow motion as in a dream. Her raging words come slowly like a record on the wrong speed, "GO ... HOME ... YOU ... FUCKIN' ... PERVERT!" Deep, distorted, echoing, each word reverberates through his mind like the tortured roar of a caged lion. Bathsheba flies off the bed—in slow motion. Disappointment, like a sucking tide, engulfs Jim pulling him into the black waters of dismay. His senses shut down. Becki blazes hot, snarling, spitting, clawing with her eyes, but he hears nothing. The room grows dim, indistinct.

Jim drowns in dark shock. But then a breaking swell of awareness sweeps him back into Becki's wrath: "MY BLUE PANTIES AREN'T HERE! YOU TOOK 'EM DIDN'T *YOU*! YOU'RE A REAL SICKO! I thought I put 'em in my basket, but now I know you took 'em 'cause they're not here! You're oversexed! You're disturbed. You oughta be locked up! GET OUTA MY SIGHT, YOU PANTY-SNIFFING *PER*VERT!" Blue flames rage in Becki's eyes. She angrily pushes her hair back.

Shock gives way to fury. Jim's wounded soul erupts like an awakening giant, "WHAT THE FUCK IS THIS! YOU TAKE A WEEKLY COUNT OF YOUR UNDERPANTS! YOU'RE THE SICK ONE, NOT *ME*!"

Growling, snarling, showing their fangs, Jim and Becki square off like two jackals fighting over a piece of meat. Face to face, they slowly rotate, jockeying for position. "I hate your dirty mind, Jimmy!" Becki declares hotly. "Sex, sex! That's *all* you think about! You don't care about me! You're just obsessed with my genitals!" Hot onion breath accompanies her hot words.

"No way, Becki! You got it wrong! I'm obsessed with your heart! I love you, you ungrateful bitch! What a fuckin' curse!"

Becki punches the air as if pounding on an invisible door. "Yeah, right! Well, my heart's not between my legs! I see you lookin'! You just wanna fuck me! That's all! That's been your goal all along! You just want a young cunt! You're nothing but a horny old bastard! If I was old, like thirty, you wouldn't even want me around!" Tomato red and mottled, her face swells with hot blood as if about to burst.

Fury, fury, fit of fury. Jim grabs Becki by the shoulders and shakes her like a rag doll. "WELL, WHAT ABOUT *YOU*! WHY'D YOU TAKE OFF YOUR PANTIES ANYWAY, YOU TWO-FACED WHORE! You started it! You were loose and dirty-mouthed the whole night. You pulled up your skirt on the sofa! Whaddeya call that! Then you walk in on me and play with my dick! If your mom hadn't called, you woulda been on my lap, and not for a bedtime story. SO DON'T CALL *ME* HORNY!"

Becki breaks free, turns away. "I got nothing more to say. Just go home, Shanley! I don't want you around me!" Burning tightly, she retreats into her silent-turtle pose.

Coughing, panting, Jim moves in to challenge her defenses. She scowls fiercely and tucks her chin. She fidgets nervously with her hands. "Why doncha turn around and talk instead of sulking like a spoiled child!" he exclaims into the side of her head. He's so close he can smell, almost taste, her lilac-scented shampoo. "I hate it how you go into your fuckin' shell! I hate it how you look down and act bothered and pick at your fingers like a *damn* retard! I hate how you shuffle your feet and step all over yourself like you got ants in your pants, and how you wag your head and do that stupid bouncy walk. I hate your bratty sourpuss look! And while I'm at it, I hate how you smack your fuckin' gum! And how you burp and fart and chew with your mouth open, and how you always show off with your corny wit! And how you keep all your clothes on one fuckin' chair!"

Jim maneuvers trying to yell into Becki's face but she rotates like the mouse on her music box to avoid him. So he goes on shouting into her chocolate mop of hair, "I hate how you say 'wicked' this and 'wicked' that! You don't even know the fuckin' language and you're supposed to be a teacher! It's like you have a twenty-year-old body and the personality of a fuckin' five-year-old!" He gestures vehemently as if chopping wood with each arm. "But most of all I hate your fuckin' mood swings! How you flirt with me then slam the door like a smart-aleck little prick-teaser! How you get wild and naughty until your panties are wet then you turn frigid and scream at me like you've got no sex drive, like you've got no cunt! But you're a liar! A *damn* liar!"

Jim gulps a breath then demands answers, "Come *on,* Rebecca Lea, let's get honest! Tell me you didn't like it in the bathroom on Christmas Eve!"—no response. "Tell me you didn't like it on the couch!"—no response. "Tell me you didn't like kissing me!"—no response. "Tell me you weren't goin' crazy to fuck me when you dropped your panties to the floor!"—no reponse. "Doncha realize I love you whether we do it or not!"—no response. "Doesn't our love mean *any*thing to you!"—no response. "If our love means nothing, then why'd you give me that Tootsie Pop in my office!"—no response. "If I said good-bye forever, would that mean anything to you!"

Becki slouches away like a cold museum statue. She sneers and gives a bothered I-don't-care shrug, but says nothing.

Jim kicks the laundry basket. It flies off the bed crashing against her dresser. Clothes spill all over the floor. He grabs Becki and spins her around. He tries to lift her chin but she turns away again. "I'M SICK AND TIRED OF YOUR SCOWLING!" he howls right into her ear. "DO YOU LOVE ME, OR NOT!"—no response. *KA-WHAP!* He slaps her. Her face jerks back. *KA-WHAAAP!* He slaps her again, knocking her onto the bed. But Becki doesn't stay down.

Shrieking, crying, scattering laundry all over the room, she fights back like a wounded wolverine, "NOBODY HITS ME! I'LL *KILL* YOU FOR THAT!" Panting, screeching, hitting, clawing, shooting pain, hot blood. Becki sinks her fingernails into Jim's face, into his neck, gouging out hunks of flesh, ripping the side of his nose.

Jim frantically pushes her off then grabs her wrists and holds tightly.

Berserk with fury, Becki fights to free herself, jerking, twisting, bawling, shrieking, kicking. "YOU LET GO OF ME! YOU'RE *DEM*ON POSSESSED! I'LL KICK YOUR BALLS OFF!"

She misses his crotch but nails his knee, then his shin. Pain, pain, sharp pain. Jim grabs her foot but her unlaced boot comes off in his hand. Free to swing, she lands a vicious punch on his mouth. Bells, stars, flashing color. His lip bursts like a pulpy grape. Stunned, stunned. He staggers. Becki dashes into the bathroom. Blood, blood, Jim tastes blood. He gives chase.

"DON'T YOU *DARE*!" Becki screams through the closed door. "I GOT A RAZOR IN MY HAND! I'LL CUT YOUR *FUCKIN'* COCK OFF!" Rabid, raging, she bawls, she screeches. "I'LL CALL THE POLICE! YOU GET OUTA MY HOUSE!"

Jim grabs some paper towels and holds them to his bleeding face. He hobbles out and down the stairs. He hears Becki slam and bolt the door behind him.

Crushed, cold, desperate, dying, Jim drives around Hadley Hill, but he can't leave. Tears blur his vision. He sobs, coughs, wheezes, chokes. He tastes blood and salt. The wad of paper towels in his hand looks like a used Kotex. His lower lip continues to swell. Bloody, pulpy, split wide-open. He feels gobs of loose skin with his tongue. His gut aches with hurt feelings and nausea, while burning spots of pain sear his face, his neck, his nose. He hates himself.

Back up Front Street, up the driveway. Jim parks behind the Escort. *O Jesus,* he sobs to himself, *I hit her, I hit her. Oh, Becki, I'm sorry. I didn't mean it. You're right. It is perverted. Forgive me. I messed everything up Christmas Eve ... and it's still messed up.* Blood, snot, and tears cover his face, his neck, his shirt, his tie, his jacket, and his sweater-vest.

\* \* \*

Becki stands at the sink, half turned and silent, and nervously picking her thumbnail. Jim sits at the kitchen table. Red whelp, swollen, bleary: her eye is closing. It will be black by morning.

Jim wheezes, sniffles, and coughs. He wants to move closer but he doesn't dare. It took thirty minutes of begging and crying and apologizing at Becki's door to get back in, and he doesn't want to press his welcome. Instead, he goes on apologizing, his voice pitiful and broken, "I didn't mean it, Becki Lea. I love you. I'm so sorry. I feel like shit. I'll never hit you again, I *swear*. I hate it too, what happened Christmas Eve. I just want to be with you. I do, I do. I love you. I'm sorry. I'll do *any*thing to be with you. We can do outreach. I'll be good now. It'll be different. We'll be a team like before ... and no more fooling around, and no more suggestive talk. I promise. I'll do anything. I just don't want you to go away. I'll die without you. I *love* you."

Becki does not reply but Jim senses a truce. He coughs. He snuffles. He buries his head in his hands.

When he looks up, she's in the bathroom. He stares out the window. The winter sun hangs low to the southwest, a bright blurry orb beyond the trees, beyond the reservoir. Long brushstrokes of amber-gold warm the snow-covered meadow between groping fingers of black and gray shadow. Evening is descending but the waning rays of sunshine make the transition seem less cold.

Suddenly: mercurochrome, cotton swabs, Band-Aids, a wet cloth, a clean towel, and Becki's pouty face. She dabs and swabs and bandages Jim's cuts. His coughing and sniffling gradually subside. Her girlish hands move skillfully like a mother, but she says nothing. The pungent odor of mercurochrome permeates the kitchen until it smells like Dr. Clay's office back in Gilmer where Jim got stitches after falling off the henhouse when he was nine.

Finally, the hint of a smile trembles over Becki's lips. Jim's heart rises from the dead. "You fight dirty," he kids her. "You claw like a wild animal."

Becki's hint of a smile grows into a blushing grin, "I fight to *win*," she quips. "And I did." After cleaning off the table, she takes the first-aid items back into the bathroom.

A bit later, Becki comes out with two clean washcloths. She opens the fridge, empties a tray of ice into a bowl, and makes up two ice packs, one for Jim's lip, one for her eye. "I'm sure not goin' to church tonight," she says. "What are you gonna say to everybody, Jimmy, I cut myself *shav*ing?"

Becki laughs as does Jim, but his laugh quickly turns into a wheezing cough.

* * *

Saturday morning. Prayer meeting will start in twenty minutes. Becki and Jodi and the other regulars are having coffee and donuts in the kitchen. Pastor Jim and Russ are talking in Jim's office.

The week passed quickly. Becki stayed home two days until

her black eye went down. At midweek service Tuesday night no one mentioned the cuts on Pastor Jim's face except Sharon. He told her the truth, at least the Becki-scratched-me part. He also told her that he'd changed his mind about ending his outreach ministry with Becki, that he and she were still going to be a team since Dr. Logan said it was okay.

Sharon didn't yell—that surprised Jim—but simply gave an exasperated shrug and said, "You deserve to have your face scratched. You're spineless, Jim. One week, you're full of faith, ready to end it, and the next, you're right back under her spell. You always end up bowing down to that conniving bitch. You'll get *no* sympathy from me."

Jim tried to persuade her that things were going to be different but Sharon didn't buy it, "Don't give me *that* line, James David. I've heard it too many times. You'll never change."

Nonetheless, Jim and Sharon did not have a prolonged fight about it. In fact, a resigned peace rules at the Shanley house, things having settled back into the old routine as if the events of Christmas week never occurred.

Jim sips his coffee then takes a letter from his in-box; it came yesterday from Nashua. In the letter Dr. Logan sympathizes with the BFBC budget crunch, and tells Jim to take as many months as he needs to balance his books locally before resuming monthly donations to home base. Logan also lauds Jim, again, for having the fastest-growing LBI branch.

Jim hands the letter to Russ. After reading it, Russ relaxes back into the LA-Z-BOY recliner. For a long moment he stares blankly into his coffee mug. Finally, he looks up and gives a wry grin. "Like I say, Jim ... Dr. Logan is a *shrewd* businessman."

# Chapter Thirty-two

A rooster tail of muddy spray chases Pastor Jim's Mustang
down Reservoir Road. Sunny, mild, melting snow, wet
streets. Jim adjusts his sunglasses against the glare. After
a brief stop at the post office, he proceeds to Flanagan's lot where
he parks facing Mill Street between two dirty mountains of old
snow. He looks for Cathy Rosinski but he doesn't see her.

*Flanagan's,* he says to himself. *I'm sure she said to meet her
in Flanagan's parking lot.*

February 23, 1984. Thursday morning. February school-
vacation week (for the public schools, and BFCA). Sharon and the
kids are in Cobleskill—due back Sunday afternoon.

Fear has driven Jim's life back into a safe rut, fear of change,
fear of losing Rebecca. Since their violent fight the first week of
January, he, like Chamberlain at Munich, has sought peace at any
cost: peace with Becki, peace with Sharon, peace with Stan, peace
with the flock, peace with Nashua, peace with his passions. Mas-
tering the art of suppression, Jim and Becki have banished eros to
the dungeon of their souls. They've had no more prurient talks or
touching or kissing. Yet they do more outreach than ever, and
outwardly they seem devoted to the ministry and contented with
no-touch love as if God has finally delivered them from lust. But in
truth, sexual desire tempts and torments more than ever, Jim
anyway, and he suspects that it's the same for Becki. Their platonic
pretense makes him feel false, frustrated, unsated, like sitting down
for dinner and not eating, yet professing fullness. At times Becki is
warm and kind, but more often she's bitchy, moody, manipulative.
She knows she can put Jim down and he won't fight back, and so
far she's right; they've had no big fights for seven weeks.

No balls, no boldness. Jim plays it safe out of the pulpit, in the
pulpit. His preaching has degenerated into a bland mix of sentimental homilies and "how to" sermons. Life has become vapid, predictable, routine—like the weather in LA. Sex with Sharon is his only
display of passion. He and Russ talk. He and Jodi talk. Truth stirs
but never makes it out into the light of day, just as a movie inspires
but you lose the fire in the rush to the parking lot.

Despite the cessation of BFBC donations, Dr. Logan has
treated Pastor Jim like a crown prince. The Shanleys have been
going to Nashua regularly for the Wednesday night service at
Moody. Logan has twice called Jim up on stage to give an
introductory sermon. Likewise, Ed Landreth sent a nice letter
thanking Jim for the many months of support and saying he

understood the budget situation. At BFBC normalcy reigns: school days, school plays, Sunday services, new members, better offerings, teen ministry, potluck suppers, Sunday school programs. The church hums like a well-oiled machine as everyone accomplishes their assigned duties without friction. Barry leads songs. Even Russ and Stan seem to be working together. If a bomb is ticking, Jim doesn't hear it. War seems far far away—as far away as his heart.

Jim waits. He looks across toward Pauline's Variety Store, then down High Street. He sees children and teenagers in shirtsleeves, eager for spring. He sees older folks in winter coats—they know better. But he doesn't see Cathy Rosinski. The Mustang is warm like a greenhouse. He slips out of his jacket and rolls down the window. Cool air wafts in along with the din of midmorning traffic and the dank smells of downtown: dirty slushy snow, silt, salt, garbage, damp brick, damp stone.

Yes, normalcy reigns at BFBC and normalcy has its usual downside as New Year's resolutions and vows of repentance surrender to February reality. Frank Cahill made it to one Monday night class but later that night he was arrested for DWI. Russ bailed him out—so much for Frank's rededication to the Lord. Doris has been staying home every eight to ten days, her usual winter drinking schedule. Barry goes to Nashua once a week, for more than preaching, but he utters not a word about it. Like Jim, he's back in the closet. But Barry's closet has more than fantasy fucks. On a sad but not surprising note, Calvin McClusky broke up with Joanne and moved back to his parents. He's never recovered from losing Baby Shane. Blaming himself, as does Joanne's family and others, Cal's been on a two-month drunk which has cost him his job at Prescott Paper. Leslie Burton found a new copy of *Hustler* magazine hidden in Gerald's dresser. Pastor Jim's Christmas message didn't change him after all. The same week she caught Wendell masturbating in their basement. She put him on the Nashua prayer list—under teen depression.

In Nashua, Project Malachi has—in ten months—brought in $240,000 from a growing list of wealthy donors. The Bible college is filled to capacity as the LBI membership skyrockets worldwide. And the EDGE video program is catching on in all the LBI branches—faster than expected. Logan's cash flow has improved greatly. So much so that the loss of BFBC tithes is hardly noticeable. But all is not rosy at home base. According to Doris, Tom Hudson has left Mary Beth, over the Michael Montanaro thing, and has taken a room at the villa. And Dr. Logan has recalled his nephew from Lawrence and has suspended Mary Beth from her teaching position. Sharon still goes to Nashua every Tuesday, but of course, she never talks about Tom and Mary Beth. Jim still wonders about Sharon and Tom, but he's not about to bring it up—for the sake of peace.

Still no Cathy. But next door to Pauline's, the town's most dedicated drunks are punching in at Clancy's Pub. The glare from the sun hurts Jim's eyes, even with sunglasses. He pulls down the visor then picks up the church mail and thumbs through it. Comfed Savings Bank: mortgage on the church. Aetna Life & Casualty: insurance on the church. Nashoba Fuel & Gas: an oil bill. A copy of *Choose Ye This Day*: Logan's quarterly magazine. And lots of junk mail. Billy Graham: solicitation of funds. *Songtime* radio network: solicitation of funds. Teen Challenge Ministries: solicitation of funds. A flyer for a *Petra* concert at Grace Chapel in Lexington: Saturday, March 10, 7 p.m., $10 advance/$12 at the door. A brochure for *JESUS '84* Christian Festival at Mt. Union, PA, June 22-24: $99 per person, group discounts. A flyer for an Agape Consultants seminar: "Marketing Strategy for Your Church," Sheraton Boston, Thursday, April 5, $79 per person, call 1-800-266-3131, *VISA*/MasterCard welcome. A brochure from Jerry Falwell's Liberty University, Lynchburg, VA: "Shake the World for Jesus Christ," call for a catalog, 1-800-522-6225. A flyer from Zig Ziglar: "Church Goals: How to Set Them, How to Reach Them," six cassettes, $59.95, *VISA*-MC, call 1-800-323-5552.

*This is all marketing bullshit,* Jim sighs disgustedly to himself as he tosses the mail into the backseat. *It has nothing to do with love or heart, or the God I hope for.* The freshening breeze feels cool on his arm; he rolls up the window all but a crack.

Jim spots a faded denim jacket by the pay phone in front of Pauline's. Faded denim, short sugarplum physique, mouse-brown hair—wispy, wind-fluffed, brushed back from a soft Polish face. He beeps and Cathy hustles across Mill Street, dodging the potholes. She steps lightly in her white slip-ons, but with enough hip sway to toss her blue waitress skirt from side to side. A gray camera-bag purse bounces at her waist.

Fresh, nubile, sweet bloom of youth. Mustang door, swish of cotton. Curvy calves, white socks, skirt riding up, chunky thighs rolling above rounded knees. She hops in and quickly pushes down her skirt. Shampoo, perfume, hint of nervous BO. Flushed cheeks, tear blotches, black smudges of mascara. Bleary-eyed sadness clouds her countenance. She sags into the seat as if misfortune has snuffed out all her dreams. Jim removes his sunglasses, placing them on the dash. He then gives Cathy an affectionate pat on the shoulder. Still sniffling, she pulls a wrinkled white hankie out of her purse and dabs her nose, her cheeks. She carefully averts her eyes.

Not only is Cathy R. built like Becki, but she also emits Becki-like vibes around Pastor Jim. *I bet she'd fuck me,* he brags to himself. *And without all the hell I've been through with Becki. God, her thighs are scrumptious—what the fuck am I thinking? She's here because she's in trouble and I'm lusting—as usual.*

Jim quickly cleans up his thoughts then says, "I could've come to your house, Cath?"

She gives him a shy side-glance. "I know, but I gotta go to work anyhow at ten. Besides, Verna's at home, and she's bitchy and hung over." Cathy's voice is soft, wistful, thick from weeping; her gray-flecked blue eyes are vacant, spent, cried-out.

"So you just got the word?" Jim asks.

"Yeh, yesterday. But it's no surprise; I been puking for three weeks."

Jim pushes his seat back. "So why'd you call me?"

Cathy twists her handkerchief on her lap. "Uum ... I needed to talk? I needed to talk to a grown-up who won't preach at me or nuthin'." Her voice wavers but she fights back her tears save for one which spills over onto her cheek like a drop of morning dew. She dabs it away with her hankie smearing more of her mascara.

"How d'you know I won't preach at you?" Jim asks.

"'Cuz you're different," Cathy replies between sniffles. "You're not like Verna."

"So your aunt hasn't been very supportive I take it?"

*"Phewh,"* Cathy snorts scornfully. "That's an understatement? She calls me a bed bunny and says I'm easy—jus' like my mom. But she's a *liar,* and she's got no room to talk the way she bows down to Angelo. That scumbag's in her bed most ever' night and she helps him peddle his low-grade pot. I wouldn't touch his stuff.... Shit, Verna's no help; she makes everything worse."

Jim fingers his mustache. "And Kevin, what does he say?"

Cathy blows her nose then wads her damp handkerchief in her hand. She speaks down toward her feet, "He says we gotta own up to it an' get married."

"So?"

"How's he gonna support a family?"

"He's got a job, doesn't he?"

"Yeh, right. He delivers pizza part-time ... for Nicky Poulos." Cathy wipes her eyes; her sniffles are subsiding.

Jim has no ready reply. He stares across Mill Street at the old three-story brick building on the corner. Its grimy smoke-stained bricks are now more black than buff. Four pairs of apartment windows stare down from the top two stories like drunk half-lidded eyes. The rusty fire escape seems more likely to fall on a pedestrian than to save anyone. Under the fire escape, Pauline's cluttered display window gathers dust at street level. Inside the window a time-faded Pepsi poster shows a slender brunette in a pink suit and pillbox hat; she holds a poodle in one hand and a bottle of Pepsi in the other. The caption says: Be Debonair. *Be Debonair,* Jim quotes silently. *Who the fuck says that anymore? I bet Pauline hasn't changed that window in twenty-five years.*

Cathy sighs shifting a bit in her seat. Jim's thoughts come back into the car, back to her situation. "So, Cath, do you love Kevin?"

"I dunno," she replies. "I'm not sure." An unruly tendril of hair unravels onto her forehead; she pushes it back. "I like him okay, and we have fun, but—" Cathy stops midsentence.

"But what?" Jim prods.

"Well, he gets selfish a lot ... like a big baby. At first he was nice to me. We used to talk an' smoke weed together. But he wanted sex most of all, so he kept bugging me about it. Finally, I gave in and we did it. Now sex is all we do, and it's no great thing, least not to me"—*She must not get off with him,* Jim interjects quickly to himself; *maybe she hasn't discovered orgasm yet? O Jesus*—"and we never talk or nuthin', and Kev won't get stoned with me anymore, and now I'm pregnant with his baby, and I always swore this would never happen to me. Don't get me wrong, Pastor Jim, I love babies and I do want a kid of my own, but later, after I have a home and a husband."

Jim has no golden advice, so he says, "Well, Cath, what do *you* want to do?"

Dropping her hankie on her lap, Cathy flattens her palms against her waitress skirt. "I dunno," she sighs. "I dunno." She gazes straight ahead.

Jim starts to reply but stops abruptly as a Brendon Falls garbage truck lurches down Mill Street like a drunk mastadon, and screaks to a stop in front of the Mustang. Frank Cahill, like a footman on a royal carriage, rides dignifiedly on the back. An overlarge John Deere cap dwarfs his grimy face and gaunt Tweety-bird physique.

The green truck backs, groaning, creaking, smoking, into the alley behind Pauline's and Clancy's. Frank spots Pastor Jim and waves proudly. Greasy gloves, grungy coveralls. He leans off the rear of the truck, rolling his arm like a brakeman backing a freight train. The truck halts. He hops off and hooks onto the dumpster.

Grinding, squalling, groaning steel. The hydraulic lifter hoists the battered metal box and dumps it into the compactor. Barflike dumpster bilge splatters like fetid rain onto the cobblestones, along with tomatoes, lettuce, chicken bones, pull-tabs, coffee grounds.

As the truck lowers the dumpster, the steel lid slams down with a resounding *BANG!* Unlike most towns, Brendon Falls still picks up its own refuse but the rusted-out trucks have long outlived their useful service. After unhooking the dumpster, Frank hops aboard and the humpbacked behemoth roars-coughs away leaving a cloud of oily smoke in its wake.

Cathy, wide-eyed and wistful, watches the truck as it lumbers out and turns down High Street. After it disappears, she shrugs resignedly and gives Pastor Jim an oblique insecure glance. She looks down. She rubs her lower lip with her finger. She starts to speak then hesitates, then starts again, "Umm, what about abortion?"

"What about it?" Jim replies, fluttering his fingers on the top of the steering wheel. *I figured this was coming,* he adds silently to himself.

"D'you think God would hate—"

"I don't think God likes it," Jim cuts in. "But I doubt He'll hate you or damn you ... else we'd all be damned." Jim shifts more toward Cathy and rests his arm on the back of her seat.

She again stares wide-eyed over the dash. "Haley, she told me there's one in Worcester."

"One what?" Jim asks.

"You know, a clinic place ... where they do it."

Jim caresses her shoulder in a fatherly manner. "Well, Cath, I guess you hafta do what you hafta do, but I'd hate to be all snug in my mom's womb, and have some doctor suck me out and cut me up. I could never do it myself."

Cathy's face blanches as if Jim has slapped her. She angrily shoves his hand away from her shoulder and withdraws behind a sullen scowl. "So you're sayin' it's a *sin* against God, huh?"

Jim retracts his arm but not his opinion, "No, it's a sin against the baby."

New tears spill down Cathy's cheeks. "Life sucks enough awhready," she sobs. "Now I gotta deal with this, an' I can't even get stoned. Fuckin' Aunt Verna took my last ten bucks. She says I owe for food. I *hate* this fuckin' town! I *hate* my fuckin' life!"

Cathy hangs her head. Brown on white, the wayward lock of hair tumbles again onto her forehead. This time she leaves it. She wheezes. Watery mucus gushes from her nose; she sponges it with her hankie. "Now *you're* preachin' at me," she says between snuffles, "and I didn't think you would or nuthin'." Her tears pepper her denim jacket, making dark spots.

Crying eyes, mottled face, wayward curl. A crushed rosebud who's never had a chance to bloom. Jim is moved. He tries to

473

comfort her but she jerks away from his touch. *She thinks I'm condemning her,* he says to himself. *Or maybe—shit, how do I know what she thinks? I've never been a girl. Their emotions are wired different.*

Jim wrings his hands then a burst of affection roars out of his heart on a wave of anger, "What the fuck, Cath! I'm not gonna lie to you! If you get an abortion, you'll regret it your whole life!" He slaps the dash for emphasis. Cathy jumps. Compassion, concern. His voice softens. "But even if you have ten of 'em, I'll still be your friend. This is just a tough time, and there are many tough times and ugly days on our calendar. It would be nice if we had a road map around them, but we don't. Not even the Bible tells us how to avoid the shit of life, not really."

Jim takes her hand. This time she doesn't jerk away. He speaks tenderly, like a father, "You've got some hard choices, Cathy, or then again, maybe you have no choices at all, but whatever happens, I'll always like holding your hand and seeing you smile. I like it when you talk with me and share your true feelings. You have a kind and sensitive heart. I trust you, Cathy."

Cathy falls sobbing into his arms. Warm, warm, womanly bosom. Soft hair, blue denim, cheap perfume. Jim strokes her head, holds her close. Her tears dampen his sweater-vest. He feels her body relaxing, the tension releasing in her arms, her shoulders, her neck. Sobs give way to sniffles.

Minutes pass, maybe three. Finally, Cathy sits up, wipes her tears, pulls a makeup kit out of her purse, and gives her face a quick fix. As she puts the kit away, she gives Jim a shy grin. He smiles back. Her grin breaks wide showing her dimples. "You really have a way with women, don'tcha, Jim? Well, I have an idea. Why don't *you* take me in? That'll solve my problem."

"Yeh, right. That's all I need, another woman, and a new-born."

Cathy fingerfluffs her hair in front of the visor-mirror. Her blue eyes spark with mirth. "But, Jim, you're a together guy," she quips. "I'm sure you can handle three wives."

*"Three?"*

"Yeh, me 'n Sharon ... and *Becki.*" Girlish giggles. Cathy blushes and giggles.

"You think you know everything, huh?"

"I guess I do. Least, I know you like Becki more than you let on." Snickers, blushing, laughing, laughing—both of them.

Jim tries to tickle her ribs. But Cathy breaks free and hops out. "I gotta go," she chortles. "I gotta call Kevin."

She hurries across Mill Street to the pay phone, regaining a measure of poise as she goes. No booth, just a phone on a pole. There used to be a booth. Jim puts on his sunglasses. *God, does she ever look like Debra Winger. But her body ... she's shaped like Becki except her knees are fatter.* As Cathy talks, she gestures as if Kevin can see her. She seems much happier and antimated.

*Why the mood change?* Jim wonders. *I didn't solve her problem? She's still poor and pregnant, and barely seventeen. She has a year and a half of school. She'll never graduate. She'll likely end up on welfare, and if the pattern plays out, she'll become an alcoholic like Verna, like her mom.* After hanging up, Cathy scampers across High Street then up the sidewalk on the other side, her hand bouncing on her camera-bag purse as if she's listening to good-time rock. Jim watches until she disappears into Bergson's.

He checks his watch—10:02 a.m. *Hafta get Becki at eleven,* he reminds himself. He pushes the watch back into his Levi's then reaches into the backseat for the LBI magazine. On the back cover is an ad for the college. Three wholesome-looking LBI students with happy smiles. Young, handsome, holding Bibles. Two girls and a guy, in front of the Priscilla Logan Memorial Chapel:

> ... At LBI, you'll experience a more fruitful spiritual life and you'll be progressively transformed into the image of Jesus Christ. We will inspire you with the moral, intellectual, and spiritual vision of orthodox, historic, Bible-believing Christianity. Heed the call of God and make a difference in your world. Make your life count for Christ. Come! Catch the LBI spirit! We are eager to hear from you. For a free LBI catalog, call 1-800-HE LIVES (fully-accredited with VA & SS benefits).

*Sounds like the Army,* Jim thinks as he rolls up the magazine. *Like, "Be all you can be." Somehow I can't see Jesus recruiting his disciples with glossy full-page ads and 800 numbers. He got down into real life, into smelly fishing boats, into the squalid bars of Capernaum, into the seamy brothels of Magdala.*

*Logan, Campbell, modern Christianity. It's a fuckin' bill of goods. Blessed are the poor, blessed are the meek—fuck! There's no place for the meek and the poor, except as shame-faced pew-sitters who add numbers to quarterly reports and march in the ranks behind their infallible pastors and masters. There's no place for the Cathy Rosinskis of this world.*

Jim hits the dashboard with the rolled magazine. *Maybe it's time to*—he kills the thought. *No way. The stakes are too high.*

He sighs, letting go of his aggravation. Black coat, gray hair, walrus shape. Agnes Hanratty waddles out of Pauline's with a shopping bag in one hand and a colored piece of paper in the other.

It looks like a Mass. Daily Numbers ticket. She stuffs the ticket into
the pocket of her ragged coat then lurches over to the pay phone. *I
bet she's calling her son in Cleveland,* Jim surmises. *I doubt he
gives a shit about her, but who does?* She talks five minutes then
grabs her shopping bag and waddles up Mill Street.

Farther up the hill: a black face under a wide-brimmed straw
hat. It's T. Willy Jones. Dirty white shirt, red suspenders, baggy
pants. Leaning heavily on his cane, he hobbles down the crumbling
sidewalk toward High Street. Roots and frost heaves have ravaged
the Depression-era WPA sidewalk, pitching and canting the concrete slabs like a collapsed freeway in a California earthquake. As
T. Willy passes Aunt Agnes, they stop and chat a moment. She
takes her lottery ticket out of her coat and shows it to him. He
smiles, flashing his white teeth and white eyes, then tips his straw
hat and continues down the hill to the pay phone.

T. Willy makes a quick call, as if placing a bet with a bookie.
Next, he heads across Mill Street toward Flanagan's to get his daily
supply of wine. His buttonless suit vest hangs open around his huge
belly. He doesn't see Pastor Jim in the Mustang. Unshaven,
unkempt, mostly unnoticed, T. Willy seems to move without
conscious intent, like so many Vietnam veterans who came home
to America only to become aimless alcoholics.

Jim feels hot again; he rolls his window all the way. Many of
the people who live on Mill Street have no telephone, so the pay
phone in front of Pauline's is a popular spot. After T. Willy, a fat
Puerto Rican mother steps up to the phone with two hyper kids
pulling on her like guy wires. Wearing a tan tentlike poncho, she
jabbers loudly in Spanish. She's new in town. Jim doesn't know
her. Next, comes a big ripe-bodied blond of about thirty who's just
pulled up to the curb in a beat-up Volkswagen Rabbit. She pushes
in a half-dozen coins. Jim recognizes her as the night clerk at
Flanagan's Liquor Store. Everybody calls her "Babe." She wears a
Budweiser sweat shirt and a bolero vest, and while she gabs, she
chomps vigorously on a wad of gum.

After Babe, the Candy Man. Scarfaced, thin, clad in black, he
slithers out of the alley behind Pauline's like a snake coming out of
his hole. Fidgety, furtive, he places a quick call and returns to the
alley. Angelo DeSantis, a nickel- and dime-bag potpusher. They
also call him: The Blade. Young, maybe 25, but looks older. Jim has
talked with him at Harry and Judy's. Despite his profession, and
creepy looks, Angelo is a regular guy—certainly not as bad as
Cathy R. makes him out to be.

Five minutes, no one, then long black hair, high heels, and red
lips. It's Rosie Rivera. Some say she's Dominican, some say she's

a Salvadorian, but everyone knows she's a professional. Clad in blue under a cinnamon cape, she makes a curt businesslike call. A few minutes later, a sixtyish gentleman in a silver Volvo drives up and whisks her away. After Rosie: barking and laughing and a wagging tail—a mangy white mutt and two Black girls, two well-stacked teenagers in tight jeans and short pigtails.

*I've seen them at the teen center,* Jim says to himself. *What are their names? Estella, Serina, something like that? They're no older than Heather but they're built like grown women. Why do colored girls develop so early? But most of 'em are ugly with that broad African nose and thick lips and kinky hair.* One girl goes into Pauline's, the other makes a call. The dog pisses on the parking meter by the pay phone. Soon, they're sashaying back up the hill, with two boxes of Cracker Jacks and a begging pooch.

Pimply face, Celtics cap; twenty-inch wheels, high-rise handle-bars, a skidding BMX bike. It's Billy McArthur coming down Mill Street, but not to use the phone. The Blade comes out of the alley just in time to give him a small bag in exchange for a wad of money—Angelo makes a bundle when school is out. Billy stashes the weed in the leg pocket of his fatigue pants then whips off two quick wheelies and accelerates up the hill. *That took ten seconds,* Jim remarks to himself. *It's no wonder the war on drugs is a failure.*

After Billy, Cathy's Aunt Verna: she doesn't get a bag from the Candy Man but a kiss and a piece of paper—evidently a list. Verna helps Angelo set up drug deals with teenagers and he gives her a small cut—plus his dick. That's how Verna gets her booze money, in addition to the room and board she gets from Cathy. A squat ruddy woman with a hound-dog face and blazing hair the color of chili powder, she looks nothing like her niece. She's in her late 30s, but with her alky face and wattled neck, she looks fifty-five. List in hand, she wobbles down to the phone. *How does Angelo stand sleeping with her? She's disgusting. I guess it's the unwritten law of copulation: uglies have to fuck uglies.*

Jim unrolls Logan's magazine and looks once more at the squeaky-clean students on the back. *Look at those goody-goody smiles,* he declares scornfully to himself. *They look so happy and devout and above it all, as if they never hurt or cry or get horny, as if their biggest dream is to glide around on clouds and play sermon tapes on hand-held recorders. It's sick and out of touch, far away from what I see in my heart, or in this town.* Jim looks up just in time to see Verna hang up and totter into Clancy's. He gives a resigned sigh and takes his pen out of his shirt pocket. He then reaches into the backseat and grabs the bill from Nashoba Fuel & Gas. On the back of the envelope he scrawls a verse:

> *IF JESUS LIVED ON*
> *MILL STREET TODAY, HE WOULD HANG*
> *OUT WITH THE PEOPLE*
> *WHO USE THE PAY PHONE IN FRONT*
> *OF PAULINE'S VARIETY STORE.*

\* \* \*

59 Front Street. 10:58 a.m. Jim leaves his coat in the car. The mild 60° air encourages his heart, but not his head. Mrs. Courtney is sweeping the porch in her sunbonnet. Her turquoise eyes bright with vigor, she peers up at Jim through her little James Joyce glasses: "Eh, young man, 'tis a rattlin' fine day to be let out, an' for a body to be aworkin'. I daresay it's warm for February."

*Mrs. C. knows,* he thinks as he goes up the stairs. *She has to? I'm over here every day.*

"Come on in," Becki yells in response to Jim's knock. "It's not locked."

He goes in. The sunlit kitchen smells of coffee, cat food, and Beckiness. Bathsheba is busy at her dish eating a late breakfast. Rebecca, still in her yellow bathrobe, sits at her kitchen table clipping coupons from the *Worcester Telegram & Gazette.* The sash to her robe is tied at her side like a giant terry-cloth shoelace.

"How come you're not dressed?" Jim asks apprehensively as he pours a mug of coffee.

"Because I just got up twenty minutes ago," Becki replies without looking up.

Pang of disappointment. Jim notes indifference in her voice, in her disposition. He sips his coffee and moves over to the table. *Shit, she knew I was coming,* he complains to himself. *I told her eleven o'clock. She's more interested in finding Stop & Shop specials than being with me. Next thing, she's gonna tell me she doesn't want to go on outreach at all.*

Standing behind and to her left, he watches as Becki cuts out the coupons with a pair of blunt-nosed scissors, the type her 1st- and 2nd-graders use at school. Her disheveled haystack of honey-brown hair spills onto the collar of the robe, parting just enough in the back for him to see the white nape of her neck showing through. He longs to kiss that sweet spot of flesh, and all of her neck. But he quickly suppresses the wish. He's only kissed her romantically on one occasion, on Christmas Eve, and that wild night has long since been disavowed. He doubts he'll ever kiss her again. At best, he hopes for fun times when she's playful with him and mirthful, but even that seems like a long shot on this Thursday morning.

Becki sips some coffee then goes on clipping: Solo Laundry Liquid, 64 oz., $2.39—Idlenot Orange Juice, 79¢/half gal—Folger's Special Roast Coffee, $1.39/lb—Boneless Rib Eye Delmonico Steaks, $3.49/lb—Nabisco Chips Ahoy, $1.89 for 18 oz. pkg. She puts the cutout coupons in a 6" x 9" clasp envelope.

"So this's why you have the Worcester paper delivered to your door?" Jim remarks, a hint of testiness and condescension in his voice. "I've never seen you read the *front* page?"

Becki seems to ignore his peevish comment as she carefully cuts out another coupon: California White Potatoes, 5 lb. bag, $1.39. But after placing the coupon in the envelope, she responds matter-of-factly, "I save ten bucks a week doing this, sometimes fifteen. That's more important than the front page if you ask me. Besides, I get all the news I need on TV."

*Fuck, she makes me feel like I'm bothering her,* Jim declares silently. Anger gathers in his mouth. *I hate <u>this</u>. I hate it when she's indifferent. I'd rather have her yell at me.* He wants to rip up the newspaper, but he doesn't; he simply sips from his mug then swallows the urge along with the coffee—for the sake of peace.

"Well, Becki, it's past eleven o'clock," Jim says out loud, finally addressing his true concern. "We're doing hospital visits today, remember?"

Becki turns the page of the newspaper. Her response is perfunctory, "I'm not going on outreach today. I have shopping to do, and laundry. I don't even have a clean pair of jeans."

Jim's stomach sinks. *There it is,* he laments to himself. *I knew it.* Yet he persists, not with hope of persuading her but to vent his hurt and frustration, "Well, what about Elmer? We hafta see Elmer. He's out of intensive care, you know?"

"I'm still not goin'," Becki replies through a yawn as she scans the CVS Pharmacy section at the bottom of the page. "I've got too much to do."

Jim moves around the table and pushes his coffee mug toward her pouty face. "Well, it *is* your job, you know?"

Becki's dark eyebrows slant into a deeper frown. "Not on *Thurs*day it's not," she rebuts, her tone of voice showing a bit of irritation. "Especially this week. This is school vacation; this is my time off ... and we already did outreach on Monday. That's enough. Besides, why visit a man in a coma? It's super *bor*ing, and gross."

"It's not a coma," Jim nitpicks. "Elmer's semiconscious, in and out."

She clips a coupon for Crest Toothpaste but does not reply. Jim feels like screaming but instead, he puts his mug, still full, on the counter, then steps over and looks out the east-facing window. Sun-washed rows of boxy houses descend away from him down the northeast slope of Hadley Hill. *O God, why do I put up with this?* he asks himself. *I've been playing it safe ever since I slapped her, and she takes advantage. I'm pussy-whipped but I get no pussy. I don't even get a kiss. Why can't I let go and be happy with Sharon and the kids?—but I can't. It's a curse. I'm addicted.*

Jim comes back to the table. He presses her, "So you don't wanna go, huh?"

"I can't," Becki affirms. "I *said* I have things to do."

"Well, who decides anyway? I *am* the pastor, you know?"

"Well, whoopie-*do*. Then you go. I'm goin' shopping, and I hafta wash my hair later." Becki now seems more occupied than irritated, as if she enjoys toying with his emotions. And she knows that nonchalance annoys him most.

Jim feels like slapping her, but quickly kills the impulse as Bathsheba rubs against his leg. The cat looks up at him with her yellow feline eyes as if to say, "What the fuck, Shanley? Every day you and Becki fight your feelings, your instincts, and cover with lies. We cats have no such hang-ups about mating. But it's no wonder. Your whole species is neurotic over sex." After giving her assessment of the situation, she bounds onto the table, struts over to the window sill, and assumes her sunbasking position. *Bathsheba's right,* Jim says to himself, *even if I just imagined it.*

He chews his annoyance a bit longer then moves closer and spits it into the side of Becki's face, "So didyuh *up*date the Sunday school outreach cards?"

"No, I didn't get around to it," Becki says without emotion, without looking up.

"Well, you've had *all* week?"

"So ... they'll be done in time. We never visit Sunday school parents until Saturday." Becki cuts around a coupon for Control Cat Litter.

Like an insecure child with hurt feelings, Jim has become intentionally difficult. He no longer cares about peace; he wants her attention even if it means a fight. "That's just like you, Rebecca Lea," he harps. "You always wait 'til the *last* minute. You've wasted this whole week. We haven't made five visits. If I'd known this, I would've gone to Cobleskill with Sharon. Why d'yuh think I stayed home? We planned to do outreach every day, re*mem*ber?"

"Well, I changed my mind. This is my vacation. I wanna take it easy."

"So you think I should pay you *mon*ey for doin' nothing?"

"Stop testing me, Shanley."

"Well, maybe I'll just stop *pay*ing you. I don't see how you deserve it."

"Suit yourself," Becki replies nonchalantly as she scans another page. Jim feels like firing her on the spot, but instead, he reaches down and pulls one end of her robe sash until the bow knot is untied. "Knock it *off,* Jimmy," she snaps in a motherly tone but short of losing her temper. "Stop pestering like a little kid."

But Jim persists anyway. "You've got it pretty easy, Becki, you know that?"

"Howso?" Becki asks.

"How many twenty-year-olds have someone to take care of them?" Jim replies.

"Oh, you're *so* kind and *so* fatherly," she mocks. "I don't need your money, or your concern. If you died today, I'd do fine."

Hurt, hurt. Her mocking indifference stings Jim's heart. He wants to cry—no, he wants to grab her, shake her, slap her, until she's thankful for love. But he doesn't. *Shit, this is hopeless,* he sighs resignedly to himself. *There's no way to change her mood. She's so fuckin' stubborn. Maybe things'll be different tomorrow but this day is lost.* He turns to leave but unexpected temptation stops him. Becki has shifted sideways in her chair. Her robe is open almost to her crotch. Unable to resist, Jim runs his eyes up between her sumptuous bread-loaf thighs until he runs out of light. But he wants more. He can't help it. He moves closer and slips his hand between her legs. She spreads wider—NO, NO. He just imagines it, but the thought drives him nuts. *Why can't we go into the bedroom and finish what we started on Christmas Eve? I know she likes sex better than clipping those fuckin' coupons.*

As if reading his thoughts, Becki lifts her pouty face and silently accuses him with her sleep-filled eyes. Jim expects condemnation or at least a cutting remark, but instead, she softens into a smile and says, "Lighten up, Shanley. There's more to life than outreach, you know?"

Becki looks down again but Jim continues to stare, at her downturned face. A renewed sense of hope begins to unravel the tangle of hurt feelings in his gut. A moment later she comes up beaming, blushing. "Stop it, Jimmy," she gushes. "Stop looking at me." She gives her scrunchy face then grins from ear to ear in spite of herself. Jim grins back, his heart recovering like a wounded fowl taking flight. Without another word, Becki gulps down her coffee, gets up, and disappears into her room.

Jim soon hears *T. Rex* and "Bang A Gong" on her stereo. The suggestive lyrics and loud percussive guitar chug through her closed door like a charging locomotive:

Well, you're dirty and sweet, clad in black,
Don't look back, and I love you.
You're dirty and sweet, oh yeah.
Well, you're slim and you're weak,
You got the teeth of the hydra upon you.
You're dirty sweet and you're my girl.

Two minutes later, Becki comes out wearing boots, gray cords, her *Pink Floyd* sweat shirt—and a teasing smirk. "Bet I can beat you to the lake," she taunts as she bolts out the door.

Mood change. Mood change. Rush of adrenaline. Jim runs after her. Around the house, up the hill into the meadow. Becki, her short legs pumping like pistons, churns through the mud, melting snow, and dead grass. Jim reaches the summit just in time to see her highballing for the stone fence. He pants; he wheezes; he pursues. Burning, burning, his lungs are burning. Without breaking stride, Becki tears into the woods, into the shadows. Crunch, crunch, ahead and below, four boots running in slushy snow, granular, melting, but still deep: a lunatic flight across a giant snow cone. Trees, shadows, spotty sun. Chugging, chugging, they zoom down the path, then through the picnic area, across the tracks, and down the embankment to the gravel beach.

Becki, red-faced and huffing, bends over hands-on-knees to catch her breath, while Jim coughs, wheezes, sucks in the south wind, and collapses on the fallen oak tree. His heart pounds in his chest, in his head. He feels hot inside his sweater-vest; he rolls up the sleeves of his flannel shirt.

Warm, no snow on the sun-drenched beach, but a sickly sheet of gray ice still stretches south over the reservoir. Getting her second wind, Becki collects a handful of rocks and throws them one by one onto the frozen lake. The stones do not bounce or *zing* or *ping* but rather *ka-plaush* into the mushy melting ice.

Seconds tick by, then a minute. Jim's breathing settles, and his pulse, but not his emotions. The beach setting normally soothes his soul, but not when Rebecca's wagging her moonish rump in front of him—in skintight corduroys which are threadbare and faded. *O Lord!* he cries in his heart. *Do something. I can't take this roller-coaster ride. I can't stand looking at her without having her.*

Her moppy brown hair blowing in the wind, she throws the rest of the rocks then hops-skips over and plops down on the old oak. Facing Jim, she straddles the tree as if riding a horse. Dimples, ruddy cheeks. A flirty grin bows her cupid mouth. She leans back on her hands. Her blue eyes flash amber like heat lightning on a summer night.

Spirited, vivacious, full of spunk, Becki opens and closes her legs as if bursting with sexual energy. That in itself takes Jim's breath, but when she spreads wide—oh, sweet smile of pink cotton—her plumpish haunches have split the crotch seam of her cords exposing her pink panties. She doesn't seem aware of the tear, or at least, she's not in a hurry to hide it.

Lust, heat, frustration. Jim's heart lurches at the door of its cell; his swelling prick lurches inside his fly. Tempting thoughts, *Oh shit, I wanna slip my finger inside that ripped seam. I can't stand it.* But fear fights back—to preserve the peace. His conscience, wielding the cold machete blade of his hardened will, slashes, swipes, hacks at the temptation until it falls bleeding and quivering onto the ground beside the old oak tree.

But Becki quickly resurrects it. Two months, too long. Giving a naughty-girl smirk, she launches a spicy conversation—from a rather peculiar angle, "Whaddeya think, Shanley? Was Mary Magdalene good in bed, or what?"

"Wah ... w-wah—what?" Jim stutters. "Why are you asking about her?"

"She was a hooker, right?"

"Yeh, I guess ... according to the Bible anyway."

"Well, I was just thinking."

"Thinking what?"

Becki blushes and arches her eyebrows coquettishly. "Well, she must've gotten wicked wild pleasure, you know, with all those demons?" Before Jim can reply, she giggles then adds a prurient punch line, "And I sure don't want *my* demons cast out. I need 'em I tellyuh!" Back to the water. Rebecca hops up and executes several repetitions of her happy-girl quickstep, then sashays back to the edge of the ice, where she resumes throwing rocks.

*I don't believe this,* Jim cries in his soul. *How can she go from clipping coupons to spreading her haunches and talking about Mary Magdalene's orgasms? I haven't seen her this frisky—shit, it's been a long time. Maybe she's tired of platonic pretense? Maybe this is the day? Maybe she'll pull down her pants and sit right on my lap, right on this log?*

After hurling a number of rocks, Rebecca picks up a shiny piece of quartz and flips it casually from hand to hand. Her soul beckons—or so Jim thinks. Instantly responding, he goes over and stands next to her. She says nothing. She seems entranced by the rock as it flies back and forth. But he's entranced by Rebecca. She thrills him, intoxicates him, draws him, yet terrifies him. His will is shut down. Her wanton butt-wiggling mood, the first since Christmas Eve, has blown away his peace-at-any-cost policy like a grass hut in a hurricane.

*O God, she wants me to kiss her,* Jim tells himself. *I feel it. I feel it.*

His pent-up heart breaks open like a great egg and runs out all over the beach. Though eros rages, he speaks tenderly, "I love you, Becki Lea. It turns me on when you flirt and get suggestive. I love it, and I want your body more than ever, but it's so much *more* than physical. I want you *with* me forever. I love you. I want to know you, and know you. I've been holding back for two months. But now I have to say it. I love you, *all* of you."

Becki seems touched by his amorous words. She tosses the rock at her feet then looks down shyly. The love vibes between them now seem more poetic than erotic. She sketches a circle about the fallen quartz rock with the toe of her boot. Oh, Becki, Becki. She looks puppyish, inviting, yet somehow sad.

Jim can't resist; he must kiss her. He can already taste her cinnamon lips. Stepping closer, he gently lifts her chin—but Becki slaps his hand away, not with anger but with mild irritation as if she's swatting a mosquito. "*Stop it,* Jimmy," she admonishes. "You've been doin' good since Christmas. Don't spoil it *now.*"

SHOCK, SHOCK, NUMB. Becki's rebuke sucks the air out of Jim's lungs, the electricity out of his nerves. Numbness spreads over him as if he's been injected with Novocain. He feels nothing. The rest of her words rumble like distant thunder, "When I get sexually buzzed, it's not *you,* Shanley. You know that. Nothing has changed. I think about sex. I have my eyes on a few guys, but not *you.*" Her tone is nonchalant and condescending as if his offense is worthy of correction but not of passion. She steps away from him toward the lake, and resumes throwing rocks.

No more Novocain, just naked pain. It rips and tears the entrails of Jim's soul as if Becki flogged him with barbed wire then wrapped him in it. Hurt, hurt, fiery hurt, searing, cutting, shredding, wounding. It ignites his rage which explodes again and again, trying to break out of his barbed cocoon—but to no avail. *O God, how can she flirt like that and not want me! Things haven't changed! Nothing will ever change!*

Jim fears his teeth will blow out of his mouth, but his anger cannot break through his hurt. The lake and sky shimmer before him, a blurry mist of gray and blue and distant purple. Hot tears well up but none escape. He does not hit, he does not yell, nor does he protest or accuse; he simply gives a dead chuckle and says, "I'm sorry."

"No harm done," Becki replies in the same nonchalant tone. She tosses rocks onto the ice. She seems unconcerned as if the whole episode means nothing. "There's no sense crying over spilled milk. You just have a problem. I'm used to it. It's nothing new."

"I guess so," Jim agrees meekly like a scolded hound with his tail—and his deflated dick—between his legs. She doesn't reply.

Becki's silence threatens, making Jim suddenly panicky and insecure. "But we can still be a team, and be friends?" he asks. His tone is pitiful, pleading.

"Why not?" Becki replies. "We've dealt with this plenty of times."

She picks up more rocks. Jim stares out at the sickly sheet of ice. His panic subsides leaving a mixed feeling of anguish and consolation. Things will be the same forever he figures. Lies, pretense, sexual frustration, bowing to her demands, saying I'm sorry when she ought to be saying it. Their relationship will go on as it is. He'll not lose her, but he'll never have her either.

Finally, he sighs resignedly and says, "I'm goin' to see Elmer. Are you coming with me?"

The question makes Becki scowl. "No, I said *no*. How many *times* do I have to say it? I'm not goin' on outreach today." She seems more upset than when he tried to kiss her.

"Okay, okay," Jim replies, turning to go. He feels wounded, castrated, but safely back into his rut. As he trudges up the path, a squirrel scurries up a naked maple in front of him and chatters sharply; even the animals seem annoyed with him.

Becki's shout halts him at the top of the embankment, "Oh, Jimmy!"

"What!" he yells back down the hill.

"Are you gonna pick me up tomorrow!"

"What for!" Jim asks.

"Outreach, of course!"

"Tomorrow's Friday!"

"I know! But we're doin' outreach all week, right!"

"I guess ... be ready at ten!"

Jim turns to go but Becki yells again, "Jimmy! Oh, Jimmy!"

"Yeh!"

"One other thing!"

"What!"

"I need my rent check early this month—I'm wicked low! Can you bring it tomorrow!"

# Chapter Thirty-three

Like a glass tit, and serving the same purpose, an i.v. bottle hangs upside down over Elmer's bed. Russ stares out the window. Pastor Jim tries to make contact, "Elmer"—no response. "Elmer, it's Pastor Jim"—nothing. Gust of revulsion.

Elmer's unresponsive face is uglier than ever. Puckered, purple-gray, and withered, he looks like a giant testicle with a nose. After a few more tries, Jim takes Elmer's toadlike hand and mutters a short superficial prayer. He's long since given up on God doing miracles but he prays anyway out of a sense of duty.

On the way out, he and Russ inquire at the nurses' station. A droopy-eyed nurse checks a computer monitor and says that Elmer is slated to go to the stroke unit at the Bedford VA Hospital, that his nephew from Lynn had completed the paperwork.

After the nurses' station, the elevator, then through two sets of glass doors to the outside. The midafternoon sun bathes the hospital grounds with dazzling light. The south wind is stronger. It smells like wet wood, almost sweet. The snow is rapidly disappearing from the landscaped lawns. Hinton Regional Hospital: modern, concrete and glass, but rather boxy and unimaginative. It sits on the summit of Greeley Hill like a five-story parking garage. Jim likes the old Greeley Hospital better: two stories, purple brick, quaint porticos, white trim, less institutional. But it now cowers as an auxiliary wing behind the new edifice. "I'm glad to get out of there," Jim sighs as he hitches up his Levi's.

"I'll say," Russ replies. "When my time comes, I hope I go quickly while I'm walking in the woods." His Red Sox hat cocked back on his head, Russ saunters along with his hands in the belly pouch of his sweat shirt. His grease-stained work pants are too short and they flap like flags about his ankles. "Doctors are okay. They know their stuff, like airline pilots, but hospitals give me the creeps. I hope I die outside. There's just something right about sun and wind and blue sky. Just look at it." Russ squints up into the bright turquoise sky and inhales the fresh air. "If I ever get like Elmer, Jim, I want you to shoot me." They both laugh—insensitively, as people laugh about death when it seems far away.

The laughing, and Russ's presence, soothes Jim's anguish a bit, anguish over trying to kiss Becki. His amorous advance accomplished nothing except to make him feel humiliated and small. Nothing has changed. He's still a slave to her capricious flirting. After the rebuff at the reservoir, he drove home, fed Sam, then started for the hospital but he felt too deflated to go alone, so he went to McD's to eat then swung by and waited for Russ to get home from work. In truth, Jim didn't want to go to the hospital at all—not without Becki. He knew that seeing Elmer would be a nothing experience, as she had said, but he stubbornly went anyway, hoping the dutiful visit would lift his self-esteem.

To the parking lot. Jim and Russ cross the main roadway which circles the hospital like an asphalt moat. The pedestrian crosswalk is painted fluorescent green between wide yellow stripes. "It's a shame," Russ says shaking his head.

"What is?" Jim asks.

"Hospitals ... how they hide the truth behind forced smiles and hi-tech equipment, and phony antiseptic environments."

"You mean how they hide death and blood and pain?"

"Well, that too, but mainly I mean the money thing ... how hospitals and insurance companies are sucking us dry. It's bad enough being sick, but now you have to give your *last* fucking penny to pay for your own death, and it looks like we'll be giving our last penny before we hit fifty, just to pay the insurance premiums. Fuck, there's talk at work about making us pay twice the percentage, and the plan they're proposing provides less coverage. The higher-ups at Stromberg, they're not dumb. They know the cost of medical care has the whole fucking economy by the balls. Unless you're filthy rich, it's better to be a *fuck*ing alcoholic like Elmer than to work everyday. If you're in the middle, you get fucked over your whole life, and especially when you die."

Russ uses "fuck" every other sentence. He never says it around Stan, or the church regulars, and he used to tone down around Jim, even last year, but their deepening friendship and mutual dislike of evangelical masks has changed that, not to mention Jim's own increased use of profanity—partly because of Becki, partly because of his rebellious spirit coming out, partly because he needs high-octane adjectives to describe his roller-coaster life.

The Mustang is on the far side of the lot next to a modern-style lamppost that looks like a lollipop with a broken neck. "Sounds like you're down on the American dream," Jim kids as they get into the car. "Of course, most people would say you just have a negative attitude because you don't like to work." He puts the key in the ignition but doesn't start the engine.

"That's for sure," Russ chuckles. "I plead guilty on *both* counts." He then becomes seriously cynical again. "I hate the fucking treadmill ... how I have to crawl out of bed and get on it every morning just to make a living. It's like having a gun at my head. But I doubt I'm the only one with a negative attitude. If people were honest, you'd hear a great *fuck*ing wail go up all over America.

Let's face it, Jim; this country is finished, caput, c'est fini. We're just running out the clock. Of course, all the politicians, least those in office, profess optimism, while they cover the putrid sores and stink of death with smiles and flag-waving. That bastard Dukakis makes great promises then robs us blind to support his wild spending. People say, 'Be glad you live in America and not in Russia.' Well, maybe our system *is* better than communism, but that's not saying much. Capitalism just works better in a human race full of greedy assholes. But all the 'isms' are flawed if you ask me. And Reagan, he's just as bad. He talks about how he ended the recession and how we can look forward to an era of unprecedented prosperity. But his philosophy is spend-now-pay-later. He gives his fat-cat friends a huge tax break but has to borrow billions to run the government. The national debt will be two trillion dollars if this keeps up. He says, 'It'll *tric*kle down.' But it never trickles down, not to *me* anyway. It's like the rich are partying with our kids' money. But he'll be re-elected come November. He's got that fucking kind-grandfather look that people love. I doubt I'll even vote. It's all the same ... Republicans, Democrats, hospitals, banks, lawyers, real estate agents ... even the *fuck*ing Red Sox—"

"Now I know you're serious," Jim cuts in, grinning.

Like a horse snorting, Russ blows out a spluttering gust of disdain. "Guys used to play hard with team spirit ... Ted Williams, Dom Dimaggio, Jimmy Piersall, Mel Parnell, even Yaz in the early days, but now they're all greedy bastards with money-hungry agents, and the owners are just as greedy. They raise ticket prices each year and sell TV rights for astronomical figures. And a fucking two-bit pitcher like Bob Stanley wants a *million* a year. Baseball's a great game, but they've ruined it. And they make kids pay five bucks for autographs. It's enough to make you *vom*it."

Jim gives a quick laugh. "I must say, Russ, I haven't seen you this worked up in a while. You must've had a worse day than me."

"I doubt that after what you told me about you and Becki, but I've been piss-faced all week. Becki's prick-teasing fickleness is just another example of how sucky things are. I can usually joke about the shittiness of life, but not lately. Maybe I'm just getting old, huh?" Russ shakes his head and gives a resigned grin. "When I was younger, I was hopeful about things, but hardly ever anymore. Now every day is boring and shitty if you ask me. Wanting and not having is the *story* of life from the moment you come screaming out of your mother's womb looking for a nipple to suck, and if you survive to puberty, you spend the rest of your life looking for a pussy to fuck. And none of us volunteered to come. But God sent us anyway. When I first came to church, I figured God had a purpose to it all and would make things better in time. But that's now a fairy-tale hope. In fact, I'm beginning to wonder if He's involved at all, and if He is, I wonder what the fuck He's up to."

Russ takes off his Red Sox hat, combs his fingers through his thinning rusty-brown locks. "To hell with love and heart, and honest feelings. You have to get it up daily. Go to work, fake it, please your boss. It's survival of the fittest, and money rules. The owners expect each worker to sell his soul to the company. 'Love thy neighbor' ... *no fucking way!*" Russ gives another spluttering snort, this one shorter, more abrupt, like a fart out of his mouth. "The verse for the '80s is: 'Get the edge on your neighbor before he gets the edge on you.' Losers are not tolerated. Profits, profits. Everyone's pushing and selling, trying to squeeze more golden eggs out of the goose, and they don't care if the goose dies as long as they get their eggs *now*. Money, money, wealth, and fame. Hype, glitz, lotteries, theme-park mania. It's like the whole country has turned into Las Vegas. And the money merchants don't care about heart or truth, or anything substantial. They just care about impressions and perceptions, and poll numbers—computerized marketing bullshit that helps them sell, sell, sell. And advertising hype is how they do it. Hype, hype, lies, and lies. We get bombarded with it. Just watch the news! They stuff commercials in and keep stuffing. There's ten of 'em between the weather and sports: Smith Barney, Delta Airlines, State Farm, Toyota, McDonald's, Midas, Budweiser, Digital, Converse, Calvin Klein, Nynex ... Diet-Pepsi. Or open *Time* magazine, they have more ads than news, and foldouts and coupon offers on every other page. Fuck, I hate it!"

Russ sighs gustily then settles a bit.

Jim opens his window. A breeze whips through refreshing the car. He reaches into the backseat and grabs the latest issue of *Choose Ye This Day*. "Speaking of advertising," Jim says. "Take a look at this." He hands the LBI periodical to Russ.

Placing his hat on the dash, Russ studies the glossy ad on the back cover. He strokes his auburn whiskers. His eyes spark with bawdy mirth—he can always joke about sex no matter his mood. "I don't know what to say, Jim, except I'd sure like to bang that broad on the left and make her confess she likes to fuck. And that gal in the middle, she's a lost puppy if I ever saw one, but look at her sweet young tits, how they lift up inside her dress." They both snicker as Jim nods his agreement. "And the guy looks so squeaky clean. You could never imagine him reading *Playboy* and pulling his pud ... but I bet he does."

Russ puts on his hat then sniffs the air as if he smells shit. His scornful mood returns, chasing the mirth in his eyes. "When Mom and Daddy Christian see this, they'll send *little* Bobby and *little* Susie to Nashua so they'll be protected from *world*liness. Logan's a fucking master salesman. He knows that fear is the big motivator with parents. That bastard is the biggest liar of all. He and Garrett and all of 'em, they're not only greedy and power hungry, but they profess to be different. They preach that Christ is the way out, that he'll deliver us from this sucky life. Logan says get saved, get right, give money, lay down your life, go to Bible college, and the Lord will deliver you from the mammon rat race and give you a new happy life far removed from all the evil and ugly things. People know the world is fucked up with lies and sin and money power, so when they hear Logan's God-pitch, they fall for it."

Russ rolls the magazine and whaps it against his open palm. "Society condemns religious cults, like the Moonies or Jim Jones, because they brainwash people using fear and false promises and mass psychology, and turn people into religious robots even to the point of drinking poison, but no one ever condemns modern Christianity—they don't dare, least not in America—but it's the *biggest* cult of all, especially the evangelicals, and more dangerous than the wacko cults if you ask me, because the mind-control is subtle and hidden, and the poison they give is highly regarded, even while it paralyzes the heart and robs people of their true identities, and separates people in the name of God. Logan says, 'Come out from the world. Don't associate with the unsaved. Don't trust your feelings or instincts. Submit to the leaders appointed over you. And God will bless you and accept you and invite you to live in his house.' It's just a ploy, a power play, to gain followers, to exploit them, and to cut them off from all influences that might turn them away. It's no different than *any* cult, except that evangelical doctrines are traditional and deep-rooted in the American psyche, so Logan and his peers are accepted and applauded for their spiritual tyranny. He says, 'Pray, believe, and claim the promises, and the Holy Spirit will fill you with love and make you a beautiful person, and will bless your marriage, your home, your finances.' It's all hype, Jim, a *fuck*ing sales pitch, a come-on!"

Russ gargles, spits out the window, giving Jim opportunity to respond, "Well, I been preaching a lot of the same things for nine years, and it's written in our tracts."

"I know," Russ acknowledges, whacking the air with the magazine. "We may spout the same verses but we're different, at least you and me and a few others. We're not into exploiting people, not like Logan. He takes advantage of discontent and loneliness. He promises love and joy, then uses guilt and peer pressure to enslave people. Let's face it, Jim; *no*body gets honest about our desperate human plight, how we ache to be loved beyond duty and ulterior motive, and how we're hurtling out of control toward death—with no fucking answers. No one dares talk about it. Truth doesn't sell very well. People don't want to hear it. They don't want to hear that we're desperately dependent on a God that we're not sure of ... and starving for love that exists only in fairy tales. People want assurance. They want it in writing. They're afraid of pain and loss and the black oblivion of death, so they go to leaders and preachers, and mothers and gurus, for propped-up promises and concocted explanations. They're afraid of losing love so they put it in a nice white house in suburbia and secure it with vows and legality and social acceptability. They want to know it'll be there when they get home from work—but it *rarely* is.... Shit, *I'm* afraid too, but I don't want sugar pills and placebos. I don't want false assurance from some hyped-up evangelist. God *is* our only hope, but no way can I say for sure what He's going to do. I hope there *is* something good after death. Fuck, I hope there's something good *before* death. But what I've seen so far doesn't make me starry-eyed with faith."

Russ slings the magazine into the back. He's in rare form and he's not done. "People don't want an awesome God who's bigger than the Bible, who acts outside the limits of their doctrinal boxes. They don't want childlike wonder and awe, or any doubt or fear. They want to cover *all* the bases. They want happy answers. They want a predictable God they can control. They want to know they're *saved* and going to heaven when they die. They want security. They want flag-waving and faldaral and *razz*matazz, even if it means death to honesty, death to an open mind, death to the heart!"

Green fire. Russ's eyes blaze. He gestures with short outward thrusts of his arm like an MP directing traffic. "They want preachers who say, 'You can be *sure,* if you study and pray and obey, and apply yourself, and make correct choices, and come to every service.' It's no wonder that evangelicals are into persuading and propping up. They're no different than Madison Avenue. They just want to create godly impressions and favorable perceptions. They don't give a shit about truth! They just want to win followers with clever ads and witty lines and gusts of rhetoric! And Logan and Garrett and Beckman, they're fucking good at it, the *best* I know!"

"Now *that's* what I should preach on Sunday," Jim responds enthusiastically, his spirit stirred by Russ's caustic tirade. "But I—" He gives a resigned sigh. "I've got no balls when I preach. For two months, I've been giving safe sermons right out of my LBI class-notes. My heart is nauseated each week, but I don't dare preach what I feel. It's such a lie. People need to hear what you're saying, Russ ... right from the gut."

"Well, it's easy to vent my feelings here in the car, Jim, but I don't talk like this with anyone else, not really, and I certainly wouldn't preach this at church."

Russ rests his elbow out his open window and drums his fingernails on the roof of the Mustang. It sounds to Jim like a pigeon walking on a tin roof. He remembers the sound from his days in the barnyard back home. Whenever he went out to feed the chickens, the pigeons would swoop down from the barn and land on the henhouse looking for a handful of corn, and they usually got it.

Silence. Seconds tick by. Ten, twenty, thirty. Jim feels a pang of schedule anxiety. "I guess we should go see Calvin; I told him we'd come by. He's ashamed to come to church, you know?"

The mention of Cal McClusky sets Russ off again; his voice cracks with sardonic weariness. "Now he's a perfect example, Jim. He bought the whole born-again package—at least, he did for two years. He got saved, joined up, prayed daily, studied the Bible, tithed faithfully." Russ gives a derisive snort and gestures with a broad sweep of his arm as if addressing the valley below them. "He even got married in the church, and became a deacon, but where did it get him? God didn't take away his laziness or his alcoholism or his debts ... or his poor opinion of himself. In fact, God didn't take any of the *shit*. He just took his son, and now his wife. He ripped *love* right out of his life. Of course, Stan says it's Cal's fault because he didn't give up his sins, but what the fuck is a guy supposed to do? He gave it his best shot. It just didn't *work*. He traded his soul for a ticket on a plane ... that won't fly."

Russ sighs, settles. Jim leans against his door sticking his elbow out the window. The distant shrieks of playing children waft across the hospital parking lot, blowing on the frisky springlike wind. "It's hard to figure," Jim says. "It sure looks like God dumped on Cal. His life is ruined and he's only twenty-six. Everyone looks at him as a loser, as a backslidden alcoholic, and they blame him for Baby Shane's death. It's no wonder he doesn't show his face at church anymore ... and we talk about the church being a family, and we preach about the mercy and forgiveness of God. We talk about loving each other in Christ. Truth is, Russ, I love maybe ten people in the church. Oh, I have affection for a lot more but I don't really know them, not heart-to-heart, like I know you. And many I just tolerate, and some I despise."

Jim sits up, grabs the key, but doesn't turn it. Instead, he pushes his seat back, sags once more against the door, and stares over the steering wheel at the painterly panorama before them. Hazy blue bleeds down into reds and violets and buffs and browns and grays, and dirty white and evergreen. Hazy sky bleeds down onto dormant smokestacks and railroad tracks and old buildings, and streets and houses and piles of snow and naked trees, and the dam and the river and traffic moving on Route 72. A thin plume bends northward from the Prescott stack, tenuous and thin like cigarette smoke. Jim gazes wide-eyed until the hues and shapes before him go out of focus and run together like wet watercolors. Greeley Hill, some three hundred feet higher than Hadley Hill, offers the best view of Brendon Falls. The Shanleys live halfway down as does Russ, but Angela and Larry live near the summit; they have the same view from their living room. Such are the benefits of being on top in America—"Fuck it!" Jim suddenly exclaims, slapping his thigh for emphasis. "I don't wanna do it!"

"No biggie," Russ replies. "We can see Cal another time."

"I don't mean Calvin, I mean Logan."

"Logan?"

Jim shifts to face more toward Russ. "Yeh, I don't want to send another damn dollar to Nashua. As far as I'm concerned, there'll be no resumption in March or April ... or any month."

Russ seems a bit startled by the suddenness of Jim's words but not by their meaning. He grins knowingly and crosses his legs, left foot on right knee. "Well, I sort of figured this was coming sooner or later," he replies when finally comfortable. "But, Jim, *later* might be wiser than *sooner*. Breaking with Nashua is not a decision to make in the heat of Logan-bashing. We're talking about hitting a big hornet's nest with a big fucking stick. Why don't you think on it a bit and see if you feel the same when I'm not around?"

Pastor Jim sweeps the back of his hand toward Russ. "It's not because of you. I've been thinking about it for two months. It's just coming to a head today. I'm ready to declare independence. My preaching, my whole ministry, it's all built on lies and half-truths. I can't bow down to Logan anymore. I realize we may get severely stung over this, and I don't look forward to it.... But this is nothing compared to my *biggest* problem."

"You mean Becki?" Russ says, his tone more declarative than interrogative.

Jim picks a white thread off his jeans, rolls it into a little ball, and stares at it with squinted eyes as if it's a diamond. After a long moment he flicks the ball of thread out the window. "You got it," he replies. "All my lies lead back to her. I love her beyond reason. I ache and yearn for her all day, all night. I think about her constantly. I want to be with her all the time. I want to live with her and sleep with her. To have her as my lover is my greatest dream. To lose her is my greatest dread. I don't give a shit about the church anymore, not really, at least not compared to Becki. I don't believe in Logan or LBI or evangelical Christianity. I'm not sure I ever did. I'm not sure I believe in anything, except I know love is the greatest thing that ever happened to me. Love is the only God I want, Becki-love, real love, love that moves me—and to continue to pastor one of Logan's churches is too much of a lie. I'm tired of doing things out of a sense of duty, of maintaining appearances."

Burst of anger. Jim slams the top of the steering wheel with the heel of his hand. "Like coming here to visit Elmer, it's a lie! Elmer's a dis*gust*ing little drunk. I don't give a *shit* about him. I'm supposed to love all the sheep, but God never gave me love for Elmer, no matter how much I prayed and I don't pray for it anymore. If he dies, *good riddance!* I don't wanna see his ugly fuckin' face, yet here I am coming to visit. It's fuckin' dishonest! I don't know what's gonna happen, but I'm sick and tired of lying. Lying to make Logan happy. To make Campbell happy. To make Sharon happy. To make the flock happy. Lying so I look good ... and most of all, lying so I can be with Becki—always pretending that outreach and church is the reason we're together. I've been walking on eggshells all year, and especially these past two months, just so we can spend time together. I even retracted my feelings I shared with her this morning, like I told you before, and today was the first time I shared my heart since Christmas Eve. She knows I'm petrified of losing her and she takes full advantage. She shows me no respect. She treats me like a toy or a pet ... like I'm a naughty dog."

Jim sucks a quick breath then hits the steering wheel again. "I can't do it anymore! I'm gonna declare my love openly and honestly without backing off. I'm gonna lay it on the line with Becki. If she wants to be my lover then she'll have to come out of her fuckin' closet. But if she has no romantic feelings for me, if Christmas Eve was nothing but misdirected passion as she now claims, then fine! She can get the fuck outa my life! And I'm gonna tell Sharon, and everyone ... *all* my feelings, *all* my heart! I can't stand it anymore! I'm *sick* of playing it safe!"

"So, I guess the bomb is ticking after all," Russ replies—the biggest understatement of the day. He chuckles. He pushes his hat back on his head. "I figured things weren't as peaceful as they appeared on the surface but it's no wonder. How can you be in love with a woman without wanting to kiss her and fondle her and take her to bed? You can only play the fucking platonic game for so long. A showdown was inevitable ... just like a showdown had to come with Logan. I had a hunch we'd never resume payments to Nashua—as did some other people, I fear."

"Oh yeh?" Jim asks curiously, his emotions cooling a bit.

"I told you Matt Garrett came by yesterday with Barry Buford

**494**

to drop off Sheila's skis that she left on the bus after the teen ski at Crotched Mountain."

"Yeh, you said something about it on the way up, but my mind was on Becki."

"Well, Garrett was asking subtle questions. He was friendly and unobtrusive yet he was feeling me out. But once he realized I wasn't a Judas, he backed off. But believe me, Jim, I don't think your decision will surprise Garrett, or Logan ... that is, if you really intend to go through with it?"

"I do ... I do," Jim replies, now speaking calmly but with conviction. "Maybe I'm right, maybe I'm wrong, but I know I'm different from Logan. I can't play his game anymore—or Becki's. I have to express my true heart. If my heart is wicked then I'm wicked, but I can't change. I can't make my heart conform to Logan's doctrines. Nor can I make it fit Becki's expectations, or Sharon's, or Stan's. I'm tired of trying. I'm tired of lying. I'm tired of wearing a different mask for every person in my life. From now on, Becki's gonna get the *real* me. And when I preach, I'm gonna pour out my heart, all my hopes and fears and dreads and doubts. If people want assurance, they'll not get it from me, not anymore. I can't be honest and certain at the same time."

Russ caresses his oily boot as it lies on his knee. He lifts his gaze into the distance. His eyes brim with awareness but he does not reply. Shifting in his seat, Jim also looks into the distance toward the pine-covered hills on the other side of the river. For a time he feels an exhilarating sense of freedom and transcendent knowing, but reality soon presses back upon him. He shudders as a chill goes up and down his spine, not from cold but from premonition.

Jim wrings his hands anxiously. "Shit, Russ, I feel like I'm up on a gallows with a hood over my head and a noose around my neck, just waiting for the door to drop under me. I'm putting everything on the table, and I don't have shit for cards. When I pull the covers back, Becki's gonna run like hell, and Sharon too. But I can't stand it anymore. I can't take another day like today."

"Who knows what will happen?" Russ counsels calmly. "I'm no quixotic dreamer to be sure, and I'd say you do have a noose around your neck with little chance of escape, at least based on what I've seen so far in this saga. But then again, who can say which way the hornets will go when you whack a hornet's nest, or who'll get stung? Who knows, Jim? Maybe this will turn a lot of things around. Maybe we'll discover a lot of kindred spirits and we can launch a new ministry based on love and honesty where intimacy is the highest good. And who knows about Becki? If she's pushed to the edge, she may run, or then again she might confess her love and stop treating you like shit and you two can be together without hiding. And who can say what Sharon will do if you really tell her the truth? It'd be a miracle to keep 'em both, or even one of them, but who the fuck knows when it comes to women?"

Russ's words settle Jim's anxiety a bit; he feels less panicky. "Of course, we may lose our building and our budget," he points out to Russ as the conversation shifts to the less critical yet practical consequences of getting honest. "And Logan will defrock me for sure."

"So we've never been part of LBI, not really? It was just a matter of time. If we have to fight to get our message out then so be it. It's hard to call. Logan's got us three-to-two on the board, but it's the members that count and a lot of 'em love you, Jim. It'll be a fucking floor fight if our people vote their hearts. But Campbell can't even call a meeting without giving thirty days' notice. So they can't do anything until the end of March. And even if we lose the building and three-fourths of our flock, we'll still end up with a church of twenty people. There may be a lot of blood on the battlefield but I think we may survive ... in one form or another."

"So how should we break this news to Stan, and to Nashua?" Jim asks.

"We won't have to," Russ replies, his eyes sparking with intensity as if he can't wait to take on Logan. "If you open up to Becki and begin to preach your heart from the pulpit, and we don't resume our monthly payments ... believe me, *they'll* be breaking the news to *us*."

\* \* \*

"Whaddeya mean barging in here!" Becki snarls. "It's almost midnight. Can't you see I'm in my *night*gown?" She scowls fiercely, showing her fangs like a she-wolf with cubs.

"I don't give a *shit* what you're in!" Jim exclaims short of shouting. "I've got some things to say, then I'm outa here."

Johnny Carson's voice coming from the TV tells him that she was not sleeping, as does the fact that the pump-handle lamp on her dresser is still on.

Passion colors Rebecca's face like ink bleeding into a blotter. Hands on hips, eyes wet with anger, she stands defiantly in the doorway to her room, but Jim marches boldly past her.

"Get the fuck outa my bedroom!" she protests. "You can't come in my room when I'm not dressed. And *what*ever you got to say, it can wait 'til tomorrow."

"That's what I thought too. But I couldn't sleep. I hafta tell you now."

"Well, I don't wanna hear it!" Becki growls, snapping off the TV and turning on her stereo as high as it will go. "The Long Run" by the *Eagles* blasts through the apartment.

"WELL, YOU'RE *GONNA* HEAR IT!" Jim rages, his pent-up emotions erupting. He kicks the stereo plug out of the wall killing the *Eagles*. Astonished silence stings the room—and Rebecca.

Startled, she steps back, drops her eyes, and picks at her thumbnail. She fidgets on the carpet with her white stocking feet, clenching her toes as if trying to pick up a marble. Her freshly blown bangs hide her scowling face. Bathsheba, realizing that a show-down is at hand, scampers off the bed and escapes to the kitchen. Only the Coca-Cola clock ignores Shanley's outburst as it groans painfully toward the top of the hour.

"You treated me like shit today!" Jim shouts, cleaving the air with his hand. "But I'm not here about that. I'm here to get honest, honest about *us*!"

Becki flinches, cringing away as if he's going to slap her, but Jim has no desire to hit or to hurt, except to pierce her heart with a sabre of truth. "First off, Becki Lea, I'm firing you as my helper. You can still teach if you want and I'll pay the rent. But the whole outreach setup is a sham! You didn't come here to be a missionary. You haven't witnessed to a single person this whole year, not really. You came here because you *love* me! This 'team' thing is a fuckin' lie! Love is the reason, not duty! I'm sick of hiding under the guise of outreach and ministry work, and always pretending that we're comrades for the Lord! We're not comrades, we're *LOVERS*!"

"I don't wanna hear—"

"SHUT UP! Let me finish! I love you, Becki Lea, more than life itself! I've loved you since I first laid eyes on you. I loved you that first day, and I've loved you every day since, and I'll love you on every tomorrow. I love everything about you: how you look, how you smile, how you walk, how you talk, how you smell, how you sleep, how you fidget and shuffle your feet, or stand on one leg and cant your hips!"

Jim gestures like a possessed artist, painting home his feelings with powerful fluid strokes. "I even *love* the stuff I said I hated! I love your face, even when you're pouty or puckering or smacking your gum. I love to watch you eat, even when you chew with your mouth open. I love how you get milk on your upper lip. I love that crazy stiff-legged way you skip-hop around, wagging your head and swinging your arms. I love it that you're coltish and impetuous, and offbeat and spontaneous, and awkward and adolescent, and not boring and polished and sophisticated, and socially correct. I love

497

it when you're witty and funny and laughing. I could listen to you forever and never get tired! Your blue eyes are the *most* enchanting and beautiful of any woman anywhere, and when you're happy, I see heaven in your eyes. But not just your eyes, I love your snubby nose and how you wrinkle it when you scrunch up your face like you do. You're so adorable, and cute—with your blushing cheeks and dimpled smirks. My heart goes crazy. I love you *so*! All of you! I love your hands and your feet. I love your hair, to touch it, to feel it against my cheek. I even love your pimples and your crooked teeth!"

Jim seeks her face but Becki turns, hunching her shoulder against his words. But her nervous hands—she's peeled the cuticle back on her thumb, tearing it on both sides—show that his words are hitting home. "I love your soft squeezable body. I'm glad you're not lean and hard and self-disciplined like some yuppie fitness nut. I'm glad you *pig out* on potato chips and cookies. I love your flab, your bulges, your baby fat. I even love your sweat and burps and farts! Fuck it to God! I love you, Becki Lea! I love you like you're part of me! And when you tease and flirt and get turned on, I shake inside. I love your juicy-ripe sexuality. I love your tits and your hips. And your thighs are so luscious it makes me weak to look at them—and your pussy is the most holy place in the entire universe. I love it! I want it! I picture it every time I look at your crotch! And I'm not *ashamed* of it—NOT *ANYMORE*!"

Jim gulps a breath. He throws his arms upward, outward as if proclaiming his heart to God and all the holy angels. "Oh, Becki Lea, I want you! I want to have beautiful sex with you! Sex that's long and slow and dreamy, then wild and hot and sweaty, again and again until we're hysterical with pleasure! Christmas Eve was no accident! You're not a naive little girl. You're twenty years old. You *knew* what you were doin' that night. You love sex. You crave it. You love how it blows you away. That's why you get so prurient and talk about it all the time. And you especially want it with me— because you *love* me! You lust and fantasize. You flirt to the edge but it doesn't fit, so you run like hell. You become mean and pious and icy cold. You lie and deny—like on Christmas Eve, or even this morning on the beach. And I've been running too. Well, I'm not running anymore! I'm gonna be me! I'm gonna tell the truth! I want to kiss you, Becki! I want to hug you and fondle you every day, and make you come a thousand times until you *black out* from ecstasy!"

He moves closer. She retreats toward the green chair until she can go no farther. Lilacs, lilacs, sweet Becki-nectar. The springlike fragrance of her freshly shampooed locks intoxicates Jim. His voice softens. He still speaks firmly but his words are velvet-edged, anointed with affection. "I can't explain love. I love Sharon. I have cozy love for Angie, for Cathy Rosinski, for a few others, but I never loved *any*one like I love you, Becki Lea. I want to be with you forever. You make me feel happy and alive in a world of duty and death. I long to talk with you, to walk with you, in the woods, in the rain, in the sunshine. I long to hold your hand, to run with you in the meadow, to laugh and giggle and have fun like little kids. I want to live with you and eat with you and sleep with you. I want to cuddle in your arms and wake up and have breakfast together ... with sleepy eyes and messy hair."

His eyes warm with feeling, Jim gazes at Becki. She tucks her chin, puts on her bothered I've-heard-it-before look, but her blanched face and fidgeting fingers tell him that she hasn't heard it before— not *this*. His reckless abandon is stripping her cover.

Silent seconds tick by then Jim's emotions erupt again, hotly, furiously, "What about Sharon you say? Well, what about her? This is between you and me, Becki Lea, not *Sharon!* And what about the Bible! You're always throwing it in my face during our fights! Well, *FUCK* THE BIBLE! Love never fits into the Bible, least not how Logan interprets it. And fuck Logan too! I've got no desire to follow Nashua, or to bow down to evangelical shit. I don't care if I have their approval. I don't care if it's right or wrong, or whether it fits. I just know that you're the center of my universe, Becki, and I'll never stop loving you, not in a million years! I can't pretend any longer! I wanna be with you every day but it's not *out*reach! We're not a *team*! Pull your head out, Becki! Get honest! It's *love*! That's why we hang around together! I'm tired of bowing down to lies and giving in to your bullshit and always apologizing for wanting you! It's not a lust problem! IT'S *LOVE,* DAMMIT! It's a fuckin' mystery! I can't explain it! I just know it's beautiful and big, bigger than anything, and you feel it too! I've been holding this in for so long because I was afraid that you'd get mad and leave, but I can't stand it anymore! So if you want to go, THEN *GO,* DAMMIT! Pack your bags! Get the fuck outa here! I'd rather be honestly apart from you than to be dishonestly together! So if I pick you up in the morning, I pick you up because we love each other and for no other reason! The choice is yours!"

Silence, save for panting and pounding. Jim pants for breath; his heart pounds inside, outside his bosom. His face feels feverish, his temples throb. He stares at Becki; he embraces her with his soul.

Becki, as if feeling this embrace, lifts her blue eyes into his gaze. Blank-faced, she looks at him from way inside herself, like a wounded animal looking out from the deepest woods. Jim senses her love, her passion: hot, palpable, yearning, yet unconfessed. He senses her hurt, her sadness. Azure eyes, sad eyes, haunting, pleading, filling. Too much. Becki looks down, dropping into her usual frown. Feathery torrents of chocolate hair hide the top of her face as her fluffy bangs fall forward. She clenches her jaw as if killing a sob in her throat. Hips cocked, weight on one foot, she slouches before him in her buff-colored gown.

Jim's heart melts, his eyes blur with tears. *O Lord Jesus, I love her so. I need her so. Why does it—I don't understand? I love her and I feel her loving me. Why can't we get into her bed and into each other? I feel it. I taste it. It's all around. What is it, this love? O God, why show yourself, if we can't have you? All of you?*

He aches to hold her but instead speaks tenderly, his voice near to breaking, "I wish I had the answers, Becki, but I don't. I can't explain our lives. I can't explain this year. I just know it's the most wonderful year I ever had, though I've been scared and confused and crazy most of the time."

The faintest hint of a smile flickers on Rebecca's mouth but she quickly kills it with her frown, as Jim goes on, "I just want you to be happy, Becki. I love it when you laugh. I love it when you tease and giggle and play like a little girl ... and when you smile at me, you open a heavenly window in my heart, and I see us walking in paradise among flowers and green grass and leafy trees, and birds and clouds, like that day we stopped and looked at the blue flowers. And there's no death, no guilt, no jealousy—nothing to end it. I know it's hard to follow love in a world built on fear and greed and ulterior motive, and I can't say much for sure anymore, Becki Lea. But there's one thing I *am* sure of. I want to be as close to you as I can be. I have no desire to change you or to own you, or to rape you, or to boss you around. I don't want to label you, corral you, or regulate your life. I just want to warm myself by the hearth of your precious heart. I yearn to be free with you, like two birds flying and frolicking, like two kids playing in a sandbox."

Her head still bowed, Rebecca softens; her frown fades into wistful yearning as if she wants to cry in Jim's arms. Her hands tremble. She nervously moistens her dry lips. She speaks in a broken whisper, "I-I ... I wish. I just wish...."

Her voice trails off. *Oh, Becki Lea,* Jim silently prods. *Don't stop. You're so close. I feel your heart at the door ... at the very door.*

But Becki does stop. Reining in her heart, her tears, her confession, she girds herself with resolve. She tosses her head haughtily. She eyes Jim with cold triumph. "You got it wrong, Jimmy," she rebuts, her voice firm and final, her brow furrowed with determination. "What did I just tell you this morning? What have I been telling you all year? Okay, so maybe I'm not so keen on the ministry, but still, I didn't come here to have a romance with you. I came to get away from Mom and Nashua. And working in the church is a lot better than Burger King. But *dammit,* can't you get it through your head! I like you as a *friend* only!" She whips the air with her loosely fisted hand, as if swatting a fly with a flyswatter. "I don't wanna marry you ... or sleep with you. What happened on Christmas Eve or other times, it's just physical, just pent-up frustration and boredom, and hormones coming out. If I had a steady guy, Christmas Eve would've never happened."

Becki sashays over to her dresser and begins to brush her hair. Jim follows. She speaks toward her frowny reflection as it stares back at her from the mirror, "I should've never shared such personal stuff with you, 'cause you twist it and take it as a come-on. You know too much about me. That's why you won't let up 'til you get me goin', 'til I say things and do things I don't mean. You take advantage. You don't love me with God's love, least not anymore. You're sexually obsessed with me. You just wanna rule over me. It's just a selfish *macho* thing. If you'd kept your eyes where they belong, this would've never come up. I thought you were mature enough to accept my feelings, what I told you last April, but I guess I was wrong. You just kept on pushing and pushing. Now you've messed things up *wick*ed bad!"

Becki pulls loose hair from the bristles of her brush. She gives a bothered sigh. "Anyway, I'll keep my teacher's-aide job until school's out in June. Then I'm leaving. I'll go live with Amelia ... or maybe my dad. I'll continue to come to church, for the sake of appearances, but I don't wanna do anything with you. I'm glad you fired me as your outreach assistant. I was ready to quit anyway. So forget about picking me up tomorrow, or ever again. You got it all wrong, Jimmy. I don't want a romantic relationship with you. Maybe you'll believe me now?"

"You're a damn liar, Rebecca Lea," Jim refutes, his voice strong but calm. "*Hor*mones? Fuck, you sound like Sharon—but I've said all I came to tell you. I've got no more to say."

No reply. But as Jim marches out, Becki gives a derisive snort accompanied by a disgusted backhand slap of the air behind her as if to say, "Good riddance."

Scarcely touching the gas, Jim coasts down Front Street. 12:08 a.m. Thursday has just turned into Friday. A raw north wind whistles about the Mustang; an evening squall of rain and sleet chased the warm weather. Now the clouds have gone south as well leaving cold starry skies and a slice of old moon over Hadley Hill. Lukewarm heat blows on Jim's legs.

His heart trembles with trepidation but a rush of expectancy stirs hope at the same time, *O God, she almost broke. I know she loves me. She can't live without me. I can't live without her. She has to come to me? If she doesn't, I'll die. But she has to?*

Danger, risk, adventure, high stakes. No map, no assurance. Now recklessly abandoned to pouring out his whole heart, Jim does feel like Columbus, as Joe said almost a year ago. Columbus sailing west to glory—or to perish at the edge of the earth. But if he's to be with Becki, he'll be with her openly. If he's to have a church, it'll be a new and radical ministry where people can truly be themselves.

He hopes for both but he's sure of neither, and there's no turning back. The fuse is lit. His only authority is the love that reigns in his heart. The possibilities thrill him, terrify him, suck his breath away, yet he feels rooted and anchored, and right and good and gutsy and solid. For the first time since he was a child, Jim isn't hiding or lying, or twisting his feelings to promote himself. He feels honest and substantial, like how a freshly sawed oak log smells in the fall, or how a sledgehammer feels when you swing it, or how a T-bone steak tastes when you're hungry. It's a feeling he can sink his teeth into.

But he also knows he's outside the camp—and outnumbered.

\* \* \*

The gray and gusty morning groans against the windows. Tears dribble down Pastor Jim's face. Bowed heads, muffled sobs, sniffles, wet handkerchiefs. Leslie and Carl are white with shock. Longing hearts, frightened hearts, a few cold stares. Becki huddles in her chair like a mouse. Stan appears concerned but not shaken.

Sunday, February 26th. 11:33 a.m. "I can't pretend anymore," Jim confesses, his voice breaking. "I can't pretend to be strong and full of faith—not anymore. I can no longer profess what I don't know. I can't do it the Bible way. I can't live up to rules and doctrines. I've tried for ten years. I have to *know* it in my heart. I have to *feel* it in my gut. I have to live from within. If my heart is wicked then I'm wicked, but I can't change, I can't. Some days I sense that I'm part of God's grand purpose and all is working together for good, but other days I feel doomed and life seems meaningless and absurd ... and sometimes I wake up in the night and tremble at the thought of dying."

Jim moves to the front of the dais. "But this is *me*. This's how I really am. I've studied and prayed for years but I still don't have sure answers to the big questions. I don't know what happens when we die. Oh, I know what the Bible says about heaven. But I need more. Truth is, I don't know who's goin' to heaven or who's goin' to hell ... and I don't know if salvation means anything. I hope we all go to a beautiful and happy place, but I can't say for sure. How can I know things that are *impossible* to know? I can't see beyond the curtain. I doubt anyone can, but I *know* I can't. That's one thing I *am* sure of. God is still my only hope. That hasn't changed—in fact, I don't see any other hope for anyone on this earth—but I don't know much about God, not really, least not as much as I've professed to know. I hope He loves us and has a purpose for all the pain and suffering of life. I hope He'll be there when we die. But I don't know for sure. And I don't know if Jesus is God, or if he rose from the dead or what. I just know I like what he said about love: 'This is my commandment that you *love* one another as I have *loved* you.' To me, love flowing in our hearts is the highest authority above any pastor or doctrine. I hope it's the same river Jesus speaks of when he says, 'Out of your belly shall flow rivers of living water.' I just want to love and be loved. I want to know the kindred spirits in my life ... to know them and know them until there are no walls. This is my dream. But it seems impossible because honest love never fits the labels and rules set up by religion and society."

Burst of passion. Pushing back his tears, Jim preaches louder, nailing each sentence as if he has a hammer in his right hand, "I'm tired of trying to build a big church! I'm tired of raising money and counting converts! I'm tired of persuading people to believe things I'm not sure of myself! I'm tired of ulterior motives like knocking on doors in hopes of filling seats at church, just so our attendance and money figures will go up! Jesus says that a little child is the greatest in the kingdom, but I don't know a single child who likes to sit in church. Now that's a contradiction if you ask me. Others can do what they want, but I'm tired of putting on coats and ties every Sunday. And I'm sick and tired of getting dressed up for all the damn faldaral in Nashua! I'm *sick* of it! It means *nothing* to me! Big crowds, big offerings, new buildings, missionary teams, save the lost! I'm tired of it! It doesn't mean a *damn* thing to me!"

Silence. Pastor Jim's tears well up again. The sanctuary is quieter than the tomb of Christ on the 2nd day. The north wind whistles against the building. A few snowflakes tick against the window panes.

"Love is the only thing that touches me," Jim goes on, his voice tender but tearful. "It's always touched me since I was a little boy. I can't explain love ... but I can always sense it, and it makes me weep for joy inside when I see love happening in this world of liars and pretenders and con artists. True love breaks me inside whether it's happening to me or to others. Whether it's happening

503

in real life or in a movie. It's beyond words but it's my only reason for living—even if it's just a fairy-tale hope. I hope God *is* love—not religious love we work up and falsely profess, but *real* love we feel in our hearts, our souls, our bodies. That's my only hope. I can't prove it, but when I look at the stars, or I watch birds flying, or kittens playing, or I hear the wind blowing through the trees, I feel a presence bigger than us that is somehow connected to the love inside of me. But at other times, life hurts so bad, I fear that God doesn't care for us at all.... Anyway, from here on, I have nothing to offer you except myself."

Jim hands the mike to Barry then exits the sanctuary.

Stan follows Jim into the hallway. His dark-blue eyes speak before his lips, more with pity than condemnation. "Pastor Jim, we gotta talk."

"How about tomorrow evening, before Bible class?" Jim replies.

"Okay, I'll be here," Stan says, as he wraps his huge hand around Jim's. He holds the handshake as if Jim is suffering from battle fatigue and just needs reassurance.

Around the corner, past the kitchen—eyes, eyes, misty brown eyes, red from crying; it's Sylvia Cahill emerging from the ladies' room. Tear-blotched and whimpering, she collapses into Pastor Jim's arms. "Oh, Jim, what you said today. I had to leave. I was crying so hard. What you said was so right. It's how I've always felt and I never—I can't, I just can't tell anyone. I'm too ashamed to say I don't have assurance, that I don't know for sure about Jesus and God. I'm just too ashamed."

Jim doesn't reply but holds Sylvia tightly to his bosom until voices down the hall send her back into the ladies' room.

After a quick stop at his office, Jim exits the church through the back door.

# Chapter Thirty-four

**M**onday afternoon, late. Breezy, cold, distant clouds. Pastor Jim slams the trunk of the Mustang. Chunks of rust sprinkle onto the bumper from the corroded trunk lid. Russ picks up Jim's Air Force Academy B-4 bag and heads into the house. Jim follows, a suitcase in one hand, a clothing bag over his shoulder; he's moving in with Russ.

Jim's ears are still ringing from Sharon's screaming ultimatum, after she and the kids returned from Cobleskill yesterday afternoon: "YOU WANT TO GET HONEST! FINE! DISAVOW YOUR LOVE FOR BECKI OR *GET OUT*! IT'S ME OR HER! YOU HAVE TO CHOOSE!" Breaking glass and Corning Ware, blond tempest, blazing eyes. Sharon swept the dirty dishes off the table then hurled the coffeepot past Jim's head into the sink. "You're sick, James David! How *dare* you preach about God! You're a liar and a cheat! You ruined my life! You be*trayed* the kids! Becki's a devil! She doesn't love you, yet you say you love her more than *life*! You're *sick*! GET OUT OF MY HOUSE YOU FUCKING FORNICATOR! Go ahead and chase that fat-assed little whore but you'll never get her! And I'll never come to church again as long as *you're* the pastor!"

Sitting, sobbing, collapsing, stormy shag of blond. White neck, pink collar, Norwegian sweater. Sharon buried her face in her folded arms on the kitchen table. Grief, humiliation, heaving, shuddering. Jim had no defense, no plea. Finally, she came up. Sniffles, blotchy face, a choking but sober voice, "If you love her, Jim, I can't live with you. You have to leave. I can't be your wife unless it's *me,* and *on*ly me. I won't share you with that conniving bitch. I let this go *too* long. I should've thrown you out last fall!" Erin and Heather, after watching it all, ran sobbing upstairs, but Chris crawled up next to his brokenhearted mommy—like a little man.

After unloading his stuff at the Bradleys', Jim heads back to the church and walks down to the lake, to the beach; he needs some time alone before his meeting with Stan. Gentle waves, dark-green, almost black. The ice has retreated from the rocky north shore leaving a wide channel of open water. At school, in his office, Jim hurt all day. Only Jodi came to see him. He saw Becki in the hall but she didn't speak to him. She seemed poised, pious, and uninvolved—as if she never knew Jim Shanley, as if she has nothing to do with what is happening. Angie, the others, seemed curious but shy and apprehensive as if Jim has a terminal disease—as if they know a big change is coming but they don't dare talk about it.

Jim kicks the gravel with the toe of his boot. He sucks in the freezing air, pure, astringent, crystal clear, like breathing the highest sky. The waning wind whimpers through the pines, and rustles the oak leaves, dead leaves from last fall. Purple haze, Worcester Hills, gathering clouds. The evening lies back against the day. Feathery brushstrokes of cirrus arch overhead painting the sky with the fiery hues of sunset—red, orange, rosy pink, and ever-changing violet. Warm color rains down on the cold water reflecting on the black waves like pink twinkling stars.

Silence, save for the rustling leaves and the droning of a small plane above the far shore. A chill runs up Jim's spine; he huddles into his jacket. He wishes he could cry but tears won't come. *Four days of raw honesty and I feel beaten to a pulp. And I fear the worst is yet to come. Maybe I'm just getting what I deserve, or maybe not? But either way, I'm out of control. My life's falling apart. It's like I'm in a new place and I can't go back. Oh, Becki, don't leave me now. But she has left me, and Sharon too, and I'm hurting the kids.*

*O Jesus, I poured out my heart and Becki rejected it. I miss her. I miss her so. And this time I've burned my bridges. Life is so empty without her ... even if she is a conniving bitch, even if she doesn't love me. It still hurts and hurts. I wish I was a kid again so I could run to Mama and cry, like when I had a nightmare and crawled into bed with her. Mama always loved me ... no matter what.*

Jim's sense of loss deepens as he thinks of his mother's death. He sees the cemetery; he smells the sweet fragrance of new grass; he feels the lump in his throat all over again. A hazy smudge of sun dapples through the clouds casting weak shadows among the granite and marble tombstones. A minister is praying.

On both sides of the small graveyard, the rolling meadows gush yellow with milkweed, while bursts of bluebonnet and red clover border the dirt road where the line of cars is parked. Lazy butterflies wing their way from blossom to blossom, unperturbed by the spectacle of human death. A warm breeze ripples through the oaks and cottonwoods. The trees are just unfurling their new leaves, soft, tender, bright liquid green—so bright, they fill the wooded hollow with an eerie phosphorescence. A small crowd is gathered about the flower-draped coffin which is under a green canopy. The blond-haired man stands at the front with his two sons. The oldest stands on his right. He's no longer a child but a broad-shouldered young man. His sandy cowlicked hair is darker, the sand color more brown than blond. Heads bowed, the people are crying softly and dabbing their faces with handkerchiefs.

Back to the present. Jim stares at the waves. He gives a resigned sigh. Night is drawing down about him like a black cowl. Peace, peace, he feels a strange peace drawing down with the night.

Whisper of wind on receding waves, breathing, breathing, rippling gently. The open channel of icy water stretches east and west before him like a sleeping woman under the veiled twilight sky. It's the 27th of February, and there is no moon.

\* \* \*

EDGE video at seven, Pastor Jim teaches at eight. To the kitchen and the aroma of coffee and corn muffins. Stan unhooks the swinging door; it creaks shut. The TV troops have just gone down to class. No muffins left, just crumbs, but plenty of coffee. Jim pours a mug and one for Stan, then hops up and sits on the butcher-block counter, dangling his short denim-clad legs. Campbell sits at the table, his greasy size-fourteen boots angled on the floor like frog's feet. Massive, chiseled, and oaklike in a black batik shirt, he reminds Jim of a piece of Elizabethan furniture, fragrant Elizabethan furniture. As always, Stan smells of Aqua Velva.

"'Fore we talk I jus' wanna read a few passages of scripture," Stan says after they exchange a few pleasantries—though the mood is hardly pleasant. With a sweep of his huge paw, he opens his large-print Bible, whips the marker ribbon out of the way, but as he starts to read, he coughs and wheezes. He fumbles in his pocket then twists a benzedrine inhaler up his hairy nostril, then up the other.

*This must be a new dispensation,* Jim says silently. *Stan's actually got a cold.*

After pocketing the inhaler, Stan reads, his bassy voice raspy, toned-down, yet still authoritative. He flips from passage to passage:

A friend loveth at all times, an' a brother is born for 'versity.

Now the Spirit speaketh 'spressly that in the latter times, some shall 'part from the faith givin' heed to seducin' spirits an' the docturns of demons.

A man shall leave his father 'n mother, an' shall cleave to his wife an' they two shall be one flesh. What therefore God has joined together, let no man put asunder.

Flee fornication. Ever' sin that a man doeth is without the body; but he that committeth fornication, sinneth against his own body.

There is a way which seemeth right unto a man ... but the end thereof are the ways of death.

Stan gives a fawning grin and lifts his huge hands over the open Bible as if warming them over a fire. "First off, Pastor Jim, this is jus' between you 'n me. You're the pastor so it's not my place to correct you. But as a brother, I gotta encourage you 'cuz I love you in Christ. We been friends a long time. If it wasn't for you leadin' me to the Lord, I'd still be a hellbound sinner." Stan coughs then spits into a paper napkin and tosses it into the trash. He wipes his nose with another napkin and leaves it wadded on the table. "Now I been hearin' stuff all year, Pastor Jim, yet I been 'luctant to come to you 'cuz a man has to walk 'fore the Lord. But the Spirit speaks 'spressly that some shall 'part from the faith ... an' after your wild messages yesterday an' Sharon's call, I fear the devil's pressin' you with lies an' you're drownin' in a sea of 'ception."

Stan pats his open Bible emphatically. His brow knits with concern. "So I gotta throw you a rope, an' the only rope we got is the Bible. All we need to know about life is in this book. If it's not in here, it's a *lie*." He curls his hammy forefinger through the handle of his coffee mug and takes a long swig. He then leans forward onto his elbows and stares down at the Bible as if studying for a sermon. His freckled biceps flex against his tight short-sleeved shirt.

Jim, his back against the wall—literally and figuratively—cuddles his mug to his stomach. He's sitting near the door where there are no cabinets over the counter. As he waits for Stan to continue, the anxiety he felt earlier returns to torment him, *So Sharon talked to Stan. Maybe she and Stan talked to Becki? I wish I was inside Becki's head. What the fuck is she gonna do? I should— no, she has to come to me. My life is like a bomb exploding in slow motion. Everything's up in the air—especially me and Becki—and I don't know where it's gonna come down. I wonder if she'll come to class tonight. I doubt it. I usually pick her up. I wonder if she thinks about me. It's been four days.*

Stan steeples his thick fingers over his Bible, phallic fingers, ten hard cocks, five facing five. He looks up at Shanley and gives another obsequious grin. Calm, in control. He seems meek and sincere, but Jim smells the stink of self-righteous contempt.

"That's why I give you verses, Pastor Jim," Stan explains, his voice filled with humility. "I jus' wanna share what *God* says, not what I think or feel. We can't lean on our own understanin' 'cuz our hearts are 'ceitful 'n wicked. I'm nuthin' myself. I'm jus' a sinner saved by grace an' a soldier for Christ ... but, Pastor Jim, you're the rankin' man on the battlefield. If Satan makes you doubt, then he can 'moralize the troops. Now 'a friend loves at all times,' an' 'a brother is made for 'versity.' That's why I gotta tell you the truth from the—"

Front door, hurried footsteps, kitchen door, frog eyes under a tight bun. "I'm late as usual," Leslie Burton declares breathlessly. "Gerald didn't get home 'til a quarter of. I don't know what I'm going to do with him. He's always—" Leslie stops abruptly, realizing she's barged into a summit meeting. For a moment she stands there awkwardly, but she quickly recovers, then apologizes, backs out, and departs for the EDGE video class.

Stan sits back and stretches. He opens his cavernous mouth into a wide yawn showing his gray teeth—and enough amalgam to set off a metal detector. "I jus' can't b'lieve what I'm seein' in this church," he says shaking his head indignantly. "The wives got no respect for their husbands. Leslie treats Gerald like a little boy. No wonder he's lukewarm. It's not Bible. How can he be the head, if she don't submit to his authority?"

Leslie's interruption shunts Stan onto his favorite tangent, but after a cough and a sip from his mug, he gets back on the main track. "Now, Pastor Jim, you know we gotta 'cept God's Word. Lucifer's the 'nointed cherub. He's got a war plan. It's no quincidence that Becki Reinhold came here." Stan still doesn't have her name right. "Now she came with a pure heart an' you loved her in the Lord, but Satan knows our weaknesses, 'specially how to tempt us with lust, an' if it was jus' lust, it wouldn't be so bad, but Lucifer didn't stop there. He's got you b'lievin' it's *good,* that it's *love*. Now that's the 'ception. That's why you got up there yesterday an' surrendered to the devil, an' gave in to your fears."

Jim burns with rebuttal but he has no desire to piss against Campbell's pious counsel. He wants to hear it all before he responds. Raised mug, purple lips. Stan's pale-granite face seems more pale than usual, perhaps from his cold. He gestures with his lifted mug. He speaks with increasing fervor, his air of humility giving way to an odd mingling of wariness and reproach, "Pastor Jim, I gotta tellya ... 'cuza Becki, you let Lucifer get 'minion in your thoughts. That's why you're afraid of death in the night an' preachin' your fears to the flock, an' sayin' we should follow our hearts. That's why you're jeopardizin' our standin' with home base an' chasin' a woman who's no more than a child. Now lust is a common sin for a man—I gotta fight it *my*self—but to b'lieve it's love, that's the *lie*. That's Satan's device! God made us male 'n female, an' what God joins together, no man can put asunder. You got a faithful Christian wife an' three kids. You can't leave 'em! You mus' set the sample for the flock!"

Stan closes his Bible and shoves it aside. Flash. Anger. Sudden anger. He throws up his hands, his fists balled like sledgehammer heads, then crashes them onto the table bouncing his mug. Coffee shoots into the air. "NO *WAY* CAN IT BE!" he shouts. "God never gives roman'ic love outside of marriage! He can't deny his Word! 'Specially with a kid half your age!"

Fierce indignation pumps hot into Stan's rocklike face; his cheeks stain pink, a sickly salmon-pink. "She's got a callin' to be a mission'ry, like her mom! She needs prayer an' Bible trainin', not no 'fair with a married man! It's the *devil,* Pastor Jim! He's tryin' to destroy your fam'ly! He's tryin' to destroy your 'fectiveness on the battlefield, an' your reputation! He's tryin' to destroy the church! An' he wants to cripple Becki with confusin' 'motions. Sharon says Becki doesn't want you. An' that's the truth. She can't want you as a man. You *got* a wife. God's not the author of confusion. He's got a social order, an' it's all here in the Word. That's why we gotta preach the Bible! You can't jus' go into the pulpit an' preach your heart! That's heresy, Pastor Jim!"

Campbell pulls back his thick shoulders and lifts his chin as if he's challenging the devil to hit him. Proud, truculent, face like flint, he looks like a Civil War colonel in a high school history textbook, and he holds the arrogant pose for some time as if an angel has arrived from heaven to photograph him. *This is fuckin' bizarre,* Jim declares to himself. *Stan condemns my personal life when his own background is shady enough to qualify for the Irish Mafia. Moreover, he divorced Paula to marry Doris who's seventeen years younger, just like Becki. Of course, that's before he was saved. You can't charge a believer for sins committed before salvation, but once saved, we're fair game.*

Loud hawking noise. Stan clears his throat. Loose phlegm rumbles raucously like food scraps in a garbage disposal. He spits into a napkin then purses his lips warily. He looks up at Pastor Jim as if expecting a confession, a rebuttal, or at least an explanation.

Jim sips his coffee, slowly bangs his dangling boots, one against the other, but says nothing. Puzzled at Jim's reluctance to respond, Stan cocks his head like a curious bird—no, no, Stan could never look like a bird—no, he tilts his massive skull awkwardly like a dinosaur, like a tyrannosaurus. He waits. He hawks. He sops his spilled coffee with the wadded napkin in his hand. Finally, after tossing the napkin into the trash, he becomes plaintive like a distraught father pleading with a wayward son, "My heart breaks, Pastor Jim. I 'member how you preached that God blessed you with a lovin' wife an' precious children, an' now you're sayin' you love another woman. It's *not* God. It can't be. You know that. It's against the Word. It's a *lie* from the devil."

Leaning back in his chair, Stan rests his monstrous hands on the table. To Jim, they seem disconnected like empty industrial gloves. Stan gazes right at Jim with his dark sapphire eyes. Jim searches these eyes for a flicker of warmth, of heart, but he discerns nothing except pious contempt and condemnation.

"I know you're goin' through a lot of guilt an' agony," Stan goes on, his plaintive voice seemingly near to breaking. "But we have a great God an' great promises in the Word, like 'let us reason together; though your sins be scarlet, they shall be white as snow.' That's a *sure* promise, Pastor Jim. The devil's got no power over a 'pennant heart. If we con*fess* our sins, He is 'faithful and just to forgive us.' You know the promises. Trust 'em, Pastor. You can bounce back. We can still beat the devil and...."

Jim stares at the death's-head tattoo on Stan's arm, but closes his ears to his words. *What's the point of being born-again?* he asks himself. *It just puts you on the defense stand. You must justify yourself daily. And someone's always telling you how God feels, and how they must tell you because they love you. Now if I was just a fuckin' factory worker with a skull on my arm, and I was shacking up with Ruthie at night, I wouldn't be getting the third degree, at least not like this. I wish I was a nobody and Becki too.... And Stan's always talking about the devil. Who the fuck is the devil anyway? Right now he's the devil as far as I'm concerned.*

Muted, distant, Stan's voice drones like a TV playing in another room. Jim slowly drinks his coffee. He looks across at the grimy smoke hood that once sheltered the deep-fat fryers in the old Legion kitchen. When BFBC bought the building, they removed the units, but not the hood. Off the hood at the wall hangs a small red fire extinguisher labeled with green words: "PURE HALON, Flame Fighter." Moving down, Jim gazes wide-eyed at the almond-colored refrigerator until it distorts psychedelically and divides, like a microbe under a microscope.

"If you con*fess* your sins, Pastor Jim, you'll be restored," Stan declares, his deep voice returning full force as Jim tunes back into the audio. His tone is no longer plaintive but demanding as if speaking down from a throne. "I warn you. You *must* repent now, 'fore it's too late. You must repent of your love for Becki an' go back home. You must repent of your unbelief. You must repent of your false preachin'. We gotta fight the devil an' make him flee! God will *never* honor adult'ry no matter how you feel in your heart. I pray God'll deliver you from this heresy. You gotta step back an' see how you've changed this year. You need a rest! You need to be loved an' neutered by the body!"

*You got that right,* Jim chuckles to himself. *That's exactly what the Church does to every man ... including Jesus.* Dusting his hands together, Campbell gives a smug smile and strikes an heroic pose as he waits for Jim's response. Eyes, eyes, his sapphire eyes are now more condemning than ever as if Stan, in true Logan fashion, is trying to bring Jim to his knees with his eyes. *What the fuck is this? He just wants me to confess, to give in to shame, like a good LBI'er. He doesn't give a shit about love or righteousness— not really. He just wants the bended knee!*

Pastor Jim throws his mug to his mouth, drinking the last of his coffee. He puts the mug down, pushing it away toward the sink. He grips the countertop on both sides of him until his knuckles turn white. Hot emotion rises from deep within him. "You can quote verses all night, Stan," he declares, "but it won't change *anything*. Maybe I *am* deceived? Maybe not? But either way, I'm goin' with my heart! I've always felt like this, but I was afraid to say it. I have no desire to argue with you, or to persuade you to see things as I do. I can't anyhow. We've worked side by side in this church for a long time, but I can honestly say I've never felt close to you. I've pretended to be friends with you, to agree with you, because of fear and guilt, and to keep the church going. But hear this, Stan: I'm not afraid of you anymore! From here on, I plan to preach my *true* feelings without pretense or propping up. If you're for me, so be it! If you want to call a meeting and try to vote me out, so be it! But I'll be *damned* if I'll ever preach, or live, to please you or Logan again! And you can bank on it, buddy, 'til fuckin' hell freezes over!"

Campbell blanches like a soldier who just got his dick shot off. He averts his eyes. He clenches his jaw against the knowing. His smug smile turns rueful then flat—as flat as a heart monitor on a dying patient. He tries to hold onto his air of authority but it escapes like quicksilver through his grasping fingers. He tries to hide his chagrin with a fit of coughing—but with little success.

And Jim gives him no opportunity to recover. "As for Rebecca Lea, you're right, Stan. She *is* the reason for the change in me. Loving her has opened my eyes. I used to be ashamed of it, but no more! Loving Becki is the most real thing in my life! I don't have to work it up with verses and vows and will power! It's always there, like a river at floodtide! Yet it's tender and warm and compassionate, and so beautiful that it makes me weep. You say she doesn't love me, and right now it appears that way, but even if she doesn't, I still love her. You say it's the devil. Well, it doesn't matter. I can't stop this love even if it is the devil. And if my Becki-love *is* of the devil, then I love the devil more than God—at least your God. Just to think of her makes my heart pound. I want to hold her and hug her and cuddle her in bed. I want to give her sexual pleasure until she goes crazy with ecstasy. I haven't but I'd love to. But it's more than sex. Even if she was invalid for life, I'd stay with her and feed her and read to her, and care for her every day."

Passion heats Jim's face; he pounds the counter. "I don't hafta justify myself to you or anyone! So from here on, Stan, my personal life in none of your damn business! AND I DON'T WANNA HEAR BECKI'S NAME ON *YOUR* FUCKIN' LIPS AS LONG AS YOU WALK THE FUCKIN' EARTH!"

Backpedal. Backpedal. Stan quickly retreats to his obsequious Uriah Heep persona. He holds up a callused hand in a gesture of reassurance, like an Indian seeking peace. "Awh, Pastor Jim," he says in his meekest voice, "don't get me wrong. A friend loveth at all times. I didn't mean to suggest I was gonna turn against you. I still b'lieve in you. It's not like you actually committed adult'ry. I b'lieve you when you say you haven't. You're jus' goin' through a hard time, an' I'm concerned about you. I hope you 'n Sharon patch things up. I hope nuthin' happens to split us away from Dr. Logan. But I'm no Bennick Arnold. I can't turn on you, Pastor Jim. You're my brother in the Lord. I jus' wanna help you get your faith back. I'm with you in the battle. When you look back, I'll be there. Nuthin's gonna change. I'll keep doin' my job. I jus' had to share my feelin's on this, that's all."

After swigging down the dregs of his coffee, Stan hoists himself out of his chair, shakes Jim's hand, without looking up, then heads for the door. "I gotta help Barry put the TV stuff away," he says as he leaves. "I'll see you at eight o'clock class."

* * *

With a froglike flick of her tongue, Jodi licks a flake of sugar from the corner of her mouth. Crew-neck sweater, Calvin Klein's, lanky legs, brunette pageboy. She rolls off the recliner, reaches into the bag for the last donut, and places it on Pastor Jim's open calendar book.

"No more," Jim says, lifting his hands in a don't-shoot pose.

"Well, just sit and look at it then," Jodi quips as she brushes crumbs off her gray sweater. Moving over to the windows, she stretches into a lengthy yawn, like a waking cat, then fingerfluffs her pageboy. Finally, she returns to the big question in a voice out the window, "But I would say this about Becki." Her tone is now serious, intuitive.

"What's that?" Jim queries, his heart springing to attention.

"I'd say, Jim, she's hurting just as much as you."

"How d'you know?"

Jodi smacks her lips as if to reply but she doesn't; she seems occupied with the blue sky and fleecy clouds. The weather has improved after a night of drenching rain. Jim sips his coffee and waits anxiously.

Passion in the pulpit. Naked, naked, no holding back. On Sunday night, Monday night, and Tuesday night, Jim continued to preach his heart, especially Tuesday when he declared: "As far as I'm concerned, being in love like Romeo and Juliet is the *great*est human experience. It's the only God I seek. I don't want self-sacrificing religious love that makes me kill my heart in the name of Christ. It's a *lie!* I don't want any such God! I want *real* love! Love that knits me to another, that makes me feel alive and takes me beyond the drudgery of our existence. To me, to know another heart is to know God! Yet it seems we only get a glimpse of this love then we live out our lives with broken hearts, like Adam aching for his rib, for his Eve. Perhaps we'll be happy in heaven, but I can't get excited about heaven. I ache for love to win in *this* life!"

Many were touched. Some cried. But others stared at Pastor Jim with accusing eyes. Mary LeBlanc even called him a heretic and stormed out. But Stan sat sober-faced, and said nothing to Jim afterward. Mary's outburst didn't bother Jim, but Becki's absence did; she hasn't been to church since Sunday morning.

Except for Jodi and Russ, and Mary LeBlanc—and Stan during his kitchen counseling session—no one in the church has spoken to Jim about his radical free-spirited sermons, and there hasn't been a peep out of Nashua. The BFBC regulars act friendly around Jim but they only share pleasantries or ministry business. Life in the church seems strangely normal, absurdly normal. Yet Jim senses an undercurrent of tension and skittishness, as one senses in a barnyard before an approaching storm. On the home front, he hasn't spoken to Sharon since their Sunday showdown, but Tuesday afternoon, he took Erin, Heather, and Chris to McDonald's. They kept it light until they got back to the car and Chris said, "Daddy, howcum you hab to sleep at Sheila's house? If you don't like your bed in Mommy's room, you can hab my bed." Jim broke, and they cried and hugged and loved each other.

Now it's 9:30 on Wednesday morning, and Jodi slouches at the window, canting her compact hips—her usual posture when standing. "Come on, Jodi, you're worse than Russ," Jim prods, after killing off his coffee. "How d'you know Becki's hurting?"

Jodi replies to the clouds, "'Cause I see her every day. She misses you something awful."

"How canyuh tell?" Jim asks; he wants evidence.

Jodi comes back over and settles hipshot against Jim's desk. She picks up the wooden mug of pens and pencils and stares into it

# MARTIN CASSITY

as if looking for a particular pen. The smell of nicotine wafts from her sweater like a faint but noxious perfume. Her face clouds; she sighs. Jodi, Jodi, the real Jodi. Compassionate, troubled, innately sad. "Becki's like a bird with a broken wing," she replies to Jim's question. "At lunch she picks at her tuna fish sandwich. During spelling drills, she gazes wide-eyed out the window instead of helping the kids. She comes in each morning with sleepy eyes and messy hair, and she mopes around during recess like a wallflower at a teenage dance. Her smiles and witty remarks are forced. I know her, Jim. I see the hurt. Besides, she knows that people are whispering. I don't see how she can go on like this. She's not good at maintaining appearances. I feel her heart crying out like a child lost in the dark. The kids sense it too. They gather around her like she's a sick puppy but she refuses to let on ... at least to me."

Becki-love floods Jim's bosom. His heart rises on this tide of emotion becoming a lump in his throat; his eyes fill. He wants to run to Jodi's classroom and gather Becki into his arms. But he doesn't. Instead, he picks up the donut on his desk, takes a bite, then replies in a pastry-clogged voice, "Yeh, I figure she's gonna leave, and a lot sooner than June. But she doesn't seem sad to me. When I ran into her in the hall earlier, she gave me nothing but a haughty toss of her head—with her flags flying."

Jodi pulls a red felt-tip pen from the mug. "Well, what do you expect?"

Jim takes another bite of donut; flakes of glazed sugar rain onto his lap. "I'm not sure, but if she misses me so?" He brushes the sugar off his pants.

Jodi uncaps the pen and studies the naked tip. "She can't help it, Jim."

"Can't help what?" Jim asks.

"As long as you had a reason, a ministry ... it was tolerable."

"*It?*"

"Being in love ... but you made it intolerable." Jodi speaks toward the pen as if it's listening.

Jim stuffs the rest of the donut into his mouth. After swallowing, he shakes his head and says, "*Me?* I just told the truth?" He licks the stickiness off his fingers.

Closing the pen, Jodi drums it on her open hand. "You like to take walks, don't you, Jim?"

"Yeh, I guess I do, but what's that got to do with anything?"

"Did you ever spy a rabbit sitting in the grass?"

"Lots of times," Jim replies.

"As long as you keep your distance, the rabbit sits still, right?"

"Right."

"But if you approach boldly?" Jodi asks.

"Well, he huddles down, wiggles his nose, then breaks at the last minute."

"To you, or away from you?"

"Away, of course, but rabbits are naturally afraid of humans?"

"Exactly," Jodi affirms, dropping the pen back into the wooden mug.

Jim gestures palms up as if feeling for rain. "You mean she's afraid of me?"

"Not really."

"Well, what *d'you* mean?"

No reply. Jodi returns to the windows and stares out at the last day of February. Jim waits. He sits back; he stretches his legs. After a minute, Jodi shrugs and speaks one word: "Chicago."

"What?" Jim asks, sitting forward to make sure he heard right. "Chicago."

"*Chicago?* What the fuck are you talking about?"

"I'm going to Chicago to live ... me and Brenda."

"Whaa ... what? You're *what*? You're gonna—when?"

"I don't know exactly, but soon."

"What about your kids, your class?" Jim asks anxiously. But he's not anxious about her class, but about her leaving *him* when he's in such a precarious situation.

Jodi spits her answer out the window, "I don't know."

"Why Chicago? Whaddeya gonna do out there?"

"I'm not sure. My cousin asked me to come. I have a few possibilities."

"So you think we're going under, huh?"

"Well, we're not going up, but that's not why."

"So why then?" No answer. *This is all I need,* Jim laments to himself, steepling his hands against his mustache. *I have two kindred souls and one of them is going to fuckin' Chicago. How can we have a new church without Jodi? And who else can I talk to?*

"Shit, it's *all* coming apart," Jim sighs aloud, his discontent surfacing.

"I really don't know why I want to go," Jodi says. "I guess—"

The office door opens. Red hair, freckles. Liz Claiborne glasses. Angie breezes in trailing a plume of Windsong perfume and witty remarks. Jodi jokes with her a moment then departs.

Wearing a beige-and-blue sailor dress and a dutiful smile, Angie places a folder on Pastor Jim's desk. "Just the end-of-month stuff, plus Stan's EDGE report," she chirps in her reedy voice. Leaning forward at his side, she quickly reviews the reports and correspondence.

Jim scarcely hears Angie's words, but he feels her womanly presence. Warm, fragrant, Sharon-like. He runs away into his mind, into his old bed. Dusty-blue eyes dilated with want. Sex with Sharon: he wonders if it will ever happen again. She's on top of him, sighing, moaning—no, no, it's Becki Lea riding his naked body. Then it's Angela fucking him on the LA-Z-BOY. Lust grows in Jim's mind but is born dead in his flesh. He's too hurt to get hard. He has no phallic potency except in his nightdreams. His unplugged penis hangs limp in his pants.

"... him a check?" Angie's question finally brings Jim back.

"Whaw ... what?" he asks, just catching the last half of the question.

"You're really with it today," she kids, shaking her head. "I said Barry needs a $25 check for Friday night when he took the teenagers bowling. He had to gas up the bus with his own money." Angie seems her normal self as if nothing is happening in the church—or so Jim thinks.

He sighs and gives a silly grin. "Oh, yeh, fine, whatever he needs. Sorry, I was thinking about something else."

Jim's face warms with embarrassment as if Angie knows his thoughts. If not his thoughts, she certainly knows his grin. She's most Sharon-like in that respect as well.

"So I affect you that much, huh?" she teases, giving a blushing smirk of her own. They begin to banter but Angie quickly sobers as if disturbing thoughts have come into her mind. Jim senses tension between them. She strides to the door but doesn't open it. Instead, she turns back and says, "I'll bring your mail as soon as I sort out the teachers' stuff." Routine words, but green eyes full of entreaty tell him that she wants to talk—to talk about her fears, and his.

"Oh, by the way, speaking of mail," Jim says. "We won't be sending any money to Nashua this month, or ever again." This remark pushes Angie beyond talk into angry apprehension. Jim's carefree tone helps to light the fuse. His heart is far from carefree, but his words seem indifferent, almost flippant.

Angie looks down; she caresses her chin. "Oh, I see," she replies mockingly. "You're breaking up with Nashua, and Sharon, all in the same week?"

"Well, I'd hardly compare Sharon with Nashua," Jim responds, his tone more serious. He wants to share his heart, his Becki-pain, but he knows that she's in no mood to hear it. He senses Sharon-like rage as if Angela is his wife, another jealous wife—one of many, he fears.

Hands on hips, head thrust forward, she comes back toward the desk, toward Jim. Fire ignites in her eyes. Her brow furrows, her lips thin. She rails at him, "A lot of people are affected, I have you to know, not just *YOU!*" A swift shadow sweeps over Angie's countenance like a diving hawk. Her voice rises an octave to a raucous screech. "YOU'RE SO *DAMN* SELFISH, JIM SHANLEY! I DON'T BLAME SHARON FOR KICKING YOU OUT! You're messing everything up for all of us! Just because you think you're in love with that spoiled brat! It's insane, Jim! It's an obsession! No man in his right mind would choose Becki over Sharon! Becki's rude and crude and stuck on herself! And she walks around here like a prima donna, because she's the *pas*tor's pet!"

Angie flails the air with her hands. Her small nostrils flare under her pointy nose. Her face is redder than her hair.

Jim recoils back; his swivel chair emits a metallic moan. But he doesn't respond. He simply looks on with a peculiar mingling of hurt and foreboding and compassion and awe—and a measure of guilt, not over loving Becki, but over hurting Angie and the others.

Angie takes several deep breaths. She calms a bit. She twists her hands anxiously in front of her. "I'm sorry, Jim, for shouting. But it's the truth. Becki gets paid *way* too much for what she does. She's supposed to teach, but she can't even *spell,* and half the time she acts like a smart-aleck high school kid. And she treats you like shit. I see it all the time, Jim. Okay, so maybe you do love her—only God knows why—but you could at least be a little more dis*creet* about it. You don't have to flaunt it and throw it in everybody's face, and let it destroy your marriage and affect your preaching and split up the church. This isn't an f-ing love movie, this is *real* life! You can't have things exactly as you want them, Jim. In real life, you have to be content with *half* a loaf!"

Jim crashes his desk chair forward. His reply is cruel and sarcastic, "It figures you'd say that, Angela, since you're *married* to 'half a loaf.'"

He immediately regrets but it's too late. Breaking into tears, Angie removes her glasses and turns away, her hands clenched at her side—so tightly it seems she'll break her frames. Jim hops up to console her but before he can, she wheels and sobs out her hurt, "You're right, Jim. My marriage *is* shit. That's why I love this church. We're different. We love each other like family—at least, some of us do—but what's going to happen now? Stan and Dr. Logan, they're going to blow the whistle on you, Jim. And I'll never work for Stan or some new LBI pastor." Tears streak down Angie's freckled face; she sucks a snuffly breath. "This church is different, and it's *all* I have. All my friends are here. Coming here is my only happiness. And now you're putting everything at risk, all because of Becki. And we won't be able to talk anymore, you and me. I love you, Jim—like a best friend. Don't you *know!*"

Heaving and sobbing, Angela buries her face in her hands. Jim tries to put his arm around her, but she shrinks away and runs out of the office.

Fear, worry, confusion. Jim feels anxious for Angie, but moreso for himself. He plunks down on his broken recliner, but before he has time to ponder, the intercom buzzes.

He wheels up and grabs the phone. "I'm sorry, Jim," Angie apologizes, still sniffling. "I just don't have any faith anymore. I'm worried all the time. I can't concentrate on my work. I don't think I trust God at all, at least not this week. I'm sorry for putting Becki down so hard. Actually, I like her most of the time. I just hate it ... what's happening with you and Sharon."

After hanging up, Jim sighs then picks up the folder of paperwork that Angie left on his desk, but he has no desire to read or sign anything. He grabs his calendar book but only to close it. Piles of neglected work, but he has no motivation. He can no longer put "new wine into old wineskins." The dam is breaking; his river is crashing out of the LBI lake, out of his secure and familiar boundaries, rushing in torrents—to who knows where?

* * *

Jim pulls a pack of Peanut M&M's from his jacket pocket and plops down at his desk. After lunching alone at McD's, he stopped at Cumberland Farms to replenish his supply of candy. *It's almost one-thirty,* he says to himself. *Becki'll be goin' home soon, without me again.* He wiggles out of his coat and unfolds the morning newspaper. He rips open the M&M's and shakes several into his mouth as if drinking them. He sighs and scans the headlines:

*BRENDON FALLS BANNER,* **Wednesday, February 29, 1984.**
**GARY HART WINS! UPSETS MONDALE IN NEW HAMP-**
**SHIRE. DUKAKIS APPLAUDS HART AND MONDALE, SAYS**
**DEMOCRATS WILL UPSET REAGAN IN NOVEMBER. LAST**
**OF MARINES LEAVE BEIRUT. TRUDEAU RESIGNS IN**
**CANADA. MBTA RAIL PLAN IGNORES BRENDON FALLS.**
**FITCH ROAD PROJECTS JEOPARDIZED BY REAGAN CUTS.**
**PASTOR JIM SHANLEY FACES SHOWDOWN—**

NO, NO. Jim's life never makes the headlines, but it's the only story that grips his soul. As he munches and reads, his mind drifts, *Chocolate-covered peanuts, I love the taste, but they're hardly a substitute for sex. Shit, I may never have sex again, with Sharon, Becki, or any woman? Basketball? Heather's game? Does she have a basketball game today? I missed her last one. I should call Gary Bob. His birthday's coming. Hard to believe he'll be thirty this year. I should get the oil changed on the Grenada. I wonder what Sharon's making for supper. I should clean out the garage this week—WHAT THE FUCK AM I THINKING! I don't even live there any more! I'm losing it. I hafta get out of here!*

Jim grabs his parka and his Crusader softball cap and heads for the lake. The picnic area is wet, squishy, and covered with that dank winter detritus that remains after the snow melts. Across the tracks, up the muddy embankment, but he goes no farther. Blue sky above, blue sky below. The wide channel of open water, strangely calm after last night's storminess, lies like an elongated mirror before him. But beyond the open water, mushy melting ice still covers most of the reservoir; the ice seems out of place on this sunny springlike day. *The cat is certainly out of the bag,* Jim thinks to himself. *I wonder if Stan has said anything to Logan. But Carl seems so supportive, and Leslie. I can't figure it. But what does it matter? I just want Becki by my side. How can she reject me after being so close all year? Maybe she is hurting, but when I see her, she acts like she doesn't know me, as if we never met.*

Angela's outburst seemed to break the silence among the church regulars. All morning they came, they called.

After Angela, Beverly Bradley: "My concern is for the kids, Jim. Whatever happens, we must preserve the academy. I personally think you're being shortsighted and foolish, and certainly unfair to Sharon. This is breaking her heart, and it hurts me because she's my friend. I hope you two get back together, but I'm not taking sides, and you can stay at our place as long as you need to. It's funny, the timing. It was just two weeks ago that we finished converting the garage into an extra bedroom—good thing."

Then Janet Buford: "How can you fuck over Sharon like this? Wives always get a raw deal. If men had the babies, this would *never* happen, and what about school? I'm not letting Campbell or any LBI asshole near *my* kids. You're the only pastor I want, Jim, so you better not quit. If it comes to a showdown, I'll vote for you, even if you are a lousy husband, even if you are overcharged with testosterone."

Then Doris on the phone—in the midst of her third straight stay-at-home drinking day—"Jim honey, I tol' you. I'm for you. You know that. I tol' you. I'll keep our secret. I won't tell about Becki. Ever'thing ish gonna be okay. I'm jusha lil' shick today. I'll be in tomorrow ... an' I'll treat you to lunch."

Next, Melissa Baker, weeping on the phone: "It hurts me, Pastor Jim, to see what's happening. I love you and Sharon. I feel bad for your kids. I think you should go back to Sharon and reconcile your marriage. That's what the Bible says. That's what God wants. But whatever happens, I'll stand with you, Pastor Jim. You've always given me love and grace. You'll always be my pastor."

And Carl, calling from work: "Pastor, I just want you to know that you have my full support. I pray that God will save your marriage. I pray that God will give you wisdom in your personal life. But, Pastor, I still believe in our church, in our vision of reaching people for Christ. And after some deep soul-searching, I've concluded that honesty *is* best. But I pray that God will renew your faith. Still, I admire your courage to share your honest doubts. And remember, if there's anything Melissa and I can do to help, just give a call ... *any*thing."

Then Joanne McClusky, calling from her lonely apartment: "In spite of all I hear, I still believe in you, Jim. I'll never forget that night at the hospital, and all of our talks. Life is *so* full of disappointment and pain, but wherever you go, I will follow. I'm with you. I love you."

Finally, Leslie B., whispering in the hall as Jim left for McDonald's: "Pastor, I knew all along since the third week she was here. I think you're wrong, but it doesn't change anything. We're saved by grace and mercy, and *that's* what I'm going to give you. I hope you stay with Sharon, and that's how I'm praying, but either way, I'll be in the teen center on Friday nights, as always."

Jim hears footsteps behind him. He turns and sees white sneakers hopping through the black cinder muck, across the rotting ties, the rusty rails. Mirrored sunglasses, dark hair, dimpled chin: Larry Thornton. *Oh shit,* Jim curses under his breath. *I really need this. What the fuck is he doin' here?* Larry ascends the embankment with the sure grace of a young buck. Slim, tan, dressed in a primrose pullover and tartan-plaid seersucker trousers, he looks like he just jumped ourt of a Filene's ad. And his Adidas jogging shoes are so new they seem luminescent in the bright sunshine.

"So what brings you down to the church?" Jim asks after exchanging greetings and comments about the splendid view; his tone is friendly but forced. "You didn't go to Boston today?"

Larry flashes his cocky Ivy League smile. "I had to see a client in Marlboro ... but I've been wanting to talk to you, Jimbo, so I decided to come here this afternoon instead of going to the office. My wife said I'd probably find you out here by the lake."

Jim can't stand Larry's obnoxious Wall Street personality. He wishes Larry would leave so he can miss Becki by himself. But he replies nonetheless, "Fat city; your job, I mean?"

"I can't complain. I can set my own schedule, as long as I take care of my people. That's one of the advantages of being a broker in a bull market...."

While Larry goes on bragging about his job, Jim reaches down, picks up a small pine branch, and snaps off the twigs until he has a stick about two feet long. He turns off his ears, tries to ignore Larry's presence, but he cannot be ignored. He exudes an odor of success and self-satisfaction, along with the scent of perfumed soap and exotic cologne. To Jim, he smells like citrus punch. A puff of wind blows up from the water bringing a welcome whiff of lake air. Jim much prefers the wild-fishy-algal smell. He drums the stick against his hand like a riding crop. *How does Larry do it?* he wonders to himself. *I haven't been that trim since plebe year. I hate his fuckin' android personality, but I must admit he does take care of his physique. He must spend hours each day on his Exercycle and I doubt he's had a doughnut since he was a kid, if he ever was? And he's so fuckin' tan. My chest is whiter than his damn sneakers.*

Sudden cawing snaps Jim out of his self-deprecating thoughts. A pair of crows flap playfully overhead then fly up the railroad cut toward the trestle. Larry quickly shifts from bonds to birds. "Just think," he observes in his dulcet hi-tech voice. "Those crows evolved from reptiles. It's truly a*mazing*, Jimbo, how mutation and natural selection have given us such a va*riety* of creatures." Larry gives a smug grin as he always does when promoting his arrogant brand of atheism.

Jim sweeps the pine crop toward the reservoir. "Yeh, Larry, it's amazing all right. A lizard just happened to be born one day with wings and hollow bones and feathers, and he flew up into the sky over a grassy meadow, and it just *so happened* he ran into a female who had evolved that very same summer. So they got married and lived happily ever after and had *many* babies. Truth is, Larry, I don't have the foggiest idea where crows came from. But neither do you. You atheists and evolutionists are just as close-minded as any Bible-thumping evangelist, and I've had enough of both."

Jim smiles without humor. "But, Larry, you didn't come to debate about evolution, didyuh?" Jim looks right at Larry, but instead of Larry, he sees his own bulbous nose, two of them, reflected in the twin mirrors on Larry's face.

"Now, now, Jimbo, I didn't mean to set you off," Larry patronizes.

*Like hell you didn't, you upward mobile asshole!* Jim retorts silently. His skin crawls with aggravation. Larry makes him feel old, ugly, and out of style, and hopelessly out of Becki's league— and he hates being called "Jimbo." Jim grips the pine branch as if it's a nightstick. He feels like jerking Larry's glasses and smashing his face, but instead, he reins in his anger, and waits for the pitch. He knows Larry has one; he never comes around without pushing some sort of moneymaking venture.

Larry reaches up and gently pats his wavy dark locks which are carefully combed back Jim Palmer-style, then he gets right to the point, "Well, Jimbo, to make a long story short, I've come to offer you a job." He extends an upturned hand as if the job is a gold nugget resting on his palm.

Jim hurls the pine stick toward the lake. It flies end over end, coming down on the beach where it bounces several times short of the water. "I have a job," he replies to Larry.

Larry gives his cocky Ivy League smile, but now it seems more smart-ass than Ivy League. "Come on, Jim; get *real.* You're a married minister involved with a college freshman. You're separated from your wife and ready to break ranks with your denomination. I'd have to say your days as a pastor are numbered."

*He's done his homework,* Jim thinks to himself. *I'll say that for him, with Angela's help no doubt.*

"Go on, Larry, I'm listening," he replies aloud as he dusts his hands. "I'm not interested, but I'll listen." Jim slouches, placing his weight on one leg, while Larry stands at casual attention, head high, up on his toes, as if practicing good posture.

Giving an openhanded "why not?" gesture, Larry moves quickly into his pitch; he sounds almost evangelical, "You see, Jimbo, Baines & Clarendon has authorized me to take on a full-time assistant and to open a branch office in Stow, so we can take full advantage of this booming bull market."

Jim takes off his softball cap and fingers the bill. "You can hire anyone you want?"

"Well, sort of. My selection has to be approved in Boston, but with your credentials, I could hire you today ... with one phone call."

"Why me?" Jim asks. "I'm sure you could find someone more experienced."

"More experienced, yes; more qualified, no. When it comes to selling, Jimbo, you're a natural. You have the gift. You see, selling investment packages, well"—Larry tips his head humbly as if to apologize—"I don't mean to belittle your faith, but it's like selling God. People need financial security just like they need to feel good about their soul, and people trust you, Jim. You're a good ol' country boy. You can sell anything. It's not the product but the salesman."

Jim's soul brims with disgust but he doesn't let on. Larry is confirming what he's always known in his heart. "So, Larry, what do *you* get out of it?" he asks.

Larry lifts his hands like a begger. "I'll get a percentage on all your accounts, and you'll help me man the new office. I can't do it by myself. But we must move quickly before the horse is out of the barn. We'll never see opportunity like this again. The Dow's going to hit 2000 for sure, and maybe 3000. We're living in the '80s, Jimbo. We've got a supply-sider in the White House. Reagan is *our* boy. The American dream is happening all around us. Business is booming again, and investment money is flowing like beer at a fraternity party. Let's get going, and get our share of it."

Jim smirks cynically. "So what do *I* get?" He holds out his baseball hat as if it's an offering basket.

Larry opens his arms wide to the sky like an Indian beseeching the Great Spirit. "Whatever you sell, Jim. The sky's the limit. I see you making thirty thou the first year, and if you sell stocks and mutual funds as hard as you sell Jesus, you'll be at six figures in five years. You'll make more than you ever made as a minister, or as a meteorologist for that matter, and you'll practically be your own boss—moreover, you'll be helping people at the same time."

Jim puts his hat back on his head. *You mean soaking people,* he rebuts, but only to himself.

Larry moves to close his sale. "The key to success, Jim, is knowing when to buy, when to sell, when to get in, and when to get out. Life is a series of decisions. Victory goes to those who decide wisely. You have a gift to sell, but I doubt you'll be selling Jesus much longer. With all the rumors and gossip and controversy flying about you, I'd say your stock as a pastor is down to junk-bond status, and it's closing lower each day. Before you know it, you'll be back at the weather station working those midshifts like when you first started the church. Why settle for a dead-end job when you can secure your future? You have to think of your kids. This is a chance to turn adversity into opportunity. And if you want to marry the younger woman, you can. I hate to see you and Sharon split up, but it's no big deal in the world of—"

*BWEEP-BWEEP-BWEEP-BWEEP!* A beeper sounds on Larry's belt.

He lifts his shirt and presses a button. "I have to call the office," he explains. "I'll give you a few days to think on this, Jimbo. I'll be in touch."

With that, Larry lopes down the embankment, crosses the tracks, and disappears into the woods.

"Don't bother," Jim mutters under his breath as he turns back toward the lake. "I'd work at Cumberland Farms before I'd work for you."

A freshening and chilly wind has blown away the calm. He zips up his parka. He gazes out over the blue-green channel of open water which is now covered with waves.

Jim feels a vague foreboding, as you feel when you walk alone in the woods in the evening and hear the sorrowful whistle of a whippoorwill.

*Where I ache to go is so far beyond selling and money and choices,* he sighs to himself. *And beyond hope, I fear?*

# Chapter Thirty-five

**R**ocks and sand and black sky. Pastor Jim flees before the thundering herd. His lungs burn. His heart pounds. His long shadow runs ahead of him across a vast rocky desert—red, brown, gray, pockmarked with craters. The sun hangs low behind him, a small orange ball, while in the black starry sky ahead, the Earth hangs blue and white, like a full and distant moon.

Thunder, thunder, thundering hooves. Jim glances over his shoulder. Closer, closer. The billowing cloud of red dust is drawing nearer. Closer, closer. Enraged bull-like creatures, snorting, breathing fire. Closer, closer. Jim stumbles then tumbles headlong, ripping his jeans and his knees. Terror, terror. He pants. He gasps. Dust chokes his nostrils. It smells like banana oil and sweat, mingled with exotic incense. It smells like Becki's body. He coughs, he screams, he scrambles to his feet. Bleeding, bleeding, lungs on fire. Near to fainting—but he runs and runs.

All at once, Jim comes to a high cliff above a lake of fire, bubbling, boiling, spewing, roaring, a lake of blue-hot molten rock, a seething volcano. Smoke and ash and chunks of lava spew upward into the darkness. Geysers of blue fire singe Jim's hair and scorch his face. A tempest rages, sucking him toward the edge.

Behind him, galloping hoofbeats approach, shaking the ground like an artillery barrage. No mercy. No mercy. Jim staggers back from the edge of the cliff and collapses on the hot sand. Thunder, thunder, black bellowing thunder, deafening roar, blinding dust. Becki, Becki—"O GOD! HELP ME! HELP ME!" Pounding pain, falling bricks, stars, stars. He covers his head. The crazed Minotaurs stampede over him and plunge like lemmings over the cliff into the lake of blue fire. A thousand knives of pain stab Jim's broken body. He quivers. He tastes blood. He chokes.

Broken but alive, he lifts his head. Distant dust: a plume approaches—an army jeep with heart insignias on the doors. Behind the wheel: a pith helmet, a safari jacket, and a toasty Scottish smile. Russ Bradley braves the hot tempest and lifts Jim into the jeep. Leaving the smoke and fire behind, they speed across the plateau, dodging rocks and craters. Desert sand, utter desolation, then suddenly out of the black starry sky a spaceship descends. Gray, shiny like glass, it hovers overhead—NO, NO. It's not a flying saucer, but a light fixture in the Bradleys' guest room.

*What the fuck!* Jim exclaims to himself. *What a crazy nightmare! Another bull-monster dream?* He rolls over and grabs his watch off the night table; it's 6:55 a.m. "Uughh," he groans. "It's time to get up. It's Friday. I've been here all week."

* * *

After wrestling with the lights, Pastor Jim slips out of his jacket, and moves to the windows. The thermometer says 18°. Wednesday's warmth froze on Thursday, and Friday's cold gray start promises no thaw. He stretches-yawns then sits down at his desk. Angie soon arrives with coffee and the mail. "Good Morning," she mumbles, looking at Jim with sleepy eyes. "Feels more like January than March out there, but never mind the weather, I'm just glad it's Friday. I can't take another week like this—oh, don't forget, Mr. Cranston from the school committee is coming for his annual inspection this afternoon. I called Stan and he's getting off work early so he can walk through with you."

Jim sips his coffee. "Oh yeh, Cranston. He can be a real pain, and I hafta sign the same paperwork every year. I hardly feel like dealing with the town today."

"Tell me about it," Angie replies. "He bosses me like I'm working for him. He's coming at one o'clock so make sure you're back from lunch, or he'll just leave and hold up our recertification, like he did two years ago."

"Don't worry, Angie, I'll be here," Jim assures as she slips out the door. *Don't worry,* he says again, this time to himself. *My afternoons are all free, and empty, now that Becki goes home alone.... How long can she stay, with this tension and whispering and gossip? Maybe she does love me like Jodi says, but she's still gonna leave. She won't hang around 'til June, no way. She can't endure* this *spotlight.*

He gives a weary sigh. *School, church, inspections, certifications. It all seems so pointless now. I don't even know if I'll be here next year. How long can this go on, this silent standoff between me and Stan? I wonder if Dr. Logan knows about my sermons. He must, but why hasn't he acted? Beckman usually hops on disloyalty like a junkyard dog on a nighttime intruder.*

Jim sorts through the mail. He finds an official-looking letter from the law offices of Wilcox and Barton. Inside is a draft separation agreement; he scans it: *$1400 alimony-child support, plus the house and the Grenada, plus, plus....* He exhales an exasperated breath. *God, she's not wasting any time.* He tosses the letter on the desk, then rocks back swiveling his chair toward the windows.

Yesterday (Thursday) brought more expressions of concern and vows of allegiance from the flock, but nothing from Stan or

Nashua. Frank Cahill called Thursday morning, full of high-pitched promises: "You know Syl and I, we're gonna stand with you *all* the way, Pastor. I'm sure God will bring you and your wife back together. He won't allow the devil to break up your family, or this church. This is just a test of your faith. Sylvia and I are prayin', and I'm gonna be helpin' more with the grounds and the building, and I'm gonna be helpin' Barry on the buses."

Sarah Johnson came by in the afternoon to see Bev about Jennifer's report card. Afterward she stopped by Jim's office: "Doncha fret none, Pastor Jim. Jesus ain't gonna for*sake* yuh even if you're adoin' a might poorly. I knows, on account he done showed me in a dream. I seen a baby in the wild. I reckon no more than a year ol', a mighty pretty lil' boy, but this here bear was acomin' an' the chil' commence to hawler, but 'fore the bear et the chil', a giant eagle come aswoopin' down an' the bear lit out. Then the eagle done right good an' took a holt of the baby an' flew higher an' higher 'til the angels came an' fetched the chil' to *glory*. I seen 'em."

Barry Buford also came by yesterday afternoon, with nervous hands and a sheepish smile: "Well, Jim ... I-I, well, all I can say is we been friends a long time. Nothing can change that. I think you should go back to Sharon. It's the right thing according to God's Word. But you didn't condemn me back in December, so I'm not condemning you now. We *must* give each other love and grace and continue on. We *must* continue the work that God has given us."

But now it's Friday morning, March 2, 1984. It's been a year since Becki came back into Jim's life, a year that has changed him forever—yet he only has an inkling of how much. He gets up and goes to the windows. He comes back to his desk. He sits down. He gets up. He goes to the kitchen for more coffee then back to his office. He reads the paper. He paces. Finally at nine-thirty, he calls Sharon. "So what's this thing from Sam Barton?" he asks her.

"Just my way of making sure," Sharon says in a businesslike voice.

"Making sure of what?"

"That you fulfill your responsibilities, until the divorce."

"You're filing for divorce?"

"Well, one of us has to, but it's *your* choice, Jim, not *mine*?"

"How come you went to Barton instead of old man Brenner?"

"He doesn't represent his employees. Besides, it's none of your business."

"So it's come to *this,* huh?"

"I don't want to talk about it, Jim, not about *us*. The kids miss you, but I don't. I'm making a new life. I'm not fighting Becki *any*more. You can have that little fat-assed bitch if she'll take you.

I doubt she wants you but that's between you and her. I'm out of the triangle now. I can't believe I took your shit so long!" Sharon goes on a minute venting her rancor, then she calms and they shift to practical matters: utility bills, credit cards, bank accounts, Jim's mail, Erin's new braces, time with the kids. Jim says he'll take them once a week, to eat out, to do fun things. Now comes silent breathing. Sharon seems to waver, but she quickly recovers and says good-bye, her voice just as businesslike as before.

Jim hangs up. He feels a lump of regret in his throat. Sitting back, he sips his coffee and stares out at the frozen ugliness of early March. The winter-weary pines sway to and fro in the wind, tossing their uplifted arms like sea kelp in an undertow. He wishes it were warmer so he could go to the big rock or walk by the lake. Instead, he takes off in his mind, *I guess Shar means it this time but I can't blame her. No wife would put up with my Becki-love. It's got to be one or the other, not both—at least in this life.* Jim sighs. He shakes his head. *Telling the truth is like pulling out your dick at church. No way can you come out of it looking good.... Oh, Becki Lea, I miss you. It's torture. Everything I see reminds me of our special times. Even if we never go to bed, or even kiss again. Oh, Becki, I miss eating with you and laughing and kidding. I don't have answers. I just want to be with you. I want to take care of you and stand with you, in good times and bad. But I doubt it'll ever happen—not now. I scared you away good. Where I'm at is too hot of a place.*

After another sigh, his thoughts drift, *I should pay room and board but Russ'll never take it. I'll give it to Bev. But I can't stay there forever. I gotta get my own place.... $1400 a month to Sharon. If they vote me out—shit, I'll be in the poorhouse. I should call Ralph at the weather station. Maybe I'll end up working for Larry— no way, I'll move back to Texas before I do that.... I wish things would resolve. I hate this fuckin' uncertainty—what is that? Shit! It looks like dried ketchup on my vest. I should've worn my blue one. I must get the rest of my clothes, but where am I gonna put them? Why do I keep dreaming about bull-monsters and blue fire? I wonder if God speaks through dreams. I wonder if God speaks at all. I wonder if*—a knock interrupts his question.

PINK DENIM AND A POUTY FACE! Whoosh! Wham! Becki, Becki. Heart rush! Shock! Jim's heart lurches, turns over, pounds up into his throat. A million volts surge through him firing every nerve, stirring every emotion. Wistful eyes, wispy bangs, Moonlight Lace, beige blouse, embroidered trim. Becki has come into his office for the first time since their midnight showdown eight days ago. Like a tree struck by lightning, Jim's psyche explodes in flames. Hope and dread clash hotly in his cheeks.

Heaven and hell war in his brain. Without a word she drops a pile of report cards on his desk and turns to leave. She pauses momentarily then heads for the door. Jim's mind races then brakes then accelerates. His thoughts stop and go like traffic in downtown Boston, locking, unlocking, then tearing in all directions.

Finally, his panic-stricken mind hurtles out of the office, crashing through the windows and fleeing into the woods—but his pounding heart stays, leans forward, and says, "Becki Lea?"

Becki freezes like a movie on "pause." Jim holds his breath; he waits ten lifetimes. Movement. Becki turns around, looks down shyly; she fidgets with her hands. Riding boots, bare legs, sassy skirt. She slouches near the Canon copy machine; she seems lost and sad. A wave of love and compassion sweeps Jim out of his chair. He closes the door. He moves toward her but she shrinks away. His heart slips, begins to sink, but then a tiny glow becomes a burst of pink. Strawberry lips, toothy smile, she comes up blushing like a child—and melts into his arms.

Warm, warm, gush of relief. Breaking dams, floods of feeling. They cry. They snuggle close. Jim whispers tearful words of affection into Becki's hair. Bountiful love wraps them like a baby's bunting. He rocks her tenderly back and forth. Sniffling, sighing, Becki blows hot breath on his neck. Magic, awe, unspeakable elation. Jim drowns in her brunette ocean with its dark-caramel depths and honey-maple waves. Brown, brown, softly fluffed, and feathered. He inhales her lilac-sweet locks, her scented neck, her blouse, her tears, her fears—her nervous perspiry glow.

Dark and blissful silence. Warm, warm, cozy warm. Becki snuggles closer, closer, her head on Jim's shoulder. He opens his eyes. He gazes lovingly at her tear-stained cheek: rosy, round, *so* angelic. He caresses her hair, her back. She sighs happily then comes up like the sun, giving him a radiant smile: cupid lips, crooked teeth, dimples, pimples, blotchy face. Smudgy mascara rings her big blue eyes—blue, blue, sky-blue, and yearning. Enraptured by her eyes, Jim sees no spot or blemish. He sees her as beautiful and perfect and precious. Her chunky body presses hot against him. Soft, squeezable, girlish, yet nubile, spirited, and raging with life.

"Oh, Shanley, I love you!" Becki gushes in a tearful whisper. "I've been waiting *so* long for this. Every time I went down the hall, I wanted to run in here and hug you and kiss you. I tried so hard to kill my feelings, but I can't. I miss you wicked bad!"

"Oh, Becki, I missed you too!" Jim exlaims joyfully. "I love you more than ever. I can't believe this is happening."

"Oh, me neither, but hold me, Jimmy. Just hold me. Make me believe it." He hugs her to him, tighter, tighter; she gasps. Breasts,

breasts, Becki's breasts. They press hot against his bosom until they seem to be his own. "Oh, *Shan*ley," she confesses further, after sucking a breath, "I can't hide it anymore. I just about died this week. I've been going crazy since Christmas. I've been going crazy all year. But I can't run anymore. I love you *so*. I want you to move in with me. I don't *care* about church. I don't *care* what people say. I don't *care* what they think. I want you with me. I love you! I love you! I can't pretend anymore! It's torture to be without you."

Kissing, kissing. Becki kisses Jim with her eyes, then her lips, then her tongue. Dark lashes, dark nostrils, cute snubby nose. Coffee breath, cinnamon lips, spicy tongue, salty tears. Breathless, floating. Jim's soul soars and spins, as if out of his body. Dizzy, dizzy, falling. He closes his eyes. He feels her heart thudding against his. She kisses him again and again, grinding her lips and body into his. She groans. Jim devours her, sucking her tongue, her lips, her crooked teeth. *O God, Jesus, God!* he cries ecstatically in his heart. *I love her so! I'm gonna die!* He grabs her moonish hips— *Oh, such wanton heft*—and pulls her to him until her legs are wrapped around his thigh, until her crotch is pressed against his resurrected prick, now a throbbing tent peg in his pants. Jim's heart races. His knees shake. Lips, hips, entwined bodies. Wild currents of sensation rip through him: cinnamon, spice, Moonlight Lace, lilacs, salty bananas. They sway in sexual rhythm. They hug and grind and kiss and kiss, like two kittens nursing at the same tit.

Hot, hot. Hot sensation. Becki caresses Jim through his dress slacks. "Oh, Jimmy, you're *bigger* than Christmas," she sighs, giving a lustful grin. Her body quivers. Lightning flashes in her eyes. "I can't stop thinking about that night, how close we came. Oh *fuck,* I feel like taking my clothes off." Drunk, drunk. Her aggressive words make Jim drunk with anticipation; he reaches back and locks the door. But Becki has a better idea. "No, not here. Let's go to my place. I'll meet you there in ten minutes. I just have to mail a P.E. packet for Jodi. Then she won't need me the rest of the day." She gives Jim another yummy kiss. "O *Jesus,* Shanley, I can't wait—and *this* time I'm unplugging my phone." She clasps her hands together like an eager child then departs.

Jim's heart whirls and skids around the office until he's too dizzy to stand up. He collapses onto the recliner and looks up at cobwebs and fluorescent lights. Bliss, bliss, euphoric bliss. He savors Becki's smile, her body, her wanton touch. His mind comes back from the woods just in time to exult with his soul, *O Lord Jesus! Thank you! Thank you! This is it. We won, we won. Love has won! Being honest, it's the only way. It's more than worth it—all the pain, all the shit. Oh, Becki, Becki, you scared the hell out of me, but I knew something good was coming when I smelled your Moonlight Lace. You went back to your old scent.*

*O God, I don't believe it. She wants me! She loves me! We're on our way. Now we can live and love and preach the true gospel!* Jim's penis patiently draws back, but his heart rages near orgasm as if he's falling into a black hole of ecstasy—beautiful, rapturous, transcendent, yet somehow like death. His lips still burn from Becki's hot kisses. He takes a slow breath to calm himself then exhales a sigh of happy relief. *I better get going. I have to warm up the Mustang. I can't wait. O God, thank you! Thank you!*

\* \* \*

The cold gray day fogs the windows at 59 Front Street. Bathsheba sleeps on the back of the green chair seemingly unconcerned about the steamy aromas of sex wafting up from Becki's bed. Jim pads back in from the bathroom. Becki, still floating from her second orgasm, looks up at him with that serene dreamy-eyed look that only a rush of endorphins can give. The blue in her eyes swells then breaks, like an ocean wave on a summer day, peaceful, yet potent and uninhibited. Her winter skin is so white that her naked body seems almost luminous in the diffuse daylight coming through the foggy windows. Knees up, legs spread, her breasts shapeless mounds of mammary flesh, she lazily fingers her pubic hair as if showing off her genitals which are still red and swollen. To Jim, the sight of her dark bush and womanly cunt against the backdrop of her fair and girlish body is irresistible—even after sex.

Set like a mysterious other face between the milky-pale rolls of her relaxed adductors, Becki's vulva seems to convey all her secrets without words, as if this swarthy vestibule between her legs does indeed lead to her heart, to her true and unfathomable self. Her burnt umber bush is shaped like a tree with two trunks. As Jim looks on, she combs her fingers through the crown of this tree, a ferny square of pubic hair that covers her fleshy pubis like an unkempt beard. It's thick and curly, but not tightly kinked, with many wayward tufts that spiral and jut in all directions giving her bush a stormy wildness like the squally underside of a thundercloud. Dropping down from this ferny crown, the two trunks frame her pussy like sideburns, not thick but shadowy and wispy.

Tawny-pink and tumescent, her large outer lips are shaped like a lady's slipper orchid in full bloom but the pink of her cunt is darker than the orchid, more like the redness of a sore. These greater lips are slowly closing about her female foreskin, her inner lips, which straddle the entrance to her vagina like a pair of swollen rose petals damp with morning dew. Above, where these petals come together, her clitoris, like a clammy little penis, is slowly deflating and folding back into its hairy hiding place. To Jim, it looks like a puckered embryo curling back into a fetal position. The birthmark on her left thigh leaves no doubt that this cunny burrow belongs to Rebecca Reinhardt.

*O Lord, it's so big,* Jim declares to himself. *It's like her crotch fills the whole bed.* Dark, enchanting, almost sinister; yet wondrous and majestic and holy. For him, Rebecca's aroused cunt is the ultimate revelation— like seeing the face of God.

After locating his jockey shorts under Becki's blouse on the floor, Jim puts them on and rejoins her in the bed.

"So, Shanley, you like what I have between my legs?" Becki sports, her whispery voice still husky from heavy breathing.

Jim curls his right arm under her head and hugs her to him. "I'll say I do. Your pussy is the sexiest I've ever seen, especially when it's wet and wide-open."

"Well, that says a lot," she quips. "You've only seen two: me and Sharon."

He playfully tweaks her nose. "You don't know how many I've seen?"

"Yes, I do," she chortles. "I know you. You've been square since you left Texas." They both laugh then Becki's laugh becomes a blissful sigh. "Oh, Jimmy, it was wicked wild getting off with you. I feel so good, like all over." Her face becomes radiant with awe as if she's speaking of God. "I love how sex feels. There's nothing else in life that compares to it. It's wicked amazing how it grabs me and won't let go. I just *love* it, how it builds and builds until I'm buzzed out of my mind, and when it comes, O *Jesus,* it's like my soul is too big for my body and it bursts out of me again and again—oh, what a re*lease.* Then I feel hot all over and light-headed, like I'm floating and slowly coming down ... like right now. Oh, Shanley, you make me *so* happy! Just hold me now, hug me close."

After a year of fantasies, denials, and frustrating near-misses, Jim and Becki's first real sex was certainly passionate and satisfying, but a video of their coupling would hardly qualify as movie material. On his way over, Jim had visions of a long erotic encounter, of leading her to orgasm again and again while holding his own passion. But upon his arrival, he lost all control, as did Becki. She may've had amazing will power during their many flirting sessions and prurient talks, but on this Friday morning she had none.

Lips, tongues, kissing, kissing. Desperate to satisfy her lust, as a drowning soul is desperate for air, she locked onto Jim at the door and didn't let go. To the sofa bed, Jim on top. They thrashed and awkwardly tore at each other like teenagers in a backseat mating frenzy. Becki, clumsily shifting and pushing, managed to lift her skirt and to wiggle her panties over her knees. Jim jerked wildly on his belt buckle which was pinned between them. Gasping, groaning, mewing, she writhed under him, her spread haunches humping uncontrollably. Awkward, awkward. But after several fumbling tries, he shoved his pants down to his thighs. Male, female, turgid flesh, hairy and hot. Naked, naked, nothing in between. Panting, panting, he punched into her bucking pussy.

O God! O God! Glory, glory, shouts of ecstasy, blinding pangs of pleasure, but short-lived. Like an excited dog peeing on himself, Jim ejaculated prematurely, thirty seconds after entry.

"Oh *fuck,* I can't stop now!" Becki cried. "I'm just gettin' to the wicked good feeling." Jim tried to forge on, but his erection had lost the throbbing hardness she needed. So he withdrew and fingered her clit. Panting, moaning, to the top, and over. She quickly came in a series of short firm thrusts, like a fish flipping.

After catching their breath, they shed the rest of their clothes and he fondled her to the edge of number two. Then she took over and masturbated herself to the howling, kicking, bed-shaking release that she craved and didn't quite get on her first climax.

Jim feels Becki's soft chunky body pressing into his. Heaven, heaven. He loves the feeling. *O Jesus, is this really happening?* he asks God and himself. *It's only ten-thirty in the morning and she's already lifted me from hell to the highest heaven.* Flesh to flesh: hot, clammy, closer, closer, cuddling, snuggling. For a long blissful moment Jim hears no sound save for Becki's breathing and the popping of the radiator. He inhales her presence, her perfume, her perspiry glow, her salty-banana scent.

"I like it when you lie on you side," Jim says, as they finally relax their embrace.

"Why is that?" Becki asks curiously as she props her pillow under her head. Her disheveled brunette locks tumble onto the pillow and over the side of her face. He doesn't reply but gently pushes her hair back from her pretty eyes. Her makeup, what little she has, is messy from tears and wet kisses. Her mascara is smeared; her peach cover-up is blotchy-smudgy on her chin. Becki, Becki. Angelic, adorable, high-schoolish. Chipmunky, kittenish, cute.

Love, love, warm love. Becki gazes adoringly at Jim, a smile of happy contentment overtaking her features. Enraptured, Jim's soul dives into her gaze, down, down, deeper, deeper, until he knows he's drowning in her azure depths—as in his phantasmal Becki-vision of a year ago. But now the vision has come to life. Glory, glory; the realization blows through him like a rushing wind.

He feels giddy as if his stomach is flying up through his body, like how you feel in an elevator when it goes down fast—suddenly, he's racing down a corridor in his mind approaching that mystical corner of awareness around which lies the full and terrible knowing of Becki and himself, but from which there is no return.

Too much, too intense. Becki must feel it as well, for she gives a silly two-syllable laugh breaking the spell. She then repeats her previous question, "So, Jimmy, why d'you like it when I lie on my side?"

"Oh yeh," Jim says, giving a snorty laugh of his own. "It's your tits. I like the way they look ... how the top one hangs and the bottom one rests on the bed."

"That's because they're bigger-looking when I'm on my side. They disappear when I lie on my back. You can't even tell I'm a girl when I'm on my back. I look like a flabby-chested boy."

"No, you don't. You have really nice breasts. Any guy would say they're sexy."

"Yeah, any guy who likes floppy lemons."

"Come on, yours are way bigger than lemons." Jim lifts her top breast cupping it in his hand. "In fact, I'd say you've grown since Christmas."

Becki looks down at her breast as Jim cups it. "No, I'm just getting fat. That's the only time my boobs get bigger, but look at the rest of me. When I took a shower this morning, I weighed 128. My fat ass will hardly fit into my jeans, and my thighs are too big." She wrinkles her nose and twists her mouth, giving her patented scrunchy face, then lifts her naked leg. "Look at that flab. *Yech.* It's dis*gust*ing."

"Not to me," Jim rebuts, running his hand over her hip and down her thigh. "I love your legs like they are, your butt too. I love your whole body. You may be a bit plumpish but you're not fat. Besides, I like a gal with a little heft in her haunches, so when you hump you hold your ground, like today. You gave me quite a ride, young lady. Believe me; I knew I was inside a real woman."

"So you liked it, huh?" Becki asks, smirking with pride in spite of herself.

Jim gives a boyish grin. "O God, it was *great.* I'm just sorry I let go so quick. I usually have more control, but I was going nuts. I was high as a kite."

"Oh, me too," Becki confesses. "When I fantasize, I hold back to make the horny feeling last, but today I couldn't wait. I was *wick*ed out of my mind. I lost my hips before I got my panties down. I couldn't have stopped even if my mom walked in. It just takes me longer to come, that's all, 'cause I'm a girl. It takes women longer, you know?"

"Is that so," Jim teases. "You know *all* about it, d'you?"

"Yeah, it takes some women thirty minutes to get a climax. I read about it in *Ladies' Home Journal* ... at the laundromat while I was waiting for my stuff to dry." Becki smirks and playfully punches Jim's paunchy gut. They both snicker.

Becki, Becki. Cozy, carnal, uninhibited. Jim loves her post-orgasmic earthiness, how she shares her most intimate thoughts without shame: "Guess we'll have to learn to cool it a bit, huh, Shanley? But no way could I cool it today. I just wanted you in me, in me. I was crazy to get there. But considering how long this has been building, I'd say we did pretty good—thank God for fingers. In fact, I'm still shaking inside." She gives a deep sigh of sexual satisfaction then squints into her cute detective look. "So, Jimmy, tell me ... was it as good as your first time with Sharon?"

Jim brushes back a last wayward wisp of hair from Rebecca's cheek. "Oh, much better. Our honeymoon was—don't get me wrong, we've had lots of fantastic sex, especially since Sharon got her tubes tied, like I toldjuh last summer when you and I first got into heavy flirting and had those spicy conversations."

Becki grins coquettishly. "Yeah, those talks were nice. Shit, every time we got naughty like that, I wanted to unzip you. My demons were at the door, especially that night at the diner. But I wasn't a*bout* to admit it. Of course, we would've made it Christmas Eve if Mom hadn't called. What a disaster that was—but go on, Jimmy. Finish answering my question. What were you saying about your honeymoon? I got you off track."

"Yeh, our honeymoon. We were starry-eyed newlyweds, me and Sharon, but the sex was ... well, let's say, we didn't exactly score that week."

"Well, it hurts when you're a virgin," Becki explains with an air of clinical authority as if she's a middle-aged sex counselor instead of a youngish 20-year-old who's had intercourse fifteen times, if that. "Even if you're horny, it still hurts when you break your cherry. When I did it with Manny, he didn't get in enough to make me bleed until the second time, and I didn't get off until the fourth ... but after that, oh fuck, I couldn't get enough, 'til he left— and especially *aft*er he left." She rolls her eyes and gives a silent whistle that becomes a *"whew."*

"He was that good, huh?"

"Good enough to take me on some wild fantasies, I tellyuh ... you know, like a single girl needs now and then." Pink color warms Becki's face. She teases Jim, "Especially when I have impure thoughts about this *other* particular guy and I need my Manny-memories to distract me."

Her smirk answers his question, but he asks it anyway, "What *other* guy?"

"I'm not saying, except he's wicked old and he has monkey legs, and when he talks he says 'thang' and 'cain't' ... and he has a potbelly like a fat fish when he lies on the bed."

"I do not," Jim banters, his face breaking wide under his mustache.

"Yes, you do," Becki banters back.

"Well, you're not exactly shaped like an hourglass, Miss Reinhardt. You've got a little pot of your own. I love it. It's cute, but you shouldn't be talking." Jim playfully fingers her navel. "I sure don't see your bellybutton sticking out."

Becki giggles and pulls in her custardy midriff. "Just look at your stomach, Jimmy, compared to mine." She pats his paunch. "See how your fat belly lies over on the bed like a fish, while mine stays up." Her voice is tight, full of air, as she strains to hold in her gut.

They banter a bit longer about his belly, then he shifts back to Manny, "So, Becki, tell me ... d'you like Manny better in person or as a fantasy lover?"

"Whaddeya think?" she quips. "I may have a good imagination and a wicked fast hand—I guess you noticed—but sex without a penis is like a meal without a *main* course." Witty, ribald: Becki humor. Dimples, crimson cheeks, crooked teeth. She laughs heartily then gives Jim a nibbling kiss on the side of his mouth. "But after today, things are gonna be different. Hallelujah and thank you, Jesus. This girl's wait is *over*.... I hope your pecker's in good shape, Shanley, because I'm gonna *wear* you out. As a matter of fact, I may be hungry again by lunchtime." She playfully grabs his prick through his jockey briefs and gives it a quick fondle.

"O God, I *love* it," Jim chortles. "You're a hot little lady, Becki Lea. You really are into the flesh. But I always figured you'd have an insatiable appetite for sex."

"What made you think that?"

"Oh, how you couldn't sit still when you were younger. You always had to move your leg or tap your foot, and when you ran or walked, you wiggled your butt like a filly horse, like you were lifting an invisible tail. And this year—shit, you drove me nuts with your dirty jokes and erotic dreams and *Penthouse* stories. Who would believe it, especially when you act so *shy* and *whole*some like a sweet little missionary? The contrast makes you irresistible."

"So you find me irresistible, d'you?" Becki asks proudly, as *if* she doesn't know.

"Well, young lady, I'd say my loss of control fifteen minutes ago already answered that question, but you've been driving me nuts all year, how you flirt and flirt, then flip and deny your passion, but even when you deny, you have that look."

"What look?"

"You know, that crazy melting glow that women get when they have a naughty yearning between their legs."

Becki gives a sporty grin and pulls back the elastic waistband on Jim's shorts. She checks out his floppy retracted penis all comfy in its cottony cocoon. "Just because you have one of *these* between your legs, you think it's all a girl wants. You think you know *so* much about women."

"Well, Miss Reinhardt," Jim responds, smirking sassily, "I don't know about *all* women, but I'd say it's what *you* think about most. God must've put an extra measure of eros in your hormones. You're even more penis-crazy than Sharon—O Jesus, I love it."

Becki turns onto her back and places her hands behind her head; she looks lazily at the ceiling. "Well, Mom always said I was oversexed, especially after she caught me with Maria's *Playgirl* magazine. That was our first year in Puerto Rico. I was in tenth grade. She also found a racy paperback in my school bag. She tore it up and yelled at me, and said it was sinful and unhealthy to read 'such trash,' that good Christian girls would never do such a thing, and that a woman's passions should never come out except in response to her husband in the marriage bed—course, she was no great example. She lost her cherry when she was fifteen, at least according to Amelia."

"What was the name of the dirty paperback?" Jim asks.

"*The Huge Bedroom,* something like that—no, *The Enormous Bed,* that's it. It was an old book, but it had a wicked lot of romance and raunchy sex scenes."

Jim playfully jabs her shoulder. "I guess you're more literate than I thought. Sounds like you've gone a bit beyond *Jane Eyre* and *Ann of Green Gables*?"

"That's for sure," Becki affirms, giving a naughty-girl smirk. "Maria had a bunch of sexy novels and I read most of 'em. She got 'em from her uncle who ran a smutty bookstore in San Juan. That's also where she got her magazines and pictures and stuff. Some of her books were in Spanish and I had to read them with her so she could translate. But the ones in English, I took home. I didn't care if it was sinful or unhealthy or what. Those erotic love stories excited my imagination and opened my eyes. I learned a lot about sex that year, short of actually doing it."

Her confession is stirring Jim's carnal curiosity. "So you were in the tenth grade when you learned how to ... uh, well, found out how it—"

"How it feels?" she says, finishing his question. "I'll say I did. It was right before Christmas; it happened in the bathtub. I came so hard I sloshed half the water out." Becki folds her lips then puts on a smirky face; her expression is "hot ticket," somewhere between proud and dirty-sweet.

"God, I wish I could've been there," Jim replies kiddingly, but there's a sense of wonder in his voice.

"Well, what about you, Shanley? Now that I've confessed, I think you should too. When did you start playing with yourself?"

"Oh, I never did," he declares tongue-in-cheek. "I was a good boy—"

"Get outa here, Jimmy! You're the *last* person I'd believe that from."

They both snicker then Jim tells her the truth, "It was my friend Jason Barnett. He taught me how to jack off when I was in seventh grade—actually it was the summer before eighth grade. I was thirteen I think, or close to it."

"Oh, you mentioned him before. Wasn't his sister Betty Lou the first girl you ever kissed, and you played with her boobs, then lost your nerve?"

"It was Betty *Sue,* but this was three years before. Jason had this clubhouse behind his house in Gilmer. It was by the tracks. It was actually an old abandoned railroad shack. But we used to go there and tell dirty jokes, and Jason had playing cards with naked girls on them. And one day, while he was looking at the cards, he pulled down his pants and jerked off. Then I tried it. I was embarrassed as hell because I was just beginning to get hair, and I looked really young compared to Jason. The first few times were duds, but after a few days I got the hang of it—and *how.*"

More snickers and chuckles. Becki's naked midriff jiggles like gelatin. Jim, still lying on his side, stares at her laughing tummy, at her deep belly dimple as it shakes mirthfully. He loves looking at her flesh; he's addicted to it.

Now more confessing from Rebecca—she speaks upward toward the Capiz shell light fixture, "Ever since I was a little girl, I knew there was something special about my pussy because when I touched myself down there, it felt tingly 'n good, sort of a warm electric feeling. I figured that feeling had to lead somewhere but I never heard about getting off until my friend Mell told me about it when I was eleven. She even showed me her mother's marriage book, a medical book—that was a year before we got into reading sex magazines in her basement—and we snuck it out of the house and read it in the bushes behind her garage. It talked about the clitoris and female climax. I felt ashamed for reading it and I didn't *dare* talk about this to anyone. But shortly after that I checked out my vagina with a mirror to see if I had everything. I was wicked curious and fascinated, and I soon started fondling myself but I never got beyond a buzzed feverish feeling until that day in the bathtub. After that—oh fuck, it was all I thought about, well almost all. I knew it was a bad sin. But it was a million times more exciting than worshiping God, at least the God I learned about in church." Becki rolls her eyes and sighs contentedly. "Maybe I *am* over-sexed? Maybe I did get extra eros in my hormones? I hope so. I want as much eros as I can get. There's *nothing* like it, I tellyuh."

Her hands still clasped behind her head, Becki shifts her buttocks to get more comfortable, and crosses her legs. Her bulbous thighs overlap her crotch. Jim props his head on his hand to get a better view. Now half hidden, her pubic bush tufts up amid the slabby shelves of milky-white flesh like a furry animal coming out of its hole. Dark brown on white, the contrast is breathtaking. With his finger he traces the faint line of peach-fuzzy abdominal hair that runs from her bush up to her belly dimple. Becki sighs in response to his touch. *O God, I can't believe I just fucked her twenty minutes ago,* Jim thinks happily. Drunk, drunk, buzzed on Beckiness. He scarcely remembers the agony that tortured him all year—even an hour ago in his office. *And all this time, in all our fights, she's been denying her desires for me. It's never been platonic. But I must say, she's a fuckin' good actor!* He chuckles at the thought.

Becki gives a curious smirk. "What's so funny?" she asks.

"Oh, I was just thinking," he replies as he probes her belly dimple. "What was all that bullshit all year about 'I don't love you like that' and 'I never fantasize about you' and 'You're too old for me' and 'Christian girls don't play with themselves' and 'I just came to Brendon Falls to do God's work'?"

"I guess I lied," Becki confesses, her smirk no longer curious but coquettish.

Jim walks his fingers up between her breasts. "I'll say, but it's hard to believe you're actually admitting it. Getting off must release a truth serum in your brain."

"No kidding. All my sinful secrets are out. I'm completely naked now."

"I'll say you are ... from head to toe."

They both snicker mirthfully then Becki yawns stretching her arms toward the ceiling. "It's really amazing, Jimmy," she reflects after replacing her hands behind her head. "It's amazing to think that we actually went all the way ... after fighting and fantasizing about it so long."

"Yeah, think of all the agony you've put me through," Jim kids, playfully punching her shoulder. "I've been turned on to you since you were fourteen."

"*Fourteen?* Shit, I wanted you when I was twelve, before I had boobs, before I even knew what I wanted. I just knew I wanted to kiss you and see your penis. But no way was I gonna admit to such impure longings. That was my *biggest* secret."

"You little flirt, you. No wonder you wiggled your tail like a wild filly." They both laugh. Becki's laugh shakes her cute paunch drawing Jim's attention back to her belly button then to her bush as it adorns the apex of her crossed legs like a pubic bow tie. "Well, young woman, I must say your body proves the rule."

"What rule?"

Jim lies back, placing his head on his pillow. "You know, the rule that says your cunt hair is the same color as your eyebrows."

"No shit," Becki wisecracks. "I knew that since I got my first fuzz in seventh grade. It's darker than yours; that's for sure. Guess that means I'm more sexually potent, huh?"

"No," Jim sports, "you're just *meaner,* that's all."

Becki giggles and rolls into Jim's arms. He hugs her then relaxes his embrace as she lies back into the crook of his arm. "Oh, Becki, you're too much," he declares with boyish delight. "Sex makes you bawdier than ever. I *love* it. You make me laugh." She gives a simpering grin but no reply. "You know, kiddo," he says shifting to a practical concern, though his tone is still mirthful. "If my calculations are correct, you're right in the middle of your cycle. And your pimple patch is just starting to heat up."

"God, you keep up with me more than I thought. But you don't know everything, Shanley." Becki puckers then twists her mouth, her grin becoming a smirk, more coy than silly.

"How's that?" Jim asks curiously.

"Well, I *am* in the middle of my cycle, but I won't be getting pregnant."

"How d'you know?"

Rebecca rolls her eyes and flutters her lashes. She gives her sassy contorted face then dimples into a toothy smile. "Because I've been on *the pill* since January."

"You sly *ras*cal, you!" Jim exclaims as he grapples with Becki, tickling her ribs and her thighs. "You knew this was gonna happen, huh?"

Squealing and squirming with delight, she rolls away from him onto her stomach. "You know I'm always one step ahead of you, Jimmy Shanley," she quips, her voice muffled by the pillow.

"I wasn't about to let on, but while you've been running scared, I've been looking at realities. It was just a matter of time. I guess today proves me right, huh?" Becki gives a teasing snicker. "Not that I don't want a kid. I do, but we can wait until we're married."

"Sounds like you have it all figured out ... our future, I mean?"

"Well, you're the one that proposed. I think that sermon you gave me a week ago would qualify as a proposal ... you know, that night you barged into my room?"

"Oh, I'm not reneging," Jim says as he runs his finger across her back following the pinkish and still-fresh impression left by her bra strap. "I'd marry you today if I wasn't married to Sharon. She's divorcing me, but it'll take a while ... maybe a year?"

"No biggie," Becki replies, her tone fait accompli. "We'll live together 'til your divorce is final, then we can make it official."

Jim dances his fingers over her back and shoulders, touching her lightly with his fingernails. "Oh yes, *finger*nails," she sighs, responding to his touch. "That feels *wicked* good. I like having my back scratched. Do my hips too, and my legs."

His heart swelling with affection, Jim scoots closer so he can reach all of her body. Becki sighs. She purrs. And after a minute or so, she speaks, "So, Jimmy, what d'you think is gonna happen? D'you think Pastor and Stan and everyone will vote you out?" Her voice, still pillow-muffled, is now relaxed, liquid, almost sleepy.

"I expect so. But so far not much is happening. Still, I can't see Stan, or Logan, putting up with my new honesty in the pulpit for very long, especially when Leslie and Carl and all the LBI'ers find out I'm moving in with you. Russ and Jodi will accept us, and maybe a few others, but no way a majority. To any good Christian clone, this is *way* out of line, what we're doing. No way can the LBI'ers accept us as lovers, or any born-again church for that matter. If we wait until we get married to live together, then perhaps we'd have more support. But I don't want their fucking approval anyway. I'm sick of bowing down to doctrines and religious traditions. We'll start a new church, you and me and Russ. We don't need a lot of people or money. I'll work at the weather station again. We can meet at Russ's house. I always wanted a small church anyway, one that's based on love and honesty. We won't put impossible rules and fearful doctrines on people. We'll let people share their feelings and be themselves. We can even have rock music and movies, and we'll talk about real things. And you and me, we can make love anytime we want without having to hide it."

"Now that sounds like *my* calling," Becki chuckles into her pillow as Jim lightly combs his fingers over her beefy buttocks. "Sure sounds *better* than handing out tracts on High Street, I tellyuh, especially the you 'n me part—oh, Jimmy, that feels *good* when you do my bum. I'm getting goose bumps." She closes her eyes into an expression of sweet serenity.

*O Jesus!* Jim thinks joyfully. *I never saw her so happy and released. But I feel it too, like I'm inside of her feeling what she's feeling. It's like I've been raptured fifty times in fifty minutes. I can't believe how fast things have changed.* Magic. Magic, magic bubbles burst in his brain. To touch her body, to satisfy it, to soothe it, to explore it, to know it, especially those private regions that a woman hides, fills him with exceeding wonder.

Like Sharon, Rebecca's hips are large and moonish, but her gluteal fat is firmer, more girlish, like a puberty butt. But the backs of her chunky thighs are much like Sharon's: soft, spongy, bulbous at the top—with a few diffuse patches of pink and violet pigment which add warm and cool accents to her ivory-vanilla flesh. Faint freckles and blemishes dapple Becki's back and shoulders, but her adolescent ass cheeks are fish-white and clear except for a few pimply red spots near the top of her gluteal fold. Jim's dancing fingers have raised up goose bumps on her hips and upper thighs like hundreds of tiny tits. These swollen skin papillae are topped by little blond hairs that are otherwise hard to see. But for him, the most provocative feature lies at the base of Becki's bum where the four-way intersection of her gluteal fold, her gluteal furrows, and the cleavage between her thighs forms a perfect four-pointed star, like a cross, with a dark diamond-shaped cave in the center. A few tufts of pubic hair, squeezing up within the fatty walls of this cave, tell Jim that it's actually the "doggie" entrance to her cunt.

"Oh, that feels nice," Becki coos as he dances his fingers down her thighs, over the backs of her knees, and onto her gracefully tapered cheerleader calves—which are bristly with leg whiskers. "*Yeah,* do my calves and my feet." Jim gazes and gazes at her naked body. He's so fascinated by her female physique that he knows he could look upon her and explore her and touch her forever without getting bored, that he could traverse her every curve and cave and hillock and valley, again and again, without exhausting the new-ness of her, that he could map her every freckle and pimple and blemish and hair, without losing his sense of awe.

"I feel a chill," Becki says, pulling the sheet up over both of them as she turns onto her side and snuggles close to Jim. Silence. No more teasing, no more bantering. Their intimacy has become quiet and tender and blissful, as if the bed sheet is a new skin that wraps them into one body, mind, and heart. Their sweet commun-ion feels more real and holy to Jim—there's no comparison—than any Eucharist service he's ever participated in, as if knowing

Becki's body and soul is to eat the true flesh of God.

He gently caresses her cheek. She sighs but does not open her eyes. Yet a tender smile curves her mouth. To look upon her face stirs worship in his heart—more than any Christ.

Wondrous words gather in Jim's bosom, but Becki speaks them for him. The velvet-edged words ride her warm breath as if she's talking in her sleep, as if she's sighing up out of a rapturous dream, "Oh, *Shan*ley, you make me *so* happy. I've loved you since that first time you came to my house, when I showed you the baby rabbits in the cardboard box. Every night when I went to bed I wished you were with me, so we could snuggle and talk, and be cozy and huggy—like right now. I've yearned for you *all* my life— even before I met you—and especially this year. I don't care if it fits. I don't care if it's sin. I don't care what people think. I love you, Jimmy Shanley. I just want to give myself to you again and again. Oh, I can't *wait* for you to move in with me."

"Me too, Becki honey," Jim replies tenderly. "I can't wait to hold you like this every night."

"Oh, Shanley, I *love* it when you call me 'honey.' It makes me feel like I'm part of you, like I'm your wife already."

"You *are* ... to me, and in the eyes of God—at least the God I hope for."

Quietness. Seconds pass, then a minute, then two. "I'm getting sleepy," Becki whispers as she briefly opens her heavy-lidded eyes. "Just hold me, hold me close." Jim takes a breath as if to speak but instead gives a long contented sigh. She has already said it all. Cozy bliss radiates outward from his heart filling his bosom with an elation that he's never known. Exulting in joy, his happy thoughts billow upward like cottony clouds on an August afternoon.

* * *

"It's ten to one; we must've dozed off," Jim says to Becki as he hurriedly puts on his pants. "I've gotta go to the church, like I said before, but I'll be back in an hour. I just hafta show a guy through the building and sign some papers for the school committee."

Rebecca, her naked breasts jouncing, rolls out of bed and pulls on her yellow robe. She gives Jim a sleepy grin but no reply. To her dresser. She brushes her brunette locks in front of her mirror. To the bathroom. Bathsheba bounds off the green chair and follows her. Next, the hissing tinkle of Becki peeing.

*God, things have certainly changed,* Jim says to himself. *She didn't even close the door.*

After brushing her teeth and pouring Friskies for Bathsheba,

Becki gives Jim a long toothpasty kiss at the door then blows a wet whisper into his ear, "You better hurry back, mister, 'cause I'm *hot* for you. When you get here, I'll go with you to get your stuff at Russ's house, then we'll come back here and pick up where we left off. We'll make it last all night, all weekend, like a fuckin' honeymoon. We'll only get outa bed to eat."

"Pinch me," Jim chuckles buoyantly. "I think I've been dreaming the past three hours." Becki quickly responds to his request. "Owh!" he exclaims. "Not *there*."

She laughs and chortles. "I just wanted to make sure you still got it, 'cause that little fellow's gonna get a workout later, I tellyuh." Her eyes are cobwebby, gritty, from sleep, but the blue in them sparks with coquettish mirth. "Oh, Jimmy, I feel like undressing you again right now. I can't get enough of your body, especially your penis. I love your cock. I wish you had an extra one for me to keep in my purse, so I can play with it and stare at it whenever I want. There's nothing like a hard dick. It's the ultimate."

"Becki Lea, you're too much. Your mom's right. You *are* oversexed."

"You better believe it. But you love it, don'tcha, Reverend? Well, you haven't seen *anything* yet. Shit, I'm ready now. My clit's halfway down to my knees." Becki cocks her hips back and forth saucily. Jim tries to tickle her, but she runs into the bathroom closing the door all but a crack. As he waves good-bye, she blows French kisses at him, darting her sassy tongue in and out.

\* \* \*

Flying, floating, giddy. Stoned on Beckiness. 1:03 p.m. Into the church. The 5th period bell is ringing. Pastor Jim combs his hair then wolfs down a coffee and three corn muffins in the kitchen, finishing just as Stan and Mr. Cranston arrive. After escorting Cranston through the building, Jim escapes to his office while Stan takes Cranston to Angie's office to get the certification packet from last year.

Jim kept a sober face during his official business, but now he gives a beaming boyish grin. *Russ will never believe it,* he declares happily to himself as he skips-floats over to the windows. *He'll shit when he sees Becki and me drive up, especially when I tell him I'm moving in with her.... Come on, Cranston, you asshole. If you and Stan will just hurry, I can sign your fuckin' papers and be back at Becki's by a quarter of two. O God, I can't wait. She loves me. She loves me. But this time we're gonna take it slow. But it's more than sex. I love talking and touching and knowing her heart. She's so*

545

*uninhibited. She tells me her every thought. It's like we have the same brain. She loves me. She wants me. And now I'm moving in. O God, I feel drunk. I love her. I love her so. Our dream is coming true.*

1:31 p.m. and 32°. Gray, cold, gloomy. The day is still wintry outside but not in Jim's mind. Sunshine, blue skies, fluffy clouds. He feels a warm breeze. He hears robins singing. He sees green fields and purling pools and gurgling streams. Pretty flowers, sweet fragrances. Daffodils and dandelions, and violets and mayflowers, and marsh marigolds. Yellows, whites, purples, and blue—blue hepatica play peek-a-boo from behind mossy rocks. The pine trees dance with delight. Rebecca, like a rose in bloom—Jim's "wild" prairie rose—has transformed the winter world into a spring garden. Beauty, beauty, all around—and everywhere he looks, he sees her face, even in the mirror. Happy, happy. Happy butterflies flit in his stomach.

\* \* \*

1:58 p.m. 59 Front Street. Love, love, beautiful love. Blue eyes, creamy thighs. Tits and hips and waiting lips. Jim roars up the driveway, parks behind the Escort. He doesn't see the gray sky; he doesn't feel the cold wind; he doesn't notice the walk, the oak tree, the porch, the stairs, just the number four on Becki's door. He shakes with joyful anticipation. He knocks. *Oh, Becki, I love you so. I can't wait to hold you.* He knocks again—no answer. He chuckles into a playful smile. *Now she's flirting, playing games.*

"Becki! Becki Lea! It's me. Cut out the teasing or I'm gonna tickle you good!" Still no answer. *She has to tease, always has to tease. Life with her is gonna be a crazy trip. I may not live through the first weekend.* He knocks a third time—silence.

He pounds harder. "Come on, Becki! Cut it out!" *She's hiding so she can jump out and scare me.* "Okay, gal, I'm coming in, and when I find you, you're gonna get it!"

Jim pulls his key. "You better hide," he kids as he swings open the door. "Because you're asking for it"—Bathsheba, but no Becki. He checks her closet, the shower, even under the bed: no Becki. Still smiling but puzzled, he surveys the scene. Becki's room still smells of love and sex, and looks much the same: unmade bed, covers on the floor, disheveled pillows, wadded tissues on the night table, radiator wide-open and popping. He sees nothing different except her yellow robe now lies crumpled on the bed, her clothes have disappeared from the floor, and the *telephone* has been reconnected; it now sits on the arm of the open sofa bed.

The phone, the phone. A chilly gust of fear blows Jim's smile away. *She's been talking on the phone. Who to? Where the fuck is she?* A cold fist of foreboding knots in his gut killing the happy butterflies; he feels suddenly sick. *But the Escort is here? Who'd pick her up? Jodi's still at school?* He hustles downstairs and checks with Mrs. Courtney, but she sheds no light on Becki's whereabouts. Back upstairs. He plops down at the kitchen table to think. Bathsheba mews, rubs against his leg. *Don't overreact,* he counsels himself. *Maybe Jodi needed her and she walked to the church? But why? She has the car? Maybe she went to the lake or the big rock, but why? She knew I'd be back at two?* Jim sighs, looks out the window at the frozen meadow. The snow is gone except for a few crusty drifts. The grass is matted, still dead, grayish in color. *Wherever she went, she can't be gone long. I'll wait.*

He gets up, pours Friskies for the cat. He paces. He sits. He paces. He munches from a bag of Fritos. He sits. He paces. 2:10, 2:20, 2:30, 2:35 p.m. "OH FUCK!" he shouts, gesturing up toward the fluorescent ceiling fixture. "SOMETHING'S GOIN' ON!"

Perspiring, panting, Jim peels out the driveway, roars back to the church. He meets Jodi on her way out and quickly relates his situation, but she has no news, just a witty quip: "Well, the way Becki left in such a heated rush this morning, I sort of figured you two had more on your mind than outreach." But Jodi quickly sobers, her brow knitting with mild concern. "But I have no idea where she is, Jim. She's probably so excited she had to get some air. She can't have gone far. Love makes us go crazy, but there's no reason to panic ... not yet."

To his office. Jim calls Becki's apartment—no answer. He gets up. To the windows. Back to his desk. He paces. He sighs. He sits down. He calls again—no answer. He repeats the cycle fifty times—or so it seems. He sighs. He anguishes. He chews the tip off a Bic pen. He feels dread, then hope, then silly, then angry. 2:55 p.m. He can't take it.

He zooms back to 59 Front Street. To the meadow, walking fast, running. To the big rock then down through the woods to the tracks. He falls ripping his knee, ruining his dress pants. He huffs. He limps. His bare hands are freezing in the cold. He hurries down the tracks to the gravel beach then back up through the picnic area, up the path, to the meadow—no sign of her. Desperate, sweating, burning lungs, white breath, welling tears. Back to the house. The Escort is still in the driveway. He goes inside: still no Becki, just Bathsheba asleep on the back of the green chair.

As Jim catches his breath, a pang of hot terror shoots through his heart like a bullet out of hell: *O God, something's wrong! Bad wrong! She'd never stand me up like this unless—O God, Becki, you wouldn't? But where are you?*

3:15 p.m. Panic, panic. Like a fear-stricken animal, Jim rushes to the Mustang and roars downtown. Familiar sights race by in a tearful blur. He searches everywhere: McDonald's, the diner, the streets, Flanagan's parking lot. Every young brunette makes his heart leap—but no Becki. He checks with Cathy Rosinski at Bergson's. She has news—she and Kevin are getting married—but nothing on Becki. He stops at Harry Hinton's. Harry and Judy give him a quick donut, but no word on Rebecca. Back to Front Street— nothing, no change, except the Coca-Cola clock is groaning toward four o'clock. The fear of the unknown knots and writhes like a serpent inside Jim's gut. His mind races, *She was mugged and raped in her driveway, and thrown in the river? Her dad arrived unexpectedly, or Amelia? Papa Chavin died, or Oma? She's having second thoughts about us? She called her mother? O God, never! She could never flip that much in less than an hour?*

Torment, torment. Jim races to Greeley Hill. He pulls into Russ's driveway, collapses behind the wheel. Russ's Fairmont is parked in front of him, under their new carport. Jim's undershirt, wet with nervous sweat, clings to his skin like Saran Wrap. When he doesn't go in, Russ comes out, still clad in his work clothes; he joins Jim in the Mustang. Fighting tears and panic, Jim pours out his roller-coaster day.

Russ strokes his beard. His words are gentle and logical, "It's hard to keep calm when a dream-come-true seems to be turning into a nightmare, but, Jim ... there has to be a reasonable explanation. And there's no point in racing around town like a mad dog. Come in, gather your senses. Bev'll be making supper soon. We'll keep calling. If we don't get Becki by ten o'clock, I'll go back with you, and we'll try to get to the bottom of this."

Soothed by Russ's words, along with a shower and a soft flannel shirt, Jim's boiling anxiety drops back to a hot simmer.

\* \* \*

10:20 p.m. Russ turns his Fairmont onto Front Street. Jim called at five, seven, eight, and ten. No answer. No Becki. Pellets of sleet ping off the windshield. Ragged and ruddy clouds scud low over Hadley Hill along with a billowing plume from Prescott Paper. Together they create an eerie glow in the eastern sky. The cold March night has snow on its breath but so far has spit nothing but a few bursts of sleet and freezing rain. "*Look,* her lights are on," Jim declares as they go up the driveway. "She must've just gotten home?" Raw cramping grips Jim's stomach. Hope and dread fight for his mind tangling his thoughts. There's now a full contingent of cars in the parking nook, but the Escort sits as before, looking more silver than red as it shivers under a thin coat of glaze and sleet.

The wind buffets the midsized Ford. Jim feels like an airborne-ranger at the door of a C-130. "If you're not back in fifteen," Russ says, patting him on the shoulder, "I'll assume all is well and go home. But if you have to make a run for it, I'll be here; but I uh—" Russ gives his warm Scottish grin. "I hope I don't see your fucking face until tomorrow."

Jim shrugs, cracks a nervous laugh, then plunges out into the night. An icy gust bites his face, takes his breath.

He steps gingerly up the frozen walk; the thin layer of sleet crunches like dry toast under his boots. *Maybe somebody called and fucked with Becki's mind, and she's been with them? No, no, I'm jumping to conclusions. Why am I so nervous about seeing her? I'm sure she has a good reason. O God, let it be the same as this morning.* Inside, up the stairs. The hallway is filled with the smell of popcorn and the happy beat of good-time rock 'n roll, not Becki's, but from Sergeant Brown's apartment.

Jim knocks on number four—no response. He knocks again—silence, save for the muffled beat of Chuck Berry and "Johnny B. Goode" coming from behind him.

*What the fuck!* Jim exclaims in silent panic. *Her light is on? That light wasn't on before?* He quickly inserts his key and opens the door. No Rebecca! No Bathsheba! NO *NOTHING*! EMPTY! VACANT! NO FURNITURE! Just the phone, a note, and Becki's key. Shock, shock. Jim's every nerve leaps, shudders, then shuts down. A strange benumbing trance protects him as if he's trapped in a time warp between lightning and thunder, between flash and confirmation. The telephone lies dead in the corner, its cord disconnected. The note is folded on the kitchen counter under the key. It's written on Rag Tag Teddies stationery, white paper with bears at the bottom—two teddy bears on a merry-go-round horse:

```
JIMMY,
    WHAT HAPPENED TODAY WAS WRONG AND DISGUST-
ING. WHAT WE HAVE IS NOT GOD'S LOVE. IT'S JUST
AN OBCESSIVE SEXUAL THING. YOU FINALLY GOT YOUR
WAY WITH ME, SHANLEY, BUT IT'S NOT GOD'S WAY. I
HATE WHAT HAPPENED TODAY. IT MAKES ME SICK TO
THINK HOW WORLDLY I WAS—BUT NO MORE. I REPENT OF
EVERYTHING I DID WITH YOU AND EVERYTHING I SAID.
LUCIFER USES LUST TO DECIEVE CHRISTIANS AND
```

*YOU'RE STILL DECIEVED, JIMMY. YOU CAN'T FOLLOW
YOUR HEART. THE HEART IS SELFISH AND FILLED WITH
INIQUETY. WE MUST FOLLOW GOD'S WORD. I PRAY
YOU'LL REPENT AND RETURN TO CHRIST. BUT I DON'T
LOVE YOU AND I DON'T WANT YOU. IT'S BEEN MY FLESH
ALL ALONG. AND YOU DON'T LOVE ME EITHER, NOT WITH
GOD'S LOVE. IN FACT, YOU TOOK ME AWAY FROM GOD.
I DON'T WANT TO EVER SEE YOU AGAIN. DON'T COME
AFTER ME BECAUSE I'LL NEVER COME BACK.*

*BECKI R.*

Her loopy high-schoolish words—a few misspelled—sear the screen of Jim's mind like an epitaph on his tombstone, but the message does not register. Thoughts form and whoosh through his brain, but they have no center of reference, no coherent unity, as when you try to conceive of reality outside the universe. He pockets the note, douses the lights, and departs; he calmly descends the stairs and exits into the freezing night.

The storm door doesn't catch, and the wind blows it open with a screak. Jim goes back to—TRUTH! TRUTH!

And the truth consumes him like fire, as if he's been doused with gasoline and set aflame. PAIN! PAIN! Shotgun blasts of pain crush his senses. BRAIN! BRAIN! His mind slams against his skull again and again like a battering ram, thundering, crashing, trying to escape this terrible knowing—but to no avail. HEART! HEART! His stunned heart pounds, staggers, then breaks with a sharp *CRACK!* as if it's his arm and the devil has snapped it over his knee.

Blinding white pain blares like an air horn in Jim's head, then turns hot and red. He gasps. He chokes. He grabs his throat. He staggers off the porch toward the oak tree. Ice, ice. He slips on the ice. He falls. He flounders. He claws for air like a man buried alive. Russ hurries out of his car.

But Jim catches a desperate breath, rolls to his feet, and tears past Russ around the house. He flees panic-stricken up into the meadow. Sleet stings his face. Tears blur the red sky. Ripping up from the pit of his gut, the scream starts as a guttural moan, becomes an anguished howl, then rises into a shrill warbling wail that slashes open the fabric of the night; it echoes across the valley like the keening bray of a British police siren.

Jim falls. He gets up. He sobs. He staggers. He clambers. He falls again. He crawls to the top of the hill. The frozen earth, like jagged concrete, rips open his gloveless hands. Sobbing, wailing, choking, he swallows despair and pain until the anguish in his gut becomes a sick and fiery gnawing.

As if beating the face of God, Jim angrily pounds the frozen turf until his fists are bloody. Gasping, burning, his lungs gulp the icy air along with the wild aromas of grass and dirt and imminent snow. But wildness quickly gives way to hot and fetid stink. Shrieking like a demon, he vomits and vomits. He heaves and dry heaves. He retches out his broken soul. Near to swooning, he collapses into the reeking puke. He quivers. He whimpers. He begs for death. Russ bends down but Jim, with a choking cry, jerks away from Russ's touch. He wants no consolation. He wants to die. Love has taken him from highest heaven to deepest hell.

Instead of holding Becki, he lies face down in vomit, hugging a frozen hill. The red and blaring horn in his head slowly subsides to a raw and distant buzz. Sinking, sinking—all is lost.

\* \* \*

The long pitiless night grays into snowy dawn. Pastor Jim stares blankly out the bay window in the Bradleys' living room. A fluffy mantle of white cloaks the lawn and shrubs. A few lazy snowflakes are still drifting down; the storm is dying and so is Jim—at least, that's how he feels. He slouches in a rocking chair, his throat aching with grief. Russ dozes on the divan. A bitter sense of loss lies naked in Jim's cried-out eyes. He knows it's over, a fate worse than death. Deep sobs, dry sobs, gushing, wailing, primitive sobs. He cried most of the night. Russ has been by his side, but they've talked little. Jim has said nothing except, "God's a *fuckin'* asshole. I quit. I'll *never* preach again."

Russ has shared no hype or cheery bullshit, but he did relate his conversation with Mrs. Courtney. He talked with her before departing 59 Front Street, while Jim whimpered in the car. She said that Becki moved out about six p.m., that two people helped her, a short-haired thirtyish woman and a large grayheaded man who came with a Ryder truck. Mrs. C. said they were in a rush and Becki would only divulge that she was moving out, nothing more. Russ and Jim immediately knew the grayheaded man had to be Stan Campbell, and Russ surmised the woman was Leslie Burton since she thinks like Stan and wears her hair up in a bun. But Jim still has no clue as to what happened to Becki during that critical hour between one p.m. and two p.m. yesterday afternoon, since Stan and Leslie were both at the church. What happened to make her flip so completely? to make her leave so suddenly? Nor does he know where she's gone. He suspects Nashua but has no confirmation.

Wide-eyed and vacant, Jim gazes into Saturday morning: 6:30, 7:30. Russ snoozes. The snow sifts down, diminishing, then stopping altogether. Jim blows his nose. His hankie looks like a blood-soaked bandage from a war wound, and smells worse.

Finally at 8:00 a.m., Jim retires to the guest room to hide and sleep. After a few hours of fitful dozing and garish dreams, he gets up and takes a shower, but doesn't shave. No one is home: Russ, Bev, or Sheila. Jim is glad. He doesn't want anyone to see him, except Russ who's at the church he figures. As Jim drives down South Meadow Road, the sun breaks through the clouds but not through the miasmal shroud that cloaks his soul. He can still smell the faint stink of vomit on his suede jacket, though Russ sponged away most of the smell when they got home last night. Jim feels groggy, cobwebby, hung over from grief. His eyes burn. He coughs. He clears. But he cannot swallow the lump in his throat.

He finds Russ waiting at the church but everyone else is gone. Russ, as Jim suspected, went to Saturday prayer meeting—not to pray, but to keep his eyes and ears on Stan Campbell and Leslie and the other Loganites. While Russ makes fresh coffee, Jim calls Sharon. *Maybe she knows where Becki went?* he thinks as he dials. *Or maybe she'll be relieved and want me back?*

No, on both counts. Sharon's voice is sharp with rancor, "I have no idea. I hope she went to *hell!* But it serves you right, James David. God's dealing with you. You're reaping what you've sown, and regardless of where she is, if you still love her—well, it's no different. I want nothing to do with you, as long as you have feelings for her."

Russ returns with two coffees, two pieces of buttered toast—for Jim—and a kind but wistful grin. As always, he moves without haste as if underwater. "You have to eat, Jim," he says as he places Jim's coffee and toast on the pullout shelf. Jim dunks then nibbles the toast. Coffee drips onto his blue sweater-vest but he doesn't care.

Russ sits sideways on the broken LA-Z-BOY. Hunched forward, elbows on knees, he clutches his mug with both hands. The steam from his coffee curls up into his face. His belly seems ready to pop the buttons on his denim work shirt. "So that was Sharon, huh?" he says knowingly. Jim nods then tells Russ what she said. Russ sips his coffee and slowly shakes his head. Finally, he shrugs and replies, his tone resigned yet undefeated, like Lincoln after Bull Run, "Becki loves you, Jim, and Sharon too, but it sure looks like you lost 'em both ... and maybe for a *long* time."

A lachrymose sigh escapes Jim's lips; tears well up. He fights them back. He tries to respond but chokes on his words. He pulls out his hankie, a clean one, and blows his nose. Russ, after pushing his Red Sox hat back on his head, shifts to what happened at prayer meeting, "It's hard to figure, Jim, what people are thinking or what they know. Stan's a master at smoothness and humble pretense. In front of the others he seems just as supportive of you as always— but he's a two-faced *ass*hole. I felt like ripping his balls off, that deceitful *fucker*. But I played dumb. I didn't let on about last night except to Jodi ... and she's heard nothing from Becki. The meeting itself was routine, though I did sense an undercurrent of anxiety."

Jim washes down a bite of toast, barely getting it by the lump in his throat. "Who else was there?" he asks, his voice thick with hurt.

"Not many ... Stan, Barry, and Carl, and Jodi. Let's see ... and Angela."

Jim coughs then wipes his runny nose with his hankie. "So, did Stan ask about me?"

"Not openly. But he talked to me after. He didn't seem angry, just disturbed. He says your emotional attachment to Becki is unhealthy and unbiblical, and that it's corrupting your preaching and crippling your leadership. He says the idea of breaking with Nashua is straight from Satan, and that God'll never allow us to have a church outside of Dr. Logan's authority. I guess he found out from Angie that you've decided to end all payments. He warned that if we try to break from LBI, we'll split the church, and lots of people will flee to Valley Baptist or to the Assembly of God, and all our hard work will be in vain. But he said nothing about calling a special meeting. In fact, he talks calmly like this storm is going to blow over. But he's not about to tip his hand to me. I suspect he fully intends to take over this ship, but I think he'd like to avoid a messy fight. He'd much prefer to have you resign."

Burst of emotion. Russ vents his Campbell-rancor: "All Stan cares about is *power* and pro*duc*tion. More members, more programs, larger crowds, larger offerings ... anything to keep the fucking schedule going. But he doesn't give a *shit* about feelings and intimacy and affection. That blind bastard wouldn't recognize *love* if a legion of angels wrestled him to the ground and made him look right at it. How can he? He has no fucking *heart!* He's so high and mighty in his Bible righteousness that he thinks nothing of playing God with your personal life and Becki's. He thinks nothing of helping her move. And anyone that hears about it will applaud him for standing up for Christian morality. Yet I doubt that's the reason. I doubt he thought much about righteousness or Becki's walk with God, not really. He just sees her as a problem that threatens the growth of the church. It doesn't matter that you and Becki love each other. If it can't be defined with doctrines, and measured with dollars and numbers and labels and job descriptions, it doesn't exist in Stan's world. No *wonder* he sees the heart as evil.

He can't make it fit. He can't buy it, sell it, label it, give it orders ... or place it on his organizational chart!"

Russ sips his coffee and calms a bit. "That's why we can't quit, Jim. We have a pure message of love, and you can preach it because you're living it. Besides, we want to have something for Becki to come back to after she gets sick of trying to kill her heart. Stan hasn't posted any notice, so we have a month, maybe more, to change this church, or at least to form a nucleus for a new church. But if you throw in the towel, we'll be handing everything to Stan and that's exactly what he's hoping for. He'd like to get rid of you without openly opposing you, as would Logan. I don't want you to keep preaching to please me, but I would ask you one thing."

"What's that?" Jim asks.

"That before you make a decision, you'll get away for a few days and think about it. Go someplace where you can be alone with your thoughts, where no one can call you or find you. I'll cover for you as best I can, but you must get away from this shit before you go insane. You must let your emotions settle. Then you can...."

Jim gazes at the office door. Russ's voice trails off into the *drip-drip* of melting snow and the distant rumble of the daily freight train. A flash flood of Becki-memories drown Jim's senses. Blue-eyed little girl, lost puppy, sweet daughter, doting, following, laughing, laughing, growing, growing—into a woman. Becki, Becki, teasing, flirting, loving, kissing, moaning, hugging sweetly in her bed. Love, purpose, living together. He smells her toothpasty breath, her perspiry glow, her perfume, her shampoo. He sees her beefy buttocks, her thighs, her tits. He brushes her hair back from her big blue eyes and cherub cheeks. Cute, cute, kittenish face. She looks at him adoringly. Heaven, heaven—but now it's *hell.*

The totality of his loss roars over him again, like an M-60 battle tank. The lump in his throat swells with hurt. He tries to swallow, to fight the swelling sorrow, but instead plunges into a gulf of despair. Defeat and fatigue ooze from his every pore. Jim swivels his chair toward the windows. His eyeballs scream with hot pain as if impaled on ice picks. No sunshine, no color. He sees nothing outside but black and gray. The pine trees are charred like after a fire. The ground is covered with ashes. Hadley Hill lies stark and bleak through the burned-out trees, like the battlefield at Verdun.

Jim smells vomit and death. He gasps, he breaks, he screams, "I'LL BE FUCKIN' *DAMNED* IF I'M GONNA PREACH FOR GOD! HE'S THE BIGGEST LIAR AND DECEIVER OF ALL! I WASN'T LOOKING FOR THIS!"

He crashes his chair back toward Russ, grabs his coffee mug, and hurls it violently against the wall by the door. White ceramic explodes all over the office. Coffee bleeds down the wall like monstrous black fingers. Heaving, sobbing, Jim collapses onto his desk; tears and snot run all over his open calendar book.

Minutes pass. Jim's sobbing gradually gives way to sniffles and snuffles. Russ cleans up the mess then retires to the kitchen. A bit later, he returns. Jim looks up. Russ has fresh coffee for both of them, and a white envelope. He places the envelope on the pullout shelf next to Jim's coffee mug, but says nothing. He simply sits back into the recliner and sips his coffee.

"What's this?" Jim asks, picking up the white envelope.

Russ chuckles and gives a wry half-grin. "Just a little something."

Jim opens it and finds six $50s plus ten $20s. "Thanks," he says to Russ, his voice weepy and hoarse. "Maybe I will get away for a couple of days and think about things, but I still doubt you'll ever see me in the pulpit again." Russ doesn't argue. Jim blows his nose. He feels better. Each crying fit, like an earthquake aftershock, releases a little more tension and hurt, helping him to accept the reality of his nightmare despite the continuing horror of it.

Jim makes a trip to the men's room, then he and Russ turn their attention to solving the who? and whereto? of Rebecca's departure. First, a long shot—Becki's dad is concerned but knows nothing of her whereabouts. Then, Becki's Aunt Amelia—but there's no answer. Next, the safest bet—Nashua. Jim calls each of the women's dormitories, Finney Hall, Edwards, and Stowe, but none of the dorm mothers are available and the student-assistants know nothing about Becki.

Finally, he plays his last card. He calls Alison in Puerto Rico, but he doesn't get Alison; he gets Ed, and Ed solves the mystery in less than ten seconds: "No, Jim, Alison's not here. She's in Nashua; she flew back on Thursday."

"Ahah!" Jim exclaims to Russ as he hangs up the phone. "It wasn't Leslie with Stan; it was Alison. Alison was the short-haired thirtyish woman. She must've cut her hair, and she does look thirtyish, though she's almost forty; and Mrs. Courtney sees everyone as younger than they are anyway."

Jim rings the dorms again, and this time uses his pastoral authority, demanding to speak to the dormitory mothers. The dorm mom at Stowe Hall finally confirms his fears, "Yes, Pastor Shanley, she's here. She's moving in right now. Her mother's helping her. Becki says she'll call you back in about thirty minutes."

Jim and Russ wait, but Becki never calls back.

# Chapter Thirty-six

Through a scrim of cold mist, Jim Shanley's broken heart beats westward out of Elkhart on Amtrak train #49, the *Lake Shore Limited.* Outside the window of his roomette, the ugly backside of an urban neighborhood glides by on the high ground above the tracks. The closely packed three-decker houses crouch on the mucky slope like a row of shivering hoboes. At their feet, junk and litter line the railroad right-of-way: broken sofas, rusty hot-water heaters, TV sets, mattresses, refrigerators, industrial spools, cinder blocks, soggy pieces of Sheetrock, shopping carts, dozens of tires, and plastic bags of trash that have been disgorged and scattered by dogs. Jim also sees living things: anemic trees, gray sparrows, gray weeds, a prowling cat, two excited mutts, and three Black kids waving in muddy coats.

Jim wasted no time in taking Russ's advice. He boarded Saturday evening in Framingham leaving the Mustang in the MBTA lot. He could've driven or flown to find solace, but a long train ride seemed to offer the best chance for peace, especially since he likes riding trains, and hadn't slept on one since 1957 when his dad took him to St. Louis to see Stan Musial and the Cardinals play. The regular rocking of a train usually calms Jim's spirit. But this time, even the clickity-clack of wheels on track failed to alleviate his Becki-agony.

Cloistered with his sink, bed, and toilet, he found solitude but no solace. Rocking, swaying, turning, sighing, he lay all night in thorns of despair, and filled his valley with tears of anguish. No phone, no schedule, no duties, no escape, just him and his nightmare. Torment, torment. Becki's pouty face, a haunting specter in his mind, uttered the words of her "Dear Jim" note again and again, keeping time to the rhythm of the rails: *clickity-clack,* "I'll never come back," *clickity-clack,* "I'll never come back." Springfield, Pittsfield, Albany, Syracuse. Darkness, darkness, lights ripping by, more darkness and stars, then clouds. Buffalo, Erie, foggy daybreak in Cleveland. French toast, bacon, and coffee in the dining car, a chat with a little bald man from Elyria. Lake Erie out the window, a service stop in Toledo, then out of Ohio into Indiana.

Underpasses, overpasses, graffiti-covered walls. A gray Catholic church, an asphalt playground, teenagers playing basketball. Faster, faster. Crossing gates, flashing lights, clanging bells: *DING! DING! DING! DING! Ding. Ding*—fading, gone. Now suburbia. Highways, shopping centers, little league fields. New schools, new churches, new homes. Pulling, pulling, a pair of red-silver-and-blue blunt-nosed diesels throb and whine westbound into the morning, blasting long sorrowful cries against the gray murk. No more Elkhart, just Indiana farmland and the rushing clatter of switchovers and girdered bridges, and *WHAWOOOM!*—the deafening roar of a passing freight. *Rip-rip-rip,* telegraph poles zip by like a picket fence. Old wires hang frayed and slack from ancient Coke-bottle insulators, while a modern Conrail signal cable rises and falls between the poles like an unending sinusoidal wave.

Sunday, March 4th. 11:18 a.m. Jim feels better, not good but resigned. Like a slow acting tranquilizer, the cradlelike rocking of the train is finally lulling his troubled soul, as does the incessant clack and whir of the rails echoing up through the toilet. A soothing drowsiness is overtaking him as he gazes at the patchwork hues of the late-winter countryside. Grays and blacks, new greens and browns, and passing Indiana towns—Osceola, Mishawaka, South Bend, New Carlisle, La Porte, Otis, Burdick, Chesterton, but the *Lake Shore* stops only at South Bend. Jim's '50s-era Heritage Class roomette—sitting room by day, bedroom by night—though cramped, is comfortable, private, and complete.

His pillow behind his head, he props his denim-clad legs against the wall. Drowsy, drowsy. He's drifting off, but a startling change in scenery snaps him back from the edge of sleep. Smoke, fire, blast furnaces. Switching yards, drawbridges, ship channels, huge hangerlike structures. It's the Gary USX steelworks, still active but an exception. The other mills along the Conrail tracks lie brown and black and oxide-orange amid weeds and shrubby trees, now just overgrown gardens of crumbling concrete and rusted steel. Midday in mid-America, not dead but dying. Unlike highways, trains catch America in the raw without her pretty clothes or makeup, whether the raw beauty of nature, or the raw ugliness of what man has done to nature. The steelworks give way to sand dunes and Lake Michigan. The drizzle has stopped but the sky, like Jim's heart, is still a dense slab of lead. *Oh, Becki,* he thinks wistfully. *We touched heaven, but now it's gone. I hafta face it. Maybe I'll move back home and help Dad and Gary Bob?*

Chicago, South Side. Jim doesn't see a single white person, but he does see Comiskey Park and the Sears Tower sticking up into the clouds. The *Lake Shore Limited* backs into Chicago Union Station. Tracks, trains, a beehive of activity. He sees other Amtrak trains arriving, departing, Amtrak cars being serviced and washed, and old green-and-white Metra commuter diesels: round-nosed, humming, waiting. As the train backs into the dark bowels of the station, he sees mail cars, express cars, baggage cars, crumbling concrete walls, grimy stone and brick, naked lightbulbs, steel columns, steel beams, thousands of rivets, and peeling paint. The train slows, screaks, then jerks to a halt.

Jim, bag in hand, follows the other sleeping-car passengers off the train. Clamor, suitcases, baggage carts. Diesel fumes, diesel engines: roaring, throbbing, deafening. Bodies, bodies, anxious bodies, fast walking, loud talking; wheel chairs, children holding tightly to adult hands. This fast-moving stream of disembarked passengers sweeps Jim toward the station—and into it, into more hustle and bustle, and stentorian voices growling train information, and redcaps pushing hand trucks piled high with luggage.

The lower concourse is like a little mall with souvenir shops, newsstands, bookstores, vending and newspaper machines, rows of pay phones, and a half-dozen eateries. The fumes and engine noise follow Jim in from the tracks, but quickly give way to people noise—and people smells: perfume, unbathed flesh, pizza, hamburger, coffee, pastry, urine, popcorn, cigarettes. People, people, all about him. Nervous, hurried, milling, moving—like excited ants. Greeting friends, hugging relatives, rushing in and out of rest rooms, talking, laughing. But some walk alone, long-faced—like himself. *What is this?* Jim thinks. *This place is more crowded than Logan Airport. I didn't think people rode trains anymore?*

After stopping at a stand-up lunch counter where he downs a hot dog, a coffee, and a donut, he heads for the main concourse on the upper level. High, vast, sunlit. Voices, echoes, hardwood benches. What a difference: it's a cavernous hall with marble walls, marble stairs, marble floors, everything of marble. High vaulted ceilings, skylights, fluted Corinthian columns, acanthus capitals, statues of gods and goddesses. It reminds Jim of a Greek temple. At the information kiosk in the center of the concourse, he checks the TV monitors: *Train #5, California Zephyr, departing 3:20 p.m. That's it. Lots of guys at the academy rode that train, but I never did. Now, after all these years, I'm finally doing it ... but all by myself.*

The *Zephyr* crawls out of the station ten minutes late, trundles southward past the Amtrak and Metra service facilities, then at 16th Street swings sharply to the west onto Burlington Northern tracks which will take it all the way to Denver. Faster, faster, the Amtrak Superliner picks up speed. The Chicago skyline recedes. Jim unpacks, making himself at home in economy bedroom #3. Modern and bi-level with a plastic "new" smell, the Superliner sleeping car seems more like an airliner than a Pullman. A bit larger than a roomette, his room has a picture window with pull curtains, a pull-out table, a full-length closet, but no sink or toilet. The rest rooms are airplane-style, downstairs. Two facing seats, mauve to match the curtains, convert into a bed at night. There's another berth that folds down from above for a traveling companion—but Jim has none.

He settles back, gazes out the window. Suburbs, suburbs, traffic-clogged highways. But greater Chicago gradually gives way to corn-belt farms. Plowed fields stretch into the distance like nut-brown corduroy. *I hope I don't have to piss in the middle of the night,* Jim thinks as he pulls off his Dingo boots, *but this train is not bad. I like looking out the window. There's something so soothing about it, if only Becki*—a surge of hope surprises his heart. Perhaps the holiday atmosphere and the first class accommodations have triggered his fairy-tale side which he figured was dead. But the feeling quickly succumbs to fatigue, then hunger.

To the diner. Jim has a six p.m. first-call reservation. Steamy aromas. The diner is crowded. The steward seats him with three college guys headed for the University of Nebraska at Lincoln. Jim marks his menu. He looks out at Galesburg, Illinois; he sighs to himself, *These fellows look so eager and optimistic, and ready to tackle the world—oh, cruel deceit of youth. I remember those days when I was the "captain of my soul" and "the master of my fate."*

Jim feels like telling them that life is going to crush their ambitions and break their hearts, but he knows they'll just laugh it off as he did when he was their age. So instead, he eats his salad and joins their small talk. Soon the dumbwaiter rings, bringing their food up from the kitchen below, and their red-vested Amtrak waiter, balancing his tray against the sway of the train, brings it to the table. Prime rib, broccoli, baked potato—no silver or china, or crystal or linen, but the food is good, and the price.

Jim tops off his supper with coffee and pecan pie, pays his bill of $9.75, and goes back to his room, just in time to see the Mississippi River as the train trundles across it on a long bridge that leads into Burlington, Iowa. The wide river looks black and flat in the cloudy last light of day.

As last light fades into full dark, Jim fades with it. He buzzes for Sonny, the sleeping-car attendant, a smiling middle-aged Negro with crisp curly hair, salted gray. While Jim visits the rest room, Sonny makes up the bed, leaving two mint candies on the pillow. Jim tips him three dollars then turns in for the night. Ottumwa, Creston, Omaha, Lincoln. The *Zephyr* races across the Great Plains. Hastings, McCook, Fort Morgan. Clouds give way to stars.

Monday morning: Jim wakes to clear skies and a red glow in the east; he feels rested and senses a newness of spirit. At 7:15 a.m. (Mountain Standard Time) Sonny brings coffee and a *Denver Post*. Jim drinks his coffee and looks out the window. Tumbleweed, dusty-brown prairie, windmills, water troughs, thousands of white-faced Herefords, some grazing, some in livestock pens. Snow-covered mountains loom on the western horizon. He hasn't laid eyes on the Rockies since he graduated from the Air Force Academy in 1968—he's a most inactive alumnus.

* * *

1700 miles, and two time zones, to the east, Alison and Becki have just entered Dr. Logan's Blantyre office for a counseling appointment. "You both look so lovely," Dr. Logan says as he escorts them from the double oak doors to the marble fireplace. Becki walks shyly behind her mother; she has butterflies. Her mom seems so relaxed around Pastor, but she feels exposed, ashamed, as if wearing no clothes. She feels inferior to her mother. She dreads this meeting. Dr. Logan gives his V-shaped victory smile. "Rebecca, you've grown up to be such an attractive young woman. I remember when you were this high"—he indicates with his hand—"but even when you were in Sunday school, I knew you'd blossom one day into a beautiful woman of God, just like your mother." Becki blushes, smiles politely, then averts her eyes; she doesn't feel beautiful or godly. "And, Alison, I must say you look ten years younger. Puerto Rico must agree with you. You look tan and healthy. And your hair is so pert and pretty. I like it short."

"Oh, thank you, Pastor," Alison replies fawningly. "I do feel good, and I've never been happier. Ed and I ... well, the Lord has blessed us beyond what we dared to dream or pray. We prayed for a building to house our school, and the Lord has given us five buildings and twenty acres of land."

"That's what I hear," Dr. Logan says. "I understand it's an old Catholic boys' school. Ed told me about it when he called last week. I do think that property will fit into our plans."

Alison gives a cheery smile and a triumphant toss of her head. "It's up in the hills," she bubbles, "on the road to Cavey, and the view of the ocean is fabulous. It's perfect for our team. I'm sure the Lord will use it mightily."

Logan nods but does not reply. After an awkward moment of silence, Alison shifts to her motherly voice, "Pastor, I appreciate you taking time to get personally involved with this matter. Rebecca and I have had several heart-to-heart talks since I arrived, and I now feel much better about everything. I can see God's hand in all of this." As she speaks, Alison nervously fingers the lapel of her blue gabardine suit.

The doctor picks up a brass-handled poker from beside the fireplace. "No problem," he assures Alison. "This is why I'm here.

I'm glad you and the fellow from Brendon Falls—"

"Stan, Stanley Campbell," Alison says, interrupting him to supply Stan's name.

Logan reaches over the screen and stirs the fire. "Yes, Stan Campbell. I'm glad you both brought this to my attention. I'm sure God will make it work together for good."

"Oh, I know He will," Alison affirms, smoothing her short bob of brunette hair. The brown of her hair is lighter, warmer, full of tropical sun, and her auburn highlights are almost blond, a deep strawberry blond. "Becki's ready to put all this behind her. There comes a time when we must grow up in the Lord. On the way over, God gave me a verse for comfort from 1st Corinthians 13: 'When I was a child, I spoke as a child, I understood as a child, I thought as a child; but when I became a man, I put away childish things.'"

Becki stands demurely next to Alison. She feels self-conscious as if she's back in 8th grade at an LCA guidance-counseling session. She hates it when her mom talks about her as if she's not there; it's humiliating. Nonetheless, she knows it *is* time to "put away childish things."

"Yes, I love that verse," Dr. Logan replies as he replaces the poker and dusts his hands. "The Lord's way of teaching and molding us is not often the way we would choose, yet it's always perfect. In fact, let's have a brief prayer together, to put this entire matter into his hands." They join hands and Logan prays.

"Yep, the Lord's way is always perfect," Alison echoes after Logan finishes his prayer. "How well I know. I remember when I was twenty. God does have a marvelous way of opening our eyes— but that's enough motherly analysis. I'll leave you two to talk." Alison gives her daughter a kiss on the cheek and departs.

Monday, March 5th. 9:20 a.m. Becki has been in the dorm for two days, and now she's alone with Pastor Logan, the one person, next to Christ himself, who makes her feel most guilty and ashamed. Yet like a spider caught in its own web, she is resigned to the fact that she must have godly counsel and pastoral care if she's to escape the entanglements of her own foolishness.

"Rebecca, my dear, do have a seat," Dr. Logan instructs as he leads Becki to the business end of his office. "Would you like a cup of coffee or a Danish?"

"No thank you, I'm fine," she replies respectfully, her voice small and contrite. She sits down in one of the yellow Louis Phillipe armchairs in front of Logan's desk. Her hands on her lap, she sits forward in rehearsed repose. She feels out of place in such an elegant chair as if her lowly presence will corrupt it. She feels the same about the office. She's only been in Logan's office once before, when her fifth-grade Sunday school class came to have their picture taken with Pastor because they had the best attendance for the year.

Dr. Logan sits down at his desk and slips on his reading glasses. His grainy voice is relaxed, "Your mother says you're all moved in?" As he speaks, he looks at Becki over his glasses which ride low on his large patrician nose.

"Yeah, I came up Friday night, and moved in Saturday."

"Finney Hall?"

"No, Stowe for now. There's no room at the freshmen dorm."

"So your mother helped you?"

"Yeah, and Stan Campbell, he drove the truck."

"Yes, Stan Campbell. He seems very concerned for you."

"Oh, he is. He helped me get my thinking straight. And he's letting me store a lot of stuff at his house, and his wife is keeping my cat, until my aunt can come from Boston to get her."

The doctor leans back in his chair. He adjusts his suit vest. "Well, I'm glad we have an elder in Brendon Falls who's firmly rooted in the Word. My heart breaks over Pastor Shanley. It always hurts when a brother falls into unbelief, but especially with Jim, because I love him dearly and I have such high regard for his ministry." At the mention of Jim's name, a stab of feeling jolts Becki's heart shaking her repose, but she quickly recovers, firming her countenance with pious resolve. "But, Rebecca, the reason I wanted to see you this morning, I uh ... well, your mom and I, we want the best for you. We want you to experience the full joy of Christ. The fact that you've returned to Bible school shows you've already rededicated your life to the Lord. But I wanted to personally assure you that I'm interested in your continued growth and happiness as you pursue your calling."

Logan picks up a letter from his desk. Becki isn't close enough to tell what it is, but it looks official. He looks at the letter a moment then puts it down, and removes his glasses. "But speaking of Pastor Jim," he says, moving abruptly from generalities to specifics. "I just talked with him on the phone a few minutes ago, and he tells me that you left because your relationship with him has turned into a romance." Logan gestures toward Rebecca with his glasses. "Jim says that you've fallen in love with him."

"That's not *so!*" Becki declares vehemently; her tone is suddenly pious, indignant, defensive.

"So you have no romantic feelings for him?"

"*No,*" Becki asserts, confirming her denial; but her conscience won't allow her to leave it there. "Not really," she adds. Heat steals into her face; her stomach clenches tight.

Logan raises his thick eyebrows. "*Not really?* What do you mean, Becki?" Her repose shattered by his bull's-eye questions, she doesn't reply. Fear, pain, guilt, shame. Her indignation gives way to disturbing emotions. Pastor Logan places his glasses on the desk and gives her a fatherly smile but his dark eyes are disconcerting.

Becki shrinks from his eyes. She looks down at her riding boots then at a circle of sunlight on the red carpet. Her cheeks burn hot. She wrings her hands anxiously. She wishes she could hide.

"I know it's personal and painful," Logan consoles. "And you certainly don't have to tell me, but anything you say is just between you and me and the Lord, and remember our purpose is not to condemn or to assign blame, but to help you and Pastor Jim get back into the fullness of Christ. Jim's going through a crisis in his faith, and in his marriage. Of course, you know that. We want to help him recover from all this so he can be reconciled with Sharon and the children, and so he can again serve the Lord with the fervor that he had before. Isn't that what you want, Rebecca?"

Becki's hands feel clammy. She pushes them down her pink-denim skirt. She replies toward her hands, her voice wavering, to her dismay, "I do. I-I, I uh ... I want everything to be right. I feel bad for Sharon and the kids—but it's *him,* not *me.* I never did anything. He's the one that wants a romance, not me. I never did, and I *still* don't. I told him, and told him."

She swallows hard. Her eyes fill until the circle of sunlight on the carpet becomes blurry. She fears she'll break and make a scene. She bites her lower lip, fighting back the tears, then she goes on, "Lately, he's been flirting with me all the time, and last Friday he came on to me. We were getting ready to go on hospital visitation like we do, and we were joking and laughing in a friendly sort of way. That's when he got wicked obnoxious and out of line, and started saying suggestive stuff. He hugged me hard. He said he wanted to undress me, but I didn't let him. I told him to leave but he wouldn't go ... so I told him I was gonna call my mom. When he saw me dialing the phone, he finally left."

Becki glances up to see Pastor's reaction. Nodding his head slowly, he seems satisfied with her concoction of lies, truths, and half-truths. She averts her eyes. She waits. She smells the fire in the fireplace; it reminds her of Papa Chavin's woodstove. She wishes she was a little girl again sitting on Papa's lap—back when love was simple and not complicated by sex and God's will.

Logan smooths his thinning hair, still more ginger than gray. "Fine," he finally replies. "I didn't mean to accuse you of sexual misconduct. I know you're not that kind of girl. I just wanted to hear your side of things.... Would you like to tell me more?"

Becki nervously picks her fingernails with her thumb. "Jimmy, I mean Pastor Shanley, he's changed. Not just his preaching, but with me. He used to respect me like a daughter, like a sister in the Lord, but the last few months he's been looking at me the wrong way, and he always wants to hug me, but not like a brother ... and he jokes about lewd things, and behaves like a flirt."

"He behaves like a flirt? What does he do? I think I know from what your mother said, but I'd like to hear it from you." Becki senses carnal curiosity in Pastor's voice but she doesn't dare attribute prurient motives to him. The very fact she could think such a thing demonstrates her depravity and desperate need for help.

"Well, like I said," she replies, "I never did it with—"

"I don't mean fornication. Of course, you didn't, but tell me about the lewd talk and sexual advances, and the flirting. What did he do?"

Becki looks up. She feels herself blushing but not burning. Her emotions center between embarrassment and contempt. "Well, he talked about wet dreams and stuff. And he tried to get me to confess about my sexual experiences."

Logan leans forward attentively elbows-on-desk. He squints his eyes until they look like gun slots on an armored vehicle. "Well, what did you tell him?"

"Nothing," Becki replies, looking down again, "I told him it was personal. Besides, I don't have anything to tell anyway ... not really."

"I see.... Well, did he try to kiss you?"

"Yeah, a few times, but I didn't let him. And he always wanted to touch me. He'd touch my face and my neck and my hair, and I always had to push him away ... and one time, when we were sitting on my sofa, he started touching my legs, and tried to pull up my skirt."

"And what did you do?" Logan asks.

"I pushed him away and told him to leave," Becki replies.

"Did that happen recently?"

"No, it was uh ... that was back in December. Uh ... Christmas Eve, I think? I should've left then, but I thought if I made my feelings clear, he'd stop and we could continue with our ministry, but I guess I was wrong."

Dr. Logan swivels his chair toward the Palladian windows. After a long pause he replies in a voice out toward the terrace, "Rebecca, you are most assuredly the innocent party in this unfortunate situation but I'm afraid you do bear some responsibility— not because of sinful intent but because of spiritual immaturity." The doctor holds his head arrogantly back; his tone is now judicial.

"Even though you never had romantic intentions toward Pastor Jim, the very fact that you left Bible school and went to Brendon Falls, and spent many hours a week alone with a married man, gave the devil opportunity. And he took *full* advantage. He deceived you, then used you to draw Jim away from his calling, and...."

Becki stares at the back of Pastor's head, at the nape of his neck where his hair spills a bit over the stiff French collar of his pinstriped dress shirt. She listens with a vague sense of unreality as if her life is no longer her own, as if she's been swept into a new place by overwhelming circumstances beyond her control. For a moment she doesn't sense the responsibility he speaks of, or the guilt she felt only a minute ago.

But her reprieve is short-lived as Logan swings his chair back and gazes right at her, impaling her with his hypnotic eyes. Becki wants to look away but she doesn't dare. Pastor seems high and lifted up as if he's looking down at her from the very throne of Christ. His eyes grow larger and darker until they become great black ovals with holy auras like two suns in eclipse. Blood pounds in her temples. Her face feels hot and tight. Tension clots the mucus in her throat. She shakes inside from shame as if he knows her every sin, her every lie. She clenches her hands together, so hard that her nails cut into her palm. Shame, shame. She abhors herself.

"We must *always* be on guard because Lucifer is very cunning," Logan admonishes as he continues his counsel. Becki hears his voice as if it's coming up from her own conscience. "He knows how to capitalize on our poor choices. He knows how to turn fatherly affection into something ugly and sinful. He knew you were close to Jim back in the old days, back when Jim was a student. I remember you, Rebecca, when your mom first came. You were such a spirited child and we all loved you dearly, but I also worried about you, that you'd have to learn much the hard way, and I guess you have—"

"No *kidding,*" Becki interrupts, eagerly agreeing with his counsel. Logan laughs good-naturedly then gives her an open-handed gesture of acceptance and reassurance. She laughs too. As she does, she feels trust and loyalty for Pastor welling up within her together with a profound sense of relief and peace.

Breakthrough. It's done. No more inner turmoil, no more wrestling with her passions. Regardless of her feelings, she'll go with the Word of God, and Dr. Logan will shepherd her. Becki feels an irresistible almost-sexual desire to do whatever he tells her to do, anything to please him—to please God.

Logan sobers and again captures her with his eyes. He speaks with his hands as well as his lips, "I don't say this to condemn,

Becki, but to encourage you and to show you how great God is. Greater is he that is in us, than he that is in the world. The fact that you've returned to your calling shows this to be so. And you now have a chance to love Pastor Jim in the truth, in the Holy Spirit. You can turn Satan's treachery into a triumph for God."

"That's all I want, Pastor," Becki replies. "I just want God's perfect will to be done."

"Well, I must say you've learned faster than most. But if you really love Jim in the Lord, and his family and his church, and if you really want to help restore him to a full life, here's what you must— now are you sure you're ready to obey Christ?"

"Yes, I am. I have no desire but to seek the face of God, and to follow you, Pastor, as we serve in his kingdom."

Dr. Logan turns on the full power of his eyes. "It's your decision of course, but if you mean business with God, Rebecca, you must cut it off completely with Jim Shanley. It sounds cruel but the Word commands us to flee youthful lusts. You must not talk to him or communicate with him in *any* way. You must show him that he has *no* future with you. You must love him with 'tough love' so he'll face the truth and return to Christ, and to his wife and children ... so he'll repent of his heretical preaching and return to his calling. You must put your relationship with Jim behind you once and far all, so you can train diligently for missionary service. There *will* be personal pain, but you must remember that God's love is not selfish but self-sacrificing, as Jesus showed us on the cross. You must let the Word of God govern your life, so Lucifer will never again use your emotions to lead you astray. Youthful passions are temporary and deceitful, Becki. You can *never* trust them!"

Pastor sweeps the air over his desk as if slapping Satan with the back of his hand. "The Lord wants to make you a devout woman of God who'll lead many to Christ. He wants to give you peace and self-control and purity, and someday a loving husband and children of your own.... But if you disobey and turn again from your holy calling, God will chastise you severely, as any father must. The stakes are high, but I'm confident you'll put God first from this day forward. And as your overseeing pastor, I cherish your soul, and I look forward to fellowshipping with you during your college days here in Nashua.... Now, before you go, I need you to sign this statement."

\* \* \*

After a one-hour service stop in Denver, the *California Zephyr* resumes its journey westward on the tracks of the Denver & Rio

Grande which assault the front range of the Rockies head-on. Roaring, roaring, full power. The *Zephyr* ascends higher, higher, coiling, cutting back: a great silver snake gleaming in the bright morning sun. Looking back, Jim sees Denver lying below them in a blanket of smog. Beyond the city, the flat Colorado plains stretch forever eastward like a vast inland sea. It's like taking off in an airplane, just slower. Two quick tunnels, then another, and another; finally, tunnel #8, and no more Denver. The *Zephyr* has penetrated the eastern massif. Climbing, climbing, but slowly. 25 mph, then 20. Tight turns, tunnels, tunnels, 29 tunnels. The train winds back and forth on narrow ledges, among crags and crevices, then enters South Boulder Canyon running high on the snow-covered south wall. Faster, faster, 40 mph. Next comes Plainview, Crescent, Pine Cliff, Rollinsville, not really towns, just railroad maintenance sites, except for Rollinsville which has a dozen houses.

As the *Zephyr* climbs toward the continental divide, Jim's spirit rises as well, ascending like a phoenix out of the ashes of his broken heart: *I'm not gonna quit. I'm gonna fight. I'm not goin' back to Texas—fuck that! I'll move in at 59 Front Street myself. The apartment's already in my name. I'll be damned if I'll let Logan and Campbell take our building and steal our people. Russ is right. Becki's not gonna come back to a middle-aged loser moping around on his father's farm. We've got the true message. I'm not gonna hide it. We'll build a church based on love and freedom, and honesty, and heart intimacy.*

Sudden darkness. Amtrak #5 enters the Moffat Tunnel which runs directly under the continental divide. The tunnel is 6.2 miles long and 9200 feet above sea level. For ten minutes Jim sees nothing but blackness outside his window, then sudden bright light, deep snow, people skiing; it's Winter Park Ski Resort. The day is now cloudy, and frigid compared to Denver, but still bright after being in the tunnel. Now descending, the *Zephyr* coasts to a halt in the town of Fraser. The Amtrak station, an alpine-style log structure, is buried in snow and is partially obscured by clouds of white exhaust hissing out from the two F-40 diesels. Three dozen skiers get off and board blue resort buses.

The train pulls out resuming its westward trek. Jim feels invincible. He rides the rest of the way fantasizing about victory as if he's MacArthur returning to the Philippines. Westward, westward, descending, descending—along the Fraser River to Granby, then the Colorado River and Byers Canyon and Gore Canyon, no more snow. Bond Junction, Glenwood Canyon, Glenwood Springs, Grand Junction, no more Colorado River. Into Utah, through

Helper, then nightfall and Soldier Summit; finally, Jim's destination: Salt Lake City—at 10:07 p.m. (MST).

\* \* \*

Brendon Falls—four hours earlier. Dr. Logan scans the faces of the BFBC members who've assembled for a special meeting. Matt Garrett, who's sitting to Logan's left on the small dais, leans over and whispers, "I know you've met a lot of Shanley's people, Doctor, but to refresh your memory ... the potbellied fellow in the third row, in the argyle sweater, that's Russ Bradley. We don't have a chance with him. He's more loyal than Lassie. Same goes for Jodi Donovan. She's the lanky brunette in the back, the one in jeans."

Garrett brushes, with a limp-wristed sweep of his hand, a bit of lint off his stylish cashmere cardigan, then goes on, "And the chubby mulatto in the cook's uniform, he'll vote for Jim regardless. But our people are here too. There's Carl Baker on the front row, and Leslie Burton just came in. And we have others who didn't come with Stan to Nashua last week, like Mary LeBlanc; she's right behind Leslie, the little one with a witch's nose. She's the one who called last Wednesday about Jim's sermons, and—"

Rich Beckman interrupts, speaking into Logan's other ear, "Stan says we have 38 people here, out of 51 on the list. Do you want to start?"

Logan checks his watch: 8:10 p.m. "Yes, go ahead," he says.

Beckman gives a thumbs-up signal. Stan hoists his massive frame out of his chair and steps to the lectern. He picks up the microphone, but before he can speak, Russ Bradley stands and objects, "This meeting is illegal. You can't call a meeting to discuss the dismissal of a pastor unless you give thirty days' notice. Besides, it's outrageous to meet while Pastor Jim's away." Jodi Donovan echoes Russ's objection. A contentious murmur spreads through the sanctuary.

Carl Baker rises from his front-row seat to challenge Russ. He gestures weakly with his bony praying-mantis arms; his voice is passionless, like a recorded weather forecast, "As a deacon in this church, and as clerk of the BFBC corporation, I must respectfully disagree. I have the pertinent bylaw right here in my briefcase, and—" A chorus of heated voices, pro and con, interrupt Carl.

"Looks like we have a hung jury," Dr. Logan whispers to Rich Beckman. "I guess we're going to need the tape after all."

Beckman cants his lipless mouth into a cunning half-grin. "No problem, Pastor. Molly has it in her office bag right here on the front row. But let's keep it up our sleeve until our backs are against the wall."

"Hold it! Hold it!" Stan exclaims from the pulpit. "Let's calm down an' do things decent an' orderly, like God says in the Word. An', Russ, why don't you come up an' sit on the stage with the other board members. We have a seat for you right here." Stan indicates with his brawny Bunyanesque hand.

"No thank you," Russ responds, giving an adverse grin. "I'll stay right here."

"Suit yourself," Stan replies to Russ, a bit of bite in his voice, then shifting to his stentorian preaching timbre, he addresses the whole group, "Let's have a time of prayer so the Holy Spirit can calm our 'motions: O Father, we come tonight with griefous hearts. We all love Pastor Jim, an' we pray that what we do here tonight will be accordin' to your vision for this church. We pray for Pastor Jim. We pray for his marriage, for his kids. We pray...."

As Campbell prays, Dr. Logan looks around the small BFBC sanctuary. He looks at the low ceiling and the naked fluorescent lights, at the stacking chairs and the forty-plus bowed heads. "Dick, doesn't this remind you of Pastor Chase's church in Gorham?" he whispers to Rich Beckman. "You know, the basement at Bethel Baptist where we used to meet on hot summer nights, and Pris would play the piano?"

Beckman strokes his pocked face. "Yeah, that's where you preached your first sermon back in '59. It's hard to believe we were ever involved with something so small." Stan prays on; he holds his left hand high in a holy salute to God. "So what's bugging Amy?" Beckman asks Logan as they continue their hushed conversation. "She hardly said a word all the way down. Does she still have her nose out of joint over Molly's promotion?"

"I'll say. She's been acting like a jealous adolescent. She says if we don't get engaged this year, she's leaving."

"Not to worry. She's been saying that since Priscilla's funeral. Women are so damn emotional and possessive. They hiss and fuss like cats when another broad comes into their territory—remember her tirade over Teri?—but they won't leave if they're getting fed well." Beckman gives a whispery cackle as does the doctor.

Stan finally concludes and recognizes Russ, who speaks from the floor, "I too want things to be done decently and in order. Therefore, I move that this meeting be adjourned until April 5th which is one month from tonight."

"I second the motion," Jodi Donovan adds from her seat in the back row. Murmurs of agreement and disagreement ripple through the body of believers, but after Stan's prayer the chorus of controversy is more subdued, like the dry buzz of summer insects.

"Okay," Stan says, "the motion's made 'n seconded. Is there any discussion?"

"Yes," Carl Baker announces. Stan instructs Carl to come up.

Beckman leans over to Logan again. "This's exactly the scenario that Stan predicted. I must say, Pastor, he's a loyal soldier. It's too bad he's so uneducated and rabble-mouthed. He clips his words like he grew up on the rough side of the tracks."

"I'm sure he did," Logan chuckles. "And he dresses tackier than the folks in Biddeford. That gray suit looks like it came off the bargain rack at Anderson-Little. I'd never put this guy on TV, but he's exactly what we need here in Brendon Falls, especially if we give this pulpit to Tom Hudson."

After pulling several papers out of a clasp envelope, Carl picks up the microphone and begins, "As clerk of the BFBC corporation, I would like to read bylaw 4:22, paragraphs E and F:

> No BFBC pastor shall be dismissed until, and if, a two-thirds majority of the BFBC members vote for dismissal at a special meeting of the BFBC corporation. Such a meeting cannot be held unless a majority of the directors vote to have such a meeting, and they notify the pastor and the membership in writing thirty days prior to said meeting. The thirty-day notice *can* be waived, but only if the pastor has been accused of behavior so deviant that it jeopardizes the church itself. Such behavior falls into three categories: criminal acts, acts that indicate emotional breakdown, and lewd and lascivious acts.... In the case of lewd and lascivious acts, the board must have at least two sworn affidavits that the pastor has indeed committed such acts.

Carl adjusts his glasses then sweeps his hand back over his bald dome as if pushing back invisible hair. "We have two sworn affidavits which charge Pastor Shanley with lewd and lascivious acts." Whispery "ew's" and "aah's" of surprise issue from the gathered members. "Since neither party is present tonight, I shall read them to you." Carl starts, but Russ again objects—to no avail. Stan, and the flock, want to hear them. Stan instructs Carl to continue. "First, I have an affidavit from Doris Campbell. I read:

> Pastor Shanley often comes to visit when my husband is gone. Sometimes he flirts with me, and one day when I had just come out of the shower, he grabbed me and kissed me, and tried to reach inside my robe. Jim Shanley has been a good pastor and he has a caring heart, but he has a weakness for women. I love him as a dear brother in Christ, but I also love his wife and family. I pray that he'll seek counseling for this "thorn in the flesh."

A buzz of reaction rushes through the room, but when Carl announces that the second affidavit is from Rebecca Reinhardt, quiet quickly returns. Drama, expectancy, not a sound. Carl reads:

Last Friday (March 2, 1984), Pastor Shanley tried to seduce me in my apartment. He hugged me aggressively and told me that he wanted to kiss me and fondle my breasts. He then tried to undress me, saying he wanted to have sex with me. I broke from his grasp and resisted his advances. His language was lewd and obscene. I told him to leave but he became obnoxious and began to swear at me with four-letter words. I told him I was going to call my mother. When he saw me dialing the phone, he finally left. This was the worst but not the only incident. Over the past four months, Pastor Jim has harassed me sexually on numerous occasions. He flirts with me using seductive words that have prurient connotation. He tells me dirty jokes and stories from dirty magazines. I repeatedly told him that I have no romantic feelings for him, and I certainly did not encourage his advances in any way. But whenever I objected to his improper behavior, he would threaten to fire me from my job. I felt trapped. Several other times he tried to kiss me, and one time he pulled up my skirt and touched my leg. He even sneaked into my closet and took a pair of my dirty panties from my laundry basket. I came to Brendon Falls to minister for Christ, and to prepare for the mission field, but this continuing sexual harassment makes it impossible for me to stay. I've learned a lot from Pastor Shanley. He's a gifted evangelist, but he has a serious problem. I pray that he will seek professional help.

Silence gives way to hushed clashing of opinions: "That's a lie"—"I told you so"—"I don't believe it"—"I knew it all the time." Stan calls for order but the flock goes on talking, arguing.

During the commotion, Dr. Logan compliments Rich Beckman, "You did a good job on those affidavits, especially Becki's. This place is buzzing like a beehive. You have a creative way of making things sound more severe than they are."

"True," Beckman whispers conceitedly. "But I've had a lot of practice. And Alison helped; in fact, she wrote most of it."

"From the look on Becki's face in my office this morning, I doubt she's as innocent as she professes," Logan remarks hushedly. "Especially when I told her that I'd just talked with Pastor Jim, and that he said she was in love with him. She blanched then turned pink. She's not telling us the *whole* story."

"But Jim's gone?" Beckman replies curiously. "His secretary doesn't even know—oh, oh, I get it." Beckman snickers under his breath. "Well, Pastor, I'd say you're just as creative as me. Moreso when it comes to counseling the guilty, especially impressionable young college girls." The doctor also snickers—behind a cough.

"But we don't know anything for sure," Logan cautions. "We

can't put words into her mouth, at least not too many—of course, compared with Lucas in Lewiston, this is *mild*. Remember, he was the teen pastor and they got pictures of him porking a high school honey in the choir loft? And we had to sneak him out of town, then wheel and deal to get the negatives." They both chuckle. "X-rated, we could've sold those shots to *Hustler*. But Lucas knew better than to bite the hand that feeds him."

The hubbub finally settles and Stan recognizes Russ, who again argues that the meeting is illegal, but to no avail; his motion to adjourn loses by a vote of 31 to 13.

"I didn't wanna call this meetin' myself," Stan says apologetically after the vote. "But as head elder I had to, not jus'cuz of the af'davits but also 'cuz of other charges I'll 'dress in a moment, but first I wanna interduce Dr. Logan, our overseein' pastor. He's also a member of our board—Dr. Logan."

Applause fills the hall, but as Logan stands at the oak pulpit, he also notices a number of cold stares. He takes a sip of water then addresses the gathering: "Even though Pastor Beckman and I are members of the BFBC board and we're concerned about Pastor Shanley's preaching and conduct, I want to assure you that we didn't come to Brendon Falls to persuade you one way or the other. The decision to dismiss or to retain Pastor Jim is *strictly* a local matter. It was only after lengthy discussion with your head elder, Stan Campbell, and others of you here in Brendon Falls, that I reluctantly agreed to this special meeting. So Pastor Beckman and I will not participate in the arguments, nor will we vote. We at home base feel that the relationship between a branch pastor and his flock is a sacred one, and we shall never violate it or interfere with it. I know this is a very trying and heartrending time in your church. I know that you love Pastor Jim dearly, and so do I. I just pray that each of you will let God"—Logan says "Gawd"—"be your guide and that'll you'll remember the words of our Lord in Matthew eleven: 'Wisdom is justified by her children.'"

"Beautiful job of fence-sitting, Pastor," Rich Beckman chuckles hushedly as Logan sits down. "You should be a politician. I couldn't have done better myself."

Matt Garrett helps the doctor slip out of his suit coat. "This may cost more than it's worth," Logan whispers to Garrett as Matt folds the garment over the back of the chair. "Jim's gifted at winning the trust of his people. It's a shame to lose him. It'll take us two years to build the offerings back up. If he'd just play ball and get off this *bull*shit honesty kick."

"Yeah, but the bullshit's already out of the barn," Matt quips. "Jim's so damn quixotic and uncompromising. You can't deal with him, especially now that he thinks he's in love. I had a hunch we were headed this way ever since Campbell alerted us about Becki back in September."

Stan, back at the pulpit, reads several Bible verses that relate to accusing an elder then says, "I have before me the official list of al'gations. Now the first charge, of bein' lewd 'n 'civious, is the reason we didn't hafta wait thirty days—"

Sudden loud crying interrupts him, but he quickly deals with it. "Sylvia, I must ask you to take her to the nurs'ry. This meetin' is no place for a small child. Teri 'n Jennie, they're watchin' the kids, an' please hurry 'cuz this is important."

Stan picks up where he left off, "Like I say, the first charge is the reason we didn't hafta wait thirty days, but there are also five other charges." He starts to read them, then stops to put on his glasses. "Excuse me," he says, giving an embarrassed chuckle, "this typin's too small. Now I'll read 'em: One—Pastor Shanley has been lewd 'n 'civious toward the opp'site sex. Two—Pastor Shanley has been unfaithful to his wife, if not in deed, certainly in his 'tentions 'n 'peerances. Three—Pastor Shanley no longer b'lieves the Bible to be the highest authority. Four—Pastor Shanley no longer accepts the LBI statement of faith. Five—Pastor Shanley no longer sees Dr. Logan as our overseein' pastor. Six—Pastor Shanley justifies his actions by sayin' the human heart is naturally good, that it's a higher authority than the Bible, which directly counterdicts the docturn of the 'fall of man.'"

After removing his glasses, Stan goes on, "Now we've already heard two sworn af'davits, one from my wife an' another from Becki Rheinhold, but 'fore we vote on the issue of dismissal, let's hear what the rest of us have to say. An' since I'm already up here, I'll start.... First off, let me say that Pastor Jim Shanley is my friend, an' it breaks my heart what's happenin'. We got a crisis, not 'cuz he's sinnin', we're all sinners, but it's 'cuz he's been deceived by the devil into thinkin' it's right."

Becoming fervent, Campbell chops the air in his awkward Frankensteinian manner. "Pastor Jim now preaches that we should follow the 'victions of our heart even if they go against the Bible. Now we all know that's heresy! In Jer'miah the Bible says, The heart is deceitful an' desper'ly wicked! We hafta put the Bible *above* our hearts. I think that Pastor Jim is stressed-out an' 'sausted. He's near to a breakdown. So it's our duty to save this church ... an' to help him get right. We can't be sentimental. We gotta love him with 'tough love' 'til he repents. I don't see him as a bad person. I see him as a soldier who's sufferin' from battle fatigue. He must step down for a season to rest, to 'gain his faith ... for his sake, for his fam'ly's sake. An' someday he'll thank us for it. We're Christians. We *must* obey the Bible." Stan's supporters applaud loudly. Stan acknowledges, tipping his hoary head as if to say, "You know I'm right."

After Stan, Carl Baker comes to the pulpit; he speaks meekly, his voice inflectionless as if teaching a theology class, "I have profound admiration and affection for Pastor Jim ... but we have to put the Word ahead of personal loyalties. Feelings are unstable and fleeting but the Word of God is forever. Until the past two weeks, Jim Shanley preached that the Bible is the highest authority. I have a hundred sermon tapes. But now he says to follow your heart. This is false teaching; I refute this teaching. What if your heart wants to commit adultery, or murder, should we follow it? This new ultralibertarian doctrine is nothing more than the promiscuous philosophy of the hippies in the '60s: 'If it feels good, do it.' No Christian can condone such teaching. 'God is not separate from his Word,' in Psalm 138:2. 'Whosoever keepeth the Word, in him is the love of God perfected,' in 1st John 2:5. Likewise, 1st John 1:5-9 tells us that no redeemed person can live in sin and have the fellowship and blessing of God, and Romans 6:1 and 6:15 warn us that the grace of God does not grant us license to live outside the absolute standards of holiness set forth in scripture. The future of our church is at stake. If our light goes out, depraved human hearts will multiply in this area until every soul is under the dominion of Lucifer's cosmic system. This is why we can no longer support Jim Shanley as our pastor. We must ask Dr. Logan to appoint a new shepherd, a pastor who will honor God's Word, who will—"

"This whole affair is just a clash of *male* egos!" Janet Buford shouts, her voice hot with rancor. "If women were allowed to be pastors and elders, we'd settle things in a more harmonious way. I'll be *damned* if I'm staying to listen to this juvenile bickering!"

"Now she's a feisty bitch," Rich Beckman whispers to Dr. Logan as Janet storms out of the auditorium. "And the best-looking broad I've seen in this town. But she's wrong. If the women-libbers ever take over the church, we'll have more fights than ever, and a lot of emotional weeping and moaning and social action ... but *no money.*" Beckman laughs, as does Logan, but the doctor covers with a cough.

Carl, seemingly flustered by Janet's outburst, gathers his notes and leaves the stage. Jodi Donovan speaks next, from the back row. Her voice brims with outrage: "Bible verses don't touch me at all. I came here because I was lonely and my life was on the rocks. Well, my life is still on the rocks. I can't say I've changed at all, but I have found a *true* friend. Jim's my friend. He loves me without a scorecard. Now he's goin' through a rough time and we're ganging up behind his back. It's like we expect him to be super perfect, whatever that means? If we judged *our*selves this way, we all would've been voted out long ago. Besides, how can you know about his personal life, just from two signed statements? Did you ever stop to think that he and Becki have been close for *ten* years? And now they're supposed to stop loving each other just because they got into an impossible situation? It's not fair. Jim's a human being; he's one of us. He laughs with us. He cries with us. He pulls us out of bars in the middle of the night. He's always got time to talk. He listens to our hopes and fears and failures, mostly failures. And he never gets preachy and pious. He never claims to have all the answers, but I don't want answers! I want what he's got. I want honesty! I want love!"

"I couldn't agree more," Lelsie Burton declares after coming up to the lectern; she speaks in the spirit of Hera but she sounds like Zeus. "Pastor Jim has been a friend to all of us and I love him as a brother in the Lord. But God has shown me that a minister *must* live above the common level of life; he *must* set the example for the flock. How can we teach our young people to obey God's laws concerning sexual purity when the pastor of the church is chasing a 20-year-old? And I'm sorry to say this, but it's not just college women. I've seen him looking at the girls at the teen center. Pastor Jim has an obsessive attraction for young women. It's called the 'Virgin Mary' complex. My heart breaks to think he has such a wordly problem. I speak as a concerned mother. When I consider my Wendell and Tommy and Lisa, I shudder to think what they must face as the world turns away from God. They face more demonic temptation than any previous generation ... drugs and alcohol and homosexuality and pornography, and movies and TV, and now the plague of AIDS which God has sent to judge sexual sin. Even a year ago we'd hardly heard of it, but now it's an epidemic. We're in the *last* days! We must have a pastor who's strict and morally upright. We can't trust our children to a man who lusts after young girls, and has the gall to say he's following love!"

Next, Beverly Bradley, looking over her half-eye glasses and speaking in a let's-be-reasonable tone: "I share Leslie's concerns, but I think we're overreacting. Jim Shanley has never advocated sexual promiscuity, nor does he live in a playboy spirit. He's always been very serious about love and intimacy, sexual or otherwise. Perhaps his new doctrines make him unsuitable to serve as a pastor in an evangelical church, but we should wait until school is out to decide this matter. We shouldn't make big changes during the school year."

"I don't care what *nobody* says," Barbara Sims declares from the second row. "I *know* Pastor Jim loves God, an' nuthin's gonna change my mind. I'm stickin' up for him, an' I got a dozen people outside who wanna speak for him too, but they're not members or nuthin'."

After a brief discussion on stage, Stan says, "This is highly 'reg'lar. Nonmembers can't participate in corp'rate proceedin's, but we'll hear two of 'em, but the rest hafta stay outside."

Barbara disappears out the door and soon comes back with Harry Hinton and Judy Kerrigan. She escorts them to the front of the sanctuary, not onto the stage but in front of it.

"Now there's a couple of *Deadheads*," Matt Garrett whispers to Dr. Logan. "I haven't seen hippie hair and headbands like that since I lived in Greenwich Village, back when I was going to cooking school. With that skull and crossbones on his back, he looks like he just stepped off a *Black Sabbath* album cover, and she looks like a flower child."

"Shanley really got in with the street people," the doctor whispers back. "Only trouble is, he never got 'em to cut their hair and to join the church. In fact, I'm afraid they converted him."

Harry Hinton speaks slowly, and without guile, "I don't know what Pastor Jim has done, and I've got no quarrel with you folks, but he's the only preacher that ever treated me like ... well, he never looks down on me like a lot of people. You know, he comes over and we eat donuts and pizza. And he never gets heavy on me about coming to church. I don't recall any other priest ever wanting to be my friend, like Pastor Jim. I think this town needs him."

Then Judy, her voice shaking from shyness, "Uh ... well. I-I, I'm not used to talkin' in front of people or nuthin' ... but I like Pastor Jim. When my cousin Jodi first tol' me she was goin' to this church, I didn't know what to think 'cuz my sister Ruthie said Pastor Jim was jus' another religious bast—creep. An' all my life since I was a lil' girl, I was afraid of priests 'n nuns. Then I met Pastor Jim in person. He was downtown, an' he gave me a blue card with verses on it, but he didn't preach at me or nuthin'. Then I started seein' him more, an' he remembered me, an' that made me feel good. An' he didn't make me feel guilty like a priest or a nun. Then we invited him for coffee an' he came, an' later he brought Becki, an' I liked her too 'cuz she's like him. I don't know shit— pardon my French. I don't know nuthin' much 'bout God, or what's goin' on in this church, but I do know Pastor Jim, an' I like him."

As Harry and Judy depart, Beckman nudges Logan with his bony elbow. "It never fails," he whispers. "A pastor gets into trouble and his die-hard supporters always show how he cares for the down-and-outers. My heart *bleeds*."

"I want to do the godly thing," Sylvia says, speaking from her seat, her dark tresses flowing over her shoulders. "But I feel for Pastor Jim. It's not hard to see why his faith is weak. His marriage is breaking up, and his life has turned upside down. I'm sure he feels guilt and pain and regret. Besides, I think a pastor *should* be honest about his feelings; maybe not every Sunday, but he shouldn't be afraid to confess his doubts. And how do we know for sure about his relationship with Becki? How do we know that he thinks it's good to go against the Bible, or to dishonor Dr. Logan? We all have times of doubt. I can't vote tonight. I need time."

"Me too," Angela agrees, her reedy voice trembling just short of breaking. "How can I vote on this? This is *too* sudden. We must wait and pray. We must let Pastor Jim tell his side."

Next, Barry Buford from his usher's station in the back. He sounds fat and anxious, "I agree with Stan that we must ask for a new pastor. But like Angie and Sylvia say, we're rushing this. If we vote tonight, I'm going to abstain."

"As you know, I'm on Jim Shanley's side all the way," Russ says speaking from the stage but without the mike. "Now I don't have much to add since Jodi and Harry and Judy have said it all. But I will say this again. Jim should have a *chance* to hear these charges and to offer a defense. I don't care what the bylaws say. We shouldn't let a few overly excited zealots ram through a quick action.... But it looks like taking a vote is the only way to end this meeting. I doubt there's a two-thirds majority against Jim, but let's find out. Let's not drag this out *any* longer. Let's do it and go home. I call on you to vote for Pastor Jim. I move that we vote now."

As Russ talks, Logan speaks hushedly to Beckman, "This guy's dangerous, even more than Jim. He's a *damn* rebel and he's filled with pride. He shows no humility toward delegated authority. He's got no respect for the kingdom of God. But he's right about the vote; we'll never get two-thirds on the first ballot."

"Not to worry," Beckman reassures. "After the votes are tallied, we'll have Stan announce that he has new evidence. That'll set off a storm, but when Stan tells them that the new evidence is a tape of Pastor Jim confessing, they'll all want to hear it, regardless of where it came from. And after they hear it, they'll be ready to *hang* him." Beckman snickers arrogantly under his breath.

*   *   *

Tuesday, March 6th. 5:55 p.m. The sun is just settling behind the pine trees. Pastor Jim drives into the church. Deserted, no cars, nothing in the parking lot, but puddles and potholes. After spending the night in Salt Lake City, at Howard Johnson's on South Temple Street, he boarded United flight #151 and recrossed the country '80s-style—above it all. He landed at Logan, took the T to South Station, then commuter rail to Framingham to get his car. He stopped for a Whopper at Burger King, then launched into rush-hour traffic. Despite jet lag, his adrenaline is flowing. He feels like a boxer before a title fight; he can't wait to preach his heart, to proclaim his hopes. He parks behind the church and hustles inside.

*What the fuck is this?* he asks himself upon finding his office door locked. *I never lock this door?* He fumbles for his key. *I never use this key. It's not even the right one. It doesn't fit.*

Back outside. Tires on wet gravel, white Fairmont, Red Sox cap, Stromberg coveralls. Russ rolls his window and says, "I figured you'd come here. Follow me to the diner. I've got news."

Down Reservoir Road. Jim feels concern but no panic. A valley fog has formed along the river and has spread its tentacles over the town. Jim and Russ descend into this somber murk. Jim turns on his headlights. Chilly memories of winter circulate among the houses and buildings and trees and streetlights. The old factory town looks like the setting for a Sherlock Holmes mystery.

Russ parks behind the diner facing Walnut Street. Jim gets into Russ's car. Russ gazes down at the steering column. He speaks slowly with a resigned sense of loss as if he just came from a funeral, but his eyes smolder with indignation. "Well, Jim, I don't know what you decided on your trip, but either way, it's pretty much academic. Instead of Bible class last night, Stan, he called a corporation meeting. It's over, Jim. They fired you; they voted you out."

Dismay, disappointment. Jim deflates like a punctured balloon but Russ's words do not devastate. After the trauma of Becki's departure, even the worst news can only register as an aftershock. No reply, nothing, no talk, just the low roar of the diner's ancient refrigeration units. Outside Jim's window, a beat-up dumpster overflows with trash bags and cardboard boxes. Beyond the dumpster, a nasty maintenance shed crouches like an ogre in the fog. Jim stares at it. The corrugated steel shed, no bigger than an outhouse, is locked with a padlock and is black with grime up to the lock. He feels hot; he opens the window a crack. Dank air drifts in along with kitchen aromas and the stink of garbage, and the adhesive rip of tires on wet asphalt which modulates the groaning of the refrigeration units. Dismissal: probable, even expected, but not the suddenness of it. He feels the stabbing pain of knives in his back but moreso he feels cut off. The foggy night seems filled with unresolved conflict as if Jim has entered a field of battle only to discover that the enemy has withdrawn beyond the range of his guns. His emotions run from hurt to outrage to anxiety to resignation. He lifts his gaze to the streetlight on Walnut Street. It hovers, diffusely haloed in the fog, like an illumined teardrop.

"I thought they had to give thirty days' notice?" Jim says, finally responding to Russ's news.

"Me too," Russ replies, raising his hands in concession. "They fucking outfoxed us ... me anyway. As it turns out, our bylaws state that a meeting can be held immediately if the elders have two sworn affidavits that the pastor has committed lewd acts. It's a fucking loophole. I never look at that shit anyway. Let's face it, Jim; religious assholes can always find something written down to justify their actions as they murder love."

Russ gives a scornful snort that turns into "Shit." Then he goes on with his analysis, "They got us with a low blow, Jim, a bunch of low blows, starting all the way back when Logan gave you the green light with Becki. It's clearer now ... how it was a setup. He knew you'd follow Becki across many forbidden lines until your Christian reputation was in jeopardy which would give him insurance against you. I figure that Logan and Garrett have been suspicious about our allegiance to Nashua for a year or more, and Campbell, that hoary-headed bastard, kept them well informed. If we'd continued to suck Logan's dick, he would have covered you, regardless of his suspicions. But when you went wild in the pulpit and it become apparent that we weren't going to resume our payments to Nashua, he decided to act. I'm sure they would've preferred to have you repent or resign, but when you blasted Stan in your kitchen talk last Monday ... I guess that convinced them that they'd have to expose you, not because they cared about the purity of our pulpit—fuck, Logan doesn't give a *shit* about your righteousness—but he had to drive a wedge between you and the body in Brendon Falls. He knew you were popular with your flock, and he and Stan could never gain control unless you were discredited. I'm sure there's a lot more that went on behind the scenes. But this is how I figure it.... Now Becki's sudden departure, with Stan's help—and I'm sure his help went well beyond loading the truck—and your three-day absence gave them a window of opportunity, so ... bang, bang, they drew up the affidavits, and called the meeting. Of course, if they'd seen you crying in your office Saturday, they might've held off in hopes that you'd quit on your own, but those bastards don't know anything about broken hearts."

"So I guess Becki signed one of the affidavits?" Jim says.

"Yeah; she wasn't there but she signed a statement saying you harassed her and made uninvited advances."

Jim sighs ruefully. "That figures ... and who was the other?"

"Doris Campbell—"

"Doris!" Jim exclaims, rolling his head back. "Whaa—you're kiddin'? What'd she say about me?" Another knife of betrayal, this one longer like a sword, runs him through, back to stomach. Chagrin and resentment rush in through the wound to join the Becki-hurt and disappointment already in his gut.

"She said you tried to seduce her at her house."

Jim shakes his head and gives a snort of exasperation. "She got that *back*wards, I think. Shit, she's the *one* who undressed. Besides, that was a year ago. I told you about it. What the hell got into her? That doesn't sound like Doris. Stan must've grilled her then made her sign it.... But Becki wasn't at the meeting, huh?"

"No, I doubt they want her out of Nashua until they brainwash her good."

"How about Sharon?"

"Nope."

"So who else was there?"

"Most of our regulars ... and the assholes from Nashua, Logan and Garrett and Beckman. And Logan brought his sweet-assed secretary bitches."

"So who voted for—"

"Hold it; there's an easier way." Russ nods his head toward the backseat. "I have a tape."

"Tape?" Jim asks curiously.

"Yeah. Before the meeting I popped a long-play cassette into the master deck in the side closet. I got it all, just like a Sunday sermon, at least everything loud enough to register on the main mike, and I'll fill you in on the rest." Russ grabs a Sony tape recorder from the backseat. Jim shifts to get more comfortable, crossing his legs ankle-on-knee. Russ places the recorder between them on the front seat. "I think you'll recognize the voices." He pushes the play-button. Time ticks by. The tape plays. Russ interprets. Five minutes, ten, twenty, and thirty. Hurt, hurt, hot and lacerating. Jim's sense of loss and betrayal grows until his heart is a hot fist of pain in his bosom, especially after hearing Carl Baker read Rebecca's affidavit. Though he figures her piously worded statement was prepared for her, the words still cut deep, not like her note on Friday night, but enough to reopen the gash in his heart.

"Shit!" Jim exclaims as Russ pushes stop after playing most of the tape. "Fuckin' Campbell makes it sound like he's doing me a favor, like he's sending me on R-and-R. He double-crossed me. Yet he wants applause for it."

"And he's going to get applause and a lot of it," Russ declares. "He's standing up for the Bible and godly morality. He's advocating discipline and 'tough love' in the Lord. He comes on like your savior, but in truth, he's a fucking Judas, and Logan and Garrett bought him for thirty pieces of silver. They probably promised him a diploma or even ordination." Russ slashes the air with his hand. "Outwardly, they're making a big deal over you and Becki, and your preaching, and your battle fatigue, but the *real* issue is allegiance. You've broken ranks. You won't bow down anymore. Logan sees you as a renegade who will lead others to rebel against his authority. But they don't want to look bad. So they say they *love* you, that you're really a good guy, just exhausted and having sort of a breakdown. They want to look godly. They want to be commended for nailing you. It's *sick!* But it's consistent with Logan's whole evangelical program—look loving, talk loving, be kind, be gentle, quote verses. Sell, sell, sell, make good impressions!"

Jim doesn't reply but gives a sigh that grows into a moan. His Becki-pain turns toward tears, but his grief catches on the way up becoming a lump in his throat. Russ, his anger subsiding, probes the fog as if Logan's sinister motives are lurking in the misty darkness. The soupy murk shrouds the Fairmont with cold cushiony silence. The passing cars, the groaning of the refrigeration units seem distant, like echoes in a dream. The lump in Jim's throat slowly dissolves as a wet scab forms over the wound in his heart.

"So Janet actually walked out, huh?" he asks Russ.

Ghosts, ghosts. Before Russ can reply, two phantasmal figures appear in front of the car, floating in the copper-colored cone of fog under the streetlamp. The ghostly figures come closer. Saucy skip, orange glow of a cigarette. Skinny slouch, Boston Celtic cap. Jim rolls down his window to cherry lips and Poindexter glasses. Two faces peer in, one pretty, the other pimpled; it's Haley Cameron and Billy McArthur.

"Mom told me that Mr. Campbell fucked you over," Haley remarks with her usual saltiness. "He's a regular shithead. I never liked him; he yells at me. If I'd been there, I woulda told him a thing or two, but I had to babysit for Paul 'n April. Besides, I'm just seventeen, so I can't be a member or nuthin', but it doesn't matter now, 'cuz I'll never set foot in that fuckin' church again."

"I don't even want to go to the teen center anymore," Billy adds in his croaky used-to-be-squeaky voice. "Mrs. Burton is always on my case 'bout whether I'm saved, 'n the fat guy, Barry, he used to be wicked nice, but now he says I can't wear my *AC-DC* sweat shirt."

Pastor Jim tells them that he's glad to have them as friends because he doesn't have many left. Haley then softens and says, "Well, I like bein' your friend. I don't care if you're a sinner or what. I don't care what people say." After saying that, she gives Jim an affectionate pat on the shoulder, and she and Billy take off across the parking lot.

Jim rolls up his window then gazes into the fog as another hush settles over the car. The naked maples on the other side of Walnut Street look surreal as if they're dismembered hands reaching up into the murk. Becki ebbs and flows in his mind as fatigue sweeps over him. Jet lag, time change, he almost dozes, but instead sits up with a start as a calico cat jumps up on the overfull dumpster and disappears under the partially open lid. Emerging a minute later with a morsel of food, she jumps down and scampers across the street toward the vacant lot.

Russ drums his fingers on the dash. No more anger, as lazy laughter plays in his eyes. "Janet left all right," he says as he finally responds to Jim's question. "Marched right out. We all should've done it. She's got balls for a girl. She's always pushing women's rights, but that's a bunch of shit. She just needs a man who can melt her hard edge. I bet she's an animal in bed, and fucking Barry's in love with Garrett, and Garrett's running Nashua, and he and Logan and Stan are condemning you for loving Becki ... and Janet hates Stan. What a *fucking* soap opera. How'd she end up with Barry anyway?"

Jim gives his first grin of the night. "I've been asking that question ever since I did their wedding."

They both chuckle then Jim says, "So, Russ, are you gonna keep me in suspense all night? What happened when the vote was taken? Are you gonna play the rest?"

"Let's see," Russ replies after sobering, "it was 17 against, 15 for you, and 12 abstentions, counting Janet."

"Don't they have to have two-thirds?" Jim asks curiously. "I thought we lost?"

"No, we won on the first go. But Stan quickly huddled with Garrett and Beckman and then announced he had new evidence."

"New evidence?"

"Believe me, this was the *lowest* blow. Listen to it." Russ starts the recorder:

**(Crowd noise, muffled male voices, shuffling papers, clunking, then Stan Campbell—his pious voice tinged with anxiety.)** "Hold it! Hold it! This meetin's not 'churned. Please sit down. We got new evidence, new information. We got a tape that'll answer a lotta questions an' move a lotta doubts. It's a tape of Pastor Jim talkin' with

Dr. Logan, in Dr. Logan's office at Blanter Castle."

**(Clamor, crowd noise, anxious voices, muffled voices, loud clunking, then Russ Bradley speaking with passion.)** "Wait a minute, Stan! Let me have the mike. You mean Pastor Jim was taped in Logan's office? What the hell is this! Watergate! There's nothing in the bylaws about tapping phones and bugging offices!"

**(More clamor, hubbub, and muffled voices, then the soothing voice of Matt Garrett.)** "Whoa, whoa, please. Let me explain. This has nothing to do with bugging or electronic surveillance. This tape is merely an excerpt from the daily office reels. We tape all counseling sessions at Blantyre. This is not unusual. This is common and accepted practice in all ministries, as well as in secular counseling. But this is your meeting. If you want to play the tape, fine. If not, that's also fine. It's up to you."

**(A reedy voice shouts, probably Frank Cahill.)** "Let's hear it!"
**(Jodi Donovan counters.)** "No way! It's confidential. It's not admissible!"
**(Next, Carl Baker's monotone.)** "We must hear it. We must know the truth."
**(More clamor, hubbub, and muffled voices.)**

"What the fuck!" Jim exclaims excitedly. "What tape of me and Logan? How uh ... so what happened next?"

Russ stops the tape recorder. "Hold on; let me explain." He unfurls his fingers touching them one at a time as if counting. "Let's see; Stan called a vote on whether to play the tape. The motion carried by a landslide. Everyone was so fucking curious. There was no way they were going to leave without hearing it. Anyway, Barry played the tape through the deck in the back of the auditorium. So I got that too, since I was recording on the master."

"You got it, then let's hear it."

"Okay, we'll pick it up where Stan is introducing the tape."

"Now this tape was made in Nashwa on December 20, 1983. Okay, Barry, let her roll:

*(Logan)* "So, Jim, tell me, are you in love with Rebecca Reinhardt?"
*(Shanley)* "Yes, I am."—**(Gasp from the flock.)**
*(Logan)* "Have you had intercourse with her?"
*(Shanley)* "No, I haven't."
*(Logan)* "Do you want to?"
*(Shanley)* "Yes, I love her deeply, all of her."—**(Loud gasp from the flock.)**
*(Logan)* "Do you fantasize about her? I mean in a sexual, lustful way?"
*(Shanley)* "Yes, I do."—**(Another gasp from the body.)**
*(Logan)* "You know what the Word says, Jim. So tell me ... what do

you think you should do, when the Bible says to *flee* youthful lusts?"
*(Shanley)* "I don't know. I just know I love Becki."
*(Logan)* "Do you believe that the Bible is the Word of God?"
*(Shanley)* "Well, I uh ... I guess, but I trust my heart more."
*(Logan)* "If I, as your pastor, tell you that you must break off your relationship with Becki, will you do it?"
*(Shanley)* "No, I won't."—**(A female voice yells, "O LORD, SAVE US!")**
*(Logan)* "Why not?"
*(Shanley)* "Because I love her too much."
*(Logan)* "You love her more than the Word of God?"
*(Shanley)* "Yes, yes ... I trust my heart more."—**(Another gasp from the flock.)**
*(Logan)* "So you see this relationship as good ... as a godly thing?"
*(Shanley)* "Yes, I do. I feel really sure about it."

"Kill it, kill it!" Jim exclaims. "I've heard *enough.*" Russ pushes stop. "I don't fuckin' believe it! That's the day Sharon and I went to talk to Logan before Christmas. Those two-faced *bas*-tards! They even edited it, to move and repeat key phrases. This confirms nine years' worth of suspicions!"

Fire flares in Jim's gut. Hot blood heats his face. But there's nothing he can do. He feels like a cat who knows that a rat is right outside on the step—but no one will open the door.

"So, what happened after that?" Jim asks, after settling a bit.

Russ sighs, then replies, "Mob psychology took over, and the flood gates opened. Let me run it forward."

As voice after voice rises against him, Jim stares at the streetlight which is now just a diffuse smudge of copper radiance in the thick fog.

# Chapter Thirty-seven

The first rays of morning sun creep over the window sill into Jim's face. He rolls over on his makeshift bed. Agony, anguish, pounding hurt. Becki-pain engulfs him, throbbing inside him as if his heart is a huge abscessed tooth. Nightmares no longer come at night but with the first light of day, as if he's waking up into a terrifying William Blake watercolor, into a Dante's *Inferno* where he swirls forever as a tortured lover in the *Circle of the Lustful*. He closes his eyes trying to escape back into sleep, but he can't. During his nightdreams, Becki loves him, smiles at him, laughs with him, and frolics with him in the meadow. But each morning the full impact of her absence smashes into his senses again and again, breaking, shattering: a jackhammer in his head.

*I hate waking up,* he cries in his thoughts. *I've called five times. She's busy. She's at class. She's in the cafeteria. She'll call you back.... She's not gonna call, no way.* The pain builds until he fears he'll faint, then it breaks like a wave and recedes as if running back into the sea. He sighs, but more waves come like labor pains. Finally, after ten minutes or so, they diminish into the gnawing ache that stays with him all day.

Thursday, March 8th. Jim has just spent his first night at 59 Front Street. *I should've never moved in here. Or maybe it's best? I gotta face it, accept it. Who the fuck knows? She really stripped this place, or Alison did? Even took the shades. I feel like I'm in a greenhouse.... I still don't believe it, 36 to 4, with 4 abstentions. Logan's tape turned them into a lynch mob.* Only four voted for Pastor Jim—Jodi, Russ, Barbara Sims, and Herschel Hightower. The rest pulled their knives like Brutus and joined the assassination, even Angela and Sylvia. But four didn't vote: Beverly B., Sarah Johnson, and Joanne McClusky—and Janet, who left early.

Jim starts to get up, but when he lifts his "brownboy," an icy draft chills him so he curls back into bed. His brownboy is a thick khaki-brown comforter he acquired in 1966 when he visited West Point for cadet-exchange week. Warm, cozy, filled with down, it's like an arctic sleeping bag with no zipper. At West Point the brownboy has a long tradition and many cadets refer to it as their "wife," but Jim never thought of his in such an intimate way—until now.

The thermometer by the window—the only thing Becki left behind—says 22°. *Can't be that cold, can it? It looks warm out.... I should pay Mrs. Courtney today. Fuckin' Becki took the March rent money with her. I bet Alison used it to check her in at school? And Sharon, $1400 per—I gotta call Ralph at the weather station.*

*I've got six thou at Comfed, and half goes to Sharon, and she's still got my MasterCard? And my mail's still goin' to Greeley Hill or to the church. I must change that, and the phone. I can't have it listed under Reinhardt? Angie'll probably throw my mail away. She hardly talked to me when I cleaned out my office—used to be my office.*

Jim groans, turns onto his back, and stares at the Capiz shell ceiling fixture, then at a psychedelic water stain directly above him; it looks like a family of amoebas. *I guess we'll move the church to Russ's house ... all five of us, and fuckin' Jodi, she's goin' to Chicago. Shit, my life's goin' down—and no more sex? I'll never have a woman again. Cutoff at 37. This place smells like a litter box, fuckin' Bathsheba. Gotta scrub the kitchen. I need a mop and Spic and Span, and a broom, all that shit. No TV, no tape deck, no toaster. And I need shades and sheets and towels. And my clothes are dirty. I hate laundromats. Gotta get food. I can't live on peanut butter and jelly.... I should call Dad. No, he'll just lecture me and say, I told you that LBI church was too big. I'll write him. I can explain it better—oh fuck, I need to piss.*

He rolls off his piled-mattress bed then hoists himself into a standing yawn. He stretches into his ragged red robe and steps into his slippers. He cranks the knob on the radiator then trudges to the bathroom. By habit he stands at the side of the toilet—not necessary since the lid cover is gone and the seat stays up on its own.

Becki-memories assail him: *"Be sure and shake it good, Reverend.... Oh, it's cute, Jimmy; I wanna touch it."* Torture every time he takes a leak. Jim sighs resignedly. Into the kitchen. He looks above the fridge to check the time, but the Coca-Cola clock is gone. Another pang of hurt, and more Becki-words, warm and recent: *"Oh, Shanley, I love it when you call me 'honey.' It makes me feel like I'm your wife already. I love you. I can't wait for you to move in with me."* Ache, ache, Jim's heart aches.

He plods back into Becki's—no, no; it's now his room. He fumbles in his jeans for his watch—7:55 a.m. He surveys the mess around him: boxes, books, shirts, shoes, paper bags, plastic bags, pictures of the kids, the mirror from his office, his briefcase, a suitcase, a duffel bag, his B-4 bag, his toolbox. No more green chair. Jim's old recliner—from his office—is in the corner, while his butcher-block desk and computer worktable are in front of the old fireplace where Becki had her stereo. And his bookshelves and dresser are against the west wall where she had her chest of drawers. Sharon also let him take two lamps, three folding chairs, a green-and-white lawn chair, and two mattresses which he hauled down from the attic. He piled the mattresses under the north windows where Becki's sofa bed used to be. He also has a dingy well-used sofa—from Beverly—which he placed under the east window; it's so gray with grime that the floral pattern looks like camouflage. She also gave him an old kitchen table with one matching chair. It came from their basement where Russ used it as a workbench; the blue formica is scratched, and stained with yellow paint.

Off with his robe and pajama top. On with a sweat shirt. Jim then kicks off his pajama pants and hauls on his Levi's. He puts on his sneakers but doesn't tie them. To the kitchen. He boils water—in a sauce pan—for instant coffee. He munches cornflakes and milk out of a cup. He has bowls but they're still buried in a box or a bag somewhere. Back to the bedroom, coffee in hand. He sips. He sighs. He sets the coffee on his dresser and gets to work. He gathers the brownboy and spreads it like a bedspread over his piled-mattress bed. He fluffs the naked pillows and puts them at the head.

Next, he unpacks his Apple computer components and places them on his desk and worktable. He arranges them. He rearranges them—four times. He wrestles with cables and connectors, and paper feeds and extension cords. Finally, after forty-five minutes, he's all set. He powers up and puts in a startup floppy. *Beep. Beep.* Now the program disk. It boots up okay, but when he tries to output a test file onto his Imagewriter, it won't print. Frustration. He checks all the connections. He tries again: still nothing. He grabs the manual and turns to the troubleshooting page—*RRRRRRING!*

It's the telephone. Jim's heart leaps, *Becki? She's finally calling back.* The phone is on the floor by the LA-Z-BOY recliner. He pounces on it like a cat on a bird.

No Becki, but it is a young woman; her clipped voice is vaguely familiar: "Is this Pastor Shanley?"

"Yes, it is," Jim replies.

"This's Molly Gibson callin' for Dr. Logan." *I knew I recognized that voice,* Jim interjects to himself. "Please hold jus'a minute while I buzz him." A sense of injustice stings Jim's soul. *Molly, Molly, I doubt Logan gives a shit about you, yet you stay with him. I truly love Becki, and she flees. It's not fair.*

"Jim, Jim," comes Logan's sandpapery voice. "Forgive me; I was on the other line. I just got back from doing chapel, and I had two calls waiting. But I've been thinking of you." The doctor pauses. He clears his throat; his voice drops a decibel. "I must say, Jim, you're being a good sport about all this."

"Well, I'm alive," Jim responds calmly, but his thoughts flame hot, *What the fuck! The bastard talks like I lost a softball game!*

Logan's tone is conciliatory: "We should talk, Jim. We need to clear the air. So much has happened, and I haven't had a chance to share my heart with you. We got your new number from your secretary—your former secretary."

Jim suppresses his rage but remains reserved. "I don't know. I'm not too keen on coming up to Nashua."

"No, no, I don't mean for you to come up. I know you're busy tying up loose ends, but I have to be in Brendon Falls all afternoon. I'll take you to lunch, say 11:30?" Jim reluctantly agrees and gives him directions.

*Why'd I say yes?* he thinks after hanging up. *I don't wanna see that pious two-faced asshole ... yet on the other hand, I may glean some news about Becki. He must be coming to do damage control, to meet with Stan and Carl, to reorganize the board. Logan, Campbell, Baker. If there is a devil, they're in his corner. They're not with God, least not the God I hope for. And Logan's the master liar.* For the first time ever, Logan's aura of spiritual authority does not intimidate Shanley. Despite his wounded heart and ruined life, and the hassle of moving and living alone, he feels a strange sense of relief, a sense of newness and liberty and honesty. The doctor no longer makes him feel guilty or inferior. Jim has learned, like Janis Joplin, that "freedom is having nothing left to lose."

\* \* \*

Perfume, cologne, polished wood, hot rolls, charbroiled beef. Lunchtime aromas. Bancrofts' Steakhouse. Yankee decor, plank floors, husky oak table. A nosegay of yellow cowslips, a flickering oil lamp, three filet mignons, and one prime rib—for Jim. Dr. Logan sits on Jim's left, Tom Hudson on his right, Jerry Crenshaw across the table. Jim figures that Crenshaw came along to set up a new donation schedule with Stan, but Tom Hudson: he has no idea. Tom seems eager but out of place. He reminds Jim of a scoutmaster for the Hitler Youth, especially with his handsome Aryan features, but he's dressed like Peter Falk on *Columbo*. His cheap wrinkled sport coat looks especially tacky next to Logan's and Crenshaw's expensive tailored suits. But Jim is even more casual—jeans, flannel shirt, sweater-vest, suede jacket. No more gray pinstripes. Things have *surely* changed.

As they eat, Logan expounds—like an expert—on various subjects with echoes from Hudson and Crenshaw. The Red Sox, the Celtics, the traffic on 495. Reagan and the Russians. Jerry Falwell and the Moral Majority. He also talks shop. EDGE and Malachi, the Moody mortgage, Easter Week. The leaky roof at Blantyre, Michael Montanaro's great sermon last night, horror stories about flying in the new Cessna, but not one word about Brendon Falls. The LBI'ers act as if nothing has happened, as if Pastor Jim is still "in the club." To Jim, it all seems absurd like when you dream that you're back in high school. He eats quietly. He has no illusions about Logan's motives. He has no desire to be "in the club."

With a last backhand bite, Logan finishes his filet. He wipes his mouth, unbuttons his suit vest, and leans back into his chair. His white-shirted potbelly balloons up out of his vest like Moby Dick breaking water. His tie is too short and slopes down onto his fat stomach like a red ski jump. He looks fatter, grayer, more wrinkled: his thinning hairline shows more forehead.

Dessert, time for dessert. Their young dark-complected waitress takes the order: four coffees, three pineapple cheesecakes, one chocolate cream pie—for Jim. Pretty Hispanic face, blue-checked dress, white pinafore, shapely buttocks. Jim doesn't know the waitress but he recognizes her from Juanita's wedding. Back to the kitchen. She sashays among the tables like the Chiquita-banana girl. Jim likes her hip sway. But Logan seems even more locked on. The doctor watches her all the way, until she disappears through the swinging doors.

Hips, haunches, hairy mound—humping, thrusting, going for orgasm. Between the background pangs of Becki-hurt, Jim thinks about sex and Sharon. The waitress's provocative hips and Tom Hudson's presence combine to take his thoughts in this direction, *I bet Shar can't wait for Tuesday? To get fuckin' high on Hudson, with his handsome face and all-American build. I bet she goes home and fantasizes about his Ayran cock, or maybe Tom's already screwing her? He doesn't have Mary Beth anymore. Maybe Sharon hangs onto his desk and Tom pulls up her dress and bangs her from the back? Spread hips and cunt lips ... like last summer in the backyard after church—goin' crazy, thrashing, moaning, hanging onto the picnic table. I never saw pantyhose and underpants come down so fast, and she jerked so hard she pulled the table up into the air—shit, I can't fantasize about this. I'm too horny. I didn't think I had enough emotion left to feel sexual desire, but I guess—*

Logan's gritty voice snaps Jim back, "Like I said on the phone, Jim, I wanted to get together with you and—oh, I hope you don't mind Tom and Jerry joining us—but I think I've got some good news for you." The doctor steeples his hands against his chin; he gives his patented V-shaped victory grin.

Jim's sexual stirring quickly gives way to indignation; anger heats his face and his thoughts, *Good news my ass! It won't be good news to me unless you tell me that Becki's on her way back to me.* He's ready to blast Logan but instead sips his water, collects himself, and replies calmly, though his voice brims with obvious scepticism, "I doubt it'll be good news to me ... but go ahead."

The doctor pats his frosted ginger-brown hair which is combed straight back on his head. He starts to explain but pauses as the pretty waitress returns with their coffee and dessert. "Well, Jim, to get right to the point," Logan goes on, after a round of sugaring, creaming, stirring, "I think I can salvage this whole situation. I'd like to offer you a staff position in Nashua."

"It's truly amazing how 'all things work together for good' in the family of God," Tom Hudson chimes in, with a Bible verse; he gestures with his spoon.

"So true," Crenshaw echoes, waving a bite of cheesecake on his fork. "Prayer and creative leadership can always transform adversity into opportunity."

Tom and Jerry: the names seem most appropriate to Jim. Their servile fawning before Logan's pompous ego makes him want to call for a barf bag. But he replies to Logan with sarcasm rather than disgust, "You mean, after going behind my back and pulling the rug out from under me, you want to put me on staff?"

Logan leans forward, cup in hand. "Now, now, Jim, you got it all wrong." His long patrician face seems benign, concerned.

"How's that?" Jim asks around a bite of chocolate pie. The pie is dark and rich and sumptuous, but the storm gathering in his gut keeps him from enjoying it much.

Hudson, abandoning his dessert after three bites, heads for the men's room. Jim figures that he ordered cheesecake only because Logan did. "First off, Jim," Logan explains after Tom has departed. "I'm truly sorry about you and Sharon. I pray daily for your reconciliation. But as for the split in your church, it was your man Campbell. He's been complaining about you since September." The doctor puts down his coffee and gestures palms up as if to show his hands are clean. "I stood up for you, Jim, but after your radical sermons last week, Stan came up to Nashua with that bald-headed fellow, and uh ... the big-eyed woman, forgive me—"

"Carl Baker and Leslie Burton," Crenshaw interjects, cocking his Howdy Doody head toward his notepad—he gives a fawning I'm-a-good-doggie grin.

Logan knits his brow with concern. "And others came too. They all said you'd lost your faith, that you were preaching licentious heresies and confessing fears and negative feelings ... and that you were involved in an immoral relationship."

"So you told them to stick with me, huh?" Jim replies scornfully.

Logan takes a huge bite of dessert, leans back in his chair; his voice is thick with cheesecake, "Not hardly. They played your sermon tapes. I had to agree with them. Yet I told Stan to be sensitive, to take a wait-and-see attitude. I told him that patience was the wisest course. But he called again last Friday. No, it was—"

"Saturday night," Crenshaw chimes in again. "It was Saturday night."

Logan takes another big bite of cheesecake. A piece of pineapple tumbles down his tie: a fallen skier. The pasty cheesecake swirls about in his half-open mouth. The doctor's country roots are showing; he chugs some coffee. "That's right, Jerry. It was Saturday night. I was preaching in Portland.... Anyway, Campbell said he wanted to call a special meeting of the body in Brendon Falls. I tried to get you, Jim, but you were gone."

Jim takes a bite of pie, washes it down with coffee. "What about the tape of you and me? That sure wasn't local?" This hot potato sets off a flurry of quick exchanges.

"I never knew the tape existed," Logan says, dabbing his tie with his napkin.

"Come *on*," Jim rebuts. "You don't expect me to believe *that*?"

"I never tape our conversations, Jim. I don't counsel you. We talk as friends. Matt must've accidently turned it on ... but *I* never knew about it, until last week."

Crenshaw pushes his half-eaten dessert away and pulls a folded memo from his zippered portfolio. "I can shed some light on that, Doctor," he says speaking in his glib *Nightline* voice. "I've got a note here from Matt. He says the problem was in Amy's access module—in her new office. Whenever she dialed, she started the main recorder. It was repaired right after Christmas."

"So if it was such a mistake," Jim counters, "why did Garrett bring it?"

"Oh, it wasn't Matt," Logan explains. "It was Rich Beckman."

"Oh, how con*venient*," Jim replies, his words brimming with contempt, but he holds back the storm that is brewing within him.

"Dick's our bad cop so to speak," Logan goes on. "You know that, Jim."

"So it was *his* idea to bring it?" Jim asks the doctor.

"I don't know; I just know he likes to cover all the bases."

Jim gives an indignant snort. "I'll *say* he does."

"No need to get overly excited, Jim," Logan counsels. "Your church didn't split because of the tape. Perhaps it was the spark, but not the cause."

Jim sips then gestures at Logan with his coffee cup. "So what *is* the cause?"

"Very simple," Logan answers. "Your flock didn't like your

new liberal message ... or your relationship with Alison's daughter."

Jim puts down his cup then asks the key question, the only reason he came, "So whaddeya know about Becki, and her sudden departure from Brendon Falls?"

Logan gives a detached shrug. "I know nothing, Jim, nothing at all ... except what her mother told me, and what Becki said in her affidavit."

"So you talked to Alison?" Jim inquires as he prepares to listen between the lines.

"Just on the phone," Logan explains. "She called me last week from Puerto Rico and said she was flying back to check on Becki ... because she was concerned."

"Concerned?" Jim replies.

"About Becki's relationship to you, Jim. I gather that Campbell's wife, Doreen, had called Alison." Logan has not done his usual homework on names.

"And what did you tell Alison?" Jim asks.

"I counseled her to pray and to follow the leading of the Holy Spirit," Logan replies matter-of-factly. "I told her that it was a mother-daughter issue, not a pastoral matter."

"And that's *all* you know about Becki?" Jim presses him.

"Well, I know she's back on campus. But I haven't seen her or talked with her, except I said hello to her after chapel yesterday morning. I don't know her plans ... and I have no desire to influence her either way."

"For the record, Doctor," Crenshaw comes in, reading from his notepad," Miss Reinhardt registered this past Monday as a second-semester freshman. She enrolled in the two-year missionary-associate program."

Logan pats Jim's hand in paternal fashion. "I'm sorry, Jim," he consoles, his voice softening. "I know Becki is dear to you. But from her sworn statement, I'd say she left because she loves you as a spiritual father, not as a lover ... and she's evidently not sympathetic to venturing outside the boundaries of Bible doctrine and Christian values."

Jim lifts his cup. "But *you* are? At least enough to offer me a job?"

"Let's just say I'm more patient about these things," Logan explains.

Jim sips his coffee. "So you think in time I'll repent of my wayward ways?"

Clasping his hands behind his neck, the doctor rolls his head back as if getting a crick out. "In due season you will, Jim. Local-church politics, loss of faith, fleshly passions, problems with women ... we all go through it."

"We do?" Jim asks.

"I would say so," Logan affirms. "I'm twenty years older remember. I went through it at Biddeford. I was wild. I thought Pris was going to leave me. For a time I hated Baptists. But I learned from that split; it was a growing experience."

A busboy clatters by pushing a cart heaped high with dirty dishes. The wheels go *clunk-clunk* over the uneven joints in the old plank floor. Logan takes a last swig of coffee, wipes his mouth, then stares at Jim from under his thick tobacco-colored brows, his hypnotic eyes now bright with darkness.

Jim feels the pull, the black entrancing power, the temptation to believe, to trust, to give in. Too much—Jim looks away. *I don't believe it,* he declares to himself. *Logan's got bewitching power in his eyes. It's like resisting a horny woman with her panties off. I know he's lying. Why do I want to believe the fucker? His words are smooth as butter. He can twist anything to his favor. He could've gotten Hitler off the hook. He's not satisfied with defeating me. He wants me to pat him on the back and to sign on as a whore in his brothel. He wants no enemies left lurking in the shadows.*

Jim looks toward the front of the restaurant, toward the brown ceiling fan which is slowly churning the air over the main entrance. He gazes wide-eyed at the slow-moving paddles until they became a hazy blur—suddenly, Tom Hudson: "I met this guy in the men's room. I gave him a tract. He seemed open but he's a Catholic. He doesn't go to Mass anymore, but he's still hung up on penance and sacrifice. You know how Catholics have a hard time accepting justification by faith?"

Tom sits down drawing Jim's attention back to the table. Hudson's return breaks Logan's spell but not his confidence. Ignoring Tom's evangelical comments, the doctor strokes his bristly beard and regards Jim carefully, as if searching for signs of surrender in his body language. Seemingly satisfied that he has Jim on the ropes, he relaxes back and interlaces his hands over his paunch. A smug grin of expected triumph tugs at the corners of Logan's mouth, like the foxy grin that a good salesman flashes right before he closes a deal. Jim too sits back in pretended repose, but rage roars hot inside him. Logan has misread Jim; the doctor's attempt to seduce has failed.

A long moment passes, perhaps a half minute, then Logan spreads his hands expansively. He speaks slowly, calmly, in his most pragmatic voice, "But anyway, Jim ... it would be a shame to lose someone as gifted as you over local-church politics or an unwise relationship. You've been a dedicated soldier for the Lord, one of our best, and despite our recent differences, I'm sure you still want your life to bring glory to Christ. We have a great God, Jim. We have abundant forgiveness. We have a worldwide vision. And I believe in taking care of my people. So, I want to give you an opportunity to wipe your slate clean and to move on to bigger things"—then the doctor speaks to Crenshaw, "Jerry, would give Pastor Jim the details."

Crenshaw pulls a typed file card from his portfolio. "We have a position in Project Malachi. Until now this initiative has been covered by Tom and Pastor Beckman, and myself, with help from Bob Logan, but we each have escalating duties outside of Malachi, so it's imperative that we designate a full-time LBI representative to visit each of our faith partners on a regular basis. You will also identify new prospects and solicit their support. Compensation is 10% on new partners, and 3% on renewals. Based on projections from our current Malachi donor-base, you'll receive about $25,000 your first year—not to mention room and board which includes a suite at the Villa. And this will go up, of course."

"This will give you an income," Logan quickly adds, "without too much visibility ... the two things you need right now."

"You're offering me a job as a fund-raiser?" Jim calmly replies. He continues to hold back his anger, but it now takes a supreme act of his will to do so.

Logan again gives his foxy-salesman grin. "To put it bluntly, yes. You'd be perfect for the job, Jim. You're educated. You can talk their language. People trust you. And you can convince people of the worthiness of our worldwide vision because you've lived it. Oh, I know you have doubts and differences—at least for now—but I'm sure you still want to see the world won for God."

*Fuck, he sounds like Larry Thornton,* Jim thinks as he listens to Logan's pitch. *Straight commissions, no risk to LBI ... but Larry's a novice compared to Logan. This scheme is masterful. He can neutralize a threat and gain a good salesman at the same time. He never gives up. Ten years in LBI: what a fuckin' education ... and today is my final exam.*

Logan gestures with wide sweeps of his arm. "You know how to relate to upscale people, Jim. You're an academy grad, an Air Force officer. You have a master's degree. They'll take you seriously. You'll be very successful. And you'll have a chance to get away from the maddening crowds until you recover and things cool down a bit. Then we can ease you back into preaching and even let you head an overseas team if you'd like, but uh ... there is one thing." The doctor wraps his arms around his barrel chest and gives a sigh, then explains as if giving the disclaimer at the end of a TV commercial, "I must ask you to get up at Moody and apologize to the body."

"What?" Jim snaps, ready to ignite, but he waits to hear it all.

Logan sighs again, throwing up his hands in seeming concession to some higher authority as if he's talking about some unreasonable bureaucratic requirement beyond his control. "Oh, it's not *me,* Jim. I know your heart, but for the body's sake, we should smooth things over. You don't have to confess like a sinner. Just let everyone know that this whole ugly episode is behind you, without mentioning names of course. A one-shot deal and you'll be on your way ... and I'll give you a solid vote of confidence the same night."

Jim shakes his head in disbelief. He gives a contemptuous snort. A hot scowl takes his face. He does not reply, but little lightning bolts of worry darting in Logan's eyes tell Jim that the doctor is getting the message. Logan's air of confidence evaporates. His color drains. He waves his hand in a gesture of exasperation. Pretense now aside, he stares angrily at Jim, their eyes locking in open warfare. Crenshaw and Hudson cringe away. Logan's black gaze becomes hard and cruel and pitiless. "You disappoint me, Jim," he declares acridly. "Your stubbornness is going to be your ruin. You can only *spurn* the hand of God so many times."

No reply. Silence, silence. Black silence engulfs the table. Dark, dark, and ominous. Jim's enraged soul is like the seismic epicenter of an 8.5 earthquake just before it breaks loose—then all at once, Logan retreats. He tries to backpedal to a posture of peace. "I'm sorry, Jim, but you *know* I speak as a friend. You *know* I love you as a son. Pride is our mutual enemy. I have to deal with it daily. We all have to apologize and go humbly before the Lord to repent of our foolishness." Logan pats Jim's shoulder in a paternal gesture—*BAAWAAAAAGHHH!* His touch sets off the earthquake.

Jim slams the table with both his fists. The dishes jump. He explodes to his feet. "I'LL GO TO *FUCKIN'* HELL BEFORE I APOLOGIZE TO YOU OR TO ANYONE! I REPENT OF NOTHING, EXCEPT FOR PRETENDING AND LYING AND BOWING DOWN TO YOUR *BULL*SHIT FOR TEN YEARS! I detest everything you stand for! I should've declared my feelings long ago! You're a degenerate and greedy old man! You don't give a shit about me or anyone! You're a liar and a con artist! You talk about love and you act so humble and concerned, and your words are so enticing! But you don't *love* people! You ex*ploit* them to get power and wealth and prestige! You're no different than Hitler, except you murder souls instead of bodies! In fact, you're worse because you do it in the name of *God*! You're always scheming and buying and selling to prop up your empire! You use fear and guilt to intimidate! You shame people into bowing down! WELL, I WANT *NO* PART OF IT! AND IF YOUR GOD RULES HEAVEN, THEN I HAVE *NO* DESIRE TO GO THERE!"

Jim turns his attention to Hudson and Crenshaw. "And as for you two yes-men stooges, you don't even exist! I'LL *NEVER* BE LIKE YOU! YOU REPRESENT THE LOWEST FORM OF HUMANITY!" White, white. Logan blanches. Hudson and Crenshaw seem to have no face at all. Jim's fury freezes the entire restaurant. Every eye is fixed on him. But before anyone moves, or breathes, he hurls his napkin at Dr. Logan and storms out.

* * *

Friday, March 9th. 9:25 a.m. Jim Shanley, a mug of coffee in his hand, looks out the kitchen window. Gray, gray, cloudy and cold. He gazes wistfully at the dead meadow, at Mrs. Courtney's dead garden. Dead, dead, all is dead, including his life. *One week ago,* he sighs to himself, *just one week ago, Becki and I were lovers, in her bed, in this apartment. O God, I feel so—RRRRRRING!* The phone interrupts his lamentation. To his room. He answers.

It's Pastor Rich Beckman calling from Nashua. After a curt exchange of greetings, he gets right to the point: "I must give you formal notice, Pastor Jim.... Unless you recant your heretical teachings, the LBI board will have no choice but to rescind your ordination. Pastor Logan has been very patient with you. As your shepherd, he's concerned for you. He loves you in the Lord. He prays for you. But if you persist in your ambition to form a church outside of his authority, God will deal with you swiftly as He did with Korah in Numbers 16:32. Rebellion is the sin of Lucifer, and a sin 'unto death.' God *must* crush it. If you continue to live as a spiritual renegade, then I fear for your very life. I pray you'll return to the fold."

* * *

Dr. Logan takes a drink of water then moves aggressively to the front of the small dais. He holds the microphone in his left hand. He chops the air with his right. "Jim Shanley has for*saken* the Bible and the authority of the body! He has re*jected* the grace of God and is now living in open sin without shame! His 'follow the heart' heresy is dangerous to all, especially to our young people! He now condones homosexuality, free sex, and the use of drugs! He seduces teenage girls. He keeps them like concubines. He associates with degenerate sinners and street people, hippie-types, drug-pushers, prostitutes!"

Thursday evening, March 15th. Special closed meeting of the BFBC membership. The meeting was called ostensibly to approve the appointment of Tom Hudson as the new pastor, but has turned into a "Jim Shanley roast."

The doctor stops center stage. He gazes soberly at the flock. He sees devout faces. He senses a spirit of humble obedience. No more rebels. Pastor Jim and his band of heretics are gone. The loaf is purged of its leaven.

Logan's voice becomes hushed and grave: "If you love Pastor Shanley in the Lord, you must not support or befriend him in *any* way. To do so will only encourage him to continue on his path of deception. He has forsaken the anointing. He's no longer ordained to speak for God. He's now energized by oppressing demons. You must not attend his unauthorized house-meetings. If you do, God will *chas*tise you severely. If you even *talk* with him, you risk being deceived by Satan. Pastor Shanley's salacious ultralibertarian doctrines will entice your flesh and beguile your mind, leading you away from Christ into his licentious lifestyle. We're in the *last* days. This is a critical moment in our warfare against evil. You must support your new branch pastor, Tom Hudson, as he works with Stan Campbell and the other local leaders who've remained loyal to God through this trial of faith."

# Chapter Thirty-eight

Tuesday, May 22, 1984. The soft spring morning drifts through the open window, its breath sweet with the fragrances of new grass and flowers. The curtains stir ever so slightly. Yes, Jim has curtains: pecan-brown, pleated, no tiebacks. Erin and Heather picked them out. He also has window shades, a toaster, a television, and a stereo—he's now well established at 59 Front Street. He pulls on his jeans and his old USAFA gym shirt. The gurgle of the coffeemaker sounds from the kitchen. Sharon let him have their old Procter-Silex. Jim has felt no serious heartache for two days, no Becki-dreams at night. *Maybe I'm healing?* he thinks as he plops down on his old recliner to put on his sneakers. *Maybe there is life after Rebecca?*

Back to the kitchen. Jim puts bread in the toaster and pours coffee into his black M.I.T. mug. He's assembled—from Sharon, Bev, Kmart, and Jodi—an odd assortment of dishes, pots, pans, knives, forks, spoons, and other utensils. He slaps some honey and peanut butter on his toast, puts the toast on a plastic Le Menu plate, grabs his coffee, and returns to his room which is also his office. He flips on the TV which sits on a stand next to his butcher-block desk. He then sits down and scans his calendar. Sound bites. The television cries for his attention; he gives it half:

> ... the exact details won't be unveiled until tomorrow but Mayor Flynn says the new master plan will go a long way toward solving Boston's educational and racial problems ... on the Central Artery, but the Southeast Expressway is jammed up at East Milton. Granite Avenue is your best alternate. The tunnels and bridges are moving except for the Tobin which is backed up well past ... Cambridge Eye Doctors can fit you with Marchon Auto-Flex frames. You must look like a winner to be a ... no mortgages. We have strict cost control. I can sell you a new Olds for less because my costs are less. My name is Ernie Boch! Come on down! ... one wide stroke, twenty-four hour protection. Nothing is going to beat you. Power Stick from ... Look years younger with Loving Care. Really now, is there a choice? Gray hair or Loving Care? ... Yes, we'll show you 35 ways to buy foreclosed properties without cash. So plan to attend this important seminar on Sunday, May 27th, at the....

"Commercials, commercials," Jim complains. *It's not worth it to watch the news.* He snaps the TV off. He takes a bite of toast; a shower of crumbs rains onto his calendar book. *Looks like this day is wide-open until I go to the weather station. Glad I did all of Mrs. C.'s chores yesterday. I don't feel like working for her today. Maybe I'll go sit by the lake. I'll use my new path. I have no desire to desecrate Stan's holy picnic grounds.* Jim stares up at the brick chimney, then at a cobweb underneath the oak mantel. *Shit, I should dust under there, but not today.... Should be slow at work tonight with this hot weather. It seems like August. Maybe I'll call Jodi on the WATS line. She didn't waste any time moving to Chicago, but who can blame her? Only three on Sunday night. If we're gonna usher in a revolution of love, it's sure off to a slow start. Of course, who wants to come to a house church to hear a defrocked minister— especially when you get blacklisted for coming?*

He drops his gaze a bit to the dirty-white plywood covering the fireplace. He notices some faint pencil marks like graffiti. *How the fuck did I miss this?* He leans closer. It's Becki's high-schoolish handwriting, half cursive, half printing, rounded, fat, and feminine—as if each letter is pregnant. No doubt. He knows her hand as well as his own. And the words are festooned with her little flowers, birds, and stars. Morevover, it's from her favorite rock album:


> HEY YOU . . . OUT THERE IN THE COLD,
> GETTING LONELY, GETTING OLD,
> CAN YOU FEEL ME?
> HEY YOU . . . STANDING IN THE AILE
> WITH ITCHIE FEET AND FADEING SMILES,
> CAN YOU FEEL ME?
> HEY YOU . . . DON'T HELP THEM TO BURY THE
> LIGHT. . . DON'T GIVE IN WITHOUT A FIGHT.


Jim loves her loopy scrawl, even her misspelled words. A knife stabs his heart. The blood of his soul pours out, agony mingled with affection. Memories, memories, once glorious but now torturous. The words go blurry. Love, love, waves of longing. His eyes fill; he senses Becki's spirit crying out. Time has not diminished his love. On the contrary, it grows stronger each day.

*Oh, Becki, Becki,* he cries in his heart, *I wonder what you're doing right now, and what you're thinking. I wonder if you daydream about me in class. I wonder if you think of me when you go to bed at night. I know you love me. I know it. Yet I fear I'll never see your sweet smile again. I miss you so much. I miss your big blue eyes. I miss your witty jokes. I miss your naughty prurient side. I miss holding you and kissing you and lying in bed with you—oh, did that really happen or was it just a beautiful dream? I even miss your pouty face and your stubborn-turtle pose and your temper tantrums. I see all the places we used to go, and I live where you used to live, but you're no longer in these places.*

Jim's "wild rose" is now wilting in a garden of fear. Becki has been in Nashua for eleven weeks, and despite brief moments of solace, his heart has not healed. Far from it—getting over Becki is a lie, a myth, a mind trip, just as Adam followed Eve to the Tree of Knowledge to try and fill the emptiness where God had ripped her out of him. But reason can never replace a living rib.

Hurt, hurt, no escape. Jim chokes back tears. He feels for a moment as if he's dying. His Becki-life flashes before him, culminating in a nightmare worse than death. March, April, May. Clawing, clawing, clawing at the wall—until his fingers are ripped raw. He's called Becki's dorm many times but she's never there, and she never returns his calls. He's written her letters, sweet letters, love letters, hate letters, begging letters, erotic letters, perplexed letters, apologetic letters, but she's never written back. Finally last Wednesday the 15th of May, he called her at work. She works as a waitress at Denny's near the Nashua Mall off Route 3. Her supervisor called her to the phone. She said hello, but when Jim spoke her name—*CLICK*, she hung up. Down, down, crushing weight. No breath, no light, no hope. Unbearable. The sharp teeth of his torment tore his heart to shreds. Falling, falling, no legs. He collapsed on the floor and cried, hugging the phone to his bosom.

Later that same evening he called Puerto Rico. Panic, panic, cold-sweat panic. He called in the desperate hope that if he could smooth things with Alison, it might open a door to Becki. But Alison was just as hateful as her daughter and almost as abrupt: "You let me down, Jim. I trusted you with Rebecca Lea, and you betrayed me. If you don't stop pursuing her, we'll go to the authorities for a restraining order. I'm sorry, but I fear you've had a breakdown; you're acting irrationally; you're emotionally unstable. Becki has no romantic intentions toward you. How could you think *such a thing*? You're obsessed and deluded. Lucifer has deceived you and led you away from truth. You need Christian counseling. I shouldn't even be talking to you"—*CLICK*.

The screaking brakes of a garbage truck outside his window jerk Jim back to the present. He goes over to the east-facing window, actually northeast-facing. He doesn't see the truck—it's on the other side of the house near the driveway—but he does see a utility pole and wires and a faded black transformer box, and beyond the pole, a larger scene. Shingled roofs, brown, gray, and buff, fall away down the slope of Hadley Hill amid trees bursting green with new leaves. More distant three-decker houses, tossed like wood crates along the many winding streets, are nested about the grid of downtown buildings. Beyond the town, beyond the river, olive-colored hills shimmer in the morning sunshine. A sepia haze hangs over the rooftops, the brick smokestacks, the abandoned factory towers, giving the old mill town the appearance of a sun-bright 19th-century daguerreotype.

Warm, almost hot, just a faint breath of wind. A thin wisp of smoke rises from the Prescott stack but quickly fades into the haze. Jim sips his coffee. Despite the twitter of happy birds, the soul of the town seems sad as always. Sadness in Jim, around Jim, as if he's in a new dimension where happiness is only a distant remembrance to which he can never return.

Yet his new life is also a life of simplicity and honesty where he'll never again have to lie to Sharon about his feelings or his whereabouts, where he'll never again have to lie and deny to Becki to keep her from leaving, where he'll never again have to profess to know things about God that he doesn't know, and where he'll never again have to bow down to Dr. Logan. Heart freedom does not lessen his Becki-pain, but it does make the sadness sweet at times like how you feel when you walk alone in the country and look up at the stars. You're alone, but you know you're beyond the world of liars and pretenders. You know you're in a realm where love can live if two souls can ever meet there. Jim takes a drink of coffee, gives a weary sigh, and returns to his desk.

Becki disavowed with silence, with distance, but many spoke openly as February oaths of allegiance changed quickly to condemnation in March. A chorus of sanctimonious voices rose up against Pastor Jim, most behind his back—most heeding Dr. Logan's warning about talking directly to him—but a few he heard.

"Pastor, I've agonized over whether to call you, but now I must," Leslie Burton declared over the phone on Monday, March 19th. "The Lord spoke to me during Pastor Hudson's message last night. I fear for you, Pastor Jim, not for your salvation, I know you're saved, but for your judgment at the Bemas Seat. I don't speak of your sin with Becki Reinhardt, but I speak of your sins as a pastor." Leslie spoke rapidly, as usual, and formally as if reading a prepared text. "Because of your loose attitude toward sin, many have followed their hearts into illicit affairs during this past year. I won't mention names, but you know who they are; their names pass my lips only in my prayers. But your sin has hurt *real* people, people that you professed to love. And your loose preaching has undermined the godly foundation in many homes. My Gerald is once again obsessed with pornography and my son Wendell cannot control himself. I can't blame you for their fleshly weaknesses, but if you had preached harder against lust, perhaps they, and others, would have gone to the cross before their sins became habitual. I pray that you'll confess and return to Dr. Logan. He's a *great* man of God; he cares for you. And I'll always be your friend ... but *only* in the Lord."

Barry Buford also phoned that Monday, his voice nervous, "Jim, I-I ... I repent of everything I told you. Your counsel to me was not Biblical. I-I, I was living in sin and you should have told me. You've departed from the faith. Your preaching is off. You're deceived. You need counseling. You *must* go to Dr. Logan ... but *I* can't talk to you anymore."

Three days later Doris Campbell called crying on the phone—but not drunk, "You probably hate me for signing that paper, but I had to do it, Jim, for your sake. Becki doesn't love you, not *that* way. She doesn't want to sleep with you. She told me right here at my kitchen table. Pastor Logan is right. We *must* forsake our wicked ways. That goes for me, as well as you. This whole painful experience has made me examine my own life. I've rededicated myself, Jim. I've given up drinking and smoking and gossip. I love you, Jimmy, but you must look at what you're doing. You *must* come back, and repent, and reconcile with the body of Christ. I can't be your friend until you do."

On Sunday afternoon, March 25th, Carl and Melissa came to visit at 59 Front Street. Humble and meek, they stood there, holding hands like newlyweds. Carl, looking down and fidgeting his foot as if putting out a cigarette on Jim's carpet, spoke first, "I don't know what to say, Pastor Jim, except to share Proverbs 27:6, Faithful are the wounds of a friend, but the kisses of an enemy are deceitful. You know what I mean, and you know I love you."

"We're just doing what you taught us, Pastor Jim," Melissa explained in a wavering voice, her blue eyes filling. "You always said that no matter what, we should put the Bible first."

Later that same Sunday, Sylvia Cahill called: "I know he's right, Jim. Dr. Logan's right. My heart is so wicked. God has given me a faithful husband and I'm so unthankful. My desires are so worldly—I don't dare tell anyone. I love you, Jim, but this has to be my last call. I must give myself *totally* to the Lord—oh! there's Frank; I have to go."

And not just BFBC regulars. One afternoon, as Jim left the house, he ran into Ruthie and Kyle coming up the porch steps. Kyle moved in with Ruthie after Jodi and Brenda left for Chicago. "I'll be *fuckin'* damned," Ruthie taunted, her punk-style haircut sticking out like the mane on a chow dog. "If it ain't the preacher man? So yuh got caught foolin' 'round with that little nun, an' your wife kicked you out, an' yuh got *ex*communicated. An' now yuh had to move into this dump. Well, it serves you right." Kyle looked on, sullen but silent. That was Saturday the 7th of April.

Ten days later, on April 17th, Ernie Johnson blasted Pastor

Jim in front of the post office. Hot with fury, he charged up as if to punch Jim, but instead, he shouted, "I used to be plum proud of you, but now you done for*sook* the Lord on accounta that little prick-teasin' whore! Older men achasin' young cunts! It's the ruination of the worl'. An' you was doin' a powerful good work in this town. Now you done left your wife an' youngins, an' you got some *fool* notion 'bout follerin' your feelin's! They ain't no earthly way God's gonna bless 'ceptin' you stay with the Bible. Folks ain't gonna do right lessin' you preach the fear of God into 'em. I ain't got no right to talk since I been a rotten sinner mosta my life, much worse than you, but I believed in *you*! An' I knowed from a chil' that the Bible is God's Word! It's a sorry sight ... so much sin agoin' on. Jus' like Kevin's done knocked up Cathy. They both need a good lickin', and so do *you,* Pastor Jim! I'm movin' back to West Virginny, an' I'm powerful glad of it!"

Throughout March and April, while Jim's former flock was condemning him, shunning him, Dr. Logan blazed hot against his hope that the heart is the highest authority. On radio and TV, from the pulpit, in college classes, the LBI chief attacked the idea as the "great heresy." Now as May moves toward June, Pastor Jim is cut off and going down—he has a half-dozen followers—and hardly poses a threat to the LBI empire. Nonetheless, Logan continues to rant against him as do Stan Campbell and Tom Hudson. To maintain a show of evangelical propriety, Logan does not attack Jim by name in open forum—though everyone knows of whom he speaks—but privately, at rap sessions, at staff meetings, over meals, he warns against any association with Jim Shanley or his band of "outlaw" Christians. Russ keeps abreast of Logan through Bev who finds out from Doris who's now privy to all the inner-circle gossip in Nashua. She goes up weekly with Stan and spends time with Pam Garrett, Tricia Logan, and Molly Gibson.

Tom Hudson spends three days a week in Brendon Falls. Otherwise, Campbell runs the church while Tom oversees from his office in Nashua—the blind leading the proud. For the sake of the academy, Beverly Bradley is staying on until June. She's never been fond of Dr. Logan, and his vitriolic attacks on Jim and Russ have made her like him even less. She has even voiced her dissatisfaction with the new BFBC regime, and she doesn't attend the BFBC services. Anyone else would've been blacklisted for such a stance, but Stan and Tom need Bev to finish out the school year. Yet on the other hand, she's not an ardent supporter of Jim and Russ's renegade house-ministry. In fact, she goes to Valley Baptist to worship. Moreover, she has remained Sharon's friend and feels that Sharon and the kids are the innocent victims of Jim's reckless choices. Nonetheless, Bev still talks to Jim and treats him kindly.

A rumbling vibration shakes the house. Like a familiar friend, the morning freight train growls westward beyond the meadow, beyond the pines. The rolling rumble rattles the windows like a mild earth tremor. The passing of that old train is one of the few things that remains the same in Shanley's life. He sighs and takes his last sip of coffee. He pulls open his file cabinet and takes out a bunch of letters bound with a rubber band. Becki has never written but he's received plenty of mail, most of it bad. He looks again at his de-ordination notification which is signed by Rich Beckman. Logan always avoids the dirty work. He then sorts through the personal notes and letters. He rereads a few:

WED, 3-14-84

DEAR PASTOR SHANLEY,
AS A CONCERNED HUSBAND AND FATHER, I MUST INSTRUCT YOU TO NO LONGER CALL MY WIFE OR TO SPEAK TO MY GIRLS. I AM NOW CONVINCED THAT YOUR INTENTIONS ARE LESS THAN PURE.

FRANKLIN DELANEY CAHILL

- - - - - - - -

March 19th

Jim,
I'll be forever grateful to you for being with me during my greatest trial. I know that Jesus has chosen me to suffer for him. Your new teachings confuse me ... so I can't be part of your new ministry at Russ's house. I've decided to go back to Valley Baptist where my parents worship. They feel that I should start over and get away from the things that confuse me ... and that remind me of Shane. Good-bye, Jim. You'll always be in my prayers.

Joanne M.

- - - - - - -

Mon, 3-26-84

Dear Pastor Jim,
Pastor Hudson is coaching the team this year. When he cleaned out the softball locker in the teen center, he found your

*shoes, your glove, and your warm-up jacket.
If you want these items, you'll have to come
get them. But please arrange with Stan to
come in the evening, because I don't want to
see you. I don't hate you, Jim, but you're
a bad influence. I've decided to go all the
way with God, and I don't want any distrac-
tions. You've always caused problems in my
thinking. I want to put it all behind me. I
pray that you'll give up your craziness and
come back to reality. Fairy tales are not for
this life.*

> *Love in Christ,
> Angela Thornton*

- - - - - - - -

*Sunday  4/15/84*

*Dear Jim,
    Upon our return from church this morn-
ing, I called Sharon. I was so disheartened
I spent the afternoon typing out a very sad
story. I ask you to read it:*

### THE SAGA OF JAMES DAVID SHANLEY

Born in 1946 in a small Texas town, Jim Shanley was the first-
born of David and Elizabeth Shanley. Lizzie loved her boys and spent
much time enjoying them. She was especially fond of her oldest who
was a stubborn rascal but very intelligent. But as a young man his heart
was shattered as he lost his mom, but with his dad's encouragement, he
recovered to become an honor student and a star athlete. In 1964, he
received an appointment to the Air Force Academy. In the spring of his
third year, he traveled east with the baseball team. During the trip, he
met the girl of his dreams, Sharon Pedersen. They were married in 1968
and she followed him across the country and overseas as he served as
an officer. During this time two lovely daughters were born (later they
would have a son). After his discharge, they settled in Massachusetts
where Jim worked as a meteorologist, but the Lord called and he went
to Bible school and soon had his own church in the town of Brendon
Falls—but Lucifer had other plans for this gifted young preacher.

New England was a playground for Satan. Families were broken,
children were insolent, adultery was rampant. Jim and his born-again
group were a threat, so Satan attacked. First he impressed on Jim that
he was nearly 40 years of age, that half his life was over, then he hit the
most vulnerable spot—his lust. A young lady whom he had taken under
his wing as a daughter figure began to appeal to him sexually. Gone was
the memory of his vow to be true to his wife. If only Jim could get rid
of his family, he could live his life again. If he could get the young girl,

he would feel twenty-one again.

And he fell right into the devil's trap. First, his sermons took a turn to justify his sin. Then he abandoned his family in his heart. Finally, his elders and supporters who'd loved him for many years could not tolerate his perverted preaching, and they voted him out. But Jim, true to his old Adamic nature, was going to do what _he_ wanted to do. He started a new ministry where he could preach his own self-glorifying gospel. What now? Who will keep Jim company as he enters the latter years of his life? Do you think the young woman he lusts for will care for him? NO! She has _never_ indicated in any way that she loves him as a husband. Why would she want a man old enough to be her father? This young woman will _never_ be in Jim's life again, for she has gone to serve the Lord and to find a young husband with whom she can share her youth. Jim has lost his church, his family, and his friends, all because he turned away from God and the Bible: "I will bless those who love me until the third and fourth generation, and I will curse those who turn from me." Sharon will doubtless marry again and be a happy and contented wife and "her children will rise up and call her blessed." But what of Jim? What will become of him? He faces a bleak lonely future, away from God and all the good things in life ... POOR JIM!

_Jim, please consider this story prayer-fully. It doesn't have to have a sad ending. Repent of your love for Becki. Return to the truth. I pray for you._

_Gretta Pedersen_

- - - - - - - -

_CAW! CAW!_ The raucous cries of a pair of crows disrupt Jim's reading, drawing his attention to the window. Large, chunky, and glossy-black, they perch on the crossarm of the utility pole. They seem to be brimming with mischievous energy as if planning a series of pranks like Heckel and Jekyll, the cartoon magpies. But Jim suspects the two scavengers are scanning down Front Street to see what the garbage truck has left behind. Spirited, spontaneous, almost majestic in self-esteem, they jump jauntily about on the crossarm, cocking their heads this way and that. They behave as if being a crow is the highest possible estate, as if the entire cosmos was created for them. The two birds are so glossy-black they seem almost purple in the hazy sunlight. After another fit of cawing, they flap their wings and take off down Front Street.

As they fly away, Jim wishes he'd been born a crow: _I'd rather be a crow than a Christian. If people were like crows, life would be a lot better._

* * *

Wild caramel locks, dilated eyes, pale-blue panties on the floor. Now she drops her skirt as well. Jim sits back on the toilet, his thick cock straining toward the ceiling. She squats over him spreading her haunches. Her cushiony thighs jiggle. Her custardy midriff bulges forward. Her raspberry nipples hang deliciously, bumpy and begging to be sucked. She lowers her sweet muff toward his pulsing pole. Swollen pussy, hot and hairy and wet. Closer, closer—"Oh, Becki Lea, I can't wait!" Jim cries as he wakes up. He turns on his side and finishes his wet dream. Panting, pumping, panting, pumping. Ten pumps with his hand then a muted shout; he ejaculates all over the sheets, onto his stomach, onto his gym shirt. He feels the hot semen on his bulbous gut. Erotic high, feverish, peaceful, drifting, drifting.

Jim lies naked on his piled-mattress bed. Naked, sweaty, melting penis. The steamy Tuesday afternoon wraps his body like a hot wet blanket. His floating orgasmic high quickly gives way to Becki-ache. He no longer feels guilty about masturbation, but wet Becki-dreams torture his psyche, taking him up into heavenly fantasy only to let him plunge back to reality, back to despair.

The drone of a school bus wafts in through the open windows along with the excited yells of liberated youngsters—then silence, save for the lazy buzz of a housefly occasionally punctuated by the distant blare of a Conrail diesel. *Now I'm gonna be blah and groggy at work. I should've never gone to sleep. I should've stayed at the lake. It's fuckin' hot in here, and it's not even June.* He looks up at the ceiling. *Look at those cobwebs, and there must be ten years' worth of bugs in that light. Shit, that fixture reminds me of Becki. I remember looking at it right after we made love. We were so happy and talking about forever. But maybe it never happened? Maybe that was just a wet dream as well?*

A last cloudy glob of jism oozes out of Jim's thumby deflated penis and drips onto his groin. *God, I stink like a mildewy fish. Cum is disgusting, especially compared to the smell of a woman. Oh, to inhale Becki's pussy, or Sharon's. I love how a cunt smells. It's exciting and exotic, so much better than the blah smell of semen. Fuck, I feel wet and hot and fat. My bellybutton is buried so deep I can't find it. I should start doing sit-ups and cut out the chocolate chip cookies. Nana's right. Why would Becki want me when she can get a young hunk to "share her youth with"?* Jim hears light footsteps coming up the stairs. *That must be Bobbie Rae. She's skinny and not that pretty but she's certainly woman enough. I wish she would've walked in about two minutes ago. She must get horny at times with her husband at Ft. Devens all day—fuck, what am I thinking? I've been here ten weeks and I've scarcely said hi to her or to her husband. What is his name? Harvey? Henry? I should be more neighborly. I'm turning into a recluse.*

Jim strips off his gym shirt and uses it as a cum rag; he wipes his dick, his stomach, the sheets. He starts to get up but instead reaches over and pulls his watch from his Levi's on the floor—2:25 p.m. *No panic; I have a few minutes yet.*

Since February, Jim's sex life has gone from bad to better to worse. At first he got off only in dreams. His emotions were too hurt to consciously ejaculate. But as the weeks passed, he began to see sexy women everywhere: Stop & Shop, the post office, in front of Pauline's, walking, riding bicycles, the tellers at the bank, the reception girl at the weather station. Jim longed to initiate but he couldn't. But he did undress them in his mind. And every time he pulled in the driveway, it seemed that Ruthie was just ahead of him shaking her cowgirl hips up the sidewalk. By the end of March he'd rediscovered the frustration of being a single male. His sex drive fully recovered, he began to masturbate regularly, getting off over *Penthouse* and *Playboy* and *Hustler*. Porno girls, but he saw them as Becki or Sharon; he also fantasized about Angela and Sylvia, and Janet and Cathy R., and Molly Gibson—even Ruthie.

Jim resigned himself to solitary sex, but then his disengagement with Sharon took an odd twist. After their breakup, Sharon was angry and hurt and humiliated, and filled with pious LBI resolve. She shunned Jim as an unfaithful husband and unrepentant sinner—or at best, as an emotionally sick person. For seven weeks she didn't talk to him except about Erin, Heather, and Chris, or about money and practical matters. But that changed, and how, on the second Sunday in April.

Jim had taken the kids to the aquarium in Boston and they got back late. After ushering the kids to bed, Sharon asked him to stay for coffee, and before he knew it, she had his clothes off and they were fucking on the kitchen floor.

They made love often; she would call him, at home, at work, always after ten p.m: "Oh, James David, I can't wait." He never saw her so horny and wild: "I hope you're ready, mister, because I'm going to screw you to the wall"—"Oh, Jim, I just want to touch your penis. I miss it. I love it when it's big and red and bumpy"—"I know I'm giving in to my flesh, but I can't live without it. I love sex more than *anything*." By day Sharon was a model LBI Christian, taking care of her kids, working downtown, working in Nashua, going to BFBC services with her Bible under her arm, but when horny at night, she disregarded Logan's blacklist, and went crazy on her heretic husband.

But Jim's respite from celibacy ended just as quickly as it began. On a rainy Friday night, the 11th of May, he was restless and horny, and couldn't get to sleep. Sex with Sharon appealed to him much more than masturbation. Though she hadn't called him, he headed to Edsel Road anyway, unannounced. He arrived just before midnight and found the lights off and Tom Hudson's white Chevy in the driveway—Jim knew the car from Nashua and from seeing it parked at BFBC when he drove by. But the clincher was the New Hampshire vanity plate on the back which said: MALACHI.

Sharon never confessed she was screwing Tom. She just politely cut Jim off: "Jim, we can't do it anymore. A relationship has to be more than sex. We can't pretend any longer. We have the kids, but that's all we have in common." She asked for his key. He gave it to her. No anger, no crying, just a handshake to signal the end—he knew it was their last fling.

Giving a resigned sigh, Jim finally rolls off his piled-mattress bed and hauls his blah sexually drained body into a standing position. *It's no wonder that Sharon cut me off,* he tells himself as he yawns and stretches. *She craves it, but she has to justify it. As long as she's just screwing one man at a time, it fits her conveniently adjusted Christian morality. And since they're talking marriage, she has to go with him instead of me, the long term for the short term ... and the long prick for the short prick. It took them long enough to get into fucking, but now that Tom's in town a lot, they're making up for lost time. She's not missing my puny penis, that's for sure. No wonder that wood-headed bastard wanted the BFBC pulpit. But as for me, it's back to being a monk. What a fucking downer.*

Jim grabs some clean underwear then plods wearily to the bathroom. As he runs the shower to get the water hot, he looks down at the faded black floor. *Right there ... that's where Becki dropped her panties. It wasn't a dream. It actually happened. I saw it with my own eyes.*

# Chapter Thirty-nine

Bluebirds and butterflies on fine china, crocheted tablecloth. Country-kitchen aromas: fried eggs, fried sausage, hot buttered biscuits, cream gravy, fresh coffee spiked with Bailey's. Puckers, wrinkles, motherly cackling. Turquoise eyes, granny glasses, a fussy grin between rouged cheeks, a peach-red pinafore faded pink—and one hungry heretic with a heavy heart. Halfway through her breakfast, Mrs. Courtney stands up and expresses her intention of going for the mail. "No, no, you sit down," Jim quickly intercedes. "I'll run down and get it."

"Hear, hear!" Mrs. C. scolds. "You eat away now. I been gettin' me own mail every mornin' eh ... since I been here; I daresay mor'n twenty years. I don't need some young *whipper*snapper treatin' me like an invalid. Goodness me! It's a splendid summer day. Now you *mind* yourself and eat your breakfast, or I'll have a crow to pick with you! Eat away now; and I'll get your mail as well." She gives a snorting, "Humph," and pulls her sunbonnet over her silver-white hair. She then totters out of the kitchen, brushing the air in front of her as if sweeping away spiderwebs.

May, June, July: not a peep from Becki, yet Jim's love for her has grown each day, along with his woe. Halfway heeding Alison's warning, he hasn't called Rebecca anymore, but he's written more letters than ever, scorching the paper with love, eros, hurt, and anger. He's also driven several times to Nashua and watched her walk into work at Denny's. He goes with the intention of talking to her, but always chickens out. Insane behavior, yes, but he can't help himself as his pain-weary Becki-emotions rush from peace to panic to brokenness, and back again. Yet he's never gone to her dorm, or sought to find her on campus. He has no desire for a confrontation with the LBI faithful who for the most part see him as an emotionally disturbed apostate who preaches the "doctrines of devils" and debauches young women.

The situation in Brendon Falls is not much better as most of Jim's former parishioners shun him as if he has AIDS. If they see him on the street or in a store, they walk the other way. Sharon, her hots for Jim cooled by Tom Hudson's cock, again relates to him only on parental and money matters. He's an outcast, a leper. He's learning what Isaiah means when he says: "... despised and rejected of men, a man of sorrows, and acquainted with grief, and we hid as it were our faces from him."

His newfound liberty and honesty, though good and right in his mind, offer little solace to his broken heart. Sleepless nights. He often writhes in his bed unable to escape the agony of Becki's absence. Yet his worst nightmares still come with the morning light. On occasion, Jim blames himself and is tormented by regret as he wishes he could relive the past eighteen months. But most of the time, he feels betrayed by love, by life, and he curses God in his prayers.

Jim's friendship with Russ has deepened like an oak rooting into the ground. Russ can't take away the Becki-agony but his resigned presence soothes Jim's spirit. Russ has lived through it with him. He shares Jim's hurt and sense of outrage. He believes in Jim. He believes in Rebecca. Like Jim, he saw beyond her bratty selfish side, beyond her pious religious side. He saw the heart behind the pouty face—and the hurt. He saw the mirthful bantering, the affectionate teasing, the childlike yearning in her eyes.

Yet Russ offers no prophecies but one: "Becki can give outward obedience to Logan, but never her heart. She may serve in his army the rest of her days but it will always be a lie." Jim cannot bear the thought of Becki denying him forever. He can't imagine, in fact, his nightmare lasting even to the end of the year.

Russ's continued friendship with Jim has earned him a prime spot on Logan's blacklist. Like Shanley, Russ is learning what it means to be "despised and rejected." In the eyes of the Loganites, Russ is a treacherous agent of Lucifer sent to support Jim's lustful appetites and renegade ambitions.

Jim knew Russ would stick with him, but Mrs. Courtney's friendship, and support, has been an encouraging surprise—as if she's an angel sent to keep him from jumping off the dam. He'd often seen a magic sparkle in her eyes but he never dreamed that she believes in fairy-tale love. As always, Mrs. C. loves to talk, but now more than ever. She invents reasons to come up to Jim's apartment. She makes breakfast for him one day a week, and Sunday dinner as well when she isn't at her daughter's. She takes him into her special room, once a bedroom but now a personal museum-library where she keeps old books and photo albums, and trunks full of letters and old newspapers and keepsakes. She delights in telling Jim about her childhood and about the history of Brendon Falls.

For the most part, she mothers him, fussing and preaching at him, but when Jim speaks of Becki Lea, Mrs. C.'s eyes light up with affection—she's always been fond of Becki—and she'll say, "You love her sorely now, don't you, lad? An' quite right you do. I know your heart's abroodin' over. I wish I could buck you up, but I feel like cryin' me-self, such a pretty little lass. I knew jolly well from the first that she loved you with a love born in heaven. Your tale is for everyone, Jim ... and I daresay it's not over. One day, God's gonna rescue Miss Becki from those *low-lived* religious bastards an' bring her home to you."

Myths, magic, legendary tales. Mrs. Courtney has shared many Irish fairy tales with Jim that back up her prediction. They all have the same story line: happy lovers and God, then evil, then separation and grief; finally, reunion against all odds, and a show-down with evil. Castles, kings, princes, princesses. Peasant girls, pretty slave girls, pirate ships. High cliffs, misty moors, raging seas, dark forests. Christ, the Holy Grail, the Virgin Mary, witches, wizards. Evil mystics, dragons, fairy people, knights on horseback. Her stories, though set in legendary Ireland, mirror Jim's life. The idea that his life is a fairy tale in progress seems an absurd long shot to Jim, but he enjoys the fantasy nonetheless. It surely sounds better than the "Poor Jim" saga he got in the mail from Nana Pedersen.

Mrs. C. talks about everything, even sex: "Eh, young man, humpin' is *no* miracle. Jus' takes a horny lad an' a horny lass, an' a bang up to the barn for a frolic in the hay—but true love, eh ... that's a *gift* of God." Her earthy language shocked Jim at first, but he's now grown fond of her salty side. Mrs. Courtney is an unexpected champion of the heart, and except for Russ, his only confidant—plus Jodi over the phone. And on a practical note, he does all the outside chores for Mrs. C. In return she's reduced his rent to $125 per month. Money, money, just enough. Jim's return to meteorology has been okay on the whole, though he works as a filler—he fills the holes in Ralph's forecaster schedule. Some weeks he works thirty hours, other weeks, sixty, mostly swings and mids. He makes just enough to pay his bills, mainly Sharon.

Russ and Mrs. Courtney have kept Jim from going under but there have been a few other friendly overtures amid the chorus of condemning voices. In early June, Mary Beth Hudson called and told Jim that she believes in his Becki-love and agrees with his views on spiritual authority, but she doesn't have the courage to go all the way with her convictions and that's why she repented before the body in Nashua. The last week of May, Mary Beth gave a testimony of repentance and rededication at a Moody service, doing for Dr. Logan what Jim had refused to do. Logan rewarded her by hiring her to edit his sermons, a low-visibility staff position in return for a loyalty declaration, a familiar scenario. She said she and Tom are still divorcing and that Tom is a baby and a rock-brained boor and she feels sorry for Sharon if she marries him. Confessing that she'd once more sold her soul to Nashua, Mary Beth declared she'd never again run off the cliff of love until she knows for sure that God is with her. She told Jim that she still loves Michael Montanaro but she must openly deny it, yet she hopes that "love" will win in the end, for her, and Jim. After the call, he knew Mary Beth was his friend, his only friend in Nashua, even though their friendship would be secret and passive.

Also on the plus side, Sharon's grandmother (Mor) sent Jim a friendly note, not supportive, not condemning, but understanding of the dilemma of being human. Likewise, Jim's dad responded favorably to his son's break with LBI—and without an I-told-you-so lecture. But Jim's break with Sharon saddened his father's heart; the elder Shanley is fond of Sharon, as is Gary Bob.

But Jim and Sharon's separation has hurt Erin, Heather, and Chris the most. The kids don't take sides or talk about it much but Jim can tell that the breakup of the family has opened their eyes to the dark and woeful realities of life, previously known only in nightmares. He is honest with the kids about his feelings but he doesn't preach to them. He figures that Erin and Heather see Becki as the villain, but they don't openly condemn her. The girls go to BFBC services with Sharon, yet they now see through a lot of the LBI hype—their eyes have also been opened to the realities of religion. They likewise know that their mom's interest in Pastor Hudson is more than ecclesiastical. Chris is sad over his dad's departure but he's too young to accuse or to assign blame—or to understand the grown-up world of love and lying, and selling God.

Yet despite all, the kids have been a comfort to Jim and he to them. They usually go out to eat once a week or to the movies or some such thing. They always laugh a lot, Jim included, and the kids like to come to 59 Front Street. The girls fret over their dad like mother hens: "Dad, you must start eating better. You can't live on TV dinners"—"When do you do your laundry?"—"Don't wear that shirt; it's out of style"—"Dad, you need some plants in here, or a puppy or a kitten." As always, Chris teases his sisters and hogs the TV. He now has new front teeth; they look big and round and rabbitlike in his mouth. The girls like to make supper for Jim, usually hot dogs or tuna fish or French toast.

But now it's Wednesday morning the 18th of July, and Jim is finishing his sausage as he waits for Mrs. Courtney. He hears the screak of the storm door. A moment later she totters in. Sparking eyes, smirking face. She hands him a letter with a Nashua postmark.

Yellow envelope, no return address, but the handwriting looks like Rebecca's. Jim's heart races upstairs with his mind and body rushing right behind it. He scarcely hears Mrs. C.'s squawking about eating the rest of his biscuits and gravy. *Becki, Becki, it's from Becki,* he declares to himself as he spills into his apartment. He closes the door, rips open the envelope:

JULY 16, '84

JIMMY,
        I HATE YOU FOR THE LIES YOU TELL! I NEVER
LED YOU ON. I NEVER WANTED TO MARRY YOU. IT'S NOT
MY FAULT WHAT HAPPENED BETWEEN YOU AND SHARON OR
IN THE CHURCH. YOU SHOULD HAVE REPENTED AND GONE
BACK LIKE I DID. DON'T SEND ANY MORE LETTERS.
THEY'RE DISGUSTING. YOU HAVE NO RIGHT TO SAY SUCH
INTIMATE AND PERSONAL THINGS TO ME. YOU HAVE NO
RIGHT TO CONDEMN ME. YOUR LOVE FOR ME IS NOT OF
GOD. IT'S SINFUL! ALL I HAVE TO DO IS READ MY
BIBLE. YOU TRIED TO POSESS ME AND TO POISEN MY
MIND AGAINST NASHUA. YOU JUST TOOK CARE OF ME
BECAUSE YOU WANTED TO CONTROL ME. THERE WAS NEVER
ANY LOVE WHEN I WAS IN BRENDON FALLS. IT WAS ALL
A LUSTFUL FANTASY THAT STARTED IN YOUR TWISTED
MIND. I BELIEVED IN YOU AS MY PASTOR AND YOU TOOK
ADVANTIGE. YOU NEED HELP, JIMMY. YOU MUST COME
TO PASTOR FOR COUNSELING. PASTOR IS YOUR FRIEND.
HE'LL TELL YOU THE TRUTH FROM GOD'S WORD.
        I'M PUTTING CHRIST FIRST NOW AND FOREVER!
I'VE FOUND TRUE HAPPINESS HERE IN NASHUA. I DON'T
WANT TO EVER SEE YOU OR HEAR FROM YOU AGAIN. LET
ME ALONE. LET ME LIVE MY LIFE THE WAY I WANT. LET
GO OF YOUR SICK FANTASIES, JIMMY, BECAUSE I'LL
NEVER CHANGE. I NEVER WANTED YOU, NOT REALLY, AND
I DON'T WANT YOU NOW! SO LET ME ALONE! TIME WILL
PASS BUT I'LL NEVER CHANGE! DO NOT WRITE ANYMORE
OR I'LL REPORT YOU TO THE POLICE!

                        REBECCA REINHARDT

*   *   *

Hot, humid, sweltering: 95° or close to it. Heat waves ripple
up from the black asphalt in front of Denny's. *Whoosh.* Jim whips
open the glass door. *Whoosh* again. He pulls open the second door.
He smells fried beef and cheese and french fries and floor wax. The
refrigerated air feels refreshing after the drive to Nashua. The
hostess, a tall buxom redhead, seats him in a tiny booth for two.
Yellow envelope, blue shirt. Becki's letter sticks out of the pocket
of his short-sleeve shirt. A skinny pimple-faced girl soon arrives
and takes his order: a BLT and a Coke. But Jim isn't there to eat.
Love, rage, and anguish roar inside him, three hungry beasts
waiting for opportunity to pounce, and they don't have to wait long.
    Perfume, perfume, Moonlight Lace. He catches a whiff. A

short brunette waitress strides by, going the other way with a tray. Heart! Heart! Jim's heart pounds to the ready. No mistaking, he knows that walk. He springs to his feet and calls her name.

Becki whirls around. The scene freezes like a Polaroid snapshot—as do the beasts inside Jim. Five seconds seem like five minutes. Rosy-pink lips, a patch of pimples, angel cheeks full of sun and freckles. Mouth half-open in surprise, fear and yearning in her eyes. And she wears her hair the same. The sun has bleached it a soft summer brown somewhere between honey-maple and toffee. Adorable, huggable, irresistible. Happy memories race up into this muted moment. Love! Love! Jim longs to take her home with him.

Without speaking, Becki calls; without moving, Jim gathers her to him. Outside of time, their spirits couple and soar above the day. He sees unquenchable love in her sky-blue eyes.

Gazing, gazing, he gazes upon her with bated breath. The frozen slice of time grows larger like the circular panorama in a widening camera angle. Suntanned arms, a tray held high. Pert uplifted bosom under a checkered bib. Canted buttocks under a dark-brown skirt. White-cotton socks, and sneakers gray with grease. Melting softness, short maidenly body. Full, full, ripely full. Jim feels faint. His attention is focused on Becki but his peripheral awareness diffuses outward to capture a distorted halo of brown booths and tan wallpaper and three-piece chandeliers with green globes, and shoppers and salesmen and families on vacation—all grabbing a late lunch. Too much. Time can hold no longer; Jim speaks, "Becki Lea, we need to talk."

Becki, caught off guard by the return of reality which confirms Jim's unexpected presence, casts her eyes downward; hot color stains her face. A tremor of expression plays on her lips but she quickly erases it. He expects her to tuck away into her porcupine pose, but instead, she sucks a breath, lifts her chin, and summons all the haughtiness she can muster. "I-I ... I can't talk." Her voice wavers then becomes firm and harsh. "Can't you see I'm busy? I got *tables*." She shifts her weight impatiently from foot to foot. Her mouth tightens, her jaw sets like rock. She glowers at Jim. Her dark eyebrows, like slash marks, jut fiercely downward into the bridge of her nose. Her eyes are now cold and contemptuous—blue ice.

A shock wave of hurt bolts like lightning from Jim's brain to the pit of his stomach. His glimpse of love is over, his cause is lost, but he still pleads pitifully, "Please, Becki, I *hafta* talk to you. Please; I'll wait outside until you get a break. I'll come back when you get off. You name a time?"

"Go *away, Shanley!*" Becki snarls reproachfully. "I meant it, what I said in my letter. I want *nothing* to do with you! If you don't go, I'll call my supervisor."

Love, rage, anguish, no more begging. The wild beasts charge out of Jim's soul; he punches the air; he screams into Becki's face, "I CAN'T BELIEVE YOU SOLD OUT TO FUCKIN' LOGAN! YOU'RE ON ONE *HELL* OF A GUILT TRIP! YOU MUST REALLY HATE YOUR—"

"That's *enough*!" Becki sharply counters, cutting him off. "I don't wanna hear your shit! You're acting like a baby! Now go away, or I'm gonna call my *super*!" Florid with indignation, she turns to march away but Jim halts her escape with a firm hand on her shoulder. "DON'T YOU *DARE* TOUCH ME!" she shouts. "YOU'RE *SICK*!" Jerking free, she strides away again.

Love, rage, anguish, no holding back. Attack! Attack! Jim swings hard, not to hit Becki but the tray—and he does not miss. Time continues but in slow motion. Food, food, flying food, and dishes. Hamburger buns, beef patties, ketchup, french fries. Plates, cups, bowls, glasses. Milk, soft drinks, lettuce, tomatoes, mayonnaise. Mushrooms, cucumbers, Russian dressing. Spinning, twirling, crashing, splashing. All sound slows as well, distorting and dropping several octaves. Becki's shrill scream comes out like the bellow of a bull, while the crash of dishes resounds like thunder.

Gooey glops of ketchup and salad dressing cover her like bloody birdshit. Shocked customers stare. The hostess and the manager, in a paper chef's hat, rush toward Jim, but they move as if running in knee-deep molasses. Jim jerks the letter from his pocket, throws it angrily at Becki, then gallops away taking long slow-motion strides. He beats them to the door, to the Mustang, and roars away—as time returns to normal speed.

Too angry to feel pain, or to look back, Jim drives straight home and calls Russ. As he hangs up the hurt hits him. He collapses on his bed; he sobs and sobs. Later, he goes down and has a tearful talk with Mrs. Courtney. Her assessment says it all: "I daresay, young man, you do love her sorely. I never laid eyes on a chap so screwed with craziness."

\* \* \*

Tuesday, August 7, 1984. Alison Landreth gestures plaintively toward the gray-robed lady magistrate who looks down at the proceedings from her lofty bench. "I fear for my daughter's safety," Alison declares. "I'm on a missionary post in Puerto Rico. I'm not here to watch over her. What happened on July 18th was not an isolated act. Mr. Shanley is ob*sess*ed with Rebecca, and he's been pursuing her for six months."

Alison, prim and proper in a cotton-twill shirtdress of burnished gold, stands next to Becki who is seated at a table. A picture of concerned motherhood, she tosses her head indignantly then sniffs the air. Despite her short stature, she commands the courtroom with her pious presence and condemning words, "My daughter has made it very clear that she has no romantic feelings for this man. How could she? She's *only* twenty years old. She simply wants to complete her education and to pursue her evangelical calling. Yet she cannot live in peace because he torments her. He calls, he follows her to work, he writes letters ... love letters, obscene letters, hate letters, bizarre letters; you've read them. I have no bad feelings toward Mr. Shanley. As a matter of fact, I pray for him daily; I pray he'll seek professional help for his problem. He's emotionally unstable and driven by fantasy. He has an unhealthy fascination for young women, like a Lolita complex, and I uh ... I hate to say it, but I feel that he's potentially dangerous, sexually and otherwise. It breaks my heart to bring—I mean for my daughter to bring—charges against a former family-friend, but we have no choice; we *must* put a stop to this; we can't let it go on. Rebecca is afraid to open her mail. She's afraid to go to work, to answer her phone. She's afraid to...."

Hurt feelings churn in Jim's gut; he feels nauseated. He can't take any more, so he escapes into his own thoughts, *This is the worst day of my life—no, the day she left was the worst, but this is close. Fuck, Alison's making me out to be another John Hinckley. Becki knows I'd never hurt her. God, I just love her. If she would've talked to me, even one time, I would've never gotten into such a lather. Besides, I'm the one who's been raped, not her.*

He gives a silent sigh. He looks up at the lady judge. She, like Beverly Bradley, wears half-eye glasses propped well down on her nose. Matronly and fortyish with dark gray-peppered hair, she looks over her glasses with reproach as she listens to Alison's testimony; Jim knows the reproach is for him.

Above and behind the lady magistrate are shelves of legal books—no, "book" is too light of a word. They are massive legal volumes, heavy cloth- and vellum-bound tomes, old and tan and red and green with gold lettering. They give the judge's bench an aura of fearful authority. Jim feels condemned and small as if he's at the Bemas Seat of God. He lifts his gaze higher to the chalky-white ceiling then at the side wall which is decorated with fluted pilasters topped by Corinthian capitals and a Greek-style frieze and fancy fretted molding, much like Dr. Logan's office at Blantyre. Finally, he drops his attention to the uniformed bailiff by the door who seems asleep with his eyes open.

Not a trial, but a show-cause hearing to see if a complaint will issue on the charges of assault and accosting. No lawyers, no jury, no cross-examination of witnesses, just Becki and her mom on one side, and Jim on the other; they sit at polished walnut tables. Russ watches from the gallery as does Becki's supervisor from Denny's along with a small LBI rooting section: Rich Beckman, Lucas Simpson, Katie Reinhardt, Tricia Logan, several other LBI ladies, and Ed Landreth's cousin Randy Scowcroft. Alison and Katie flew in from Puerto Rico, but Ed didn't come.

Prepared statements, questions from the judge: Becki spoke first, then her supervisor, then Jim, and now Alison. Jim didn't have much to say except that he loves Becki, but love has no weight in a court of law. Rebecca read her statement—it was much the same as her mother's—from a notebook. Her voice was quiet and reserved. A few times she stumbled, and Alison had to coach her. She seems brainwashed, tranquilized, and she looks sexless, shapeless in her baggy overlarge floral-print dress. Her dress is three sizes too big, as if Alison wants to make sure that Jim doesn't see her hips and bustline, like keeping booze away from an alcoholic.

As Alison concludes her scathing testimony, pain squeezes Jim's bosom like a vise. No breath. His heart cries out, *There's no way! Just my luck to get a fuckin' lady judge, but it's not luck. My whole life's going this way.* He unbuttons his suit vest. But as quickly as it gripped him, the crushing pain lets go and a strange peace settles over him—either shock or surrender, or both.

Alison sits down. The lady magistrate shuffles through the papers before her. She adjusts her glasses; she clears her throat. Finally, she delivers her opinion: "After hearing the testimony and reading Mr. Shanley's letters, I have concluded that there *are* sufficient grounds for a complaint to issue on both charges." She speaks in a high judicial tone as if she's Sandra Day O'Connor, but her spirit seems to be that of a disturbed mother as if Alison is still speaking—but through her. "Miss Reinhardt's statement and that of her supervisor clearly substantiate the assault charge, and I think that Mr. Shanley's letters speak for themselves." She picks up Jim's letters and gestures with them. "They're excessive, bothersome, and intimidating, and in some cases, lewd, indecent, and bi*zarre,* bordering on obscene. It is my view that Mr. Shanley has indeed accosted Miss Reinhardt through the mail." As it turns out, all of Jim's letters were intercepted at the LBI mail room—with Becki's permission—and sent straight to Blantyre where copies were made before the originals were sent on to Becki.

The lady judge now speaks directly at Jim as if scolding him, "You have frightened this young woman to such a degree that she's afraid to open her own mail, and she's afraid to go to work. You have *no* right to interfere with her life in such a manner. She has made it very clear that she no longer wants a relationship with you ... of *any* sort. Yet you have continued to harass her."

Giving a sigh of seeming disgust, she looks over her glasses at Jim, and down her nose. "But, Mr. Shanley, I have a compromise to offer. If you're wise, you will accept. After all, you're an educated man and a professional. You *cer*tainly don't want to go to trial on these charges, especially when there's a better than even chance you'll be convicted—at least in my view. But even if you're acquitted, the testimony will be most damaging to your reputation. So I have a compromise that will put this all behind us. If you agree to have no contact with Miss Reinhardt from this day forward, then no complaint will issue, but if you write one letter, make one call, or approach her in any way, then you'll go to trial. This court can only enforce such a condition for one year, at which time the complaint will be dismissed. However, I strongly advise that you observe this restriction for the *rest* of your days."

Resignation, letting go, no more fight—against the tide. Jim quickly agrees, and the hearing is adjourned. Russ joins Jim and they wait at his table while Becki and the others file out. When Jim and Russ finally exit the courthouse, they find Alison and Becki and their band of LBI rooters gathered in quiet celebration on the steps. Her chin held high, Alison eyes Jim with an expression of cold triumph. Becki gives him a blank look; her blue eyes seem unfeeling, showing no evidence of farewell—or even recognition. But neither looks long at him as they quickly turn back to receive the kudos and congratulations of their LBI peers.

Jim and Russ walk quickly past without a word then across the street to Russ's Fairmont. The August sun glares hot upon them but not like July; the days are already getting shorter.

# Chapter Forty

Thursday, September 27, 1990. Hazy sky, warm sun, yet so different than summer. The air is filled with that indefinable sense of autumn that makes the blood tingle with accelerated life. Jim Shanley, his heart yearning, strides past the parking nook, around the house, then up toward the meadow. Muffled music. Rock music. The old barn resonates to the whine of Joe's guitar and the percussive chug of Haley's bass track. Jim carries a blue loose-leaf book, a journal. He loves it, but he can't read it without crying. In an ACCO binder, it feels heavy in his hand like a dictionary.

Knee-high grass, nodding goldenrods, piney woods. Jim walks briskly. Reaching the big rock, he plops down and dangles his sneakers over the edge. The midafternoon sun throws his shadow on the lower tier of rock. The day started frosty but has warmed to the mid 70s. The dam hovers before him like a monstrous mirage while the river, dark-blue and glistening, flows below him. The hills across the river present a preview of fall color but green still dominates the auburns, ambers, and yellows. Jim adjusts his old softball cap and pushes up the sleeves of his sweat shirt. *It's been six years,* he sighs to himself as he opens the hefty journal. *Why can't I let go?* He pulls his glasses from the pouch of his shirt and begins to read—not every entry but a goodly number:

Ltr #1, Wed 8-8-84, 11:13 a.m. (159 days). Dear Becki, no hope, no hope. After yesterday's hearing, I'm resigned to the fact that I can't communicate w you. Even if I disobey the court, my letters won't get to you. So when I feel like talking to you, I'll type a letter into my computer. At the end of each month, I'll print them out & put them in a notebook like a diary. (159 days) means 159 days since you were last friendly to me—that heavenly Friday back in March. To write unsent letters is fucking insane but at least I can say what I want w/o getting charged w accosting! & believe me I will. I don't plan to edit or censor my entries. ◊ I have your picture taped to my monitor, your high school graduation picture that you gave me last year. √ js

- - - - - - -

Ltr #3, Sat 8-11-84, 10:10 p.m. (162 days). Hurt, hurt! Becki, my heart is ripped to shreds. I still hear your words in court: "Mr. Shanley has weird sexual fantasies about me; he scares me." It cuts like a knife when people say I'm dangerous/perverted, but it hurts most from your lips. ◊ This morning I ate w Russ at the diner. He has no answers either. √ js

--------

<u>Ltr #5, Tue 8-14-84, 4:42 p.m. (165 days).</u> Becki, you're a cold bitch! Cold, cold, and hateful! You deny our love, accuse me, & come out pure & clean = a little Christian rosebud. You sanitized yourself as if you spent the whole year sorting outreach files. If you have no love for me as you now profess, you're the biggest heart criminal in history, & I lost all for a fucking fantasy! √ js

--------

<u>Ltr #6, Wed 8-15-84, 4:19 p.m. (166 days).</u> Becki, I'm numb today, no emotion. ◊ My job's OK. I work 40-50 hrs/wk. I make just enough to live & pay Sharon. She's nice as long as she gets her $$. She's going w Tom H. Guess you know that. ◊ Sharon says Barry & Janet are in Nashua, & Barry's working for Garrett for his campus job—no big surprise. ◊ Russ & I are making new tracts that say that following love is the highest good. We meet at his house on Sun nites. We call our new church "The Remnant" = Herschel, Barbara S, Harry & Judy, & a few others. ◊ Tonite I'm eating Stouffer's Salisbury steak. I'm tired of TV dinners. √ js

--------

<u>Ltr #8, Mon 8-20-84, 5:44 p.m. (171 days).</u> Sunny, breezy, warm. Becki, I just got back from the meadow. I saw a chipmunk on the stone fence. You always said the animals liked us & wanted to talk to us. I choked up as I thought of the times we spent there, you & me. It's so hard to accept this as reality = the door is bolted = not even a "hi" after being so close. On the way back I talked w Mrs. C. while she worked in her garden. She got this twinkle in her eyes, like she does, & said that you ran because you were terrified of your love for me. Makes sense, but how can I know? √ js

--------

<u>Ltr #10, Thur 8-23-84, 7:43 a.m. (174 days).</u> Becki, I just got home from the weather station. I worked mid shift last nite. Pissed! Pissed! Unfair! No justice! Logan labels me a heretic, tells everyone to never talk to me again or God will punish them. And you say I tried to poison your mind. FUCK THAT! Logan secretly tapes people in his office and has girls all over him. Yet you reject me & bow down to him like he's fucking God! & your mom never talked to me. She just zoomed back from Puerto Rico w her guns firing, & Logan's Gestapo agents intercepted my love letters to you & you allowed it = wicked = a knife in my back. YOU'RE A FUCKING LIAR, BECKI! You can take me to court & banish me from your presence but you can't take your heart to court & banish it from your bosom. √ js

--------

Ltr #15, Sat 9-8-84, 8:44 p.m. (190 days). Becki, I got a letter from Mary Beth Hudson today. She keeps me posted on you = you still live at Stowe Hall & work at Denny's. Your new roommate is your step-cousin, Linda Scowcroft = Randy's younger sister. You both waitress in Logan's Blantyre dining room for campus duty. Looks like Alison has you well placed & surrounded. √ js

--------

Ltr #18, Thur 9-13-84, 9:44 p.m. (195 days). Dear Becki, when I get the mail I expect a letter from you & when the phone rings, I hope for your voice & when I drive downtown, I look for you on every corner, I cry out to God, but He seems distant, cold, & cruel. Sharon says, "You can't blame God, Jim. It was your choice to love Becki. You must let go. You must love God more than Becki." Fuck that! If loving you, Rebecca, is not loving God, then I'll never love God! ◊ I got a note from Stan Campbell, after 6 mos. He's praying for me & no hard feelings = easy for him to say. ◊ Earlier tonite I took Erin, Heather, & Chris to McD's. √ js

--------

Ltr #28, Mon 10-8-84,1:37 p.m. (220 days). Becki, we only had six at Russ' house last nite, not good after handing out 400 tracts. ◊ Yesterday, I helped Mrs. C. fix the barn door. Afterward we sat in her old Packard and talked. It was like she was reliving her past. The car smells musty but the inside is still very plush. ◊ Jodi called Fri. She lives with her cousin in Elmwood Park & she works at a restaurant in Addison. She makes twice her teacher's salary, but Brenda doesn't like her new school. √ js

--------

Ltr #34, Wed 10-24-84, 9:13 p.m. (236 days). Dear Becki, tonite I heard the song "Longer" (Dan Fogelburg). You like that song. I cried. I went to the meadow & looked up at the stars. The north wind chilled my face. I felt you near me. √ js

--------

Ltr #35, Thur 10-25-84,11:38 p.m. (237 days). Life sucks, Becki! Sucks, sucks, sucks! My woeful state grates on me like gravel in my bed. ◊ I got into a shouting match with Ruthie tonite. She had her stereo so high the fillings in my teeth were vibrating, & she was playing Ozzy Osbourne = no redeeming value. Since Kyle moved in, they stay home and drink. √ js

--------

Ltr #36, Fri 10-26-84, 6:55 p.m. (238 days). Dear Becki, Russ came by on his way home. He says Sylvia & Angie left BFBC to go to Valley

Baptist along w Freddie & Juanita, & Thelma H. According to Bev, there's a lot of dissatisfaction with Tom Hudson's strict LBI regime, and the church is down to 35 members. I hope it dwindles to nothing! Those fuckers! √ js

- - - - - - - -

Ltr #40, Wed 11-7-84, 00:35 a.m. (250 days). Dear Becki, I just got home from the wx station, takes 30 min. on Rte 62. Reagan crushed Mondale but what does it matter? The girl, Geraldine, she's all right but I doubt anyone wants an emotional female a heartbeat away from the White House. ◊ I got a letter from Ernie Johnson. He and Sarah live in Ripley, West Virginia where he works for his brother at the local Agway outlet. He apologized for yelling at me last April but he still calls my love for you, foolishness. √ js

- - - - - - - -

Ltr #46, Sat 11-17-84, 9:15 a.m. (260 days). Dear Becki, bad news. Mrs. C. got the flu & she couldn't breath. Her daughter Connie came & took her to the hospital. √ js

- - - - - - - -

Ltr #50, Wed 11-28-84, 9:15 a.m. (271 days). Torture! Torture! Oh, Becki, I hurt. I hurt. I love you. I miss you. No escape, except when I sleep. ◊ Mrs. C. is doing better. She has an oxygen tank by her bed. She has emphysema. Her spirit is spunky but her body's weak. She says it's because she used to smoke a lot before the war—even cigars. I believe it. √ js

- - - - - - - -

Ltr #55, Sun 12-9-84, 4:58 p.m. (282 days). Blustery but not freezing. This aftn, Becki, I went to the big rock. I saw the train going across the trestle. It made me sad since we used to watch it together. The blue engine looks old & forlorn as if it knows its days are numbered. On the way back, I stopped in the meadow & watched the sunset. It gets dark early now. I felt you near. √ js

- - - - - - - -

Ltr #71, Mon 1-14-85, 8:13 a.m. (318 days). All is ice, and still silence of death. The lake is frozen. The snow is old & crusty. I look forward to nothing. ◊ Mrs. C. had a bad spell yesterday & had to go back to the hospital. ◊ Nobody came to our meeting at Russ' house last nite. C'est fini. We decided to quit. Herschel works every Sun, & Harry & Judy were never into church. And Barbara is leaving Curt & taking the kids to California (with a soldier from Ft. Devens). Russ says, "I'll never go to any fucking church again." I agree. Besides, no church would have me. ◊ Sharon says I'm going through male menopause. That's Nana's latest explanation for my behavior the past two years. √ js

--------

**Ltr #76, Fri 1-25-85,11:07 a.m. (329 days).** Dear Becki. Bad news. Mrs. Courtney died at four o'clock this morn. God's an asshole! He's fucking good at taking my friends away! √ js

--------

**Ltr #84, Thur 2-14-85, 11:21 a.m. (349 days).** Oh, Becki, my heart breaks. I just heard the song, "The First Time Ever I Saw Your Face" (Roberta Flack). It made me weep. So many songs remind me of you. I wish I had no memory, yet memory is all I have. I no longer expect you to write, or expect your voice when the phone rings. You're so gone from my life. ◊ Mrs. Courtney left the house to Connie. She left me the clock on her mantel & her '38 Packard. Connie says she's going to sell the house & asked me to manage/maintain it until she does. I no longer have to pay rent. √ js

--------

**Ltr #88, Fri 2-22-85,9:17 a.m. (357 days).** Becki, I'm tired. I just got off 6 straight mids. ◊ Sharon says she saw you at Wed nite service, & you look so grown-up & ladylike. She always says how well you're doing (w/o me). You're flying high all right! = living in the dorm & bowing down to all the religious rules & routines = what you hated & would never do? √ js

--------

Suddenly, pigeons: a dozen pigeons, flying as one. Jim stops reading and watches them. Gray, white, brown, and mottled, they swoop down toward the river and land on the trestle. The birds now have the rusty steel structure to themselves. No trains since '86. The abandoned trestle gives Jim a sad and vague sense of loss. After a long moment of reflection, he returns to the journal:

**Ltr #92, Sun 3-3-85,9:23 p.m. (366 days).** Cathy Rosinski (Johnson) came by this aftn w Chad, her baby boy. She & Kevin are moving to West Virginia to be near Ernie & Sarah. Kevin is going to work with Ernie at Agway. ◊ Russ & I ate at the diner yesterday. We talked about "destiny" for the 100th time = Is God a loving artist & history a grand painting? Or is God a holy referee & victory up to us = wise choices + effort + prayer +luck? It seems to me, Becki, if there's no eternal plan, no plot-twist that leads to a just triumph for love, then Babylon rules forever & "might makes right" & people will go on hiding and supressing their feelings because they fear "Big Brother." And anyone who openly loves is a fucking fool, like me! What's the point? Maybe there is no point? Maybe love is no more than an emotion that makes us mate & propogate, then we die into dust, into cold darkness forever, like the back side of the moon? √ js

- - - - - - - - -

<u>Ltr #108, Mon 4-1-85, 6:48 p.m. (394 days).</u> Dear Becki, for supper I made pork chops with Shake & Bake, + baked potato, green beans, & sliced peaches. I cook now, but I still eat weird at work = Fritos, donuts, & McD's. ◊ My sex life is much worse = none for 10 mos. Lust, lust. Every woman I see is all tits & ass. Sharon's still w Tom, of course. She treats me like a backslidden brother. She says I should meet new women but right now I can't. So I jerk off & think of you, Rebecca. How's your sex life? Do you still "do your wash by hand"? I'm sure you'd never admit it. No sweet Spirit-filled LBI girl would dare admit that she lusts for hard cock and fingerfucks herself. Oh fuck, Becki, you drive me nuts, even w/o seeing you. I can't type. I have to jerk off—right now. √ js.

- - - - - - - - -

<u>Ltr #121, Wed 4-24-85, 11:32 p.m. (417 days).</u>  Dear Becki. Carl & Melissa came over tonite. They encouraged me to come to church— if not BFBC then to some Bible church. They say Tom H. & Stan are preaching w fervor & BFBC has recovered to 70 members (means 45). As they left, Carl says, "We love you in Christ, Jim"—FUCK THAT! I don't want to be loved "in Christ." I want to be loved period! Like heart to heart! √ js

- - - - - - - - -

<u>Ltr #129, Wed 5-8-85, 4:37 p.m. (431 days).</u> Well, Becki, I guess my days here are numbered. Connie put the house up for sale. She's asking $160,000. Seems a lot for such a run-down place but real estate is skyrocketing. With the barn & 5 acres, maybe it's a deal, especially since it abuts on state land. She came over w her husband & took all of Mrs. C's furniture & stuff. ◊ I got a letter from Jodi = she's still working as a waitress & Brenda's happier = she has a boyfriend (he's 19 & has a rich father). √ js

- - - - - - - - -

<u>Ltr #131, Sat 5-11-85, 2:08 p.m. (434 days).</u> Warm, almost summer-like. My windows are open. Oh, Becki, the sweet fragrance of the meadow grass reminds me of the times we chased each other on the hill—Fuck! Why do humans regulate love with rules, vows, labels— wife, husband, wedlock, honeymoon, certificate, ceremony, in-laws, young, old, virgin, Christian, "thou shalt not," family, home, "until death do us part"? It makes people behave in a dishonest fashion based on duty & guilt & ulterior motive. Love can't flow in a closed vessel. Is it any wonder that marriage leads to lying & loneliness? There's no category for us, Becki = LOVE w no credentials = we can't be together. But it's OK & applauded to buy candy for your wife on Valentine's Day—even if it's not in your heart. √ js

- - - - - - - - -

<u>Ltr #136, Tue 5-21-85, 7:27 a.m. (444 days).</u> Shock! Unexpected! Gary Bob just called. Dad died in his sleep last nite of a heart attack. He was only 66 & in good health. He still worked part-time. I'm flying to Dallas this aftn. I must pack. √ js

- - - - - - - - -

<u>Ltr #141, Sat 6-15-85, 4:36 p.m. (469 days).</u> I just got back from Texas. My brain is shot from jet lag. I feel cobwebby and blah. I've been down 3 times in 3 wks. It's sad, but it's not like the hurt of losing Mom, or the trauma of losing you, Becki. ◊ But I did get a surprise at the lawyer's office on Thursday = Dad left Gary Bob & me the farm as expected, but he also left us $260,000. I never knew he had so much saved up. So I now have $139,800 in my Comfed acct = I'm rich. But I'd give it up w/o a thought to be w you, Becki Lea. √ js

- - - - - - - - -

<u>Ltr #142, Mon 6-17-85, 12:10 p.m. (471 days).</u> Dear Becki. Guess what? I'm buying 59 Front St. for $150,000 (80 down & graduated mortgage payments starting at $496/mo). √ js

- - - - - - - - -

<u>Ltr #147, Tue 7-1-85, 1:02 a.m. (485 days).</u> Dear Becki. Curious news = Ruthie came up for 3 hours tonite w/o Kyle. She was sober & friendly. Her bangs are longer. She dimples when she smiles just like Judy & Jodi—I never saw her smile before. I suspect she wants to get on my good side since I'm buying the house but she also seemed lonely. We had Pepsi & Fritos—& she smoked her Virginia Slims. She was raw & honest : "My stepfather started fuckin me when I was 14 so I split.... My marriage to David was OK 'til that cocksucker, Stan Campbell, messed it up. Doris was my friend but Stan ruined that too. Kyle's lazy & he hits me, but I feel sorry for him since Jodi & everyone rejected him.... I hate my job at Nypro. I run a machine that makes plastic milk bottles. It's fuckin dull." √ js

- - - - - - - - -

<u>Ltr #160, Wed 7-24-85, 10:52 p.m. (508 days).</u> Dear Becki. Shar & I went to court this morning for the divorce. She cried & hugged me afterward, but she left with Tom. ◊ Sgt. Brown & Bobbie Rae moved out this aftn. They're out of the Army & going back to Ky. Ruthie & Kyle are the only ones left and I don't feel like inviting new tenants. Ruthie was up again last nite. She laughs & cuts up like Jodi. ◊ I Got a letter from Joe L. He's still in St Louis & plays in a local band, but not much $$. He works as a security guard to get by. √ js

- - - - - - - - -

Ltr #164, Thur 8-1-85, 10:13 a.m. (516 days). Oh, Becki. Unexpected action last nite. When I got home from swing shift, Ruthie was waiting on the porch. She came up. She kissed me. She took off her clothes. Jutting breasts, beer-bloated paunch. Her naked body doesn't look as good as it does inside her jeans and pullover shirts, and her tobacco breath was disgusting. But she still turned me on. I was hard as a rock until she spread her legs then it melted, and I couldn't get it back—maybe it was her sour breath—so I fingered her off then she gave me a blow job. That's one thing I never got from Sharon. (Perhaps Nana Pedersen's contention that all sodomites and fags are damned beyond redemption had something to do with it.) Afterward, Ruthie and I made coffee & talked. She says she never saw me as a regular guy before. The sex part was frustrating. I never had trouble getting it up before. But just getting off w a girl was quite a release after so long. I like Ruthie okay, but she can never heal my heart. √ js

- - - - - - - - -

Ltr #171, Wed 8-14-85, 1:46 p.m. (529 days). Hot = 91°. I'm sweating. ◊ Sharon & Tom have set a date = 1st week of Feb. Despite Logan's ranting against divorce and remarriage, he's doing the wedding, in his office, on Feb. 8th. Russ is right. At LBI, allegiance is the bottom line. ◊ Life is heavy. I have no energy. My job at the weather station is getting to me. I had to go in 3 hrs early yesterday. I work so much overtime. We have lots of new clients but no increase in staff. Mr. Watkins (the owner) wants to handle the increased forecast load thru increased efficiency. With $58,000 in the bank, I don't feel like killing myself. ◊ Ruthie & Kyle are moving to New Jersey on Sat. Nypro was bought out by Poly Plastic Corp. They laid off half the workforce—fuck! every time I get to know someone they die or go away. I'll be here by myself now & I have no energy to be a landlord. ◊ I'm nuts to write letters that you'll never see. √ js

- - - - - - - - -

Ltr #183, Tue 9-10-85, 9:46 a.m. (556 days). Dear Becki. On Sunday evening, I took a walk to the lake with Erin & Heather & Chris. It was warm & humid. When we got back, we sat out front under the oak tree & listened to the doves. They perch on the wires and give a hollow mournful cry— like the cry of my heart. ◊ When I took the kids home, Sharon told me that your sister Katie is in Nashua now & her campus job is right at the top = typing for Matt Garrett. Rebecca Lea, now Katie Marie. Your mom certainly has her daughters on the inside track to greatness in the kingdom of God—"Yay! Great job, Alison!" √ js

- - - - - - - - -

Ltr #197, Mon 10-14-85, 8:32 a.m. (590 days). Oh, Becki, you turn me on! Last night I had a wet dream about you. We were at the diner.

You were so horny you pulled down your jeans and showed me your pussy under the table, then fingered off. Just as you were coming, your mom came in, and you opened a door—our booth had a door like a car door—and ran away.  √ js

- - - - - - - - -

<u>Ltr #216, Sun 11-17-85, 2:43 p.m. (624 days).</u> 59 Front St. is a lonely place, Becki. No voices, no footsteps, just a blue Mustang in the driveway. I could move down to Mrs. C's apt = 5 rooms, or I could open the whole house, but what's the point? I only need two rooms. Besides, it's special to live where you lived. I've never been this alone but somehow it seems right despite the pain = a time for the old leaves to fall inside of me & for the pure death of winter to take my soul. I just hope winter doesn't last forever. √ js

- - - - - - - - -

<u>Ltr #217, Tue 11-19-85, 8:23 a.m. (626 days).</u> Becki, I got into it w Ralph about overtime. He said he did me a favor when I needed a job & I should be thankful. I'm not! ◊ Last nite I went to a singles bar w Russ = Jerry's Lounge in Worcester. We sipped beer & tried to pick up girls, but it was a fucking disaster = embarrassing. The whole alcohol-bar scene turns me off. As bad as I hurt, I still like being sober. I want to be <u>me</u>. ◊ Russ says Freddie & Juanita are getting a divorce = no big surprise. I'm sure Leslie B. will blame it on me. √ js

- - - - - - - -

<u>Ltr #230, Fri 12-13-85, 11:03 a.m. (650 days).</u> Dear Becki. I quit yesterday. I can't take it anymore! Ralph had me scheduled 27 days this month so everyone else can have time off for the holidays. Fuck that! I don't have to take his shit, not with $56,000 in the bank. ◊ Last nite I took the kids to Searstown & let them pick out their Xmas presents from me. When we got back, I told Sharon that I quit my job. She didn't react in front of the kids but walked me out to my car where she nailed me: "You haven't changed, Jim! You just think of yourself! You lay around feeling hurt because that little bitch rejected you! Well, you're not the 1st person to hurt from unrequited love! Grow up! I told you all along she didn't want you! You're letting it destroy you & you're depriving your kids! YOU'RE THE MOST SELFISH MAN I KNOW! All you have is hot air and a hot penis! I should've known better 17 years ago! You have that whole house & could bring in $2000 a month on rent! You have degrees & credentials! You could make fifty thou if you'd get off you ass & get a decent job!" Such is my ongoing relationship with Sharon Pedersen Shanley, soon-to-be Hudson. I felt like throwing her in the car & fucking the anger out of her but she'd never do it, not now. She has a new vision for her life—just like you, Becki Lea. √ js

----------

<u>Ltr #233, Thur 12-19-85, 10:34 a.m. (656 days).</u> Down, down. I haven't shaved for a week. I need a haircut. I gaze out the window. I write seed poems. But mostly I think of you, Rebecca. You're the air I breathe. You're the water I drink. You're the food I eat. Your presence falls with the snow & covers the land about me, & when I sleep, I dream into your waiting arms. You're my eternal curse—& my only salvation? √ js

----------

Jim puts down his diary, hauls himself to his feet, then goes to the far end of the rock and pisses over the edge. As the yellow stream splatters on the ledge below, he thinks, *Becki took a pee up here with Joe. He said she had a big butt and pissed like a cow. He got that right. Oh, Rebecca, you're a wild one; there'll never be another you.* Chuckling, Jim returns to his rocky perch, and resumes reading:

<u>Ltr #252, Mon 1-27-86, 10:57 a.m. (695 days).</u> Dear Becki. Got a note fm Mary Beth Hudson. She says you're completing the two-year missionary program in May & going to Puerto Rico to join your mom's team. But Sharon says you're going on a new team to Angola? What does it matter? You're already gone! ◊ M.B. also says that Dr. Logan rarely talks about me anymore except as an example of a Pastor who turned from the true gospel to a salacious gospel which he uses to seduce young women—I WISH! ◊ Russ was over yesterday to watch the Super Bowl. The Bears crushed the Pats 46-10. Russ has to work overtime for 6 wks, so I won't see him much. ◊ Oh, this aftn I went to Sears & bought a VCR. √ js

----------

<u>Ltr #253, Tue 1-28-86, 9:36 p.m. (696 days).</u> Dear Becki, it's hard to believe the shuttle blew up. I feel bad for the teacher, Christy McAulife. She was a guinea pig in NASA's push to get more $$. Must be horrible to fall 10 miles = 50 seconds of free fall. NASA says they died instantly. I doubt it. NASA's like LBJ = pure Babylon. They lie to protect the organization. √ js

----------

<u>Ltr #256, Wed 2-5-86, 10:14 p.m. (704 days).</u> Frigid, 11° out. The wind's howling. I watched 2 movies today—Sophie's Choice & Romantic Comedy. I like the happy ending to the Dudley Moore flick but Sophie's Choice (Meryl Streep) seems more honest. There's a new video store, ZOOM VIDEO, at Coachlace. Movies = $1.75/nite,

except new-releases cost $2.75. √ js

- - - - - - - -

<u>Ltr #258, Sun 2-9-86,10:32 a.m. (708 days).</u> Becki, I'm sick. Coughing, wheezing. Can hardly get out of bed. ◊ Guess you know Sharon & Tom were married at Blantyre yesterday. Bev was there. Saves me $600/mo alimony, but what a cruel twist = Hudson screwing <u>my</u> wife in <u>my</u> house, & living w <u>my</u> kids, & pastoring <u>my</u> church—but I hurt much more over you, Becki Lea. √ js

- - - - - - - -

<u>Ltr #272, Tue 3-11-86, 9:17 p.m. (738 days).</u> Oh, Becki, what a frustrating afternoon. Doris came over, drunk on wine. She undressed. I kick myself for going along. I fondled her. She tried to respond, but her pussy was drier than Melba Toast. My prick shriveled to a thumby thimble. Giving up, she lit up a Salem Light, & confessed in a wine-slurred voice, "Oh, Jimmy honey, I'm 32 an' I never had a climax. Stan says I'm frigid, yes, he doesh. He saysh the Catholic Church meshed me up. But I love you, Jimmy honey, you know that." Then she suddenly shifted, "Oh, Jimmy, this ish wrong, you know ish wrong. Stan, he saysh—you know it, honey, I love you, I tol' you, but you know we're not supodz to talk." She quickly dressed & left, leaving a cloud of smoke behind her. √ js

- - - - - - - - -

<u>Ltr #279, Thur 3-27-86, 2:43 p.m. (754 days).</u> So, Becki, how does it feel to be 22? ◊ Sharon called last night. As usual, she needs money. Chris has an ear infection & went to the doctor 3 times and my BC/BS doesn't cover it. She also shared some hot gossip = Logan & Amy B. are getting married. It's unannounced but Sharon knows. No big surprise, except Logan waited 11 yrs? √ js

- - - - - - - -

<u>Ltr #280, Fri 3-28-86, 5:48 p.m. (755 days).</u> Cloudy, chilly, gloomy. I took a walk today. I heard no birds. Sad. Sad. I sat on the big rock & watched the river. No more trains, just rusty rails and rotten ties. B&M sold out to Guilford & they closed down the line. The abandoned tracks give me a strange sense of absence & absurdity = like my life = disconnected & adrift on a sea of tears. I'm the bearded man in the boat in the Andrew Wyeth painting. Old, ugly, rejected. No hope. My life is like cello music. I weigh 165 = most ever. ◊ According to Mary Beth, LBI is growing fast = 45 branches in the U.S. & 23 overseas teams. And BFBC is growing again as well. Tom Hudson has 80 out on Sunday mornings (means 55). Fuck it! The cold-blooded killers of love prosper & grow while I twirl down, down, drifting on the wind like a dead October leaf. And you're in their victory parade,

Becki Lea. Betrayal! Betrayal! I hate God! √ js

· · · · · · · ·

Ltr #289, Sun 4-20-86,10:43 p.m. (778 days). Dear Becki, Stan was ordained in Nashua this aftn—as you know I'm sure. What a farce! Sharon says Dr. Logan wants to make Stan the head pastor in Brendon Falls, not right away but in a year or two. She says it's good since Tom would like to be the pastor in Pittsfield eventually. Sounds more like a Sharon-scheme to get closer to Cobleskill. √ js

· · · · · · · ·

Ltr #306, Thur 5-29-86,10:15 a.m. (817 days). Yesterday I saw 3 movies, Somewhere in Time, Crimes of Passion, & Against all Odds. Each shows the war between love & self-hate. I've seen 70 movies since Jan. I never watch regular TV except news & weather. I hate commercials. Some movies are bombs but many touch my heart. I think movies & novels & artists & poets & musicians, now & thru the ages, say more about God & life than any Bible preacher. Of course, you told me that many times, Becki Lea? √ js

· · · · · · · ·

Ltr #310, Sat 6-7-86, 9:15 a.m. (826 days). Dear Becki, I got a note from Mary Beth Hudson. She confirmed that Logan & Amy are getting married. It's still a secret, but it leaked out in the office, & Molly Gibson had a crying fit & left the ministry & moved back to Boston. She had one year to go on her degree. ◊ Mary Beth also says you're preparing to go to Puerto Rico, Becki, that Dr. Logan is increasing the PR team by 3 = you & Linda Scowcroft & her brother Randy = a fucking family reunion. Where did Sharon get that shit about Africa? √ js.

· · · · · · · ·

Ltr #319, Fri 6-27-86, 5:15 p.m. (846 days). Dear Becki, Sharon says you left for Puerto Rico last Tuesday. I guess Mary Beth was right. Yay Rebecca! Rah! Rah! Rah! I'm sure Alison is prouder than a peacock. You're now a missionary and a witness for Christ—but I disagree. To me, to be a witness for God doesn't mean to hand out salvation tracts or to teach the young and insecure and guilt-ridden how to escape hell, but it means to openly declare your true heart & to undergo the crucifixion which always follows. √ js

· · · · · · · ·

Ltr #336, Sun 8-10-86, 5:45 p.m. (891 days). Dear Becki. Happy Birthday to me, but it's hardly happy. I'm 40, but I feel 80. It's hot &

humid, & my spirit is heavier than the sultry air. The lawn is knee-deep but I don't care—but I did accomplish one task this week. I got my watchband fixed after three years. ◊ So you're back in Guayama where you said you'd never go as a missionary. Do you ever see Maria or Manny? I doubt it. You no longer associate w such worldly people. √ js

- - - - - - - -

Ltr #351, Mon 9-22-86, 8:57 p.m. (934 days). Becki, I bought a woodstove at Aubuchon. Russ & I set it up on the hearth in front of the fireplace—we cut away the carpet—& ran the stovepipe into the old chimney. I moved my desk over to the east window, & Bev's sofa into the kitchen. ◊ Russ says Joanne McClusky is partially paralyzed, that she has a neuromuscular disorder. She's at a special hospital in Maryland. And Cal lives w his parents but spends most of his time at Clancy's. God has really answered their prayers. √ js

- - - - - - - -

Ltr #354, Mon 9-29-86, 4:57 p.m. (941 days). Becki, I can see the meadow as I type. Happy memories torment me. The shadows are long like that warm autumn day in '83 when we hugged by the blue flowers. I looked them up. They're called Fringed Gentians = rare & cannot be picked. I often go back to the spot but I've not seen them again. ◊ Got a note from Mary Beth Hudson—it's good to have a spy at Blantyre. She says you're teaching kindergarten, Becki, that you love the kids, but you're bored, & you live w Alison & Ed in a big Spanish-style house on the new LBI property. Mary Beth must talk with Katie to know so much. Of course they're both working in Logan's office. ◊ I had a fight with Sharon on the phone last nite. She asked how I was. I told her life sucks, especially celibacy. She says, "How can you get a wife when you have nothing to offer except depression & self-pity?" I said I wanted a woman who'll love me as I am. She retorted, "You won't get one as you are." ◊ I watched a movie earlier = Paris, Texas = love loses, but I like the bluesy slide guitar & Harry Dean Stanton, the way he talks so slowly & sadly. It's like my spirit is in him. √ js

- - - - - - - -

Ltr #355, Tue 9-30-86, 8:23 p.m. (942 days). Today I broke down & wrote you a real letter. I mailed it this aftn. Maybe your mail won't be intercepted now that you're out of Nashua. √ js

- - - - - - - -

Ltr #358, Wed 10-8-86, 10:54 a.m. (950 days). Nerves, nerves, anxious. Oh, Becki, you must have my letter by now. I've picked up the phone 10 times but I can't call. My heart roars. I feel like flying down & rushing to you, but I'm too scared. Why is it taking so long?

Just to know you don't despise me will save my life. I can't sleep. I'm anxious for a reply. I'm going nuts. √ js

--------

Ltr #361, Fri 10-17-86, 11:51 a.m. (959 days). Oh, Becki, my heart leaps when the mail truck comes then sinks when I find nothing. Why do you treat me as an enemy or worse = you ignore me? ◊ The trees blaze with fall color but I see no reds, oranges, yellows. All is gray & growing dark. Why can't I let go? Why do I love you so? I hate this torment = not one crumb of response in 959 days. ◊ I guess you know Logan & Amy were married on Sat. Sharon says it was magnificent like Prince Charles & Diana—FUCK 'EM! ◊ I'm down to $42,000. It's scary to watch it run out. Getting a job is a heavy thought. Fuck it! I'll sell first. I've got 80 thou sunk into this house. √ js

--------

Ltr #363, Mon 10-27-86, 9:32 a.m. (969 days). Dear Becki, I just checked the mail = no letter. It's been a month. Sad. Sad. I hurt so bad—I can't type. I have to go back to bed. I hate life! √ js

--------

Ltr #364, Sat 11-1-86, 11:44 a.m. (974 days). Why Becki, why? Still nothing? I'm a basket case. I don't shower or shave. I scarcely eat. My hair is shaggy & long. I'm dying. I tried to call you but I got some guy jabbering in Spanish. Guess Ed's phone # is changed at the new school. So I wrote you again. I just mailed it. I thought I was cured of clawing at the wall after the hearing, but I'm still crazy in love w you. This is what I said: "If you have no love for me, Becki, why'd you come to Brendon Falls & spend every day with me? Why'd you show me your dolls & your special stuff? I don't know why you shut me out of your life? Is it because our feelings got too intense? But how can love be too intense, if God is LOVE? I have problems, you have problems. But isn't LOVE bigger? Why can't we talk to each other—just talk? It kills me, Becki, that we never talked. You just slammed the door & left me crying outside & I'm still crying after 2 1/2 yrs. I love you, Becki! I make no demands on you! Just a "hi" from you across the miles would be like the sun rising on a new day." √ js

--------

Ltr #365, Sat 11-8-86, 4:38 p.m. (981 days). Death! Death! I beg for death! Oh, Becki, I've been wailing & sobbing all day. My heart is gone. My eyes are so blurred, I can hardly see to type this. This morning my last letter came back unopened with "return to sender" scrawled on it in your handwriting. Fuck it, Becki! I'll never write you again. I give up! √ js

--------

Ltr #366, Mon 11-10-86, 8:35 p.m. (983 days). No control! Becki, I'm addicted to you. This afternoon I sent you 3 big post cards, so you'll have to read what I have to say. √ js

- - - - - - - -

Ltr #369, Sat 11-22-86, 9:52 a.m. (995 days). Dear Becki, No letter from you, but I got one from your mom & Ed = a warning. I'm pasting it in for the record:

November 19, 1986

Dear Jim,

Your emotional attachment to Rebecca is not God's love. It's sad that your fatherly affection went over the line into obsessive infatuation. Becki has no romantic feelings for you. That's why she doesn't respond. That's why she asked us to reply to your recent barrage of letters. You must accept reality, Jim. We've watched with regret as Lucifer used this obsession to corrupt your preaching and to lead you away from your calling. You must go for counseling, if not to Dr. Logan then to another born-again pastor. Becki has no desire to live in the past. She can't be your friend because it only fans the flames of your infatuation. She has a new life now. If you send another letter, we'll have no choice but to get a court order to stop you.

We pray for you, Jim, that you'll return to Christ and do something good with your life. It's a shame to see such a gifted man of God sink so low. We love you in the Lord.

Ed & Alison

- - - - - - - -

Ltr #370, Sun 11-23-86, 6:10 p.m. (996 days). I was fucking insane to think I could get thru to you, Becki. Maybe it's true what your mom says, but the thought is cold & hellish & voids my being. ◊ I showed the letter to Russ. He shrugged & said, "How can Alison know Becki's heart? She loved you in '83. I saw it. We all touched a special intimacy, you & Becki & me & Syl & Jodi & Angie & Joe & others, but maybe it was a dream? Who the fuck knows?" √ js

- - - - - - - -

Ltr #378, Tue 12-9-86, 4:23 p.m. (1012 days). It's snowing, Becki. The meadow is windswept & frozen. My wood stove keeps this place toasty, & cozier than the radiators. I have a woodbin in here but my main supply is in the barn. The big things in my life today = a pot of peas, a hamburger, a baked potato, a Snickers bar, a new Penthouse from Russ. My only passions = eating & masturbating & crying over sad movies. I'm turning into a fat couch potato. I weigh 170. I have no energy. I feel like crawling into bed & hibernating. √ js

- - - - - - - -

Jim stands, stretches, then paces up and down the rock ledge. Heavy despair. *Why do I read this? If I'd known in '86 what I know now, I would've jumped off this cliff.* He checks his watch—3:26 p.m. The shadows are lengthening but the wind is still warm. He sucks in the fallish air, gives a weary sigh, then sits down and continues:

Ltr #384, Thur 1-1-87, 10:21 a.m. (1035 days). Dear Becki, Sharon's right. Your mom's right. I can't live in a fantasy. You say you don't love me. Okay, I accept it. There are millions of cute women on the earth. I'll find someone else & get you out of my heart. Fuck! It's time to take control of my life! √ js

- - - - - - - -

Ltr #385, Fri 1-2-87, 11:04 a.m. (1036 days). Snow, snow. A snowstorm is raging. My stove is roaring. I just got out of the shower. I'm exhausted but I feel good. I ran-hiked through the snow to the big rock, then down to the tracks, then west to the beach, then up the path to the meadow. When I got back, I did 25 sit-ups & 25 push-ups—just about killed me. This is my new routine, & no more cookies or candy or fatty foods. I unplugged the VCR = no more movies to feed my fantasies. I'm sick of reading porno & making love to my brownboy. It's time to get over you, Becki, & to find a good woman—the right way. √ js

- - - - - - - -

Ltr #386, Mon 1-5-87, 3:10 p.m. (1039 days). Dear Becki, I joined VDP (Video Dating for Professionals), 6 mos = $295. I go to Framingham to see the videos. I pick, they accept—or vice versa. I lied during my taping. I said I was working as a meteorologist, but it won't be a lie if I can get back on at the wx station. I'll call Ralph in the morning. ◊ I also got a haircut & $300 worth of new clothes = shirts, sweaters, Dockers, & a new suede jacket = gray. √ js

- - - - - - - -

Ltr #388, Sat 1-17-87, 7:41 a.m. (1051 days). Just back from jogging. I've lost 8 lbs. ◊ Last nite I went out w my first VDP date = Debbie from Acton = 36 & divorced = OK, but chubby. No wonder they just showed her face on the video. ◊ No luck at the wx station, but I have a meeting w Larry Thornton when he gets back fm the Bahamas. I have $$, but I need the prestige of a professional position. √ js

- - - - - - - -

<u>Ltr #390, Sat 1-24-87, 8:21 a.m. (1058 days).</u> Frigid, windy, -3°. The snow is old & icy like gray rock. I had another VDP date last night = Carol = attractive but older = 45. She psychoanalyzed me the whole nite. Fuck, I felt like I was out w Sharon's mom. √ js

- - - - - - - -

<u>Ltr #392, Thur 2-5-87, 7:30 a.m. (1070 days).</u> Dear Becki, I went out w Kimberly last nite—out to eat. She has a sassy butt & a cute face, but when she found out I was against abortion, she hardly said another word. No big loss. I don't need a fucking feminist. Can't get discouraged. I must maintain a positive attitude. I'll find someone to love. I'll get you out of my mind. You wait and see. √ js

- - - - - - - -

<u>Ltr #393, Mon 2-9-87, 6:56 a.m. (1074 days).</u> Becki, the sky is red. It's blustery with a few spits of snow. The Prescott plume is blowing up into the clouds. Saturday nite I went out w Eilene = tall leggy blond w sleepy eyes. We met at Bancrofts'. Afterward, she got into my car & kissed me. Then she unbuckled me & fondled my dick but I only got semihard. Finally, she gave up & said, "Maybe we should've waited a bit longer"—no kidding. ◊ I told Russ. He chuckled & said, "Jim, I guess you can't fuck outside of love." √ js

- - - - - - - -

<u>Ltr #403, Sun 3-15-87, 7:15 a.m. (1108 days).</u> Dear Becki. I'm taking the kids to the Boston Museum of Science today. I just got back from running. I'm down to 153. I'm tired, but not bored. I met 4 girls this week = Betty on Mon, Sue on Wed, Jan on Thur, & Carla last nite. Carla, I like = 33, dark hair, bangs, cute face, smart & witty, & she has a nice low-hung butt, like yours, Rebecca. ◊ I talked w Larry Thornton about selling investments. He has a temporary guy thru May, but I can start in June. & he asked me to play on his company softball team. Practice starts in April. New job & softball & I just met a girl who turns me on = I'm on my way back! Up. Up. Things are looking up! I can even think about you, Becki, w/o hurting! Yay! √ js

- - - - - - - -

<u>Ltr #409, Sat 4-11-87, 5: 17 p.m. (1135 days).</u> Dear Becki. Big night. I'm going to the movies w Carla = our 4th date. I like her. I think I'm healed. I'm over you = no more weeping! ◊ I practiced w Larry's softball team this aftn. I'm the best player. Most are younger than me, but they're bush-leaguers & out of shape. Larry's in shape but he's no ballplayer. It feels good to be on a team again. I'm back into the mainstream. Things are cooking now! You can make things

happen—if you get off your ass. I have no time to write in this book. √ js

- - - - - - - -

Ltr #410, Sun 4-12-87, 1:23 p.m. (1136 days)! O God! What a fucking disaster! I brought Carla home last nite. We lay on the brownboy in front of the stove. She was going crazy but I melted on entry. We dressed & made coffee. She said, "You do have kids right?"√ js

- - - - - - - -

Ltr #414, Wed 4-29-87, 1:34 p.m. (1153 days). Dear Becki. We had a spring snowstorm overnight = 14" of heavy wet snow. The power just came back on. My stove is going. I've been sick for two weeks = weak & congested & coughing. I have no voice. ◊ I called Carla again last nite. This time she leveled w me = she's no longer available; she found a steady guy (w a steady dick I'm sure). ◊ Larry T. called Mon = more bad news = his temporary guy is staying on, & he said he submitted the softball roster to the league & since I'd been sick & I wasn't on the team last year, it wasn't fair to the others to put me on it .◊ Fuck it! Life sucks again! My good fortune has suddenly turned to shit! I called Russ to share my woes. He just says, "It's looking more & more like we're not in control." √ js

- - - - - - - -

Ltr #417, Thur 5-14-87, 7:35 p.m. (1168 days). Hopeless! Hopeless! It's no use! Oh, Becki, I miss you so! I love you so! I quit the dating service. I've loved you all along! I'm not over you! No matter how I try I can't disconnect my penis from my heart! I can get up w Sharon, or maybe Angie or Cathy R = women I know & love, but not w the girls from VDP. I can't fuck strange flesh!—& I'm sick of lying & pretending & shaving & perfuming myself & dressing nice—I hate Dockers & dress slacks, & cleaning the Mustang. I'd rather jerk off & think about you & wear blue jeans & my old gym shirt. Oh, Rebecca, my heart aches for you. All the pain & hurt is back—not just back but a hundred times worse. Everyone says, "Jim, you can't live in the past." Well, Becki, I can't escape the "you" of my past anymore than a tree can escape its roots, & a million counselors cannot convince me otherwise. I love you! I love you! I'm hooked forever! I have no control of my heart. √ js

- - - - - - - -

Ltr #419, Sat 5-16-87, 2:22 p.m. (1170 days). Hurt, hurt. Oh, Becki, I cry for you in the nite. Loving you is like being in the belly of a whale, like Jonah. God is my only hope & it's agony to be utterly dependent on a God I don't trust. At times I feel an inkling of hope but I don't call it "faith." I don't want faith = pious lying = claiming to know what we don't know to deal w our fears. I can't fake it. If I don't know, THEN I DON'T FUCKING KNOW! I crave honesty, even if I have to stare into despair & dire possibilities. ◊ I'm down to $26,650. My 4-month fling took a chunk out of my account. √ js

- - - - - - - -

<u>Ltr #428, Thur 6-27-87, 9:54 a.m. (1212 days).</u> Becki Lea, it's raining out today. I can't get your naked hips out of my mind. What does a single Christian teacher do in Puerto Rico when Eros calls? I bet you have some wild fantasies. Oh, Becki, everyone sees you as so demure & devout, but I bet you think more about fucking than winning the lost. √ js.

- - - - - - - -

<u>Ltr #433, Wed 7-15-87, 7:52 a.m. (1230 days).</u> On my desk, Becki, I keep a yellow legal pad, I write down seed thoughts. Here are some of them: I hate religion but God is my only hope. ◊ If kids are the greatest in the kingdom, why don't they like church? ◊ My most profound thoughts always come when I'm taking a piss at 4 a.m. ◊ I don't fear Lucifer but I greatly fear the fear of Lucifer. ◊ Investing in a person's life to gain a desired result is slow prostitution. ◊ Every flower is an open cunt with a built-in cock. ◊ Evangelical Christianity is the antithesis of orgasm. They would've never created the universe w a "Big Bang." ◊ The corn is wilted & dead but still standing. It reminds me of people I know. ◊ As long as you have status, you never know if you have love. ◊ Most people never speak, they just echo. ◊ I'm so free from fear that it scares me. ◊ Truth only emerges against the backdrop of death, just as stars only come out in the black of night. ◊ In this life I've seen a lot, but I never saw a cat smoke pot. ◊ Born-again Christianity is an insane asylum of contradiction because they have God & Satan mixed up. √ js

- - - - - - - -

<u>Ltr #436, Sat 7-25-87, 7:17 p.m. (1240 days).</u> Hot & muggy. This aftn, Becki, I went down to the lake. No more RR tracks, just a cinder path. Guilford crews took up the rails & ties last week but left the track on the trestle. On the way back I sat in the meadow & watched a storm coming up, like we used to do—but now we're so cut off, yet our love seems unresolved. It's like reading a book and halfway through all the pages become blank, or like throwing stones into the air & they never come down? ◊ A piece of curious news today = my brother Gary Bob called & said a guy from Koch Oil Co. was coming to do seismic tests on the Gilson farm next door. √ js

- - - - - - - -

<u>Ltr #438, Sun 7-26-87, 9:27 p.m. (1241 days).</u> Dammit! Dammit! Shitty news! Sharon says she saw you, Becki, at summer conference & you were sitting w Randy Scowcroft & you two are going out. How fucking sweet! You're dating Ed's squeaky-clean, milquetoast cousin = pretty face & nice bod, but he's pure party line. He epitomizes everything you used to hate! Next thing you'll be getting married. After all, you're 23 & you've always wanted a baby, not to mention

**638**

what your hungry haunches are aching for—& marriage is the only way to fuck in Logan's empire. After Sharon told me, I ripped your picture into fifty pieces—but later I taped it back together. √ js

--------

Ltr #442, Mon 8-10-87, 3:40 p.m. (1256 days). Becki, it's hot & humid, & hazy. I feel sweaty, sticky. I hurt. I have no energy. I haven't shaved in 2 weeks. My hair is over my ears. The lawn is knee-high. All I do is watch movies & pig out. I'm back up to 165 lbs. I feel forsaken, finished, forgotten—& useless. Why do I have to go on w the curse of loving you = slow torture! Oh, Becki, I should've stayed in hiding in '84. I should've kept my mouth shut. Honesty has no place in this life. To get anything, to keep anything, you've got to lie & play the whore. ◊ Last nite I saw 2 Woody Allen flicks: Annie Hall & Manhattan = honest = he asks the same painful questions I ask. √ js

--------

Ltr #447, Tue 8-25-87, 9:40 a.m. (1271 days). Becki, the way the light is hitting your picture, the Scotch tape looks like cracked glass over your face. When I woke up this morning, I felt you near. I could almost taste your presence. Oh, to see you walk around the room, or to watch you fix your hair, or to see your stuff scattered about: your jeans & shirts & sweaters & sneakers & boots & kneesocks & your little mice & nic nacs. I miss you so. But I have peace about it this morning, a strange peace, like I sense the beauty of your heart. I don't think you rejected me to hurt me, but you honestly felt it was best for both of us. I hope you're wrong, but today I see your motives as pure. Whatever you do, you always do it "all the way." I just hope we end up with the same God = LOVE. √ js

--------

Ltr #450, Mon 8-31-87, 7:07 p.m. (1277 days). Cunt, cunt, tits & ass. Oh, Becki, this aftn I went on a solitary sexual rampage = me & my brownboy & 3 Penthouse magazines, but you're on every page. Sex, sex, Eros. I got off 3 times and each time I was loving you, satisfying you. My penis is sore, my body drained, but I feel no guilt, just sadness—it's all a fantasy. √ js

--------

Ltr #453, Mon 9-7-87, 3:45 p.m. (1284 days). Rainy, gloomy. The trees seem sad in their gray & misty clothing. I feel just as sad. To write letters you'll never read is such a farce. People say, "Repent & God will bless." Fuck that! If I perish, I perish, but I'll perish loving you, Becki, & it surely appears I'm sliding into a black hole of oblivion, while you go on w a happy life filled w people & popularity & Randy S. ◊ Russ was over last nite. He says Jerry Crenshaw left LBI to take a position w Kenneth Copeland in Ft Worth, & Dr. Logan praised him

**639**

at a Moody service—but rumor has it that he & Logan had a big blowout over Jerry's salary demands. ◊ My eyes are going. These words are blurry on my monitor. I need glasses. Nana's right. Why would you want a man who has no youth to share? √ js

--------

<u>Ltr #465, Thur 10-8-87, 7:39 a.m. (1315 days).</u> The meadow glistens with dew this morning. The leaves are turning & will soon fall. The seasons pass but the wall remains. All my life, if I wanted something, I went all out for it, & got it, through hard work & perseverance, but not with you, Becki. You've shown me that no amount of effort can make love connect. ◊ LBI is so far away from the God I hope for, & Logan is small compared to Falwell & Jim Bakker & Swaggart & Oral Roberts & Pat Robertson. The PTL empire is tottering. Falwell & Swaggart are helping shake it (w secret glee—Christians always profess prayerful concern when other believers falter, but they secretly rejoice = gives them an edge) Robertson is running for president & promising a return to Godly morality in America, yet he admits his son was conceived out of wedlock. Of course that was before he was saved. The moment he invited Christ into his life his sex drive became obedient to scripture = so much bullshit! Christians have no more answers than anyone. I don't want to be a "Christian"! I'm just a "human being." If we need any more credentials than that, we're all fucked forever. √ js

--------

<u>Ltr #469, Sun 10-18-87, 8:10 p.m. (1325 days).</u> Lonely, crushed, barren, hopeless, bleak, empty, cold, hurt, confused, afraid, useless, down, forgotten, broken, wasted, cut off, betrayed, faithless, finished, old, sinking, ugly, heartsick, helpless, trapped, defeated. That's how I feel today, Becki. I miss you. I need you. I love you. But you're gone gone—you're gone forever = hell for me. √ js

--------

<u>Ltr #470, Mon 10-19-87,11:34 p.m. (1326 days).</u> Becki, the stock market fell 508 pts—so what? I'm lower than any stock market as I sit in the ruins of my bombed-out heart & wait for death. ◊ Tonite I wrote a poem about you, Becki, but it could also be about God—or the Love Goddess:

<u>I WAIT ALONE ...</u>

No hope moves on my horizon.
No hint of dawn in my night.
Nothing, nothing, nothing new,
O ... how could she ever come?

Pierced my heart with slow cold stroke.
My life oozed out in her hands.

Nothing, nothing, nothing new,
O ... how could she ever come?

Fear closed in, I clawed at death,
'til fingers, ripped raw, hung limp.
Nothing, nothing, nothing new,
O ... how could she ever come?

Can't get out, I claw no more.
I wait alone 'til the end.
Nothing, nothing, nothing new,
O ... how could she ever come?

--------

Ltr #475, Wed 11-18-87, 11:07 a.m. (1356 days). Dear Becki, on the way back from the post office, I was tuning the car radio and came across Logan's LBI Hour: "The Lord is coming soon. Will he find you believing or will he find you doubting & faithless? It takes courage to believe the Bible, to pray w/o ceasing, to stay in your marriage. Anyone can praise God & obey the scriptures when things are going good, but it takes courage to profess victory & to live a holy life when you have no evidence"—I snapped off the radio. Fucking Logan & all preachers. They use the 2nd coming of Christ as a threat. And Logan makes lying—he calls it professing faith—sound so pious. But no evangelical preacher would dare preach honestly = "I'm not sure of the Bible. I'm not sure of the 2nd coming, or even what it means. I'm not sure of God." They'd be cast out—like me. √ js

--------

Ltr #480, Fri 12-4-87, 11:36 p.m. (1372 days). Dear Becki. Snow is falling thru the streetlight outside. There's something so calm about a gentle snowfall like it's rooted in peace & isn't striving. And I had a resigned peace for two days after Sharon told me the news, but now I'm dying. I thought I was as low as I could go, but now you're getting married in the spring. You love Randy & reject me. Torture, torture. This is it. You've killed your heart & me w it. You said you'd never change, & you've not wavered. Now you're giving your body, your time, your smiles, to Randy Scowcroft, & you two will eat together & sleep together & live together & flirt & giggle & fuck = torture to me. I feel so LEFT OUT! You'll go places together & pool your money & he'll see you naked & your dirty clothes will be mixed w his. Logan & your mom & all the LBI'ers can proudly proclaim that God's Word has prevailed! = Jim loses = "Jim, how could you expect otherwise? She made it so clear that she didn't love you LIKE THAT!" Sharon seemed almost gleeful over the news. Everyone is so right & wise, but I'm on God's shitlist forever! But it doesn't change my heart, Rebecca. I love you more each day! √ js

--------

Ltr #481, Sat 12-5-87, 11:17 a.m. (1373 days). Dear Becki. The news of your upcoming wedding hits me again & again, like I'm on the ropes & God's beating the shit out of me. I know paperwork can't change hearts, & most marriages sour quickly but it's just like God to give you happiness & great sex w no problems. But even if it's terrible, you'll stick it out to maintain <u>your vows against me</u>. It's not that I want you to be unhappy, but I just feel so REJECTED = crushed, betrayed, used, abused, & discarded. It kills to know my enemies = Logan's LBI pretenders are applauding you & Randy over my dead heart, & they will all support you & expect you to stay together in the name of Christ = you'll be setting up your nice little nest w babies & in-laws & LBI friends & it'll go on for fucking ever!—Don't get me wrong. I know you love kids, & will be a good mother—& I don't hate Randy. I just wish I could be included somehow. √ js

- - - - - - - -

Ltr #483, Mon 12-7-87, 2:12 p.m. (1375 days). I bet your mom is ecstatic. You got a pious missionary pastor, & Ed's cousin to boot. Oh, Rebecca, you've really got your life together for God. But I know your wild carnal side—how you love "high noon cock" and crave the "wicked good feeling." You always wanted a cute & hunky guy to kiss & fuck & fondle, & to stare out. Of course, that has nothing to do with your decision to marry Randy. I'm sure your main concern is his vision for the lost—HA, HA. ◊ I saw 2 movies tonight: Officer & a Gentleman & Blue Lagoon. The last one turned me on like a porno flick. I jerked off & thought about you fucking Randy—SHIT! I feel so left out = down, down, down. Life sucks. I hate God! √ js

- - - - - - - -

Ltr #488, Wed 12-16-87, 2:55 p.m. (1384 days). This morning I exploded with rage. I turned over the kitchen table, broke dishes, put my fist through two cabinet doors, ripped the bathroom door off its hinges, threw soggy cereal against the wall, & threw a chair halfway thru the window breaking one of the panes. I then collapsed on the floor & cried. Oh, Becki, 1400 days have passed & now you're getting married = final nail in my coffin. After 45 min. of sobbing, I got up, cleaned up the mess, & put the cabinets back together with masking tape & glue. I thought I was over the anger & bitterness & insanity, but I guess I'm not. I called Russ. He said he'd come over on Friday & help me fix the bathroom door & the window. √ js

- - - - - - - -

Ltr #489, Thur 12-17-87, 9:24 a.m. (1385 days). Dear Becki, I feel better today—no not better, but surrendered. It's sad how vows make walls around us. ◊ I got a Xmas card from Jodi = no change in Chicago. I wrote her back & told her about your engagement. √ js

--------

<u>Ltr #490, Sat 12-19-87, 1:25 p.m. (1387 days).</u> Dear Becki, this morning when I went for wood, I found a kitten in the barn. She was cold & shivering & thin, & crying w a pitiful meow. My brain said, "You don't need a cat," but my heart won out. I brought her in & gave her milk & hamburger. I'm calling her Rusti. She's a beautiful kitten w dark tiger stripes, but she's not gray like most tiger cats but tawny & amber & beige as if an artist brushed warm shades into her coat. On her neck & face she's lighter, almost white. Her tail is ringed like a racoon. You'd love her, Becki. √ js

--------

<u>Ltr #491, Wed 12-23-87, 11:35 p.m. (1391 days).</u> Dear Becki, I spent the aftn w Erin, Heather, & Chris. We went to Searstown = usual Xmas routine = I gave them $$ so they could buy their own presents. & I got presents from them. Erin gave me a sweater, Chris, a book on the Red Sox, & Heather, a U2 tape = Joshua Tree. Erin & Heather are both into rock but Tom H. won't let them play it at home. I just played the U2 tape. It stirs my soul. Do you ever hear their songs, Becki, or have you eradicated music along w your heart? How do you do it Becki? How long can you, "Weep w/o crying, talk w/o speaking, & scream w/o raising your voice?" √ js

--------

<u>Ltr #492, Fri 12-25-87, 9:37 p.m. (1393 days).</u> Becki, I spent Christmas alone w Rusti, my new kitten. I didn't see a single person. Russ is in Maine. My kids are in Cobleskill, of course. But I don't feel any lonelier than on regular days. I ate my dinner at 4:30 = steak, home fries, green beans, applesauce, bread, a glass of milk, & Oreo cookies & coffee for dessert. I fed Rusti in a saucer by the foot of my chair. She ate the steak of course, but also potatoes & bread = a strange cat. She eats cat food too, but only as a last resort. I'd say she's 4 or 5 mos. old. She's so innocent & very attached to me. √ js

--------

<u>Ltr #499, Sat 1-9-88, 9:24 a.m. (1408 days).</u> Early this morning as Rusti & I lay in bed (she sleeps at the foot), I listened to the wind roaring against the house & I felt a comforting peace, not the peace of knowing but the peace of being a child. If I have no power over the wind, who am I to pretend I can move God w pleas or prayers or religious performance? Either He loves me or He doesn't—& I can't change him. If I could, it wouldn't be LOVE. Letting go = peace. √ js

--------

<u>Ltr #501, Wed 1-13-88, 10:06 p.m. (1412 days).</u> Dear Becki, Rusti's asleep on top of my bookcase. She always finds a high place to sleep.

It's rainy & foggy out. The street light has a fuzzy halo about it. ◊ This morning the old furnace in the basement gave out. 2 guys fm McClellan Plumbing & Heating installed a new one = $2100. I have my stove but I need the main system for the whole house. (My account is dropping = $13,100 left.) √ js

- - - - - - - -

Ltr #502, Thur 1-14-88, 8:05 a.m. (1413 days). Bitter cold = -12°. The wind whistles & this old house moans & creaks. My stove is going full blast. Rusti's sitting in the window in front of me. She eats like a horse. She's no longer thin. When I sat down to type, she jumped up & attacked my hands = her usual play routine. Finally she hopped on my desk, knocked all my pencils & pens onto the floor, then to the window where she's grooming herself & taking in the view. She has a box of toys = ping-pong balls, string, wads of paper, rubber bands, but she prefers to play w me. She acts like royalty—just like Bathsheba. She wants to go outside but I'm keeping her in 'til spring. I have a litter box downstairs on the back porch. I keep my door open & Mrs. C's so Rusti can get to her box. √ js

- - - - - - - -

Ltr #504, Wed 1-20-88, 7:32 p.m. (1419 days). Becki, I've felt nauseous all day. I have chills. I can't get warm. I hate this feeling. ◊ I got papers fm Gary Bob that authorize Koch Oil to drill. They're drilling on the Gilson place but it's close to our line. We'll get a small % if they hit. But they may not start 'til the fall. ◊ I got 2 pair of cheap reading glasses at CVS. Guess I'm officially middle-aged. My life is like the weather = cold & old & dry w no change in sight. √ js

- - - - - - - -

Ltr #506, Fri 1-29-88, 4:32 p.m. (1428 days). Becki, it's cold & blustery out. I went nowhere today. I saw no one. I'm reading books like 2 per week since Xmas. I still watch movies but books penetrate deeper into my soul. I go to the big library in Worcester or buy them at Waldenbooks = fiction, non-fiction, all kinds—but especially novels about the agony & ecstasy of love. √ js

- - - - - - - -

Ltr #508, Thur 2-4-88, 10:45 a.m. (1434 days). Becki, I took the kids to McD's after school yesterday. When I arrived at the house, they weren't home yet. Sharon made coffee & bantered playfully w me. I told her she still has a nice butt. She blushed & sported some more, but quickly caught herself, & snapped, "Sex, sex, that's all you think about, Jim." I asked why not love me & Tom both & she shot back, "Because I'm married to Tom & I'd never hurt him like that. I'm not a slut, you know." I felt like a stray dog trying to get in on a cold night.

I don't miss Shar like I miss you, Becki, but I do miss her a lot, especially sex and cuddling in bed. Why does marriage mean you have to stop loving all others? √ js

---------

Ltr #509, Fri 2-5-88, 9:34 a.m. (1435 days). Snowed 7" yesterday. The meadow is a winter fairyland. I took Rusti out while it was snowing. She was so cute. She chased & batted the snowflakes. Rusti's the only warm soul to come into my life in 4 yrs. A kitten is small consolation but I've grown to love her like a dear little friend. She's growing fast. She sleeps on my lap when I'm reading or watching a movie. She snuggles close & purrs when I pet her. And when I come home, she's always excited to see me. √ js

---------

Ltr #512, Sat 2-20-88, 11:34 p.m. (1450 days). Dear Becki, I got a letter from Mary Beth Hudson. She says you're getting married in Nashua during Easter Week. Whoopie Do! She also says that Molly Gibson was arrested in Boston. Her boy friend was selling cocaine out of her apartment. So much for her new life in Christ. ◊ I've read 15 books in 2 mos. Fiction = Andrew Greeley, John Updike, James Joyce, D H Lawrence, George Macdonald, Kahil Gibran. Non-fiction = Matthew Fox, Noam Chomsky, Emerson, Thoreau, Blake, Voltaire, Sartre. Poetry = Frost, Whitman, Poe, Shelley, Byron, Rilke, & Camus. Some I read before in high school & college but now they have much more meaning because my heart is plowed up with pain. √ js

---------

Ltr #514, Mon 2-22-88, 8:23 p.m. (1452 days). So, Becki, Sharon says your wedding is going to take place at Priscilla Logan Chapel on Sat. April 2nd. I don't want details but she gives them anyway. Just think, a storybook wedding to go with your storybook life = "Devout woman of God to marry handsome missionary pastor." ◊ Sharon & I also had a fight about Erin's college. I said I'd give $2500/yr but she wants more so she can send Erin to Houghton College = an expensive Bible college in Houghton, NY = $13,000/yr = much more tradition and evangelical status than Logan Bible Institute. (Nana of course recommends it). I told Sharon a secular state college is just as good since Erin wants to be a teacher. Sharon called me a "lazy bum" & said if I didn't pay half, she'd take me to court. Perhaps I am a bum but no court will make me send an adult daughter to college—especially a college I don't approve of. √ js

---------

Ltr #516, Thur 3-3-88, 1:34 p.m. (1462 days). Down, down, lethargy, melancholy. I have no energy. My life = sighs & moans & groans. It's all I can do to wash dishes or to feed Rusti. The house needs paint &

**645**

a new roof. It leaks into the attic then into the hallway. My apartment is a mess—looks like the monkey cage at a zoo. Sharon says I need professional help, but why should I pay someone $60/hr to tell me to forget you, Becki, when 1462 days of experience show I can't do it. But I am nuts to type these unsent letter after all this time. ◊ It's sunny & mild out. Spring is near—but I feel like a November tree. √ js

- - - - - - - -

Ltr #524, Mon 4-4-88, 6:04 p.m. (1494 days). Dear Becki. Sharon confirmed all my fears. She told me about your wedding. She said you looked stunning in your white dress. Well, fuck you, Becki! Fuck Randy! Fuck Sharon! Fuck all the Loganites! I hate life! I hate God! Life sucks! My heart has no standing in this world! I truly love you Becki but you won't even talk to me! = rejected, damned forever! √ js

- - - - - - - -

Ltr #527, Sat 4-23-88, 1:13 p.m. (1513 days). Oh, Becki, this has been a horrible month, but today I feel a glimmer of hope. I just finished an Andrew Greeley novel called Ascent into Hell. It's about a man & woman who love each other for many years. They're separated by time & distance & marriage vows. Yet against all odds they come back together & when they do, Greeley calls it, "Christ has risen" = the only resurrection I ache for. I want no part of a celibate heaven. √ js

- - - - - - - -

Ltr #532, Tue 5-17-88, 11:33 a.m. (1537 days). Becki, I just got back from Stop & Shop & unloaded my stuff = 2 Delmonico steaks, 4 pork chops, 2 Swanson Great Start Breakfasts (French toast), 1 bag Chips Ahoy cookies, 1 gal milk, 1 Lb. Land O Lakes butter, a six-pack of Scott tissue, 2 cans Del Monte green beans, 2 cans Green Giant Niblets corn, 2 LeMenu TV dinners (Salisbury steak), a liter bottle of Pepsi, 2 jars of Sunsweet prunes, 2 pkgs of Thomas' Toast-R-Cake corn muffins, 1 loaf Nissen oatmeal bread, 1 doz. eggs, 5 Lb. potatoes, 1 Lb. Oscar Meyer bacon, & about 10 cans of cat food (Nine Lives, Friskies Buffet, Fancy Feast). It came to $48.33. Shopping alone is sad. No one cares what I buy except Rusti. She jumps into each bag to check out the contents. √ js

- - - - - - - -

Ltr #533, Wed 5-18-88, 7:35 a.m. (1538 days). Foggy, drizzly = another gloomy day. Of course, Becki, I'm sure it's sunny for you & Randy, as you happily serve the Lord—& get high on legal sex? There's no sun in my life—or sex. I'm null & void. I expect nothing, I get nothing. ◊ My money's getting lower, but I'll stretch it as far as I can, but even then I'll sell this house before I bow to Babylon. ◊ I fixed a cat door on the back porch so Rusti can come & go. She loves it outside. √ js

--------

<u>Ltr #535, Tue 5-24-88, 8:24 a.m. (1544 days)</u>. Dear Becki, I moved my $$ to FSB. Russ says Comfed is secretly in trouble because of bad RE loans. ◊ Most people have exciting changes in their lives during May & June but not me. Each day = same routine = get up, stagger to bathroom, take a leak, brush teeth, feed Rusti, start fire in stove (winter only), make coffee, get dressed (flannel shirt, old Levi's, old boots), tuck bed, spread brownboy on top, get coffee in black M.I.T. mug, sit, gaze out window, jot thoughts on pad, type journal letter to you, or simply consider chores for the day & how to put them off until tomorrow. I still shower but in the aftn after I walk or do outside tasks. I shave once a week. I write lots of seed poems but rarely finish them. I scarcely know the day, the date, the hour. I sense time passing in the chunks & cycles of solitary life = I use the last paper towel. I rip open a new roll of toilet paper. The litter box fills up (faster in winter). The wood rack is empty, the ash can is full (both in winter). I pour the last of the milk. My laundry basket overflows, I take the trash to the dumpster. The toilet stinks. I clean it (I wait until it hits me like smelling salts). The soap in the shower goes from big to small. The toothpaste goes from fat to flat. The lawn grows & my fingernails & toenails & mustache—I clip them. Day blurs into day. My hair grows. I get a haircut. Mrs. C's German clock keeps good time on my mantel, but I need no clock or calendar to tell me that death is approaching—or maybe life? √ js

--------

<u>Ltr #537, Mon 5-30-88, 11:32 a.m. (1550 days)</u>. Dear Becki, Rusti's sitting on my desk staring at me. Her eyes are big & yellow w vertical black slits. She's purring so loud, she sounds like an electric razor. ◊ I've read many great thinkers this year, yet I've found no religion, philosophy, or worldview that explains what I've been through, or what I see about me. Christianity, Protestant, Catholic, born-again, Islam, Buddism, the Mormons, the cults, communism, capitalism, humanism, nihilism, Freudian psychology—the list is endless. Yet in each case they have to twist reality to make it fit their model. Even my hope = "intimacy is the highest good" becomes corrupt when I try to codify, classify, & define a system of good & evil. There's only one clear & absolute truth, Rebecca = I LOVE YOU! All else changes like a kaleidoscope. √ js

--------

Jim stops reading and checks his watch. It's 4:17 p.m. Shadows cover him—from the trees behind the big rock—but sunshine still plays on the hills across the river. The breeze has lost its warmth. He pushes down the sleeves of his sweat shirt.

# Chapter Forty-one

"**J**im; oh, Jim," Angie yells down from the woods behind the big rock.

Jim twists around and smiles up at her. "Yeh, what is it?"

"Jodi's inviting everyone to eat with her and Tony. Nothing fancy, just hamburgers and beans. If you'd like to join us, we're eating in thirty minutes."

"Tell her thanks, but I'll eat later. I'm into some heavy reading."

Angie gives a teasing grin. "So you're spending the evening with Becki?"

"Now, Angela, you don't know *every*thing about me?"

"When it comes to Rebecca Reinhardt, I do." They both laugh, then Angie says, "We'll save you a plate anyway, in Jodi's oven. You can't stay here all night."

Angie heads back toward the house. Jim returns to his journal:

Ltr #538, Tue 6-7-88, 9:10 a.m. (1558 days). Dear Becki. My window's open. I feel a warm & gentle breeze as I type. The meadow is soft & green. I love you so much today, I can scarcely get my breath. The song "The Rose" (Bette Midler) is on the radio. It forms you in my mind. Your honey-brown hair blows in the wind. Your cheeks glow warm & ruddy. Your blue eyes sparkle. Oh, Becki, I love your arms, your hands. I could sit for days & watch you draw or write or cook or fold laundry. I love the way you wiggle your toes when you put on your sneakers. I love how you wrinkle your nose & scrunch your face. You're a princess. It doesn't matter that you're married. √ js

- - - - - - - -

Ltr #539, Mon 6-13-88, 11:14 a.m. (1564 days). Dear Becki, I got a note from Mary Beth. She says that you & Randy live in a cottage next door to Ed & Alison. How homey & sweet? Do you really love him, Becki? Do you feel a thrill when he comes home? Do you miss him when he's gone? Is it your life, you're living, Rebecca, or is it your mom's & Randy's & Dr. Logan's? ◊ Erin graduated on Sat. It's hard to believe she's out of high school. ◊ Speaking of graduation, Sharon says that Barry graduated & the Lord is leading him to stay in Nashua to work full-time as Garrett's assistant. What else is new? No Christian ever says I want to do this or that = too selfish. It's always, "The Lord is leading," or "The Lord told me." What a crock of shit! It's the Lord all right! It's fucking Garrett = Barry's new God! I feel sorry for Janet & Pam Garrett. ◊ I'm down to $5100. Guess I'll sell in Sept. & move to Texas & live w Gary Bob. √ js

- - - - - - - -

<u>Ltr #542, Tue 6-21-88, 4:53 p.m. (1572 days).</u> Dear Becki. I just ate my early supper. After 4 yrs I'm used to the routine = 1 plate, 1 glass, 1 fork, 1 knife, 1 spoon, 1 baked potato, 1 slice of bread, 1 dish of corn, 1 bowl of peaches, but 2 pork chops—& a saucer on the floor for Rusti w a bit of each, except she doesn't like peaches. ◊ I got a letter from Joe L. His band is breaking up. He may move to Memphis. I wrote him back, told him about your marriage & Brenda's boyfriend. I'm full of good news. √ js

- - - - - - - -

<u>Ltr #546, Thur 6-30-88, 10:32 p.m. (1581 days).</u> Dear Becki, I just finished a George Macdonald romance = The Portent. In the end, the heroine, Barbara, has a dream = all hearts cuddle inside of Christ. = "Father, I pray that they might be one." I wonder about oneness. How close can we get to others? My dream is to be one w you, Becki, & yet somehow love isn't complete unless it includes everyone we love = orgy of kindred spirits = hard to imagine since I think of orgies in the Caligula sense, the dirty X-rated sense. Maybe we all ache for "Barbara's dream"—Russ thinks so—but I can't fathom such a miracle. I can't even believe you & I will ever talk again. √ js

- - - - - - - -

<u>Ltr #547, Tue 7-5-88, 11:30 a.m. (1586 days).</u> Lonely, defeated, hopeless. I feel old, Becki. I hate being alone. I hate how you rejected me & how Sharon rejected me. I hate masturbating over Penthouse. I hate it when people say, "Have faith in God." Fuck that! You & Sharon may have faith, but God's a cruel & sadistic asshole! Logan says, "Heaven will be better." Fuck that! I don't even know if there is a heaven! Besides, he's not waiting for heaven to enjoy himself. Money, power, young wife. He lives like a fucking king! √ js

- - - - - - - -

<u>Ltr #548, Sat 7-9-88, 2:30 p.m. (1590 days).</u> Heavy, heavy, blah, no energy. Oh, Becki, I hurt, I hurt. I've been in bed all week. I sweat, I stink, I hide in my brownboy. I'm living on stale bread & peanut butter & hot Pepsi. I feel like Mickey Rourke in Barfly = lethargic, unshaven, shaggy, disgusting—except I'm sober. Rusti's the only soul who wants to share my bed, my life. She knows I'm sad & licks my face. I sleep in fits but I always wake up drowning in an ocean of ache = you're married & happy & on your way. You left me dying by the side of the road, & never looked back—like I was a discarded McDonald's cup. ◊ Russ called this morning. I told him I have no hope of seeing you again. He just sighed & said, "That's old news, Jim. Besides, you never expect snow in July." √ js

- - - - - - - -

<u>Ltr #549, Sun 7-10-88, 10:30 p.m. (1591 days).</u> Becki, I feel better tonite. I rented a movie = To Kill a Mockingbird. There's something so right about that movie, the way the little girl tells the story, the way Gregory Peck (Atticus Finch) is so kind—yet resigned. √ js

- - - - - - - -

<u>Ltr #550, Tue 7-12-88, 10:43 a.m. (1593 days).</u> Thunder & lightning overnight but it's still hot & humid. Sharon called w sad news = Mor died in her sleep. She was 85. I liked her. ◊ I have $2650 left. My days are numbered. I must put this house up for sale. ◊ Rusti's my only comfort. When I lie on my back on the bed, she gets on my chest & licks my chin. I rub her back & ears & when I stop she puts her paw on my cheek to tell me she wants more. When I walk across the room, she'll jump out from behind my dresser & attack my feet & run into the kitchen & we'll chase each other all over the house upstairs & down. When I pick her up she snuggles her head under my chin & purrs into my shoulder. She stays out all nite & comes in at sunrise. I worry but there's no way I can keep her in. She's a hunter. I find mouse heads & hind legs on the back steps, or a dead mole. She eats mice but never moles. √ js

- - - - - - -

<u>Ltr #554, Fri 7-22-88, 6:27 p.m. (1603 days).</u> Dear Becki, a strange day. This morning Angela called. She was crying. She said she can't stand it w Larry & she hates the phony crowd at Valley Baptist. We talked an hour. Sylvia was there & she talked as well = "Frank's a fucking wimp." (Syl was drunk). They said they missed me & wanted to see me. I felt good. But this afternoon, Angie rang back & coldly declared she shouldn't have called, that it wasn't "in the Spirit." ◊ I told Russ. He said, "It looks like their house of cards is falling & they're scrambling to prop it up. People panic when their fig leaves fall off." √ js

- - - - - - -

<u>Ltr #556, Wed 7-27-88, 10:26 a.m. (1608 days).</u> Rusti didn't come home this morning. I'm worried. I was never so attached to a cat. I looked all over, the meadow, the barn, up & down Front St., but no sign of her. She's big now, 6 lbs & still growing, but she's just a year old & hardly street-smart. I feel like a mom who lost her baby. Fuck it God! Rusti is all I have. √ js

- - - - - - - -

<u>Ltr #557, Wed 7-27-88, 11:56 a.m. (1608 days).</u> Relief! Good news ! Rusti returned—but not alone. She had a mouse in her mouth = still alive. She dropped it at my feet like a gift. It ran under the fridge. Rusti stalked the fridge for 15 min. then gave up & ate her Nine Lives tuna.

Now she's on my bookcase proudly preening herself. √ js

- - - - - - - -

**Ltr #562, Wed 8-10-88, 10:26 p.m. (1622 days).** Hot again today = 93°. This has been a brutal summer. Today 's my 42nd birthday, Becki, but it was no different than most days. In fact, I saw no one but Rusti. I made scrambled eggs & sausage. I made extra for Rusti & served it to her in a cereal bowl. The moment she saw me take out the eggs, she was rubbing all over my legs & mewing. She goes crazy over scrambled eggs—I know this cat so well. √ js

- - - - - - - -

**Ltr #565, Tue 8-16-88, 9:52 p.m. (1628 days).** Dear Becki. A cool front finally arrived last nite after 20 straight days of 90+ temps. ◊ I sold Mrs. C's old Packard to Harry Hinton's cousin who collects old cars. I got $2900. Gives me a little more time. ◊ I got a reference form in the mail yesterday, from the Brendon Falls Banner regarding Angela Thornton. Guess she's bored at home again. I gave a glowing report, but it hurts when all I am to my old friends is a job reference. I wish Angie would come talk to me, walk w me, eat w me, & fuck me. I'm sick of celibacy. √ js

- - - - - - - -

**Ltr #566, Wed. 8-17-88, 11:52 a.m. (1629 days).** Dear Rebecca, I woke up very early this morning. I must've had an encouraging dream. I don't remember it but I woke up feeling strangely hopeful. So much so, that I went out to the meadow & watched the sun come up. The air was warm & softly sweet. I felt you near me, Becki. When I got back I wrote this poem:


### OUR RISING SUN

Fingers of shadow and light
dance forth to brush in our day,
toasting your leaves orange and red,
stretching my fields black to green,

tinting pink then blue your sky
lighting up my lark to sing.
Fingers of shadow and light
splash our canvas with color.

- - - - - - - -

**Ltr #568, Sun 8-21-88, 9:43 p.m. (1633 days).** This evening, I took my lawn chair & sat out back by Mrs. C's long-neglected garden = weeds & daisies & waist-high rhubarb, gone to seed. The house needs painting. The lawn is overgrown—but I don't care. Rusti chased bugs & ran around my chair teasing me, trying to get me to chase her. She's too much. The setting sun always draws me. I like the sky, the trees, the birds, the breeze. Oh, Rebecca, I feel you most in the evening as the shadows gather. Wildness, animals, weather, the cosmos. It surrounds me with raw integrity that I rarely sense in humans. As I sat there, I felt a kinship with all that was about me even the old house itself, & the barn—as if age has made them part of nature. I stayed until the mosquitos drove me inside. √ js

- - - - - - - -

<u>Ltr #571, Sun 9-4-88, 10: 18 a.m. (1647 days).</u> Dear Becki, Rusti didn't come home yet. I guess she's after another mouse. She usually comes in early to eat. √ js

- - - - - - - -

<u>Ltr #572, Sun 9-4-88,12:58 p.m. (1647 days).</u> SHOCK! SHOCK! MY HEART! MY HEART! Oh, Becki! I hurt! I cry! I sob! I just found Rusti dead by the back steps. She was evidently hit by a car & struggled to get home but couldn't make it up to her door. There were no gaping wounds or mangled limbs, just blood oozing from her mouth. She looked like she was sleeping on the grass. I buried her in the woods by the stone fence. I cried & cried as I laid her in the hole & covered her w dirt. God is such a fucking asshole! He even takes the little creatures I love. She was so innocent & trusting. It's not like losing you, Becki, but it shreds what little heart I have left. Why is life so merciless & cruel? I didn't ask to be born.√ js

- - - - - - - -

<u>Ltr #573, Mon 9-5-88,10:22 p.m. (1648 days).</u> Becki, I put away Rusti's bowls & toys, & I cleaned her litter box for the last time. I cried over her things as if I'd lost a child. I never cried over a pet before, but Rusti's different. She was like a friend & the only living soul that wanted to be with me & eat w me & play w me. My apartment, the whole house, seems so empty w/o her. ◊ I called Russ and told him all about it. He replied, "I just wonder, Jim, how many more Rusti's do you have to go thru?" ◊ Logan always warns, "You have to face God." But after the past 4 yrs, I say, "God, you have to face me." √ js

- - - - - - - -

<u>Ltr #574, Thur 9-8-88, 7:15 p.m. (1651 days).</u> Oh, Becki, this place is so lonely especially when I come home. I miss how Rusti always ran to meet me when I came in. I find myself looking for her. Then it hits me—SHE'S DEAD! When I eat I expect her to appear—she always came into the kitchen when she heard me getting dishes out. I'm always glancing over at my bookcase as if I'll see her sleeping there. She was such a cuddly cat, yet spirited & excited to be alive & filled

with energy & trust as if the whole universe was made for her. But she was CUT OFF, just like my heart in '84. Life sucks! √ js

- - - - - - - -

Jim removes his glasses, wipes the tears from his eyes. He stares wistfully at the hills. The trees blur into a wash of green and red and gold. He blows his nose and goes on with his story:

Ltr #576, Sat 9-17-88, 9:44 p.m. (1660 days). Fear, terror, panic. Oh, Becki, in the shower just now I had a horror-of-death experience like I was being buried alive = I realized that I too must fall into the chasm of death = no control, no way out. The blue shower curtain turned black and shrouded me. No way out! no way out!—I shook w fear. But as I dried w the towel, a resigned peace came over me = I'm desperately dependent on God, as w all humans. But I don't pretend to know all about him like I used to. √ js

- - - - - - - -

Ltr #579, Sun 9-25-88, 10:53 p.m. (1668 days). Becki, I took Heather & Chris out to eat this aftn. Erin's at college (Houghton of course). When we got back to Greeley Hill, Heather stayed in the car & said, "Dad, you seem wicked depressed. I want you to cheer up. Things'll get better. You should forget Becki & all that." She meant well but she was repeating Sharon, & no sooner did she get out, but Sharon got in: "Jim, my heart breaks to see you suffering. I'm sorry about your cat, & I know it hurts that Becki's married & I'm w Tom—but what's done is done. Becki's gone, accept it, she's happily married. She has her own life & you'll never be part of it. You & I are divorced. I can never be your lover again. You must accept that too. But I still care for you, Jim. Your agony is self-inflicted. You're still obsessed w Becki & you feed it each day by living in that creepy house & by talking w Russ. I feel sorry for Bev. He runs around, you know. Doris said—never mind, I won't get into that. But he reinforces your fantasies & endorses your bizarre lifestyle. You just lie around & feel sorry for yourself & think about losing Becki, then you write weird poems about it. No wonder people see you as strange. You don't work, you spout unorthodox views about God & family & marriage & sex. You must get away from that house. Get a job. Get back into life. There are many sweet & respectable women who'd love to be w you if they knew the Jim that I once knew." √ js

- - - - - - - -

Ltr #580, Mon 9-26-88, 8:34 a.m. (1669 days). Becki, I got a note from Mary Beth Hudson = you & Randy had a big fight = you want a baby & he wants to wait. Mary Beth & Katie have grown to be friends over the months. They talk a lot in the office & your sister gossips about you. But fighting over when to get pregnant is no marriage-breaker. Most couples fight about it. √ js

- - - - - - - -

**Ltr #586, Wed 10-12-88, 6:22 p.m. (1685 days).** Fuck it! I give up! My star has flickered out. You denied our love, Becki, & threw it away as if it were a dirty Kotex. I was nuts to think something good would happen. Sharon's right. I've got to get out of here. I'm putting this place up for sale. I'll be gone in a few months. Why do I write in this insane journal? √ js.

- - - - - - - -

**Ltr #587, Thur 10-13-88, 11:37 p.m. (1686 days).** Dear Becki. I've been here 4 years & except for the stove, my room's exactly the same = butcher-block desk, Lazy-Boy recliner, piled-mattress bed—& today I stayed in bed wrapped in my brownboy. I saw 3 movies = all bombs = P.K. and the Kid, Rumblefish, & Shanghai Surprise. Finally, I jerked off. I pictured your big cunt as you lay on your bed, your legs spread, right after our one & only fuck = my most erotic memory of you. You torment me but what can I do? I curse the day I took you into my heart. ◊ As usual, the rush of endorphins to my brain was the high point of my day. After I got off, I was blah, hopeless, hungry. I had 2 hot dogs, a bag of Fritos, a mug of Pepsi. √ js

- - - - - - - -

**Ltr #588, Mon 10-17-88, 1:42 p.m. (1690 days).** Pussy, pussy. I can't stand it! I want your pussy, Becki! I want Sharon's! Any ripe & juicy cunt. Young cunt. Creamy thighs! Hairy cunt! I want to see a hairy cunt. I want to fuck it & fuck it. I've been horny all week. √ js

- - - - - - - -

**Ltr #589, Mon 10-17-88, 10:06 p.m. (1690 days).** I got so horny earlier, I called SALLY'S GIRLS in Boston—I got the # from Russ. They had a girl here at 6:00 p.m. = Mandy (22), a cute redhead w green eyes, nice hips, nice tits—& her cunt was a sight for horny eyes—but her bush was light, like amber-blond. Dark-haired cunts, like yours, Becki, are more erotic. I was nervous = 1st time I was ever w a whore. But she turned out to be sweet & down-to-earth, though hardly passionate = no different than any professional woman doing her job. It cost $275 for 2 hrs. She says she became a call girl so her son could have the best. He's four. She gave me a back rub then stroked my cock 'til I was hard, but as usual I melted at the door. So I jerked off & stared at her crotch = a living Penthouse pose. ◊ Later I called Russ. He replied, "Sounds like an LBI church service. You have to pump it up to get off." We both laughed then talked more seriously about spiritual prostitution = if Jesus had to <u>pay</u> a price ($$, blood, or whatever) so I can go in w God, then my relationship w God is prostitution, & Christianity is whoredom & every church, a brothel, &

every preacher, a pimp—& such a system of purchased favor can never reveal true love & intimacy. ◊ I feel so shitty. Life sucks. √ js

--------

<u>Ltr #590, Sun 10-23-88,10:51 p.m. (1696 days).</u> I've been a lazy horny bum for 10 days, but tomorrow I'm calling a realtor. I can't put it off any longer. I'm going to Texas. I give up! This is my last entry. √ js.

--------

<u>Ltr #591, Wed 10-26-88,11:43 a.m. (1699 days).</u> Dear Becki. News. News. I had no intention of writing any more letters in this journal, but Joe Lareux showed up yesterday in his old green Buick. He moved into the apartment across the hall. He's going to pay 25% of expenses as soon as he gets a job. I'll still have to sell this house but this gives me more time, a month or two, & a lot to think about. We talked all night. After 5 years, Joe gave up trying to be a Christian and to make things fit. He says he must live from within = no choice. I shared about you, Becki, & he talked about Brenda = he still loves her after 5 yrs of nothing—sounds familiar. I asked Joe why he went to Logan about you & me back in Dec. of '83. He said he never talked to Logan. Fucking Garrett set me up, & I fell for it. √ js

--------

<u>Ltr #592, Tue 11-1-88, 8:53 a.m. (1705 days).</u> Dark, rainy, cold. The meadow is gray. The trees loom in the distance like dark ranks of soldiers. The whole world is silent, Becki, except for the rain dripping off the roof. I have my stove going. It smells good. Joe's working for 1st Security & he's not smoking pot. I told him I didn't want it on the property. He says he hopes for bigger things than a drug high. He feels that people are ready to break free from the shackles of religion. I told Russ—Russ says he'll believe it when he sees it. √ js

--------

<u>Ltr #595, Wed 11-9-88, 7:54 a.m. (1713 days).</u> Dear Becki, I love you so much this morning it makes me weak. I can hardly sit in this chair. Joe's return has rekindled a glimmer of hope in my heart. I'm not sure I want it. ◊ Bush beat Dukakis, but compared to—Fuck it! Politics is nothing. ◊ Russ & I went to McDonald's last night. He said Frank Cahill left Sylvia, took the girls & went to his mother's in Allentown, Pa. Russ called Sylvia but she wouldn't talk to him except to say that our "follow the heart" message had ruined her life. √ js

--------

Ltr #597, Fri 11-18-88, 11:53 a.m. (1722 days). Dear Becki, I went for a walk this morning. The fallen leaves underfoot are no longer red & yellow but dirty-brown on their way to dust. ◊ Joe & I talked last nite. He hopes God will raise up a ministry of love and liberty that will expose & challenge Logan's empire. I told him it would have to be <u>God</u> because I'll never again hand out tracts or knock on doors—nor would I take offerings or put ads in the yellow pages. Joe replied, "My vision is a '60s-style rock band w a guitar, a bass, a keyboard, drums, a vocalist, maybe tambourines & harmonica, but everyone'll be part of it whether they play or not, & we can do all kinds of music: straight rock, soft rock, metal, good-time rock 'n roll, blues, country, boogie, heavy, light, acoustic—whatever we need to bare our souls. We'll do our own songs, plus cover tunes, & you can preach, Jim, between songs." I replied that it sounded great but it's hard to have a band w one musician. Joe laughed, agreed it would be a miracle & that he'll never again recruit band members or play for $$. I also told him God doesn't have much time because I'm selling the house when my bank acct. runs out = no later than Jan. √ js

- - - - - - - -

Ltr #599, Mon 11-21-88, 11:35 p.m. (1725 days). This aftn Joe set up his amplifiers and speakers and shit in Mrs. C's old apt, in front of the plugged fireplace. He also has two tape decks, a drum machine, and a Fender keyboard. ◊ Tonight, we watched a great movie = Room with a View = shows how this girl, Lucy Honeychurch—she reminds me of you, Becki—runs from her heart & lies to cover herself. It's an E. M. Forster story = he knows the war of heart vs. fear so well. √ js

- - - - - - - -

Ltr #600, Thur 11-24-88, 9:55 p.m. (1728 days). Thanksgiving Day. Joe & I went for Chinese at Debbie Wong's in Worcester then he went to work. He's a guard at Digital in Hudson. Joe writes letters to Brenda but she never writes back. Sounds familiar, Becki. He says, "Brenda is the life of my music. I sing to her in my songs. If she was w me, I could give people heaven on earth, but as it is I can only share my ache." It's curious how Joe & I are in the same boat. √ js

- - - - - - - -

Ltr #604, Sat 12-10-88, 2:55 p.m. (1744 days). Dear Becki. I spoke w Sharon last nite. Logan is sending Tom to Pittsfield (in mid January) as Sharon had hoped. But they'll be moving to Cobleskill to live w her parents. Nana's idea of course, now that Mor's gone. Tom will commute to Pittsfield from Cobleskill. Heather is glad to leave Brendon Falls. Chris has given no opinion. But I bet Stan Campbell's ejaculating all over himself. I guess he'll finally be head pastor at BFBC after waiting all this time. ◊ I got a Xmas card from Jodi. She says Tony called. I guess love isn't completely dead. √ js

--------

Ltr #606, Sun 12-18-88, 11:55 a.m. (1752 days). Becki, we just saw Logan's Sun service from Moody on TV (Chan 27). I don't watch the bastard, but Joe wanted to check out the "enemy camp" as if we're having a showdown next week—what a laugh! We have 3 people & LBI has 10,000. Logan preached his usual mixture of promises & warnings, & the body roared their approval. Nothing has changed in 4 years except Crenshaw's gone & Robert Logan leads songs, & fucking Barry Buford took the offering & proudly proclaimed the ongoing success of the LBI vision = 52 branches in the U.S. & 31 missionary teams. √ js

--------

Ltr #607, Thur 12-22-88, 9:17 p.m. (1756 days). Dear Becki, I guess you heard about Pan Am flight 103 = exploded over Lockerbie, Scotland. What a way to go, but who knows how it feels to die whether in a bomb or in your bed. Who knows about the soul, or where it goes? People want sure answers to the big questions & Christians profess to have them but I like what Voltaire says: "Doubt is not a pleasant condition, but certainty is absurd." √ js

--------

Ltr #608, Sat 12-24-88, 11:55 a.m. (1758 days). Dear Rebecca, after Joe got home fm work last nite we played tapes 'til 5 a.m. = Led Zeppelin, Aerosmith, The Doors, Janis Joplin, Queen, Pink Floyd, The Beatles, Stevie Nicks, Jimi Hendrix, B.B. King, Hank Williams, Ray Charles, Fats Domino, 2nd Chapter of Acts, Amy Grant, Oakridge Boys. Joe talks about chords & riffs & frets & dynamics & key & pitch & bass tracks & back beats & fills. He says, "Every true song, Jim, is a painting. The instruments are brushes in the hand of an artist. The notes & chords are colors, shapes, tones. The lyrics speak to the mind but the music takes the message to the soul. I like to check out what different groups are doing but most bands these days are like matches. They flare up w passion but quickly burn out leaving smoke but no flame. They start as artists but quickly become whores w agents for pimps. The record companies & sponsors suck their essence & produce lip-sync videos & hyped-up concerts. They're like Logan & LBI. They exploit their fans for profit, fame, & power. But we're different, Jim, we see people as part of us. We want their hearts w/o ulterior motive. We'll never have to hype it w marketing campaigns & missionary tactics. People have been abused long enough. It's time for love to move." I reminded Joe that we have no band and no ministry, except for him and me and Russ. He laughed and said, "Well, we can dream can't we?" √ js

--------

Ltr #612, Thur 1-5-89, 9:24 a.m. (1770 days). Becki, Joe's reading my poems & seed thoughts. He says I have a gift for writing lyrics. He plays his guitar for hours. He acts like we're going to be here forever. I told him again that we had to sell the house. He just shrugged and said, "Let's live one day at a time." √ js

- - - - - - - -

Ltr #614, Fri 1-13-89, 12:22 p.m. (1778 days). Frigid out = -2° this morn. But still no snow. I'm out of cash, Becki. I borrowed $1200 on my Master Card. Ms. Blakely from Century 21 is coming over Monday. I could get an equity loan, but what's the point of prolonging the inevitable = more payments, more interest. It's more realistic to sell & go to Texas = reasonable & sane. ◊ Jodi called last nite. She said Tony came to see her. She tried to play it down, but she couldn't hide her excitement. She also said Brenda moved in w her boy friend = thrilling news for Joe. ◊ Sharon also called about child support—I'm two wks late. √ js

- - - - - - - -

Ltr #615, Sat 1-14-89, 10:49 a.m. (1779 days). Dear Becki, last nite Joe & I saw a movie: The Breakfast Club = charged w erotic yearning. Joe says Ally Sheedy turns him on = reminds him of Brenda. Afterward, we went down & played tapes = John Lennon, Mama's & Papa's, J. Geils Band, Elton John, Bob Seger, Prince, Wilson Pickett. Between tapes, we talked about the war of LOVE vs. FEAR = how Babylon, like George Orwell's "Big Brother," wants to suppress orgasm (any ecstasy of spirit, body, mind that makes you lose control) = they want order at any cost. The things we talked about are still popping in my head like popcorn = questions: Why must I be a no-name whore chained to profit & efficiency—just to get my daily bread? ◊ Why am I a faceless body in my marriage bed? ◊ Why do I put on my mask & go to the masquerade each day? ◊ Why do I pretend to love people I don't love? ◊ Why am I so ashamed of my sex fantasies? ◊ Why do I think nothing of saying, "I'm hungry" yet I'd never say, "I'm horny." ◊ If God is LOVE, why is LOVE losing? √ js

- - - - - - - -

Ltr #616, Sun 1-15-89, 3:35 p.m. (1780 days). Joe just left for work. Before he left, he said, "I'm going to teach you to play the drums, Jim. I doubt you'll be great, but I can teach you well enough to give me a back beat." As usual, he was bluntly honest—but he did say our heart connection will make us unique. Think of it, Rebecca—me, a "rock drummer." Now Logan will say I'm demon-possessed. But I bet you'd secretly like to join our movement—why do I give way to such fantasy? You don't even think of me. You're too busy fucking Randy. Besides, there's no movement around here—except for my morning bowel movement. ◊ Tom & Sharon moved to Cobleskill yesterday. But there's been a change in orders fm Nashua. Things are going so well in Brendon Falls (good monthly donations to home base no doubt) that Logan wants Tom to remain as head pastor at BFBC for at least another year. So he'll be coming to Brendon Falls each week instead of Pittsfield. Stan will continue to be his assistant. So much for Stan's aspirations, & Logan's promises. √ js

- - - - - - - -

<u>Ltr #617, Mon 1-16-89, 1:21 p.m. (1781 days).</u> Dear Becki, I guess Joe's serious about the drums. He bought a used set of CB-700's & set them up for me = a snare, a bass, a floor tom, 4 mounted toms, a hi-hat, and 2 Zildjian cymbals. ◊ I ate w Russ at McD's last nite. He says Sylvia went to an alcoholic treatment center in Brattleboro, Vt. She's been on a binge ever since Frank left w the kids. Russ called the hosp but she wouldn't take his call. I know that feeling. ◊ On a brighter note: as we left McD's, Russ handed me an envelope & said, "Wait 'til next month to sell the house." In the envelope were twenty $50 bills = $1000. √ js

- - - - - - - -

<u>Ltr #619, Sun 1-22-89, 7:40 a.m. (1787 days).</u> Inch of snow & sleet overnite. The meadow is finally white. Joe's teaching me the basics = keeping a tempo on the hi-hat, exercises on the snare, & yesterday he showed me the straight rock beat = bass-skip-snare-skip = 1 & 2 & 3 & 4 & 1, etc, w snares on 2, 4, & bass on 1, 3. I feel awkward as a newborn colt = hard to get my arms & feet in sync. √ js

- - - - - - - -

<u>Ltr #621, Fri 1-27-89, 7:27 a.m. (1792 days).</u> Dear Becki, good news on $$ front. Gary Bob called & said the Koch Oil crew has a producing well on the Gilson place just 50 yds east of our property line. Too early to be precise, but we should get $1000 each/mo. So, Becki, maybe I won't have to sell our house after all—What the fuck's wrong w me, calling this place "our" house. √ js

- - - - - - - -

<u>Ltr #624, Mon 2-13-89, 11:05 a.m. (1809 days).</u> Becki, last nite Joe played more tapes. He has music in his blood. He lives it, breathes it. His comments are still dancing in my mind—on AC-DC, "These guys overdo it w the noise. Heavy metal is dynamite in small doses, but they're pushing it & distorting out the beautiful chords." On ZZ Top, "This is Billy Gibbons. He's an old fart. He does a bluesy Texas rock." On Dire Straits & 'So Far Away,' "That's a heartache song. It's been my cry to Brenda for 5 yrs." On INXS, "These are Australian guys. They have lots of energy, & a sweet sax—but they don't say much. On the Steve Miller Band, "These guys do boogie blues w a hot harmonica." On Joe Walsh & 'Rocky Mountain Way,' "This guy fucks w his guitar." On Bryan Adams & 'Going Home,' These are beautiful lyrics that I'd

love to sing to Brenda." On Simon & Garfunkel & 'Scarborough Fair,' "I love how he repeats like 2 voices. It's like a holy wedding w nature— Paul Simon has turned into an egotistical asshole but his early music was great—I like how he says 'tell her to meet me' like me telling God to have Brenda come here—when I get stoned, I can believe it—but let's make our songs mean something. Let's paint a musical picture that shows a place that's beautiful, yet it's for everybody, I want to make people feel what they've never felt before. I don't want to entertain, I want us to bleed w truth!" √ js

- - - - - - - -

Ltr #625, Tue 2-14-89, 8:52 p.m. (1810 days). Becki, I spend hours on the drums. I have blisters on my hands. I wear batter's gloves. The rock beat is 2nd nature now. I play along to Joe's drum machine & to songs that have a straight beat like "Talk to Me" (Stevie Nicks), "The Long Run" (Eagles), "Old Time Rock & Roll" (Bob Seger), "Tuesday Afternoon" (Moody Blues)—& lots of others. I love to get lost in the rhythm. Joe says, "I don't give a shit about fancy drumming, I just want a steady beat to lay my guitar on. Rolls & cymbals are important, but only when they truly add to the dynam- ics—usually, Jim, the best songs are the simplest songs." √ js

- - - - - - - -

Ltr #626, Fri 2-17-89, 9:10 p.m. (1813 days). Tonite I stood in the meadow & gazed at the stars. I saw the northern lights. They pulsed thru the heavens like rippling curtains of amber radiance. I felt you near. Oh, Becki. I miss you as the night misses the dawn, as the frozen meadow misses the butterflies & buttercups, as old men miss their youth. But now, as I sit here at my desk staring out at the darkness, I must face reality & drink it like poison = you're married, established, & you'll never come to me. It hurts & hurts, but I have to drink it until my heart no longer cries for justice. √ js

- - - - - - - -

Ltr #627, Sun 2-19-89, 4:43 p.m. (1815 days). I practiced 3 hrs this morn. Joe taught me the blues beat = bass-bass-skip-bass-snare-skip w different variations = odd-based (3's, 6's) as opposed to the straight beat which is even (2's, 4's). He also showed me a few simple fill-ins & cymbal crashes. √ js

- - - - - - - -

Ltr #629, Mon 2-20-89, 4:07 p.m. (1816 days). Rainy, foggy. I can barely see the meadow. I have a cold. I'm coughing. ◊ Despite Joe & the drums, my outlook is still dark & gray, like the gloom outside. You vowed in '84 that you'd never be w me, Becki, & you've kept that vow for 1816 days. ◊ I ate w Russ at Bergson's last nite. He asked if Joe's smoking pot. I told him no. Russ replied, "Joe has an eager-puppy

660

heart. I always saw it even in the old days when he used to sleep on our couch on weekends, but I fear his high hopes may lead to a crushing letdown. A guitar player & a novice drummer & me watching is hardly a revolution." ◊ Sharon called to remind me I haven't sent Feb's $$. She said Erin's going with a senior at Houghton, a nice Christian guy, but she hopes they don't get serious since Erin's just a freshman. I told Shar I was playing the drums. She laughed, "Oh, Jim, you <u>are</u> desperate to regain your youth." √ js

--------

<u>Ltr #630, Tue 2-21-89, 3:35 p.m. (1817 days)</u>. Becki, I guess you heard the LBI Cessna crashed last nite in the fog. Russ just called. Logan wasn't aboard, but Mike Montanaro & Pam Garrett were killed, & the pilot—yet miraculously, Matt Garrett walked away w/o a scratch. He <u>is</u> a Rasputin. √ js

--------

<u>Ltr #631, Fri 2-24-89, 10:48 a.m. (1820 days)</u>. Dear Becki, Russ was over last nite. We talked about the plane crash & prayer = I'm sure they prayed before they took off—at LBI you pray for everything—but they still crashed. Logan says pray, & God will grant your request if you pray fervently & you're not living in sin. Yet believers still have disasters & accidents & broken hearts. They lose their jobs, get divorced, get cancer, have strokes, grow old & die like all humans. But when something good happens they say, "That's an answer to prayer!" Russ summed it up well, "I can see pouring out our hearts to God, but the idea that we can persuade God to do what we want doesn't jive with reality. We used to pray all the time, Jim, but I doubt it changed anything; it just gave us a false peace about the future. People want an 'edge' on life; they don't want God, or the devil, to get out of their control, & prayer is a way of controlling God. Logan doesn't call it that, of course. He calls it 'moving' God which sounds more humble & pious. I can't see God scrambling about & changing his plans every day to make sure the universe runs in response to Christian prayers. He's got to be bigger than that." √ js

--------

<u>Ltr #634, Sun 3-12-89, 11:45 a.m. (1836 days)</u>. Dear Becki. I got a letter from Mary Beth. She's still in shock over the plane crash. She says she knew deep in her heart that she & Michael would never be together in this life. I guess I could say the same about me & you, Becki. ◊ M.B. also says she doesn't know how much longer she can put up with Logan's bullshit. √ js

--------

<u>Ltr #635, Tue 3-14-89, 8:45 p.m. (1838 days)</u>. Becki, I got my 1st

check from Koch Oil = $3127 = two-months' worth. The well is producing more than we expected. I sent my overdue child support to Sharon & paid off half of my MC debt = things are looking up financially. ◊ Joe & I jam for hours every day. I play a straight beat or blues. I love Joe's guitar. He can make it wail like a banshee, chug like a train, whine like a puppy, warble like a siren, rumble like an 18-wheeler, growl like a wildcat, snort like a hog, squeal like a piglet, honk like a Model T, twang like a Jew's harp, whimper like a weeping child—and everything in between. He never went to music school, but he knows a lot. He tried to explain chords to me = something about 3 notes at once. I'm glad I don't have to know much to play the drums. Joe has a rich baritone voice but he doesn't like to sing & play at the same time except w his acoustic. He wants a female vocalist for our band = another wild dream. Joe says I'm not bad for a beginner = I keep a steady beat but my sixteenth notes are sloppy. He says I have to feel them. It's not a mathematical mind thing. ◊ My life is different now. I don't lie around & watch movies & read Penthouse, but I still get horny thinking about you, Becki. O God, would I love to see the rolls of wanton flesh inside your soft thighs = insane fantasy = you're married & happily fucking your husband = I'm nuts = out of touch w reality! √ js

- - - - - - - -

Ltr #636, Thur 3-16-89, 4:33 p.m. (1840 days). Dear Becki, Joe & I got into a big fight this afternoon. I've been practicing my sixteenth notes for 2 days. Joe listened to them today & in his usual blunt way said, "They're sloppy. You're not getting it. That'll never do." I exploded & called him a "PERFECTIONIST BASTARD!" I turned over the drums & threw one of my sticks so hard that it punctured the wall. Joe roared back, "DAMMIT, JIM! YOU'LL NEVER BE A DRUMMER IF YOU PLAY WITH YOUR FUCKING EGO!" Then he cooled & said, "It doesn't matter if you get sixteenth notes. Our victory has nothing to do with talent. Finally, we stared at each other & started laughing, so hard that we collapsed on the floor. √ js

- - - - - - -

Jim chuckles. He takes off his old Crusader softball hat and runs his fingers through his hair. The cap is so sweat-stained that the white part looks yellow like strong piss. No more sun, except on the topmost trees across the river; afternoon is fading into evening. After replacing his hat, he turns his attention back to the journal:

Ltr #639, Wed 3-22-89, 6:15 p.m. (1846 days). This afternoon Joe made beans & franks & invited me over. He says he dreams of a family of heart & love & poetry & music = a spiritual commune = a music ministry = w me & you, Becki, & him & Brenda, & Russ, & maybe 10 others. Then the love-starved souls in LBI will see our joy & similar cocoons of love will spring up throughout Logan's empire as "love casts out fear" & LBI will collapse. I love the thought but Joe's fucking mad = worse than "Don Quixote." √ js

- - - - - - - -

<u>Ltr #647, Sat 4-29-89, 10:31 a.m. (1884 days).</u> Dear Becki, Joe says my fills are OK = I'm finally getting sixteenth notes. Now he's teaching me offbeats & double-bass beats & a slow beat with qtr notes on the hi-hat. ◊ Russ came over last nite to watch the Red Sox. He still wears his old Red Sox hat & hunter's vest & he's just as laid-back as ever = he never hypes our chances. If we ever have an outbreak of heart & Russ is part of it, I'll know it's real. Joe's not into baseball but he joined us after the game & we talked about how Logan & other Bible preachers cause most of the sexual hang-ups in our society = strange fetishes, frigidity, sado-masochism, fucking animals, incest, child abuse, urinating-defecating = it all comes from people hating & suppressing their sex drive til it comes out in perverted ways. Joe brought up the subject of gays. Russ says homosexuals are frustrated men in hiding. I said I didn't know but some seem to be born gay, like Garrett who moves & gestures as if he has a female spirit inside his male body. We came to no conclusion & our talk shifted to the plane crash & how we felt sorry for Pam, but we agreed that she might be better off dead? √ js

- - - - - - - -

<u>Ltr #648, Mon 5-1-89, 9:15 a.m. (1886 days).</u> Yesterday, Becki, we moved the band stuff to the barn. Russ helped us build a low stage & knock out 2 old stalls to give us a large open area. The floor is wood plank. There's already electricity & lights & one water faucet, but we'll have to put in some kind of heat & a bathroom. Joe & I played out there this afternoon. The acoustics are expansive = more like a church w the high ceiling & loft in the back. √ js

- - - - - - - -

<u>Ltr #653, Sun 5-21-89, 10:48 a.m. (1906 days).</u> Becki, I went to see the kids yesterday = 1st time since they moved to Cobleskill. Nana was polite but distant. Pop was friendly but quickly escaped to his barn office. Harry & Grover are dead, but he has a new mutt, "Ulysses Grant." People never change—not really. ◊ I took the kids to Albany for the aftn. Erin's home from college. She broke up w her boy friend. She gave the right reasons = he lives in Cincinnati, she has 3 yrs to go, etc—but she was echoing Sharon. Heather's graduating next Sat. She's been accepted at Houghton but she now says she's not going—a battle looms. ◊ Sharon says your sister Katie is now Matt Garrett's personal secretary. After typing for him & Barry for 3 yrs she's moved up to top dog. Hurrah for Katie! Hurrah for Alison! ◊ Russ says that Sylvia is out of the hospital, that she went to Long Island to live with her sister, & Frank has custody of the girls. Russ says that Frank's a

pious ass-kissing actor, that he was a model father while the custody hearings were going on. √ js

- - - - - - - -

Ltr #654, Mon 5-22-89, 11:53 p.m. (1907 days). Joe, Russ, & I had a thought-provoking talk tonite = we got real honest & listed the women we'd most like to screw & you were high on each list, Becki, as were Sylvia & Brenda & Sharon & Janet Buford. We then debated the big question: "Does it violate love to share lovers or is it necessary for true oneness?" I told about "Barbara's Dream" from George Macdonald's novel. Joe says he's seen a few swinger parties where people get drunk & fuck each other in chairs, on tables, on the floor, but it's like a bunch of loose meat hanging out w no heart. Russ offered practical wisdom (his gift), "I think ultimate oneness means heart, soul, & body, but I doubt we'll see it in this life. We're a lot freer than the LBI crowd but I expect we'd still feel self-conscious in a group-fuck & that would cut off our hearts & make it a performance like a porno film." √ js

- - - - - - - -

Ltr #664, Fri 6-30-89, 11:15 a.m. (1946 days). News. News. Big news, Becki! A gray Dodge van pulled in yesterday aftn = surprise = Jodi & Tony. They moved into Mrs. C's old apt. Brenda stayed in Chicago w her boyfriend. (I'm asking Jodi & Tony to pay 40% of expenses = $350/mo. Joe will pay 20% & I'll pay the final 40%, & I'm buying a washer & dryer for the basement.) Joe asked them if they sang or played. They laughed & said no. So what? I like having Jodi & Tony w us—band or no band. √ js

- - - - - - - -

Ltr #666, Thur 7-6-89, 10:32 p.m. (1952 days). Jodi got a waitress job at Bancrofts' & Tony still works for the YMCA in Leominster. Perhaps a new ministry is being born = good, yet also sad w/o you, Becki. √ js

- - - - - - - -

Ltr #667, Mon 7-10-89, 10:23 p.m. (1956 days). Dear Becki, Jodi came up tonite. Tony & Joe were working. She brought donuts. I made coffee. She laughed & said, "Just like old times, huh, Jim?" She talked about Tony = their love is up & down & scary & she never knows what to expect, but it's still the best thing that's ever happened to her. Jodi's hair is grayer & her crow's-feet are more evident & she still has rings around her eyes, but she acts younger than 38, whereas before she seemed older than her age. Perhaps it's just that she smiles more & seems alive & no longer heavy-laden. I talked about you, Rebecca = 1956 days of pain. Jodi ate, sipped, & smoked her Winstons. Finally, she said, "Becki loved you in '84, Jim.

I never saw such yearning in a young woman." I gave a painful chuckle & reminded her that it's been 5 years, & I've given up. But Jodi held her ground, "5 years is a long time, Jim, but it takes considerably longer for an oak tree to get completely out of an acorn. The strongest love is usually the last to be seen?" √ js

- - - - - - - -

Ltr #670, Wed 7-19-89, 9:23 a.m. (1965 days). Dear Becki, Joe & I jammed 3 hours last nite. I play different beats & Joe plays his riffs & parts of songs. Jodi & Tony came out too. Joe's teaching them how to run the speakers, mikes, & tape deck thru the Peavey mixer. Joe talks as if we're going on the road in 3 days—hard to do w a two-man band. Afterward we went inside & Jodi served coffee & cake & we talked half the night. Tony's got a warm little-boy heart & he laughs w a deep laugh. √ js

- - - - - - -

Ltr #672, Wed 7-26-89, 9:30 p.m. (1972 days). Becki, I traded the Mustang in on an '87 Tempo. My finances are stable now thanks to my oil checks & sharing of expenses around here. ◊ I like having Jodi & Tony w us, but this place will never be the same. Tony's deep voice booms through the whole house & when Jodi & Tony fight I hear every word not to mention when they make love. Things are surely changing, I wonder where we're headed? √ js

- - - - - - - -

Ltr #676, Sat 8-12-89, 7:55 p.m. (1989 days). Dear Becki. The shit finally hit the fan in Cobleskill. Heather called = she won't go to Houghton. She wants to go to secretarial school in Albany & get an apartment w her girl friend from high school. I supported Heather, so Sharon got on & we had our own fight, but she finally agreed if I help Heather buy a car & pay half her tuition. ◊ Note from Mary Beth—she says it's a riot about me playing the drums. She also says that Logan mentioned me at staff meeting as an example of a pastor who abandoned "categorical doctrine & sanctification in favor of salacious subjectivity & concubinage w young women." Fucking Logan, he always uses big words to lift himself above people. √ js

- - - - - - - -

Ltr #679, Sun 8-20-89, 9:10 p.m. (1997 days). Dear Becki, we were doing a blues beat this aftn & Joe started singing made-up lyrics about a brokenhearted fellow who's too sad to get out of bed. Afterward, he said, "Now if Jesus played the guitar, he'd play 12-bar blues. The blues beat is God's big cock that penetrates hearts. The blues get down to the common everyday guy. I mean we can do songs like this & the whole house can be part of it. I'd like to have video cameras all around so we can capture real life, not phony fellowship like in Nashua. Then we'll put it all together w a blues song & we'll have a video that'll touch hearts." √ js

- - - - - - - -

**Ltr #680, Mon 8-21-89,11:15 a.m. (1998 days).** Hazy, hot, humid = dog days of summer. Our cocoon is growing, Becki, but not our band. Billy McArthur arrived yesterday. He can't take it living with his mother anymore. I told him he can stay in the attic but no drugs on the property & he has to pay his share of expenses = 60/4 =15%. Everyone, Joe, Jodi, Tony, will now pay 15%. (I'll still pay 40%.) Billy works at Poulos Pizza & has no musical talent, but he's got a sensitive & eager heart. He still looks slim & boyish, but w less pimples. √ js

- - - - - - - -

**Ltr #686, Thur 9-14-89, 8:23 a.m. (2022 days).** Dear Becki, we're renovating the barn so we can play out there all year, & it'll gives us a bigger place for all of us to congregate, like a big living room. We're putting in insulation, plasterboard, & a bathroom. We're doing a lot of the work ourselves but we have a plumber doing the pipes & fixtures, & connecting to the main sewer. We have an electrician putting in radiant-heat units & upgrading the circuits to give us more lights & outlets. While we're at it, we're painting the house, & a roofing guy is putting on a new roof. I got a home improvement loan for $10,500. √ js

- - - - - - - -

**Ltr #691, Sun 10-1-89, 6:53 p.m. (2039 days).** Just got back from a walk. The dry-sweet smell of fall is in the air. ◊ This aftn we all ate together in Jodi's apt. We eat there almost every Sun & share the food costs. ◊ Russ says that Sylvia's back in town. She's staying w the Thorntons on Greeley Hill, & she's sober. √ js

- - - - - - - -

**Ltr #693, Wed 10-4-89, 7:56 p.m. (2042 days).** Dear Becki. Sharon called this aftn, upset & near tears. Erin dropped out of college, went to Cincinnati & got an apt w her boyfriend (his name is Ronnie & he works at his dad's pharmacy). Nana says it's my worldly influence on Erin that caused her to forsake her calling & her chastity. As far as I'm concerned, Erin is following her calling. ◊ This morning, Joe & Tony & I painted the new walls in the barn = light brown, & Jodi put blue curtains on the windows. Jodi & Tony also got 4 old sofas from a garage sale. We arranged them around our practice area. A lot of work for a two-man band. ◊ I bought a microwave today. I always said I'd never get into the yuppie microwave routine. But I have no time to cook. √ js

- - - - - - - -

Ltr #697, Thur 10-19-89, 8:36 a.m. (2057 days). Went to Bergson's last nite w Russ & Jodi. We laughed & cut up. The only serious subject = the rotten state of born-again Christianity = Jim Bakker's in jail. Tammy's on drugs. Swaggart got caught with a whore = a brother turned him in. But Russ reminded, "Despite the media hype, these bad apples are not what make the barrel rotten. It's the clean assholes, the Falwells & Logans & Pat Robertsons, & the highly respected local preachers, who enslave souls the most." √ js

- - - - - - - -

Ltr #700, Wed 10-25-89, 3:31 p.m.(2063 days). Joe just left for work. He was down. He says, "I came w a vision but God has brought no one for the band. I spent 10 mos. teaching you, Jim, but for what? God doesn't give a shit. Nothing happens in life unless you pour money into it. Well, I'm not waiting on God. Forget the amplifier & drums, I'll play my acoustic & sing simple songs, & you can read your poems & preach." Joe's frustrated but I feel a resigned peace, Becki. We're on a train w no exits, I hope to a good place. Only God can gather hearts that are wild & terrible—yet tender. I'm not qualified to do it. √ js

- - - - - - - -

Ltr #705, Mon 11-13-89, 11:58 p.m. (2082 days). Tonight we gathered in the barn (the 5 of us + Russ). Joe did an original song = "Salvation" on his acoustic guitar = from my poem of the same title which satirically compares Christianity to prostitution. He also did a few of his own songs. After that we sat around on the old sofas & shared our hearts. I told the whole saga of you & me, Becki (back to '75). Jodi & Tony shared their own roller coaster story. Billy said he loves Haley C. (in California) but never had the guts to tell her. √ js

- - - - - - - -

Ltr #707, Thur 11-23-89,7:20 p.m. (2092 days). Snow & cold. Six inches of snow. It's Thanksgiving, Becki, but it looks like Xmas. ◊ The Berlin Wall is coming down. Who would've believed it? The Russians are now our friends. Communism is falling apart, but political freedom is not the freedom I ache for. I want more than a level playing field on which to compete for money & goodies. I ache for the walls of fear & self-hatred to come down, so hearts can run to each other—so you can run to me, Becki. √ js

- - - - - - - -

Ltr #709, Wed 11-29-89,11:20 p.m. (2098 days). Cherry lips. Strawberry hair. Bass guitar. Guess who showed up today, Becki? Haley Cameron & she plays bass guitar. She learned it in Calif. Billy almost fainted, & Joe believes in God again. He can't believe she plays bass.

She hugged me like a long-lost daughter. She came back because her mom's moving to Oregon w a new boyfriend (Barbara hasn't changed = new guy every 3 yrs = not bad for <u>zero</u> sex appeal). Haley's face—she's now 22—has lost its adolescent softness. She's getting that dry, seasoned, dark-eyed look that smokers get in their 20s, like Jodi's face ten years ago. She's taking Ruthie's old apartment = same deal as the others. ◊ Tonite we got back to drums, amplifiers, etc. Joe got all excited & said, "Haley, you're good for a <u>girl</u>!" Haley laughed, shot back, "You're not fucking bad yourself—for a <u>guy</u>!" She's just as brash & foulmouthed as ever. ◊ Good things are happening but they can't really be good w/o you, Becki. I wish you were here to be part of this—whatever it is? √ js

- - - - - - - -

Ltr #710, Fri 12-1-89, 3:31 p.m. (2100 days). Jodi got Haley a busgirl job at Bancrofts'. Now we have two women in the house. I love them both but not sexually—oh, I doubt I'd kick them out of my bed. But Jodi still seems like a sister, & Haley, I'm not sure what it is. She's pretty enough & she's got a nice shape despite her small breasts = she's built like her mom. That's probably it. She reminds me of her mom & I've never been turned on to Barbara. Or maybe it's just my aversion to kissing cunts that smoke, like Doris, like Ruthie—anyway, when I masturbate, it's you, Becki, 80% of the time. The other 20% = Sharon, Angie, Cathy R, Brenda, Janet B. √ js

- - - - - - - -

Ltr #713, Sun 12-10-89, 8:22 a.m. (2109 days). Dear Becki. We now have six (7 counting Russ) in our cocoon of kindred spirits, but we have no party line. We're so different from the orchestrated harmony in Nashua where no one shares their true feelings, but must keep it safe, doctrinal—& dead. Yet we have no phony bar-room hype either like the Michelob scene. In fact, we don't drink at all except a beer now & then. We simply share our "selves" = our experiences, hopes, dreads, ideas—& you're part of it, Becki. It's the same love. It's just most intense between me & you. It's like gravity = all stars attract each other, but those that are closest attract each other the most. But 59 Front St. is no utopia. Joe yelled at Haley for using up the hot water. Billy got pissed at Jodi because his sweat shirt came back pink (Jodi does our laundry). Joe & Billy got upset w me when I refused to relax the pot rule, & Tony & Jodi have at least one good fight a week—& none of us agree on theology. ◊ Haley & Billy are together all the time. I guess he told her. √ js

- - - - - - - -

Jim takes off his glasses, rubs his eyes. He gazes at the hills across the river. The splotches of color have faded into various shades of gray. The sun is hidden by Hadley Hill behind him. *Six years,* he sighs to himself. *No one comes back after six years. Two years, four years, perhaps? But not six? Yet this story seems so unresolved as if the last reel of the movie is somehow missing?* He checks his watch—5:25 p.m. He continues to read:

Ltr #715, Thur 12-21-89, 9:10 a.m. (2120 days). Dear Becki. last nite our session in the barn lasted 'til 1:00 a.m. We did some cover tunes and a few of Joe's songs from St. Louis. We also did a new song about the hypocrisy & heartache of Christmas that Joe adapted from one of my poems. Afterward we talked and talked. We're getting a lot closer to each other. √ js

‑‑‑‑‑‑‑‑

Ltr #716, Sat 12-23-89, 10:47 a.m. (2122 days). Dear Becki, it's -6° outside = coldest Dec. ever. What happened to global warming? ◊ This morning I ran into Haley coming down fm Billy's room. I smiled, she blushed. I'm happy for them. Our house is a far cry from LBI! √ js

‑‑‑‑‑‑‑‑

Ltr #717, Tue 12-26-89, 6:03 p.m. (2125 days). Chugging, chugging, rock 'n blues. We're now into serious jamming. Haley does her bass routines. Joe plays riffs/leads. We do good-time rock for practice = "Johnny B. Goode," "Smokin in the Boys' Room," "Help Me Rhonda." & bluesy rock = Fats Domino shit. Joe's teaching Billy the drums—to back me up. ◊ This aftn Haley moved her stuff up w Billy = lightning & thunder to the attic. √ js

‑‑‑‑‑‑‑‑

Ltr #718, Wed 12-27-89, 3:55 p.m. (2126 days). Dear Becki, sad news = a real tragedy = Molly Gibson died of a drug overdose in a Dorchester tenement (Russ heard fm Bev who heard fm Doris). Molly was a lost puppy w a hungry heart. Perhaps she's lucky. Most of Logan's victims don't die physically, but live on in "soul death" = slaves to self-hate—like you, Becki. Fuck Christianity! Fuck it all! Protestant, Catholic, born-again. The institution is applauded & respected, but to me it's the most diabolical force in the world & far removed from the kind & loving man we call "Jesus." For 1700 years, Church leaders have taken advantage of desperate souls to gain power & wealth & fame = tyranny = worse than all the "Hitlers" = they've enslaved minds & caused hatred, division, & wars. √ js

‑‑‑‑‑‑‑‑

Ltr #721, Thur 1-4-89, 10:46 a.m. (2134 days). Dear Becki. I got a note from Mary Beth lamenting Molly's death. She says that Molly needed someone to look up to, that she couldn't cope w/o a God-figure in her life. ◊ M.B. also says, "Your new ministry, Jim, is bothering Dr. Logan. He ignores you publicly, but in private, he says you're running a house of sin, a free-sex commune, that you lead young women away from God & turn them into concubines to satisify your lecherous appetites." Logan & his "fuck stories." The way he tells it I've had hundreds of sweet young cunts in my bed in the past 5 years. If only it were true—I might believe in God more. Mary Beth also says that Logan calls me a hippie cult leader. Maybe I'm a hippie but I'd hardly call 7 people a "cult." √ js

. . . . . . . . .

Ltr #724, Mon 1-22-90, 7:53 a.m. (2152 days). White, white, soft & beautiful. It's snowing, Becki. I got up early & took a walk. A pristine hush reigns in the woods. Virgin snow—it's like "first love." All is new. All is pure. All invites discovery. The trees bow in silent worship. Feathery flakes drift down down down. When I got back, I went out front by the oak tree & looked down the street toward town, toward the roar of snowplows, the whir of snow throwers, & the scraping of snow shovels. Babylon wastes little time. Snow gets in the way of commerce. It's no wonder Thoreau liked Walden Pond better than New York City. √ js

. . . . . . . . .

Ltr #725, Tue 1-23-90, 8:18 a.m. (2153 days). The clouds are racing over the meadow. The Prescott plume is white & blowing up river toward the dam. We have 14" of snow. ◊ More news, Becki! At the height of the storm yesterday, Angela & Sylvia arrived in Angie's Volvo. They're going to share Ruthie's old apt. When Sylvia moved in w Angela back in Sept, the Thornton house became a war zone until Larry finally ordered Sylvia out—so Angie left w her. Sylvia's face shows the ravages of alcohol yet she still has wild & beautiful eyes. Angie's 42, but looks the same. ◊ I called Russ. He said, "Something's up. I just hope God's not teasing us"—so do I. √ js

. . . . . . . . .

Ltr #727, Thur 2-1-90, 1:23 p.m. (2162 days). Dear Becki. We now have a complete band. Sylvia's voice is so enchanting = rich & dark & earthy, & wet w yearning, calling to kindred hearts. Her every song is an orgasm of soul. Sometimes Joe plays his acoustic, & he & Sylvia sing together. Angie's hot on the keyboard. I feel good on the drums as long as I don't try to get too fancy. Jodi & Tony & Billy are sound experts. They do all our hookups & volume levels. We practice as much as we can, especially on Mon & Tue nites when most everyone is off work. Joe's vision for a group has surely come to pass, but we still have no following, except Russ. Joe refers to Russ as our "road manager" as if we have a tour coming up. We have no name. We considered different names, but Russ said, "Fuck this! We don't want a buzzword name like naming a new deodorant. When it's time, we'll know our name." √ js

- - - - - - - -

<u>Ltr #729, Thur 2-8-90, 8:41 p.m. (2169 days).</u> Just talked w Erin in Cincinnati = she's pregnant. She was timid about telling, but I said it didn't matter about vows & paperwork, not to me. I asked how Sharon reacted. She said, "Well, Dad, it wasn't as bad as I thought. Mom's happy for us & she's coming to help when the baby arrives— but Nana says we must get married for the baby's sake." Erin then kidded me about being a grandfather = no joke when I'm in love w a 26-year-old woman = you, Rebecca (Reinhardt) Scowcroft. √ js

- - - - - - - -

<u>Ltr #730, Fri 2-9-90, 11:50 p.m. (2170 days).</u> Busy, busy. Oh, Becki, this house is a beehive. Jodi, Syl, Angie—they do the laundry. Billy takes out the trash for Tue pickup & sweeps the barn. Tony & Joe shovel snow, help me w repairs & outside chores. Haley gets & distributes the mail each morning, & she vacuums the hall, sweeps the stairs. Sometimes we eat family-style in Jodi's apartment, but usually we cook for ourselves. I still pay 40% of expenses = I can, thanks to my oil checks. Everyone else pays 7.5% = $75/mo. = quite a deal. But we all pitch in for extras—i.e. refreshments in the barn, or the folding chairs, or the old upright piano we got for Angie. Russ also helps—but no offerings. I'll never pass a basket again! ◊ Syl & Angie are home a lot = good for the band. Syl works Fri-Sat-Sun at CVS. Angie works 3 mornings a week in the classified dept at the Banner. Besides, she has $$ in the bank. √ js

- - - - - - - -

<u>Ltr #736, Sun 2-25-90, 9:32 p.m. (2186 days).</u> Dear Becki. We're developing songs = "Heart Cry" & "Rebel Soul" = 2 of Joe's songs from St Louis (hard-charging rock), & Joe worked out chords for 5 more of my poems = "Our Rising Sun" (acoustic), "Land Beyond the Sea" (blues chords), "I Wait Alone" (sad blues), "Empty Tomb?" (slow rock), & "Weep O Angels" (Pink Floyd rock = chords like "Hey You"). & we have new cover tunes: "Talk to Me" (Stevie Nicks), "Nikita" (Elton John), & "Rocky Mtn Way" (Joe Walsh). ◊ Russ & Sylvia are together a lot. He says Bev is pissed & jealous, & she feels our barn ministry is too radical. She doesn't damn it to hell like Sharon, but she's only been over a few times. I think Bev likes our songs but she despises Sylvia. I doubt many can deal w this house = heart, heart, soul freedom = revolutionary = beautiful—but scary too. √ js

- - - - - - - -

<u>Ltr #737, Tue 2-27-90, 9:41 a.m. (2188 days).</u> Cloudy, mild. The snow is gone. The meadow is gray & dank. We had new people at our jam session last nite = Harry & Judy & Herschel Hightower. Afterward we pitched in for pizza. Billy got a special deal fm his boss, Nicky Poulos.

Things have certainly changed—except for you, Rebecca. You're still gone. That sad fact ripped my heart as I crawled into my lonely bed at 1:00 a.m. Oh, Becki, you've done it. You've pushed me so far back into your memory that I'm hidden among great aunts, school teachers, pet birds, & goldfish. Perhaps you never loved me at all as you declared in '84. But not so w me. You're still the center of my universe. How can my heart be so out of touch w reality? How can something so big in me be nothing in you? √ js

- - - - - - - -

**Ltr #739, Thur 3-1-90, 9:53 p.m. (2190 days).** Becki, we jammed 2 hours this aftn. Joe talked to us afterward: "Making music is like making love. It bursts up from within. The instruments are just a way of making our invisible music visible. It's already there, playing inside us. It's our passion, our yearning—our inner fire. It's not the instrument that plays the music but the music that plays the instrument ... yet love & yearning must flow back to us or we quickly go to empty— we don't have ego energy to sustain. But if they give their souls, we take off. There's no performance, no audience. We all soar together. This is why we're different." √ js

- - - - - - - -

**Ltr #740, Sun 3-4-90, 11:16 a.m. (2193 days).** Hugging, kissing, humping. Guess I'm not impotent after all! It's cold outside but it's been hot in my apartment—all nite. Angela came up at 10 p.m. I made coffee & talked about you, Rebecca, & my 6 yrs of hell. Angie said, "After seeing you go down for Becki, Jim, I understand better. Now I see that you love her beyond what any of us realized." I also told her about my sex failures w other women. That loosened her up & we began to flirt. I got hard in my pants. Angie saw it & teased, "You look pretty healthy to me, Jim." We blushed-laughed & the next thing I knew she was standing w a smirk on her face & her clothes on the floor. Her bush is copper-blond like buttered toast. After years of curiosity, I finally saw it. She led me to the bed. Afterward, we lay breathless as my prick wilted inside the rubber she just happened to have in her purse. "Oh, Jim, I can't believe this finally happened," she sighed. "I've wanted you since the first week I worked for you ten years ago." She then went on to confess about her sexual frustration with Larry, & how it led her into an affair with Herschel Hightower, "After I moved to Valley Baptist, Jim, Thelma & I became friends & I got to know Herschel. One thing led to another until one night we made passionate love—while Thelma was at prayer meeting. But I felt so guilty after that I shunned him 'til last fall, but now we meet at the Holiday Inn in Worcester each week." Angie laughed. "I'd probably be there now but he & Thelma are in New Jersey for 2 weeks. Who'd believe it, me screwing two men outside of wedlock—guess I'm a liberated woman, huh, Jim?" She laughed again. I grinned at Angie but expressed no shock. After knowing Sharon & you, Becki, nothing shocks me when it comes to women & sex. After 70 months of

**672**

celibacy, Angie was a wet-dream-come-true but I wish it had been you, Becki Lea. √ js

- - - - - - - -

Ltr #741, Mon 3-5-90, 8:16 a.m. (2194 days). 24°, 4" of snow. The meadow is white again. I ate w Russ at Bergson's last nite. I told him about Angela. He smiled & said, "I know. I was w Sylvia 'til 4 a.m. Maybe we're oversexed sinners, Jim, but I know I'll never be monogamous or follow a celibate Jesus. I'm not talking about the "swinger" scene or one-night stands. I'm talking about real love w more than one woman. I love Sylvia, I love Bev. I love a few special women, not strangers at a bar, but women I know & cherish. I can't choose one & reject all the others. Any preacher, most people for that matter, would call it sin, but I think the passion breaking out among us is more genuine than in most marriages. Vows can never generate love or Eros. Fire can't burn in a closed stove." √ js

- - - - - - - -

Ltr #742, Wed 3-7-90, 10:47 a.m. (2196 days). Becki, I wrote a poem/ song about a life w/o love. It could be about you. It could be about any of us. Joe set it to a blues beat:

### MONDAY

monday cuts my face like ice on fire
burning red pain but no heat
and no bus
feet are gone
boots full of novocaine
anchor my weary heart against the wind
colors and shapes rush by on black whirls
well-dressed slaves racing for the starting line
but no bus
just blank nameless eyes
staring at america through clouds of winter breath
why the rush little girl twenty-six years
hearts are still distant like the stars
like the bus
no time to make my bed
who could ever know
all is blurry now
must be the wind in my eyes

- - - - - - - -

Ltr #743, Sun 3-11-90, 11:46 p.m. (2200 days). Dear Becki, good news—I think? Our family continues to grow. Cathy Rosinski (Johnson) arrived today w Chad (5). Jodi & I picked them up at the Amtrak station in Worcester. They're moving into the spare bedroom in Jodi's apartment = the room where Mrs. C. kept her old stuff. Cathy says that Kevin left her, & moved in with his girlfriend, a 17-yr-old clerk at the Agway store. But he does send $$ for Chad. She hopes to get back on at Bergson's. She's older (23) but she still has those sad lost-puppy eyes. She's heavier, almost plump—but still very sexy-looking. Little Chad is all Kevin = a warm & friendly kid who likes to tease. He has brown eyes & dark hair like his dad, & a hillbilly drawl. He says, "I reckon" & "ain't" & "this here." √ js

---------

Ltr #744, Thur 3-15-90,10:19 a.m. (2204 days). Angie slept w me again last nite (3rd time). She climaxes like Sharon = stiffens & emits a series of short gasping cries. I asked when Herschel's due back. She said Sunday night. I asked if she'll still come up after he's back in town. She didn't answer. She just smirked & turned the question around = what would happen if you came back, Becki? I said, "That's a fairy tale, but if she did, I doubt we'd be lying her like this, unless you & Becki do me at the same time." Angie laughed & said, "I'm not ready for that." Oh, Becki, why do I joke about you wanting me? It's fucking insane. √ js

---------

Ltr #746, Tue 3-20-90, 9:33 a.m. (2209 days). Happy Birthday, Becki = #26. ◊ Everyone adores little Chad. He's so cute & curious & wants to be involved w everything from playing the guitar, to turning the mixer knobs, to taking out the trash, to squirting Haley's hair spray, to typing into my computer. When he saw your picture on my monitor, he asked, in a most innocent voice, "Is she your friend?" That's my question, Becki Lea, for 2209 days. √ js

---------

Ltr #751, Tue 3-27-90, 11:13 a.m. (2216 days). Pussy, pussy. No longer celibate. The fuck stories about me are finally true. Last nite after our session in the barn, Jodi & Cathy came up w 3 beers & a bag of pretzels. We talked 'til 1 a.m. I went to bed. The house grew quiet—then a soft knock. Cathy was back, in a sheer nightgown. She crawled into bed & we cuddled like 2 stacked chairs w her hefty butt against my rising dick. I fantasize about Cathy. I couldn't believe she was w me. I caressed her arms, her shoulders, her hips, her legs. She took my hand inside her gown. Her tits are like yours, Becki = cuddly bunnies on her chest. She turned over & slid under me. She said nothing except, "Don't worry, I'm on the pill." I finished but she didn't. She said, "I never come. I've only had one orgasm in my life, last month by myself on our couch. O Jesus, it was nice. I never knew what I was missing. Jus' thinkin about it made me want to sneak in here w you, but I don't think I can come with a man. I'm too self-conscious." She then talked about her lousy marriage, her in-laws, her Aunt Verna, & the time we talked in the Mustang & how she loves

Chad so much. Finally she fell asleep in my arms like an overfed kitten. Cozy & soft & so nice, but it made me miss you even more, Becki. She's so like you—w/o being YOU. √ js

- - - - - - - -

Ltr #752, Thur 3-29-90, 8:13 p.m. (2218 days). Joe & I wrote a new song = "Lay Low My Sweet Child." It talks about the child within us aching for love, & how we hide this child. Joe worked up chords for it = similar to the U2 song, "Running to Stand Still." ◊ Joe is glad about the band, but his heart is heavy: "Things are moving, Jim. If only Brenda was w us, I'd be on fire, but as it is I'm running on 2 cylinders." Tell me about it. Without you, Becki, I'm running on fumes—like for six years. √ js

- - - - - - - -

Ltr #753, Tue 4-3-90, 11:58 p.m. (2223 days). Dear Becki. We had 16 people in the barn tonight = us & Russ, + Harry & Judy & Herschel (he's back), & he brought T. Willy & "Slick Dick" Washington. We did 10 songs. We're so different from BFBC = no outreach, no prayer, no promises, no fearful exhortations, no offerings, no membership, no paid staff, minimal organization, no statement of faith, no Sun School (Chad gets into the music more than us). ◊ I guess Joe & Tony are serious about making a video. They got a camcorder at Sears this aftn, then went w Angie & got a 2nd video camera from her house on Hickory Lane. "Larry will never miss it," she said. √ js

- - - - - - - -

Ltr #754, Wed 4-4-90, 11:13 a.m. (2224 days). Tony & Joe mounted the TV cameras in Tony's apt so they can get us eating together. They plan to move the camcorders around the house & barn to get lots of Candid Camera style footage. We all agreed to be on the video as long as it's not X-rated. Joe kidded, "Well, you better stay under the sheets." We all laughed. √ js

- - - - - - - -

Ltr #755, Thur 4-5-90, 11:56 p.m. (2225 days). Becki, we're doing 3 songs for the video. The 1st = "Lay Low My Sweet Child," & the 2nd = my villanelle, "Salvation," that Joe put to music last fall, but for the video we redid it w the full band to a blues rhythm. The 3rd is an anti-church sonnet that I wrote. Joe & Sylvia sing it together w his acoustic guitar. The music is similar to Simon & Garfunkel's "Bleecker Street." Here are the words:

675

## GOD IS TALKING NOW

While Mary Anne colors her barnyard story,
the pastor preaches down from his big black book.
"Straight is the gate that leads us to glory!"
He pounds, he paces, but Mary does not look
up from her crayons, for such dreadful gloom
cannot yet darken her colorbook days.
"Wide is the road that leads to Lucifer's room
and you secretly crave to walk in his ways!
Repent of passion pleasure and carnal lust!
Cast your foul flesh under the cleansing blood!"
Some fall to their knees, others just feel crushed,
but Mary chooses pink above the damning flood.
"Mommy, Mommy, look at my pretty pink cow!"
"Be still, Mary Anne. God is talking now."

- - - - - - - -

Ltr #756, Sat 4-7-90, 9:22 a.m. (2227 days). Action, action, naked female flesh. I can't believe how things have changed. Cathy came up again last nite. She was Charmin soft, cozy as a teddy bear. Her hair smelled like flowers. I aroused her slowly. I asked her to describe how it felt when she masturbated on the couch last month. At first she was shy, but after a bit she became very prurient until she couldn't talk w/o panting. I stroked her clit. She rolled her hips slowly until she got close then she went berserk, thrusting wildly as if hornets were stinging her pubis—until she shuddered w ecstasy. She didn't scream but grimaced & bit her lip—'til it bled. If Sharon & Logan & Campbell could see me now—or even you, Becki—they'd declare me to be reprobate = never saved. But I've long since given up trying to preserve my reputation before God or man. To me it's good & right to love & to be loved, & to fuck & be fucked. √ js

- - - - - - - -

Ltr #758, Thur 4-12-90, 11:14 p.m. (2232 days). Dear Becki, Russ & I, and Billy, we expanded the parking nook this afternoon & spread two truckloads of crushed stone on it. We have so many cars around here, especially for our barn sessions, that there's no place left to park. ◊ While we were working on the parking area, Joe & Tony went to a guy in Stow to edit the video. They made 20 copies. We simply call it "59 Front St" = 11 min. of music & video scenes. ◊ Angie came up tonite but only to talk. She knows about Cathy, & Herschel's back. She laughed & said, "One lover at a time is enough." I don't know about that? √ js

- - - - - - - -

Ltr #759, Sun 4-15-90, 4:22 p.m. (2235 days). We ate together this aftn & watched our video = many scenes = Joe comes home in his old

Buick. He looks like a cop in his 1st Sec. uniform. Chad helps Billy sweep the barn. We pig out on spaghetti in Jodi's apt. Haley scowls as she vacuums the hall. Joe complains about the noise. Haley gives him the finger. Angie's sick in bed. Sylvia brings soup to her. I shave in my undies. My paunch is evident. Billy spills a bag of trash on the stairs & yells, "FUCK!" (you can read his lips). Tony & Jodi frolic in the nude = no close-ups. Joe writes "BRENDA" on a poster board. Haley serves Billy fried eggs. He pushes them away. A fight ensues but ends w tears & a tender hug. Cathy cuddles in bed w Chad. Sylvia kisses Russ under the oak out front. You can't tell it's Russ. Haley sits on her bed in her waitress dress & puts on her sneakers & shows a lot of leg. Tony pulls an empty six-pack fm the fridge & snaps at Jodi. Jodi wheels, snarls, & throws a wet rag at Tony—then exits. Cathy & Jodi fold laundry in the basement. Tony plays catch w Chad by the barn. Jodi & Haley leave for Bancrofts' wearing their waitress outfits & I-don't-want-to-go-to-work frowns. Haley finds a little white moth in the hall, cups it in her hands, lets it go on the front porch. Angie takes a shower = brief shots of hips & lathered tits. Cathy in bed w me = just sleeping, w her tawny-brown locks tumbling over her face. All of us on the big rock = we cut up/make faces, then run like kids to the meadow. Haley & Billy stroll hand & hand on the path. Russ naps on Jodi's sofa under his Red Sox hat. Jodi & Angie make a tossed salad in Jodi's kitchen. We all gather in the barn and sing along to the last song = "God Is Talking Now." √ js

- - - - - - - -

A gust of wind swirls up from the river. A shiver runs up Jim's spine. *I feel a chill,* he says to himself, *but it's not that cold. Must be my age. I'm going on 45. I'm a grandfather. It's crazy—Becki would never. It's nuts to read this and it's getting late but I may as well finish, but why? I know the ending. It's always the same.*

Ltr #760, Tue 4-17-90, 10:20 a.m. (2237 days). We had 20 in the barn last nite. Cal McClusky showed up as did a carload fm BFBC/LBI = Doris, Melissa, Janet B, & Tricia Logan. They also brought David Myszak & Nina Ramirez. We did 5 songs & showed our video 3 times. We gave free copies to anyone who wanted one. Afterward we had refreshments & lounged around. We rapped for an hour then a mood of carefree abandon came over us like being drunk w/o alcohol. Joe put on a Buddy Holly tape & we danced '50s-style & laughed & hugged like at a junior high slumber party. There was such love among us & it was very soulish and sensual = touching, hugging, ruddy faces, perspiry glow, pretty hair, nubile curves, & legs & breasts & hips—but we didn't take off our clothes. √ js

- - - - - - - -

Ltr #761, Sat 4-21-90, 4:08 p.m. (2241 days). Rainy, gloomy. Got a call fm Mary Beth. She says Dr. Logan & Rich Beckman are furious about the LBI'ers coming to 59 Front Street, especially about Tricia L. = Logan's daughter-in-law. (I'm sure Stan is just as furious about Doris.) M.B. wanted to come herself but she feels she'll be more valuable to us in Logan's office. She says Stan Campbell gave Logan a copy of our video (I bet he took it fm Doris) & Logan showed it to Beckman & Garrett & his closest staff, & attacked it as "soft porn that tempts the flesh thru visual suggestion & devilish music." He told Garrett to lock it away, & said he doesn't want 59 FRONT STREET mentioned on campus or in any branch ministry. But M.B. loves the video. She says the '60s-style music & lyrics & the creative real-life scenes stir love & hope in her heart more than any sermon. ◊ Later I had lunch at McD's w Russ, Joe, Tony, Jodi, & Angie. I told them about Logan's reaction to our video. Russ said, "Well, I guess we know our name now & it's simple to remember because it's our mailing address—but Logan's fucking paranoid. Why would a pastor w 10,000 devoted disciples be disturbed by 15 people in a barn? It's amazing how a few naked hearts can make big-time liars nervous." √ js

- - - - - - - -

Ltr #762, Mon 4-23-90, 10:22 a.m. (2243 days). Got a letter fm Janet Buford. Barry screamed at her for coming to Brendon Falls = "Jim's house is no 'house of God' but a 'den of iniquity'! Anyone who goes there will be seduced by demons of lust." Barry smashed her copy of the 59 FRONT STREET video & gave the ruined cassette to Rich Beckman. But Janet got another from Tricia Logan & she's showing it (secretly) on campus. People either love it or hate it. √ js

- - - - - - - -

Ltr #763, Fri 4-27-90, 5:14 p.m. (2247 days). Windy, warm. Feels like spring, Becki, & things are moving. Mary Beth called again & said her friend Marcia (the same Marcia Logan hooked over the radio in '83) is involved with a group of disenchanted LBI'ers in Lawrence, & they saw our video & loved it. M.B. says they want us to come & do a concert in Lawrence. I told Joe. We called a house meeting, then Russ called Mary Beth. It's on for Tue, May 8th. √ js

- - - - - - - -

Ltr #764, Sat 4-28-90, 9:29 a.m. (2248 days). Dear Becki. Cathy came in again last night. She's such a sexual creature now = normal if you ask me. During our pillow talk she shared some curious news = she likes our barn gatherings because she gets to see other people whereas back in West Va. she never saw anyone. She said, "I talk w Cal a lot & he took me & Chad to McDonald's. He's sober now. He went for treatment." ◊ Russ bought a pickup yesterday—a red '84 Ford w a cap on the back—to haul our equipment. √ js

- - - - - - - -

<u>Ltr #766, Sun 5-6-90, 9:03 p.m. (2256 days).</u> At dinner this aftn, Russ briefed us on our trip to Lawrence: "They said they'd pay us. I said no. They said they'd take an offering. I said no. They said they'd feed us afterward. I said great." We all laughed, especially Tony. He sounds like a tuba. Then Russ said, "We'll share the road expenses but it's only an hour drive. We'll take my truck, the van, & Jim's car, & remember, we're not going to persuade them that we're good & Logan's bad. We're going to share ourselves, our feelings, & we hope they'll get out of their heads & into our hearts. It's love that binds us, not opposition to LBI." ◊ Later I took a long lonely walk. I don't go to the meadow as much & I miss it. The wind was fresh & cool. The sun set bright & blinding w/o the usual red haze. Oh, Becki, why can't I forget you, w all that's happening? Cathy cuddles me twice a week & people are hungry for our heartbeat. But, Rebecca, you're the inspiration for all I say or do. How can our "house of hearts" be real— if my heart is out of touch, if "you & I" are not real? √ js

- - - - - - - -

<u>Ltr #767, Wed 5-9-90, 11:02 a.m. (2259 days).</u> Dear Becki. 10 people came out last nite in Lawrence, plus 11 of us. We met in an old VFW hall. We did "Empty Tomb"—"Weep O Angels"—"God Is Talking Now"—"Our Rising Sun"—"I Wait Alone" —"Salvation," & "Monday," & cover tunes. Sylvia's voice drew us all into the music. Her voice is so rich & filled w breath. She sings like Chrissie Hinds. Later, as we ate, I shared between bites:

> It seems to me that human beings, & especially Christians, are ashamed to be human. We're ashamed of our fears, our frailties, our passions, our needs, our happiness, our hurts. We're ashamed of our dreams. ◊ We long for true love, love that's fresh & alive & childlike—yet we hide the child within & prop up our lives to convince others & ourselves that we're winners w God. We must maintain a successful Christian identity if it kills us. We must look strong, wholesome, healthy, pretty, & poised. No wonder we're cutoff & stressed-out. We prop up our marriages, our moods, our reputations, & especially our faith. We must not confess doubts. Instead, we bow to preachers who soothe our fears & doubts w dogmatic certainty. If we challenge their authority we forfeit our stature in the church. If we persist, they threaten us with divine judgment & blacklist us. So we dare not question the pulpit. But how can we love & be close if we simply spout doctrine like a recording? Must I deny my heart to follow God? I hope not. ◊ I can't soothe your fears & I don't want your allegiance. I just want to <u>know</u> you as best I can. Forget the labels, we're all human, & whether we like it or not, we're desperately dependent on a God we're not sure of. I hope God <u>is</u> LOVE & that He'll be w us at death, but I have <u>no</u> guarantees. All I know for sure is what I feel inside, & most of the time I feel sad

because the person I love most is not w me. ◊ What about the Bible? Well, it's a fascinating anthology of ancient writing but I no longer fear it or submit to it blindly. I trust my heart above the Bible. ◊ I can't promise you victory, but I have a dream. I dream of a society w/o walls or ulterior motive where intimacy is the highest good, where LOVE casts out fear & hearts soar on the wind w/o shame—not an elitist heaven just for Christians, but a transcendent realm for all of us. ◊ Is such a dream possible? It's a fairy tale, yet at unexpected moments, I get a fleeting glimpse—at the ocean, under the stars, in a song, in a face, in a movie, in a memory, in a touch. Is this what Jesus meant by the 'kingdom of God'? I don't know, but I yearn for an outbreak of LOVE—LOVE in all its wildness & tenderness, that'll take us beyond fear & self-hatred, beyond lies & props, beyond money & profit, beyond bigotry, greed, competition, & control. I have no plan or prayer to make it happen—it's too big. LOVE must bring down the walls. √ js

- - - - - - - -

Ltr #768, Sat 5-12-90, 11:07 a.m. (2262 days). Cathy came in late last nite. Afterward—as usual—I talked about you, Becki. Cathy flew into a rage, "BECKI! BECKI! THAT'S ALL YOU TALK ABOUT! You fuck me then you talk about her. I thought I could handle it but I can't. You're selfish, Jim. You want me & Angie & others to sleep w you, but your true love is Becki." She grabbed her nightgown & stormed out naked, whipping her fat ass w indignation. She came back this morning & apologized, but said, "I can't do it w you, Jim, knowing you want Becki, but we can still be friends." ◊ 6 yrs, Rebecca, & you're still a fucking albatross around my neck! I can't have you, & because of you, I can't have anyone else. √ js

- - - - - - - -

Ltr #769, Sun 5-13-90, 7:41 a.m. (2263 days). Big news, Becki. Brenda broke up w her boyfriend & flew in from Chicago yesterday. Angie took Jodi to pick her up at Logan Airport. As of now, she's camped out in Jodi's living room but Jodi says she's going to stay w her grandmother across town. Brenda's hair is longer, & her womanhood is in full bloom = nice ripe bosom & breeder hips, but her eyes still twinkle like a teenager. Joe's excited but scared. He came over to talk late last night. He says the butterflies in his gut feel like "humming birds." He said he helped Brenda w her luggage & she acted bashful around him, & didn't say much. √ js

- - - - - - - -

Ltr #775, Sat 6-9-90, 6:47 a.m. (2290 days). I got up early to collect my thoughts. Gray wisps of fog drift over the meadow like ghosts who've lost their way. I'm now celibate again. Angie & Cathy are still special but they no longer share my bed. Angie's w Herschel &

Cathy's hooked up with Cal. I'm glad for Cath & Cal after all the shit they've seen, but I feel more deprived than ever. Angie & Cathy reminded me of how heavenly sex can be when two people have more than bodies to share. It makes me miss you, Becki, all the more. ◊ I have little time to write in this journal. LBI splinter groups are forming all over. In 4 weeks, we've played in Fitchburg, N. Adams, Gardner, Springfield, & Merrimack, NH, in YMCAs, Grange halls, VFWs, even in a Unitarian church. The rebel groups are small but hungry for freedom. Three of our concerts turned into dance parties = wild, especially since Logan says dancing is "of the devil." ◊ Our talent is average, but our chemistry is extraordinary. We're like one person. Joe's guitar is our voice, & Sylvia's voice is our soul, & they cry out together. Angie plays the keyboard as if she has an orchestra at her fingertips. Haley & I are wedded in rhythm as if we're fucking (not a bad thought—she turns me on more, now that I'm celibate again). & Billy plays too, we take turns. (He knows Haley's tempo best of all.) ◊ But the biggest news = Brenda & Joe = she moved in w him Thur nite. They're together all the time. Joe's teaching her a dance routine & the tambourine. A lot has happened since she got back a month ago. ◊ Joe was over last nite. He's out of his mind with happiness. He says, "Brenda takes me higher than any drug. I'll never need pot again. Our dream is coming true, Jim, except for Becki. Our victory can't be complete while your ache goes on"—what more can I say, Rebecca? Joe said it all = our band, our ministry, our cocoon of love, it's like a beautiful archway—but w no capstone. √ js

--------

Ltr #776, Sun 6-10-90, 11:37 p.m. (2291 days). Dear Becki, I went to Cobleskill today for Erin & Ronnie's wedding = a very private ceremony in Nana's living room. Erin looks like she swallowed a watermelon. Everyone's relieved that the baby will be born in wedlock—what the fuck does it matter! But don't ask me, I'm from another planet! ◊ The kids seemed supportive of my new music ministry, even Ronnie who's a free-thinker = unusual for a Houghton grad. But Sharon, of course, had a different view. She said little to me until I was going out the door: "Jim, you're living a fantasy. Who do you think you're kidding? I know all about Angela & Sylvia & Cathy. You're trying to go back to the '60s, to free love & radical lifestyles w a cult of musicians & poets & pleasure seekers, & Bev says you let them live there for nothing—& it's all tied to Becki. Well, the '60s gave us nothing but drugs & AIDS. The devil ruled that decade. God never intended for us to mate like dogs, & God won't let this go on. If you don't straighten out, Jim, He's going to deal w you! and"—too much. I cut in and shouted, "KNOCK IT OFF SHARON! WE'RE NOT MARRIED ANYMORE! In case you haven't noticed!" I then threw the Tempo into gear & roared out of the driveway. Whatever happened to the Sharon who got off in the car on Route 2, & said, "Oh, James David, tell me a naughty story.... I love young guys who are sweaty & strong & well-hung. I want them to fuck me & fuck me. Fucking, screwing, there's nothing like it! I live for this feeling. O God, I love it when it's sinful & I fight but fail." √ js

--------

<u>Ltr #777, Mon 6-11-90, 11:55 p.m. (2292 days).</u> We had 30 people in the barn tonite. Janet B. & Tricia L. brought 2 carloads of LBI students, & Amy B. (Logan). I was surprised to see Amy, but not shocked. Doris & Melissa were also back. During our last song, "Rocky Mtn Way," everyone yelled & danced & gyrated their hips, like in the movie Dirty Dancing. √ js

--------

<u>Ltr #778, Tue 6-12-90, 11:04 a.m. (2293 days).</u> Oh, Becki, I can't get over last nite. Think of it—Logan's wife & daughter-in-law, & Campbell's wife too, all dancing & going crazy. And what Jodi shared afterward was also amazing. After the music stopped, we settled on sofas, chairs, on the floor, & Jodi preached. This is what she said, as I recall:

> I like what Jesus says about the wind—If you're born of the Spirit, you're like the wind that blows thru the trees, & nobody knows where you came from or where you're going. But in churches people have to know where you came from & where you're going, & whether you're 'naughty or nice.' It's such a contradiction. The Church is petrified of the wind & preaches security & structure & good behavior, & control & predictability. Everybody wants to be proper & safe. But it just makes us lonely & miserable, because what we really want is LOVE—& LOVE is not orderly or secure or safe, or predictable. It's risky & stormy & out of control, & it blows our nice Christian life away! I was a good mother & wife. I cooked & cleaned & taught in a Christian school. I went to church. I put up w my husband's drinking. I pinched pennies to make ends meet—but in my heart I longed for LOVE, for passion, I longed to break loose & really <u>live</u>. The gap between what I felt inside & what I saw around me grew & grew until I felt I would split in two. Then I met Tony & he scared the shit out of me. He makes me wail w joy & weep like death. I have no control w him. I lose my breath. My heart races like I'm diving off a cliff. I shake w fear, but then we get drunk on joy. Our life is never predictable. We touch heaven but it slips thru our hands like mercury. We argue, we fight, we touch heaven again, but we can't keep it. We have no vows to prop us up. We just have LOVE & I'm risking all to follow it. That's why I like what Jesus says about the wind. That's the only God I'll ever follow. I give myself to LOVE, to the WIND blowing in my heart. People say I'm on a road to disaster. I don't care. I don't want to play it safe! I want to ride the WIND! I WANT TO <u>LIVE</u>! √ js

--------

<u>Ltr #779, Thur 6-14-90, 6:57 p.m. (2295 days).</u> Hazy, hot. I took a

walk, Becki. The meadow was alive w buttercups & butterflies. As I returned, I saw two men by the barn, one in a dark suit, the other in a cool madras pullover. I soon recognized Rich Beckman's reptilian face & Matt Garrett's charming smile. I have no office, so we talked in the barn. Garrett relaxed on a sofa. Beckman pulled up a folding chair. I sat on the stage in front of my bass drum.

Beckman made the pitch: "Pastor has never stopped caring for you, Jim. He prays for you often, but your new ministry is causing unrest in our branch churches. As always, we've been patient with you, but you've violated a sacred tradition by proselytizing among our people. But we come not as enemies, but as friends in the hope we can bury our differences. We see a place for your music in the LBI vision. At the same time we can help you reach your full potential. We'll promote 59 FRONT STREET as a front-line Christian band. We'll make you bigger than Petra or White Heart. We'll give you 40% of all offerings & admissions, & we'll put you on TV & help you connect with a record company, & all we ask, Jim, is that you concentrate on the music, & cut down on the preaching & partying, & that you openly declare your band to be affiliated with LBI—that despite your differences, you believe in Dr. Logan's vision."

"Come on, Dick," I replied with rancor in my voice, "I can't work for you guys. I despise your whole operation. It's a lie. You exploit people in the name of God. It took me ten years to get out of your program, & I don't want back in. So you may as well stop trying to buy me off. You don't have what I want. You never did! What I want is not for sale!"

No more nice guy. Beckman's ugly pockmarked face heated with rage. "OK, Jim, I tried to be nice. But if you want to play fucking hardball, we'll tell it all—how you associate with gays & whores & druggies, & how you have a different girl in your bed every night, & how your house is filthy with fornication & pornography.... & know this, Jim, we'll fight you until your devilish heresy is stamped out! Believe me, God's going to deal with you!"

"Now, now, Dick, don't get angry," I mocked. "That's the difference between you & us. We're not fighting at all. I got here by GIVING UP. We have no reputation or empire to protect."

Beckman stood, reached into his coat—as if for a gun—pulled out a videocassette, shoved it into my hand, & snarled, "Watch this & feel good!" He then stormed out. Garrett left as well, but with a smile. √ js

- - - - - - - -

<u>Ltr #780, Fri 6-15-90, 10:57 a.m. (2296 days).</u> Oh, Becki, why is Logan so worked up? He sends Beckman & Garrett to try to make a deal w me. He should know me better by now. Besides, we're no threat to anything but his pride. We've never had more than 30 in the barn & all the LBI dissidents combined don't total more than 150 out of 10,000, & they would've left anyway. ◊ But what bothers me is the cassette Beckman gave me. It's your wedding video, Becki. I started to watch it earlier, but it was too painful. √ js

--------

**Ltr #781, Sun 6-17-90, 12:17 p.m. (2298 days).** Dear Becki, we watched Logan's service on TV this morn (Joe, Brenda, Jodi, & I). His ranting attack still echoes in my head:

> I rarely name names from the pulpit, but when the danger is great, the shepherd must warn the flock. I've loved Jim Shanley since he came here to Bible school back in the mid '70s, & I still care for him deeply. We all regret his departure from the faith 6 years ago, & we've all prayed for his return & waited with open arms. But he has refused all our overtures, even as recently as this week. As most of you know, he has a new ministry in Brendon Falls. This ministry, I regret to say, is very dangerous. Some of our people, especially in our branch churches, have been enticed by Shanley's smooth words & soulish music. I must warn you that 59 FRONT STREET is a cult of Lucifer, a worldly rock band, & a hippie commune where fornication is practiced openly. They deny the scriptures in favor of feelings as they pursue a licentious lifestyle. They mock God with wild parties & dirty dancing. The devil is using Shanley's band to lead believers away from the body of Christ. I WARN YOU TO FLEE FROM THIS TERRIBLE HERESY! "In the last days perilous times shall come," Paul tells us in 2 Timothy 3:15. "For men shall be lovers of their own selves ... traitors, heady, high-minded, lovers of pleasures more than lovers of God ... from such turn away." YOU MUST TURN AWAY FROM THIS SATANIC CULT! YOU MUST FLEE THIS WICKED MOVEMENT! If you attend even one of his concerts, your faith will be corrupted, & if you attend regularly, God will punish you severely. There is no greater sin than to join in a rebellion against the kingdom of God. Be not deceived. God will surely bring down 59 FRONT STREET! Thus saith the Lord! √ js

--------

**Ltr #782, Mon 6-18-90, 11:41 a.m. (2299 days).** Dear Becki. Tom Hudson & Stan also blasted us on Sun morning. Doris says she never saw Stan so angry. I'm sure all of LBI is crucifying us. Russ says Valley Baptist is attacking as well—as will any born-again church that knows about our movement. √ js

--------

**Ltr #784, Tue 6-26-90, 9:38 a.m. (2307 days).** Dear Becki, Logan's attack has backfired so far. He's given us front-page exposure throughout LBI, since every LBI branch watches Logan's Sunday service from Moody, either live or by tape. The barn was packed last nite. We have road concerts lined up through the summer, & the 1st week of Oct, we have a 3-day trip to Maine. In addition we've given out over 50 copies of our video. Cocoons of disenchanted LBI'ers are forming throughout Logan's empire, especially in New England. But there is no central authority to our movement. I have no desire to turn this into a new religion. I abhor the thought. ◊ God seems to be moving for everyone—but me. I won't say that God is moving until I see you, Becki, coming toward me. √ js

- - - - - - - -

Ltr #785, Wed 6-27-90, 10:24 p.m. (2308 days). Tonite I got a strange call from Matt Garrett. He says he's sorry Rich Beckman reacted so angrily when they came down 2 weeks ago, & that he'd like to talk with me alone & explore our common ground. I told him we had no common ground, to which he replied, "You'd be surprised, Jim. I think you & I see things the same—more than you imagine." Despite his provocative words, I still declined—yet it's a mystery. Why would he call & be so friendly after Logan & all of LBI have been blasting me for 10 days? But Garrett has always been an enigma to me. I can never tell if he's acting on orders from Logan, or on his own. ◊ I called Russ & told him about the call. Russ replied, "Garrett's a sly rascal. He's thinking about his own power. He wants to cover all the bases, even the possibility that our movement will grow so large that Logan's star will fall—a fucking long shot—but Garrett doesn't want to burn his bridges to us, just in case it does. He's shrewd, but he doesn't get it—what we're really about." √ js

- - - - - - - -

Ltr #787, Sun 7-8-90, 2:41 p.m. (2319 days). Agony, anguish. Oh, Becki, I'm sick w hurt. Raw cramps grip my gut. I finally watched your wedding video from 1988 = you, so pretty & fair like a magnolia blossom in your white dress, & Randy, so handsome & wholesome & pious. & Logan & everyone was there applauding you & kissing you. Oh, I should've never watched, but I had to = masochistic curiosity. Your vows to Randy will forever echo in my mind as the final testimony to my defeat. Your voice was soft & quiet, but emphatic: "Randy, I thank God for you; I take you as my husband 'til death do us part. You have completed me as Christ completes the Church. From a child I prayed for a godly & kind husband, & God has answered my prayers. I promise to honor you & obey you as God leads us in our home & on the mission field. I trust Christ in you. I give my heart & soul & body to you." FUCK IT, BECKI! I give up! I'll never write in this book again. No matter if hearts connect in this house & people hear & embrace our music, I still lose w/o you, Becki = I'm alone = I hate what God has done to me = so close, but still, I lose. Because w/o you, I cannot know my heart is good. I cannot know I'm valid as a person. I cannot know that all the precious times we had were real. Having a band is better than suicide, but it's a cruel cross to bear. Go on; live your life with Randy. Do the right thing! I GIVE UP, REBECCA. LIFE SUCKS! √ js

- - - - - - - -

<u>Ltr #788, Wed 7-11-90, 9:57 p.m. (2322 days).</u> Oh, Becki, I love you so. I just got back from the meadow. The sweet fragrances of summer grass & blooming flowers lifted my spirits. A soft breeze caressed my face. Love overwhelmed me until I was faint. I can't close this journal on a sour note. I'll never write in this book again, but if you could hear me tonight, I would tell you this: "It doesn't matter that you're married. It doesn't matter that we haven't talked in 6 yrs. I know I've hurt you & you've hurt me, but that doesn't matter either. You're still my best friend, & I would do <u>anything</u> for you. The love I have for you is the greatest love I have ever known. I wish I could be in your life. I wish I could see your dimpled smile. I wish I could hold your hand & talk to you. But whatever happens, wherever you go, just know this, Rebecca: I can <u>never</u> forget you. I see you in the sunrise. I feel your spirit blowing in the wind. Your blue eyes fill the sky w color. You live in my heart. I love you forever. Good-bye, Becki Lea." √ js

- - - - - - - -

Jim closes the book, removes his glasses, and wipes the tears from his eyes. Haloed streetlamps now glimmer here and there on the hills across the river. *It's been three months since I wrote in this journal, but still nothing. She's gone forever whether I write in it or not?* He stands, stretches, then trudges up the hill behind the big rock, and through the woods back to the meadow. At the top of Hadley Hill, he pauses to gaze at the pink cirrus clouds beyond the Worcester Hills. He feels a pang of hope, but quickly quenches it with a sigh.

# Chapter Forty-two

**S**oap, water, silence. After turning off the shower, Jim pushes his wet hair back off his face and gazes for a moment at the shower curtain, now more gray than blue from age, mold, and mildew. Water drips off his naked body—then silence.

He sighs and steps out of the tub. Hot-water steam fogs the mirror, sweats the walls, beads up on the toilet tank. Sunday, October 7, 1990. Columbus Day Weekend. The band, the entire house, left this morning for three days of concerts in Maine— they'll be gone until Tuesday night—but at the last minute, Jim decided to stay home. Last night he watched Becki's wedding video again, and it put him into a slough of lethargy and melancholy.

Just up from a fitful afternoon nap, he now feels even worse. He feels all alone as if he's back in '87, '88—no band, no ministry, no cocoon of kindred spirits; it's just him and the house.

As he pulls on his undershorts, Becki-memories, fiery darts from the past, attack his mind. Sad eyes laughing, blue eyes yearning, tender eyes turning wild and loving him all the way. *Almost seven years, but I still see her eyes brimming with affection and happiness. I can't forget that Christmas Eve ... or that Friday in March. I can't forget her bashful blush, her teasing smirks, her soft white flesh, the calling of our hearts, but now she's gone forever to be with Randy. O God, it doesn't matter if people come to hear us. I don't believe in fairy tales. It doesn't matter if Logan curses me weekly. I've been cursed since I met the Love Goddess in '74.*

Jim rubs the fog off the mirror and examines his two-day beard. He gives a weary snort. *I look like shit, like wrinkled middle-aged shit. I got bags under my—fuck it; looks don't matter either, not for me. So I'm paunchy and getting wrinkled—so what? Who sees me naked? Who sees me up close? Vows, vows, fucking vows. Becki must honor her vows, and Sharon too, even Angie & Cathy— they just have different vows. I'm fucking cutoff forever.*

After halfheartedly combing his hair, Jim thinks of shaving but quickly dismisses the idea as a waste of energy. To his room. Levi's, plaid flannel shirt. He pulls on his clothes then plops down on the LA-Z-BOY recliner to put on his sneakers. Up again, he flips on the radio. He spreads, smoothes the brownboy on top of his piled-mattress bed. No music, just the 5:30 p.m. news headlines:

> ... while jogging at Camp David today, President Bush declared that the UN sanctions against Saddam Hussein are working, and he reaffirmed that the mission of the Desert Shield deployment is to defend Saudia

Arabia. He says the U.S. buildup is defensive in nature, and that's why the operation is called "Desert Shield," but if Iraq does not—

Jim kills the radio. *Shit, I don't wanna listen to this,* he declares to himself. *I don't give a damn about Saddam, or Kuwait ... or Bush. Military might, Middle East oil: it means nothing to me.* The old house is suddenly silent, as silent as his hopes. He goes to the window; he stares out at the grassy meadow. Trees, falling leaves, the lake, the river: they beckon to him; he grabs his windbreaker.

He hikes up the well-trod footpath into the meadow. His discontent gives way to resignation; his step becomes lighter, more leisurely. Above him, the hazy evening sky billows blue against an orange ball of sun, while twittering birds soar and glide on the south wind. The same breeze caresses Jim's face and softly nods the goldenrods. A few late-season butterflies flit among the tall yellow flowers. He inhales the smoky sweetness of October. The air is pleasantly cool but he feels warm after walking up the hill; he takes off his jacket. Wraparound color: red, auburn, gold, green. Autumn woods surround the grassy knoll like stadium walls. Falling leaves and pine needles flutter down: glitter on the breeze.

To the big rock. His long shadow strolls eastward ahead of him, lazily, leisurely—there's no rush. His jacket thrown over his shoulder, Jim slouches at the edge of the granite ledge and gazes reflectively at the dark river running below him. He sighs. He moves on. Down to the railroad right-of-way, west to the gravel beach, then back to the path that runs through the woods. He takes in all the familiar scenes—familiar, yet so alive with change, change that somehow invigorates, inspires, and renews his soul. He's taken the same walk a thousand times, but he never tires of it. The mystery of wildness is his only solace.

Back to the meadow. Jim tarries to watch the sunset. Time ticks by; seconds become minutes. Cirrus clouds stream overhead: milky white, fancy as hat plumes, delicate as filigree. The breeze feels cooler; he puts on his windbreaker. The sun, no longer orange but Day-Glo pink, balances on the horizon like a great fluorescent egg. All is silent save for the distant droning of a truck and the dry chirping of crickets, not the incessant chorus of summer but enough to stir life rather than death. Hope wells up in Jim's heart.

He tries to quench it, but to no avail; it grows and grows until he's faint with Becki-love. His eyes fill. He feels her near as he has so often over six-and-a-half years. The sun, now blurry and cherry red, slowly sinks behind the hills, down, down. He watches until it diminishes to a point of haloed red light, like a railroad signal on a foggy night—THEN A VOICE: "Shanley?"

BURST OF JOY, THEN FEAR! Jim dares not look. His heart lurches. His stomach knots. But his mind denies, *O Jesus, am I ever insane. I meet her on this hill as if I'm courting a ghost.*

But the voice speaks again, "Shanley, what are *you* doing here?"

NO DREAM, BUT REAL! Panic, jubilation, shock, sheer terror. Jim's emotions riot inside him. His heart thunders and shakes. BECKI! BECKI! BECKI! There she is, coming toward him from the woods, from the path. He gasps, then all his breath expels in one explosive rush. Nausea, butterflies, weak knees. His thoughts race. He tries to answer, "I uh ... I-I...."

"Relax," she teases, dimpling and extending her hand. "I'm not going to bite you." He shakes her hand. A warm shiver shoots to the quick of his soul. Becki acts calm but nervous excitement plays in her blue eyes. Jim notices and she quickly averts them.

Pink knit top, beige poplin jacket, shirred hip skirt, charcoal gray. She looks healthy, wholesome—and very evangelical. A handsome calfskin bag hangs from her shoulder. No more jeans on Sunday night, but she does have white socks and sporty sneakers— low-cut Connies. A swirl of wind brushes a wayward wisp of hair onto her cheek. She pushes it back. Styled the same, like a helmet with bangs—and just a bit longer—her brunette locks are stiff under a net of hair spray. Her honey-blond highlights, full of tropical warmth, are as blond as they ever get. Her face is firmer, her body fuller, and she looks older, but hardly twenty-six.

"So, Shanley, what *are* you doing here?" Becki asks again, this time accenting the "are" instead of the "you." Her voice is still soft and moist, but more grown-up, more like Alison.

"I-I ... well, whaddeya think?" Jim stammers, his body trembling, his brain near to shutting down. "I still live here ... over there. I think you know. I thought Puerto Rico?"

Tucking one leg under her, Becki plops down onto the grass. "We're up for a week of fund-raisers," she replies. She scrunches her face and gives a moth-wind flutter of her hand as if to indicate that missionary fund-raisers are boring affairs. "Pastor Hudson and Stan are having a thing for us tonight. Mom 'n Ed had to stay in Nashua, so Randy's gonna speak and show our team video, then there's a spaghetti supper and we'll be taking pledges and stuff. Randy's at a staff meeting now, with Stan and everybody. I had an hour to kill, so I decided to take a walk." Becki drops her eyes and shrugs wistfully as if to say no one will miss her.

Jim sits down beside her but his heart soars over the meadow, *She came to see me. She's lonely. She loves me.* But reason quickly brings him back to earth. *No way. She just likes the woods and the meadow better than a BFBC staff meeting, that's all. This is pure coincidence.*

Silence, silence, unbearable silence. Rebecca lifts her eyes, gazing up at the feathery clouds which are no longer white but amber-violet edged in pink. Her prettiness is still utterly common, but to Jim, she's more adorable than ever as the soft shadows of evening accent her countryish features. Her suntanned face looks much the same, just a bit more adult, less kittenish. Her cheeks, though still cherubic, are not so chipmunky, not so chubby. Summer freckles and blemishes dapple her sunny complexion which is more ruddy than brown. She has no makeup except mascara and peach cover-up on her chin where her monthly pimple patch is scabbed and drying. Except for her oversprayed hair, she seems fresh and clean, as if she showered but didn't wash her hair.

Perfume, powdered flesh, clean clothes, hair spray, calfskin leather, faint salty-banana scent. *Oh, sweet Becki,* Jim exclaims to himself as he inhales her most feminine presence. *I don't believe this, that you're actually sitting here after so many years.* Butterflies, anxious, anxious. His pulse pounds.

Becki drops her gaze to the grass beside her. She seems to sense Jim's eyes loving her. A soft enchanting smile curves her cupid mouth. Hope, fear, memories, magic, surges of affection, pangs of anxiety. Jim's heart melts; his mind gropes. She thrills him so, scares him so. He aches to hug her, but he doesn't dare. The attraction between them grows like a charging electric field. His mouth goes dry. He nervously buttons and unbuttons his windbreaker. She plays with the strap on her shoulder bag. She has on a gold watch which makes her wrist look delicate and womanly.

Jim longs to take her hand, but fear holds him back. Becki steals an oblique glance. A fresh surge of pink stains her cheeks. He gulps. Passion kindles, but before lightning strikes, she smirks and retreats to teasing, "Jimmy Shanley, you need a shave."

"Well, I would've if I'd known you were coming," Jim jokes, glad for the release of the building tension between them; her mirth encourages and relaxes him. "But I didn't expect you until tomorrow." She gives a girlish giggle, he, a snickering laugh.

For a while they spar and banter, then Becki kids, "I guess you know, Jimmy, you're making quite a name for yourself."

"How's that?" Jim asks.

"You know, with your band. I still can't believe it. When I heard that you were playing drums in a rock band, I just about died."

"Why is that?"

"Because you were the biggest square around."

"Well, I guess we've changed places, huh? Now *you're* the

square."

"Oh, you know all about me, do you, Shanley?" Becki replies. She crinkles her nose sassily then dimples into a grin. Her sassy scrunchy-faced expression is so familiar that it seems to Jim that no time has passed, as if six years have diminished to a day, an hour, a minute.

He leans forward and hugs his knees; he gives a mischievous smirk under his mustache. "Well, Becki Lea, let's just say I have my sources."

She doesn't reply, but rests her chin on her hand; a playful glint sparks in her eyes.

"So how's married life?" Jim asks, boldly shifting the spotlight onto her. "As good as you thought?"

"Wouldn't you like to know?" Becki quips.

"Yeh, I'm curious. What's it like to marry a missionary pastor?"

Flirty grin. Her blush deepens. "Better than being single, I tellyuh."

Memories, fantasies, swell of anticipation. Jim's pulse quickens again. Love, passion, carnal curiosity. Churning, churning. They churn in his gut along with fearful apprehension. His palms feel sweaty; he dries them on his jeans.

But Rebecca relieves his inner turmoil—no, she sends it spinning the other way. Her face clouds; her coquettish grin gives way to a pensive downward gaze. "Actually, my marriage is lousy," she confesses after a lengthy pause. "Oh, it was good the first year, but now we've sort of drifted apart. Some days we hardly even see each other."

She nervously picks at her thumbnail. She sighs then adds the clincher, "As a matter of fact, Randy's been sleeping on the couch for the past five months."

*God, she is lonely,* Jim gulps to himself in response to this most personal disclosure. *Maybe she was on the way to my house.* Casting propriety to the wind, he probes further, "You mean you haven't—" He pauses midsentence.

"Not since April," Becki laments, answering his uncompleted but obvious question. "I may as well be a nun or a—"

She abruptly stops as if alarm bells are sounding in her conscience. Her color drains; she knits her brow assuming her familiar pouty face—also unchanged over six years.

PANIC! Jim tries to rescue their reunion but his words catch in his throat. He coughs. He clears. But he cannot speak. The churning in his gut becomes a deafening roar. A dark and awful horror grips his soul, *O Jesus, here it comes, the knife. I know it.*

Becki swallows hard, firms her jaw determinedly. She squares her shoulders, narrows her eyes—then jerks to her feet. "I can't talk about this," she declares piously as if scolding herself. "I shouldn't be talking to *you* at all. I can't be here."

She quickly stalks off toward the woods, toward the path. Sinking anguish, sheer black terror. Jim jumps up, cries after her, but no sound comes out of his mouth. The cold blade of death pierces his chest, but stops short of his heart, as Becki stops short of the stone fence. She faces away; she stands motionless—as still as Lot's wife.

Jim's heart jolts upward lodging in his throat. Waiting, waiting. His brain freezes into blankness. Cosmic night sucks up the sky, the meadow, the birds, the trees, the clouds. Dark. Dark. All creation gasps, holds its breath.

Dark. Dark. Holding, holding—now the MIRACLE! Becki turns, runs back, and collapses sobbing into Jim's arms.

YES! YES! THE ANSWER IS *YES*! JOY! JOY! FIRE AND LIGHT! A starburst of light extinguishes the darkness. Hugging, hugging, desperately hugging, they sob and weep until hot tears melt all their fears—all their anger and misgivings and hurt feelings. Relief, reconciliation, unspeakable happiness.

Heaven opens. A howling wind swirls down from glory filling Jim's soul with great exultation. He holds Becki snugly; he rocks her gently. She lifts her face; she finds his lips. The abyss of Adam opens. She fills it to overflowing.

Raptured by love, they soar on the wind, back through the meadow, back to the house, back to *their* house, to *their* room.

Becki kisses him tenderly, lovingly, then hotly and passionately. She undresses him in the soft light from his desk lamp; her girlish hands tremble. Her azure eyes are wide and awestruck, even frightened, at the prospect of what they're about to do. But her spirit seems eager, resolute. Logic versus libido. Jim's knees shake. He feels self-conscious about his potbellied middle-aged body. Yet he watches with incredulous delight as Becki quickly sheds her own clothes: sneakers, shirt, skirt, and bra.

He can scarcely believe his eyes as she drops her brassiere and stands before him clad only in hip-hugger briefs and white socks—and her gold watch. Her deep belly dimple peers cutely over her panty waistband.

Becki, Becki. Oh, Becki. She blushes with delicious embarrassment. Naked female flesh, lusty, adult, yet tender, softly full, and girlishly smooth: warm custard. She looks a bit chunkier but oh, so ripe and succulent. Her midriff is paunchier, her thighs, thicker, more cushiony, yet she's still not roly-poly. In fact, her hip-heavy figure seems much the same as Jim remembers, except her skin has browned in the Puerto Rico sun, not dark, but tawny brown. Her breasts though are still ivory-white, the color of vanilla ice cream. White gibbous moons of nubile flesh: a bit larger, more heft, more hang, but still youthful, high-perched, and *proud.*

Inhibition quickly gives way to instinct. Erotic magnetism charges the air calling them to couple quickly, to satisfy their unsated love in a heated rush, like their first and only fuck six years ago. But this time they hold back their passion allowing their excitement to grow and grow. For a long moment, they adore and arouse each other without touching, save with their eyes.

Seconds pass, perhaps a minute. Too much. Rebecca's rouge-colored nipples begin to bud—swelling raspberries. The sight intoxicates Jim. No more self-consciousness. His penis stiffens. He no longer feels fat or middle-aged but powerful, manly, beautiful, and unashamed. Becki gazes hungrily at his growing erection. Her lips droop sensually. Her eyes flare with lust as when you squirt charcoal lighter on hot coals.

"Oh, *Shan*ley, I want you," she sighs, her voice thick with eros. "It's you. It's always been *you.* I'm married, but I fucked you a thousand times in my mind. O God, I tried to stop. I prayed. I dedicated. I made vows. I gave my body to Randy, but not my heart—oh fuck, am I ever horny. I need a man. I need *you.* My panties are soaked." Her language is now raw and unrestrained like the Becki of six years ago—far removed from evangelical propriety.

Can't wait. Can't wait. Becki fondles Jim's prick, then lifts it as if to suck it. But instead, she comes up and sucks his mouth, attacks his lips. Hot fury. Wild woman. She takes his breath away. She grinds her body into his. Becki, Becki, biting, kissing. Hot breath, coffee breath, sugar lips, wet lips, spicy darting tongue. Perfume, soap, hair spray, salty-banana flesh. Hot heaving midriff, damp bristly armpits, whiffs of nervous BO. Jim drowns in a swirling sea of Becki-sensation. He feels her. He smells her. He tastes her. He hears the dark beast roaring up from between her legs. Pussy, pussy, panty-clad pussy. Ravenous pussy, ferocious untamable cunt. Becki's cunt. He wants to fuck it and fuck it until the beast howls and shrieks and dies.

But for now he fucks her mouth with his tongue. He swabs her crooked teeth then thrusts deep. Becki moans. Now in a delirium of anticipation, she pulls back panting for air then attacks again, kissing and biting his lips, his cheeks, his chin. Electric nibbles. Flickering wetness. She kisses down his neck, his shoulders, his chest; her wild locks fly from side to side. Delicious shudders heat Jim's body; he gasps.

But as quickly as Becki attacks, she stills. Body talk. They agree—without words—to slow the pace, to prolong their passion, to postpone the hot and terrible frisson of ecstasy, so they can charge it with greater potency, so they can drink until drunk the sweet but torturous anticipation of its most certain coming.

Jim lightly touches her neck, her chest. The skin above Becki's breasts has an oily sheen and is dotted here and there with pimply blemishes. He moves lower. He circles her pink areolas teasing her fully-budded nipples. She sighs and sinks down onto his piled-mattress bed. Jim drops to his knees in front of her.

Flushed, feverish, eyes down, Becki studies her crotch as if admiring the adult darkness looming inside her white-cotton panties. Her youthful breasts hang wantonly in the pale-yellow light— ripe pears, ready to mother, ready to nourish. A soft umbra and penumbra shadow her left bosom like the moon in eclipse.

Love, eros, aroused female flesh. As she sits on the bed, her naked fullness overwhelms Jim's psyche; even her tummy folds are awesome. He can hardly believe that he lay hopeless and alone on this same bed less than ninety minutes ago.

A sweet Mona Lisa smile graces Becki's lips. She cants her head spilling her disheveled locks onto her shoulder.

"Oh, Becki Lea, I love you *so*," Jim declares happily. "I can't believe you're here." No reply just a blissful sigh. *O God, to be a sculptor and capture your pose forever,* he adds, to himself.

He lifts each of her razor-stubbled calves and pulls stinky socks off her girlish toes. He moves closer. He parts her knees exposing her plumpish thighs and panty-clad mound. The pungent aroma of her aroused pussy wafts out to him: smoky, perspiry, female, feral—similar to her dirty socks, yet enticingly sweet like vanilla extract.

Jim's cock is so erect he fears it will break away from his body and fuck her without him, yet he does not rush. He fondles, caresses her inner thighs. She sighs and mews. Becki, Becki, womanly Becki. Her flesh feels hot, spongy, squeezable—like freshly baked angel food cake. Her breathing is labored. Her dilated blue eyes devour his every move.

Slowly, deliberately, Jim moves higher, higher. Reaching her groin, he slips his fingers under the elastic of her panties. He feels hot and hairy wetness amid clammy folds of excited flesh.

"Oh yes, right there," Becki sighs breathlessly as she spreads wide and goes up on her toes to give him full access to her clitoris. "Yes, yes. Oh, Shanley, that feels *so* good. Oh fuck! Squeeze it. Oh yeah! Oh, that's fuckin' nice! Fuckin' *nice*! I love sex, how it feels. I wanna feel it forever. I wanna—O God, don't stop."

But Jim has to stop to remove her underpants. As Becki lifts one cheek then the other, he awkwardly tugs but her panties twist underneath her. So she quickly stands, slides them off, and plunks her butt back down onto the piled-mattress bed.

Now naked where it counts, she leans back on her hands and smiles dreamily as if buzzed on a drug. She opens her chunky thighs like the doors of heaven, proudly displaying her swarthy aroused genitals.

Tan lines, milky-pale flesh, burnt-umber pubic hair, tawny-pink petals: parted and swollen. Becki's cunt looks the same as Jim remembers, like a beautiful flower, like a lady's slipper orchid in full bloom. The birthmark on her left thigh, like a tattoo on a whore, accents her muliebrial beauty and sexual prowess.

Jim goes up as far as he can, but her position on the edge of the bed is still too high. He quickly grabs a pillow and places it under his knees adjusting his height until his wild stallion is pawing and bucking inches away from her yearning deepness. Molten shafts of desire arc between them, pulsing, drawing, burning with erotic potency.

Panting, slow panting. Becki breathes like she just ran up a flight of stairs. Her eyes flare with want yet she remains back on her hands. Her erect clitoris swells even bigger before Jim's eyes until it's blood-red and rigid and near to bursting with unsated lust, like a little cannon cocked and ready to fire.

"Oh, *Shan*ley, your dick is *so* nice," she raves. "I love how a man's cock lifts up and the knob swells and turns purple and has a neck like the head of a fuckin' snake. I see it pulsing now, the neck."

Penis hunger. Months of pent-up penis hunger. Too much. Becki's thighs begin to quiver. "Oh, Jimmy, let's *go*. Put it in. Oh, fuck me now! O Jesus! I want your cock in me! It's been too long! I want you!"

Teasing, flirting, Jim spreads her cunt lips with his purple knob until it's oozy wet, then he pulls back.

"No!" Becki pants. "Don't stop. I need it *now*." Her hips begin to move. She tucks her chin; she tries to rein in her haunches but her muscles ripple uncontrollably. She sucks in a long shuddering breath which comes up as ragged whimpers of sheer need, "Oh, Jimmy, do it. Fuck me. Fuck me *now!* O Jesus, I can't wait! I gotta come! I hear the roar!"

Her pubis bucks out of control. She reaches for his cock but he pulls back, tantalizing her, making her wait. But she can't wait. She falls back on the bed and frantically masturbates. Tremors of rapture shake her whole body. Her breaths come in panicky gasps. But she can't seem to get there; she cries for help.

Jim takes over. He squeezes then strongly strokes her clit.

Becki quickly responds to his rhythm. Desperate to come, she gyrates her hips like she's doing the twist. Faster, faster. Wild frenzy. She flails her arms. She whips her head back and forth. Her gold watch herks and jerks above her grimacing face like a crazed bumblebee. Her tongue flickers from side to side then curls over her front teeth. She clenches her toes. She kicks, thrashes her legs, then squeezes them together swallowing Jim's whole hand between her bulbous thighs. She grinds her pussy against his moving fingers until he has no strength left in them.

But just as fatigue demands he stop, she sucks a gasping breath and stretches her legs full-length to the floor. She gives a silent scream, her body becoming rigid as if frozen in time, but not for long as her breaking dam sends hot shudders of satisfaction through her naked flesh. Cascading ecstasy. Hot spasms of relief. She comes and comes until she knows she's got it all, then, sobbing and panting, she becomes limp as a rag doll and spirals down into the lingering euphoria of female orgasm.

Jim lies down beside her. She wraps her arms around him and sobs into his breast, "Oh, Jimmy, I love you! I love you! That was *so* good." She sucks a breath. She wipes her nose with the back of her hand. Limp, loose, relaxed. Her body seems fluidly supple as if a lifetime of tension has gone out of it. Release, release: uninhibited and complete.

Jim is still on fire with his own desire, but for the moment, he's more than content to soar on Becki's high—and he doesn't want to rush things anyway.

"Oh, Shanley," she goes on excitedly. "I feel so happy. That was so nice. I've dreamed about being with you, but I never thought it would actually happen."

Becki inhales deeply then gives a slow satisfied sigh as if exhaling cigarette smoke. Her voice is whispery, dreamy with afterpleasure. "I love you, Jimmy. I've never stopped. I love you, all of you. I love your body, and especially your cock. It's so beautiful. I want it to fuck me and fuck me. I wanna go all night ... just as soon as I get my strength back. Oh, Jimmy, you've got a strong hand. Oh, that felt *so* nice. The "good feeling" got so big I didn't think I was gonna get it out. It's been too long. I thought I'd never stop coming. At home I get off in the tub, but with all the traveling and busy schedules, I haven't had a chance to do my thing." She gives a sniffling laugh. "But I never dreamed I'd be getting off with you. And that's not why—well, I didn't plan this at all. I can't believe I'm here. But I'm so happy. I'm so glad. Oh, Jimmy, I love you! I love you so much!"

Becki's eyes brim with affection. Jim hugs her hot nakedness. He tastes her salty tears. His hand smells of vanilla and smoke.

Minutes pass. He can't wait any longer and she's ready for more. She turns Jim onto his back and mounts him. After a few moments of awkward shifting, probing, and cooperative effort, she seats his glans into her sweet spot and pushes her juicy sheathe down onto his full shaft. Her face takes on a dreamy look of wonder as she savors his presence inside her. Jim savors her as well.

Cunt, cunt, Becki-cunt. Young, hot, horny around him. The grip of a young woman's pussy, grabbing, sucking, pulpy yet abrasive, expanding to receive, yet firmly tight. To Jim, there's no feeling like it. No movement, just heavenly anticipation.

Becki gives him a playful squeeze with her sphincter muscle. As she does, she teases, "I must say, Jimmy, you've acquired re*mark*able restraint. At least compared to last time."

He grins up at her. "More than *you* anyway. You go fuckin' wild when you need to come—O Jesus, I love it. But I thought you could control your demons?"

"I can," she quips. "You just caught me in a bad way, that's all. Just wait; *you*'ll see."

Burnt umber on hazel brown, Becki's pubic bush meshes with Jim's. The sight is erotic and fierce and X-rated.

Leaning forward on her hands, Becki stares back between her pendulous breasts and feasts on their dark union. Her honey-maple hair hangs in his face. "Now *that's* a sexy sight," she sighs, her voice thick with renewed desire. "That's enough to turn a girl on, even a shy missionary wife."

They both laugh, but teasing quickly gives way to passion as their labored breathing and slowly heaving abdomens remind them that they're in the midst of intercourse.

Jim fondles her pendulous tits. Her aroused nipples jut out stiffly. He twists them as if tuning a radio. Becki sighs, lifts her head. He moves down and fingers her cunt lips as they grasp the root of his cock like a hungry mouth. Then he slides up a finger's width and strokes her clit.

Becki moans, begins to move. She humps slowly then faster and faster to meet Jim's phallic thrusts. Eyes closed, mouth open, she mews and groans. Faster, faster. She bares her teeth. Her tongue lolls as dead. Jim feels the tumult rising, rising—but then she stops, abruptly stops.

Spasms of near-orgasm ripple through their coupled genitals. Becki heaves and pants but holds back her eruption. Clawing, clawing. She claws for control and manages to regain a precarious balance on the high cliff above the chasm.

"Come *on,* Becki," Jim pants in breathless protest. "We're too close to stop." But she's on top. He can't move without her.

"Now we'll see who has will power," she sports. Her words are heavy and slurred. She can scarcely talk, but she wants to drink the hot and awful pleasure just this side of letting go. "Oh fuck, Jimmy, *this* is the best feeling of all! I wish we could stay here forever. Oh, I *love* it. I could *die* here!"

Seconds pass that seem like hours. Sweet agony takes them higher and higher, but no one has the will power to ascend to the top of that precipice, not even Becki Reinhardt. Finally, she gives a catlike growl and hurtles them into the abyss.

Humping, humping, Becki digs her nails into Jim's shoulders. She fucks him savagely. He frantically grips her beefy hips as she pumps furiously back and forth on his thrusting cock. They now jerk as one, locked in lust, an untethered beast charging to its own death. Her tits jounce to and fro. Her hair flies wildly about her head. She cries openly, sobbing Jim's name. Her sweaty midriff folds and unfolds like an accordion. Her hefty haunches advance and retreat, driving Jim into her, again and again—deeper, deeper, harder, harder. Her hot wetness soaks his belly.

Deeper, deeper, he plunges into the hot core of her. Deeper, deeper, yet beyond the horizon. Heart, mind, body. Origin and destiny. Jim and Becki loving. Jim and Becki fucking—pulling, pumping, sobbing, moaning, drowning, closer, closer.

Yes! Yes! Closer, closer. NOW IT COMES!

A primal scream pierces the night as they stiffen in shuddering ecstasy—as they stiffen as ONE in the mystery of love and lust and mating.

# Chapter Forty-three

2:20 a.m—Sunday has just turned into Monday. The house is quiet save for the droning of the refrigerator and Rebecca's regular breathing, and dark save for the bathroom light.

*This has to be a dream?* Jim thinks as he watches Becki sleep. Her weedy mop of oversprayed hair cutely hides half her face. Her lips are parted and faintly smiling. Jim's exhausted but too entranced to close his eyes. He drinks in the blissful silence; he feels wonder and thanksgiving. Becki lies snuggled in his arms, her fetal position backed into his; her naked buttocks dominate the bed. Flannel and flesh, cozy warm under the sheets, under the brownboy: he, in his pajamas; she, in his old softball jersey.

*O God, I believe in you,* Jim declares happily in his heart. *I believe in love. I do, I do.* Becki's breathing is regular but shallow. Her chest slowly lifts and falls. Her pillowy bosom presses hot against his arm; he feels her heart beating. As she sleeps, she holds his hand like a little girl. Heaven has come down to 59 Front Street.

The whole night has been a fairy-tale-come-true. Jim thinks back reliving each joyous moment—love, sex, unspeakable ecstasy. After Becki rides him to a mind-blowing mutual climax, culminating their torrid reunion, she collapses near to fainting at his side. Panting, panting, they soar and glide on the wings of post-orgasmic euphoria. The feeling is hot and buoyant yet penetrating, like a fever turned inward. Jim tenderly enfolds her in his arms and pulls the brownboy over them. They float down, into sweet tranquility. Two hearts, one body. Becki snuggles so close that he feels their flesh merging. Blissfully happy, they breath in unison; their hearts couple. Their peace is bottomless. Time seems suspended. There's no talk except for sweet whispers of love.

8:55 p.m. Practical concerns; reality returns. Becki calls her husband at the church; she stands naked near the butcher-block desk. Her weight on one foot, she sassily cocks her beefy buttocks, giving Jim his first good view of her 26-year-old ass. No more puberty butt: from the back, Becki is *all* woman. Becki hips, breeder hips, still moonish, low hung, but more heft than before, more saddlebag fat, yet more provocative than ever—sexually potent, furious, heavy with conviction, as if her hips anchor her soul as well as her body. Her fish-white gluteal flesh, more adult, more doughy in texture—like the texture of brown 'n serve rolls before you brown them—seems even whiter, brighter against her tanned back and legs as if a spotlight is focused on her bare bottom.

Jim will never forget her pose, or her words: "I'm at Jimmy's house.... That's right, Jimmy Shanley.... I know, Randy; I know it's nine o'clock.... I know; I couldn't. You were in a meeting—but let me talk; I have serious news. I can't do it anymore. What we have is not a marriage. I'm not going back with the team. I'm moving in with Jimmy. We'll come to Nashua tomorrow to get my suitcase and things. I'll send for the rest of my stuff after you get back to Puerto Rico.... No, that's not it.... Look, I don't wanna get into it—but yeah, we did.... I know, I know. But it's not you, Randy; it's *me*.... I know, I know.... Okay, so it's partly you. But it's much bigger than sex. It just isn't working. Even if you move back into the bedroom, it wouldn't change anything.... No, that's not true. It's not my flesh; I'm not trying to escape. I'm just being honest, *finally*. I can't pretend anymore. No.... No.... No, I don't dislike you, Randy, but we don't love each other enough to live together."

For several minutes they go on arguing. Becki turns sideways. She shifts her weight from foot to foot. She scrunches her face. She wraps the telephone cord about her finger—then a vehement exchange, but the outburst of emotion is brief.

After hanging up, Becki fingerfluffs her hair, grabs Jim's softball shirt off the closet door, and wiggles into it. He watches from the bed. Large and white with blue shoulder stripes, the old Crusader jersey hangs to her thighs, just covering her haunches like a baby-doll nightgown. Becki's cheeks are red and raw from beard-burn, and her dirty hair sticks out in tufts and tangles despite the fluffing. She looks like a little jock after a tough game and her body still exudes the perspiry smells of lovemaking. But to Jim, she's adorable, a princess, enchanting, irresistible, a precious child inside a sexually seasoned woman.

On the back of the jersey, the numeral "18" declares their age difference, while on the front, script writing spells out "Crusaders" over Becki's uptilted breasts. Her braless tits are now bashful and relaxed, a pair of cute hillocks under the cotton fabric. Her presence overwhelms Jim as does the realization that she's moving in. He didn't ask her but there's nothing he wants more. No request, no reply, just a shared knowing. That's how it is on this heavenly night as he and Becki wed in heart and spirit, without vows, without ceremony, and without official sanction.

Barefoot to the bathroom. Rebecca cat-washes and brushes her teeth—with his toothbrush. Next comes the hiss of female piss spraying into the toilet—a most wifely sound that warms Jim's heart—then the screak of the tank lid and the flush, together with her bantering voice: "I see you haven't fixed the toilet in six years. What am I gonna do with you, Jimmy Shanley? This place needs a woman's touch. The whole apartment looks boring. We need plants and pictures and stuff. I have a lot of things that'll be coming up from Puerto Rico, but we hafta go shopping too." Becki seems right at home as if she never left. Likewise, in keeping with her pack-rat instincts, she's already turned the LA-Z-BOY recliner into a catchall for her things: her skirt, her shirt, her jacket, her underwear, her calfskin shoulder bag—even her dirty socks.

Out of the bathroom into the kitchen. Becki sets about preparing a late supper. As she works, she yells comments to Jim who's still in bed: "Hot dogs and beans all right with you? What happened to my cabinets? Two of the doors are broken? That sofa used to be at Sheila's, right? And the table was in her basement, in Russ's workshop? And you got Sharon's coffeemaker? Who picked out your curtains? Not you I'm sure? They're nice and homey, but they need to be washed." Jim loves her voice. It's velvety soft and angelic, and her every word reminds him that his impossible dream is coming true. Woman, woman, a wife. He's ached for years; he's yearned to have a woman in his life, even after giving up on Becki. But now *she's* in his kitchen. Becki, Becki, in his kitchen, cooking, chirping. He believes in God again; he believes in destiny.

A bit later she comes back into the bedroom, but just long enough to grab her socks and Jim's raggedy robe—the bedroom is warm from body heat but the kitchen is chilly on this early autumn night—and to pop a cassette into Jim's tape deck: *U2* and the *Joshua Tree* album. She boldly assumes his things as her own. They are. True love is like that. As the music plays, Jim's heart dances a jig around the room. He feels like a kid again, a little boy on Christmas. And now every day will be Christmas. He pulls on his shirt and jeans, visits the bathroom, then joins Becki at the kitchen table. Beans and franks, bread and butter. Campbell's "Pork & Beans." And she found a bag of Chips Ahoy cookies.

Becki does most of the talking. No inhibition. She speaks as if conversing with her own heart—in a food-clogged voice: "No, it's just hurt pride. I understand his reaction. I feel for him, but he *knew*. He had to. We haven't touched each other since our second anniversary.... Randy's not a bad person, not really. He sees the bullshit but he's got no balls. He's so intimidated by Mom 'n Ed, and Pastor. Fuck, he can't do anything without official instructions—I can't believe I'm sayin' 'fuck' again. I haven't talked like this since I left here. See what you do to me, Shanley. You're a *fuckin'* bad influence, I tellyuh!"

They both snigger and laugh, then Becki stabs a piece of hot dog and pops it into her mouth. After swallowing, she goes on, "But me 'n Randy, we never really knew each other, not in a deep way. How could we? The ministry was everything. We could never be ourselves except briefly in bed ... and our sex life was pretty good the first year. Nothing spectacular"—she rolls her eyes as if to say, Like to*night*—"but it was still better than being single and bored. But we didn't have deep-rooted love for each other. I knew when I married him, but I thought God would give it in time, since we had dedicated our lives to serving Christ. But it never changed, how I felt. Oh, I like Randy okay, and he's cute and has a nice bod. That's what attracted me to him, but I never get that excited rush around him. Don't get me wrong; I can turn on to his sex appeal when I'm horny and he wants it—course, it's been a while since *that* happened—but I never get that electric feeling, like butterflies, when he walks in the room ... like with *you*, Shanley."

Becki laughs then scrunches her face teasingly. "You mess me up, you know? I can never think clearly around you. Guess that's why I'm here, huh?"

She gives another quick laugh then sobers and sops her beans with a piece of bread. But instead of eating it, she pushes it toward Jim to emphasis her words: "So when the newness of our marriage wore off, and sex became less satisfying—no, not less satisfying, but less frequent—there was nothing left for Randy and me. The rest of our life was lousy, the ministry and all that. We were *always* busy, too busy. Randy had to raise money and do ministry shit all the time, even at night, and I had to teach and take care of the cottage and help Mom with the women's fellowship. We had to go to conferences and seminars. We had to travel a lot, he more than me. I wanted a baby, but babies got postponed. Randy was cranky and stressed-out all the time. He showed less and less desire for romance. In fact, he hardly noticed me at all ... and before long, I was sleeping alone. Now we hardly ever talk, except about money and church business."

Becki sighs then pops the bean-soaked bread into her mouth. As she chews, her face warms into a happy glow. "But all that's be*hind* me now. I feel so good and free, like I just broke out of jail. I've been dreaming about coming back ever since I left but I never believed in myself enough. I've been to Brendon Falls a lot of times, to Stan's church. I always wanted to take off and come over here but I never had the courage. And today I didn't plan it or anything. I was just waiting for Randy like I always do, then all of a sudden, I was out the door and headed up the path. Randy says I'm just giving in to my flesh because I'm sexua.ly frustrated. He says I just wanted a 'walk on the wild side.' But that's not it. This is not a one-night fling I tellyuh. Oh, I've been horny a lot and starving for romance and affection, and it's hard when you're a missionary *wife* and you have to be quiet about such feelings and pretend to have pure and righteous thoughts all day. But today was different. I wasn't seeking sex, or romance, or *any*thing—at least not consciously. It's like something unlocked inside me and I knew I was gonna walk up the path to the meadow. It's not like I thought any further than that."

Becki shakes her head and chuckles. "I still can't believe I did it, that I'm *act*ually here.... Mom's gonna kill me for this, especially since Pastor's foaming at the mouth over your music ministry. He says the devil's using you, Jimmy. But I'm not bowing down, never again. I love Mom, but she has to accept me as I am. Besides, I think the devil's using Pastor Logan, if there *is* a devil."

The chugging beat and melodic slide guitar of *U2*'s "Running to Stand Still" sounds over the stereo. Jim's heart exults, his hopes soar—for him and Becki, for the band, for the prospect of love breaking loose in the land. His long nightmare is over. The wall is gone. He and Rebecca are together in a new and wonderful place. They're no longer "running to stand still."

Becki rips open the chocolate chip cookies. "Truth is, Jimmy, I never liked Pastor, even when I was a kid. Yet I was afraid of him since I knew I was a sinner ... and Mom always said he was 'God's man,' and anointed and all that. I never trusted my feelings before—least not for long—but now I know what really goes on in the ministry. I guess you have to go through it. I see all the lies now, and how people are two-faced, and how *money* is the big thing, bigger than God. And I'm tired of suppressing my heart, and calling it sin when my feelings don't fit."

Jim can hardly believe his ears; she sounds like Russ, like Jodi—like himself. She wolfs down a cookie, washes it with several gulps of milk. He kids her as she lowers her glass, "Becki, you still eat like a teenager, like you're thirteen."

Becki dimples and gives a blushing smile. "I do *not*," she playfully rebuts.

"Yes, you *do*. You still get that milk mustache on your upper lip."

She quickly wipes her lip with her paper towel—Jim has never stocked paper napkins. "Cut it out, Shanley. I'm going on 27, and I act more grown-up than you. You're just a big tease that's all. You haven't changed."

They both laugh, then Jim shifts, "So Logan says I'm of the devil, huh?"

Becki arches her eyebrows. "I'll *say;* I never saw him so mad at anything."

Jim eats a cookie, swigs some milk. "Well, do his sermons bother you ... when he blasts me and the band?"

"No, I already knew," Becki replies.

"Knew what?" Jim asks.

Becki smirks then gushes, "That you're *of the devil.*"

She giggles. He laughs almost choking then declares, "You're too much, Becki Lea." His heart overflows with gladness. She's witty and wild and childlike again, but no longer naive or innocent. Six years as a soldier in Logan's army has opened her eyes— something his pleas and accusations never accomplished.

"So, Jimmy, you decided to believe me, huh?" Becki chortles around a mouthful of cookie.

Jim gestures with his milk glass. "Believe what?"

"Well, I always said rock music touches people more than anything. I guess you had to learn the hard way, huh?" Becki shakes her head; she gives a chuckling sigh. "I can't believe I threw away all my tapes."

Jim doesn't reply. Becki sobers, becomes still. Seconds tick by. Her blue eyes fill with "I'm sorry" as if she wants to talk about the long war that separated them, but the moment becomes too intense, too immediate. They have much to talk out but it's not the time. So instead of talking about it, she gets up and pours more milk into their glasses while Jim stuffs another cookie into his mouth.

"I saw your music video," Becki says as she sits down. "Katie showed me at summer conference. She snuck it out of Matt Garrett's desk. Katie's curious, but she thinks like Mom. She says you've gone crazy, Jimmy—but that's hardly news." Becki gives a snorting laugh, laughing through her nose. "But I like the songs, and especially the camera work, like how it shows real-life shots of everyone like Joe and Angie and Jodi—and like *you* in bed with Cathy Rosinski." She rolls her eyes then purses her lips in a coy fashion. "But I'm not worried about other women 'cause I know you can't resist me, Shanley. Besides, you're old. You don't have the strength for two lovers ... but me, I'm in my prime. I could handle a dozen—and *how.*"

Unable to resist her flirting, Jim hops up, tries to tickle her. But Becki, blushing and giggling, breaks free and scampers into the bedroom, with him in hot pursuit. Frolic, frolic, flirting and frolic. They fall onto the piled-mattress bed. Laughing, giggling, teasing, tickling, they wrestle until drunk on fresh desire.

After consummating their love again, she cleaves to him purring on his shoulder. He pulls the sheet and brownboy over them. He strokes her face and softly kisses her lips; she smiles, loving him with dewy eyes. Floating, floating, as in warm water, they snuggle deep into *their* bed—like twins in a mother's womb.

* * *

As the first rays of morning sun shine through the window, the phone rings. It's Alison. Her voice is stern, her message brief: "Please tell Rebecca that Randy and I are coming to talk this morning. We'll be there at nine o'clock."

Becki, squinty-eyed and scowling inquisitively, looks up at Jim. He relays Alison's curt message. She gives a yawn that becomes a grumbling sigh. She drops her pouty face back into the pillow. Adulthood has not changed her morning countenance. Finally, she cranks her head from under her dirty haystack of hair and says, "I could've figured as much, not Randy but Mom. I knew she wouldn't accept this without a fight." Becki's voice is thick with sleep.

The sun is now above the trees. Too bright: Jim pulls the shade. On the mantel Mrs. Courtney's clock says 7:14 a.m. After a visit to the bathroom, he heads into the kitchen but doesn't get far as Becki calls, "Oh, Shanley, let's stay in bed. We have plenty of time." Quickly changing from morning grouch to morning lover, she wears Jim out, but he's never known such heavenly fatigue. She seems insatiable—quite a difference from Christmas Eve of '83 when Alison's call threw her into a frenzy of guilt.

At eight-twenty they finally get up. While Becki showers, Jim makes coffee and toast then puts on his clothes, the same clothes he wore yesterday. His hair is clumpy and unruly. It has that slept-on look, especially his cowlicked bangs. So instead of combing, he covers it with his grubby softball hat. As H-hour approaches, he refills his M.I.T. mug and heads down to the front porch. Rebecca is still in the bathroom making do with his limited toiletries plus what she has in her purse. Jim senses the electricity of coming confrontation but he has a relaxed peace about the outcome.

He plops down sideways on the top porch step and props his back against the post; he pushes his hat back on his head. Coffee in hand, he sips and waits. Messy hair, faded jeans, scraggly mustache, three-day beard: Jim could certainly pass for a '60s cult leader, but he feels more like a prince or a king.

Beautiful fall day in Brendon Falls. Bright sunshine has chased the chilly dawn. Now the morning feels almost warm—more like early September than October. A drab and smoky haze veils the old mill town and the hills beyond. Autumn has painted the hills misty orange and rusty red. Above Jim, a few sparrows chirp happily on the utility wires while a gentle but frolicking breeze stirs the leaves of the oak tree. The air is alive with country smells—damp grass, pine trees, fallen leaves, dank earth. The front lawn is still wet with morning dew which sparkles on the weeds and wounded grass like silver sequins. Fallen leaves lie about but not from the oak. The old tree is greener than the grass with just a hint of auburn showing in its thick crown. Columbus Day: no school, no work for many; it's like Sunday morning on Hadley Hill.

*I wonder how it's going in Maine,* Jim thinks. *O God, am I ever glad I didn't go. Russ and Joe, they'll never believe this, nor will Jodi or Cathy or Angie. They're gonna shit when they get back!* His heart exults as a gust of joy bursts up and becomes a laugh.

But his laugh is cut short as a beige Lincoln limousine turns onto Front Street, roars aggressively up the hill, and up the driveway. Logan, Logan, pang of fear. Jim's body becomes tense; he sits forward. Lucas Simpson is driving with Rich Beckman riding shotgun. Logan sits in the back with Alison, but Pastor Scowcroft is not in the car. *What the fuck!* Jim exclaims to himself. *Looks like Alison brought the big guns instead of Randy.* Another pang of fear grips his gut, but apprehension quickly gives way to resignation.

After what he's seen in the meadow, in his room, in his bed, Jim doubts that Logan has any power at 59 Front Street, but even if he does, even if Becki buckles, there's nothing Jim can do. No battle plan, no need of one, he'll never try to hold her again. He leans back against the post and drinks the last swig of his coffee. He sets the black mug beside him on the porch. His peace returns; he feels bold yet unburdened.

Beckman and Simpson remain in the limo, but Dr. Logan and Alison get out; Logan wears a blue business suit, Alison, a tan blazer over a maroon skirt. Devout Christians decked out for battle, full of faith and piety and righteous indignation. After a brief huddle beside the car, probably for last-minute prayer, they march zealously up the sidewalk like bounty hunters for God—Alison's midheel slingback shoes resound rhythmically on the concrete, as if she's counting cadence. Heads high, they exude an air of evangelical assurance as if they know their prayers and words will quickly deliver Rebecca from Jim Shanley's "house of sin."

Jim leans lazily against the porch post; his legs block the steps. Alison marches ahead of Logan. She gives Jim a tight little smile, but he senses fury lurking underneath. She reminds him of a dog baring its fangs before a fight. Her hands clasped in front of her like fig leaves, she stands rigidly erect as if the Star Spangled Banner is playing. Everything about her seems hard, tense, wound tight, like the inside of a golf ball, her face, her eyes, her hair, her body language, her official-sounding voice: "We're not here to see you, Jim. Kindly step aside. We don't want any—" Alison stops midsentence as the front door opens and Becki steps out.

Silence, save for the lazy squeak of the storm door and the

creaking of the wooden planks under Becki's sneakers. Ruddy-faced, freshly showered, and wearing her pink top and gray skirt, but no jacket, she stands on the porch next to Jim as he sits on the first step. Her just-shampooed hair is wet and straight but neatly combed; her damp bangs adorn her forehead like the fringe on a lamp shade. "Pastor and I came to help you, Rebecca Lea," Alison says, looking up at her daughter. "We're not her to judge or to condemn. We just want to talk. Why don't we go sit in the car?" Inching closer to Jim, Becki declines her mom's invitation.

Jim feels Becki's leg touching his shoulder. He glances up at her. Their eyes briefly meet. He feels her loving him, trusting him; his heart melts.

But then his anger kindles as Alison advances closer almost onto the porch steps, so close that he smells her perfume. *Fuckin' Alison,* he declares to himself. *She's cunning as a witch. I feel like grabbing her by the neck and throwing her off the property.*

But he restrains himself as Alison continues her motherly appeal: "It's okay, Becki. We can talk here if you prefer. I just want to tell you my heart....We love you, honey. You've come so far. We're so proud of you 'n Randy. You're an inspiration to all of us. But you *must* consider what you're doing. You've worked so hard to get where you are. You can't let an emotional flight of fantasy destroy your marriage and your ministry. You're a woman of God. You can't desert your husband. You have a holy calling together. I understand how you feel. We all have sacred duties. We're all on the front lines fighting the forces of evil. It's not easy. We're in the *last* days. Wickedness is rampant on the earth and the devil's attacking on all sides. We all feel the stress. We all have fleshly weaknesses. I feel like running away *my*self at times. It's nothing to be ashamed of, but we cannot forsake the Lord. Please, Becki, consider your ways and come back with us, back to your family. Come back to the body of Christ. I love you. Pastor loves you. We love you with *God's* love, not the love of the world."

Becki looks down shyly and picks at her thumbnail, but does not reply. Yet her firm jaw and defiant eyes tell Jim that she feels the same contempt that he feels.

Alison steps back. Logan steps forward. He looks first at Jim. The doctor's dark eyes are filled with a strange mixture of pious indignation and paranoia. He despises Shanley as a heretic yet he's petrified of Jim's nakedness. Heart honesty poses a personal threat to Logan, as it does to Alison, and all evangelicals. Ostensibly, the LBI chief has come to 59 Front Street to rescue Becki for the Lord, to save her from sin, and to preserve her marriage. But in fact, he's come to challenge her heart, her freedom, her love for Jim, because she's a prized possession who has fled his LBI trophy case. She's a living testimony that he does not win the hearts of his LBI followers, but builds his Popelike power on fear and shame and lies and manipulative schemes. The doctor has worked with maniacal fervor to package and sell himself as a kind and devout "man of God," but Rebecca's break from LBI threatens to exposes his true spiritual impotence, and he fears exposure to the point of madness, exposure before his people but moreso before his own conscience. So regaining Becki's allegiance is vital to preserve his delusion of grandeur. At least, this is how Jim Shanley sees it on this sunny Monday morning.

For a moment Jim thinks that Dr. Logan will address him, but the doctor quickly turns his attention to Rebecca as if afraid to acknowledge Shanley's presence. Logan's eyes fill as if his heart is breaking with concern for Becki, who is still looking down shyly. Palms up, he gestures with beseeching hands and begins his well-measured pitch—his sandpapery voice seems kind and fatherly— "Like your mother says, Becki, we're not here to condemn you, or even to question your motives. I know you love the Lord. I know you have no sinful intent. But as your friend, and as your shepherd, I *must* remind you, as I have in the past, that Satan uses our emotions to draw us away from truth."

Logan pauses and glances nervously at Jim as if he expects him to intervene, to rebut. Reproachful disdain burns in Jim's gut but he says nothing. The same miracle that brought Becki will have to engineer their victory; it's too big for him to fathom much less command. So he merely fingers his mustache and relaxes more fully against the post.

"Our passions cannot be trusted," Logan goes on, now reaching out plaintively toward Becki. "They change like the weather. True love is not a feeling, but a decision, a commitment in Christ, as you and Randy made to each other when you exchanged your vows. Rebecca, you're a grown woman now, and I respect you deeply. I've loved you from a child. We all have. You've grown up in the church. But I *must* tell you the truth. I know from experience that fleshly passion never lasts. Only the wisdom of God endures, as Solomon teaches: Trust in the Lord with all thine heart and lean not unto thine own understanding, be not wise in thine own eyes; fear the Lord and depart from evil...."

*Why was I ever afraid of this guy?* Jim asks himself as he tunes out for a moment. *He's nothing but a charlatan and a bullshit artist, and now the years are catching up.* Up close, the doctor does indeed look his age, like a man in his sixty-fourth year. He's wrinkled, gray, squat, and balding, and has large liverish pouches under his eyes. He reminds Jim of a loathsome toad.

"Becki, you're a soldier of the cross," Logan implores. "We're in a *great* army. God has commissioned us to preach salvation to the world, to march against Lucifer and to defeat him. The Lord is with us. We shall not fail. A cloud of witnesses watches from heaven, Christian soldiers who through the centuries have carried the banner of Christ to the nations. Think of your heritage. Think of the martyrs who gave their lives for the gospel. I beg of you, dear Becki, please be reasonable. Jesus loves you and reaches out to you. Don't let one night of foolishness ruin your marriage and rob you of your calling. I know it hurts to lay down your life for the kingdom, but just think of Jesus and how he died for us at Calvary. Standing with Christ is painful and humbling, but it's *right*. So come with us. We love you. We want the *best* for you. No one will hold this against you. We've all been though it. It's only through falling and getting up that we learn to walk in the Spirit."

Suspense, electric tension, time slows to a crawl. Alison and Logan project an air of confidence as they await Rebecca's response. Their body language conveys poise and faith in the Lord. But their eyes betray their seeming cool. Anxious eyes. The two LBI'ers look warily from one to the other like lawyers waiting for the jury's verdict. Jim senses the high-stakes tension about him but a peaceful almost carefree spirit still reigns inside him. No apprehension or necessity to act: for once, he senses that destiny is on *his* side. He picks up his coffee mug and fondles it nonchalantly. He can scarcely believe it. His fairy-tale showdown with Logan has finally arrived and he'll not have to lift a finger or say a word.

It's Becki versus LBI. Half hidden behind Jim, she fidgets with her hands and shuffles her feet, shifting her weight from foot to foot. Yet, despite her nervous energy, Jim senses that her soul is at the ready, like a surfer waiting for a perfect wave.

Seconds tick by—they seem like minutes. Jim shifts his butt on the concrete step. Birds twitter on the wires above. The morning sky is high and blue over Hadley Hill. A playful gust of wind swirls about them rustling the oak leaves and blowing a wispy curl of hair onto Alison's cheek. She pushes it back brusquely as if impatient with her daughter. But she doesn't have to wait much longer.

Becki lifts her eyes. She draws a breath. She gazes defiantly upon her adversaries. Before she says a word, the verdict of her heart is apparent to all. Logan quickly drops his friendly facade and glares sternly at her, intimidating and accusing with his hypnotic eyes. Young and shy and far from eloquent, and less than a day out of the LBI camp, Rebecca Lea hardly seems a match for Dr. Charles Logan. But such are the ways of destiny.

Like David before Goliath, Becki puts a smooth stone in her sling and lets fly, her voice furious with contempt, "You say you love me and you act so sincere, but in truth, I don't even know you, least hardly at all. I'm sick of your party line! We never really talk. We never say out what we feel. I want to know the *real* you, how you *really* feel! I've tried it your way, always doing the right thing and forcing myself to live up to doctrines and sermons, and calling it God. Well, it doesn't work! You never changed me. You just made me feel guilty. I CAN'T DO IT ANYMORE! IT'S A LIE! You never loved me! Not the *real* me! You just used me and made me feel ashamed of my heart like it belongs to the devil! WELL, I'M *NOT* ASHAMED! I DON'T WANT TO CHANGE! I LIKE HOW I AM! I JUST WANT TO BE *ME*! I trust Jesus, but I don't trust you! You want to control me and make me afraid of God! You're all following the worms! Born-again Christians are phonies and liars! AND LBI IS NO DIFFERENT! YOU TAKE ADVAN- TAGE OF TRUSTING SOULS! YOU MAKE ME *SICK*! YOU'RE ALL LIARS, A BUNCH OF *FUCKIN'* LIARS!"

Shock! Shock! Stunned by her irreverent outburst, Logan and Alison blanch with dismay and chagrin as if Becki has ripped off their clothes—and she's far from finished. Red-faced and furious, she preaches on; she rolls her hands wildly in front of her as if she's dog-paddling. "You say you love people then you make them afraid of God so you can get their money and make them bow down! You say come to Christ, and he'll make you happy, and deliver you from alcohol and drugs and immorality—BUT YOU NEVER CHANGE *ANY*ONE, NOT REALLY! YOU JUST SCARE THEM UNTIL THEY *ACT* RIGHTEOUS!"

Jim remains silent but his heart roars with Rebecca: "You don't make the world better, you make it worse! You don't save anyone, you just make people hate themselves in the name of Christ! Even those who never come to church! You make people suppress their feelings until they're bombs of emotion ready to explode! You shame people and make them hide their true selves until they feel lonely and cutoff. Is it any wonder that life is a rat race and people are cruel and deceitful and angry and resentful! Is it any wonder they hate each other and murder and abuse each other, and take drugs to escape! YOU DON'T SOLVE *ANY*THING! IN FACT, *YOU'RE THE PROBLEM*!"

Becki drops a decibel but her words remain sharp and lacer- ating: "I came to Nashua seeking God, but I never found God. I felt sad each day, but I had to pretend to be happy. I can't do it anymore! I'm tired of living a lie! I'm tired of saying I believe the Bible just 'cause I'm supposed to. I'm tired of playing at marriage when it's not. I'm tired of raising money and saying it's God. I'm tired of goin' to services and conferences. I'm tired of scaring people about hell then telling them they're saved just because they pray. It's a *lie,* like selling tickets to heaven! I want to go to heaven, but it's a lie to tell people things we don't know for sure. You talk like you know everything about God. But you don't know any more than me or anybody! And who the fuck are *you* to tell me how to live? You don't care about my happiness! You just want me to bow down! You say let's be reasonable, but you reject anything that doesn't fit your rigid doctrines. I'm *sick* of it, I tellyuh!"

Her blue eyes blazing, Becki hacks the air as if breaking a trail with a machete. Her words burn with conviction, piercing to the soul: hot bullets. "I'm not a*fraid* of you anymore! You say don't talk to Jim or God will chastise. Well, if your God punishes people for loving and being happy, then I *reject* your God! I *love* Jim Shanley. I've always loved him, since I first knew him! And I want to be with him. I love him! I love him! I do! It's the most real thing in my life! I don't want your dry, no-touch, religious love that you act out as a duty. Your love is a *lie*! It's a heavy burden like a ball and chain. I want *real* love! I want love I can *feel*! I want love that makes me come alive, love that's magical and beautiful and out of control. Love that's erotic and wild yet warm and true. You tried to kill my love. I tried to kill it. But it wouldn't *die.* I STILL LOVE JIM! I DO! AND BEING WITH HIM MAKES ME HAPPY AND GLAD! IF YOU REALLY CARED ABOUT *ME,* YOU'D BE GLAD TOO, INSTEAD OF TRYING TO PUT ME BACK INTO YOUR *FUCKIN'* CAGE!" Jim's body still sits on the porch step, but his heart soars on Rebecca's words until he feels like he's above the house, above the oak tree, looking down on the scene.

White, white, stunned white, no words. Becki's scathing attack seems to have stunned Logan and Alison, rendering them speechless. But they quickly recover as righteous indignation devours their dismay and chagrin. Now comes the counterattack.

Alison, chin up, arms folded tight as a gate, steps forward. Severe face, motherly scowl. She glares at her daughter, her brown eyes hot with reproach. Becki boldly stares back, cocking her buttocks hipshot against the porch post like a sassy cowgirl. An equally sassy grin tips the corners of her mouth. Her impertinence ignites Alison like a match to dry tinder: "HOW *DARE* YOU SHOW SUCH DISRESPECT TO ME, AND TO PASTOR! You may be 26, Rebecca Lea, but you're *still* my daughter! The Lord doesn't take it lightly when a young person shows disrespect to her elders, or when a missionary wife cheats on her husband! Why must you always learn the hard way! A holy God cannot allow you to flaunt such fleshly sins in his face!"

Rebuke and condemnation. Recognizing their cause is lost, and smarting from Becki's verbal assault, Alison has shifted to accusation and threats of judgment, the Christian tactic of last resort to preserve ego and pride when evangelical entreaties are strongly rebuffed or successfully refuted—in this case Becki has done both. Alison goes on, her voice trembling with rage, "You've always been a rebellious child, Rebecca, with sinful tendencies, especially when it comes to sexual sins! You're a loose woman. You're obsessed with carnal things. And it's no mystery why you don't change! You won't let Christ change you! You love fleshly pleasures more than God! You've never given your heart to the Lord, not *really*! And now you're involved with a worldly backslider who leads people away from the body of Christ. God will *never* allow this, Rebecca Lea! IF YOU DON'T REPENT, HE'LL DEAL WITH YOU SEVERELY—AND *YOU TOO,* JIM!"

Jim quickly comes down to earth as Alison turns her rancor upon him. She's so close that she fans his face with coffee breath. "I hope your satisfied, Jim! It's really your fault, you know! All of this! Not only have you messed up your own life, but now you're ruining Becki's as well! YOU'RE A DECEIVER! A DE-BAUCHER! AND A DEGENERATE TOO! GOD WON'T LET YOU GET AWAY WITH THIS! YOU WAIT AND *SEE*!"

Now it's Dr. Logan's turn. He steps closer as Alison retreats. He holds his head arrogantly back as if sniffing—he and Stan Campbell are masters at this pose. He glowers at Becki, his eyes hard and cold and pitiless, like black holes in his pouched face. His patrician nose is blotchy-white and flaring. He speaks slowly, his tone grave and pharisaical. He arches his arm upward gesturing at the house. "Becki, this is a house of sin. It's a den of vipers and the seat of rebellion against the kingdom of God. You *must* repent and come back to your husband and to your calling. You *must* honor your vows. God will surely judge this house, and if you're here, He'll judge you as well." Advancing almost on top of Jim, Logan thrusts his head toward Rebecca. The doctor's wattled neck, loose, leathery, and wrinkled, hangs in ugly folds above his tie, like the neck of an iguana. He too smells of coffee breath, but unlike Alison, he has no perfume, just his usual Mennen aftershave.

Becki moves forward as well, leaning out as far as she can without stepping on Jim's legs which still block the steps. Sancti-monious rage scalds up into Logan's face, rising like the red in an overheated thermometer. Showdown. Showdown. Becki, her hands on her hips, lifts her chin defiantly and meets his accusing gaze. She doesn't flinch. Face to face, they glare at each other. The LBI chief holds back his wrath, yet he seems more venomous than ever: a cobra coiling to strike. He wags his finger at Rebecca. "You're on very dangerous ground, young lady," he warns. "But for the grace of God and the atoning blood of Christ, you'd be stoned to death as an adulteress outside the—"

"FINE, LET HIM WHO HAS NO SIN CAST THE FIRST STONE!" Becki shouts, attacking with the swiftness of a cheetah— she cuts Logan off, turning his sword back upon himself. "You pretend to be so holy, but I know *all* about you! Katie tells me everything!" She thrusts her finger into Logan's face; his countenance freezes into stone and turns gray as death. "Katie told me all about you and Molly and Cheri, and how you *fool around* with the girls in your office, and about the secret late-night parties at the villa, and about your girlfriends in Florida, and how you *lie* to Amy! I know all about the ministry money you spend on yourself, and how you tape all your calls so you can *black*mail people! And everybody says you're a *man of God*! What a fuckin' joke! You're nothing but an insecure old man! You just want power and money, and you lie and manipulate to get it! You just want everybody to be afraid of you so you can feel like a big shot! WELL, YOU'RE *NOT*! YOU'RE A *FAKE*! YOU'RE DELUDED AND HALF CRAZY! AND THE WORMS HAVE EATEN YOUR BRAIN!"

Lightning, thunder, crashing bolts of truth. Becki's words charge the air. Hot blood, hot blood, no more gray. Logan's face boils with hot blood; he shakes like an addict in need of a fix. The pulsing veins on his temples seem ready to explode; they don't, but he does, "REBECCA SCOWCROFT, 'YOU HAVE BEEN RE-BELLIOUS AGAINST THE LORD' in Deuteronomy 31:27! '*WOE* TO THE REBELLIOUS CHILDREN WHO TAKE COUN-SEL BUT NOT OF ME' in Isaiah 30:1!" Hot Bible verses spew out of his mouth, riding a spray of hot spittle.

As he rants, Logan flails his arms crazily like a baby bird trying to fly. "'He that despised Moses' law died without mercy under two or three witnesses! Of how much *sorer* punishment ... shall he be thought worthy, who hath trodden under foot the Son of God' in Hebrews 10:29! YOU'RE A *STIFF*-NECKED INSO-LENT WOMAN, REBECCA! YOUR PROFANE IRREVER-ENCE FOR MY OFFICE SHALL BRING YOU TO *RUIN*!"

Scarcely pausing, the doctor shifts his assault onto Shanley, "The *same* goes for you, Jim Shanley! I've been your friend despite your mutinous spirit! I've offered you opportunity to repent again and again, but you re*fuse* the grace of God! You blaspheme the Lord with worldly music and heretical preaching! 'An evil man seeketh only rebellion' in Proverbs 17:11! You stir up rebellion and unbelief everywhere you go!" Logan sucks a quick breath. He jabs the air in front of Jim's face; he bobs down like a boxer; he comes up bellowing. "YOU PLANT SEEDS OF DISCORD AND DISSENT IN THE KINGDOM OF GOD! YOU HINDER THE PREACHING OF THE GOSPEL! YOU LEAD THE SHEEP ASTRAY! YOU DE*BAUCH* YOUNG WOMEN! YOU TURN SOUL-WINNERS INTO RENEGADES AND HIPPIES AND *WHORES*! AND *NOW* YOU TAKE A YOUNG MISSIONARY WIFE AND BRAINWASH HER AND SEDUCE HER, AND STEAL HER FROM HER HUSBAND! I'VE HAD IT WITH YOU, JIM! EXCEPT YOU REPENT, I *MUST* CALL UPON GOD TO DEAL WITH YOU, AND YOUR DEVILISH CULT!"

Gulping air, Dr. Logan steps back. Jim shrugs, lifts his coffee mug impassively toward the doctor, but says nothing.

This carefree gesture throws Logan into a final vitriolic tantrum. He slams his fist repeatedly into his open hand; he screams upward as if he wants heaven to hear, "THUS SAITH THE LORD! IF YOU DON'T RE*PENT,* THE FATE OF HANANIAH WILL COME UPON YOU in Jeremiah 28:16! 'BEHOLD, I SHALL CAST THEE FROM OFF THE FACE OF THE EARTH! THOU SHALT *DIE* BECAUSE THOU HAS TAUGHT REBELLION AGAINST THE LORD!' THUS SAITH THE LORD TO YOU, JIM SHANLEY, AND TO YOU, BECKI SCOWCROFT: UNLESS YOU RE*TURN* TO THE BODY OF CHRIST, GOD SHALL TAKE YOU HOME EARLY! 'THERE IS A WAY WHICH SEEMETH RIGHT UNTO A MAN BUT THE END THEREOF ARE THE WAYS OF *DEATH*'!"

There it is, the threat of death, Logan's desperate and final card. But there's no response from Jim or Becki. Jim stares wide-eyed into his black M.I.T. mug. Becki stands sober and silent on the porch. Alison, burning with self-righteous indignation and pumped up by Logan's decree, steps forward and stands shoulder to shoulder with her pastor as he seals his prophecy, "So be it, Jim and Rebecca! God offered you *life,* but you have chosen *judgment*! You have no one to blame but your*selves*! Thus saith the Lord: You're bringing the wrath of Almighty God onto your own heads. We hereby shake the dust off our feet before this cursed house!"

Logan storms to the car. Alison follows. Firing up the limo, Lucas Simpson jerks it forward, turns around in the parking nook, and guns out of the driveway, spewing gravel and rocks, and sending a cloud of dust into the air. The limo zooms down Front Street. Screeching tires. They turn and disappear. The cloud of dust follows, drifting slowly down the street.

Hazy blue sky. Singing birds. Peace has returned to Hadley Hill. The south wind sighs through the oak tree. The leaves flutter, turning this way and that.

\* \* \*

Becki lies on the bed; she gazes at the ceiling. "It doesn't surprise me that Randy didn't come," she reflects. "He has no stomach for confrontation. Besides, I bet Mom 'n Pastor counseled him to stay in Nashua. They knew things were gonna get nasty. Randy's so damned submissive and insecure ... but he's not a pharisee. He's a victim like me, like most of us. I escaped but I doubt he ever will. Mom 'n Pastor didn't come here this morning 'cause they care about me, or Randy. They just can't stand it that I ran away to be with you, Jimmy."

The LBI'ers have been gone for twenty minutes. Becki, her hair now dry and downy soft but no longer neat, lies on her pillow, her hands behind her head. Jim, his legs crossed ankle-on-knee, sits at his butcher-block desk. He fiddles with his sneaker laces. A rope of sunshine, having slipped in around the window shade, runs from Rebecca's arm to the pillow, then to the brownboy and onto the floor. Becki's complexion is still blotched with emotion, but her sassy boldness has given way to sober contemplation. Her pouty face now seems more wounded than defiant. She breathes in long slow breaths, her bosom lifting and falling inside her pink shirt.

Her eyes fill. She lifts her hands and examines her nails as if to distract herself; she bites her lower lip. A tear dribbles down her cheek. She trembles. Jim moves quickly to her side, sinking to his knees before the piled-mattress bed. She comes up sobbing into his arms. He holds her tightly. After a minute of hard crying, she calms. "Did he scare you?" Jim asks, whispering into her freshly washed hair. "I mean Dr. Logan?"

"No, I'm not afraid of his shit," Becki replies into Jim's breast, her voice thick from crying. "He doesn't know what God thinks anymore than me."

"What uh ... was it the shouting and fighting, and all the viscious words?"

"No—well, sort of. It just fuckin' hurts that's all. It hurts to know they can be so mean and narrow, especially *Mom*."

Becki shifts her butt and snuggles closer to Jim, pressing her face into the hollow between his shoulder and neck. She sniffles and coughs then swallows hard. He gently smoothes her hair. She clings to him like a child seeking comfort. His heart overflows with love and compassion. He speaks tenderly, "I guess you got your

**715**

suspicions confirmed the hard way, just like me?"

"No shit; it's like I knew, but I didn't."

"It's amazing how they resort to fear when they have no rational argument."

"I'll say," Becki agrees. "Pastor always preaches that heaven is such a glorious place, and to die and go there is a blessing. But now he uses death as a threat, like it's the worst punishment."

"Of course, he may mean hell for us, but that contradicts once-saved-always-saved, and he always says, 'God's gonna take you *home* early.' *Home* is not hell. It's a fuckin' contradiction."

"I've heard about others who got threatened like this," Becki replies, "but it's different when it happens to you."

Jim caresses her back. "So you didn't expect them to be so vicious?" he says as he massages the tension out of her shoulder.

"Not to me, not my *mom*—oh, I guess I did in a way. Pastor always brings out her cruel side. But I never thought they'd get to me, and set me off into an emotional rage like they did."

"Fuck, I think you were great. I wish I had it on tape."

"But, Jimmy, it makes me shake inside, like everything's happening so fast."

A flea of doubt bites Jim's heart. "So you have second thoughts about—"

"No way," Becki interrupts, wrapping her arms tightly around him; the flea dies instantly.

"So you're glad about last night?"

"Best thing I ever did ... but still, it's a big fuckin' change."

"Like being *born again,* huh?"

Becki looks up at Jim with a tear-stained but grinning face. "I'll say," she replies to his pun. "It's no wonder that babies cry when they come out." They both laugh then she burrows again into his embrace.

Closeness, closeness, intimate closeness. Heart-to-heart, body-to-body: Becki sitting, Jim kneeling. Hugging, holding one another, they seem welded together. Her breath feels hot and wet on his neck. No doubt, Becki Lea is back, more than back. The dreaded wall is truly gone. Logan's scare tactics no longer have power over her. Fear made its final stand last evening in the meadow—and lost to love. Rush of elation. Jim's heart rejoices at this realization. Becki's skin is warm and baby fresh. Her newly washed hair presses softly against his cheek. She smells of Ivory soap and DeMoulas balsam shampoo. *She did okay with my cheap shit,* he says to himself. *But I bet she'll be glad to get her own stuff. O Lord, I can scarcely—too much! She's gonna live with me. This is heaven.*

Becki snuffles. Jim hands her a roll of toilet paper from the floor by the bed, where it's been since their early-morning lovemaking three hours ago. She blows her nose then wads the tissue in her hand. Jim gently brushes a tear-matted tendril of hair off her cheek. An enchanting smile curves her mouth as she loves him with bleary but happy eyes. His heart melting with affection, he gets onto the bed with Becki, and they scoot up and lie on the pillows, he on his back, she on her left side facing him.

Jim slips his arm around her and pulls her close; her cozy heft heats his flesh, thrills his soul. She touches his face with her finger, tenderly tracing his cheekbone, his jaw. He's unshaven and shaggy but she seems overjoyed to look upon him, to touch him. Her soft voice overflows with feeling, "Oh, Jimmy, all those months, I wanted so much to reach out to you, but I couldn't. I just couldn't."

"I know, honey. It uh ... well, it was bigger than us, like out of our hands."

"When you called me at Denny's that time and I hung up, I almost died. I couldn't do my tables. I went to the ladies' room and cried. And that day you came and we had the fight, I wanted to go with you *so* bad, but I was scared because you made me go crazy inside. That's why I took you to court. I was ashamed and afraid, so I did what Mom 'n Pastor told me to do. I had no self-confidence, so I denied my feelings, to you, to Mom, to everyone. I tried to be like them."

Becki gently smoothes Jim's eyebrows; he closes his eyes. Her touch is intoxicating but he still manages a reply, "Well, gal, you certainly convinced me."

"No kidding. I had everybody convinced, especially Mom 'n Ed, and then Randy, but I never felt like I belonged. Everybody praised God and sang four-part harmony, but I never felt anything, not really. Besides, there was a lot of gossip about my year in Brendon Falls, about how I worked for you, and how I had to leave, and you were dismissed and the church split, and all that. And the stories were all blown out of proportion. I never confessed, and no one spoke to me openly about it, except Dr. Logan, but a lot of people accused me in their minds. I could feel it; they looked at me funny as if I had a scarlet 'A' tattooed on my forehead. I felt guilty and spiritually inferior. I tried to fit in, but I felt like an outsider."

Becki kisses Jim's cheek then sighs happily. She again runs her finger lightly over his face. His eyes are still closed but he feels her adoring him. A minute passes, perhaps two. She runs her fingers through his hair. She chuckles playfully. "You're not bad-looking, Shanley ... for an *old* guy. I like your hair when it's wild and uncombed and sort of long just over your collar. It's more sexy, and your cowlick is cute." Compliments from Becki. Things have *certainly* changed. Jim feels himself blushing. Opening his eyes, he gives her a boyish grin. "Oh, *Shan*ley," she gushes in a burst of girlish exuberance. "I love you so much, I can't stand it. I could *eat* you up. It's like I was born to be with you, and I've been waiting my whole life for it to happen." Her blue eyes spark with inexpressible emotion. She again kisses his cheek, then his ears, then his neck. Her nibbling lips tickle him. He squirms and laughs and grabs her ribs which leads to more laughing and squirming and squealing.

Finally, they sober and settle back into their previous positions. Jim stares up at the amoeba-like water stains on the ceiling. Back, back: six years. "So, Becki, what actually happened on that Friday after I left? What made you move out and leave Brendon Falls so suddenly? Did your mom get to you? or Stan? or what?"

Becki sighs reflectively. "Well, I guess they both did, but it was really my conscience. I started feeling guilty about Sharon and the kids. I thought about my mom and what everyone would say if you moved in. I felt fucked up and sinful for coming on to you and being so wild. It was heavenly that morning, being with you, Jimmy. But after you left, my conscience took over and I crashed. I felt dirty and slutty, like a whore. I felt ashamed for liking sex so much, and for loving you and going crazy over you. I needed to talk to someone who would understand. I tried to call Amelia but she wasn't home. I tried to call Jodi but Angie said an inspection was going on, that I should call back in an hour. I took it as a sign that God was disgusted with me, that He didn't want me to hear anything that would condone my sin. And just when I was condemning myself, Mom drove up. It was perfect timing like *God* planned it. She'd flown up the day before. She took me to McDonald's. I told her you were making unwanted sexual advances. Then we went to Stan's house. When he got home, he counseled me and showed me a lot of Bible verses. I felt more ashamed than ever. So when he said it was God's will that I go back to Nashua, I quickly agreed and we went to Worcester to rent a truck. It happened fast."

"No *kid*ding," Jim agrees emphatically.

Becki massages Jim's chest and his shoulders. The touch of her hand is almost unbearable with tenderness, as is the tone of her voice. "When I got to Nashua, Pastor said if I cared about you 'n Sharon and the kids, and about God, I had to put it all behind me. That's why I signed that paper and sent you that mean letter. I feel so *bad* sometimes when I think of what I put you through, Jimmy. You had every right to reject me and to forget me altogether."

"Oh, Becki, I could *never* forget you," Jim replies, speaking up toward the ceiling. "I was pissed to the point of hating you, but I could never get you out of my mind. I hated you and loved you at the same time, but I couldn't ignore you. You were with me each day. Oh, I tried to kill my heart, but I couldn't. In fact, I loved you more each day for six years. It was torture, but now it seems worth it, like it was somehow necessary to bring us to this place."

"Yeah, I think God wanted us together," Becki says. "I think this was all planned. I do."

"Well, God kept me at home anyway. Our reunion would've never happened if I'd gone to Maine with the band."

Becki turns onto her stomach and hugs Jim, placing her head on his chest; her eyes are sleepy, heavy-lidded. He fingers a loose lock of hair that has fallen over her face. She seems ready to doze off, but she doesn't. Instead, she sighs lazily and shifts from the past to the present, "You seem different, Shanley. Not like a different person, but more laid-back, like how you didn't get uptight about Mom 'n Pastor. Before, you always seemed driven and ready to fight, like everything was up to you."

"I guess it comes from giving up," Jim explains. "All my life, I got what I wanted through planning and hard work and perseverance, but with you it was different. I tried so hard to keep you from leaving, but still, you left. Then I fought desperately to get you back, but nothing worked. Finally, I had no strength to fight, so I gave up. I knew I had no control. It was a scary realization, but a comforting release as well ... like facing death."

Becki doesn't reply as she again seems on the verge of dozing off. Jim gently strokes her hair. She closes her eyes but soon opens them again. "I hear it," she says; her voice is still lazy but no longer serious.

"What?" he asks. "I can't hear anything?"

"I *cain't* hear any*thang*," Becki mocks teasingly as she lifts her head. "You still talk like J.R. At least, I *thank* you do." She giggles girlishly. "You still sound like a damn Texan."

"Come on, Becki, I'm not *that* bad. Besides, you talk like a teenager."

"No, I don't. I outgrew that long ago. I haven't said 'wicked' or 'yech' since I've been here. Not once have you heard me." Becki laughs then wrinkles her nose at him, giving her cocky contorted expression.

"Come to think of it, you haven't," Jim concedes. "But I notice you still make that sassy scrunchy-face of yours. You've been giving me that look since you were a teenybopper."

"So, I can't help it around you, Shanley. You bring out my sassy side—and *how*." They both snicker then Becki again rests her head on his chest. "There, I hear it again," she says after a bit.

"This is where I came in," Jim kids. "Whaddeya hear?"

"Your heart, silly. It goes ka-thump, ka-thump. I like to put my head on your chest especially when you have on a flannel shirt. You feel cozy but solid, and I like hearing—*oh,* that feels good," Becki purrs as Jim begins to massage her back. "I love it when you do my back, like that morning after we first made love. That was six years ago but it seems the same, like no time has passed, like it's still the same day and we've been lying here all the time and everything else was just a bad dream—oh *yeah,* do my shoulders and neck."

Becki's eyes grow heavy again and slowly close. Silence, silence, beautiful quietness. *O God,* Jim cries in his happy soul. *Let this moment last forever.* It doesn't last forever, but it does last five heavenly minutes until a car honking down the street reminds him that they're still in the world. The line of sunlight has advanced off the bed. The clock on the mantel says 10:31 a.m.

"Guess we better get up, kiddo," Jim says as he gives Becki a playful swat on her skirt-covered ass which commands the bed like the summit of a roundtop mountain. "Remember, we have to go to Nashua and get your luggage and stuff?"

Becki wags her head. "Not yet," she sighs sleepily. "We hafta give 'em time to get back and get cleared out of the guest house. Mom knows we're coming. I doubt she or Randy or Ed want to see us." Eyes, eyes, big blue eyes. Becki seems suddenly awake. A coy smirk twists her mouth. "Besides, I got something *better* to do."

"What's that?" Jim asks.

She answers with a kiss. Hot lips, darting tongue. She locks him into a long kiss then unbuckles his Levi's. Next thing she's on her back, hips, legs, sneakers in the air, skirt up just enough. They fuck with their clothes on except Becki's beige panties are around her left ankle. As for Jim, only his erection is naked—out the fly of his underpants. Their late-morning lovemaking is brief but furious, like a quick torrential downpour on a day of gentle rain.

\* \* \*

Tuesday, October 9th. 9:15 a.m. Becki's in the kitchen making pancakes. Twenty-four hours have passed since the showdown with Logan. Sleepy eyes, chewing gum, unmade face, stone-washed jeans; socks, but no shoes, and no bangs. Her hair is up in a Nike sweatband. She's also appropriated one of Jim's old dress shirts, pale-yellow, untucked, collar up, sleeves rolled halfway, a new "bum around" shirt.

Jim stands in the doorway to the bedroom and watches with a sense of wonder as she takes plates and mugs and glasses from the cabinets, milk and orange juice from the fridge, and utensils from the drawers, as she pours batter into the skillet, water into the coffeemaker, and juice into the glasses—all accompanied by the soft patter of her stocking feet on the pea-green linoleum.

Becki suddenly notices his attention and blushes into a simpering grin, as does Jim. For a time, they gaze at each other. *"What?"* she finally gushes, her grin breaking wide, her face dimpling. Inviting, irresistible, such a little queen. Jim gathers her into his arms. Cozy warmth, tender elation. Love raptures them. She feels downy soft and moist: her body, her hair, her clothes. He kisses her; her lips taste of toothpaste and Wrigley's Doublemint gum—she's given up Big Red for the more adult brand.

After the kiss, Becki looks up with squinty inquisitive eyes and says, "Why were you staring at me just now?"

Jim gives her an adoring smile. "Because I can't help it. I love to watch you do things. I love how you move, how you walk, how you reach up, and bend over. I love how you bounce with energy, and how your sexy ass sways and rolls. I love how you do things with your hands, and how you nod and wag your head. I love how you chew your gum and fold your lips and wrinkle your nose. I could watch you for days, for years, and *never* get tired. You're the most *awe*some creation of God."

Becki beams; her eyes grow large and brim over with gladness, but no words. None are needed; she simply melts back into his embrace—heaven. "Oh, Becki," Jim declares happily, "you're so much the same yet so different. You've always been funny and cute, but now you're kind and caring and sensitive. I love you *so*."

Blissful silence, then he chuckles. "I always knew you had a good heart, even when you were an insolent adolescent *brat*."

"Maybe I still am," Becki teases without looking up. "You haven't seen me get mad yet." She laughs, but her laugh quickly becomes a contented sigh.

Despite some apprehension, their trip to Nashua yesterday afternoon was uneventful. The guest house was deserted as was the campus—not unusual for Columbus Day. They saw no one except a few students walking across the quadrangle.

Upon their return, Becki changed into jeans and ran out of the house with Jim in hot pursuit. Through the meadow, through the woods, she beat him to the big rock where she lamented the lonely trestle, "I'm gonna miss that blue train. That was the best thing about coming up here—well, almost the best." She went on to talk and laugh about the day she got stoned with Joe and peed on the ledge. Back in the meadow, she picked goldenrods and chased butterflies while Jim chased her. Finally, they sprawled laughing onto their backs and watched the chimney swifts, chippering, spurting, sailing through the air—twinkling crescents cavorting in the waning sunshine. After watching the birds, they bantered and flirted and wrestled, then made love in the sweet autumn grass. Higher, higher—above the birds—hot whoosh of ecstasy. Then they drifted back to earth, sobbing with happiness.

Last night, Jim took Becki out for dinner, to celebrate their "heart marriage." Before they left, he watched as she fixed her face, her hair, then dressed and perfumed herself. Anything she does fascinates him, intrigues him, as if it's the only thing happening in the universe—even the smallest things, such as covering the crusty pimple on her chin. Gray crinkled-silk blouse, navy cummerbund-waist skirt, pantyhose—a rarity for Rebecca—dark midheel pumps: she looked angelic, but very much like a missionary.

Bancrofts' Steakhouse, flickering oil lamp, not enough light. Jim couldn't read the menu so he put on his glasses. Becki grinned and quipped, "So, Shanley, your eyes are goin' too, huh? I must say you *are* middle-aged ... wearing glasses and sleeping in pajamas. You're definitely out of the '50s." They both laughed as he playfully squeezed her thigh under the table.

Back at 59 Front Street, they propped pillows on the bed and watched TV: *Designing Women* and *The Trials of Rosie O'Neill*. Becki's long religious odyssey did not diminish her appetite for prime-time TV. Jim never watches regular TV, and he didn't watch much last night as he fell quickly asleep. Becki had worn him out, spirit, soul—and especially his body.

Stink, stink, smoky stink. Burning batter. Becki breaks from Jim's arms and quickly moves the skillet off the burner. "Oh, Jimmy, look what you made me do." She tosses the blackened pancake into the trash. Now she concentrates on her cooking, making more pancakes, about a half dozen. She pops some frozen sausage patties into the microwave. Jim pours the coffee. Finally, they sit down to eat.

The morning is cool and rainy, so after breakfast they stay inside. Back to the bedroom. Becki tunes the radio to classic rock, WCLX, keeping the volume low. Jim plops into the recliner—after removing her rat nest of clothes and things, which has grown larger since she unpacked yesterday. He's given her two of his dresser drawers until her furniture arrives but a lot of her stuff went right from her travel bag to the LA-Z-BOY. As Jim relaxes, Becki wanders about the room like a cat exploring and marking new territory. She asks curious questions. She gives her appraisal of things. She investigates his closet, his dresser, his desk, his computer equipment, his file cabinets, his bookshelves. As she checks out the bookcase by his dresser, she gives a whoop of delight,

"Ahah, what have we here? 'Dear Becki' ... 'Dear Becki.' This looks like a diary of some sort. Now *this* may prove interesting."

She sprawls on the unmade bed and opens the thick journal of unsent letters, letters to her. Jim watches with loving eyes. He feels vindicated, validated. The many lonely outpourings of his heart were not in vain. Head on hand, she reads the letters eagerly, not all of them, but jumping from page to page. Some she reads aloud, others to herself. Some make her laugh, some inspire wisecracks, some make her pensive, some turn her on, some turn her off, and a few make her sad near to tears, but each entry helps fill in the lost months and years. As the rain pitters off the roof, they reminisce about the court hearing, Jim's anger, his hurt, Becki's confusion, her fear, her roommate Linda—now her sister-in-law. They talk about Mrs. Courtney, Jim's dad, Jim's weather job, Becki's boredom, her decision to go to Puerto Rico; about Jodi and Joe, and Russ and Sheila, and listening to tunes and doing fun things; about Mary Beth Hudson and Molly Gibson and Barry Buford, and Logan and Amy and Stan and Doris. About *Pink Floyd* and the *Eagles;* about Erin, Heather, and Chris, and Sharon and Tom.

Jim crosses his legs and leans back in the recliner placing his hands behind his head. As the minutes pass, he becomes more of a listener than a talker.

"Mom isn't against me, not *really*," Becki explains after finding an entry that blasts Alison. "She's not really a religious prude, not deep down—course, you know that from the old days. She's just afraid to be herself, especially now that she's a leader on the Puerto Rico team and has a godly reputation. She has to make everything fit into Pastor's bullshit. But she does want the best for me. We just disagree on what *best* means. I can't do it her way, but if she calls me, I'll be friendly—if she stays off my case."

Becki reads on, talks on. Jim devours her words as her soft voice reveals secrets and details about her life he's always longed to know. He feels a sense of wonder. He loves how she shares her true and most intimate thoughts with him as if their minds are having sex. She elaborates on her life as a missionary-teacher, on her courtship with Randy, on her wedding, on the stress of being a pastor's wife. She also comments about her sister, "Katie knows it's big business and built on lies, but she's quiet and submissive when it comes to authority, like Randy. And she spouts the LBI line better than Mom. Katie knows all the ministry dirt but she'll never split. She's in tight with Matt Garrett now. I wouldn't be surprised if they marry someday. She knows he's gay. She knows about Barry and other guys, but she wants security more than romance."

When Becki reads about Rusti, her eyes fill. "That's a sad

723

story, Jimmy. I feel bad for your kitten; she sounds like Bathsheba. I gave Bathsheba to Amelia, you know. We must go to Boston and see her." Becki wiggles her hand to wake it, then replaces it under her head. She comments on Jim's poems and songs, then becoming more adamant, she speaks about the band, "I can't sing or play, but I'm looking forward to seeing everybody again, and I want to be part of it. I want to see Pastor's lies tremble before the truth. I want to see love win. I want to see the whole *world* change."

After perusing an entry in which Jim quotes Russ's convictions about people having more than one lover, Becki teases Jim, "Now this sounds like a *good* way to live. I'd like two or three dicks in my life, especially when yours is tired and droopy, Jimmy, like last night." She snickers but quickly sobers. "But seriously, I think Russ is right, at least partly. I don't like the Christian way, how married couples are private and cutoff from others. I don't mean sexually so much, but there's no honest sharing of feelings or problems. There's nothing but party-line fellowship. It's like living in a steel box and you can only spend time with certain people. That's why I'm glad we'll be living here with everybody and doing things together, and saying out our feelings, not that I actually want to fuck around, but I don't want to be told I can't. Christians are *so* paired off and bound up in vows and duties and appearances. It messes things up, like with me and Randy."

"What's this?" Becki says after reading an entry about her wanting a baby. "Mary Beth knew everything about me. Katie must've let her read my letters. But it's true. I do want kids. Maybe not right away since we're like brand-new together, but pretty soon, don'tcha think?" She blushes and gives Jim a smirky grin. "It's a good thing I just got over my period. Otherwise, pretty soon would be *now,* I tellyuh: after Sunday night and yesterday. O Jesus, I never did it *this* many times in two days ... 'cept maybe with Manny back at the beachhouse, when I was eighteen."

The mention of fucking after sixteen hours of abstinence seems to excite Rebecca, and her mood quickly becomes prurient. She now turns her attention to the letters with sexually explicit content as if she's been saving them for last so she can satisfy her naughty-girl appetite for erotica all at once. "You're worse than me, Shanley," she flirts. "This journal is *X*-rated, and I thought *I* was oversexed. God, you were into *Penthouse* every day." Her carnal curiosity aroused, she asks about his brief affairs with Angie and Cathy, then she teases him about his impotence with Ruthie and Doris and Carla, and the hooker from Boston. "Serves you right, Jimmy Shanley, for trying to get me out of your mind."

But Becki seems most interested in those entries that surmise about her own sexual adventures. "I must say," she confesses, "you do have good insight when it comes to my Bible school experiences. If you could've looked in on me, you would've got a good education, I tellyuh." Becki squeezes her tight denim-clad thighs up into her crotch. Her words become whispery and wanton. "My best times at Bible college were in the shower or after lights-out. After my one time with you, I didn't have real sex again for four years, until my wedding night—I didn't *dare*—but I sure got good at fantasizing, not so much at first, but later after I gave up trying to suppress it."

Jim gives Becki a seductive grin. "You gave up?" he asks curiously. Her mood change excites him. He loves her prurient side. He feels his pulse quickening, his penis stirring. A good night's sleep has rested his dick and renewed his desire.

"Well, when I left here and went to Nashua, I hated my emotions especially my sex drive. I saw myself as oversexed and different from the other girls who seemed so prim and proper and pure. I saw lust as the root of all my sins and problems, all the way back to when I looked at smutty magazines in Mell's basement. So I prayed and dedicated my body to God, like Pastor preached from the pulpit. I tried to set my affections on spiritual things and to stop thinking about you or Manny, or anything erotic. I tried to live like a nun. But I couldn't get sex out of my mind. In fact, the harder I tried the *more* I wanted it. I lusted after every good-looking guy I saw on campus. I'd wonder what his pecker looked like. I'd picture myself unzipping his fly and pulling it—oh, *Shanley*, I better stop talking about this or I'll never finish reading these letters."

But Becki doesn't stop. She's too far into her favorite subject. "Even the young pastors when they preached, I imagined them naked with hard-ons. In fact, that's how I got attracted to Randy. I prayed and resisted, and I could go a long time, but I always ended up giving in to my flesh. It made me feel cheap and ashamed, and I'd repent and vow to have pure thoughts. Sometimes I went for weeks, or even a month, but—O Jesus, no *way* could I stop. So after six months or so, I gave up trying. I still felt guilty but I just accepted it as a weakness, my sinful weakness. And that's how it was until I got married. I felt like I had a guy's weakness, because Pastor always yelled at the men for lusting and masturbating, and he taught that the woman was the responder, not the initiator, when it came to the marriage bed. At the time, I couldn't imagine the other girls having aggressive sexual desires, much less getting so horny they had to come. I really felt like a hussy and a hypocrite. But looking back on it, I'm sure some of them fingered off like me. But that's one sin we *never* confessed."

Becki's misty velour voice is now arousing Jim to no end. He knows that she's salivating in her panties. His rejuvenated prick is up and ready. Her inclination toward prurient talk and sexual confession has always turned him on, but now it makes him shake with anticipation for he knows it won't end in frustration.

"So when you were trying to be a nun, you actually went a month without getting off?" he asks, whetting her appetite further—and his.

"Fuck, I went six weeks once," Becki brags, giving a coquettish grin and a sassy toss of her head. "I was so horny I could taste it, but I refused to give in to lust. I took cold showers. I prayed for hours. I denied my flesh through will power. And I thought I had victory ... until one night when I went to a summer-league softball game. The air was warm and sweet, and all these well-hung jocks are running around in tight spandex pants. I couldn't get back to my room fast enough."

"So that temptation made you fail, huh?"

"Oh, did I ever *fail.* Afterward I felt like shit, like a slut, like I wasn't even saved. I couldn't even look at people in the face. But not while I was getting off—oh fuck, my mind went wild. Raw. Triple-X. *Way* out for an LBI girl. I fantasized that the pitcher—he was the cutest—was slowfucking me on the infield grass, then faster and faster as the crowd cheered him on, then the catcher, then the shortstop. I took on the whole team and outlasted them all, ten hairy sweaty guys. It was purely physical, and *so* sinful, but it sure got me where I wanted to go, like three times—O Jesus, it felt so fuckin' good to *come,* after resisting so long. And that's why it was so good with you Sunday night. I was horny out of my mind. If I go a long time without getting off, like two weeks or more, then I can really *pop my cork,* I tellyuh."

Too much. Jim unbuckles. Becki quickly strips from the waist down. Before he can get his pants past his knees, she's on his lap on the recliner. "Don't move," she says in a suffocated whisper as they merge into physical union. "Let's see who can go the longest."

She grips his prick with her vagina, teasing him, but there's no gyrating or pumping as she holds onto her hips. Deeper, deeper. Her pussy contractions excite his cock, drawing him deeper into her. Jim feels his erection growing, lifting inside her, until his throbbing glans seems like a second heart beating in her chest.

Time ticks by. Becki gazes at Jim, her blue eyes wide, wanton, fully dilated. He returns her gaze, staring into the dark depths of her: swirling fires, vast blackness, terrible tenderness. Her untamed soul envelops him like the starry heavens of a tropical night. Love, lust, rapture, awe. Jim feels wobbly and weak as if on the ledge of a skyscraper looking down at the street below. He aches to know her, all of her, to know the magnificence and mystery of Rebecca Reinhardt. It's his "raison d'etre," yet he realizes he can never fully explore her inner universe, nor comprehend the love that rules it, not in a thousand eternities.

"Dog & Butterfly" by *Heart* plays softly on the radio. Becki closes her eyes as if meditating. Labored breathing, flushed cheeks, but no movement. Drunk with wonder, Jim devours her with his eyes, his heart, his spirit—as she devours his malehood with her young womanly body. What makes him love her so? What draws him to this utterly ordinary girl who to most has more detractive traits that attractive ones? Is it the unspeakable majesty of her secret self, or is it his love that crowns her a princess? He suspects the former, yet only a few, perhaps only he, have eyes to behold her hidden beauty—and the keys and the chemistry to open her door. Spiritual Becki, so beyond the carnal, so beyond male-female, yet there can be no entry to her heaven save through the swollen flower of her womanhood, save through the deep throat of her dark underneath. To truly find Rebecca Reinhardt, you must love her in wildness, in Eros, in the whole truth.

Jim looks down at the curly pelts of pubic hair that darkly shroud their pulsing union, hazel brown meshed into burnt umber, hers darker than his. The sight stirs him and stirs him; his penis screams for permission to thrust, to fuck her. But he refrains.

A long minute passes. The throbbing between them grows and grows—"Oh, I *can't!*" Becki gasps. She rocks urgently back & forth. It takes her no more than ten seconds—she gives an ecstatic cry, stiffens, and slumps panting upon Jim. But he holds back.

A minute or so later, upon getting her second wind, she leads him to the bed where she gets on her hands and knees, lifts her imaginary tail, and offers her cunt like a horse in heat. Her pussy is so swollen and open and lubricated that it looks like it's turned inside out. Jim pumps her like a stallion fucking a wild mare; her bucking ass brutalizes his belly. Becki takes longer this time— fighting the fire to prolong her pleasure—but when she finally comes, she arches her back so violently he fears it will snap, but Jim still postpones his own climax.

Now to the shower where he finally lets loose with the help of Becki's hand—and lips. "Oh, *Shan*ley, I've been wanting to suck you since Sunday night!" she exclaims, pulling back just as he shoots his load into the tub. "Oh, I love to watch a man come. I love how it fires out in stringy spurts and how your cock is so thick and hot, and how you come out of the same hole you pee out of. It's a*maz*ing. I love it! I love your hard cock! It's God! It's God! It's my

God. It's gotta be ... because it excites me more than *anything*. I wanna love it, and serve it, and worship it. I wanna hold it and eat it, and fuck it forever. I love to see it come."

Lust, lust, love, and lust. Hearts on fire. Wanting, wanting, years of wanting all of each other. Growing, growing, long unsated, long denied—except for March of '84 which only made the wanting more—growing, growing, until finally exploding in two days of orgasmic fireworks. Once, twice, three times—not enough. Night, day, night, day. Shrieks of relief, melting sweetness. Each act of copulation lasts but minutes, each climax, but seconds, yet the aftershocks and aftershudders swirl inside them all day, all night, and fresh lust stirs at the slightest touch or tease.

Coming, coming, coming out. Father, farther, they ache out together, wretching out their deepest caves of self, drinking to the dregs the red wine of passion that gushes like hot blood from the dark side of the soul. Yet only this wine can free their spirits to love and snuggle without fear on the white side of their being.

Happy lovers in the shower. Jim and Becki soap and admire each other. He washes her breasts and bulgy midriff while she plays with his penis as it deflates underneath his potbelly and pudgy pubis. "Oh, Jimmy, it's so cute when it's little and floppy. I always wanted one." They stay in the shower until the hot water runs out. Their skin is lobster red. The bathroom is steamier than a sauna.

Becki gets out and dries herself with a brown towel. But Jim remains in the tub, hands on hips. He watches her. He adores her. Becki, Becki. He's addicted to her naked flesh, especially from her waist down. All women have cunts, with lips and clits and pubes, but no two look alike. Becki's is unique with its own peculiar folds and features and hair, like a second face, and Jim now knows it as well as her first one, her pouty one. Her pussy will forever stand out in a crowd.

Yet, as she dries, he senses a mystique about her that goes beyond genitals, hips, and tits. To him, Becki is God's greatest creation, a poetic work of art even down to her girlish toes. He loves how her pretty neck is more slender than a man's, how her collarbones are shorter and less curved, how her shoulders are gently rounded, not square, how her arms and wrists and hands are graceful and swanlike, how her waist curves in despite her cute paunch and her waistline is above her navel instead of below it. He loves how her flank fat conceals the crests of her hips, how her chunky thighs take an oblique course inward to her knees, how her calves are nubily curved, her ankles, rounded and fluid, how her small feet are almost as graceful as her hands, and how her body is so smooth and hairless compared to a man. Solomon describes her well—at least, Jim thinks so:

> Behold, thou are fair, my love ... Thou hast doves' eyes within thy locks ... Thy lips are like a thread of scarlet ... Thou art beautiful, O my love, as Tirzah, comely as Jerusalem, terrible as an army with banners ... O prince's daughter! The joints of thy thighs are like jewels, the work of the hands of a cunning workman. Thy navel is like a round goblet, which wanteth not liquor; thy belly is like a heap of wheat set about with lilies. Thy two breasts are like two young roes that are twins ... thine eyes, like the fishpools in Heshbon ... the fragrance of thy breath, like apples, and the roof of thy mouth, like the best wine.

\* \* \*

Becki gives Jim a peck on the cheek. "I'm glad you shaved," she says, grinning happily. "I like your face when it's smooth and smells of Old Spice."

She then kicks up her heels and romps ahead of Jim, rollicking, frolicking, wagging her head, swinging her arms, swiveling her moonish hips: an adult version of her old happy-girl *ENERGIZER* quickstep.

Joy, joy: Jim exults as he watches this wonderfully endearing Becki-routine. He loves her romping exuberance. He loves to see her happy childlike heart bursting forth—spirited, flying, free from adult fetters.

Reaching the top of the hill, Becki waits for Jim. He gathers her into his arms. Warm, warm—heaven. They hug, they kiss, they sport, they laugh. Finally, they continue walking, southward toward the woods, toward the opening in the rock fence.

The wet meadow grass soaks their sneakers and the cuffs of their jeans. Not cold but cool. They're both wearing jackets against the chilly dampness. The sun shines in their hearts but the sky above Hadley Hill is low and dark and full of gray scud. Fog obscures the Worcester Hills. The murky afternoon mutes the fall colors as if an artist has scumbled them over with washes of gray and purple.

Jim and Rebecca, gladhearted and carefree, coo and tease as lovers do when all things are new and magical. Hand in hand, they pass through the stone wall and head down the path into the woods. The rain has given way to a light drizzle but the woods are still wet. *Drip-drip, drip-drip.* The trees shed their water slowly like thousands of leaky faucets. The path is soft with sodden leaves and pine needles.

"Oh look, Jimmy," Becki says as she spies a chipmunk. It sits cutely on its hind legs and chirps like a bird. They crouch and watch the little critter for some time.

Out of the woods and across the old railroad ravine. They descend to the gravel beach. A gray gloom shrouds the reservoir but it cannot dispel the sunny aura about Jim and Becki; they're living at the end of the rainbow.

A flotilla of mallard ducks swims out from the cattails. The females are tawny brown and mottled. The males have shiny green heads. As the ducks swim out toward deeper water, Becki laughs and calls to them as if they're pets. In the calm water near the cattails, she spots a water strider and they watch it as it scurries about dimpling but not breaking the skin of the water. Finally, they cuddle close and gaze out over the lake. Further out, a breath of wind whispers across the water blowing black ripples gently toward the shoreline. Fog, mist, cushioning silence.

Tuesday afternoon, late, almost evening. Together forty-eight hours—and Jim and Becki's honeymoon bliss has increased with each passing hour, as if angels have been escorting them from one romantic experience to the next. Unspeakable joy. Jim is happier than at any time in his life. Life, life, new life; all is new; it doesn't seem like Earth life at all.

A verse from 2nd Corinthians comes into his mind, *If any man be in Christ, he is a new creation; old things are passed away; behold all things are become new.* He's not sure if they're "in Christ" or "out of Christ" but things have certainly "become new," as if he and Becki have hatched out of an egg into a new world.

The honking of geese breaks the silence. After circling over-head, the large birds splash down out beyond the mallards. As Jim watches the geese bobbing in the misty fog, he thinks about the future, his thoughts shifting from the blissful memories of the past two days. A slight tremor of unease slips over his joy like a small cloud slipping over the moon, *Everybody's coming back tonight. What's it gonna be like for me and Becki after being alone like this? Life is always changing.*

As if sensing his thoughts, Rebecca looks up. Jim cups her chin and searches her upturned face. He sees nothing but peace and gladness; her blue eyes brim with affection. No words. She just smiles sweetly and snuggles into his breast. He kisses her hair tenderly. He caresses and pets her back. He feels her shoulder blades through her jacket. The tremor of unease disappears as quickly as it came, leaving nothing but soft still happiness.

# Chapter Forty-four

"**H**oney, I'm goin' inside," Becki says to Jim. "It's getting cold out here. The wind's starting to blow."

"Okeydoke," Jim replies. "I'll be there in a minute."

"Don't be long," she reminds in wifely fashion. "Jodi's making popcorn and cider for all of us." With a springy bounce, Becki hustles up the walk and into the house. Her khaki parka looks yellow under the porch light. The storm door does not latch and the wind blows it open with a screak.

Monday, November 12, 1990. Jim is standing in the driveway at 59 Front Street. He and Rebecca have just returned from a brisk walk in the meadow. The gathering in the barn has ended. Everyone has departed save for the house regulars who've moved from the barn to Jodi's apartment. Above the house a fishy piece of moon scuttles along among the clouds. After a mild October which continued into November, the weather has finally turned. The branches of the oak tree heave to and fro in the gusty north wind.

*Sixty people in the barn tonight,* Jim says to himself as he pulls his jacket around him, *and fifty in Lawrence last Tuesday, five times more than our first trip, and tomorrow night we're going to North Adams. Things are really perking.*

October, November. Lowell, Fitchburg, Pittsfield, Springfield, Boston, Lawrence. The band plays in the barn on Mondays and travels on Tuesdays. Becki shares her story after the concerts. Her remarks are never eloquent and never more than ten minutes, but her words—as well as her presence—cut right to the heart making the music and message of *59 Front Street* come alive.

Disenchanted LBI'ers: cocoons of kindred spirits have formed throughout New England, in every town where Logan has a branch church. This growing response to Jim's heartbeat is shaking up Nashua and the Blantyre inner circle. Dr. Logan condemns *59 Front Street* in every sermon, at every staff meeting, calling them, "Hippies and whoremongers and agents of Anti-christ."

Tom Hudson, Stan Campbell, and all the LBI branch pastors echo Dr. Logan's attacks. Yet the more Logan rants, the more the "heart revolution" grows. To add insult to his infuriation, Logan's wife and daughter-in-law have joined Jim's renegade ministry. Now living off-campus in a Nashua apartment, Amy and Tricia work secretly with Mary Beth and their many LBI contacts to arrange concerts for the band and to distribute tapes and videos throughout LBI. They also come to Brendon Falls on Monday nights, usually leading a caravan as more and more LBI students come to check out *59 Front Street*. Rich Beckman sends spies along to take names, and he also collects the names of the LBI branch members who attend Jim's road concerts. As a result, many students are being suspended, and many branch members are being admonished, some blacklisted, which only stokes the fire.

Stan Campbell gave Doris an ultimatum to stop attending the barn concerts or to "get outa my house." So Doris left. Janet Buford broke up with Barry under similar circumstances. She and Doris have taken up temporary residence downstairs from Harry and Judy on Mill Street. They bring carloads of local people to Hadley Hill each week: Harry, Judy, T. Willy, Slick, David Myszak, Nina R., Freddie B., and many others. There's also a sizable young-adult contingent, Haley and Billy's friends (used-to-be teenage townies, now in their 20s) whom Jim had befriended back in the early '80s. Melissa Baker also comes and brings local LBI'ers from BFBC. Melissa is still with Carl, but he rails at her, calling her a traitor.

The main conflict rages within LBI, but other Bible churches are also attacking Jim's music ministry as some of their members join the movement. Locally, a half dozen come from Valley Baptist, mainly friends of Angie and Sylvia and Herschel. A few radio talk shows have invited Jim to tell his story, so far, stations in Nashua, Lowell, and Lawrence. The talk-show hosts are interested in the music, the libertarian vision, and Jim's stand against Logan, but most callers are enraged evangelicals who condemn Jim and his band as sinners and heretics and blasphemers. Once aware of the *59 Front Street* ministry, people either love it or hate it.

The LBI empire is hardly in danger of toppling, but as autumn turns toward winter, it appears that Joe Lareux's vision is coming to pass. Jim Shanley's house of poets and musicians and lovers is growing into a '60s-style movement as they lift up the banners of love, liberty, and honest intimacy. Logan still outnumbers them twenty to one but their dream of a "love revolution" no longer seems crazy or quixotic. In fact, on this blustery November night, Jim sees anything as possible. Perhaps in due season, they'll actually take Logan's fangs away, or even change the whole world. Why not? Rebecca has come back—against all odds.

* * *

Jim pours hot coffee into a styrofoam cup; a plume of steam rises. Sugar, milk. He stirs with a plastic spoon. Chips, dip, cheese and crackers, cider, soda, a six-pack of Bud Dry. Jodi has more than popcorn on her kitchen table. Now comes the toasty-buttery aroma of fresh-baked cookies—it's Angela with a platter and a teasing quip, "Okay, Jim, control yourself. I know you like chocolate chip cookies better than sex."

"I don't remember eating cookies with you, Angie?"

"Oh, I know," she replies, giving him a sporty smirk. "But Becki, she tells me all about you." They both laugh then he gives her a quick hug and a playful tickle to her ribs. She giggles, twists away, and escapes to the living room. Jim grabs a handful of her cookies and follows.

The gathering is a far cry from Logan's afterservice rap sessions. The house regulars sit and sprawl about in blue jeans, faded cords, stocking feet, sneakers, sweat shirts, and sweaters, amid an assortment of jackets, coats, and boots, all tossed about. The room smells of popcorn, perfume, beer, and cigarettes, even faintly of Mrs. Courtney's honeysuckle-scented air fresheners—though they've been gone for years. Haley sits next to Billy on the large braided rug. Tobacco smoke circles her strawberry hair like the rings of Saturn. On the sofa behind Haley, Jodi is also puffing a Winston. Tony, feet up, boots off, lies lengthwise, his head on Jodi's lap; he reminds Jim of a mocha-colored porpoise. Cider in hand, Joe and Brenda sit on the adjacent sofa while Angie and Herschel and Calvin McClusky lounge on the floor opposite Billy and Haley. Russ and Sylvia sit in folding chairs in front of the boarded-up fireplace. No Becki. But Jodi informs Jim that Becki and Cathy just carried Chad back to bed, that the little fellow fell asleep on the rug. Jim settles onto the floor next to Russ's chair.

The eleven o'clock news is going on the television. Channel five, Chet Curtis: "Secretary of Defense, Dick Cheney, confirmed today that President Bush will be sending an additional 200,000 troops to Saudia Arabia...."

"I can't believe it," Jodi remarks as she picks up an ashtray from the coffee table and mashes out her cigarette. "Fuckin' Bush is actually serious about goin' to war, but nobody's attacked us? This is all over oil and money."

"Well, it's better to stop Saddam over there than to fight him over here," Calvin rebuts, hugging his knees. "Remember what happened with Hitler?" During his six months with the group, and with Cathy, Cal's self-confidence has increased markedly. No longer a sheepish hayseed, he shares his feelings openly. Recovered from alcohol, he works at Prescott again—part-time. He still lives with his parents but comes over every day.

"I can't stand the thought," Sylvia says, tossing her head and brushing the air with her hand. "I think war's insane. I just think of innocent kids getting bombed and burned up." As she talks, her long hair spills over the side of her face; she pushes it back.

Now comes Tony's tubalike voice, "I think we should assassinate the motherfucker. Saddam is ruthless. He gassed his own people and he's making a nuke and—"

"But war's a fuckin' waste," Haley cuts in, a wooly plume of smoke accompanying her words. "It's just a macho thing."

Jim munches a cookie and drinks his coffee. He listens but says nothing. The standoff between George Bush and Saddam Hussein is hardly a high priority in his mind.

Rebecca's been back for five weeks. The honeymoon is over, then again it isn't. The sexual firestorm has calmed a bit. Sometimes they even skip a day, three when she had her period. Not that desire has diminished—on the contrary, their carnal excitement is renewed with each coupling, often hitting new peaks of fulfillment as they get to know each other's sexuality better and better. But no pair of mortal bodies could keep up the torrid pace of Columbus Day Weekend. Besides, they're both busy with the band and the everyday responsibilities of life.

Nonetheless, the return of their housemates has not dampened the joy of loving and discovering each other. Jim and Becki still spend a lot of time alone together, watching TV, watching movies, going out to eat, taking walks. Becki loves the woods more than ever, and the lake and the river and the chipmunks and the ducks. And on many afternoons, they escape to their bed to cuddle in the brownboy. Jim's life is now so beautiful and different, he feels like a butterfly after six years as a caterpillar.

Elation, exhilaration, action, fatigue. Sweet peace, silent emotion, clash of wills, but never of heart. Becki no longer hides her feelings—affection, anger, or anything in between. The wall of fear is gone and she no longer withdraws and sulks down like a turtle, but her moods are still erratic, her temper hot, her complaints fierce. She goes from teasing to laughing spells, from angry outbursts to crying, from pensive reflection to times of tenderness—and when lust stirs, she loves to be the aggressor.

All of Jim's previous times with Becki only gave him a hint of her pervading and consuming presence. Sometimes she needs to be held like a little girl, but she also needs space and independence for her own projects. Sometimes she takes off shopping with Jodi or Angie, or spends time visiting around the house with Brenda or Joe or Haley or whomever. She spends a lot of time with Cathy and has become attached to little Chad. Becki takes him for walks and brings him up for milk and cookies. And she often babysits Chad when Cathy's at work or out with Calvin. The fact that Cathy has been in Jim's bed doesn't seem to threaten Becki.

Jim hardly recognizes the apartment, as Rebecca's rat-nest

decor is back in full force. Clothes, books, boxes, bags. Boots, sneakers, knickknacks, stuffed animals. Pictures, plants, but no posters. She gave Randy most of her furniture, but her sofa bed and green chair are back, along with her stereo and a new dresser.

Choked, crowded. Jim feels like he's living in a garage sale but he cherishes the orderly clutter for it immerses him in beautiful "Beckiness." He loves seeing her tangle of clothes on the green chair, her feminine toiletries in the bathroom, the jumble of jars and tubes on her dresser, her panties and bras in the laundry—her underwear mixed with his. Hallelujah! He loves smelling her perfumes and powders and scented soaps. He loves watching her walk around the apartment in her underpants, her big round butt shaking, jiggling with each step. Her ass, her ass. Becki's ass. Seeing it, loving it, fucking it. That's the proof, the crowning testimony that she's *with* him—living with him like a wife.

After six years of dreaming, Jim drowns daily in the glory of discovering her: her personality, her psyche, her private routines and habits she's formed from a child, those singular and intimate patterns of her personal life that make her uniquely "Becki." She's likewise learning about his most private ways and habits. Idiosyncrasies, eccentricities—distinctive strands of raw life, different, diverse, some beautiful and pleasing, some vulgar and disgusting, strands which clash and contradict in false relationships, but in the magic of true love, twine together to form one rope.

Becki loves to snuggle after sex and to have long pillow talks, but when ready for serious sleep, she anchors her ass in the center of the bed and curls away from Jim. She never wears panties under her nightgown unless she has her period. She also has pink shorty pajamas but they often spend the night on the floor—she rarely puts them back on after lovemaking. She never snores but her breathing is always noticeable because she breathes through her mouth and drools.

She wakes up with sleep in her eyes, a frown on her face, and a frog in her throat, and her morning breath is like a sour Santa Ana wind. Once out of bed, she goes to her dresser for a few quick strokes with her hairbrush and a check of her pouty face, then she plods sleepily to the bathroom. Shy and modest, she dresses in the corner by the closet with her back to Jim—in stark contrast to her uninhibited display of flesh when sexually aroused. She rarely smiles or says much until after her first cup of coffee, at which point her mood can go in any direction. She likes having the radio on or a tape playing but never before coffee. She prefers long bubble baths, but she usually settles for a quick shower. She hates any deadline that does not originate with her and grumbles about it even if they're just going out to eat. She rarely wears a dress or even a skirt and when she does, she complains about the hassle. Jim wonders how she kept her sanity as an LBI missionary wife, with the impossible schedules and dress codes.

"That's for sure," Jodi says, gesturing with a can of beer as the discussion of the Gulf crisis continues. "Bush has to prove he has balls like he's fuckin' *Ram*bo but it won't be Bush dying for oil in the desert—or his kids. The rich have no great risk. Our army's made up of poor people, and those that come back will be messed up for life. War fucks people up ... like what Vietnam *did* to Kyle."

"You got that right," Herschel agrees, scrubbing his knuckles into his tightly kinked cap of Negro hair. "And Blacks are bearin' the burden. We'll be doin' the fightin' while the rich *hon*kies and the *A*-rabs sit back and watch."

Tony gives a ponderous laugh. "Don't gimme that shit, Professor. I doubt there'll be much fighting. If we attack, Saddam's soldiers will run all the way back to Bagdad. But as for brothers bearing the burden, you know the army's done more for Blacks than *any*body. Just look at Colin Powell. He started out just like you, in the streets of Newark, and—"

"Yeah; just think, Hersh," Angie interjects teasingly. "If you'd joined the army, you'd be *famous* instead of running morning shift at McDonald's."

Everyone laughs, including Jim, though he's still thinking about Becki—Becki, Becki; oh, Becki. So puppyish, so poignant, so adorable, yet volatile, unpredictable, and at times, impossibly petulant and stubborn. No one can possess her tempestuous spirit. Constrained by love and want, she gladly intertwines her body, her soul, her life with Jim's, but she's never deeded herself to him as property. She doesn't mind domestic chores: shopping, cooking, laundry, taking care of the apartment. For that matter, she likes caring for Jim and doing special things, like baking cookies to have as a treat during a movie—that is, until he asks her to do something in a tone that suggests it's her duty: "I'm not your *damn* maid, Shanley; how the fuck did you live six years by yourself?"

Becki bristles against any infringement of her sovereignty, against any curb of her freedom. Jim often fights her stiff-necked independence. But in truth, he loves her feral spirit, her unsubmitted womanhood, for it's her allegiance to her own instincts, to her own passions, together with her rebellious nature, that ultimately brought her back to him—and makes her different from Randy, from Alison, from Katie, from Barry B., from Carl Baker, from all of Logan's sycophants. Rebecca is a living expression of Jim's own heartbeat. To know Becki Lea is to know the hope of his house, his band, his "heart revolution."

Yet, paradoxically, she thinks nothing of bossing Jim, not in a high-handed fashion, but in little "wifely" ways: "Come *on,* Jimmy, you've been on the phone all day and I still have groceries in the car"—"Honey, I need you to hang these pictures"—"Jimmy, would you please stop clipping your mustache in the sink. Your bristly hairs are all over. They're dis*gust*ing"—"Honey, I think Joe's wrong. You should tell him. I think we should sing 'Weep O Angels' in Lowell and show our new video too"—"You must call Heather; it's her birthday"—"Shanley, clean up these wood chips. You make a mess every time you load that stove and I just va*cuumed* in here"—"I think Joe should listen to Angie more. After all, she *is* a trained musician. You should stand up for her, Jimmy"—"Let's not go to Cobleskill this weekend"— "Tell Billy he spilled trash in front of our door and I had to clean it up."

Becki boldly refers to Jim's oil checks as "our" money as if the checks are gifts from God to both of them, which in a way they are. She talks about getting a job but never seriously, and Jim never pushes. Truth is, he's glad she doesn't have to work; he wants her with him as much as possible, despite the craziness. Besides, she has a frugal Alison-missionary mentality when it comes to spending. She still saves grocery coupons, for example.

Though she despises orders, even subtle ones, she pours her soul into any task she sets out to do. She works as hard as anyone in the house. Not only does she take care of Jim and the apartment— she's a better-than-average cook when she takes the time, though more often than not she pops something into the microwave—but she also helps Jodi with the laundry and Haley in the hallway. She even helps Joe and Tony with the outside chores, not to mention the hours she spends doing ministry tasks.

When it comes to the band, Becki does anything and everything, except play or sing. She helps set up in the barn, on the road. She helps Jodi and Tony at the mixer board, mixing and adjusting sound levels. She drives the van; she drives the Tempo. She helps Jodi and Angie with refreshments for the barn crowd. She helps Tony and Joe send out tapes and videos. She works with Russ maintaining address files and making coordination calls to Amy Logan and Tricia. She talks secretly with her sister Katie and with Mary Beth Hudson, gleaning intelligence information on Logan's battle strategy. After the showdown at 59 Front Street, Logan told Matt Garrett to fire Katie for gossiping but Garrett, in his masterful way, smoothed things over. Katie, of course, is not crazy about her sister's involvement with Jim or the *59 Front Street* ministry but she is wholeheartedly supportive of Matt Garrett and he seems much more tolerant of Jim's renegade band than Logan.

Back to Jodi's living room. A question from Billy M. draws Jim out of his thoughts into the ongoing discussion. "Whaddeya think, Jim? Is this Iraq thing the beginning of the end that the Bible talks about? Is it the beginning of Armageddon?" Billy gives a curious smirk. His half-twisted mouth and curious eyes peering through his Poindexter glasses remind Jim of how he used to look when he'd ask questions back in Flanagan's parking lot.

"Well, the Bible says a lot about a lot of things, Billy," Jim replies to the question. "But I'm not sure how to interpret much of it, or how true it is, particularly when it comes to tying prophetic scripture to current events ... but it seems like something big has to happen sooner or later."

Billy straightens his skinny grasshopper legs as if they're asleep. "Well, the book of Revelation says the final war's gonna be in the Middle East ... you know, the showdown with the devil and the second coming of Christ, and his kingdom?"

Jim eats his last cookie, washes it down with coffee. He gestures toward Billy with his styrofoam cup. "Very true; and Daniel and Isaiah also speak of a final war and disasters, and a coming kingdom, and Jesus preaches about it too. But it's not just the Bible that talks about calamity and upheaval on the earth. Everybody's talking about it: Christians and Jews and Eastern gurus, and astrologers and New Agers, even the Hopi Indians ... and scientists and economists, and of course, Nostradamus. They all talk about a catastrophic change coming. Babylon's so *top*-heavy with wealth and so propped up with propaganda, and uh—well, who knows, maybe we're part of the change? Who the fuck can say? I *sure* can't. I just hope good things keep happening to us."

"We have to *nail* Saddam," Calvin reiterates. "If we hit him hard now, we can stop Armageddon. We must destroy his nerve gas and his military machine, and stop him from making atomic bombs. Then we'll have peace."

Brenda gives a sleepy disgusted sigh as she sits close to Joe, her head resting on his shoulder. "I get sick of hearing about it," she says. "Let's change the subject."

"If I was president," Russ remarks. "I'd keep it simple. Either do nothing or drop a nuke on Saddam's palace. Anything in between and we'll get another fucking Vietnam." Russ leans back and locks his hands behind his head. "But Bush talks about good and evil, like kicking Saddam's ass is a crusade for God. Fuck *that*. Wars are fought to preserve wealth and power, whether it's squeaky clean presidents like Bush or ruthless dictators like Saddam ... but like Brenda says, it's not worth talking about. It has nothing to do with love. We don't make the headlines, but what we're doing is far more important. At least, I think so. People on this earth are starving for love, for someone to be with, to live with, to talk to, to sleep with. What we're doing is beyond money and political power. Touching hearts, exposing Logan ... this is the Armageddon I care about. And Logan and Garrett and Beckman, they're worse than fucking Saddam, if you ask me."

On the TV, the news is over and Dick Albert is talking about the colder air coming in. Jodi picks up the remote and zaps off the television. The debate about Iraq and Bush and Armageddon disintegrates into numerous smaller conversations.

*It's not what we talk about,* Jim says to himself as he crumples his empty styrofoam cup and tosses it into a trash basket which sits on the hearth in front of the plugged fireplace, *but that we share our feelings without fear of rejection. That's what makes us different. Logan's crowd of evangelical brown-nosers would never dare to make anti-Bush statements or*—Jim abruptly loses his train of thought as Cathy R. comes into the living room and plops down next to Calvin. *Where the fuck is*—a flushing toilet answers his thought before he completes it.

A few seconds later, Becki comes in and sits down in front of Jim. She extends and crosses her corduroy-clad legs and leans back into him as he wraps his arms about her. Her knit shirt is open at the top giving him a good view of her white bunnylike breasts as they nestle inside her bra. He inhales her lilac-scented shampoo. He tunes out of the room and into Rebecca, *O God, I love her more than ever. She turns me on more than ever—and now she lives with me and sleeps with me. This is too good to be true but it keeps happening and happening.*

Finally unfettered and united in purpose, Jim's heart and mind and body are now devoted to loving and satisfying and discovering Becki. No longer a torment, his love constrains him, propels him, inspires him. His joy derives from hers. He's dreamed of making her happy like a little girl—now he has. He's dreamed of wrapping her up in the strength of his malehood—now he has. He's dreamed of arousing and satisfying her wanton side, of meeting and mating the wild woman within—now he has. He's dreamed of seeing the majesty of her liberated female soul—now he has. He's dreamed of living with her, of having her like a wife—now he has. No guilt, no shame, no taboos. Jim and Becki are getting to know the miracle of being truly human and truly in love—and that you can never experience one without the other.

Jim's mind, like an anchored rowboat rocking on gentle waves, rolls back and forth lullingly as he enjoys the sweet peace of Becki's presence. The others come through in jumbled bits and pieces: "Which tire?"—"We're not against the family"—"He cut you back 'cause you won't work on Tuesday?"—"Aunt Verna says we're a cult"—"Right rear. We have to replace it"—"Ever'body needs a family but it has to be real"—"I hated California"—"She says I'm *brain*washed"—"Maybe, but Bob doesn't like me either"—"No, the red mike"—"Sex is more than penis and vagina"—"No, Chad's got an upset stomach"—"I used to pray to God, but He never talked back"—"I couldn't stand my mom's *boy*friend. He's a fuckin' sonavabitch"—"It cut out twice on Sylvia"—"He pigged out on chips 'n dip"—"Sex starts with the eyes"—"Logan's fuckin' insane"—"We're beatin' the van to death"—"A good mike costs sixty bucks"—"I still talk to God, but I don't call it prayer"—"Too rich for a six-year-old"—"We need *each other* more than answers"—"He hurls threats like Saddam Hussein"—"So, d'you pool your tips or what?"—"I never smoke it anymore"—"I feel it inside me. Maybe it *is* God"—"Frank's such an asshole"—"Fuck, I'm out of cigarettes"—"Things are crazy enough with Brenda"—"Jodi, lemme have a smoke"—"Look who's talkin'"—"Here, hand me my guitar."

Jim feels drowsy near to dozing. The confusion of voices diminishes until he hears nothing but Rebecca's breathing. Soothing color floods his mind: shades of blue and green, water and pine trees and sky. Softly floating, he lets go of time and drifts away on the lapping waves. Next thing he knows, Joe is playing his guitar and Sylvia is singing:

> ... over and over, and I can't believe it's true. A life almost forgotten can still shine through. The dying embers are fading, but hope still lights my eyes. I can only sit here waiting. Will love arrive? I see the eagle he flies. He soars so freely, in the sky. I see my wings, they are tied. My life without love, it will die. Lay low, lay low, my sweet child. Over and over I've walked through this space and time, all so long, scraping and clawing, the wall is unyielding....

Everyone is now on the floor, gathered closely together on the braided rug in front of Joe as he sits between Brenda and Sylvia. They normally do this song with amplifiers and the whole band, but the chords on the acoustic seem to perfectly match the music in Jim's heart. Sylvia's soulful voice draws everybody into the song and into each other. Becki lies back into Jim's breast as if part of him, and he feels the others as well—Haley's thigh, Billy's elbow, Cathy's shoulder, Calvin's knee, and Jodi's foot behind him. They're all huddled close and touching, hearts, minds, and bodies, as if they're in a small life raft cast upon a tranquil sea.

Sylvia pauses but Joe continues to play—softly. He speaks in a tender voice, "There's a child inside each of us. At first, she rocks to sleep in Mommy's arms. She knows only love and warmth. She is congratulated when she goos or smiles or when she wiggles her little arms. And when she says her first words, she is wonderful. When family and friends see her discovering her body, her fingers, her toes, her tummy, she is beautiful, and when she cries, her tears are loved away ... and Mommy and Daddy often bring her into their bed. But as she grows older, she sleeps alone with no arms to hold her. Instead, she cuddles her teddy at night. Family, friends, and others no longer give her favorable attention, unless she does well in school, in sports, at church, at her part-time job, unless she's well-dressed and fixed up pretty, unless she behaves and says the right things. Though she aches to follow the light within her, society pushes her onto the treadmill of life and in her innocence she trusts and marches away to the drumbeat of adulthood."

As they all listen to Joe's words, love binds them together like atoms in a molecule with Jim and Becki as one atom. Adult differences and defenses melt away. Hearts are full and near to breaking. The feeling is warm and heavenly yet sensual as if they're moving toward group sex, yet it's somehow beyond the physical like an experience from another realm. Joe's eyes brim. He sighs above the sound of his guitar then finishes the story, "There's no longer any recognition for the child within. When she speaks from her soul, she's counseled to calm down. Her body is no longer beautiful since it gives rise to feelings that interfere with the death of the heart. She is told to control her emotions so she can succeed and do well in life. Now when she cries, she cries alone. There are no arms to love her tears away. She has to be strong. She must ignore the soft whimpers of the child within. She must conform to what is expected of adults ... but the child does not die. That's the *good* news. And to me, it's the *gospel* of Christ. 'I can't believe it's true. A life almost'"—Joe sings. Sylvia joins him:

> —forgotten can still shine through. The dying embers are fading, but hope still lights my eyes. I can only sit here waiting. Will love arrive? I see the eagle he flies. He soars so freely, in the sky. I see my wings, they are tied. My life without love, it will die.... Lay low, lay low, my sweet child....

Closer, closer, kindred hearts draw closer, touching, knitting, *feeling* each other. Singing, singing, spirit, soul, and body. No fearful exhortation to "get right," to improve, to change; no call to arms; no call to rally around a flag, a cause, a plan. Jim and his cohorts can never fight uphill again. They can do nothing except to let go, to *be* who they were born to *be*—which is the only *true* liberty. Their closeness does not derive from doctrinal agreement or allegiance to a charismatic leader but from a yearning to discover and share the child within, a child who is glorious, not depraved or "fallen." If the child is "born in sin" as orthodoxy declares, they have no hope. But as Joe and Sylvia sing, hope seems near. The dream seems to be coming true. A feeling of brokenness, compassion, and overflowing affection wells up inside Jim's bosom, *No wonder Jesus said, "Except you be converted, and become as little children, ye shall not enter into the kingdom of heaven." I've always known it, but now it seems so simple, so clear. Conversion has nothing to do with changing or attaining or confessing sin. It simply means to free the child within.*

Coming, coming, coming together. Lovers, housemates, kindred souls, Adam and Eve. Everyone in Jodi's living room has become *one* person, "one child," innocent, needy, playful, trusting, vulnerable—constrained only by love. Jim's heart rejoices, his eyes fill. Overwhelmed with love and elation, he senses Becki rising with him, and in him. Touching, feeling, everyone in the room seems to rise as one into an orgasm of heart, higher, higher—*whoosh!* They break; they weep unashamedly. They hug and hold each other; they give whimpers of sheer happiness.

Not a stitch of clothing is shed, not a word is said, but they express love to each other beyond any spoken language. Time stands still, then bows in awe.

* * *

12:55 a.m. The apartment is dark save for a narrow crack of bathroom light. The north wind whistles, rattling the storm windows. Though it's still autumn, the sounds of winter surround Jim and Becki as they cuddle close under the bedcovers, immersed in the cozy fragrances of clean sheets and toothpaste, and soft flannel and face cream. Jim can just see Becki's eyes; they are deep and dark and full of soul.

"Oh, Shanley," she whispers, "that was *so* beautiful, what happened downstairs. I never felt so ... well, it's like our hearts were knit and we all felt it and nobody was ashamed. I never cry in front of people, but tonight it was so right, like how Christians are supposed to feel at church, but I never did, not once."

Cupid lips, cute and full. He gives Becki an affectionate peck on the side of her mouth; she smiles. Love, love, bountiful love. Waves of love rush out of Jim's heart flooding his bosom. He starts to speak but before he can, she asks a question, "Honey, d'you think this might be the beginning of the kingdom of love that Jesus talks about?" Her question is like the one Billy asked earlier but from a different perspective. "You know, what people have longed for all through the ages: a coming together of all hearts that will end war and greed and money-power, and will bring peace and love to the earth, like the wolf dwelling with the lamb in the book of Isaiah? It seems like something's going on. Love is happening all over, with you 'n me, and here at the house, and wherever we go to play. It's like hearts are coming out. I never believed in happy endings, but now it seems possible."

Jim sighs with happiness. He looks at Becki adoringly. "Oh, Becki Lea, you're such a tender flower. I love you so, beyond all words." He hugs her to him, so tightly that she squeals with delight. He feels a current of warm joy flowing from her flannel-clad flesh into his. He whispers into her sweet-scented hair, "I don't know if this is the kingdom of God happening, if what Jesus spoke about is coming to pass. I just don't know. God is such a mystery, and the future's impossible to predict. But right now, things are moving and God seems good and kind, like the Love Goddess I've always talked about. If God truly is *love,* then it seems that love has to win over fear and guilt and money and wars and competition, and deceit and hatred and death. But whether this is it or not, I don't know."

Jim kisses Becki on the cheek, then goes on, "Perhaps in time, tomorrow, someday, the river of love that brought us together against all odds, and is freeing so many in New England, will flood the whole world? At least, that's my hope, honey, and I don't see any other hope for *us* or the human race. I feel like something big has got to happen, but I can't say when. We'll just have to wait and see. God's plan is so big and beyond ... and yet so inside of us."

"Sometimes when you talk gently to me," Rebecca responds, her voice breaking, "like right now, it makes me so happy I feel like I'm gonna cry."

Jim starts to reply, but before he can, he hears his soul speaking from her lips, "Oh, honey, I just want to tickle and tease and play with you every day and make you laugh and blush. I want to feel my heart beating in your bosom. I just want to get high on love and hug and flirt and fuck 'til we go crazy. I just want to feel your nakedness all over me. I want to live with you and laugh with you and have babies with you. I want to hear your voice loving me tenderly in our pillow talks—like right now. Oh, Shanley, *this* is my calling. *This* is Christ to me." Blissful feelings, loving words. They go on talking until the moaning of the wind lulls them to sleep.

\* \* \*

Crying, moaning, closer, closer. Frenzy, fire, hot vortex of desire. Becki whips her head violently. Clawing for completion, she digs her nails into Jim's neck. The bed shakes, the frame squeaks. Finally, with a stammering scream of rapture, they climax together. A cascading shudder shakes Becki's sweating body. She groans. She dismounts. She collapses onto her back beside Jim.

Panting, falling, floating, they drift down into a warm pulsing afterglow. Faint gray light gives shape to the east-facing window, signaling the approach of dawn. Open scratches burn Jim's shoulders, his neck, his back. "What the fuck got into you?" he asks breathlessly. "I feel like I've been mauled by a tiger?"

"Oh, Jimmy, O Jesus. Dream ... I-I, I had a—O God! Oh, honey, *what* a dream!" Becki is breathless and euphoric as if she just snorted two lines of cocaine and ran to the woods and back.

"So that's it? You just woke out of a wet dream, and finished it on me?"

He playfully squeezes her chunky thigh—it feels hot and spongy like homemade bread just out of the oven—but she squirms away, pulling down her nightgown.

"Come on, Shanley," she protests between breaths as a hint of testiness tarnishes her elated state. "I'm not talking about a horny *fuck* dream ... like I used to have back at Bible school when I was trying to suppress my sex drive. This was more than lust and horny hormones coming out.... Oh, it was sexual all right, but this dream was different, *way* different."

"You mean like spiritual?" Jim asks.

No reply, just postorgasmic panting gradually relaxing into regular breathing. Finally, Becki says, "I gotta pee." Yawning, she heads to the bathroom.

Jim feels cold. He reaches for the bedcovers but they're hopelessly tangled at the foot of the bed and the brownboy is on the floor. So he gets up and puts on his pajama pants then lights a fire in the stove—the wood is already laid.

To the bathroom. He goes in as Becki comes out. Back to the bedroom. He rejoins her in the bed. They pull the brownboy over them and reassume their supine positions. For a time they watch the fire through the glass-windowed stove door as the eager flames dance and snap and pop, filling the room with the cozy aroma of pine kindling and hickory logs—certainly a more pleasant sensation than the clanking of a radiator.

Becki, after glancing over to make sure that Jim is sober-faced, responds to his question about her dream, beginning with a question of her own, "Honey, you know that painting of the rapture that shows everybody goin' up to heaven, with angels and clouds and all?"

"You mean the one in Priscilla's Chapel?"

"Yeah, that's the one, where everyone's going up into the clouds and Jesus is waiting." Becki lifts her hands and flutters her fingers as if they're people going up. "Well, in my dream we were in Jodi's living room and Sylvia was singing, and we started weeping and hugging, like last night, then all of a sudden, we were up in the clouds, way up in the sky, and we were filled with love and joy and gladness, like on our way to heaven, but—"

"But what?" Jim asks.

Becki sighs, then replies, "This angelic voice, a woman's voice, shouted, 'Yes! Yes! Yes!' She shouted real loud but her tone was friendly and kind, not harsh. The next thing I knew we were all cuddled inside this big warm cloud, like a giant sleeping bag except it wasn't dark. There was a cozy yellow glow sort of like firelight, sort of like how the stove looks right now, and we were snuggling together like newborn kittens, then uh ... we uh—"

"Go on; what happened?" Jim prods curiously.

"I can't describe it. My heart was overflowing with feeling. I just wanted to hug and kiss and cuddle everyone. It was spiritual but also fleshly. Our love was genuine and from the heart but also uninhibited and *so* sexual. I knew I was gonna come. But not just my body. It was like my whole being was gonna climax. The 'love high' was *over*whelming, more than I ever felt, and we all felt it together."

"You mean like an orgy?"

"Yeah, but it wasn't dirty or anything. We were naked but our bodies were different—no, not exactly different, but more beautiful. It was *so* right and perfect, and somehow you 'n I were coming again and again with each other, but at the same time our souls were making love with the others, like a guy with me and a girl with you, until we did it with everyone: Russ 'n Sylvia and Joe 'n Brenda, and Tony 'n Jodi and Cal 'n Cathy, all of 'em ... and you 'n I, we felt everything together like we had the same brain. The love feelings got stronger and stronger, and we went higher and higher, and we didn't get tired—O Jesus, it's be*yond* words!"

Becki, her face aglow with wonder, caresses the air with her hands as if she's caressing an invisible body, an invisible face. Her voice is filled with astonishment and awe. "And the music wasn't harps or hymns or religious shit. It was *ZZ Top*'s new song about Mississippi. It was raunchy and lustful, yet *so* heavenly, and we all moved to the beat like one body, like a giant worm wiggling. And we didn't hafta talk. It's like we all knew what everyone else was thinking, and we all were thinking thoughts of love and togetherness and giving to each other. We were like little kids. Nobody was jealous or afraid, and nobody felt sinful or guilty about hugging and kissing, and having sexual pleasure. And we weren't ashamed of our nakedness. It makes me tremble to talk about it. It was so different, so *wonder*ful and *glor*ious, like the heavenly love people talk about in near-death experiences. I never felt such love and joy and lust and ecstasy. It was *so* beautiful yet so erotic, and it grew and grew like an atomic bomb until I thought I was going to explode. Then I woke up."

"No wonder you went wild on me."

"Oh yeah, that was nice. But, O Jesus, my dream. It's like we can't get there by ourselves, Jimmy, not where we were in the clouds. Somehow we need the others."

They turn onto their sides with Becki facing away toward the window which is now a pink rectangle of predawn sky. Jim pulls her into him as they assume their usual butt-to-gut double-fetal position. "So you think we should have orgies?" he asks.

After adjusting her pillow, Becki sighs and settles as if thinking. "It wouldn't be the same," she answers after a long moment. "It was different in my dream. It's like we were immersed in liquid love. I could touch it and taste it and breathe it ... and nobody was nervous or self-conscious or scared. I can't describe it, except whatever we did, we did it together. We felt it together and nobody said, 'Don't do that,' and nobody got hurt or felt left out."

"So you think your dream is a foretaste of heaven?"

"I don't know," Becki replies, "but I sure hope so. Mom says there's no sex or boy-girl love in heaven and that's what Pastor teaches. I tried to believe it, but it made heaven seem like such a dry and dreary place. If love and romance and sex excite us the most and make us so happy, like the *great*est feeling on earth, it seems like God would have it in heaven, or it wouldn't be *heaven*?"

"I hope so too," Jim says. "It seems like the true body of Christ should be knit together with the most powerful passions that humans possess, as opposed to doctrines and church hierarchy."

"I uh—well, it sure was in my dream. It's like the love was sexual yet holy at the same time. It was *so* beautiful. I don't have words to describe it. Mom always said Jesus' love was high and pure while sexual love was a temporary thing, for marriage and having babies, and we had to control it because it was a fleshly passion. It made sense in a way, what she said about having one husband and having babies, and being a family and all that, but still,

I never liked it because it made me feel selfish and guilty for
wanting sexual pleasure, especially after I learned how to get an
orgasm in tenth grade. When I got horny, I didn't think about babies
or weddings or God. I fantasized about hunky guys and hard cocks
... wild sinful stuff that I could get off on. Then I'd feel ashamed
afterward like it was the worst sin of all, like God was disgusted and
offended. But if He made us this way, why would He condemn us
for wanting sex? And why would He kick it out of heaven? If He
created us as sexual creatures and we're his bride, then everybody
coming together sexually should be a glorious part of heaven, and
just as spiritual as hugging?"

Becki gives a delicious sigh. "Besides, how can sex be bad
when it feels *so fuckin'* good?" She snickers at her pun, and Jim too.

The eastern sky now blazes toward sunrise but the fire in the
stove has settled back to lazy flames. The bedroom is toasty warm.
For some time, Jim and Becki go on discussing her dream. He tells
her that it sounds a lot like "Barbara's dream" in George Macdonald's
novel. He wraps his arms about her pulling her as close as he can,
until her hot buttocks seem melted into his midriff. He inhales her
soft locks. He loves her, he knows her—like no other.

Finally, as the first rays of sun dapple the wall above Becki's
dresser, they doze off—together.

\* \* \*

Pursued by the waning moon, the Dodge van descends from
Westminster into Fitchburg. Wednesday, November 14, 1990.
2:40 a.m. Route 2, no traffic, and no weather except for radiation
fog in the valleys. "Cecilia" by *Simon & Garfunkel* plays softly on
the tape deck. Road signs and exit signs strobe into the headlights
then flash rapidly by like low-flying phantoms.

Almost back from North Adams, half hour to go. Billy drives.
Haley sits next to him. Tony rides shotgun. Becki dozes on Jim's
shoulder. Jodi sleeps to Becki's left. Joe and Brenda snooze in the
third seat, in the rear. Cigarette smoke, garlic breath, tired bodies,
drained emotions. Their triumphant chatter has given way to
stillness and slumber, but Jim rarely sleeps in the car. Normally, he
takes the Tempo but his muffler is going, so he and Becki are riding
in the van. Ahead of them are two pairs of cherry-red taillamps:
Angie's Volvo, Russ's pickup.

Tuesday night concert, packed Grange hall, 70 people. A
dozen songs: guitar, bass, keyboard, drums, and Sylvia, so tender
yet awe-inspiring. They played as one, they loved as one, and hearts
melted together, as in Jodi's living room. No performers, no

audience, no walls, no one left out. LBI rebels and other hungry souls came from all over: North Adams, Williamstown, Bennington, Adams, Pittsfield, along with carloads from Greenfield, Brattleboro, and Northampton. Amy and Tricia brought a bunch all the way from Nashua, and Heather came over from Albany with several of her friends. Afterward, everyone ate together: hot rolls and spaghetti, then coffee and donuts. Many stayed past midnight, talking with Jim and Becki and their renegade family from 59 Front Street.

Falling, flowing. Destiny is gathering kindred spirits as gravity gathers raindrops to the earth then collects them into puddles, ponds, lakes, streams, torrents—and now into a river of "living water." Jim senses that this "river of life" is ready to break loose and flow to the ocean. He stares past Tony's head at the highway as it rushes under them; he thinks happily about the future, *Maybe it's true what Becki and I were talking about in bed? Maybe this is the beginning of a great change on the whole earth? It's still a fuckin' fairy tale but who would've predicted what's goin' on now? Two years ago I was by myself, with no hope at all.*

As the *Simon & Garfunkel* tape clicks to the other side, the van zooms by the Searstown mall then veers to the south on Interstate 190. Into the homestretch. Billy goes faster as if responding to the cruising beat of "Baby Driver," the next tune on the tape.

Becki stirs and looks up sleepily at Jim. No words, but she dimples and loves him with her eyes. He pulls her closer. She snuggles again into his shoulder. He studies her cupid face, her angelic glow. *O Jesus,* he declares joyfully in his heart. *It keeps getting better and better. No matter what happens with the band, the "revolution of love" has already taken place in my life. Just being with Becki is heaven on earth. I need nothing more.*

Jim's spirit soars. He looks out at the cresent moon as it races along on their right, hazy and dingy and skirting the treetops—then veiled and diffuse and gone. Valley fog.

"Low beams," Tony says, as Billy slows the van a bit to deal with the reduced visibility.

No more moon, no more trees, just low-beam headlights fighting the fog. The monotony of it makes Jim sleepy; his eyes burn with fatigue. He closes them as the lyrics of "The Boxer" dance in his nodding head—*BANG! Thump! Thump! Thump!*

"Oh shit!" Billy exclaims. "We just lost a tire." He pulls the van over to the shoulder. He kills the tape deck.

Jim wakes with a start as do the others. "It's that fuckin' bald mother on the right rear," Tony declares in his tubalike voice as everyone yawns and stretches. "It would have to go ten minutes from home. But no sweat. I'll change this mother in two minutes."

Tony gets out. Jim slides open the right-side door and hops out to help him—*VAA-ROOHMM!*

Jim never sees the tire, or the tanker truck. He just sees the fire: FIRE! FIRE! EXPLODING BLUE FIRE!

The concussion knocks Jim into the ditch. He shrieks! He screams! "O GOD, NO! BECKI! BECKI! OH FUCK! O GOD! BECKI! BECKI! HELP HER! HELP HER! O GOD, HELP HER!"

PANIC! PANIC! Jim tries to get up but he can't move. *MY LEG! MY LEG! I CAN'T GET UP! NO! NO! IT CAN'T BE!* He chokes. He sobs. He faints from pain and shock.

* * *

Russ breaks the news at the hospital, but Jim knew from the moment he heard the crash, from the moment he saw the ball of blue fire. He knew that no one in the van made it out alive.

# Chapter Forty-five

Sunday afternoon, November 19, 2006. Warm for late autumn and cloudy. An oily smog blankets the valley. No wind. The grimy air smells like New York City.

Jim Shanley, wincing, climbs over a low place in the stone fence and follows Russ down through the trees. The throbbing pain below his left knee slowly subsides. His leg was burned and broken in the accident, but except for a slight limp, it functions okay. It only hurts in cold weather, and when he goes up and down stairs—or over stone walls. The big rock is covered with leaves and pine needles and acorns and pine cones. Jim plops down in his usual place and hangs his feet off the upper ledge. Russ sheds his shabby hunter's vest and plunks down beside him.

"Hard to believe it's been sixteen years?" Russ reflects, giving a sigh.

"No kidding," Jim replies. "I'm sixty years old. Look at the fuckin' gray in my hair." Jim lifts his baseball cap and runs his fingers through his salt-and-pepper locks. His Crusader hat has long since worn out. He now has a Red Sox cap like Russ; in fact, Russ bought it for him when he got a new one for himself.

Jim pulls a pack of Peanut M&M's out of the kangaroo pouch of his sweat shirt. He opens it and gives Russ a handful. Silence, save for the munching of candy and the distant cawing of a crow. Jim stares at the hills across the river, at the November trees, some naked, some mocha brown, some evergreen. The dam and the river look much the same, but the trestle is gone save for the footings. And no smoke from the Prescott stack—the paper mill closed ten years ago, back in '96.

After the accident, Jim's ministry disintegrated faster than a sand castle at high tide. No band, no Becki, no hope for this life. It all ended that fateful night. Despite tearful vows to carry on, the survivors returned to their old lives within weeks as if there had never been a gathering of kindred souls at 59 Front Street. Angie went back to Larry, Cathy to Kevin, Herschel to Thelma, Calvin to Clancy's, Sylvia to Long Island. Tony Liggons, unhurt in the crash but crushed emotionally, moved to Philadelphia to live with his brother. Throughout LBI, dissent disappeared as the many "cocoons of heart" fell apart. The rebels repented, rededicated, and returned to Logan. In like manner, Doris returned to Stan, Janet to Barry, Amy to the villa, Tricia to Robert, and Melissa repented before the BFBC body—and before Carl.

Mary Beth Hudson also retreated to the safety of evangelical orthodoxy, cutting off her secret liaison with Jim. Even Harry and Judy and Jim's friends downtown shied away from him. Only Russ has stayed with him through the years, but Russ too lives much as before, working at Stromberg Tool—now known as Stromberg-Nishimoto, Inc—and living with Beverly on Greeley Hill.

As for Jim, he again leads a solitary life at 59 Front Street. No women, no wife, no sex. He's tried to connect with a few. He even tried to rekindle things with Cathy, with Angie, but to no avail. Doris calls him occasionally to pour out her drunken monologues, mainly gossip and heartaches, but she never comes over. He sees no one except Russ, and sometimes his kids and grandkids. Oil prices are up but his checks are down—according to Gary Bob, the wells on the Gilson farm have dropped to "stripper" status. But Jim still receives enough to cover expenses.

He lives simply: reading books, writing poetry, watching movies, doing his chores. On occasion, he plays his drums—by himself. He walks in the woods, in the meadow, to the lake. He often feels Becki near as memories, and dreams of eternity, devour the present. Never in a hurry, he often walks downtown as well, rather than drive. He has no desire to participate in the Babylonian rat race where winning is everything and true love has no more status than the hordes of homeless on the streets of Boston. He now accepts his lonesome destiny, just him, the house, and Chinook, his cat—a black-and-white tomcat, now old and cantankerous, who's been a comfort through the many years.

Russ is Jim's only true friend. He has seen it; he knows what Jim knows. Russ understands why Shanley can never again be part of this world. Jim followed the goddess within and love ravished him on the "mountain of myrrh," on the "hill of frankincense." He gazed upon the vehement flame "from the top of Amana, from the top of Senir and Hermon, from the lions' dens, from the mountains of the leopards." But destiny, in a few horrible seconds, ripped happiness out of his hands and hurled him from paradise into the pit. He experienced the utter desolation of Orpheus and Eurydice at the gates of Hades. He looked upon the "pale priest" and lived, despite his wishes to the contrary. Nothing, nothing, nothing left, save for Becki-memories, beautiful yet torturous.

For two years Jim hardly left the house. Shell-shocked, bereft, and inconsolable, he inhaled misery with every breath and awoke each morning choking on torment. In one fiery moment, he had lost his heartmate, his reason for living, and his housemates, Joe and Jodi and Brenda and Haley and Billy, five kindred spirits, not to mention the band, the ministry. Yet as horrible as it was, it did not crush Jim as in 1984, because Becki died loving him. He has no answers except one, and that answer is YES! Yes, Rebecca Reinhardt does love Jim Shanley, and against all odds, she came back to him in 1990. Alison and Randy took her body and her belongings but they can never take the truth of her love. Jim is different, now and forever, because of Becki Lea.

He pours the last four M&M's into his hand, two reds, two yellows. He offers them to Russ who takes one of each and pops them into his mouth. Russ then hops down onto the lower ledge. Thrusting his hands into the back pockets of his paint-splattered corduroys, he saunters out to the edge. "It's a fucking shame about the trestle," Russ says, speaking over the edge. "It's not the same without it, and with the price of gas and the gridlocked highways, plus all this pollution and global-warming shit, we should be adding rail lines, instead of abandoning them."

"That's been obvious for twenty years," Jim replies, "ever since they tore up the tracks. But who plans for the long term? There's no money in it." He speaks with detached contempt, his usual tone when addressing the affairs of this life.

Russ rolls up the sleeves of his khaki work shirt and ambles back to where Jim is sitting. He leans hipshot against the face of the rock. He sighs and pushes his Red Sox hat back on his head. He looks much the same except his paunch is bigger, his head balder. He still has hair, even on top, but his ruddy dome is quite visible when he removes his hat. Russ picks up an acorn and fingers it delicately: he studies it with squinted eyes as if it's a priceless ruby. To Jim, the acorn looks like a little head capped with a beret. "Sixteen years and not a *fuck*ing thing has changed, least not for us," Russ remarks as if speaking to the acorn. "It still amazes me, Jim, how they took Becki and did the funeral in Nashua, and fucking Logan, he praised her and just talked about her service on the mission field, as if she never left the LBI camp."

Russ and Jim have been over this ground a thousand times but it still dominates their conversations. Jim wads the empty M&M's pack and stuffs it into the front pocket of his Levi's. "But people knew," he replies to Russ. "No one saw it as an *ac*cident, what happened to us that night. They saw it as *God* who sent that truck hurtling down the hill in the fog, especially after all of Logan's warnings and threats."

"No shit," Russ says. "But Logan and Beckman, and *fuck*ing Garrett, they were sly, like foxes. They were coming all over themselves with excitement, but they acted so calm and concilia- tory and sorrowful and humble. They knew the accident put the fear of God into everyone but they never came right out and said it was God who took her, yet they never denied it either. They played it well, and everybody ran like hell back to Logan as if he was fucking *Noah* and another flood was on the way and—"

"But he *did* say it later, in private anyway," Jim interjects. "He warned his staff and the branch pastors about the dire consequences of disloyalty and rebellion and sexual permissiveness. He said God would deal swiftly with any leader who defies church authority or who flouts the rules of decency and Christian morality ... at least, that's what Doris said. Of course, you know that."

Russ shrugs, gives a resigned grin, and tosses the acorn into the underbrush behind them. "It's no fucking wonder there hasn't been a single peep against Nashua in all this time. At least, I haven't heard of it?" Folding his arms over his chest, Russ turns toward the river and relaxes back against the wall of stone.

Jim stares wistfully into the distance. He bangs his boots slowly against the granite. "I think about it a lot," he says to Russ. "Why'd Becki hafta go when we were so happy? And we were helping people to love themselves. I think what we were doing was right. It's the only time I ever saw people getting out of their hang-ups so they didn't hate their instincts and innermost feelings. People were coming out and connecting with others. It was *beautiful*. Why'd it hafta end? Why did hearts hafta bow down again to shame and repression and lies? I don't know. I just don't know. Yet in all these years, I never felt that it was divine judgment that took Becki, or that Logan called it down." Jim crosses his legs, left boot on right knee. He looks at Russ, but Russ doesn't reply. He just gives a contemplative snort and a weary wag of his head.

After Rebecca's death and the demise of Shanley's ministry, Dr. Logan prospered like never before as a revival of fervent and blind obedience swept through all of LBI. The doctor declared the 1990s to be the decade of "divine blessing" and it appeared to be just that. By 1998, he had doubled his worldwide membership with 106 churches stateside and 63 missionary teams, and his radio-TV ministry covered every state and much of the world. He expanded the Nashua campus with new dormitories and classroom buildings, and he built "Agape Towers," a grand convention-center-hotel complex that dwarfs Moody Coliseum. The LBI chief became a man of renown in all evangelical circles and received a $5,000 honorarium wherever he went to speak, and he had many invitations. In like manner, Alison and Ed prospered in Puerto Rico, and Katie even moreso in Nashua. In 1993 she married Matt Garrett as Becki had predicted.

While preaching on Easter Sunday 1999, Dr. Logan died of a heart attack. Body members swore they saw angels flocking around their fallen leader. Others said they saw his soul rise gloriously to heaven. All over the world, his followers declared that his Easter death was the final confirmation of his holy office and calling. His passing set off a brief power struggle between Robert Logan and Rich Beckman, but a sealed videotape in Logan's safe quickly ended the dispute. In the tape, Logan declared that God had spoken to him, directing that upon his death, the anointing and mantle of authority would pass to Matthew Garrett—"Thus saith the Lord."

Success, success, more evangelical success. In the years since Logan's death, Garrett has taken LBI to even greater heights. He has diversified the ministry to include Christian counseling centers, hospitals, nursing homes, Christian resorts, retirement villages, recreational areas, camps, retreat centers, even Christian ski areas. On west campus he built an LBI historical park to honor Dr. Logan. The park includes the Charles R. Logan Memorial Library, an evangelical museum, an LBI pavilion, a small theme park, plus bookstores and gift shops.

To squeeze even more out of the evangelical sponge, Garrett established "Charis Products," an Amway-style pyramid enterprise. He also built a new media center that turns out state-of-the-art video shorts and commercials, along with Christian movies and programs. His polished marketing campaigns insure a positive image for LBI within Christendom, and before the general public. And the LBI church services are now seen by millions on his new "Worldreach" satellite TV network.

Garrett has called Jim several times—and has visited him once—asking him to help develop a contemporary music ministry and other projects. Though Jim declines of course, Matt is always friendly and speaks to Jim as if he never left LBI.

Preaching only on TV, and Sundays at the new Agape Towers complex, Garrett, now "Dr. Garrett," conducts himself like a CEO, and lets Rich Beckman run the evangelical side of the ministry. But Garrett does come to BFBC often, like once a month. He and Barry Buford have a special affinity for the old mill town. Barry of course, as Garrett's chief of staff, loves to flaunt his high station in front of Stan Campbell. But there's a bigger reason. Barry maintains, at a renovated rowhouse on Water Street, a local covey of young men, mostly Hispanics and Orientals, who entertain Garrett on his trips to town. This is a well-kept secret but Doris Campbell knows, and therefore so does Bev, and Russ, and Jim.

BFBC, riding the wave of LBI prosperity, has tripled in size in 16 years. Stan Campbell, despite his advancing years—he's now 71—is still going strong but has never attained his goal of becoming head pastor in Brendon Falls. When Tom Hudson finally departed in 1993 to take the LBI pulpit in Pittsfield, Logan recalled Randy

Scowcroft from Puerto Rico and appointed him to the BFBC pulpit. Rumor has it that Ed and Alison engineered this appointment with Katie's help. Nonetheless, Stan has served zealously as Pastor Scowcroft's assistant, with much evangelical success. In addition to increasing the membership threefold, they've expanded the Christian academy to K-12, added a new wing to house the high school, and established a fully-staffed branch of the Bible college, LBIBF (Logan Bible Institute, Brendon Falls).

Sharon and Tom carry on in Cobleskill, as Tom pastors in Pittsfield. Sharon's dad died in 1997 but Nana lives on as the Pedersen matriarch. After Pop's death, Erin and Ronnie moved to Cobleskill with Jim's three grandchildren, two boys and a girl. Nana added on two rooms to accommodate them. Ronnie works for Nana, maintaining the house and grounds, and he also has a part-time position with a local pharmacy. Heather, divorced with no children, still resides in Albany where she works as a secretary. Unmarried and quiet, Chris lives at home. He teaches chemistry and physics at Cobleskill High School, and helps Ronnie take care of the Pedersen property.

"Like I say, Jim," Russ finally replies breaking the silence. He speaks over the cliff into the sooty smog. "If Logan was such a holy prophet, how come you're still around? He twice declared that God was going to take you, but you out*lived* the bastard? And fucking Rasputin came out on top. I can't say what God is like, but I don't want Logan's God, or Garrett's, not in a million years. I don't want a God I have to prop up and lie about, a God I have to defend and explain every day—and raise money for. Who knows why Becki had to die so young, and the others, and our ministry? Maybe it was bad luck, or maybe God has a beautiful hidden purpose, or maybe God's an *ass*hole? Who the fuck knows? But regardless of the reason, it's like we've always said ... love and freedom never seem to last, but fear and lies and money, they bury the truth, and hypocrisy prevails year after year, and guilt and intimidation and ass-kissing—yet we saw it, Jim. We saw people loving and coming together without bullshit and party masks, but it was over in a flash."

"I'll say," Jim agrees. "Our hopes and dreams exploded and fell out of the sky faster than the *Challenger* space shuttle. I guess we didn't win the world, huh?"

Russ runs his finger over his lower lip. "But did we lose?"

"I don't know. I sure lost Becki ... at least for this life."

"But did they win?"

"I don't know. Did they?"

Now comes Russ's toasty smile; lazy laughter twinkles in his gray-green eyes. Through it all, he's never lost his laughing eyes; they're more seasoned and aware but the laughter is still there. "Well, Jim, they may've won in a lot of ways, but they didn't win *us*. I haven't been to fucking church in twenty-two years and I don't feel guilty or deprived. In fact, I feel more spiritual than ever, or at least more honest about God and life and death, and love and hurt. I don't have to act happy when I'm not. I don't have to say 'I love' when I don't. God is still my only hope, but I don't have to profess assurance about things I can't *poss*ibly be sure of. People can go to church if they want, but it's nothing to be *proud* of. I don't want some foamy-mouthed preacher telling me how great God is just to make me *feel* good—especially when he knows no more about God than I do. And I'm fucking glad to be free of the stress of trying to make my life fit the Bible or the latest bullshit from the pulpit."

Russ pops his fist against his open hand. "I trust my instincts more than I trust any preacher or any scripture. And I don't have to pretend that I know how God feels about everything, or pretend that I can control him through prayer ... or control anything for that matter. Logan attacked and intimidated us with every weapon in his arsenal, but when the fucking smoke cleared, we were still standing—bloody and brokenhearted to be sure, but *un*bowed. We may be unhappy and uncertain and out to pasture, but *love* is still the highest good in our lives. We'll never be intimidated by religion again, or serve pious causes because of shame. Let's face it, Jim, we're *rare* birds. Maybe we're fucked? But I like how we are."

"You're right about that," Jim chuckles. "I'm a *rare* bird all right. So rare that few people ever see me, even with binoculars. Course, who wants to be around an old fart who says exactly what he feels and has a reputation of being a heretic and whoremonger?" They both laugh as Jim slides down joining Russ on the lower tier of rock, but Jim quickly sobers. "I may be free from religion, and pretense, and all that shit, and I agree that it's better than where we used to be, but still, I hafta live each day without Becki, and maybe forever—depending on what happens after death? So what good is it to be my true self? Not that I have any choice; I could never go back, anymore than a frog could go back to being a tadpole. But what good is it, if I have no lover to share my*self* with?"

No response. Russ moves out close to the edge as if he didn't hear Jim. After stretching and rubbing the ague out of his neck, Jim follows him to the edge. Below them the Nashua River runs black and wide under the gray sky. They watch the water flowing and flowing. Russ seems lost in thought as if fascinated by the dark coursing water. After a while, he says, "I like rivers."

"Why is that?" Jim asks. No response, so he asks again.

Finally, Russ gives a wry grin and replies, "Because they never go *up*hill."

\* \* \*

An hour later: Jim and Russ head back through the meadow toward the house. Like its owner, the old house has an aura of comfortable deterioration. The years of wind, rain, sun, and cold have weathered the paint, blown away shingles, loosened the clapboards, and filled the yard with high grass and weeds. 59 Front Street, laid-back, detached, different from the other homes on Hadley Hill, has taken on Shanley's reclusive disposition as if the glorious events that happened there hallowed the house and set it apart as a place for solitude and memories of Becki. A few years ago a thunderstorm snapped off the old oak tree at the Y of the trunk, but the other half survives, maimed and lopsided—but alive. Jim identifies with the tree.

He and Russ head around toward the driveway but stop instead at the barn with its sprained doors hanging ajar. Jim rarely goes into the barn—he moved his drums into the house long ago—but on this Sunday afternoon they browse inside.

Disuse, disuse, years of disuse. Dark and dank, the old practice room smells of dust and mildew and has more cobwebs than Miss Havisham's wedding chamber. Many generations of spiders have decorated the beams, rafters, and posts, embellishing every nook and cranny with their delicate and wispy works of art. No guitars, amplifiers, speakers, or keyboard. No band, no crowd of happy souls. The stage is empty save for a patina of dirt and Angie's old upright piano, long out-of-tune and pushed against the far wall. No conversation, Jim and Russ simply give a few shrugs and rueful sighs. There's nothing to add, the room says it all.

Back outside, they cut across to the driveway walking through weedy shrubs and head-high pines that have taken over the old parking nook. Russ's car is parked behind Jim's, two old Fords from the previous decade, from the previous century. They hop into Russ's Taurus and proceed slowly down Front Street.

"Sure you don't want a ride back?" Russ asks some five minutes later as they arrive at Cumberland Farms on the near side of the Coachlace shopping center; he seems less than enthusiastic about going home.

"Nawh," Jim replies as he gets out. "I like walking. If I wanted a ride back, I would've taken my Escort."

After a quick exchange of sighs, smiles, and good-byes, Russ heads for Greeley Hill while Jim goes into the convenience store.

He buys milk, eggs, and bread, plus two cans of cat food, and two packs of Peanut M&M's. It comes to $9.85. He pays with a ten. He could use his ETF card but he prefers old-fashioned cash. The young woman at the scan-checkout is cute and gives a pleasant smile. But Jim scarcely notices her or the others in the store. Though he still has sexual desire and longs to cuddle, to hug, to be held, to be loved and accepted and befriended, he's given up trying to break through the facades and pretense. People now seem programmed and soul-less to him, like smiley-faced robots.

Carrying the bag of groceries, Jim departs Coachlace, walks under the Union Street railroad overpass, and takes a right onto Reservoir Road. He heads up the sidewalk on the west side. A smutty pall of darkness is gaining on the gray November afternoon. Night stalks the day, and always wins.

Jim saunters slowly along. For him the game is over. He's just running out the clock. The mournful bleat of a P&W diesel stops him halfway up the hill. (Conrail sold their branchline through Brendon Falls to the Providence & Worcester in 1992.) He turns and looks back as an eastbound coal train trundles through the old mill town on its way to the new NEPCO power plant in Boxboro. The train, pulling a long string of hopper cars heaped high with coal, winds its way toward the river like a giant black centipede. Jim watches until the flashing light on the last car disappears into the smog. P&W, the only railroad left in the valley, but no commuter service, no Amtrak service. No train stops in Brendon Falls, not even freight trains. The switching yard west of town has been closed for eight years.

Jim gazes at the empty tracks, then at the town. Amber street-lamps push at the gloom. Ancient smokestacks poke up into the murk. Abandoned factories and commercial buildings huddle in the fading light like ruins from a previous civilization. There is no downtown in the old sense of the word. Except for Flanagan's and Clancy's, every business on High Street is boarded up, even Pauline's and Bancrofts'. The only pulse of downtown life emanates from the rows of dilapidated houses, now inhabited by people of color: Latinos, Blacks, Asians, Arabs, along with a sprinkling of poor whites. An aura of pathos shrouds the scene, so palpable, Jim can almost grip it and wring it out with his hands. It seems thicker than the smog. Despite his abhorrence of Babylon and its ways, he has a lingering fondness for Brendon Falls, but only in the sense that the dismal soul-stiffling town has nothing to look forward to—but death. Jim knows the feeling very well.

*Why does life have to be so sad?* he asks himself as he resumes his trek up Reservoir Road. *It seems like the true and honest hearts end up desolate and boarded up, just like this fucking town. Why does it*—the sound of a slowing car interrupts his plaintive musing.

Silver limousine, hum of a power window. Ice-blue eyes, self-assured smile, a graceful hand holding a thin cigarette. It's Matthew Garrett. "How are you doing, Jim?" he asks, his tone congenial and relaxed. "You want a ride? We'll be glad to swing by and drop you off?"

Jim feels some surprise but little emotion. "No thanks, Matt. I like walking." In the old days, the sudden appearance of an LBI limo would have intimidated him and set his heart to pounding, but those times are long gone.

Well-preserved for a man in his 50s, Garrett seems little changed except he's given up his trendy apparel for a conservative gray suit. But he still indulges in the "sin" of smoking—at least in the privacy of his inner circle. Jim shakes Matt's hand then exchanges greetings and introductions with the others. As he moves closer to the fancy Lincoln, he gets a strong whiff of evangelical prosperity—moist perfume, Sunday dresses, wool suits, rich upholstery, all mixed with Garrett's tobacco smoke.

Garrett sits in the back with Katie at his side. Now in her late 30s, she looks just like her dad as if Derek Reinhardt is sitting there with shoulder-length hair. To Katie's left on the plush purple seat is a young trimly-built woman with a Bible on her lap. Blond and demure with a fawnlike face, she looks no older than twenty. She seems new and eager and naive, most likely an LBI freshman—the cycle continues. In the front seat, a student chauffeur is behind the wheel while Barry Buford rides shotgun. Barry is cranked around looking into the large passenger compartment; his heavy-jowled head turns on his shoulders like a globe rotating on a pivot. Now middle-aged, he resembles Jackie Gleason more than ever. The student chauffeur is a handsome young man with a square jaw and a swarthy face—no surprise to Shanley. Katie is cordial to Jim, but her heart is out of sight. Ditto for the others.

What a contrast: Jim, in tattered jeans, faded sweat shirt, Red Sox hat, and a three-day beard, next to this swanky LBI limo with darkened windows, not to mention the bag of groceries on his hip.

"So I take it you're going up the hill to spend the evening with Stan and Pastor Scowcroft?" Jim says to Garrett.

Garrett flicks, with smug nonchalance, a bit of burned tobacco out the window. "Right you are, Jim. I must say you're still very discerning." Matt's feigned friendliness has given way to suave cockiness and condescending wit.

Unperturbed, Jim parries Garrett's barb and probes behind his pretty evangelical mask, "Perhaps so, Matt, but there is one thing I haven't discerned."

"What's that?" Garrett asks, giving a girlish limp-wrist gesture as if aiming his cigarette at Jim; he holds the thin European-looking cigarette delicately between his index and middle fingers. There's now a hint of hostility in Matt's voice and a tinge of suspicion in his eyes.

Jim shoves his baseball cap back on his head. "Oh, I was just wondering why you come to Brendon Falls so much. It puzzles me. With a hundred other branch churches and all your many responsibilities, it seems like you'd have other things to do ... instead of coming *here* once a month?" Jim gives a knowing smirk.

Garrett takes a long pull on his cigarette then exhales a tumbling stream of smoke out the window, but he does not reply. Instead, he gazes intently at Jim with his Nordic eyes as if trying to intimidate, but to no effect. Jim has long since lived in another realm. But as they stare at each other, Jim poses another question in his mind, *What the fuck is Garrett doing in the backseat with the women when Barry and the handsome young driver are up front?*

Suddenly unnerved, Garrett answers both questions with one response, as if he can read Jim's thoughts, "Things are never what they seem ... are they, Jim?" His tone is sharp, his manner brusque, and he gives no time for a reply as he quickly withdraws into the car, buzzes up his window, and the limo roars away.

*In thirty years, that's the first time I ever saw him lose his cool,* Jim remarks to himself as he watches the limousine speed up the hill toward BFBC. *"Things are never what they seem." That's Garrett's favorite fuckin' line ... but I sure hope it's true.* He watches until the taillights become a haloed smudge of red against the gray and somber dusk. He then gives a shrug, shifts his groceries to his other arm, and continues up the hill.

Garrett and his entourage are on their way to a packed church where they'll be lauded and applauded, embraced and revered. Jim Shanley is on his way home to scrambled eggs and toast. There will be no embrace, no applause, no congregation, just an empty house, an aged tomcat—and memories of Becki.

Jim turns off Reservoir Road and tramps up the narrow winding streets that lead to the top of Hadley Hill. The streets are dark except for copper cones of streetlight which guard the corners like military sentries: silent, hatted, and tall.

Up, up, he goes, finally reaching Front Street. The old house, silhouetted against the fading twilight, waits patiently at the end of the street—as if expecting him.